Francie

Karen English

A Sunburst Book   Farrar Straus Giroux

The excerpt from "Dreams" is reprinted by permission of Alfred
A. Knopf, Inc., from *Collected Poems* by Langston Hughes.
Copyright © 1994 by the Estate of Langston Hughes

Library of Congress Cataloging-in-Publication Data
English, Karen.
    Francie / Karen English. — 1st ed.
        p. cm.
    Summary: When the sixteen-year-old boy whom she tutors in
reading is accused of attempting to murder a white man, Francie
gets herself in serious trouble for her efforts at friendship.
    ISBN 0-374-42459-4 (pbk.)
    1. Afro-Americans—Juvenile fiction. [1. Afro-Americans—
Fiction. 2. Race relations—Fiction. 3. Schools—Fiction.
4. Friendship—Fiction.] I. Title.
PZ7.E7232Fr 1999
[Fic]—dc21
                                                98-53047

For my mother

Contents

Francie

Treasure

I did something to that cat, I admit it. But that cat did something to me first.

All year we've been washing clothes every weekend at Miss Beach's Boarding House for Colored—Mama and I. All year that cat's had something against me.

Saturday morning, we went there to wash the linens. I could see Miss Beach sitting on her porch glider as we came up the hill toward her large white three-story house. She had that cat on her lap. Treasure. He'd scratched me four times already.

There he sat with his fat orange caterpillar tail swishing slowly back and forth as if he was fanning flies, his mouth stretching in a wide yawn so that I could see all the way down his pink little throat, past that pink

spade tongue and mouth full of tiny razor teeth. Miss
Beach nodded at us, then rose and let him spill from
her lap.

"Hurry and round up the linens, Francie," she said,
squinting at the sky. "I feel a storm coming up."

Mama and I headed out back, Mama to get the tubs
ready and me to take the back stairs up to the rooms. I
started with Mr. Ivory's room, gathered his sheets, sniffed
some of his colognes and hair ointments, and then made
my way to my teacher Miss Lafayette's room. I liked her.
Sometimes she left books on her bed for me to borrow
and then discuss with her later. Sometimes she left a
cologne packet from her beauty order. She'd had to go
down to Louisiana Friday night for two weeks to take care
of some mysterious business, so I knew I wouldn't be seeing her that day—or Monday neither. I frowned, thinking
of having Miss Lattimore, the principal, who always substituted for Miss Lafayette.

I studied myself in the bureau mirror. I was waiting to
look like I was of some age, but I still seemed nearly
as young as my brother, Prez, and he was ten. Prez's
real name was Franklin, after our last President. Mama
always said I had nice eyes. Now I looked at them closely.
She said God had blessed me with my daddy's thick eyebrows and long lashes. I supposed that she was right.

I checked Miss Lafayette's gallery of porcelain-framed
photos on the bureau—all of them light-skinned folks like
her—and ran her silver-handled brush through my hair.

Then I carefully plucked out my wiry strands from her silky ones.

As I was turning to go, having had my fill of fiddling with other people's belongings, I heard a noise. There was Treasure coming out from under the bed, doing that little wiggle cats do when they're getting ready to pounce. I wondered how he'd gotten to the room without me seeing him.

"Fool," I said, liking the feel of the forbidden word in my mouth. But before I could get it out good, before I could sashay on out of there, that cat ran at me and swiped my leg, drawing a line of blood. It was just through pure reflex that I was able to grab hold of him before he could get away. He twisted and turned in my clutch and tried to reach back and nip at my hand. He pawed at the air with his bared claws, making me even madder.

I marched him into Miss Beach's room at the end of the hall, shoved him into the bottom of the wardrobe, and slammed the door shut. I stood there a moment, breathing hard but feeling triumphant. I wanted to laugh. I wanted to shout.

Then I pushed my deed to the back of my mind and finished gathering the linens from the other rooms. I made my way down the back stairs and said nothing about my stinging leg, though I wanted to show it to Mama—just for any sympathy I might wring out of her. But I bit my tongue on my pain and just dumped my load near where Miss Beach stood in the middle of the kitchen sorting the piles with the tip of her shoe and telling Mama which laundry needed bleach and bluing, which collars and cuffs needed extra attention, and on and on and on and on, like the drone of a pesky fly. She paused long enough to glance over at me and say, "I hope you weren't up there meddling."

"No, ma'am," I mumbled. She stepped away from the piles of laundry and nodded at me to take over. I squatted down to finish the sorting, kind of puffed-up and satisfied and smiling to myself.

Miss Beach was of a suspicious nature. She didn't even believe we were moving to Chicago in a few months when Daddy sent for us. He'd gone up there a little over a year ago to work on a passenger train as a Pullman porter. It was hard work, he'd told us on a visit, serving white folks, even polishing their shoes and ironing their clothes, but if that's what it took to get his family up to Chicago, it was worth it.

Once I heard Miss Beach warning Mama not to get her hopes up. Maybe we wouldn't be going to Chicago, after all. She'd heard of menfolk all the time promising their families they were going to send for them and never doing it. And Pullman porters had some of the worst reputations. Some even kept two families, one down South and one up North. Her words made me have a bad dream about Daddy getting another family up in Chicago and giving them the life he was supposed to give us.

Miss Beach had told Mama that Beulah Tally never left to go nowhere, and after her husband had promised. "Don't count on going to Chicago, Lil. It might not happen." Mama didn't say a word.

Now, when Miss Beach turned her back to reach for the bowl of sugar on the sideboard to sweeten her tea, I stuck my tongue out at her.

By noon Mama and I had gotten the first load of laundry ready to be wrung out and hung on the lines. The sky was clear and blue. Miss Beach's "feeling" about a storm had only meant to hurry us up. We sat down on Miss Beach's back steps to eat the lunch we'd brought: cold yams and lemonade. Miss Beach crossed in front of us, her hand shielding her eyes against the bright sun, and I knew the consequences of my deed were soon to be met. She went back and forth across the lawn, then disappeared around the corner of the house. I raked my front teeth along the inside of the yam skin to get every last bit.

We worked the rest of the afternoon getting everything washed, rinsed, and wrung out for the line. In the late afternoon Mama sent me home to get dinner ready for Prez. I passed Miss Beach stepping out onto the veranda, fanning a face full of woe. "You seen Treasure?" she called out.

"No'm," I called back. It was true. I hadn't *seen* him—lately.

Mama came home fuming. I was sitting on the porch with a letter from Daddy balanced on my knees, the afternoon's events neatly tucked away in a far-off, hazy place in my mind, when I saw her shadowy form moving down Three Notch Road toward our house almost in a trot.

I stopped petting Juniper, our dog, and he raised his head, his ears perking up as if he sensed danger barreling toward him as well.

"Mama looks mad," Prez said from behind me. I hadn't noticed him come out to the porch. "Why you think, Francie?"

"How'm I to know?" I said, my mouth suddenly dry.

Mama marched up to the porch steps, and stood with her feet splayed in the dirt. Her nostrils flared in the dying light as she said breathlessly, "Go get me a switch."

My eyes welled up. Prez sucked in air loud enough for me to hear. I could picture his eyes wide with fear that he was the one who was going to get it.

"Move it!" she growled.

I moved it to the sweet-gum tree on the side of the house, and barely able to see through my tears, I searched the lower branches for a switch that would please Mama. I didn't dare bring her one that wouldn't.

She was in the house, pouring water in the basin, when I came in with a knotty branch dangling from my hand. It felt like a whip. I set it on the table. Mama splashed some water on her face. "Go on in the other room," she said over her shoulder after patting her face dry with a towel.

My lower lip began to tremble at the calmness she'd taken on. I walked toward the bedroom as if I was walking to my death. I had barely crossed the threshold when I felt the first burning lash cut across the back of my calves. My fresh cat scratch caught fire. I jumped and yelped at the same time.

"Mama . . ." I cried, bending to grab my leg. *Whop!* That next blow caught my hand. The pain shot up my arm to the shoulder.

"Have you lost your ever-lovin' mind?" she said, her voice tight through clenched teeth. *Whop!* "You trying to make me lose one of my jobs?" *Whop! Whop!* "I'll beat you till you can't sit down!" *Wham!* The switch came across my behind to help her make her point.

She hit me until I guess her arms got tired. Then she said, "Francie Weaver, why you want to hide that woman's cat?"

It was hard to speak around my fit of hiccups. "I don't know." It was true. I didn't know why'd I do something that was bound to get me in trouble.

"She might not let you come around no more," Mama said. "You sit on that bed and think about what you did." She went out of the room.

I hobbled over to the bed I shared with Mama, the letter now balled in my hand. I hadn't had a chance to give

it to Mama. I slipped it in my dress pocket, bitterly deciding to keep it to myself.

I sat and sat, inhaling the scent of the greens and corn
bread I'd cooked for me and Prez. I would have to sit
there until Mama felt I'd seen the error of my ways.

At one point, she passed the door and said, "You better
pray to God for your soul." I knew she was right. Every
once in a while I did some hateful things and I just didn't
know why.

Our Side of Town,
Their Side of Town

The next morning when I woke up, the unread letter was still in the pocket of my dress I'd draped over the chair. My eyes were swollen from crying all night. Mama had left without me, still angry, I guessed, because she didn't even say goodbye. She left word with Prez that I was to come to Mrs. Montgomery's by noon to help set up for her monthly tea. Aunt Lydia, Mama's sister, usually helped at these teas, but her time was close and she'd been troubled with swollen ankles. I thought about the new baby coming soon and hoped for a girl. I was tired of Prez having our cousin Perry to play with and me having no one. Though I knew it'd be a long time before a baby would be a friend.

I fed the chickens and swept the yard. Prez left to go to

the Early farm to help plant cotton with Perry. I started off toward Mrs. Montgomery's. Up ahead Mr. Grandy, in his battered old pickup truck, was heading in the same direction. I could've run ahead to catch a ride with him, but I decided to take my time.

"Francie . . ."

It was Miss Mabel, Three Notch Road's moocher, up on her porch, beckoning me over to her.

I pretended not to hear and kept on walking.

"Hey," she called.

I gave up and headed over to her sagging porch steps, glancing around her unswept yard at the parched weeds. My feet felt hot in the shoes Mama made me wear when I had to go into town. I longed to take them off.

"You goin' by Green's anytime tomorrow?" Miss Mabel asked quickly, grinning and showing off her missing teeth. Half her hair was braided and half hung loose.

"Maybe." I could feel her thinking how she was going to con me as she sat there with her lap full of snap beans, a pot at her feet, and right next to her, her snuff can. She rearranged the wad of tobacco in her lower lip.

"Can you pick me up some snuff? I'm 'bout to run out." She leaned over and aimed a stream of brown juice at her can.

"Green don't let kids buy snuff."

"He will if'n you tell him it's for me."

I dug the tip of my shoe into the dry dirt. I looked out toward the Grandy pasture, at the black and brown cows in a cluster, some grazing, some stupidly staring off. I'd be so glad to leave this road—and Miss Mabel and her cunning ways. I was sick of cows, sick of Miss Mabel, sick of work, work, work. I counted the days I had left in Noble.

A while ago she'd got me to pick up a pound of coffee and put it on Mama's tab. I nearly got a beating for that one. "You watch," Mama said. "That old woman's gonna have more excuses than the law allows. We ain't never gonna get the money for that coffee."

Three days in a row I'd come by to get the money and she come up with three different excuses.

"You never paid for that coffee I bought for you," I said now.

Miss Mabel let her mouth droop in a brooding way. "Go on, then, if you don't think I'll pay you." She made a shooing motion with the back of her hand. She didn't have to tell me twice. I backed out of the yard and was on my way.

I sang a little tune, then dug in my dress pocket to get Daddy's letter. *Ha, ha, ha,* I thought as I opened it. I might not ever read it to Mama.

It began the usual way—no news after the "I hope this letter finds you well" stuff and the part about sending for us before summer's over. I did like the last paragraph:

When you all get up this way, Francie and Prez, all you going to have to do is go to school. And Francie, I'm going to find you a

piano teacher and Prez, I'm going to find you a baseball team to
play on. It gets real cold in Chicago. There's plenty of opportunity.
This is the place where you just have to work hard and you can do
anything!

Love, Your Daddy

Piano lessons. I loved just looking at a piano. The
thought of learning to play . . .

I folded the letter and put it back in my pocket and
continued on to Mrs. Montgomery's tea in Ambrose Park,
the white section of town. When I reached the house, I
followed the footpath around to the back porch, pausing
to pet Portia, Mrs. Montgomery's cocker spaniel. I could
hear Mama's busy sounds in the kitchen through the
open window.

I stood there a moment, not wanting to go in. Clarissa,
Mrs. Montgomery's niece from Baltimore who'd come to
live with her because her parents were going through a
divorce, was sitting cross-legged on a blanket under the
Chinese elm, her nose stuck in a book. She glanced at me,
pushed up her glasses, and then went back to her reading. I didn't like her, because she was all the time sneaking a peek at me. I stepped into the kitchen.

"What took you so long?" Mama said, looking over at
me from the sink. Last night's beating came back to me
and my mouth drooped. "Come here and let me look at
you." She squinted. "You wash your face?"

"Yes'm."

"Mmm." She pulled a handkerchief from her dress pocket. "Here. Wet this on your tongue and go around your mouth. Looks like you left some breakfast on your face."

I sighed and did as I was told.

"Now." She nodded at the sink full of dirty dishes. "Get those washed, dry those punch cups." She indicated a bunch of cups upended on a towel on the counter. "And iron that basket of linens over there."

With dread I followed her pointing finger. There must have been fifty napkins, damp and balled up. I sighed again and went over to the sink. At least the kitchen had indoor plumbing and a double sink. At least there was an ironing board and an electric iron with five heat settings.

I went over to the radio, turned on *Homemaker's Exchange,* and started in on the dishes while I listened to the recipe for coffee sponge jelly. The last time I'd listened, it had been mayonnaise cake, and the time before, green-tomato pie. We didn't eat like white folks, that was for sure.

Mama caught that faraway look in my eye, and said, "Pay attention to your work, Francie." Clarissa came in then, licking the icing off of one of Mama's petit fours. She snuck a look at me and went over to the refrigerator to get herself a tall refill of lemonade. I felt her eyes on the back of my legs and turned to catch her studying them with interest. I went to work on a stain on the stove top with the Dutch Boy. When I finally stopped and checked behind me, she was gone. Mama caught me and pointed at the basket of linens.

As we walked home in the late afternoon, I slipped my hand in my pocket and ran my finger along the folded edge of Daddy's letter. Just a few more months, I thought.

School

I still carried my school shoes, at least to the school yard, before putting them on. Daddy had sent them from Chicago in December and to me they were still new and special and too good to be getting dust or mud on them. I didn't care about the snickers I got from the Butler boys every morning as they joined me and Prez and Perry on the road.

"Why you carryin' your shoes, Francie?" Bertrum Butler asked me.

"Cause I don't want no dust on them."

"Cause they from *Chicago* . . ."

"Maybe."

"You always braggin' about movin' to Chicago. Bet you ain't even goin'."

"Think what you want. It's no matter to me."

We entered the school yard and I went straight over to the pecan tree across from Booker T. Washington, the white clapboard building that was our school. Miss Lattimore came out onto the porch then to ring the bell.

I sat down under the tree and brushed off my feet, slipped on the new shoes, and stood up to admire them.

Oxfords. I loved them. Nobody had shoes like mine. I turned my foot this way and that. When I looked up, there was Augustine Butler staring at me from across the yard. She whispered something to her sister Mae Helen, and they both burst into laughter.

I didn't care nothin' about them—or any of their mean-spirited siblings. The Butlers were a large, angry family who sharecropped out near the county line. The boys and girls both were spiteful and always on the verge of a fight. You had to give them wide berth or wind up at the end of a fist. Their father was a known drunk who'd trade his mule for a bottle. All the kids stuck together like a pack of dogs. Augustine and Mae Helen, especially.

Today they were wearing thin cotton dresses with the waistlines heading up toward their armpits, and scuffed, laceless shoes. I straightened my shoulders and crossed the yard, eased past them where they were trying to crowd the doorway. The Butler brothers were taking seats in the back. I sat down at the desk next to my friend, Serena Gilliam, who smiled at me. She'd been over in Florida helping her sister take care of her new baby for the last two weeks. Serena was a good friend but I only got to see her at school, I had so much work to do all the time.

"Hey, Serena."

"Hey, Francie. We got Miss Lattimore today."

"Ugh."

Just at that moment, as if our thoughts had served her up, Miss Lattimore bustled in, carrying a bulging leather case that she grasped under the bottom and by the worn handle at the same time. She ignored us while unloading the bag onto her desk: workbooks, thermos, coffee mug . . .

On the chalkboard, in big expansive strokes like she was painting the side of a barn, she wrote the date. Finally, she whipped out a handkerchief from her pocket and mopped at her face.

"Let me tell you this right off." The sudden sound of her deep, booming voice made everyone jump. Serena's brother Billy, who'd been busy whittling on a piece of pine, looked up and dropped his mouth open. "I won't take no mess from none of y'all. And if you know what's good for you, you won't test me."

I frowned.

"Something wrong with you?"

It took a minute for me to realize she was talking to *me*. "Ma'am?"

"You look like somethin's botherin' you." Augustine and Mae Helen snickered.

"No, ma'am."

Miss Lattimore continued and I let out my breath slowly. "I want to see where you all are in your studies. Do these problems I put on the board." She began to cover it with arithmetic problems. Then she pointed directly at me. "You. Get on up there and do the first problem."

It was long division. A snap. *Daddy Mama Sister Brother*, I thought to myself—Divide, Multiply, Subtract, and Bring down. I finished it in a flash, because I knew my multiplication tables and division tables without hardly thinking about them.

She called Forrest Arrington next. He labored through a subtraction problem, but he got the right answer, and when Miss Lattimore said "Correct!" he beamed.

When she got to Augustine Butler, only the easiest problems were left. Slowly and heavily Augustine made her way up to the chalkboard like she was going before a firing squad. She stood a moment, facing the problem. Then, as if it might bite her, she reached for the chalk. It was three-column addition. I found myself running down the ones column in my head. Easy. With the tip of the chalk, Augustine touched the first digit, then tapped the second, lingering. With her left hand, down by her side almost hidden in the folds of her skirt, she tried counting her way to an answer.

There's nothing more pitiful than a big bully of a person being revealed as lumbering and stupid. The beads of sweat on her neck and her oil-stained collar made her meanness all the more pathetic. I almost felt sorry for her.

"You're too big and too old to be countin' on your fingers, missy," Miss Lattimore barked. "You should know your facts. They should come to you as fast as this!" She snapped her fingers. "Sit down. I have no patience for laziness."

Augustine made her way back down the aisle, her eyes on the floor until she passed my desk. At that point, she glanced at me, a quick flicker filled with awful intent. She hated that I was smarter though a year younger.

As usual, the Butlers had no lunch. The boys and their baby sister, Ernestine, played while the rest of us opened our pails and dug into our corn bread, butter beans, and grits. Augustine and Mae Helen sat off by themselves on the tire swings, twirling themselves this way and that to show they didn't care. No past effort on Miss Lafayette's part had got them to accept a handout. They were poor but proud. Long ago I'd even tried to share my lunch with them—but they wouldn't have it. I'd learned that wasn't the way to go with the Butlers.

Augustine Butler was hissing at me. I was pretending not to hear. Miss Lattimore sat at her desk at the front of the class, correcting papers. Every once in a while, her head snapped up, so she could snag anyone who was crazy enough to cheat on her math test.

"Number *four* . . ." Augustine whispered. I stopped writing for a few seconds, then stubbornly went on with my test, an awful anger growing in me. I was determined not to turn around.

Miss Lattimore stood up. "Do I hear talking?" We all held our breath. She squinted at us suspiciously, then sat down slowly.

I handed in my test first, picked up the class dictionary off the bookshelf, and went back to my desk. The only free-time activity Miss Lattimore allowed was reading the dictionary. As I began to get lost in the words, I felt a hand on my arm. Serena was slipping me a note—not from her, but from Augustine, who sat behind her.

Your gon to get it, I read. I folded the note, slipped it in my pocket, and glanced up at Miss Lattimore. She'd be of no help. I looked back at Augustine. She sat there glaring at me.

"Time's up. Francie, collect the papers in your group. Ernestine, collect the papers in yours."

Augustine held on to her test a second, then gave me a slow nod full of threat. Her paper was smeared with pencil smudges and erasures.

After dismissal, I washed down the blackboard, watered Miss Lafayette's plants—I wanted to keep them healthy and happy while she was away—and clapped the erasers out the window, all the while looking around the school yard for Augustine, but she wasn't among the kids who were playing before heading home.

"Come on, Francie," Prez said from the doorway. "I'm ready to go."

"Then go on," I said.

"Mama wants us to walk together."

That was a stupid rule, always having to walk with Prez. I could tell he was mad because Perry had gone ahead without us. I thought of something. "Come here, Prez." He took his time getting over to me, sensing I needed him. "Go see where Augustine is and come back and tell me."

"She's gone home."

"How do you know?"

"I seen her leave."

"How do you know she ain't somewhere waitin' on me?"

"I don't."

Miss Lattimore looked up from her desk and I lowered my voice.

"You go on," I urged.

"You comin'?"

"Git!"

"Well, where you going, Francie?"

"Never you mind." I knew where I wasn't going—down that road toward home so Augustine could jump out at me from behind a bush.

Prez looked at me a second longer, shrugged, and turned to go.

"Anything else you need done, Miss Lattimore?" I had

swept the floor and dusted the shelves. I had corrected
the math tests and straightened the books.

"I think you done all there is to do, Francie."

I left the schoolhouse and stood for a moment looking
up the road as if it led directly to hell. I walked in the opposite direction. Toward town.

I kept meaning to turn around and go the other way
—where Mama's chores were waiting for me, where
there was dinner to cook and the house to clean—but I
couldn't. I couldn't. The farther I walked, the more I was
resolved not to take any chances.

Town felt strange. Walking along Lessing Street, I just
then realized I'd never been there before on a weekday
during the school year. Clusters of white schoolchildren
took up the walk. I had to step off the curb for children
who barely noticed me. I stopped at Diller's Drugs and
looked in the window, past the display of electric irons
and mixers and toasters, to the pictures of malteds and
french fries above the counter.

I wished I had some money. I wished I'd thought to get
a nickel out of my savings in the can under my bed. I
could go sit in the colored section and have me a Coke. I
could sit there all relaxed, forgetting my cares. If I was
rich and had money to spare I could get me another *Nancy
Drew*, since I'd soon finish the one Miss Lafayette had
given me. If only I had me seventy-five cents.

Clarissa Montgomery stood with a bunch of other girls

at the comic-book carousel. Holly Grace, Mrs. Grace's blond, butter-wouldn't-melt-in-her-mouth daughter, said something to Clarissa, then moved over to the cosmetics aisle. She lifted a lipstick out of a socket display, opened it, and ran the tube across the back of her hand. She stared at her hand for a moment, looked around, then re-capped the lipstick and slipped it into her pocket.

My mouth dropped open. Did I see what I thought I saw? Holly Grace—that Mama all the time had to be hearing about when she served at Mrs. Grace's biweekly book club? Holly's piano recitals, Holly's citizenship awards and perfect attendance—stealing lipstick?

I left the store and moved on, feeling funny about my aimlessness but also a little excited by my newly discov-ered information. I wished I could be at that next book-club meeting. I wanted to be like a fly on the wall and watch Holly put on her usual airs. I wanted to hear Mrs. Grace brag on her.

As I walked along, I daydreamed, my thoughts finally returning to Mama. She wouldn't be back from the Mont-gomerys' until just after dark. If I beat her home, I could say I was sick and couldn't get the dinner and chores done because of that.

Naw, I decided. That wouldn't work. I didn't have a fever and Mama could always tell when I was lying, any-way.

Two little white girls came toward me, holding hands. I stepped sideways to get off the walk. That's when I saw

Mama coming out of Penny's Grocers walking behind Mrs. Montgomery, loaded down with two brown sacks. It was too late for me to get out of sight. Mama looked me dead in the face with no expression at all.

I dragged myself over to her with slumped shoulders.

"Excuse me, Mrs. Montgomery," she said. She looked down at me. "Where's Prez?"

"He's at home."

"Why ain't *you* home?"

Before I could answer, she said, "Come on."

We sat in silence in the back seat of Mrs. Montgomery's big black sedan. When we pulled into the driveway, Mama gathered the packages and got out without a word. I knew to follow her into the house.

"Sit down," Mama said. She began to move briskly around the kitchen, putting away the contents of the sacks. When she was finished, she called to Mrs. Montgomery that she was going, got her hat off the hook by the back door, and put it on.

"Let's go," she said.

It would be a long, quiet walk, because Mama didn't reprimand in public. You acted up in town and she just dug a thumb in your forearm and whispered a promise of a whipping in your ear. Mama could wait hours before she acted, and the whole time you lived with an awful dread.

Prez looked from Mama to me. "Where you been, Francie?" he asked me—to gain Mama's favor, anyone could see.

I ignored the question.

"Francie went to town," Mama said. "Now the chores ain't done and we don't have no supper."

"I was afraid," I said quickly.

"Afraid of what?" Mama looked at me full of suspicion. Neither one of us had sat down.

"Augustine Butler was mad cause I didn't give her an answer on our math test." I pulled the note out my pocket, glad that I had saved it. "She passed me this."

"What's it say?" Mama asked. She didn't read.

" 'You're going to get it.' "

"Come on over here, Prez, and read that note. Tell me if that's what it says."

Prez squinted at the note and nodded his head. "That's what it says, Mama."

"And you didn't write it yourself, Francie?"

"No, ma'am."

"Francie didn't write that note, Mama. 'Going' ain't even spelled right. It's spelled g-o-n."

Mama thought about this. She was quiet. Then: "You're not to go into town no more. You gonna have to figure out how to handle that ol' bully, but I want your behind to come straight home—with Prez—after school. *Straight home.*"

There was nothing to say to that. It gave me no answer to my problem, but I could tell by the tired way Mama took off her town hat and went to the basin to wash up that I wasn't going to be punished.

I woke up the next morning with my head filled with

schemes of how to avoid Augustine. I'd start out early and cut through the woods. If she saw me already at school helping Miss Lattimore, she'd just think the teacher asked me to come early.

Prez was trying to spoil my plan by not hurrying, determined to be hard to wake and slow about eating his oatmeal.

"Come on!" I said, pushing his book bag at him.

"I am," he said, squeezing his foot into his shoe. "I ain't even finished my breakfast good."

"I'll let you have some of my lunch."

"What about Perry?"

"We ain't got time to wait for Perry. He'll have to walk to school by himself. Now, come on!"

The woods actually slowed us. We had to cross the creek by walking the flat stones without slipping in, and that took time and care and Prez's constant bellyaching. "She ain't got it in for me. Why I gotta go through the woods instead of on the road?"

"Shut up." Fear made me irritable.

I thought of ways of doing Augustine in. I thought of beating her over her ugly head with a stick, or ripping her hair out, or pushing her off a cliff. Though we didn't have any cliffs around, I could imagine the satisfaction I'd feel in my hands as I sent her over one.

I peeked out from the deep coziness of the forest edge. The school yard was empty.

"Come on," I said, pulling Prez by the arm. We crossed

the yard quickly to the classroom door. It was locked. I tried it twice, my heart sinking. Prez ran around to the window. He had to jump up to peek in.

"She's in there," he said.

"Who?"

"Miss Lattimore. She's in there at her desk."

"What's she doing?"

He jumped up again. "Nothin'."

"Nothing?"

"Just drinkin' a cup of tea or coffee or somethin'."

I went back to the door and tapped lightly. I waited, listening. When the door opened, I stepped back, speechless. Miss Lattimore, with a steaming cup in her hand, looked annoyed.

"What is it, Francie?"

"I just wanted to know if you needed any help?"

"Can't say I do—right now. You go on and play."

How was I supposed to go and play? I sat down on the steps, feeling miserable. Prez was happy—he had the tire swing all to himself.

Then I noticed someone coming up the road. I could tell by the loping walk it wasn't Augustine. I shaded my eyes against the morning sun and closed my mouth, which had dropped open. It was a boy. A big boy. He walked right into the school yard, stopped for a few seconds to look around, and walked over to me, bold as you please.

His kinky hair was brushed back and packed down like

it had been under a stocking cap all night. His overalls
and shirt were tattered but clean. He was darker than
me, a reddish kind of dark. He didn't look me in the eye.

"What time this school start?"

"In a little while," I said. He put one foot on the bottom step and looked off like he was trying to cover up
some embarrassment. Prez hopped off the swing and
came over to stare at him. He was still young enough to
get away with it.

"Who are you?" Prez said.

"Jesse Pruitt."

I was secretly happy that Prez was so outright nosy.

"I ain't never seen you before. Where you from?"

"Over in New Carlton." He stopped to give Prez the
once-over. Then something seemed to smile in his eyes
but not on his lips. "Ain't no school in New Carlton."

"Everybody know that."

"Yea," he said. Then there was silence all around.

As soon as the yard began to fill up, Jesse went over to
a tree stump to sit and wait. Finally, Miss Lattimore came
out and rang the bell. I dashed inside.

From the safety of my seat, I watched my classmates
file in, the strange boy hanging back, I noted, in the doorway. Each person looked up at him as they passed, wondering who he was and why he was there. Augustine
finally arrived, and she stared openly at him even after
she sat down, seeming to have forgotten all about me.

Miss Lattimore took her seat, shuffled some papers,

then looked over her glasses at the boy. "You here for school?"

He didn't look her in the eye.

"Yes'm."

"What's your name?"

"Jesse Pruitt."

"Pruitt. I ain't heard that name before. Where's your people?"

"We stay up by New Carlton," he mumbled.

"How old are you, Jesse Pruitt?"

He didn't answer right away. She waited, tilting her head to the side, like she was expecting him to lie. He said nothing. Augustine and Mae Helen snickered behind their hands. "Well, Jesse Pruitt, can you hear? I asked you a question."

"Sixteen," he said quietly. So quietly that I didn't know if I heard him right. Yes, there was something older about him and there was something serious, something weighing on him.

"Come again?" Miss Lattimore said. Jesse would be in an age group all by himself.

"I'm sixteen," he repeated, his voice loud now as if he had a point to prove. I felt sorry for him standing there like he had no kin, no friends, not a soul in his corner.

"You're a big boy. Take that seat in the back. I don't want you to be blocking the view from the little ones. Pass out the readers, Francie."

I got up to do as I was told. Augustine took hers out

of my hand with a little snatch. I placed one on Jesse Pruitt's desk and gave him a smile to encourage him. He looked at the book's cover, leaving it as I had put it. Upside down. I knew at that moment he was like Mama. He couldn't read.

Miss Lattimore got the lower grades practicing their printing, the middle grades their cursive, then she had us turn to *Hiawatha* in our books. Reading aloud was the most boring thing I had to endure every morning, because Mae Helen, Augustine, and several others who'd never learned to read too good would take ten years to drag through one sentence. The teacher had to tell them every other word. Then the next morning they would repeat the very same mistakes. Some of them were thick as posts. My turn would be over before I knew it, after waiting all morning for the teacher to get to me.

This time was different, because Miss Lattimore was making her way down the row to Jesse Pruitt. He came after Serena's brother J. Dean, who took minutes and minutes to limp through five lines. Then: "Okay, Jesse Pruitt, let's see what you can do. Take it from there."

I looked back. His book was still closed and upside down. He touched it but did not open it. "I ain't learned to read," he said, loud enough for there to be no doubt about what was said. Everyone whipped around then. Even the poor readers, probably glad that there was finally someone worse off than them.

"You don't read . . ." Miss Lattimore adjusted her

glasses, trying to figure out what to do with this big person who never learned to read. "You can't read at all?"

"I never went to school regular."

"I see. Well, you comin' here after school's been in session for months. I don't have time to coddle you. Francie's a good reader. Maybe she can help you. Maybe she can't." She looked over at me. "Francie?"

"Yes, ma'am, I'll help him." I looked back at Jesse and smiled, but he was sitting there staring at his hands.

"Now, you know your alphabet?"

"My ABCs?"

"Yea—your ABCs." Jesse Pruitt and I had stayed behind after everyone had been sent home. Miss Lattimore was grading quizzes at her desk, not seeming to pay any mind to us.

"My mama taught me."

"You know the sounds of the letters?"

"No—I don't think so."

I looked at him. It was going to be a long, hard row to hoe, I decided.

By the time I'd taken him through the sounds of the consonants so that he could remember them, I'd changed my mind. Jesse Pruitt wasn't no dummy, and I was going to teach him to read. The idea gave me butterflies in my stomach.

I looked out the window. The school yard was nearly empty now, and Miss Lattimore was packing up to go.

Prez was kicking a pebble around. He was soon going to grow tired of waiting on me every day. I wished Perry would stick around with him.

"How come that boy never went to school?" Prez and I were hurrying home to get there in time to do our chores.

"Mama never went," I said.

"How come Mama never went?"

"She had to take care of all her brothers and sisters when her mama died."

For a moment, I felt sad for Mama—her never going to school. But then my sadness vanished as soon as I remembered I was teaching someone to *read*. I quickened my pace, determined to keep Mama satisfied with my work so I could keep staying after school, helping Jesse Pruitt. I was feeling so good, thinking about this, I forgot all about Augustine.

And suddenly there she was. Augustine stepped in front of me with Mae Helen right behind her. She wore her ugly grin on her face, like this was something she'd been planning all day. I was more surprised than scared. Then I felt a prick of anger. Prez looked from me to her.

Without a word, I tried to go around her, but Augustine blocked me, and Mae Helen joined her to widen the barrier.

"You think you so cute, don't you—just cause you think you movin' up to Chicago." Augustine turned her head and spit on the ground. "Shoot, it ain't so special. I got a cousin up there and it ain't so hot."

"Yea," Mae Helen said, inching closer. She was bigger than Augustine, with a halo of unruly hair that stood out all around her face. I weighed her role in this, deciding I couldn't fight one of them—let alone both.

"I never said it was special and I don't think I'm cute," I said, my voice breaking and sounding frightened to my own ears.

"You shoulda give me that answer."

"Miss Lattimore would've torn up my paper," I said.

"So?"

Augustine didn't care about no answer. She just didn't like me. She was simply giving herself something to go on—giving herself a reason to beat me up.

I stepped back, knocking into Prez. Augustine, taller than me, leaned forward, her arms behind her a bit, her chest out. She brought her face close to mine. It was like a dance. She'd said her ugly words, and next she'd be giving me a hard shove. I braced myself for it, so when it came, it took more effort than she expected to knock me down. But Augustine outweighed me by about twenty pounds. I fell hard on my elbows, scraping them on the gravel. Both girls laughed. When I tried to get up, Mae Helen pushed me down.

"Come on—get up. Ain't you gonna get up?" Mae Helen looked at Augustine, I guess for instructions on what to do next.

Prez began to cry, taking Mae Helen's attention off me for a second. I hurried to stand up. "Aw, no you don't," Augustine said, readying herself to shove me again. But just then Jesse, appearing out of nowhere it seemed, grabbed her from behind, nearly lifting her off her feet before setting her aside. She went down on her butt hard, her eyes wide with surprise. She struggled to get up, but Jesse Pruitt held her down by the top of the head, so all she could do was get purplish with the effort to push against his big flat palm. Prez laughed, suddenly feeling brave.

I brushed the back of my dress off.

"Now," Jesse told Mae Helen, "you go on home." He turned to Augustine. "You, too," he said. He didn't even sound angry.

Mae Helen helped her sister to her feet. They started up the road—slowly, shooting mean stares back at me to pretend they weren't scared, anyhow. I met every one of their stares. To show I wasn't scared, neither.

"You okay?" Jesse asked.

"Where'd you come from?"

"I followed you."

"How come?"

"I heard them talking about all they were going to do to you. I thought it was just talk. But I decided to see for myself. So I come this way, stayin' behind you." He looked past me.

"I'm fine," I said.

"I'ma go, then."

I brushed away more dirt and twigs that were clinging to my dress. "Thanks," I said and watched him walk away. Me and Prez started for home.

More important things came into my thoughts, though. I'd have to really hurry now. With all the delays, it was going to be nearly impossible to rush through everything I needed to get done before Mama arrived home hot, tired, and irritated.

I tutored Jesse every day the rest of the week. Miss Lattimore, busy with her teaching and principal duties, bustled in and out of the classroom and hardly seemed to notice us. I liked teaching Jesse for two reasons: I liked watching his progress, and he kept me safe from Augustine.

I surprised myself. I could tutor Jesse for thirty minutes, run home, and get every one of my chores done and the dinner on the stove by the time Mama was walking up the road toward home. Course, that first night Mama had caught sight of my scraped elbows and said, "What happened to you?" I was in a pitiful state, like someone always doing battle and getting a new wound every time she turned around. Cat scratches, welts from a whipping, and now scraped elbows that promised to crack and sting fiercely whenever I bent my arms.

"I hurt myself," I'd said simply and Mama was too tired to question me further.

"What's that?" Jesse asked me the following Monday.

"What?"

"That," he said, laying his finger on the picture of an orange grove. Slowly and painfully, he was making his way through *The Little Red Hen*. I had to bite my tongue to keep from yawning. It took a lot of patience not to correct him, to wait and let him sound the words out himself. Sometimes I had to tell him. Then he'd repeat it four or five times, even closing his eyes while he said it to see it in his mind. But I never had to tell him that word again.

"That's what you call an orange grove. We don't have any here." I looked out the schoolhouse window at the trees we grew here. Pine and pecan, peach and sweet gum. No orange.

"Where they have orange groves?"

"They have them in Florida and California."

"Where's this California?"

"On the other side of the country. Right where the Pacific Ocean is."

"Where's that?"

I looked in his earnest face. He didn't know where the Pacific Ocean was. I got up and checked the hall toward the small room Miss Lattimore used as an office. Then I got the atlas off the front desk and opened it to the map of the United States. Jesse leaned over me. "We're here," I said, showing him where Alabama was. "And the Pacific Ocean is here." I ran my finger slowly across the map to show what a big country it was we lived in. "It's two thousand miles away."

"Two thousand miles," he repeated and pulled at his sleeve. "I'ma go there one day—where they grow oranges on trees." He thought about his own words for a moment.

Then he gave a short nod, like he was settling it in his mind.

He stood and started for the door, just as he did every day, saying that was all the time he could spare.

The next day, Jesse was late for the first time. In the middle of multiplication drills, he entered, head down. Some of the kids stared as he slunk to his seat, waiting to see if he'd get yelled at. But Miss Lattimore didn't miss a beat. She just went on calling on us and snapping her fingers if we hesitated. She didn't call on Jesse and he didn't volunteer. It seemed she was letting him make his way.

The next day, Miss Lattimore had him listen to the second-graders read *Little Red Hen* and follow along as best he could. Later, she gave him a slate to practice writing letters from his penmanship book and only called on him when she couldn't avoid it. Any giggling was met with a piercing stare over her glasses.

Finally on Friday I asked Jesse a question that had been nagging at me. "How do you get all the way here from New Carlton?"

"I walk."

I thought about this. New Carlton was six or seven miles away. He'd have to start out at sunrise to get here on time.

"Why did you want to go to school? Now?"

"I always wanted to go." His eyes left the window and settled on me almost defiantly. "My daddy needed me to work in the fields. I'm the oldest." He shrugged. "My mama always wanted me to go, too."

"You going for your mama."

His mouth quivered and he lowered his eyes. "She died."

"You don't have a mama?"

He seemed to be struggling to compose himself. Finally, he managed to say, "She died last winter—and I always promised her I'd get some schooling. So that's why I come here."

"Who do you live with now?"

"My daddy and my younger brother and younger sister."

"Who takes care y'all?"

"We all take care of ourselves."

That was the loneliest thing I'd ever heard. Even with all the work I had to do, I never thought I was the only one taking care of me.

"I want you to come home with me—for dinner."

He looked surprised. "I can't do that."

"Why?"

"I'm expected at home. I gotta get there before the sun go down. I got a lot of work that has to be done yet." He stood then. "Or my daddy will stop me from comin' for sure."

Miss Lafayette

Mama argued my case and I was allowed to return to Miss Beach's on Saturday.

All the way there, I had to hear Mama's lecture. "I need your help, so stay out of the way of that cat and just do your work."

"Yes, Mama," I said, though I was hardly listening. Miss Lattimore had announced that Miss Lafayette would be back on Monday, so my mind was on seeing her, telling her about Jesse. Maybe she even had a present for me.

"Are you listening to me, Francie?"

"Yes'm."

Miss Beach was up on her porch as usual—Treasure curled on her lap, enjoying Miss Beach's long and slow strokes down his back. When we got within earshot, Mama called out brightly, "Mornin', Miss Beach! Nice day for doin' laundry, ain't it?"

Miss Beach looked up, nodded, then narrowed her eyes at me.

"Francie's got somethin' she wants to tell you," Mama said, nudging me.

"I'm really sorry, Miss Beach, for what I did to that cat." Mama elbowed me in the side. "And I'm never going to put him in your wardrobe again."

Miss Beach, who was busy checking something in Treasure's fur, looked up. "You better not," she said. Then, as if she'd just thought of it, she said, "And don't go pestering Miss Lafayette."

I said nothing, but I felt as if I would burst with joy. Miss Lafayette was really home!

I hurried around the back and started up the stairs. I listened for a few seconds at Miss Lafayette's door, then tapped on it.

"Come in, Francie."

I stepped in, feeling suddenly shy. Miss Lafayette was still in bed. I'd never seen her in a nightgown before. Her pecan-colored hair, always up and out of the way, was hanging down over her shoulder to her waist. She sat propped against pillows in a white gown with tiny roses around the neck and wrists. She looked as fragile as a china teacup. She had a book face-down on her lap.

She smiled at me. I stayed near the door, my hand

still on the knob. "Hello, Miss Lafayette. I'm glad you're back."

"Have you all been showing Miss Lattimore you have some home training from ol' Miss Lafayette?"

"You're not old."

She pulled a flat package out from somewhere under the covers, wrapped in brown paper. "Been waiting for you." I pressed my lips together to hide my pleasure. "Here." She held it out to me.

I walked to her bedside. "You sick?"

She waved the question away. "Sit down," she said, patting the strip of space next to her, and I eased down on the edge, feeling funny about sitting there.

She chuckled. "I'm not going to bite you, Francie. Here," she said again.

Carefully, I took the package out of her hand and unwrapped it, trying not to tear the paper.

It was a book. I knew it would be. Miss Lafayette knew how I loved books. She knew I'd started my own little library with the books she'd given me.

The Dream Keeper by Langston Hughes.

"The poet," I said.

Miss Lafayette looked at me closely and recited:

> "Hold fast to dreams
> For if dreams die
> Life is a broken-winged bird
> That cannot fly."

I flipped through the pages. "I'ma read it on my hill."

"While you wait for the train to go by?"

"No, I eat my Scooter Pie while it goes by. Then I read."

She laughed.

"Thank you, Miss Lafayette." I ran my hand over the cover.

"What have you been up to?"

"We got a new boy, Miss Lafayette. His name is Jesse Pruitt and he's sixteen and he can't read."

"Oh?" She cocked her head with interest.

"I'm teaching him."

"Are you doing a good job?"

"I think so."

"Good."

I heard my name being called then. Miss Beach—calling up to see what was taking me so long. Miss Lafayette nodded toward the laundry bag hanging on the bedpost. I looked back at her before going out the door. "Will you be at school on Monday?"

She winked at me.

"Is she gonna be there?" Prez said as we walked with Perry to school Monday morning.

"I said she was."

"You know for sure?" Perry asked.

"Don't no one ask me again."

We turned into the yard just as Miss Lafayette stepped

out to ring the bell. Prez and I grinned at each other at the same time.

How different the two teachers were. In her smooth, gentle manner, Miss Lafayette leaned on the edge of her desk, looked us over, and said, "I've missed you so."

"Why were you gone so long?" Perry burst out, and I could have smacked him for his rudeness.

"It really wasn't that long—only two weeks." Miss Lafayette blushed almost crimson.

"Felt like a long time," Bertrum mumbled.

Miss Lafayette looked at her watch. "Let's get busy. Bertrum, please pass out the readers."

I sighed. Just then Jesse arrived—late as usual, but this time I knew why.

He stopped in the doorway, not knowing what to think about Miss Lafayette's presence. Carefully he made his way to the back of the room.

"Are you Jesse?" Miss Lafayette asked.

He was just sinking into his seat. Now he stood up quickly. "Yes, ma'am."

"Are you always late, or is this an exception?"

"I'm late almost every day, ma'am."

"May I ask why?"

Jesse stood blinking at Miss Lafayette, not knowing how to take such politeness coming from an adult.

"I come from New Carlton and I can't leave as early as I need to, cause I got chores to do."

I'd been looking from one to the other. Now I switched back to Miss Lafayette. She frowned, slightly.

"That's a long way you walk."

"Yes, ma'am."

Noticing he was empty-handed, she asked, "Where's your lunch?"

Jesse didn't answer. He looked out the window, then back at her, then down at the floor.

"Never mind. Please sit down."

I'd tried to share my lunch with Jesse when after a day or so I noticed he had nothing. But he always acted like he wasn't a bit hungry. Then on Friday I'd pretended to be full, with corn bread left over. He took it then, just so it wouldn't "go to waste."

At midday, Miss Lafayette dismissed us for lunch but held Jesse back. I knew she'd try to coax him to take some of her lunch. And I was sure he wouldn't take it. He'd be just like those proud Butlers—pretend he wasn't hungry. I'd ask him to come to our house for dinner again.

Miss Lafayette quietly corrected papers at the front of the class while I tutored Jesse in the back. I bit my lip to stay alert while he struggled through a paragraph, putting his finger on each word as he went along at a pace that was torture. I still loved the notion of teaching someone to read, but it sure did take patience.

"Jesse," I said, when he stopped to take a breath. "Can you come for dinner on Friday?"

He stared at the page he'd been reading.

"Friday. Cause you don't have to go to school on Saturday—maybe you can put some things off?"

I felt a little anger rise up in him and immediately regretted being so pushy.

"Why you always askin' me to do something I can't. It just makes me feel bad." He hadn't looked up yet. He clenched his fists. "I said I can't do it." His voice rose enough for Miss Lafayette to look up and watch us a moment.

"I'm sorry," I told him.

"I can't do it." He got up quickly then. "Time for me to go," he said, pulling himself up out of his chair. He didn't even bother closing the book before he walked out of the room.

Mr. Pruitt came the last Monday in April to take Jesse out of Booker T.

J. Dean had led the Pledge of Allegiance and we'd just sat down to work on our readers when a strange man appeared in the doorway in work overalls, holding his hat. Jesse had arrived on time and sat hunched over his book, seemingly with no thoughts of nothing else. The man wore a hard expression on his face. He looked directly at Jesse. Jesse must have felt eyes on him because he glanced up, and immediately flinched. The man lifted his chin, just a little, but it was enough to have Jesse scrambling out of his chair and making his way up the aisle. He didn't even get to the door good when his daddy—it didn't take long for me to realize he was Jesse's daddy—reached out and grabbed his arm. He gave him a hard shove and Jesse, looking as weak as a sick kitten, let himself be pushed out the door and down the steps. We all watched them through the window hurrying along the road. Miss Lafayette stood and watched with us, saying nothing.

Then she sighed heavily. "Let's get back to work," she said.

"Who was that?" Serena whispered to me.

"His daddy, I'ma bet."

For the rest of the day I hoped to see Jesse walk back through our classroom door, but when 3:00 came and he still hadn't returned, I feared he wasn't ever coming back.

For the rest of the week I watched for him. I'd frequently check the window, picturing him loping up the road like the first time I saw him. Then I'd imagine him coming through the door after we'd all settled with our readers. He didn't come.

His absence wasn't lost on Augustine. Toward the end of the week, she squatted down beside me while I was waiting my turn to play the winner in a game of jacks. "Where's your friend?"

I didn't answer.

"He comin' back?"

"Sure. When he can get away." She considered this, checking me closely to see if I was lying. "It's planting time," I continued. "He's gotta help his daddy right about now. But he's coming back and he's my friend."

She stood up and looked down at me. She snorted. "Betcha he ain't comin' back," she said.

I swallowed and put my eyes on Serena and Viola's game like I didn't care one way or the other. But I did care—a lot.

Diller's Drugs

"Mama," I said on Saturday, as we were hurrying along to Miss Beach's.

"What, baby?" She had that far-off look in her eye. She'd gotten a letter from Daddy and this time she'd fished it out the mailbox first and had me read it to her.

It was full of the usual promises. Promises that he was going to send for us. That he was going to set us up in Chicago with our own house. That Mama wouldn't have to do day work and laundry no more cause he didn't want that for a wife of his, and how Prez and me were just going to have to go to school. No more scrubbing other people's clothes and serving at people's parties for me and no more planting and picking cotton for Prez. And, on top of that, I was going to get those piano lessons I was wanting for a long, long time. I knew the promises by heart because I'd been hearing them since a year ago March, when Daddy left the pulp mill to go up to Chicago, but sometimes I didn't know how much I believed them.

When my chores were done and I could go sit under my pecan tree up from the railroad tracks to read, then I'd think about the promises and life up North.

This time, money had come. Mama had given me and Prez a nickel apiece. I knew what I was going to do with mine. I was going to buy me a Scooter Pie, get my *Nancy Drew* from home, and go read and wait for the train to come roaring through.

But now something else was on my mind. Commencement. Miss Lafayette had reminded us on Friday that it was coming up. I'd almost forgotten all about the eighth-grade ceremony commemorating the end of grammar school. Now I thought about the commencement dress Daddy's sister had sent from Chicago. White organza with a dropped pink sash. At first, I'd hung it on the back of the bedroom door, just so I could sit on my bed and look at it. But for the past few weeks I hadn't given that dress a thought or barely a look. Now, since Miss Lafayette put commencement back on my mind, I thought of Mama's rhinestone clip-on earrings.

"Mama," I said, hoping that she was going to grant my request.

"What is it?" She glanced over at me with annoyance.

"I was wonderin'—for my commencement, can I please wear them earrings Daddy sent you last fall?"

"My birthday earrings?"

"Please, Mama." I waited. She was squinting into the distance, actually thinking about it. That was a good sign, because when Mama said no right off, it was settled—as settled as could be.

"Okay," she said. Just like that. I couldn't believe it had been so easy. I kept my mouth closed, not wanting anything I said to change her mind.

"Thanks, Mama," was all I chanced a few moments later.

Miss Beach was on her porch, sipping her morning coffee and gliding gently back and forth. Treasure lay at her feet, his eyes closed to slits. I did not like that cat.

Miss Beach nodded good morning to us.

I started around back.

Before I could get down the stairs good, Miss Beach was asking me, "Were you up there meddling?"

"No, ma'am." I'd hoped to see Miss Lafayette. She'd made me feel better about Jesse's departure, telling me he'd probably be back—as soon as his farm workload lightened up. But her room was empty and there was no sign of her.

I dropped the laundry on the floor, then squatted down to sort it. Miss Beach stood over me for a minute, giving me the usual instructions. Finally, she left the room. I loaded my arms with the whites and took them out to Mama.

"Miss Beach wants these to go through two boiling tubs, Mama," I said, relaying Miss Beach's instructions.

Mama sighed. "If I don't know that by now, I must be a dimwit."

I smiled and then remembered the nickel I had in my pocket. I could taste the Scooter Pie I was going to buy with it as soon as I could get over to Green's. I just needed to get to my hill in time to see the local race by on its way up to Birmingham to make its connection to the Illinois Central. I loved watching that train. I was gonna be taking that route one day, on my way to Chicago. Daddy had promised.

Things went off without a hitch. Mama and I wrung and wrung the sheets, we hung the wash, and Miss Beach stayed out of our way. That horrid cat kept out of our way, too. Mama finally said I could go.

"You be home by the time I get there, missy," Mama said.

I quickly calculated that I'd have less time than I was counting on, but I was in such a good mood that it gave me only a pinprick of disappointment. I could make that up if I ran all the way to Green's.

I stopped at our house. Prez was gone down to Perry's. Good, I thought. He won't be pestering me to let him come along. I quickly went to get the *Nancy Drew* I was in the middle of reading.

I kept all my books on a little shelf above me and Mama's bed. She kept her earrings up there in a little box. I had to keep my books away from Prez. He liked to thumb through the pages and pick out the words he knew, his dirty hands smudging my pages. Miss Lafayette had given me a beautiful feather, dyed shocking pink, from an old hat, to use as a bookmark. I loved it. I always left it on my shelf to keep from losing it when I took a book out of the house.

"Page 58," I said to myself as I slipped the feather from between the pages and placed it carefully on the shelf.

Green's was nearly empty. Good, I thought. I wouldn't have to wait while white folks were helped before me.

"Hey, Francie," Vell said, coming out from the back and heading for the porch with a broom. He was Mr. Green's retarded nephew.

"Hey, Vell." I went directly to the counter where Scooter Pies were kept in their own display box. The box was empty. There was the jar of penny candy but no Scooter Pies. I checked every inch of the counter. The big jar of pickles—the jar of pickled eggs—no Scooter Pies. Naw, I thought. Couldn't be. Mr. Green sat behind the register, reading his paper and smoking his Old Gold. He flicked an ash into a jar lid.

"Mr. Green," I said politely. He looked up. "Don't you have any Scooter Pies?"

"You see any Scooter Pies, Francie?"

"No, sir."

He went back to his paper. "Then I don't have any. We're out."

I searched the counter again. It wasn't that I didn't believe him—I just had to be sure. Fingering my smooth nickel in my pocket, I walked to the porch and looked up the road toward town. I hadn't gotten permission to go there, though.

I knew Diller's Drugs would have Scooter Pies. A stack of them by the register. Sitting on my hill waiting on the local wouldn't be the same if I didn't have one to nibble on.

I skipped down the porch steps and headed for town. I tucked my book under my arm and put a little bounce in my step, determined to stay happy.

Diller's was empty enough, so I decided to look around a couple of minutes before I got my Scooter Pie. Mr. Diller was putting new magazines in the rack and taking out the old ones.

Eugene and Jimmy Early were sitting cross-legged on the floor, reading *Buck Rogers* comics.

"Excuse me," I said, trying to get around them, and when they ignored me and I had to squeeze past, one laughed. Then I felt something hit my back. It was a piece of wadded paper. I looked back at the boys. They held their comic books an inch from their noses, pretending innocence.

I went on my way, turning down the cosmetics aisle. Lined up on the shelves were creamy lotions and bath salts in the most wonderful colors. I sniffed at a closed bottle of cologne, too afraid to take the top off. I was careful to put it back exactly as I'd found it. There were pretty tortoiseshell combs and hairnets in all colors. I wished I could get one for Mama. She would like that.

I heard giggling behind me and turned to see Clarissa Montgomery, Verdie Johnson, and Holly Grace arriving at the lunch counter. I knew from overhearing Clarissa talking with her friends that they were giggling at Mr. Diller's son Joe. He'd just come home from the army and was working at the drugstore. Verdie and Clarissa reached for menus, but Holly slid off her stool and went over to the carousel that held all the copies of *Nancy Drew* and *Hardy Boys* and *Bobbsey Twins*. She gave it a twirl and withdrew one volume.

I made my way to the front for my Scooter Pie.

I took one from the display, set it carefully on the counter, then waited for Mr. Diller to finish writing things in what looked like a ledger. Finally, with a sigh, he ambled over to me.

"Eighty cents," Mr. Diller said.

"Pardon me?" I thought I hadn't heard right.

"Eighty cents," he repeated and tapped the counter with his nails.

I looked at my Scooter Pie. I wanted it—but not for

eighty cents. Maybe it was a price just for me. Maybe he aimed to keep colored out of his store. Whyn't he just put up a sign? I felt everyone watching me, hoping something was about to spice up their dull afternoon.

I thought about my words carefully, as I was accustomed to doing. "Sir, I was thinking Scooter Pies were a nickel." I avoided Mr. Diller's eyes.

"Yea, but that *Nancy Drew* you got tucked under your arm so's I can't see it . . ." He reached over and snatched it from under my arm and slapped it on the counter. "That there is seventy-five cents." He laid his meaty hand on top of it like a weight. There was no way I'd reach across that counter and try to remove that big hairy hand off my book.

I heard snickers coming from two directions. Holly and Verdie had turned on their stools and were grinning ear to ear. Clarissa's face showed no expression. She kept her head down and sipped on her soda, as if she didn't want to see what was happening.

I looked back at Eugene and Jimmy Early's stupid faces. "I didn't get that book from your store, Mr. Diller. I had it when I come in."

He squinted at it then. He removed his hand, picked the book up, and held it out in front of him, his eyes darting to his audience at the lunch counter. He turned the book this way and that.

"You trying to tell me you brought this book in with you?"

"Yes, sir. *The Secret of the Old Clock.* That's the truth."

"Why, it looks brand-new to me." He held it up to show the Early boys. "Don't it to you boys?"

"I think she stole that book," Jimmy Early piped up.

"She ain't had no book. I seen her come in empty-handed," Eugene said with scorn.

I met his eyes squarely. He blushed red with his lie. Jimmy kept his mouth shut, unwilling to get too bad a mark on his soul.

"He's lying on me, Mr. Diller."

"Is he, now?"

"Yes, sir."

Eugene, I guess believing his lie by now, stared back. "Mr. Diller, I seen her come in empty-handed. That's the truth." He inched toward me, but Mr. Diller put up his hand.

Holly had slid off her stool and come up for a closer gander, still sipping on her soda.

"Let me get this straight. You calling Eugene here a lie?" Mr. Diller asked.

I felt the trap he was laying for me. How could a colored call a white a lie?

"I'm saying I brought that book in here with me."

Mr. Diller came from around the counter and with a purposeful stride went right over to the carousel, counted the copies of *Nancy Drew*, and glanced back at me like I was cow manure.

"I just ten minutes ago put five new copies on that

carousel. I had five already, and that makes ten! Guess how many I got now?"

I said nothing, because in the middle of his count-ing—and he made quite a show of it—I knew there'd be one missing. He'd be short one, because Holly took it.

"Cat got your tongue?"

"No, sir."

"You want to guess, then?"

"No, sir." I looked directly at Holly. She gazed back at me level and confident.

"I got nine," he said, coming down hard on *nine*. He glanced around at the onlookers—from one to the other. "I got *nine*." He seemed to be speaking only to them, like he was expecting them to bear witness.

I turned to Eugene. "You saw me take a book off that carousel?"

"I sure did," he said quickly.

"Did you see me with your own eyes?"

He seemed not to know how to answer that. Then: "Yea, I did."

"What I do with it?"

"Put it under your arm."

"I didn't open it and read it?"

"No, you just hid it under your arm and went right up to the register," he said.

"Okay." I turned back to Mr. Diller. "If you open up that book to page 58 you'll probably see a bit of pink feather in the binding. I use a feather as a bookmark, but I left it at home cause I didn't want to lose it."

He studied my face, then the book in his hand. He flipped to page 58. The bit of pink feather stood out on the page for everyone to see. Mr. Diller blew on it and it floated to the floor.

"Where's that missing book, then?" Eugene said.

I answered, just as calm as you please—though I don't know what could have prompted me to say such a thing— "Whyn't you all ask Holly. I seen her steal lipstick right off that display not too long ago." I pointed to the cosmetics aisle. "Maybe if you searched her purse . . ." I could hardly get the words out, she came at me so fast, jaws clenched.

"How dare you, you little pickaninny," she sputtered, enraged. Her slap sent my head spinning. She went to hit me again, and I ducked in time, so that her hand glanced off the back of my head, the palm side of her fingers connecting in a way that was probably more painful for her than me. Still, I actually saw little exploding lights in front of my open eyes. The place on my cheek where her hand had made contact had a fierce ringing sting. If I hadn't been dark, I figured I'd be wearing her palm print for days. "You want to stand there, you little black pickaninny, and call me a thief?"

Her face was as red as mine would have been if it could show. She reared back to strike me again, but Mr. Diller caught her hand.

"That ain't necessary, Holly." Joe Diller, who'd been in the back room, came out now to stop the ruckus. "Let me take care of this." He turned to me. "You get on out of here, and don't let me see you set foot in Diller's Drugs again."

I looked at my book in Mr. Diller's hand. My eyes started to fill with tears, but I willed them away. That man knew in his heart that the book belonged to me. But he was gonna stand there and act like I'd done something wrong, just to save face. I didn't understand white folks sometimes. I'd be too scared to be so mean.

I stepped out into the bright sunshine, which now seemed to mock my earlier good feeling. I was innocent, but the world had decided to make me guilty. Why did I feel so guilty? I walked toward my hill.

The ground trembled beneath me. I could hear the distant rumble of the train. I gazed in its direction as it came at me. I stood and waved at it. I was going to be on that train one day. I was going to get out of Alabama, God willing.

Commencement

On Monday, after the flag salute, after roll was called, after Miss Lafayette wrote down the problem of the day on the board and we grabbed our slates to start working it, she turned around and said, "Put your slates down for a moment."

She gazed around the room and then settled on our eighth-grade section, though all had to listen.

In her soft voice she began. "Now, you know, the end of the school year is right around the corner. Commencement is at the end of the month. Y'all will be going on to Thomas Jefferson." She stopped and closed her eyes. "I so much want you to use every opportunity that comes your way. There are scholarships to our Negro colleges and any one of you can get one of those scholarships and go on to become a teacher, or a lawyer, or a doctor even." She stopped and searched our faces. Already I felt a little buzz of excitement in the pit of my stomach. Even though I wouldn't be going to Thomas Jefferson, and didn't know where I'd be going up in Chicago. I just loved the thought of *possibilities*. It could almost make me forget Diller's on Saturday and everything I'd experienced like it.

Just as we started our lunches, Miss Lafayette called Augustine over to her desk, and we all guessed why. Augustine's sad expression as she walked out of the classroom and went straight into the woods served as proof.

"She knows she's gonna be held back," Serena said.

"Yea, she knows," I added, feeling a strange new sympathy for Augustine.

She didn't come back the rest of the day. The next morning she sheepishly entered the classroom with welts all up and down the back of her legs. Miss Lafayette didn't scold her for skipping out on school, and I knew she wouldn't. She just gave her a sympathetic smile. One of Augustine's little brothers or sisters must have told their daddy on her. Whatever the case, the wind seemed to be out of her sails. She hardly gave me a glance. For the rest of the day, when I saw her hunched over an arithmetic problem or mouthing words during silent reading time, a knot formed in my throat. Poor Augustine Butler. God had blessed me with knowing I could fight my way out of my circumstances, if need be. But she didn't know that like I did. No wonder she was so mean.

"Jesse's over at the Early farm, helping with the planting," Prez said two days later when he got home from working after school at the Early farm.

I stopped in my tracks. "You seen him there?"

"This very day."

"Jesse?"

"I said he's there."

"What'd he say?"

"He didn't say nothin'."

"He didn't ask about me?"

"What for?"

I shrugged. I didn't know what for.

For the rest of the evening, I thought about Jesse working over at the Early farm.

"Turn," Mama said to me, a spray of pins clenched in her teeth. I turned. "Not that much." I turned a bit the other way. "Stop. Hold still."

I nearly held my breath. She was hemming the white organza and taking a long time. A free Saturday—Miss Beach was down in Mobile and had told us to skip this day, since she wouldn't be there to supervise. I'd arranged to take a lunch to Prez and Perry. I wanted to see Jesse. But for now I was stuck standing uncomfortably on a kitchen chair.

"I just don't know . . ." Mama muttered to herself.

"When can I get down, Mama?"

"Not till I'm done."

She wasn't done until a half hour more of pinning, frowning, taking it out. As soon as she was satisfied, I hopped down, changed back into my regular clothes, grabbed the lunch pails, and ran out the door.

When Prez and Perry saw me, they dropped their hoes and left them lying on the ground. Prez looked back over his shoulder to see what Mr. Early's boss man Bellamy was doing. He was walking to the woods.

I held up the buckets and they made their way over.

"Why'd you take so long? We done missed our dinner-time," Prez whined.

"Now we'll have to work and eat at the same time," Perry said, his mouth in a pout.

"Mama held me up, hemming my dress." I set the buckets down. "Where's Jesse?"

"Bellamy has him cutting some wood," Prez said. He pulled up a drooping overall strap.

Jesse just then came out of the woods, carrying a stack of logs. I had to resist the urge to shout his name. He dumped them on the edge of the field and went back.

"Jesse ain't got time for company," Perry said. "He been in trouble already. Bellamy pretendin' Jesse's not workin' fast enough for his size. He lookin' to cut his pay."

"That ain't fair."

"Betcha he gon' do it."

Jesse came out with another load, his head down. I waved anyway, but he went back into the woods without looking up.

Miss Lattimore mopped her forehead in the hot sun and began reading from her notes. Commencement day had finally arrived. We'd rehearsed the way we'd shake with one hand and take our diploma with the other, all week. Already sweat was running down my neck and making my dress stick to my back. But I didn't mind. Here I was, wearing Mama's earrings! I sat in the first row on our little makeshift stage: a thick piece of plywood on bricks. Serena, in her homemade dress of beige muslin, sat beside me. A mosquito landed on my arm and I swatted at it just in time.

Mama sat in the second row in the swept school yard, next to Aunt Lydia, who had suddenly seemed to blow up even bigger with child. Perry, in clean, pressed overalls, sat next to her, then Uncle June in his black going-to-meeting suit. Prez wore new dungarees Daddy had sent him and a white shirt. Perry and Prez would be going up to Benson with Uncle June later that evening for a week-long visit. Uncle June had been there working in a turpentine factory, planning to move his family after Auntie had her baby.

Auntie had told Mama she looked forward to the quiet

not having Perry underfoot would bring. I looked forward to the peace as well.

Miss Lattimore's voice lifted to reach the back rows. Prez squirmed and ran a finger around his collar to loosen it. Mama began to fan. Miss Lafayette looked over at me from the side of our stage and smiled. Finally, Miss Lattimore got to the last page of her notes and with another mop of her face sat down.

It was time for Miss Lafayette to give out the awards. Serena got the penmanship award. J. Dean got the attendance. I got the award for academic achievement. When Miss Lafayette handed me my certificate in my left hand and reached out to shake my right, I could have floated right up into the clouds. Mama beamed. She was proud. A smile was all I was going to get, but I didn't care. I knew what was in her heart and mind, and her smile was worth more than gold.

Sunday at the
Montgomerys'

"You're going to have to go to Mrs. Montgomery's, Francie, and start those cakes." Mama adjusted her hat in front of the little cracked mirror hanging over the basin stand where we washed our faces. "I'll be down the street at Mrs. Grace's, since I promised I'd get her floors waxed for her book-club meeting tonight."

My heart sank at the memory of Holly Grace and the sting of her slap. I hoped Mama wouldn't find out about it. Mama took her hat off and hit it against her thigh, then set it on her head again and twisted it a bit. She frowned at herself in the mirror. "When we get up to Chicago, I'm sure getting me a brand-new town hat—I'm so sick of this one."

She turned to me. "Okay, as soon as you get to Mrs.

Montgomery's, start on the icing. I want it nice and chilled by the time I get there. You can go on and make the cakes, so they can cool, too. You listening to me?"

"Yes, ma'am."

All the way to Mrs. Montgomery's I dreaded the thought of seeing that priss, Clarissa. Maybe she'd gone back home to Baltimore. I hoped.

"I'm on the phone," Mrs. Montgomery told me as she let me in the back door. She hurried out of the room, leaving me standing there in her cool, spotless kitchen. "Help yourself to the radio," she called.

I started setting out all the things I was going to need. I had two kinds of sheet cake to make, with three kinds of icing, and if Mama was really late, I'd have to cut the cakes into diamonds and hearts and squares like Mrs. Montgomery always wanted for her teas, with cherries on some and nuts on the others.

"Stay out of them nuts, Francie," Mama had warned. "I know how you like to nibble as you go."

I found the jar of pecans in the cupboard, opened it, and popped one in my mouth. Pausing at the window, I noticed someone fixing the busted bottom step on the backyard gazebo. I reached for another pecan. There was something familiar about that man, though I couldn't see his face. I screwed the lid back on the jar and set it down.

The morning sun was warm on my shoulders as I

headed across the lawn. I don't think he even heard me coming. I walked over to him and looked down. "Hey, Jesse."

He squinted up at me. "Hey, Francie."

"Been wondering what happened to you."

"Workin' here and there." He reached for a nail.

"You left and never came back."

"I couldn't. I had to help my daddy with the late plantin'."

"We had our commencement."

"I wouldn't have been part of no commencement, no-how." I saw the tiny hurt in his eyes.

"You were learning pretty fast."

He looked down at the hammer in his hand. "No mind."

I asked carefully, "You still reading?"

"Some." He fiddled with his hammer.

"You going to school, *ever* again?"

"Ain't got time for school. I gotta work. My daddy run off and it's just me."

That stopped me. I'd heard of people's daddies running off. My daddy wasn't around, but he sure hadn't run off.

"What about your brother and sister?"

"They with relatives."

I didn't know what to say.

"I better go, Jesse."

He nodded and I headed back to the house.

.   .   .

"You got everything you need," Mrs. Montgomery said, eyeing the table.

"I believe I do."

She pursed her mouth. "Okay, I'll leave you to your work."

As I worked, I listened to *Homemaker's Exchange* on the radio. A lady was discussing the three danger zones of a woman's face—under eye, nose, and throat—and the wonderful rejuvenating qualities of Dorothy Gray emollient.

I'd just started measuring out the flour for the first cake when a voice from behind me said, "Hi." I turned around and there was Clarissa Montgomery standing in the kitchen doorway, her hands behind her back.

"Hey," I answered, turning to face her. I waited.

"What are you doing?"

"Making cakes."

"You know how to make a cake?"

Was she funning me? Who couldn't make a cake? "Yea," I answered. She moved into the room and I stiffened, neither of us saying a word. Finally, she held something out to me.

I stared down at my book. My *Nancy Drew—The Secret of the Old Clock*. She laid it on the table. "I bought it—but it was always yours."

I felt my face grow hot, remembering the shame of being accused though innocent. I hadn't even confided that horrible incident to Serena. Now I found my voice and said, "I wouldn't steal no book. My teacher gave me that book."

"I believe you." She didn't explain why she didn't come to my defense, and I didn't care to ask her about it. I never expect a white to take up for me, anyway. I was mostly glad to get my book back.

"Thank you."

Clarissa sat down. I started in on my work, trying to ignore her.

"I was waiting to give that book to you."

"I appreciate it," I said again and continued working.

She watched in silence for a moment. "What's that?" she asked.

I looked at the object in my hand. "A sifter."

"What's it for?"

"For *sifting*."

"What's sifting?"

How could she not know about sifting? "Mixing stuff together and making them powdery," I said. I handed her the sifter. "Here. I'll let you do it some."

She took it and began to squeeze the handle. "You have to hit the side with the palm of your hand from time to time." She hit it and I sat down.

"That boy outside," I started. "How long has he been working for you all?"

"Jesse Pruitt? Awhile," Clarissa answered. "Aunt Myra hired him to get the gazebo ready for her outdoor brunch coming up." She switched hands.

"I used to tutor him," I said, not knowing why.

"Oh?" She looked toward the window. "In what?"

"I was teaching him to read."

"Didn't he know how to read?" She stopped and shook her hand. "My hand hurts."

"Not much." I picked up the sifter and took up where she left off.

Suddenly she looked over at the stove clock. "Oh no! I'm supposed to be dressed. Aunt Myra's going to kill me." She was gone in a flash.

The cakes were in the oven, the icing was in the refrigerator, and I was alone with my thoughts. I swished my hand in the warm sudsy water in the sink and began washing the dishes, so they wouldn't pile up.

Suddenly Clarissa was back and standing in the doorway, shyly holding another book. "Please give this to Jesse. Aunt Myra has all of Cousin Victor's books still up in his old room and I found this one." She held out the book. "He's been gone to college for two years now. Don't think he's still interested in books he read as a kid."

It was a copy of *Aesop's Fables*. Miss Lafayette had lent me that book last spring and I'd read every one of them fables. Jesse would like it. I dried my hands and took the book. I opened it. The stories were short, I was reminded, and simple.

"He can have it?"

"Why not? Auntie was getting ready to donate it to the library fund-raiser, anyway."

I looked out the window, imagining Jesse bent over his work, sweating in the hot sun.

"Thank you," I said. "I know he'll be happy to have it."

She left me alone then. I went back to work on the dirty dishes.

Mama didn't get there until after one. "Mrs. Grace had me do some *light* ironing," she said. "I couldn't refuse." She looked over at the iced cakes and sighed. She tied on an apron and went to the sink to wash her hands. She kind of moved me over with her hip and went to work, pulling crusts off bread for the finger sandwiches, chopping onion for the salmon mold. I watched, then wandered over to the window to check on Jesse, but I didn't see him. The step looked finished, except for needing paint. Jesse was probably in the work shed right then, mixing some.

Mama started to sing "Sweet By and By," which meant she was already lost in her work. I could disappear for a few minutes. I slipped out the door and across the yard, around to the shed. It was padlocked. I'd been all prepared to see his smile when I gave him the book, and now I was too late. He'd already gone. I felt like I was in a deep pit. The kind you drop down into from a place of high hopes.

"Mama, Clarissa Montgomery did something nice for me." We were walking home in the late afternoon.

"Mmm." Mama was tired and she didn't talk much

when she was tired. But I wasn't feeling tired at all. I wanted to tell Mama the whole story, but I couldn't. I'd get myself into trouble for going into town without permission and for tutoring Jesse instead of coming straight home every day. "That was good of her."

"That's what I was thinking."

Then Mama looked me over, narrowing her eyes. "Don't you be too fooled by that. I've seen 'em friendly one minute and turn just as fast the next. Depending on their mood."

I'd seen the same thing. Soon as you began counting on white folks to be one way, they'd remind you of your place. I didn't care. I had my book back.

The sun was sinking behind the trees and Mama and me were walking step-in-step and I was feeling satisfied. How was I going to get *Aesop's Fables* to Jesse? Mentally, I made a list right then of all the books I wanted him to read. Miss Lafayette would help me find a way to keep teaching him. I only had to convince Jesse. We'd take him on as our project. He was motherless and fatherless. He was without even his little brother and sister. I knew Miss Lafayette felt nearly as sorry for him as I did.

Janie Arrives

Janie's early arrival spiced things up a bit. We were expecting her at the end of the month, but in early June, long after everyone had been good and asleep, there was a banging on the door. I sat up with a start and Mama jumped out of bed and ran around, trying to find her robe. "Auntie's time must be here," she said.

Prez beat me to the door, letting in the night air and the hum of crickets. Perry stepped in.

"Mama's getting ready to have her baby," he said. "You gotta come now, Aunt Lil."

"Sure, baby." Mama looked over at Prez. "You and Perry run down and get Granny." Granny was the midwife. She delivered everybody's baby.

"Can I come, Mama?"

Mama looked me over, calculating if I was old enough. "For a little bit," she said, not wanting to promise more. Then we were out the door, rushing up the road toward Auntie's in the pitch-black night, with only a lantern lighting the way.

The gravelly crunch of our hurrying feet seemed loud in the still night. I had thrown on Daddy's big nightshirt over my gown. I ran after Mama, who was taking huge strides. All the way there, I thought: No Miss Beach, this day.

As we stepped into the house, we could hear groans coming from the back room. Auntie Lydia was rolling around on her bed in pain. I stopped short and stared.

"Stop, Lydia," Mama scolded. "You know rolling around makes it worse."

Auntie just raised her pitiful face to Mama and there were tears in her eyes. "I can't do this," she said.

"Don't be silly. You ain't got no choice in the matter." Mama sat down and helped her turn over on her side. "Breathe slow," she said, rubbing Auntie's back.

"I can't."

"Come on, now. You done it before."

"I can't," she cried, and the cry rose up, ending with a gasp. She shrieked as if the pain surprised her.

"That makes it worse, Lydia," Mama said. But Auntie just began to writhe again, moaning, her face covered in beads of sweat.

Mama found a rag and threw it to me. "Go outside and

wet this at the pump. Then wring it out and bring it back."

I hurried out onto the dark porch, pausing there a moment, blind in the moonless night. I had to feel for the pump. It took four or five good pumps before cool water began to flow. I held the rag under it for a while, wrung it, and turned to go inside.

At the same time, something rustled nearby. A small crackling sound that cut off sharp, not dying away as if it was all in innocence. I squinted in its direction. All was suddenly too still, a silence filled with guilt. I waited, listening. Nothing. A possum maybe, scrounging for food.

Quickly, I made my way to the bedroom with the wet rag. Mama took it and dabbed at Auntie's forehead. Auntie clutched at her hand. "How far apart are your pains, Lydia?" Mama asked her.

"Every time I catch my breath, seem like." The next wave hit her, in answer, and Auntie rolled away from Mama and began to groan miserably.

Mama checked the door, her brow frozen in a worried line. I knew she was hoping to see Granny there. "I sent Prez and Perry to get Granny. She should be here any minute." Mama loosened Auntie's grip and helped her lie back to rest in the space between pains.

Granny came through the door then. "Here I am," she said. Mama sighed. "I sent Prez and Perry on to your place, Lil." Wearing her faded kerchief, long loose dress, and apron with deep pockets that held all sorts of necessities, Granny hurried into the room, carrying a washbasin and a cloth bag. From it she pulled a sheet, a square of quilted material, and an ax. She handed the ax to me. "Here, missy. Slip this under the bed to cut the after-pains. Lift your hips, Lydia." Granny helped Auntie while positioning the quilted square under her. Then she clapped her hands once. "Help me tie the ends of this sheet"—she held out the sheet to me—"to the bedposts. This poor chile's gonna need something to pull on." After I had tied the ends in place, she asked me, "Are they good and tight?"

I pulled at them. "Yes, ma'am."

"Good. Go on, now. We ain't gonna need you around here. Go tend to your little brother and cousin."

Mama nodded in agreement. Granny was in charge now.

Disappointed, I left Auntie's and stepped out into the weak, milky light of early morning. More time had passed than I'd thought. A thin fog had settled across the fields and road, blurring every sharp edge. In the new light I scanned the overgrown shrubbery by the side of the house, where I'd heard the strange rustling. Nothing. I searched the road and the fields, looking in the direction of the woods. Nothing. It must have been a possum making that noise, like I thought.

I walked home slowly, wondering about childbirth and why it had to hurt so much. Prez and Perry were already asleep when I got back. I was glad to crawl into bed, but it felt empty without Mama next to me.

I fell into a deep sleep.

Mama stayed down to Auntie's and let Prez and Perry and me sleep in. It felt good to wake up in my own time—and with a happy thought of a brand-new baby. I hurried into my clothes, threw some water on my face, and rushed down the road to Auntie's. Mama met me at her door.

"Shhh. Auntie and the baby are asleep."

"What'd she have, Mama?"

"A girl." Mama smiled. "She named her Janie."

"Janie."

"You go on home and come down later. I want you to write to Uncle June and tell him the news and that everybody's fine. Then you'll need to stop by Mrs. Beach's and tell her why we ain't comin' today." Mama reached into her pocket. "Here." She put some money in my hand. "Go by Green's, too, and get me a pound of coffee. You can get yourself and Prez a Scooter Pie. I'ma be down here awhile."

I looked at the money. It was like a ticket to heaven. I had a free day.

Granny stopped by our house a little later, after Perry went back home, to tell us about the baby. Janie had come fast when she decided to make her appearance, hollering right away.

"I'ma need a cup of tea, Francie," she said to me. "Some black cohosh if you have any."

Later, she sat there sipping away while she filled me and Prez in on everything. She leaned back and squinted her eyes. "Let me tell you. That baby's going to be something, being born between the two lights like she was." Daybreak and sunrise, she meant.

Granny believed a host of superstitions. Mama hated superstition, so I had a little guilty thrill sitting there listening to her. "Betcha she ain't gonna have no problem making it to her second birthday. You watch."

I hoped Granny would get started telling me some stories about haints and ghosts. She slept with a fork under her pillow, and when the "witches rode her," she slept with a sifter under her bed, so they'd have to go through every hole before they could bother her. I wanted to hear the story about her waking up to see a haint sitting right on the foot of her bed watching her sleep. That gave me nightmares the first time she told me.

"That's pure ignorance," Mama always said when I asked her about such. "Just some old stuff from slavery times." I waited, but Granny wasn't up to her stories this morning. She was so tired she started to doze right there over her tea.

Scooter Pie . . .
at Last!

After Granny left, Prez went down to Perry's to see if he wanted to go fishing, and I wrote a short letter to Uncle June, put a stamp on it, and left it in our mailbox. Then I walked over to Miss Beach's, then to Green's to get Mama's coffee and me and Prez Scooter Pies. Mama always bought Chase & Sanborn. I put the can of coffee and the Scooter Pies on the counter, but no one was around, not even Vell. Finally, he came shuffling out of the storeroom, carrying a box of canned goods.

"Where's Mr. Green?" I asked.

"Out back, talkin' to some men."

"Well, I want to buy this coffee and these Scooter Pies." I jingled the money in my pocket and looked at my treat with longing. "Can you go get him?"

"Naw."

"Why?"

He looked down, embarrassed like he didn't know what to say. "He's back there with them other men and they're talking like they're mad."

"About what?"

"I ain't gonna go interruptin' them, neither."

"Well, can you take the money for these?"

I put the money on the counter. He looked at it. "I better not," he said.

"Come on, Vell. Mr. Green won't mind."

"He might get mad."

"Not if you get the right amount."

He pinched his lips together, thinking.

"He ain't gonna get mad, Vell." I pushed the money toward him. He stepped back like he was afraid of it. Then he slapped his hand down over it quick. I grabbed my coffee and Scooter Pies just as fast, before he could change his mind.

I dropped the coffee off, set Prez's Scooter Pie on our table, fetched my *Nancy Drew*, and made it to my hill with time to spare. The sun was scorching. In the direction the train would approach, all was still, like nothing moving was ever going to come that way. The tracks, shimmering a gleaming silver, wound out of sight where the woods met the gully running next to the tracks' incline. I pushed my bare feet into the cool grass and slowly tore the cellophane wrapper off my Scooter Pie. Once all of it was off, I held the pie up and turned it slowly, studying it with anticipation. I scraped a bit of the hard chocolate frosting on the edge of my teeth and let it melt on my tongue. I had my book once again and my pie—I was happy.

Just then I heard someone singing behind me, at the bottom of the hill—riverside. I could hear a banjo, too. I crept to the other side of the hill and lay flat on my stomach. There was a hobo camp down by the river—by the viaduct. I knew about hoboes. Sometimes one would come to the door for a handout, and if Mama thought he was harmless, she'd hand him out a sweet potato or some hot-water corn bread.

There were about six or seven of them, both black and white. Someone had built a lean-to out of an old packing crate, and two men were cooking some food over a fire right in front of it. The music was coming from the one sitting by the river's edge. He was singing along with his banjo and then he closed his mouth and let his fingers fly, making a lively tune, making himself feel good, I guess—for a time. I was blessed to have picked just this time to watch for my train. It was almost as good as a picture show, looking at them. One was mending a shirt, another tying his bedroll, and there was another sitting on a flat rock just staring out at the water. Probably thinking about what a miserable turn his life had taken.

The lonely little figure who'd been gazing out at the

river stood up. Something strange about that one, but I couldn't put my finger on it. He began to climb the hill in my direction. When he drew closer, I saw that he wasn't a *he* at all. He was a *she*—dressed in men's clothes. She had a sharp birdlike face, with sad, startled eyes. She was colored, caramel skin. Adjusting the man's cap, she turned and shaded her eyes in my direction. She clutched a lumpy satchel like she wasn't ever gonna let it go.

I sat up and let myself be seen. She jumped a little and stopped in her tracks.

"Hey, you," she called out. "What you doin'?" She climbed closer, grabbing at a bush with her free hand to pull herself up.

She came right up to me and squatted down. She set her bag in front of her and looked at it as if measuring whether it was safe so close to a stranger. She was skinnier than I'd thought, her arms wiry and ropy with veins. Her lean face, all sharp chin and cheekbones, showed that she was older, as well. As old as twenty-five, maybe.

"What's your name?" she asked.

"Francie."

"My name's Alberta—after my daddy."

"Alberta . . . There was a character named Alberta in a book I read once."

She studied my face to see if I was lying, it seemed. Then she shoved some stray hair back under her cap. "You read?" she said.

"Course."

Her mouth flicked down at the corners like Prez's when he was trying not to cry. But she recovered quickly and said, "I never got to go to school."

"Why?"

"Never mind."

She sat there silent for a while. I kept quiet too. Her eyes dropped to my Scooter Pie with the one bite out of it and I saw her swallow.

"You hungry?"

"Naw."

"Me neither. Here, take my Scooter Pie." Mama had told me you shouldn't ever let someone go hungry if you had something to share. It was sinful.

She shrugged and took it. She ate it quickly, almost choking on it. She licked the inside of the wrapper. "I came up here to look for some place—away from them mens—to go to the bathroom."

"Do they know you're a girl?"

"I don't know. I keep to myself and they don't bother me none." She licked her fingers.

"You traveling with them?"

"I'm traveling on my own. I'm going to New Orleans, then hopping a freight out to California."

"California?"

"It seem like the place to go. Land of opportunity . . ." Her voice drifted off and she had that getting-ready-to-cry look again.

"Where are your people? Where's your folks?"

"Here and there."

I stared at her in wonder. Imagine traveling alone like that. Just picking a place and deciding to go.

She stood up and looked around. "I'ma go behind them bushes over yonder. You tell me if anybody be comin'." She slipped and slid down a bit of incline to a row of thick brush. Then she disappeared behind it. I checked the camp at the base of the hill again, deciding her privacy was safe.

Suddenly it was coming. The local heading to Birmingham . . . The ground trembled beneath me and a faint curl of white smoke plumed above the trees beyond where the tracks curved out of sight. It was coming! I could hear its whistle and that sh-sh-sh sound of steel wheels on steel track.

Finally, a thunderous roar brought that big black round face of the engine into view. I hadn't stood up good before it was racing by and I was counting cars and squinting at the windows to see the people in them. I waved and waved until it was out of sight.

"What you doin'?" Alberta said from behind me.

"Waving to my train."

She stood there with me looking down the empty tracks. "I do like trains," she said. "Cause they're full of possibility."

That was just how I felt. They took you to places of *possibility.*

Alberta started down the hill. Halfway, she turned

around and waved. I waved back. Although I wanted to see my new cousin, I wasn't ready to go home yet. I felt sleepy. I lay down, right there, and using my arms for a pillow, closed my eyes for a nap.

I dreamed someone was watching me—from the woods. Someone was standing there at its edge, just out of reach of the open light, staring at me. I woke with a start, whipped my head around in all directions, then sat there for a while barely breathing, listening as hard as I could. For what, I don't know.

I sighed, got up, brushed off the backside of my cotton dress, and started down the small hill toward the road, my bare soles relishing the places where the grass was slick and cool. I was going to see a new baby girl.

Clarissa's Room

"Want to see my room?" Clarissa said on Tuesday.

I couldn't look at no room. I had work to do. I wiped the sweat off my forehead with my apron. I was down on my knees, rolling up the heavy area rug in the living room. Me and Mama had come to wax the floors. "I can't," I said. "I gotta roll up the rugs."

"I can help you."

"No you can't, neither."

"Why?"

She looked funny with her sunburned face peeling across the nose, her face round and plain as the moon. Her pink shirred sundress showed off red shoulders.

"Cause my mama wouldn't like it. Your aunt neither."

"Well, come up then, for just a bit."

I looked toward the dining room, where Mama was working. Maybe I could sneak up for just a little while.

"I was going to show you my books."

I looked toward the dining room again. I thought about them books.

"Okay," I said, standing quickly.

Clarissa led the way and I tiptoed up the stairs behind her, while she chattered on. "Aunt Myra decorated this room for me because she thought I needed cheering."

"Do you need cheering?" I asked. Such a thought was unknown to me. I couldn't remember anyone concerned with cheering me up.

"Not much anymore," Clarissa said, throwing open the door. Stepping aside, she allowed me to go in ahead of her. It was like something I'd never seen. One whole wall was nothing but bookshelves like a library. I'd never really been in a library, but when I moved to Chicago, I was going to find me one.

I cocked my head sideways and began to read the titles: some I'd read already, some I ain't never heard of. I'd read *Silas Marner* in seventh grade. And *David Copperfield* last winter.

Clarissa was pulling back her curtains over a window seat covered in the same fabric. "I picked this fabric myself. Aunt Myra and I got it in Mobile."

It *was* pretty. I liked cornflowers. What was it like to wake up in a room like this every morning, I wondered. I pictured myself sitting in the gazebo on a summer evening, with a glass of lemonade with shaved ice and a good book.

"Can you keep a secret?" she asked suddenly.

"I guess . . ." I said slowly.

"First"—she squinted at me—"how old are you?"

"Almost thirteen." I already knew Clarissa was fourteen.

"Skinny little thing like you? Is your growth stunted?"

"Mama said I take after her people, small and wiry."

Clarissa seemed to consider this. "What grade you in?"

"I just had my eighth-grade commencement."

"And you ain't even thirteen yet?"

"I'll be thirteen soon—at the end of summer."

"I guess you're old enough to keep a secret."

She went to the bed, bent down, and pulled out a notebook from underneath. She patted the bed beside her. I crossed the room and sat down.

Her eyes were bright as she searched my face. "I'm writing a book."

"How you doing that?" I asked. I'd never heard of a person writing a book before, though I guessed someone had to.

"I'm writing a little each day. It's going to take me a long time, because I want it to be longer than *War and Peace.*" She stopped. "You've heard of that book?"

"I know it's real long. I haven't read it yet, though."

"So far, it's my favorite book. In fact, I've decided to name my first girl Natasha because of it."

"Natasha . . ." It sounded like a sneeze.

"My book is going to be better than *War and Peace*," she said, like just uttering the words would make it so.

"My mama says it's not nice to brag."

"I'm not bragging if it's true."

"You can brag about things that are true."

Suddenly Mama was calling up the stairs. I looked at Clarissa and hurried out to the landing. She came after me. And before I could look down into Mama's angry face, Clarissa pushed a big, thick book in my hand. "I finished this a while ago. You can have it."

I took it because I didn't know what else to do. It was heavy in my hand. "Thanks," I murmured before I rushed down the stairs to Mama's scolding.

"Girl, if you don't get your behind down here . . . You think Mrs. Montgomery is paying for you to visit with her niece?" I set the book on the hall table. Mama didn't notice.

As I scooted by Mama to get back to the living room, she popped me on the head with her knuckle.

Just when I thought we were finished, after Clarissa had skipped out the door and down the walk with her friends, Mrs. Montgomery came into the kitchen, where Mama and I were putting away the cleaning supplies, and stood there wringing her hands and smiling.

"I hate to ask this, but can you two stay and polish the silver? I've got unexpected company coming tomorrow."

She smiled and shrugged. I looked at Mama but Mama didn't meet my eyes.

"Course, Mrs. Montgomery. I'd be happy to. But I gotta send Francie on home so she can look in on Lydia. She just delivered a short while ago and still needs help."

"And the upstairs linen. I forgot to ask you to change it," Mrs. Montgomery said, as if her mind had never left her own concern.

"I'll get right on it." Mama turned and left the room. I went over and picked up the book Clarissa gave me. It was *War and Peace*.

Daddy's Coming

I went right over to Auntie's and spent the rest of the day cleaning and washing for her, so she wouldn't have anything to do but take care of Janie. Mama came by to pick me up and we were walking down Three Notch together when we noticed the flag was up on our mailbox. "Run over to the box and get our mail," Mama said, climbing the porch steps heavily.

We hadn't heard from Daddy in weeks. I pulled the single letter out of the box and immediately checked the postmark. Chicago. I marched the letter to Mama.

She took it out of my hand and leaned it against the sugar bowl on the table. She still had to wash her face.

"That from Daddy?" Prez asked, coming over to look at it.

"Yea, and don't you touch it."

Mama finally sat down. She picked up the letter, opened it, and held it for a moment. Then she handed it to me to read. I read it aloud word for word, then raced to reread the part about him coming home. Sunday. Four days from tomorrow. Mama took it back and looked at it. "Where does it say that?"

I pointed to the words. We all sat almost holding our breath and finding it hard to believe. It'd been over a year since Daddy had left us. He was tired of being without his family. When Mama said, "I'ma go on down and see how Auntie's doin'," I knew she was just trying to get away to hide her excitement. "You two go on and heat up the supper. We gonna have a lot to do between now and Sunday."

I knew what I was going to do. I was going to go buy Daddy a present. A pipe, God willing, because he'd look handsome smoking a pipe. I saw one at Green's, so I wouldn't even have to go into town to get it. I wouldn't have to go to the place I'd been practically run out of.

I woke up with a buzz of planning in my head early the next morning. I went to the outhouse and met Prez on the way. He'd already made his trip.

"Perry was just here. He said he came to get Mama at dawn. Auntie's not feeling well. She's sick. Mama wants you down there as soon as you can get dressed."

He looked smug with this news and I could have popped him. With Mama distracted with caretaking

Auntie, I knew he and Perry would be off to the fishing hole.

"What about you?"

"Me and Perry are workin' over at the Early farm today."

Mama probably had plans to use up most of my morning, but if I hurried I could get down to Green's by early afternoon.

Auntie had visitors. Nola Grandy and her daughter, Violet, were there with a potato pie and a bouquet of black-eyed Susans. Granny was there, having come with a sugar tit for Baby Janie and some catnip tea. She brought a chicken feather tied in red flannel for Auntie to hang around the baby's neck, but Mama had stepped in—taking it from Granny and dropping it in her pocket.

"I ain't puttin' that nasty thing around Baby Janie's sweet little neck," Mama whispered to me when Granny wasn't looking.

Auntie looked tired and pale and I knew Mama was worried about her getting childbirth fever. Women died from it all the time. Mama had tightly braided Auntie's hair into two thick cornrows that pulled her face to show her cheekbones. She looked pretty, but it was a tired pretty. Janie nursed at her breast.

Two loud knocks sounded on the front door. Before anyone could say anything, Miss Mabel stepped into the room.

"I'm comin' to see that new baby," she announced. She walked straight across the room to stare down at Janie. "My, that's a fine baby." She scooped Janie out of Auntie's arms just as Auntie was settling her after burping her. Before Auntie could protest, she carried Janie to the window.

"Mabel . . ." Mama said, standing.

"Aw, I ain't gonna steal her." She squinted at Janie. "Bright like her daddy's people." She lifted a tiny hand to the light. "But the rims around her fingers are pretty dark. She's gonna be brown." Mama and Auntie exchanged uneasy looks. "She got a whole lotta hair, I see. It's gonna be kinky."

Mama rescued Janie out of Miss Mabel's arms and returned her to Auntie. "You don't know that, Mabel."

"Yea, sure I do. Ain't that right, Granny? You seen a bunch of babies and how they turn out." Granny didn't answer, just sat there, arms crossed.

Miss Mabel got herself a comfortable seat at the table with the other women. "You heard about that boy they after."

"Sure did," said Nola.

Mama glanced over at me and gave a little quick nod that was meant to convey something to them. They all turned to stare at me then. I'd found a little corner to sit in, hoping to just sit and catch some grownup conversation, which was always interesting. "Go on, Francie, and get to washing them diapers," Mama said now. "Auntie's gonna need some before you know it."

"They offerin' a reward," Miss Mabel said as I walked out into the blistering-hot morning.

A pile of wet diapers and sheets sat at my feet. One by one, I pulled them out of the basket, shook them, and pinned them to the line. It had taken all morning to wash them, and now the sun beat ferociously on my back and biting flies were making mad dashes at my arms. The baby was sleeping peacefully and the company had gone home to start their dinners.

I grabbed a sheet and sunk my hot face into its cool, clean scent, almost missing a bright flash of red skirting the edge of the woods. If I'd blinked, I would have missed it. I squinted, staring at the place until I wondered if I'd imagined it. Just trees and undergrowth stared back. I finished hanging up the laundry, put the basket up against the porch, and skipped out of there. I had money from my can under the bed. I smiled, thinking of Daddy's pleasure when I gave him his present.

Run, Jesse, Run

Some white farmers stood just inside the door at Green's, huddled in conversation. When I squeezed by, they stopped talking until I passed. I found the rack of pipes. I chose a shiny black one with a white mouthpiece. At the register, Mr. Green leaned on the counter, picking his teeth with a toothpick and watching the group by the door.

I put my pipe on the counter. Mrs. Early came up then with boxes of Musterole and Triscuit Shredded Wheat. She set her items on the counter and with the back of her hand moved my item to the side.

I looked up at her sagging chin and limp hair the color of mud. She started up some talk with Mr. Green about the hot humid weather. I waited. I whistled "Camptown

Races." My eyes drifted to the wall behind the register. Something pasted up there made me stop dead.

It was a black-and-white "wanted" picture of Jesse Pruitt. My lips parted and my heart pounded and my hands shook. My mouth went dry. I nearly spoke his name: *Jesse* . . .

The photograph was hazy, as if it had been part of a group picture once and someone had cut out his face and made it bigger. But the straight brow and hesitant eyes were unmistakable. Under it were the words:

WANTED: *A colored boy who goes by the name of Jesse Pruitt for the attempted murder of Mr. Rosco Bellamy, the foreman for Mr. Robert Early. Use precaution. He is considered armed and dangerous. Reward offered.*

"What you starin' at, Francie?" Mr. Green asked me.

I looked down, feeling like I'd been caught stealing candy.

"Nothin', Mr. Green."

"You seen that boy?" he asked.

"No, sir," I was able to answer honestly.

"Well, if you do, you let me know directly, you hear?"

I said nothing.

"You hear me?" he said louder.

Mrs. Early narrowed her eyes at me, making her face ugly and mean. "What's wrong with you?" she asked.

"Nothing, ma'am."

"Then what's taking you so long to answer Mr. Green, here?"

"Yes, sir," I said quietly. Mrs. Early gathered up her purchases, dropped her change in her pocketbook, and snapped it shut.

"You takin' up smokin', Francie?" Mr. Green laughed at his own joke.

"It's for my daddy. He's comin' home on Sunday." I paid and stepped out onto the sidewalk in time to see Mrs. Early making her way across the road, where her husband was starting the engine of their car, his straw hat pushed to the back of his head and his fringe of hair plastered to his red forehead in dark sweaty points. He slowly scratched the back of his neck. I felt a deep abiding fear, watching after them.

He gunned the motor then, and they took off in a cloud of red dust.

"I know that boy," Vell said suddenly from behind me.

I whirled around.

"I seen him."

"Where, Vell?"

"I was out looking for my dog in the woods out by your place and I seen him. And he run from me." He paused and his lower lip drooped. "He didn't have to run from me. I wasn't after him."

I believed Vell. "You gonna tell?"

"Naw. Cause I know him and I like him."

"Don't tell—please." I felt I had to say it. "It's real important that you don't tell nobody, Vell, please. Please."

He looked insulted. "I told you I wasn't," he said and walked back toward the store.

When I got home, I did a few chores, then I waited on the porch for Prez. Juniper slept at my feet, twitching through a dream. Prez wouldn't be getting back from the Early farm until the sun was nearly touching the trees.

Finally, I could see two little figures making their way up the road. I got up and began to pace. They seemed to be taking so long I ran to meet them.

"When was the last time you seen Jesse?" I said, starting right in.

Prez shrugged his thin little shoulders. I looked to Perry. "Jesse's in trouble," he said.

"When you seen him last?" I repeated.

"Before we went up to Benson visiting Uncle June," Prez said. "Now everybody after him, sayin' he tried to kill Mr. Bellamy." Prez looked like he was going to cry. "Are they gonna catch him, Francie?"

I didn't answer. I didn't want to think about it.

I turned away and walked slowly back up the road to our house. I had supper to get on.

Jesse filled my mind—so much so I couldn't get to sleep that night, and when morning came, I couldn't tell if I'd done more than doze. I'd talked Mama's ear off with my fears and suspicions that he was hiding out nearby, until she turned over and said, "Francie, there ain't nothin' we can do about that poor boy but pray and hope for the best. I think he's long gone anyway. Now go to sleep. We got tomorrow's work plus gettin' ready for your daddy's homecomin'."

I let out a last shuddery sigh and kept my lips pressed together against all that I was feeling.

Serving on a Budget

At breakfast the next day Mama reminded me that we had the Grace tea to serve. I hadn't wanted to think about it. Mama would be needing me all day, to wax and polish and get the finger foods together.

I stopped in the middle of dishing up Prez's oatmeal. He opened his mouth to say he wanted more, but I was protesting before he could get the words out.

"Mama, I don't want to serve at Mrs. Grace's."

"Get a move on, Francie," Mama said, busy at the mirror getting her hat on, and not listening. "You gonna have to grab a couple of biscuits cause you ain't got time for oatmeal. We gotta go."

"Mama, I don't want to serve at . . ."

Mama looked over at me. "What?"

I thought about telling her why but decided against it. "Nothing, Mama."

Holly Grace was nibbling on a cookie as she opened the back door. She looked me and Mama up and down, then turned and walked away. "Mother," she called out, "the colored girls are here."

I checked Mama to see what she thought about being called a girl, but she acted like she hadn't even heard it. She pushed open the screen door and stepped into the kitchen. I followed her. I'd helped Mama at the Graces' before and knew where things were kept. I started collecting what we'd need, while Mama went to get special instructions from Mrs. Grace. I could hear their voices in the dining room on the other side of the kitchen door.

Just then, Holly Grace came through the door and stood staring at me coldly. I pretended not to notice.

"Don't you be spreading lies about me."

I said nothing.

"Cause if you do—I'ma make sure you get in *big* trouble."

I didn't know how she'd do it, but I figured she had something in mind.

"You listening to me?" She tossed her hair. I measured the flour into a mixing bowl for monkey bread.

When Holly Grace reached the door, she gave me a look meant to seal her words on my mind, I was sure. I just went on with my work. But I was thinking: *thief, thief, thief.*

"Now, Lil," Mrs. Grace was saying to Mama over the platter of shrimp wheels me and Mama had just finished making. "I'm counting on you to make sure no one gets more than two of these shrimp wheels."

A whoop of laughter sounded from outside. Holly and her friends were sitting at the outdoor table under the big live oak playing cards. "Now, once you've determined a guest has had her two, Francie, you only go over to them with the tuna fingers." Mrs. Grace checked my face closely. "You understand that, Francie?"

"Yes'm." Mama frowned at me. "Yes, ma'am," I corrected myself. Mama didn't like me to sound slack around grownups.

Mrs. Grace sighed, patted her hair, and swished out.

"You need to take these out to them girls." Mama handed me a tray of glasses of iced tea. She noted my pout. "Go on, now. This is heavy."

Slowly, I took the tray from her. Mama stepped in front of me and held the door open. I made my way carefully down the back steps and the sloping lawn to where the girls sat fanning themselves and concentrating on their cards.

I placed a glass beside each of the four girls. Only one, Eva May Holland, murmured, "Thank you."

As I turned to go, Holly said, "Wait a minute. This needs more sugar." She held the glass out to me.

She was shielding her eyes at me and cocking her head. I took the glass, then made my way back up the slope to the kitchen. I put a teaspoon of sugar in her glass, stirred it, and tasted it. It tasted fine, but I dumped another teaspoon in it just in case.

Then I took it back to Holly, deposited it into her waiting hand, and started back to the kitchen. "Hold on, now," she called after me.

I looked back and caught her slyly smirking at one of her friends. "Not enough sugar still."

"Pardon me?"

"It's not sweet enough. Take it back."

"Did you give it a stir?" I'd put spoons and napkins on the table with the iced tea.

"What's that got to do with the price of rice in China?"

Betty Jo Parnell burst into giggles at this. I glanced over at her fat, sweating face.

"Well, the sugar has probably sunk to the bottom. If you stir every once in a while—"

"If you'd just put enough sugar in it in the first place, I wouldn't have to worry myself with stirrin' it all the time." Holly Grace held it out to me. I took it and went up the sloping lawn again. Once in the kitchen, I counted to twenty, then took it right back out to her.

She took a sip, smacked her lips, and announced, "Now, that's better." Then, with a whisk of the back of her hand, she waved me away.

I went back up the hill, grinning.

Mama put a tray of shrimp wheels in my hands as soon as I came into the kitchen, and directed me toward the dining-room door. "Remember, no more than two per customer. They pretty big, so ain't nobody gonna be able to take more than two. Most'll take just one, so you have to remember who took two and who took one when it's time to go around again." Mama opened the door for me and nodded her head toward the waiting guests. The tray was heavy, but Mama was needed in the kitchen to get the tuna fingers ready to go.

I advanced toward Mrs. Montgomery first—a familiar face.

"Thank you, Francie," she said, plucking a shrimp wheel off the tray, then resting it on a napkin on her palm.

I went to Betty Jo Parnell's mama next. She was deep in conversation, with her back to me. There wasn't room to get around her. Besides, the lady she was talking to, Miss Rivers, was bound to notice me. Then I could offer them both the tray.

"He knocked him out stone-cold, don't you know," Mrs. Parnell said.

"I hope they catch that boy soon."

"Oh, they will, I'm sure. My Henry is on it and they've enlisted some men up in Benson, too." She took a sip of punch. "Oh, he'll be caught. It's just a matter of when."

Miss Rivers noticed me then and gave Mrs. Parnell a little warning nod. She whirled around, all bright smiles,

and said, "Well, don't mind if I do." She took a napkin
and two shrimp wheels, stacking one on top of the other.

"I'ma need your mama a week from Saturday, Francie," Miss Rivers said. "Please tell her."

"Yes, ma'am." I made my way to the next cluster of
white ladies, with my ears tuned to talk of Jesse. By the
time I got back to the kitchen with the empty tray, there
was a pain in my heart. Mama had a sandwich ready for
me and I ate it standing at the kitchen counter, though
with every bite I kept thinking: through the door are the
wives of men who might think nothing of killing Jesse if
they so decided. I was serving them finger food and grinning and being polite. I hated this. I wished I was on my
train, leaving this place forever.

Mrs. Grace poked her head in the door just then to tell
me to take a tray of shrimp wheels down to Holly and her
guests.

With the heavy tray, I made my way down the slope.
Betty Jo Parnell, her plump body squeezed into her
shirred-bodiced sundress, took a slow sip of her tea.
Selma Sutter, the richest of the group—her father owned
Sutter Pulp Mill down near the river and half the land of
the county, it seemed—had her brow furrowed over her
cards. Eva May Holland, the beauty of the group, was
watching Selma closely, her lips holding back a tiny smile.

A plan formed in my mind and with every step it took
shape. With every step I grew excited by its perfection. It
would work, God willing, if I did it just right. Did it in

such a way that I could not be blamed. All I had to do was act stupid—act just the way they expected.

"Oh—Mama's shrimp wheels," said Holly Grace when I reached them. "Listen, you all, these are an absolute delight. Wait until you taste them."

"Two for each," I said, all sweetness and light.

Holly gave a little snort, looked over at Selma like I was some ninny, and said, "We'll certainly have as many as we like." She placed first one on her napkin, then another, then started to reach for a third. But I moved the tray to the side before she could do it. She looked up, her eyes blinking with astonishment. "What do you think you're doing?"

She had swam right to my bait and clamped down hard. "I'm doing what your mama told me to do and I gotta take my instructions from her." I started serving the other girls, which infuriated Holly.

"What in the world are you talking about?" She glanced first at Eva May Holland, then at Selma Sutter. Fat Betty Jo she didn't worry about. "We can have as many as we darn well please."

"I don't want to get in no trouble. I'ma have to tell your mama that you wouldn't listen that you all was to get only two each."

"That's ridiculous—you idiot—you must be making that up."

"No, ma'am. Your mama is serving on a budget and she said to make sure that nobody at this tea gets more than two shrimp wheels. She just can't afford it since your daddy messed up a lot of his money on a bad investment." I stopped short. I was saying too much and it might make her suspicious. She started to rise out of her chair. I backed up a little.

Holly caught her breath and a blush began from her neck to the top of her head until everything rising out of her bodice was bright crimson. Her lips moved but nothing came out. She checked her guests. They stared back. Betty Jo slowly set her own shrimp wheel down, looking slightly mortified.

"For Pete's sake, Betty Jo, you're not believing such foolishness, are you?" She shot a look to Selma, then to Eva May, who were also putting their shrimp wheels on their napkins and pushing them away. "I can't believe you all would pay any kind of attention to this simpleton."

Selma stared at her hands. Eva May looked off toward the house. An embarrassed silence filled the air. Finally Betty Jo, who wasn't as bright as the others and therefore too straightforward, said in a whining voice, "Well, Holly, let's face it—everybody knows your daddy did have that spell of financial—*bad luck*, so—"

"Shut your mouth, Betty Jo. That just ain't so."

"Actually, Holly," Eva May piped up, "I really think I'm allergic to seafood anyway. The last time I had lobster, I broke out in hives." Holly whipped around in her direction and just stared. Her eyes narrowed with disdain.

"You stupid idiot," she said, her attention back on me.

"Take them things back up to the house. We don't want any." Holly Grace sat down. When I hadn't moved, she blew up. "Take 'em!" she said. I returned each to the tray, noting all the while how each girl seemed embarrassed and uneasy. Holly picked up her cards and took a sip of tea, in an attempt to put the whole thing right out of her mind.

But as I made my way back up the hill to the kitchen, I knew she wouldn't be able to. Like I was gonna remember that slap, she'd remember this—always.

Waiting on Daddy

"What you doin'?" Prez asked, coming up behind where I sat on the porch steps in the twilight, staring at the woods. Juniper was darting in and out of the edge, chasing some poor creature for fun. Mama had washed my hair in castile soap. We all had our baths in the big tin tub in the kitchen. Now I sat on the steps, letting my hair dry in the last of the sun's heat. As it dried, it slowly grew into a woolly bush around my face. Mama was going to straighten it after she finished baking Daddy a welcome-home cake. Prez soon brought out a bowl and was licking a wooden spoon full of chocolate icing.

"Here," he said. "You get half."

I picked up the other spoon and licked some of the chocolate off. Prez drew a line with his finger down the center of the bowl. "This my side and this yours," he said, pointing to the two halves. I ran my finger along my side and came up with a nice helping of chocolate frosting.

"Whatcha doin' out here?" Prez asked.

"Watching the woods."

Prez had on his overalls and no shirt, his arms all coppery from the sun. He was what people called rhiny, with sandy hair bleached lighter at the temples. He had the same hazel eyes as Daddy's mama, who died when I was ten and Prez was seven.

"What for?" he said.

"Because Jesse Pruitt's in our woods."

"How you know that?"

"I feel it."

"Then they'll come down here and get him," he said, running his finger around the top of his side of the bowl, stopping exactly at the line he'd drawn.

"Right. And we gonna get some food to him and some money so he can get on. We gonna help him get away."

Later on, Mama took out the hot comb and heated it on the stove. She sat me in the kitchen chair.

"Bend your head and hold your ear," she said when she thought the comb had heated enough. I held my ear and my breath at the same time. When the heavy iron comb was that close to my face, I was afraid to breathe. It sizzled as Mama slid it through a place where the hair was still damp. "This part ain't dry enough," she said.

I stayed quiet. I wasn't going to chance a word. I'd been burned on the ear too many times from making an unexpected move. "Bend your head way down," she said. "Touch your chin to your chest."

I arched my head down as far as I could and felt the heat close in on the nape of my neck. The *kitchen*, Mama called it. The hardest part to straighten. Each time the heat moved away—the comb being placed on the fire again—I exhaled deeply and relaxed until Mama reached for it again to hold against the cloth to see if it was too hot, hot enough to leave brown teeth marks on the cloth. Then she waved it slowly through the air to cool it, her eyes far-off and patient. Thinking of Daddy coming tomorrow, I bet.

That night, in bed, I smelled vanilla. Mama must have put a couple of dabs behind her ears.

The morning was full of anticipation. While Mama pumped the water for boiling feathers off the chicken, she squinted up the road. As she stoked the fire in the stove, a noise outside made her move quickly to the porch to look out. She sewed a new patch on Prez's pants, and her eyes were constantly moving to the open door to look down Three Notch Road. Each time she turned from the door, or the window, or stepped back into the house, a flash of disturbance showed on her face that I didn't like.

I watched her closely and carried the weight of Mama's waiting as well as my own. Soon I couldn't stand it any longer. I had to get out. I'd go and pick flowers for the Sunday pitcher. Mama used it as a vase because it had a chip on its lip. "Get the watermelon out the creek," Mama called after me as I skipped down the steps. She had me put one in there the day before, so it could get cool.

Prez came along and we walked in silence. Then he piped up with, "What you think Daddy is gonna bring us from the road?"

"I don't know." I was busy wondering if maybe we should take this opportunity to search around for Jesse.

"You think some of them red swizzle sticks with the little monkeys on them?"

"I said I didn't know." He was quiet then, sulking. "Maybe some of them little soaps shaped like seashells like he brought us once," I said to make him feel better.

"I don't want no soap."

We closed in on the place where wildflowers grew in abundance. We picked black-eyed Susans and coneflowers and some goldenrod. Just as I was leading the way into the woods for some nice fern, Perry called out to us from the road. He had his fishing pole and a bucket of bait. Without even a word to me, Prez laid his flowers at his feet and started to trot off toward Perry.

"You better ask Mama about going fishing," I called after him. I was angry that he was running off and deserting me.

"Mama won't care."

"Ask her, then."

He was only a few minutes in the house. Then he was out again, running up the road with Perry, laughing and waving back at me. I could have slapped him. The only reason Mama was letting him go, I knew, was because she was wound up and she wouldn't have the quiet of mind she needed, having Prez underfoot asking when was Daddy coming.

Dry grass whipped at my ankles as I climbed down a small slope that led to some flowers I wanted that grew at the bottom. I forgot what they were called, but I loved how each green thistle shot out its furl of lavender like a bright promise.

The sun's rays warmed me and made me thirsty. My hair was still rolled in the rags from the night before. Now it was getting all sweated out. If I didn't get out of the sun, it wasn't going to be pretty as I'd planned for when Daddy got home. I looked at the stand of pine ahead. I'd go on and get that watermelon, and some fern, too, while I was at it.

Carefully, I laid my bouquet down and entered the woods, following the footpath that led to the creek. Soft pine needles felt good to my bare feet, as did the cool damp clay beneath that. I could hear Prez and Perry in the distance on their way to the pond. Light filtered through the changing pattern of leaves above, and an odd smoky scent in the air grew stronger as I neared the creek.

Someone had made a cooking fire, I thought. I slowed and stopped, scouring the dense growth around and ahead. I listened for some shift in the air, then continued toward the creek.

I ran into Prez and Perry sidetracked by the creek and all it had to offer. With pant legs rolled up, they shared the flattened top of a boulder. Prez was skipping pebbles over the water's surface. Perry was hunched forward, watching. They looked over at me.

"We came to get the watermelon, but someone ate it," Perry said.

"A hobo got it," Prez said stupidly.

"Or was it you two?" I asked.

"You just put it in the creek yesterday. How we have time to eat a whole watermelon?"

"What you think happened to it, Francie?" Perry whined.

I didn't bother to answer. I looked around. Everything seemed right. But there on the ground, hidden under the cover of damp leaves, were shiny black watermelon seeds and several wedges of rind. "Jesse Pruitt was here."

"Where!" both boys said at once.

I took a deep breath. "I smell his fire."

They followed suit, expanding their chests. Prez squinted. "I do smell it, too."

"And he didn't hit no Bellamy," I said.

"How you know?" Perry asked.

"Jesse wouldn't be that stupid."

"He supposedly knocked him out," Prez said, skipping a pebble.

"I don't believe it."

"I think they gonna get Jesse," Perry said.

"Shut up, fool," I said. He was making me mad.

"I'ma tell you said 'fool,' " Prez threatened.

"Tell. I don't care." I pretended to be looking up at the branches overhead. But I held my head back to keep the tears at bay. "Anyway, I think Jesse will get to the Southern Pacific and it will take him all the way to California.

"We'll take care of him until he can get away. I'll give him the money I got saved, and we'll bring him food." Both boys looked at me with admiration, which made me feel clever.

It was time to get back. Daddy might be there already and wondering where we were. I had to get the flowers in the Sunday pitcher and the rags out of my hair. I had to tell Mama that we didn't have no watermelon. "You all still going fishing?"

"Yea," Perry said quickly.

"Naw," Prez said, shaking his head. "I want to see if Daddy's come."

As soon as we stepped out of the woods and I looked across the open field to our house, I knew it held disappointment. Perry and Prez ran ahead. I hung back and slowly made my way over to where I'd laid down my bouquet. Mama would probably be on the porch by now, driven there by a waiting that no longer could be contained inside the house. She'd be shelling peas or shucking corn, but her eyes would be mostly on the road. And her thoughts would be full of preparing for disappointment. We'd been disappointed enough times before, so that by now I always held back some of my happiness at good news, and I knew Mama did, too.

Course she'd be preparing for him, too. Just in case.

It was early afternoon. There had been no set time for Daddy to arrive. Last summer, after he'd been gone for three months, he just showed up late one night. I'd woken up, hearing his voice coming from the kitchen. As soon as I was sure it was not part of a dream, I'd gotten out of bed and found him sitting at our table across from Mama, sipping a steaming cup of coffee. How wonderful my daddy looked. How wonderful it had been to crawl into his lap, to breathe his smell of tobacco, Old Spice, and sweat.

I had been glad that Prez, sound sleeper that he is, was still snoring away, unaware of anything but some silly dream he was probably having, and for a few minutes, while Mama had busied herself making Daddy a late supper and before she could think to shoo me back to bed, I had had Daddy all to myself.

Mama wasn't on the porch. She wasn't in the house. Maybe she was down to Auntie's, trying to get her mind off the waiting. Auntie was feeling stronger, we were happy to know. Daddy's homecoming cake sat in the middle of the kitchen table and the stove was crowded with good food. Corn bread and fried chicken, greens and corn on the cob. I was suddenly hungry. We seldom got such good food all at once.

I went over to the pantry, opened the door, and checked the jars of fruits and vegetables. I put a couple of jars of turnips into our croker sack, and a jar of beets. I snuck a jar of Mama's special pickled peaches and said a little prayer that she wouldn't notice.

"Take this and hide it by the outhouse," I said to Prez, handing him the sack. "We'll take it in the woods as soon as we can."

"I Gotta Help Him"

Mama didn't get back from Auntie's until just before dinnertime. Her face was as readable as a stone. She walked over to the pantry and got out a jar of pickled peaches and set it on the table.

"Wash up for dinner," she said. I let out the breath I'd been holding when Mama went into the pantry.

We ate in silence—neither Prez nor me having the nerve to ask any questions. We only spoke to ask that things be passed. I snuck a look at the cake now on the pantry counter, wanting some but afraid to ask. Besides, just because Daddy hadn't showed yet didn't mean that he wasn't going to show at all.

.   .   .

I awakened the next morning in a warm glow of expectation that lasted for a few seconds, until I remembered. Daddy had not come in the night. I felt his absence even before I slid out of bed for my trip to the outhouse. I met Prez on the way back. "Daddy didn't come," he said, his mouth sagging with disappointment. It always took Prez a while for things to sink in.

"No—he ain't coming, I guess."

"I should've gone fishing."

I had nothing to say to that.

I got dressed, put a couple of cold biscuits in my pocket, splashed some water on my face, and walked down to Auntie's. I climbed the steps to her door and heard Miss Mabel's voice coming from inside.

"Let me tell you, Lil and Lydia, I ain't never been so scared in my life."

I stood on the porch and listened.

"I was in the woods goin' after my headache leaf and I heard this noise that weren't no animal noise. Liked to scare me to death. I looked where that noise come from and there was that colored boy all hunched down in the bushes."

"What you do, Mabel?" Mama asked.

"I got outta there as fast as I could. That's what I did."

I peeked through the door.

"It won't be long before they come this way looking for him and it be best if we didn't give them folks no cause to get mad at us people on Three Notch," Miss Mabel said. I turned and tiptoed down the steps. I was going to the woods. I was going to find Jesse.

It was quiet. I got the jars Prez had hidden by the out-house and set them beside the creek, then sat on the boulder, listening. I aimed my face at the shaft of light cutting through the network of branches overhead and saw it alive with tiny white flies. Jesse was close. I could feel it.

I wanted to call out his name, but I didn't know who else might be nearby. I threw my head back and closed my eyes. This was fine for now. I'd brought food. That'd be a help to him. I'd bring money as well. And maybe I could ask Miss Lafayette for advice. I slipped off the boulder and sloshed back to the creek bank, squatting to con-ceal the jars in the brush, but not too hidden that Jesse wouldn't see them.

There was a rustle nearby, but all I saw was a rabbit making a break for it.

Tuesday, Miss Beach and Treasure watched me and Mama come up the hill. Not our usual day, but Miss Beach needed us. She picked up Treasure from her lap, set him aside, and went into the house. She met us in the kitchen with her list of special instructions. One boarder wanted special attention paid to his collars and cuffs; an-other wanted light starch in his shirts, another wanted heavy. I watched Mama record these requests in her head and wondered how she could remember them all.

As soon as Miss Beach finished with my instructions—I was to polish the parlor furniture that day as well—I slipped upstairs. Just as I was about to knock on Miss Lafayette's door, she opened it. Her face registered surprise.

"Francie," she said, putting her hand to her chest. "I didn't even know you were coming today. How's Lydia doing and that fine baby girl I heard she had?"

"She's better now."

"Good, Francie."

"My daddy was supposed to come Sunday, but he didn't show," I blurted out.

Miss Lafayette frowned. "You must be disappointed."

"He's done that before."

"But still . . ."

"Miss Lafayette," I said, jumping ahead. "They're after Jesse."

"I know." She'd just gotten back into town, yet she'd already heard.

"They said he hit ol' Bellamy out at the Early farm."

She'd been standing. Now she sat down on the edge of the bed. "I don't believe it," she said.

"I don't believe a word of it either, Miss Lafayette. But they're after him and I think he's hiding out in our woods."

She sighed, thinking.

"I left him some food. By the creek."

"Francie." She pulled me down beside her and looked at me closely. "Listen to me. What you're doing is dangerous. Do you know what they'd do to your family if it was discovered you were aiding that boy in any way—what would happen to the colored community around here?"

"I gotta help him."

"You might not be able to."

"I have to." Tears filled my eyes. I grabbed her laundry bag and hurried out.

Mama and I got the linen and things washed, wrung out, and hung up by noon. Then I went to work on the parlor. When I got around to the old piano, I raised the lid carefully and placed my fingers on the keys. I wondered if Daddy was really gonna get me piano lessons. I wondered if I could count on him.

Signs in the Woods

I hadn't planned to go to the woods. My feet just guided me there. As soon as the idea took hold, I almost danced across Miss Beach's wide lawn to the road. I had to check my jars.

As I neared our house on Three Notch in the late afternoon, I saw Prez standing in the middle of the road, looking at me. I could sense his excitement.

"You got something to tell me?" I said right off.

He just looked at me with his eyes big and his mouth pressed together as if he had to clamp it shut on his news until he thought about how he'd say it. He jumped a little in place, then fell into step with me.

"You can't come with me," I said. I didn't want him tagging along.

"I been to the creek and I seen the jars." It seemed to spill out against his will. He looked surprised as soon as the words were said. "Me and Perry went to the woods after our time at the Earlys'."

"What are they saying over there?"

"Nothing to us." He kicked at a rock in the road.

"You seen Bellamy?"

"Yea, and I can't tell that anything happened to him. He's just fine and as mean as ever."

"What'd you see in the woods, Prez?"

"They empty!" He stopped walking and gave me a big loony grin.

"Come on."

First we had to stop by the house. I went straight for the pantry to get something new to take to the woods. Prez stood behind me, watching me make my decision.

"I'm gonna give him another jar of Mama's pickled peaches."

"You better not. Mama'll miss 'em."

"She got ten jars," I said, not really convinced that that would keep her from missing two. I rearranged what was left behind the jars of last year's summer squash and tomatoes. "She might not remember how many jars she had in the first place." I looked at Prez to see if he believed me. He looked as doubtful as I felt.

"Mama counts 'em," he said.

"She'll think she counted wrong."

Prez didn't say anything else. His lower lip quivered. He could be such a scaredy-cat.

"Prez, you wanna give him something to eat, don't you? Remember how pitiful he was? Big ol' boy and he couldn't even read . . ."

"Mama can't read."

"Mama's grownup. Lots a grown folks can't read," I said, trying to decide if I should take *Aesop's Fables* off the little shelf over my bed and leave it with the food. No, I decided. It would get messed up or carried off by animals or something.

"Come on. We need to get back before Mama gets home."

The woods in late afternoon had a mysterious dream-like light that made me hurry ahead.

"Wait up," Prez whined.

I slowed and let him catch up. He took my hand. I let him do that, too. We reached the creek and I knelt down and searched the brush until my hand felt the first cool glass jar. I lifted it up and saw it really was empty! A second one, too! Hmmph! I thought. I replaced the jars with the one I'd brought, carefully placing the empty ones in my sack. I looked over at Prez and couldn't help the big smile sliding over my face. "I knew it." I threw my head back. "Jesse's in our woods!"

Mama was sliding jars around in the pantry and muttering softly to herself. I could hear her counting behind my back as I sat at the kitchen table reading *The Dream Keeper.* Prez was quietly drawing—off in his own world. I nudged him under the table with my foot and he looked up, frowning at me, until he realized I was lifting my chin to draw his attention behind me. His eyes widened. I could feel him thinking: Uh-oh.

Mama's muttering grew louder. "One, two, three, four . . . five . . . I know I had ten jars of pickled peaches, ten jars of turnip greens, and I'm missing some black-eyed peas, for sure."

I felt Mama look over at me. I kept on reading.

"You two been in them peaches?"

I didn't say anything.

"Did you hear what I asked you?"

"We didn't eat any, Mama," I said truthfully.

"What happened to 'em, then?"

"We borrowed them."

Mama came around the table and gazed down at me, ignoring Prez. "And the turnips and greens?"

"It's for that boy they're after. I *know* that boy, Mama. He was in my class for a while last year." I closed the book over my finger and watched her closely, trying to read her face for what she was going to do to me. She sat down heavily, looking more perplexed than angry. She shook her head slowly.

"Mama, I know he's there and I know he's hungry."

"Francie, what am I going to do with you? What you're doing is dangerous, pure and simple. You can't be leaving food off in the woods for those white men runnin' around huntin' for him to find. They gonna look right to us cause those are our woods. We all gonna get in trouble, if they find that food. You get them jars out of there as soon as mornin' comes. You hear me?"

I didn't argue.

"You understand me, Francie?"

"Yes, ma'am." And I wasn't lying. I did understand Mama's point.

"We'll pray that boy's long on his way and it's just some hobo's been eatin' my food."

"What about what Miss Mabel said. That she seen him."

"Miss Mabel just wants attention. And she'll say anything to get it."

Mama got up then, took her sweater off the hook by the door, and slipped it on. There was the smell of rain in the air. Past her through the open door I could see dark clouds had gathered and now hung low. I shivered, thinking of Jesse out there in the woods.

"I'm going down to sit with Auntie. Give her some company. You remember what I said, Francie."

"Yes, ma'am." I'd remember it, but I wasn't going to heed it—not yet.

Sheriff Barnes

The next morning, I woke up to a long list of chores.
Mama was already washed and dressed and twisting her
hair into a knot. She jabbed it with a hairpin and it
stayed. "I'm working for a friend of Mrs. Montgomery's
today. You need to stop by Mrs. Grandy's and pick some of
that headache leaf she got growin' by her house, for
Auntie. Perry came down to tell me that she's feeling
poorly again."

She walked over to me. "And needs her cow milked,
too." She pushed at my shoulder, thinking I'd gone back
to sleep.

"I'm awake, Mama."

"Auntie needs some things washed and ironed, and have
Prez and Perry round up some kindling. She's runnin' low."

It seemed that Mama was going to go on and on forever. I was happy to see her walk out the door. "But you
get them jars before you do anything," she said over her
shoulder. I rolled my eyes, sitting there among the rum-
pled sheets. The sun was hardly up.

Mama had left some cold biscuits on the table and a
saucer of maple syrup. I sat down, dropped a biscuit in my
shift pocket, and ran the edge of another through the
syrup. I nibbled on it as I padded barefoot down the hall
to wake Prez. He was curled up, his bedclothes kicked
onto the floor, his mouth gaping open, and his snore a
light whistle. I gave him a hard shove. He muttered
something and swatted at his face. I pushed him again.

"Stop that!"

"You gotta get up." I was feeling mean.

"Why?"

"Cause you gotta get over to Auntie's and milk her
cow." I didn't say: *Mama said.* If he thought so—it wasn't
my fault.

He pouted. "Why can't Perry do it?"

"You know he's been too scared to, since Millie kicked
him."

"It ain't fair."

"Too bad." I pushed at his shoulder. "Get up!"

Perry was playing Jack in the dirt by the porch as we
walked up. "Come on, Jack, get on the stick," he said,
peering down in a hole.

"You got one?" Prez asked.

"Got more than one. And there's another one down there."

"Here, let me try," Prez said, reaching for the thin jonquil branch that Perry was carefully twirling in the hole.

"Naw—you gotta wait until I'm good and finished." He turned the stick. "There," he said, pulling it out slowly with a jack bug clinging to the end. Perry raked it into a mason jar to join two others. He twisted the top, then held it up so he could examine his bugs more closely.

Prez and I leaned in for a better look. "I'm next," Prez said. He spit on a clump of dirt and mixed it with the twig until it was the right thickness to stick to the end. Carefully he lowered it into the hole and began to turn it gently. We held our breath. Then something far off disturbed the quiet air.

A car was approaching. I shielded my eyes and squinted at the distant cloud of red dust.

"It's the sheriff," Perry said. We watched as the big, shiny black roadster turned down Three Notch and crept toward us. Two men in wide-brimmed hats sat in the front.

We stood up. I nudged Prez's elbow with my own as the sheriff got out of his car and made his way over to us. He looked back at his deputy, whose eyes seemed to be boring into the woods with suspicion.

"How y'all doin' today?" His eyes slid over the boys, then settled on me.

"We're fine, Sheriff," I said.

"Whatcha all doin'?"

"Playin' Jack," Prez offered before I could answer.

I shot him a sideways glance. I didn't want him to start running his mouth. He could be careless.

"How you do that?"

"We catch 'em on this here twig," Prez said, unaware of my signal.

Sheriff Barnes wasn't paying any attention, however. He was looking toward the house.

"Where's your mama?" he said to Perry.

Perry looked back. "In the house."

"What about your daddy. He over at the Early farm?"

"No, sir. He work over in Benson."

Now the deputy—Withers was his name—stepped out of the car and was wiping the back of his neck with a red handkerchief oily with dirt and sweat. He pulled a piece of paper out of his back pocket and unfolded it carefully. It was that same picture of Jesse that I saw posted behind the register at Green's.

"You seen this boy?" Jesse Pruitt's sorrowful face stared back at us. I stiffened and felt Prez and Perry stiffen, too. The deputy must have picked up on it. "Don't you lie, now." He squinted down at us.

I didn't have to lie. "We ain't seen him," I said.

The deputy looked over at Sheriff Barnes, then back to me. "You know who he is?" he asked.

"He was in my class in the spring for a few weeks."

"You know him, then," Sheriff Barnes said, perking up.

"Yes, sir. He was in my class."

"But you ain't seen him."

"No, sir."

He let a few seconds go by. "You sure?"

"Yes, sir. I'm sure I ain't seen him," I said firmly and shook my head.

Withers kept his eyes on me as he folded up the paper and tucked it into his back pocket. He turned and started for the house, leaving Sheriff Barnes rubbing his chin and looking around.

As he passed Prez and Perry, he chucked them on the back of the head, playfully but hard—both boys winced from the pain.

Withers had to pound on the door for what seemed like a long time. Finally, Auntie cracked the door, holding her robe up at her neck. She leaned on the doorjamb. They showed her Jesse's picture. She took the paper out of the deputy's hand and held it in her trembling hand. She shook her head slowly from side to side, then handed the paper back. Sheriff Barnes, now on the porch, said something to her while Withers folded his precious paper, turned his head toward the steps, hocked, and spit.

They didn't drive toward town when they left. They made their way slowly up Three Notch and for some reason passed Miss Mabel's and stopped in front of our house. They banged on the door a few times, then tried the knob. Finding it unlocked, they went in.

"They going in our house," Prez said.

"I can see," I said.

Before long, Sheriff Barnes came out with a hunk of Daddy's cake in his hand, his mouth so full it was pushing out both cheeks.

"He's eatin' Daddy's cake," Prez said.

I went over to the deputy's glob of spit and kicked dirt over it.

They circled back to Miss Mabel's next. "She's gonna tell 'em something," I said. I could feel it.

"Maybe not," Prez said hopefully.

I snorted at this. "I should have listened to Mama and got those jars out first thing. But I wanted to give Jesse a chance to discover them." I kicked at the dirt. "I'm going as soon as they leave. Prez, you go milk Millie. Perry, go on down to Mrs. Grandy's and get your mama some headache leaf. Stay out of the woods and let me take care of things."

Miss Mabel was now on her porch. All three figures leaned over the railing, focusing on the woods. "I knew it," I said.

"You think they gonna get the bloodhounds?" Perry asked.

I looked over at him, not liking him much right then. "Just go do what I said." The sheriff drove off toward the Grandys'. After a short while, the men were back in their car, driving in the direction of the woods. We stood open-mouthed as they stopped their car, got out, and began walking. Soon the woods swallowed them up.

"Francie," Prez whimpered. "We gon' get it."

"Would you stop it? I gotta think."

"We gon' get in trouble. We gon' get the whole road in trouble," he insisted.

"Go do your work," I said.

I thought about Mama's jars, jars with Mama's labels on them. The ones I'd carefully written, myself: *From Lil's Kitchen*. I'd seen similar labels on Mrs. Montgomery's canned goods. "They're not going to find them," I said.

"How you know, Francie?"

"I got a feeling."

I did have a feeling. But that didn't keep me from looking for Sheriff Barnes and Withers to come out of the woods as I went about doing my work. It didn't keep my heart from sinking a little every time I looked up and saw that big black car still parked there.

Finally, just as I was setting up the washboard and tub to wash diapers, I spotted them getting into their car and driving off, empty-handed and alone.

With my heart in my mouth, I left the washboard in the tub, dried my hands, then went down the splintered steps and across the hot, dusty yard. I hurried along, but it didn't feel nearly fast enough.

The Bascombs

Once I was on the path to the creek, my fear grew. I decided to try a shortcut, pushing through brush and leaping over tree roots, until I heard something that stopped me as still as a frightened deer. Men's voices. Up ahead. Carefully, I made my way through the undergrowth.

White men. Two of them. I pictured Mama's mason jars lined up neatly by the creek, all nicely labeled. My breath came fast and shallow as I suffered through the thunderous sound of every rustling leaf.

Maybe I had imagined it. I waited, then continued, stepping even more cautiously. Those voices again. Not the sheriff and his deputy; other voices, steadily getting closer. With terror taking hold, I looked for a place to hide, all the time pushing down the urge to cry.

In back of me was brush dense enough to hide in. I ducked behind it and hunched down, struggling to hear what the voices were saying. To my horror, I heard Prez's voice—whimpering. Pleading. Then Perry's pleading in the same tone. I knew then what it meant to feel as if all your blood had drained away. I felt faint.

Gently, I parted small branches until I could see. Four figures came into view and I clamped my mouth with my hand. A small animal, perhaps, rustled the bushes and Billy Bascomb, gripping Prez by the arm, nearly lifted him off the ground, jerking his head around. Billy's eyes narrowed and bored into bushes near me. He slowly raised a palm.

"Wait . . ." he said, and Jack Bascomb, his arm wrapped around Perry's head, forcing him along that way, stopped.

"Thought I heard something."

"A rabbit . . ." Jack said. Billy searched in my direction—too high, thank God—but the moment hung there until he turned away.

I'd seen those two over the years. Billy's wife, Mary Jo, sometimes came by the Montgomerys' for a handout. Everybody knew Billy didn't hardly work if he could help it. They'd gotten to our woods and come upon Prez and Perry. I felt a stab of anger. I *told* those boys to stay out of the woods, and now their hardheadedness had gotten them square in this situation.

"Mister, honest—I didn't do nothing," Prez wailed.

"You comin' with us anyway. Now stop that blubbering. We takin' you to jail for aidin' and abettin'."

"We didn't do nothin'," Perry cried, sounding as if he was lying.

"Shut your mouth," Billy said through gritted teeth. "You was up to somethin' and we all know it."

For a frantic moment, I nearly rushed out from my hiding place, but fear paralyzed me. With repugnance, I saw Perry's whole shirtsleeve had been nearly ripped off. There was a bloody gash on his arm. I buried my face in my hands and squeezed my eyes tight, willing myself not to make a peep until their sounds faded away completely. *Perry was hurt.* I stood up, my legs nearly buckled, but I knew I had to get home.

I ran to the clearing and the bright afternoon light. There was Auntie's house. No cars, no sign of anything amiss. I looked down toward Mama's. Nothing to see but our small house vacant and alone.

"That you, Francie?"

"Yes, Auntie."

"Where you been?" She was struggling toward me, holding on to the wall. "Perry ain't come back yet with that headache leaf. Can you go down to Nola's and get me—"

"Auntie, they got Perry and Prez!" I blurted out before I could think about fixing up the words a little first.

"What?" Auntie continued toward me.

"Here, Auntie." I took hold of her and tried to direct her back to bed, but she pulled away and pushed past. She almost fell into the kitchen chair, then sat for a moment, catching her breath.

I paced a little, not wanting to tell her.

"Francie, what you sayin'? Out with it."

"I was in the woods . . ."

"What for?"

"I had to do something—real important."

Auntie just stared at me, perplexed.

"They were coming at me. And I had to hide behind some bushes . . ."

"Who? What are you talking about?"

"I seen the Bascomb brothers taking Perry and Prez out of the woods."

"Why would they be taking them *anywhere*?" Her face was full of confusion.

I hesitated.

"Francie, you tell me, now!" Janie woke up and began to cry from the bedroom. Auntie ignored her.

"We left some food for Jesse Pruitt. It was my idea, Auntie," I said quickly. "I had to wait until the sheriff come out of the woods and drove away before I could get the jars back—that's what I'd been leaving—some of Mama's canned goods. They'd see them with Mama's labels on them and we'd get in trouble." My words were coming out in a rush. "Perry and Prez were just supposed to do their work. I told them to stay out of the woods."

"Francie, I'm confused. What is it you're sayin' to me?"

I sat down. "They got the boys because they think they were helping Jesse. The Bascomb brothers."

Auntie's eyes grew big with horror. "They got those babies? Where they takin' them?"

"I don't know, Auntie," I lied.

Auntie ran her hands through her hair and searched the tabletop. "Where they takin' 'em!" she said, her voice rising with hysteria. Janie began to cry louder. Auntie's face drained of color. "Francie, you get them into this?"

I nodded weakly.

"You did somethin' that foolhardy?"

I nodded again.

"Where your brains, girl? Why not give them men an invitation to get mad at all the coloreds and burn us out just to make their point? Why not just put up a sign?"

I began to cry.

"Oh, my God . . . Where would they be takin' 'em?" she whispered into the air, as if that was all she could manage.

I looked away for a second. It was hard to bear the expression on her face. "They taking them to jail, Auntie," I finally admitted.

"To jail? Them two little boys? Was they hurt?" She asked this like she was afraid of the answer.

I thought of Perry's torn sleeve and his hurt arm, but I couldn't bring myself to relate this situation to Auntie.

"No'm," I said, feeling worse for it.

She slumped down in the chair and put her face in her hands. "How on earth am I going to get through this?"

I was crying in earnest now. I cried for myself because this was my fault, I cried for Perry and Prez and what they must be feeling, and for Mama, who was gonna be real scared and mad—when she found out.

Mama looked at me as if she hadn't heard. I'd been pacing the room for the last hour and looking out the window up the road for the first sign of her. Auntie had all that time sat immobile at the table, her face in her hands.

Mama now put her hand over her mouth, as if preventing herself from screaming out.

"We gotta do something. We gotta do something quick. Come on." She had taken off her town hat and set it on the table. And now, for some reason, she plucked it back up, plunked it on her head, and started for the door. Auntie went and picked up the now sleeping Janie and I followed her outside. But Mama stopped short at the bottom of the porch steps and said, "I don't know what we can do."

"Mama," I offered, "maybe Mr. Grandy can help us." Folks were always looking to Mr. Grandy for help. He was smart, he had his own land, and he was there with his family rather than off working the railroad or up in Benson working away from his family. And he seemed to always know what was happening behind the scenes.

Without a word, we made our way up the road toward the Grandys'.

I could tell by his face when he opened the door that Mr. Grandy didn't know what to think. We stood huddled there, crying on his front porch.

"Lil . . . Lydia? What's *wrong*?" Janie began to whimper as if on cue.

Mama spoke first. "O.C., Francie done a stupid thing and now they got our boys."

This didn't give Mr. Grandy any real information, but he motioned us inside. Mrs. Grandy and her daughter, Violet, who were sitting at the dinner table, stood up.

"Lil, what you talkin' about?" Mrs. Grandy said, coming forward and taking Mama by the shoulder. Violet helped Auntie into a chair, then Mama, for Mama seemed barely able to move at that point. She was stiff and her eyes were filled with fear. Violet went to get them both a drink of water. I started crying anew and Mama looked at me with disgust. The others took no notice of my personal misery. All were focused on Mama, and finally, too, Auntie with Janie in her arms.

"You tell us, now," Mr. Grandy said calmly. "You tell us what happened."

Mama took a deep breath and told them the story. When she finished, they turned their stunned faces to me. I looked down at my feet.

"Sheriff was out here this mornin'," Auntie added, "with a picture of that boy. Then Perry and Prez musta got it into their heads that they had to go get them jars of food out the woods before they were found—bringin' trouble on all us."

"I told them not to, Mama," I said, pleading my case. "I was going to take care of that myself. I knew I could do it without getting caught. But they didn't listen."

"That ain't the point, Francie!" Mama said, losing her temper, and I knew if we weren't at the Grandys' and Mama wasn't so scared, I would have gotten a back hand across the face for sure.

"So the sheriff caught 'em?" Mr. Grandy asked, putting Mama's tirade at me on hold.

"No," Mama said. "The Bascomb brothers were in the woods, probably hopin' they'd get a jump on them others the sheriff was roundin' up. They goin' after that reward money." Mama put her head down on her folded arms. "I pray they don't hurt our boys."

Auntie, who'd been looking back and forth between Mama and Mr. Grandy, watching how he was taking everything in, now said, "What can we do?"

Everyone turned to him then. Even Mrs. Grandy and Violet. He seemed to be searching for an answer, while a grave silence filled the room. We waited. Mama's eyes swept desperately back and forth between Mr. and Mrs. Grandy.

At once, the rumble of what sounded like a hundred cars began to approach from the distance. Mr. Grandy went quickly to the window and looked out.

"Kill that light," he said.

Violet leaned over the kerosene lamp and blew. The room instantly slipped into blackness.

Headlights played on the far wall. Before Mama could stop me, I was at the window peering out at the procession moving along the edge of the woods. I flinched at the flurry of yelps and snarls from Mr. Early's dogs. He was proud of those hounds. They were used to tracking. "They *love* it," Prez had heard him bragging one time. "You see, nigras got a particular smell and they can find one and zero right in."

"Where's my baby?" Mama said behind me. She was looking over my head, talking more to herself than to me.

"What's happening out there ain't got nothin' to do with those boys," Mrs. Grandy reassured Mama.

"That's right," Mr. Grandy agreed. "Them boys are probably in jail right now, gettin' a good scare."

Mama didn't answer. Her mind seemed to be on something else. Suddenly I felt her tense up. "Come on," she said all at once. "We gotta get home."

Before I knew it, we were on the small back trail, rushing toward home, with the Grandys watching us from their back porch, knowing there was no changing Mama's mind.

"They could've found their way home, somehow," Mama told us. "Could've learned their lesson and now they're wonderin' where we are."

With every step, our hopes grew. Until we came upon

the dark house with not one sign of life. Still, we hurried up the steps with the hope that perhaps the trucks and dogs and loud, drunken men had scared the boys into darkness and quiet.

Mama called out Prez's name as she went through the door. Silence was the dismal answer.

"They ain't here," Aunt Lydia said. Janie stirred in her arms as if she was disappointed, too. Mama wasn't afraid of light. She lit the kerosene lamp on the table, illuminating the sad room.

"What happened here?" she asked, pointing to the half-eaten cake sitting on the counter.

"Wasn't none of us, Mama. The sheriff and his deputy come by today while we were down to Auntie's. They had a picture of Jesse to show us. They came down here and went right in our house—and just took what they pleased."

Mama listened without a word. Then she took the cake platter over to a bag by the sink and, with a knife, raked what remained into it. Every last crumb.

"I'll make another," she said, but it was an empty promise. It had taken us long enough to save for the ingredients for the one she'd just thrown out.

"Maybe they got away and are hiding in the woods," Auntie said.

Mama shook her head solemnly. "They wouldn't be in no woods at night. They're both scared of their own shadows."

Auntie started to stand then, just to do something, but

Mama gently pulled her back down. "Please don't get yourself worked up . . ."

Auntie rocked and cried softly. "What are we going to do?" she said over and over.

"We just gonna wait."

But our wait was disturbed by snarls and the stubborn yelps of Mr. Early's excited hounds. Voices shouted back and forth for the next hour.

That hour passed slowly and painfully. Several times I wanted to put my head down on the table. I didn't dare. I was scared I'd fall asleep. Mama paced. Auntie wept with fear. From time to time, we joined hands and prayed.

I must have slept at some point. The next thing I knew, there was the sound of tires driving slowly around the side of our house. Mama and Auntie were at the window just as I was lifting my head from the table.

"What on earth . . ." Mama was saying.

"What on earth . . ." Auntie repeated. I squeezed in between them and looked out.

A shadowy figure sat behind the steering wheel of a long black car parked in our backyard. Something about it seemed odd. I squinted at the car window. Who *was* that? The door opened and Clarissa Montgomery got out and started for the door. Before she could knock, Mama had opened it and stood waiting, dumbfounded.

"Clarissa," I said.

"I've got your brother and cousin in my uncle's car," she said simply.

Mama rushed past her to the car. I stood there, peering into the night.

"Where are they?" I asked.

"In the back, on the floor. When I saw the men and heard the dogs, I cut my lights and told them to get down." Clarissa looked over her shoulder.

Mama yanked open the door and pulled out of the back seat, first Prez, then Perry. Frightened and huddled, they stumbled up the steps. Auntie grabbed Perry and drew him to her.

"Mama, I'm okay," he said, slipping out of her grasp.

She grabbed him and hauled him into the house. Prez, between Mama and Perry, followed meekly. Mama settled them both at the table, then just stared down at them for seconds. She and Auntie took in their bedraggled condition. Perry's shirt was torn, with only a scrap of sleeve hanging from the shoulder. His bare arm was wrapped in a dish towel. Blood showed through.

"My God . . ." Auntie cried, gently touching his arm. "What happened to you?" Perry began to cry, his attention back on his sorry state.

Prez was almost as bad. His hair was matted with leaves and his clothes were caked with dirt. He started sobbing, as if in sympathy.

Finally, between hiccups, Perry managed to get out, "I cut it trying to get away from one of them Bascomb brothers."

"What happened?" Mama asked.

"They was trying to haul us off to jail."

I looked over at Clarissa, who was surveying our front room. The sink pump, the kerosene lamp, Mama's Diller's Drugs calendar . . . She sat down without being asked and listened to Prez's story as if she'd never heard it before. Auntie interrupted him. "Girl, how'd you drive your uncle's car out here?"

"Prez told me a back way," Clarissa said.

"No. I mean, your uncle let you drive his car?" Auntie asked.

"I waited until I knew he was asleep. Then I rolled it down the driveway." Mama and Auntie studied her. "I saw the boys in the gazebo earlier in the evening, trying to hide, but I had to wait until everyone was asleep before I could go down and see what was going on."

She stopped and let that sink in.

"What were you doing in the Montgomerys' back-yard?" Mama asked Prez. Prez always got tongue-tied when frightened.

"We were hiding there."

"Prez—don't try my patience. I know you were hiding there. Why? How?"

"We were just trying to get the jars after the sheriff came out, so nobody'd get in trouble," Prez cried. "Those Bascomb boys were gonna take us to jail!"

I cut him off to try and salvage my good name. "And I told you to just do your work. You know I did."

He only glanced at me. He was more interested in getting his side over to Mama.

"We decided to hide them instead. We hid them good, too," he said to me in particular. "We dug a hole . . ."

"But they run across us," Perry added, "and they said we looked suspicious and stuff. Then they grabbed us. 'Cept I got away for a minute, but I fell and hurt my arm. I scraped it real bad—else Jack Bascomb wouldn'ta caught me." He looked over at Prez. "Billy Bascomb already caught Prez." He took a breath.

"Only cause I fell, too," Prez said.

Auntie, standing behind Perry, had been rubbing his shoulders. Now she leaned down and looked at him closely.

"They threw us in their car, Mama. They said they were taking us to jail for"—he hesitated—"aidin' and abettin' a fugitive."

"They said all that, huh." Mama was getting angry.

"We got away when they stopped at the filling station."

"I think they let us get away," Perry cut in.

"Did not!" Prez insisted.

"I saw 'em laughing at us when we ran."

"Then whyn't you just walk on back, then? Tell me that!" Prez demanded.

"Don't start arguing among yourselves now," Auntie said on her way out of the room to see about Janie, who'd awakened for her midnight feeding.

"We was over on Cypress and Prez said they was gonna come after us and put us in jail for sure."

"I didn't say no such thing."

"Tell the truth and shame the devil," Perry said.

"You was the one who was runnin'." Prez turned to Mama. "He was the one who started runnin' in those white folks' backyards—hidin' out and such."

"Wasn't—"

"Shut up, both of you," Mama said quietly. She sighed and got up, went into the other room, and came back with the brown bottle of peroxide and some strips of muslin. "Let me see that," she said to Perry.

He drew back.

Clarissa, who'd been sitting with her chin in her hand for some time, perked up.

"Naw, Auntie. It's gonna hurt."

"Boy, if you don't give me that arm—you are gonna be hurt for sure."

Perry submitted. He scrunched his face and squeezed his eyes shut in preparation for pain.

"Ow, ow, ow . . ."

"Shut up now, you big baby—you know I ain't hurtin' you." Quickly Mama washed the wound and wrapped it in clean muslin. She bit the end of the strip and ripped it down the middle. She tied the bandage closed.

Perry seemed to slump then. "I'm tired, Mama."

Mama turned to Clarissa. "I want to thank you for bringing our boys back to us. But you go on home. Your people've probably discovered you gone by now and are worried sick."

Clarissa got up slowly and, it seemed, reluctantly. She

moved to the door. Mama reached past her and opened it for her. "Be careful, now. I sure thank you," she said again.

Clarissa gave her a little nod and slipped out.

"They're packin' up," Mama said. She'd not left her post by the window since Clarissa left. Sure enough, we could hear the motors being revved up. I joined her and looked out. A train of headlights was snaking up the road, heading our way. A pickup filled with loud, whooping men gunned past. Something cracked against the side of the house and we heard it shatter. An empty beer bottle, I was sure. Mama and I ducked down and waited until the sound of every car and truck had died away.

Auntie had snuck home with Perry and Janie, and Prez lay sound asleep in his bed when Mama said, "Bet they didn't get him."

"How do you know?"

"I got a feelin'."

When the night settled into its quiet, we crawled into bed and fell immediately to sleep.

Jesse

I let Prez sleep through the morning while I worked on some pillow slips Mama was having me do for Auntie. I peeked in on him just to make sure he was still there. Before Mama had left for an emergency situation at the Montgomerys'—they were having unexpected overnight guests—she had told me not to let Prez out of my sight. I was excused from helping her.

A storm seemed promised for late morning. I had swept the yard and then sat on the porch, finishing the slips Mama had made me rip out and start over. "Your stitches are long and lazy. You know better than to get in a hurry," she said. I sat on the porch and watched rain clouds gathering.

I thought about Juniper. We hadn't seen him in days,

but I wasn't worried. He often went on excursions in the woods, only to emerge days later, hungry and full of ticks. I was really going to miss him when we moved, however. We couldn't take him with us, so Perry'd be getting him.

As if he'd read my mind, I spied Juniper running along the edge of the woods and disappearing back into it. I sewed a line of tiny stitches, then stopped to admire my handiwork. Mama was not going to make me rip these out, I thought. When I checked to see if I could glimpse Juniper again, I saw a man walking slowly across the field toward our house. Not Juniper.

It was Jesse, moving as if his legs weighed a ton, but not caring that he was crossing the open field in broad daylight. Reminding me of the first time I laid eyes on him last spring at school.

He walked right to the steps and stared at me without a word. I stood up and held the door open for him and he went inside. I took a good look at him then. His hair was caked with leaves and twigs and clumps of mud. His shirt was in tatters and he'd either lost his shoes or didn't have any on when he first went into hiding.

"I thought you were gone for good. How'd you hide from them dogs?"

"I ran along the creek for a good mile or two and came out when I thought I'd gone on long enough. Then I hid out till this morning."

"Why'd you try to beat up a white man?" I asked.

He sunk down into our kitchen chair.

"Can I have some water?" he asked. "And a little somethin' to eat?"

I got him the water and some of the corn bread left over from the day before. He pushed the corn bread into his mouth with filthy hands. Then, while his mouth was still full, he began to gulp down the water, his eyes nearly closed. I watched the rising and falling of his Adam's apple. He wiped his mouth with the back of his hand. "I'd like some more—if you don't mind."

I brought him another glass.

"Got any shoes I can have?"

I looked down at his muddy feet. "My daddy has some old shoes about your size." I went into the other room. "He's a Pullman porter now," I called out as I dug around in the bottom of the wardrobe. "They gave him a full uniform and new shoes. He wouldn't wear these now." I returned to the front room and set them down by his feet. He slipped his dirty feet easily into them and tied them up. I felt full of accomplishment, looking at his feet in my daddy's shoes.

"Did you do that fool thing that they said you did?" I asked, taking my seat across from him.

"I didn't go after nobody." His eyes were filled with anger. "I ain't crazy."

"Bellamy going around saying you did."

"Cause he lied on me." Jesse drank from his glass. "To save face."

I waited.

"The man ain't never paid me honestly. He was short-changing me. Laughing at me behind my back. I suspected as much, but I didn't know it until I heard one of the white workers laughing about how stupid I was. That I couldn't cipher. When I asked Bellamy about it, real polite like, he got mad and called me uppity. Told me there was plenty men who'd be glad to get my job."

Without warning, tears welled up in Jesse's eyes. He wiped them away. "I didn't say nothin' more about it— just did my job. But he fired me."

Silence settled between us while I tried to understand this different version. "I just took what was mine. One night I snuck in the Early henhouse to get a chicken. I figured that was what he owed me—at least. Bellamy come in before I could get away. I only run past him, s'all. And he fell. I got away. He must have decided he was gonna get me back. I heard what he sayin'—I assaulted him. But I didn't touch that man."

He stared at his hands. "I got me a plan," he said. "It's just gonna take me a few days to put it into motion, but . . ."

The sound of a car pulling up in front of the house interrupted him. It seemed to come out of nowhere. Jesse put a hand on my arm. I moved away and went quickly to the window in time to see the sheriff, alone, getting out of his car.

I was outside before he got to the steps to the front door. He'd parked in my freshly swept yard. Leisurely, and with deliberate slowness, I thought, he came over to stand at the bottom step. He flicked a cigarette butt in Mama's flower bed.

"Where's your brother?"

"Prez's asleep, sir."

"Go get him."

I backed into the house and did what I was told. The kitchen was deserted; Jesse had disappeared. I couldn't even imagine where. Mama had all her boxes of quilting scraps under Prez's bed. The pantry was too small. The bed me and Mama slept in stood so high nothing could be hidden under there. I dared not try to find him.

"Get up, Prez," I said, shaking him. "The sheriff wants you."

He sat up at once and started whimpering. "Why's he want me?"

"He didn't tell me." I looked around the room. "Hurry up."

Prez threw on his clothes and wiped the sleep out of his eyes. We hurried down our small hallway and came upon the sheriff standing in our kitchen. I stopped short. I looked around. Prez slipped his hands in the back pockets of his overalls and cast his eyes to the floor.

The sheriff stared down at him. "What were you doin' in the woods yesterday?"

"We was just going after kindling for my auntie, Sheriff," Prez said in a muffled voice.

"Speak up when I talk to you," the sheriff bellowed.

Prez looked up with fear, but he did not look in the man's eyes. "That's the only reason we was there, sir."

"Jack Bascomb said he caught you in the woods up to something."

"No, sir."

"You callin' him a lie?"

"No, sir," Prez said quickly. "I'm just saying we was only going after kindling."

"By the creek."

"We got to playing, sir." Prez's voice caught, and I knew he was struggling to hold back the tears.

"You weren't in them woods to help that boy we're after?"

"No, sir! I don't know nothin' about no boy." He broke down over his lie then. The sheriff looked down on him like he was disgusted and yet found Prez funny at the same time. He glanced over at me. "I need me some water."

Quickly, I moved to the pump and filled the glass Jesse had used and handed it to him. He downed the water and handed the glass back. He looked at me with a puzzled expression, as if it had just occurred to him to wonder about my part in this.

Suddenly my eye caught Daddy's boots, through the open door down the hall, in the dark space between the hem of the wardrobe curtain and the floor. My heart thumped in my chest. I turned toward the window, thinking my expression would surely give me away.

And if that didn't, my pounding heart. I felt my face flush hot.

"What's wrong?" the sheriff asked.

"I just remembered I ain't seen my dog for a while and I was hoping he didn't get torn up by one of those hounds last night."

The sheriff angled his head back and looked at me for a long time. Finally, he moved to the door. "I better not learn you two been up to something. You'll be sorry if I do." He shook his finger at us. A thick slab of a finger. "Don't let me find out you was lyin'."

As soon as he was gone, I brought my finger to my mouth and pointed down the hallway. Prez followed my pointing finger and his eyes grew big. He ran to the window and watched until the sheriff's car pulled away. "He's going down to Auntie's to talk to Perry."

Jesse stepped out of the wardrobe and wiped his sweating face. "I'ma go."

Prez's mouth dropped open. "We gonna get in trouble, Francie!" he cried.

"No, we ain't," I said. I turned to Jesse. "Where you going?"

He drew up, like he was trying to fill himself with confidence. "I'm gettin' down to New Orleans. I can catch a freight out to California from there."

For a second I envied him and wished I could hop a freight to California myself. Where the sun always shined and oranges grew on trees and the ocean was in your backyard. "Where you going to be until then?"

"Where I been."

"It ain't safe."

I took his hand and led him to the window. I pointed over to Miss Mabel's house. "You see that house down there? The woman who lives there saw you in the woods, and I know she told the sheriff and his deputy. I know it."

"She ain't gonna see me."

"Yes, she will. Because she's in the woods all the time, going after her plants. She'll know you're there. And if she thinks she can get something out of it, she'll tell."

He seemed to think about this.

"You can hide out in our shed."

"Uh-uh, Francie," Prez said. "We'll get in trouble."

I ignored him and just waited for Jesse's response.

"Okay," he said. He had no choice.

"The sheriff's gonna find out and he's gonna arrest us!" Prez whined.

"Be quiet, Prez. You don't know what you're talking about." I was moving around the room, gathering up what I thought he'd need. A blanket, some biscuits, a quart jar of water. I screwed the lid on tight and put everything in his arms. I got my own pillow off my bed and put it on top. Then I remembered the book Clarissa had given me for Jesse. I ran and got it.

"Here, take this, too. It's *Aesop's Fables*. The shed is out back. You can go get some sleep." We all looked out the window to see where the sheriff's car was. There was no sign of it. I opened the door and Jesse went through it, crossed my yard, and disappeared into the shed.

Then I watched that shed. While I rolled dough for biscuits and made hominy and gravy, I kept my eyes on it as much as possible. When Prez started for the door, I checked him. "Where you going?"

"Down to Perry's," he said, all innocent.

"No, you aren't. Mama told me you had to stay home."

"Down to Perry's is practically stayin' home."

"You just want to tell him about Jesse."

He didn't say anything and I knew I was right. He went out the front door and stood on the porch.

"Don't you leave the yard," I said.

Just like I thought, a storm hit by early evening. Before I could worry about Mama getting soaked on her walk home, I heard a car approaching. The same car from last night. Dr. Montgomery had driven Mama home. Now she jumped out of the car and ran for the porch, calling her thanks over her shoulder.

She came in shaking her hat and wiping her wet face. "Hi, Mama," I said and began to set the table. Prez came out from the back room. "Hi, Mama," he said sheepishly.

"Boy, don't you know I could hardly work today, thinkin' about last night?" She sat down heavily at the table and I brought her her dinner. Prez went to the win-

dow and looked toward the shed. Then he looked pointedly at me. Mama felt our tension.

"What's with you two?"

"Nothing," I said, and shot Prez a warning look.

"Get your rest tonight, Francie. We got Miss Rivers'
house in the morning."

Mentally, I sighed. I'd left Jesse alone all day, thinking
he was exhausted from the night before. But I'd sure
planned to sneak him some dinner before Mama got back
from the Montgomerys'. Because of the storm, she'd gotten back sooner than expected. Now she was going to
make sure I got into bed early.

"Prez," I said, pulling him aside as soon as I could,
"when Mama and I leave in the morning, you take Jesse
something to eat."

He stared at me stupidly. "Don't forget," I said.

"Get your clothes on, Francie. And hurry."

I sulked all the way there. When we had stepped out
into the yard, I snuck a quick peek at the shed. Oddly, I
felt no sense of Jesse. It was almost as if he wasn't there.

"Put that lip back in, missy. I ain't gonna have you
walk around all morning with a long face, spoilin' everybody's happiness."

Miss Rivers taught history at the white high school.
She had a regular maid, Burnette, who was all the time
putting on airs. She pointedly called herself a house-

keeper. And she thought she was a step up from us because she was lighter and Miss Rivers had taken her along to Paris a few summers back.

She'd come back practically thinking she was French. All the time slipping in little tidbits about "gay *Paree*" and how the men thought of her as exotic. "Exoteek," as she said it. "They didn't think I was no African, neither," she'd said to me and Mama on one of our workdays there at Miss Rivers'.

Burnette opened the back door and gave us the full inspection. We wouldn't have to serve at this function; we'd just be doing the cleaning and cooking. Which was fine with me because then I could eat a little bit as I prepared things. It was easier than serving. More relaxing. And Bea Mosely was there already and she always kept me and Mama in stitches.

We stepped through the door. Burnette shook her head. "Didn't you bring something to put on your hair?" Mama pulled off her hat and smoothed her hair.

"I'll just have to find you something. You can't prepare food with your hair uncovered. It's not sanitary." She sashayed out of the kitchen. Miss Bea looked back at me and Mama and we all burst into laughter. "I guess she told you," Miss Bea said.

"I guess she did," Mama agreed, not caring a whit.

"Well, I'm glad you're here, because she like to drive me out of my mind."

"So now she can drive us all out of our minds."

Burnette came back with two kerchiefs. Mama and I tied them on and then followed her to the dining room to get the rug up and outside. It was heavy and hard to get over the railing evenly. Once I had it up there, Mama handed me the broom and told me to sweep the porch.

As I neared the end of the back side of the porch, I heard Sheriff Barnes's voice coming from around the corner.

"I'ma get going, Miss Rivers."

"Well, tell Mrs. Barnes we're sure going to miss her today and we're sorry she's down with that cold."

"Will do. Just as soon as I get back from out Three Notch way."

I stopped sweeping the porch.

"What do you have to do out there?" Miss Rivers asked.

"I'm not satisfied with our search yet. I want to check some sheds and chicken coops and under a few corncribs . . . I got me a hunch."

"Well, I suppose you've got to go with a hunch. They usually pay off."

I heard the sheriff go down the steps, and peeked around the corner just as he was getting in his car. I watched him ease out of Miss Rivers' driveway, then I looked back at Mama—the edge of her scarf already a dark ring of sweat—and knew what I was going to do. I quickly swept around the corner of the porch and out of sight. Mama had glanced over at me once, but her mind seemed to be on something else. I leaned the broom against the porch railing, and went down the steps and across the front lawn toward the road. Then I ran.

I'd been walking for some time and still had a long way to go when a horn made me jump. I was afraid to turn around until I heard a friendly voice. "Where you going so fast, Francie?" It was Mr. Grandy. I hurried to the cab of the truck, gripping the windowsill.

"Something's come up and I need a ride back home, Mr. Grandy."

"Well, hop in."

"Thank you, sir."

Mr. Grandy began to speak the moment I settled in the seat. "You over your fright by now? Shame how those boys put you through all that—"

"Yes, Mr. Grandy," I said, cutting him off. "But that's done now."

We rode along in silence for a bit. Then I thought of something. "Mr. Grandy—that hobo camp—is it still down there by the viaduct?"

"I wouldn't know. I ain't been down that way."

I thought about Alberta and her cap pulled down to her eyebrows. Mr. Grandy was wearing the same kind of cap. I felt a small desire to dress up in men's clothes and be gone myself. I wouldn't need to take much, neither. Just some of my books. I was so tired of working and having no friends to be with and nothing ahead of me each day but drudgery . . . But it wasn't myself I was thinking of when I asked about the hoboes. That Alberta girl—she seemed to know all about hopping freights. She could help Jesse get to California.

Mr. Grandy pulled in front of my house and I jumped out. "Thank you, Mr. Grandy. I appreciate it." I waited until he drove away before I headed for the shed.

The door was ajar. That in itself signaled that something was amiss. I eased the door open and peered in. Mama's quilt, the pillow, the book, the jars of food—all of it was gone. There was no sign of hurry or struggle.

I looked around in the shed and the house for something that would give me a clue as to where Jesse'd gone. There was nothing, no footprints on the shed's dirt floor, none of the things I'd given him left behind. He'd just up and left. Went back to the woods, I guessed. I felt a mixture of relief and disappointment. What was I supposed to do now?

I'd have to make that long trek back to Miss Rivers' and face Mama's wrath. I had a good mind to go to my hill with a book. If I was going to get in trouble, I might as well really deserve it.

But I didn't. I turned up the road toward Ambrose Park. I'd barely gotten past Miss Mabel's when I heard her screen door slam and my name called.

"You missed all the excitement," she yelled.

I stopped in my tracks and went to stand in front of her porch steps.

"Pardon me, Miss Mabel?"

"Sheriff Barnes was out here." She smacked her lips a bit, taking her time. "Searching for that boy." She took a bite of biscuit. I waited while she gummed it. "Went over to your place and looked in your shed."

"They go in?" I asked, remembering the smooth floor.

"I know he looked in. Looked under the corncrib, too. Then he came on down here. Course he know better than to think I'd be hidin' anybody. I got some sense."

I wondered briefly if she knew that Jesse Pruitt had slept in our shed.

"Then he went on down to the Grandys'," Miss Mabel was saying.

I looked in that direction in search of the sheriff's car. It wasn't there.

"Oh, he ain't down there now. He was heading down to the Tallys' last I saw. Probably go on down to the Darnells' next. Where you off to?" she asked quickly before I could get away.

"Mama's cooking over at Miss Rivers' in Ambrose Park. I gotta go," I said. "She's waiting on me." That wasn't a lie. She was probably waiting on me, all right— with her belt.

I got back just as Mama was coming out to empty a bucket of sudsy water in the bushes. Mama glanced in my direction, then did a double take.

"Francie Weaver!" She caught me by the shoulder and dug her nails into my flesh through my shirtsleeve.

"Just where have you *been*! You had me worried sick—just leavin' the broom leanin' against the rail without even a by-your-leave." She pushed me along. "I ain't got time to beat your butt now, but know this—your behind is mine!"

Which meant I had to spend the rest of the afternoon working in the awful knowledge that I had a whipping ahead of me. No matter how fast and efficiently I did my job for the rest of the day, I was going to get what I was owed, so everything seemed pretty useless. Burnette gave me a whole tray of glasses back, saying I'd left lint in them and they weren't fit to return to the china cabinet.

I used my hip to open the door to the kitchen and eased into the room with the heavy tray. Bea Mosely, standing at the sink, looked over her shoulder and said, "What you bring those back for?"

"Burnette said I left lint on them."

Bea Mosely rolled her eyes at that. "Leave 'em. I'll take care of it. Your mama's waitin' on the porch for you anyhow."

I set the tray on the table and slowly slipped off my apron and kerchief.

"Bye, Miss Bea," I said before going out the door.

Mama was sitting on the back steps, staring off toward Miss Rivers' rose garden. "I always wanted me a rose garden," she said as she got up heavily. She seemed to have lost all her anger.

We started up Parker Street, then turned down Mrs. Montgomery's street. Clarissa was playing cards with some girls on her porch. One lifted her clinking glass of iced tea to her lips and took a long sip. The heat and stagnant air felt burdensome. Mama and I had a long, long walk ahead of us home to Three Notch. I would have waved to Clarissa—she'd been so nice to me, then Prez and Perry, too—but her back was to me.

Mama's voice dispelled the silence between us, surprising me. "I believe you must've had some good reason to run off that way. I'ma listen to what you have to say before I decide whether or not to give you your whippin'." She looked over at me, waiting.

"I had to go back home, Mama."

"I know you gonna tell me why . . ."

"I heard Sheriff Barnes telling Miss Rivers he was going out our way to search barns and corncribs and such."

"What's goin' on, Francie . . ."

"I hid Jesse in the shed."

Mama stopped in her tracks.

"I had to, Mama. He was so pitiful when he came out of the woods, and I was so glad to see that he wasn't hurt bad or dead."

Mama began walking again. "Where's he now?"

"I don't know, Mama. I think he left before the sheriff ever got there. I got a ride home with Mr. Grandy and there wasn't not one sign of Jesse in that shed. I think he's gone."

We walked on in silence.

"What if Daddy don't ever send for us, Mama?" I knew

I was breaking an unspoken rule, saying that, but I had to ask.

Mama was silent.

"He didn't come when he said he was," I persisted. "How we know he's gonna send for us just cause he said he would? We don't even have a date. People probably think we ain't going nowhere."

"Those are the jealous folks. They're like crawdads in a barrel. They don't want no one gettin' out if they can't."

"But, Mama—"

"You got to be patient," Mama said. "God willing, we're moving . . ."

"Mama, I think only you believe that."

"Just have faith."

I didn't get the promised whipping. When we reached home, she told me to go on in and start supper, she was just going to sit on the porch swing and rest a bit.

Prez hadn't gotten home yet from down to Auntie's. He was supposed to be helping Perry fix the chicken coop, but I knew they'd probably done just as much play as work, and they'd be in a rush to get something finished before the sun set.

I got the dinner going and came out to sit by Mama. She was staring at the mailbox. "I'm so sick of workin' on Sundays. Wish I had me one Sunday where I could go to church and pray to God. The white ladies make sure they go, before they have their teas and luncheons and book clubs . . ."

I studied Mama's wistful face. I almost never saw her looking like this. And talking about what she wished for. Mama just worked—all the time. Her harsh words probably came out of her weariness, mostly. Mama loved us, I knew. "Tonight, before we go to bed—we'll say a special prayer to God for Jesse."

"Mama."

"Yes, baby."

"God will hear us, no matter where we pray."

"That sure is true."

It was then that we noticed the flag up on the mailbox. How could we miss it? We both looked at it for a bit. "We got mail," Mama said. "Go see what we got."

Word from Daddy

I already knew it was from Daddy. I didn't feel good about it, for some reason. I carried it back to Mama and held it out. She must have felt it, too, because she was slow to take it out of my hand. I followed her to the house. We settled at the table. "Go on—read it," she said, sighing.

I opened it and a ten-dollar bill fell out. My throat grew tight over the first few sentences.

Dear Family:

I pray this letter finds you all in good health and doing well. I'm sorry I couldn't get word to you that I wasn't able to come like I planned. I sure hope this letter gets to you directly and you didn't go to too much trouble. I know it must have been a disappointment. Family, this letter brings bad news. We're going

*to have to put off your move up here for a little while longer. I
think I'll have the money to get you up here by spring . . .*

I stopped reading then. Spring was past. The spring he
was talking about was next *year*! *Next year!*

I threw the letter down on the table. Tears collected in
my eyes, then rolled down my cheeks. It wasn't fair . . .

"Finish reading, Francie," Mama said.

I finished all the pointless stuff about how hot and humid Chicago was, how hard Daddy's last run was. How
tired he was. And I thought, maybe he did have another
family. Mama held out her hand. I put the letter in it and
watched her fold it in half. She got up and put it on the
pantry shelf in the little box with all the others.

It had been so long since we'd seen him. I closed my
eyes, trying to picture his face. I couldn't see it.

Prez cried when he heard the news later. His wails
did the job for me and Mama both, I was certain. It
wasn't until I was in bed that I cried so hard I thought
I'd make myself sick. I could hear Mama out on the
porch. The slow creaking of the swing sounded sad and
hopeless.

Mama let me sleep. When I woke, my face felt swollen
from a night of determined crying. I sat up and tried to
remember when and how I'd finally fallen asleep. I had no
memory of Mama coming to bed. I had no memory of
Mama getting up to fix breakfast. Yet the table was laid

out with all our favorites when I dragged myself into the kitchen.

Mama sat at the table. "Are you hungry?"

I shrugged. I was hungry, having refused dinner the night before—but I didn't want to admit it. Prez came in then, his eyes red and watery.

"We ain't never movin' to be with Daddy," he said.

Mama just got up and dished grits onto our plates and scrambled eggs and biscuits with butter and peach preserves. I began to eat hungrily. I wasn't going to care. What was the point? I was too angry to worry about Jesse, who was probably long gone anyway, who knew where. Jesse hadn't cared enough to say thank you or even goodbye—so why should I care?

"Francie, what's taking you so long?" Mama stood at the bottom of Miss Beach's back stairs, calling up to me. I ignored her first call and hovered over Miss Lafayette's dresser some more. She'd gone into town, so I didn't even have her to talk to.

She had a new photograph up there and I was studying it. Her beau, I decided. Her fiancé. He was going to marry her and take her away from Noble. Judging from his clothes, I decided he was a man of means and intelligence and education. Just the kind of man I hoped to meet and marry one day, God willing. He wouldn't be no railroad man.

" 'Bout time," Miss Beach said to me nastily, her face

full of suspicion as she watched me drop the load of clothes and sheets onto the floor with the other loads. "What were you doing up there, anyway?"

"Nothing. Just getting the linens."

"Took you long enough. You better not have been up there messing in people's things."

Mama looked over. "Francie knows better not to mess with nothing that don't belong to her," she said, sending a tiny jolt of guilt through me.

Treasure trotted by and rubbed his back on Miss Beach's leg, signaling to be picked up. She brought his tiny face close to hers and began cooing at him almost nose to nose until her teakettle went off. Then she let him slip back to the floor. He leaped right into the middle of Mama's pile of whites, nestled down, and settled his head on his paws. He blinked up at me. Mama frowned at him.

"Scoot," she said and motioned with her hand.

He squinted at me again and yawned. "Go on, cat," Mama said and waved at him again. Miss Beach stood at the stove, slowly dunking her tea bag in her cup.

"Come on, now . . ." Mama said and pulled a little at the corner of the top sheet. It only budged him momentarily from his roosting post. He wiggled back to it stubbornly. I hated him more than ever. Miss Beach continued stirring her tea, with her back to us. Around and around went her spoon.

Real fast, I yanked the corner of the sheet, sending the

cat sailing across the kitchen, then landing with a wonderful thud. Miss Beach whirled her fat self around then, her eyes popping out at Treasure heaped in the corner of the kitchen. He unfurled, stood up, and gave himself a little shake.

"What did you do to my cat?" she gasped.

"Just moved him off the sheet," I said, pleased with myself.

"You did more than that." She watched him wobble to the table and scamper underneath it. "I see why he doesn't like you. You're mean and evil to him."

"He scratches me for no good reason."

"I don't believe that for a second. If you'll steal, you'll lie."

"When did I steal?"

"One half can of smoked salmon."

"I never stole no salmon."

"Last week I left a half can on the sideboard for my lunch. I left the room and when I came back it was finished off."

"It was probably that crazy cat of yours." I shook with anger. I looked over at Mama, but she was just sorting the clothes, keeping her eyes on her task.

"You think cause you're moving North that you can do whatever you please . . . Well, let me tell you, Miss Ann."

"That ain't true," I said back. "Cause we ain't even going." I said it quickly before thinking, then immediately wished I could pull those words out of the air and put them back in my mouth.

Miss Beach latched onto that, lifted an eyebrow—looked from me to Mama and back to me, her lips a quivering little smile. "Oh?"

Mama threw me a scathing look.

"What's this? No move to Chicago? I knew it! Course I didn't want to say anything, with you all being so sure and all." She sat down to get comfortable. Mama just continued to sort. "Well, what happened, Lil? What happened to the big move?"

Without looking up, Mama said, "It's been delayed."

"Delayed." Miss Beach brought her cup to her lips and blew. "I see. Well, I'm sure it's just as well. Things can be hard up there—for country folk. It ain't the paradise people say it is and . . ." She stopped then. Mama had gathered the first load and was heading out the door.

"Why'd you tell that woman we weren't going?" Mama growled at me as we were wringing the sheets.

"It just came out."

"Yea? Well, now it's going to be *out* all over town."

We got the laundry hung on the lines and settled on the porch steps to eat our lunch. Miss Beach opened the door behind us. "Since you aren't movin' anywhere, I'm gonna need you in a few weeks to get at my attic. It'll be a major job. Maybe take a week or two." When Mama didn't say anything, Miss Beach said, "You'll be able to do it, won't you?"

"I can't be sure, Miss Beach." I looked over at Mama, surprised. Mama didn't refuse work unless she was sick or someone in the family needed her. "I can tell you next week—about September."

About September. What did Mama mean by that.

I could tell Miss Beach was puzzled, too. She just sputtered. "Well, I must know by next week at the latest—I have to make my plans, you know."

"God willing, you'll know by next week."

Crawdads

A bleak week followed. I could hardly go through the motions: Tuesday, helping serve at Mrs. Montgomery's book club; Wednesday, serving at a tea at some friend of Mrs. Grace's; Thursday, cooking and doing laundry at Auntie's. She continued to feel better, but still needed help. Every once in a while, I'd look up from stirring the diapers over the open fire outside and check the woods and think: Where are you, Jesse—where are you? Not knowing was nearly unbearable. The thought of staying in Noble for almost another year was nearly as unbearable. God, please help me get through all of this, I prayed.

Mama must have seen the sad look on my face. Friday, she gave me a day off. I had to go to my hill. It had been days and days since I'd been there.

.   .   .

The hoboes were cooking one of their stews. Its strong aroma drifted up the hillside where I sat with my Scooter Pie in my lap still in its cellophane wrapper. I didn't want to eat it yet. Sometimes the moment just didn't seem right and I liked to wait.

I was watching Alberta, anyway, wondering if she'd ever had a chance to get away. She was squatting by the river, washing a shirt with a slow, tired rhythm. She wrung it, stood up, and with her dripping garment in one hand and her other hand shading her eyes, she looked right up at me and smiled brightly. There was a small shadow in her mouth like she'd lost a tooth. She began the climb up to me.

"Hey," she said when she reached me. It was a front tooth, but I wasn't going to ask her about it and embarrass her. "You lookin' for your train?"

"Yea . . . " I squinted up at her in her man's cap. "They don't know you're a girl yet?"

"I guess they do—but they don't pay no attention to me." She sunk down beside me.

I sat up straight and stared at her. "Weren't you going to California?"

"I didn't make it. I just come back from New Orleans."

"Why'd you come *back*?"

"Just wanted to."

I wondered what was the real reason.

"I was workin', too, in a big house there. I earned me some money."

"Alberta, don't you have family?" I had to ask her this, though I feared it would make her feel funny.

"I have family." Her eyes hardened. "I just didn't get along with my stepdaddy. He was mean—especially when he drank."

As casually as possible, I asked, "Have you seen a colored boy around here looking to get down to New Orleans?"

"The one they're after?" she answered, surprising me. She looked at me sharply. "Why?"

"I know him. And—I want to know if he's okay."

She waited so long I didn't think I was going to get an answer. "I ain't seen him," she finally said.

We sat quietly for a while. Someone down there had picked up a harmonica and music reached up to us. Alberta tapped her booted foot.

"I might go back down to New Orleans. It's nice."

"Ain't you ever going to settle down?"

"Yea. When I get good and ready." She stood up and brushed off the back of her trousers. "I gotta go," she said, then started back down the hill.

I watched her, thinking how easily she left people. No goodbye. Just like Jesse. He never did say goodbye, he always just left.

"Here, take this out to the back porch and sweep it good," Burnette said to me. It was Saturday. We were back at Miss Rivers' for heavy cleaning, and Burnette was being particularly bossy. I felt her watching me as I started for the door. "Wait a minute."

I looked back at her, waiting.

"I hear you ain't going up to Chicago after all—least not anytime soon . . ." A smile played on her lips. I went out the door without speaking and started my sweeping. Miss Rivers was visiting with her sister. They sat at a little table under her big live oak, having tea and cake. What was it like to wake up every morning and have only pleasantness to fill your day? To have not a speck of work to think of? To have money enough to hire people to take care of all that you didn't want no part of? I might as well have wondered what it was like living on Mars.

After sweeping, I went in, so Burnette could tell me what my next task would be. Mama had sent me to Miss Rivers' in her stead, saying she had things to do. Strange behavior for Mama. What could she have to do? Auntie was feeling better, Baby Janie was fine. I thought about her being born between the two lights, and almost slipped into ignorance and superstition before I could catch myself.

"Come on in here, Miss Ann," Burnette said, motioning to me from her comfortable seat at the table. She was sipping iced tea. She tinkled the ice cubes in her tall glass while she thought. "You need to get started on the parlor windows." She nodded at the supplies lined up on the counter. "You need to take your time and don't leave streaks."

"Yes, ma'am."

"Why'd your mama send you, anyway? Miss Rivers wanted your mama, not you."

"She said me coming was okay."

"But what's your mama got to do that so important that she couldn't come herself?"

"I don't know."

"Or you don't want to say." She took a sip of tea and cocked her head to the side. "Your mama better be careful to keep people like Miss Rivers happy. Looks like she's gonna be dependin' on her for *employment* for a little while longer."

"Yes, ma'am," I said, gathering the bucket and vinegar and newspapers. The sooner I got those windows done and got out of there, the better.

I took my time going home. I felt no rush. Why should I? What was there? I looked through the heat shimmering just above the road ahead of me. My throat closed and tears came to my eyes. Nothing ever went right for long. Just like Jesse. I remembered the sad sight of his back moving away from me as he made his way toward our shed. He'd stopped then to readjust his load and for a moment I'd considered calling out just to prolong the sight of him. You never knew if you'd never lay eyes on a person again.

When I last saw Daddy—last summer—and he kissed

me goodbye and said "See you soon," I believed I'd see him soon. Not that a whole year would go by. He might as well have stayed at the pulp mill. He might as well have never promised to go up there to Chicago and pave the way for our new life.

I heard my name called then. I was coming up to Miss Mabel's. She sat back in the shadow of her porch, almost hidden. I wanted to keep going, but home training made me turn into her yard. I put my hands behind my back.

"Hey, Miss Mabel. How are you this evening?"

"Mmmm," she started, thinking. And I knew she was going to list her ailments. "I've done better, but I don't like to complain." Her chair scraped. "Come on up here and visit awhile."

"I gotta get home and start supper."

There was a moment of dead silence in which I sensed her caginess.

"I hear you all ain't going up there to Chicago. I hope you don't mind me telling you—I never did think you were going anywhere. Men always telling their family they gonna go on ahead to get things situated, and they don't ever do nothin' but keep 'em hangin' around the mailbox looking for train tickets that ain't never gonna come." She licked her lips and nodded. "I seen it happen over and over."

All the time she was talking, I felt my heart hardening into stone and an awful pain starting in my head. Before I could stop myself, harsh words poured out of my mouth.

"You just the meanest ol' woman I ever knew—saying those awful things to me. I believe you love other folks' misery. I believe it makes you happy. What kind of God-fearing woman are you to be so happy about our disappointment . . ."

"Why, you hateful, hateful child," she called out to me as I walked toward our house. The words were hitting my back, but I didn't really feel anything. My legs felt heavy as lead. I didn't even know I was crying until the tears were tickling my chin. Not even when Daddy didn't show did I feel this bitterly disappointed.

I couldn't go in the house when I reached it. It was empty and sad. Prez had yet to come home from the Early farm and Mama had said she'd be gone all day. Maybe she was over at Auntie's by now. I sat on the top porch step and stared at our mailbox with its flag down. No mail. No nothing.

In the last light, I saw Mama coming up the road. She had on her town hat—which she wouldn't have worn to Auntie's—and a big box under her arm.

"Evenin', Francie," she said, climbing the steps and going past me into the house.

I barely got out an "Evenin', Mama." Something was up.

I followed close on her heels. She took off her hat and hung it on its hook, then looked around. "You ain't started supper."

"I was just getting to it."

"Prez ain't back yet?"

"He's been hanging out at Auntie's after he gets done at the Earlys'."

Mama sighed. She went over to our bed and slipped the big box under it. Before I could ask her what was in it, she said, "How was it at Miss Rivers'?"

"Burnette was happy to lord it over me. I think she even gave me some of her chores, since you weren't there to know what was her work and what was yours. I did the parlor windows, swept and washed the whole veranda. Waxed the parlor floor and the entire staircase and—"

"What's done is done," Mama said. "You weren't there to wax no floors, but I'll straighten that out with Miss Rivers before we move."

Move. What was Mama talking about? *Move.* She smoothed her skirt and went over to the basin to wash her face and hands.

"First thing Monday," she said, patting her face dry, "you're going to go down to Green's—you and Prez—and you're going to bring back as many boxes as you can carry. We got some packin' to do. We giving everything we're not taking to Chicago to Auntie."

Mama's Got Plans

I had not heard her right. I stared at her, waiting for further explanation. How could we just up and move before Daddy had arranged for us to come?

"But, Mama . . ."

"Don't ask me no questions—I'm not gonna be answering any." She got busy then, starting our supper. I kept quiet, happy Mama had the energy to get supper and relieve me.

"What you think she's gonna do, Francie?" Prez asked me. We were sitting on the porch, watching Juniper lap furiously at his bowl of water. He'd just gulped down a moth and it must have been hot like pepper. I laughed, then Prez joined in. Juniper looked so pitiful.

"She's not saying. And when Mama says she's not saying . . . she's *not* saying."

"How can we move up there when Daddy ain't sent for us?"

"She's got *something* in mind. I know it."

We were coming back with our boxes. I got Vell to give us all that we could carry. We could hardly see for what was stacked in our arms.

"Where you going with them boxes?" It was Miss Mabel. Was there a nosier woman on earth?

"We movin'!" Prez shouted out before I could jab him in the side.

"Movin'!" Miss Mabel got up off her chair then and came to the edge of the porch. She held on to her post and watched us, her mouth hanging open.

"Shut up," I hissed at Prez.

"We movin' to Chicago, *anyhow*!" Prez shouted.

"That's it. I'm telling on you. I'm telling Mama you telling the whole world our business."

He didn't care. He was revved up. I might as well have said nothing.

We stacked the boxes on our porch, then I looked down toward Auntie's house. "Stay out here," I ordered Prez. "And watch for Mama." I wanted to see what was in that box under the bed.

I pulled it out and stared down at it for a few seconds. I lifted off the top and saw something soft and blue peeking out from the tissue paper it was wrapped in. I peeled back one corner of the paper. Rhinestone buttons glittered in a row down a bodice front. The skirt was folded underneath. It was a new dress for Mama. I'd never known her to buy one.

Mama came home after dark. I was surprised to see her in her work dress. She hadn't said anything about working.

Still wearing her hat, she walked over to the table and placed a shiny fifty-cent piece in the middle of it. "That's yours, Francie."

"For what?"

"That extra work you did at Miss Rivers'. I collected what was owed."

I slipped it in my pocket. I wasn't going to buy any Scooter Pies with it, either. I was saving it for Chicago. No telling what I'd want to buy up there.

"Now come here, you two. I got something to show you."

She led us over to the bed and reached down and pulled out her box. She set it on the bed, carefully lifted off the lid, and pushed back the paper. "It's the dress I intend to wear up to Chicago. The one your daddy's gonna see me in first off." She held it up to her chin and smiled happily. I'd never seen her smile like that before. Prez and I looked at each other.

"It's real pretty, Mama," Prez said first.

"It's real pretty," I agreed.

She went over to the wardrobe and opened the curtain. She fished around on the bottom of it and pulled out two more boxes. One she handed to Prez—then one to me. I almost stopped breathing. Prez dropped to his knees and ripped off the top. "New pants and shirt!" he cried. "Can I try 'em on?"

"Not till you have a bath."

I sat down on the edge of the bed to open my box. My heart pounded, my eyes welled up. I felt such happiness and fear all mixed up. We *were* going . . . but how? I pulled a yellow eyelet dress out. It was so beautiful. My favorite color.

"You like it?" Mama asked.

I could only nod.

"Good. We're leaving on Saturday."

"How, Mama?"

"By train."

"Daddy sent the tickets?"

"No. I went and bought them myself—with money I been settin' aside." She pulled herself up straighter. "Now don't ask me any more. Just do as I tell you."

Everything was a whirl thereafter. Prez was down to Perry's night and day; they suddenly were joined at the hip, realizing they would soon be parted. And Mama was down there, too, helping Auntie get ready for her move up to Benson.

Mama had sent a telegram to Daddy to tell him we were coming and he just better get ready for us. And he better meet our train. Pulling in Sunday morning.

Lots of stuff we were giving to Auntie, who was going to have a larger household up in Benson. The furniture was staying because it wasn't ours. It all belonged to the white family we rented from. But that didn't matter none. When we got to Chicago and finally moved into our own house, we'd be buying all new.

Moving Day

We'd been in a rush all morning, scared we were going to miss the local for sure—and our connection in Birmingham. I'd never seen Mama in such a state. She paced. She stammered out instructions. "Prez, you need to get Juniper over to Auntie's before Uncle June gets here. Francie, don't take them rags out of your hair until the last minute. Prez, don't walk so hard—you gonna make Daddy's cake fall."

She'd fried a chicken for the trip, then worried that the grease smell had gotten into her hair. She'd yelled at me for having my nose stuck in my book of poetry by Langston Hughes, even though there wasn't really anything that she had for me to do. We'd done it all. She'd made up her face twice, but the sweat was still pouring off in little streams down her powdered cheeks. Finally, she decided to just scrub her face, dab on a little lipstick, and let it be.

In the excitement of the past few days, Mama had been eating like a bird and had lost weight from her nerves. Now, at last, she sunk down at the kitchen table and sipped coffee, her eyes glassy with tears.

I went over to her and hugged her. "It's gonna be okay, Mama." The few suitcases and parcels we were taking were out on the porch, waiting on Uncle June. Mr. Griffin, our landlord, had already come by to look at the house and determine that we weren't leaving it any worse for wear and we weren't hauling off any of the few sticks of furniture that had come with the house. He had stomped off grim and in a bad mood. He hated to lose a tenant who'd always had that rent money in his hand on the first of every month, rain or shine.

Mama got up to pace some more. "Uncle June's gonna make us late for our train for sure if he don't get here soon," she said, staring out the window, then turning her worried face back to me. I felt calm, though I could hardly imagine not spending any more of my life within these walls. I felt guilty that I wasn't sadder than I was.

Prez, in his excitement about Chicago, was only sad about leaving Perry and Juniper. He'd finally gone to take poor Juniper down to Auntie's, and then he'd be coming back with Uncle June.

I got up and moved to our bed to sit on it for the last

time. My throat got tight and my eyes welled. While I sat on the bare mattress, I dropped my face in my hands and cried.

We were leaving *everything*. And what were we going to do? What if we couldn't get used to such a big place? What if Chicago coloreds laughed at us? We wouldn't talk like them or dress like them.

And Daddy had already told me I'd be going to school with white children. Sitting right next to them in the classroom—learning what they were learning. I couldn't imagine such a thing.

I ran my hand over the mattress. My last time sitting on this bed . . . my last time.

A loud horn sounded. "Uncle June's here!" Mama called out from the porch, where she'd gone to check on our belongings. "Hurry, Francie—we gotta get going. Help me get our things out to the car."

Mama was bending over the bulging bags and cases on the porch and rearranging stuff. The cake and fried chicken and potato salad and pickled peaches and jars of lemonade were boxed and tied with string. I'd left out the *War and Peace* Clarissa gave me. I planned to start it on the train. I should have said goodbye to her. And to Serena and Miss Lafayette, too. I was as bad as Jesse and Alberta—just moving on like I was. Just pointing all my attention on what was ahead and almost forgetting about who and what I was leaving behind. Even the jars still in the woods. We'd be long gone by the time anyone found them.

I had on my new yellow dress. I'd pulled the rags out of my hair, and greasy curls that I wasn't to comb out until just before we reached the station covered my head. Prez and Perry leaned their heads out of the car. Auntie, with Janie on her lap, scooted close to Uncle June to make room for Mama. Prez jumped out and shouted, "Come on and get in, slowpoke."

Uncle June, in clean overalls and a big-brimmed hat, got out and opened the trunk for our belongings. "Hey, Miss Priss." He smiled down at me. "You ready to leave Noble?"

"I think so," I said, my voice sounding uncertain to my own ears.

"We sure gonna miss you," he said.

I smiled and got into the car, pushing Prez on the shoulder so he would give me more room. The car started up with a noise that was like a loud horse's snort. We moved out over the bumpy road. I looked out the window at the fields beginning to race by. The woods whizzed goodbye.

"We going on a train!" Prez said, punching Perry in the shoulder softly. The grownups in the front seat laughed. I looked out the back window then to say goodbye to the house on Three Notch Road, secretly.

Mr. Grandy was coming up behind us. He honked.

"Uncle June, Mr. Grandy wants us," I said. "Uncle June, pull over."

Uncle June stopped the car and all of us looked back

and watched Mr. Grandy climb out of his truck and walk over to us. "I thought that was you, June." I noticed a small envelope in his hand. "How you doin' up there in Benson?"

"Doin' pretty good. Finally movin' my family up there."

"I heard. We all gonna miss Lil and Lydia, and the children, too."

My eyes latched onto the envelope he was using to gesture with. "How you doin'?" he asked Mama and Auntie.

"Fine," Mama said, speaking up first. "Just trying to get to our train before it go off and leave us."

"Oh, sure," Mr. Grandy said, bringing the letter up near his eyes. "I saw this being put in your mailbox right after you pulled away. Francie almost missed it." He handed it to me while everyone turned their puzzled faces to me. I checked the postmark, just as puzzled. California. My breath quickened. All waited. Mama and Auntie and Uncle June had practically turned all the way around in their seats.

"It's from California," I said.

"California," they said together.

Mama recovered first. "Open it, Francie. See who it's from."

I knew who it was from. Even before I tore off the end of the envelope, blew in it, and let the contents fall in my lap. Prez tried to grab the postcard that had fallen out, but I was quicker.

It was just a picture postcard. Of an orange grove. For the second time that day, my eyes filled with tears, and I looked out the window to hide my face, then realized Mr. Grandy was out that window, looking right at me.

"Who's it from?" Mama said impatiently.

I brought the envelope up to my face as if I didn't know and had to read the return address. Of course there wasn't one. My name was written in a child's script, full of struggle, it looked like. Then: Three Notch Road. Then: Noble, Alabama. Jesse hadn't been in school long enough to learn to write. Someone must have helped him.

"You gonna tell us who that postcard's from, Francie?" Uncle June asked.

"It's from Jesse Pruitt," I said.

Mama opened her mouth, but nothing came out. Auntie looked at Uncle June, and Prez and Perry said "Wow!" at the same time.

"He got himself out to California," I said.

"Well, why you crying?" Mama asked.

"I didn't think he ever would . . ."

Mama smiled at me. Mr. Grandy backed away from the car and let us get going. He waved at us and we waved back. I slipped the postcard in my *War and Peace*, deciding I was going to use it for my new bookmark. That way, I'd be looking at that picture of oranges growing on trees for a long, long time and thinking about Jesse *making it* and deciding—I could, too.

FOR CATHOLIC READERS

From the early days of the Church Fathers to the present day the Catholic Church has urged its members to learn about Christ and to grow in faith through the reading of the scriptures. "Ignorance of the scriptures is ignorance of Christ," proclaimed St. Jerome, the first translator of the Bible into Latin. In our own time Pope Pius XII, in his famous encyclical Divino afflante Spiritu (1943), exhorted Catholics to increase their knowledge of the sacred writings through prayerful study. This call was echoed by the Second Vatican Council in The Constitution on Divine Revelation. That document stated that the Council "forcefully and specifically exhorts all the Christian faithful, especially those who live the religious life, to learn 'the surpassing knowledge of Jesus Christ' by frequent reading of the divine scriptures" (25).

Today the possibility of deepening one's knowledge of the Word of God is enhanced enormously by the existence of many excellent modern trans- lations, including the New International Version that was published in 1973. In the years since it first appeared, the New International Version has been praised by Catholic scholars for the clarity of its language and the depth of its scholarship. It has frequently been used as a study-text in Catholic colleges and universities. This edition of the New International Version includes teaching and discussion materials that bring the study of the New Testament within the reach of individuals and small groups, whether Catholic or Protestant, or mixed ecumenical groups. It is hoped that this edition will help to promote a knowledge of God's Word and a love for his Son among Catholics and Christians everywhere.

Serendipity House
of Littleton, Colorado 80160
and
Paulist Press
of Mahwah, New Jersey 07430
have published this work
by special arrangement
with Zondervan Publishing House
under the title:
SERENDIPITY NEW TESTAMENT FOR GROUPS.
The Zondervan title is
THE SERENDIPITY BIBLE STUDY BOOK.

This special edition has been published by special arrangement
between Zondervan Publishing House, 1415 Lake Drive S.E.,
Grand Rapids, Michigan 49506 and Paulist Press, 997 Macarthur
Boulevard, Mahwah, N.J. 07430.

ISBN: 0-8091-2863-2

Printed in the United States of America.

86 87 88 89 90 91 / 10 9 8 7 6 5 4 3 2 1

SERENDIPITY NEW TESTAMENT FOR GROUPS

FOR GROUPS

NEW INTERNATIONAL VERSION

PAULIST PRESS
NEW YORK · MAHWAH

GENERAL EDITOR
Lyman Coleman, Littleton, Colorado

ASSOCIATE EDITORS
Denny Rydberg, Seattle, Washington □ Richard Peace, South Hamilton, Massachusetts □ Gary Christopherson, Tucson, Arizona □ Dietrich Gruen, Madison, Wisconsin

OTHER CONTRIBUTORS
GOSPEL OF MATTHEW and MARK: Jim Singleton, San Antonio, Texas; Mary Naegeli, Menlo Park, California and Dietrich Gruen, Madison, Wisconsin. □ GOSPEL OF LUKE: Carol Detoni, Arcadia, California □ GOSPEL OF JOHN: Bill Tucker, Dallas, Texas and Bill Cutler, Auburn, Maine □ ACTS and ROMANS: Bill Cutler, Auburn, Maine □ 1 CORINTHIANS: Mark Horton, Bethel, Connecticut □ 2 CORINTHIANS: Bill Cutler, Auburn, Maine □ GALATIANS and COLOSSIANS: John Crosby, Glen Ellyn, Illinois; Bill Cutler, Auburn, Maine; Dietrich Gruen, Madison, Wisconsin □ EPHESIANS, JAMES, PHILIPPIANS, 1 & 2 THESSALONIANS, TITUS and PHILEMON: John and Faye Winson; Steve and Betty Crowe, Beverly, Massachusetts; Dietrich Gruen, Madison, Wisconsin □ 1 & 2 TIMOTHY: Judy Johnson and Dietrich Gruen, Madison, Wisconsin □ 1 & 2 PETER: Mark Shepard, Easton, Massachusetts and Dietrich Gruen, Madison, Wisconsin □ 1, 2, 3 JOHN: Bill Tucker, Dallas, Texas, and Dietrich Gruen, Madison, Wisconsin □ REVELATION: Dietrich Gruen, Madison, Wisconsin □ SPECIAL QUESTIONNAIRES: Jim Singleton, San Antonio, Texas and Mary Naegeli, Menlo Park, California.

ART/DESIGN
Steve Eames, Colorado Springs, Colorado

HOW TO USE THE QUESTIONS IN THE MARGIN FOR EVERY PASSAGE IN THE NEW TESTAMENT

1. OPEN: Designed to break the ice in the group. Smile. Relax. Get ready for the Bible study. Questions about your childhood that relate to the Bible passage and give you a chance to share your own "story" with the group. Important stuff—like "where did you go fishing" and "what was the biggest fish you caught?" Watch out for laughter. A group is never so vulnerable to the Holy Spirit as when it is laughing!

2. DIG: Designed to help you scratch, sniff, sift and search for clues in the Scripture passage. Questions are planted like timebombs to go-off just at the right moment in the group—like "what's going on here" or "why do you think..." or "what is Jesus really saying?" Always open-ended to give the group a chance to talk about their own point of view—where no one is "right or wrong."

3. REFLECT: Designed to take personal inventory. Share on a deeper level. Questions like "how would you have reacted in that situation"... "what is your own experience of this..." or "what is God saying to you in this Scripture passage?" Here's the chance to share your own spiritual journey. Turning points. Struggles. Goals. And where you need the support of the group for the next step in your life.

Mark

1.

OPEN: If John the Baptist tried to do his job in the twentieth century what would he wear? eat? sound like?

DIG: 1. How did the substance of what John preached prepare the people for Jesus? **2.** What does it really mean to 'repent'? **3.** Why do you think the crowds responded to John as they did?

2.

REFLECT: 1. Who played the role of John the Baptist in your life to prepare you for Jesus? **2.** In what areas of your life do you need to hear God's word of forgiveness right now?

3.

OPEN: What is the best thing about a desert? the worst?

DIG: 1. What might have been the significance of the dove and the voice for Jesus? **2.** How do you feel about the fact that it was the Spirit who sent Jesus into the desert?

REFLECT: Have you found "deserts" often follow "highs"?

OPEN: Describe the best day that you ever had fishing.

DIG: 1. What do you suppose was this "good news of God" which Jesus was proclaiming? **2.** What was the same in Jesus' message as in John's (verse 4)? What was different? **3.** Why is it important to both repent and believe? **4.** What was Jesus offering in his invitation to the disciples?

REFLECT: 1. What first attracted you to begin following Jesus? **2.** What did you have to leave when you followed Him? **3.** How did your family respond? **4.** What does it mean for you to have the self-identity of a "fisher of men"?

John the Baptist Prepares the Way

1 The beginning of the gospel about Jesus Christ, the Son of God.*

²It is written in Isaiah the prophet:
"I will send my messenger ahead of you,
who will prepare your way"*—
³"a voice of one calling in the desert,
'Prepare the way for the Lord,
make straight paths for him.' ".

⁴And so John came, baptizing in the desert region and preaching a baptism of repentance for the forgiveness of sins. ⁵The whole Judean countryside and all the people of Jerusalem went out to him. Confessing their sins, they were baptized by him in the Jordan River. ⁶John wore clothing made of camel's hair, with a leather belt around his waist, and he ate locusts and wild honey. ⁷And this was his message: "After me will come one more powerful than I, the thongs of whose sandals I am not worthy to stoop down and untie. ⁸I baptize you with* water, but he will baptize you with the Holy Spirit."

The Baptism and Temptation of Jesus

⁹At that time Jesus came from Nazareth in Galilee and was baptized by John in the Jordan. ¹⁰As Jesus was coming up out of the water, he saw heaven being torn open and the Spirit descending on him like a dove. ¹¹And a voice came from heaven: "You are my Son, whom I love; with you I am well pleased." ¹²At once the Spirit sent him out into the desert, ¹³and he was in the desert forty days, being tempted by Satan. He was with the wild animals, and angels attended him.

The Calling of the First Disciples

¹⁴After John was put in prison, Jesus went into Galilee, proclaiming the good news of God. ¹⁵"The time has come," he said. "The kingdom of God is near. Repent and believe the good news!"

¹⁶As Jesus walked beside the Sea of Galilee, he saw Simon and his brother Andrew casting a net into the lake, for they were fishermen. ¹⁷"Come, follow me," Jesus said, "and I will make you fishers of men." ¹⁸At once they left their nets and followed him.

¹⁹When he had gone a little farther, he saw James son of Zebedee and his brother John in a boat, preparing their nets. ²⁰Without delay he called them, and they left their father Zebedee in the boat with the hired men and followed him.

*1 Some manuscripts do not have the Son of God.   *2 Mal 3.1   *3 Isaiah 40.3
*8 Or in

Mark 1:-1-8
JOHN THE BAPTIST PREPARES THE WAY

LOOKING INTO THE SCRIPTURE/25 Minutes. Read Mark 1:1-8 and discuss. Answer YES, NO or MAYBE to these situations:

1. JOHN THE BAPTIST WAS THE KIND OF GUY THAT I WOULD LIKE TO . . .

Y	N	M	take shopping
Y	N	M	rock me to sleep
Y	N	M	get stuck with in an elevator
Y	N	M	invite to a black tie dinner
Y	N	M	drive with for 500 miles keeping within the speed limit
Y	N	M	send to convert my hard-hearted sister in the hospital
Y	N	M	sit with at an all-you-can-eat buffet

2. Why did the people flock to John the Baptist instead of avoiding him?
   a. he was the first prophet in 300 years
   b. he was more interesting than a circus
   c. anyone will come to see a fire burn
   d. he spoke to the reality of their hearts
   e. he talked about sin and forgiveness

3. In modern words, what was the message of John?
   a. you can have it all
   b. look out for number one
   c. turn or burn
   d. you only go around once, so reach for the gusto
   e. pay me now or pay me later
   f. there's a new day coming

4. Why was the establishment so upset with John?
   a. his popularity
   b. his simple life
   c. his preaching
   d. his attack on sin
   e. his call for change

5. What role did John the Baptist play in the overall plan of God?
   a. shake up the establishment
   b. bridge the Old to New Testament
   c. prepare folks for coming of Jesus
   d. baptize Jesus
   e. alert sinners to the need for a Savior

MY OWN STORY/20 Minutes. Read Mark 1:1-8 again and share your experience.

1. If John the Baptist came to your town with this message, how would he be received?
   a. the media would love it
   b. people would flock to him
   c. church people would be polite
   d. everybody would run for cover
   e. people would ignore him

2. Who played the part of John the Baptist in your life—who "prepared the way" for Jesus?
   a. my parents
   b. a Sunday school teacher
   c. a coach/counselor/teacher
   d. a special friend
   e. a whole lot of people
   f. nobody yet

3. How would you describe your relationship with Jesus right now?
   a. just beginning
   b. nowhere
   c. holding
   d. struggling
   e. roller-coaster
   f. going great

4. What would it take to move you on in your relationship with God?
   a. a little support
   b. a deeper commitment
   c. some spiritual discipline
   d. a big change
   e. a miracle
   f. a strong belief that God loves even me

HOW TO USE THE READY-MADE QUESTIONNAIRES ACROSS FROM THE PASSAGE ON 48 BIBLE STORIES

1. LOOKING INTO THE SCRIPTURE

Questions with multiple-choice options built in. Structured to walk you through the Bible story step by step—pausing along the way to "smell the flowers." Look "between the lines" in the Bible story for the meaning, motives, feelings of the principle characters. The questions flow from easy to not-so-easy, and the options from outrageous to a little revealing. No "easy answers." No "right or wrong." Just a good way to force you to relive the story for yourself. Laugh a little. Think a lot.

2. MY OWN STORY

Now it is your turn. Questions with multiple-choice options built in. Structured to relive your own spiritual journey. Look at the significant turning points. Take inventory. Check out your own feelings, motives, fears, hopes and dreams. Share your "story" with your group and pray for one another. Watch out for the last question in the questionnaire. It can get deep...and beautiful. In one short questionnaire, the pendulum swings from the "child" to the "spirit."

HOW TO CHOOSE FROM 10 READY-MADE COURSES FOR SPECIAL INTEREST GROUPS

BUILT INTO THIS NEW TESTAMENT.
No need to buy separate little booklets. Here they are. Ten courses covering ten major areas of interest. All you need to do is pick one of the courses and follow the outlines here.

EACH COURSE HAS SIX SESSIONS.
Just enough to get acquainted with the subject and with one another. If you wish to continue as a group, choose another course and renew your covenant. There are enough courses here to keep you studying for years.

EACH COURSE HAS TWO LEVELS.
If you are a beginning group (don't know each other), use the Gospel Studies in the second column with a questionnaire across from the Bible passage to help you get acquainted. If you are an advanced group (you know each other or have been together for a while), use the Epistle Studies in the third column.

COURSE AND SIX SESSION TOPICS	FOR BEGINNING GROUPS TO GET TO KNOW EACH OTHER	FOR ON-GOING GROUPS TO GO DEEPER IN STUDY

Course One: DISCOVERING MY IDENTITY

SESSION	(A) GOSPEL STUDY	(B) EPISTLE STUDY
1 My Values	Rich Fool/Luke 12:13-21 (167)	1 John 2:15-17 (460)
2 My Strengths	The Talents/Matt 25:14-30 (75)	2 Tim 2:14-26 (408)
3 My Desires	Mary-Martha/Luke 10:38-42 (163)	Phil 3:12-4:1 (379)
4 My Self-image	Sinful Woman/Luke 7:36-50 (153)	Phil 4:10-13 (380)
5 My Faith	Peter's Confession/Matt 16:13-28 (57)	Eph 1:3-14 (368)
6 My Tomorrow	Walk on Water/Matt 14:22-33 (53)	2 Tim 3:10-4:8 (409)

Course Two: WORKING THROUGH MY HANG-UPS

SESSION	(A) GOSPEL STUDY	(B) EPISTLE STUDY
1 Self-worth	Zacchaeus/Luke 19:1-10 (183)	2 Pet 1:3-11 (453)
2 Escapes	Pool Paralytic/John 5:1-15 (213)	Jam 5:13-20 (442)
3 Quitting	Road to Emmaus/Luke 24:13-35 (195)	1 Cor 9:19-27 (333)
4 Rejection	Jesus' Hometown/Luke 4:14-30 (143)	1 Pet 1:3-12 (445)
5 Fear of Failure	Ask, Seek, Knock/Matt 7:7-12 (39)	Heb 11:1-40 (430)
6 Will Power	Gethsemane/Mark 14:32-42 (123)	Phil 2:12-18 (377)

Course Three: DEALING WITH MY PROBLEMS

SESSION	(A) GOSPEL STUDY	(B) EPISTLE STUDY
1 Headaches	Water to Wine/John 2:1-11 (205)	Jam 1:2-18 (438)
2 Hassles	Unforgiving Servant/Matt 18:21-35 (61)	Eph 4:25-32 (371)
3 Stress	The Storm/Mark 4:35-41 (99)	2 Cor 4:1-18 (348)
4 Moral Dilemmas	Jesus before Pilate/Matt 27:11-26 (83)	1 Pet 1:13-2:3 (445)
5 Worry	Do Not Worry/Matt 6:25-34 (37)	Phil 4:4-9 (379)
6 Chronic Illness	Roof Paralytic/Luke 5:17-26 (147)	1 John 1:5-10 (459)

Course Four: LEARNING THE BASICS

SESSION	(A) GOSPEL STUDY	(B) EPISTLE STUDY
1 Jesus	Samaritan Woman/John 4:1-26 (209)	Col 1:15-23 (383)
2 New Birth	Nicodemus/John 3:1-21 (207)	Phil 1:3-11 (376)
3 Temptation	Temptation/Matt 4:1-11 (29)	1 Cor 10:1-13 (334)
4 Prayer	Lord's Prayer/Matt 6:9-13 (35)	1 Tim 2:1-7 (401)
5 The Cross	Jesus' Death/Matt 27:45-56 (85)	Rom 3:21-26 (306)
6 Lordship	Jesus' Call/Matt 16:13-28 (57)	Heb 12:1-13 (432)

Course Five: HANDLING CRISES

SESSION	(A) GOSPEL STUDY	(B) EPISTLE STUDY
1 Failure	Peter Disowns Jesus/Matt 26:69-75 (81)	1 Pet 2:4-12 (446)
2 Grief	Lazarus' Death/John 11:1-44 (227)	2 Cor 1:3-11 (346)
3 Panic	Road to Emmaus/Luke 24:13-35 (195)	Heb 5:11-6:12 (424)
4 Starting Over	Adulterous Woman/John 8:1-11 (220)	1 John 2:28-3:10 (461)
5 Risk Taking	Walk on Water/Matt 14:22-36 (53)	Heb 11:1-40 (430)
6 Despair/Hope	Doubting Thomas/John 20:24-31 (247)	1 Cor 15:1-58 (340)

Course Six: FACING THE ISSUES

SESSION	(A) GOSPEL STUDY	(B) EPISTLE STUDY
1 Money	Expensive Ointment/Mark 14:1-11 (120)	1 Tim 6:3-10 (404)
2 Success	Rich Fool/Luke 12:13-21 (167)	1 Cor 4:8-13 (328)
3 Social Concern	Good Samaritan/Luke 10:25-37 (161)	2 Thes 3:6-15 (396)
4 Corruption/Abuse	Temple Cleansing/Mark 11:12-19 (115)	Rom 13:1-7 (318)
5 Judgmental Eye	Adulterous Woman/John 8:1-11 (220)	Rom 14:1-23 (319)
6 World Vision	Feeding 5000/Mark 6:30-44 (103)	Eph 6:10-20 (373)

Course Seven: BECOMING A CARING COMMUNITY

SESSION	(A) GOSPEL STUDY	(B) EPISTLE STUDY
1 Getting Acquainted	Jesus' Call/Luke 5:1-11 (145)	1 Thes 1:2-10 (390)
2 Sharing Our Story	Nicodemus/John 3:1-21 (207)	Eph 2:1-10 (369)
3 Being Real	Tax Collector/Luke 18:9-14 (181)	Jam 5:13-16 (442)
4 Caretaking	Roof Paralytic/Luke 5:17-26 (147)	Heb 10:19-39 (429)
5 Accountability	Peter Restored/John 21:15-25 (249)	Gal 6:1-10 (365)
6 Body Ministry	Footwashing/John 13:1-17 (233)	Rom 12:1-21 (317)

Course Eight: RESHAPING MY LIFESTYLE

SESSION	(A) GOSPEL STUDY	(B) EPISTLE STUDY
1 Turnaround	John the Baptist/Mark 1:1-8 (91)	Heb 12:1-11 (432)
2 Mental Attitude	Beatitudes/Matt 5:3-10 (31)	Phil 2:1-11 (377)
3 Moral Issues	Temple Cleansing/Mark 11:12-19 (115)	Col 3:1-17 (385)
4 Priorities	Mary-Martha/Luke 10:38-42 (163)	Rom 13:8-14 (318)
5 Possessions	Do Not Worry/Matt 6:25-34 (37)	1 Tim 6:3-10 (404)
6 Control	Gethsemane/Mark 14:32-42 (123)	Rom 6:15-23 (309)

Course Nine: FAMILY RELATIONSHIPS

SESSION	(A) GOSPEL STUDY	(B) EPISTLE STUDY
1 Roots	First Temple Visit/Luke 2:21-40 (137)	2 Tim 1:3-7 (407)
2 Growing Pains	Second Temple Visit/Luke 2:41-52 (139)	Eph 6:1-4 (373)
3 Parent Expectations	Mother's Request/Matt 20:20-28 (65)	1 Pet 5:1-11 (449)
4 Parents in Pain	Prodigal Son/Luke 15:11-31 (175)	1 Thes 2:7-16 (390)
5 Forgiveness	Unforgiving Servant/Matt 18:21-35 (61)	Phil 2:12-18 (377)
6 Ultimate Love	Footwashing/John 13:1-17 (233)	1 Cor 13:1-13 (337)

Course Ten: DISCOVERING THE DEEPER LIFE

SESSION	(A) GOSPEL STUDY	(B) EPISTLE STUDY
1 Promise	Great Banquet/Luke 14:15-24 (173)	Eph 1:3-14 (368)
2 Yearning	Transfiguration/Mark 9:2-13 (109)	Rom 8:18-39 (312)
3 Abiding	Vine-Branch/John 15:1-17 (237)	Col 1:24-2:5 (384)
4 Asking/Receiving	Ask, Seek, Knock/Matt 7:7-12 (39)	1 John 5:13-21 (463)
5 Fruits	The Sower/Mark 4:1-20 (96)	Gal 5:13-26 (365)
6 Gifts	Loaves and Fish/Mark 6:30-44 (103)	1 Cor 12:1-13:13 (336)

HOW TO CREATE YOUR OWN COURSE FROM THESE READY-MADE QUESTIONNAIRES ON CHRIST'S LIFE

How about a special course for groups during Lent or Pentecost? How about a special course on stewardship or discipleship or spiritual healing? Here's a chance for you to design your own small group course, using the questionnaires across from the Bible passage on the 48 stories in the life of Christ. All you need to do is choose the events in the life of Christ.

HOW TO OVERCOME THE 8 DEADLY DISEASES OF BIBLE STUDY GROUPS

1. JITTERS AFFLICTION

SYMPTOMS: Palms sweat. Mouth turns to sawdust. Armpits drip blood. Voice sounds like a squeak or nothing at all comes out when "it is your turn."

PROBLEM: Fear of groups, often caused by a "bad experience" in groups.

PRESCRIPTION: Divide the large group into foursomes and ask each foursome to enjoy "table fellowship"— 4 at the dining table, 4 at the kitchen table, etc. Begin every session with an "Open" question, designed to break the ice and get the group talking before moving into Bible study. Food permitted. But no talking with your mouth full.

THE FEARLESS FOURSOME

2. COURTSHIP FAILURE

SYMPTOMS: Communication breakdown. Surface chatter about "football" or "the weather." Group sits like in a poker game with cards held close to chest. Feelings never shared. Or, if somebody does "open up," nobody "hears it." Nobody cares or "gets close."

PROBLEM: No group building. No bonding. No trust.

PRESCRIPTION: Spend the whole first session and the first few minutes of every session getting to know each other. Covenant together (see #8). Share your "God story" with each other. Your spiritual ups and downs. Hopes and dreams. Fears and failures. And where you are struggling right now. The group that plays together stays together. No fair having fun without letting the other guy in on it.

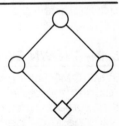

KOINONIA COMMUNITY

3. DEFORMITY

SYMPTOMS: Grotesque, distended group body. One of the parts larger than the rest: either a mammoth brain or heart or tongue that saps all the energy, leaving the rest of the body deformed and deficient. Hideously out of balance. Distorted. Disfunctioning.

PROBLEM: Imbalance of the three necessary ingredients of a healthy group.

PRESCRIPTION: Picture a healthy group with all three "legs" in balance. Have regular "checkups" by a group doctor to see that the group is staying healthy. If not, prescribe some mid-course corrections. If you need a "fourth leg" to stand on, try worship. But don't bring too much joy to God—you might never again need a doctor.

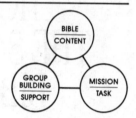

THREE LEGGED STOOL

4. INFANTILE PARALYSIS

SYMPTOMS: Baby talk. Baby diet. Baby concerns ... even after years together as a group. Dependent upon an "authority" figure. No signs of growth. No sense of drive, initiative, concern for others or reproduction.

PROBLEM: Stagnation. Growth arrested at infancy.

PRESCRIPTION: Have a clear picture of the stages of group development and expect a group to develop within a year to the completion level. First phase (6-12 weeks) major on group building. Second phase (12-24 weeks) major on Bible study and gift awareness. Third phase (24-36 weeks) major on finding your mission and starting a new group (with the support of the old group).

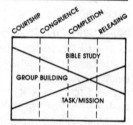

STAGES OF DEVELOPMENT

5. IN-GROWN SYNDROME

SYMPTOMS: Self-centeredness. Exclusiveness. Deliberate "closing the door" to outsiders because of fear—fear that someone from the outside might ruin the "closeness" or "betray your confidence."

PROBLEM: Clique complex. Anemic mission.

PRESCRIPTION: Envision the church as a place where "sinners" are accepted. Expect your Bible study to energize your vision into reality. Use an empty chair to remind your group that it is always "open" for one more "sinner" in search of God. When you pray, ask God to fill it by the next week. Then pull up more empty chairs.

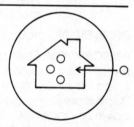

THE EMPTY CHAIR

6. BURNOUT

SYMPTOMS: Feeling "tired" of the group. Chronic absence. Loss of interest. Feeling guilty because you have lost interest, but don't know how to say "goodbye."

PROBLEM: How to quit gracefully.

PRESCRIPTION: Follow the 3-phase lifecycle (see #4) for one year. If the group wants to continue, shift into "overdrive" where you don't consume as much energy. Meet once a month for a pot-luck meal as a reunion group. After the second year, meet occasionally to keep in touch. Here's the principle: the longer the group lasts, the less intensive should be the experience, so that each group member is free to start a new group.

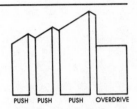

PUSH   PUSH   PUSH   OVERDRIVE

ALUMNI SUPPORT GROUP

7. DEATH BY OVERDOSE

SYMPTOMS: Feeling worn-out. Burdened. Overworked. Heavy. Used. Put-upon. Stressed-out. killed-off.

PROBLEM: 10% of people in the church are killed off by leadership overdose. 30% are used as helpers. 60% are too "worldly," so never asked.

PRESCRIPTION: Start a pilot group with the 60%ers. (Jesus did.) Look for the "Galilean fringe," not the "Jerusalem establishment." Wanted: Only prodigals; no elder brothers. With their friends mostly outside the church, fringe members are dangerous. Watch out for church growth. And "let the dead bury their dead."

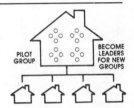

PILOT GROUP   BECOME LEADERS FOR NEW GROUPS

PILOT GROUP

8. FLABBY COMMITMENT

SYMPTOMS: Ill-defined expectations. Unmet goals. No mutual accountability. No basis for evaluating progress.

PROBLEM: Group has yet to "covenant" together.

PRESCRIPTION: Ask not what the group can do for you... Ask what you can do for the group. Verbalize and mobilize your commitment with these sentences:
1. The purpose of our group is....
2. Our specific goals are....
3. We will meet _____ hours, every _____, at _____'s place, for _____ weeks, then we re-evaluate.

We will accept 7 of the following group disciplines:
☐ Regular attendance ☐ Strict confidentiality
☐ Full participation ☐ Mutual accountability
☐ Shared leadership ☐ Scriptural authority
☐ Outreach to _____ ☐ Prayer partner with _____
☐ Homework ☐ Other _____

GROUP COVENANT

"For where two or three
come together
in my name,
there am I with them."

Matthew 18:20 NIV

PREFACE

THE NEW INTERNATIONAL VERSION is a completely new translation of the Holy
Bible made by over a hundred scholars working directly from the best available Hebrew,
Aramaic and Greek texts. It had its beginning in 1965 when, after several years of exploratory
study by committees from the Christian Reformed Church and the National Association of
Evangelicals, a group of scholars met at Palos Heights, Illinois, and concurred in the need for
a new translation of the Bible in contemporary English. This group, though not made up of
official church representatives, was transdenominational. Its conclusion was endorsed by a large
number of leaders from many denominations who met in Chicago in 1966.

Responsibility for the new version was delegated by the Palos Heights group to a self-
governing body of fifteen, the Committee on Bible Translation, composed for the most part of
biblical scholars from colleges, universities and seminaries. In 1967 the New York Bible Society
(now the International Bible Society) generously undertook the financial sponsorship of the
project—a sponsorship that made it possible to enlist the help of many distinguished scholars.
The fact that participants from the United States, Great Britain, Canada, Australia and New
Zealand worked together gave the project its international scope. That they were from many
denominations—including Anglican, Assemblies of God, Baptist, Brethren, Christian Reformed, Church of Christ, Evangelical Free, Lutheran, Mennonite, Methodist, Nazarene,
Presbyterian, Wesleyan and other churches—helped to safeguard the translation from sectarian
bias.

How it was made helps to give the New International Version its distinctiveness. The
translation of each book was assigned to a team of scholars. Next, one of the Intermediate
Editorial Committees revised the initial translation, with constant reference to the Hebrew,
Aramaic or Greek. Their work then went to one of the General Editorial Committees, which
checked it in detail and made another thorough revision. This revision in turn was carefully
reviewed by the Committee on Bible Translation, which made further changes and then released
the final version for publication. In this way the entire Bible underwent three revisions, during
each of which the translation was examined for its faithfulness to the original languages and for
its English style.

All this involved many thousands of hours of research and discussion regarding the meaning
of the texts and the precise way of putting them into English. It may well be that no other
translation has been made by a more thorough process of review and revision from committee
to committee than this one.

From the beginning of the project, the Committee on Bible Translation held to certain goals
for the New International Version: that it would be an accurate translation and one that would
have clarity and literary quality and so prove suitable for public and private reading, teaching,
preaching, memorizing and liturgical use. The Committee also sought to preserve some measure
of continuity with the long tradition of translating the Scriptures into English.

In working toward these goals, the translators were united in their commitment to the
authority and infallibility of the Bible as God's Word in written form. They believe that it
contains the divine answer to the deepest needs of humanity, that it sheds unique light on our
path in a dark world, and that it sets forth the way to our eternal well-being.

The first concern of the translators has been the accuracy of the translation and its fidelity
to the thought of the biblical writers. They have weighed the significance of the lexical and
grammatical details of the Hebrew, Aramaic and Greek texts. At the same time, they have striven
for more than a word-for-word translation. Because thought patterns and syntax differ from

language to language, faithful communication of the meaning of the writers of the Bible demands frequent modifications in sentence structure and constant regard for the contextual meanings of words.

A sensitive feeling for style does not always accompany scholarship. Accordingly the Committee on Bible Translation submitted the developing version to a number of stylistic consultants. Two of them read every book of both Old and New Testaments twice—once before and once after the last major revision—and made invaluable suggestions. Samples of the translation were tested for clarity and ease of reading by various kinds of people—young and old, highly educated and less well educated, ministers and laymen.

Concern for clear and natural English—that the New International Version should be idiomatic but not idiosyncratic, contemporary but not dated—motivated the translators and consultants. At the same time, they tried to reflect the differing styles of the biblical writers. In view of the international use of English, the translators sought to avoid obvious Americanisms on the one hand and obvious Anglicisms on the other. A British edition reflects the comparatively few differences of significant idiom and of spelling.

As for the traditional pronouns "thou," "thee" and "thine" in reference to the Deity, the translators judged that to use these archaisms (along with the old verb forms such as "doest," "wouldest" and "hadst") would violate accuracy in translation. Neither Hebrew, Aramaic nor Greek uses special pronouns for the persons of the Godhead. A present-day translation is not enhanced by forms that in the time of the King James Version were used in everyday speech, whether referring to God or man.

For the Old Testament the standard Hebrew text, the Masoretic Text as published in the latest editions of *Biblia Hebraica*, was used throughout. The Dead Sea Scrolls contain material bearing on an earlier stage of the Hebrew text. They were consulted, as were the Samaritan Pentateuch and the ancient scribal traditions relating to textual changes. Sometimes a variant Hebrew reading in the margin of the Masoretic Text was followed instead of the text itself. Such instances, being variants within the Masoretic tradition, are not specified by footnotes. In rare cases, words in the consonantal text were divided differently from the way they appear in the Masoretic Text. Footnotes indicate this. The translators also consulted the more important early versions—the Septuagint; Aquila, Symmachus and Theodotion; the Vulgate; the Syriac Peshitta; the Targums; and for the Psalms the *Juxta Hebraica* of Jerome. Readings from these versions were occasionally followed where the Masoretic Text seemed doubtful and where accepted principles of textual criticism showed that one or more of these textual witnesses appeared to provide the correct reading. Such instances are footnoted. Sometimes vowel letters and vowel signs did not, in the judgment of the translators, represent the correct vowels for the original consonantal text. Accordingly some words were read with a different set of vowels. These instances are usually not indicated by footnotes.

The Greek text used in translating the New Testament was an eclectic one. No other piece of ancient literature has such an abundance of manuscript witnesses as does the New Testament. Where existing manuscripts differ, the translators made their choice of readings according to accepted principles of New Testament textual criticism. Footnotes call attention to places where there was uncertainty about what the original text was. The best current printed texts of the Greek New Testament were used.

There is a sense in which the work of translation is never wholly finished. This applies to all great literature and uniquely so to the Bible. In 1973 the New Testament in the New International Version was published. Since then, suggestions for corrections and revisions have been received from various sources. The Committee on Bible Translation carefully considered the suggestions and adopted a number of them. These were incorporated in the first printing of the entire Bible in 1978. Additional revisions were made by the Committee on Bible Translation in 1983 and appear in printings after that date.

As in other ancient documents, the precise meaning of the biblical texts is sometimes uncertain. This is more often the case with the Hebrew and Aramaic texts than with the Greek text. Although archaeological and linguistic discoveries in this century aid in understanding difficult passages, some uncertainties remain. The more significant of these have been called to the reader's attention in the footnotes.

In regard to the divine name *YHWH*, commonly referred to as the *Tetragrammaton*, the translators adopted the device used in most English versions of rendering that name as "LORD" in capital letters to distinguish it from *Adonai*, another Hebrew word rendered "Lord," for which small letters are used. Wherever the two names stand together in the Old Testament as a compound name of God, they are rendered "Sovereign LORD."

Because for most readers today the phrases "the LORD of hosts" and "God of hosts" have little meaning, this version renders them "the LORD Almighty" and "God Almighty." These renderings convey the sense of the Hebrew, namely, "he who is sovereign over all the 'hosts' (powers) in heaven and on earth, especially over the 'hosts' (armies) of Israel." For readers unacquainted with Hebrew this does not make clear the distinction between *Sabaoth* ("hosts" or "Almighty") and *Shaddai* (which can also be translated "Almighty"), but the latter occurs infrequently and is always footnoted. When *Adonai* and *YHWH Sabaoth* occur together, they are rendered "the Lord, the LORD Almighty."

As for other proper nouns, the familiar spellings of the King James Version are generally retained. Names traditionally spelled with "ch," except where it is final, are usually spelled in this translation with "k" or "c," since the biblical languages do not have the sound that "ch" frequently indicates in English—for example, in *chant*. For well-known names such as Zechariah, however, the traditional spelling has been retained. Variation in the spelling of names in the original languages has usually not been indicated. Where a person or place has two or more different names in the Hebrew, Aramaic or Greek texts, the more familiar one has generally been used, with footnotes where needed.

To achieve clarity the translators sometimes supplied words not in the original texts but required by the context. If there was uncertainty about such material, it is enclosed in brackets. Also for the sake of clarity or style, nouns, including some proper nouns, are sometimes substituted for pronouns, and vice versa. And though the Hebrew writers often shifted back and forth between first, second and third personal pronouns without change of antecedent, this translation often makes them uniform, in accordance with English style and without the use of footnotes.

Poetical passages are printed as poetry, that is, with indentation of lines and with separate stanzas. These are generally designed to reflect the structure of Hebrew poetry. This poetry is normally characterized by parallelism in balanced lines. Most of the poetry in the Bible is in the Old Testament, and scholars differ regarding the scansion of Hebrew lines. The translators determined the stanza divisions for the most part by analysis of the subject matter. The stanzas therefore serve as poetic paragraphs.

As an aid to the reader, italicized sectional headings are inserted in most of the books. They are not to be regarded as part of the NIV text, are not for oral reading, and are not intended to dictate the interpretation of the sections they head.

The footnotes in this version are of several kinds, most of which need no explanation. Those giving alternative translations begin with "Or" and generally introduce the alternative with the last word preceding it in the text, except when it is a single-word alternative; in poetry quoted in a footnote a slant mark indicates a line division. Footnotes introduced by "Or" do not have uniform significance. In some cases two possible translations were considered to have about equal validity. In other cases, though the translators were convinced that the translation in the text was correct, they judged that another interpretation was possible and of sufficient importance to be represented in a footnote.

In the New Testament, footnotes that refer to uncertainty regarding the original text are introduced by "Some manuscripts" or similar expressions. In the Old Testament, evidence for the reading chosen is given first and evidence for the alternative is added after a semicolon (for

Preface

example: Septuagint; Hebrew *father*). In such notes the term "Hebrew" refers to the Masoretic Text.

It should be noted that minerals, flora and fauna, architectural details, articles of clothing and jewelry, musical instruments and other articles cannot always be identified with precision. Also measures of capacity in the biblical period are particularly uncertain (see the table of weights and measures following the text).

Like all translations of the Bible, made as they are by imperfect man, this one undoubtedly falls short of its goals. Yet we are grateful to God for the extent to which he has enabled us to realize these goals and for the strength he has given us and our colleagues to complete our task. We offer this version of the Bible to him in whose name and for whose glory it has been made. We pray that it will lead many into a better understanding of the Holy Scriptures and a fuller knowledge of Jesus Christ the incarnate Word, of whom the Scriptures so faithfully testify.

The Committee on Bible Translation

June 1978
(Revised August 1983)

Names of the translators and editors may be secured
from the International Bible Society
144 Tices Lane, East Brunswick, New Jersey 08816.

MATTHEW

INTRODUCTION

The Synoptic Gospels

The word "synoptic" means, literally, "able to be seen together." It refers to the first three gospels — Matthew, Mark and Luke — which cover the same events in Jesus' life, often in the same way. A parallel reading of the first three gospels makes it clear that there is some sort of literary connection between them. For example, even the parenthesis in the story of the healing of the paralytic — "He said to the paralytic" — is in the identical place in each account. Compare Matt. 9:6, Mark 2:10, and Luke 5:24.

The nature of this connection is not absolutely certain, but generally it is assumed that Mark was the first gospel, that Matthew and Luke had Mark's text before them when they wrote, and that they included some of Mark's material in their own compositions. One reason scholars conclude this is that of the 105 sections in Mark, all but 4 occur in Matthew or Luke. In fact, Matthew uses 93 of these 105 sections (nearly 90%), including not just the general story but in 51% of the cases Mark's very words.

While it might be argued that Mark merely summarized Matthew and Luke (and so was the *last* synoptic Gospel and not the first), this seems less probable because Matthew and Luke tend to polish up Mark's harsher writing style. Further comparison indicates that Matthew and Luke drew mainly narrative material from Mark — stories about what Jesus did. However, Matthew and Luke also share some two hundred verses not found in Mark, most of which consist of the teachings of Jesus. This discussion material may have come from an early (but now lost) collection of Jesus' teaching.

In any case, it is clear that when the gospel writers put together their accounts, they did so with a clear purpose in mind. Each selected some stories and left out others to produce an account of Jesus' life that would answer the questions and concerns of his particular audience. Mark probably wrote for Christians in Rome who were suffering under Nero's persecution, and so he told about Jesus who was the suffering servant. Luke wrote about the son of Man who came to seek and to save the needy, the lost, the outcasts. Matthew wrote to a Jewish audience and told the story of King Jesus, the Son of David, who came as the long-promised Messiah to claim his throne.

Author

Nowhere is the author named within the first gospel. There is however a long tradition that has assigned it to Matthew, the tax collector who became an apostle. Indeed, Bishop Papias wrote (around A.D. 125) that "Matthew composed the Logia in the Hebrew tongue" — though this reference is not unambiguous or without problematic features.

Little is known about Matthew except that he was a tax gatherer. As such he would have been bitterly hated by the general populace in Israel — with good reason. For one thing, tax collectors worked for Rome, the oppressor, and therefore were seen as traitors to Israel. For another, tax collectors made their living — and many were quite wealthy — by charging above and beyond what Rome required (only the tax collector knew what was owed). Matthew the tax collector stands in contrast to the poor and middle-class fisherman who composed the main body of the disciples.

It has been suggested that it took Matthew's logical accountant's mind to produce a precisely organized gospel such as this one. It is interesting to note that in telling the story of paying tribute, only the gospel of Matthew uses the precise word for the coin involved instead of the more common word (which Mark and Luke used).

Characteristics

Matthew is the most Jewish of all the Gospels. It was written by a Jew to other Jews to convince them that Jesus was, indeed, the Messiah foretold by Old Testament Scripture. Thus the author cites numerous Old Testament prophecies which were fulfilled by Jesus. He uses the phrase "All this took place to fulfill what the Lord had said through the prophets" some sixteen times.

The Jewishness of the gospel is also seen in the fact that Matthew mentions Jewish customs without explanation (e.g., "phylacteries" in 23:5), that he has a very high view of the Law (5:17-20), and that even when recording Jesus' denunciations, he shows more respect for the teachers of the Law and the Pharisees than any other gospel writer (23:2).

Yet one of the most interesting features of Matthew is that although he is so Jewish in his concerns, in his book we discover the universal nature of the gospel — that it is for all the peoples of the world. This emphasis emerges right at the beginning when the Gentile Magi bring gifts to the baby Jesus, and it runs through to the end when Jesus sends His followers out to "make disciples of all nations."

Other features of Matthew include his interest in the church (this is the only gospel to use the word "church") and his concern about the end times — the Second Coming of Jesus, the end of the world, and the final judgment (his is the fullest account).

Structure

It has been said that Matthew is the most orderly in structure of the four gospel accounts. After an introductory section, the material is organized into five blocks of narrative alternated with five blocks of discourse or teaching. We can see that this is not an accidental arrangement, because Matthew ends each teaching section with a similar formula (compare 7:28; 11:1; 13:53 and 26:1).

Overview Study Questions

1. Quickly skim the whole gospel, watching for the divisions noted above. What picture of Jesus emerges from this account?
2. Read about Matthew in the New Testament: Matthew 9:9-13; Mark 2:13-17; Luke 5:27-32; Mark 3:18; Acts 1:13. What picture of this man emerges?

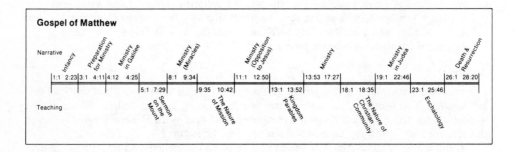

Matthew

The Genealogy of Jesus

1 A record of the genealogy of Jesus Christ the son of David, the son of Abraham:

²Abraham was the father of Isaac,
 Isaac the father of Jacob,
 Jacob the father of Judah and his brothers,
³Judah the father of Perez and Zerah, whose mother was Tamar,
 Perez the father of Hezron,
 Hezron the father of Ram,
⁴Ram the father of Amminadab,
 Amminadab the father of Nahshon,
 Nahshon the father of Salmon,
⁵Salmon the father of Boaz, whose mother was Rahab,
 Boaz the father of Obed, whose mother was Ruth,
 Obed the father of Jesse,
⁶and Jesse the father of King David.

David was the father of Solomon, whose mother had been Uriah's wife,
⁷Solomon the father of Rehoboam,
 Rehoboam the father of Abijah,
 Abijah the father of Asa,
⁸Asa the father of Jehoshaphat,
 Jehoshaphat the father of Jehoram,
 Jehoram the father of Uzziah,
⁹Uzziah the father of Jotham,
 Jotham the father of Ahaz,
 Ahaz the father of Hezekiah,
¹⁰Hezekiah the father of Manasseh,
 Manasseh the father of Amon,
 Amon the father of Josiah,
¹¹and Josiah the father of Jeconiah*a* and his brothers at the time of the exile to Babylon.

¹²After the exile to Babylon:
 Jeconiah was the father of Shealtiel,
 Shealtiel the father of Zerubbabel,
¹³Zerubbabel the father of Abiud,
 Abiud the father of Eliakim,
 Eliakim the father of Azor,
¹⁴Azor the father of Zadok,
 Zadok the father of Akim,
 Akim the father of Eliud,
¹⁵Eliud the father of Eleazar,
 Eleazar the father of Matthan,
 Matthan the father of Jacob,
¹⁶and Jacob the father of Joseph, the husband of Mary, of whom was born Jesus, who is called Christ.

OPEN: 1. Where did your parents grow up? **2.** What are a couple of things that you remember about your grandparents? **3.** What do you know about your genealogy? What would you like to discover about it? **4.** Who's the historian in your family? **5.** If you could design a coat of arms for your family, what animal would you choose? Why? What other symbols would you choose?

DIG: 1. What title does Matthew assign Jesus in verses 1 and 16? What is the meaning of each title? What would each mean to Matthew's audience? **2.** Which people do you recognize in this genealogy? What do you remember about each of these people? Which people on the list are the most signifigant in establishing who Jesus is? **3.** Which women are named? Why do you think women were named when it was not the Jewish custom to include women's names in genealogies? What do you know about these women? **4.** Into what three sections does Matthew divide his genealogical table? What great event climaxes each section? **5.** If Luke's genelogy (Lk 3:23-38) goes all the way back to Adam to emphasize the universality of the gospel, what is Matthew's point in beginning with Abraham? What does this account of lineage say to Matthew's Jewish readers? **6.** Matthew's gospel says more about Joseph than any other—how is that evident?

REFLECT: 1. Who are the signifigant people in your spiritual upbringing? What has been passed on to you spiritually from your forebearers? **2.** If you have children or plan to have them, what would you like to pass on to them? How would you pass these things on?

---

a11 That is, Jehoiachin; also in verse 12

[17]Thus there were fourteen generations in all from Abraham to David, fourteen from David to the exile to Babylon, and fourteen from the exile to the Christ. [b]

The Birth of Jesus Christ

[18]This is how the birth of Jesus Christ came about: His mother Mary was pledged to be married to Joseph, but before they came together, she was found to be with child through the Holy Spirit. [19]Because Joseph her husband was a righteous man and did not want to expose her to public disgrace, he had in mind to divorce her quietly.

[20]But after he had considered this, an angel of the Lord appeared to him in a dream and said, "Joseph son of David, do not be afraid to take Mary home as your wife, because what is conceived in her is from the Holy Spirit. [21]She will give birth to a son, and you are to give him the name Jesus,[c] because he will save his people from their sins."

[22]All this took place to fulfill what the Lord had said through the prophet: [23]"The virgin will be with child and will give birth to a son, and they will call him Immanuel"[d]—which means, "God with us."

[24]When Joseph woke up, he did what the angel of the Lord had commanded him and took Mary home as his wife. [25]But he had no union with her until she gave birth to a son. And he gave him the name Jesus.

The Visit of the Magi

2 After Jesus was born in Bethlehem in Judea, during the time of King Herod, Magi[e] from the east came to Jerusalem [2]and asked, "Where is the one who has been born king of the Jews? We saw his star in the east[f] and have come to worship him."

[3]When King Herod heard this he was disturbed, and all Jerusalem with him. [4]When he had called together all the people's chief priests and teachers of the law, he asked them where the Christ[g] was to be born. [5]"In Bethlehem in Judea," they replied, "for this is what the prophet has written:

[6]"'But you, Bethlehem, in the land of Judah,
are by no means least among the rulers of Judah;
for out of you will come a ruler
who will be the shepherd of my people Israel.'[h]"

[7]Then Herod called the Magi secretly and found out from them the exact time the star had appeared. [8]He sent them to Bethlehem and said, "Go and make a careful search for the child. As soon as you find him, report to me, so that I too may go and worship him."

[9]After they had heard the king, they went on their way, and the star they had seen in the east[i] went ahead of them until it stopped over the place where the child was. [10]When they saw

---

OPEN: 1. What was your father like when you were growing up? **2.** What does your name mean? **3.** How did you first learn about "the birds and the bees"?

DIG: 1. What kind of man was Joseph? What did he plan to do? Why? **2.** What is the signifigance of the word that Joseph heard from the angel? **3.** What is the first reason Matthew gives as to why Jesus was born (v. 21)? **4.** Apart from fulfilling prophecy, why do you think Jesus' virgin birth was necessary? Likewise, Joseph's legal paternity?

REFLECT: 1. If you were Joseph or Mary—unmarried, pregnant, and a teenager—how would you have felt? what would you have said to each other? To God? To family and friends? **2.** In your experience, does God still speak via dreams? What is the value of dreams? Their danger? How does one know if it is God speaking? **3.** How is "God with us" today?

OPEN: 1. What is your favorite Christmas story **2.** Who are three "Magi" or wise men to whom you look for input into your life today?

DIG: 1. What do you know about Bethlehem? Why was it important that Jesus be born there? **2.** Why do you think that the Magi left everything behind to follow a star? **3.** Why was Herod so concerned that the baby be found? **4.** What kind of messiah does the prophecy from Micah portray? **5.** Trace the responses of the Magi upon seeing Jesus. How is that similar to the response that Christians make to Jesus? How is it different? **6.** Why didn't the Magi return to Herod? **7.** What do the star, the Magi, the gifts, the homage, the hostility, and the prophecy teach about the nature and significance of Jesus?

REFLECT: 1. If your father came to you and said that he had seen a new star and was going to follow it, what would you think? **2.** What "star" are you following right now? Where is it taking you? **3.** In your "journey" toward God, how are you like the Magi? Unlike them? How far along that journey are you? **4.** What is the "gold, incense and myrrh" in your life? How much of

---

[b]17 Or Messiah. "The Christ" (Greek) and "the Messiah" (Hebrew) both mean "the Anointed One."   [c]21 Jesus is the Greek form of Joshua, which means the LORD saves.   [d]23 Isaiah 7:14   [e]1 Traditionally Wise Men   [f]2 Or star when it rose   [g]4 Or Messiah   [h]6 Micah 5:2   [i]9 Or seen when it rose

the star, they were overjoyed. [11]On coming to the house, they saw the child with his mother Mary, and they bowed down and worshiped him. Then they opened their treasures and presented him with gifts of gold and of incense and of myrrh. [12]And having been warned in a dream not to go back to Herod, they returned to their country by another route.

The Escape to Egypt

[13]When they had gone, an angel of the Lord appeared to Joseph in a dream. "Get up," he said, "take the child and his mother and escape to Egypt. Stay there until I tell you, for Herod is going to search for the child to kill him."

[14]So he got up, took the child and his mother during the night and left for Egypt, [15]where he stayed until the death of Herod. And so was fulfilled what the Lord had said through the prophet: "Out of Egypt I called my son."[j]

[16]When Herod realized that he had been outwitted by the Magi, he was furious, and he gave orders to kill all the boys in Bethlehem and its vicinity who were two years old and under, in accordance with the time he had learned from the Magi. [17]Then what was said through the prophet Jeremiah was fulfilled:

[18]"A voice is heard in Ramah,
    weeping and great mourning,
Rachel weeping for her children
    and refusing to be comforted,
because they are no more."[k]

The Return to Nazareth

[19]After Herod died, an angel of the Lord appeared in a dream to Joseph in Egypt [20]and said, "Get up, take the child and his mother and go to the land of Israel, for those who were trying to take the child's life are dead."

[21]So he got up, took the child and his mother and went to the land of Israel. [22]But when he heard that Archelaus was reigning in Judea in place of his father Herod, he was afraid to go there. Having been warned in a dream, he withdrew to the district of Galilee, [23]and he went and lived in a town called Nazareth. So was fulfilled what was said through the prophets: "He will be called a Nazarene."

John the Baptist Prepares the Way

3 In those days John the Baptist came, preaching in the Desert of Judea [2]and saying, "Repent, for the kingdom of heaven is near." [3]This is he who was spoken of through the prophet Isaiah:

"A voice of one calling in the desert,
    'Prepare the way for the Lord,
        make straight paths for him.' "[l]

[4]John's clothes were made of camel's hair, and he had a leather belt around his waist. His food was locusts and wild

j15 Hosea 11:1   *k18* Jer. 31:15   *l3* Isaiah 40:3

---

this (time, talent, riches or whatever) have you offered to Jesus?

OPEN: 1. If you could pull up stakes and go to another country, where would you go? Why? **2.** In your group, who has come the closest to dying as a child?

DIG: 1. How is baby Jesus preserved from Herod's wrath (vv. 12-16)? **2.** From Joseph's responsiveness, what do you learn about faith and obedience? **3.** From Isaiah's and Jeremiah's prophecy what do you learn about God's involvement in human affairs?

REFLECT: 1. What empathy do you have for Herod? When you are outwitted, how do you react? **2.** When is "flight" better than "fight"? Give an example from a recent crisis in your life. **3.** Generally, how do you hear God speak? How long would it take you to say "yes" if God asked you to move on with him? Why the delay?

OPEN: Would you ever go back to your birthplace to live now? Why or why not?

DIG: What relocation options face Joseph? How did God use prophecy, dreams, faith and circumstances to guide him?

REFLECT: What did God use in determining where your family grew up? How did your hometown shape you for a future ministry?

OPEN: 1. If John the Baptist tried to do his job in the twentieth century what would he wear? Eat? Sound like? **2.** Who in your group or community would you cast in that role? Why?

DIG: 1. How much time elapsed between Matthew 2:23 and 3:1? **2.** What was John the Baptist like? Why would anyone go out of their way to hear this radical preacher (v. 7)? Who did they think he was (see also 2 Kings 1:8)? **3.** What does it mean to "repent"? What is the "kingdom of heaven"? **4.** Why was John's message to the Pharisees and Sadducees so negative? What special privilege did they claim? Why was that fruitless? **5.** What do these images of judgment each mean: "The coming wrath"? "The ax"? "The fire"? "His winnowing fork"? "Burning up the chaff"? **6.** How do the ministries of John and Jesus compare?

REFLECT: 1. What people have been like John the Baptist in your life? How did they prepare you to meet Jesus? **2.** In whose lives have you served as John the Baptist? **3.** How often is the call to repentance included in today's popular evangelism? What part should repentance play in salvation?

OPEN: When were you baptized? When did that mean something to you?

DIG: 1. Why did Jesus, who was without sin, want to be baptized? What "righteousness" did he thereby fulfill (see Isaiah 53:12)? **2.** In the context of Matthew 3 and 4, what do you think the events of Jesus' baptism meant to him? To others?

OPEN: If an agent from a foreign power wanted you to turn over state secrets, how might he or she attract your attention and get you to listen?

DIG: 1. For each of the three temptations: (a) Where does it take place? (b) What is the nature of the temptation? (c) What potentially might appeal to Jesus? (d) What price would there be were he to yield? (e) How does Jesus respond in each instance? What is the source of his response? **2.** What links these temptations with the baptism of Jesus (vv. 1, 3, 6)? **3.** Of these three, which temptation feels most legitimate? Which one is shrewder? Which one is basic to them all?

REFLECT: 1. What is the human need at the heart of each of the three temptations? How do you see these needs manifested in your life? How does Satan use these to tempt you? **2.** What have you found most helpful in resisting temptation? **3.** What is your greatest temptation right now? How can others help you resist it this week?

honey. [5]People went out to him from Jerusalem and all Judea and the whole region of the Jordan. [6]Confessing their sins, they were baptized by him in the Jordan River.

[7]But when he saw many of the Pharisees and Sadducees coming to where he was baptizing, he said to them: "You brood of vipers! Who warned you to flee from the coming wrath? [8]Produce fruit in keeping with repentance. [9]And do not think you can say to yourselves, 'We have Abraham as our father.' I tell you that out of these stones God can raise up children for Abraham. [10]The ax is already at the root of the trees, and every tree that does not produce good fruit will be cut down and thrown into the fire.

[11]"I baptize you with[m]water for repentance. But after me will come one who is more powerful than I, whose sandals I am not fit to carry. He will baptize you with the Holy Spirit and with fire. [12]His winnowing fork is in his hand, and he will clear his threshing floor, gathering his wheat into the barn and burning up the chaff with unquenchable fire."

The Baptism of Jesus

[13]Then Jesus came from Galilee to the Jordan to be baptized by John. [14]But John tried to deter him, saying, "I need to be baptized by you, and do you come to me?"

[15]Jesus replied, "Let it be so now; it is proper for us to do this to fulfill all righteousness." Then John consented.

[16]As soon as Jesus was baptized, he went up out of the water. At that moment heaven was opened, and he saw the Spirit of God descending like a dove and lighting on him. [17]And a voice from heaven said, "This is my Son, whom I love; with him I am well pleased."

The Temptation of Jesus

4 Then Jesus was led by the Spirit into the desert to be tempted by the devil. [2]After fasting forty days and forty nights, he was hungry. [3]The tempter came to him and said, "If you are the Son of God, tell these stones to become bread."

[4]Jesus answered, "It is written: 'Man does not live on bread alone, but on every word that comes from the mouth of God.'[n]"

[5]Then the devil took him to the holy city and had him stand on the highest point of the temple. [6]"If you are the Son of God," he said, "throw yourself down. For it is written:

" 'He will command his angels concerning you,
    and they will lift you up in their hands,
    so that you will not strike your foot against a stone.'[o]"

[7]Jesus answered him, "It is also written: 'Do not put the Lord your God to the test.'[p]"

[8]Again, the devil took him to a very high mountain and showed him all the kingdoms of the world and their splendor. [9]"All this I will give you," he said, "if you will bow down and worship me."

----

[m]11 Or in   [n]4 Deut. 8:3   [o]6 Psalm 91:11,12   [p]7 Deut. 6:16

LOOKING INTO THE SCRIPTURE/20 Minutes. Read Matthew 4:1-11 and discuss.

1. What is the longest you have ever gone without food?
   a. three hours
   b. one day
   c. three days
   d. I've never been hungry

2. What were the circumstances?
   a. I was on a diet
   b. I was stranded on a mountaintop
   c. there was no food in the house
   d. I decided to fast and pray

3. How did your hunger affect your:
   a. will power
   b. emotions
   c. attitude
   d. reasoning

4. How would you describe the power struggle going on here?
   a. this is the classic struggle between good and evil
   b. Satan is trying to conquer Jesus when he seems weak and powerless
   c. this power struggle is no different than those we face daily
   d. Satan is trying to conquer Jesus by tempting him on the physical, intellectual, emotional and spiritual levels

5. What is the devil trying to do with Jesus?
   a. kill him physically
   b. play "mind games" with him
   c. get Jesus to worship him
   d. enlist Jesus as an ally

6. What tactics does Jesus use to conquer Satan?
   a. call on angels to help
   b. quote Scripture to refute claims
   c. appeal to higher authority
   d. tell Satan to "beat it"

7. In verse 3, why did the devil challenge Jesus to change stones into bread?
   a. to see if Jesus could do it
   b. to exercise control over Jesus
   c. to mock and dare Jesus
   d. to attack where Jesus was vulnerable

8. In verse 6, what do you learn about Satan?
   a. he knows Scripture too
   b. he can change tactics as circumstances dictate
   c. he is easily frustrated
   d. he tempts at the weakest point

MY OWN STORY/25 Minutes.

1. Which of these temptations would be the hardest for you to resist?
   ☐ Chocolate: All you could eat
   ☐ Skipping work on a nice day
   ☐ Sleeping in on Sunday
   ☐ Taking that long needed vacation
   ☐ Taking a Porsche for a joy ride
   ☐ Never passing up a "bargain"
   ☐ Sneaking into a ball game
   ☐ Taking a book to bed

2. How would you compare your own temptations with the temptations that Jesus faced?
   a. different, but just as real
   b. not quite so big
   c. not quite so obvious
   d. I've never been tempted

3. When do you find yourself most vulnerable to the tempter?
   a. when I'm tired or under stress
   b. when I'm alone or away from home
   c. after a spiritual high
   d. when I'm not expecting it
   e. when I let my mind dwell on certain things

4. What has helped you to overcome temptation when it comes?
   a. Scripture (my special passage is . . .)
   b. telling a friend about it
   c. prayer
   d. talking myself out of it
   e. fleeing/change of scene

5. What has made you feel good about resisting temptation?
   a. avoiding hurt
   b. just knowing I did the right thing
   c. I've gotten stronger as a Christian
   d. nothing. Given the chance again I'd go for it

¹⁰Jesus said to him, "Away from me, Satan! For it is written: 'Worship the Lord your God, and serve him only.'ᵠ"

¹¹Then the devil left him, and angels came and attended him.

Jesus Begins to Preach

¹²When Jesus heard that John had been put in prison, he returned to Galilee. ¹³Leaving Nazareth, he went and lived in Capernaum, which was by the lake in the area of Zebulun and Naphtali— ¹⁴to fulfill what was said through the prophet Isaiah:

¹⁵"Land of Zebulun and land of Naphtali,
the way to the sea, along the Jordan,
Galilee of the Gentiles—
¹⁶the people living in darkness
have seen a great light;
on those living in the land of the shadow of death
a light has dawned."ʳ

¹⁷From that time on Jesus began to preach, "Repent, for the kingdom of heaven is near."

The Calling of the First Disciples

¹⁸As Jesus was walking beside the Sea of Galilee, he saw two brothers, Simon called Peter and his brother Andrew. They were casting a net into the lake, for they were fishermen. ¹⁹"Come, follow me," Jesus said, "and I will make you fishers of men." ²⁰At once they left their nets and followed him.

²¹Going on from there, he saw two other brothers, James son of Zebedee and his brother John. They were in a boat with their father Zebedee, preparing their nets. Jesus called them, ²²and immediately they left the boat and their father and followed him.

Jesus Heals the Sick

²³Jesus went throughout Galilee, teaching in their synagogues, preaching the good news of the kingdom, and healing every disease and sickness among the people. ²⁴News about him spread all over Syria, and people brought to him all who were ill with various diseases, those suffering severe pain, the demon-possessed, those having seizures, and the paralyzed, and he healed them. ²⁵Large crowds from Galilee, the Decapolis,ˢ Jerusalem, Judea and the region across the Jordan followed him.

The Beatitudes

5 Now when he saw the crowds, he went up on a mountainside and sat down. His disciples came to him, ²and he began to teach them, saying:

³"Blessed are the poor in spirit,
for theirs is the kingdom of heaven.
⁴Blessed are those who mourn,
for they will be comforted.
⁵Blessed are the meek,
for they will inherit the earth.

OPEN: If your spiritual mentor was suddenly removed from the scene, how would you feel? React?

DIG: 1. How does Jesus react to the news of John's imprisonment? 2. In what way had the people been "living in darkness"? 3. What was the nature of Jesus' message? What is the relation between repentance and the kingdom of heaven?

REFLECT: 1.When have you suffered the loss of a close friend in the ministry? What did you do to recover the loss and pick up the slack? 2. What part of your ministry is concerned with the coming kingdom? With repentance?

OPEN: When did you leave home for the first time? What for?

DIG: What invitations does Jesus give to these fishermen? What seems unusual about their response? What prior knowledge of Jesus do you think they had (see vv. 13, 17)? How might Zebedee have felt?

REFLECT: Spiritually, are you going to fish or cut bait? How soon?

OPEN: Only some kinds of illness can be healed spiritually—T or F?

DIG: How is Jesus' ministry expanding: Wider area? Whole person? Larger crowds? More commitment? Why? What seems to be Jesus' criteria for healing?

REFLECT: What one thing would you like Jesus to heal in your life?

OPEN: If there were all star teams for certain character traits (All-Humble Team, All-Thoughtful Team, etc.) for which team would you be nominated?

DIG: 1. What is the connection between Matthew 4:23-25 and 5:1-2? 2. What eight qualities ought to characterize kingdom people (vv. 3-12)? How would you describe the opposite of each of these eight? 3. What is the specific promise associated with each quality? Will these promises come about in the

ᵠ10 Deut. 6:13   ʳ16 Isaiah 9:1,2   ˢ25 That is, the Ten Cities

30

LOOKING INTO THE SCRIPTURE/25 Minutes. Read Matthew 5:3-10 and measure yourself on these mental attitudes—1 being LOW and 4 being HIGH.

POOR IN SPIRIT: I have come to the place where I feel accepted by God when I feel most unacceptable to myself. I recognize my need for God and know that I do not have to earn His love with wealth, status or spiritual sophistication.

LOW 1 2 3 4 HIGH

MOURN: I have come to the place where I can really feel the empty places in my life. I can let others know when I am hurting and share the grief of others without embarrassment. I can weep like Jesus did.   LOW 1 2 3 4 HIGH

MEEK: I have come to the place where I don't have to be the strong one all the time. I can be tender and gentle with people. I've given the control of my life to God and I don't have to "win" all the time.   LOW 1 2 3 4 HIGH

SPIRITUAL HUNGER: I have come to the place where I want to know God and His will for my life more than anything. I am more excited about God's will for the world than my own financial gain, success in my career, or acceptance by my peers. I long for God's perspective in my decision-making.   LOW 1 2 3 4 HIGH

MERCIFUL: I have come to the place where I can enter into the feelings of someone who is hurting, lonely, or distressed and feel alongside them in their pain. God has given me a sensitivity for the suffering of others.   LOW 1 2 3 4 HIGH

PURE IN HEART: I have come to the place where I can be completely open and honest with God and others—transparent because I have nothing to hide. I don't have to put on "airs," or pretend to be what I'm not.   LOW 1 2 3 4 HIGH

PEACEMAKER: I have come to the place where I really work at keeping the channels of communication open between me and those around me. I deal with anger and disagreements immediately and don't allow them to fester. I encourage those around me to work out their differences without hurting one another.   LOW 1 2 3 4 HIGH

PERSECUTION: I have come to the place where I know what I am living for, and for this cause I am not afraid to suffer and, if need be, die. I am willing to "take the heat" and stand alone for what is right. I can take criticism without feeling self-pity or self-righteous.

LOW 1 2 3 4 HIGH

MY OWN STORY/20 Minutes.

1. In what area (beatitude) have you made the most progress in the last year? How have you experienced the "blessing"?

2. In what area do you need to work on something? How could the group help you grow in that area?

3. Below is a list of qualities based on the Beatitudes. In silence, think about the members of your group and jot down their initials next to the beatitude paraphrase where you see each person as strong. (For instance, you might put Bob's initials next to "gentleness".) Then, ask one person to sit in silence while the others explain where they put this person's name. Then, take the next person and do the same until everyone has been affirmed.

☐ SELF-ACCEPTANCE: The ability to accept yourself and your imperfections, and to enable others to be more self-accepting.

☐ EMPATHY: The ability to feel what others feel; to laugh and cry with others.

☐ GENTLENESS: Ability to be tender because you are inwardly strong and to lead without overpowering others.

☐ SPIRITUALITY: Ability to maintain spiritual priorities and to cause others to seek a deeper walk with Christ.

☐ SENSITIVITY: The ability to pick up on the hurt and pain of others and be "present" without being pushy or nosey.

☐ TRANSPARENCY: The ability to be yourself without any pretenses and allow the presence of Christ to radiate through you.

☐ PEACEMAKING: The ability to harmonize differences between others without causing either person to "lose."

☐ ENDURANCE: The ability to stand up for what you believe without getting defensive or compromising your principles.

present? Or the future? **4.** Is Jesus *describing* who his followers *are*? Or *prescribing* what they must *do*? Why? **5.** How does this section of Scripture begin to explain the nature of the kingdom?

REFLECT: 1. How do these promised blessings compare with what most people in the world prize? Would kingdom people be admired in your society? Why or why not? **2.** Of these eight qualities, which two do you desire most in your life? Why? Who in your group or family do you associate with each? Desired quality? **3.** How does Jesus embody and enable the qualities you desire?

_____

OPEN: Are you more likely to curse the darkness, or light a candle? Why?

DIG: 1. Consider salt and light: How do they function? Become useless? What prevails in their absence? **2.** How then do Christians penetrate society? Or become useless?

REFLECT: Is your lifestyle salty or saltless? Covered or open? Why?

_____

OPEN: As a kid, what family rule did you just love breaking? Why?

DIG: 1. Why might Jesus have to explain his position on the Law and Prophets? **2.** How might Jesus "fulfill" the Prophets and "accomplish everything" in the Law? **3.** In the kingdom, what makes one "least"? "Great"?**4.** How does one obtain this "surpassing righteousness" (v. 20): Living by law? By the Sermon on the Mount? By grace?

REFLECT: Which righteousness are you practicing and teaching?

_____

OPEN: 1. "If looks could kill", how many of your friends would be dead by now: 10? 100? What friends? **2.** What gets your goat most often: Tardiness? Laziness? Clumsiness?

DIG: 1. How are these particular commandments (5:21-48) related to each other and to the previous section (vv. 17-20)? How is Jesus like a "New Moses"? **2.** What new standard of right and wrong is Jesus creating here (vv. 21-26)? How are murder, anger, reconciliation and

⁶Blessed are those who hunger and thirst for
   righteousness,
  for they will be filled.
⁷Blessed are the merciful,
  for they will be shown mercy.
⁸Blessed are the pure in heart,
  for they will see God.
⁹Blessed are the peacemakers,
  for they will be called sons of God.
¹⁰Blessed are those who are persecuted because of
   righteousness,
  for theirs is the kingdom of heaven.

[11]"Blessed are you when people insult you, persecute you and falsely say all kinds of evil against you because of me. [12]Rejoice and be glad, because great is your reward in heaven, for in the same way they persecuted the prophets who were before you.

Salt and Light

[13]"You are the salt of the earth. But if the salt loses its saltiness, how can it be made salty again? It is no longer good for anything, except to be thrown out and trampled by men. [14]"You are the light of the world. A city on a hill cannot be hidden. [15]Neither do people light a lamp and put it under a bowl. Instead they put it on its stand, and it gives light to everyone in the house. [16]In the same way, let your light shine before men, that they may see your good deeds and praise your Father in heaven.

The Fulfillment of the Law

[17]"Do not think that I have come to abolish the Law or the Prophets; I have not come to abolish them but to fulfill them. [18]I tell you the truth, until heaven and earth disappear, not the smallest letter, not the least stroke of a pen, will by any means disappear from the Law until everything is accomplished. [19]Anyone who breaks one of the least of these commandments and teaches others to do the same will be called least in the kingdom of heaven, but whoever practices and teaches these commands will be called great in the kingdom of heaven. [20]For I tell you that unless your righteousness surpasses that of the Pharisees and the teachers of the law, you will certainly not enter the kingdom of heaven.

Murder

[21]"You have heard that it was said to the people long ago, 'Do not murder,[t] and anyone who murders will be subject to judgment.' [22]But I tell you that anyone who is angry with his brother[u] will be subject to judgment. Again, anyone who says to his brother, 'Raca,[v]' is answerable to the Sanhedrin. But anyone who says, 'You fool!' will be in danger of the fire of hell.

[23]"Therefore, if you are offering your gift at the altar and

---

t21 Exodus 20:13   *u22* Some manuscripts *brother without cause*   *v22* An Aramaic term of contempt

there remember that your brother has something against you, [24]leave your gift there in front of the altar. First go and be reconciled to your brother; then come and offer your gift.

[25]"Settle matters quickly with your adversary who is taking you to court. Do it while you are still with him on the way, or he may hand you over to the judge, and the judge may hand you over to the officer, and you may be thrown into prison. [26]I tell you the truth, you will not get out until you have paid the last penny. [w]

Adultery

[27]"You have heard that it was said, 'Do not commit adultery.' [x] [28]But I tell you that anyone who looks at a woman lustfully has already committed adultery with her in his heart. [29]If your right eye causes you to sin, gouge it out and throw it away. It is better for you to lose one part of your body than for your whole body to be thrown into hell. [30]And if your right hand causes you to sin, cut it off and throw it away. It is better for you to lose one part of your body than for your whole body to go into hell.

Divorce

[31]"It has been said, 'Anyone who divorces his wife must give her a certificate of divorce.' [y] [32]But I tell you that anyone who divorces his wife, except for marital unfaithfulness, causes her to become an adulteress, and anyone who marries the divorced woman commits adultery.

Oaths

[33]"Again, you have heard that it was said to the people long ago, 'Do not break your oath, but keep the oaths you have made to the Lord.' [34]But I tell you, Do not swear at all: either by heaven, for it is God's throne; [35]or by the earth, for it is his footstool; or by Jerusalem, for it is the city of the Great King. [36]And do not swear by your head, for you cannot make even one hair white or black. [37]Simply let your 'Yes' be 'Yes,' and your 'No,' 'No'; anything beyond this comes from the evil one.

An Eye for an Eye

[38]"You have heard that it was said, 'Eye for eye, and tooth for tooth.' [z] [39]But I tell you, Do not resist an evil person. If someone strikes you on the right cheek, turn to him the other also. [40]And if someone wants to sue you and take your tunic, let him have your cloak as well. [41]If someone forces you to go one mile, go with him two miles. [42]Give to the one who asks you, and do not turn away from the one who wants to borrow from you.

justice linked here? Who is the Judge most to be feared (v. 25)? Why?

REFLECT: What Brother (see Heb. 2:11) enables you to be reconciled to your other "brothers" (vv. 22, 23, 24)? Who has paid the "last penny" to set you free? How then shall you live?

OPEN: If your group collected "a penny for your thoughts" everytime you lusted, how rich would they be?

DIG: How does one guage lustfullness? What is Jesus' point in using such exaggerated language (vv. 29-30)?

REFLECT: Who does adultery hurt? Likewise, lust? Why?

DIG: How does Jesus sharpen the focus of Moses' law on divorce (also 19:3-9)? How is divorce linked with adultery?

REFLECT: How has divorce touched your life?

OPEN: What would you love to have different about your hair?

DIG: 1. Why are promises to God so important? 2. What should replace oaths and vows? Why?

REFLECT: 1. How would your parents or children evaluate you on this passage? 2. How could you grow in this area of your life?

OPEN: 1. When you were a child, what fights did you get into? 2. How would you describe yourself in those fights: Muhammad Ali? Chicken Little? Who?

DIG: 1. What was the original intent of "eye for eye", and "tooth for tooth"? 2. What was Jesus' intent in saying, "Do not resist an evil person"? Do you think Jesus is exaggerating here as he did in Matthew 5:29-30? Why or why not?

REFLECT: 1. Is this teaching of pacifism intended for individuals only? Nations also? Both? 2. Would Jesus resist Hitler? If so, how? If not, why? 3. What modern-day examples can you cite of this pacifist ethic?

[w]26 Greek kodrantes   [x]27 Exodus 20:14   [y]31 Deut. 24:1
[z]38 Exodus 21:24; Lev. 24:20; Deut. 19:21

OPEN: As a kid, who was your Public Enemy No 1? Why? Today, who is toughest for you to love? Why?

DIG: 1. In this context, what does love involve: Prayer? Action? Unconditional positive regard? Perfect grace from God? **2.** Who is the object of love in Leviticus 19:18? In verses 44-47? Why the shift?

REFLECT: Have the directions in this chapter been encouraging or overwhelming for you? Why?

OPEN: What is noticeable about someone "religious"? Why is that?

DIG: 1. What does hypocrisy in giving look like? Sound like? Feel like? What is its reward? **2.** What is the opposite? What is the reward of giving in "secret"?

REFLECT 1. What would it feel like to give in secret? **2.** Where do you need growth in the area of giving?

OPEN: 1. What do you remember from your childhood about prayer? What were you taught to pray? By whom? **2.** What "hang-ups" do you keep in your closet?

DIG: 1. What did Jesus tell his listeners to avoid in prayer? **2.** How do hypocrisy and verbosity go together? How does each diminish prayer? **3.** In Jesus' model prayer (vv. 9-13), to whom did he pray? What three concerns, related to God, did he pray about first? **4.** What concerns follow? What three personal concerns are to be the subject of prayer? **5.** How do prayer and forgiveness go together? **6.** What is significant about the plural pronouns and adjectives in this prayer? **7.** If our Father knows what we need before we ask (v. 8), why do we need to pray? **8.** How does Jesus' directive concerning "closet prayer" (v. 6) reconcile with Jesus' encouragement of "group prayer" (see Mt. 18:20)?

REFLECT: 1. What bad habits have you acquired in prayer? **2.** How can you experience a "break through" in prayer? Will this take more time? More words? More forgiveness? More closet space? **3.** From Jesus' model prayer, what do you want to practice and pass along to your family?

Love for Enemies

43"You have heard that it was said, 'Love your neighbor^a and hate your enemy.' 44But I tell you: Love your enemies^b and pray for those who persecute you, 45that you may be sons of your Father in heaven. He causes his sun to rise on the evil and the good, and sends rain on the righteous and the unrighteous. 46If you love those who love you, what reward will you get? Are not even the tax collectors doing that? 47And if you greet only your brothers, what are you doing more than others? Do not even pagans do that? 48Be perfect, therefore, as your heavenly Father is perfect.

Giving to the Needy

6 "Be careful not to do your 'acts of righteousness' before men, to be seen by them. If you do, you will have no reward from your Father in heaven.

2"So when you give to the needy, do not announce it with trumpets, as the hypocrites do in the synagogues and on the streets, to be honored by men. I tell you the truth, they have received their reward in full. 3But when you give to the needy, do not let your left hand know what your right hand is doing, 4so that your giving may be in secret. Then your Father, who sees what is done in secret, will reward you.

Prayer

5"And when you pray, do not be like the hypocrites, for they love to pray standing in the synagogues and on the street corners to be seen by men. I tell you the truth, they have received their reward in full. 6But when you pray, go into your room, close the door and pray to your Father, who is unseen. Then your Father, who sees what is done in secret, will reward you. 7And when you pray, do not keep on babbling like pagans, for they think they will be heard because of their many words. 8Do not be like them, for your Father knows what you need before you ask him.

9"This, then, is how you should pray:

" 'Our Father in heaven,
    hallowed be your name,
10your kingdom come,
    your will be done
        on earth as it is in heaven.
11Give us today our daily bread.
12Forgive us our debts,
    as we also have forgiven our debtors.
13And lead us not into temptation,
    but deliver us from the evil one.'^{c}

14For if you forgive men when they sin against you, your heavenly Father will also forgive you. 15But if you do not forgive men their sins, your Father will not forgive your sins.

---

^{a}43 Lev. 19:18 ^{b}44 Some late manuscripts *enemies, bless those who curse you, do good to those who hate you* ^{c}13 Or *from evil;* some late manuscripts *one, / for yours is the kingdom and the power and the glory forever. Amen.*

LOOKING INTO THE SCRIPTURE/20 Minutes. Read Matthew 6:9-13 and evaluate your own prayer life against the model here.

ADORATION OF GOD: *"Our Father in heaven, hallowed be your name."* I spend time praising God for who he is, both holy Lord and compassionate Father.

1. I know God is holy and compassionate by what I see:
   a. in history
   b. in creation
   c. in my relationships
   d. in Jesus Christ

LONGING FOR HIS REIGN: *"Your kingdom come, your will be done on earth as it is in heaven."* I spend time welcoming God's influence into my life and into my world.

2. I would like to know God's will for my life in the following area:
   a. family problems
   b. political issues
   c. life planning
   d. ethical questions

DAILY NEEDS: *"Give us today our daily bread."* I have confidence to ask that today's needs will be provided.

3. How would praying "just for today" change my petitions?
   a. no change
   b. change the quantity of my petitions
   c. change what I ask for
   d. change how often I pray
   e. make me more specific

RELATIONAL HEALING: *"Forgive us our debts, as we also have forgiven our debtors."* In my prayer time, I ask for and experience God's forgiveness. I consciously recall the relationships where I have been hurt or have hurt others and ask for forgiveness.

4. What is my typical method for responding to those who hurt me?
   a. hold a grudge/seek revenge
   b. talk it out
   c. get angry and blow up
   d. forget it

STRENGTH FOR THE SPIRITUAL BATTLE: *"And lead us not into temptation, but deliver us from the evil one."* In my prayer time, I allow God to speak to me about the areas where I am struggling or treading on dangerous ground. I express dependence upon God for the ability to resist temptation.

5. I experience yielding to temptation somewhere on this scale:
THE DEVIL MADE   1   2   3   4   5   6   7   8   9   10   I WALKED INTO IT
ME DO IT   WITH BOTH EYES OPEN

MY OWN LIFE/20 Minutes.

How balanced are you in your prayer life, based on the model in the Lord's prayer of the five elements of prayer? Take the first element (Adoration of God) and ask everyone in your group to respond by using one of the Options below. Then, go around again on the second element (Longing for His Reign), etc., until you have gone through all five elements.

OPTION 1
1. This is *difficult* for me because:
   a. I have trouble believing God cares about this
   b. I feel God is powerless to change this
   c. I struggle with the cooperation I need to give in this prayer
   d. I can't picture the end goal of this
   e. I want to take the credit for success in this area

OPTION 2
2. This prayer element is *easy* for me because:
   a. God's blessing has already been so real in my life
   b. I recognize only God can help me here
   c. I am ready to go where God sends me
   d. I know God has my best good at heart, despite the present circumstances

OPEN: How long could you make it without ice cream?

DIG: What is fasting? Pharisaical fasting? Christian fasting? Why fast? How does this teaching fit in with the rest of chapter 6?

REFLECT: How do you keep your fast "secret", from everyone?

OPEN: If Jesus was not your treasure, what would be?

DIG: 1. What alternatives, does Jesus propose with respect to treasures, (vv. 19-21) bodily conditions (vv. 22-23), and masters (v. 24)? **2.** What would be valuable in heaven that isn't valuable here? **3.** What is the link between treasure and heart? Heart and eye? Eye and body? Body and master? Master and money? How is that cycle broken?

REFLECT: How has this TV culture affected your view of treasure?

OPEN: How would your best friend describe your clothing selections? Moth-eaten? Well-feathered? Only one tunic? Dressed to kill?

DIG: 1. How does your choice of treasure, master, and sight (vv. 19-24) affect your attitude toward life (vv. 25-27)? **2.** What does God's care for the birds and lillies teach you? How does God release us from materialistic preoccupations? **3.** How does the work ethic fit into this passage? How does faith?

REFLECT: 1. Why pray, when you can worry? What causes you the most worry? **2.** What gives you the greatest sense of security? **3.** How can you measure whether you are seeking the kingdom first (or second or third)? Which is to say, how do you measure your character (5:3-12), influence (5:13-16), righteousness (5:17-48), and religious activities (6:1-18), as well as your material concerns (6:19-34)?

OPEN: Would you be a better insurance adjuster or baseball umpire?

DIG: 1. In distinctively Christian relationships, how do you discern wrong-doing and erroneous doctrine? Is Jesus calling for "no" judgment? Or "fair" judgement? Or "self" judgement? Or "divine" judgement only? Why? **2.** In Jesus' day, who were the "dogs" and "pigs" and what are the "pearls" (v. 6)?

Fasting

[16]"When you fast, do not look somber as the hypocrites do, for they disfigure their faces to show men they are fasting. I tell you the truth, they have received their reward in full. [17]But when you fast, put oil on your head and wash your face, [18]so that it will not be obvious to men that you are fasting, but only to your Father, who is unseen; and your Father, who sees what is done in secret, will reward you.

Treasures in Heaven

[19]"Do not store up for yourselves treasures on earth, where moth and rust destroy, and where thieves break in and steal. [20]But store up for yourselves treasures in heaven, where moth and rust do not destroy, and where thieves do not break in and steal. [21]For where your treasure is, there your heart will be also.

[22]"The eye is the lamp of the body. If your eyes are good, your whole body will be full of light. [23]But if your eyes are bad, your whole body will be full of darkness. If then the light within you is darkness, how great is that darkness!

[24]"No one can serve two masters. Either he will hate the one and love the other, or he will be devoted to the one and despise the other. You cannot serve both God and Money.

Do Not Worry

[25]"Therefore I tell you, do not worry about your life, what you will eat or drink; or about your body, what you will wear. Is not life more important than food, and the body more important than clothes? [26]Look at the birds of the air; they do not sow or reap or store away in barns, and yet your heavenly Father feeds them. Are you not much more valuable than they? [27]Who of you by worrying can add a single hour to his life[d]? [28]"And why do you worry about clothes? See how the lilies of the field grow. They do not labor or spin. [29]Yet I tell you that not even Solomon in all his splendor was dressed like one of these. [30]If that is how God clothes the grass of the field, which is here today and tomorrow is thrown into the fire, will he not much more clothe you, O you of little faith? [31]So do not worry, saying, 'What shall we eat?' or 'What shall we drink?' or 'What shall we wear?' [32]For the pagans run after all these things, and your heavenly Father knows that you need them. [33]But seek first his kingdom and his righteousness, and all these things will be given to you as well. [34]Therefore do not worry about tomorrow, for tomorrow will worry about itself. Each day has enough trouble of its own.

Judging Others

7 "Do not judge, or you too will be judged. [2]For in the same way you judge others, you will be judged, and with the measure you use, it will be measured to you.

[3]"Why do you look at the speck of sawdust in your brother's eye and pay no attention to the plank in your own eye? [4]How can you say to your brother, 'Let me take the speck out of your

[d]27 Or *single cubit to his height*

LOOKING INTO THE SCRIPTURE/15 Minutes.

1. If you could have three wishes, which three would you choose from the list below:
   - □ Win the lottery: Never have to work again.
   - □ Secure job: Lifetime guarantee with benefits.
   - □ Stress-free life: No pain. No struggle. No tension.
   - □ Close family: No hassles. Lots of love and support.
   - □ Good health: Long life full of vigor and vitality.
   - □ One deep abiding friendship: Someone who will stick forever.
   - □ Happiness: A life full of joy and surprises.
   - □ Success: Fame and recognition in your chosen field.
   - □ Direction: To know what you want to do with your life.
   - □ Strong, spiritual faith: Deep, satisfying relationship with God.

2. Read Matthew 6:25-34. What does this mean? "Do not worry about your life . . ."
   a. everything will be okay
   b. don't sweat the small stuff
   c. God will bail you out
   d. get out of the fast lane
   e. get your act together

3. "But seek first his kingdom. . . ." What does this mean?
   a. get rid of your Porsche
   b. put God first and keep your Porsche
   c. check it out with God first
   d. Volkswagen buyers are smarter

4. What is Jesus saying here? "Therefore, do not worry about tomorrow. . . ."
   a. don't plan ahead
   b. plan ahead so you don't worry
   c. live for today
   d. take it as it comes
   e. trust God with things you can't control

5. What is the spiritual principle of this passage?
   a. slow down and live longer
   b. if you can't take the heat, get out of the kitchen
   c. Christians never have problems
   d. if it causes worry, check it out
   e. relax. God is in control

MY OWN STORY/25 Minutes.

1. Code the list of concerns below with these symbols in the margin.
   P=My parent's biggest concern
   −5=My biggest concern 5 years ago
   +5=My biggest concern 5 years from now

   X=Something I can do nothing about
   †=Something I can give to God and forget about
   ★=My biggest concern right now

   _____ Children: Doing OK in school
   _____ Parents: Getting old
   _____ Job: Finding or losing it
   _____ Money: Not having enough
   _____ Advancement: Getting ahead
   _____ Older children: Not making it

   _____ Transition: Starting over
   _____ Midlife: Failing my expectations
   _____ Health: Can't work/pay bills
   _____ Retirement: Feeling useless
   _____ Future: Being left alone
   _____ Accidents: Loved one getting hurt

2. If you were to take seriously the Scripture passage, how would it effect your list above?
   a. it would change everything
   b. it would change a few things
   c. it would change the way I view things
   d. it wouldn't change a thing

3. How do you feel after taking this personal inventory?
   a. relieved
   b. angry, because these concerns do not go away
   c. frustrated, because I know I should not be this way
   d. I'll have to think about this

REFLECT: When have you had a judgmental attitude? How can one grow out of that? How can your group help you do that?

OPEN: What house or room do you remember having the most doors, none of which led outside?

DIG: 1. What does Jesus actually promise? What is the nature of his argument? 2. Would God give you anything you asked for? If you asked for a snake, would he give it? What is the guiding principle?

REFLECT: How do we really know God is good and not some "scrooge"?

DIG: What is the point of the two gates, roads, destinies, crowds? Why is one road less traveled?

REFLECT: Why doesn't God make the gate to life wider?

OPEN: What is your favorite fruit?

DIG: 1. How do these warnings (vv. 15-20) relate to the narrow gate (vv. 13-14)? 2. How does one tell a good tree? A good person (also Mt. 3:8, 10)? 3. What is wrong with a mere verbal profession of faith? What more is needed? 4. Why are the people ultimately banished as "evil-doers"?

REFLECT: How does Jesus' warning make you feel: Sheepish? Wolf-like? Barren? Fruitful? Sour grapes? Dispossessed? Possessed? Thankful? Why? What's at stake for you?

OPEN: If you could build a dream home, what would it look like? Where would it be?

DIG: 1. What are the similarities and differences between these two houses and their owner-builders? 2. What does this passage suggest about the kinds of people who face storms? 3. What kind of commitment is Jesus calling for here?

REFLECT: 1. Why would anyone build with a weak foundation? 2. At this point in your life, is your pressing need to learn more, or to prac-

eye,' when all the time there is a plank in your own eye? ⁵You hypocrite, first take the plank out of your own eye, and then you will see clearly to remove the speck from your brother's eye.

⁶"Do not give dogs what is sacred; do not throw your pearls to pigs. If you do, they may trample them under their feet, and then turn and tear you to pieces.

Ask, Seek, Knock

⁷"Ask and it will be given to you; seek and you will find; knock and the door will be opened to you. ⁸For everyone who asks receives; he who seeks finds; and to him who knocks, the door will be opened.

⁹"Which of you, if his son asks for bread, will give him a stone? ¹⁰Or if he asks for a fish, will give him a snake? ¹¹If you, then, though you are evil, know how to give good gifts to your children, how much more will your Father in heaven give good gifts to those who ask him! ¹²So in everything, do to others what you would have them do to you, for this sums up the Law and the Prophets.

The Narrow and Wide Gates

¹³"Enter through the narrow gate. For wide is the gate and broad is the road that leads to destruction, and many enter through it. ¹⁴But small is the gate and narrow the road that leads to life, and only a few find it.

A Tree and Its Fruit

¹⁵"Watch out for false prophets. They come to you in sheep's clothing, but inwardly they are ferocious wolves. ¹⁶By their fruit you will recognize them. Do people pick grapes from thorn-bushes, or figs from thistles? ¹⁷Likewise every good tree bears good fruit, but a bad tree bears bad fruit. ¹⁸A good tree cannot bear bad fruit, and a bad tree cannot bear good fruit. ¹⁹Every tree that does not bear good fruit is cut down and thrown into the fire. ²⁰Thus, by their fruit you will recognize them.

²¹"Not everyone who says to me, 'Lord, Lord,' will enter the kingdom of heaven, but only he who does the will of my Father who is in heaven. ²²Many will say to me on that day, 'Lord, Lord, did we not prophesy in your name, and in your name drive out demons and perform many miracles?' ²³Then I will tell them plainly, 'I never knew you. Away from me, you evildoers!'

The Wise and Foolish Builders

²⁴"Therefore everyone who hears these words of mine and puts them into practice is like a wise man who built his house on the rock. ²⁵The rain came down, the streams rose, and the winds blew and beat against that house; yet it did not fall, because it had its foundation on the rock. ²⁶But everyone who hears these words of mine and does not put them into practice is like a foolish man who built his house on sand. ²⁷The rain came down, the streams rose, and the winds blew and beat against that house, and it fell with a great crash."

LOOKING INTO THE SCRIPTURE/20 Minutes. Read Matthew 7:7-12 and discuss.

1. My initial reaction to these promises is:
   a. it's too good to be true
   b. there must be a catch somewhere
   c. God must be crazy to give a blank check
   d. if it's really true, WOW!

2. What does this mean? "Ask and it will be given to you; seek and you will find; knock and the door will be opened to you."
   a. God is waiting for us
   b. you get what you ask for
   c. you have to persevere with God
   d. here's a promise you can't refuse

3. What is the point in the two questions about bread and fish?
   a. God knows best
   b. God has our best interest in mind
   c. God always answers but not always the way we want
   d. God wants to give anything we ask

4. What is God promising to give us?
   a. all the bread and fish we need
   b. whatever we ask in all cases
   c. whatever we need, but he decides
   d. what is best for us

5. What slogan or bumper sticker comes the farthest from the Golden Rule (v. 12)?
   a. I'm easy to get along with as long as you do it my way
   b. If you don't like the way I drive, get off the sidewalk
   c. Treat others like dirt and you'll be the one to get hurt
   d. Who said you can't have it all?
   e. Go ahead. Make my day.
   f. _____

6. What is the Golden Rule really saying?
   a. look out for number 2
   b. never think of yourself
   c. if you love yourself, you will also love others
   d. put yourself in their shoes
   e. be a doormat for God

MY OWN STORY/25 Minutes.

1. If it were my house instead of Dorothy's, my door to the land of Oz would open to reveal:
   a. heaven itself
   b. Oz without the wicked witch
   c. unlimited opportunity for advancement
   d. a yellow brick road with no detours, dead ends, or booby-traps

2. When it comes to prayer, what do you need to do?
   a. find out what I want to pray for
   b. separate my wants from God's desires
   c. separate the "urgent" from the "important"
   d. learn how to pray

3. How do you think of prayer?
   a. enjoying God's presence
   b. getting my marching orders
   c. tapping into God's resources
   d. sitting down for a feast with God
   e. bringing my needs to God

4. When do you get serious about prayer?
   a. when I'm in trouble
   b. when someone I love gets sick
   c. on special occasions
   d. hardly ever
   e. when I am at a crossroads

5. If you were to take God seriously and ask him for one thing now, what would it be?
   a. better relationships at home
   b. to know what he wants me to do
   c. to show me how to cope with where I am
   d. to get me out of this situation
   e. to give me peace of mind

6. What would it take from you for God to answer this prayer?
   a. showing a little patience
   b. taking time off to think through the situation
   c. dealing with a sour relationship
   d. redoubling my efforts
   e. having complete faith that God is at work

7. How would you describe your openness to God right now? Put a dot on the line somewhere between the two extremes.

I AM KNOCKING ON GOD'S
DOOR RIGHT NOW _____

I'M AT GOD'S DOOR BUT I'M
AFRAID TO KNOCK

tice what you have already learned? **3.** How is Jesus' teaching different than anything you've heard?

OPEN: Who "hogs the shower" in your family?

DIG: What did being a leper in Jesus' day mean—physically, socially and religiously? What is signifigant about the leper's request? About Jesus' touch? Why the need for official certification?

REFLECT: Who are the lepers in your world?

OPEN: Who is one of the greatest people of faith you've ever met? What touched you about that person's life?

DIG: 1. What is a centurion? What is his citizenship? **2.** Why is Jesus' offer to go the centurion's house a remarkable thing? What does it tell you about Jesus? **3.** Why is the centurion's faith important to Jesus? How does he use it to teach his followers? **4.** In verses 11-12, who are the "many"? Who are the "subjects of the kingdom"? What is Jesus' point in sharing this with a Jewish audience? **5.** What is remarkable about the manner in which Jesus healed?

REFLECT: 1. What delights you in this passage? **2.** What challenge does it provide for you?

OPEN: If you are married, what do you like best about your mother-in-law? If you are unmarried, who amoung your acquaintances would be an ideal mother-in-law? Why?

DIG: 1. What power does Jesus demonstrate in this passage? **2.** What does Peter's mother-in-law do upon being healed? Why is that significant? **3.** Who else was healed? Of what? How did this fulfill prophecy?

REFLECT: How is your healing and your service to Christ related?

---

²⁸When Jesus had finished saying these things, the crowds were amazed at his teaching, ²⁹because he taught as one who had authority, and not as their teachers of the law.

The Man With Leprosy

8 When he came down from the mountainside, large crowds followed him. ²A man with leprosy^e came and knelt before him and said, "Lord, if you are willing, you can make me clean."

³Jesus reached out his hand and touched the man. "I am willing," he said. "Be clean!" Immediately he was cured^f of his leprosy. ⁴Then Jesus said to him, "See that you don't tell anyone. But go, show yourself to the priest and offer the gift Moses commanded, as a testimony to them."

The Faith of the Centurion

⁵When Jesus had entered Capernaum, a centurion came to him, asking for help. ⁶"Lord," he said, "my servant lies at home paralyzed and in terrible suffering."

⁷Jesus said to him, "I will go and heal him."

⁸The centurion replied, "Lord, I do not deserve to have you come under my roof. But just say the word, and my servant will be healed. ⁹For I myself am a man under authority, with soldiers under me. I tell this one, 'Go,' and he goes; and that one, 'Come,' and he comes. I say to my servant, 'Do this,' and he does it."

¹⁰When Jesus heard this, he was astonished and said to those following him, "I tell you the truth, I have not found anyone in Israel with such great faith. ¹¹I say to you that many will come from the east and the west, and will take their places at the feast with Abraham, Isaac and Jacob in the kingdom of heaven. ¹²But the subjects of the kingdom will be thrown outside, into the darkness, where there will be weeping and gnashing of teeth."

¹³Then Jesus said to the centurion, "Go! It will be done just as you believed it would." And his servant was healed at that very hour.

Jesus Heals Many

¹⁴When Jesus came into Peter's house, he saw Peter's mother-in-law lying in bed with a fever. ¹⁵He touched her hand and the fever left her, and she got up and began to wait on him.

¹⁶When evening came, many who were demon-possessed were brought to him, and he drove out the spirits with a word and healed all the sick. ¹⁷This was to fulfill what was spoken through the prophet Isaiah:

> "He took up our infirmities
>   and carried our diseases."^g

---

^e2 The Greek word was used for various diseases affecting the skin—not necessarily leprosy.   ^f3 Greek *made clean*   ^g17 Isaiah 53:4

The Cost of Following Jesus

¹⁸When Jesus saw the crowd around him, he gave orders to cross to the other side of the lake. ¹⁹Then a teacher of the law came to him and said, "Teacher, I will follow you wherever you go."

²⁰Jesus replied, "Foxes have holes and birds of the air have nests, but the Son of Man has no place to lay his head."

²¹Another disciple said to him, "Lord, first let me go and bury my father."

²²But Jesus told him, "Follow me, and let the dead bury their own dead."

Jesus Calms the Storm

²³Then he got into the boat and his disciples followed him. ²⁴Without warning, a furious storm came up on the lake, so that the waves swept over the boat. But Jesus was sleeping. ²⁵The disciples went and woke him, saying, "Lord, save us! We're going to drown!"

²⁶He replied, "You of little faith, why are you so afraid?" Then he got up and rebuked the winds and the waves, and it was completely calm.

²⁷The men were amazed and asked, "What kind of man is this? Even the winds and the waves obey him!"

The Healing of Two Demon-possessed Men

²⁸When he arrived at the other side in the region of the Gadarenes,ʰ two demon-possessed men coming from the tombs met him. They were so violent that no one could pass that way. ²⁹"What do you want with us, Son of God?" they shouted. "Have you come here to torture us before the appointed time?"

³⁰Some distance from them a large herd of pigs was feeding. ³¹The demons begged Jesus, "If you drive us out, send us into the herd of pigs."

³²He said to them, "Go!" So they came out and went into the pigs, and the whole herd rushed down the steep bank into the lake and died in the water. ³³Those tending the pigs ran off, went into the town and reported all this, including what had happened to the demon-possessed men. ³⁴Then the whole town went out to meet Jesus. And when they saw him, they pleaded with him to leave their region.

Jesus Heals a Paralytic

9 Jesus stepped into a boat, crossed over and came to his own town. ²Some men brought to him a paralytic, lying on a mat. When Jesus saw their faith, he said to the paralytic, "Take heart, son; your sins are forgiven."

³At this, some of the teachers of the law said to themselves, "This fellow is blaspheming!"

⁴Knowing their thoughts, Jesus said, "Why do you entertain evil thoughts in your hearts? ⁵Which is easier: to say, 'Your sins

ʰ28 Some manuscripts *Gergesenes;* others *Gerasenes*

OPEN: On a scale of 1-10 (one lowest—ten highest) how would you rank yourself as an excuse-maker? What's your excuse for procrastination?

DIG: Why did Jesus answer his questioners this way? What answers do you think they were expecting?

REFLECT: 1. How much does it cost to be a follower of Christ? **2.** When you came to Christ did you understand the cost?

OPEN: When caught in a storm without shelter, what do you do?

DIG: 1. What is Jesus teaching the disciples by sleeping through the storm? By rebuking the storm? **2.** Why is Jesus upset? **3.** In this story, what emotions hinder faith? Accompany faith? Why?

REFLECT: When clouds darken your life outlook, is the Son still shining? Or does he seem asleep? How do you know?

OPEN: If this healing of the two demoniacs had happened in your community, how would the local TV station have covered the story?

DIG: 1. How do you think that the disciples were feeling as they continued across the lake? When they arrived to meet these men? Who is more afraid of whom? Why? **2.** What do you learn about Jesus' authority and demon-possession from this story? **3.** Why did the people want Jesus to leave?

REFLECT: Are people or "pigs" (one's livelihood) more important in your culture? In your church? In your life?

OPEN: Where do you call "home"? Why?

DIG: 1. Where does this story take place? **2.** What did the people expect Jesus to do for the paralytic? Why did Jesus forgive the man's sins instead? Do you think the man was happy about this? **3.** Why would Jesus' statement be considered blasphemy by the teachers of the Law? **4.** Popular Jewish thought held that illness was caused by sin. How did Jesus demonstrate that he had indeed forgiven the man's sin? How did the people respond?

REFLECT: If Jesus really does forgive sin, why do many Christians struggle so with their forgiveness?

OPEN: Judging from the company you keep, what's your reputation?

DIG: 1. In Jesus' choice of Matthew, what is surprising? Offensive? To whom? Why? 2. How does Jesus respond to the Pharisees' indirect criticism? What is the irony here?

REFLECT: 1. What would be different about your life if Jesus had come to call "righteous" people instead of "sinners"? 2. How willing are you to associate with the kind of people that Jesus came to call?

OPEN: As a kid, did you outgrow your clothes, or wear them out?

DIG: 1. In this context, why do Jesus' disciples not fast? When will they? 2. How do unshrunk cloth and new wine relate to fasting, the bride groom, and the kingdom?

REFLECT: 1. How might the old practices of separatedness in eating (vv. 9-13) and fasting be old cloth mixing with the new wine of Jesus' call? 2. Does one need to fast to follow Jesus? Why?

OPEN: If "children are better seen and not heard"," what about demanding sick folk?

DIG: 1. What feelings or faith do you think prompted the ruler to approach Jesus? 2. If you were the woman, how would you feel just before you reached out to touch Jesus? Just afterward? How was her faith evident? 3. What new thing does Matthew reveal in this story? What is most signifigant about it? 4. What part does the ruler's intensive desire and the crowd's disbelief play in the raising of the dead girl? What is significant about their representative responses?

REFLECT: 1. The ruler and the woman were desperate. What is the relationship between desperateness and faith? 2. What is Jesus' role in healing today? What is the role of faith? Of touch?

are forgiven,' or to say, 'Get up and walk'? [6]But so that you may know that the Son of Man has authority on earth to forgive sins. . . ." Then he said to the paralytic, "Get up, take your mat and go home." [7]And the man got up and went home. [8]When the crowd saw this, they were filled with awe; and they praised God, who had given such authority to men.

The Calling of Matthew

[9]As Jesus went on from there, he saw a man named Matthew sitting at the tax collector's booth. "Follow me," he told him, and Matthew got up and followed him.

[10]While Jesus was having dinner at Matthew's house, many tax collectors and "sinners" came and ate with him and his disciples. [11]When the Pharisees saw this, they asked his disciples, "Why does your teacher eat with tax collectors and 'sinners'?"

[12]On hearing this, Jesus said, "It is not the healthy who need a doctor, but the sick. [13]But go and learn what this means: 'I desire mercy, not sacrifice.'[i] For I have not come to call the righteous, but sinners."

Jesus Questioned About Fasting

[14]Then John's disciples came and asked him, "How is it that we and the Pharisees fast, but your disciples do not fast?"

[15]Jesus answered, "How can the guests of the bridegroom mourn while he is with them? The time will come when the bridegroom will be taken from them; then they will fast.

[16]"No one sews a patch of unshrunk cloth on an old garment, for the patch will pull away from the garment, making the tear worse. [17]Neither do men pour new wine into old wineskins. If they do, the skins will burst, the wine will run out and the wineskins will be ruined. No, they pour new wine into new wineskins, and both are preserved."

A Dead Girl and a Sick Woman

[18]While he was saying this, a ruler came and knelt before him and said, "My daughter has just died. But come and put your hand on her, and she will live." [19]Jesus got up and went with him, and so did his disciples.

[20]Just then a woman who had been subject to bleeding for twelve years came up behind him and touched the edge of his cloak. [21]She said to herself, "If I only touch his cloak, I will be healed."

[22]Jesus turned and saw her. "Take heart, daughter," he said, "your faith has healed you." And the woman was healed from that moment.

[23]When Jesus entered the ruler's house and saw the flute players and the noisy crowd, [24]he said, "Go away. The girl is not dead but asleep." But they laughed at him. [25]After the crowd had been put outside, he went in and took the girl by the hand, and she got up. [26]News of this spread through all that region.

[i]13 Hosea 6:6

Jesus Heals the Blind and Mute

²⁷As Jesus went on from there, two blind men followed him, calling out, "Have mercy on us, Son of David!"

²⁸When he had gone indoors, the blind men came to him, and he asked them, "Do you believe that I am able to do this?"

"Yes, Lord," they replied.

²⁹Then he touched their eyes and said, "According to your faith will it be done to you"; ³⁰and their sight was restored. Jesus warned them sternly, "See that no one knows about this." ³¹But they went out and spread the news about him all over that region.

³²While they were going out, a man who was demon-possessed and could not talk was brought to Jesus. ³³And when the demon was driven out, the man who had been mute spoke. The crowd was amazed and said, "Nothing like this has ever been seen in Israel."

³⁴But the Pharisees said, "It is by the prince of demons that he drives out demons."

The Workers Are Few

³⁵Jesus went through all the towns and villages, teaching in their synagogues, preaching the good news of the kingdom and healing every disease and sickness. ³⁶When he saw the crowds, he had compassion on them, because they were harassed and helpless, like sheep without a shepherd. ³⁷Then he said to his disciples, "The harvest is plentiful but the workers are few. ³⁸Ask the Lord of the harvest, therefore, to send out workers into his harvest field."

Jesus Sends Out the Twelve

10 He called his twelve disciples to him and gave them authority to drive out evil ʲ spirits and to heal every disease and sickness.

²These are the names of the twelve apostles: first, Simon (who is called Peter) and his brother Andrew; James son of Zebedee, and his brother John; ³Philip and Bartholomew; Thomas and Matthew the tax collector; James son of Alphaeus, and Thaddaeus; ⁴Simon the Zealot and Judas Iscariot, who betrayed him.

⁵These twelve Jesus sent out with the following instructions: "Do not go among the Gentiles or enter any town of the Samaritans. ⁶Go rather to the lost sheep of Israel. ⁷As you go, preach this message: 'The kingdom of heaven is near. ⁸Heal the sick, raise the dead, cleanse those who have leprosy,ᵏ drive out demons. Freely you have received, freely give. ⁹Do not take along any gold or silver or copper in your belts; ¹⁰take no bag for the journey, or extra tunic, or sandals or a staff; for the worker is worth his keep.

¹¹"Whatever town or village you enter, search for some worthy person there and stay at his house until you leave. ¹²As you enter the home, give it your greeting. ¹³If the home is deserving, let your peace rest on it; if it is not, let your peace

---

ʲ1 Greek *unclean*   ᵏ8 The Greek word was used for various diseases affecting the skin—not necessarily leprosy.

OPEN: If you were blind, what would you miss seeing the most? If you talked less, who would that please?

DIG: 1. Who did the blind men perceive Jesus to be? What does this title mean? **2.** Why did he warn them against telling people about the healing? **3.** Why do you think the healed men disobeyed Jesus' warning? **4.** How did the crowds react to Jesus' power? How did the Pharisees react?

REFLECT: 1. When, if ever, have you been unable to keep your mouth shut about Jesus? **2.** In what ways might you still be partially blind and partially dumb spiritually? How can Jesus help give you fuller sight and speech?

OPEN: If forced, would you be a shepherd or a tractor driver? Why?

DIG: What does Jesus see in the crowds? In the harvest field? And so, what does he urge?

REFLECT: 1. In today's harvest are there enough workers? Too many? Too few? Why? **2.** Then will you pray, send or go? When?

OPEN: 1. What has been one of your all-time greatest adventures? **2.** The next time you embark upon a spine-tingling adventure, which four people do you want in your tent? **3.** Who was one of the more unusual house guests you or your family ever entertained?

DIG: 1. What did Jesus do before sending out his men? How does what the disciples will be doing compare with what Jesus had been doing (Matthew 8-9)? With what Jesus has seen (9:36)? With what Jesus has prayed (9:38)? **2.** Which disciples have you already met in the Book of Matthew? What do you know about them: Which are related? Which are from the same town? What were their former occupations? Which disciples do you know nothing about? **3.** What does a "zealot" sound like? Is it odd to you that Jesus would have one of those? How do you think Matthew and Simon would have gotten along if they had not been on the same team? **4.** What limits did Jesus put on their ministry (v. 5)? Why? **5.** What was to be their message? What were they to do? **6.** Why do you think that Jesus told them to

43

take nothing more than the clothes on their backs? **7.** Why do you think their mission excluded Samaritans and Gentiles? Do you think the disciples were disappointed that these groups were excluded? Why? **8.** What was the basic point of Jesus' preparation speech to the disciples? What problems would they (and future disciples) face? How were they to respond to each problem? **9.** What does it mean to be "like sheep among wolves", "as shrewd as snakes", "as innocent as doves"? **10.** Who would persecute them? Why? In times of persecution, what could they expect from God? **11.** How might Christ's truth divide a family? What kind of commitment does Jesus call for? **12.** Why is the believer worthy of Jesus (vv. 37-39)? What does verse 39 mean to you? **13.** How were the disciples to understand their reception (vv. 40-42)? What confirming authority does Jesus bestow upon his disciples at the end of his discourse (v. 40), as well as the beginning (v. 1)?

REFLECT: **1.** If Jesus called you to participate in a ministry, what do you think he would say to you in light of your own personality and needs? **2.** How has Christ's teaching united the members of your family? Divided them? **3.** How are you both "shrewd" and "innocent" in your dealings with the world? **4.** If asked, would you go on a journey like this to neighboring towns? To foreign countries? Which would be easier for you? Why? **5.** If the disciples came to your house, would they be welcomed? Or would they need to shake the dust off their feet? **6.** How can you tell your neighbors this week that the kingdom of heaven is near? **7.** What, besides dust on your feet, will stick with you from this passage?

return to you. ¹⁴If anyone will not welcome you or listen to your words, shake the dust off your feet when you leave that home or town. ¹⁵I tell you the truth, it will be more bearable for Sodom and Gomorrah on the day of judgment than for that town. ¹⁶I am sending you out like sheep among wolves. Therefore be as shrewd as snakes and as innocent as doves.

¹⁷"Be on your guard against men; they will hand you over to the local councils and flog you in their synagogues. ¹⁸On my account you will be brought before governors and kings as witnesses to them and to the Gentiles. ¹⁹But when they arrest you, do not worry about what to say or how to say it. At that time you will be given what to say, ²⁰for it will not be you speaking, but the Spirit of your Father speaking through you.

²¹"Brother will betray brother to death, and a father his child; children will rebel against their parents and have them put to death. ²²All men will hate you because of me, but he who stands firm to the end will be saved. ²³When you are persecuted in one place, flee to another. I tell you the truth, you will not finish going through the cities of Israel before the Son of Man comes.

²⁴"A student is not above his teacher, nor a servant above his master. ²⁵It is enough for the student to be like his teacher, and the servant like his master. If the head of the house has been called Beelzebub,ˡ how much more the members of his household!

²⁶"So do not be afraid of them. There is nothing concealed that will not be disclosed, or hidden that will not be made known. ²⁷What I tell you in the dark, speak in the daylight; what is whispered in your ear, proclaim from the roofs. ²⁸Do not be afraid of those who kill the body but cannot kill the soul. Rather, be afraid of the One who can destroy both soul and body in hell. ²⁹Are not two sparrows sold for a pennyᵐ? Yet not one of them will fall to the ground apart from the will of your Father. ³⁰And even the very hairs of your head are all numbered. ³¹So don't be afraid; you are worth more than many sparrows.

³²"Whoever acknowledges me before men, I will also acknowledge him before my Father in heaven. ³³But whoever disowns me before men, I will disown him before my Father in heaven.

³⁴"Do not suppose that I have come to bring peace to the earth. I did not come to bring peace, but a sword. ³⁵For I have come to turn

> " 'a man against his father,
> a daughter against her mother,
> a daughter-in-law against her mother-in-law—
> ³⁶ a man's enemies will be the members of his own
> household.' ⁿ

³⁷"Anyone who loves his father or mother more than me is not worthy of me; anyone who loves his son or daughter more than me is not worthy of me; ³⁸and anyone who does not take his cross and follow me is not worthy of me. ³⁹Whoever finds his life will lose it, and whoever loses his life for my sake will find it.

ˡ25 Greek *Beezeboul* or *Beelzeboul*   ᵐ29 Greek *an assarion*   ⁿ36 Micah 7:6

40"He who receives you receives me, and he who receives me
receives the one who sent me. 41Anyone who receives a prophet
because he is a prophet will receive a prophet's reward, and
anyone who receives a righteous man because he is a righteous
man will receive a righteous man's reward. 42And if anyone gives
even a cup of cold water to one of these little ones because he
is my disciple, I tell you the truth, he will certainly not lose his
reward."

Jesus and John the Baptist

11 After Jesus had finished instructing his twelve disciples,
he went on from there to teach and preach in the towns
of Galilee.[o]

2When John heard in prison what Christ was doing, he sent
his disciples 3to ask him, "Are you the one who was to come,
or should we expect someone else?"

4Jesus replied, "Go back and report to John what you hear
and see: 5The blind receive sight, the lame walk, those who have
leprosy[p] are cured, the deaf hear, the dead are raised, and the
good news is preached to the poor. 6Blessed is the man who does
not fall away on account of me."

7As John's disciples were leaving, Jesus began to speak to the
crowd about John: "What did you go out into the desert to see?
A reed swayed by the wind? 8If not, what did you go out to see?
A man dressed in fine clothes? No, those who wear fine clothes
are in kings' palaces. 9Then what did you go out to see? A
prophet? Yes, I tell you, and more than a prophet. 10This is the
one about whom it is written:

" 'I will send my messenger ahead of you,
who will prepare your way before you.'[q]

11I tell you the truth: Among those born of women there has not
risen anyone greater than John the Baptist; yet he who is least
in the kingdom of heaven is greater than he. 12From the days
of John the Baptist until now, the kingdom of heaven has been
forcefully advancing, and forceful men lay hold of it. 13For all
the Prophets and the Law prophesied until John. 14And if you
are willing to accept it, he is the Elijah who was to come. 15He
who has ears, let him hear.

16"To what can I compare this generation? They are like
children sitting in the marketplaces and calling out to others:

17" 'We played the flute for you,
and you did not dance;
we sang a dirge,
and you did not mourn.'

18For John came neither eating nor drinking, and they say, 'He
has a demon.' 19The Son of Man came eating and drinking, and
they say, 'Here is a glutton and a drunkard, a friend of tax
collectors and "sinners." ' But wisdom is proved right by her
actions."

[o]1 Greek *in their towns* [p]5 The Greek word was used for various diseases affecting the skin—not necessarily leprosy. [q]10 Mal. 3:1

OPEN: 1.(For married): When did you know that the person you married was "the one"? What tipped you off? (For unmarried) What is the sign you look for in a mate to tell you "this is the one"? **2.** When you church shop, what do you look for in a prospective pastor? What signs would authenticate his ministry?

DIG: 1. Having instructed his disciples in the nature of ministry (10:1-42), what does Jesus now do (v. 1) that models the same? What is significant about that? **2.** Who questions Jesus (v. 2)? Where is John? How did he land in prison (see 14:1-5)? **3.** How might prison have given rise to John's doubts (v. 3)? **4.** Does Jesus answer John more with promises or with evidence? Why? How might John, who knew the Old Testament well, have interpreted Jesus' reply (see Isaiah 35:5-6, 61:1)? What encouragement does Jesus add for John in verse 6? **5.** How was John different from a swaying weak reed or a well-groomed politician? What does Jesus say about John? **6.** How does John fulfill Old Testament prophecy (see Malachi 3:1, 4:5-6)? In what way does he exhibit the faith of the Old Testament? **7.** In what way is a New Testament believer greater than John (see Matthew 18:3-4)? **8.** How do the people respond to John? To Jesus? How were the people like the children pictured here?

REFLECT: 1. What kinds of "prisons" tend to bring out doubts for you regarding Jesus? **2.** In those periods of discouragement and doubt, what most renews your courage and faith? **3.** In what specific way can you be an encourager to someone in church leadership? In your family? Among your friends?

OPEN: 1. What is your most favorite city? Your least favorite? Why?

DIG: 1. What judgment does Jesus pass on each city mentioned? Why are they guilty? Why will their judgment be worse than that of the pagan cities of Tyre, Sidon, and Sodom? **2.** If an individual, city, or nation rejects the revelation of Jesus and his miracles, what is the pronounced judgment?

REFLECT: Now that you have read the works of Jesus, will God's judgment be "more bearable", or less?

OPEN: What childhood belief have you since abandoned in adulthood?

DIG: 1. Why is it good that the gospel is hidden from the "wise and learned"? **2.** Who truly knows God and how is that knowledge shared? **3.** What does Jesus offer to all who take up his "yoke"?

REFLECT: 1. How are you like the "wise and learned"? Like the "little children"? **2.** What is the significance of Jesus' invitation for you?

OPEN: 1. As a child, what was Sunday dinner like? What do you like best about Sundays now? Least? **2.** What would you miss doing most if you lost your best hand?

DIG: 1. Which commandment are the Pharisees trying so hard to keep (see Deut. 5:12-15)? How have the Pharisees defined "work" (see vv. 2, 10, 14)? **2.** Why does Jesus use examples from the Scriptures to argue with the Pharisees? What was the point of the story about David (see I Sam. 21:1-6)? How did priests break the literal Sabbath Law by doing what God commanded (Nu. 28:9-10)? **3.** What do the words "I desire mercy, not sacrifice" mean? How had the Pharisees misunderstood that point? **4.** What is lawful to do on the Sabbath (v. 12)? **5.** What does Jesus say and do to show that he is the authoritative interpreter of the law? **6.** Consequently, how do the Pharisees respond?

REFLECT: 1. How does God want you to spend your Sabbath day? Are you obeying his intention? **2.** How important are your needs to God? How important are other

Woe on Unrepentant Cities

²⁰Then Jesus began to denounce the cities in which most of his miracles had been performed, because they did not repent. ²¹"Woe to you, Korazin! Woe to you, Bethsaida! If the miracles that were performed in you had been performed in Tyre and Sidon, they would have repented long ago in sackcloth and ashes. ²²But I tell you, it will be more bearable for Tyre and Sidon on the day of judgment than for you. ²³And you, Capernaum, will you be lifted up to the skies? No, you will go down to the depths.ʳ If the miracles that were performed in you had been performed in Sodom, it would have remained to this day. ²⁴But I tell you that it will be more bearable for Sodom on the day of judgment than for you."

Rest for the Weary

²⁵At that time Jesus said, "I praise you, Father, Lord of heaven and earth, because you have hidden these things from the wise and learned, and revealed them to little children. ²⁶Yes, Father, for this was your good pleasure.

²⁷"All things have been committed to me by my Father. No one knows the Son except the Father, and no one knows the Father except the Son and those to whom the Son chooses to reveal him.

²⁸"Come to me, all you who are weary and burdened, and I will give you rest. ²⁹Take my yoke upon you and learn from me, for I am gentle and humble in heart, and you will find rest for your souls. ³⁰For my yoke is easy and my burden is light."

Lord of the Sabbath

12 At that time Jesus went through the grainfields on the Sabbath. His disciples were hungry and began to pick some heads of grain and eat them. ²When the Pharisees saw this, they said to him, "Look! Your disciples are doing what is unlawful on the Sabbath."

³He answered, "Haven't you read what David did when he and his companions were hungry? ⁴He entered the house of God, and he and his companions ate the consecrated bread—which was not lawful for them to do, but only for the priests. ⁵Or haven't you read in the Law that on the Sabbath the priests in the temple desecrate the day and yet are innocent? ⁶I tell you that oneˢ greater than the temple is here. ⁷If you had known what these words mean, 'I desire mercy, not sacrifice,'ᵗ you would not have condemned the innocent. ⁸For the Son of Man is Lord of the Sabbath."

⁹Going on from that place, he went into their synagogue, ¹⁰and a man with a shriveled hand was there. Looking for a reason to accuse Jesus, they asked him, "Is it lawful to heal on the Sabbath?"

¹¹He said to them, "If any of you has a sheep and it falls into a pit on the Sabbath, will you not take hold of it and lift it out? ¹²How much more valuable is a man than a sheep! Therefore it is lawful to do good on the Sabbath."

ʳ23 Greek *Hades*   ˢ6 Or *something*; also in verses 41 and 42   ᵗ7 Hosea 6:6

¹³Then he said to the man, "Stretch out your hand." So he stretched it out and it was completely restored, just as sound as the other. ¹⁴But the Pharisees went out and plotted how they might kill Jesus.

God's Chosen Servant

¹⁵Aware of this, Jesus withdrew from that place. Many followed him, and he healed all their sick, ¹⁶warning them not to tell who he was. ¹⁷This was to fulfill what was spoken through the prophet Isaiah:

¹⁸"Here is my servant whom I have chosen,
the one I love, in whom I delight;
I will put my Spirit on him,
and he will proclaim justice to the nations.
¹⁹He will not quarrel or cry out;
no one will hear his voice in the streets.
²⁰A bruised reed he will not break,
and a smoldering wick he will not snuff out,
till he leads justice to victory.
²¹ In his name the nations will put their hope." ᵘ

Jesus and Beelzebub

²²Then they brought him a demon-possessed man who was blind and mute, and Jesus healed him, so that he could both talk and see. ²³All the people were astonished and said, "Could this be the Son of David?"

²⁴But when the Pharisees heard this, they said, "It is only by Beelzebub,ᵛ the prince of demons, that this fellow drives out demons."

²⁵Jesus knew their thoughts and said to them, "Every kingdom divided against itself will be ruined, and every city or household divided against itself will not stand. ²⁶If Satan drives out Satan, he is divided against himself. How then can his kingdom stand? ²⁷And if I drive out demons by Beelzebub, by whom do your people drive them out? So then, they will be your judges. ²⁸But if I drive out demons by the Spirit of God, then the kingdom of God has come upon you.

²⁹"Or again, how can anyone enter a strong man's house and carry off his possessions unless he first ties up the strong man? Then he can rob his house.

³⁰"He who is not with me is against me, and he who does not gather with me scatters. ³¹And so I tell you, every sin and blasphemy will be forgiven men, but the blasphemy against the Spirit will not be forgiven. ³²Anyone who speaks a word against the Son of Man will be forgiven, but anyone who speaks against the Holy Spirit will not be forgiven, either in this age or in the age to come.

³³"Make a tree good and its fruit will be good, or make a tree bad and its fruit will be bad, for a tree is recognized by its fruit. ³⁴You brood of vipers, how can you who are evil say anything good? For out of the overflow of the heart the mouth speaks. ³⁵The good man brings good things out of the good stored up

ᵘ*21* Isaiah 42:1-4   ᵛ*24* Greek *Beezeboul* or *Beelzeboul*; also in verse 27

people's needs to you? **3.** When is it right to break the law? When, for example, do legalistic systems value property over people?

OPEN: Where do you go when life gets too heavy for you? Why?

DIG: 1. How could too much publicity harm Jesus' ministry? **2.** How does Jesus fulfill prophecy in his reaction to the Pharisees' hostility (v. 14)? **3.** What does this passage say about Jesus' identity? **4.** How does Jesus treat broken and weak people?

REFLECT: 1. How do you respond when people are hostile to you? How does Jesus' example encourage your self-restraint? **2.** In telling others about Jesus, what use of the Old Testament do you make? **3.** In what ways has Jesus mended your life?

OPEN: 1. Would you rather be blind or mute? Why? **2.** Using a fruit or vegetable as a metaphor, how would you describe your life this week (dried fig, ripe cantaloupe, smashed banana)?

DIG: 1. What were the two main reactions to the healing of the blind and mute man? Who did the people suppose Jesus to be? Who did the Pharisees suspect Jesus to be? Why are Jesus' miracles open to such various interpretations? **2.** What three defenses does Jesus give in answer to the Pharisees' accusations (see vv. 26, 27, 29)? By implication what is Jesus saying about his inauguration of God's kingdom (v. 28)? **3.** What does this passage say about neutrality to Jesus? Is it possible? Why or why not? **4.** What is meant by "blasphemy against the Spirit"? How have the Pharisees committed this sin? Since forgiveness necessitates people asking for it, why is it impossible for "blasphemy against the Spirit" to be forgiven (vv. 31-32)? **5.** What meaning does Jesus give for the Pharisees' growing hostility to his message and ministry (see v. 34)? How fair is it for Jesus to judge the Pharisees according to their words? How does it feel for you to be judged according to your words?

REFLECT: 1. What real difference does Jesus' power make in the day to day struggles against evil? **2.** What does this passage say about honesty before God concerning our feelings and motives? **3.** What have you learned about the importance of our words in God's eyes?

OPEN: What is the funniest bumper sticker or sign you have seen?

DIG: 1. Why do you think the Pharisees wanted to see a miracle? **2.** How does Jesus feel about "this generation"? Why? **3.** What is the "sign of Jonah"? How is Jesus greater than Jonah? Than Soloman? How might the Pharisees have interpreted this? **4.** How do the Ninevites and the Queen of the South condemn Jesus' generation? **5.** A person who is reformed but neglectful of God's presence is prey to even greater evil. How do Israel's leaders exemplify this principle?

REFLECT: 1. Do you think a new sign from God would convince members of contemporary culture to believe in Jesus? Why or why not? **2.** What more does Jesus want besides a heart "swept clean and put in order"? What protects a believer from such unwholesome occupancy (see John 14:15-17)?

OPEN: What non-relative is as close to you as kin? Why?

DIG: 1. Why were Jesus' mother and brothers eager to speak with him (see Mark 3:20-21)? **2.** What relationship should have highest priority?

REFLECT: What "family ties" do you have to Jesus? To your group?

OPEN: 1. What is one of your most pleasant memories of a farm? **2.** What kind of luck have you had raising a garden? Is your crop yield small, average, or humongous? What is your secret?

DIG: 1. As a teachable moment for his kingdom parables (chapter 13), what is significant about their context in Matthew's gospel: Growing opposition to Jesus' ministry (11:1-12:50)? Growing popularity with the crowds (13:2)? **2.** What is a parable? **3.** What four types of soil did Jesus mention? What characterizes each? What happens to the seed in each kind of soil? **4.** What does Jesus' explanation of the parable (vv. 18-23) reveal about the

in him, and the evil man brings evil things out of the evil stored up in him. ³⁶But I tell you that men will have to give account on the day of judgment for every careless word they have spoken. ³⁷For by your words you will be acquitted, and by your words you will be condemned."

The Sign of Jonah

³⁸Then some of the Pharisees and teachers of the law said to him, "Teacher, we want to see a miraculous sign from you."

³⁹He answered, "A wicked and adulterous generation asks for a miraculous sign! But none will be given it except the sign of the prophet Jonah. ⁴⁰For as Jonah was three days and three nights in the belly of a huge fish, so the Son of Man will be three days and three nights in the heart of the earth. ⁴¹The men of Nineveh will stand up at the judgment with this generation and condemn it; for they repented at the preaching of Jonah, and now one*greater than Jonah is here. ⁴²The Queen of the South will rise at the judgment with this generation and condemn it; for she came from the ends of the earth to listen to Solomon's wisdom, and now one greater than Solomon is here.

⁴³"When an evil* spirit comes out of a man, it goes through arid places seeking rest and does not find it. ⁴⁴Then it says, 'I will return to the house I left.' When it arrives, it finds the house unoccupied, swept clean and put in order. ⁴⁵Then it goes and takes with it seven other spirits more wicked than itself, and they go in and live there. And the final condition of that man is worse than the first. That is how it will be with this wicked generation."

Jesus' Mother and Brothers

⁴⁶While Jesus was still talking to the crowd, his mother and brothers stood outside, wanting to speak to him. ⁴⁷Someone told him, "Your mother and brothers are standing outside, wanting to speak to you."*

⁴⁸He replied to him, "Who is my mother, and who are my brothers?" ⁴⁹Pointing to his disciples, he said, "Here are my mother and my brothers. ⁵⁰For whoever does the will of my Father in heaven is my brother and sister and mother."

The Parable of the Sower

13 That same day Jesus went out of the house and sat by the lake. ²Such large crowds gathered around him that he got into a boat and sat in it, while all the people stood on the shore. ³Then he told them many things in parables, saying: "A farmer went out to sow his seed. ⁴As he was scattering the seed, some fell along the path, and the birds came and ate it up. ⁵Some fell on rocky places, where it did not have much soil. It sprang up quickly, because the soil was shallow. ⁶But when the sun came up, the plants were scorched, and they withered because they had no root. ⁷Other seed fell among thorns, which grew up and choked the plants. ⁸Still other seed fell on good soil, where it

*w*41 Or *something*; also in verse 42   *x*43 Greek *unclean*   *y*47 Some manuscripts do not have verse 47.

produced a crop—a hundred, sixty or thirty times what was sown. [9]He who has ears, let him hear."

[10]The disciples came to him and asked, "Why do you speak to the people in parables?"

[11]He replied, "The knowledge of the secrets of the kingdom of heaven has been given to you, but not to them. [12]Whoever has will be given more, and he will have an abundance. Whoever does not have, even what he has will be taken from him. [13]This is why I speak to them in parables:

"Though seeing, they do not see;
    though hearing, they do not hear or understand.

[14]In them is fulfilled the prophecy of Isaiah:

" 'You will be ever hearing but never understanding;
    you will be ever seeing but never perceiving.
[15]For this people's heart has become calloused;
    they hardly hear with their ears,
    and they have closed their eyes.
Otherwise they might see with their eyes,
    hear with their ears,
    understand with their hearts
and turn, and I would heal them.'[z]

[16]But blessed are your eyes because they see, and your ears because they hear. [17]For I tell you the truth, many prophets and righteous men longed to see what you see but did not see it, and to hear what you hear but did not hear it.

[18]"Listen then to what the parable of the sower means: [19]When anyone hears the message about the kingdom and does not understand it, the evil one comes and snatches away what was sown in his heart. This is the seed sown along the path. [20]The one who received the seed that fell on rocky places is the man who hears the word and at once receives it with joy. [21]But since he has no root, he lasts only a short time. When trouble or persecution comes because of the word, he quickly falls away. [22]The one who received the seed that fell among the thorns is the man who hears the word, but the worries of this life and the deceitfulness of wealth choke it, making it unfruitful. [23]But the one who received the seed that fell on good soil is the man who hears the word and understands it. He produces a crop, yielding a hundred, sixty or thirty times what was sown."

The Parable of the Weeds

[24]Jesus told them another parable: "The kingdom of heaven is like a man who sowed good seed in his field. [25]But while everyone was sleeping, his enemy came and sowed weeds among the wheat, and went away. [26]When the wheat sprouted and formed heads, then the weeds also appeared.

[27]"The owner's servants came to him and said, 'Sir, didn't you sow good seed in your field? Where then did the weeds come from?'

[28]" 'An enemy did this,' he replied.

seed? The various soils? The fruit? The farmer? **5.** How might the parable help the disciples understand what was happening in their ministry? **6.** Why do you think Jesus used parables as his teaching device? What do parables accomplish that simple and direct speech lacks? **7.** How does Jesus' challenge in verse 9 help explain verses 11-12? How does faith open you up to more and more spiritual insight? **8.** How does the quotation from Isaiah (vv. 14-15) explain verse 13? Why don't people understand parables? **9.** In verses 16-17, Jesus gives a new beatitude. What have the disciples seen and heard that the prophets longed to see and hear? Are we included in this blessing, or was it only for the disciples? **10.** Can we see and hear Jesus at work in today's world? If so, how? **11.** How would you explain this parable to a bunch of city kids who had never seen a field? What modern analogy would you use?

REFLECT: **1.** Why might a person not understand the Christian message? **2.** What helps a believer have deep "roots" which prevent one from falling away? What gives you roots? **3.** What worries have potential to choke your growth in Christ? How can you free your life from the "thorns" of wealth? **4.** What "crop" does Jesus want believers to yield? How does one increase their crop productivity?

OPEN: On a scale from 1 to 10, how much delight do you derive from pulling weeds?

DIG: **1.** In this parable, who is the sower? What does the wheat represent? The weeds? The enemy? (See also vv. 36-43), **2.** In what way can premature judgments cause harm to a community of believers? What is the harvest?

REFLECT: What is your responsibility in the church community regarding "wheat" and "weeds"?

[z]*15* Isaiah 6:9,10

"The servants asked him, 'Do you want us to go and pull them up?'

²⁹" 'No,' he answered, 'because while you are pulling the weeds, you may root up the wheat with them. ³⁰Let both grow together until the harvest. At that time I will tell the harvesters: First collect the weeds and tie them in bundles to be burned; then gather the wheat and bring it into my barn.' "

The Parables of the Mustard Seed and the Yeast

³¹He told them another parable: "The kingdom of heaven is like a mustard seed, which a man took and planted in his field. ³²Though it is the smallest of all your seeds, yet when it grows, it is the largest of garden plants and becomes a tree, so that the birds of the air come and perch in its branches."

³³He told them still another parable: "The kingdom of heaven is like yeast that a woman took and mixed into a large amount*ᵃ* of flour until it worked all through the dough."

³⁴Jesus spoke all these things to the crowd in parables; he did not say anything to them without using a parable. ³⁵So was fulfilled what was spoken through the prophet:

"I will open my mouth in parables,
I will utter things hidden since the creation of the world."*ᵇ*

The Parable of the Weeds Explained

³⁶Then he left the crowd and went into the house. His disciples came to him and said, "Explain to us the parable of the weeds in the field."

³⁷He answered, "The one who sowed the good seed is the Son of Man. ³⁸The field is the world, and the good seed stands for the sons of the kingdom. The weeds are the sons of the evil one, ³⁹and the enemy who sows them is the devil. The harvest is the end of the age, and the harvesters are angels.

⁴⁰"As the weeds are pulled up and burned in the fire, so it will be at the end of the age. ⁴¹The Son of Man will send out his angels, and they will weed out of his kingdom everything that causes sin and all who do evil. ⁴²They will throw them into the fiery furnace, where there will be weeping and gnashing of teeth. ⁴³Then the righteous will shine like the sun in the kingdom of their Father. He who has ears, let him hear.

The Parables of the Hidden Treasure and the Pearl

⁴⁴"The kingdom of heaven is like treasure hidden in a field. When a man found it, he hid it again, and then in his joy went and sold all he had and bought that field.

⁴⁵"Again, the kingdom of heaven is like a merchant looking for fine pearls. ⁴⁶When he found one of great value, he went away and sold everything he had and bought it.

OPEN: What small childhood dream has grown into reality for you (example—married Prince Charming, became a brain surgeon)?

DIG: 1. What aspects of Jesus' ministry seem small? What is the promise if the small seed is sown? **2.** How does the "kingdom of heaven" message and lifestyle affect the surrounding environment? **3.** How is prophecy thus fulfilled?

REFLECT: How have you seen the "yeast message" or "mustard seed faith" at work—something small making a great impact in your life? In the life of your church? In society?

OPEN: If you were in charge of designing a ride called *Hell* for a major amusement park, how would you make it unbelievably miserable?

DIG: 1. Why does this parable so puzzle the disciples? Why is patience and tolerance toward unbelievers difficult for them (and for you)? **2.** What does this passage teach about church purity? Divine patience? Human accountability? End of the age?

REFLECT: 1. What accountability are you now feeling for yourself? For others? To God? **2.** What are you "hearing" God call you to do as a reslut?

OPEN: 1. What three events in your life brought you the greatest joy? **2.** With the proceeds of garage sales, what worthy item are you saving for or bought and still own?

DIG: What do these parables teach about the value of the kingdom of God? With what emotion and energy should it be pursued?

REFLECT: What does it mean to "sell everything" for the kingdom? Is it strictly monetary? What else could you "sell" for this worthy cause?

ᵃ33 Greek *three satas* (probably about 1/2 bushel or 22 liters)   *ᵇ35* Psalm 78:2

The Parable of the Net

47"Once again, the kingdom of heaven is like a net that was let down into the lake and caught all kinds of fish. 48When it was full, the fishermen pulled it up on the shore. Then they sat down and collected the good fish in baskets, but threw the bad away. 49This is how it will be at the end of the age. The angels will come and separate the wicked from the righteous 50and throw them into the fiery furnace, where there will be weeping and gnashing of teeth.

51"Have you understood all these things?" Jesus asked.

"Yes," they replied.

52He said to them, "Therefore every teacher of the law who has been instructed about the kingdom of heaven is like the owner of a house who brings out of his storeroom new treasures as well as old."

A Prophet Without Honor

53When Jesus had finished these parables, he moved on from there. 54Coming to his hometown, he began teaching the people in their synagogue, and they were amazed. "Where did this man get this wisdom and these miraculous powers?" they asked. 55"Isn't this the carpenter's son? Isn't his mother's name Mary, and aren't his brothers James, Joseph, Simon and Judas? 56Aren't all his sisters with us? Where then did this man get all these things?" 57And they took offense at him.

But Jesus said to them, "Only in his hometown and in his own house is a prophet without honor."

58And he did not do many miracles there because of their lack of faith.

John the Baptist Beheaded

14 At that time Herod the tetrarch heard the reports about Jesus, 2and he said to his attendants, "This is John the Baptist; he has risen from the dead! That is why miraculous powers are at work in him."

3Now Herod had arrested John and bound him and put him in prison because of Herodias, his brother Philip's wife, 4for John had been saying to him: "It is not lawful for you to have her." 5Herod wanted to kill John, but he was afraid of the people, because they considered him a prophet.

6On Herod's birthday the daughter of Herodias danced for them and pleased Herod so much 7that he promised with an oath to give her whatever she asked. 8Prompted by her mother, she said, "Give me here on a platter the head of John the Baptist." 9The king was distressed, but because of his oaths and his dinner guests, he ordered that her request be granted 10and had John beheaded in the prison. 11His head was brought in on a platter and given to the girl, who carried it to her mother. 12John's disciples came and took his body and buried it. Then they went and told Jesus.

OPEN: What needs sorting out in your garage right now? Is there more trivia, trash or treasure to be found here?

DIG: 1. What does the parable of the net teach about the kingdom of heaven? 2. How does it compare with the parable of the weeds? 3. Who are the teachers of the old law who have been instructed in the new gospel (v. 52)? How has Matthew been that for you?

REFLECT: Why do Jesus' disciples (then and now) need to understand these parables? Which ones are still unclear? All too clear?

OPEN: What do people still say about you in your childhood hometown: An angel? A brat? A brain?

DIG: How does the hometown crowd receive Jesus? How does their relation differ from most other Israelites? What do these neighbors "know"? How does their knowledge impede his ministry?

REFLECT: What might this teach us about assuming that we know all that there is to know about Jesus? What relation does our faith have to Jesus' ability to be at work?

OPEN: 1. When you were growing up, who was the neighborhood bully? What made that person so frightening? 2. If promised "anything you ask for" at your next birthday, what would you want?

DIG: 1. What is Herod's fear after hearing reports of Jesus? What was Herod's fear during the life of John the Baptist? 2. Why did Herod behead John? What does this say about his character? 3. What does Herod seem to fear most: The fame of Jesus? The ghost of John? The reaction of John's followers? The oath he took? The exception of his dinner guests? The woman behind the throne?

REFLECT: 1. What is one area in your life where your actions are likely to be governed by your fear of what others think? How could Jesus help you in this one area? 2. What would be the most effective ministry to someone like a Herod?

OPEN: **1.** After a busy day, how do you like to unwind? **2.** If you had to feed five thousand people at a picnic, what would you serve?

DIG: **1.** Why does Jesus withdraw? How does he react to the interruption? **2.** What sensitivity do the disciples show initially? How might they have felt after Jesus' statement in verse 16? **3.** What is their likely reaction after the miracle? What new power do the disciples discover in Jesus? **4.** What is the lesson in the feeding of the multitude?

REFLECT: **1.** How do you react to interruptions of planned rest? **2.** How do you feel when Jesus is urging you to a ministry which is too large for you? **3.** What will "stick to your ribs" from this story?

OPEN: **1.** Of all your adventures in life, which was your most daring? What risk was involved? **2.** Of all your boating experiences, which is your most memorable? Why? **3.** What figures from literature or the movies do you associate with "ghosts"?

DIG: **1.** Why did Jesus dismiss the disciples so abruptly? Why didn't he want the disciples there? Why do you think Jesus wanted to pray alone? How might Jesus be tempted by his mounting popularity and the crowds clamour for a king (see John 6:15)? **2.** How does this temptation and Jesus' response to it resemble that of the temptations in Matthew 4:3-10? **3.** Meanwhile, what happens out on the lake to rock the disciples' boat? To stir up their fear? To encourage their faith? **4.** What do Peter's actions reveal about his character? **5.** Why do you think Jesus told Peter to come? What do we learn about Jesus' hopes for us in this passage? When did Peter begin to sink? Why then and not earlier? **6.** What do the disciples conclude about Jesus as a result of this faith-stretching experience? **7.** Once on land, how is the word about Jesus spreading?

REFLECT: **1.** Would you be more likely to stay in the boat, or step out of it? Why? Which do you think is the best course of action? **2.** What do you see in your own life that parallel's Peter's attempt to walk on water?

Jesus Feeds the Five Thousand

[13]When Jesus heard what had happened, he withdrew by boat privately to a solitary place. Hearing of this, the crowds followed him on foot from the towns. [14]When Jesus landed and saw a large crowd, he had compassion on them and healed their sick.

[15]As evening approached, the disciples came to him and said, "This is a remote place, and it's already getting late. Send the crowds away, so they can go to the villages and buy themselves some food."

[16]Jesus replied, "They do not need to go away. You give them something to eat."

[17]"We have here only five loaves of bread and two fish," they answered.

[18]"Bring them here to me," he said. [19]And he directed the people to sit down on the grass. Taking the five loaves and the two fish and looking up to heaven, he gave thanks and broke the loaves. Then he gave them to the disciples, and the disciples gave them to the people. [20]They all ate and were satisfied, and the disciples picked up twelve basketfuls of broken pieces that were left over. [21]The number of those who ate was about five thousand men, besides women and children.

Jesus Walks on the Water

[22]Immediately Jesus made the disciples get into the boat and go on ahead of him to the other side, while he dismissed the crowd. [23]After he had dismissed them, he went up on a mountainside by himself to pray. When evening came, he was there alone, [24]but the boat was already a considerable distance[c] from land, buffeted by the waves because the wind was against it.

[25]During the fourth watch of the night Jesus went out to them, walking on the lake. [26]When the disciples saw him walking on the lake, they were terrified. "It's a ghost," they said, and cried out in fear.

[27]But Jesus immediately said to them: "Take courage! It is I. Don't be afraid."

[28]"Lord, if it's you," Peter replied, "tell me to come to you on the water."

[29]"Come," he said.

Then Peter got down out of the boat, walked on the water and came toward Jesus. [30]But when he saw the wind, he was afraid and, beginning to sink, cried out, "Lord, save me!"

[31]Immediately Jesus reached out his hand and caught him. "You of little faith," he said, "why did you doubt?"

[32]And when they climbed into the boat, the wind died down. [33]Then those who were in the boat worshiped him, saying, "Truly you are the Son of God."

[34]When they had crossed over, they landed at Gennesaret. [35]And when the men of that place recognized Jesus, they sent word to all the surrounding country. People brought all their sick to him [36]and begged him to let the sick just touch the edge of his cloak, and all who touched him were healed.

[c]24 Greek *many stadia*

LOOKING INTO THE SCRIPTURE/25 Minutes. Read Matthew 14:22-36 and discuss.

1. If you had been in the boat with the disciples when they saw someone walking on the water, what would you have said?
   a. I think I ate too many anchovies
   b. where's Jesus?
   c. I'm seeing things
   d. absolutely nothing
   e. let me out of here
   f. how does he do that?

2. What was Jesus saying when he cried out, "Take courage. It is I. Don't be afraid"?
   a. get yourself together
   b. Yoo-hoo! It's only me
   c. relax . . . believe in me
   d. why are you surprised? . . . you saw me feed 5,000 people today

3. When Peter replied, "If it's you, tell me to come to you on the water," what was he asking for?
   a. to have the same power
   b. to see a little proof
   c. to risk
   d. to show off
   e. to get to Jesus
   f. to test his own faith

4. What was the tone in Jesus' voice when he said, "you of little faith . . . why did you doubt?"
   a. disappointment: When are you ever going to learn?
   b. concern: What happened? You almost drowned!
   c. anguish: Oh Peter! I know what you are going through.
   d. anger: Don't ever do that again!
   e. reassurance: You almost made it. And with a little more faith, you will.

5. If Jesus knew Peter was going to sink, why did he invite him to "come"?
   a. to teach him a lesson
   b. to encourage him to take risks
   c. to test his faith
   d. to let him fail

6. If you could put in a good word for Peter, what would you say?
   a. at least he was willing to step out
   b. he learned
   c. he's my kind of person
   d. he had guts

MY OWN STORY/20 Minutes.

1. If you had to compare your strong point and weak point in terms of bones, what would be your strongest bone and weakest bone?
   a. crazy bone
   b. ham bone
   c. neck bone
   d. back bone
   e. wish bone

2. When it comes to risking, how would you describe yourself?
   a. cautious—hedge my bets
   b. impulsive—quick to leap
   c. calculating—play the odds
   d. procrastinating—put it off
   e. apprehensive—scared to death

3. If you had been Peter, how would you have responded if Jesus invited you to "Come"?
   a. fainted on the spot
   b. jumped at the chance
   c. asked for a guarantee bond
   d. said, "I'll go second."
   e. asked to think about it

4. Where do you feel that God is inviting you to "get out of the boat" right now?
   a. in my job/career—trying something risky
   b. in my family—starting over with someone
   c. in my spiritual walk—putting God first
   d. in my future planning—doing what I've been afraid to try

5. If God could help me deal with this situation, what would he do?
   a. be very gentle with me
   b. give me a push
   c. assure me that it is okay to fail
   d. give me a lot of support people
   e. get out of the boat with me

6. How could the group you are in help you?
   a. support me
   b. share their own risky plans
   c. hold each other accountable
   d. let me alone
   e. pray for me

OPEN: 1. What is one family tradition which you have observed as a child, still do now, and have even instilled in the next generation? **2.** Which person in your family washes their hands the most often? **3.** On what recent project have you felt like you were "the blind leading the blind"?

DIG: 1. Compare and contrast the different manner in which Jesus addresses each of the groups in this passage (identified in vv. 1, 10, 12). Who is Jesus harshest with? Why? **2.** Where do Jesus' opponents come from in this passage? **3.** Why do you think they have come looking for Jesus? Why would they begin with this issue (v.2)? **4.** What does hypocrisy sound like? Look like? Feel like? How does Jesus support his charge of hypocrisy against his accusers? What does Isaiah say to the Pharisees (vv. 7-9)? To all religious people? **5.** Why does Jesus call them "blind guides"? What's their apparent relationship with God? **6.** List three good things about traditions or rules. How might these good things help to blind the Pharisees? **7.** How is "uncleanness" understood by the Pharisees? By Jesus?

REFLECT: 1. What did your church consider "unclean" 30 years ago? Nowadays? How do you feel about these rules and rituals defining "holiness"? **2.** What do you like best about what comes from your mouth and heart? What do you like least? How do you see God making you more clean? **3.** In what area do you tend to place too much emphasis on the letter of the law or tradition? What will you do to reverse this tendency?

OPEN: For what would you walk one mile? 100 miles? Why?

DIG: 1. What is signifigant about Jesus going to the region of Tyre and Sidon? What would his accusers in 15:1 have thought about this? **2.** How does Jesus' teaching in Matthew 15:1-20 relate to this trip? **3.** What does the label "Canaanite" say about this woman? What do we learn about her character and her faith in this passage? **4.** What do you learn about Jesus from his response to this woman?

REFLECT: 1. When, if ever, have you acted like the woman in this story? Like the disciples? Like

Clean and Unclean

15 Then some Pharisees and teachers of the law came to Jesus from Jerusalem and asked, [2]"Why do your disciples break the tradition of the elders? They don't wash their hands before they eat!"

[3]Jesus replied, "And why do you break the command of God for the sake of your tradition? [4]For God said, 'Honor your father and mother'[d] and 'Anyone who curses his father or mother must be put to death.'[e] [5]But you say that if a man says to his father or mother, 'Whatever help you might otherwise have received from me is a gift devoted to God,' [6]he is not to 'honor his father[f]' with it. Thus you nullify the word of God for the sake of your tradition. [7]You hypocrites! Isaiah was right when he prophesied about you:

[8]" 'These people honor me with their lips,
   but their hearts are far from me.
[9]They worship me in vain;
   their teachings are but rules taught by men.'[g]"

[10]Jesus called the crowd to him and said, "Listen and understand. [11]What goes into a man's mouth does not make him 'unclean,' but what comes out of his mouth, that is what makes him 'unclean.' "

[12]Then the disciples came to him and asked, "Do you know that the Pharisees were offended when they heard this?"

[13]He replied, "Every plant that my heavenly Father has not planted will be pulled up by the roots. [14]Leave them; they are blind guides.[h] If a blind man leads a blind man, both will fall into a pit."

[15]Peter said, "Explain the parable to us."

[16]"Are you still so dull?" Jesus asked them. [17]"Don't you see that whatever enters the mouth goes into the stomach and then out of the body? [18]But the things that come out of the mouth come from the heart, and these make a man 'unclean.' [19]For out of the heart come evil thoughts, murder, adultery, sexual immorality, theft, false testimony, slander. [20]These are what make a man 'unclean'; but eating with unwashed hands does not make him 'unclean.' "

The Faith of the Canaanite Woman

[21]Leaving that place, Jesus withdrew to the region of Tyre and Sidon. [22]A Canaanite woman from that vicinity came to him, crying out, "Lord, Son of David, have mercy on me! My daughter is suffering terribly from demon-possession."

[23]Jesus did not answer a word. So his disciples came to him and urged him, "Send her away, for she keeps crying out after us."

[24]He answered, "I was sent only to the lost sheep of Israel."

[25]The woman came and knelt before him. "Lord, help me!" she said.

---

d4 Exodus 20:12; Deut. 5:16   *e4* Exodus 21:17; Lev. 20:9   *f6* Some
manuscripts *father or his mother*   *g9* Isaiah 29:13   *h14* Some manuscripts
guides of the blind

²⁶He replied, "It is not right to take the children's bread and toss it to their dogs."

²⁷"Yes, Lord," she said, "but even the dogs eat the crumbs that fall from their masters' table."

²⁸Then Jesus answered, "Woman, you have great faith! Your request is granted." And her daughter was healed from that very hour.

Jesus Feeds the Four Thousand

²⁹Jesus left there and went along the Sea of Galilee. Then he went up on a mountainside and sat down. ³⁰Great crowds came to him, bringing the lame, the blind, the crippled, the mute and many others, and laid them at his feet; and he healed them. ³¹The people were amazed when they saw the mute speaking, the crippled made well, the lame walking and the blind seeing. And they praised the God of Israel.

³²Jesus called his disciples to him and said, "I have compassion for these people; they have already been with me three days and have nothing to eat. I do not want to send them away hungry, or they may collapse on the way."

³³His disciples answered, "Where could we get enough bread in this remote place to feed such a crowd?"

³⁴"How many loaves do you have?" Jesus asked.

"Seven," they replied, "and a few small fish."

³⁵He told the crowd to sit down on the ground. ³⁶Then he took the seven loaves and the fish, and when he had given thanks, he broke them and gave them to the disciples, and they in turn to the people. ³⁷They all ate and were satisfied. Afterward the disciples picked up seven basketfuls of broken pieces that were left over. ³⁸The number of those who ate was four thousand, besides women and children. ³⁹After Jesus had sent the crowd away, he got into the boat and went to the vicinity of Magadan.

The Demand for a Sign

16 The Pharisees and Sadducees came to Jesus and tested him by asking him to show them a sign from heaven. ²He replied,ⁱ "When evening comes, you say, 'It will be fair weather, for the sky is red,' ³and in the morning, 'Today it will be stormy, for the sky is red and overcast.' You know how to interpret the appearance of the sky, but you cannot interpret the signs of the times. ⁴A wicked and adulterous generation looks for a miraculous sign, but none will be given it except the sign of Jonah." Jesus then left them and went away.

The Yeast of the Pharisees and Sadducees

⁵When they went across the lake, the disciples forgot to take bread. ⁶"Be careful," Jesus said to them. "Be on your guard against the yeast of the Pharisees and Sadducees."

⁷They discussed this among themselves and said, "It is because we didn't bring any bread."

⁸Aware of their discussion, Jesus asked, "You of little faith, why are you talking among yourselves about having no bread?

ⁱ2 Some early manuscripts do not have the rest of verse 2 and all of verse 3.

Jesus? **2.** Jesus walks 100 miles out of his way to heal this person. **3.** How has God done that in your life? In others through you?

OPEN: 1. What kind of food leaves you completely satisfied? Why this food? **2.** What kinds of things (names, birthdays, umbrellas, etc.) do you tend to forget most often?

DIG: 1. What ministry is Jesus doing along the Sea of Galilee (vv. 29-31)? How does that compare with Jewish expectations of the Messiah (see Isaiah 35:3-6)? **2.** How does the feeding of this multitude compare with the previous one (see 14:13-21)? **3.** What then seems shocking to you about the disciples lack of insight and faith (v. 33, compare 14:15)? **4.** What seems familiar about Jesus' compassion for the crowd?

REFLECT: 1. When you face overwhelming situations, how well do you remember God's provision for you in the past? **2.** What would stimulate your memory of God's mercy? **3.** How helpful is it for you to hear the stories of how God has worked in the lives of other Christians? Why?

OPEN: If you could ask Jesus for super dramatic sign of his reality, for what would you ask?

DIG: What do you think that the Pharisees and Sadducees actually were hoping to see in the sky? How convincing would a sign have been for these religious leaders?

REFLECT: What part do external signs play in your faith in Jesus?

OPEN: Which would you rather have homemade and hot out of the oven: Hot bread with butter? Chocolate chip cookies with cold milk?

DIG: 1. How does Jesus use the disciples' forgetfulness to teach them about the Pharisees and Sadducees? **2.** What was Jesus' point in the series of questions? What does he want to teach them? **3.** Why do the disciples appear so dull in

55

understanding Jesus? **4.** How might they have felt about themselves at this moment?

REFLECT: **1.** How often do you feel like you're missing the point of what Jesus is trying to teach you? **2.** What gives you the courage to persevere and break out of your spiritual dullness?

OPEN: If we polled five good friends from your late teen years, "who" would they say you were?

DIG: **1.** Why did people think that Jesus was John the Baptist, Elijah, or Jeremiah? **2.** What was significant about Peter's confession? What does the title Christ (Messiah) mean? **3.** What did the first century Jews expect of the Messiah? **4.** How do you interpret the insight (v. 17), power (v. 18), and authority (v. 19) given to Peter? What are the "keys" of the kingdom? What do they "bind" and "loose"?

REFLECT: Have you made Peter's discovery for yourself? When? How?

OPEN: If you could indeed "gain the world", where would you place your summer and winter castles?

DIG: **1.** Why do you think Jesus changes the direction of his teaching at this point? **2.** Based on his response in verse 22, what kind of messiah do you think Peter was expecting? **3.** Why was Jesus' response to Peter so strong? How does Matthew 16:22-23 compare with Matthew 4:1-11? **4.** How does Jesus' response to Peter in verse 23 compare with his response in verse 17? **5.** What is a "stumbling block"? **6.** What activities and attitudes are at the heart of Christian discipleship? **7.** How does a Christian forfeit his life? What "things of men" (v. 23) or worldly gain (v. 27) might tempt people to lose their life or exchange their soul? **8.** What did Jesus mean by his statement in verse 28?

REFLECT: **1.** Where do you think that your life might be a stumbling block to other believers? **2.** Over what do you often trip in your life of discipleship? **3.** What does it mean specifically to you to (a) deny self, (b) take up your cross, and (c) follow Jesus?

⁹Do you still not understand? Don't you remember the five loaves for the five thousand, and how many basketfuls you gathered? ¹⁰Or the seven loaves for the four thousand, and how many basketfuls you gathered? ¹¹How is it you don't understand that I was not talking to you about bread? But be on your guard against the yeast of the Pharisees and Sadducees." ¹²Then they understood that he was not telling them to guard against the yeast used in bread, but against the teaching of the Pharisees and Sadducees.

Peter's Confession of Christ

¹³When Jesus came to the region of Caesarea Philippi, he asked his disciples, "Who do people say the Son of Man is?" ¹⁴They replied, "Some say John the Baptist; others say Elijah; and still others, Jeremiah or one of the prophets."

¹⁵"But what about you?" he asked. "Who do you say I am?" ¹⁶Simon Peter answered, "You are the Christ,ʲ the Son of the living God."

¹⁷Jesus replied, "Blessed are you, Simon son of Jonah, for this was not revealed to you by man, but by my Father in heaven. ¹⁸And I tell you that you are Peter,ᵏ and on this rock I will build my church, and the gates of Hadesˡ will not overcome it.ᵐ ¹⁹I will give you the keys of the kingdom of heaven; whatever you bind on earth will beⁿ bound in heaven, and whatever you loose on earth will beⁿ loosed in heaven." ²⁰Then he warned his disciples not to tell anyone that he was the Christ.

Jesus Predicts His Death

²¹From that time on Jesus began to explain to his disciples that he must go to Jerusalem and suffer many things at the hands of the elders, chief priests and teachers of the law, and that he must be killed and on the third day be raised to life.

²²Peter took him aside and began to rebuke him. "Never, Lord!" he said. "This shall never happen to you!"

²³Jesus turned and said to Peter, "Get behind me, Satan! You are a stumbling block to me; you do not have in mind the things of God, but the things of men."

²⁴Then Jesus said to his disciples, "If anyone would come after me, he must deny himself and take up his cross and follow me. ²⁵For whoever wants to save his lifeᵒ will lose it, but whoever loses his life for me will find it. ²⁶What good will it be for a man if he gains the whole world, yet forfeits his soul? Or what can a man give in exchange for his soul? ²⁷For the Son of Man is going to come in his Father's glory with his angels, and then he will reward each person according to what he has done. ²⁸I tell you the truth, some who are standing here will not taste death before they see the Son of Man coming in his kingdom."

ʲ16 Or *Messiah*; also in verse 20   ᵏ18 *Peter* means *rock.*   ˡ18 Or *hell*
ᵐ18 Or *not prove stronger than it*   ⁿ19 Or *have been*   ᵒ25 The Greek word
means either *life* or *soul*; also in verse 26.

Matthew 16:13-28   **PETER'S CONFESSION/JESUS' PREDICTION**

LOOKING INTO THE SCRIPTURE/20 Minutes. Read Matthew 16:13-28 and discuss.

1. If you were to ask the average person where you work, "Who is Jesus Christ?" what would he say?
   a. a religious nut
   b. greatest man who ever lived
   c. Son of God
   d. a swear word
   e. an enigma (mystery)

2. "You are the Christ." When Peter answered this, what did he mean?
   a. long-awaited Messiah
   b. ruler of a new Israel
   c. sacrifice for sin
   d. answer to his deepest quest

3. Why did Peter get so upset when Jesus explained the cross?
   a. he didn't understand prophecy
   b. he didn't want Jesus to suffer
   c. he didn't want to suffer
   d. he didn't want to lose his leader
   e. he was just acting tough

4. What is Jesus saying? "If anyone would come after me, he must deny himself and take up his cross and follow me."
   a. following Jesus is no rose garden
   b. if you've got reservations, now is the time to get out
   c. it's gonna cost you everything
   d. shape up or ship out

5. What is Jesus saying here? "What good is it for a man to gain the whole world, yet forfeit his soul?"
   a. it's a question of personal priorities
   b. why pay the ultimate price for temporary happiness?
   c. it's all or nothing
   d. someday you'll have to answer for your choices

6. How do you think Peter felt after this experience?
   a. confused
   b. depressed
   c. scared to death
   d. ready to go

MY OWN STORY/25 Minutes.

1. For each period of your life, put a symbol to indicate how you experienced Jesus.

   ☐ K=Jesus is someone to KNOW about   ☐ L=Jesus is someone to LEARN about
   ☐ F=Jesus is someone to FOLLOW   ☐ A=Jesus is someone to AVOID

CHILDHOOD	TEENS	COLLEGE AGE	YOUNG ADULTHOOD	MIDDLE AGE	RETIRE-MENT	SENIOR CITIZEN

2. How would you compare where you are in your spiritual journey to a ball game? Are you right now . . .
   a. a spectator—in the grandstand
   b. a benchwarmer
   c. playing on the offensive team
   d. playing defense
   e. on the injury list

3. How would you describe your response to Jesus' call to deny yourself, take up your cross and follow him?
   a. I'm not ready for this
   b. I've got a long way to go
   c. I've come a long way
   d. There's a lot more to it than I bargained for
   e. Ask me tomorrow

4. For you, what would taking the next step in your spiritual life mean?
   a. remedial work in the basics—prayer, Bible reading, etc.
   b. turning to Jesus for guidance in daily decisions
   c. deeper commitment to the people in my small group
   d. reevaluating my goals and priorities

5. How can other members of your group help you?
   a. give me a kick in the pants when I need it
   b. pray for me
   c. keep quiet on discipleship while I think it through
   d. give me the support I need
   e. hold me accountable

The Transfiguration

17 After six days Jesus took with him Peter, James and John the brother of James, and led them up a high mountain by themselves. [2]There he was transfigured before them. His face shone like the sun, and his clothes became as white as the light. [3]Just then there appeared before them Moses and Elijah, talking with Jesus.

[4]Peter said to Jesus, "Lord, it is good for us to be here. If you wish, I will put up three shelters—one for you, one for Moses and one for Elijah."

[5]While he was still speaking, a bright cloud enveloped them, and a voice from the cloud said, "This is my Son, whom I love; with him I am well pleased. Listen to him!"

[6]When the disciples heard this, they fell facedown to the ground, terrified. [7]But Jesus came and touched them. "Get up," he said. "Don't be afraid." [8]When they looked up, they saw no one except Jesus.

[9]As they were coming down the mountain, Jesus instructed them, "Don't tell anyone what you have seen, until the Son of Man has been raised from the dead."

[10]The disciples asked him, "Why then do the teachers of the law say that Elijah must come first?"

[11]Jesus replied, "To be sure, Elijah comes and will restore all things. [12]But I tell you, Elijah has already come, and they did not recognize him, but have done to him everything they wished. In the same way the Son of Man is going to suffer at their hands." [13]Then the disciples understood that he was talking to them about John the Baptist.

The Healing of a Boy With a Demon

[14]When they came to the crowd, a man approached Jesus and knelt before him. [15]"Lord, have mercy on my son," he said. "He has seizures and is suffering greatly. He often falls into the fire or into the water. [16]I brought him to your disciples, but they could not heal him."

[17]"O unbelieving and perverse generation," Jesus replied, "how long shall I stay with you? How long shall I put up with you? Bring the boy here to me." [18]Jesus rebuked the demon, and it came out of the boy, and he was healed from that moment.

[19]Then the disciples came to Jesus in private and asked, "Why couldn't we drive it out?"

[20]He replied, "Because you have so little faith. I tell you the truth, if you have faith as small as a mustard seed, you can say to this mountain, 'Move from here to there' and it will move. Nothing will be impossible for you. *"*

[22]When they came together in Galilee, he said to them, "The Son of Man is going to be betrayed into the hands of men. [23]They will kill him, and on the third day he will be raised to life." And the disciples were filled with grief.

P20 Some manuscripts you. [21]But this kind does not go out except by prayer and fasting.

The Temple Tax

²⁴After Jesus and his disciples arrived in Capernaum, the collectors of the two-drachma tax came to Peter and asked, "Doesn't your teacher pay the temple tax⁹?"

²⁵"Yes, he does," he replied.

When Peter came into the house, Jesus was the first to speak. "What do you think, Simon?" he asked. "From whom do the kings of the earth collect duty and taxes—from their own sons or from others?"

²⁶"From others," Peter answered.

"Then the sons are exempt," Jesus said to him. ²⁷"But so that we may not offend them, go to the lake and throw out your line. Take the first fish you catch; open its mouth and you will find a four-drachma coin. Take it and give it to them for my tax and yours."

The Greatest in the Kingdom of Heaven

18 At that time the disciples came to Jesus and asked, "Who is the greatest in the kingdom of heaven?"

²He called a little child and had him stand among them. ³And he said: "I tell you the truth, unless you change and become like little children, you will never enter the kingdom of heaven. ⁴Therefore, whoever humbles himself like this child is the greatest in the kingdom of heaven.

⁵"And whoever welcomes a little child like this in my name welcomes me. ⁶But if anyone causes one of these little ones who believe in me to sin, it would be better for him to have a large millstone hung around his neck and to be drowned in the depths of the sea.

⁷"Woe to the world because of the things that cause people to sin! Such things must come, but woe to the man through whom they come! ⁸If your hand or your foot causes you to sin, cut it off and throw it away. It is better for you to enter life maimed or crippled than to have two hands or two feet and be thrown into eternal fire. ⁹And if your eye causes you to sin, gouge it out and throw it away. It is better for you to enter life with one eye than to have two eyes and be thrown into the fire of hell.

The Parable of the Lost Sheep

¹⁰"See that you do not look down on one of these little ones. For I tell you that their angels in heaven always see the face of my Father in heaven.ʳ

¹²"What do you think? If a man owns a hundred sheep, and one of them wanders away, will he not leave the ninety-nine on the hills and go to look for the one that wandered off? ¹³And if he finds it, I tell you the truth, he is happier about that one sheep than about the ninety-nine that did not wander off. ¹⁴In the same way your Father in heaven is not willing that any of these little ones should be lost.

---

q24 Greek the two drachmas to save what was lost. *r10 Some manuscripts heaven. ¹¹The Son of Man came*

OPEN: What is the wildest "fish story" that you ever heard?

DIG: 1. What was the temple tax (see Exodus 30:11-16)? Who was required to pay it? For what purpose was it used? **2.** Why would Jesus say he was exempt from the tax? (Who is the King worshiped in the Temple?) **3.** What lesson was Jesus teaching Peter by paying the tax anyway?

REFLECT: 1. Which freedoms do you enjoy most as a Christian? **2.** What is at stake when we offend someone? Why is it often better to pay even when we don't owe?

OPEN: Of the following, which "woe" would be the worst way to go: a) Canoe going over a surprise 250-foot waterfall; b) Parachute failing to open; c) Running out of gas in outer space; d) Being a late night snack for a pride of lions?

DIG: 1. Why might the disciples want to be "the greatest"? What does this say about their understanding of the kingdom? **2.** What does it mean to humble oneself like a child? Why do you think this is important for Jesus' kingdom? **3.** Why is causing a child to sin such a serious offense? **4.** Although evil is inevitable (vv. 7-9), we are still morally responsible to care for our own and other's spiritual welfare. How so?

REFLECT: 1. In what ways are you still childlike? No longer childlike? Why? **2.** Which areas of your life might be encouraging others to sin?

OPEN: 1. What do you believe about angels? **2.** What are you like when you've lost something?

DIG: What does the parable in verses 12-13 teach about God's attitude toward "little ones"? Who might these straying sheep be?

REFLECT: 1. How might a "guardian angel" have protected your life when you were a child? When you were defenseless? Weak in faith? **2.** What has God taught you here about your attitude and actions toward all little ones—children and the weak and powerless in the world?

OPEN: How did your parents settle fights between you and your siblings?

DIG: 1. Jesus addresses this teaching to whom (vv. 1, 15, 20)? About what? For what desired result? **2.** This reconciliation process involves what four stages? **3.** What obstacle frustrates the process? What authority (vv. 18-20) is given to Jesus' followers to aid this process?

REFLECT: 1. Have you ever followed this four step reconciliation process? What happened? **2.** When you do get up the courage to confront, how do you avoid being vindictive or hurtful in return?

OPEN: What was one of the worst things your brother or sister did to you when you were growing up?

DIG: 1. The rabbis of Jesus' day said if a man offended you, you should forgive him three times. But if he did it a fourth time, he did not need to be forgiven. What might Peter expect of Jesus when he asked his question? **2.** What does Jesus mean when he says to forgive seventy-seven times? What does this say about forgiveness in the kingdom? **3.** How does the parable of the unmerciful servant extend Jesus' teaching on forgiveness (vv. 23-35)? In refusing to be merciful to others, what do we deny ourselves (vv. 31-34)? **4.** How does Jesus' point in verse 35 compare with 6:12? Do we forgive others so God will forgive us? Or does God forgive us, so that we will have a forgiving attitude? Why? **5.** Based on this parable is God's forgiveness of us limited or unlimited? Conditional or unconditional? Likewise, our forgiveness of others? Why? **6.** In summary, what did Jesus teach in chapter 18 about the nature of the kingdom? In what ways was his teaching expected or unexpected?

REFLECT: 1. Who has extended the most forgiveness to you? **2.** To whom have you offered much forgiveness? **3.** Whom do you need to forgive right now? **4.** What is the best way to forgive people who don't know they have wronged you? How should you forgive someone from the distant past who hurt you deeply? **5.** How important is forgiveness to health and personal wholeness? Why? **6.** What will you take home from Matthew 18?

A Brother Who Sins Against You

¹⁵"If your brother sins against you,ˢ go and show him his fault, just between the two of you. If he listens to you, you have won your brother over. ¹⁶But if he will not listen, take one or two others along, so that 'every matter may be established by the testimony of two or three witnesses.'ᵗ ¹⁷If he refuses to listen to them, tell it to the church; and if he refuses to listen even to the church, treat him as you would a pagan or a tax collector.

¹⁸"I tell you the truth, whatever you bind on earth will beᵘ bound in heaven, and whatever you loose on earth will beᵘ loosed in heaven.

¹⁹"Again, I tell you that if two of you on earth agree about anything you ask for, it will be done for you by my Father in heaven. ²⁰For where two or three come together in my name, there am I with them."

The Parable of the Unmerciful Servant

²¹Then Peter came to Jesus and asked, "Lord, how many times shall I forgive my brother when he sins against me? Up to seven times?"

²²Jesus answered, "I tell you, not seven times, but seventy-seven times.ᵛ

²³"Therefore, the kingdom of heaven is like a king who wanted to settle accounts with his servants. ²⁴As he began the settlement, a man who owed him ten thousand talentsʷ was brought to him. ²⁵Since he was not able to pay, the master ordered that he and his wife and his children and all that he had be sold to repay the debt.

²⁶"The servant fell on his knees before him. 'Be patient with me,' he begged, 'and I will pay back everything.' ²⁷The servant's master took pity on him, canceled the debt and let him go.

²⁸"But when that servant went out, he found one of his fellow servants who owed him a hundred denarii.ˣ He grabbed him and began to choke him. 'Pay back what you owe me!' he demanded.

²⁹"His fellow servant fell to his knees and begged him, 'Be patient with me, and I will pay you back.'

³⁰"But he refused. Instead, he went off and had the man thrown into prison until he could pay the debt. ³¹When the other servants saw what had happened, they were greatly distressed and went and told their master everything that had happened.

³²"Then the master called the servant in. 'You wicked servant,' he said, 'I canceled all that debt of yours because you begged me to. ³³Shouldn't you have had mercy on your fellow servant just as I had on you?' ³⁴In anger his master turned him over to the jailers to be tortured, until he should pay back all he owed.

³⁵"This is how my heavenly Father will treat each of you unless you forgive your brother from your heart."

ˢ15 Some manuscripts do not have *against you.*   ᵗ16 Deut. 19:15   ᵘ18 Or *have been*   ᵛ22 Or *seventy times seven*   ʷ24 That is, millions of dollars   ˣ28 That is, a few dollars

Matthew 18:21-35   THE PARABLE OF THE UNMERCIFUL SERVANT

LOOKING INTO THE SCRIPTURE/25 Minutes. Read Matthew 18:21-35 and discuss.

1. Do you suppose Peter had a special reason for asking how many times he needed to forgive his brother and, if so, what was it?
   a. he was the type to keep score
   b. he couldn't forgive someone
   c. he was easily hurt
   d. he just wanted to know

2. What is the parable that Jesus told really about?
   a. how to deal with someone who owes you money
   b. how to deal with your own anger when you've been wronged
   c. how to keep your relationship with God fresh
   d. how to avoid getting trapped in grudges
   e. how to say thanks for God's forgiveness

3. How would you describe the attitude of the servant toward the one who had wronged him?
   a. business is business
   b. an eye for an eye
   c. don't let the scoundrel off the hook
   d. let him suffer

4. What's the principle for you as a Christian in dealing with someone who has wronged you?
   a. you can't out-forgive God
   b. scorekeepers end up getting hurt
   c. God expects you to be a "pushover"
   d. if you don't forgive others, God is going to refigure what you owe him
   e. unforgivers wind up in their own chains
   f. only the forgiven know how to forgive

MY OWN STORY/20 Minutes. Study the case history below and share how you would deal with the situation.

LITTLE BROTHER: You have been putting up with your little brother for years. When you were growing up, you had to share a bedroom, where he kept "his side" like a pig pen. He "borrowed" your clothes without asking, left the car a mess when he used it, and never thought of filling the tank with gas. Now, the two of you run the family business, but you have to keep the books, pay the bills, and come in on Saturdays while he coaches a Little League team. Recently, your doctor told you that you have an ulcer, and it is caused by deep-seated anger against your little brother.

1. What do you do?
   a. decide it's not worth getting sick over
   b. complain to his wife
   c. call your father and tell everything
   d. sweep it under the rug
   e. have it out with him
   f. take off for six months and leave the business to him

2. What have you found helpful in dealing with sour relationships?
   a. keep short accounts
   b. write a letter but don't mail it
   c. ask someone else to mediate
   d. have it out—right now
   e. sleep on it
   f. get away from the situation
   g. break off the relationship

3. Who is the easiest and hardest person for you to forgive?
   a. brother/sister
   b. spouse
   c. parents/kids
   d. neighbor/friend
   e. stranger
   f. yourself

4. How could you pass on God's forgiveness to those who have wronged you?
   a. pray for them
   b. think first about whether I've done anything wrong myself
   c. hold them accountable for the consequences of what they have done
   d. drop the issue and let them know it's past history
   e. look for ways to show kindness to them

OPEN: What makes good marriages "work"? What would your spouse, if any, say is the key?

DIG: 1. What were the Pharisees trying to do by asking this question about divorce? 2. How would it have benefitted the Pharisees to trick Jesus into opposing Moses? 3. Instead of debating the law, on what did Jesus focus his attention? What was the central point of his quotations from Genesis? What, then, was Jesus' answer to the Pharisees? 4. Did Moses "command" or "permit" divorce (vv. 7-8, see Dt. 24:1)? What was Moses' real intention in allowing divorce? 5. What was Jesus condemning: All frivolous divorces? All divorces not properly resolved with a certificate of rights? All divorces except on the grounds of infidelity? All divorce? All divorcees? 6. To what extent does "unfaithfulness" (v. 9) extend Jesus' point? Why this exception? Are there any others? 7. How do the disciples show that they now view marriage most seriously (v. 10)?

REFLECT: 1. How has divorce influenced your life or family? 2. What advice would you give to a couple contemplating marriage on how a marriage stays together?

DIG: Why would parents bring their children to Jesus? Why do the disciples discourage this? What is Jesus' view of children and the kingdom (see also 18:1-14)?

REFLECT: What can you begin doing this week to approach Jesus in the same way a child would?

OPEN: 1. If your house were on fire, what three items (not people) would you try to save? 2. What do you think would be the ideal salary? What would make this salary ideal?

DIG: 1. What seems to have been this young man's view on how one obtains eternal life? 2. Is there a difference between the young man's concern ("eternal life") and Jesus' concern ("life")? 3. Which of the Ten Commandments did Jesus leave out (see Exodus 20)? What is the general subject of the first four commandments? Which one of the last six commandments did Jesus omit? Why? Which commandment did Jesus add which was not part of the original ten? 4. Had the man kept the commandments in his own

Divorce

19 When Jesus had finished saying these things, he left Galilee and went into the region of Judea to the other side of the Jordan. [2]Large crowds followed him, and he healed them there.

[3]Some Pharisees came to him to test him. They asked, "Is it lawful for a man to divorce his wife for any and every reason?"

[4]"Haven't you read," he replied, "that at the beginning the Creator 'made them male and female,'[y] [5]and said, 'For this reason a man will leave his father and mother and be united to his wife, and the two will become one flesh'[z]? [6]So they are no longer two, but one. Therefore what God has joined together, let man not separate."

[7]"Why then," they asked, "did Moses command that a man give his wife a certificate of divorce and send her away?"

[8]Jesus replied, "Moses permitted you to divorce your wives because your hearts were hard. But it was not this way from the beginning. [9]I tell you that anyone who divorces his wife, except for marital unfaithfulness, and marries another woman commits adultery."

[10]The disciples said to him, "If this is the situation between a husband and wife, it is better not to marry."

[11]Jesus replied, "Not everyone can accept this word, but only those to whom it has been given. [12]For some are eunuchs because they were born that way; others were made that way by men; and others have renounced marriage[a] because of the kingdom of heaven. The one who can accept this should accept it."

The Little Children and Jesus

[13]Then little children were brought to Jesus for him to place his hands on them and pray for them. But the disciples rebuked those who brought them.

[14]Jesus said, "Let the little children come to me, and do not hinder them, for the kingdom of heaven belongs to such as these." [15]When he had placed his hands on them, he went on from there.

The Rich Young Man

[16]Now a man came up to Jesus and asked, "Teacher, what good thing must I do to get eternal life?"

[17]"Why do you ask me about what is good?" Jesus replied. "There is only One who is good. If you want to enter life, obey the commandments."

[18]"Which ones?" the man inquired.

Jesus replied, " 'Do not murder, do not commit adultery, do not steal, do not give false testimony, [19]honor your father and mother,'[b] and 'love your neighbor as yourself.'[c]"

[20]"All these I have kept," the young man said. "What do I still lack?"

---

y4 Gen. 1:27   *z* Gen. 2:24   *a12* Or *have made themselves eunuchs*
b19 Exodus 20:12-16; Deut. 5:16-20   *c19* Lev. 19:18

²¹Jesus answered, "If you want to be perfect, go, sell your possessions and give to the poor, and you will have treasure in heaven. Then come, follow me."

²²When the young man heard this, he went away sad, because he had great wealth.

²³Then Jesus said to his disciples, "I tell you the truth, it is hard for a rich man to enter the kingdom of heaven. ²⁴Again I tell you, it is easier for a camel to go through the eye of a needle than for a rich man to enter the kingdom of God."

²⁵When the disciples heard this, they were greatly astonished and asked, "Who then can be saved?"

²⁶Jesus looked at them and said, "With man this is impossible, but with God all things are possible."

²⁷Peter answered him, "We have left everything to follow you! What then will there be for us?"

²⁸Jesus said to them, "I tell you the truth, at the renewal of all things, when the Son of Man sits on his glorious throne, you who have followed me will also sit on twelve thrones, judging the twelve tribes of Israel. ²⁹And everyone who has left houses or brothers or sisters or father or mother*d* or children or fields for my sake will receive a hundred times as much and will inherit eternal life. ³⁰But many who are first will be last, and many who are last will be first.

The Parable of the Workers in the Vineyard

20 "For the kingdom of heaven is like a landowner who went out early in the morning to hire men to work in his vineyard. ²He agreed to pay them a denarius for the day and sent them into his vineyard.

³"About the third hour he went out and saw others standing in the marketplace doing nothing. ⁴He told them, 'You also go and work in my vineyard, and I will pay you whatever is right.' ⁵So they went.

"He went out again about the sixth hour and the ninth hour and did the same thing. ⁶About the eleventh hour he went out and found still others standing around. He asked them, 'Why have you been standing here all day long doing nothing?'

⁷" 'Because no one has hired us,' they answered.

"He said to them, 'You also go and work in my vineyard.'

⁸"When evening came, the owner of the vineyard said to his foreman, 'Call the workers and pay them their wages, beginning with the last ones hired and going on to the first.'

⁹"The workers who were hired about the eleventh hour came and each received a denarius. ¹⁰So when those came who were hired first, they expected to receive more. But each one of them also received a denarius. ¹¹When they received it, they began to grumble against the landowner. ¹²"These men who were hired last worked only one hour,' they said, 'and you have made them equal to us who have borne the burden of the work and the heat of the day.'

d29 Some manuscripts mother or wife

eyes? In Jesus' eyes? What would account for this difference (see also 5:21-22, 27-28)? **5.** On what basis (vv. 20-21) does Jesus call for "perfection"? With what revealing response (v. 22)? Had the young man truly loved his neighbor (v. 19)? What does the young man love more? **6.** Why is it so difficult for the rich to enter the kingdom? On what basis is it possible for anyone—rich or poor—to enter (vv. 26-30)? **7.** According to verses 16-30, how are these four connected: being saved, becoming a disciple, entering the kingdom of heaven, and inheriting eternal life? What surprises might there be in heaven (v. 30)?

REFLECT: 1. Jesus hit this man where it hurt—in his wallet. If Jesus were to address you where it hurts, what would his topic be? **2.** Why is Jesus so tough on riches? Is it really a spiritual problem? **3.** What have you given up to follow Jesus? How is your life different?

OPEN: 1. Which category of persons do you believe works the hardest: a) mothers of young children; b) attorneys; c) door to door salesmen; d) high school teachers; e) preachers? Why? **2.** Have you ever experienced difficulty landing a job? Explain.

DIG: 1. To what is the kingdom of heaven compared? Why is the parable told here (see 19:30 and 20:16)? **2.** What wage does the landowner offer the first workers hired? What wage does he offer the others? Why are they identical? **3.** Why do many people stand around all day doing nothing (v. 7)? Whose initiative led to their employment? **4.** In what order are the workers paid? Who is discontent and why (vv. 10-12)? Is the landowner's practice unjust, or generous, or both? Why? **5.** How does this parable apply to the kingdom and to 19:30? Who gets any less of God: The "eleventh hour" converts (Gentiles)? Or those who should have known God all along from the "first hour" (the Jews)?

REFLECT: 1. If you had been one of the first people hired, how might you feel about the landowner's wage system? **2.** If you have lived a fairly moral life, does it bother you when those who haven't will get the same benefits as you in the kingdom of God? **3.** Would you recommend that people wait until just before they die to come to Christ, so that they won't have to work so hard or give up so much? Why?

_____

OPEN: When do you avoid the subject of death?

DIG: What does Jesus predict? Why on this occasion? Why once again for these disciples (see 16:21)? What about Jesus' prediction does not mesh with their view of the kingdom?

_____

OPEN: When you were a child, what did your parents want you to be when you grew up? What did you want to be?

DIG: 1. Who were the sons of Zebedee (4:21)? 2. What does their mother want? Why? Of what is she ignorant (v. 22)? 3. In order to share in his kingdom, what must the disciples share with Jesus? What "cup" is Jesus to drink soon (vv. 18-19)? 4. Why were the other ten disciples so outraged? Were their reactions any more commendable? 5. What contrast does Jesus set up between how the Gentiles rule and how authority is exercised in God's kingdom? How does Jesus model this new way?

REFLECT: How signifigant do you feel in relation to God's kingdom? In what specific ways can you serve people using Jesus as your model?

_____

OPEN: If you had to beg for your living, what location would you beg from and what kind of approach would you use? Why?

DIG: 1. How would you compare the blindness of these men with the blindness of the disciples in verses 20-28? 2. How does this incident fit with the crowd's agenda (v. 31)? With Jesus' agenda (see 19:30, 20:16)? 3. Why are these two singled out for healing? Once healed, what do they do? Why?

REFLECT: 1. In what ways do you feel spiritually blind? In what ways are you less blind than you were six months ago? 2. If Jesus said to you, "What do you want me to do for you"? How would you answer?

[13]"But he answered one of them, 'Friend, I am not being unfair to you. Didn't you agree to work for a denarius? [14]Take your pay and go. I want to give the man who was hired last the same as I gave you. [15]Don't I have the right to do what I want with my own money? Or are you envious because I am generous?'

[16]"So the last will be first, and the first will be last."

Jesus Again Predicts His Death

[17]Now as Jesus was going up to Jerusalem, he took the twelve disciples aside and said to them, [18]"We are going up to Jerusalem, and the Son of Man will be betrayed to the chief priests and the teachers of the law. They will condemn him to death [19]and will turn him over to the Gentiles to be mocked and flogged and crucified. On the third day he will be raised to life!"

A Mother's Request

[20]Then the mother of Zebedee's sons came to Jesus with her sons and, kneeling down, asked a favor of him.

[21]"What is it you want?" he asked.

She said, "Grant that one of these two sons of mine may sit at your right and the other at your left in your kingdom."

[22]"You don't know what you are asking," Jesus said to them. "Can you drink the cup I am going to drink?"

"We can," they answered.

[23]Jesus said to them, "You will indeed drink from my cup, but to sit at my right or left is not for me to grant. These places belong to those for whom they have been prepared by my Father."

[24]When the ten heard about this, they were indignant with the two brothers. [25]Jesus called them together and said, "You know that the rulers of the Gentiles lord it over them, and their high officials exercise authority over them. [26]Not so with you. Instead, whoever wants to become great among you must be your servant, [27]and whoever wants to be first must be your slave— [28]just as the Son of Man did not come to be served, but to serve, and to give his life as a ransom for for many."

Two Blind Men Receive Sight

[29]As Jesus and his disciples were leaving Jericho, a large crowd followed him. [30]Two blind men were sitting by the roadside, and when they heard that Jesus was going by, they shouted, "Lord, Son of David, have mercy on us!"

[31]The crowd rebuked them and told them to be quiet, but they shouted all the louder, "Lord, Son of David, have mercy on us!"

[32]Jesus stopped and called them. "What do you want me to do for you?" he asked.

[33]"Lord," they answered, "we want our sight."

[34]Jesus had compassion on them and touched their eyes. Immediately they received their sight and followed him.

Matthew 20:20-28   **A MOTHER'S REQUEST**

LOOKING INTO THE SCRIPTURE/20 Minutes. Read Matthew 20:20-28 and discuss.

1. If you had been the mother, how would you have felt about Jesus' response to her question?
   a. confused
   b. disappointed
   c. angry
   d. insulted
   e. inspired

2. What do you think motivated the mother to ask a favor of Jesus?
   a. mother's love
   b. ambition for her sons
   c. she knew they would be best
   d. she wanted the best for her sons

3. What was the mother really wanting when she asked if her sons could "sit at your right . . . and left hand . . ."?
   a. close relationship with God
   b. power and position
   c. special recognition
   d. her own satisfaction
   e. spiritual security

4. What was Jesus really saying, "You don't know what you are asking"?
   a. you're embarrassing your sons
   b. you've got to be kidding
   c. your sons don't deserve it
   d. what you ask is impossible
   e. it's not my decision

5. What is Jesus referring to when he said, "Can you drink the cup I am going to drink?"
   a. royal silverware
   b. divine authority
   c. suffering and death
   d. God's plan for Jesus
   e. unreasonable expectations

6. What values did Jesus turn upside down when he met with the disciples?
   a. always listen to a boy's mother
   b. God gives special favors
   c. heaven rewards the powerful
   d. the great are the ones who are served
   e. get what you can out of life

MY OWN STORY/20 Minutes. Take a moment and share your experience.

1. Do/did your parents put any expectations on you?   ☐ Yes ☐ No ☐ Sometimes

2. Are/were you able to live up to those expectations?   ☐ Yes ☐ No ☐ Sometimes

3. Do/did you put any expectations on your children?   ☐ Yes ☐ No ☐ Sometimes

4. What would you desire for your children? (Top three)
   ☐ good health
   ☐ college education
   ☐ good friends
   ☐ spiritual fulfillment
   ☐ success in their field
   ☐ secure job
   ☐ lasting marriage
   ☐ life full of surprises
   ☐ star on athletic team
   ☐ amount to something
   ☐ good grades in school
   ☐ leader in school
   ☐ happiness
   ☐ life free of hardship
   ☐ financial independence

5. If you could pass on to your children three things, what would they be?
   ☐ moral courage
   ☐ sense of humor
   ☐ faith in God
   ☐ respect for country
   ☐ family pride
   ☐ lots of initiative
   ☐ good self-image
   ☐ money
   ☐ opportunity to get ahead
   ☐ your own values
   ☐ love of adventure
   ☐ concern for the poor
   ☐ peace of mind
   ☐ basic honesty
   ☐ hard work

OPEN: How would you arrange for Jesus to have maximum exposure in your town: What parades? What escorts? What TV talk shows or radio call-in programs? Where would he eat? Stay the night?

DIG: 1. To what town has Jesus come? Why? **2.** Jesus comes on a donkey and not on a stallion. What kind of Messiah does that portray? **3.** Why such a large crowd at this time of year? What did they shout? Why? **4.** What kind of kingdom, and king were the people expecting? How do their wishes compare with the reality of Jesus? **5.** How might that discrepancy account for the same crowd later on shouting, "Crucify him"?

REFLECT: 1. Would the request of Jesus for the disciples to get the donkey be a hard one to keep? If someone had questioned them while getting the donkey, how convincing would be the line which Jesus offered them to speak? **2.** How might you have reacted had you been there to greet Jesus riding into town? Do you jump on other political or religious bandwagons today? Why or why not? **3.** How much do you comprehend at this point about who Jesus really is?

OPEN: 1. Would you classify yourself as a collector or a cleaner—do you keep accumulating more things or are you always throwing stuff out? **2.** "Children say the darndest things": What recent examples come to mind?

DIG: 1. Where does Jesus go first upon arrival in Jerusalem? **2.** What actually upset him so much in what he saw there? What once-useful role did these merchants perform for out-of-towners? **3.** In this passage, which groups of people did, and did not recognize the significance of Jesus? How do you explain that? **4.** Why do you suppose Jesus did not spend the night in Jerusalem?

REFLECT: 1. Today, is it easier for children or adults to recognize Jesus? Why? **2.** If Jesus were to visit your church, are there any areas where he might begin "turning over tables"? What about in your life? **3.** What will you remember most from this passage? What difference do you expect it to make in your life?

The Triumphal Entry

21 As they approached Jerusalem and came to Bethphage on the Mount of Olives, Jesus sent two disciples, [2]saying to them, "Go to the village ahead of you, and at once you will find a donkey tied there, with her colt by her. Untie them and bring them to me. [3]If anyone says anything to you, tell him that the Lord needs them, and he will send them right away."

[4]This took place to fulfill what was spoken through the prophet:

[5]"Say to the Daughter of Zion,
    'See, your king comes to you,
gentle and riding on a donkey,
    on a colt, the foal of a donkey.' "[e]

[6]The disciples went and did as Jesus had instructed them. [7]They brought the donkey and the colt, placed their cloaks on them, and Jesus sat on them. [8]A very large crowd spread their cloaks on the road, while others cut branches from the trees and spread them on the road. [9]The crowds that went ahead of him and those that followed shouted,

"Hosanna[f] to the Son of David!"

"Blessed is he who comes in the name of the Lord!"[g]

"Hosanna[f] in the highest!"

[10]When Jesus entered Jerusalem, the whole city was stirred and asked, "Who is this?"

[11]The crowds answered, "This is Jesus, the prophet from Nazareth in Galilee."

Jesus at the Temple

[12]Jesus entered the temple area and drove out all who were buying and selling there. He overturned the tables of the money changers and the benches of those selling doves. [13]"It is written," he said to them, " 'My house will be called a house of prayer,'[h] but you are making it a 'den of robbers.'[i]"

[14]The blind and the lame came to him at the temple, and he healed them. [15]But when the chief priests and the teachers of the law saw the wonderful things he did and the children shouting in the temple area, "Hosanna to the Son of David," they were indignant.

[16]"Do you hear what what these children are saying?" they asked him.

"Yes," replied Jesus, "have you never read,

" 'From the lips of children and infants
    you have ordained praise'[j]?"

[17]And he left them and went out of the city to Bethany, where he spent the night.

---

[e]5 Zech. 9:9   [f]9 A Hebrew expression meaning "Save!" which became an exclamation of praise; also in verse 15   [g]9 Psalm 118:26   [h]13 Isaiah 56:7   [i]13 Jer. 7:11   [j]16 Psalm 8:2

The Fig Tree Withers

¹⁸Early in the morning, as he was on his way back to the city, he was hungry. ¹⁹Seeing a fig tree by the road, he went up to it but found nothing on it except leaves. Then he said to it, "May you never bear fruit again!" Immediately the tree withered.

²⁰When the disciples saw this, they were amazed. "How did the fig tree wither so quickly?" they asked.

²¹Jesus replied, "I tell you the truth, if you have faith and do not doubt, not only can you do what was done to the fig tree, but also you can say to this mountain, 'Go, throw yourself into the sea,' and it will be done. ²²If you believe, you will receive whatever you ask for in prayer."

The Authority of Jesus Questioned

²³Jesus entered the temple courts, and, while he was teaching, the chief priests and the elders of the people came to him. "By what authority are you doing these things?" they asked. "And who gave you this authority?"

²⁴Jesus replied, "I will also ask you one question. If you answer me, I will tell you by what authority I am doing these things. ²⁵John's baptism—where did it come from? Was it from heaven, or from men?"

They discussed it among themselves and said, "If we say, 'From heaven,' he will ask, 'Then why didn't you believe him?' ²⁶But if we say, 'From men'—we are afraid of the people, for they all hold that John was a prophet."

²⁷So they answered Jesus, "We don't know."

Then he said, "Neither will I tell you by what authority I am doing these things.

The Parable of the Two Sons

²⁸"What do you think? There was a man who had two sons. He went to the first and said, 'Son, go and work today in the vineyard.'

²⁹"'I will not,' he answered, but later he changed his mind and went.

³⁰"Then the father went to the other son and said the same thing. He answered, 'I will, sir,' but he did not go.

³¹"Which of the two did what his father wanted?"

"The first," they answered.

Jesus said to them, "I tell you the truth, the tax collectors and the prostitutes are entering the kingdom of God ahead of you. ³²For John came to you to show you the way of righteousness, and you did not believe him, but the tax collectors and the prostitutes did. And even after you saw this, you did not repent and believe him.

OPEN: What are you likely to curse: The weather? Your luck? "It"? Why?

DIG: 1. How is the fig tree incident a parable about what has happened in the temple and what is to come for Israel (see Hosea 9:10-17)? **2.** What does this dramatized parable teach about faith? Prayer? Judgment? Jesus?

REFLECT: 1. How might the promise of verse 22 be abused? **2.** What great prayer would you like to see answered in your life right now?

OPEN: When in high school, with what big authority figure did you run into trouble? Why?

DIG: 1. Where does Jesus go now? While teaching with what issue is Jesus confronted? By whom? Why? **2.** What possible answers could Jesus have given? How would these answers have trapped him? **3.** How did Jesus counter-question force the issue? **4.** How was Jesus' authority linked to John's authority? What had John said about Jesus?

REFLECT: 1. Ultimately, who is your chief authority figure now? **2.** When it comes right down to it, whose opinion do you care about more—God's or people's?

OPEN: As a child, what kind of worker were you? How much did your parents have to yell and scream to get you to work?

DIG: 1. What links this parable with Jesus' encounter with the chief priests and elders (vv. 23-27)? **2.** To whom is the parable directed? **3.** Describe the story. What is the father's request? What does each son say? What does each son do? The first son repented. What did the second son do? **4.** Which group is like which son? In what ways? **5.** How do you suppose the religious leaders responded to this story (especially v. 31)?

REFLECT: 1. Which son's story is most like your own story of salvation? **2.** In what ways might this story be helpful in sharing the gospel with a nominal (in name only) Christian?

If you could journey anywhere in the world, money being no problem, where would you go and why? **2.** If you were an absentee landlord, and had to find trustworthy tenants, what would you look for? **3.** Have you ever entrusted your place to a house-sitter? Anything "eventful" happen while you were gone?

DIG: 1. In this parable, who is represented as the landowner: The vineyard? The tenants? The servants? The son? What corresponds to the son's death? What corresponds to the removal of the wretched tennants? **2.** What is the main point of this parable (vv. 42-44)? **3.** At whom does Jesus direct the parable? What does he say to them? Why don't they arrest him? Why don't they repent and follow Jesus? **4.** In what ways are the last three parables (Matthew 20:1-16, 21:28-32, 33-43) similar?

REFLECT: 1. At different times in your life, how have you received Jesus? **2.** How would you rewrite this parable to reflect twentieth-century situations? **3.** In your life, is Jesus like a capstone (the highest point in your building)? Or is he like a millstone (a weight that drags you down)? In what ways? **4.** With whom do you identify in this story? Why? **5.** How could your group encourage you to be more faithful in stewarding the responsibilities and resources God has given you?

OPEN: If you could choose one unusual way to redo your wedding, or plan the one to come, what would you chose: Recite your wedding vows while parachuting? Hold the service underwater? Dress everyone up to look like penguins? Let your imagination soar!

DIG: 1. Why is this banquet held? **2.** What do you learn about those originally invited? How do they snub king and his son? **3.** Who was the king subsequently brought to the banquet and why? **4.** What is the problem with one guest (vv. 11-12)? What does it mean to be in the king's presence "without wedding clothes"? Why is this ill-clad guest banished? **5.** What does this parable suggest about how one is first invited and then qualified for the kingdom? **6.** Had you been one of

The Parable of the Tenants

³³"Listen to another parable: There was a landowner who planted a vineyard. He put a wall around it, dug a winepress in it and built a watchtower. Then he rented the vineyard to some farmers and went away on a journey. ³⁴When the harvest time approached, he sent his servants to the tenants to collect his fruit.

³⁵"The tenants seized his servants; they beat one, killed another, and stoned a third. ³⁶Then he sent other servants to them, more than the first time, and the tenants treated them the same way. ³⁷Last of all, he sent his son to them. 'They will respect my son,' he said.

³⁸"But when the tenants saw the son, they said to each other, 'This is the heir. Come, let's kill him and take his inheritance.' ³⁹So they took him and threw him out of the vineyard and killed him.

⁴⁰"Therefore, when the owner of the vineyard comes, what will he do to those tenants?"

⁴¹"He will bring those wretches to a wretched end," they replied, "and he will rent the vineyard to other tenants, who will give him his share of the crop at harvest time."

⁴²Jesus said to them, "Have you never read in the Scriptures:

" 'The stone the builders rejected
    has become the capstone*ᵏ*;
the Lord has done this,
    and it is marvelous in our eyes'*ˡ*?

⁴³"Therefore I tell you that the kingdom of God will be taken away from you and given to a people who will produce its fruit. ⁴⁴He who falls on this stone will be broken to pieces, but he on whom it falls will be crushed."*ᵐ*

⁴⁵When the chief priests and the Pharisees heard Jesus' parables, they knew he was talking about them. ⁴⁶They looked for a way to arrest him, but they were afraid of the crowd because the people held that he was a prophet.

The Parable of the Wedding Banquet

22 Jesus spoke to them again in parables, saying: ²"The kingdom of heaven is like a king who prepared a wedding banquet for his son. ³He sent his servants to those who had been invited to the banquet to tell them to come, but they refused to come.

⁴"Then he sent some more servants and said, 'Tell those who have been invited that I have prepared my dinner: My oxen and fattened cattle have been butchered, and everything is ready. Come to the wedding banquet.'

⁵"But they paid no attention and went off—one to his field, another to his business. ⁶The rest seized his servants, mistreated them and killed them. ⁷The king was enraged. He sent his army and destroyed those murderers and burned their city.

⁸"Then he said to his servants, 'The wedding banquet is

ᵏ42 Or *cornerstone*   *ˡ42* Psalm 118:22,23   *ᵐ44* Some manuscripts do not have verse 44.

ready, but those I invited did not deserve to come. [9]Go to the street corners and invite to the banquet anyone you find.' [10]So the servants went out into the streets and gathered all the people they could find, both good and bad, and the wedding hall was filled with guests.

[11]"But when the king came in to see the guests, he noticed a man there who was not wearing wedding clothes. [12]'Friend,' he asked, 'how did you get in here without wedding clothes?' The man was speechless.

[13]"Then the king told the attendants, 'Tie him hand and foot, and throw him outside, into the darkness, where there will be weeping and gnashing of teeth.'

[14]"For many are invited, but few are chosen."

Paying Taxes to Caesar

[15]Then the Pharisees went out and laid plans to trap him in his words. [16]They sent their disciples to him along with the Herodians. "Teacher," they said, "we know you are a man of integrity and that you teach the way of God in accordance with the truth. You aren't swayed by men, because you pay no attention to who they are. [17]Tell us then, what is your opinion? Is it right to pay taxes to Caesar or not?"

[18]But Jesus, knowing their evil intent, said, "You hypocrites, why are you trying to trap me? [19]Show me the coin used for paying the tax." They brought him a denarius, [20]and he asked them, "Whose portrait is this? And whose inscription?"

[21]"Caesar's," they replied.

Then he said to them, "Give to Caesar what is Caesar's, and to God what is God's."

[22]When they heard this, they were amazed. So they left him and went away.

Marriage at the Resurrection

[23]That same day the Sadducees, who say there is no resurrection, came to him with a question. [24]"Teacher," they said, "Moses told us that if a man dies without having children, his brother must marry the widow and have children for him. [25]Now there were seven brothers among us. The first one married and died, and since he had no children, he left his wife to his brother. [26]The same thing happened to the second and third brother, right on down to the seventh. [27]Finally, the woman died. [28]Now then, at the resurrection, whose wife will she be of the seven, since all of them were married to her?"

[29]Jesus replied, "You are in error because you do not know the Scriptures or the power of God. [30]At the resurrection people will neither marry nor be given in marriage; they will be like the angels in heaven. [31]But about the resurrection of the dead—have you not read what God said to you, [32]'I am the God of Abraham, the God of Isaac, and the God of Jacob'[n]? He is not the God of the dead but of the living."

[33]When the crowds heard this, they were astonished at his teaching.

[n]32 Exodus 3:6

the chief priests and elders to whom this parable was addressed, how would you react (see v. 15)?

REFLECT: 1. When did Jesus first call you to the banquet? How did you initially respond? How many other times did he invite you? 2. With whom in this story do you most easily identify? Why? 3. What can you do this week to encourage "attendance" and "proper dress"?

OPEN: If you emptied your pockets and pocketbooks on the floor, what priorities would that reveal? Try it.

DIG: 1. How would the crowd respond if Jesus said simply, "Pay Caesar"? Why? How would the ruling government respond if Jesus said, "Don't pay"? 2. What does Jesus mean by his answer (v. 21)? What is it that should be given to God? What is he teaching about the relationship of church and state? Which obligation do you think Jesus considers primary? Why?

REFLECT: 1. What belongs to Caesar in your life? To God? 2. How well are you giving what belongs to each side?

OPEN: In heaven, who or what on earth would you miss most?

DIG: 1. Who now questions Jesus? What do they believe? 2. How does their question appear: Mocking? Serious? Scriptural (see Dt. 25:5-10)? A trick? Full of error (v. 29)? 3. What aspects of their question does Jesus answer? 4. Why no marriage in heaven? (Note: There's no need for procreation in heaven if people are like angels and never die.) 5. How does the Exodus 3:6 quote "prove" the resurrection? (Note: "I am" implies a present tense, ongoing relationship with God for these patriarchs.)

REFLECT: 1.How do you feel about the fact that there will be no marriage in the resurrection? 2. As you ponder going to heaven, what do you anticipate missing from your earthly life? What excites you about heaven? 3. What hope does the fact of the resurrection give you? What one question would you like to ask Jesus about life after death?

OPEN: Who are the three people in this world who love you the most?

DIG: How are these three loves related to each other? To the Law and the Prophets (see Dt. 6:5 and Lv. 19:18 in context)? To "situational ethics" today? Is love the only absolute?

REFLECT: By Jesus' definition, what kind of "lover" are you?

OPEN: Would you rather ask questions or answer them? Why?

DIG: 1. Were the Pharisees expecting the Messiah to be human or to be divine? What problem with this view does Jesus point out? 2. Why would it take Jesus' death and resurrection to show that the Messiah is more than just David's son?

REFLECT: 1. How important is it to understand "the Christ"? 2. How has your view of Jesus changed through the weeks of your group study in Matthew?

OPEN: 1. Growing up, what "hot buttons" did you push to get your parents mad? What "hot buttons" do your kids, if any, use on you? If married, what do you do or say that pushes your spouse to get mad? 2. If you were asked to be a guest preacher on any subject you wished within your experience, what would you choose to speak on? Besides sex and sin, what would you speak on? Why that subject?

DIG: 1. What was the seat of Moses? Given Jesus' remarks about the Pharisees in chapters 21-22, what is surprising about his remarks in Matthew 23:3? How does he limit his commendation of the Pharisees? 2. As Jesus sees it, what is the main evil of the Pharisees? How are the disciples to avoid falling into the same evil? Why would it be important that the disciples not allow themselves to be called rabbi (remember that Jesus was called rabbi)? What distinction was Jesus trying to make between his followers and the Pharisees? 3. Compare the path to greatness followed by the Pharisees with that taught by Jesus (vv. 5-12). What do these two views of greatness teach us about the two views of the kingdom? 4. Make a list of the seven

The Greatest Commandment

³⁴Hearing that Jesus had silenced the Sadducees, the Pharisees got together. ³⁵One of them, an expert in the law, tested him with this question: ³⁶"Teacher, which is the greatest commandment in the Law?"

³⁷Jesus replied: " 'Love the Lord your God with all your heart and with all your soul and with all your mind.'*° ³⁸This is the first and greatest commandment. ³⁹And the second is like it: 'Love your neighbor as yourself.'*ᵖ ⁴⁰All the Law and the Prophets hang on these two commandments."

Whose Son Is the Christ?

⁴¹While the Pharisees were gathered together, Jesus asked them, ⁴²"What do you think about the Christ*? Whose son is he?"

"The son of David," they replied.

⁴³He said to them, "How is it then that David, speaking by the Spirit, calls him 'Lord'? For he says,

⁴⁴" 'The Lord said to my Lord:
"Sit at my right hand
until I put your enemies
under your feet." 'ʳ

⁴⁵If then David calls him 'Lord,' how can he be his son?" ⁴⁶No one could say a word in reply, and from that day on no one dared to ask him any more questions.

Seven Woes

23 Then Jesus said to the crowds and to his disciples: ²"The teachers of the law and the Pharisees sit in Moses' seat. ³So you must obey them and do everything they tell you. But do not do what they do, for they do not practice what they preach. ⁴They tie up heavy loads and put them on men's shoulders, but they themselves are not willing to lift a finger to move them.

⁵"Everything they do is done for men to see: They make their phylacteriesˢ wide and the tassels on their garments long; ⁶they love the place of honor at banquets and the most important seats in the synagogues; ⁷they love to be greeted in the marketplaces and to have men call them 'Rabbi.'

⁸"But you are not to be called 'Rabbi,' for you have only one Master and you are all brothers. ⁹And do not call anyone on earth 'father,' for you have one Father, and he is in heaven. ¹⁰Nor are you to be called 'teacher,' for you have one Teacher, the Christ.ᵠ ¹¹The greatest among you will be your servant. ¹²For whoever exalts himself will be humbled, and whoever humbles himself will be exalted.

*°37 Deut. 6:5   *ᵖ39 Lev. 19:18   ᵠ42,10 Or Messiah   ʳ44 Psalm 110:1
ˢ5 That is, boxes containing Scripture verses, worn on forehead and arm

¹³"Woe to you, teachers of the law and Pharisees, you hypocrites! You shut the kingdom of heaven in men's faces. You yourselves do not enter, nor will you let those enter who are trying to.¹

¹⁵"Woe to you, teachers of the law and Pharisees, you hypocrites! You travel over land and sea to win a single convert, and when he becomes one, you make him twice as much a son of hell as you are.

¹⁶"Woe to you, blind guides! You say, 'If anyone swears by the temple, it means nothing; but if anyone swears by the gold of the temple, he is bound by his oath.' ¹⁷You blind fools! Which is greater: the gold, or the temple that makes the gold sacred? ¹⁸You also say, 'If anyone swears by the altar, it means nothing; but if anyone swears by the gift on it, he is bound by his oath.' ¹⁹You blind men! Which is greater: the gift, or the altar that makes the gift sacred? ²⁰Therefore, he who swears by the altar swears by it and by everything on it. ²¹And he who swears by the temple swears by it and by the one who dwells in it. ²²And he who swears by heaven swears by God's throne and by the one who sits on it.

²³"Woe to you, teachers of the law and Pharisees, you hypocrites! You give a tenth of your spices—mint, dill and cummin. But you have neglected the more important matters of the law—justice, mercy and faithfulness. You should have practiced the latter, without neglecting the former. ²⁴You blind guides! You strain out a gnat but swallow a camel.

²⁵"Woe to you, teachers of the law and Pharisees, you hypocrites! You clean the outside of the cup and dish, but inside they are full of greed and self-indulgence. ²⁶Blind Pharisee! First clean the inside of the cup and dish, and then the outside also will be clean.

²⁷"Woe to you, teachers of the law and Pharisees, you hypocrites! You are like whitewashed tombs, which look beautiful on the outside but on the inside are full of dead men's bones and everything unclean. ²⁸In the same way, on the outside you appear to people as righteous but on the inside you are full of hypocrisy and wickedness.

²⁹"Woe to you, teachers of the law and Pharisees, you hypocrites! You build tombs for the prophets and decorate the graves of the righteous. ³⁰And you say, 'If we had lived in the days of our forefathers, we would not have taken part with them in shedding the blood of the prophets.' ³¹So you testify against yourselves that you are the descendants of those who murdered the prophets. ³²Fill up, then, the measure of the sin of your forefathers!

³³"You snakes! You brood of vipers! How will you escape being condemned to hell? ³⁴Therefore I am sending you prophets and wise men and teachers. Some of them you will kill and crucify; others you will flog in your synagogues and pursue from town to town. ³⁵And so upon you will come all the righteous

charges Jesus makes against the Pharisees and the teachers of the Law (vv. 13-32). How do they relate to what Jesus says in verses 2-7? Do you find anything common to all seven charges? Which picture described by Jesus is the funniest to you? **5.** How do each of these affect the common people? **6.** How have the religious leaders corrupted the practice of evangelism (vv. 13-15)? The practice of oath-making (vv. 16-22)? The practice of tithing (vv. 23-24, see Micah 6:6-8)? The practice of integrity, where public image matches inner reality (vv. 25-28)? **7.** How are these religious leaders condemned to repeat the past because of their failure to learn from their forefathers (vv. 29-36)? How is the punishment in verses 33-36 appropriate to the crimes? **8.** Could any of these seven charges be leveled against your world? Choose one and paraphrase it to fit your world. **9.** What emotion does Jesus display in verses 37-39? How do you think he felt as he was teaching? Why?

REFLECT: **1.** Where did Jesus catch your attention in this passage? What practices touch close-to-home in your life? **2.** How can you avoid making it hard for others to grow spiritually? **3.** What about today's church do you lament over (as Jesus did over Jerusalem)? **4.** From reading this passage, what, if anything, would you like to see your church do differently? Are there any topics here you'd like to see your pastor specifically address? Which? **5.** Do you feel Jesus is a little tough on the Pharisees? Why or why not? **6.** How can you best avoid what is preached against in this passage?

---

¹13 Some manuscripts *to.* ¹⁴*Woe to you, teachers of the law and Pharisees, you hypocrites! You devour widows' houses and for a show make lengthy prayers. Therefore you will be punished more severely.*

blood that has been shed on earth, from the blood of righteous Abel to the blood of Zechariah son of Berekiah, whom you murdered between the temple and the altar. ³⁶I tell you the truth, all this will come upon this generation.

³⁷"O Jerusalem, Jerusalem, you who kill the prophets and stone those sent to you, how often I have longed to gather your children together, as a hen gathers her chicks under her wings, but you were not willing. ³⁸Look, your house is left to you desolate. ³⁹For I tell you, you will not see me again until you say, 'Blessed is he who comes in the name of the Lord.'ᵘ"

Signs of the End of the Age

24 Jesus left the temple and was walking away when his disciples came up to him to call his attention to its buildings. ²"Do you see all these things?" he asked. "I tell you the truth, not one stone here will be left on another; every one will be thrown down."

³As Jesus was sitting on the Mount of Olives, the disciples came to him privately. "Tell us," they said, "when will this happen, and what will be the sign of your coming and of the end of the age?"

⁴Jesus answered: "Watch out that no one deceives you. ⁵For many will come in my name, claiming, 'I am the Christ,ᵛ' and will deceive many. ⁶You will hear of wars and rumors of wars, but see to it that you are not alarmed. Such things must happen, but the end is still to come. ⁷Nation will rise against nation, and kingdom against kingdom. There will be famines and earthquakes in various places. ⁸All these are the beginning of birth pains.

⁹"Then you will be handed over to be persecuted and put to death, and you will be hated by all nations because of me. ¹⁰At that time many will turn away from the faith and will betray and hate each other, ¹¹and many false prophets will appear and deceive many people. ¹²Because of the increase of wickedness, the love of most will grow cold, ¹³but he who stands firm to the end will be saved. ¹⁴And this gospel of the kingdom will be preached in the whole world as a testimony to all nations, and then the end will come.

¹⁵"So when you see standing in the holy place 'the abomination that causes desolation,'ʷ spoken of through the prophet Daniel—let the reader understand— ¹⁶then let those who are in Judea flee to the mountains. ¹⁷Let no one on the roof of his house go down to take anything out of the house. ¹⁸Let no one in the field go back to get his cloak. ¹⁹How dreadful it will be in those days for pregnant women and nursing mothers! ²⁰Pray that your flight will not take place in winter or on the Sabbath. ²¹For then there will be great distress, unequaled from the beginning of the world until now—and never to be equaled again. ²²If those days had not been cut short, no one would survive, but for the sake of the elect those days will be shortened. ²³At that time if anyone says to you, 'Look, here is the Christ!' or, 'There he is!' do not

OPEN: 1. When you were growing up, what were you like with building blocks (Lincoln logs, Tinker toys, etc.): Were you meticulous in following the instructions step by step? Were you innovative in designing your own structure? Were you mischievous in destroying someone else's creation? How are you like that today? **2.** When do you think the world will end? Why then?

DIG: 1. What prompts Jesus' next lesson? **2.** What bombshell of information does he explode on his disciples? What do you know about the temple? How do the Jewish people (including the disciples) feel about the temple? How must the disciples have felt when they heard Jesus' words in verse 2? **3.** What three questions do the disciples ask? **4.** What events might mislead the disciples into thinking the end had come (vv. 4-7)? **5.** What would happen to the church after that (vv. 9-12)? What does Jesus promise for those who endure and don't give in? What must the church continue doing (v. 14)? **6.** What event would signal the start of the great distress? What does "the abomination that causes desolation" mean? (see Dan. 9:27 and 11:31 in context)? **7.** What should Christians do when this happens (vv. 16-20)? Why? **8.** Against what dangerous deceptions would Christians need to guard (vv. 23-26)? Why would believers be susceptible to such rumors then? **9.** In contrast, what will mark the coming of the true Messiah (vv. 27-29)? What will his second coming be like (vv. 30-31)? **10.** What is the lesson from the fig tree? How does it apply to the disciples' question (v. 3) and Jesus' answer (vv. 33-35)?

REFLECT: 1. If you knew the world was going to end in six months, what would you do? How would your lifestyle change? **2.** What bothers you most about the end of the world? **3.** What do you like best about the second coming? **4.** If you could ask Jesus one question about

ᵘ39 Psalm 118:26   ᵛ5 Or *Messiah*; also in verse 23   ʷ15 Daniel 9:27; 11:31; 12:11

believe it. [24]For false Christs and false prophets will appear and perform great signs and miracles to deceive even the elect—if that were possible. [25]See, I have told you ahead of time.

[26]"So if anyone tells you, 'There he is, out in the desert,' do not go out; or, 'Here he is, in the inner rooms,' do not believe it. [27]For as lightning that comes from the east is visible even in the west, so will be the coming of the Son of Man. [28]Wherever there is a carcass, there the vultures will gather.

[29]"Immediately after the distress of those days

" 'the sun will be darkened,
    and the moon will not give its light;
the stars will fall from the sky,
    and the heavenly bodies will be shaken.' [x]

[30]"At that time the sign of the Son of Man will appear in the sky, and all the nations of the earth will mourn. They will see the Son of Man coming on the clouds of the sky, with power and great glory. [31]And he will send his angels with a loud trumpet call, and they will gather his elect from the four winds, from one end of the heavens to the other.

[32]"Now learn this lesson from the fig tree: As soon as its twigs get tender and its leaves come out, you know that summer is near. [33]Even so, when you see all these things, you know that it[y] is near, right at the door. [34]I tell you the truth, this generation[z] will certainly not pass away until all these things have happened. [35]Heaven and earth will pass away, but my words will never pass away.

The Day and Hour Unknown

[36]"No one knows about that day or hour, not even the angels in heaven, nor the Son,[a] but only the Father. [37]As it was in the days of Noah, so it will be at the coming of the Son of Man. [38]For in the days before the flood, people were eating and drinking, marrying and giving in marriage, up to the day Noah entered the ark; [39]and they knew nothing about what would happen until the flood came and took them all away. That is how it will be at the coming of the Son of Man. [40]Two men will be in the field; one will be taken and the other left. [41]Two women will be grinding with a hand mill; one will be taken and the other left.

[42]"Therefore keep watch, because you do not know on what day your Lord will come. [43]But understand this: If the owner of the house had known at what time of night the thief was coming, he would have kept watch and would not have let his house be broken into. [44]So you also must be ready, because the Son of Man will come at an hour when you do not expect him.

[45]"Who then is the faithful and wise servant, whom the master has put in charge of the servants in his household to give them their food at the proper time? [46]It will be good for that servant whose master finds him doing so when he returns. [47]I tell you the truth, he will put him in charge of all his possessions. [48]But suppose that servant is wicked and says to himself, 'My

either the second coming or the end of the world, what would you ask? How do you think he would answer it? **5.** Do you see some of these signs being fulfilled? How do you feel about this? **6.** What will you remember most from this passage?

OPEN: 1. When you were a child, what was your favorite time of day? Day of the week? Time of the year? Why were these favorite? **2.** What would your day be like if you never once looked at your watch or a clock? How would you know when you were hungry? Sleepy? In need of a break?

DIG: 1. In what ways is the Flood like the second coming of Christ? **2.** What are the practical implications of not knowing when Jesus will return? What does it mean to be ready for Jesus' return if we do not know when he will come? **3.** In view of Christ's second coming what does the story of the faithful and wise servant teach your about readiness? Stewardship? Judgement? Responsibility for serving and witnessing to others? **4.** How does this story relate to verses 1-31? To 32-35? **5.** What is one thing you can say for certain about the day and the hour of the second coming of Christ?

REFLECT: 1. Specifically, how are you preparing for the second coming? **2.** How would you explain the end times and the second coming to a searching person? **3.** Over what has God given you stewardship?

---

[x]29 Isaiah 13:10; 34:4   [y]33 Or *he*   [z]34 Or *race*   [a]36 Some manuscripts do not have *nor the Son.*

How do you think he would feel about how you have watched what he left in your care?

———

OPEN: What is one of your classic memories of being late and missing something important?

DIG: 1. To what event in history does this parable apply? How does it relate to Matthew 24? **2.** In what ways were the ten girls alike? Different? What unexpected event takes place (vv. 5-6)? With what embarassing consequence (v. 8)? Being caught short and going for more oil, what awful event occurs (vv. 10-12)? **3.** What then is the point of this parable? (see also 24:42)? **4.** Why is readiness so important in regard to the second coming?

REFLECT: 1. What unexpected event has happened in your life in the past six months? Were you ready to handle it? **2.** What is the "oil" that keeps your "lamp" lit? **3.** Who are you most like in this story? Why? **4.** At the final wedding banquet, where will you be standing? Why?

———

OPEN: 1. Who was one of the most talanted people you knew in school? What happened to that person? **2.** What were you known for in school—what talents did people recognize in you? **3.** If you had $8,000 and wanted some people to "work it" while you were gone, to whom would you give $5,000, $2,000 and $1,000? Why these three?

DIG: 1. In this parable, who does the master represent? The journey? The talents? The servants? **2.** What happens to the two servants who doubled their investment? To the one servant who hides his talents? On what basis were they rewarded? **3.** How does the master's treatment of the one-talent servant seem to you: Fair? Harsh? Lenient? Why? **4.** Why do you think Jesus thought it necessary to repeat his point so many times and in so many different ways?

REFLECT: 1. What are some of your talents? How have you worked

master is staying away a long time,' ⁴⁹and he then begins to beat his fellow servants and to eat and drink with drunkards. ⁵⁰The master of that servant will come on a day when he does not expect him and at an hour he is not aware of. ⁵¹He will cut him to pieces and assign him a place with the hypocrites, where there will be weeping and gnashing of teeth.

The Parable of the Ten Virgins

25 "At that time the kingdom of heaven will be like ten virgins who took their lamps and went out to meet the bridegroom. ²Five of them were foolish and five were wise. ³The foolish ones took their lamps but did not take any oil with them. ⁴The wise, however, took oil in jars along with their lamps. ⁵The bridegroom was a long time in coming, and they all became drowsy and fell asleep.

⁶"At midnight the cry rang out: 'Here's the bridegroom! Come out to meet him!'

⁷"Then all the virgins woke up and trimmed their lamps. ⁸The foolish ones said to the wise, 'Give us some of your oil; our lamps are going out.'

⁹" 'No,' they replied, 'there may not be enough for both us and you. Instead, go to those who sell oil and buy some for yourselves.'

¹⁰"But while they were on their way to buy the oil, the bridegroom arrived. The virgins who were ready went in with him to the wedding banquet. And the door was shut.

¹¹"Later the others also came. 'Sir! Sir!' they said. 'Open the door for us!'

¹²"But he replied, 'I tell you the truth, I don't know you.'

¹³"Therefore keep watch, because you do not know the day or the hour.

The Parable of the Talents

¹⁴"Again, it will be like a man going on a journey, who called his servants and entrusted his property to them. ¹⁵To one he gave five talents*ᵇ* of money, to another two talents, and to another one talent, each according to his ability. Then he went on his journey. ¹⁶The man who had received the five talents went at once and put his money to work and gained five more. ¹⁷So also, the one with the two talents gained two more. ¹⁸But the man who had received the one talent went off, dug a hole in the ground and hid his master's money.

¹⁹"After a long time the master of those servants returned and settled accounts with them. ²⁰The man who had received the five talents brought the other five. 'Master,' he said, 'you entrusted me with five talents. See, I have gained five more.'

²¹"His master replied, 'Well done, good and faithful servant! You have been faithful with a few things; I will put you in charge of many things. Come and share your master's happiness!'

²²"The man with the two talents also came. 'Master,' he said, 'you entrusted me with two talents; see, I have gained two more.'

ᵇ15 A talent was worth more than a thousand dollars.

Matthew 25:14-30   **THE PARABLE OF THE TALENTS**

LOOKING INTO THE SCRIPTURE/25 Minutes. Read Matthew 25:14-30 and discuss.

1. My opinion of the master is that
   a. he was too harsh with his servant
   b. he was not hard enough on the servant
   c. his reaction was justified
   d. I'm glad I don't work for him

2. When Jesus talks in this parable about "talents," what is he referring to?
   a. ability to make something of money
   b. natural abilities
   c. special spiritual gifts
   d. capital for investment

3. How would you have felt if you were the one to receive only one talent?
   a. jealous of the others who got more
   b. resigned to a life of obscurity
   c. relieved to have less responsibility
   d. invigorated to invest it wisely

4. What happened to the two servants who doubled their investment?
   a. they kept the profit
   b. they felt good about themselves
   c. the master split the profit with the servant that did nothing
   d. the master rewarded them

5. Why did the servant with one talent hide his talent?
   a. he was lazy
   b. he was afraid of his master
   c. he had no initiative
   d. he had low self-confidence

6. What was Jesus saying to the two servants who doubled their investment?
   a. I am proud of you
   b. you'll get your reward in heaven
   c. my investment in you paid off
   d. I can trust you with bigger things

7. Why was the master so hard on the servant who hid his talent?
   a. he didn't take responsibility for what was given him
   b. he wasted his opportunity
   c. he wasted his master's goods
   d. he wallowed in self-pity
   e. he did absolutely no good to anyone

MY OWN STORY/20 Minutes.

1. One of the best ways to figure out what God wants you to do with your life is to take a look at your abilities and assets. Finish the sentence by checking three or four things: "I am good at . . ."

☐ working with children   ☐ motivating/leading   ☐ working with old people
☐ listening/caring   ☐ getting others involved   ☐ playing ball
☐ helping behind the scenes   ☐ crusading for a cause   ☐ making people laugh
☐ playing an instrument   ☐ peacemaking/reconciling   ☐ sticking it out
☐ problem solving   ☐ cooking/homemaking   ☐ cheering others on
☐ coaching/teaching   ☐ teaching the Bible   ☐ hanging out with kids
☐ organizing/administering   ☐ running a business   ☐ being sensitive to others
☐ acting/singing   ☐ helping others start a   ☐ raising money
☐ sharing my faith   business

2. Let the others in your group add two more things you are good at.

3. Now imagine how those abilities could be used to share Christ's love and do God's work in your circumstances. Be specific as you apply your strengths to "kingdom business."

4. What is your favorite excuse for not using your talents?
   a. I don't have any
   b. I'm tired
   c. I'm afraid I might fail
   d. I'm not as talented as . . .
   e. I've got a hang-up
   f. I want to be humble
   g. I don't have the time

5. What do you need to get you started?
   a. guarantee from God that I'll be successful
   b. self-confidence
   c. my priorities sorted out
   d. lots of support from friends
   e. a personal call from God
   f. energy
   g. a gentle push from group members

at developing them? What kind of responsibility do you feel toward God regarding your talents? **2.** When, if ever, have you observed that the more you used a talent, the more talents God gave you? **3.** If the Master returned today, what would he say about how well you have been using what he gave you? **4.** What will you do this week with the talents God has given you to prepare for his coming? What can your group do to help you in this regard?

OPEN: 1. If you were ever without food for a long period of time, what is the first thing you would crave to eat? **2.** What for you is the creepiest thing about a hospital about a barnyard? About prison?

DIG: 1. Does this story seem more like a parable or a prophecy? Why? **2.** What coming event is being considered here? What is the purpose of this event? **3.** List the six actions Jesus will use as the basis of judgment. What kinds of acts are these? For whom are they done now and ultimately (v. 40)? How do they benefit the doer? **4.** How are those who don't do the acts and those who do them similar? Different? **5.** What does this section teach about Christian responsibility? Who, besides those mentioned here, might be considered "the least of these"? **6.** In summary, what did Jesus teach in chapters 23-25? How were Jesus and his opponents different in actions and attitudes? **7.** Is the judgment note in this section consistent with your view of Jesus? Why or why not?

REFLECT: 1. When have you been hungry, thirsty, a stranger, in need of clothes, sick or imprisoned and someone reached out to you? **2.** When have you reached out to people in those areas? **3.** In these six areas, where do you find yourself serving most naturally? In which areas do you have the most trouble reaching out? **4.** Of these six areas, is there one where you would like to get more involved (prison ministry or hunger prog-

23"His master replied, 'Well done, good and faithful servant! You have been faithful with a few things; I will put you in charge of many things. Come and share your master's happiness!'

24"Then the man who had received the one talent came. 'Master,' he said, 'I knew that you are a hard man, harvesting where you have not sown and gathering where you have not scattered seed. 25So I was afraid and went out and hid your talent in the ground. See, here is what belongs to you.'

26"His master replied, 'You wicked, lazy servant! So you knew that I harvest where I have not sown and gather where I have not scattered seed? 27Well then, you should have put my money on deposit with the bankers, so that when I returned I would have received it back with interest.

28" 'Take the talent from him and give it to the one who has the ten talents. 29For everyone who has will be given more, and he will have an abundance. Whoever does not have, even what he has will be taken from him. 30And throw that worthless servant outside, into the darkness, where there will be weeping and gnashing of teeth.'

The Sheep and the Goats

31"When the Son of Man comes in his glory, and all the angels with him, he will sit on his throne in heavenly glory. 32All the nations will be gathered before him, and he will separate the people one from another as a shepherd separates the sheep from the goats. 33He will put the sheep on his right and the goats on his left.

34"Then the King will say to those on his right, 'Come, you who are blessed by my Father; take your inheritance, the kingdom prepared for you since the creation of the world. 35For I was hungry and you gave me something to eat, I was thirsty and you gave me something to drink, I was a stranger and you invited me in, 36I needed clothes and you clothed me, I was sick and you looked after me, I was in prison and you came to visit me.'

37"Then the righteous will answer him, 'Lord, when did we see you hungry and feed you, or thirsty and give you something to drink? 38When did we see you a stranger and invite you in, or needing clothes and clothe you? 39When did we see you sick or in prison and go to visit you?'

40"The King will reply, 'I tell you the truth, whatever you did for one of the least of these brothers of mine, you did for me.'

41"Then he will say to those on his left, 'Depart from me, you who are cursed, into the eternal fire prepared for the devil and his angels. 42For I was hungry and you gave me nothing to eat, I was thirsty and you gave me nothing to drink, 43I was a stranger and you did not invite me in, I needed clothes and you did not clothe me, I was sick and in prison and you did not look after me.'

44"They also will answer, 'Lord, when did we see you hungry or thirsty or a stranger or needing clothes or sick or in prison, and did not help you?'

45"He will reply, 'I tell you the truth, whatever you did not do for one of the least of these, you did not do for me.'

⁴⁶"Then they will go away to eternal punishment, but the righteous to eternal life."

The Plot Against Jesus

26 When Jesus had finished saying all these things, he said to his disciples, ²"As you know, the Passover is two days away—and the Son of Man will be handed over to be crucified."

³Then the chief priests and the elders of the people assembled in the palace of the high priest, whose name was Caiaphas, ⁴and they plotted to arrest Jesus in some sly way and kill him. ⁵"But not during the Feast," they said, "or there may be a riot among the people."

Jesus Anointed at Bethany

⁶While Jesus was in Bethany in the home of a man known as Simon the Leper, ⁷a woman came to him with an alabaster jar of very expensive perfume, which she poured on his head as he was reclining at the table.

⁸When the disciples saw this, they were indignant. "Why this waste?" they asked. ⁹"This perfume could have been sold at a high price and the money given to the poor."

¹⁰Aware of this, Jesus said to them, "Why are you bothering this woman? She has done a beautiful thing to me. ¹¹The poor you will always have with you, but you will not always have me. ¹²When she poured this perfume on my body, she did it to prepare me for burial. ¹³I tell you the truth, wherever this gospel is preached throughout the world, what she has done will also be told, in memory of her."

Judas Agrees to Betray Jesus

¹⁴Then one of the Twelve—the one called Judas Iscariot— went to the chief priests ¹⁵and asked, "What are you willing to give me if I hand him over to you?" So they counted out for him thirty silver coins. ¹⁶From then on Judas watched for an opportunity to hand him over.

The Lord's Supper

¹⁷On the first day of the Feast of Unleavened Bread, the disciples came to Jesus and asked, "Where do you want us to make preparations for you to eat the Passover?"

¹⁸He replied, "Go into the city to a certain man and tell him, 'The Teacher says: My appointed time is near. I am going to celebrate the Passover with my disciples at your house.' " ¹⁹So the disciples did as Jesus had directed them and prepared the Passover.

²⁰When evening came, Jesus was reclining at the table with the Twelve. ²¹And while they were eating, he said, "I tell you the truth, one of you will betray me."

²²They were very sad and began to say to him one after the other, "Surely not I, Lord?"

²³Jesus replied, "The one who has dipped his hand into the bowl with me will betray me. ²⁴The Son of Man will go just as

ram)? What steps will you take this week to get involved?

OPEN: Which death in your family would affect you the most? Why?

DIG: Why was Passover an appropriate time for these events to unfold? Why might the timing be risky?

REFLECT: What does the crucifixion mean to you?

OPEN: If you had a year's wages to blow on one special gift, what would you buy and for whom?

DIG: 1. What is significant about the setting for this woman's gift to Jesus? (Note: It was forbidden to asociate with lepers.) 2. What context in Jesus' life (vv. 11-12) justifies this woman's act (also 25:35-36)? 3. Why are the disciples indignant? 4. What is Jesus trying to teach his disciples, then and now, about priorities?

REFLECT: What "beautiful" thing could you do this week for Jesus (or "the least of these")?

DIG: What part does Judas play in Jesus' life? How could he do it?

REFLECT: What will you do, and not do, for money? For what causes are you an "opportunist" like Judas? Like the woman (v. 7)?

OPEN: 1. What has been one of your all-time favorite dinner parties? What made it so good? 2. As you were growing up, what were mealtimes like in your family? Where did everyone sit around the table? Who got to sit by dad? For misbehavior at the table, what were the consequences?

DIG: 1. What do you know about the Feast of Unleavened Bread? 2. Why do you think Jesus was so secretive about his arrangements for the Passover meal? 3. In what stages does Jesus reveal his betrayer (vv. 21, 23, 25)? Is Jesus warning Judas not to go through with his scheme? Or is Jesus predicting what will happen when he does? 4. What two parts of the supper does Jesus single out to give new, symbolic meaning? Why does Jesus make this connection and his prediction (v. 29)? What does blood have to do with forgiveness? **5.** Are the disciples singing their final hymn together (v. 30) in a major or minor key? Why do you think that?

REFLECT: 1. What does Communion mean to you? **2.** How steadily do you know God's forgiveness of your sins? Why is it that many Christians struggle with guilt if Jesus provides the forgiveness of sins? **3.** What impresses you most about Jesus at the Lord's Supper?

OPEN: What most sincere promise did you once make but failed to deliver on: To clean up your room? Marry the one you first loved? Etc.

DIG: What emotions and motives accompany Jesus' next prediction (vv. 31-32)? Peter's vow (v. 33)? Jesus' reply (v. 34)? Peter's follow-up vow (v. 35)?

REFLECT: 1. When, have you felt betrayed? How did you deal with it? **2.** When, if ever, have you felt like you betrayed Jesus? How did you and Jesus resolve that issue?

OPEN: What is the longest night of your life: Delivering your first child? Waiting up for your teenager? Deciding to call it quits?

DIG: 1. What are the various emotions Jesus must have felt in Gethsemane? What did he ask of them? **2.** What does he ask of God? What is God's will (vv. 39, 42)? What model for our prayers does Jesus provide here? **3.** What obstacles to prayer does Jesus face? Likewise, his disciples? What is meant by "the spirit is willing, but the flesh is weak"?

REFLECT: 1. Where has been your Gethsemane—a place where you really wrestled with God? What was the issue? **2.** Who would you want to "watch and pray" with you next time you face a "Gethsemane"? **3.** What do you learn from Jesus' prayers? How then would you like to change your prayer style? **4.** What do you most appreciate about Jesus from this story?

---

it is written about him. But woe to that man who betrays the Son of Man! It would be better for him if he had not been born."

²⁵Then Judas, the one who would betray him, said, "Surely not I, Rabbi?"

Jesus answered, "Yes, it is you."ᶜ

²⁶While they were eating, Jesus took bread, gave thanks and broke it, and gave it to his disciples, saying, "Take and eat; this is my body."

²⁷Then he took the cup, gave thanks and offered it to them, saying, "Drink from it, all of you. ²⁸This is my blood of theᵈ covenant, which is poured out for many for the forgiveness of sins. ²⁹I tell you, I will not drink of this fruit of the vine from now on until that day when I drink it anew with you in my Father's kingdom."

³⁰When they had sung a hymn, they went out to the Mount of Olives.

Jesus Predicts Peter's Denial

³¹Then Jesus told them, "This very night you will all fall away on account of me, for it is written:

" 'I will strike the shepherd,
and the sheep of the flock will be scattered.'ᵉ

³²But after I have risen, I will go ahead of you into Galilee."

³³Peter replied, "Even if all fall away on account of you, I never will."

³⁴"I tell you the truth," Jesus answered, "this very night, before the rooster crows, you will disown me three times."

³⁵But Peter declared, "Even if I have to die with you, I will never disown you." And all the other disciples said the same.

Gethsemane

³⁶Then Jesus went with his disciples to a place called Gethsemane, and he said to them, "Sit here while I go over there and pray." ³⁷He took Peter and the two sons of Zebedee along with him, and he began to be sorrowful and troubled. ³⁸Then he said to them, "My soul is overwhelmed with sorrow to the point of death. Stay here and keep watch with me."

³⁹Going a little farther, he fell with his face to the ground and prayed, "My Father, if it is possible, may this cup be taken from me. Yet not as I will, but as you will."

⁴⁰Then he returned to his disciples and found them sleeping. "Could you men not keep watch with me for one hour?" he asked Peter. ⁴¹"Watch and pray so that you will not fall into temptation. The spirit is willing, but the body is weak."

⁴²He went away a second time and prayed, "My Father, if it is not possible for this cup to be taken away unless I drink it, may your will be done."

⁴³When he came back, he again found them sleeping, because their eyes were heavy. ⁴⁴So he left them and went away once more and prayed the third time, saying the same thing.

ᶜ25 Or *"You yourself have said it"*   ᵈ28 Some manuscripts *the new*
ᵉ31 Zech. 13:7

⁴⁵Then he returned to the disciples and said to them, "Are you still sleeping and resting? Look, the hour is near, and the Son of Man is betrayed into the hands of sinners. ⁴⁶Rise, let us go! Here comes my betrayer!"

Jesus Arrested

⁴⁷While he was still speaking, Judas, one of the Twelve, arrived. With him was a large crowd armed with swords and clubs, sent from the chief priests and the elders of the people. ⁴⁸Now the betrayer had arranged a signal with them: "The one I kiss is the man; arrest him." ⁴⁹Going at once to Jesus, Judas said, "Greetings, Rabbi!" and kissed him.

⁵⁰Jesus replied, "Friend, do what you came for."ᶠ

Then the men stepped forward, seized Jesus and arrested him. ⁵¹With that, one of Jesus' companions reached for his sword, drew it out and struck the servant of the high priest, cutting off his ear.

⁵²"Put your sword back in its place," Jesus said to him, "for all who draw the sword will die by the sword. ⁵³Do you think I cannot call on my Father, and he will at once put at my disposal more than twelve legions of angels? ⁵⁴But how then would the Scriptures be fulfilled that say it must happen in this way?"

⁵⁵At that time Jesus said to the crowd, "Am I leading a rebellion, that you have come out with swords and clubs to capture me? Every day I sat in the temple courts teaching, and you did not arrest me. ⁵⁶But this has all taken place that the writings of the prophets might be fulfilled." Then all the disciples deserted him and fled.

Before the Sanhedrin

⁵⁷Those who had arrested Jesus took him to Caiaphas, the high priest, where the teachers of the law and the elders had assembled. ⁵⁸But Peter followed him at a distance, right up to the courtyard of the high priest. He entered and sat down with the guards to see the outcome.

⁵⁹The chief priests and the whole Sanhedrin were looking for false evidence against Jesus so that they could put him to death. ⁶⁰But they did not find any, though many false witnesses came forward.

Finally two came forward ⁶¹and declared, "This fellow said, 'I am able to destroy the temple of God and rebuild it in three days.'"

⁶²Then the high priest stood up and said to Jesus, "Are you not going to answer? What is this testimony that these men are bringing against you?" ⁶³But Jesus remained silent.

The high priest said to him, "I charge you under oath by the living God: Tell us if you are the Christ,ᵍ the Son of God."

⁶⁴"Yes, it is as you say," Jesus replied. "But I say to all of you: In the future you will see the Son of Man sitting at the right hand of the Mighty One and coming on the clouds of heaven."

OPEN: Who was your favorite adventure hero in your growing up years? How did that character respond to danger?

DIG: 1. What kind of leader was the large, armed crowd expecting to arrest? What does this say about their expectations of the messianic leader? **2.** What kind of messiah was the disciple with the sword expecting? Which do you think the other disciples would be more willing to do: Physically defend Jesus? Or go peacefully with him to death? Why? What do they do instead? **3.** How does Jesus respond to Judas' kiss? To the armed crowd? To the fighting disciple? Why does Jesus respond as he does and not as expected?

REFLECT: 1. Knowing yourself, how do you think that you would have reacted if you had been with Jesus in this scene? **2.** How does your view of what a messiah should be correspond to the view of Jesus in this passage?

OPEN: 1. Share a memory you have of being present at a function or event when you clearly wanted to be somewhere else (do not list your wedding). **2.** When, if ever, did someone lie about you when you were growing up? What happened? How did you feel?

DIG: 1. What do you know about the Sanhedrin? **2.** Why was Jesus taken to the house of the high priest? Why do you think Peter followed? Why do you think the priests were willing to accept false evidence? What was their strategy? **3.** What is unusual about Jesus' defense of himself? What does this say about his view of the proceedings? What does it say about his view of the kingdom of God? What is blasphemy? Why would the priests think Jesus' statement blasphemous? **5.** Do they actually pass sentence on Jesus? Why not?

REFLECT: 1. What impresses you most about Jesus in this story? **2.** If Jesus were not the Messiah, how would you feel about him? **3.** When, if ever, have you had to defend your faith? How well did you do? **4.** What would you need to do to give a bet-

---

ᶠ50 Or "Friend, why have you come?"   ᵍ63 Or Messiah; also in verse 68

ter answer for the hope you have (I Peter 3:15-16)? **5.** How do you know when to keep silent and when to talk?

OPEN: What is the best word of advice you have ever heard regarding failure?

DIG: 1. So far in Matthew, what character traits has Peter exhibited? Here, how do his actions typify his character? Which character trait dominates this story? **2.** When did Peter realize what was happening? Why then? Why cry?

REFLECT: 1. When, if ever, have you felt like Peter must have felt? What was the situation? What was the "rooster" in your life that caused you to realize what was happening? How did you make a comeback? What part did God play in your comeback? What was your role? **2.** What would be your advice to people who have failed miserably in a spiritual sense?

OPEN: What do you think is the all-time worst way to die? The best way to die? Why?

DIG: 1. Why do you think Judas is suddenly seized with remorse? Do you think that he was expecting a different outcome? Why or why not? **2.** How were the actions and reactions of Judas and Peter similar? Different? **3.** What in verse 4 helps to explain the priests' actions in verses 1-2? Why do you think they avoid taking direct responsibility for Jesus' death? **4.** Do you think that what Judas did placed him beyond redemption? How do you think Judas felt about this?

REFLECT: 1. Both Peter and Judas caved in under pressure and betrayed their Lord. Yet history has treated each very differently. Why is that? **2.** If you had met with Judas right after he had thrown the money into the temple, what would you have said to him? **3.** Have you ever felt like you were beyond redemption? Why? To whom did/can you turn in this situation?

⁶⁵Then the high priest tore his clothes and said, "He has spoken blasphemy! Why do we need any more witnesses? Look, now you have heard the blasphemy. ⁶⁶What do you think?"

"He is worthy of death," they answered.

⁶⁷Then they spit in his face and struck him with their fists. Others slapped him ⁶⁸and said, "Prophesy to us, Christ. Who hit you?"

Peter Disowns Jesus

⁶⁹Now Peter was sitting out in the courtyard, and a servant girl came to him. "You also were with Jesus of Galilee," she said.

⁷⁰But he denied it before them all. "I don't know what you're talking about," he said.

⁷¹Then he went out to the gateway, where another girl saw him and said to the people there, "This fellow was with Jesus of Nazareth."

⁷²He denied it again, with an oath: "I don't know the man!"

⁷³After a little while, those standing there went up to Peter and said, "Surely you are one of them, for your accent gives you away."

⁷⁴Then he began to call down curses on himself and he swore to them, "I don't know the man!"

Immediately a rooster crowed. ⁷⁵Then Peter remembered the word Jesus had spoken: "Before the rooster crows, you will disown me three times." And he went outside and wept bitterly.

Judas Hangs Himself

27 Early in the morning, all the chief priests and the elders of the people came to the decision to put Jesus to death. ²They bound him, led him away and handed him over to Pilate, the governor.

³When Judas, who had betrayed him, saw that Jesus was condemned, he was seized with remorse and returned the thirty silver coins to the chief priests and the elders. ⁴"I have sinned," he said, "for I have betrayed innocent blood."

"What is that to us?" they replied. "That's your responsibility."

⁵So Judas threw the money into the temple and left. Then he went away and hanged himself.

⁶The chief priests picked up the coins and said, "It is against the law to put this into the treasury, since it is blood money." ⁷So they decided to use the money to buy the potter's field as a burial place for foreigners. ⁸That is why it has been called the Field of Blood to this day. ⁹Then what was spoken by Jeremiah the prophet was fulfilled: "They took the thirty silver coins, the price set on him by the people of Israel, ¹⁰and they used them to buy the potter's field, as the Lord commanded me."ʰ

ʰ10 See Zech. 11:12,13; Jer. 19:1-13; 32:6-9.

LOOKING INTO THE SCRIPTURE/20 Minutes. Read Matthew 26:69-75 and discuss.

1. How do you react to Peter in this story?
   a. I probably would have done the same thing
   b. he was a coward
   c. with pity
   d. disbelief that he could do something so dumb
   e. I was angry

2. Why do you think Peter followed Jesus to the scene of the trial?
   a. to satisfy his curiosity
   b. to rescue him
   c. to keep his promise
   d. to be near Jesus
   e. to record the events for the other disciples

3. What made Peter claim that he did not know Jesus?
   a. fear for his life
   b. spiritual weakness
   c. momentary insanity
   d. no guts

4. If you could put in a good word for Peter, what would it be?
   a. he meant well
   b. he couldn't help it
   c. he came back
   d. he's only human
   e. he was confused

5. After this, why do you think Jesus chose Peter and changed his name from Simon (sinking sand) to Peter (the rock)?
   a. Peter was the best one available
   b. Jesus believed in positive thinking
   c. belief that despite his flaws, Peter would do fine
   d. to illustrate the power of God

6. What impact do you think this failure had upon the future of Peter's life?
   a. it probably made him less cocky
   b. it probably made him less self-confident
   c. it probably made him a more sensitive person
   d. it probably made him into the man of God that he became

7. If Peter were the only disciple present beside Jesus during this incident, he must have shared this experience about his failure with others. Why?
   a. to get it off his chest
   b. to ask forgiveness from the others
   c. to help someone else who had done the same
   d. to show how God uses failure

MY OWN STORY/20 Minutes.

1. How do you usually react to failure?
   a. kick myself for days
   b. run away from the situation
   c. hide my feelings from everyone
   d. ask forgiveness and move on
   e. try to be extra nice

2. When you blow it, what have you found helpful?
   a. talk it over with a friend
   b. do penance
   c. forget about it
   d. try to learn from the mistake
   e. take some time off to get back on track
   f. write myself a long letter
   g. spend time with God

3. What have you found helpful in dealing with a friend who has experienced failure?
   a. keep my mouth shut
   b. share some of my failures
   c. let your friend talk it out
   d. do something crazy together
   e. refuse to let the person dwell on it

4. In the light of this lesson, how would you describe your life this past week in terms of a weather report?
   a. sunny and bright
   b. patchy fog and clouds
   c. stormy
   d. hurricane warnings
   e. cold and gloomy

Jesus Before Pilate

[11]Meanwhile Jesus stood before the governor, and the governor asked him, "Are you the king of the Jews?"

"Yes, it is as you say," Jesus replied.

[12]When he was accused by the chief priests and the elders, he gave no answer. [13]Then Pilate asked him, "Don't you hear the testimony they are bringing against you?" [14]But Jesus made no reply, not even to a single charge—to the great amazement of the governor.

[15]Now it was the governor's custom at the Feast to release a prisoner chosen by the crowd. [16]At that time they had a notorious prisoner, called Barabbas. [17]So when the crowd had gathered, Pilate asked them, "Which one do you want me to release to you: Barabbas, or Jesus who is called Christ?" [18]For he knew it was out of envy that they had handed Jesus over to him.

[19]While Pilate was sitting on the judge's seat, his wife sent him this message: "Don't have anything to do with that innocent man, for I have suffered a great deal today in a dream because of him."

[20]But the chief priests and the elders persuaded the crowd to ask for Barabbas and to have Jesus executed.

[21]"Which of the two do you want me to release to you?" asked the governor.

"Barabbas," they answered.

[22]"What shall I do, then, with Jesus who is called Christ?" Pilate asked.

They all answered, "Crucify him!"

[23]"Why? What crime has he committed?" asked Pilate.

But they shouted all the louder, "Crucify him!"

[24]When Pilate saw that he was getting nowhere, but that instead an uproar was starting, he took water and washed his hands in front of the crowd. "I am innocent of this man's blood," he said. "It is your responsibility!"

[25]All the people answered, "Let his blood be on us and on our children!"

[26]Then he released Barabbas to them. But he had Jesus flogged, and handed him over to be crucified.

The Soldiers Mock Jesus

[27]Then the governor's soldiers took Jesus into the Praetorium and gathered the whole company of soldiers around him. [28]They stripped him and put a scarlet robe on him, [29]and then twisted together a crown of thorns and set it on his head. They put a staff in his right hand and knelt in front of him and mocked him. "Hail, king of the Jews!" they said. [30]They spit on him, and took the staff and struck him on the head again and again. [31]After they had mocked him, they took off the robe and put his own clothes on him. Then they led him away to crucify him.

JESUS BEFORE PILATE

LOOKING INTO THE SCRIPTURE/25 Minutes. Read Matthew 27:11-26 and discuss.

1. Each person in this passage looked upon Jesus from a different perspective and saw a different thing. Match the people with their viewpoint of Jesus.
   - ☐ Pilate/Roman Governor
   - ☐ wife of Pilate
   - ☐ chief priests
   - ☐ Barabbas
   - ☐ crowd

   - ☐ troublemaker
   - ☐ threat to Roman Empire
   - ☐ threat to religious establishment
   - ☐ imposter
   - ☐ innocent person
   - ☐ Messiah/God's Son
   - ☐ stranger who took my place
   - ☐ yesterday's hero

2. Why did the religious authorities bring Jesus to Pilate, the Roman governor?
   a. to place the blame on Pilate
   b. they knew Pilate would give in
   c. they were afraid of the crowd
   d. their law forbade killing
   e. only the Roman governor could give the death sentence

3. Why did the Roman governor offer to release a prisoner chosen by the crowd?
   a. to avoid making a decision about Jesus
   b. to check out their motives
   c. to expose their hypocrisy
   d. to get Jesus off the hook
   e. to keep everybody happy

4. How would you describe Pilate?
   a. pragmatist—what works is right
   b. absolutist—what is right is right
   c. relativist—it all depends on the situation
   d. pantywaisted powder puff

5. How would you portray Pilate if you were a film director?
   a. smooth politician
   b. wimp
   c. victim of circumstances
   d. realist

6. Do you think Pilate knew that Jesus was innocent?
   a. it's hard to say
   b. probably so
   c. absolutely
   d. if he didn't, he was blind

7. Who ended up the biggest winner and who ended up the biggest loser in this situation?
   a. Pilate
   b. wife of Pilate
   c. chief priests
   d. Barabbas
   e. crowd

MY OWN STORY/20 Minutes.

1. How do you react to conflicting pressures from different sources?
   a. bury my head in the sand
   b. get stubborn and do my own thing
   c. listen to each one and make a decision
   d. look for more options
   e. try to avoid making a decision

2. Faced with a similar dilemma, how would you describe yourself?
   a. pragmatist—what works is right
   b. absolutist—what is right is right
   c. relativist—it all depends on the situation
   d. broad-minded escapist—there are too many issues to decide
   e. pantywaisted powder puff—whatever keeps the peace
   f. procrastinator—ask me tomorrow

3. If you had been in Pilate's shoes, what would you have done?
   a. the same thing
   b. referred the problem to Rome
   c. deferred making a decision until studying the facts some more
   d. stood up against the pressure and dismissed the charges
   e. I don't know

4. Who in this story would best describe the way you respond to the radical claims of Jesus Christ?
   a. Pilate
   b. wife of Pilate
   c. chief priests
   d. Barabbas
   e. crowd

OPEN: How "thick is your skin"—how well do you absorb insults?

DIG: 1. Who carries the cross for Jesus? How was he "recruited"? Why does Jesus need help—what shape is he in? **2.** For what "official" reason is Jesus crucified? **3.** What three groups taunt Jesus? Why these particular insults? **4.** What supreme irony do you see here in the cry that Jesus come down from the cross? If he had, would they believe? If there's no cross, would they ever be saved? **5.** How has Jesus' experience with the Tempter prepared him for such a time as this (v. 40; see 4:3, 6)?

REFLECT: 1. If Jesus came today, who would "crucify" him? What would be the charge against him? Where would you be? **2.** What part does the agony of these insults play in your appreciation of what Christ did for you in his death?

OPEN: 1. What is the saddest funeral you ever witnessed—where a friend or family member or national figure was taken suddenly and unexpectedly? How did you feel at the time? **2.** If given the choice, how would you choose to die: Accidentally? Of natural causes? Voluntarily? Heroically? Martyred for your faith?

DIG: 1. How do you view Christ's crucifixion: Necessary evil? Common tragedy? Cruel and unusual punishment? "Good" Friday? Triumph of injustice? Triumph over injustice? Why? **2.** Why does Jesus cry out in verse 46? What is the significance of this for Jesus? For you? **3.** What sympathizers attend? What do they see? Smell? Hear? Say? Feel? Do? **4.** What is the significance of each of the supernatural events accompanying Jesus' death? According to the centurion, how dramatic were these events? **5.** Where are the disciples all this time? What might they believe about Jesus just now?

REFLECT: 1. Why was Jesus separated from the Father when he was on the cross? For whose sins did he go to the cross? How willing are you to die for someone else's crime? **2.** How do you explain the necessity of Jesus' death to a nonbeliever? **3.** Is Jesus' death for you more a dispassionate fact or an emotional experience? Why?

The Crucifixion

[32]As they were going out, they met a man from Cyrene, named Simon, and they forced him to carry the cross. [33]They came to a place called Golgotha (which means The Place of the Skull). [34]There they offered Jesus wine to drink, mixed with gall; but after tasting it, he refused to drink it. [35]When they had crucified him, they divided up his clothes by casting lots.[i] [36]And sitting down, they kept watch over him there. [37]Above his head they placed the written charge against him: THIS IS JESUS, THE KING OF THE JEWS. [38]Two robbers were crucified with him, one on his right and one on his left. [39]Those who passed by hurled insults at him, shaking their heads [40]and saying, "You who are going to destroy the temple and build it in three days, save yourself! Come down from the cross, if you are the Son of God!"

[41]In the same way the chief priests, the teachers of the law and the elders mocked him. [42]"He saved others," they said, "but he can't save himself! He's the King of Israel! Let him come down now from the cross, and we will believe in him. [43]He trusts in God. Let God rescue him now if he wants him, for he said, 'I am the Son of God.'" [44]In the same way the robbers who were crucified with him also heaped insults on him.

The Death of Jesus

[45]From the sixth hour until the ninth hour darkness came over all the land. [46]About the ninth hour Jesus cried out in a loud voice, "Eloi, Eloi,[j] lama sabachthani?"—which means, "My God, my God, why have you forsaken me?"[k]

[47]When some of those standing there heard this, they said, "He's calling Elijah."

[48]Immediately one of them ran and got a sponge. He filled it with wine vinegar, put it on a stick, and offered it to Jesus to drink. [49]The rest said, "Now leave him alone. Let's see if Elijah comes to save him."

[50]And when Jesus had cried out again in a loud voice, he gave up his spirit.

[51]At that moment the curtain of the temple was torn in two from top to bottom. The earth shook and the rocks split. [52]The tombs broke open and the bodies of many holy people who had died were raised to life. [53]They came out of the tombs, and after Jesus' resurrection they went into the holy city and appeared to many people.

[54]When the centurion and those with him who were guarding Jesus saw the earthquake and all that had happened, they were terrified, and exclaimed, "Surely he was the Son[l] of God!"

[55]Many women were there, watching from a distance. They had followed Jesus from Galilee to care for his needs. [56]Among them were Mary Magdalene, Mary the mother of James and Joses, and the mother of Zebedee's sons.

i35 A few late manuscripts lots that the word spoken by the prophet might be fulfilled: "They divided my garments among themselves and cast lots for my clothing" (Psalm 22:18)
j46 Some manuscripts Eli, Eli   k46 Psalm 22:1   l54 Or a son

LOOKING INTO THE SCRIPTURE/25 Minutes. Read Matthew 27:45-56 and discuss.

1. If you were the editor of the *Jerusalem Times,* what headline would you pick to describe the events of the Scripture passage the next day?
    a. strange darkness descends
    b. earthquake rocks city
    c. temple curtain ruined
    d. dead people reported seen
    e. spiritual leader killed
    f. three thieves crucified

2. How would you describe Jesus in his obituary?
    a. prominent civic leader
    b. controversial teacher
    c. troublemaker
    d. failure
    e. innocent victim
    f. the so-called Messiah
    g. mysterious miracle worker

3. Of Jesus' own followers, how many do you think understood what was happening to Jesus on the day he died?
    a. not one
    b. maybe the women
    c. the centurion
    d. only his disciples

4. Why did darkness cover the land for three hours?
    a. just a coincidence
    b. an eclipse of the sun
    c. God was mad at the world
    d. the darkness of sin reigned

5. What caused Jesus to cry out, "My God, my God, why have you forsaken me?"
    a. the physical pain he was suffering
    b. the feeling that God had deserted him
    c. God really did turn his back on him at that moment
    d. God did not send his angels to rescue him as he expected
    e. he thought the whole world had turned against him
    f. he was angry at God

6. What is so significant about the curtain in the temple being torn in two?
    a. the barrier between God and man was taken away
    b. everyone can approach God directly now
    c. no more need for mystery
    d. fellowship restored between God and mankind

MY OWN STORY/20 Minutes.

1. When you think about the death of Jesus, what person in this story best describes you?
    a. the temple crowd—detached, cynical
    b. the one who brought the sponge—hostile jokester
    c. one of the people raised from the dead
    d. the centurion—terrified but awed
    e. women followers—sympathetic and caring

2. What remains a mystery to you about the death of Jesus?
    a. why it ever happened
    b. how God could let it happen
    c. why nobody came to his rescue
    d. why the disciples didn't understand
    e. how the earthquake and the darkness happened

3. At what point in your life did you come to realize that Jesus died for you?
    a. as a child
    b. years ago
    c. just recently
    d. don't know that I have

4. How would you describe the way the death of Jesus has impacted your life, lifestyle and whole system of values?
    a. a little bit
    b. a whole lot
    c. not as much as it should
    d. a lot more than it used to
    e. I'm not sure

The Burial of Jesus

[57] As evening approached, there came a rich man from Arimathea, named Joseph, who had himself become a disciple of Jesus. [58] Going to Pilate, he asked for Jesus' body, and Pilate ordered that it be given to him. [59] Joseph took the body, wrapped it in a clean linen cloth, [60] and placed it in his own new tomb that he had cut out of the rock. He rolled a big stone in front of the entrance to the tomb and went away. [61] Mary Magdalene and the other Mary were sitting there opposite the tomb.

The Guard at the Tomb

[62] The next day, the one after Preparation Day, the chief priests and the Pharisees went to Pilate. [63] "Sir," they said, "we remember that while he was still alive that deceiver said, 'After three days I will rise again.' [64] So give the order for the tomb to be made secure until the third day. Otherwise, his disciples may come and steal the body and tell the people that he has been raised from the dead. This last deception will be worse than the first."

[65] "Take a guard," Pilate answered. "Go, make the tomb as secure as you know how." [66] So they went and made the tomb secure by putting a seal on the stone and posting the guard.

The Resurrection

28 After the Sabbath, at dawn on the first day of the week, Mary Magdalene and the other Mary went to look at the tomb.

[2] There was a violent earthquake, for an angel of the Lord came down from heaven and, going to the tomb, rolled back the stone and sat on it. [3] His appearance was like lightning, and his clothes were white as snow. [4] The guards were so afraid of him that they shook and became like dead men.

[5] The angel said to the women, "Do not be afraid, for I know that you are looking for Jesus, who was crucified. [6] He is not here; he has risen, just as he said. Come and see the place where he lay. [7] Then go quickly and tell his disciples: 'He has risen from the dead and is going ahead of you into Galilee. There you will see him.' Now I have told you."

[8] So the women hurried away from the tomb, afraid yet filled with joy, and ran to tell his disciples. [9] Suddenly Jesus met them. "Greetings," he said. They came to him, clasped his feet and worshiped him. [10] Then Jesus said to them, "Do not be afraid. Go and tell my brothers to go to Galilee; there they will see me."

The Guards' Report

[11] While the women were on their way, some of the guards went into the city and reported to the chief priests everything that had happened. [12] When the chief priests had met with the elders and devised a plan, they gave the soldiers a large sum of money, [13] telling them, "You are to say, 'His disciples came during the night and stole him away while we were asleep.' [14] If this report gets to the governor, we will satisfy him and keep you

out of trouble." [15]So the soldiers took the money and did as they were instructed. And this story has been widely circulated among the Jews to this very day.

The Great Commission

[16]Then the eleven disciples went to Galilee, to the mountain where Jesus had told them to go. [17]When they saw him, they worshiped him; but some doubted. [18]Then Jesus came to them and said, "All authority in heaven and on earth has been given to me. [19]Therefore go and make disciples of all nations, baptizing them in [m]the name of the Father and of the Son and of the Holy Spirit, [20]and teaching them to obey everything I have commanded you. And surely I am with you always, to the very end of the age."

skeptics explain the empty tomb? **2.** What proof of the resurrection does your life demonstrate?

OPEN: What is the greatest challenge you have faced in the past year? Where did you find your resources to meet that challenge?

DIG: 1. Upon seeing the resurrected Jesus, how do the disciples respond? How is doubt mingled with their worship? What do they doubt? **2.** How does Jesus' commission here compare with his earlier one in 10:5-7? **3.** How does Jesus' authority here, gained through obedience, compare with what Satan offered through compromise in 4:8-10? **4.** Of the four actions commanded of the disciples (vv. 19-20), which one is central? How are they to make disciples? Of whom? With what resources? Toward what end?

REFLECT: 1. Is this Great Commission still valid today? For whom? For you? In what ways do you see yourself fulfilling the Great Commission? **2.** Does this passage encourage you or bring you guilt? Why? **3.** How has the Book of Matthew changed your views of Jesus as the Messiah? Of the kingdom of God? Of Jesus' ministry? Of your ministry?

---

[m]19 Or *into;* see Acts 8:16; 19:5; Romans 6:3; 1 Cor. 1:13; 10:2 and Gal. 3:27.

MARK

INTRODUCTION

Author

From the Bible, we discover that Mark's full name is John Mark, that he was the son of Mary, and that their home was used as a meeting place by the disciples. Peter went there directly after his miraculous release from prison (Acts 12:1-17). Consequently, as a young man, Mark was immersed in the life of the newly forming church.

In particular, Mark was close to Peter. Peter referred to him as "my son Mark" (1 Peter 5:13). Many hold that Mark was Peter's secretary and that his gospel reflects Peter's view of the events. Writing in A.D. 140, Bishop Papias says: "Mark, having become the interpreter of Peter, wrote down accurately all that he remembered of the things said and done by our Lord, but not, however, in order."

Mark was also connected closely with Paul. Along with his cousin Barnabas, Mark accompanied the great apostle on the first missionary journey. Mark unaccountably left the party at Perga when they turned inland to Asia. Because of this, Paul refused to allow Mark to go on the second missionary journey, so Barnabas went with Mark to Cyprus while Paul teamed up with Silas. For years Mark dropped out of sight. Tradition says he founded the church at Alexandria, Egypt. Eventually, Paul and Mark were reconciled, so much so that Mark became Paul's companion during his imprisonment in a Roman jail.

Date and Audience

The ten years between A.D. 60 and A.D. 70 when Mark wrote his gospel were not good ones for the Christians living in Rome. For a long time they had hardly been noticed — they were just another exotic religious sect. But then Nero burned down Rome in A.D. 64 and had to find someone to blame. The Christians were nominated, and an era of persecution began. Nero threw them to the animals in the coliseum and burned them as human torches at his garden parties. It is into this atmosphere of persecution, to these Christians who were dying for Jesus' name, that Mark directed his gospel.

This was the first written account of Jesus' life. Thus it was, according to William Barclay, "the most important book in the world." Mark's collection of hitherto word-of-mouth stories was widely circulated and was used by Matthew and Luke when they wrote their gospels. In fact, all but 24 verses of Mark's gospel are found in their accounts.

Characteristics

In the shortest of the gospels, Mark races breathlessly through Jesus' life by connecting together a series of little stories. His sentences are almost childlike. He makes a simple statement and then connects it to another by using "and." Yet this gospel is the richest and most vivid in eyewitness detail. For example, when speaking of Jesus blessing the children, Mark alone tells us that Jesus first took them in his arms (Mark 10:13-16).

Overview Study Questions

1. Trace, in order, the following references to Mark and then write a "portrait" of this gospel writer: Acts 12:12; Acts 12:25; Acts 13:5; Acts 15:36-41; (here Mark disappears from sight); Colossians 4:10; Philemon 24; 2 Timothy 4:11; and 1 Peter 5:13.
2. Read through all of Mark's gospel in one sitting. It won't take long. It is only the length of a magazine article. As you read, notice the major divisions of thought.
3. As you study Mark, make a detailed outline. Title each section.

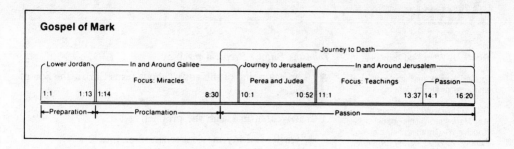

Gospel of Mark

	Journey to Death		
Lower Jordan	In and Around Galilee	Journey to Jerusalem	In and Around Jerusalem
	Focus: Miracles	Perea and Judea	Focus: Teachings — Passion
1:1 1:13	1:14 8:30	10:1 10:52	11:1 13:37 14:1 16:20
←Preparation→	←Proclamation→	←Passion	

Mark

OPEN: **1.** What kind of books do you enjoy reading? **2.** Do you like to read a book that starts off slow and easy or jumps right in?

DIG: **1.** How would you describe the way Mark starts off his gospel story: Shocking? Grabbing? Intriguing? Boring? **2.** What literary form does he use: Historical sketch? A tiny episode? A human interest story? Flash back? **3.** Why is John (the Baptist) so important to the Jesus story? How would you describe John by his dress, diet and message in modern terms? Why was he so popular with the masses? **4.** What do you learn about Jesus' background from this first paragraph?

REFLECT: If you wrote "the gospel according to you", how would you begin it and who would be the John the Baptist in your life?

OPEN: How were you "baptized" (initiated) into the work you are in?

DIG: **1.** Why did Jesus go to John, an Old Testament prophet, to be baptized? **2.** What is significant about the dove and the voice from heaven? **3.** What follows this high experience? What is the lesson here for you?

OPEN: **1.** Who's the best fisherman in your family? **2.** How did you feel the first time you left home? Where did you go? Why?

DIG: **1.** What are the elements of Jesus' message and what does each mean? Compare his message to that of John the Baptist (see vv. 4, 7-8). **2.** What might cause these four men to leave their family and occupation to follow Jesus? How do you think Zebedee felt about his son's action? **3.** What would they understand by "fisher of men"?

REFLECT: **1.** What first attracted you to begin following Jesus? **2.** What did you leave when you followed him? **3.** How did your family respond? **4.** What does it mean for you to be a "fisher of men"?

John the Baptist Prepares the Way

1 The beginning of the gospel about Jesus Christ, the Son of God. [a]

[2] It is written in Isaiah the prophet:

"I will send my messenger ahead of you,
  who will prepare your way" [b]—
[3] "a voice of one calling in the desert,
'Prepare the way for the Lord,
  make straight paths for him.' " [c]

[4] And so John came, baptizing in the desert region and preaching a baptism of repentance for the forgiveness of sins. [5] The whole Judean countryside and all the people of Jerusalem went out to him. Confessing their sins, they were baptized by him in the Jordan River. [6] John wore clothing made of camel's hair, with a leather belt around his waist, and he ate locusts and wild honey. [7] And this was his message: "After me will come one more powerful than I, the thongs of whose sandals I am not worthy to stoop down and untie. [8] I baptize you with [d] water, but he will baptize you with the Holy Spirit."

The Baptism and Temptation of Jesus

[9] At that time Jesus came from Nazareth in Galilee and was baptized by John in the Jordan. [10] As Jesus was coming up out of the water, he saw heaven being torn open and the Spirit descending on him like a dove. [11] And a voice came from heaven: "You are my Son, whom I love; with you I am well pleased."

[12] At once the Spirit sent him out into the desert, [13] and he was in the desert forty days, being tempted by Satan. He was with the wild animals, and angels attended him.

The Calling of the First Disciples

[14] After John was put in prison, Jesus went into Galilee, proclaiming the good news of God. [15] "The time has come," he said. "The kingdom of God is near. Repent and believe the good news!"

[16] As Jesus walked beside the Sea of Galilee, he saw Simon and his brother Andrew casting a net into the lake, for they were fishermen. [17] "Come, follow me," Jesus said, "and I will make you fishers of men." [18] At once they left their nets and followed him.

[19] When he had gone a little farther, he saw James son of Zebedee and his brother John in a boat, preparing their nets. [20] Without delay he called them, and they left their father Zebedee in the boat with the hired men and followed him.

---

[a]1 Some manuscripts do not have *the Son of God.*   [b]2 Mal. 3:1   [c]3 Isaiah 40:3
[d]8 Or *in*

Mark 1:-1-8   **JOHN THE BAPTIST PREPARES THE WAY**

LOOKING INTO THE SCRIPTURE/25 Minutes. Read Mark 1:1-8 and discuss. Answer YES, NO or MAYBE to these situations:

1. JOHN THE BAPTIST WAS THE KIND OF GUY THAT I WOULD LIKE TO . . .

Y N M   take shopping
Y N M   rock me to sleep
Y N M   get stuck with in an elevator
Y N M   invite to a black tie dinner
Y N M   drive with for 500 miles keeping within the speed limit
Y N M   send to convert my hard-hearted sister in the hospital
Y N M   sit with at an all-you-can-eat buffet

2. Why did the people flock to John the Baptist instead of avoiding him?
   a. he was the first prophet in 300 years
   b. he was more interesting than a circus
   c. anyone will come to see a fire burn
   d. he spoke to the reality of their hearts
   e. he talked about sin and forgiveness

3. In modern words, what was the message of John?
   a. you can have it all
   b. look out for number one
   c. turn or burn
   d. you only go around once, so reach for the gusto
   e. pay me now or pay me later
   f. there's a new day coming

4. Why was the establishment so upset with John?
   a. his popularity
   b. his simple life
   c. his preaching
   d. his attack on sin
   e. his call for change

5. What role did John the Baptist play in the overall plan of God?
   a. shake up the establishment
   b. bridge the Old to New Testament
   c. prepare folks for coming of Jesus
   d. baptize Jesus
   e. alert sinners to the need for a Savior

MY OWN STORY/20 Minutes.

1. If John the Baptist came to your town with this message, how would he be received?
   a. the media would love it
   b. people would flock to him
   c. church people would be polite
   d. everybody would run for cover
   e. people would ignore him

2. Who played the part of John the Baptist in your life—who "prepared the way" for Jesus?
   a. my parents
   b. a Sunday school teacher
   c. a coach/counselor/teacher
   d. a special friend
   e. a whole lot of people
   f. nobody yet

3. How would you describe your relationship with Jesus right now?
   a. just beginning
   b. nowhere
   c. holding
   d. struggling
   e. roller-coaster
   f. going great

4. What would it take to move you on in your relationship with God?
   a. a little support
   b. a deeper commitment
   c. some spiritual discipline
   d. a big change
   e. a miracle
   f. a strong belief that God loves even me

OPEN: Who's one of the best teachers you've had? What made that person so good?

DIG: 1. Why do you suppose Jesus started his public ministry in a synagogue? What events took place there? What impact did they have? What two things about Jesus amazed the people? Why? 2. What does it mean to teach "with authority"? What was the nature and source of Jesus' authority? 3. What characterizes this evil spirit?

REFLECT: On a scale of one to ten, how much authority does Jesus have in your life? What would he have to cast out to rate a ten?

OPEN: As a child, what was the worst sickness you ever had?

DIG: 1. How does Jesus' healing of this woman compare with his exorcism of the evil spirit? How do you know this was a miracle? An eyewitness account? By whom? 2. Why did the people wait until after sunset to bring the sick? Why are the demons silenced?

REFLECT: How do you think Jesus could use you to heal hurts today?

OPEN: Are you a "morning" dove or a night owl? Why?

DIG: 1. What about Jesus' prayer most impresses you: The hour? The solitude? His priorities? 2. What impact did prayer have on his decision (v. 38)? On his ministry (v. 39)?

REFLECT: When do you pray most effectively? Where? With whom? What decision awaits your prayer?

OPEN: What kinds of people do you resist touching?

DIG: 1. Why might the leper be unsure of Jesus' willingness to heal him? 2. Why was leprosy such an awful disease (see Lev. 13)? 3. What is significant about how Jesus healed him? 4. Why did he disobey Jesus' command to keep silent? What would you have done?

REFLECT: How has Jesus made his compassion tangible to you? When have you offered his healing touch to the "lepers" or "untouchables" in your community? Why not now?

Jesus Drives Out an Evil Spirit

21They went to Capernaum, and when the Sabbath came, Jesus went into the synagogue and began to teach. 22The people were amazed at his teaching, because he taught them as one who had authority, not as the teachers of the law. 23Just then a man in their synagogue who was possessed by an evil[e] spirit cried out, 24"What do you want with us, Jesus of Nazareth? Have you come to destroy us? I know who you are—the Holy One of God!"

25"Be quiet!" said Jesus sternly. "Come out of him!" 26The evil spirit shook the man violently and came out of him with a shriek.

27The people were all so amazed that they asked each other, "What is this? A new teaching—and with authority! He even gives orders to evil spirits and they obey him." 28News about him spread quickly over the whole region of Galilee.

Jesus Heals Many

29As soon as they left the synagogue, they went with James and John to the home of Simon and Andrew. 30Simon's mother-in-law was in bed with a fever, and they told Jesus about her. 31So he went to her, took her hand and helped her up. The fever left her and she began to wait on them.

32That evening after sunset the people brought to Jesus all the sick and demon-possessed. 33The whole town gathered at the door, 34and Jesus healed many who had various diseases. He also drove out many demons, but he would not let the demons speak because they knew who he was.

Jesus Prays in a Solitary Place

35Very early in the morning, while it was still dark, Jesus got up, left the house and went off to a solitary place, where he prayed. 36Simon and his companions went to look for him, 37and when they found him, they exclaimed: "Everyone is looking for you!"

38Jesus replied, "Let us go somewhere else—to the nearby villages—so I can preach there also. That is why I have come." 39So he traveled throughout Galilee, preaching in their synagogues and driving out demons.

A Man With Leprosy

40A man with leprosy[f] came to him and begged him on his knees, "If you are willing, you can make me clean."

41Filled with compassion, Jesus reached out his hand and touched the man. "I am willing," he said. "Be clean!" 42Immediately the leprosy left him and he was cured.

43Jesus sent him away at once with a strong warning: 44"See that you don't tell this to anyone. But go, show yourself to the priest and offer the sacrifices that Moses commanded for your cleansing, as a testimony to them." 45Instead he went out and

e23 Greek unclean; also in verses 26 and 27   f40 The Greek word was used for various diseases affecting the skin—not necessarily leprosy.

began to talk freely, spreading the news. As a result, Jesus could no longer enter a town openly but stayed outside in lonely places. Yet the people still came to him from everywhere.

Jesus Heals a Paralytic

2 A few days later, when Jesus again entered Capernaum, the people heard that he had come home. ²So many gathered that there was no room left, not even outside the door, and he preached the word to them. ³Some men came, bringing to him a paralytic, carried by four of them. ⁴Since they could not get him to Jesus because of the crowd, they made an opening in the roof above Jesus and, after digging through it, lowered the mat the paralyzed man was lying on. ⁵When Jesus saw their faith, he said to the paralytic, "Son, your sins are forgiven."

⁶Now some teachers of the law were sitting there, thinking to themselves, ⁷"Why does this fellow talk like that? He's blaspheming! Who can forgive sins but God alone?"

⁸Immediately Jesus knew in his spirit that this was what they were thinking in their hearts, and he said to them, "Why are you thinking these things? ⁹Which is easier: to say to the paralytic, 'Your sins are forgiven,' or to say, 'Get up, take your mat and walk'? ¹⁰But that you may know that the Son of Man has authority on earth to forgive sins . . . ." He said to the paralytic, ¹¹"I tell you, get up, take your mat and go home." ¹²He got up, took his mat and walked out in full view of them all. This amazed everyone and they praised God, saying, "We have never seen anything like this!"

The Calling of Levi

¹³Once again Jesus went out beside the lake. A large crowd came to him, and he began to teach them. ¹⁴As he walked along, he saw Levi son of Alphaeus sitting at the tax collector's booth. "Follow me," Jesus told him, and Levi got up and followed him.

¹⁵While Jesus was having dinner at Levi's house, many tax collectors and "sinners" were eating with him and his disciples, for there were many who followed him. ¹⁶When the teachers of the law who were Pharisees saw him eating with the "sinners" and tax collectors, they asked his disciples: "Why does he eat with tax collectors and 'sinners'?"

¹⁷On hearing this, Jesus said to them, "It is not the healthy who need a doctor, but the sick. I have not come to call the righteous, but sinners."

Jesus Questioned About Fasting

¹⁸Now John's disciples and the Pharisees were fasting. Some people came and asked Jesus, "How is it that John's disciples and the disciples of the Pharisees are fasting, but yours are not?"

¹⁹Jesus answered, "How can the guests of the bridegroom fast while he is with them? They cannot, so long as they have him with them. ²⁰But the time will come when the bridegroom will be taken from them, and on that day they will fast.

²¹"No one sews a patch of unshrunk cloth on an old garment. If he does, the new piece will pull away from the old, making

OPEN: 1. If you were in trouble in the middle of the night and needed to call on some friends, who would you call? **2.** If you knew someone could help a hurting friend, how far would you go to get your friend to this person?

DIG 1. As the events unfold in the first four verses, what does it sound like: A zoo? A TV sit-com episode? An emergency ward? **2.** What do you think was going on in the minds of the principle characters in the story: The owner of the house? The crowd? The man on the stretcher? The "teachers of the law"? **3.** Why are the teachers of the law so upset? **4.** In the Jewish mind, how are sin and the authority of God linked (see also John 9:1-3)? **5.** How did each of these people play a part in healing: The friends? The paralytic? Jesus?

REFLECT: 1. In your spiritual beginnings, who cared enough to get you to Jesus? **2.** Who do you care about in the same way today?

OPEN: What is the wildest party you have gone to in the last year?

DIG: 1. If Levi came from a good religious family (the priestly tribe), why do you think he went into the fraudulent business of "tax collecting"? **2.** Why do you think Jesus selected the "cheat" as one of his disciples? **3.** Why do you think Levi threw a party for his old friends? **4.** Do you think Jesus should have gone to the party? Do you think Jesus just made a token appearance or really enjoyed himself? **5.** What is the irony here between "tax collectors and sinners"? The "healthy" and the "sick"?

OPEN: Has your life this past week been more like feasting or fasting?

DIG: 1. Why did the Pharisees and John's disciples fast? Why was it a problem that Jesus' disciples did not? **2.** How is Jesus' teaching like the unshrunk cloth and new wine? What was the old cloth and old wineskins that he was referring to?

REFLECT: 1. Is Jesus running a "Fan Club" or a "Fun Club"? Why? **2.** What is the new wine in your life?

The old wineskins? **3.** How might fasting help you to get both fresh wine and new wineskins?

OPEN: 1. Would you "steal" food to feed your starving family? Why? **2.** If you lost your hand, what would you miss doing the most?

DIG: 1. What is the basic complaint about Jesus in these two stories? **2.** What do you know about the incident in verses 25-26 (see I Samuel 21:1-6)? How does David's story apply to Jesus' situation? **3.** What caused the tension in the synagogue (vv. 1-6)? What concerns were shared by the leaders? By Jesus? By the man with the shriveled hand? **4.** What emotion does Jesus express in verse 5? When is it right to be angry at arbitrary rules? To put people above principle? **5.** Why were their hearts stubborn? What would belief have cost these people? **6.** Review the five conflicts recorded in 2:1-3:6 and then explain the conclusion these religious leaders come to in verse 6.

REFLECT: 1. Is the Sabbath a day of freedom or restriction for you? Why? **2.** What is the best way for you to use the Sabbath? **3.** How much "Pharisee" lives in you?

OPEN: What is the largest crowd of which you were ever a part?

DIG: 1. How far were people coming to see and hear Jesus? **2.** How do you think Jesus felt about crowds? Which of their motives would have pleased him? What motives would have displeased him? **3.** What kind of commitment did the crowds have to Jesus?

REFLECT: Where do you need a "touch" from Jesus now?

OPEN: What was your first business venture and who were your partners?

DIG: 1. How might the events of verses 7-12 bring Jesus to choose the Twelve? **2.** Of the three purposes for the Twelve, which comes first? Why? **3.** Why such ordinary guys and not people with clout?

REFLECT: 1. What kind of people does Jesus need to be his disciples

the tear worse. ²²And no one pours new wine into old wineskins. If he does, the wine will burst the skins, and both the wine and the wineskins will be ruined. No, he pours new wine into new wineskins."

Lord of the Sabbath

²³One Sabbath Jesus was going through the grainfields, and as his disciples walked along, they began to pick some heads of grain. ²⁴The Pharisees said to him, "Look, why are they doing what is unlawful on the Sabbath?"

²⁵He answered, "Have you never read what David did when he and his companions were hungry and in need? ²⁶In the days of Abiathar the high priest, he entered the house of God and ate the consecrated bread, which is lawful only for priests to eat. And he also gave some to his companions."

²⁷Then he said to them, "The Sabbath was made for man, not man for the Sabbath. ²⁸So the Son of Man is Lord even of the Sabbath."

3 Another time he went into the synagogue, and a man with a shriveled hand was there. ²Some of them were looking for a reason to accuse Jesus, so they watched him closely to see if he would heal him on the Sabbath. ³Jesus said to the man with the shriveled hand, "Stand up in front of everyone."

⁴Then Jesus asked them, "Which is lawful on the Sabbath: to do good or to do evil, to save life or to kill?" But they remained silent.

⁵He looked around at them in anger and, deeply distressed at their stubborn hearts, said to the man, "Stretch out your hand." He stretched it out, and his hand was completely restored. ⁶Then the Pharisees went out and began to plot with the Herodians how they might kill Jesus.

Crowds Follow Jesus

⁷Jesus withdrew with his disciples to the lake, and a large crowd from Galilee followed. ⁸When they heard all he was doing, many people came to him from Judea, Jerusalem, Idumea, and the regions across the Jordan and around Tyre and Sidon. ⁹Because of the crowd he told his disciples to have a small boat ready for him, to keep the people from crowding him. ¹⁰For he had healed many, so that those with diseases were pushing forward to touch him. ¹¹Whenever the evil*g* spirits saw him, they fell down before him and cried out, "You are the Son of God." ¹²But he gave them strict orders not to tell who he was.

The Appointing of the Twelve Apostles

¹³Jesus went up on a mountainside and called to him those he wanted, and they came to him. ¹⁴He appointed twelve—designating them apostles*h*—that they might be with him and that he might send them out to preach ¹⁵and to have authority to drive out demons. ¹⁶These are the twelve he appointed: Simon (to whom he gave the name Peter); ¹⁷James son of Zebedee and his

---

g11 Greek *unclean*; also in verse 30   *h14* Some manuscripts do not have *designating them apostles.*

brother John (to them he gave the name Boanerges, which means Sons of Thunder); [18]Andrew, Philip, Bartholomew, Matthew, Thomas, James son of Alphaeus, Thaddaeus, Simon the Zealot [19]and Judas Iscariot, who betrayed him.

Jesus and Beelzebub

[20]Then Jesus entered a house, and again a crowd gathered, so that he and his disciples were not even able to eat. [21]When his family heard about this, they went to take charge of him, for they said, "He is out of his mind."

[22]And the teachers of the law who came down from Jerusalem said, "He is possessed by Beelzebub[i]! By the prince of demons he is driving out demons."

[23]So Jesus called them and spoke to them in parables: "How can Satan drive out Satan? [24]If a kingdom is divided against itself, that kingdom cannot stand. [25]If a house is divided against itself, that house cannot stand. [26]And if Satan opposes himself and is divided, he cannot stand; his end has come. [27]In fact, no one can enter a strong man's house and carry off his possessions unless he first ties up the strong man. Then he can rob his house. [28]I tell you the truth, all the sins and blasphemies of men will be forgiven them. [29]But whoever blasphemes against the Holy Spirit will never be forgiven; he is guilty of an eternal sin."

[30]He said this because they were saying, "He has an evil spirit."

Jesus' Mother and Brothers

[31]Then Jesus' mother and brothers arrived. Standing outside, they sent someone in to call him. [32]A crowd was sitting around him, and they told him, "Your mother and brothers are outside looking for you."

[33]"Who are my mother and my brothers?" he asked.

[34]Then he looked at those seated in a circle around him and said, "Here are my mother and my brothers! [35]Whoever does God's will is my brother and sister and mother."

The Parable of the Sower

4 Again Jesus began to teach by the lake. The crowd that gathered around him was so large that he got into a boat and sat in it out on the lake, while all the people were along the shore at the water's edge. [2]He taught them many things by parables, and in his teaching said: [3]"Listen! A farmer went out to sow his seed. [4]As he was scattering the seed, some fell along the path, and the birds came and ate it up. [5]Some fell on rocky places, where it did not have much soil. It sprang up quickly, because the soil was shallow. [6]But when the sun came up, the plants were scorched, and they withered because they had no root. [7]Other seed fell among thorns, which grew up and choked the plants, so that they did not bear grain. [8]Still other seed fell on good soil. It came up, grew and produced a crop, multiplying thirty, sixty, or even a hundred times."

[i]22 Greek *Beezeboul* or *Beelzeboul*

in this age? **2.** What does being "with him" do for you? **3.** What does being "sent out" with a mission and purpose do for you? For others?

OPEN: What is the one thing you could do that would make your family think you were out of your mind?

DIG: 1. Why do you think Jesus' family was worried about him? **2.** Why would the Pharisees connect Jesus with Beelzebub (the Devil)? **3.** How do Jesus' parables answer the charges? **4.** What sins can be forgiven? What is the sin that cannot be forgiven? (Remember: to receive forgiveness, you must ask.)

REFLECT: 1. When have you felt misunderstood by your family? How was the issue resolved? **2.** What sorts of things have you done that would seem "strange" to those without your faith? **3.** Have you ever worried about committing the "unforgiveable sin"? Explain. How does your concern prove that you are not guilty of such a sin?

OPEN: How does it feel to be misunderstood by family?

DIG: 1. What does it mean to do God's will? Is this an action or a belief? **2.** What is the basis of a "family" relationship with Jesus?

REFLECT: In what ways is your Christian fellowship like family? How do you treat those "outside"?

OPEN: 1. Who is the best "storyteller" that you have ever known. What makes them so good? **2.** What experience, if any, have you had on a farm? Raising a garden? Growing flowers? What success have you had in trying to grow things?

DIG: 1. What are the four types of soil on which these seeds fall? What kind of growth occured in each soil type? **2.** How might this crowd have responded to such a parable? **3.** Does Jesus tell parables to obscure meaning, or does the hardness of the hearts of the hearers prevent understanding? **4.** When and to whom did Jesus explain this parable? **5.** Why does the word not take root at all in some people? What causes the second plant to wither? What three things choked off the

Mark 4:1-20   **THE PARABLE OF THE SOWER**

LOOKING INTO THE SCRIPTURE/15 Minutes. Read Mark 4:1-20 and discuss.

1. If you had been in the crowd when Jesus shared this parable, how would you have felt?
   - a. what's he saying?
   - b. wonder which soil I am?
   - c. is he trying to say something to me?
   - d. who does he think he is?

2. Why do you think Jesus used this illustration to expain how people receive his message?
   - a. he was sick and tired of people tagging along and doing nothing
   - b. they were sitting in a wheat field
   - c. everybody understood farming
   - d. he deliberately wanted to keep some people in the dark

3. What is the "crop" that the seed is supposed to produce?
   - a. wheat
   - b. the lifestyle of Jesus
   - c. new converts to the faith
   - d. spirituality

4. What is Jesus really saying in this parable?
   - a. if you can't hear, turn up the volume
   - b. paint or get off the ladder
   - c. if you are not producing, it's not the fault of the seed
   - d. God is making a list and checking it twice

MY OWN STORY/30 Minutes.

1. If you had to divide your life from BIRTH to RIGHT NOW into four quarters (like the four quarters of a football game), how would you describe each quarter as far as your responsiveness to the *spiritual values* that Jesus preached and lived? On the line below, fill in the four quarters of your life—starting with CHILDHOOD as your first quarter. Then, for each *quarter,* jot down one of the four soils:

P=PATH   R=ROCKY   T=THORNY   G=GOOD

CHILDHOOD

First Quarter   Second Quarter   Third Quarter   Fourth Quarter

2. In the period of your life where you indicated the best crop, what was the contributing factor?
   - a. I was around a spiritual community of people
   - b. I was daily seeking the will of God
   - c. I had very few distractions in my life
   - d. I had my priorities in order
   - e. I was communicating with God regularly

3. In the period of your life where you indicated the poorest crop, what was the contributing factor?
   - a. I had a whole lot of problems
   - b. I didn't know anything about Christ
   - c. I knew about Christ, but I was taken up with other things
   - d. I didn't have a supportive community
   - e. I was living life my way

4. If you were to take God seriously for 30 days, what would it mean in practical terms?
   - a. plowing up the soil and starting over
   - b. removing a few rocks
   - c. doing some serious weeding
   - d. letting God do his thing

5. Which of these "farm trivia" facts would encourage you the most as you "sow" the "seed" of the gospel?
   - a. seed can germinate after being stored for centuries
   - b. a seed of grain can yield 100 times its weight
   - c. spring wheat is planted in the fall
   - d. the crop yield cannot be determined as the seed is planted

⁹Then Jesus said, "He who has ears to hear, let him hear."

¹⁰When he was alone, the Twelve and the others around him asked him about the parables. ¹¹He told them, "The secret of the kingdom of God has been given to you. But to those on the outside everything is said in parables ¹²so that,

" 'they may be ever seeing but never perceiving,
   and ever hearing but never understanding;
   otherwise they might turn and be forgiven!' "

¹³Then Jesus said to them, "Don't you understand this parable? How then will you understand any parable? ¹⁴The farmer sows the word. ¹⁵Some people are like seed along the path, where the word is sown. As soon as they hear it, Satan comes and takes away the word that was sown in them. ¹⁶Others, like seed sown on rocky places, hear the word and at once receive it with joy. ¹⁷But since they have no root, they last only a short time. When trouble or persecution comes because of the word, they quickly fall away. ¹⁸Still others, like seed sown among thorns, hear the word; ¹⁹but the worries of this life, the deceitfulness of wealth and the desires for other things come in and choke the word, making it unfruitful. ²⁰Others, like seed sown on good soil, hear the word, accept it, and produce a crop—thirty, sixty or even a hundred times what was sown."

A Lamp on a Stand

²¹He said to them, "Do you bring in a lamp to put it under a bowl or a bed? Instead, don't you put it on its stand? ²²For whatever is hidden is meant to be disclosed, and whatever is concealed is meant to be brought out into the open. ²³If anyone has ears to hear, let him hear."

²⁴"Consider carefully what you hear," he continued. "With the measure you use, it will be measured to you—and even more. ²⁵Whoever has will be given more; whoever does not have, even what he has will be taken from him."

The Parable of the Growing Seed

²⁶He also said, "This is what the kingdom of God is like. A man scatters seed on the ground. ²⁷Night and day, whether he sleeps or gets up, the seed sprouts and grows, though he does not know how. ²⁸All by itself the soil produces grain—first the stalk, then the head, then the full kernel in the head. ²⁹As soon as the grain is ripe, he puts the sickle to it, because the harvest has come."

The Parable of the Mustard Seed

³⁰Again he said, "What shall we say the kingdom of God is like, or what parable shall we use to describe it? ³¹It is like a mustard seed, which is the smallest seed you plant in the ground. ³²Yet when planted, it grows and becomes the largest of all garden plants, with such big branches that the birds of the air can perch in its shade."

³³With many similar parables Jesus spoke the word to them,

j12 Isaiah 6:9,10

third plant? 6. In the context of 1:16-3:35, how does this parable explain the various responses to Jesus? 7. How would you explain this parable to contempory city kids who have never seen a farm? What modern analogy would you use?

REFLECT: 1. What was your earliest response to the gospel which you can remember? 2. Which soil would best describe your response to the gospel right now? 3. In your circle of acquaintances, which kind of "soil" do you most often see in the their hearts? 4. What does this parable teach you about evangelism? Should we sow the gospel indiscriminately? Why or why not? What does this parable say about failure in evangelism? About the inevitability of success?

OPEN: What is under your bed now?

DIG: 1. If Jesus came to show the world what God is like, what does this parable mean (also vv. 11-12)? 2. If the saying in verses 24-25 concerns how people react to Jesus' coming, what does it mean?

REFLECT: Are you a "secret Christian"? If so, what will it take for you to go public?

OPEN: Who can make things grow in your family?

DIG: 1. What part if any, does one play in the growing kingdom? 2. How does this parable complement the one in 4:3-20?

REFLECT: With God at work, do you rest or witness more?

OPEN: As a child, where was your favorite place of shade?

DIG: 1. What does the contrast between the small seed and huge bush teach you about the kingdom of God? 2. What have the parables in verses 21-34 taught you about the kingdom of God?

REFLECT: What evidence of growth have you seen in your life in the last year?

as much as they could understand. ³⁴He did not say anything to them without using a parable. But when he was alone with his own disciples, he explained everything.

Jesus Calms the Storm

³⁵That day when evening came, he said to his disciples, "Let us go over to the other side." ³⁶Leaving the crowd behind, they took him along, just as he was, in the boat. There were also other boats with him. ³⁷A furious squall came up, and the waves broke over the boat, so that it was nearly swamped. ³⁸Jesus was in the stern, sleeping on a cushion. The disciples woke him and said to him, "Teacher, don't you care if we drown?"

³⁹He got up, rebuked the wind and said to the waves, "Quiet! Be still!" Then the wind died down and it was completely calm.

⁴⁰He said to his disciples, "Why are you so afraid? Do you still have no faith?"

⁴¹They were terrified and asked each other, "Who is this? Even the wind and the waves obey him!"

The Healing of a Demon-possessed Man

5 They went across the lake to the region of the Gerasenes.ᵏ ²When Jesus got out of the boat, a man with an evilˡ spirit came from the tombs to meet him. ³This man lived in the tombs, and no one could bind him any more, not even with a chain. ⁴For he had often been chained hand and foot, but he tore the chains apart and broke the irons on his feet. No one was strong enough to subdue him. ⁵Night and day among the tombs and in the hills he would cry out and cut himself with stones.

⁶When he saw Jesus from a distance, he ran and fell on his knees in front of him. ⁷He shouted at the top of his voice, "What do you want with me, Jesus, Son of the Most High God? Swear to God that you won't torture me!" ⁸For Jesus had said to him, "Come out of this man, you evil spirit!"

⁹Then Jesus asked him, "What is your name?"

"My name is Legion," he replied, "for we are many." ¹⁰And he begged Jesus again and again not to send them out of the area.

¹¹A large herd of pigs was feeding on the nearby hillside. ¹²The demons begged Jesus, "Send us among the pigs; allow us to go into them." ¹³He gave them permission, and the evil spirits came out and went into the pigs. The herd, about two thousand in number, rushed down the steep bank into the lake and were drowned.

¹⁴Those tending the pigs ran off and reported this in the town and countryside, and the people went out to see what had happened. ¹⁵When they came to Jesus, they saw the man who had been possessed by the legion of demons, sitting there, dressed and in his right mind; and they were afraid. ¹⁶Those who had seen it told the people what had happened to the demon-possessed man—and told about the pigs as well. ¹⁷Then the people began to plead with Jesus to leave their region.

¹⁸As Jesus was getting into the boat, the man who had been

OPEN: What is the most terrifying storm that you can remember?

DIG: 1. When did this incident take place (compare 4:1 with 4:35-36)? **2.** Which various emotions did the disciples exhibit? Do you think they were angry? **3.** How did their fear during the storm differ from their fear afterward? **4.** How is this miracle different from any other that Mark has yet recorded? What does this teach you?

REFLECT: 1. How do you react to Jesus when he seems to be asleep in your life? **2.** How does this story encourage you in those situations?

OPEN: If this healing of the demon-possessed man had happened in your community, how would the local TV station have covered the story?

DIG: 1. How do you think that the disciples were feeling as they continued across the lake? After a ride like theirs, how would it feel to be accosted by this man in this eerie place? **2.** What do we learn about demons from the actions of the possessed man? **3.** How does the healing take place? What is the man like afterwards? **4.** Why do you think the people of the region reacted as they did? Why were they "afraid" (v. 15) after seeing the man "dressed and in his right mind?" What does this story say about their values? **5.** Where was this region called Decaplis? What was the cultural or ethnic background of the people who lived there (see Bible dictionary)? How might that explain this charge to witness (v. 19), when previously Jesus ordered silence (1:43-44)? **6.** What do you suppose the demoniac said to his family and those in the Decapolis? **7.** What new thing did the disciples learn about Jesus from this incident?

REFLECT: 1. Are people or "pigs" (a person's livelihood) more important in your culture? In your church? In your life? **2.** Is "The Bay of Pigs Disaster" a good title for this story? Why or why not? **3.** What can you tell your family about what God has done for you?

ᵏ1 Some manuscripts *Gadarenes;* other manuscripts *Gergesenes*   ˡ2 Greek *unclean;* also in verses 8 and 13

LOOKING INTO THE SCRIPTURE/25 Minutes. Read Mark 4:35-41 and discuss.

1. If you had been one of these disciples, what would you have told your wife that evening?
      a. I almost got killed!
      b. that Jesus is sure a sound sleeper
      c. I can't figure Jesus out
      d. only God can do what I saw today

2. Why do you think Jesus suggested that they take a boat trip across the lake?
    a. to get a little rest
    b. to get away from people
    c. to put the disciples through this test
    d. to be alone with his disciples

3. Why did Jesus let the storm come up?
    a. he didn't. It was natural
    b. he was sleeping
    c. he wanted to teach them a lesson
    d. he didn't send the storm, but he used it to stretch their faith
    e. he didn't know what was going on

4. Why do you think the disciples awakened Jesus?
    a. concern for their lives
    b. they needed help bailing water
    c. they resented his sleeping during the crisis
    d. they expected a miracle

5. What was the tone in Jesus' voice when he said, "You of little faith. Why are you so afraid?"
    a. put down: "You scaredicats"
    b. puzzlement: "Why would you worry when I am in the boat"
    c. empathy: "I feel what you're feeling"
    d. disappointment: "You've disappointed me. I wish you had more faith"

MY OWN STORY/20 Minutes.

1. What is your typical response to storms in your life?
    a. help: What do I do?
    b. anger: Why did this happen to me?
    c. brave front: I can tough it out.
    d. turn to God: Help me out of this, Lord!
    e. punt: I give up.

2. How would you compare your life now to the storm in the Scripture?
    a. smooth sailing—enjoying the ride
    b. choppy water—rough ride
    c. cloud burst—danger signals
    d. storm over—cleaning up the mess

3. What brings storms in your life?
    a. financial difficulties
    b. hassles with relationships
    c. insecurity: job/future
    d. failure: feeling a failure
    e. tragedy: sickness/death

4. "Quiet! Be still!" For the storm you're facing, what would this mean?
    a. don't panic
    b. quit rocking the boat
    c. accept the storm as a gift
    d. don't sweat the small stuff
    e. God has it under control

5. If you have time, take and discuss this stress test. Circle those events you have experienced within the past 12 months. Total your score. If you score more than 150 points, you are probably living under a whole lot of stress.

EVENT	STRESS POINTS	EVENT	STRESS POINTS	EVENT	STRESS POINTS
Death of spouse	100	Health problem	44	Foreclosure on mort./loan	30
Divorce	73	Pregnancy	40	Change in work	29
Marital separation	65	Sex difficulties	39	Son/daughter leaving home	29
Jail term	63	Gain of new family member	39	Trouble with in-laws	29
Death of family member	63	Business readjustment	39	Major achievement	28
Personal injury or illness	53	Change in financial state	38	Wife starting/stopping work	26
Marriage	50	Death of a close friend	37	Change in living conditions	25
Loss of job	47	Change in line of work	36	Revision of personal habits	24
Marital reconciliation	45	Arguments with spouse	35	Trouble with boss	23
Retirement	45	Large mortgage taken out	31	Change in work hours	20

demon-possessed begged to go with him. ¹⁹Jesus did not let him, but said, "Go home to your family and tell them how much the Lord has done for you, and how he has had mercy on you." ²⁰So the man went away and began to tell in the Decapolis ᵐhow much Jesus had done for him. And all the people were amazed.

A Dead Girl and a Sick Woman

²¹When Jesus had again crossed over by boat to the other side of the lake, a large crowd gathered around him while he was by the lake. ²²Then one of the synagogue rulers, named Jairus, came there. Seeing Jesus, he fell at his feet ²³and pleaded earnestly with him, "My little daughter is dying. Please come and put your hands on her so that she will be healed and live." ²⁴So Jesus went with him.

A large crowd followed and pressed around him. ²⁵And a woman was there who had been subject to bleeding for twelve years. ²⁶She had suffered a great deal under the care of many doctors and had spent all she had, yet instead of getting better she grew worse. ²⁷When she heard about Jesus, she came up behind him in the crowd and touched his cloak, ²⁸because she thought, "If I just touch his clothes, I will be healed." ²⁹Immediately her bleeding stopped and she felt in her body that she was freed from her suffering.

³⁰At once Jesus realized that power had gone out from him. He turned around in the crowd and asked, "Who touched my clothes?"

³¹"You see the people crowding against you," his disciples answered, "and yet you can ask, 'Who touched me?' "

³²But Jesus kept looking around to see who had done it. ³³Then the woman, knowing what had happened to her, came and fell at his feet and, trembling with fear, told him the whole truth. ³⁴He said to her, "Daughter, your faith has healed you. Go in peace and be freed from your suffering."

³⁵While Jesus was still speaking, some men came from the house of Jairus, the synagogue ruler. "Your daughter is dead," they said. "Why bother the teacher any more?"

³⁶Ignoring what they said, Jesus told the synagogue ruler, "Don't be afraid; just believe."

³⁷He did not let anyone follow him except Peter, James and John the brother of James. ³⁸When they came to the home of the synagogue ruler, Jesus saw a commotion, with people crying and wailing loudly. ³⁹He went in and said to them, "Why all this commotion and wailing? The child is not dead but asleep." ⁴⁰But they laughed at him.

After he put them all out, he took the child's father and mother and the disciples who were with him, and went in where the child was. ⁴¹He took her by the hand and said to her, *"Talitha koum!"* (which means, "Little girl, I say to you, get up!"). ⁴²Immediately the girl stood up and walked around (she was twelve years old). At this they were completely astonished. ⁴³He gave strict orders not to let anyone know about this, and told them to give her something to eat.

ᵐ20 That is, the Ten Cities

OPEN: 1. If you could raise one person from the dead, who would it be? 2. What is the closest you have come to dying? 3. How much courage do you think it took for her to touch Jesus? 4. Why do you think Jesus makes the sick woman reveal herself: For his sake? Or for her own sake? How was her faith obvious to Jesus? 5. What is the relationship here between faith and healing? In what ways other than the physical was this woman healed and given new peace? 6. What impressions do you get of Jairus from verses 22-23? How is his situation similar to that of the sick woman? How is it different? 7. What is Jesus' reaction to the news that the child is dead? Jairus' reaction? How do we know the girl was actually dead? Why did Jesus say the child was asleep? How do we know she is truly alive again (and not just a ghost)? What part does Jairus' intense desire have in raising the dead girl? 8. What two new things did the disciples learn about the power of Jesus? Summarize their deepened understanding of Jesus from the incidents in 4:35-5:43.

DIG: 1. Of all the people pressing for Jesus' attention, two get through to him in this story—how so? 2. What impressions do we get of the sick woman in verses 25-26? (Note: This particular illness made her ceremonially unclean and thus unable to have contact with other people.) 3. What is one of the nicest things your parents ever did for you?

REFLECT: 1. Of the people in this story, whom are you most like? 2. What does it cost Jesus to be involved in your life? What does it cost you to be involved with Jesus? To be involved with others? 3. What is the role of Jesus in healing today? What is the role of faith? Of touch? 4. What people have the greatest healing influence in your life? In whose lives are you a healer? How? 5. In what area of your life will you trust Jesus to heal you?

A Prophet Without Honor

6 Jesus left there and went to his hometown, accompanied by
his disciples. 2When the Sabbath came, he began to teach
in the synagogue, and many who heard him were amazed.
"Where did this man get these things?" they asked. "What's
this wisdom that has been given him, that he even does miracles!
3Isn't this the carpenter? Isn't this Mary's son and the brother
of James, Joseph,[n] Judas and Simon? Aren't his sisters here with
us?" And they took offense at him.
4Jesus said to them, "Only in his hometown, among his relatives and in his own house is a prophet without honor." 5He
could not do any miracles there, except lay his hands on a few
sick people and heal them. 6And he was amazed at their lack of
faith.

Jesus Sends Out the Twelve

Then Jesus went around teaching from village to village.
7Calling the Twelve to him, he sent them out two by two and
gave them authority over evil[o] spirits.
8These were his instructions: "Take nothing for the journey
except a staff—no bread, no bag, no money in your belts. 9Wear
sandals but not an extra tunic. 10Whenever you enter a house,
stay there until you leave that town. 11And if any place will not
welcome you or listen to you, shake the dust off your feet when
you leave, as a testimony against them."
12They went out and preached that people should repent.
13They drove out many demons and anointed many sick people
with oil and healed them.

John the Baptist Beheaded

14King Herod heard about this, for Jesus' name had become
well known. Some were saying,[p] "John the Baptist has been
raised from the dead, and that is why miraculous powers are at
work in him."
15Others said, "He is Elijah."
And still others claimed, "He is a prophet, like one of the
prophets of long ago."
16But when Herod heard this, he said, "John, the man I
beheaded, has been raised from the dead!"
17For Herod himself had given orders to have John arrested,
and he had him bound and put in prison. He did this because
of Herodias, his brother Philip's wife, whom he had married.
18For John had been saying to Herod, "It is not lawful for you
to have your brother's wife." 19So Herodias nursed a grudge
against John and wanted to kill him. But she was not able to,
20because Herod feared John and protected him, knowing him
to be a righteous and holy man. When Herod heard John, he
was greatly puzzled[q]; yet he liked to listen to him.
21Finally the opportune time came. On his birthday Herod
gave a banquet for his high officials and military commanders

[n]3 Greek *Joses*, a variant of *Joseph* [o]7 Greek *unclean* [p]14 Some early manuscripts *He was saying* [q]20 Some early manuscripts *he did many things*

OPEN: Which story from your past does your family most like to retell when you go back home?

DIG: 1. After these four "power" miracles, where does Jesus go? What happens there? **2.** What do the four questions (vv. 2-3) reveal? Why do they take offense? **3.** Why is Jesus' ministry "limited" in Nazareth? Why limited by faith?

REFLECT: 1. Is it easier for you to live a Christian life at home or away from home? Why? **2.** How could you be more effective at home?

OPEN: Who in your family packs too much?

DIG: 1. What was the significance of the disciples' assignment for the spread of the kingdom of God? Couldn't this have been achieved by Jesus himself? **2.** Compare the disciples' message with John's (1:4) and Jesus' (1:14-15). **3.** What benefits do you think were gained by the disciples? By Jesus? By the people? By the Kingdom?

REFLECT: Where has God sent you to tell about the Kingdom? How is it going? What help do you need?

OPEN: 1. If a king came to you and said, "Ask me for anything you want and I'll give it to you", what would you ask for? **2.** What is the best party that you have ever attended?

DIG: 1. What was it that drew Herod's attention to Jesus? What was the significance of Elijah and John the Baptist to the people of Jesus' day (see Matt. 17:9-13)? Why might people mistake Jesus for John the Baptist or Elijah? **2.** Why does Herod jail John? How did Herod feel about John? **3.** What do you learn about Herodias in this passage? Trace the steps by which she is finally able to have John killed. **4.** What do you learn about the complex character of Herod from this passage? What kind of leader do you think he was? **5.** Contrast the two "kings", Jesus and Herod, in terms of their kingdoms, character, popularity, and use of power.

REFLECT: 1. What might this story say to anyone facing persecution? **2.** When, if ever, have you made a rash vow that you regretted? Is it ever right to go back on a vow or to fail to keep a promise? **3.** In this story, with whom do you identify most closely? Why? **4.** Whom do you know who is struggling with the truth and is perplexed—much like Herod? How can you reach out to that person?

OPEN: 1. After a busy day, how do you like to unwind? **2.** If you had to feed five thousand people at a picnic, what would you serve?

DIG: 1. Why might Mark have included the "flashback" to Herod in between sending out the disciples (vv. 6-13) and their return (vv. 30-31)? Compare the "banquet" Jesus serves here to the one Herod served (vv. 21-28). **2.** Why did Jesus decide to take the disciples away? What happened as soon as they left? **3.** What was the difference in the way the disciples and Jesus viewed the problem? The solution? **4.** What emotions might have been expressed by the disciples in verse 37? In verse 43? **5.** If God can multiply food, why save the scraps? **6.** What's the lesson in five loaves feeding five thousand?

REFLECT: 1. When was the last time you heard these words: "Let's go to a quiet place and get some rest"? What happened instead? **2.** How do you usually react to interruptions: Like the disciples? Or like Jesus? In what ways would you like your actions or attitudes changed in this area? **3.** When you relax, do you feel guilty? Explain. **4.** How do you react to crowds and busy activity? **5.** Where is God calling you to share what you have? What specifically does he want you to share?

---

and the leading men of Galilee. ²²When the daughter of Herodias came in and danced, she pleased Herod and his dinner guests.

The king said to the girl, "Ask me for anything you want, and I'll give it to you." ²³And he promised her with an oath, "Whatever you ask I will give you, up to half my kingdom."

²⁴She went out and said to her mother, "What shall I ask for?"

"The head of John the Baptist," she answered.

²⁵At once the girl hurried in to the king with the request: "I want you to give me right now the head of John the Baptist on a platter."

²⁶The king was greatly distressed, but because of his oaths and his dinner guests, he did not want to refuse her. ²⁷So he immediately sent an executioner with orders to bring John's head. The man went, beheaded John in the prison, ²⁸and brought back his head on a platter. He presented it to the girl, and she gave it to her mother. ²⁹On hearing of this, John's disciples came and took his body and laid it in a tomb.

Jesus Feeds the Five Thousand

³⁰The apostles gathered around Jesus and reported to him all they had done and taught. ³¹Then, because so many people were coming and going that they did not even have a chance to eat, he said to them, "Come with me by yourselves to a quiet place and get some rest."

³²So they went away by themselves in a boat to a solitary place. ³³But many who saw them leaving recognized them and ran on foot from all the towns and got there ahead of them. ³⁴When Jesus landed and saw a large crowd, he had compassion on them, because they were like sheep without a shepherd. So he began teaching them many things.

³⁵By this time it was late in the day, so his disciples came to him. "This is a remote place," they said, "and it's already very late. ³⁶Send the people away so they can go to the surrounding countryside and villages and buy themselves something to eat."

³⁷But he answered, "You give them something to eat."

They said to him, "That would take eight months of a man's wagesʳ! Are we to go and spend that much on bread and give it to them to eat?"

³⁸"How many loaves do you have?" he asked. "Go and see."

When they found out, they said, "Five—and two fish."

³⁹Then Jesus directed them to have all the people sit down in groups on the green grass. ⁴⁰So they sat down in groups of hundreds and fifties. ⁴¹Taking the five loaves and the two fish and looking up to heaven, he gave thanks and broke the loaves. Then he gave them to his disciples to set before the people. He also divided the two fish among them all. ⁴²They all ate and were satisfied, ⁴³and the disciples picked up twelve basketfuls of broken pieces of bread and fish. ⁴⁴The number of the men who had eaten was five thousand.

ʳ37 Greek *take two hundred denarii*

Mark 6:30-44   **JESUS FEEDS THE FIVE THOUSAND**

LOOKING INTO THE SCRIPTURE/25 Minutes. Read Mark 6:30-44 and discuss.

1. Which three from the following list will ruin a *restful* vacation for you the most?
   - ☐ running into acquaintances from home
   - ☐ mosquitoes/jellyfish/ants
   - ☐ car trouble
   - ☐ 7 straight days of rain
   - ☐ losing luggage
   - ☐ unfinished business at work
   - ☐ phone calls from the office
   - ☐ surprises
   - ☐ losing your wallet
   - ☐ standing in long lines
   - ☐ tight time schedule
   - ☐ having relatives along

2. "Come with me by yourself to a quiet place and get some rest." If you were one of the disciples, what would you expect?
   - a. a quiet little vacation
   - b. time to be with Jesus
   - c. a fun time
   - d. anything but people

3. Surprise. There are 5,000 waiting on the shore. How do you feel?
   - a. delighted
   - b. "Oh no"
   - c. compassion
   - d. anger/frustration
   - e. whipped

4. "You give them something to eat." Why did the disciples object?
   - a. they were "on empty"
   - b. they didn't like welfare
   - c. they were mad because their vacation was blown
   - d. they were afraid of attracting loafers

5. "How many loaves do you have?" What was Jesus asking the disciples to do?
   - a. take inventory of their resources
   - b. stop thinking of their own self-interests
   - c. see how impossible it really was
   - d. start with what they had
   - e. trust that he had a plan

MY OWN STORY/20 Minutes. Read the Scripture again and share your feelings.

1. How do you react when you are faced with an overwhelming sense of need?
   - a. panicked
   - b. inadequate
   - c. let's do something
   - d. I can't do anything
   - e. hold back and feel guilty later

2. How does it make you feel when you realize that you have special gifts to contribute to the world's needs?
   - a. lump in my throat
   - b. scared stiff
   - c. pretty responsible
   - d. eager to do something
   - e. mixed feelings
   - f. question God's choice of me

3. What is your favorite way of avoiding your responsibility?
   - a. claim problem is too big
   - b. blame everybody else
   - c. wait for someone to go first
   - d. say I can't make a difference
   - e. turn on the TV and ignore the issue
   - f. get busy with something else

4. If you could pool the resources of your group to do something about the needs of your community, what would be your biggest strength?
   - a. financial
   - b. leadership
   - c. political connections
   - d. community action
   - e. spiritual motivation
   - f. genuine concern

5. Where are you now in listening to God's call for action? (Put a dot somewhere between the two extremes).

GOD IS ON
THE PHONE
RIGHT NOW _____

I MAKE SURE
I'M NOT AT HOME
WHEN GOD CALLS

Jesus Walks on the Water

[45]Immediately Jesus made his disciples get into the boat and go on ahead of him to Bethsaida, while he dismissed the crowd. [46]After leaving them, he went up on a mountainside to pray.

[47]When evening came, the boat was in the middle of the lake, and he was alone on land. [48]He saw the disciples straining at the oars, because the wind was against them. About the fourth watch of the night he went out to them, walking on the lake. He was about to pass by them, [49]but when they saw him walking on the lake, they thought he was a ghost. They cried out, [50]because they all saw him and were terrified.

Immediately he spoke to them and said, "Take courage! It is I. Don't be afraid." [51]Then he climbed into the boat with them, and the wind died down. They were completely amazed, [52]for they had not understood about the loaves; their hearts were hardened.

[53]When they had crossed over, they landed at Gennesaret and anchored there. [54]As soon as they got out of the boat, people recognized Jesus. [55]They ran throughout that whole region and carried the sick on mats to wherever they heard he was. [56]And wherever he went—into villages, towns or countryside—they placed the sick in the marketplaces. They begged him to let them touch even the edge of his cloak, and all who touched him were healed.

Clean and Unclean

7 The Pharisees and some of the teachers of the law who had come from Jerusalem gathered around Jesus and [2]saw some of his disciples eating food with hands that were "unclean," that is, unwashed. [3](The Pharisees and all the Jews do not eat unless they give their hands a ceremonial washing, holding to the tradition of the elders. [4]When they come from the marketplace they do not eat unless they wash. And they observe many other traditions, such as the washing of cups, pitchers and kettles.[s])

[5]So the Pharisees and teachers of the law asked Jesus, "Why don't your disciples live according to the tradition of the elders instead of eating their food with 'unclean' hands?"

[6]He replied, "Isaiah was right when he prophesied about you hypocrites; as it is written:

" 'These people honor me with their lips,
     but their hearts are far from me.
[7]They worship me in vain;
     their teachings are but rules taught by men.'[t]

[8]You have let go of the commands of God and are holding on to the traditions of men."

[9]And he said to them: "You have a fine way of setting aside the commands of God in order to observe[u] your own traditions! [10]For Moses said, 'Honor your father and your mother,'[v] and, 'Anyone who curses his father or mother must be put to death.'[w]

---

[s]4 Some early manuscripts *pitchers, kettles and dining couches*   [t]6,7 Isaiah 29:13
[u]9 Some manuscripts *set up*   [v]10 Exodus 20:12; Deut. 5:16
[w]10 Exodus 21:17; Lev. 20:9

[11]But you say that if a man says to his father or mother: 'Whatever help you might otherwise have received from me is Corban' (that is, a gift devoted to God), [12]then you no longer let him do anything for his father or mother. [13]Thus you nullify the word of God by your tradition that you have handed down. And you do many things like that."

[14]Again Jesus called the crowd to him and said, "Listen to me, everyone, and understand this. [15]Nothing outside a man can make him 'unclean' by going into him. Rather, it is what comes out of a man that makes him 'unclean.'ˣ"

[17]After he had left the crowd and entered the house, his disciples asked him about this parable. [18]"Are you so dull?" he asked. "Don't you see that nothing that enters a man from the outside can make him 'unclean'? [19]For it doesn't go into his heart but into his stomach, and then out of his body." (In saying this, Jesus declared all foods "clean.")

[20]He went on: "What comes out of a man is what makes him 'unclean.' [21]For from within, out of men's hearts, come evil thoughts, sexual immorality, theft, murder, adultery, [22]greed, malice, deceit, lewdness, envy, slander, arrogance and folly. [23]All these evils come from inside and make a man 'unclean.'"

The Faith of a Syrophoenician Woman

[24]Jesus left that place and went to the vicinity of Tyre.ʸ He entered a house and did not want anyone to know it; yet he could not keep his presence secret. [25]In fact, as soon as she heard about him, a woman whose little daughter was possessed by an evilᶻ spirit came and fell at his feet. [26]The woman was a Greek, born in Syrian Phoenicia. She begged Jesus to drive the demon out of her daughter.

[27]"First let the children eat all they want," he told her, "for it is not right to take the children's bread and toss it to their dogs."

[28]"Yes, Lord," she replied, "but even the dogs under the table eat the children's crumbs."

[29]Then he told her, "For such a reply, you may go; the demon has left your daughter."

[30]She went home and found her child lying on the bed, and the demon gone.

The Healing of a Deaf and Mute Man

[31]Then Jesus left the vicinity of Tyre and went through Sidon, down to the Sea of Galilee and into the region of the Decapolis.ᵃ [32]There some people brought to him a man who was deaf and could hardly talk, and they begged him to place his hand on the man.

[33]After he took him aside, away from the crowd, Jesus put his fingers into the man's ears. Then he spit and touched the man's tongue. [34]He looked up to heaven and with a deep sigh said to him, "*Ephphatha!*" (which means, "Be opened!"). [35]At this, the

ing rules? **3.** When have you felt like "throwing in the towel" because of petty religious issues? What kept you going? **4.** What do you do to root out hypocrisy and preserve integrity, so the "your walk matches your talk" and "what you see is what you get"? **5.** What do you like best about what comes from within you? What do you like least? How can you influence what comes from within?

OPEN: When have you felt like an outsider in a group situation? What did it make you want to do?

DIG: 1. Tyre was outside of Israel. Why do you think that Jesus went to a non-Jewish territory: Was Jesus trying to dodge the crowds? Did God have a mission to accomplish in Tyre? Or both? **2.** Were Jesus' words in verse 27 harsh, or were they some kind of play on words? How does this woman take it (v. 28)? How is her reply evidence of her faith? **3.** What message is Jesus giving by healing the daughter?

REFLECT: Jesus walks a hundred miles to heal one person. How far are you willing to go for one person?

OPEN: If you suddenly went deaf, name three sounds that you would not miss at all.

DIG: 1. Where does this healing take place? Who else had been healed there (Mark 5:1-20)? **2.** Why do you think Jesus used this method to heal the man? **3.** How do the locals respond to this healing in contrast to the previous one?

REFLECT: 1. Which people in your life have cared enough to bring you closer to Jesus? **2.** Who do you know who might feel separated or alone because of a certain disability? What can you do to touch them with friendship this week?

ˣ15 Some early manuscripts *'unclean.'* ¹⁶*If anyone has ears to hear, let him hear.*
ʸ24 Many early manuscripts *Tyre and Sidon*   ᶻ25 Greek *unclean*   ᵃ31 That is, the Ten Cities

man's ears were opened, his tongue was loosened and he began to speak plainly.

[36]Jesus commanded them not to tell anyone. But the more he did so, the more they kept talking about it. [37]People were overwhelmed with amazement. "He has done everything well," they said. "He even makes the deaf hear and the mute speak."

Jesus Feeds the Four Thousand

8 During those days another large crowd gathered. Since they had nothing to eat, Jesus called his disciples to him and said, [2]"I have compassion for these people; they have already been with me three days and have nothing to eat. [3]If I send them home hungry, they will collapse on the way, because some of them have come a long distance."

[4]His disciples answered, "But where in this remote place can anyone get enough bread to feed them?"

[5]"How many loaves do you have?" Jesus asked.

"Seven," they replied.

[6]He told the crowd to sit down on the ground. When he had taken the seven loaves and given thanks, he broke them and gave them to his disciples to set before the people, and they did so. [7]They had a few small fish as well; he gave thanks for them also and told the disciples to distribute them. [8]The people ate and were satisfied. Afterward the disciples picked up seven basketfuls of broken pieces that were left over. [9]About four thousand men were present. And having sent them away, [10]he got into the boat with his disciples and went to the region of Dalmanutha.

[11]The Pharisees came and began to question Jesus. To test him, they asked him for a sign from heaven. [12]He sighed deeply and said, "Why does this generation ask for a miraculous sign? I tell you the truth, no sign will be given to it." [13]Then he left them, got back into the boat and crossed to the other side.

The Yeast of the Pharisees and Herod

[14]The disciples had forgotten to bring bread, except for one loaf they had with them in the boat. [15]"Be careful," Jesus warned them. "Watch out for the yeast of the Pharisees and that of Herod."

[16]They discussed this with one another and said, "It is because we have no bread."

[17]Aware of their discussion, Jesus asked them: "Why are you talking about having no bread? Do you still not see or understand? Are your hearts hardened? [18]Do you have eyes but fail to see, and ears but fail to hear? And don't you remember? [19]When I broke the five loaves for the five thousand, how many basketfuls of pieces did you pick up?"

"Twelve," they replied.

[20]"And when I broke the seven loaves for the four thousand, how many basketfuls of pieces did you pick up?"

They answered, "Seven."

[21]He said to them, "Do you still not understand?"

The Healing of a Blind Man at Bethsaida

²²They came to Bethsaida, and some people brought a blind man and begged Jesus to touch him. ²³He took the blind man by the hand and led him outside the village. When he had spit on the man's eyes and put his hands on him, Jesus asked, "Do you see anything?"

²⁴He looked up and said, "I see people; they look like trees walking around."

²⁵Once more Jesus put his hands on the man's eyes. Then his eyes were opened, his sight was restored, and he saw everything clearly. ²⁶Jesus sent him home, saying, "Don't go into the village. ᵇ"

Peter's Confession of Christ

²⁷Jesus and his disciples went on to the villages around Caesarea Philippi. On the way he asked them, "Who do people say I am?"

²⁸They replied, "Some say John the Baptist; others say Elijah; and still others, one of the prophets."

²⁹"But what about you?" he asked. "Who do you say I am?" Peter answered, "You are the Christ.ᶜ"

³⁰Jesus warned them not to tell anyone about him.

Jesus Predicts His Death

³¹He then began to teach them that the Son of Man must suffer many things and be rejected by the elders, chief priests and teachers of the law, and that he must be killed and after three days rise again. ³²He spoke plainly about this, and Peter took him aside and began to rebuke him.

³³But when Jesus turned and looked at his disciples, he rebuked Peter. "Get behind me, Satan!" he said. "You do not have in mind the things of God, but the things of men."

³⁴Then he called the crowd to him along with his disciples and said: "If anyone would come after me, he must deny himself and take up his cross and follow me. ³⁵For whoever wants to save his lifeᵈ will lose it, but whoever loses his life for me and for the gospel will save it. ³⁶What good is it for a man to gain the whole world, yet forfeit his soul? ³⁷Or what can a man give in exchange for his soul? ³⁸If anyone is ashamed of me and my words in this adulterous and sinful generation, the Son of Man will be ashamed of him when he comes in his Father's glory with the holy angels."

9 And he said to them, "I tell you the truth, some who are standing here will not taste death before they see the kingdom of God come with power."

OPEN: If you lost your sight, what would you miss the most?

DIG: 1. Why do you think Jesus took the man outside the city to heal him? **2.** Why do you think the man was healed in stages rather than all at once? **3.** How does this healing compare and contrast to the healing in Mark 7:31-37?

REFLECT: 1. When were your eyes opened spiritually? **2.** What have been some significant "second touches" in your life?

OPEN: Which adjective do people use most often to describe you?

DIG: 1. Of what significance is the place where Jesus asks these questions? **2.** Why is Jesus first interested in other people's assessment of him? What is the significance of Peter's reply?

REFLECT: If someone asked you who Jesus is, what would you say?

OPEN: If you could "gain the whole world", where would you live?

DIG: 1. What title did Jesus twice use for himself? What is the significance of this title? What four things does he prophesy about the Son of Man? According to Jesus, what kind of Messiah is he? **2.** Why does Peter react so strongly to Jesus' teaching? Why does Jesus react so strongly to Peter? Why does Jesus call Peter "Satan"? How is Peter like the blind beggar Jesus healed (8:22-26)? **3.** What is the essential difference between "the things of God and the things of man"? **4.** Who does Jesus now call to listen to his teaching? Why? What three things are involved in following Jesus? What is the "self" that must be denied? What are the consequences of denying Jesus instead? **5.** How does the whole tenor of the gospel shift at this point?

REFLECT: 1. When have you felt a need to advise God? **2.** In which groups do you tend to be most ashamed of Jesus' words? **3.** What "things of men", as reflected in your budget and time priorities, might tempt you? What priority has the highest "exchange" value (see v. 37) for you?

ᵇ26 Some manuscripts *Don't go and tell anyone in the village*   ᶜ29 Or *Messiah*.
"The Christ" (Greek) and "the Messiah" (Hebrew) both mean "the Anointed One."
ᵈ35 The Greek word means either *life* or *soul*; also in verse 36.

OPEN: 1. What is one of your classic moments of "putting your foot in your mouth"? **2.** Of all the places called "Gods country", which one is your favorite?

DIG: 1. What is the connection between 9:1 and this event? **2.** What does it mean that Jesus was "transfigured"? What is the significance of Moses' and Elijah's presence? Of the "voice" (see 5:37-43)? Why did Peter respond as he did? **3.** Why do you think Jesus took the three with him? Why only three? Why these three? Why did Peter respond as he did? **4.** How long would they have to keep silent? What two questions did they have? **5.** Why was the transfiguration important to Jesus? To the three disciples? **6.** Who played the role of Elijah (see Matt. 17:10-13)? With what result (recall 6:14-29)? How could John the Baptist's experience help the disciples understand the nature of Jesus' Messiahship?

REFLECT: 1. In this story, what will you remember the most? **2.** What spot is most like the Mount of Transfiguration—where Jesus appeared to you in a special way?

OPEN: When you were a child, what did you argue most about with your brothers and sisters? With your parents?

DIG: 1. While the three disciples were up on the mountain, what problem were the other nine having? How did they deal with it? What do you think the argument was about in verse 14? **2.** Describe the boy's problem? What was his father's greatest fear? **3.** Upon whose faith does the cure depend: The boy's? The father's? The disciples'? Jesus'? **4.** How could the father doubt and believe at the same time? **5.** What two commands does Jesus' issue to the evil spirit? What was the result? **6.** What part does faith play with prayer? **7.** What is the major difference between Jesus' teaching in Mark 8:31-31 and Mark 9:30-32? What is significant about this difference?

REFLECT: 1. How often in your life are spiritual highs followed by problems and temptations? **2.** Why isn't the Christian life more of a plateau experience, instead of highs and lows? **3.** Where do you learn

The Transfiguration

[2]After six days Jesus took Peter, James and John with him and led them up a high mountain, where they were all alone. There he was transfigured before them. [3]His clothes became dazzling white, whiter than anyone in the world could bleach them. [4]And there appeared before them Elijah and Moses, who were talking with Jesus.

[5]Peter said to Jesus, "Rabbi, it is good for us to be here. Let us put up three shelters—one for you, one for Moses and one for Elijah." [6](He did not know what to say, they were so frightened.)

[7]Then a cloud appeared and enveloped them, and a voice came from the cloud: "This is my Son, whom I love. Listen to him!"

[8]Suddenly, when they looked around, they no longer saw anyone with them except Jesus.

[9]As they were coming down the mountain, Jesus gave them orders not to tell anyone what they had seen until the Son of Man had risen from the dead. [10]They kept the matter to themselves, discussing what "rising from the dead" meant.

[11]And they asked him, "Why do the teachers of the law say that Elijah must come first?"

[12]Jesus replied, "To be sure, Elijah does come first, and restores all things. Why then is it written that the Son of Man must suffer much and be rejected? [13]But I tell you, Elijah has come, and they have done to him everything they wished, just as it is written about him."

The Healing of a Boy With an Evil Spirit

[14]When they came to the other disciples, they saw a large crowd around them and the teachers of the law arguing with them. [15]As soon as all the people saw Jesus, they were overwhelmed with wonder and ran to greet him.

[16]"What are you arguing with them about?" he asked.

[17]A man in the crowd answered, "Teacher, I brought you my son, who is possessed by a spirit that has robbed him of speech. [18]Whenever it seizes him, it throws him to the ground. He foams at the mouth, gnashes his teeth and becomes rigid. I asked your disciples to drive out the spirit, but they could not."

[19]"O unbelieving generation," Jesus replied, "how long shall I stay with you? How long shall I put up with you? Bring the boy to me."

[20]So they brought him. When the spirit saw Jesus, it immediately threw the boy into a convulsion. He fell to the ground and rolled around, foaming at the mouth.

[21]Jesus asked the boy's father, "How long has he been like this?"

"From childhood," he answered. [22]"It has often thrown him into fire or water to kill him. But if you can do anything, take pity on us and help us."

[23]"'If you can'?" said Jesus. "Everything is possible for him who believes."

LOOKING INTO THE SCRIPTURE/25 Minutes. Read Mark 9:2-13 and discuss.

1. What impresses you about Peter in this story?
    a. his enthusiasm
    b. quick thinking in a threatening situation
    c. willingness to act on his faith
    d. "foot in mouth" disease

2. Why do you think Jesus took time for this long trip into the mountains just a few weeks before his death?
    a. to spend time with God
    b. to prepare himself for the cross
    c. to strengthen his disciples
    d. to sort out his thoughts

3. If you had been Peter when Moses and Elijah appeared, how would you have felt?
    a. scared spitless
    b. totally awed
    c. out of place
    d. on a high
    e. like hiding

4. Why did Peter want to build three shelters?
    a. to honor Elijah, Moses, and Jesus
    b. to remember the occasion
    c. to keep the mountaintop feeling
    d. he couldn't think of anything better to do
    e. to expend nervous energy

5. What is the meaning of the words, "This is my Son, whom I love. Listen to him."
    a. shut up a minute
    b. forget about building anything
    c. "Be still and know that I am God"
    d. the splendor you have seen is proof that Jesus is my son

6. If you had been Peter after this experience, how would you have felt?
    a. subdued
    b. awed
    c. put down
    d. elated/ecstatic
    e. very special

MY OWN STORY/20 Minutes. Read the Scripture and share your own experience.

1. On the line below, put a mark and an event or place to indicate the time you remember having your first mountaintop experience with God.
BIRTH _____ NOW

2. What is your most recent mountaintop experience?
    a. years ago
    b. quite recently
    c. right now
    d. hasn't happened yet

3. What helps you to feel close to God?
    a. nature
    b. music
    c. being alone with Christ
    d. real Christian fellowship
    e. the Lord's Supper
    f. remembering His love for you

4. How do you feel when you are on the mountaintop?
    a. like being awed
    b. like the other shoe is about to drop
    c. like nothing else matters
    d. like conquering the world
    e. like staying forever

5. How would you describe your relationship with God now?
    a. on the mountaintop
    b. down off the mountain
    c. in the valley
    d. in a quandry
    e. in the desert
    f. in mid-climb

more—highs or lows? **4.** How can you live with the full reality of evil and yet with strong awareness of God's transforming power? **5.** How often do you see in yourself the reality that the father expressed in verse 24? **6.** What possibilities and what abuses come to mind when you ponder the fact that "everything is possible for him who believes" (v.23)?

24Immediately the boy's father exclaimed, "I do believe; help me overcome my unbelief!"

25When Jesus saw that a crowd was running to the scene, he rebuked the evil' spirit. "You deaf and mute spirit," he said, "I command you, come out of him and never enter him again."

26The spirit shrieked, convulsed him violently and came out. The boy looked so much like a corpse that many said, "He's dead." 27But Jesus took him by the hand and lifted him to his feet, and he stood up.

28After Jesus had gone indoors, his disciples asked him privately, "Why couldn't we drive it out?"

29He replied, "This kind can come out only by prayer.'"

30They left that place and passed through Galilee. Jesus did not want anyone to know where they were, 31because he was teaching his disciples. He said to them, "The Son of Man is going to be betrayed into the hands of men. They will kill him, and after three days he will rise." 32But they did not understand what he meant and were afraid to ask him about it.

Who Is the Greatest?

OPEN: If you could recapture one quality you had as a child, what quality would it be?

DIG: 1. Contrast the agenda of the disciples with that of Jesus. **2.** According to Jesus, what is the true measure of greatness? Why did he use a child to illustrate greatness? **3.** What does it mean to receive the weak and powerless in Jesus' name? What is the surprising outcome of such an act?

REFLECT: 1. How do you measure success? **2.** How well do you do when it comes to being a servant?

33They came to Capernaum. When he was in the house, he asked them, "What were you arguing about on the road?" 34But they kept quiet because on the way they had argued about who was the greatest.

35Sitting down, Jesus called the Twelve and said, "If anyone wants to be first, he must be the very last, and the servant of all."

36He took a little child and had him stand among them. Taking him in his arms, he said to them, 37"Whoever welcomes one of these little children in my name welcomes me; and whoever welcomes me does not welcome me but the one who sent me."

Whoever Is Not Against Us Is for Us

OPEN: What makes you jealous?

DIG: 1. What is ironic about this passage in light of Mark 9:18? **2.** Why are these other exorcists a problem for John? **3.** In verse 37-40, what does it mean to do something in Jesus' name?

REFLECT: What Christian groups would you like to shut up? Why?

38"Teacher," said John, "we saw a man driving out demons in your name and we told him to stop, because he was not one of us."

39"Do not stop him," Jesus said. "No one who does a miracle in my name can in the next moment say anything bad about me, 40for whoever is not against us is for us. 41I tell you the truth, anyone who gives you a cup of water in my name because you belong to Christ will certainly not lose his reward.

Causing to Sin

OPEN: If you ever had to give up a hand, foot, or an eye, which would you give up and why?

DIG: 1. What four things does Jesus say are "better"? What point is he trying to make? **2.** What is Jesus teaching about discipleship in this collection of sayings? **3.** What point was Jesus making when he spoke about salt? **4.** Once again Jesus uses exaggerated language (hyperbole) to make his point. Identify each instance in which he does this.

42"And if anyone causes one of these little ones who believe in me to sin, it would be better for him to be thrown into the sea with a large millstone tied around his neck. 43If your hand causes you to sin, cut it off. It is better for you to enter life maimed than with two hands to go into hell, where the fire never goes out.ᵍ 45And if your foot causes you to sin, cut it off. It is

ᵉ25 Greek *unclean*   ᶠ29 Some manuscripts *prayer and fasting*   ᵍ43 Some manuscripts *out,* 44*where* / " '*their worm does not die,* / *and the fire is not quenched.'*

better for you to enter life crippled than to have two feet and be thrown into hell. *ʰ* ⁴⁷And if your eye causes you to sin, pluck it out. It is better for you to enter the kingdom of God with one eye than to have two eyes and be thrown into hell, ⁴⁸where

" 'their worm does not die,
　　and the fire is not quenched.'ⁱ

⁴⁹Everyone will be salted with fire.

⁵⁰"Salt is good, but if it loses its saltiness, how can you make it salty again? Have salt in yourselves, and be at peace with each other."

Divorce

10 Jesus then left that place and went into the region of Judea and across the Jordan. Again crowds of people came to him, and as was his custom, he taught them.

²Some Pharisees came and tested him by asking, "Is it lawful for a man to divorce his wife?"

³"What did Moses command you?" he replied.

⁴They said, "Moses permitted a man to write a certificate of divorce and send her away."

⁵"It was because your hearts were hard that Moses wrote you this law," Jesus replied. ⁶"But at the beginning of creation God 'made them male and female.'ʲ ⁷'For this reason a man will leave his father and mother and be united to his wife,ᵏ ⁸and the two will become one flesh.'ˡ So they are no longer two, but one. ⁹Therefore what God has joined together, let man not separate."

¹⁰When they were in the house again, the disciples asked Jesus about this. ¹¹He answered, "Anyone who divorces his wife and marries another woman commits adultery against her. ¹²And if she divorces her husband and marries another man, she commits adultery."

The Little Children and Jesus

¹³People were bringing little children to Jesus to have him touch them, but the disciples rebuked them. ¹⁴When Jesus saw this, he was indignant. He said to them, "Let the little children come to me, and do not hinder them, for the kingdom of God belongs to such as these. ¹⁵I tell you the truth, anyone who will not receive the kingdom of God like a little child will never enter it." ¹⁶And he took the children in his arms, put his hands on them and blessed them.

The Rich Young Man

¹⁷As Jesus started on his way, a man ran up to him and fell on his knees before him. "Good teacher," he asked, "what must I do to inherit eternal life?"

¹⁸"Why do you call me good?" Jesus answered. "No one is good—except God alone. ¹⁹You know the commandments: 'Do not murder, do not commit adultery, do not steal, do not give

What might the outcome be if a person failed to recognize this as hyperbole?

REFLECT: 1. What sacrifices have you made for your own spiritual well-being? 2. What are the properties of salt? How potent is the "salt" in your life? 3. Do you keep your "salt" in a shaker or shake it around?

OPEN: What "born-again" marriages (once dead, but now alive) have you seen? What's their secret?

DIG: 1.Why do you think the Pharisees asked the question on divorce? 2. What was their viewpoint on divorce? 3. What is God's intention for marriage? 4. What new element did Jesus bring to the question of divorce? 5. In a culture in which males dominated, what is the significance of verses 11-12 for women?

REFLECT: 1. What, to you, is the essence of the marriage covenant? 2. How is your view of marriage similar to and different from the views of Moses? Of the Pharisees? Of Jesus? Of your contemporaries? 3. What effect does each divorce have on our belief in God's steadfast love toward us?

OPEN: What age child would you prefer to look after? Why?

DIG: What childlike characteristics do you think Jesus was commending here? How does childlikeness relate to the kingdom of God?

REFLECT: 1.How could you be more childlike in your spiritual life?

OPEN: Supposing you could climb your way to heaven by works of the law. What rung of the ladder would you be on by now: Just starting out? Stepping on people's toes? Almost to the top? Falling off?

DIG: 1. On whom did the young man's question (v. 17) place the emphasis? 2. What was his assumption about how one gains eternal life? 3. How did his view differ from Jesus' in 10:15? 4. What part of his question does Jesus initially

---

ʰ45 Some manuscripts hell, ⁴⁶where / " 'their worm does not die, / and the fire is not quenched.'　ⁱ48 Isaiah 66:24　ʲ6 Gen. 1:27　ᵏ7 Some early manuscripts do not have and be united to his wife.　ˡ8 Gen. 2:24

respond to (v. 18)? Why is that relevant? **5.** Jesus "quizzes" him on only a partial list of the Ten Commandments (v. 19, see Ex. 20:1-17)? How well might the rich ruler have performed the ones relating directly to God? **6.** Upon having his smug reply (v. 20), what two-part command does he lovingly give him (v. 21)? With what revealing response? **7.** What does Jesus say about riches and the kingdom (vv. 23-25), that broadens the scope of this inquiry (v. 26)? Why is it so hard for the rich to follow Jesus? **8.** On what basis is it possible for anyone—rich ruler or poor fisherman—to receive the kingdom (vv. 27-30)? **9.** Historically, who shall be "first" and "last" in that kingdom?

REFLECT: 1. How often do you find yourself trying to earn your salvation? **2.** If Jesus said to you, "one thing you lack", to what would he most likely point? How would you respond if he said "This has got to go"? **3.** What is Jesus saying to you in this passage about possessions and riches? Concretely, what does it mean to follow Jesus?

OPEN: What is the scariest journey that you can remember?

DIG: 1. Why would going to Jerusalem cause the disciples to be astonished and yet make the other followers afraid? **2.** What impresses you about Jesus in these verses?

REFLECT: If you had been one of the disciples, what would have been difficult for you in losing Jesus?

OPEN: What is your secret dream of grandeur?

DIG: 1. What did James and John want? How appropriate was their request? How did Jesus answer? **2.** What is "the cup" and "the baptism" and the "glory" as each applies to Jesus? As each applies to the disciples? **3.** What made the other ten disciples indignant (v. 41, also v. 31)? **4.** How does Jesus turn this rhubarb into a teachable moment? What new insights into Christ-like leadership and servanthood does he convey? **5.** How does Jesus practice what he preached? In this context what is a "ransom for many"? How is the death of Christ the ultimate service to all? **6.** How

false testimony, do not defraud, honor your father and mother.'[m]"

[20]"Teacher," he declared, "all these I have kept since I was a boy."

[21]Jesus looked at him and loved him. "One thing you lack," he said. "Go, sell everything you have and give to the poor, and you will have treasure in heaven. Then come, follow me."

[22]At this the man's face fell. He went away sad, because he had great wealth.

[23]Jesus looked around and said to his disciples, "How hard it is for the rich to enter the kingdom of God!"

[24]The disciples were amazed at his words. But Jesus said again, "Children, how hard it is[n] to enter the kingdom of God! [25]It is easier for a camel to go through the eye of a needle than for a rich man to enter the kingdom of God."

[26]The disciples were even more amazed, and said to each other, "Who then can be saved?"

[27]Jesus looked at them and said, "With man this is impossible, but not with God; all things are possible with God."

[28]Peter said to him, "We have left everything to follow you!"

[29]"I tell you the truth," Jesus replied, "no one who has left home or brothers or sisters or mother or father or children or fields for me and the gospel [30]will fail to receive a hundred times as much in this present age (homes, brothers, sisters, mothers, children and fields—and with them, persecutions) and in the age to come, eternal life. [31]But many who are first will be last, and the last first."

Jesus Again Predicts His Death

[32]They were on their way up to Jerusalem, with Jesus leading the way, and the disciples were astonished, while those who followed were afraid. Again he took the Twelve aside and told them what was going to happen to him. [33]"We are going up to Jerusalem," he said, "and the Son of Man will be betrayed to the chief priests and teachers of the law. They will condemn him to death and will hand him over to the Gentiles, [34]who will mock him and spit on him, flog him and kill him. Three days later he will rise."

The Request of James and John

[35]Then James and John, the sons of Zebedee, came to him. "Teacher," they said, "we want you to do for us whatever we ask."

[36]"What do you want me to do for you?" he asked.

[37]They replied, "Let one of us sit at your right and the other at your left in your glory."

[38]"You don't know what you are asking," Jesus said. "Can you drink the cup I drink or be baptized with the baptism I am baptized with?"

[39]"We can," they answered.

Jesus said to them, "You will drink the cup I drink and be

---

[m]19 Exodus 20:12-16; Deut. 5:16-20   [n]24 Some manuscripts *is for those who trust in riches*

baptized with the baptism I am baptized with, [40]but to sit at my right or left is not for me to grant. These places belong to those for whom they have been prepared."

[41]When the ten heard about this, they became indignant with James and John. [42]Jesus called them together and said, "You know that those who are regarded as rulers of the Gentiles lord it over them, and their high officials exercise authority over them. [43]Not so with you. Instead, whoever wants to become great among you must be your servant, [44]and whoever wants to be first must be slave of all. [45]For even the Son of Man did not come to be served, but to serve, and to give his life as a ransom for many."

is 10:45 the divine answer to the humanly unanswerable question in 8:37?

REFLECT: **1.** When do you find yourself desiring the first chair in God's orchestra? **2.** How does Jesus' model of a suffering servant influence your life? **3.** What one way could you serve this week?

Blind Bartimaeus Receives His Sight

[46]Then they came to Jericho. As Jesus and his disciples, together with a large crowd, were leaving the city, a blind man, Bartimaeus (that is, the Son of Timaeus), was sitting by the roadside begging. [47]When he heard that it was Jesus of Nazareth, he began to shout, "Jesus, Son of David, have mercy on me!"

[48]Many rebuked him and told him to be quiet, but he shouted all the more, "Son of David, have mercy on me!"

[49]Jesus stopped and said, "Call him."

So they called to the blind man, "Cheer up! On your feet! He's calling you." [50]Throwing his cloak aside, he jumped to his feet and came to Jesus.

[51]"What do you want me to do for you?" Jesus asked him.

The blind man said, "Rabbi, I want to see."

[52]"Go," said Jesus, "your faith has healed you." Immediately he received his sight and followed Jesus along the road.

OPEN: How do you typically respond when a beggar approaches you on the street? Why?

DIG: **1.** What new title does Bartimaeus use for Jesus? What is signifigant about that? **2.** How does the crowd react to Bartimaeus? How does Jesus respond? **3.** What evidence of faith does Bartimaeus display which contributed to his healing? **4.** Why no "order of silence", as in 7:36 or 8:26?

REFLECT: **1.** What has been the greatest miracle in your life? What part did your faith play in this miracle? **2.** If Jesus asked you, "What do you want me to do for you?", what would you say? What would be your part and God's part?

The Triumphal Entry

11 As they approached Jerusalem and came to Bethphage and Bethany at the Mount of Olives, Jesus sent two of his disciples, [2]saying to them, "Go to the village ahead of you, and just as you enter it, you will find a colt tied there, which no one has ever ridden. Untie it and bring it here. [3]If anyone asks you, 'Why are you doing this?' tell him, 'The Lord needs it and will send it back here shortly.' "

[4]They went and found a colt outside in the street, tied at a doorway. As they untied it, [5]some people standing there asked, "What are you doing, untying that colt?" [6]They answered as Jesus had told them to, and the people let them go. [7]When they brought the colt to Jesus and threw their cloaks over it, he sat on it. [8]Many people spread their cloaks on the road, while others spread branches they had cut in the fields. [9]Those who went ahead and those who followed shouted,

"Hosanna![o]"

"Blessed is he who comes in the name of the Lord!"[p]

OPEN: If you were the advance man for the Messiah, what kind of entry would you have planned?

DIG: **1.** How does Jesus identify himself in his request for the colt? In what ways does this request confirm his identity? **2.** How does the manner in which Jesus entered Jerusalem confirm his character? Is this what the multitudes expected? Has Jesus' life and teachings been what the people had expected? **3.** Considering what would happen to Jesus later that week, do you think the multitudes' "hosannas" were more a response of emotional feeling, or a response of true faith? **4.** What do you find most significant about the triumphal entry into Jerusalem?

REFLECT: **1.** Reflect on Jesus' Messiahship. When he rides that colt into your life, how do you respond? What other means had Jesus used to reach you? To humble you? **2.** Have you ever misunderstood Jesus' purposes, praising him one day and despairing the

*o*9 A Hebrew expression meaning "Save!" which became an exclamation of praise; also in verse 10   *p*9 Psalm 118:25,26   *q*17 Isaiah 56:7

next? What was the basis for your misunderstanding? **3.** Where is your "Jerusalem"—the destiny, the fulfillment of your life? Where are you on the road to that destination?

---

[10]"Blessed is the coming kingdom of our father David!"

"Hosanna in the highest!"

[11]Jesus entered Jerusalem and went to the temple. He looked around at everything, but since it was already late, he went out to Bethany with the Twelve.

Jesus Clears the Temple

[12]The next day as they were leaving Bethany, Jesus was hungry. [13]Seeing in the distance a fig tree in leaf, he went to find out if it had any fruit. When he reached it, he found nothing but leaves, because it was not the season for figs. [14]Then he said to the tree, "May no one ever eat fruit from you again." And his disciples heard him say it.

[15]On reaching Jerusalem, Jesus entered the temple area and began driving out those who were buying and selling there. He overturned the tables of the money changers and the benches of those selling doves, [16]and would not allow anyone to carry merchandise through the temple courts. [17]And as he taught them, he said, "Is it not written:

" 'My house will be called
a house of prayer for all nations'*r*?

But you have made it 'a den of robbers.'*'*"

[18]The chief priests and the teachers of the law heard this and began looking for a way to kill him, for they feared him, because the whole crowd was amazed at his teaching.

[19]When evening came, they*s* went out of the city.

The Withered Fig Tree

[20]In the morning, as they went along, they saw the fig tree withered from the roots. [21]Peter remembered and said to Jesus, "Rabbi, look! The fig tree you cursed has withered!"

[22]"Have*t* faith in God," Jesus answered. [23]"I tell you the truth, if anyone says to this mountain, 'Go, throw yourself into the sea,' and does not doubt in his heart but believes that what he says will happen, it will be done for him. [24]Therefore I tell you, whatever you ask for in prayer, believe that you have received it, and it will be yours. [25]And when you stand praying, if you hold anything against anyone, forgive him, so that your Father in heaven may forgive you your sins.*u*"

The Authority of Jesus Questioned

[27]They arrived again in Jerusalem, and while Jesus was walking in the temple courts, the chief priests, the teachers of the law and the elders came to him. [28]"By what authority are you doing these things?" they asked. "And who gave you authority to do this?"

[29]Jesus replied, "I will ask you one question. Answer me, and I will tell you by what authority I am doing these things. [30]John's baptism—was it from heaven, or from men? Tell me!"

---

r17 Jer. 7:11   *s19* Some early manuscripts *he*   *t22* Some early manuscripts *If you have*   *u25* Some manuscripts *sins.* [26]*But if you do not forgive, neither will your Father who is in heaven forgive your sins.*

LOOKING INTO THE SCRIPTURE/25 Minutes. Read Mark 11:12-19 and discuss.

Divide into groups of four or five and share how angry each of the following situations makes you by choosing a number from 1 to 5 (1 being NO SWEAT, 2 being MIFFED, 3 being LOW GROWL, 4 being FLARING NOSTRILS and 5 being BLOOD BOILS)

1	2	3	4	5	Getting the run-around/red tape
1	2	3	4	5	Car boils over during 5 o'clock rush
1	2	3	4	5	Political scandals
1	2	3	4	5	Mistreatment of others/bigotry
1	2	3	4	5	Criticism from your mother
1	2	3	4	5	No time left for yourself/someone intrudes on your time
1	2	3	4	5	Violation of your rights
1	2	3	4	5	God is commercialized
1	2	3	4	5	Sunday morning paper gets wet
1	2	3	4	5	Favorite sweater lost at drycleaners
1	2	3	4	5	Preacher preaches past noon
1	2	3	4	5	Cold food in a restaurant
1	2	3	4	5	Lose money in a vending machine

2. How would you describe the behavior of Jesus in this passage?
   a. politician
   b. umpire
   c. Marine sergeant
   d. pussycat
   e. tyrant
   f. bull in a china shop
   g. county sheriff
   h. superman
   i. bouncer

3. Do you think Jesus overreacted in this situation?   ☐ Yes ☐ No

4. Why did the chief priests and the teachers of the law start looking for a way to kill Jesus?
   a. he intruded on their turf
   b. he threatened their authority
   c. he exposed them as a bunch of thieves
   d. he ruined their business

5. If Jesus came to clean up your town, where would he start?
   a. city hall
   b. high school
   c. porno shops
   d. church
   e. newspapers
   f. your room

MY OWN STORY/20 Minutes. Take a moment and think about your own reaction to social wrongs or abuse.

1. How would you describe your own response to injustice, abuse, or moral corruption?
   a. pussycat
   b. bull in a china shop
   c. politician
   d. pistol-packing mama
   e. the three stooges

2. When are you more likely to get involved or take action?
   a. when my interests are threatened
   b. when my friends are involved
   c. when a moral principle I believe in strongly is involved
   d. when God tells me
   e. when I think I can make a difference

3. What have you found most effective in changing the behavior of society for the good?
   a. appeal to people's sense of fairness
   b. work on changing the heart first
   c. change the law
   d. work quietly behind the scenes
   e. overturning a few tables

4. Where is God calling you now to get involved?
   a. winning people to Christ
   b. reaching leaders in the community
   c. getting involved in community pro-grams to assist the poor, under-privileged, or abused
   d. forming a political action task force

trickery backfire on them?

REFLECT: 1. What do you think is the greater priority in your life—"the praise of men" or the honor of God? **2.** How do you grow to honor God more than your reputation?

OPEN: 1. If you owned a garden or an orchard, what would you grow? **2.** If you had to entrust your business to someone, whom would you choose? Why?

DIG: 1. What does the vineyard represent? Who is the owner? The son? Who are the tenants? The servants? What was Jesus prophesying by telling this story **2.** How does the Scripture Jesus quotes relate to the parable? Who were the builders? Who is the capstone? **3.** What impact did this parable have on its hearers? How did it answer the question about Jesus' authority (Mark 11:28)?

REFLECT: 1. When have you felt greatly rejected? Greatly accepted? Generally, how do you feel: Rejected or accepted? Why? **2.** How do you make Jesus feel welcome in your life each day? What actions of yours might make him feel unwelcome? **3.** Does Jesus seem more like a millstone (weight), or a capstone (one who holds everything together) in your life? Why?

OPEN: When *do* you feel right about paying taxes? For what?

DIG: 1. Why was this trip particularly dangerous? What would have happened if Jesus responded with a simple yes or no answer? **2.** Why do the liberal Herodians (who owed their allegiance to Rome) and the conservative Pharisees make strange partners? How was Jesus a threat to each of these groups? What did Jesus' answer probably do to their partnership? **3.** Why were they amazed at Jesus?

REFLECT: 1. If it's the coin that you give to "Caesar", what do you give to God? What often prevents you from giving to God what is God's? What happens when we hold back? **2.** Would the Church do better than "Caesar" with our taxes? Why?

³¹They discussed it among themselves and said, "If we say, 'From heaven,' he will ask, 'Then why didn't you believe him?' ³²But if we say, 'From men'. . . ." (They feared the people, for everyone held that John really was a prophet.)

³³So they answered Jesus, "We don't know."

Jesus said, "Neither will I tell you by what authority I am doing these things."

The Parable of the Tenants

12 He then began to speak to them in parables: "A man planted a vineyard. He put a wall around it, dug a pit for the winepress and built a watchtower. Then he rented the vineyard to some farmers and went away on a journey. ²At harvest time he sent a servant to the tenants to collect from them some of the fruit of the vineyard. ³But they seized him, beat him and sent him away empty-handed. ⁴Then he sent another servant to them; they struck this man on the head and treated him shamefully. ⁵He sent still another, and that one they killed. He sent many others; some of them they beat, others they killed.

⁶"He had one left to send, a son, whom he loved. He sent him last of all, saying, 'They will respect my son.'

⁷"But the tenants said to one another, 'This is the heir. Come, let's kill him, and the inheritance will be ours.' ⁸So they took him and killed him, and threw him out of the vineyard.

⁹"What then will the owner of the vineyard do? He will come and kill those tenants and give the vineyard to others. ¹⁰Haven't you read this scripture:

" 'The stone the builders rejected
    has become the capstone*ᵛ*;
¹¹the Lord has done this,
    and it is marvelous in our eyes'*ʷ*?"

¹²Then they looked for a way to arrest him because they knew he had spoken the parable against them. But they were afraid of the crowd; so they left him and went away.

Paying Taxes to Caesar

¹³Later they sent some of the Pharisees and Herodians to Jesus to catch him in his words. ¹⁴They came to him and said, "Teacher, we know you are a man of integrity. You aren't swayed by men, because you pay no attention to who they are; but you teach the way of God in accordance with the truth. Is it right to pay taxes to Caesar or not? ¹⁵Should we pay or shouldn't we?"

But Jesus knew their hypocrisy. "Why are you trying to trap me?" he asked. "Bring me a denarius and let me look at it." ¹⁶They brought the coin, and he asked them, "Whose portrait is this? And whose inscription?"

"Caesar's," they replied.

¹⁷Then Jesus said to them, "Give to Caesar what is Caesar's and to God what is God's."

And they were amazed at him.

ᵛ10 Or *cornerstone*   *ʷ11* Psalm 118:22,23

Marriage at the Resurrection

[18]Then the Sadducees, who say there is no resurrection, came to him with a question. [19]"Teacher," they said, "Moses wrote for us that if a man's brother dies and leaves a wife but no children, the man must marry the widow and have children for his brother. [20]Now there were seven brothers. The first one married and died without leaving any children. [21]The second one married the widow, but he also died, leaving no child. It was the same with the third. [22]In fact, none of the seven left any children. Last of all, the woman died too. [23]At the resurrection[x] whose wife will she be, since the seven were married to her?"

[24]Jesus replied, "Are you not in error because you do not know the Scriptures or the power of God? [25]When the dead rise, they will neither marry nor be given in marriage; they will be like the angels in heaven. [26]Now about the dead rising—have you not read in the book of Moses, in the account of the bush, how God said to him, 'I am the God of Abraham, the God of Isaac, and the God of Jacob'[y]? [27]He is not the God of the dead, but of the living. You are badly mistaken!"

The Greatest Commandment

[28]One of the teachers of the law came and heard them debating. Noticing that Jesus had given them a good answer, he asked him, "Of all the commandments, which is the most important?"

[29]"The most important one," answered Jesus, "is this: 'Hear, O Israel, the Lord our God, the Lord is one.[z] [30]Love the Lord your God with all your heart and with all your soul and with all your mind and with all your strength.'[a] [31]The second is this: 'Love your neighbor as yourself.'[b] There is no commandment greater than these."

[32]"Well said, teacher," the man replied. "You are right in saying that God is one and there is no other but him. [33]To love him with all your heart, with all your understanding and with all your strength, and to love your neighbor as yourself is more important than all burnt offerings and sacrifices."

[34]When Jesus saw that he had answered wisely, he said to him, "You are not far from the kingdom of God." And from then on no one dared ask him any more questions.

Whose Son Is the Christ?

[35]While Jesus was teaching in the temple courts, he asked, "How is it that the teachers of the law say that the Christ[c] is the son of David? [36]David himself, speaking by the Holy Spirit, declared:

" 'The Lord said to my Lord:
"Sit at my right hand
until I put your enemies
under your feet." '[d]

OPEN: What aspects of earthly life would you like to see remain the same in heaven?

DIG: 1. Considering their beliefs, why was the Sadducees' question an odd one? Why do you suppose they asked it? **2.** What did Jesus say is the source of the Sadducees' erroneous assumption? **3.** What characterizes "resurrection life"? How does Exodus 3:6 (quoted in verse 26) demonstrate the fact of the resurrection? **4.** What does this story tell us about marriage and its relation to eternity?

REFLECT: 1. What would you like to ask Jesus about heaven? **2.** Which do you know more about—the Scriptures, or the power of God? What are your hopes for growing in the other area?

OPEN: Think of one Bible trivia question that stumps your whole group: What did you come up with?

DIG: 1. Why are these two commandments the greatest? How do the Ten Commandments relate to these two commandments? **2.** How was this teacher's attitude different from that of many others whose questions to Jesus are recorded elsewhere in Mark? What does Jesus' response to this man teach you about Jesus? **3.** Why do you think Jesus' answer silenced his enemies? What else were they thinking but didn't say?

REFLECT: In the three possibilities of love relationships—with God, neighbors, and self—where are you the strongest? The weakest?

OPEN: 1. When you were a child, whom did your parents tell you to "watch out for"? **2.** When have you had the most fun at someone else's expense?

DIG: 1. What was the issue behind Jesus' question in verses 35-37? How will the answer to this one question answer all the others directed at Jesus in Mark 11:27-12:34? **2.** How would you recognize the "strut" of these teachers of the law (vv. 38-40)? By contrast, what does the "strut" of a Christian leader look like (see 10:42-45)? **3.** What "delights" you about this Jesus?

x23 Some manuscripts *resurrection, when men rise from the dead,*   y26 Exodus 3:6
z29 Or *the Lord our God is one Lord*   a30 Deut. 6:4,5   b31 Lev. 19:18
c35 Or *Messiah*   d36 Psalm 110:1

REFLECT: 1. How might showy prayers hurt the purposes of God? 2. What do you think of people who use religion to elevate themselves? 3. Can you think of any time when you did that? 4. What else have you used to evaluate yourself in the marketplace?

OPEN: What do you usually feel when an offering plate is passed?

DIG: What's the point of this comparison? When is "more" actually "less"? When is a "little" a "lot"?

REFLECT: 1. Why do you give to God's work? What do you give besides money? 2. Is it possible to out-give God? How so?

OPEN: 1. If you had to leave this earth tomorrow, what two things would you miss the most? 2. Share one instance when you've been deceived? What were the results?

DIG: 1. Why do you think that Jesus used the discussion about the temple to begin his discourse about the end of the age? What made the temple so significant for the disciples? What would its destruction symbolize for them? 2. Upon hearing this bombshell of news, what two questions do the disciples ask (v. 4)? What events might deceive them into thinking the end times had come (vv. 5-8)? Of what will these events be a sign 3. After that, what things will happen to the disciples and the church (vv. 9-13)? To governors, kings and "all nations"? What comfort and advocate will aid them in their trails to endure? 4. What dreadful event (v. 14; see Daniel 9:276, 11:31, 12:11) will bring "days of distress" unequalled in human history? What deceptive signs will accompany that distress (vv. 21-22)? 5. How will the Son of Man come (vv. 24-27)? 6. How does the "fig tree" lesson (vv. 28-29) answer the disciples' questions from verse 4? 7. What promises does Jesus give in verses 30-31? How would these words have been of comfort to the disciples? Of discomfort? What impact do they have on you, 20 centuries later? 8. How is this prophetic passage capable of multiple fulfillment? What versions in history, in the present, and in the future do you see of these various signs: "Wars and rumors of wars"? Earthquakes and famines? Trials

---

[37]David himself calls him 'Lord.' How then can he be his son?" The large crowd listened to him with delight.

[38]As he taught, Jesus said, "Watch out for the teachers of the law. They like to walk around in flowing robes and be greeted in the marketplaces, [39]and have the most important seats in the synagogues and the places of honor at banquets. [40]They devour widows' houses and for a show make lengthy prayers. Such men will be punished most severely."

The Widow's Offering

[41]Jesus sat down opposite the place where the offerings were put and watched the crowd putting their money into the temple treasury. Many rich people threw in large amounts. [42]But a poor widow came and put in two very small copper coins,[e] worth only a fraction of a penny.[f]

[43]Calling his disciples to him, Jesus said, "I tell you the truth, this poor widow has put more into the treasury than all the others. [44]They all gave out of their wealth; but she, out of her poverty, put in everything—all she had to live on."

Signs of the End of the Age

13 As he was leaving the temple, one of his disciples said to him, "Look, Teacher! What massive stones! What magnificent buildings!"

[2]"Do you see all these great buildings?" replied Jesus. "Not one stone here will be left on another; every one will be thrown down."

[3]As Jesus was sitting on the Mount of Olives opposite the temple, Peter, James, John and Andrew asked him privately, [4]"Tell us, when will these things happen? And what will be the sign that they are all about to be fulfilled?"

[5]Jesus said to them: "Watch out that no one deceives you. [6]Many will come in my name, claiming, 'I am he,' and will deceive many. [7]When you hear of wars and rumors of wars, do not be alarmed. Such things must happen, but the end is still to come. [8]Nation will rise against nation, and kingdom against kingdom. There will be earthquakes in various places, and famines. These are the beginning of birth pains.

[9]"You must be on your guard. You will be handed over to the local councils and flogged in the synagogues. On account of me you will stand before governors and kings as witnesses to them. [10]And the gospel must first be preached to all nations. [11]Whenever you are arrested and brought to trial, do not worry beforehand about what to say. Just say whatever is given you at the time, for it is not you speaking, but the Holy Spirit.

[12]"Brother will betray brother to death, and a father his child. Children will rebel against their parents and have them put to death. [13]All men will hate you because of me, but he who stands firm to the end will be saved.

---

e42 Greek two lepta f42 Greek kodrantes g14 Daniel 9:27; 11:31; 12:11 h14 Or he; also in verse 29

¹⁴"When you see 'the abomination that causes desolation'ⁱ standing where itʰ does not belong—let the reader understand—then let those who are in Judea flee to the mountains. ¹⁵Let no one on the roof of his house go down or enter the house to take anything out. ¹⁶Let no one in the field go back to get his cloak. ¹⁷How dreadful it will be in those days for pregnant women and nursing mothers! ¹⁸Pray that this will not take place in winter, ¹⁹because those will be days of distress unequaled from the beginning, when God created the world, until now—and never to be equaled again. ²⁰If the Lord had not cut short those days, no one would survive. But for the sake of the elect, whom he has chosen, he has shortened them. ²¹At that time if anyone says to you, 'Look, here is the Christⁱ!' or, 'Look, there he is!' do not believe it. ²²For false Christs and false prophets will appear and perform signs and miracles to deceive the elect—if that were possible. ²³So be on your guard; I have told you everything ahead of time.

²⁴"But in those days, following that distress,

" 'the sun will be darkened,
and the moon will not give its light;
²⁵the stars will fall from the sky,
and the heavenly bodies will be shaken.'ʲ

²⁶"At that time men will see the Son of Man coming in clouds with great power and glory. ²⁷And he will send his angels and gather his elect from the four winds, from the ends of the earth to the ends of the heavens.

²⁸"Now learn this lesson from the fig tree: As soon as its twigs get tender and its leaves come out, you know that summer is near. ²⁹Even so, when you see these things happening, you know that it is near, right at the door. ³⁰I tell you the truth, this generationᵏ will certainly not pass away until all these things have happened. ³¹Heaven and earth will pass away, but my words will never pass away.

The Day and Hour Unknown

³²"No one knows about that day or hour, not even the angels in heaven, nor the Son, but only the Father. ³³Be on guard! Be alertˡ! You do not know when that time will come. ³⁴It's like a man going away: He leaves his house and puts his servants in charge, each with his assigned task, and tells the one at the door to keep watch.

³⁵"Therefore keep watch because you do not know when the owner of the house will come back—whether in the evening, or at midnight, or when the rooster crows, or at dawn. ³⁶If he comes suddenly, do not let him find you sleeping. ³⁷What I say to you, I say to everyone: 'Watch!' "

and persecutions? Family divisions? World-wide evangelization? False Christs and false prophets?

REFLECT: 1. What is the most exciting thing about the Second Coming to you? The most distressing? Why? **2.** What questions would you like to ask Jesus about the end times? **3.** When you see biblical prophecy fulfilled in our own day, or when you see the forces of evil apparently winning, how does that make you feel? Do you feel like withdrawing from the battle and perching on your rooftop? Or rolling up your sleeves and getting into the frey?

OPEN: 1. When have you been most surprised: Birthday party? Bachelor's party? Retirement? **2.** Would you like to know the exact date of your death? Why or why not?

DIG: 1. Why do you think the Father has kept the day and the hour secret? **2.** To whom is this warning addressed (v. 37)? How is the warning equally revelant to all generations of Christians?

REFLECT: 1. "Be on guard!", "Be alert!", "Watch!" Specifically, how can you do this? **2.** How would you explain the Second Coming to someone who does not believe in it?

ⁱ21 Or *Messiah*   ʲ25 Isaiah 13:10; 34:4   ᵏ30 Or *race*
ˡ33 Some manuscripts *alert and pray*

OPEN: 1. If you had a year's wages to blow on friends, which would you choose and why: (a) a big party for all, (b) a glorious trip for a few, or (c) an extravagant gift for one? 2. What one gift you received stands out in your memory? Why?

DIG: 1. What was significant about this time of year? How might this cause the fear expressed by Jesus' opponents? 2. How does this woman's action (v. 3) strike you: Thoughtful, but misguided? Tasteful, but extravagant? Wasteful, no buts about it? Honoring to the nth degree? 3. Do you think the perfume could have been spent for better purposes? Why? How was her action justified by Jesus (vv. 6-9)? What does it mean that "she did what she could" (v. 8)? 4. What effect do you think the events in this passage had on Judas' decision in verses 10-11?

REFLECT: 1. What "beautiful thing" (v. 60) would you like to do for Jesus? 2. How do you react when you are rebuked for doing something you know pleases God? 3. For what would you like to be remembered?

OPEN: 1. What is one of your favorite places to eat? What makes it special? 2. As a kid, what were the meal times like? Who sat where around the table? 3. What favorite meal does mom prepare to celebrate your homecoming?

DIG: 1. What is the Feast of Unleavened Bread? How does it fit into the Passover (see Exodus 12)? 2. What is unusual about the disciples' preparations for this meal? Why the secrecy? What risk was involved? 3. What does Jesus say about his betrayers? How do the disciples react to that bombshell news? 4. What new meaning did Jesus give to the Passover bread? The wine? What vow did he make? 5. How much do you think the disciples understood when Jesus spoke about his body and blood? What clue to the meaning of Jesus' death and resurrection would later be provided by reference to the first Passover (see Exodus 12)? 6. Were the disciples singing their last hymn together (v. 26) in a minor key, or a major key? Why do you think so?

REFLECT: 1. How would you have felt if you had been at that meal? How would you have felt if you had foreknowledge of the things to

Jesus Anointed at Bethany

14 Now the Passover and the Feast of Unleavened Bread were only two days away, and the chief priests and the teachers of the law were looking for some sly way to arrest Jesus and kill him. ²"But not during the Feast," they said, "or the people may riot."

³While he was in Bethany, reclining at the table in the home of a man known as Simon the Leper, a woman came with an alabaster jar of very expensive perfume, made of pure nard. She broke the jar and poured the perfume on his head.

⁴Some of those present were saying indignantly to one another, "Why this waste of perfume? ⁵It could have been sold for more than a year's wages ᵐ and the money given to the poor." And they rebuked her harshly.

⁶"Leave her alone," said Jesus. "Why are you bothering her? She has done a beautiful thing to me. ⁷The poor you will always have with you, and you can help them any time you want. But you will not always have me. ⁸She did what she could. She poured perfume on my body beforehand to prepare for my burial. ⁹I tell you the truth, wherever the gospel is preached throughout the world, what she has done will also be told, in memory of her."

¹⁰Then Judas Iscariot, one of the Twelve, went to the chief priests to betray Jesus to them. ¹¹They were delighted to hear this and promised to give him money. So he watched for an opportunity to hand him over.

The Lord's Supper

¹²On the first day of the Feast of Unleavened Bread, when it was customary to sacrifice the Passover lamb, Jesus' disciples asked him, "Where do you want us to go and make preparations for you to eat the Passover?"

¹³So he sent two of his disciples, telling them, "Go into the city, and a man carrying a jar of water will meet you. Follow him. ¹⁴Say to the owner of the house he enters, 'The Teacher asks: Where is my guest room, where I may eat the Passover with my disciples?' ¹⁵He will show you a large upper room, furnished and ready. Make preparations for us there."

¹⁶The disciples left, went into the city and found things just as Jesus had told them. So they prepared the Passover.

¹⁷When evening came, Jesus arrived with the Twelve. ¹⁸While they were reclining at the table eating, he said, "I tell you the truth, one of you will betray me—one who is eating with me."

¹⁹They were saddened, and one by one they said to him, "Surely not I?"

²⁰"It is one of the Twelve," he replied, "one who dips bread into the bowl with me. ²¹The Son of Man will go just as it is written about him. But woe to that man who betrays the Son of Man! It would be better for him if he had not been born."

²²While they were eating, Jesus took bread, gave thanks and broke it, and gave it to his disciples, saying, "Take it; this is my body."

ᵐ5 Greek *than three hundred denarii*

LOOKING INTO THE SCRIPTURE/20 Minutes. Read Mark 14:1-11 and discuss.

1. When you want to give a special gift to someone you love, which kind of thing do you look for?

Totally frivolous . . . . Very practical
Something I like . . . . Something she/he would like
Expensive . . . . Inexpensive, but creative
Something you use . . . . Something you look at
Responding to current need . . . . Anticipating future need

2. Why do you think the woman spent a year's wages on perfume?
   a. to express devotion to Jesus
   b. to show off
   c. to get to heaven
   d. on an impulse

3. Why were Jesus' friends so upset?
   a. she crashed the party
   b. she wasted money
   c. she made everybody look cheap
   d. she was a known prostitute
   e. she was a little weird

4. If you had been one of the disciples, what would you have said to the woman?
   a. let's save the money for the poor
   b. do what you want—it's your money
   c. what a waste
   d. beat it!

5. What was the motive of the people who criticized the woman?
   a. concern for the poor
   b. greed
   c. jealousy toward the woman
   d. hope of embarrassing Jesus

6. What was Jesus really saying when he defended the action of the woman?
   a. extravagance is okay
   b. her motive made it okay
   c. don't worry about the poor
   d. don't judge another's motives

7. For Judas, this was the last straw. Why?
   a. Jesus fraternized with a woman
   b. Jesus didn't care about the poor
   c. Jesus predicted his own death
   d. Jesus thought himself pretty important

MY OWN STORY/20 Minutes. Read the Scripture again and share your experience.

1. When you spend money on another person, what concerns you?
   a. can I afford it?
   b. am I buying a friendship?
   c. will it do some good?
   d. will that person feel obligated to return with a similar gift?
   e. have I spent enough to show my feelings are serious?
   f. will s/he like what I got?
   g. should I have given this to someone else?

2. What is the biggest problem you have in making money decisions?
   a. never enough to go around
   b. no financial plan
   c. no clear priorities
   d. too many credit cards

3. If you had ten times the amount of money you now have to give away, would you do a better job with your giving?
   a. I would like to think so
   b. I would sure try
   c. probably not
   d. ask me tomorrow

4. When it comes to giving money, what factors do you consider?
   a. IRS deduction
   b. how great the need is
   c. how will it be used
   d. what others will think
   e. my commitment to that cause

come? Would you then try to stop the betrayer or Jesus? Why or why not? **2.** What is your focus when you partake of Communion? Why is the Communion celebration important to the body of believers?

OPEN: What is the boldest claim you ever made and couldn't back up?

DIG: 1. How does Peter see himself in relation to the other disciples? How do you think this makes the other disciples feel? **2.** Why do you think Jesus felt the need to inform the disciples (especially Peter) of their upcoming denial? What purpose did this prediction serve?

REFLECT: As Jesus knows your weaknesses and failures too, how does that make you feel? Why?

OPEN: Where do you go, or what do you do, when you're facing difficult situations? Do you prefer to be alone at these times, or in the company of close friends?

DIG: 1. Why do you think Jesus took Peter, James and John along with him to pray? **2.** Why don't the disciples share Jesus' sense of urgency? How does this relate to their statements in the previous passage? **3.** What did Jesus desire most of all? Yet how did he pray? Why? **4.** Why did Jesus specifically urge Peter to "watch and pray"? **5.** What was the most important thing you learned about Jesus from the Gethsemane story?

REFLECT: 1. When, if ever, have you faced a "Gethsemane"? What happened? **2.** What should determine for whom and what you pray? How will the Gethsemane story change the way you pray this week?

OPEN: Who would you call first if you were arrested?

DIG: 1. Who leads the lynch mob? Why so many and armed? What do they fear (v. 48)? What does this tell you about Judas' misunderstanding of Jesus' mission? **2.** Why was the anticipated rebellion a false alarm? What Scriptures were fulfilled (see Isaiah 53:7-8)? **3.** How do you account for the disciples' reactions in verses 47,50,51?

²³Then he took the cup, gave thanks and offered it to them, and they all drank from it.

²⁴"This is my blood of the *n* covenant, which is poured out for many," he said to them. ²⁵"I tell you the truth, I will not drink again of the fruit of the vine until that day when I drink it anew in the kingdom of God."

²⁶When they had sung a hymn, they went out to the Mount of Olives.

Jesus Predicts Peter's Denial

²⁷"You will all fall away," Jesus told them, "for it is written:

> " 'I will strike the shepherd,
>   and the sheep will be scattered.'*o*

²⁸But after I have risen, I will go ahead of you into Galilee."
²⁹Peter declared, "Even if all fall away, I will not."
³⁰"I tell you the truth," Jesus answered, "today—yes, tonight—before the rooster crows twice*p* you yourself will disown me three times."
³¹But Peter insisted emphatically, "Even if I have to die with you, I will never disown you." And all the others said the same.

Gethsemane

³²They went to a place called Gethsemane, and Jesus said to his disciples, "Sit here while I pray." ³³He took Peter, James and John along with him, and he began to be deeply distressed and troubled. ³⁴"My soul is overwhelmed with sorrow to the point of death," he said to them. "Stay here and keep watch."

³⁵Going a little farther, he fell to the ground and prayed that if possible the hour might pass from him. ³⁶"*Abba,q* Father," he said, "everything is possible for you. Take this cup from me. Yet not what I will, but what you will."

³⁷Then he returned to his disciples and found them sleeping. "Simon," he said to Peter, "are you asleep? Could you not keep watch for one hour? ³⁸Watch and pray so that you will not fall into temptation. The spirit is willing, but the body is weak."

³⁹Once more he went away and prayed the same thing. ⁴⁰When he came back, he again found them sleeping, because their eyes were heavy. They did not know what to say to him.

⁴¹Returning the third time, he said to them, "Are you still sleeping and resting? Enough! The hour has come. Look, the Son of Man is betrayed into the hands of sinners. ⁴²Rise! Let us go! Here comes my betrayer!"

Jesus Arrested

⁴³Just as he was speaking, Judas, one of the Twelve, appeared. With him was a crowd armed with swords and clubs, sent from the chief priests, the teachers of the law, and the elders.

⁴⁴Now the betrayer had arranged a signal with them: "The one I kiss is the man; arrest him and lead him away under guard." ⁴⁵Going at once to Jesus, Judas said, "Rabbi!" and

---

n24 Some manuscripts *the new* manuscripts do not have *twice.*   *o27* Zech. 13:7   *p30* Some early   *q36* Aramaic for *Father*

LOOKING INTO THE SCRIPTURE/20 Minutes. Read Mark 14:32-42 and share.

1. If you knew that you had only a few days to live, what would you do with the time? Choose three.

□ not tell anyone
□ straighten out my affairs
□ throw a big party
□ spend time with loved ones
□ write all my friends
□ have as much fun as possible
□ plan my funeral
□ isolate myself from everyone
□ give away all my possessions

□ travel around
□ offer myself for science
□ spend time with God
□ reminisce with my old buddies
□ go fishing
□ do what I've always wanted to do
□ gamble everything in Las Vegas
□ do nothing different
□ call friends and family to say "Good-by"

2. Why did Jesus take Peter, James, and John along with him?
   a. he needed their fellowship
   b. to test their endurance
   c. to experience his grief so they could write about it
   d. to pray for him

3. From Jesus' perspective, what was the test?
   a. to do God's will or his own
   b. to take the easy way out
   c. to keep his emotions from showing
   d. to say "no" to Satan

4. For the disciples, what was the test?
   a. to stay awake and pray
   b. to be present with Jesus in his agony
   c. to keep from giving advice
   d. to watch Jesus suffer

5. From the standpoint of God, the Father, what was the test?
   a. to stand by and let his Son make the decision
   b. to call off the mission and save his Son
   c. to keep from lashing out against Satan
   d. to stick to the game plan for saving mankind from judgment

---

MY OWN STORY/40 Minutes.

1. With what decision are you struggling at the moment?
   a. what to do with my life
   b. what does God want
   c. should I make a change in job
   d. how can I improve my marriage
   e. what should I do for my kids
   f. how can I make Christ a part of my lifestyle
   g. how can I get out of the mess I'm in
   h. how can I be a Christian and a success

2. Where are you now in this decision?
   a. still praying about it
   b. torn between several alternatives
   c. waiting on a phone call from God
   d. starting to act on my decision
   e. just barely coping
   f. not sure God is listening

3. What is harder for you?
   a. to struggle to know God's will
   b. to do what I know God wants
   c. to go through this struggle with someone I love
   d. to keep open and available to God for change of direction

4. Who do you call on when you need help in knowing God's will?
   a. no one but God
   b. someone who will listen and not give advice
   c. someone who has been through struggles
   d. someone completely objective
   e. someone good at giving advice

5. How do you know when you've identified God's will for you?
   a. I feel peaceful about the decision
   b. My friends agree with my decision
   c. Scripture tells me what is God's will in this situation
   d. Circumstances work out according to God's will
   e. I'm not sure I ever really know God's will
   f. In hindsight I can see what God's will was

REFLECT: 1. In times of provocation and crises, how do you respond: (a) Like the impulsive disciple, with sword in hand? or (b) Like the pacifist Jesus, with Scriptures in hand? or (c) Like the streaking disciple, with sword, Scriptures and clothes left behind? **2.** What empathy do you have for Judas Iscariot? How do you think he felt? Why do you think he did what he did?

OPEN: Who is your favorite lawyer or law enforcement officer on television? Why?

DIG: 1. What does the fact that Peter has followed Jesus, but at a distance, tell you about Peter's character? **2.** What sort of evidence do the chief priests initially seek against Jesus? Why do you think that Jesus, for the most part, remained silent? **3.** On what evidence is the final decision against Jesus based? Why would the chief priests feel that Jesus had committed blasphemy? **4.** What is the significance of Jesus' Messianic acknowledgement, the first direct confession recorded in Mark (v. 62; see Ps. 110:1 and Dn. 7:13)? **5.** How seriously would a charge of blasphemy be taken by the Roman authorities (see 15:14)? How does this present a problem for the Jewish authorities who jealously oppose Jesus?

REFLECT: 1. Contrast Jesus' behavior with that of the priests, elders and teachers? What does this say about the character of each? **2.** What type of situations are best handled silently? When is it best to speak up for yourself? What could a good defense attorney have done for Jesus? **3.** Like the Sanhedrin, how often do you make hasty judgments based on vested interests and conflicting testimony?

OPEN: What is a moment in your life in which you where most disappointed in yourself?

DIG: 1. Peter is brave enough to follow Jesus to the high priest's house. Why do you think he now denies Christ? Do you think he realized what he was doing? Why? When did it finally "dawn" on him? **2.** How were the three accusations and denials similar? Different? **3.** In retrospect (see 14:29-31), how does Peter feel? **4.** Do you think the situation would have been different

kissed him. [46]The men seized Jesus and arrested him. [47]Then one of those standing near drew his sword and struck the servant of the high priest, cutting off his ear.

[48]"Am I leading a rebellion," said Jesus, "that you have come out with swords and clubs to capture me? [49]Every day I was with you, teaching in the temple courts, and you did not arrest me. But the Scriptures must be fulfilled." [50]Then everyone deserted him and fled.

[51]A young man, wearing nothing but a linen garment, was following Jesus. When they seized him, [52]he fled naked, leaving his garment behind.

Before the Sanhedrin

[53]They took Jesus to the high priest, and all the chief priests, elders and teachers of the law came together. [54]Peter followed him at a distance, right into the courtyard of the high priest. There he sat with the guards and warmed himself at the fire.

[55]The chief priests and the whole Sanhedrin were looking for evidence against Jesus so that they could put him to death, but they did not find any. [56]Many testified falsely against him, but their statements did not agree.

[57]Then some stood up and gave this false testimony against him: [58]"We heard him say, 'I will destroy this man-made temple and in three days will build another, not made by man.'" [59]Yet even then their testimony did not agree.

[60]Then the high priest stood up before them and asked Jesus, "Are you not going to answer? What is this testimony that these men are bringing against you?" [61]But Jesus remained silent and gave no answer.

Again the high priest asked him, "Are you the Christ,[r] the Son of the Blessed One?"

[62]"I am," said Jesus. "And you will see the Son of Man sitting at the right hand of the Mighty One and coming on the clouds of heaven."

[63]The high priest tore his clothes. "Why do we need any more witnesses?" he asked. [64]"You have heard the blasphemy. What do you think?"

They all condemned him as worthy of death. [65]Then some began to spit at him; they blindfolded him, struck him with their fists, and said, "Prophesy!" And the guards took him and beat him.

Peter Disowns Jesus

[66]While Peter was below in the courtyard, one of the servant girls of the high priest came by. [67]When she saw Peter warming himself, she looked closely at him.

"You also were with that Nazarene, Jesus," she said.

[68]But he denied it. "I don't know or understand what you're talking about," he said, and went out into the entryway.[s]

[69]When the servant girl saw him there, she said again to those standing around, "This fellow is one of them." [70]Again he denied it.

[r]61 Or Messiah   [s]68 Some early manuscripts *entryway and the rooster crowed*

After a little while, those standing near said to Peter, "Surely you are one of them, for you are a Galilean."

[71]He began to call down curses on himself, and he swore to them, "I don't know this man you're talking about."

[72]Immediately the rooster crowed the second time.' Then Peter remembered the word Jesus had spoken to him: "Before the rooster crows twice" you will disown me three times." And he broke down and wept.

Jesus Before Pilate

15 Very early in the morning, the chief priests, with the elders, the teachers of the law and the whole Sanhedrin, reached a decision. They bound Jesus, led him away and handed him over to Pilate.

[2]"Are you the king of the Jews?" asked Pilate.

"Yes, it is as you say," Jesus replied.

[3]The chief priests accused him of many things. [4]So again Pilate asked him, "Aren't you going to answer? See how many things they are accusing you of."

[5]But Jesus still made no reply, and Pilate was amazed.

[6]Now it was the custom at the Feast to release a prisoner whom the people requested. [7]A man called Barabbas was in prison with the insurrectionists who had committed murder in the uprising. [8]The crowd came up and asked Pilate to do for them what he usually did.

[9]"Do you want me to release to you the king of the Jews?" asked Pilate, [10]knowing it was out of envy that the chief priests had handed Jesus over to him. [11]But the chief priests stirred up the crowd to have Pilate release Barabbas instead.

[12]"What shall I do, then, with the one you call the king of the Jews?" Pilate asked them.

[13]"Crucify him!" they shouted.

[14]"Why? What crime has he committed?" asked Pilate.

But they shouted all the louder, "Crucify him!"

[15]Wanting to satisfy the crowd, Pilate released Barabbas to them. He had Jesus flogged, and handed him over to be crucified.

The Soldiers Mock Jesus

[16]The soldiers led Jesus away into the palace (that is, the Praetorium) and called together the whole company of soldiers. [17]They put a purple robe on him, then twisted together a crown of thorns and set it on him. [18]And they began to call out to him, "Hail, king of the Jews!" [19]Again and again they struck him on the head with a staff and spit on him. Falling on their knees, they paid homage to him. [20]And when they had mocked him, they took off the purple robe and put his own clothes on him. Then they led him out to crucify him.

'72 Some early manuscripts do not have *the second time*.   "72 Some early manuscripts do not have *twice*.

---

if Peter heeded Jesus' command to "watch and pray" (14:38)? Why?

REFLECT: 1. When, if ever, have you felt that your failures had made it impossible for Christ ever to use you again? **2.** What "rooster" reminds you of failure and guilt? What helps them?

OPEN: 1. As a kid, would you rather have been punished by mom or dad? Why? **2.** Today, would you rather be judged by a church body or a civil court? Why?

DIG: 1. What insights into Pilate's and Jesus' character does this story offer? Why is Pilate indecisive? Why is Jesus silent? How do those two character traits interplay here? **2.** What insights into people does this stroy offer? Why do the people, after witnessing Jesus' miracles, hearing his teachings and praising him with hosannas, now demand that Jesus be crucified? **3.** Why does Pilate grant their request: Out of concern for justice? Or peace-at-any-price? **4.** What insights into the gospel do you see in the release of Barabbus in exchange for Jesus (see 8:37, 10:45)?

REFLECT: 1. In family squabbles, how are you like Pilate, selling short your convictions in exchange for peace? Give an example. **2.** In other respects, how are you like Jesus, consistently matching your actions with your convictions, never mind the consequences to yourself? Give an example. **3.** In what sense are you like Barabbus?

OPEN: What brutal mockery have you witnessed or read about? How did it make you feel toward the person mocked? What, if anything, did you do?

DIG: What mental, physical and emotional brutality do the soldiers inflict on Jesus? Why? Does their mockery stem from fear, anger, unbelief, or what?

REFLECT: 1. Why did Jesus go through this trial and torture when he could easily have used his great powers and escaped? How does this make you feel? What does it make you want to do? **2.** Have your actions ever mocked the name of Jesus? What can you do to help resist this kind of behavior?

OPEN: Have you ever sat with someone who was dying? What was it like?

DIG: 1. Who carries the cross for Jesus? How is he "recruited"? Why couldn't Jesus carry it (see 14:65, 15:15, 19)? **2.** What kinds of people were usually crucified (v. 27)? How is Jesus like them? **3.** What further insults are added to injury (vv. 29-32)? **4.** What supreme irony do you see here: In the places occupied by the robbers (see 10:37)? In the call for Jesus to save himself by coming down from the cross? In the officially posted reason for Jesus' death?

REFLECT: 1. When did you realize the full meaning of Christ's death? **3.** Read Isaiah 53:12. How does Jesus count in your life? How does this affect the way you live your life?

OPEN: Other than Jesus, which other death has affected you personally in the deepest way? Why?

DIG: 1. What aspect of the crucifixion was the worst for Jesus: The physical pain? Or the spiritual separation? Why? **2.** What causes his separation from the Father (who cannot look upon sin, Hab. 1:13)? What does this fact say about our part in his crucifixion? **3.** What indicates that Jesus' death was a voluntary act, preceeding the time when natural causes would have been fatal (vv. 37, 39, 44)? **4.** What does the iron curtain of the temple indicate (see Heb. 10:19ff)? **5.** Why do you think that only women are mentioned in verses 40-41?

REFLECT: How difficult is it for you to fathom the cross? How could a loving God abandon his obedient Son? And for *my* sins?

OPEN: What do you feel down deep at funerals and burials you've attended?

DIG: 1. Who buries Jesus? What do you learn about him here? What risks does a man of his stature take by asking for the body of a condemned criminal? Might he have also given Jesus his own grave site? Why do you think so? **2.** What is signifigant about the fact that the centurion confirms Jesus' death? The fact that there were eyewitnesses of his burial (see Mt. 28:11-15)?

The Crucifixion

[21]A certain man from Cyrene, Simon, the father of Alexander and Rufus, was passing by on his way in from the country, and they forced him to carry the cross. [22]They brought Jesus to the place called Golgotha (which means The Place of the Skull). [23]Then they offered him wine mixed with myrrh, but he did not take it. [24]And they crucified him. Dividing up his clothes, they cast lots to see what each would get.

[25]It was the third hour when they crucified him. [26]The written notice of the charge against him read: THE KING OF THE JEWS. [27]They crucified two robbers with him, one on his right and one on his left. [v] [29]Those who passed by hurled insults at him, shaking their heads and saying, "So! You who are going to destroy the temple and build it in three days, [30]come down from the cross and save yourself!"

[31]In the same way the chief priests and the teachers of the law mocked him among themselves. "He saved others," they said, "but he can't save himself! [32]Let this Christ, [w]this King of Israel, come down now from the cross, that we may see and believe." Those crucified with him also heaped insults on him.

The Death of Jesus

[33]At the sixth hour darkness came over the whole land until the ninth hour. [34]And at the ninth hour Jesus cried out in a loud voice, *"Eloi, Eloi, lama sabachthani?"*—which means, "My God, my God, why have you forsaken me?"[x]

[35]When some of those standing near heard this, they said, "Listen, he's calling Elijah."

[36]One man ran, filled a sponge with wine vinegar, put it on a stick, and offered it to Jesus to drink. "Now leave him alone. Let's see if Elijah comes to take him down," he said.

[37]With a loud cry, Jesus breathed his last.

[38]The curtain of the temple was torn in two from top to bottom. [39]And when the centurion, who stood there in front of Jesus, heard his cry and[y] saw how he died, he said, "Surely this man was the Son[z] of God!"

[40]Some women were watching from a distance. Among them were Mary Magdalene, Mary the mother of James the younger and of Joses, and Salome. [41]In Galilee these women had followed him and cared for his needs. Many other women who had come up with him to Jerusalem were also there.

The Burial of Jesus

[42]It was Preparation Day (that is, the day before the Sabbath). So as evening approached, [43]Joseph of Arimathea, a prominent member of the Council, who was himself waiting for the kingdom of God, went boldly to Pilate and asked for Jesus' body. [44]Pilate was surprised to hear that he was already dead. Summoning the centurion, he asked him if Jesus had already died. [45]When he learned from the centurion that it was so, he gave the

---

[v]27 Some manuscripts *left,* [28]*and the scripture was fulfilled which says, "He was counted with the lawless ones"* (Isaiah 53:12)   [w]32 Or *Messiah*   [x]34 Psalm 22:1   [y]39 Some manuscripts do not have *heard his cry and.*   [z]39 Or *a son*

body to Joseph. ⁴⁶So Joseph bought some linen cloth, took down the body, wrapped it in the linen, and placed it in a tomb cut out of rock. Then he rolled a stone against the entrance of the tomb. ⁴⁷Mary Magdalene and Mary the mother of Joses saw where he was laid.

The Resurrection

16 When the Sabbath was over, Mary Magdalene, Mary the mother of James, and Salome bought spices so that they might go to anoint Jesus' body. ²Very early on the first day of the week, just after sunrise, they were on their way to the tomb ³and they asked each other, "Who will roll the stone away from the entrance of the tomb?"

⁴But when they looked up, they saw that the stone, which was very large, had been rolled away. ⁵As they entered the tomb, they saw a young man dressed in a white robe sitting on the right side, and they were alarmed.

⁶"Don't be alarmed," he said. "You are looking for Jesus the Nazarene, who was crucified. He has risen! He is not here. See the place where they laid him. ⁷But go, tell his disciples and Peter, 'He is going ahead of you into Galilee. There you will see him, just as he told you.'"

⁸Trembling and bewildered, the women went out and fled from the tomb. They said nothing to anyone, because they were afraid.

[The most reliable early manuscripts and other ancient witnesses do not have Mark 16:9-20.]

⁹When Jesus rose early on the first day of the week, he appeared first to Mary Magdalene, out of whom he had driven seven demons. ¹⁰She went and told those who had been with him and who were mourning and weeping. ¹¹When they heard that Jesus was alive and that she had seen him, they did not believe it.

¹²Afterward Jesus appeared in a different form to two of them while they were walking in the country. ¹³These returned and reported it to the rest; but they did not believe them either.

¹⁴Later Jesus appeared to the Eleven as they were eating; he rebuked them for their lack of faith and their stubborn refusal to believe those who had seen him after he had risen.

¹⁵He said to them, "Go into all the world and preach the good news to all creation. ¹⁶Whoever believes and is baptized will be saved, but whoever does not believe will be condemned. ¹⁷And these signs will accompany those who believe: In my name they will drive out demons; they will speak in new tongues; ¹⁸they will pick up snakes with their hands; and when they drink deadly poison, it will not hurt them at all; they will place their hands on sick people, and they will get well."

¹⁹After the Lord Jesus had spoken to them, he was taken up into heaven and he sat at the right hand of God. ²⁰Then the disciples went out and preached everywhere, and the Lord worked with them and confirmed his word by the signs that accompanied it.

REFLECT: 1. What is the riskiest thing you have ever done because of your faith in Jesus? Why did you do it? What were the results? **2.** In what area of your Christian life do you need to be bolder?

OPEN: 1. What's the first thing you do on Sunday morning? Where do you go to read? **2.** When visiting the grave of a friend, flowers in hand, you find the gravestone missing, what do you conclude?

DIG: 1. Why do you think the women go to the tomb on the day and at the time they do? What does this say about them? Where have their thoughts been since Friday? **2.** What potential problem looms ahead? Instead, what do they find? What do they fear? Seeing the empty tomb and the man sitting beside it, what thoughts are racing through their heads? **3.** Do you think they believed the man's words? How do their actions support your answer? **4.** Why do you think the angel specifically asked them to speak to Peter? What does this tell you about Jesus' desires for Peter?

REFLECT: 1. Would you have had trouble believing the angel's words? Why or why not? **2.** Who did Jesus send to you to tell you he had risen? Did you have trouble believing that person? How were you finally convinced of Jesus' resurrection? **3.** To whom is Jesus sending you with this message? How will you accomplish this mission? **4.** Where is your spiritual life focused these days: On Good Friday? Easter Sunday? Or in between? **5.** What will you remember most from the gospel of Mark to resharpen your focus on who this Jesus really is?

LUKE

INTRODUCTION

Author

Although no author is named in the third Gospel, there is a tradition dating from the second century that Luke was the writer. There is good ground to accept Luke as author simply because he was *not* an apostle, nor was he particularly famous in the first-century church. In fact, he was a Gentile — the only non-Jewish author in the New Testament. Therefore, it is highly unlikely that anyone would have attached his name to this gospel had he not actually written it.

Internal evidence supports the testimony of tradition. For one thing, it is clear that the same man wrote both the third Gospel and the Book of Acts. Both books are dedicated to Theophilus. The books are similar in style, language, and interests. The author of Acts begins by saying, "In my former book," which is surely the Gospel. Since Acts was traditionally associated with Luke, the evidence that both books came from the same pen strengthens the tradition that Luke wrote the gospel bearing his name.

It is also interesting to note that the author of the third Gospel uses the language we would expect from a doctor (Luke was a physician). He describes illnesses with more precision than is found in Matthew and Mark (4:38; 5:12). He also omits the comment in Mark 5:26 that the woman who was subject to bleeding "had suffered a great deal under the care of many doctors and had spent all she had, yet instead of getting better she grew worse." Professional ethics prevailed in that day as well as in our own!

Little is known about Luke from the New Testament except that he was a doctor beloved by Paul (Col. 4:14) and that he was a coworker with Paul (2 Tim. 4:11; Philem. 24). However, in the Book of Acts, Luke describes experiences he shared while traveling with Paul (in the so-called *we* passages), though even here it is Paul, not Luke, who is front and center. One early non-canonical document the *Prologue to Luke* states that Luke was a physician, that he was unmarried and childless, and that he died at the age of 84. Beyond this, we know Luke only through his two eloquent documents published in the New Testament.

Date

There is no strong evidence as to when Luke's gospel was written. Many scholars date it between A.D. 75 and 85, although this is by no means conclusive. In fact, since Acts ends with Paul awaiting trial in Rome (probably before A.D. 67), if Luke wrote his gospel before he wrote Acts, then a date in the early sixties is likely.

Audience

Luke was a Gentile who wrote the story of Jesus for other Gentiles. This fact about the third Gospel gives it its distinctive flavor. The Gentile character of the manuscript begins in the preface, in which Luke dedicates the book to Theophilus, probably a high-ranking Roman government official (this title "most excellent" was normally reserved for such officials). Luke then dates the conception and birth of John the Baptist and Jesus with reference to the Roman rulers governing at the time (1:5; 2:1-2). Throughout the book, Luke makes a habit of translating Hebrew words into their Greek equivalents so that his Gentile readers will understand. For example, Luke never refers to Jesus as "Rabbi," the Hebrew title for a teacher, but always by the Greek equivalent, "Master." Luke identifies the place where Jesus was crucified not as *Golgotha*, its Hebrew name, but as *Kranion*, the Greek equivalent for "the place of the skull."

The Gentile character of the third Gospel is also seen in its identification of Jesus' lineage. Luke traces him back to Adam, the founder of the human race, and not, as Matthew does, back to Abraham, the founder of the Jewish race. Also in contrast to Matthew, Luke seldom quotes the Old Testament or demonstrates how Jesus fulfills Old Testament prophecy. This is a Gentile book about the Jewish Messiah who died for the whole world.

Characteristics

Luke's account of the life of Jesus is a unique document. For one thing, it is the longest book in the New Testament. Therefore, it contains more information about Jesus than any other book in the Bible. For another thing, Luke's gospel is extraordinarily joyful. It begins and ends with rejoicing (1:46-47 and 24:52-53), and in the account itself, Luke uses the words "joy" (6:23), "laughter" (6:21), and "celebration" (15:23, 32). Luke is also the only writer to record the four great canticles of joy and worship: *Magnificat* (1:46-55), *Benedictus* (1:68-79), *Gloria in Excelsis* (2:4), and *Nunc Dimittis* (2:29-32).

Why is Luke so filled with joy? He is overwhelmed with the thought that Jesus is the Savior of the whole world. He is astonished that Jesus came to seek and to save not just his kinsfolk, the Jews, but all people regardless of race, age, or culture.

Jesus came, for example, for the Gentiles. This is clear in Luke's gospel. In Luke, we hear Simeon prophesy that Jesus will be "a light for revelation to the Gentiles" (2:32). We hear Jesus praise the widow in Zarephath and Naaman the Syrian, two Gentiles whose stories are told in the Old Testament (4:25-27), and we hear Jesus single out the faith of a Roman centurion as an example of how people should respond to him (7:9).

Jesus came even for the hated Samaritans. As we see in the parable of the Good Samaritan (10:25-37), he places them on a par with the Jews in regard to God's kingdom. Luke has a lot to say about social outcasts in general. Women, children, and the poor—often treated badly by first-century society—are treated with special compassion by Luke. It is not accidental that Luke alone recounts the birth narratives from *Mary's* point of view. Luke mentions thirteen women not named in other gospel accounts. His special concern for children is clearly seen in his careful record of Jesus' childhood; Luke is the only gospel writer to record this information. As for the poor, Luke makes it clear that Jesus came to minister to them (4:18; 7:22; see also 1:53; 6:30; 14:11-13; 21; 16:19-31). Luke also takes great pains to warn about the danger of riches (1:53; 6:24; 12:1-34; 16:1-31; 18:18-30; 19:1-10; 21:1-4). From Luke's perspective, then, it does not matter who you are—you are welcome in God's kingdom. How well this is expressed in the beloved parable of the Prodigal Son (15:11-32), which occurs only in Luke's gospel. In Jesus' own words: "People will come from east and west and north and south, and will take their places at the feast in the kingdom of God" (13:29).

In addition to Luke's universality (Christ has come for all people) and his fascination with people (especially the outcasts), several other themes distinguish Luke. For example, Luke records more of Jesus' teaching about prayer than is found anywhere else in the Bible. He records nine of Jesus' own prayers. Luke also has more to say than the other gospels about the Holy Spirit (4:1, 14; 10:21; 24:49). He will pick up and expand on this emphasis of the Holy Spirit's active ministry in the companion volume to the third Gospel, the Book of Acts.

Structure

Luke was obviously well-educated, as we would expect a doctor to be. His training is reflected in his style.

Language

His prologue (1:1-4) is a fine example of first-rate classical Greek. Luke is capable of this quality of writing. The rest of chapters 1 and 2, however, have a strong Jewish flavor to them, almost as if Luke is translating from Jewish sources as he describes Jesus' birth and infancy. Then in chapter 3 he begins to write in the language of the people—good *koine* (popular) Greek.

Historical Detail

Luke writes very carefully. As he indicates in the prologue, his aim is to produce "an orderly account" (1: 3), which is exactly what he does. This book gives evidence of his meticulous research. For example, he dates the beginning of John the Baptist's ministry by reference to *six* historical facts (3:1-2). Another example of Luke's care as a historian is his practice of stating the exact titles of various Roman officials, even though these were notoriously difficult to get straight. Sir William Ramsay, the famous British scholar, once undertook to reseach the accuracy of Luke's writing. When he began he thought that Luke was a poor historian. His research, however, convinced him that exactly the opposite was true. He wrote:

> No writer is correct by mere chance: or accurate sporadically. He is accurate by virtue of a certain habit of mind. Some men are accurate by nature: a permissible view that a writer is accurate occasionally and inaccurate in other parts of his work which is produced by his moral and intellectual character. . . . The present writer takes the view that Luke's history is unsurpassed in respect of its trustworthiness. (W. Ramsay, *The Bearing of Recent Discovery on the Trustworthiness of the New Testament,* p. 80).

Zest

Yet for all the author's care and meticulous nature, Luke's gospel is no dry, pedantic document. It sparkles with life and vitality. Luke's portraits of people are particularly vivid and compassionate. People like Zacchaeus and Cleopas, Mary and Martha, Elizabeth and Mary the mother of Jesus all spring to life through his talented pen. Luke's gospel tells a rare and unforgettable story.

Outline

Luke's prologue to Theophilus (1:1-4) is followed by the comparatively long infancy narratives (1:5-2:52). Jesus' baptism and temptations are presented in the section on his preparation for ministry (3:1-4:13). Next come three sections on Jesus' ministry, divided according to location: ministry in Galilee (4:14-9:50), from Galilee to Jerusalem (9:51-19:44), and ministry in Jerusalem (19:45-21:38). Luke's gospel concludes with an account of Jesus' death and resurrection (22:1-24; 53).

Overview Study Questions

1. Write a short biography of Luke using the references found in the New Testament. These include three from Paul's writings (Col. 4:14; 2 Tim. 4:11; Philem. 24) and the so-called "we-sections" in Acts, when Luke accompanied Paul (Acts 16:10-17; 20:5-21:18; 27:1-28:16).
2. Skim through Luke, using the outline above to guide you. What themes do you detect? What are the major points Luke makes about Jesus?
3. Luke's account contains four great canticles (hymns) of praise. These have often been set to music and used in prayer books. Read them over and use them to write your own worship service. Perhaps you will also want to write music for one of them; draw a picture (abstract or realistic) inspired by a canticle; paraphrase the words; or pray them as part of your own worship. These canticles are: the *Magnificat* (1:46-55), *Benedictus* (1:68-79), *Gloria in Excelsis* (2:14), *Nunc Dimittis* (2:29-32).

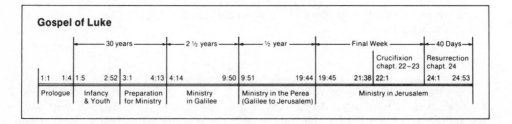

Gospel of Luke						
	30 years	2 ½ years	½ year	Final Week		40 Days
					Crucifixion chapt. 22–23	Resurrection chapt. 24
1:1 1:4	1:5 2:52	3:1 4:13	4:14 9:50	9:51 19:44	19:45 21:38 22:1	24:1 24:53
Prologue	Infancy & Youth	Preparation for Ministry	Ministry in Galilee	Ministry in the Perea (Galilee to Jerusalem)	Ministry in Jerusalem	

Luke

Introduction

1 Many have undertaken to draw up an account of the things that have been fulfilled[a] among us, ²just as they were handed down to us by those who from the first were eyewitnesses and servants of the word. ³Therefore, since I myself have carefully investigated everything from the beginning, it seemed good also to me to write an orderly account for you, most excellent Theophilus, ⁴so that you may know the certainty of the things you have been taught.

The Birth of John the Baptist Foretold

⁵In the time of Herod king of Judea there was a priest named Zechariah, who belonged to the priestly division of Abijah; his wife Elizabeth was also a descendant of Aaron. ⁶Both of them were upright in the sight of God, observing all the Lord's commandments and regulations blamelessly. ⁷But they had no children, because Elizabeth was barren; and they were both well along in years.

⁸Once when Zechariah's division was on duty and he was serving as priest before God, ⁹he was chosen by lot, according to the custom of the priesthood, to go into the temple of the Lord and burn incense. ¹⁰And when the time for the burning of incense came, all the assembled worshipers were praying outside.

¹¹Then an angel of the Lord appeared to him, standing at the right side of the altar of incense. ¹²When Zechariah saw him, he was startled and was gripped with fear. ¹³But the angel said to him: "Do not be afraid, Zechariah; your prayer has been heard. Your wife Elizabeth will bear you a son, and you are to give him the name John. ¹⁴He will be a joy and delight to you, and many will rejoice because of his birth, ¹⁵for he will be great in the sight of the Lord. He is never to take wine or other fermented drink, and he will be filled with the Holy Spirit even from birth.[b] ¹⁶Many of the people of Israel will he bring back to the Lord their God. ¹⁷And he will go on before the Lord, in the spirit and power of Elijah, to turn the hearts of the fathers to their children and the disobedient to the wisdom of the righteous—to make ready a people prepared for the Lord."

¹⁸Zechariah asked the angel, "How can I be sure of this? I am an old man and my wife is well along in years."

¹⁹The angel answered, "I am Gabriel. I stand in the presence of God, and I have been sent to speak to you and to tell you this good news. ²⁰And now you will be silent and not able to speak until the day this happens, because you did not believe my words, which will come true at their proper time."

²¹Meanwhile, the people were waiting for Zechariah and wondering why he stayed so long in the temple. ²²When he came out,

---

OPEN: Who read to you at night when you were a child and/or heard your prayers?

DIG: 1. Why did Luke, the author, write this gospel? To whom? **2.** Where did Luke get his stories?

REFLECT: Who first told you about Jesus? When did Jesus become more than just a name to you?

OPEN: 1. How many children do you want to have? Boys or girls? Do you want to have your children early or after a little while? Why? **2.** Do you know of any couple that wanted children but couldn't? Do you know of any that had given up and then "it" happened? **3.** What is the best story in your own family of God sending a "surprise"? What happened?

DIG: 1. From what you learn about Zechariah and his wife (vv. 5-7), what stands out? **2.** For what special task was Zechariah chosen? What do you know about the significance of this task? **3.** What happened to Zechariah while fulfilling his duties (v. 11)? What was Zechariah's response (v. 12)? **4.** What was the angel's message to him? What did he say would happen? What would this event do to Zechariah and Elizabeth? How would it impact others? What did he say about the son who would be born? What was the mission assigned to John the Baptist? What was to be the nature of this greatness (v. 15)? **5.** How did Zechariah respond to the angel's words (v. 18)? Why did he doubt? How did Gabriel answer Zechariah's question? **6.** In the meantime, how were the people feeling (v. 21)? What did they think when Zechariah emerged mute from the temple? **7.** How did Elizabeth react to her pregnancy?

REFLECT: 1. In your family tree, how far back can you go? Who is the most colorful character? Any "horse thieves"? **2.** Any ancestors whom you take pride in and say: "Spiritually, this person had a great impact upon our family"? What are some of the stories that are told about this person: Any idiosyncrasies? Any "old fashioned" ways? **3.** In the same way that God used the parents of John the Baptist to "prepare the way" for Jesus, what are you doing

---

a1 Or been surely believed   *b15 Or from his mother's womb*

to "prepare the way" for generations to come in your family?

OPEN: 1. What is the most unusual birth announcement you have ever received? **2.** If God told you that you were to be a parent 9 months from now, how would you feel?

DIG: 1. What does Gabriel say to Mary? How does that compare with what he said to Zechariah (1:13-17)? **2.** How does Mary respond (vv. 34, 18) differently than Zechariah (vv. 12, 18)? **3.** How is this miracle to take place (v. 35)? Why do you think God chose a "virgin birth" to fulfill his plan? **4.** How does Elizabeth's pregnancy encourage Mary? **5.** Comparing Luke's account to Matt. 1:18-25, what else do you learn about Jesus? About Joseph?

REFLECT: 1. (Females) If an angel of the Lord asked you to become pregnant before marriage, what would you say to the angel? To your parents? To your boyfriend? (Males) If you were unmarried and your girlfriend informed you, "I'm pregnant by the Holy Spirit", what would you feel? Say? Do? Why?

OPEN: Who do you call first when you have special news to share? Likewise, when you are in trouble?

DIG: 1. Who does Mary call first? Why? **2.** How does Elizabeth and her baby respond? **3.** How is Mary "blessed" and encouraged? **4.** What role had the Holy Spirit played thus far (vv. 15, 35, 41)?

REFLECT: When you last shared your special or troubling news, what happened?

OPEN: 1. What songs do you sing in the shower? What is your favorite religious music? **2.** Have you ever felt inspired to write poetry or music? What inspires you?

DIG: 1. How do praise and humility go together in Mary? **2.** How do reward and punishment go together in God's actions (vv. 51-53)? How will Jesus accomplish this in the

he could not speak to them. They realized he had seen a vision in the temple, for he kept making signs to them but remained unable to speak.

²³When his time of service was completed, he returned home. ²⁴After this his wife Elizabeth became pregnant and for five months remained in seclusion. ²⁵"The Lord has done this for me," she said. "In these days he has shown his favor and taken away my disgrace among the people."

The Birth of Jesus Foretold

²⁶In the sixth month, God sent the angel Gabriel to Nazareth, a town in Galilee, ²⁷to a virgin pledged to be married to a man named Joseph, a descendant of David. The virgin's name was Mary. ²⁸The angel went to her and said, "Greetings, you who are highly favored! The Lord is with you."

²⁹Mary was greatly troubled at his words and wondered what kind of greeting this might be. ³⁰But the angel said to her, "Do not be afraid, Mary, you have found favor with God. ³¹You will be with child and give birth to a son, and you are to give him the name Jesus. ³²He will be great and will be called the Son of the Most High. The Lord God will give him the throne of his father David, ³³and he will reign over the house of Jacob forever; his kingdom will never end."

³⁴"How will this be," Mary asked the angel, "since I am a virgin?"

³⁵The angel answered, "The Holy Spirit will come upon you, and the power of the Most High will overshadow you. So the holy one to be born will be called ᶜ the Son of God. ³⁶Even Elizabeth your relative is going to have a child in her old age, and she who was said to be barren is in her sixth month. ³⁷For nothing is impossible with God."

³⁸"I am the Lord's servant," Mary answered. "May it be to me as you have said." Then the angel left her.

Mary Visits Elizabeth

³⁹At that time Mary got ready and hurried to a town in the hill country of Judea, ⁴⁰where she entered Zechariah's home and greeted Elizabeth. ⁴¹When Elizabeth heard Mary's greeting, the baby leaped in her womb, and Elizabeth was filled with the Holy Spirit. ⁴²In a loud voice she exclaimed: "Blessed are you among women, and blessed is the child you will bear! ⁴³But why am I so favored, that the mother of my Lord should come to me? ⁴⁴As soon as the sound of your greeting reached my ears, the baby in my womb leaped for joy. ⁴⁵Blessed is she who has believed that what the Lord has said to her will be accomplished!"

Mary's Song

⁴⁶And Mary said:

"My soul glorifies the Lord
⁴⁷ and my spirit rejoices in God my Savior,
⁴⁸for he has been mindful
of the humble state of his servant.

ᶜ35 Or *So the child to be born will be called holy,*

From now on all generations will call me blessed,
49 for the Mighty One has done great things for me—
holy is his name.

⁵⁰His mercy extends to those who fear him,
from generation to generation.

⁵¹He has performed mighty deeds with his arm;
he has scattered those who are proud in their inmost
thoughts.

⁵²He has brought down rulers from their thrones
but has lifted up the humble.

⁵³He has filled the hungry with good things
but has sent the rich away empty.

⁵⁴He has helped his servant Israel,
remembering to be merciful

⁵⁵to Abraham and his descendants forever,
even as he said to our fathers."

⁵⁶Mary stayed with Elizabeth for about three months and then returned home.

The Birth of John the Baptist

⁵⁷When it was time for Elizabeth to have her baby, she gave birth to a son. ⁵⁸Her neighbors and relatives heard that the Lord had shown her great mercy, and they shared her joy.

⁵⁹On the eighth day they came to circumcise the child, and they were going to name him after his father Zechariah, ⁶⁰but his mother spoke up and said, "No! He is to be called John." ⁶¹They said to her, "There is no one among your relatives who has that name."

⁶²Then they made signs to his father, to find out what he would like to name the child. ⁶³He asked for a writing tablet, and to everyone's astonishment he wrote, "His name is John." ⁶⁴Immediately his mouth was opened and his tongue was loosed, and he began to speak, praising God. ⁶⁵The neighbors were all filled with awe, and throughout the hill country of Judea people were talking about all these things. ⁶⁶Everyone who heard this wondered about it, asking, "What then is this child going to be?" For the Lord's hand was with him.

Zechariah's Song

⁶⁷His father Zechariah was filled with the Holy Spirit and prophesied:

⁶⁸"Praise be to the Lord, the God of Israel,
because he has come and has redeemed his people.

⁶⁹He has raised up a horn ᵈ of salvation for us
in the house of his servant David

⁷⁰(as he said through his holy prophets of long ago),

⁷¹salvation from our enemies
and from the hand of all who hate us—

⁷²to show mercy to our fathers
and to remember his holy covenant,

⁷³ the oath he swore to our father Abraham:

ᵈ69 *Horn* here symbolizes strength.

---

future? **3.** What other actions and attributes does Mary praise God for? **4.** Why do you think Mary stayed so long with Elizabeth (v. 56)? What would a diary from that 3-month visit reveal?

REFLECT: **1.** Why do you spontaneously break out in praise, glorifying and rejoicing in God: When things are going well? While walking in the woods? Listening to the "Hallelujah Chorus"? **2.** What music best suits your lifestyle today: Heavy rock? Punk? Blues? Mellow "elevator" music? Dissonant modern stuff? Simple gospel music? All of the above? **3.** What could you do this week to improve your praise life?

OPEN: How did your parents decide on your name? What name did your friends give you at school?

DIG: **1.** How did John's birth fulfill the words of the angel in verses 13-17? **2.** What happened on the eighth day? Why did Elizabeth want to name the baby John (see v. 13)? How did the neighbors and relatives respond? **3.** How does Zechariah solve the problem? What happens to him? **4.** How do the neighbors react to all of this? How does all of this begin to promote the gospel?

REFLECT: **1.** What are you going to name your children? **2.** What are some dreams you have for your kids? What are you doing to help those dreams come true?

OPEN: **1.** When you were born, what did your father do to celebrate the occasion: Write a song? Paint a picture? Pass out cigars? Faint in the delivery room? **2.** What would it take to get you to write a song?

DIG: **1.** What does Zechariah do when he can finally speak (v. 67)? What power enables him to do this? **2.** In verse 68, what two things does he praise God for? What's the significance of each? **3.** In verses 69-75, what primary activity is he praising God for? **4.** What does he say about his son in verses 76-79? What else does he say?

REFLECT: **1.** Of the promises listed in this song, which one means the most to you at this stage in your life? Why? **2.** Have you ever felt that God was preparing the way for your life, just as he was preparing the way for Jesus through John the Baptist? Who has helped prepare the way for God in your life? **3.** Have you ever felt like God was preparing you for a special task? When, like John the Baptist, has God led you into "the desert" to prepare you for the future?

⁷⁴to rescue us from the hand of our enemies,
and to enable us to serve him without fear
⁷⁵ in holiness and righteousness before him all our days.

⁷⁶And you, my child, will be called a prophet of the Most
High;
for you will go on before the Lord to prepare the way
for him,
⁷⁷to give his people the knowledge of salvation
through the forgiveness of their sins,
⁷⁸because of the tender mercy of our God,
by which the rising sun will come to us from heaven
⁷⁹to shine on those living in darkness
and in the shadow of death,
to guide our feet into the path of peace."

⁸⁰And the child grew and became strong in spirit; and he lived in the desert until he appeared publicly to Israel.

The Birth of Jesus

2 In those days Caesar Augustus issued a decree that a census should be taken of the entire Roman world. ²(This was the first census that took place while Quirinius was governor of Syria.) ³And everyone went to his own town to register.

OPEN: Where were you and your dad born? Why there?

DIG: **1.** What do these historical, political and geographical details mean here? How would a very pregnant lady survive this long trip? **2.** Where does Mary give birth? Why such a humble birthplace (see Micah 5:2)? **3.** What does this story say about God's control of political affairs and "closed doors"?

REFLECT: What were Mary and Joseph pondering when their long journey ended with "no room"?

⁴So Joseph also went up from the town of Nazareth in Galilee to Judea, to Bethlehem the town of David, because he belonged to the house and line of David. ⁵He went there to register with Mary, who was pledged to be married to him and was expecting a child. ⁶While they were there, the time came for the baby to be born, ⁷and she gave birth to her firstborn, a son. She wrapped him in cloths and placed him in a manger, because there was no room for them in the inn.

The Shepherds and the Angels

⁸And there were shepherds living out in the fields nearby, keeping watch over their flocks at night. ⁹An angel of the Lord appeared to them, and the glory of the Lord shone around them, and they were terrified. ¹⁰But the angel said to them, "Do not be afraid. I bring you good news of great joy that will be for all the people. ¹¹Today in the town of David a Savior has been born to you; he is Christ^e the Lord. ¹²This will be a sign to you: You will find a baby wrapped in cloths and lying in a manger."

OPEN 1. Growing up, when did your family put up the Christmas tree? Who decorated it? **2.** What Christmas traditions do you still keep? **3.** What do you remember about the manger scene and shepherds?

DIG: **1.** Now who is visited by an angel? Under what circumstances? How specific is the message? How does the shepherds' experience compare to that of Zechariah (1:8f) and Mary (1:26f)? **2.** What does all this angelic fanfare say about the importance of Jesus' birth? **3.** Consequently, what do the shepherds do? And after their discovery? After they return? **4.** How does Mary respond to all of this (v. 19)? **5.** Of all the people the angels could have visited, why do you think God sent them to the shepherds?

REFLECT: **1.** God appeared to Zechariah, to Mary and now to the shepherds when they were just doing their jobs, being themselves. How has God spoken to you

¹³Suddenly a great company of the heavenly host appeared with the angel, praising God and saying,

¹⁴"Glory to God in the highest,
and on earth peace to men on whom his favor rests."

¹⁵When the angels had left them and gone into heaven, the shepherds said to one another, "Let's go to Bethlehem and see this thing that has happened, which the Lord has told us about."

¹⁶So they hurried off and found Mary and Joseph, and the baby, who was lying in the manger. ¹⁷When they had seen him,

^e11 Or *Messiah*. "The Christ" (Greek) and "the Messiah" (Hebrew) both mean "the Anointed One"; also in verse 26.

LOOKING INTO THE SCRIPTURE/20 Minutes. Read Luke 2:8-20 and discuss.

1. What do you remember about Christmas time when you were a child? Ask the first person in your group to answer the first question. The second person the next question, etc., until you have answered all of the questions below.

☐ Where were you living when you were seven years old?
☐ What was the weather like around Christmas time?
☐ Who did most of the decorating of the tree?
☐ What special tradition did your family observe at Christmas?
☐ What is your earliest memory of a Christmas morning?
☐ When and where did you open your presents?
☐ What Christmas present stands out in your memory?
☐ Who was the person in your family who made Christmas special?
☐ What tradition would you like to continue with your children?

2. Why do you think God chose to announce the birth of his Son to shepherds?
  a. only ones listening
  b. lowliest of people
  c. lived close to nature/God
  d. they were open and receptive

3. What do you think the good news, "a Savior has been born . . . Christ the Lord," meant to the shepherds?
  a. very little
  b. something special
  c. the long-awaited Messiah had arrived
  d. life will be different
  e. there was hope for them
  f. God was alive

4. How would you have felt if you had been there when a "great company of heavenly angels appeared . . ."?
  a. totally awed
  b. scared to death
  c. blown away
  d. like crawling in a hole

5. Do you think Mary and Joseph understood the cosmic significance of the child they had just given birth to?
  a. probably not
  b. they must have
  c. Mary could have
  d. up to a point
  e. they couldn't have

MY OWN STORY/20 Minutes.

1. How would you announce the birth of your kids?
  a. chocolate candy and cigars
  b. telegrams and phone calls
  c. throw a party
  d. big banner on the front door
  e. save the money for college

2. When did the Christmas story take on real significance for you?
  a. when I was a child
  b. years ago
  c. quite recently
  d. not sure it ever has

3. How would you compare your spiritual awakening to the shepherds?
  a. not quite so dramatic
  b. different, but just as real
  c. more intellectual
  d. just as confusing
  e. more gradual

4. How would you describe your relationship to God right now?
  a. nowhere
  b. up and down
  c. in a holding pattern
  d. on the injured list
  e. great
  f. doing better

recently in the ordinary flow of life? **2.** Other people apparently didn't see the star or hear the angels? Why? Are you open to God's serendipity in your life?

OPEN: 1. When you were growing up, what teacher, coach or relative made you feel special. How did that person make you feel so good? **2.** Who helps you feel special now?

DIG: 1. Why is Jesus presented in the temple at this time: Circumcision? Christening? Purification? Dedication? What Mosaic laws are hereby fulfilled (see Lev. 12:1-8, Ex. 13:2, 12, 13; Nu. 18:15, 16)? Why the name Jesus? **2.** What does this temple ceremony reveal about the parents of Jesus: They were very poor? Religious? Proud? Dedicated? Fearful of their salvation? **3.** How could Simeon possibly know this baby Jesus was the long-promised Messiah (vv. 25-28)? In Simeon's prophecies (vv. 29-32, 34-35), what was he predicting about the work of Jesus? The fate of the nations? The pain of the parents? **4.** Of whom does Anna remind you? How does she complement Simeon's prophecy? **5.** What impact would these startling predictions by Simeon and Anna have on "all" who were listening that day? On the parents of Jesus as they returned home (vv. 33, 39)? On Jesus as he was growing up (v. 40)? **6.** In summary, what do you learn about Mary and Joseph in this passage? About Jesus? About God? About godly people?

REFLECT: 1. How did your parents dedicate you to the Lord, if at all? How do you feel about the fact that you were or weren't dedicated? How did your parents help you mature spiritually? **2.** When has God brought along someone to confirm something in your life, like Simeon and Anna did for the parents of Jesus? How did this make you feel?

they spread the word concerning what had been told them about this child, [18]and all who heard it were amazed at what the shepherds said to them. [19]But Mary treasured up all these things and pondered them in her heart. [20]The shepherds returned, glorifying and praising God for all the things they had heard and seen, which were just as they had been told.

Jesus Presented in the Temple

[21]On the eighth day, when it was time to circumcise him, he was named Jesus, the name the angel had given him before he had been conceived.

[22]When the time of their purification according to the Law of Moses had been completed, Joseph and Mary took him to Jerusalem to present him to the Lord [23](as it is written in the Law of the Lord, "Every firstborn male is to be consecrated to the Lord"[f]), [24]and to offer a sacrifice in keeping with what is said in the Law of the Lord: "a pair of doves or two young pigeons."[g]

[25]Now there was a man in Jerusalem called Simeon, who was righteous and devout. He was waiting for the consolation of Israel, and the Holy Spirit was upon him. [26]It had been revealed to him by the Holy Spirit that he would not die before he had seen the Lord's Christ. [27]Moved by the Spirit, he went into the temple courts. When the parents brought in the child Jesus to do for him what the custom of the Law required, [28]Simeon took him in his arms and praised God, saying:

[29]"Sovereign Lord, as you have promised,
　　you now dismiss[h] your servant in peace.
[30]For my eyes have seen your salvation,
[31]　which you have prepared in the sight of all people,
[32]a light for revelation to the Gentiles
　　and for glory to your people Israel."

[33]The child's father and mother marveled at what was said about him. [34]Then Simeon blessed them and said to Mary, his mother: "This child is destined to cause the falling and rising of many in Israel, and to be a sign that will be spoken against, [35]so that the thoughts of many hearts will be revealed. And a sword will pierce your own soul too."

[36]There was also a prophetess, Anna, the daughter of Phanuel, of the tribe of Asher. She was very old; she had lived with her husband seven years after her marriage, [37]and then was a widow until she was eighty-four.[i] She never left the temple but worshiped night and day, fasting and praying. [38]Coming up to them at that very moment, she gave thanks to God and spoke about the child to all who were looking forward to the redemption of Jerusalem.

[39]When Joseph and Mary had done everything required by the Law of the Lord, they returned to Galilee to their own town of Nazareth. [40]And the child grew and became strong; he was filled with wisdom, and the grace of God was upon him.

---

f23 Exodus 13:2,12　　*g24* Lev. 12:8　　*h29* Or *promised, / now dismiss*
i37 Or *widow for eighty-four years*

Luke 2:21-40   **JESUS PRESENTED IN THE TEMPLE**

LOOKING INTO THE SCRIPTURE/20 Minutes. Read Luke 2:21-40 and discuss.

1. What does this story reveal about the parents of Jesus?
   - a. they were very poor
   - b. they were religious
   - c. they were very young
   - d. they knew their son was very special

2. Why do you suppose this was such a meaningful occasion for Simeon?
   - a. he had waited so long for this moment
   - b. he expected to see the Christ (God's Anointed One)
   - c. God had not forgotten his promise
   - d. he marvelled at how God could use a baby to bring his salvation

3. Put yourself in Joseph and Mary's shoes. How would you have felt if two old people came to you and gave startling predictions about your son?
   - a. proud
   - b. scared
   - c. confused
   - d. overwhelmed

4. In Simeon's prophecy about the child, what was he predicting?
   - a. Roman Empire would collapse
   - b. Israel would reject God's Messiah
   - c. national bloodshed
   - d. the parents would experience pain

5. Do you think the parents of Jesus understood what was going to happen to their son?
   - a. maybe a little
   - b. probably not
   - c. not at first
   - d. his mother probably did
   - e. I would like to think so

6. What strikes you as significant about Anna and Simeon?
   - a. they were both old
   - b. they both spent all their time at the temple
   - c. they were very close to their God
   - d. they lived life expecting to see God at work
   - e. they were both concerned about the welfare of Isreal
   - f. they recognized their need for a Savior

MY OWN STORY/25 Minutes.

1. Briefly tell your "roots," what your parents were like when you were born:
   - a. financially
   - b. religiously
   - c. socially

2. What do you know about your baptism or dedication as an infant?
   - a. don't know anything about it
   - b. I have a certificate/pictures in my baby book
   - c. we did not go to church then
   - d. it was a big family affair

3. Do you think your parents understand what is going on in your life now?
   - a. I hope not
   - b. probably
   - c. maybe a little bit
   - d. for sure
   - e. no, but I'd like them to

4. Do you think God has a plan and purpose for your life like he did for Mary and Joseph?
   - a. not at all
   - b. in a way
   - c. maybe, but not the same plan
   - d. definitely

5. How open are you to God's will for your life at the moment?
   - a. a little bit
   - b. a whole lot
   - c. just don't send me to Africa
   - d. ask me tomorrow

6. What would be the crowning joy for you in your old age?
   - a. to see my children's children
   - b. to strike it rich
   - c. to look back on a life full of surprises
   - d. to leave the world a better place to live in
   - f. to feel I have done God's will

OPEN 1. What was one of the best trips you ever took with your family? **2.** Can you remember ever getting lost as a child? What happened?

DIG: 1. What was this feast that was an annual tradition with Jesus' parents (see Ex. 23:15, Dt. 16:1-6)? **2.** How do the parents and the boy Jesus end up separated? For how long (vv. 44-46)? **3.** What was Jesus up to: No good? Others' good? Too much good? **4.** How do the people and his parents react? **5.** What does Jesus' answer (v. 49) reveal about his understanding of his future? About his empathy with his parents anxiety? **6.** Likewise, what does Jesus' subsequent action (v. 51) reveal? **7.** How is Mary profiting from these experiences (v. 51)? Likewise, the boy Jesus (v. 52)?

REFLECT: 1. Growing up, what year did you have the most difficulty communicating with your parents? When did things start getting better? **2.** What are you going to do differently with your kids?

OPEN: 1. If you were an advertising executive and your firm had been chosen to prepare the way for Jesus' arrival in your country, what would you do? What kind of campaign would you develop? **2.** If you were producing a family play and had to cast someone in the role of John the Baptist, who would you cast in that role and why?

DIG: 1. How long is the probable time gap between appearances of John the Baptist here and in 1:80? What do you suppose John the Baptist was doing in those intervening years? Why? **2.** Why does Luke bother to list all the political and religious figures in verses 1-2? **3.** What is John the Baptist like? What's the basic content of his message? What more can you learn about John, his message and his style in Matthew 3:1-12, Mark 1:1-8 and John 1:6-8, 19-28? **4.** Why would you go out of your way to hear a message of repentance from this radical preacher (v. 7)? **5.** What's so radical about John's message? What does the "root" and "fruit" signify? Is he advocating social upheaval? Or inner transformation? Is he "preaching" or "meddling"? Why? **6.** Who is John castigating and why (vv. 7-9)? **7.** What other groups does John address (vv. 10-14)? **8.** How does John's message to them illustrate the kind of repentance he is calling for? **9.**

The Boy Jesus at the Temple

⁴¹Every year his parents went to Jerusalem for the Feast of the Passover. ⁴²When he was twelve years old, they went up to the Feast, according to the custom. ⁴³After the Feast was over, while his parents were returning home, the boy Jesus stayed behind in Jerusalem, but they were unaware of it. ⁴⁴Thinking he was in their company, they traveled on for a day. Then they began looking for him among their relatives and friends. ⁴⁵When they did not find him, they went back to Jerusalem to look for him. ⁴⁶After three days they found him in the temple courts, sitting among the teachers, listening to them and asking them questions. ⁴⁷Everyone who heard him was amazed at his understanding and his answers. ⁴⁸When his parents saw him, they were astonished. His mother said to him, "Son, why have you treated us like this? Your father and I have been anxiously searching for you."

⁴⁹"Why were you searching for me?" he asked. "Didn't you know I had to be in my Father's house?" ⁵⁰But they did not understand what he was saying to them.

⁵¹Then he went down to Nazareth with them and was obedient to them. But his mother treasured all these things in her heart. ⁵²And Jesus grew in wisdom and stature, and in favor with God and men.

John the Baptist Prepares the Way

3 In the fifteenth year of the reign of Tiberius Caesar—when Pontius Pilate was governor of Judea, Herod tetrarch of Galilee, his brother Philip tetrarch of Iturea and Traconitis, and Lysanias tetrarch of Abilene— ²during the high priesthood of Annas and Caiaphas, the word of God came to John son of Zechariah in the desert. ³He went into all the country around the Jordan, preaching a baptism of repentance for the forgiveness of sins. ⁴As is written in the book of the words of Isaiah the prophet:

"A voice of one calling in the desert,
'Prepare the way for the Lord,
  make straight paths for him.
⁵Every valley shall be filled in,
  every mountain and hill made low.
The crooked roads shall become straight,
  the rough ways smooth.
⁶And all mankind will see God's salvation.' "ʲ

⁷John said to the crowds coming out to be baptized by him, "You brood of vipers! Who warned you to flee from the coming wrath? ⁸Produce fruit in keeping with repentance. And do not begin to say to yourselves, 'We have Abraham as our father.' For I tell you that out of these stones God can raise up children for Abraham. ⁹The ax is already at the root of the trees, and every tree that does not produce good fruit will be cut down and thrown into the fire."

¹⁰"What should we do then?" the crowd asked.

j6 Isaiah 40:3-5

Luke 2:41-52 — THE BOY JESUS AT THE TEMPLE

LOOKING INTO THE SCRIPTURE/20 Minutes. Read Luke 2:41-52 and discuss.

1. How do you think Jesus' parents felt while they were searching for three to five days for Jesus?
   - a. hysterical
   - b. calm and collected
   - c. angry and terrified
   - d. relaxed and confident

2. When they found him in the temple, what did they say?
   - a. just wait until you get home!
   - b. you're not coming next year!
   - c. where in the world have you been?
   - d. we're proud of you.
   - e. do you realize how worried we've been?

3. What was the problem, from the parents' point of view?
   - a. Jesus wandered off in a big crowd at Passover
   - b. Jesus embarassed his parents in public
   - c. Jesus had gone too far in his religious activity
   - d. Jesus hardly seemed like their son anymore

4. What was the situation from Jesus' perspective?
   - a. his parents were too protective
   - b. he was growing up and had more important things to do
   - c. there were people here he could help
   - d. he had found his real "home" in the temple

5. As a result of this incident, what do you think changed in the relationship between Jesus and his parents?
   - a. Joseph and Mary had lots to think about
   - b. Jesus knew more than his parents, and they knew it
   - c. they were more alert to Jesus' spiritual growth
   - d. it probably happened again, but without the fireworks
   - e. they had more confidence that Jesus would grow up to be a responsible adult
   - f. they all probably had more understanding for each others' feelings

6. How do you feel about the possibility that Jesus' parents were not spared the struggle of most parents?
   - a. reassured
   - b. there's no hope for me then
   - c. more "normal"
   - d. inspired to keep going
   - e. wondering about my expectations of parenthood

MY OWN STORY/20 Minutes.

1. What kind of preparation did your parents have to raise you?
   - a. they had Dr. Spock's book
   - b. their parents were good role models
   - c. absolutely no preparation
   - d. family life classes at school

2. Do you think your parents understood what they were getting in for when they had you?
   - a. they wanted twelve children until they had me
   - b. they thought child-raising would be cheaper
   - c. they knew life was tough but had lots of love to share
   - d. they weren't counting on my teenage rebellion
   - e. they trusted God would help them through the surprises

3. What do you cherish most about your parents?
   - a. unconditional love/acceptance
   - b. old-fashioned values
   - c. spiritual direction
   - d. fun times together
   - e. closeness/togetherness

4. What are you going to do differently in raising your children?
   - a. give them more freedom
   - b. give them less freedom
   - c. spend more time with them
   - d. show more affection
   - e. enjoy them
   - f. give them more guidance

5. If you could pass on one or two things to your children, what would they be?
   - a. spiritual direction
   - b. self-respect
   - c. drive/ambition
   - d. concern/compassion
   - e. value of hard work
   - f. good memories
   - g. money/wealth

Why is John confused with Christ (v. 15, see also John 1:19-28)? By contrast, how does John differentiate himself and his ministry? What does the "wheat" and "chaff" signify? **10.** What is the beginning of the end for John's earthly ministry (vv. 19-20)? What does this illustrate about John? **11.** What do you learn about the cause (vv. 7-9, 16, 17), future (vv. 8, 10-14) and outcome (vv. 3, 15-17) of true repentance?

REFLECT: 1. Who has been John the Baptist in your life — people who have shown you the way, led you to Christ, encouraged you, and given you a kick in the pants when you needed it? What were these people like? What was their style? **2.** What would John say to your Bible study group if he showed up? Your business and community club? Your church? **3.** How is John's message like and unlike what you often hear today?

OPEN: 1. What's one of the most memorable baptism services you've ever seen or been a part of? Why? **2.** Who's the family historian in your extended family? What has he/she done to help you know more about your ancestors? **3.** If you were to explore in more detail the life of one of your ancestors, whose life would you investigate? Why? **4.** Who's the hero in your genealogy? The black sheep? Why?

DIG: 1. Why is Jesus being baptized at the same time as all the people? **2.** What three things happen at Jesus' baptism that make his baptism unlike the other people's? What meaning do you think these events have for Jesus as a 30-year old? **3.** How does this account of Jesus' baptism compare and contrast with the other three accounts found in Matthew 3:13-17, Mark 1:9-11 and John 1:32-34? **4.** If Matthew's geneology starts with Abraham to demonstsrate God's working through the chosen people (Mt. 1:1-17), what is Luke's point in going all the way back to Adam (v. 38)? (What do Adam and Jesus have in common?) Why else might Luke include this geneology (see 1:27, 32, 69)? **5.** In this genealogy, what names stand out to you? What do you remember about them? What can you conclude about Jesus' "earthly ancestory" from what you know of these people?

[11]John answered, "The man with two tunics should share with him who has none, and the one who has food should do the same."

[12]Tax collectors also came to be baptized. "Teacher," they asked, "what should we do?"

[13]"Don't collect any more than you are required to," he told them.

[14]Then some soldiers asked him, "And what should we do?"

He replied, "Don't extort money and don't accuse people falsely—be content with your pay."

[15]The people were waiting expectantly and were all wondering in their hearts if John might possibly be the Christ.[k] [16]John answered them all, "I baptize you with[l] water. But one more powerful than I will come, the thongs of whose sandals I am not worthy to untie. He will baptize you with the Holy Spirit and with fire. [17]His winnowing fork is in his hand to clear his threshing floor and to gather the wheat into his barn, but he will burn up the chaff with unquenchable fire." [18]And with many other words John exhorted the people and preached the good news to them.

[19]But when John rebuked Herod the tetrarch because of Herodias, his brother's wife, and all the other evil things he had done, [20]Herod added this to them all: He locked John up in prison.

The Baptism and Genealogy of Jesus

[21]When all the people were being baptized, Jesus was baptized too. And as he was praying, heaven was opened [22]and the Holy Spirit descended on him in bodily form like a dove. And a voice came from heaven: "You are my Son, whom I love; with you I am well pleased."

[23]Now Jesus himself was about thirty years old when he began his ministry. He was the son, so it was thought, of Joseph,

the son of Heli, [24]the son of Matthat,
the son of Levi, the son of Melki,
the son of Jannai, the son of Joseph,
[25]the son of Mattathias, the son of Amos,
the son of Nahum, the son of Esli,
the son of Naggai, [26]the son of Maath,
the son of Mattathias, the son of Semein,
the son of Josech, the son of Joda,
[27]the son of Joanan, the son of Rhesa,
the son of Zerubbabel, the son of Shealtiel,
the son of Neri, [28]the son of Melki,
the son of Addi, the son of Cosam,
the son of Elmadam, the son of Er,
[29]the son of Joshua, the son of Eliezer,
the son of Jorim, the son of Matthat,
the son of Levi, [30]the son of Simeon,
the son of Judah, the son of Joseph,
the son of Jonam, the son of Eliakim,

k15 Or Messiah   l16 Or in

140

³¹the son of Melea, the son of Menna,
   the son of Mattatha, the son of Nathan,
   the son of David, ³²the son of Jesse,
   the son of Obed, the son of Boaz,
   the son of Salmon,ᵐ the son of Nahshon,
³³the son of Amminadab, the son of Ram,ⁿ
   the son of Hezron, the son of Perez,
   the son of Judah, ³⁴the son of Jacob,
   the son of Isaac, the son of Abraham,
   the son of Terah, the son of Nahor,
³⁵the son of Serug, the son of Reu,
   the son of Peleg, the son of Eber,
   the son of Shelah, ³⁶the son of Cainan,
   the son of Arphaxad, the son of Shem,
   the son of Noah, the son of Lamech,
³⁷the son of Methuselah, the son of Enoch,
   the son of Jared, the son of Mahalalel,
   the son of Kenan, ³⁸the son of Enosh,
   the son of Seth, the son of Adam,
   the son of God.

The Temptation of Jesus

4 Jesus, full of the Holy Spirit, returned from the Jordan and was led by the Spirit in the desert, ²where for forty days he was tempted by the devil. He ate nothing during those days, and at the end of them he was hungry.

³The devil said to him, "If you are the Son of God, tell this stone to become bread."

⁴Jesus answered, "It is written: 'Man does not live on bread alone.'ᵒ"

⁵The devil led him up to a high place and showed him in an instant all the kingdoms of the world. ⁶And he said to him, "I will give you all their authority and splendor, for it has been given to me, and I can give it to anyone I want to. ⁷So if you worship me, it will all be yours."

⁸Jesus answered, "It is written: 'Worship the Lord your God and serve him only.'ᵖ"

⁹The devil led him to Jerusalem and had him stand on the highest point of the temple. "If you are the Son of God," he said, "throw yourself down from here. ¹⁰For it is written:

" 'He will command his angels concerning you
      to guard you carefully;
¹¹they will lift you up in their hands,
      so that you will not strike your foot against a stone.'ᵠ"

¹²Jesus answered, "It says: 'Do not put the Lord your God to the test.'ʳ"

¹³When the devil had finished all this tempting, he left him until an opportune time.

REFLECT: 1. What means the most to you about your own baptism? **2.** At what time(s) in your life have you felt God's special touch, as if a new ministry was beginning for you? What happened? **3.** How godly is the heritage in your ancestry? Whose names stand out as "the godly"? What kind of contribution have they made? **4.** How would you like to be remembered in your family? What are you doing to ensure those remembrances?

OPEN: 1. What's the longest time you've ever gone without eating? What do you remember about that? What's the first thing you ate when you ended your "fast"? **2.** What's one of your favorite all-time foods? How often do you eat it?

DIG: 1. Under what circumstances (vv. 1-2) is Jesus tempted? After a spiritual high? At a weak moment? Apart from God? **2.** What potentially might appeal to Jesus in the first temptation? In the second? Third? **3.** What would be the price to pay if Jesus yielded to the first temptation? The second? Third? **4.** How does Jesus resist the first temptation? The second? Third? **5.** How are the three temptations similar? Different? **6.** Why were the temptations all directed against the divine Sonship of Jesus when this had just been confirmed at Jesus' baptism (3:21-22)? Why not appeal to the human nature of Jesus? **7.** The devil does not reappear until 22:3—what do you make of that?

REFLECT: 1. When, if ever, have you experienced a spiritual high and then been hit with a spiritual low, temptation or depression? Does this seem normal to you? Why? **2.** If the devil had three "shots" at you, what three temptations would he use? What three temptations might have been used ten years ago? How have tempting influences changed as you mature?

ᵐ32 Some early manuscripts Sala   ⁿ33 Some manuscripts Amminadab, the son
of Admin, the son of Arni; other manuscripts vary widely.   ᵒ4 Deut. 8:3
ᵖ8 Deut. 6:13   ᵠ11 Psalm 91:11,12   ʳ12 Deut. 6:16

OPEN: 1. What do you like best about the hometown where you grew up? What do you like least? **2.** What was the symbol or sign of having "made it" in your hometown: (e.g., big house, star player, member of right club, be from one of the "old families")?

DIG: 1. Having been empowered to resist temptation in the desert (4:1), Jesus is now empowered by the spirit for what ministry? With what results? **2.** What is significant about the time and place (v. 16) for Jesus' discourse from Isaiah? **3.** What is Jesus' five-fold mission (vv. 18-19)? How is Jesus the fulfilment of that prophecy: Literally or spiritually? Presently or futuristically? With grace or judgment (see Is. 61:2b which Jesus did not quote)? **4.** What was the basis for the amazement (v. 22) and anger (vv. 28-29) of the crowd? **5.** What is Jesus saying through proverbs (v. 23)? Through the Elijah and Elisha stories (vv. 24-27)? Is Jesus implying the gospel might be given to the Gentiles after all? Why? **6.** What else is this passage saying about the focal point of the gospel and its reception?

REFLECT 1. Do you find it harder to be accepted and affirmed as a special person in your hometown, or among total strangers? How do you handle this? **2.** Jesus refers to five goals of his mission on earth in the Scripture passage. If all five are equally important, which area of concern do you give priority to and which do you tend to neglect: (a) "the poor". (b) "the prisoners", (c) "the blind", (d) "the oppressed" and (e) the hopeless (who need the "Lord's favor")?

OPEN: Who was your favorite teacher in high school? Why?

DIG: 1. What distinguishes Jesus' teaching here (vv. 31-32, 36, 37)? **2.** What event demonstrates Jesus' power and authority (vv. 33-35)? **3.** Is this a case of "actions speak louder than words"? Or of words mightier than illness and evil? Or "seeing is believing"? **4.** How does this healing story compare with the previous one?

REFLECT: 1. What teacher, writer, or news columnist do you look for guidance? What about this this person makes you listen? **2.** Do you

Jesus Rejected at Nazareth

[14] Jesus returned to Galilee in the power of the Spirit, and news about him spread through the whole countryside. [15] He taught in their synagogues, and everyone praised him.

[16] He went to Nazareth, where he had been brought up, and on the Sabbath day he went into the synagogue, as was his custom. And he stood up to read. [17] The scroll of the prophet Isaiah was handed to him. Unrolling it, he found the place where it is written:

[18]"The Spirit of the Lord is on me,
   because he has anointed me
     to preach good news to the poor.
 He has sent me to proclaim freedom for the prisoners
     and recovery of sight for the blind,
   to release the oppressed,
[19]   to proclaim the year of the Lord's favor." [s]

[20] Then he rolled up the scroll, gave it back to the attendant and sat down. The eyes of everyone in the synagogue were fastened on him, [21] and he began by saying to them, "Today this scripture is fulfilled in your hearing."

[22] All spoke well of him and were amazed at the gracious words that came from his lips. "Isn't this Joseph's son?" they asked.

[23] Jesus said to them, "Surely you will quote this proverb to me: 'Physician, heal yourself! Do here in your hometown what we have heard that you did in Capernaum.' "

[24]"I tell you the truth," he continued, "no prophet is accepted in his hometown. [25] I assure you that there were many widows in Israel in Elijah's time, when the sky was shut for three and a half years and there was a severe famine throughout the land. [26] Yet Elijah was not sent to any of them, but to a widow in Zarephath in the region of Sidon. [27] And there were many in Israel with leprosy [t] in the time of Elisha the prophet, yet not one of them was cleansed—only Naaman the Syrian."

[28] All the people in the synagogue were furious when they heard this. [29] They got up, drove him out of the town, and took him to the brow of the hill on which the town was built, in order to throw him down the cliff. [30] But he walked right through the crowd and went on his way.

Jesus Drives Out an Evil Spirit

[31] Then he went down to Capernaum, a town in Galilee, and on the Sabbath began to teach the people. [32] They were amazed at his teaching, because his message had authority.

[33] In the synagogue there was a man possessed by a demon, an evil [u] spirit. He cried out at the top of his voice, [34]"Ha! What do you want with us, Jesus of Nazareth? Have you come to destroy us? I know who you are—the Holy One of God!"

[35]"Be quiet!" Jesus said sternly. "Come out of him!" Then the demon threw the man down before them all and came out without injuring him.

---

[s]19 Isaiah 61:1,2   [t]27 The Greek word was used for various diseases affecting the skin—not necessarily leprosy.   [u]33 Greek *unclean*; also in verse 36

LOOKING INTO THE SCRIPTURE/20 Minutes. Read Luke 4:14-30 and discuss.

1. How would you describe the reception Jesus got in his hometown?
    a. thunderous applause
    b. faint praise
    c. mixed reviews
    d. a few snickers
    e. a change in public opinion

2. Why do you think his hometown had a problem accepting Jesus?
    a. rumors about Mary's pregnancy
    b. he came from the lower class
    c. they accepted the notion that "nothing good could come out of Nazareth"
    d. spiritual blindness
    e. they didn't understand prophecy

3. Why didn't Jesus wow them with a miracle?
    a. he was warned of this temptation by Satan
    b. they didn't have faith
    c. he was not a crowd pleaser
    d. that was not his purpose
    e. they still would not have believed
    f. he had nothing to prove

4. Why would Jesus' hometown neighbors be so furious?
    a. he discounted them
    b. he made them look bad
    c. he was just a carpenter's son
    d. he thought he was better than they were
    e. he would rather go to the non-Jews who would accept him

MY OWN STORY/25 Minutes.

1. Where do you find it hardest to be accepted as a person of worth and special value?
    a. around strangers
    b. around school/work
    c. around home
    d. around church
    e. around my friends

2. How do you deal with feelings of rejection?
    a. turn cold and indifferent
    b. get bitter and nasty
    c. crawl into a shell and mope
    d. laugh it off
    e. share openly, "I feel I have been discounted. . . ."

3. This story suggests several ways of coping with feelings of rejection. Which one(s) makes sense to you right now?
    a. I can accept the fact that my kin might praise me, but not really take me seriously
    b. there are others in the world who need me
    c. God can give me courage to do what's right despite criticism
    d. rejection might help me examine my life and make corrections as needed
    e. acceptance from my peers is not as important as God's love and acceptance of me

4. In Luke 4:18-19, Jesus applied five Old Testament promises to his mission on earth. Which of these five forms of rejection can you connect with the gospel in your life today?

☐ POVERTY (downtrodden, underprivileged): to receive hope and dignity
☐ IMPRISONMENT (physically, psychologically or politically captive): to receive freedom from bondage
☐ BLINDNESS (physical disability often meaning spiritual darkness): to receive new sight to recognize God's perspective and new life
☐ OPPRESSION (political and economic disadvantage): to receive release and new freedom from forces holding you down
☐ DEBT (every 50 years all debts were canceled): to receive the Jubilee Year's release from debt of every sort

really believe in "exorcism" today? Why? **3.** What uncontrollable craving would Jesus want to cast out of your life?

OPEN: What do you like best about your mother-in-law? Or what do you hope she will be like?

DIG: 1. Where does Jesus go now? Why? What happens to those who are healed (vv. 39, 41)? **2.** What is the significance about sunset (the day's end), Jesus' touch, and rebuking (the fever or the evil spirit)? **3.** Why does Jesus find it necessary to retreat at this time (vv. 42-44)? What are his priorities?

REFLECT: Jesus is obviously busy and in high-demand, yet he takes time to be alone. What part does solitude and quiet play in your life? How often do you go away...alone? How does God refresh you in those alone moments?

OPEN: 1. What's one of the best fish stories you've ever heard? **2.** Who's the best fisherman in your family? What kind of fisherman are you? **3.** If you could go anywhere on a fishing trip, where would you like to go and what would you like to catch? Why? **4.** What was it like the first time you "left home" for college, the military, a job, etc.?

DIG: 1. Under what circumstances does Jesus meet his first disciples? With each doing his own thing, how does Jesus capitalize on this situation? **2.** What does this preacher know about fishing? What does this fisherman know about the preaching of Jesus? **3.** What results from Simon's obedience? What then (vv. 8-10)? Why this confession of sin? What new insight did Simon and his partners have? **4.** Why do you suppose Jesus called these three and not the rest of their companions? **5.** What about Jesus makes these three fishermen leave all behind them to follow him?

REFLECT: 1. How did Jesus call you to himself and to ministry? How did he get your attention? Was it while you were doing something else or at a church service? **2.** If Jesus came to your place of work and called you to something new starting today, what would you say? What would your spouse, parents or children say?

---

³⁶All the people were amazed and said to each other, "What is this teaching? With authority and power he gives orders to evil spirits and they come out!" ³⁷And the news about him spread throughout the surrounding area.

Jesus Heals Many

³⁸Jesus left the synagogue and went to the home of Simon. Now Simon's mother-in-law was suffering from a high fever, and they asked Jesus to help her. ³⁹So he bent over her and rebuked the fever, and it left her. She got up at once and began to wait on them.

⁴⁰When the sun was setting, the people brought to Jesus all who had various kinds of sickness, and laying his hands on each one, he healed them. ⁴¹Moreover, demons came out of many people, shouting, "You are the Son of God!" But he rebuked them and would not allow them to speak, because they knew he was the Christ. ^v

⁴²At daybreak Jesus went out to a solitary place. The people were looking for him and when they came to where he was, they tried to keep him from leaving them. ⁴³But he said, "I must preach the good news of the kingdom of God to the other towns also, because that is why I was sent." ⁴⁴And he kept on preaching in the synagogues of Judea. ^w

The Calling of the First Disciples

5 One day as Jesus was standing by the Lake of Gennesaret, ^x with the people crowding around him and listening to the word of God, ²he saw at the water's edge two boats, left there by the fishermen, who were washing their nets. ³He got into one of the boats, the one belonging to Simon, and asked him to put out a little from shore. Then he sat down and taught the people from the boat.

⁴When he had finished speaking, he said to Simon, "Put out into deep water, and let down^y the nets for a catch."

⁵Simon answered, "Master, we've worked hard all night and haven't caught anything. But because you say so, I will let down the nets."

⁶When they had done so, they caught such a large number of fish that their nets began to break. ⁷So they signaled their partners in the other boat to come and help them, and they came and filled both boats so full that they began to sink.

⁸When Simon Peter saw this, he fell at Jesus' knees and said, "Go away from me, Lord; I am a sinful man!" ⁹For he and all his companions were astonished at the catch of fish they had taken, ¹⁰and so were James and John, the sons of Zebedee, Simon's partners.

Then Jesus said to Simon, "Don't be afraid; from now on you will catch men." ¹¹So they pulled their boats up on shore, left everything and followed him.

---

^v41 Or *Messiah*   ^w44 Or *the land of the Jews;* some manuscripts *Galilee*
^x1 That is, Sea of Galilee   ^y4 The Greek verb is plural.

LOOKING INTO THE SCRIPTURE/20 Minutes. Read Luke 5:1-11 and discuss.

1. What gets your attention about this first meeting of Jesus and Simon?
   - a. it was a terrific coincidence
   - b. it was more than coincidental
   - c. Jesus trusted a stranger to help him
   - d. how Jesus showed his interest in Simon's work

2. If you had been Simon Peter when Jesus asked him to "Put out into deep water, and let down the nets for a catch," what would you have done?
   - a. what Peter did
   - b. made some excuse
   - c. politely told Jesus to stick to his preaching
   - d. suggested another time when the fish were biting
   - e. gone ahead grudgingly
   - f. wondered who this person thought he was

3. When they "caught such a large number of fish that their nets began to break," how do you think Simon Peter felt?
   - a. overjoyed
   - b. terrible about what he had said to Jesus
   - c. dumbfounded
   - d. aware of who Jesus was

4. When Simon Peter said, "Go away from me, Lord; I am a sinful man!" what did he mean?
   - a. You embarrass me because you know more about fishing than I do
   - b. I feel uncomfortable being around you because of my sinful life
   - c. I know you are all that you say you are, but I am not ready to follow
   - d. Stop bugging me. Get out of my life
   - e. I'm confused. If I say "yes," I know that it will mean changing my life and I don't think I can measure up

5. "They left everything and followed Him." Why?
   - a. they wanted Jesus to become their fishing partner
   - b. they followed him in blind faith
   - c. they were confused and needed time to figure him out
   - d. they were attracted to his message
   - e. they were intrigued by the thought of becoming "fishers of men"
   - f. they were irresponsible
   - g. they knew then and there that he was the Messiah

MY OWN STORY/20 Minutes. Share some of your own spiritual journey with your group.

1. In comparison to Simon Peter's call, how would you explain your spiritual beginning?
   - a. tame
   - b. more intellectual
   - c. just as confusing
   - d. even crazier
   - e. different, but just as real
   - f. not sure

2. What is the condition of your spiritual boat right now?
   - a. sinking
   - b. out for repairs in dry dock
   - c. dead in the water
   - d. sailing at a fast clip
   - e. sailing in the wrong direction
   - f. battered by the heavy waves

3. Where do you think Jesus is, in relationship to your spiritual boat?
   - a. on the shore watching
   - b. swimming out to meet me
   - c. climbing on board
   - d. aboard, but not doing anything
   - e. casting out the nets
   - f. pulling in the catch

4. How does the idea of "putting out into deep water and letting down your nets for a catch" sound to you?
   - a. scary
   - b. crazy
   - c. okay, but . . .
   - d. fine, if someone will join me
   - e. just the invitation I've been waiting for
   - f. not sure what you mean

5. What is it going to take to get you going?
   - a. time to consider the cost
   - b. a little support from others
   - c. a good kick in the pants
   - d. time to get myself together
   - e. help to clean up my life
   - f. frankly, I don't know

OPEN: 1. What is the worst illness you had growing up? **2.** What was your family doctor like?

DIG: 1. What is leprosy? **2.** What is significant about the interaction between Jesus and this leper? **3.** Why the touch? Why the order to see the priest? Why the order of silence? **4.** What happens anyway? Was Jesus using reverse psychology? **5.** Why does Jesus withdraw?

REFLECT: When have you felt outcast like a leper? Who then "touched" you? Who are the "lepers" where you live? What would touch them for Christ?

OPEN: Who were your four closest friends in high school? What trouble did you get in together? What then? Who bailed out whom?

DIG: 1. In this story, who sits (in judgment)? Lies flat (sick)? Stands (in faith)? **2.** How is the faith of the paralytic's friends obvious to Jesus? **3.** How is the healing and forgiveness of the paralytic made obvious to others? Why do the Pharisees object? **4.** What is the *process* of healing? What part is played by faith of the friends? Forgiveness of Jesus? Power of the Lord? Obedience of the paralytic? **5.** What motivates each group (the people, friends, man, and Pharisees) to respond as they do?

REFLECT: 1. Who are you most like in this story: the paralyzed man, his friends, the crowd, the Pharisees and teachers? Why? **2.** Where are you a little paralyzed right now: either emotionally, physically, mentally, spiritually, relationally? What can be done by your friends, you and God for you to "take your mat and go home"?

OPEN: Of all those personalities you've always wanted to meet, who would you want as a dinner guest? As a close friend?

DIG: 1. What is significant in the call of Levi to discipleship? Why Levi? Why not Levi? Who celebrates this calling? Who opposes it? Why? **2.** What is Jesus' rationale for his choice of Levi (instead of others)? What is the irony in Jesus' mission statement (vv. 31-32)?

REFLECT: Are you "healthy" or "sick"? "Righteous" or "sinner"? Why? Which are your friends? Which one will you invite over today?

The Man With Leprosy

[12]While Jesus was in one of the towns, a man came along who was covered with leprosy.[z] When he saw Jesus, he fell with his face to the ground and begged him, "Lord, if you are willing, you can make me clean."

[13]Jesus reached out his hand and touched the man. "I am willing," he said. "Be clean!" And immediately the leprosy left him.

[14]Then Jesus ordered him, "Don't tell anyone, but go, show yourself to the priest and offer the sacrifices that Moses commanded for your cleansing, as a testimony to them."

[15]Yet the news about him spread all the more, so that crowds of people came to hear him and to be healed of their sicknesses. [16]But Jesus often withdrew to lonely places and prayed.

Jesus Heals a Paralytic

[17]One day as he was teaching, Pharisees and teachers of the law, who had come from every village of Galilee and from Judea and Jerusalem, were sitting there. And the power of the Lord was present for him to heal the sick. [18]Some men came carrying a paralytic on a mat and tried to take him into the house to lay him before Jesus. [19]When they could not find a way to do this because of the crowd, they went up on the roof and lowered him on his mat through the tiles into the middle of the crowd, right in front of Jesus.

[20]When Jesus saw their faith, he said, "Friend, your sins are forgiven."

[21]The Pharisees and the teachers of the law began thinking to themselves, "Who is this fellow who speaks blasphemy? Who can forgive sins but God alone?"

[22]Jesus knew what they were thinking and asked, "Why are you thinking these things in your hearts? [23]Which is easier: to say, 'Your sins are forgiven,' or to say, 'Get up and walk'? [24]But that you may know that the Son of Man has authority on earth to forgive sins. . . ." He said to the paralyzed man, "I tell you, get up, take your mat and go home." [25]Immediately he stood up in front of them, took what he had been lying on and went home praising God. [26]Everyone was amazed and gave praise to God. They were filled with awe and said, "We have seen remarkable things today."

The Calling of Levi

[27]After this, Jesus went out and saw a tax collector by the name of Levi sitting at his tax booth. "Follow me," Jesus said to him, [28]and Levi got up, left everything and followed him.

[29]Then Levi held a great banquet for Jesus at his house, and a large crowd of tax collectors and others were eating with them. [30]But the Pharisees and the teachers of the law who belonged to their sect complained to his disciples, "Why do you eat and drink with tax collectors and 'sinners'?"

[31]Jesus answered them, "It is not the healthy who need a doctor, but the sick. [32]I have not come to call the righteous, but sinners to repentance."

z12 The Greek word was used for various diseases affecting the skin—not necessarily leprosy.

LOOKING INTO THE SCRIPTURE/15 Minutes. Read Luke 5:17-26 and discuss.

1. If you had been the paralytic when your friends decided to take you up on the roof, remove the tiles, and lower you into the room, how would you have felt?
   a. reluctant: You're going to embarrass me
   b. scared: You're going to drop me
   c. dubious: You guys are crazy
   d. grateful: I appreciate your concern
   e. apprehensive: They are going to throw us out
   f. mixed: I don't think it is going to work, but I'm willing to trust you guys

2. What would it have taken for you to lower your paralytic friend down through the roof?
   a. organization
   b. courage
   c. a good sense of humor
   d. physical strength
   e. good timing
   f. desperation
   g. the right equipment

3. When the crowd heard all of the commotion on the roof and saw the paralytic being lowered into the room, how do you think the bystanders felt?
   a. annoyed: Don't these guys have any respect?
   b. amused: This is the best show in town
   c. angry: Throw them out
   d. sympathy: These guys are really concerned for their friend.

4. When Jesus said to the paralytic, "Friend, your sins are forgiven," what do you think the Pharisees and teachers of the law were thinking?
   a. who does this guy think he is?
   b. you have no right to assume his paralysis is caused by sin
   c. this Jesus ought to be sued for malpractice
   d. wait a minute. This guy has not sinned. He's just sick
   e. Jesus is trying to say that spiritual and physical illness are interrelated

5. If something like this ever happened in your church, what would the people say?
   a. this is the most excitement we've seen in years
   b. who is going to pay for the roof?
   c. whatever it takes to get someone healed is fine with us
   d. we're used to these things
   e. let's see this never happens again

MY OWN STORY/20 Minutes.

1. Take a moment and think about the major areas of your life. Then, for each area, put a dot to indicate your fitness—somewhere between ON THE INJURY LIST and PERFECT FITNESS. The midpoint on the line would be normal—you're not bad enough to ask for help, but you're not feeling great in this area either.

	ON THE INJURY LIST	PERFECT FITNESS
BODY: feeling physically fit	_____
MIND: feeling no stress/no pain	_____
SPIRIT: feeling close to God	_____
JOB/SCHOOL: doing what I like	_____
RELATIONSHIPS: getting along at home	_____
FUTURE: feeling good and secure	_____

2. What would you like to have from the group you are in right now to help you in the area where you indicated the greatest need? Go around and let each person in your group finish this sentence: "The way in which you could help me most is . . ."
   a. organization
   b. courage and faith
   c. a good sense of humor
   d. physical strength
   e. faithfulness in prayer
   f. desperation
   g. the right equipment

As a kid, did you ever split your pants or have the patch come off? What then? Today, do you prefer clothes used or new?

DIG: 1. Why is Jesus questioned about fasting? **2.** Given the festive nature of Jewish weddings and the identity of the bridegroom, how apt is Jesus' defense? When would fasting be okay? **3.** What's the point of this parable (vv. 36-39)? What is the new cloth ? Old garment? New wine? Old wineskins?

REFLECT: 1. In your life this week, are you feasting or fasting? Why? **2.** What's the new wine in your life? The old wineskins? How can you get more harmony in your life, new wine in new wineskins?

OPEN: In your family, what was special about Sunday? Was there anything you were not supposed to do "because it was the Sabbath"? **2.** What do you do well with your hands? What would you miss most if you lost one of your hands?

DIG: 1. What's the major issue in these verses? **2.** Why is corn-picking and healing so offensive to the Pharisees? **3.** How does the story of David and Abithar (see 1 Samuel 21:1-6) apply to Jesus and his disciples? **4.** How does Jesus clarify the sabbath issue (vv. 5, 9)? **5.** Why does Jesus provoke the Pharisees wrath by healing on the Sabbath? Couldn't he wait a day? **6.** What do you learn about Jesus and formalized religion in these encounters with the opposition?

REFLECT: When is it right to break the law? In your family are you more likely to treat Sunday like any other day, or be so strict that children dread to see Sunday come? How could you make Sunday more special for your family?

OPEN: What was one of the best teams you ever belonged to?

DIG: 1. How did Jesus prepare for choosing the twelve? What's significant about this to you? **2.** What do you know about these ordinary guys? Any brothers? Hometown buddies? Antagonists? Who introduced whom to Christ? Who do you know nothing about?

REFLECT: 1. In making big decisions, how much do you pray? Where do you go? What major decision is pending for you?

Jesus Questioned About Fasting

³³They said to him, "John's disciples often fast and pray, and so do the disciples of the Pharisees, but yours go on eating and drinking."

³⁴Jesus answered, "Can you make the guests of the bridegroom fast while he is with them? ³⁵But the time will come when the bridegroom will be taken from them; in those days they will fast."

³⁶He told them this parable: "No one tears a patch from a new garment and sews it on an old one. If he does, he will have torn the new garment, and the patch from the new will not match the old. ³⁷And no one pours new wine into old wineskins. If he does, the new wine will burst the skins, the wine will run out and the wineskins will be ruined. ³⁸No, new wine must be poured into new wineskins. ³⁹And no one after drinking old wine wants the new, for he says, 'The old is better.' "

Lord of the Sabbath

6 One Sabbath Jesus was going through the grainfields, and his disciples began to pick some heads of grain, rub them in their hands and eat the kernels. ²Some of the Pharisees asked, "Why are you doing what is unlawful on the Sabbath?"

³Jesus answered them, "Have you never read what David did when he and his companions were hungry? ⁴He entered the house of God, and taking the consecrated bread, he ate what is lawful only for priests to eat. And he also gave some to his companions." ⁵Then Jesus said to them, "The Son of Man is Lord of the Sabbath."

⁶On another Sabbath he went into the synagogue and was teaching, and a man was there whose right hand was shriveled. ⁷The Pharisees and the teachers of the law were looking for a reason to accuse Jesus, so they watched him closely to see if he would heal on the Sabbath. ⁸But Jesus knew what they were thinking and said to the man with the shriveled hand, "Get up and stand in front of everyone." So he got up and stood there.

⁹Then Jesus said to them, "I ask you, which is lawful on the Sabbath: to do good or to do evil, to save life or to destroy it?"

¹⁰He looked around at them all, and then said to the man, "Stretch out your hand." He did so, and his hand was completely restored. ¹¹But they were furious and began to discuss with one another what they might do to Jesus.

The Twelve Apostles

¹²One of those days Jesus went out to a mountainside to pray, and spent the night praying to God. ¹³When morning came, he called his disciples to him and chose twelve of them, whom he also designated apostles: ¹⁴Simon (whom he named Peter), his brother Andrew, James, John, Philip, Bartholomew, ¹⁵Matthew, Thomas, James son of Alphaeus, Simon who was called the Zealot, ¹⁶Judas son of James, and Judas Iscariot, who became a traitor.

Blessings and Woes

[17]He went down with them and stood on a level place. A large crowd of his disciples was there and a great number of people from all over Judea, from Jerusalem, and from the coast of Tyre and Sidon, [18]who had come to hear him and to be healed of their diseases. Those troubled by evil[a] spirits were cured, [19]and the people all tried to touch him, because power was coming from him and healing them all.

[20]Looking at his disciples, he said:

"Blessed are you who are poor,
for yours is the kingdom of God.
[21]Blessed are you who hunger now,
for you will be satisfied.
Blessed are you who weep now,
for you will laugh.
[22]Blessed are you when men hate you,
when they exclude you and insult you
and reject your name as evil,
because of the Son of Man.

[23]"Rejoice in that day and leap for joy, because great is your reward in heaven. For that is how their fathers treated the prophets.

[24]"But woe to you who are rich,
for you have already received your comfort.
[25]Woe to you who are well fed now,
for you will go hungry.
Woe to you who laugh now,
for you will mourn and weep.
[26]Woe to you when all men speak well of you,
for that is how their fathers treated the false prophets.

Love for Enemies

[27]"But I tell you who hear me: Love your enemies, do good to those who hate you, [28]bless those who curse you, pray for those who mistreat you. [29]If someone strikes you on one cheek, turn to him the other also. If someone takes your cloak, do not stop him from taking your tunic. [30]Give to everyone who asks you, and if anyone takes what belongs to you, do not demand it back. [31]Do to others as you would have them do to you.

[32]"If you love those who love you, what credit is that to you? Even 'sinners' love those who love them. [33]And if you do good to those who are good to you, what credit is that to you? Even 'sinners' do that. [34]And if you lend to those from whom you expect repayment, what credit is that to you? Even 'sinners' lend to 'sinners,' expecting to be repaid in full. [35]But love your enemies, do good to them, and lend to them without expecting to get anything back. Then your reward will be great, and you will be sons of the Most High, because he is kind to the ungrateful and wicked. [36]Be merciful, just as your Father is merciful.

[a]18 Greek unclean

OPEN: 1. What bumper sticker do you have on your car? What is another one of your favorite bumper stickers? 2. What is one of the greatest sermons you have heard?

DIG: 1. Where does Jesus preach this sermon? Who's in the crowd? Why have they come? How does Jesus meet their needs? 2. Who specifically is Jesus speaking to (v. 20)? 3. What are the four qualities that ought to characterize kingdom people (vv. 20-22)? How would you define each of these? What blessing is promised for each? When are these blessings to be experienced: Present? Future? Both? 4. What are the four warnings (vv. 24-26)? How would you define each: To whom are these addressed? 5. How does this section of Scripture begin to define the nature of the Kingdom of God?

REFLECT: 1. How do the values Jesus talks about here compare with the values you are sold everyday on TV? Which set of values do you and your family "buy" into? 2. If you could add another "blessed" and another woe to counteract the values on TV what would you add?

OPEN: 1. Who were your "enemies" when you were in school? What do you remember them doing to you? How did you get back at them? 2. What, if anything, have you had stolen? How do you feel about that?

DIG: 1: What's the significance of the shift Jesus has made in the object of love (see Leviticus 19:18)? What specifically are we to do that exhibits this love to enemies? 2. What reasons does Jesus give for this active love? 3. From this passage, does love seem like an emotion? An action? A decision? For your own kind? Why? What's the significance of that fact?

REFLECT: Who is on your "enemies" list at the moment? Why? What would happen if you "turned the tables" and sent them a kind letter? Who else could use a kind letter at this moment?

Judging Others

37"Do not judge, and you will not be judged. Do not condemn, and you will not be condemned. Forgive, and you will be forgiven. 38Give, and it will be given to you. A good measure, pressed down, shaken together and running over, will be poured into your lap. For with the measure you use, it will be measured to you."

39He also told them this parable: "Can a blind man lead a blind man? Will they not both fall into a pit? 40A student is not above his teacher, but everyone who is fully trained will be like his teacher.

41"Why do you look at the speck of sawdust in your brother's eye and pay no attention to the plank in your own eye? 42How can you say to your brother, 'Brother, let me take the speck out of your eye,' when you yourself fail to see the plank in your own eye? You hypocrite, first take the plank out of your own eye, and then you will see clearly to remove the speck from your brother's eye.

A Tree and Its Fruit

43"No good tree bears bad fruit, nor does a bad tree bear good fruit. 44Each tree is recognized by its own fruit. People do not pick figs from thornbushes, or grapes from briers. 45The good man brings good things out of the good stored up in his heart, and the evil man brings evil things out of the evil stored up in his heart. For out of the overflow of his heart his mouth speaks.

The Wise and Foolish Builders

46"Why do you call me, 'Lord, Lord,' and do not do what I say? 47I will show you what he is like who comes to me and hears my words and puts them into practice. 48He is like a man building a house, who dug down deep and laid the foundation on rock. When a flood came, the torrent struck that house but could not shake it, because it was well built. 49But the one who hears my words and does not put them into practice is like a man who built a house on the ground without a foundation. The moment the torrent struck that house, it collapsed and its destruction was complete."

The Faith of the Centurion

7 When Jesus had finished saying all this in the hearing of the people, he entered Capernaum. 2There a centurion's servant, whom his master valued highly, was sick and about to die. 3The centurion heard of Jesus and sent some elders of the Jews to him, asking him to come and heal his servant. 4When they came to Jesus, they pleaded earnestly with him, "This man deserves to have you do this, 5because he loves our nation and has built our synagogue." 6So Jesus went with them.

He was not far from the house when the centurion sent friends to say to him: "Lord, don't trouble yourself, for I do not deserve to have you come under my roof. 7That is why I did not even consider myself worthy to come to you. But say the word, and my servant will be healed. 8For I myself am a man under authority, with soldiers under me. I tell this one, 'Go,' and he goes; and that one, 'Come,' and he comes. I say to my servant, 'Do this,' and he does it."

⁹When Jesus heard this, he was amazed at him, and turning to the crowd following him, he said, "I tell you, I have not found such great faith even in Israel." ¹⁰Then the men who had been sent returned to the house and found the servant well.

Jesus Raises a Widow's Son

¹¹Soon afterward, Jesus went to a town called Nain, and his disciples and a large crowd went along with him. ¹²As he approached the town gate, a dead person was being carried out—the only son of his mother, and she was a widow. And a large crowd from the town was with her. ¹³When the Lord saw her, his heart went out to her and he said, "Don't cry."

¹⁴Then he went up and touched the coffin, and those carrying it stood still. He said, "Young man, I say to you, get up!" ¹⁵The dead man sat up and began to talk, and Jesus gave him back to his mother.

¹⁶They were all filled with awe and praised God. "A great prophet has appeared among us," they said. "God has come to help his people." ¹⁷This news about Jesus spread throughout Judea*b* and the surrounding country.

Jesus and John the Baptist

¹⁸John's disciples told him about all these things. Calling two of them, ¹⁹he sent them to the Lord to ask, "Are you the one who was to come, or should we expect someone else?"

²⁰When the men came to Jesus, they said, "John the Baptist sent us to you to ask, 'Are you the one who was to come, or should we expect someone else?'"

²¹At that very time Jesus cured many who had diseases, sicknesses and evil spirits, and gave sight to many who were blind. ²²So he replied to the messengers, "Go back and report to John what you have seen and heard: The blind receive sight, the lame walk, those who have leprosy*c* are cured, the deaf hear, the dead are raised, and the good news is preached to the poor. ²³Blessed is the man who does not fall away on account of me."

²⁴After John's messengers left, Jesus began to speak to the crowd about John: "What did you go out into the desert to see? A reed swayed by the wind? ²⁵If not, what did you go out to see? A man dressed in fine clothes? No, those who wear expensive clothes and indulge in luxury are in palaces. ²⁶But what did you go out to see? A prophet? Yes, I tell you, and more than a prophet. ²⁷This is the one about whom it is written:

" 'I will send my messenger ahead of you,
who will prepare your way before you.'*d*

²⁸I tell you, among those born of women there is no one greater than John; yet the one who is least in the kingdom of God is greater than he."

OPEN: If you were in charge, how would you change our funerals and burial practice? Why?

DIG: 1. How's this story staged: When? Where? Who? What's happening? 2. Why is Jesus so moved by this woman (vv. 12-13)? 3. What does Jesus do? Say? With what results? Impact on others? 4. Why does Luke, a Greek doctor, include so many healing stories?

REFLECT: When someone you love dies, what is the best thing you can do to give comfort? What do you do with your feelings? Bottle them up? Or let them out? Long term, what can you do to be helpful?

OPEN: (For married) When did you know that the person you married was "the one"? (For unmarried) What is the sign you look for in a mate to tell you "this is the one"?

DIG: 1. How does John receive information about Jesus? Why can't he get it firsthand (see 3:20)? What question does he ask his men to ask Jesus (v. 20)? Why? What probably is John's expectation of how a Messiah ought to act (for clues, see 3:16-17)? 2. How does Jesus answer the question (vv. 21-23)? Why doesn't he answer the question directly? What six things characterize his ministry? 3. From Isaiah (29:18-19; 35:5-6; 61:1), how might John interpret Jesus' reply? How might he take Jesus' added blessing (v. 23)? 4. What questions does Jesus put to the people? How does Jesus affirm John? 5. As great as John was, who is greater? Why? 6. What is noteworthy about the people's response to John in contrast to that of the Pharisees? In what ways are the followers of the Pharisees like "children" bickering over which game to play (vv. 31-32)? In what ways are the followers of John and Jesus like "children" proving God's wisdom is right (v. 35)?

REFLECT: 1. When did you come to the place in your own spiritual pilgrimage when you knew Jesus

The "Big" crises or the little crises? ("Big" = a death "Little" = your child gets a bad report card ... or gets caught for the third time speeding?)

b17 Or the land of the Jews *c22 The Greek word was used for various diseases affecting the skin—not necessarily leprosy.* *d27 Mal. 3:1*

151

was "the one" you were looking for? How did you come to this understanding? What difference has it made? **2.** If you could ask Jesus one question today about a decision you are facing, what would it be?

OPEN: 1. What is your favorite perfume or aftershave? Why? **2.** What do you look for in a gift for your spouse or someone you care about? What is one of the most touching gifts you have received from your kids or parents? **3.** What kind of dinner parties do you like to go to? Hate going to?

DIG: 1. Who invites Jesus to dinner? Why the invitation? **2.** Who's the uninvited guest? What do you learn about her in verse 37? What does she do? Why do you think she does it? **3.** What does the Pharisee say? To whom? **4.** How does Jesus surprise him? What story does he tell (vv. 41-42)? What's the point? What's Jesus' question? How does Simon answer? What does his answer reveal about him? **5.** How does Jesus amplify the previous story (vv. 44-47)? How does the way the woman relates to Jesus compare with the way Simon has? What does this say about Simon? The woman? **6.** What is the bottom line for the woman (v. 48)? How do the other guests react to this? **7.** What is Jesus' final word to the woman? How would these words be comforting to her?

REFLECT:1. Where do you "blow" your money? On what? Clothes? Cars? Entertainment? **2.** On whom do you find it easy to be extravagant with your gifts? **3.** When it comes to relationships, are you a "big forgiver" or a "stingy one"? **4.** When it comes to risking your reputation by sticking up for a "questionable" character, what do you do? What do you learn from this story that could apply this week?

²⁹(All the people, even the tax collectors, when they heard Jesus' words, acknowledged that God's way was right, because they had been baptized by John. ³⁰But the Pharisees and experts in the law rejected God's purpose for themselves, because they had not been baptized by John.)

³¹"To what, then, can I compare the people of this generation? What are they like? ³²They are like children sitting in the marketplace and calling out to each other:

" 'We played the flute for you,
  and you did not dance;
we sang a dirge,
  and you did not cry.'

³³For John the Baptist came neither eating bread nor drinking wine, and you say, 'He has a demon.' ³⁴The Son of Man came eating and drinking, and you say, 'Here is a glutton and a drunkard, a friend of tax collectors and "sinners." ' ³⁵But wisdom is proved right by all her children."

Jesus Anointed by a Sinful Woman

³⁶Now one of the Pharisees invited Jesus to have dinner with him, so he went to the Pharisee's house and reclined at the table. ³⁷When a woman who had lived a sinful life in that town learned that Jesus was eating at the Pharisee's house, she brought an alabaster jar of perfume, ³⁸and as she stood behind him at his feet weeping, she began to wet his feet with her tears. Then she wiped them with her hair, kissed them and poured perfume on them.

³⁹When the Pharisee who had invited him saw this, he said to himself, "If this man were a prophet, he would know who is touching him and what kind of woman she is—that she is a sinner."

⁴⁰Jesus answered him, "Simon, I have something to tell you."

"Tell me, teacher," he said.

⁴¹"Two men owed money to a certain moneylender. One owed him five hundred denarii,ᵉ and the other fifty. ⁴²Neither of them had the money to pay him back, so he canceled the debts of both. Now which of them will love him more?"

⁴³Simon replied, "I suppose the one who had the bigger debt canceled."

"You have judged correctly," Jesus said.

⁴⁴Then he turned toward the woman and said to Simon, "Do you see this woman? I came into your house. You did not give me any water for my feet, but she wet my feet with her tears and wiped them with her hair. ⁴⁵You did not give me a kiss, but this woman, from the time I entered, has not stopped kissing my feet. ⁴⁶You did not put oil on my head, but she has poured perfume on my feet. ⁴⁷Therefore, I tell you, her many sins have been forgiven—for she loved much. But he who has been forgiven little loves little."

⁴⁸Then Jesus said to her, "Your sins are forgiven."

ᵉ41 A denariusᵢwas a coin worth about a day's wages.

Luke 7:36-50　　　　　　　JESUS ANOINTED BY A SINFUL WOMAN

LOOKING INTO THE SCRIPTURE/20 Minutes. Read Luke 7:36-50 and discuss.

1. Do you think the Pharisee was aware of the social custom to greet guests with a kiss and wash their feet?
   a. yes
   b. no

2. Do you think Jesus was aware of the purification law prohibiting anyone to "touch" a prostitute?
   a. yes
   b. no

3. Why do you think the sinful woman came to the Pharisee's house?
   a. to upset the Pharisee
   b. to ruin the party
   c. to seek forgiveness
   d. to minister to Jesus
   e. to confront her oppressors

4. What made the Pharisee so upset?
   a. her reputation
   b. his reputation
   c. Jesus' acceptance of the woman

5. How did the Pharisee feel when the sinful woman "touched" Jesus?
   a. contaminated
   b. humiliated
   c. angry
   d. sympathetic
   e. hysterical

6. "If this man were a prophet, he would know who is touching him and what kind of woman she is—that she is a sinner." Which possibility comes closest to your understanding of Jesus?
   a. Jesus was not a prophet and didn't know who the woman was
   b. Jesus knew who the woman was but didn't care about the Law
   c. Jesus cared about the Law but cared about the person more
   d. Jesus, because he really was a prophet, was able to see the "sinful woman" as clean and forgiven

7. In the story about the two men who owed money, what was Jesus saying to Simon?
   a. You can't know grace because you have never thought of yourself as a sinner
   b. You are a bigger sinner than the woman but you don't know it
   c. The more you have sinned the more your love for God
   d. The more you have been forgiven the more your love for God

8. What was the tone in Jesus' voice when he said to the woman, "Your faith has saved you; go in peace."
   a. judicial: like a judge
   b. clinical: like a psychiatrist
   c. pastoral: like a priest
   d. paternal: like a father
   e. authoritative: like a sergeant

MY OWN STORY/25 Minutes.

1. Who was the prophet in your life who believed in you and saw beauty in you before you believed in yourself?
   a. my mom/dad
   b. a special teacher/coach
   c. one special friend
   d. a pastor/youth leader

2. How did this affect your life?
   a. I could deal with my own negative feelings
   b. I could accept God's forgiveness
   c. I started to believe in myself
   d. I started to act differently

⁴⁹The other guests began to say among themselves, "Who is this who even forgives sins?"

⁵⁰Jesus said to the woman, "Your faith has saved you; go in peace."

The Parable of the Sower

8 After this, Jesus traveled about from one town and village to another, proclaiming the good news of the kingdom of God. The Twelve were with him, ²and also some women who had been cured of evil spirits and diseases: Mary (called Magdalene) from whom seven demons had come out; ³Joanna the wife of Cuza, the manager of Herod's household; Susanna; and many others. These women were helping to support them out of their own means.

⁴While a large crowd was gathering and people were coming to Jesus from town after town, he told this parable: ⁵"A farmer went out to sow his seed. As he was scattering the seed, some fell along the path; it was trampled on, and the birds of the air ate it up. ⁶Some fell on rock, and when it came up, the plants withered because they had no moisture. ⁷Other seed fell among thorns, which grew up with it and choked the plants. ⁸Still other seed fell on good soil. It came up and yielded a crop, a hundred times more than was sown."

When he said this, he called out, "He who has ears to hear, let him hear."

⁹His disciples asked him what this parable meant. ¹⁰He said, "The knowledge of the secrets of the kingdom of God has been given to you, but to others I speak in parables, so that,

" 'though seeing, they may not see;
    though hearing, they may not understand.'ᶠ

¹¹"This is the meaning of the parable: The seed is the word of God. ¹²Those along the path are the ones who hear, and then the devil comes and takes away the word from their hearts, so that they may not believe and be saved. ¹³Those on the rock are the ones who receive the word with joy when they hear it, but they have no root. They believe for a while, but in the time of testing they fall away. ¹⁴The seed that fell among thorns stands for those who hear, but as they go on their way they are choked by life's worries, riches and pleasures, and they do not mature. ¹⁵But the seed on good soil stands for those with a noble and good heart, who hear the word, retain it, and by persevering produce a crop.

A Lamp on a Stand

¹⁶"No one lights a lamp and hides it in a jar or puts it under a bed. Instead, he puts it on a stand, so that those who come in can see the light. ¹⁷For there is nothing hidden that will not be disclosed, and nothing concealed that will not be known or brought out into the open. ¹⁸Therefore consider carefully how you listen. Whoever has will be given more; whoever does not have, even what he thinks he has will be taken from him."

ᶠ10 Isaiah 6:9

OPEN: 1. Who is the "green thumb" in your family? What is the closest you have come to living on a farm? What do you do: Slop the hogs? Feed the chickens? Milk the cows? **2.** What kind of luck have you had raising a garden? Is your crop yield small, average or humongous? What is your secret?

DIG: 1. What's Jesus' ministry style here (v. 1)? Who travels with him? What can you say about this "crew"? How is Jesus' ministry financed? **2.** What's the setting for this parable (v. 4)? What is a parable? **3.** What are the four types of soil? What's Jesus' main point in his parable? **4.** How would the parable help the disciples better understand what is happening in their ministry? **5.** What question do the disciples ask (v. 9)? Why? What does Jesus say is the "secret" to understanding a parable? How does the challenge of Jesus in verse 8 help to explain his words in verse 10? **6.** How does faith open up to more and more spiritual insight (see also 8:18)? **7.** In Jesus' explanation of this parable, what is the seed, the soils, the fruit, the farmer? **8.** How would you explain this parable to a bunch of city kids who had never seen a field? What modern analogy would you use?

REFLECT: 1. What kind of "soil" best represents you now? What kind of soil would have represented you five years ago? **2.** What kind of crop are you going to yield this year? If God could get his hands on you, what would he do to increase the yield? **3.** What are you having a difficult time understanding in your life now? **4.** What help do you get from this parable about sharing your faith with others?

OPEN: What do you like to hide under your bed? Why?

DIG: 1. Why shouldn't an oil lamp be covered? **2.** If Jesus and his message are the lamp of truth, what is the meaning of this parable? **3.** What is the promise for those who listen and those who don't?

REFLECT: When all that you have done in your life is revealed, how will you feel? Which of those years would you like to erase?

Jesus' Mother and Brothers

¹⁹Now Jesus' mother and brothers came to see him, but they were not able to get near him because of the crowd. ²⁰Someone told him, "Your mother and brothers are standing outside, wanting to see you."

²¹He replied, "My mother and brothers are those who hear God's word and put it into practice."

Jesus Calms the Storm

²²One day Jesus said to his disciples, "Let's go over to the other side of the lake." So they got into a boat and set out. ²³As they sailed, he fell asleep. A squall came down on the lake, so that the boat was being swamped, and they were in great danger.

²⁴The disciples went and woke him, saying, "Master, Master, we're going to drown!"

He got up and rebuked the wind and the raging waters; the storm subsided, and all was calm. ²⁵"Where is your faith?" he asked his disciples.

In fear and amazement they asked one another, "Who is this? He commands even the winds and the water, and they obey him."

The Healing of a Demon-possessed Man

²⁶They sailed to the region of the Gerasenes,ᵍ which is across the lake from Galilee. ²⁷When Jesus stepped ashore, he was met by a demon-possessed man from the town. For a long time this man had not worn clothes or lived in a house, but had lived in the tombs. ²⁸When he saw Jesus, he cried out and fell at his feet, shouting at the top of his voice, "What do you want with me, Jesus, Son of the Most High God? I beg you, don't torture me!" ²⁹For Jesus had commanded the evilʰ spirit to come out of the man. Many times it had seized him, and though he was chained hand and foot and kept under guard, he had broken his chains and had been driven by the demon into solitary places.

³⁰Jesus asked him, "What is your name?"

"Legion," he replied, because many demons had gone into him. ³¹And they begged him repeatedly not to order them to go into the Abyss.

³²A large herd of pigs was feeding there on the hillside. The demons begged Jesus to let them go into them, and he gave them permission. ³³When the demons came out of the man, they went into the pigs, and the herd rushed down the steep bank into the lake and was drowned.

³⁴When those tending the pigs saw what had happened, they ran off and reported this in the town and countryside, ³⁵and the people went out to see what had happened. When they came to Jesus, they found the man from whom the demons had gone out, sitting at Jesus' feet, dressed and in his right mind; and they were afraid. ³⁶Those who had seen it told the people how the demon-possessed man had been cured. ³⁷Then all the people of

ᵍ26 Some manuscripts *Gadarenes*; other manuscripts *Gergesenes*; also in verse 37
ʰ29 Greek *unclean*

OPEN: Which family member was closest to you in age? In trouble?

DIG: What does Jesus teach about his true family? How does one get "near" Jesus?

REFLECT: Who in your family do you consider "nearest"? Why?

OPEN: What is the worst storm you remember? When kept inside by a storm, what do you do?

DIG: 1. What is Jesus teaching his disciples by ignoring the storm? By rebuking the storm? **2.** Why is Jesus upset: Because they couldn't calm the storm? Or they didn't believe God would protect them? **3.** In this story what emotions hinder faith? Accompany faith? Why?

REFLECT: Compared to a storm, what would your life be like right now: Partly cloudy? Lightening? Raging? Clearing up?

OPEN: 1. Where do you go to "get away from it all"? What do you do for "kicks"? **2.** When did a vacation turn into something you never expected? What happened?

DIG: 1. After the events of verses 22-25, how do you think the disciples are feeling as they arrive on the other side of the lake? After verse 31? After verse 33? After verse 39? **2.** What happens when Jesus steps ashore? How does Luke describe this man in verses 27-31? What does the man say to Jesus (vv. 30-32)? **3.** How is Jesus' treatment of the man probably different than the way others have treated him? What does Jesus do for the man (vv.29, 32)? What results (v. 33)? **4.** How do the pig farmers respond? The townspeople? Why? **5.** What does Jesus ask him to do instead? What happens?

REFLECT: 1. In your life right now, what is the thing that "wears" on you, that makes you feel like there are a legion (6,000 soldiers) marching through your head, keeping you awake at night or "torn" at work? **2.** When, if ever, have you wanted Jesus to leave you alone? To get out of your life? To let you hurt yourself? **3.** Who are the "townspeople" who don't want to listen to the claims of Christ if it is going to effect their business?

---

the region of the Gerasenes asked Jesus to leave them, because they were overcome with fear. So he got into the boat and left.

³⁸The man from whom the demons had gone out begged to go with him, but Jesus sent him away, saying, ³⁹"Return home and tell how much God has done for you." So the man went away and told all over town how much Jesus had done for him.

A Dead Girl and a Sick Woman

⁴⁰Now when Jesus returned, a crowd welcomed him, for they were all expecting him. ⁴¹Then a man named Jairus, a ruler of the synagogue, came and fell at Jesus' feet, pleading with him to come to his house ⁴²because his only daughter, a girl of about twelve, was dying.

As Jesus was on his way, the crowds almost crushed him. ⁴³And a woman was there who had been subject to bleeding for twelve years,ⁱ but no one could heal her. ⁴⁴She came up behind him and touched the edge of his cloak, and immediately her bleeding stopped.

⁴⁵"Who touched me?" Jesus asked.

When they all denied it, Peter said, "Master, the people are crowding and pressing against you."

⁴⁶But Jesus said, "Someone touched me; I know that power has gone out from me."

⁴⁷Then the woman, seeing that she could not go unnoticed, came trembling and fell at his feet. In the presence of all the people, she told why she had touched him and how she had been instantly healed. ⁴⁸Then he said to her, "Daughter, your faith has healed you. Go in peace."

⁴⁹While Jesus was still speaking, someone came from the house of Jairus, the synagogue ruler. "Your daughter is dead," he said. "Don't bother the teacher any more."

⁵⁰Hearing this, Jesus said to Jairus, "Don't be afraid; just believe, and she will be healed."

⁵¹When he arrived at the house of Jairus, he did not let anyone go in with him except Peter, John and James, and the child's father and mother. ⁵²Meanwhile, all the people were wailing and mourning for her. "Stop wailing," Jesus said. "She is not dead but asleep."

⁵³They laughed at him, knowing that she was dead. ⁵⁴But he took her by the hand and said, "My child, get up!" ⁵⁵Her spirit returned, and at once she stood up. Then Jesus told them to give her something to eat. ⁵⁶Her parents were astonished, but he ordered them not to tell anyone what had happened.

Jesus Sends Out the Twelve

9 When Jesus had called the Twelve together, he gave them power and authority to drive out all demons and to cure diseases, ²and he sent them out to preach the kingdom of God and to heal the sick. ³He told them: "Take nothing for the journey—no staff, no bag, no bread, no money, no extra tunic. ⁴Whatever house you enter, stay there until you leave that town. ⁵If people do not welcome you, shake the dust off your feet when

---

OPEN: When have you been almost crushed in a crowd? What famous person did you come close to in a crowd? Did you get to "touch" this person? What happened?

DIG: 1. Of all the people pressing for Jesus' attention, two get through to him in this story—how so? **2.** Why do you think Jesus makes the sick woman reveal herself? For his sake? Or for her own sake? What does this say about Jesus' view of health? **3.** What more do you learn about her character before and after she touches Jesus' garment? How was her faith obvious to Jesus? **4.** What do you know about Jairus' daughter from verses 41-42? From verses 49, 53? **5.** Why does Jesus say she will be healed or is "only asleep" when the facts speak otherwise? **6.** Compare the reaction of Jairus to Jesus' coming with that of the mourners. What accounts for this difference? What part does Jairus' intense desire have in the raising of the dead girl? **7.** Why does Jesus sometimes order silence of people he heals (vv. 56; also 5:14), but other times orders the healed person to first go home then presumably tell all (see 5:24, 8:39)?

REFLECT: 1. When have you been as desperate as Jairus and the bleeding woman? How did Jesus touch you then? **2.** Have you ever been too frightened to come to God with a problem? Why? Have you ever felt you could not share something with anyone other than God? How about your Christian support group?

OPEN: 1. What do you pack for a trip: A toothbrush? Light bag and good book? All but the kitchen sink? **2.** Where do you stay: Posh hotel? Bed and breakfast? Relatives?

DIG: 1. What decision does Jesus make about his ministry? Why? **2.** What are the disciples told to do? **3.** What instructions does he give the disciples? Why? **4.** How does King Herod react? Why would he be perplexed?

ⁱ43 Many manuscripts *years, and she had spent all she had on doctors*

you leave their town, as a testimony against them." ⁶So they set out and went from village to village, preaching the gospel and healing people everywhere.

⁷Now Herod the tetrarch heard about all that was going on. And he was perplexed, because some were saying that John had been raised from the dead, ⁸others that Elijah had appeared, and still others that one of the prophets of long ago had come back to life. ⁹But Herod said, "I beheaded John. Who, then, is this I hear such things about?" And he tried to see him.

Jesus Feeds the Five Thousand

¹⁰When the apostles returned, they reported to Jesus what they had done. Then he took them with him and they withdrew by themselves to a town called Bethsaida, ¹¹but the crowds learned about it and followed him. He welcomed them and spoke to them about the kingdom of God, and healed those who needed healing.

¹²Late in the afternoon the Twelve came to him and said, "Send the crowd away so they can go to the surrounding villages and countryside and find food and lodging, because we are in a remote place here."

¹³He replied, "You give them something to eat."

They answered, "We have only five loaves of bread and two fish—unless we go and buy food for all this crowd." ¹⁴(About five thousand men were there.)

But he said to his disciples, "Have them sit down in groups of about fifty each." ¹⁵The disciples did so, and everybody sat down. ¹⁶Taking the five loaves and the two fish and looking up to heaven, he gave thanks and broke them. Then he gave them to the disciples to set before the people. ¹⁷They all ate and were satisfied, and the disciples picked up twelve basketfuls of broken pieces that were left over.

Peter's Confession of Christ

¹⁸Once when Jesus was praying in private and his disciples were with him, he asked them, "Who do the crowds say I am?"

¹⁹They replied, "Some say John the Baptist; others say Elijah; and still others, that one of the prophets of long ago has come back to life."

²⁰"But what about you?" he asked. "Who do you say I am?"

Peter answered, "The Christ*ʲ* of God."

²¹Jesus strictly warned them not to tell this to anyone. ²²And he said, "The Son of Man must suffer many things and be rejected by the elders, chief priests and teachers of the law, and he must be killed and on the third day be raised to life."

²³Then he said to them all: "If anyone would come after me, he must deny himself and take up his cross daily and follow me. ²⁴For whoever wants to save his life will lose it, but whoever loses his life for me will save it. ²⁵What good is it for a man to gain the whole world, and yet lose or forfeit his very self? ²⁶If anyone is ashamed of me and my words, the Son of Man will

ʲ20 Or Messiah

REFLECT: 1. Who is someone you have really admired because they dared to take off, give up all security and give their life to a mission? **2.** What is your mission in life, other than to keep food on the table? **3.** What is the one thing you would like to do if you didn't have to worry about money?

OPEN: How do you unwind when you return home from work? After a trip?

DIG 1. Why does Jesus take his disciples away with him upon their return from work? Is their purpose for this debriefing retreat fulfilled, or frustrated, by what happens next? **2.** How differently do the disciples and Jesus view the crowd? How do you account for these differences? **3.** What is the secret to Jesus' multiplying the loaves and fish: His blessing? His piece-making? His hands ("quicker than the eye") His distribution system? Why the leftovers: Did Jesus miscalculate?

REFLECT: 1. From what do you need a rest: Work hassles? Kids? Church activities? Community activities? School deadlines? **2.** How do you handle the overload of another "challenge" from God? Or the question "Guess who's coming for dinner?"

OPEN: If you asked the average street person "Who is Christ?," what answers would you get: (a) Great person, (b) A swear word, (c) Good teacher, (d) An imposter?

DIG: 1. Why might Jesus be interested in this opinion poll? What affect would that have on him? On the disciples' perception? **2.** How does Jesus focus his follow-up question (v. 20)? **3.** What does Peter's reply mean? **4.** Why doesn't Jesus want them to tell anyone he is the Christ? **5.** What lies ahead for Jesus? For his disciples? **6.** What activities or attitudes are key to following Christ (v. 23)? Not following Christ (vv. 24-26)? **7.** How do these three sections (vv. 18-20, 21-22, 23-27) flow together?

REFLECT: 1. When did Jesus become more than just a name in the history books to you? **2.** What does it mean specifically to you to (a) deny self, (b) take up your cross daily, (c) follow Christ and (d) lose your life? **3.** If you could go back and reconsider your commitment to

Jesus Christ (knowing what you do now), would you make the same commitment? Why or why not?

OPEN: If you went back-packing, where would you go? What three friends would you take along? Why?

DIG: 1. How's this story staged: When? Where? Who? What's happening? **2.** Why might Jesus take these particular disciples to witness him transfigured and speaking with Moses and Elijah? **3.** What's the connection here with Peter's confession (vv. 18-20)? With Jesus' prophecy (v. 22)? The preceeding saying (v. 27)? Moses and Elijah (see Mt. 11:13)? **4.** Why is this event misunderstood by Peter (v. 33)? Underscored by God (vv. 34-35)? Kept secret by the disciples (see Mark 9:9)?

REFLECT: 1. As on a mountain, where have you experienced God in an unusual way? What happened? **2.** When did you last take time to clarify your goals? Why not now?

OPEN: 1. When you take off a few days from work, who takes over for you? What is it like on your first day back on the job? **2.** Have you ever coached or played on a Little League team? How do you feel when the team "can't do it right"?

DIG: 1. What has evidently been going on while Jesus has been on the mountain? **2.** Who meets Jesus and the three disciples? What does the man want? How does the man describe his son? What has been his experience with Jesus' disciples? **3.** Why does Jesus seem to be impatient in verse 41? **4.** What does the boy do as Jesus approaches? What does Jesus do for the boy? The father? How does the crowd respond? **5.** As the amazement continues, what does Jesus teach his disciples? What's the significance of teaching this content at this time? How well do the disciples grasp it? **6.** What more can you learn from this story by reading it in Matthew 17:14-21 and Mark 9:14-29?

REFLECT: 1. If you had been one of the disciples who couldn't solve the boy's problem only days after you had been on a mission trip, how would you feel? **2.** What "spiritual low" has recently followed a "spiritual high" for you? Why the "highs" and "lows"? What helps even them out?

be ashamed of him when he comes in his glory and in the glory of the Father and of the holy angels. ²⁷I tell you the truth, some who are standing here will not taste death before they see the kingdom of God."

The Transfiguration

²⁸About eight days after Jesus said this, he took Peter, John and James with him and went up onto a mountain to pray. ²⁹As he was praying, the appearance of his face changed, and his clothes became as bright as a flash of lightning. ³⁰Two men, Moses and Elijah, ³¹appeared in glorious splendor, talking with Jesus. They spoke about his departure, which he was about to bring to fulfillment at Jerusalem. ³²Peter and his companions were very sleepy, but when they became fully awake, they saw his glory and the two men standing with him. ³³As the men were leaving Jesus, Peter said to him, "Master, it is good for us to be here. Let us put up three shelters—one for you, one for Moses and one for Elijah." (He did not know what he was saying.) ³⁴While he was speaking, a cloud appeared and enveloped them, and they were afraid as they entered the cloud. ³⁵A voice came from the cloud, saying, "This is my Son, whom I have chosen; listen to him." ³⁶When the voice had spoken, they found that Jesus was alone. The disciples kept this to themselves, and told no one at that time what they had seen.

The Healing of a Boy With an Evil Spirit

³⁷The next day, when they came down from the mountain, a large crowd met him. ³⁸A man in the crowd called out, "Teacher, I beg you to look at my son, for he is my only child. ³⁹A spirit seizes him and he suddenly screams; it throws him into convulsions so that he foams at the mouth. It scarcely ever leaves him and is destroying him. ⁴⁰I begged your disciples to drive it out, but they could not."

⁴¹"O unbelieving and perverse generation," Jesus replied, "how long shall I stay with you and put up with you? Bring your son here."

⁴²Even while the boy was coming, the demon threw him to the ground in a convulsion. But Jesus rebuked the evil ᵏ spirit, healed the boy and gave him back to his father. ⁴³And they were all amazed at the greatness of God.

While everyone was marveling at all that Jesus did, he said to his disciples, ⁴⁴"Listen carefully to what I am about to tell you: The Son of Man is going to be betrayed into the hands of men." ⁴⁵But they did not understand what this meant. It was hidden from them, so that they did not grasp it, and they were afraid to ask him about it.

k42 Greek unclean

Who Will Be the Greatest?

⁴⁶An argument started among the disciples as to which of them would be the greatest. ⁴⁷Jesus, knowing their thoughts, took a little child and had him stand beside him. ⁴⁸Then he said to them, "Whoever welcomes this little child in my name welcomes me; and whoever welcomes me welcomes the one who sent me. For he who is least among you all—he is the greatest."

⁴⁹"Master," said John, "we saw a man driving out demons in your name and we tried to stop him, because he is not one of us."

⁵⁰"Do not stop him," Jesus said, "for whoever is not against you is for you."

Samaritan Opposition

⁵¹As the time approached for him to be taken up to heaven, Jesus resolutely set out for Jerusalem. ⁵²And he sent messengers on ahead, who went into a Samaritan village to get things ready for him; ⁵³but the people there did not welcome him, because he was heading for Jerusalem. ⁵⁴When the disciples James and John saw this, they asked, "Lord, do you want us to call fire down from heaven to destroy them^l?" ⁵⁵But Jesus turned and rebuked them, ⁵⁶and^m they went to another village.

The Cost of Following Jesus

⁵⁷As they were walking along the road, a man said to him, "I will follow you wherever you go."

⁵⁸Jesus replied, "Foxes have holes and birds of the air have nests, but the Son of Man has no place to lay his head."

⁵⁹He said to another man, "Follow me."

But the man replied, "Lord, first let me go and bury my father."

⁶⁰Jesus said to him, "Let the dead bury their own dead, but you go and proclaim the kingdom of God."

⁶¹Still another said, "I will follow you, Lord; but first let me go back and say good-by to my family."

⁶²Jesus replied, "No one who puts his hand to the plow and looks back is fit for service in the kingdom of God."

Jesus Sends Out the Seventy-two

10 After this the Lord appointed seventy-two^n others and sent them two by two ahead of him to every town and place where he was about to go. ²He told them, "The harvest is plentiful, but the workers are few. Ask the Lord of the harvest, therefore, to send out workers into his harvest field. ³Go! I am sending you out like lambs among wolves. ⁴Do not take a purse or bag or sandals; and do not greet anyone on the road.

⁵"When you enter a house, first say, 'Peace to this house.' ⁶If a man of peace is there, your peace will rest on him; if not, it will return to you. ⁷Stay in that house, eating and drinking

---

l54 Some manuscripts them, even as Elijah did *m55,56 Some manuscripts them. And he said, "You do not know what kind of spirit you are of, for the Son of Man did not come to destroy men's lives, but to save them." 56And* *n1 Some manuscripts seventy; also in verse 17*

OPEN: Are you "the greatest" at anything among your peers? What "bragging rights" do you own? For how long?

DIG: 1. In chapter 9, how are the disciples guaging "greatness"? **2.** In Jesus' object lesson (vv. 47-48), what is greatness? **3.** In John's concern (verse 49), what's the root desire? The irony (see verse 40)?

REFLECT: As a kid, how did you picture "greatness"? How have those visions changed since?

OPEN: What's hard about crossing enemy lines? Going to jail?

DIG: How does Jesus' "timetable" meet resistance? Why from the Samaritans? Why from his own disciples? How is Jesus feeling all this time (vv. 51, 53, 54)?

REFLECT: What impresses you about Jesus in this story?

OPEN: Share one creative excuse for not doing something (e.g., "the dog ate my homework")?

DIG: How does Jesus speak to the excuses offered by these three prospective followers? In your own words, what do each of Jesus' sayings mean? What's his overall point?

REFLECT: If Jesus were to say to you "Follow me"—today—and you were to use one of your favorite excuses for putting things off, what would happen? What will it take to get you off your duff?

OPEN: 1. If you could sell anything "door to door", what would you choose: Fuller brushes? Encyclopedias? Imported jewelry? Magazine subscriptions? Family Bibles? Natural foods? Why? **2.** What territory or city would you choose: New Your City high-rises? Deep South? Appalachian mountains? California beach resorts? Why?

DIG: 1. Why does he send them two-by-two? Why does he send them ahead of him? **2.** Why is the Christian disciple like a "worker in the harvest"? A "lamb among wolves"? **3.** What was the purpose of traveling light (v. 4)? Of praying first (v. 2), going later (v. 3)? **4.** What kind of household guests are they

159

to be (v. 5)? Why does this make good sense? **5.** How are they related to the town and townspeople of which they are a part (vv. 8-12)? What is their basic message? **6.** How do the verses 1-12 show the urgency Jesus himself senses for evangelism? What is the reason for this urgency? **7.** What do you know about Korazin and Bethsaida? About Tyre and Sidon? Capernaum? How closely were the seventy-two aligned with Jesus in this mission (v. 16)? **8.** What's their report upon their return? What does Jesus say to them (vv. 18-20)? What has he seen? What does he promise? What should be their source of joy? **9.** In what emotional state is Jesus in verse 21? Why? Who is he talking to in verses 21-22? What does he say about the Father? About the situation? What does this prayer teach about the way God works and Jesus' relationship to the Father? **10.** What does he say to the disciples (v. 23)? Why are they so blessed?

REFLECT: 1. Why are so many people in our society turning to spiritual study, "meditation" Eastern religions, New Age religions? **2.** In what sense is our age "ripe" for the gospel that Jesus brought? **3.** If you invited every person on your block, apartment house or in your office to a Bible study group "to discover what Jesus Christ has to say about their life," how many people do you think would come? **4.** Do you know of one person who would be your "partner" in starting such a group? **5.** What night would be good? What book would you study? **6.** What is holding you back?

OPEN: 1. What do you remember about your neighborhood as a child? Who was the "cookie jar" neighbor? Who was the neighbor most kids feared or misunderstood? **2.** Who would you nominate for the "Good Samaritan Award" in your neighborhood for being a "good neighbor"?

DIG: 1. Who's testing whom in this story? **2.** How do the responses of the expert in the law seemingly pass Jesus' test? What counts with Jesus: Is it what you know? What you do? Who you know (as your neighbor)? Or what? Does the lawyer seem to think he has passed the test in verse 29? **3.** Why does Jesus answer with a story instead

whatever they give you, for the worker deserves his wages. Do not move around from house to house.

⁸"When you enter a town and are welcomed, eat what is set before you. ⁹Heal the sick who are there and tell them, 'The kingdom of God is near you.' ¹⁰But when you enter a town and are not welcomed, go into its streets and say, ¹¹'Even the dust of your town that sticks to our feet we wipe off against you. Yet be sure of this: The kingdom of God is near.' ¹²I tell you, it will be more bearable on that day for Sodom than for that town.

¹³"Woe to you, Korazin! Woe to you, Bethsaida! For if the miracles that were performed in you had been performed in Tyre and Sidon, they would have repented long ago, sitting in sackcloth and ashes. ¹⁴But it will be more bearable for Tyre and Sidon at the judgment than for you. ¹⁵And you, Capernaum, will you be lifted up to the skies? No, you will go down to the depths.ᵒ

¹⁶"He who listens to you listens to me; he who rejects you rejects me; but he who rejects me rejects him who sent me."

¹⁷The seventy-two returned with joy and said, "Lord, even the demons submit to us in your name."

¹⁸He replied, "I saw Satan fall like lightning from heaven. ¹⁹I have given you authority to trample on snakes and scorpions and to overcome all the power of the enemy; nothing will harm you. ²⁰However, do not rejoice that the spirits submit to you, but rejoice that your names are written in heaven."

²¹At that time Jesus, full of joy through the Holy Spirit, said, "I praise you, Father, Lord of heaven and earth, because you have hidden these things from the wise and learned, and revealed them to little children. Yes, Father, for this was your good pleasure.

²²"All things have been committed to me by my Father. No one knows who the Son is except the Father, and no one knows who the Father is except the Son and those to whom the Son chooses to reveal him."

²³Then he turned to his disciples and said privately, "Blessed are the eyes that see what you see. ²⁴For I tell you that many prophets and kings wanted to see what you see but did not see it, and to hear what you hear but did not hear it."

The Parable of the Good Samaritan

²⁵On one occasion an expert in the law stood up to test Jesus. "Teacher," he asked, "what must I do to inherit eternal life?"

²⁶"What is written in the Law?" he replied. "How do you read it?"

²⁷He answered: " 'Love the Lord your God with all your heart and with all your soul and with all your strength and with all your mind'ᵖ; and, 'Love your neighbor as yourself.'ᑫ"

²⁸"You have answered correctly," Jesus replied. "Do this and you will live."

²⁹But he wanted to justify himself, so he asked Jesus, "And who is my neighbor?"

ᵒ15 Greek *Hades*   ᵖ27 Deut. 6:5   ᑫ27 Lev. 19:18

Luke 10:25-37   **THE PARABLE OF THE GOOD SAMARITAN**

LOOKING INTO THE SCRIPTURE/20 Minutes. Read Luke 10:25-37 and discuss.

1. Do you think Jesus knew about the Samaritans—that they were social outcasts because they had intermarried with the wrong people?   ☐ Yes ☐ No

2. Do you think Jesus knew about the road from Jerusalem to Jericho—that it was the most dangerous road in Judea with robbers posing as wounded people?   ☐ Yes ☐ No

3. Do you think Jesus knew about the Old Testament rule that anyone who touched a dead person was "unclean" for several days?   ☐ Yes ☐ No

4. If there was a good chance that the wounded person was only "playing dead" in order to trap the priest and Levite, do you think they were justified in passing by on the other side?   ☐ Yes ☐ No

5. If the priest and Levite were taking the dangerous road because they were in a rush to get to their religious duties in Jericho, do you think they could be justified in passing by the wounded man?   ☐ Yes ☐ No

6. Why do you think the Samaritan stopped when the others "passed by on the other side"?
   a. he was more sensitive
   b. he didn't care about the religious problem of touching a dead corpse
   c. he knew what it meant to be a hurting person and have people pass by
   d. he didn't have much to lose

7. Why do you think Jesus told this parable in response to the lawyer's question, "Who is my neighbor?"
   a. to let the lawyer answer his own question
   b. to catch the lawyer in a moral dilemma
   c. to use a "case history" approach that lawyers use

MY OWN STORY/20 Minutes.

1. What do you do when people come up to you on a street corner asking for a handout?
   a. ignore them
   b. take a look at what they are wearing
   c. give them money without any questions
   d. get to know their situations and then decide
   e. assume I'm being conned
   f. find some excuse not to give
   g. offer to take them to the grocery store and buy what they need
   h. share the gospel with them and pray for them
   i. take them to your pastor who is better equipped to handle the problem
   j. report them to the police

2. Now that you've read this parable, who would you say is your "neighbor"?
   a. someone like me with a need
   b. anyone who approaches me with a need
   c. only reputable charitable organizations
   d. those I have reasonable hope of helping
   e. the ones I'm most afraid of helping

3. If you had to call upon someone outside of your family at 3 o'clock in the morning because of a deep personal problem, on whom would you call?
   a. my pastor/priest
   b. professional counselor
   c. my friend _____
   d. someone who had the same problem
   e. someone who had conquered this problem
   f. someone who didn't know me

of a straight cognitive answer? **4.** How might one justify the actions of the priest and the Levite? **5.** From what you know about the historic divisions between Jews and Samaritans (see John 4), what's unusual about the plot twist in this story? **6.** What is Jesus' point in using the Samaritan to exemplify brotherly love? **7.** Does Jesus get his point across? Why?

REFLECT: 1. At 3:00 AM, who do you call with a serious problem, someone you trust to just be with you, all ears and heart, no advice-giving? What about this person makes you feel as you do? **2.** What support group do you have that would accept you—warts and all? **3.** Who do you know right now that is hurting and has no one to call on?

OPEN: 1. What brothers/sisters do you have? How are you different? **2.** When unexpected company you love drops by, how do you react?

DIG: How do the two sisters differ? Why is Mary's choice better? Doesn't hospitality count, too? What is Jesus' point?

REFLECT: What, to you, are good points and blind spots of both Mary and Martha? Who are you most like - Mary or Martha? Why?

OPEN Who prayed with you when you were a child? Did you have a standard prayer that you recited? If so, how much can you remember?

DIG: 1. What motivates the disciple to ask about prayer at this time (v. 1)? **2.** In Jesus' model prayer (vv. 2-4), to whom do you pray? What two concerns related to God are you first to pray about? What personal concerns then follow? How do prayer and forgiveness relate? How does this prayer compare and contrast to the more expanded prayer of Matthew 6:9-13? **3.** What does the parable in verses 5-8 teach about prayer? How do the words in verses 9-10 relate to the parable? **4.** What three commands does Jesus give in verse 9? How are they different from one another? What is the promise he gives? **5.** What does the story in verses 11-13 illustrate? **6.** According to Jesus (v. 13), what is the ultimate good gift?

---

[30] In reply Jesus said: "A man was going down from Jerusalem to Jericho, when he fell into the hands of robbers. They stripped him of his clothes, beat him and went away, leaving him half dead. [31] A priest happened to be going down the same road, and when he saw the man, he passed by on the other side. [32] So too, a Levite, when he came to the place and saw him, passed by on the other side. [33] But a Samaritan, as he traveled, came where the man was; and when he saw him, he took pity on him. [34] He went to him and bandaged his wounds, pouring on oil and wine. Then he put the man on his own donkey, took him to an inn and took care of him. [35] The next day he took out two silver coins' and gave them to the innkeeper. 'Look after him,' he said, 'and when I return, I will reimburse you for any extra expense you may have.'

[36] "Which of these three do you think was a neighbor to the man who fell into the hands of robbers?"

[37] The expert in the law replied, "The one who had mercy on him."

Jesus told him, "Go and do likewise."

At the Home of Martha and Mary

[38] As Jesus and his disciples were on their way, he came to a village where a woman named Martha opened her home to him. [39] She had a sister called Mary, who sat at the Lord's feet listening to what he said. [40] But Martha was distracted by all the preparations that had to be made. She came to him and asked, "Lord, don't you care that my sister has left me to do the work by myself? Tell her to help me!"

[41] "Martha, Martha," the Lord answered, "you are worried and upset about many things, [42] but only one thing is needed.' Mary has chosen what is better, and it will not be taken away from her."

Jesus' Teaching on Prayer

11 One day Jesus was praying in a certain place. When he finished, one of his disciples said to him, "Lord, teach us to pray, just as John taught his disciples."

[2] He said to them, "When you pray, say:

" 'Father,'
hallowed be your name,
your kingdom come.ᵘ
[3] Give us each day our daily bread.
[4] Forgive us our sins,
     for we also forgive everyone who sins against us.ᵛ
And lead us not into temptation.ʷ ' "

[5] Then he said to them, "Suppose one of you has a friend, and he goes to him at midnight and says, 'Friend, lend me three loaves of bread, [6] because a friend of mine on a journey has come to me, and I have nothing to set before him.'

---

r35 Greek *two denarii*   *s42* Some manuscripts *but few things are needed—or only one*
t2 Some manuscripts *Our|Father in heaven*   *u2* Some manuscripts *come. May your will be done on earth|as it is in heaven.*   *v4* Greek *everyone who is indebted to us*
w4 Some manuscripts *temptation but deliver us from the evil one*

Luke 10:38-42   AT THE HOME OF MARTHA AND MARY

LOOKING INTO THE STORY/20 Minutes. Read Luke 10:38-42 and discuss.

1. Why do you think Jesus went to Martha and Mary's house?
   a. they were close friends
   b. he had nowhere else to go
   c. he liked their cooking
   d. he needed their fellowship

2. What do you think Jesus meant when he said, "Mary has chosen what is better"?
   a. Martha had her priorities messed up
   b. people who let their housework go are more spiritual
   c. people are more important than a clean house
   d. fussing over little things is a sign of spiritual immaturity
   e. spiritual matters come first

3. If you had been Martha, how would you have responded to Jesus' remark?
   a. gone to my room and pouted
   b. thought to myself: "He doesn't have to live with my sister"
   c. flown off-the-handle
   d. felt put down
   e. accepted the rebuke
   f. sat down with Jesus and let the supper burn

4. Why do you think Jesus said it?
   a. Martha was picking on Mary
   b. Martha was getting on his nerves
   c. he knew her well enough to say this without hurting her
   d. he knew he had one more week and he wanted to spend the time with them

---

MY OWN STORY/25 Minutes.

1. How do you see yourself . . . somewhere between the two extremes.

ON HOUSEWORK: dirty dishes everywhere _____ slippers at the door
ON TEMPERAMENT: easygoing _____ high strung
ON TAKING RESPONSIBILITY: little sister _____ big sister
ON ORGANIZING MY LIFE: a day late and a dollar short _____ ten minutes early
ON HURT FEELINGS: let's have it out _____ sweep it under the rug

2. If you had to choose between Mary and Martha for the following situations, who would you choose?

MARY	MARTHA	
☐	☐	For a roommate
☐	☐	For a close friend
☐	☐	To work for
☐	☐	To work for you
☐	☐	To be your next-door neighbor
☐	☐	To be the executor of your estate
☐	☐	To be your pastor
☐	☐	To go to with a problem

3. If you had Mary as a sister, what would you do?
   a. try to change her
   b. move out
   c. accept her as she is
   d. learn from her spirituality
   e. accept myself as different
   f. try to change myself

4. If you were the parents of these two sisters, what would you do?
   a. try to affirm them for their uniqueness
   b. let them keep their rooms as they wish
   c. set some rules for everybody
   d. move out and leave the house to them
   e. accept them as they are
   f. help them appreciate each other's unique temperaments

5. What would Jesus likely say to you if he dropped in on your home today?
   a. turn down the music
   b. turn off the TV
   c. reorganize your time
   d. enjoy the people in your life
   e. slow down and appreciate the little things
   f. set aside time for God daily
   g. take a look at your expectations of yourself
   h. _____

[7]"Then the one inside answers, 'Don't bother me. The door is already locked, and my children are with me in bed. I can't get up and give you anything.' [8]I tell you, though he will not get up and give him the bread because he is his friend, yet because of the man's boldness[x] he will get up and give him as much as he needs.

[9]"So I say to you: Ask and it will be given to you; seek and you will find; knock and the door will be opened to you. [10]For everyone who asks receives; he who seeks finds; and to him who knocks, the door will be opened.

[11]"Which of you fathers, if your son asks for[y] a fish, will give him a snake instead? [12]Or if he asks for an egg, will give him a scorpion? [13]If you then, though you are evil, know how to give good gifts to your children, how much more will your Father in heaven give the Holy Spirit to those who ask him!"

Jesus and Beelzebub

[14]Jesus was driving out a demon that was mute. When the demon left, the man who had been mute spoke, and the crowd was amazed. [15]But some of them said, "By Beelzebub,[z] the prince of demons, he is driving out demons." [16]Others tested him by asking for a sign from heaven.

[17]Jesus knew their thoughts and said to them: "Any kingdom divided against itself will be ruined, and a house divided against itself will fall. [18]If Satan is divided against himself, how can his kingdom stand? I say this because you claim that I drive out demons by Beelzebub. [19]Now if I drive out demons by Beelzebub, by whom do your followers drive them out? So then, they will be your judges. [20]But if I drive out demons by the finger of God, then the kingdom of God has come to you.

[21]"When a strong man, fully armed, guards his own house, his possessions are safe. [22]But when someone stronger attacks and overpowers him, he takes away the armor in which the man trusted and divides up the spoils.

[23]"He who is not with me is against me, and he who does not gather with me, scatters.

[24]"When an evil[a] spirit comes out of a man, it goes through arid places seeking rest and does not find it. Then it says, 'I will return to the house I left.' [25]When it arrives, it finds the house swept clean and put in order. [26]Then it goes and takes seven other spirits more wicked than itself, and they go in and live there. And the final condition of that man is worse than the first."

[27]As Jesus was saying these things, a woman in the crowd called out, "Blessed is the mother who gave you birth and nursed you."

[28]He replied, "Blessed rather are those who hear the word of God and obey it."

The Sign of Jonah

²⁹As the crowds increased, Jesus said, "This is a wicked generation. It asks for a miraculous sign, but none will be given it except the sign of Jonah. ³⁰For as Jonah was a sign to the Ninevites, so also will the Son of Man be to this generation. ³¹The Queen of the South will rise at the judgment with the men of this generation and condemn them; for she came from the ends of the earth to listen to Solomon's wisdom, and now one*ᵇ* greater than Solomon is here. ³²The men of Nineveh will stand up at the judgment with this generation and condemn it; for they repented at the preaching of Jonah, and now one greater than Jonah is here.

The Lamp of the Body

³³"No one lights a lamp and puts it in a place where it will be hidden, or under a bowl. Instead he puts it on its stand, so that those who come in may see the light. ³⁴Your eye is the lamp of your body. When your eyes are good, your whole body also is full of light. But when they are bad, your body also is full of darkness. ³⁵See to it, then, that the light within you is not darkness. ³⁶Therefore, if your whole body is full of light, and no part of it dark, it will be completely lighted, as when the light of a lamp shines on you."

Six Woes

³⁷When Jesus had finished speaking, a Pharisee invited him to eat with him; so he went in and reclined at the table. ³⁸But the Pharisee, noticing that Jesus did not first wash before the meal, was surprised.

³⁹Then the Lord said to him, "Now then, you Pharisees clean the outside of the cup and dish, but inside you are full of greed and wickedness. ⁴⁰You foolish people! Did not the one who made the outside make the inside also? ⁴¹But give what is inside ₍the dish₎*ᶜ* to the poor, and everything will be clean for you.

⁴²"Woe to you Pharisees, because you give God a tenth of your mint, rue and all other kinds of garden herbs, but you neglect justice and the love of God. You should have practiced the latter without leaving the former undone.

⁴³"Woe to you Pharisees, because you love the most important seats in the synagogues and greetings in the marketplaces.

⁴⁴"Woe to you, because you are like unmarked graves, which men walk over without knowing it."

⁴⁵One of the experts in the law answered him, "Teacher, when you say these things, you insult us also."

⁴⁶Jesus replied, "And you experts in the law, woe to you, because you load people down with burdens they can hardly carry, and you yourselves will not lift one finger to help them.

⁴⁷"Woe to you, because you build tombs for the prophets, and it was your forefathers who killed them. ⁴⁸So you testify that you approve of what your forefathers did; they killed the prophets, and you build their tombs. ⁴⁹Because of this, God in his wisdom

---

OPEN: What is the funniest bumper sticker or sign you have seen?

DIG: 1. How does Jesus feel about "this generation"? Why? 2. What is the sign of Jonah? How is Jesus like that? 3. Who is this Queen (1 Kings 10:1-15)? Who condemns whom? 4. What is Jesus' point?

REFLECT: 1. What kind of "sign" would it take for this generation to wake up and turn to God? 2. How are your own values influenced by and resistant to, this generation?

OPEN: Growing up, what did you do when the lights went out?

DIG: 1. What's Jesus' point in verse 33 (also 8:16f)? In this analogy (v. 34), what do the eye and body represent? How is spiritual truth perceived and blindness avoided?

REFLECT: On an eye-test, how would your spiritual sight score: 20/20? 20/80? Color blind? Why?

OPEN: 1. When you were a child, who insisted upon you "washing" your hands before meals? Who insisted upon you wearing "clean" clothes? 2. Who is your favorite lawyer or private eye on TV? How would you like to have their job?

DIG: 1. Where does Jesus go to dinner? What surprises the Pharisee? 2. How does the Lord turn the tables on his host? What is his basic point about the Pharisees (v. 39-41)? 3. In your own words, what is the meaning of these three woes directed at the Pharisees (vv. 42-44)? Given the Pharisees' view of tombs and the dead (see Numbers 19:16), what is the significance of the unmarked graves (v. 44)? 4. What is the point of these criticisms: To add insult to injury (v. 45)? 5. In your own words, what is the meaning of the next three woes (vv. 46-52)? How would this fifth woe (vv. 47-51) be especially distasteful for lawyers? In the sixth woe (v. 52), what does Jesus mean by the key of knowledge? 6. What is the main point of these accusations directed at lawyers: To intensify their opposition to him (v. 53)? Or what? 7. How does this Pharisee dinner compare with the first dinner in Luke 7:36-50?

REFLECT: 1. What are some religious practices that you think we could do without today? What are

---

ᵇ31 Or *something*; also in verse 32   ᶜ41 Or *what you have*

said, 'I will send them prophets and apostles, some of whom they will kill and others they will persecute.' [50]Therefore this generation will be held responsible for the blood of all the prophets that has been shed since the beginning of the world, [51]from the blood of Abel to the blood of Zechariah, who was killed between the altar and the sanctuary. Yes, I tell you, this generation will be held responsible for it all.

[52]"Woe to you experts in the law, because you have taken away the key to knowledge. You yourselves have not entered, and you have hindered those who were entering."

[53]When Jesus left there, the Pharisees and the teachers of the law began to oppose him fiercely and to besiege him with questions, [54]waiting to catch him in something he might say.

Warnings and Encouragements

12 Meanwhile, when a crowd of many thousands had gathered, so that they were trampling on one another, Jesus began to speak first to his disciples, saying: "Be on your guard against the yeast of the Pharisees, which is hypocrisy. [2]There is nothing concealed that will not be disclosed, or hidden that will not be made known. [3]What you have said in the dark will be heard in the daylight, and what you have whispered in the ear in the inner rooms will be proclaimed from the roofs.

[4]"I tell you, my friends, do not be afraid of those who kill the body and after that can do no more. [5]But I will show you whom you should fear: Fear him who, after the killing of the body, has power to throw you into hell. Yes, I tell you, fear him. [6]Are not five sparrows sold for two pennies[d]? Yet not one of them is forgotten by God. [7]Indeed, the very hairs of your head are all numbered. Don't be afraid; you are worth more than many sparrows.

[8]"I tell you, whoever acknowledges me before men, the Son of Man will also acknowledge him before the angels of God. [9]But he who disowns me before men will be disowned before the angels of God. [10]And everyone who speaks a word against the Son of Man will be forgiven, but anyone who blasphemes against the Holy Spirit will not be forgiven. [11]"When you are brought before synagogues, rulers and authorities, do not worry about how you will defend yourselves or what you will say, [12]for the Holy Spirit will teach you at that time what you should say."

The Parable of the Rich Fool

[13]Someone in the crowd said to him, "Teacher, tell my brother to divide the inheritance with me."

[14]Jesus replied, "Man, who appointed me a judge or an arbiter between you?" [15]Then he said to them, "Watch out! Be on your guard against all kinds of greed; a man's life does not consist in the abundance of his possessions."

[16]And he told them this parable: "The ground of a certain rich man produced a good crop. [17]He thought to himself, 'What shall I do? I have no place to store my crops.'

*d*6 Greek *two assaria*

Luke 12:13-21

THE PARABLE OF THE RICH FOOL

LOOKING INTO THE SCRIPTURE/15 Minutes. Read Luke 12:13-21 and discuss.

1. In verse 13, what was the man in the crowd really saying to Jesus?
   a. my brother is treating me poorly
   b. I want my share of the action
   c. would you straighten out this mess?
   d. my brother is greedy
   e. what does the Jewish law say about inheritance?

2. In his reply, what was Jesus telling the crowd?
   a. greed will get you into trouble
   b. I am not a judge or an arbiter
   c. money, wealth, and material goods are not important
   d. concern for money and wealth can easily get out of control

3. In the parable, what is Jesus saying about wealth and the pursuit of wealth?
   a. wealth can make us greedy
   b. wealth will make us better people
   c. wealth can be used to further the kingdom of God
   d. wealth can make us self-indulgent

4. Why is God's response to the rich man so harsh?
   a. because God is intolerant of self-indulgent people
   b. because God has so much compassion for the poor
   c. because God wanted him to use his resources more wisely
   d. because God is jealous of other "gods" such as wealth

5. What does it mean to be "rich toward God"?
   a. seek first the kingdom of God
   b. give most of your money to the poor
   c. use your abilities and resources to further God's kingdom
   d. invest in church lotteries

6. If Jesus commented on our view of wealth today, what do you think he would say?
   a. "Lifestyles of the Rich and Famous" is not the way to go
   b. you are grabbing for it all but missing the true meaning of life
   c. it is difficult to see the difference between Christian values and secular values today
   d. you have so much but you are spiritually bankrupt

MY OWN STORY/30 Minutes.

1. Where are your riches? (Name two)
   a. in my children
   b. in my friends
   c. in my bank account
   d. in my education
   e. in my job advancement
   f. in a good self-image
   g. in a strong body
   h. in some beautiful memories
   i. in my family

2. What are three priorities for your life right now?
   a. a good time
   b. a good marriage/family
   c. having nice things
   d. getting ahead
   e. being true to myself
   f. finding spiritual fulfillment
   g. making a contribution to mankind
   h. making lots of money

3. How would you like to be remembered?
   a. as the one who had a lot
   b. as the one who gave a lot
   c. as the one who built it all single-handedly
   d. as the one who enjoyed what he/she had
   e. as the one who lost it all to be rich toward God

4. Where would you like to leave your riches?
   a. to my family
   b. to a charitable cause that I believe in
   c. to build a memorial at my church
   d. to my college/school
   e. to overseas missions
   f. to the government

is he a fool? **4.** In your own words, what is the punch line of this parable (vv. 15,21)?

REFLECT: 1. In this story, do you think God is too hard on the rich man? Why? When have you been like the man in this story? Have you ever nearly "lost it all" and come back to thank God for the experience? **2.** In planning an investment portfolio to become "rich toward God", what will you do?

OPEN: Which situation would cause you the most worry: Overdrawn at the bank? Gained 10 pounds? Son doesn't make Little League team? Nobody called all weekend? Mother-in-law stays two weeks? Business goes "belly up"?

DIG: 1. How do these verses about worry relate to the preceding parable about riches? **2.** Addressing his disciples this time, what does Jesus tell them *not* to do (vv. 22, 29, 32)? Why? **3.** In contrast, what does Jesus urge believers to do (vv. 24, 27, 31, 33)? Why? What will result? **4.** What pictures illustrate his points? **5.** What does Jesus teach here about worry? About motives for the Christian? Material needs?

REFLECT: 1. On a scale from 1 to 10 (1 = "no sweat" and 10 = "panic"), what is the worry quotient in your life right now? Why? **2.** How do you specifically "seek the kingdom of God"? **3.** If you could reduce your lifestyle by moving to a smaller house with smaller monthly payments, would you? Why don't you – for your own and your family's health?

OPEN: 1. What caused you to be "grounded"? Missing curfew? A bad report card? Throwing a party when the folks were away? **2.** What would your parents do if they came home "early" and found you throwing a "party"? **3.** When is the last time you slept through an appointment? Have you ever been caught "napping" when you were supposed to be on duty?

DIG: 1. What quality is Jesus stressing to his disciples in verses 35-36? What reward will they receive (vv. 37-38)? What does this reward mean in a broader perspective? **3.** Why does Jesus say they should be ready (vv. 39-40)? Who is the thief? **4.** What does Peter want to know in verse 41? Why? How does Jesus answer that? Is he saying

[18]"Then he said, 'This is what I'll do. I will tear down my barns and build bigger ones, and there I will store all my grain and my goods. [19]And I'll say to myself, "You have plenty of good things laid up for many years. Take life easy; eat, drink and be merry." '

[20]"But God said to him, 'You fool! This very night your life will be demanded from you. Then who will get what you have prepared for yourself?'

[21]"This is how it will be with anyone who stores up things for himself but is not rich toward God."

Do Not Worry

[22]Then Jesus said to his disciples: "Therefore I tell you, do not worry about your life, what you will eat; or about your body, what you will wear. [23]Life is more than food, and the body more than clothes. [24]Consider the ravens: They do not sow or reap, they have no storeroom or barn; yet God feeds them. And how much more valuable you are than birds! [25]Who of you by worrying can add a single hour to his life[c]? [26]Since you cannot do this very little thing, why do you worry about the rest?

[27]"Consider how the lilies grow. They do not labor or spin. Yet I tell you, not even Solomon in all his splendor was dressed like one of these. [28]If that is how God clothes the grass of the field, which is here today, and tomorrow is thrown into the fire, how much more will he clothe you, O you of little faith! [29]And do not set your heart on what you will eat or drink; do not worry about it. [30]For the pagan world runs after all such things, and your Father knows that you need them. [31]But seek his kingdom, and these things will be given to you as well.

[32]"Do not be afraid, little flock, for your Father has been pleased to give you the kingdom. [33]Sell your possessions and give to the poor. Provide purses for yourselves that will not wear out, a treasure in heaven that will not be exhausted, where no thief comes near and no moth destroys. [34]For where your treasure is, there your heart will be also.

Watchfulness

[35]"Be dressed ready for service and keep your lamps burning, [36]like men waiting for their master to return from a wedding banquet, so that when he comes and knocks they can immediately open the door for him. [37]It will be good for those servants whose master finds them watching when he comes. I tell you the truth, he will dress himself to serve, will have them recline at the table and will come and wait on them. [38]It will be good for those servants whose master finds them ready, even if he comes in the second or third watch of the night. [39]But understand this: If the owner of the house had known at what hour the thief was coming, he would not have let his house be broken into. [40]You also must be ready, because the Son of Man will come at an hour when you do not expect him."

---

[c]25 Or *single cubit to his height*

⁴¹Peter asked, "Lord, are you telling this parable to us, or to everyone?"

⁴²The Lord answered, "Who then is the faithful and wise manager, whom the master puts in charge of his servants to give them their food allowance at the proper time? ⁴³It will be good for that servant whom the master finds doing so when he returns. ⁴⁴I tell you the truth, he will put him in charge of all his possessions. ⁴⁵But suppose the servant says to himself, 'My master is taking a long time in coming,' and he then begins to beat the menservants and maidservants and to eat and drink and get drunk. ⁴⁶The master of that servant will come on a day when he does not expect him and at an hour he is not aware of. He will cut him to pieces and assign him a place with the unbelievers.

⁴⁷"That servant who knows his master's will and does not get ready or does not do what his master wants will be beaten with many blows. ⁴⁸But the one who does not know and does things deserving punishment will be beaten with few blows. From everyone who has been given much, much will be demanded; and from the one who has been entrusted with much, much more will be asked.

Not Peace but Division

⁴⁹"I have come to bring fire on the earth, and how I wish it were already kindled! ⁵⁰But I have a baptism to undergo, and how distressed I am until it is completed! ⁵¹Do you think I came to bring peace on earth? No, I tell you, but division. ⁵²From now on there will be five in one family divided against each other, three against two and two against three. ⁵³They will be divided, father against son and son against father, mother against daughter and daughter against mother, mother-in-law against daughter-in-law and daughter-in-law against mother-in-law."

Interpreting the Times

⁵⁴He said to the crowd: "When you see a cloud rising in the west, immediately you say, 'It's going to rain,' and it does. ⁵⁵And when the south wind blows, you say, 'It's going to be hot,' and it is. ⁵⁶Hypocrites! You know how to interpret the appearance of the earth and the sky. How is it that you don't know how to interpret this present time?

⁵⁷"Why don't you judge for yourselves what is right? ⁵⁸As you are going with your adversary to the magistrate, try hard to be reconciled to him on the way, or he may drag you off to the judge, and the judge turn you over to the officer, and the officer throw you into prison. ⁵⁹I tell you, you will not get out until you have paid the last penny.ᶠ"

ᶠ59 Greek *lepton*

"Yes" or "No" to Peter? What makes you think that? **5.** What should be the attitude and actions of the faithful and wise manager (vv. 42- 43)? What will be his reward if he does (v. 44)? **6.** What could tempt the manager to do wrong (v. 45)? Why might a manager be punished severely (vv. 46-47)? Lightly (v. 8)? **7.** How does Jesus summarize this passage in verse 48? How would the disciples have interpreted it?

REFLECT: **1.** What do you believe about the return of Jesus Christ? What difference does your belief make in the way you live your life? **2.** On spiritual priorities, what grade would you give yourself right now: A + ? C-? **3.** What particularly has God entrusted to you as his manager? How are you taking care of this responsibility? **4.** If you knew that in 30 days time either Jesus was returning, or you were giving an account of your life to God, what would you do to get ready?

OPEN: Who was your first "true love"? What caused the break-up?

DIG: **1.** What does Jesus seem to be feeling now? **2.** Of what "fire" is he speaking? What "baptism"? What division? **3.** How does Jesus bring division? Why families? **4.** How do you reconcile this with the fact that Jesus brings peace?

REFLECT: What has Christ done for your family: Division or peace?

OPEN: **1.** In your family, who has a "nose" for predicting the weather? **2.** Who in your family has "strong" opinions about politics? Are they usually right in their forecasts?

DIG: **1.** What signs can the crowd recognize? What signs don't they recognize? **2.** Why does misinterpreting "this present time" make them hypocrites? **3.** What's wrong with leaving matters to be settled in court (vv. 57-59)? Who is the judge they don't want to meet in court? **4.** What warnings does Jesus give this crowd (vv. 54-59) that differ from the warnings he gives his disciples (vv. 35-53), as both groups must decide what to do with Jesus?

REFLECT: **1.** What signs help you interpret the times correctly? **2.** What signs in your own life indicate how you're doing? **3.** Using a weather map to describe your spiritual life, what does it forecast?

OPEN: 1. What tragedy this week in the news most caught your attention? Why? **2.** When, if ever, have you been in a "disaster" – flood, earthquake, car crash, etc.?

DIG: 1: What news gets to Jesus first (v. 1)? **2.** How does he take this news for a "teachable moment"? Likewise, the other bad news (v. 4)? What is the point of both illustrations? What does the word "repent" mean here? **3.** In verses 6-9, who does the tree represent: The owner? Farmer? Why urgency?

REFLECT: 1. What is God saying to you in the story about the "fig tree"? **2.** How would you compare your life to the "fig tree"? If God could get his hands on you, what would he do? **3.** If you had "one more year" like the fig tree to turn your life around, what would you do?

OPEN: Who is a handicapped person you admire because of the way they deal with their handicap?

DIG: 1. Is this woman's problem (v. 11) physical? Spiritual? Legal? **2.** Given the Sabbath-setting, how is that a problem for the woman? For Jesus? For the ruler? **3.** Whose view of the Sabbath prevails: Jesus' or the ruler's? Why? **4.** How does Jesus expose their hypocrisy and delight the crowd? **5.** How does this Sabbath conflict compare with the one in Luke 6:1-11?

REFLECT: Who does your church regard as a "cripple": An alcholic? Druggie? Divorcee? Parolee? If this person came to your church or small group, what would happen? If then miraculously healed, but at some offense to church tradition, what would be done?

OPEN: 1. What does "mustard" remind you of? **2.** What does freshly baked bread smell like?

DIG: 1. What does the contrast between the small seed and huge bush teach about the kingdom of God? **2.** What does yeast teach about the kingdom? About its expansion? About its proclamation?

REFLECT: 1. How has "mustard seed conspiracy" (something small making a great impact) worked in your life? In your church? **2.** When have you felt too small to matter? What do these parables teach you about significance?

Repent or Perish

13 Now there were some present at that time who told Jesus about the Galileans whose blood Pilate had mixed with their sacrifices. ²Jesus answered, "Do you think that these Galileans were worse sinners than all the other Galileans because they suffered this way? ³I tell you, no! But unless you repent, you too will all perish. ⁴Or those eighteen who died when the tower in Siloam fell on them—do you think they were more guilty than all the others living in Jerusalem? ⁵I tell you, no! But unless you repent, you too will all perish."

⁶Then he told this parable: "A man had a fig tree, planted in his vineyard, and he went to look for fruit on it, but did not find any. ⁷So he said to the man who took care of the vineyard, 'For three years now I've been coming to look for fruit on this fig tree and haven't found any. Cut it down! Why should it use up the soil?'

⁸" 'Sir,' the man replied, 'leave it alone for one more year, and I'll dig around it and fertilize it. ⁹If it bears fruit next year, fine! If not, then cut it down.' "

A Crippled Woman Healed on the Sabbath

¹⁰On a Sabbath Jesus was teaching in one of the synagogues, ¹¹and a woman was there who had been crippled by a spirit for eighteen years. She was bent over and could not straighten up at all. ¹²When Jesus saw her, he called her forward and said to her, "Woman, you are set free from your infirmity." ¹³Then he put his hands on her, and immediately she straightened up and praised God.

¹⁴Indignant because Jesus had healed on the Sabbath, the synagogue ruler said to the people, "There are six days for work. So come and be healed on those days, not on the Sabbath."

¹⁵The Lord answered him, "You hypocrites! Doesn't each of you on the Sabbath untie his ox or donkey from the stall and lead it out to give it water? ¹⁶Then should not this woman, a daughter of Abraham, whom Satan has kept bound for eighteen long years, be set free on the Sabbath day from what bound her?"

¹⁷When he said this, all his opponents were humiliated, but the people were delighted with all the wonderful things he was doing.

The Parables of the Mustard Seed and the Yeast

¹⁸Then Jesus asked, "What is the kingdom of God like? What shall I compare it to? ¹⁹It is like a mustard seed, which a man took and planted in his garden. It grew and became a tree, and the birds of the air perched in its branches."

²⁰Again he asked, "What shall I compare the kingdom of God to? ²¹It is like yeast that a woman took and mixed into a large amount^g of flour until it worked all through the dough."

^{g}21 Greek *three satas* (probably about 1/2 bushel or 22 liters)

	SINGLE	S

Customer:

ted sohn

Serendipity New Testament for Groups

Coleman, Lyman

W1-N063-E3

TU-829-010

Ex-Lib

No CD

Used - Good

9780809128631

Picker Notes:
M _____ 2 _____
WT _____ 2 _____
CC _____

34379132

1 Item   1030429772

Wednesday Singles REG SHLV   Ship. Created: 1/26/2015 8:36:00 PM

The Narrow Door

²²Then Jesus went through the towns and villages, teaching as he made his way to Jerusalem. ²³Someone asked him, "Lord, are only a few people going to be saved?"

He said to them, ²⁴"Make every effort to enter through the narrow door, because many, I tell you, will try to enter and will not be able to. ²⁵Once the owner of the house gets up and closes the door, you will stand outside knocking and pleading, 'Sir, open the door for us.'

"But he will answer, 'I don't know you or where you come from.'

²⁶"Then you will say, 'We ate and drank with you, and you taught in our streets.'

²⁷"But he will reply, 'I don't know you or where you come from. Away from me, all you evildoers!'

²⁸"There will be weeping there, and gnashing of teeth, when you see Abraham, Isaac and Jacob and all the prophets in the kingdom of God, but you yourselves thrown out. ²⁹People will come from east and west and north and south, and will take their places at the feast in the kingdom of God. ³⁰Indeed there are those who are last who will be first, and first who will be last."

Jesus' Sorrow for Jerusalem

³¹At that time some Pharisees came to Jesus and said to him, "Leave this place and go somewhere else. Herod wants to kill you."

³²He replied, "Go tell that fox, 'I will drive out demons and heal people today and tomorrow, and on the third day I will reach my goal.' ³³In any case, I must keep going today and tomorrow and the next day—for surely no prophet can die outside Jerusalem!

³⁴"O Jerusalem, Jerusalem, you who kill the prophets and stone those sent to you, how often I have longed to gather your children together, as a hen gathers her chicks under her wings, but you were not willing! ³⁵Look, your house is left to you desolate. I tell you, you will not see me again until you say, 'Blessed is he who comes in the name of the Lord.'ʰ"

Jesus at a Pharisee's House

14 One Sabbath, when Jesus went to eat in the house of a prominent Pharisee, he was being carefully watched. ²There in front of him was a man suffering from dropsy. ³Jesus asked the Pharisees and experts in the law, "Is it lawful to heal on the Sabbath or not?" ⁴But they remained silent. So taking hold of the man, he healed him and sent him away.

⁵Then he asked them, "If one of you has a sonⁱ or an ox that falls into a well on the Sabbath day, will you not immediately pull him out?" ⁶And they had nothing to say.

⁷When he noticed how the guests picked the places of honor at the table, he told them this parable: ⁸"When someone invites you to a wedding feast, do not take the place of honor, for a

ʰ35 Psalm 118:26   ⁱ5 Some manuscripts *donkey*

OPEN: To get into the opening to the attic or the crawl space under your house, how many pounds would you have to lose?

DIG: 1. Enroute to Jerusalem, what does Jesus encounter (vv. 22, 23)? **2.** How does Jesus answer the question (vv. 24-27)? How does Jesus qualify those who will make it through the narrow door and those who won't? **3.** If God wants all kinds of people (v. 29) to know him, why isn't the door wider? Why isn't eating and drinking with Jesus enough? **4.** In the end, do you think only "a few" or "many" or "all" people will be saved? Why? Who will be "first" and "last" in the kingdom?

REFLECT: 1. If Jesus is the only "door" into the kingdom, what then of other religions? **2.** How would Jesus accomodate his message to today's pluralistic university campus?

OPEN: What place do you identify with your spiritual roots? When you go back, how do you feel?

DIG: 1. What does Jesus reveal here (vv. 32-33) about his intentions? **2.** How do these intentions differ from that expected of Jesus by the Pharisees (v. 31)? **3.** About Jerusalem, how does Jesus feel and what does he prophesy? **4.** What surprises you most about Jesus' response to his opponents?

REFLECT: 1. As for the spiritual condition of your country: What most concerns you? What most encourages you? **2.** Likewise, for your community? Your church?

OPEN: 1. What is the closest you have come to being invited for dinner with one of the "rich and famous"? How did you feel? **2.** If you could have the best seats at a major public event, what would you choose: Super Bowl? Rock concert? Philharmonic orchestra? Indy 500? Royal wedding?

DIG: 1. What's the situation here: The day? Host? Atmosphere? Do you suppose the man with dropsy was planted there to trap Jesus (vv. 1-2)? **2.** What does Jesus do to heal the man and trap the Pharisees (vv. 3-5)? **3.** How do the Pharisees respond? What does their silence mean? **4.** What next societal issue and spiritual principle does Jesus address (vv. 7-11)? **5.** What does

Jesus say about invitations to meals (vv. 12-14)? What's the spiritual principle here? **6.** How does Jesus' view of honor vary from that held by others at the meal? **7.** What does this teach you about kingdom values vs. societal values and their application at the final banquet? At your next party?

REFLECT: 1. If invited to dine with one of the "rich and famous" and told "sit anywhere you like," where would you: Head table? Nearby? In the back? With the hired help? **2.** If you throw a party for the "poor", "crippled", "lame", and "blind" in your world, who would you invite?

OPEN: 1. If you were in charge of planning a reunion banquet for your school, where would you hold the banquet? What would you serve as the main course? What would you plan for entertainment? **2.** And if the invited guests didn't show, . . .?

DIG: 1. How does Jesus address this man's presumption (v. 15)? How does this parable expand on the previous story (vv. 12-14)? **2.** In this parable, who are the invited guests? Why don't they come? Who are the ones who eventually come? What happens to the original invitees? On what basis is one invited to this banquet? **3.** In sum, what does this parable teach about the kingdom? What keeps people out? What enables them to get in?

REFLECT: 1. From your own experience, how do you explain why so many say "No" to God's incredible "banquet"? **2.** What view of God does the average unchurched person have? What would it take for them to sense God's loving invitation to table fellowship?

OPEN: 1. What did your first car cost? First house? **2.** When did you start making a budget? Was it easier to stick to your budget when you had little or a lot?

DIG: 1. What does Jesus say to the crowds about family? What does he mean by "hate" in this context? Does this justify "Christian divorce"? **2.** How does one's "cross" affect discipleship? **3.** How does the tower story expand this theme? **4.** Likewise, the war story? **5.** How is verse 33 illustrated by the family, cross, tower, and war stories? **6.**

person more distinguished than you may have been invited. [9]If so, the host who invited both of you will come and say to you, 'Give this man your seat.' Then, humiliated, you will have to take the least important place. [10]But when you are invited, take the lowest place, so that when your host comes, he will say to you, 'Friend, move up to a better place.' Then you will be honored in the presence of all your fellow guests. [11]For everyone who exalts himself will be humbled, and he who humbles himself will be exalted."

[12]Then Jesus said to his host, "When you give a luncheon or dinner, do not invite your friends, your brothers or relatives, or your rich neighbors; if you do, they may invite you back and so you will be repaid. [13]But when you give a banquet, invite the poor, the crippled, the lame, the blind, [14]and you will be blessed. Although they cannot repay you, you will be repaid at the resurrection of the righteous."

The Parable of the Great Banquet

[15]When one of those at the table with him heard this, he said to Jesus, "Blessed is the man who will eat at the feast in the kingdom of God."

[16]Jesus replied: "A certain man was preparing a great banquet and invited many guests. [17]At the time of the banquet he sent his servant to tell those who had been invited, 'Come, for everything is now ready.'

[18]"But they all alike began to make excuses. The first said, 'I have just bought a field, and I must go and see it. Please excuse me.'

[19]"Another said, 'I have just bought five yoke of oxen, and I'm on my way to try them out. Please excuse me.'

[20]"Still another said, 'I just got married, so I can't come.'

[21]"The servant came back and reported this to his master. Then the owner of the house became angry and ordered his servant, 'Go out quickly into the streets and alleys of the town and bring in the poor, the crippled, the blind and the lame.'

[22]"'Sir,' the servant said, 'what you ordered has been done, but there is still room.'

[23]"Then the master told his servant, 'Go out to the roads and country lanes and make them come in, so that my house will be full. [24]I tell you, not one of those men who were invited will get a taste of my banquet.'"

The Cost of Being a Disciple

[25]Large crowds were traveling with Jesus, and turning to them he said: [26]"If anyone comes to me and does not hate his father and mother, his wife and children, his brothers and sisters—yes, even his own life—he cannot be my disciple. [27]And anyone who does not carry his cross and follow me cannot be my disciple.

[28]"Suppose one of you wants to build a tower. Will he not first sit down and estimate the cost to see if he has enough money to complete it? [29]For if he lays the foundation and is not able to finish it, everyone who sees it will ridicule him, [30]saying, 'This fellow began to build and was not able to finish.'

LOOKING INTO THE SCRIPTURE/20 Minutes. Read Luke 14:15-24 and discuss.

1. How do you feel when someone declines your invitation to dinner?
   a. no problem
   b. hurt feelings
   c. wonder what the real reason is
   d. resentment for the trouble I went to
   e. embarrassment
   f. understanding

2. To what is the "great banquet" referring?
   a. the kingdom of God
   b. deeper spiritual things
   c. Jesus himself
   d. the marriage banquet at the return of Christ
   e. restoration of the Jewish nation

3. Why did the three people who were originally invited refuse to come?
   a. they didn't like banquets
   b. too busy with other things
   c. not interested in being with God
   d. unaware of what they were missing
   e. they didn't realize this was the last invitation

4. "Go out quickly into the streets and alleys . . . bring in the poor, the crippled, the blind and the lame." Who are these people?
   a. the losers
   b. outcasts of society
   c. people hungry for spiritual things
   d. Gentiles outside of the covenant
   e. everybody who knows they do not deserve God's grace

5. "I tell you, not one of those men who were invited will get a taste of my banquet." Why?
   a. they blew their chance
   b. committed the "unforgivable sin"
   c. chose not to receive God's grace
   d. rejected Jesus as the Messiah

6. If God invited you to a banquet as his special guest (to spend time together) what would you do?
   a. probably make some excuse
   b. ask who else is coming
   c. wonder what God was up to
   d. go reluctantly
   e. jump at the chance
   f. don't know

MY OWN STORY/25 Minutes.

1. How would you describe your spiritual diet right now?
   a. baby food
   b. TV dinners
   c. meat and potatoes
   d. junk food except on Sunday
   e. dehydrated food (dried out)
   f. gourmet feast
   g. pure Bread and Wine

2. What can you expect at God's banquet?
   a. all my needs will be met
   b. the company will be interesting
   c. it's a once-in-a-lifetime event
   d. it will take commitment to stay and eat
   e. I will always be welcome
   f. in order not to get fat I will be asked to share the banquet with others

3. When it comes to experiencing God's spiritual feast, what will help you enjoy it more?
   a. spiritual hunger
   b. recognition that it is not a pot-luck— God provides all the food
   c. eating on a regular schedule rather than gorging once a week
   d. assurance that I can eat whenever I'm hungry

4. What would it take to get you to come to the banquet of God's deeper things?
   a. an adjustment in my schedule
   b. an invitation direct from God
   c. a few friends to join me
   d. lively entertainment and fun
   e. a little more spiritual hunger

How is salt a good analogy for Jesus' final point about listening and discipleship? **7.** In sum, what kingdom values are taught? Why such tough talk from Jesus?

REFLECT: According to the latest statistics, approximately 100,000 Christians are martyred every year. Many more face the loss of job, jail, or physical harm if they are caught reading their Bible or meeting for worship with other Christians. What has it cost you to follow Jesus?

OPEN: 1. Did you ever lose your pet? **2.** Were you ever a camp counselor or day-care worker and lose one of the children? How did it feel when you found the missing person?

DIG: 1. Who is in Jesus' "mixed audience"? How do they respond to him? **2.** How does Jesus' parable relate to the muttering of the Pharisees? What is Jesus' point? What should be the Pharisees' attitude? What is Jesus' attitude?

REFLECT: When did you stray from the Christian faith? What did God use to bring you back?

OPEN: How did you earn your first dollar? Ever lose big bills? How?

DIG: 1. What has the woman lost? To what extremes does she go to find it? What does she do when she succeeds? **2.** What is Jesus' point? Who is your "lost coin"?

OPEN: 1. When did you leave home for the first time? Did you ever run away from home? Where did you go and what happened? **2.** Were you the "nice guy" and stay-at-home type while your "brother" was having all the fun? How did you feel about your "brother"?

DIG: 1. What stages does the younger son go through on his pilgrimmage? What brings him to his senses? What does he realize then? With what sort of attitude does he approach his father? **2.** From your understanding of the father, what do you think he was doing while his son was away? Why do you think that? How does he receive his son? **3.** How does the older brother feel about his younger brother's return? Why? How does the father answer the older brother's objection? **4.** What's Jesus' point with

---

³¹"Or suppose a king is about to go to war against another king. Will he not first sit down and consider whether he is able with ten thousand men to oppose the one coming against him with twenty thousand? ³²If he is not able, he will send a delegation while the other is still a long way off and will ask for terms of peace. ³³In the same way, any of you who does not give up everything he has cannot be my disciple.

³⁴"Salt is good, but if it loses its saltiness, how can it be made salty again? ³⁵It is fit neither for the soil nor for the manure pile; it is thrown out.

"He who has ears to hear, let him hear."

The Parable of the Lost Sheep

15 Now the tax collectors and "sinners" were all gathering around to hear him. ²But the Pharisees and the teachers of the law muttered, "This man welcomes sinners and eats with them."

³Then Jesus told them this parable: ⁴"Suppose one of you has a hundred sheep and loses one of them. Does he not leave the ninety-nine in the open country and go after the lost sheep until he finds it? ⁵And when he finds it, he joyfully puts it on his shoulders ⁶and goes home. Then he calls his friends and neighbors together and says, 'Rejoice with me; I have found my lost sheep.' ⁷I tell you that in the same way there will be more rejoicing in heaven over one sinner who repents than over ninety-nine righteous persons who do not need to repent.

The Parable of the Lost Coin

⁸"Or suppose a woman has ten silver coins^j and loses one. Does she not light a lamp, sweep the house and search carefully until she finds it? ⁹And when she finds it, she calls her friends and neighbors together and says, 'Rejoice with me; I have found my lost coin.' ¹⁰In the same way, I tell you, there is rejoicing in the presence of the angels of God over one sinner who repents."

The Parable of the Lost Son

¹¹Jesus continued: "There was a man who had two sons. ¹²The younger one said to his father, 'Father, give me my share of the estate.' So he divided his property between them.

¹³"Not long after that, the younger son got together all he had, set off for a distant country and there squandered his wealth in wild living. ¹⁴After he had spent everything, there was a severe famine in that whole country, and he began to be in need. ¹⁵So he went and hired himself out to a citizen of that country, who sent him to his fields to feed pigs. ¹⁶He longed to fill his stomach with the pods that the pigs were eating, but no one gave him anything.

¹⁷"When he came to his senses, he said, 'How many of my father's hired men have food to spare, and here I am starving to death! ¹⁸I will set out and go back to my father and say to him: Father, I have sinned against heaven and against you. ¹⁹I am no

---

j8 Greek ten drachmas, each worth about a day's wages

Luke 15:11-32   THE PARABLE OF THE LOST SON (PRODIGAL)

LOOKING INTO THE SCRIPTURE/20 Minutes. Read Luke 15:11-32 and discuss.

1. Why do you think the Prodigal Son decided to leave home?
   a. to grow up
   b. to get away from his father's values
   c. he wasn't appreciated at home
   d. to try to make it on his own
   e. to get away from his older brother

2. What was it that caused the Prodigal Son to come to his senses?
   a. homesickness
   b. guilt for what he had done
   c. feeling sorry for himself
   d. feeling sorry for his father
   e. hunger pangs
   f. realization that he was stupid
   g. he "hit bottom"

3. When the Prodigal Son returned home, what was his father's attitude?
   a. come on in but you're grounded
   b. you have disgraced the family
   c. where's the money
   d. I don't approve of what you've done, but you are still my son
   e. welcome home, son, I love you

4. When the older brother (who had been good) heard music and dancing, what was his attitude?
   a. it's unfair
   b. don't expect me to forgive him
   c. no use being good
   d. he blew his inheritance and now he's blowing mine

5. Do you think that the father was wise to give his son his inheritance when he knew his son would probably blow it?   ☐ Yes   ☐ No

6. If the father had a pretty good idea where his son had gone, do you think he should have gone after him?   ☐ Yes   ☐ No

7. Do you think it was wise for the father to "kill the fatted calf" and throw a party when his son came home?   ☐ Yes   ☐ No

8. Do you think the father split his inheritance a second time so that the Prodigal Son could have some spending money?   ☐ I hope so   ☐ I hope not

---

MY OWN STORY/20 Minutes. Share some of your own story through this parable.

1. By temperament and experience, whom do you identify with in this story?
   a. Prodigal Son
   b. Older Brother
   c. The Father

2. If you had to compare your spiritual journey to the Prodigal's journey, where are you now?
   a. at home, but not too happy
   b. in a far country
   c. coming to my senses
   d. on my way home, but not sure what I'll find
   e. I've just arrived/feeling great
   f. enjoying the fattened calf and the party

3. When it comes to spiritual things, what is your response to God's "party"?
   a. denial: there's no party in this life
   b. party pooper: sorry, I'm too busy
   c. party lover: I'm ready, let's party
   d. wallflower: I'm there, but I can't dance

4. What's the lesson for you in this parable?
   a. you've got to let your children go, even though you know they will probably blow it
   b. God's love has no strings
   c. waiting for your children to come home is painful
   d. older brothers have trouble enjoying the party
   e. Love overcomes mistakes

this parable? What does this story teach about sin, repentance and the love of God? **5.** In summary, what part does celebration play in the three parables of chapter 15? How do these three parables answer the Pharisees' objection in verse 2? What does Jesus want to teach the Pharisees in verses 25-31?

REFLECT: 1. If you had to compare yourself to the two brothers in this story, who are you most like? Why? Whom would you have identified with ten years ago? Twenty years ago? **2.** Would you like to be more like the other son in this story? Which son do you think had the best "self image"? Which son would likely be the more healthy? **3.** How do you feel about the father in this story? Do you think he did the right thing for his younger son in giving him his "inheritance" before the son was able to handle it? Do you think he should have "thrown a party" when the son returned? **4.** If you had been the elder son, how would you feel about the father? About the younger son? **5.** Which son would make the best father when they got older? The best counselor? The best pastor? The best group leader?

OPEN: 1. Who has been one of the shrewdest businessmen or women you've ever met? What impressed you or depressed you about that person? **2.** If you could be the Chief Executive Officer of any corporation, which one would you want to manage? What do you think would be most exciting about that position? **3.** Which job would best fit your personality: Ringmaster at a circus? The owner of a video store? Construction worker? Parachute instructor? Gourmet chef? Why?

DIG: 1. To whom is Jesus addressing this parable? Why is it especially important to know to whom it's directed? **2.** In what crisis does the manager find himself? What does he say to himself (v. 3)? What plan does he concoct? **3.** In light of this deceit, why does the owner commend the manager (v. 8)? **4.** How does Jesus summarize this parable in verse 9? Is Jesus commending dishonesty? Is he commending prudently preparing and providing for the future? The use of money? Why? What do you think he's commending here? How do verses 10-12 help understand his point? How does it confuse the point for you? **5.** What's the problem with trying to

longer worthy to be called your son; make me like one of your hired men.' ²⁰So he got up and went to his father.

"But while he was still a long way off, his father saw him and was filled with compassion for him; he ran to his son, threw his arms around him and kissed him.

²¹"The son said to him, 'Father, I have sinned against heaven and against you. I am no longer worthy to be called your son. *ᵏ*'

²²"But the father said to his servants, 'Quick! Bring the best robe and put it on him. Put a ring on his finger and sandals on his feet. ²³Bring the fattened calf and kill it. Let's have a feast and celebrate. ²⁴For this son of mine was dead and is alive again; he was lost and is found.' So they began to celebrate.

²⁵"Meanwhile, the older son was in the field. When he came near the house, he heard music and dancing. ²⁶So he called one of the servants and asked him what was going on. ²⁷'Your brother has come,' he replied, 'and your father has killed the fattened calf because he has him back safe and sound.'

²⁸"The older brother became angry and refused to go in. So his father went out and pleaded with him. ²⁹But he answered his father, 'Look! All these years I've been slaving for you and never disobeyed your orders. Yet you never gave me even a young goat so I could celebrate with my friends. ³⁰But when this son of yours who has squandered your property with prostitutes comes home, you kill the fattened calf for him!'

³¹" 'My son,' the father said, 'you are always with me, and everything I have is yours. ³²But we had to celebrate and be glad, because this brother of yours was dead and is alive again; he was lost and is found.' "

The Parable of the Shrewd Manager

16 Jesus told his disciples: "There was a rich man whose manager was accused of wasting his possessions. ²So he called him in and asked him, 'What is this I hear about you? Give an account of your management, because you cannot be manager any longer.'

³"The manager said to himself, 'What shall I do now? My master is taking away my job. I'm not strong enough to dig, and I'm ashamed to beg— ⁴I know what I'll do so that, when I lose my job here, people will welcome me into their houses.'

⁵"So he called in each one of his master's debtors. He asked the first, 'How much do you owe my master?'

⁶" 'Eight hundred gallons*ˡ* of olive oil,' he replied.

"The manager told him, 'Take your bill, sit down quickly, and make it four hundred.'

⁷"Then he asked the second, 'And how much do you owe?'

" 'A thousand bushels*ᵐ* of wheat,' he replied.

"He told him, 'Take your bill and make it eight hundred.'

⁸"The master commended the dishonest manager because he had acted shrewdly. For the people of this world are more shrewd in dealing with their own kind than are the people of the

---

ᵏ21 Some early manuscripts *son. Make me like one of your hired men.*
ˡ6 Greek *one hundred batous* (probably about 3 kiloliters)   *ᵐ7* Greek *one hundred korous* (probably about 35 kiloliters)

light. [9]I tell you, use worldly wealth to gain friends for your-selves, so that when it is gone, you will be welcomed into eternal dwellings.

[10]"Whoever can be trusted with very little can also be trusted with much, and whoever is dishonest with very little will also be dishonest with much. [11]So if you have not been trustworthy in handling worldly wealth, who will trust you with true riches? [12]And if you have not been trustworthy with someone else's property, who will give you property of your own?

[13]"No servant can serve two masters. Either he will hate the one and love the other, or he will be devoted to the one and despise the other. You cannot serve both God and Money."

[14]The Pharisees, who loved money, heard all this and were sneering at Jesus. [15]He said to them, "You are the ones who justify yourselves in the eyes of men, but God knows your hearts. What is highly valued among men is detestable in God's sight.

Additional Teachings

[16]"The Law and the Prophets were proclaimed until John. Since that time, the good news of the kingdom of God is being preached, and everyone is forcing his way into it. [17]It is easier for heaven and earth to disappear than for the least stroke of a pen to drop out of the Law.

[18]"Anyone who divorces his wife and marries another woman commits adultery, and the man who marries a divorced woman commits adultery.

The Rich Man and Lazarus

[19]"There was a rich man who was dressed in purple and fine linen and lived in luxury every day. [20]At his gate was laid a beggar named Lazarus, covered with sores [21]and longing to eat what fell from the rich man's table. Even the dogs came and licked his sores.

[22]"The time came when the beggar died and the angels carried him to Abraham's side. The rich man also died and was buried. [23]In hell,[n] where he was in torment, he looked up and saw Abraham far away, with Lazarus by his side. [24]So he called to him, 'Father Abraham, have pity on me and send Lazarus to dip the tip of his finger in water and cool my tongue, because I am in agony in this fire.'

[25]"But Abraham replied, 'Son, remember that in your life-time you received your good things, while Lazarus received bad things, but now he is comforted here and you are in agony. [26]And besides all this, between us and you a great chasm has been fixed, so that those who want to go from here to you cannot, nor can anyone cross over from there to us.'

[27]"He answered, 'Then I beg you, father, send Lazarus to my father's house, [28]for I have five brothers. Let him warn them, so that they will not also come to this place of torment.'

serve two Masters (v. 13)? **6.** Who's listening in on this conversation (v. 14)? What characterizes their at-titude? How does he use the para-ble to speak to them (v. 15)?

REFLECT: If Jesus were to stop in at your home or business today and take inventory of the way you are using your resources and wealth (including all your possessions, cars, house, education, potential, etc.), what would he probably rec-ommend to you in planning for your future "estate"? Would he recom-mend that you "cut your losses" and get out of debt? Cut back on your spending? Reclarify your goals? Start doing what?

OPEN: Is your mom's childrearing manual obsolete? Why?

DIG: Did John's preaching render the law obsolete? Why or why not? What does Jesus teach here about marriage and divorce that sharpens the Old Testament law?

REFLECT: To clarify this passage, what would you ask Jesus?

OPEN: 1. Growing up, what did you think heaven was? What about "hell"? **2.** Who was the "ghost storyteller" you remember? Where would you go to tell stories? **3.** What would you do when they got scary?

DIG: 1. How do the lives of the rich man and Lazarus compare on earth (vv. 19-21)? How do they compare after death (vv. 22-24)? **2.** What request does the rich man make of Abraham? Why? What two points does Abraham make in his reply? Why can't he help? What pic-ture does this show of life after death? **3.** What is the next request the rich man makes (v. 27)? How does Abraham answer this one? How does the dialogue conclude? **4.** What is Jesus' point here? **5.** In sum, why was the rich man punished? What ought individuals be doing with their lives on earth?

REFLECT: 1. How do you rate this story for audiences: G (General)? PG (Parental Guidance)? R (Re-stricted)? **2.** How did this story make you feel? How do you feel about discussing the issue of the "the judgment" with friends? Do we need more of this teaching today? Why?

[n]23 Greek *Hades*

²⁹"Abraham replied, 'They have Moses and the Prophets; let them listen to them.'

³⁰" 'No, father Abraham,' he said, 'but if someone from the dead goes to them, they will repent.'

³¹"He said to him, 'If they do not listen to Moses and the Prophets, they will not be convinced even if someone rises from the dead.' "

Sin, Faith, Duty

17 Jesus said to his disciples: "Things that cause people to sin are bound to come, but woe to that person through whom they come. ²It would be better for him to be thrown into the sea with a millstone tied around his neck than for him to cause one of these little ones to sin. ³So watch yourselves.

"If your brother sins, rebuke him, and if he repents, forgive him. ⁴If he sins against you seven times in a day, and seven times comes back to you and says, 'I repent,' forgive him."

⁵The apostles said to the Lord, "Increase our faith!"

⁶He replied, "If you have faith as small as a mustard seed, you can say to this mulberry tree, 'Be uprooted and planted in the sea,' and it will obey you.

⁷"Suppose one of you had a servant plowing or looking after the sheep. Would he say to the servant when he comes in from the field, 'Come along now and sit down to eat'? ⁸Would he not rather say, 'Prepare my supper, get yourself ready and wait on me while I eat and drink; after that you may eat and drink'? ⁹Would he thank the servant because he did what he was told to do? ¹⁰So you also, when you have done everything you were told to do, should say, 'We are unworthy servants; we have only done our duty.' "

Ten Healed of Leprosy

¹¹Now on his way to Jerusalem, Jesus traveled along the border between Samaria and Galilee. ¹²As he was going into a village, ten men who had leprosy*ᵒ* met him. They stood at a distance ¹³and called out in a loud voice, "Jesus, Master, have pity on us!"

¹⁴When he saw them, he said, "Go, show yourselves to the priests." And as they went, they were cleansed.

¹⁵One of them, when he saw he was healed, came back, praising God in a loud voice. ¹⁶He threw himself at Jesus' feet and thanked him—and he was a Samaritan.

¹⁷Jesus asked, "Were not all ten cleansed? Where are the other nine? ¹⁸Was no one found to return and give praise to God except this foreigner?" ¹⁹Then he said to him, "Rise and go; your faith has made you well."

OPEN: As kids, who got whom into trouble? What was your favorite play? Your parents' response?

DIG: 1. In his view of stumbling blocks to sin, is Jesus a realist? Or an idealist? Why? **2.** Likewise, in Jesus' view of the limitations to forgiveness (vv. 3-4)? **3.** What are we to "watch"? Why? **4.** Which takes more faith: Being our brother's keeper? Or endlessly forgiving him? **5.** What do verses 7-10 say about the attitude Jesus' followers should have in serving him? **6.** From this passage, what are four characteristics of disciples? Can you summarize each in one word?

REFLECT: In trusting God for the "impossible", what would your "faith quotient" be on a scale of 1 to 10 (1 = "Chicken hearted", 10 = "Giant killer")? What is the biggest thing you've seen God do this year: Raise money for school? Save your marriage? Your teenager?

OPEN: 1. What is the longest you had to stay out of school because you were sick or hurt? Were your ever "quarantined" for something contagious? **2.** How are you at writing "thank you" notes?

DIG: 1. Who does Jesus encounter on the road to Jerusalem? What do you know about his disease and how lepers were treated in Jesus' day? **2.** What is their plaintive plea? **3.** How are they healed? What is Jesus' part? What is their part? **4.** How do the nine and the one respond differently? **5.** What questions does Jesus ask in verse 17-18? What does he tell the man to do? What is the key to his healing?

REFLECT: 1. Who are the "lepers" in your community? How would you feel about having one of these people over for dinner? In your group? As one of your friends? **2.** What is your favorite excuse for not associating with these people? **3.** Have you ever felt like a leper yourself? When? What happened?

ᵒ12 The Greek word was used for various diseases affecting the skin—not necessarily leprosy.

The Coming of the Kingdom of God

20 Once, having been asked by the Pharisees when the kingdom of God would come, Jesus replied, "The kingdom of God does not come with your careful observation, 21 nor will people say, 'Here it is,' or 'There it is,' because the kingdom of God is within[p] you."

22 Then he said to his disciples, "The time is coming when you will long to see one of the days of the Son of Man, but you will not see it. 23 Men will tell you, 'There he is!' or 'Here he is!' Do not go running off after them. 24 For the Son of Man in his day[q] will be like the lightning, which flashes and lights up the sky from one end to the other. 25 But first he must suffer many things and be rejected by this generation.

26 "Just as it was in the days of Noah, so also will it be in the days of the Son of Man. 27 People were eating, drinking, marrying and being given in marriage up to the day Noah entered the ark. Then the flood came and destroyed them all.

28 "It was the same in the days of Lot. People were eating and drinking, buying and selling, planting and building. 29 But the day Lot left Sodom, fire and sulfur rained down from heaven and destroyed them all.

30 "It will be just like this on the day the Son of Man is revealed. 31 On that day no one who is on the roof of his house, with his goods inside, should go down to get them. Likewise, no one in the field should go back for anything. 32 Remember Lot's wife! 33 Whoever tries to keep his life will lose it, and whoever loses his life will preserve it. 34 I tell you, on that night two people will be in one bed; one will be taken and the other left. 35 Two women will be grinding grain together; one will be taken and the other left.[r]"

37 "Where, Lord?" they asked.

He replied, "Where there is a dead body, there the vultures will gather."

OPEN: 1. Who in your group has the most speeding tickets? Anyone arrested "out of the blue"? **2.** What is the biggest natural disaster you have ever seen?

DIG: 1. In answering the Pharisees' question, what does Jesus say about the kingdom, as to when, how, or where it is? **2.** If this kingdom comes without observable signs (v. 20), how does that reconcile with Luke 21:5-36? **3.** Does Jesus view the kingdom as an inward, spiritual state of affairs "within" his audience (i.e., the Pharisees)? Or more likely an outward, social manifestation "among" them? **4.** What did Jesus mean by "one of the days of the Son of Man"? Why would the disciples long for those end-times? When rumors abound, how are they to respond? **5.** How will the days of the Son of Man be like the days of Noah and Lot (see also Gen. 7:18-19)? **6.** What aspects of this future time are illustrated in verses 30-35? How should the suddenness of that future day be anticipated? **7.** How do the kingdom of God and the day of the Son of Man differ? How are they alike?

REFLECT: 1. How would you compare the time of Noah and Lot to today? **2.** How should a person who is in the "kingdom of God" and waiting for "the Son of Man" live? Does God want you to withdraw or get even more into the battle?

The Parable of the Persistent Widow

18 Then Jesus told his disciples a parable to show them that they should always pray and not give up. 2 He said: "In a certain town there was a judge who neither feared God nor cared about men. 3 And there was a widow in that town who kept coming to him with the plea, 'Grant me justice against my adversary.'

4 "For some time he refused. But finally he said to himself, 'Even though I don't fear God or care about men, 5 yet because this widow keeps bothering me, I will see that she gets justice, so that she won't eventually wear me out with her coming!' "

6 And the Lord said, "Listen to what the unjust judge says. 7 And will not God bring about justice for his chosen ones, who cry out to him day and night? Will he keep putting them off? 8 I tell you, he will see that they get justice, and quickly. However, when the Son of Man comes, will he find faith on the earth?"

OPEN: 1. Growing up, what "strategy" did you use to get your way with your parents? **2.** If you're a parent, how do your kids attempt to get what they want from you? What have you learned through this?

DIG: 1. This parable is for whom? About what? Involving who? **2.** What is the woman's strategy? How does she wear the judge out? **3.** How does Jesus sum up the parable (vv. 6-8)? What does he promise to his chosen ones? **4.** In what ways are God and the judge alike? Unalike? **5.** How would this parable encourage a believer to persist with unanswered prayer?

REFLECT: 1. As for persistent prayer, are you more likely to "give up" or "hang tough"? Cite examples. **2.** When unsure if you are praying in God's will, how do you proceed? **3.** What unanswered prayer can you resume praying for today?

[p]21 Or *among* [q]24 Some manuscripts do not have *in his day.* [r]35 Some manuscripts *left.* 36 *Two men will be in the field; one will be taken and the other left.*

OPEN: What early prayers, prayer "bloopers" and praying "too long" do you recall from your family home?

DIG: 1. This parable is for whom? About what? Involving who? **2.** How does this parable on humble prayer complement the one on persistence (vv. 1-8)? **3.** How do the Pharisee and the tax collector see themselves and God? **4.** Who is justified before God? Why?

REFLECT: 1. In what religious practices do you secretly take pride now and then? Why? **2.** Why do more sinners go to the bartender than church for confession?

OPEN: What age child would you prefer to look after? Why?

DIG: Why are the babies coming to Jesus? Why do the disciples object? How does Jesus overrule?

REFLECT: How could you be more like a child in your spiritual life?

OPEN: If you had to give up one luxury in your home, what would be the first and the last item you would give up: Indoor toilet? Washer/dryer? TV? Stereo? Waterbed? Electric lights? Make-up vanity?

DIG: 1. What question does the ruler ask Jesus? Implying what viewpoint on eternal life? **2.** What part of his question does Jesus initially respond to (v. 19)? Why? **3.** From the partial list of the Ten Commandments cited here (v. 20), what does Jesus omit (for complete list, see Ex. 20:1-17)? Why? **4.** Upon hearing his smug reply (v. 21), what new commandment does Jesus give him (v. 22)? With what revealing response? **5.** What does Jesus say about riches and the kingdom (vv. 24-25), that broadens the scope of this inquiry? (v. 26)? Why is it so difficult for the rich to enter the kingdom? **6.** On what basis is it possible for anyone–rich ruler or poor fisherman–to enter (vv. 27-30) **7.** According to this story, how are becoming a disciple, entering the kingdom of heaven and inheriting eternal life related?

REFLECT: If not money, what would Jesus probably put his finger on in your life as an "idol" that you give priority to over spiritual things? How would you respond if he said, "This has got to go"?

The Parable of the Pharisee and the Tax Collector

⁹To some who were confident of their own righteousness and looked down on everybody else, Jesus told this parable: ¹⁰"Two men went up to the temple to pray, one a Pharisee and the other a tax collector. ¹¹The Pharisee stood up and prayed about' himself: 'God, I thank you that I am not like other men—robbers, evildoers, adulterers—or even like this tax collector. ¹²I fast twice a week and give a tenth of all I get.'

¹³"But the tax collector stood at a distance. He would not even look up to heaven, but beat his breast and said, 'God, have mercy on me, a sinner.'

¹⁴"I tell you that this man, rather than the other, went home justified before God. For everyone who exalts himself will be humbled, and he who humbles himself will be exalted."

The Little Children and Jesus

¹⁵People were also bringing babies to Jesus to have him touch them. When the disciples saw this, they rebuked them. ¹⁶But Jesus called the children to him and said, "Let the little children come to me, and do not hinder them, for the kingdom of God belongs to such as these. ¹⁷I tell you the truth, anyone who will not receive the kingdom of God like a little child will never enter it."

The Rich Ruler

¹⁸A certain ruler asked him, "Good teacher, what must I do to inherit eternal life?"

¹⁹"Why do you call me good?" Jesus answered. "No one is good—except God alone. ²⁰You know the commandments: 'Do not commit adultery, do not murder, do not steal, do not give false testimony, honor your father and mother.'ᵗ"

²¹"All these I have kept since I was a boy," he said.

²²When Jesus heard this, he said to him, "You still lack one thing. Sell everything you have and give to the poor, and you will have treasure in heaven. Then come, follow me."

²³When he heard this, he became very sad, because he was a man of great wealth. ²⁴Jesus looked at him and said, "How hard it is for the rich to enter the kingdom of God! ²⁵Indeed, it is easier for a camel to go through the eye of a needle than for a rich man to enter the kingdom of God."

²⁶Those who heard this asked, "Who then can be saved?"

²⁷Jesus replied, "What is impossible with men is possible with God."

²⁸Peter said to him, "We have left all we had to follow you!"

²⁹"I tell you the truth," Jesus said to them, "no one who has left home or wife or brothers or parents or children for the sake of the kingdom of God ³⁰will fail to receive many times as much in this age and, in the age to come, eternal life."

ᵗ11 Or *to*   ᵗ20 Exodus 20:12-16; Deut. 5:16-20

Luke 18:9-14 THE PARABLE OF THE PHARISEE AND TAX COLLECTOR

LOOKING INTO THE SCRIPTURE/20 Minutes. Read Luke 18:9-14 and discuss.

1. How do you feel about the Pharisee in the story?
   a. like punching him in the nose
   b. I agree with him
   c. I feel like putting him in his place
   d. I feel sorry for him

2. Why do you think the Pharisee acted this way?
   a. gratitude to God
   b. peer pressure from friends
   c. sincere desire to please God
   d. fear of letting anybody know what he's really feeling
   e. he was self-righteous

3. How do you feel about the tax collector?
   a. at least he's honest
   b. he's more aware of who he is
   c. I can relate to this guy
   d. after cheating us, he has his nerve

4. Why do you think the tax collector acted the way he did?
   a. he knew he had done wrong
   b. he wanted sympathy
   c. he had a poor self-image
   d. he was plea bargaining with God
   e. he felt like dirt

MY OWN STORY/20 Minutes.

1. How much of your own problems could you share with each of these people? Put a dot on the line to indicate your response.

WITH THE PHARISEE, I COULD SHARE
Everything _____ Nothing

WITH THE TAX COLLECTOR, I COULD SHARE
Everything _____ Nothing

2. For the person with whom you could share the most in the previous questions, why do you feel this way?
   a. he is more spiritual
   b. more honest
   c. more like me
   d. more like the person I want to be
   e. more likely to understand me

3. If the tax collector in the parable came to your group, how would he be received?
   a. with open arms
   b. with suspicion
   c. with disgust
   d. like a fellow-sinner

4. If the Pharisee in the parable showed up at your group, how would he be received?
   a. with open arms
   b. with raised eyebrows
   c. with a few snickers
   d. with cold stares
   e. with sympathy

5. What is the reason you have for receiving one of these people better than another?
   a. fewer surface problems to hassle
   b. less emotional healing needed
   c. we don't tolerate sinners
   d. we don't tolerate phonies
   e. one would fit into our group better
   f. there really isn't a good reason

6. What would it take for you to receive either of these people into your group?
   a. a lot of patience
   b. a thick skin
   c. compassion
   d. tough love

OPEN: With only a few days to live, what would you tell your family?

DIG: In whom does Jesus confide? Where are they going? Why? What is his extraordinary prediction? Why is this new info misunderstood (see also 9:22, 45)?

REFLECT: When facing a tough spiritual battle, who do you trust?

OPEN: If you lost your sight, what would you miss seeing the most? How would your lifestyle change?

DIG: 1. Where is Jericho in relationship to Jersalem? Why might this account for disciples' rude behavior (v. 31)? 2. What do you know about the beggar from this story? His physical handicap? His faith? His intensity? How would you compare his blindness with that of the disciples in verse 34? 3. Why then does Jesus stop? What is significant about their interaction? How is the man's faith evident and effective?

REFLECT: What are you "begging" for – what miracle? If Jesus asked, "What do you want me to do" about this, what would you say?

OPEN: 1. As a kid, what was your favorite tree to climb? Did you ever build a tree house? Out of what? 2. How do you feel about your height? If you were six inches taller, how would you feel?

DIG: 1. What is significant about Zacchaeus and his vantage point? 2. Why does Jesus want to dine with him? Why does this bother others? 3. How does this rich "sinner" differ from the rich ruler (Luke 18:18-30): In approach? In response? 4. On what basis does Jesus confirm Zacchaeus' salvation (vv. 8-10)?

REFLECT: 1. Where did Jesus first find you: Up a tree? Out on a limb? How did he get you to come down: A little coaxing? A big scare? An invitation you couldn't refuse? 3. If Jesus stopped under the tree you're climbing, what would he say?

OPEN: 1.When you play Monopoly, what is your strategy: Go for broke? Take a few chances? Play it safe? 2. With $1,000 to invest, what would you do: (a) Buy a popcorn machine and sell door-to-door with big potential profit? (b) Buy pigs and raise them, with modest but sure profit? (c) Bank the cash, collect interest?

Jesus Again Predicts His Death

[31]Jesus took the Twelve aside and told them, "We are going up to Jerusalem, and everything that is written by the prophets about the Son of Man will be fulfilled. [32]He will be handed over to the Gentiles. They will mock him, insult him, spit on him, flog him and kill him. [33]On the third day he will rise again."

[34]The disciples did not understand any of this. Its meaning was hidden from them, and they did not know what he was talking about.

A Blind Beggar Receives His Sight

[35]As Jesus approached Jericho, a blind man was sitting by the roadside begging. [36]When he heard the crowd going by, he asked what was happening. [37]They told him, "Jesus of Nazareth is passing by."

[38]He called out, "Jesus, Son of David, have mercy on me!"

[39]Those who led the way rebuked him and told him to be quiet, but he shouted all the more, "Son of David, have mercy on me!"

[40]Jesus stopped and ordered the man to be brought to him. When he came near, Jesus asked him, [41]"What do you want me to do for you?"

"Lord, I want to see," he replied.

[42]Jesus said to him, "Receive your sight; your faith has healed you." [43]Immediately he received his sight and followed Jesus, praising God. When all the people saw it, they also praised God.

Zacchaeus the Tax Collector

19 Jesus entered Jericho and was passing through. [2]A man was there by the name of Zacchaeus; he was a chief tax collector and was wealthy. [3]He wanted to see who Jesus was, but being a short man he could not, because of the crowd. [4]So he ran ahead and climbed a sycamore-fig tree to see him, since Jesus was coming that way.

[5]When Jesus reached the spot, he looked up and said to him, "Zacchaeus, come down immediately. I must stay at your house today." [6]So he came down at once and welcomed him gladly.

[7]All the people saw this and began to mutter, "He has gone to be the guest of a 'sinner.' "

[8]But Zacchaeus stood up and said to the Lord, "Look, Lord! Here and now I give half of my possessions to the poor, and if I have cheated anybody out of anything, I will pay back four times the amount."

[9]Jesus said to him, "Today salvation has come to this house, because this man, too, is a son of Abraham. [10]For the Son of Man came to seek and to save what was lost."

The Parable of the Ten Minas

[11]While they were listening to this, he went on to tell them a parable, because he was near Jerusalem and the people thought that the kingdom of God was going to appear at once. [12]He said: "A man of noble birth went to a distant country to have himself appointed king and then to return. [13]So he called ten of his

Luke 19:1-10   **ZACCHAEUS THE TAX COLLECTOR**

LOOKING INTO THE SCRIPTURE/20 Minutes. Read Luke 19:1-10 and discuss.

1. What impresses you about Zacchaeus?
   a. his wealth
   b. his agility
   c. his curiosity
   d. his flexibility
   e. his change of heart

2. What was it about Zacchaeus that Jesus singled him out?
   a. the worst sinner in town
   b. sold out to Roman authorities
   c. guilty of fraud and thievery
   d. hungry for something more in life
   e. he was so short

3. What do you suppose was Jesus' facial expression when he said, "Zacchaeus, come down immediately . . ."?
   a. stern
   b. delighted
   c. relieved to find a dinner companion
   d. sympathetic
   e. matter-of-fact

4. Why do you think Jesus invited himself to Zacchaeus' house for dinner?
   a. he felt sorry for him
   b. he wanted to talk to him about his shady business
   c. he needed a spectacular miracle to gain credibility in the town
   d. he knew he had what Zacchaeus was seeking

5. What do you think they talked about over dinner?
   a. the weather
   b. how Zach was really feeling
   c. God's plan for his life
   d. how to pay back what he had stolen from the people

6. "Today salvation has come to this house, because this man, too, is a son of Abraham...." What is Jesus saying about Zach here?
   a. Zach is a newborn person
   b. accept Zach as a brother Jew
   c. Zach has followed in the tradition of Abraham's faith
   d. Zach is no worse than any of you
   e. give Zach a chance to pay back what he has stolen

7. Do you think the meeting between Zacchaeus and Jesus was coincidental or all part of the plan and purpose of God?
   a. coincidental
   b. more than coincidental
   c. don't know

8. How do you think Zacchaeus felt when he left Jesus?
   a. loved and accepted
   b. relieved and restored
   c. clean and beautiful
   d. a part of God's family again

MY OWN STORY/20 Minutes. Suppose Jesus were to invite himself to your house. Bob Munger, in his little booklet "My Heart—Christ's Home," describes the areas of life as the rooms of a house. Take an inventory of your own life, then give yourself a grade on each room as follows: A = excellent rating; B = good rating; C = passing, but needs a little dusting; and D = barely passing, needs a lot of cleaning.

☐ LIBRARY: This room is your mind—what you allow to go into it and come out of it. It is the "control room" of the entire house.

☐ DINING ROOM: Appetites, desires, those things that your mind and spirit feed on for nourishment.

☐ DRAWING ROOM: This room is where you draw close to God, seek time with him daily, not just in times of distress or need.

☐ WORKSHOP: This room is where your gifts, talents, skills are put to work for God . . . by the power of the Spirit.

☐ RUMPUS ROOM: The social area of your life—the things you do to amuse yourself and others.

☐ HALL CLOSET: The one secret place that no one knows about, but is a real stumbling block in your walk in the Spirit.

---

servants and gave them ten minas. " 'Put this money to work,' he said, 'until I come back.'

¹⁴"But his subjects hated him and sent a delegation after him to say, 'We don't want this man to be our king.'

¹⁵"He was made king, however, and returned home. Then he sent for the servants to whom he had given the money, in order to find out what they had gained with it.

¹⁶"The first one came and said, 'Sir, your mina has earned ten more.'

¹⁷" 'Well done, my good servant!' his master replied. 'Because you have been trustworthy in a very small matter, take charge of ten cities.'

¹⁸"The second came and said, 'Sir, your mina has earned five more.'

¹⁹"His master answered, 'You take charge of five cities.'

²⁰"Then another servant came and said, 'Sir, here is your mina; I have kept it laid away in a piece of cloth. ²¹I was afraid of you, because you are a hard man. You take out what you did not put in and reap what you did not sow.'

²²"His master replied, 'I will judge you by your own words, you wicked servant! You knew, did you, that I am a hard man, taking out what I did not put in, and reaping what I did not sow? ²³Why then didn't you put my money on deposit, so that when I came back, I could have collected it with interest?'

²⁴"Then he said to those standing by, 'Take his mina away from him and give it to the one who has ten minas.'

²⁵" 'Sir,' they said, 'he already has ten!'

²⁶"He replied, 'I tell you that to everyone who has, more will be given, but as for the one who has nothing, even what he has will be taken away. ²⁷But those enemies of mine who did not want me to be king over them—bring them here and kill them in front of me.' "

The Triumphal Entry

²⁸After Jesus had said this, he went on ahead, going up to Jerusalem. ²⁹As he approached Bethphage and Bethany at the hill called the Mount of Olives, he sent two of his disciples, saying to them, ³⁰"Go to the village ahead of you, and as you enter it, you will find a colt tied there, which no one has ever ridden. Untie it and bring it here. ³¹If anyone asks you, 'Why are you untying it?' tell him, 'The Lord needs it.' "

³²Those who were sent ahead went and found it just as he had told them. ³³As they were untying the colt, its owners asked them, "Why are you untying the colt?"

³⁴They replied, "The Lord needs it."

³⁵They brought it to Jesus, threw their cloaks on the colt and put Jesus on it. ³⁶As he went along, people spread their cloaks on the road.

³⁷When he came near the place where the road goes down the Mount of Olives, the whole crowd of disciples began joyfully to praise God in loud voices for all the miracles they had seen:

¹³ A mina was about three months' wages.

³⁸"Blessed is the king who comes in the name of the Lord!"ᵛ

"Peace in heaven and glory in the highest!"

³⁹Some of the Pharisees in the crowd said to Jesus, "Teacher, rebuke your disciples!"

⁴⁰"I tell you," he replied, "if they keep quiet, the stones will cry out."

⁴¹As he approached Jerusalem and saw the city, he wept over it ⁴²and said, "If you, even you, had only known on this day what would bring you peace—but now it is hidden from your eyes. ⁴³The days will come upon you when your enemies will build an embankment against you and encircle you and hem you in on every side. ⁴⁴They will dash you to the ground, you and the children within your walls. They will not leave one stone on another, because you did not recognize the time of God's coming to you."

Jesus at the Temple

⁴⁵Then he entered the temple area and began driving out those who were selling. ⁴⁶"It is written," he said to them, " 'My house will be a house of prayer'ʷ; but you have made it 'a den of robbers.'ˣ"

⁴⁷Every day he was teaching at the temple. But the chief priests, the teachers of the law and the leaders among the people were trying to kill him. ⁴⁸Yet they could not find any way to do it, because all the people hung on his words.

The Authority of Jesus Questioned

20 One day as he was teaching the people in the temple courts and preaching the gospel, the chief priests and the teachers of the law, together with the elders, came up to him. ²"Tell us by what authority you are doing these things," they said. "Who gave you this authority?"

³He replied, "I will also ask you a question. Tell me, ⁴John's baptism—was it from heaven, or from men?"

⁵They discussed it among themselves and said, "If we say, 'From heaven,' he will ask, 'Why didn't you believe him?' ⁶But if we say, 'From men,' all the people will stone us, because they are persuaded that John was a prophet."

⁷So they answered, "We don't know where it was from."

⁸Jesus said, "Neither will I tell you by what authority I am doing these things."

The Parable of the Tenants

⁹He went on to tell the people this parable: "A man planted a vineyard, rented it to some farmers and went away for a long time. ¹⁰At harvest time he sent a servant to the tenants so they would give him some of the fruit of the vineyard. But the tenants beat him and sent him away empty-handed. ¹¹He sent another servant, but that one also they beat and treated shamefully and

---

worshipping disciples? How does Jesus reply? **6.** How does Jesus feel about the city (vv. 41-44)? What does he then prophesy?

REFLECT: 1. If Jesus rode into your town today, what kind of reception would he get: Immediately? After the people heard the message? **2.** How would the local media treat this? The elected officials? The guys in the tavern? The ladies in the bridge clubs? **3.** How do you handle praise? Rejection? Rejection by those who once praised you? **4.** Where is your "Jerusalem"—the place you yearn to see come to God?

OPEN Where do you go first when you visit a town? Why?

DIG: Where does Jesus go? Why there? Why so extreme an action? What else does Jesus do there? How does he get away with that?

REFLECT: How would Jesus react to injustice and corruption in your town? Where would he go first?

OPEN: In school, who were your three greatest authority figures?

DIG: 1. This story takes place where? When? What's happening? Who confronts Jesus? **2.** What for? What other vested interests are they trying to protect from Jesus' probing return question? For Jesus' own sake, why does he evade their question? **3.** If Jesus were linked with John, what would happen to these religious officials? To Jesus?

REFLECT: How do you handle one who's always "on your case"? On what authority do you act?

OPEN: 1. Who is your baby-sitter or who do you baby-sit for? **2.** What is your rule on allowing "parties" at your house while you are away from home? Did you ever throw a "party" when your parents were away? What happened?

DIG: 1. To whom does Jesus direct this parable (v. 9)? But who really gets the point (v. 19)? Why? **2.** What nine things does the landowner do in this parable? How do the tenants

---

ᵛ38 Psalm 118:26   ʷ46 Isaiah 56:7   ˣ46 Jer. 7:11

respond to his actions? Why? **3.** Why does the owner send his son (v. 13)? **4.** What questions does Jesus ask by way of the conclusion (v. 15)? What's the answer? What's the response of the people? **5.** In this parable, who's the landowner, the vineyard, the tenants, the servants, the son? What corresponds to the son's death? **6.** How does the scripture Jesus quotes relate to the parable? Who are the builders? The capstone? **7.** How does the parable and the quote impact the religious leaders? Why don't they act?

REFLECT: **1.** As for taking responsibility to look after God's vineyard, are you a leader or a follower? A giver or a taker? **2.** If Jesus told this parable today, who would be the tenant-farmers? **3.** Do you think today's "tenant-farmers" are trying to cheat God out of his due deliberately, or out of ignorance? Why?

OPEN: Would there ever be a case when you would feel right about paying taxes? Why?

DIG: **1.** How do the religious leaders hope to trap Jesus? What is their style? Tactics? Goal? **2.** What's the trap here: If Jesus had said, "Pay Casear," what would have happened to his crowd support (19:36, 48; 20:19)? If Jesus had said, "Don't pay", how would the rulers have responded? **3.** What's so insightful about Jesus' response? What does he mean by verse 25?

REFLECT: Do you think government spends tax money well? Would the church do any better?

OPEN: How did you prep for exams at school? If asked a "trick" question (one without a right or wrong answer), what did you do?

DIG: **1.** Who next confronts Jesus? Given their background as status quo politicians and strict materialists (see also Acts 23:8), how do the Sadducees question Jesus? With what address? Tone of voice? **2.** How seriously does Jesus treat this absurd question? What if he had ridiculed it? **3.** What does Jesus teach about life after death? Is he implying the discontinuity of all earthly relationships? Or only that there is no need for procreation in heaven to replenish the race, as no one dies? **4.** How does he then "prove" the resurrection? (Note the

sent away empty-handed. ¹²He sent still a third, and they wounded him and threw him out.

¹³"Then the owner of the vineyard said, 'What shall I do? I will send my son, whom I love; perhaps they will respect him.'

¹⁴"But when the tenants saw him, they talked the matter over. 'This is the heir,' they said. 'Let's kill him, and the inheritance will be ours.' ¹⁵So they threw him out of the vineyard and killed him.

"What then will the owner of the vineyard do to them? ¹⁶He will come and kill those tenants and give the vineyard to others."

When the people heard this, they said, "May this never be!"

¹⁷Jesus looked directly at them and asked, "Then what is the meaning of that which is written:

" 'The stone the builders rejected
     has become the capstone'ʸᶻ?

¹⁸Everyone who falls on that stone will be broken to pieces, but he on whom it falls will be crushed."

¹⁹The teachers of the law and the chief priests looked for a way to arrest him immediately, because they knew he had spoken this parable against them. But they were afraid of the people.

Paying Taxes to Caesar

²⁰Keeping a close watch on him, they sent spies, who pretended to be honest. They hoped to catch Jesus in something he said so that they might hand him over to the power and authority of the governor. ²¹So the spies questioned him: "Teacher, we know that you speak and teach what is right, and that you do not show partiality but teach the way of God in accordance with the truth. ²²Is it right for us to pay taxes to Caesar or not?"

²³He saw through their duplicity and said to them, ²⁴"Show me a denarius. Whose portrait and inscription are on it?"

²⁵"Caesar's," they replied.

He said to them, "Then give to Caesar what is Caesar's, and to God what is God's."

²⁶They were unable to trap him in what he had said there in public. And astonished by his answer, they became silent.

The Resurrection and Marriage

²⁷Some of the Sadducees, who say there is no resurrection, came to Jesus with a question. ²⁸"Teacher," they said, "Moses wrote for us that if a man's brother dies and leaves a wife but no children, the man must marry the widow and have children for his brother. ²⁹Now there were seven brothers. The first one married a woman and died childless. ³⁰The second ³¹and then the third married her, and in the same way the seven died, leaving no children. ³²Finally, the woman died too. ³³Now then, at the resurrection whose wife will she be, since the seven were married to her?"

³⁴Jesus replied, "The people of this age marry and are given in marriage. ³⁵But those who are considered worthy of taking part in that age and in the resurrection from the dead will neither

ʸ17 Or *cornerstone*   ᶻ17 Psalm 118:22

marry nor be given in marriage, ³⁶and they can no longer die; for they are like the angels. They are God's children, since they are children of the resurrection. ³⁷But in the account of the bush, even Moses showed that the dead rise, for he calls the Lord 'the God of Abraham, and the God of Isaac, and the God of Jacob.'ᵃ ³⁸He is not the God of the dead, but of the living, for to him all are alive.''

³⁹Some of the teachers of the law responded, "Well said, teacher!'' ⁴⁰And no one dared to ask him any more questions.

Whose Son Is the Christ?

⁴¹Then Jesus said to them, "How is it that they say the Christᵇ is the Son of David? ⁴²David himself declares in the Book of Psalms:

" 'The Lord said to my Lord:
"Sit at my right hand
⁴³until I make your enemies
a footstool for your feet." 'ᶜ

⁴⁴David calls him 'Lord.' How then can he be his son?''

⁴⁵While all the people were listening, Jesus said to his disciples, ⁴⁶"Beware of the teachers of the law. They like to walk around in flowing robes and love to be greeted in the marketplaces and have the most important seats in the synagogues and the places of honor at banquets. ⁴⁷They devour widows' houses and for a show make lengthy prayers. Such men will be punished most severely.''

The Widow's Offering

21 As he looked up, Jesus saw the rich putting their gifts into the temple treasury. ²He also saw a poor widow put in two very small copper coins.ᵈ ³"I tell you the truth," he said, "this poor widow has put in more than all the others. ⁴All these people gave their gifts out of their wealth; but she out of her poverty put in all she had to live on.''

Signs of the End of the Age

⁵Some of his disciples were remarking about how the temple was adorned with beautiful stones and with gifts dedicated to God. But Jesus said, ⁶"As for what you see here, the time will come when not one stone will be left on another; every one of them will be thrown down.''

⁷"Teacher," they asked, "when will these things happen? And what will be the sign that they are about to take place?''

⁸He replied: "Watch out that you are not deceived. For many will come in my name, claiming, 'I am he,' and, 'The time is near.' Do not follow them. ⁹When you hear of wars and revolutions, do not be frightened. These things must happen first, but the end will not come right away.''

¹⁰Then he said to them: "Nation will rise against nation, and

---

verb tense in this Exod. 3:6 quote and recall *when* this burning bush incident took place.) **5.** How do the teachers of the law differ in their response?

REFLECT: 1. How do you deal with a person who just wants to argue a point in the Bible? **2.** What if the person has honest questions and you don't have the answer?

OPEN: Growing up, what "hot buttons" did you push to make your parents mad? What "hot buttons" do your kids use on you?

DIG: 1. Now whose turn is it to ask questions (and push hot buttons)? What issue lies behind his first question (vv. 41-44)? What answer does this rhetorical question beg? **2.** For whose benefit (v. 45) does Jesus issue his warning about the teachers? What things do they enjoy now, for which they will suffer later? **3.** Can you feel the heat here?

REFLECT: What "hot buttons" would Jesus push in probing your professional group?

OPEN: Who do you know is the most generous? By what measure?

DIG: What does God value in those who give (also 2 Cor. 8:2)?

REFLECT: When have you given to God's work when you didn't have much yourself? What happened?

OPEN: 1. If you knew the world would end in six months, how would that fact change your lifestyle? **2.** If you had to leave this earth tomorrow, what two things would you miss most? Why?

DIG: 1. What prompts Jesus' next lesson? **2.** What bombshell of information does he explode on his disciples (v. 6)? What do you know about the temple? How did the Jewish people (including the disciples) feel about the temple? How must the disciples have felt when they heard Jesus' words? **3.** What two questions do the disciples ask in verse 7? What events might mislead them into thinking the end times had come (vv. 7-11)? Of what will these events be a sign? **4.** What nine things will happen to the disciples and the church after that (vv. 12-

---

ᵃ37 Exodus 3:6   ᵇ41 Or *Messiah*   ᶜ43 Psalm 110:1   ᵈ2 Greek *two lepta*

19)? What comfort will come in the midst of these trials? What should the attitude of the disciples be during that time? **5.** What event will signal the start of the great distress (v. 20)? Why will Jerusalem be devastated (see 11:49-51; 13:34-35 and 19:41-44)? How does Jesus describe this time (vv. 21-24)? What does he tell the people to do? Why? What else will be happening during this time (vv. 25-26)? **6.** How will the Son of Man come (v. 27)? What should be the attitude of believers when they see the Son of Man coming? **7.** What is the lesson of the fig tree (vv. 29-31)? How does the fig tree answer the disciples' question from verse 7? **8.** What promises does Jesus give in verses 32-33? How would these words have been of comfort to the disciples? Of discomfort? What impact do they have on you, 20 centuries later? **9.** In the midst of this heavy news and heavy times, how does Jesus caution his followers (vv. 34-35)? Why? **10.** During this time, what is Jesus' schedule? The schedule of the people? What is significant about these schedules to you?

REFLECT: 1. What are some "signs" occurring today that relate to the "end times"? How do you feel about the "end time"? **2.** What is the lesson for you in the parable of the "fig tree"? **3.** When you read the newspaper or listen to the evening news, how does it make you feel? In tough times, when the forces of evil seem to be winning, do you feel like withdrawing from the battle or rolling up your sleeves and getting into the frey? **4.** What causes you to feel weighed down and discouraged about the world situation today?

---

kingdom against kingdom. ¹¹There will be great earthquakes, famines and pestilences in various places, and fearful events and great signs from heaven.

¹²"But before all this, they will lay hands on you and persecute you. They will deliver you to synagogues and prisons, and you will be brought before kings and governors, and all on account of my name. ¹³This will result in your being witnesses to them. ¹⁴But make up your mind not to worry beforehand how you will defend yourselves. ¹⁵For I will give you words and wisdom that none of your adversaries will be able to resist or contradict. ¹⁶You will be betrayed even by parents, brothers, relatives and friends, and they will put some of you to death. ¹⁷All men will hate you because of me. ¹⁸But not a hair of your head will perish. ¹⁹By standing firm you will gain life.

²⁰"When you see Jerusalem being surrounded by armies, you will know that its desolation is near. ²¹Then let those who are in Judea flee to the mountains, let those in the city get out, and let those in the country not enter the city. ²²For this is the time of punishment in fulfillment of all that has been written. ²³How dreadful it will be in those days for pregnant women and nursing mothers! There will be great distress in the land and wrath against this people. ²⁴They will fall by the sword and will be taken as prisoners to all the nations. Jerusalem will be trampled on by the Gentiles until the times of the Gentiles are fulfilled.

²⁵"There will be signs in the sun, moon and stars. On the earth, nations will be in anguish and perplexity at the roaring and tossing of the sea. ²⁶Men will faint from terror, apprehensive of what is coming on the world, for the heavenly bodies will be shaken. ²⁷At that time they will see the Son of Man coming in a cloud with power and great glory. ²⁸When these things begin to take place, stand up and lift up your heads, because your redemption is drawing near."

²⁹He told them this parable: "Look at the fig tree and all the trees. ³⁰When they sprout leaves, you can see for yourselves and know that summer is near. ³¹Even so, when you see these things happening, you know that the kingdom of God is near.

³²"I tell you the truth, this generation*ᵉ* will certainly not pass away until all these things have happened. ³³Heaven and earth will pass away, but my words will never pass away.

³⁴"Be careful, or your hearts will be weighed down with dissipation, drunkenness and the anxieties of life, and that day will close on you unexpectedly like a trap. ³⁵For it will come upon all those who live on the face of the whole earth. ³⁶Be always on the watch, and pray that you may be able to escape all that is about to happen, and that you may be able to stand before the Son of Man."

³⁷Each day Jesus was teaching at the temple, and each evening he went out to spend the night on the hill called the Mount of Olives, ³⁸and all the people came early in the morning to hear him at the temple.

ᵉ32 Or race

Judas Agrees to Betray Jesus

22 Now the Feast of Unleavened Bread, called the Passover, was approaching, [2]and the chief priests and the teachers of the law were looking for some way to get rid of Jesus, for they were afraid of the people. [3]Then Satan entered Judas, called Iscariot, one of the Twelve. [4]And Judas went to the chief priests and the officers of the temple guard and discussed with them how he might betray Jesus. [5]They were delighted and agreed to give him money. [6]He consented, and watched for an opportunity to hand Jesus over to them when no crowd was present.

The Last Supper

[7]Then came the day of Unleavened Bread on which the Passover lamb had to be sacrificed. [8]Jesus sent Peter and John, saying, "Go and make preparations for us to eat the Passover."

[9]"Where do you want us to prepare for it?" they asked.

[10]He replied, "As you enter the city, a man carrying a jar of water will meet you. Follow him to the house that he enters, [11]and say to the owner of the house, 'The Teacher asks: Where is the guest room, where I may eat the Passover with my disciples?' [12]He will show you a large upper room, all furnished. Make preparations there."

[13]They left and found things just as Jesus had told them. So they prepared the Passover.

[14]When the hour came, Jesus and his apostles reclined at the table. [15]And he said to them, "I have eagerly desired to eat this Passover with you before I suffer. [16]For I tell you, I will not eat it again until it finds fulfillment in the kingdom of God."

[17]After taking the cup, he gave thanks and said, "Take this and divide it among you. [18]For I tell you I will not drink again of the fruit of the vine until the kingdom of God comes."

[19]And he took bread, gave thanks and broke it, and gave it to them, saying, "This is my body given for you; do this in remembrance of me."

[20]In the same way, after the supper he took the cup, saying, "This cup is the new covenant in my blood, which is poured out for you. [21]But the hand of him who is going to betray me is with mine on the table. [22]The Son of Man will go as it has been decreed, but woe to that man who betrays him." [23]They began to question among themselves which of them it might be who would do this.

[24]Also a dispute arose among them as to which of them was considered to be greatest. [25]Jesus said to them, "The kings of the Gentiles lord it over them; and those who exercise authority over them call themselves Benefactors. [26]But you are not to be like that. Instead, the greatest among you should be like the youngest, and the one who rules like the one who serves. [27]For who is greater, the one who is at the table or the one who serves? Is it not the one who is at the table? But I am among you as one who serves. [28]You are those who have stood by me in my trials. [29]And I confer on you a kingdom, just as my Father conferred one on me, [30]so that you may eat and drink at my table in my kingdom and sit on thrones, judging the twelve tribes of Israel.

OPEN: Who was your "steady" in high school? What happened?

DIG: What is signifigant about the time of this "Passover Plot"? Who plots against Jesus? Why the indirect plot through Judas (vv. 2, 6)? What is Judas' role in the plot? Satan's role?

REFLECT: When have you felt "betrayed"? When have you felt "trapped" to do dirty work?

OPEN: 1. Where is one of your favorite places to eat as a family? What makes the place so good? **2.** When you were growing up, what were mealtimes like? Where did everyone sit around the table? What's one vivid memory you have about each family member at this time? **3.** What kind of bread (sourdough, whole wheat, rye, homemade biscuits) best describe your personality? Why?

DIG: 1. What is the Feast of Unleavened Bread? How does it fit into the Passover? Who does Jesus send to make preparations for this meal? What is unusual about their assignment (vv. 10-13)? Why do you think it would have been dangerous for the disciples to openly seek a room for this meal? **2.** How does Jesus feel about sharing this meal with his followers (v. 15)? Why? What does he say about suffering and eating here? **3.** What two parts of the supper does Jesus single out to give new, symbolic meaning? What is the new meaning of the bread and the cup in verses 19-20? What is the connection between the Passover and Jesus' death and resurrection (see also Exodus 12)? **4.** What does he say about his betrayer? How do the disciples react to that news? **5.** What other dispute arises at the table (v. 24)? What does Jesus say about servanthood? How has his life been an example of this? What does he say about the place of the disciples in his kingdom later? **6.** What special word does he have for Simon Peter (vv. 31-32)? How does Peter react? What does Jesus predict? **7.** Finally, what message does Jesus have for his disciples (vv. 35-37)? How is this different from the way he had previously sent them out? Why does he say this? **8.** How do the disciples show their love for the Lord but at the same time their lack of understanding?

REFLECT: 1. If you were Simon in verse 31 and Jesus said to you, "Satan has asked to sift you as wheat. But I have prayed for you, Simon, that your faith may not fail," how would you respond? 2. In what ways do you feel like Satan is on your back right now "sifting" you? What is Satan's strategy for "getting to you" or causing you to cave in?

OPEN: Where do you go to get away from it all? What tough decision has kept you from sleeping?

DIG: 1. To what familiar place do they go (see 21:37)? 2. What are the disciples to pray about? What happens instead? Why? 3. What does Jesus pray about? What is "this cup"? What about the cross bothers Jesus: The physical pain? Or something else? Why? 4. How does God strengthen him? What does this teach about prayer in relation to temptation?

REFLECT: What did you "endure" this year that compares with verses 40 or 42? What finally happened?

OPEN: What actor would you choose to play Judas Iscariot? Why?

DIG: 1. Who leads this lynch mob? Why so many and armed? What do they fear? Why are their fears unfounded (vv. 54-53)? 2. What is the irony in Judas' betrayal? What is the irony in the use of the sword by Peter (John 18:10) in view of Peter's betrayal (vv. 54-62)? 3. What does Jesus mean by "your hour" (v. 53; in contrast to his own, v. 42)?

REFLECT: 1. How do you feel about Judas? How do you think he felt about himself? Why do you think he did what he did? 2. In times of provocaution and crisis, do you respond more like the impulsive Peter or the pacifist Jesus? Why?

[31]"Simon, Simon, Satan has asked to sift you[f] as wheat. [32]But I have prayed for you, Simon, that your faith may not fail. And when you have turned back, strengthen your brothers."

[33]But he replied, "Lord, I am ready to go with you to prison and to death."

[34]Jesus answered, "I tell you, Peter, before the rooster crows today, you will deny three times that you know me."

[35]Then Jesus asked them, "When I sent you without purse, bag or sandals, did you lack anything?"

"Nothing," they answered.

[36]He said to them, "But now if you have a purse, take it, and also a bag; and if you don't have a sword, sell your cloak and buy one. [37]It is written: 'And he was numbered with the transgressors'[g]; and I tell you that this must be fulfilled in me. Yes, what is written about me is reaching its fulfillment."

[38]The disciples said, "See, Lord, here are two swords."

"That is enough," he replied.

Jesus Prays on the Mount of Olives

[39]Jesus went out as usual to the Mount of Olives, and his disciples followed him. [40]On reaching the place, he said to them, "Pray that you will not fall into temptation." [41]He withdrew about a stone's throw beyond them, knelt down and prayed, [42]"Father, if you are willing, take this cup from me; yet not my will, but yours be done." [43]An angel from heaven appeared to him and strengthened him. [44]And being in anguish, he prayed more earnestly, and his sweat was like drops of blood falling to the ground.[h]

[45]When he rose from prayer and went back to the disciples, he found them asleep, exhausted from sorrow. [46]"Why are you sleeping?" he asked them. "Get up and pray so that you will not fall into temptation."

Jesus Arrested

[47]While he was still speaking a crowd came up, and the man who was called Judas, one of the Twelve, was leading them. He approached Jesus to kiss him, [48]but Jesus asked him, "Judas, are you betraying the Son of Man with a kiss?"

[49]When Jesus' followers saw what was going to happen, they said, "Lord, should we strike with our swords?" [50]And one of them struck the servant of the high priest, cutting off his right ear.

[51]But Jesus answered, "No more of this!" And he touched the man's ear and healed him.

[52]Then Jesus said to the chief priests, the officers of the temple guard, and the elders, who had come for him, "Am I leading a rebellion, that you have come with swords and clubs? [53]Every day I was with you in the temple courts, and you did not lay a hand on me. But this is your hour—when darkness reigns."

---

f31 The Greek is plural.   *g37* Isaiah 53:12   *h44* Some early manuscripts do not have verses 43 and 44.

Peter Disowns Jesus

⁵⁴Then seizing him, they led him away and took him into the house of the high priest. Peter followed at a distance. ⁵⁵But when they had kindled a fire in the middle of the courtyard and had sat down together, Peter sat down with them. ⁵⁶A servant girl saw him seated there in the firelight. She looked closely at him and said, "This man was with him."

⁵⁷But he denied it. "Woman, I don't know him," he said.

⁵⁸A little later someone else saw him and said, "You also are one of them."

"Man, I am not!" Peter replied.

⁵⁹About an hour later another asserted, "Certainly this fellow was with him, for he is a Galilean."

⁶⁰Peter replied, "Man, I don't know what you're talking about!" Just as he was speaking, the rooster crowed. ⁶¹The Lord turned and looked straight at Peter. Then Peter remembered the word the Lord had spoken to him: "Before the rooster crows today, you will disown me three times." ⁶²And he went outside and wept bitterly.

The Guards Mock Jesus

⁶³The men who were guarding Jesus began mocking and beating him. ⁶⁴They blindfolded him and demanded, "Prophesy! Who hit you?" ⁶⁵And they said many other insulting things to him.

Jesus Before Pilate and Herod

⁶⁶At daybreak the council of the elders of the people, both the chief priests and teachers of the law, met together, and Jesus was led before them. ⁶⁷"If you are the Christ,ⁱ" they said, "tell us."

Jesus answered, "If I tell you, you will not believe me, ⁶⁸and if I asked you, you would not answer. ⁶⁹But from now on, the Son of Man will be seated at the right hand of the mighty God."

⁷⁰They all asked, "Are you then the Son of God?"

He replied, "You are right in saying I am."

⁷¹Then they said, "Why do we need any more testimony? We have heard it from his own lips."

23 Then the whole assembly rose and led him off to Pilate. ²And they began to accuse him, saying, "We have found this man subverting our nation. He opposes payment of taxes to Caesar and claims to be Christ,ʲ a king."

³So Pilate asked Jesus, "Are you the king of the Jews?"

"Yes, it is as you say," Jesus replied.

⁴Then Pilate announced to the chief priests and the crowd, "I find no basis for a charge against this man."

⁵But they insisted, "He stirs up the people all over Judeaᵏ by his teaching. He started in Galilee and has come all the way here."

⁶On hearing this, Pilate asked if the man was a Galilean. ⁷When he learned that Jesus was under Herod's jurisdiction, he sent him to Herod, who was also in Jerusalem at that time.

ⁱ67 Or *Messiah*   ʲ2 Or *Messiah*; also in verses 35 and 39   ᵏ5 Or *over the land of the Jews*

OPEN: When have you felt like crawling into a hole, never to return: When you let in the winning run in a baseball playoff game? When you missed the winning field goal in overtime? When you dropped the baton in the state track meet?

DIG: 1. What character has Peter displayed so far? How is Peter still courageous here? **2.** How are the three accusations and denials similar? Different? **3.** What was more heart-rending for Peter: The cock's crow? Jesus' look? Jesus' words (v. 34)? Why such tears?

REFLECT: When have you felt like Peter? How do you handle ridicule for your spiritual beliefs? What "rooster" reminds you when you have blown it? What helps you work through guilt?

OPEN: What particular form of injustice makes your blood boil?

DIG: What brutality do the soldiers inflict on Jesus (also Mt. 27:27-31; Mk. 15:16-20)?

OPEN: 1. When you were a kid, would you rather have been punished by your mother or your father? Why? **2.** Would you rather be judged today by a religious court or a secular court? Why? **3.** In family squabbles are you closer to "peace-at-any-price" or "there-will-be-hell-to-pay"? Why?

DIG: 1. At daybreak, where does Jesus find himself? What do they tell him to do? **2.** How does Jesus initially (vv. 67-68) answer their order? Finally (v. 70) how does he? When his opponents hear this, how do they react? Why? **3.** Where do they take Jesus now (v. 1)? Why him? What powers does he have? As the Roman governor of Judea, what does Pilate want to know? **4.** What accusations do the Jewish leaders level against Jesus? How does this fit into what Pilate would be interested in? **5.** What question does Pilate ask Jesus (v. 3)? How does Jesus answer? Why doesn't this seem to alarm Pilate? How do you think Pilate feels about Jesus' guilt as the trial opens? **6.** So in verse 5, of what do the Jewish leaders accuse Jesus? How does this charge lead Jesus to be taken to Herod? **7.** What is Herod's response in seeing Jesus? Why?

How does he question Jesus? How does Jesus respond? What are the chief priests and teachers doing during this time (v. 10)? So what does Herod do with Jesus (v. 11)? What is the irony of verse 12 to you? **8.** What does Pilate conclude and tell the leaders (vv. 13-16)? How do they respond? Who is Barabbas? **9.** What is Pilate's desire (v. 20)? But how is the crowd wearing him down? What does Pilate finally do?

REFLECT: 1. If you were part of an investigation team that was appointed to find out what went wrong in the "system" that allowed such a miscarriage of justice, what would you conclude? Were the laws that protect human rights OK? Was the system in place to guarantee "fair trial"? Then, what went wrong? What is the lesson for you here? **2.** Could this same thing happen today in our system of justice? What could one person do? **3.** Should a Christian fight for justice, or withdraw and let the devil have his way? **4.** How does the story of Barabbas illustrate the meaning of the gospel? In what sense are you like Barabbas?

OPEN: 1. What is one of the worst ways you can imagine dying? **2.** What would you like carved on your tombstone? What is the statement you would like the newspaper to say about you in your obituary?

DIG: 1. Who carries the cross for Jesus? How is he "recruited"? Why does Jesus need help (see Mark 14:65; 15:15, 19)? **2.** Who follows this procession? What does Jesus say to them? What does he mean in verse 31? **3.** Where does the crucifixion take place? Who is executed with Jesus? What do you know about crucifixion? **4.** What does Jesus say to God about his executors? What do the soldiers do with his clothes? **5.** Who taunts Jesus (vv. 36-39)? What do the various people say? Do Why are the members of the crowd angry? What hopes for Jesus did they have that now seem shattered? **6.** Do you think the written notice (put there at Pilate's request) reflects a hint of sarcasm or truth on Pilate's part (v. 38)? Why? **7.** What is significant about the interchange between the criminals and Jesus?

⁸When Herod saw Jesus, he was greatly pleased, because for a long time he had been wanting to see him. From what he had heard about him, he hoped to see him perform some miracle. ⁹He plied him with many questions, but Jesus gave him no answer. ¹⁰The chief priests and the teachers of the law were standing there, vehemently accusing him. ¹¹Then Herod and his soldiers ridiculed and mocked him. Dressing him in an elegant robe, they sent him back to Pilate. ¹²That day Herod and Pilate became friends—before this they had been enemies.

¹³Pilate called together the chief priests, the rulers and the people, ¹⁴and said to them, "You brought me this man as one who was inciting the people to rebellion. I have examined him in your presence and have found no basis for your charges against him. ¹⁵Neither has Herod, for he sent him back to us; as you can see, he has done nothing to deserve death. ¹⁶Therefore, I will punish him and then release him.ˡ'"

¹⁸With one voice they cried out, "Away with this man! Release Barabbas to us!" ¹⁹(Barabbas had been thrown into prison for an insurrection in the city, and for murder.)

²⁰Wanting to release Jesus, Pilate appealed to them again. ²¹But they kept shouting, "Crucify him! Crucify him!"

²²For the third time he spoke to them: "Why? What crime has this man committed? I have found in him no grounds for the death penalty. Therefore I will have him punished and then release him."

²³But with loud shouts they insistently demanded that he be crucified, and their shouts prevailed. ²⁴So Pilate decided to grant their demand. ²⁵He released the man who had been thrown into prison for insurrection and murder, the one they asked for, and surrendered Jesus to their will.

The Crucifixion

²⁶As they led him away, they seized Simon from Cyrene, who was on his way in from the country, and put the cross on him and made him carry it behind Jesus. ²⁷A large number of people followed him, including women who mourned and wailed for him. ²⁸Jesus turned and said to them, "Daughters of Jerusalem, do not weep for me; weep for yourselves and for your children. ²⁹For the time will come when you will say, 'Blessed are the barren women, the wombs that never bore and the breasts that never nursed!' ³⁰Then

" 'they will say to the mountains, "Fall on us!"
    and to the hills, "Cover us!" 'ᵐ

³¹For if men do these things when the tree is green, what will happen when it is dry?"

³²Two other men, both criminals, were also led out with him to be executed. ³³When they came to the place called the Skull, there they crucified him, along with the criminals—one on his right, the other on his left. ³⁴Jesus said, "Father, forgive them,

---

ˡ16 Some manuscripts *him."* ˡ⁷*Now he was obliged to release one man to them at the Feast.*   ᵐ30 Hosea 10:8

for they do not know what they are doing."ⁿ And they divided up his clothes by casting lots.

³⁵The people stood watching, and the rulers even sneered at him. They said, "He saved others; let him save himself if he is the Christ of God, the Chosen One."

³⁶The soldiers also came up and mocked him. They offered him wine vinegar ³⁷and said, "If you are the king of the Jews, save yourself."

³⁸There was a written notice above him, which read: THIS IS THE KING OF THE JEWS.

³⁹One of the criminals who hung there hurled insults at him: "Aren't you the Christ? Save yourself and us!"

⁴⁰But the other criminal rebuked him. "Don't you fear God," he said, "since you are under the same sentence? ⁴¹We are punished justly, for we are getting what our deeds deserve. But this man has done nothing wrong."

⁴²Then he said, "Jesus, remember me when you come into your kingdomᵒ."

⁴³Jesus answered him, "I tell you the truth, today you will be with me in paradise."

Jesus' Death

⁴⁴It was now about the sixth hour, and darkness came over the whole land until the ninth hour, ⁴⁵for the sun stopped shining. And the curtain of the temple was torn in two. ⁴⁶Jesus called out with a loud voice, "Father, into your hands I commit my spirit." When he had said this, he breathed his last.

⁴⁷The centurion, seeing what had happened, praised God and said, "Surely this was a righteous man." ⁴⁸When all the people who had gathered to witness this sight saw what took place, they beat their breasts and went away. ⁴⁹But all those who knew him, including the women who had followed him from Galilee, stood at a distance, watching these things.

Jesus' Burial

⁵⁰Now there was a man named Joseph, a member of the Council, a good and upright man, ⁵¹who had not consented to their decision and action. He came from the Judean town of Arimathea and he was waiting for the kingdom of God. ⁵²Going to Pilate, he asked for Jesus' body. ⁵³Then he took it down, wrapped it in linen cloth and placed it in a tomb cut in the rock, one in which no one had yet been laid. ⁵⁴It was Preparation Day, and the Sabbath was about to begin.

⁵⁵The women who had come with Jesus from Galilee followed Joseph and saw the tomb and how his body was laid in it. ⁵⁶Then they went home and prepared spices and perfumes. But they rested on the Sabbath in obedience to the commandment.

REFLECT: 1. How do you view the crucifixion: Necessary evil? Common tragedy? Cruel and unusual punishment? "Good" Friday? Sacrifice for sin? Triumph of justice? Triumph over injustice? Why? 2. When did the full meaning of the death of Christ begin to make sense to you? How would you explain the necessity of the crucifixion to a non-Christian friend? 3. How do you feel about your own death and dying? About the death of members of your family? What hope does Christ's death give you? 4. Who in this story do you identify with most? With least? Why? 5. What impresses you most about Jesus in this story?

OPEN: Other than Jesus, whose death (family, friend or national figure) has most affected you? Why?

DIG: What sympathizers attend? What do they see? Smell? Hear? Say? Feel? Do? How do these special effects witness to who Jesus is? Likewise, what do the final words of Jesus reveal? What double irony do you detect here?

REFLECT: Is Jesus' death for you more a dispassionate fact or an emotional experience? Why?

OPEN: 1. If you could choose anywhere in the world to be buried, where would you choose and why? 2. Would you characterize yourself as risky or cautious? Why?

DIG: 1. Who buries Jesus? What do you learn about him from these verses? 2. How does he arrange the burial? Why is he able to get permission? How bold a move is this? 3. What does Joseph do after obtaining the body? Why does he have to rush (vv. 54-56)? 4. What do the women do? Observe? What do they do at home?

REFLECT: 1. What do you appreciate most about Joseph? 2. What's one of the riskiest things you've ever done for Jesus? What happened? What did you learn? 3. Jesus had apparently failed, but the women did not abandon him. What do you learn from this?

ⁿ34 Some early manuscripts do not have this sentence.   ᵒ42 Some manuscripts *come with your kingly power*

OPEN: 1. What time do you like to get up in the morning? **2.** When visiting the grave of a friend, flowers in hand, you find the gravestone missing, what do you conclude?

DIG: 1. Who visits the tomb? When? Why now? What does this mean? **2.** What potential problems loom ahead (see Matthew 27:60, 65-66; Mark 16:3)? Instead, what do they find? Fear? **3.** How do the angles confront the women? **4.** How do the women respond (vv. 8-10)? How are they received? Why? **5.** How does Peter try to make sense of the empty tomb and grave clothes?

REFLECT: 1. At funerals, how do you comfort those who grieve without hope? What difference does the physical resurrection make to you? **2.** Where is your spiritual life focused these days: On Good Friday? Easter Sunday? Or in between?

OPEN: 1. If you got "laid off" from work today or your job was "terminated" what would you do? Where would you go to "get yourself together"? **2.** What cause have you believed in and given yourself to that came to an abrupt and painful end? For instance, a Presidential campaign or a pennant race?

DIG: 1. How does Luke use this story to better explain the meaning of the crucifixion and resurrection? **2.** Who is going where in this story? What are they discussing on the road? **3.** How does Jesus interrupt their discussion? What does he ask them? With what emotion do they answer Jesus' questions? Why do you think Jesus asks them these questions when he already knows the answers? **4.** How do they explain what has happened? How do they explain their hope? What the woman found? What conclusions have they drawn at this point from all the information they have? Why? **5.** How does Jesus give them clarity in verses 25-27? **6.** How much further does Jesus plan to go on the road (v. 28)? What do the men urge him to do? Why? **7.** How does the time at dinner open their eyes? What happens to Jesus when they recognize him? Why do you think he leaves? What do the men say to one another? Where do they go? What do they report? **8.** What role do meals play in the life of Jesus and the disciples? What do you learn from this?

The Resurrection

24 On the first day of the week, very early in the morning, the women took the spices they had prepared and went to the tomb. [2]They found the stone rolled away from the tomb, [3]but when they entered, they did not find the body of the Lord Jesus. [4]While they were wondering about this, suddenly two men in clothes that gleamed like lightning stood beside them. [5]In their fright the women bowed down with their faces to the ground, but the men said to them, "Why do you look for the living among the dead? [6]He is not here; he has risen! Remember how he told you, while he was still with you in Galilee: [7]'The Son of Man must be delivered into the hands of sinful men, be crucified and on the third day be raised again.'" [8]Then they remembered his words.

[9]When they came back from the tomb, they told all these things to the Eleven and to all the others. [10]It was Mary Magdalene, Joanna, Mary the mother of James, and the others with them who told this to the apostles. [11]But they did not believe the women, because their words seemed to them like nonsense. [12]Peter, however, got up and ran to the tomb. Bending over, he saw the strips of linen lying by themselves, and he went away, wondering to himself what had happened.

On the Road to Emmaus

[13]Now that same day two of them were going to a village called Emmaus, about seven miles[p] from Jerusalem. [14]They were talking with each other about everything that had happened. [15]As they talked and discussed these things with each other, Jesus himself came up and walked along with them; [16]but they were kept from recognizing him.

[17]He asked them, "What are you discussing together as you walk along?"

They stood still, their faces downcast. [18]One of them, named Cleopas, asked him, "Are you only a visitor to Jerusalem and do not know the things that have happened there in these days?"

[19]"What things?" he asked.

"About Jesus of Nazareth," they replied. "He was a prophet, powerful in word and deed before God and all the people. [20]The chief priests and our rulers handed him over to be sentenced to death, and they crucified him; [21]but we had hoped that he was the one who was going to redeem Israel. And what is more, it is the third day since all this took place. [22]In addition, some of our women amazed us. They went to the tomb early this morning [23]but didn't find his body. They came and told us that they had seen a vision of angels, who said he was alive. [24]Then some of our companions went to the tomb and found it just as the women had said, but him they did not see."

[25]He said to them, "How foolish you are, and how slow of heart to believe all that the prophets have spoken! [26]Did not the Christ[q] have to suffer these things and then enter his glory?" [27]And beginning with Moses and all the Prophets, he explained to them what was said in all the Scriptures concerning himself.

_p13_ Greek _sixty stadia_ (about 11 kilometers)   _q26_ Or _Messiah_; also in verse 46

Luke 24:13-35   ON THE ROAD TO EMMAUS

LOOKING INTO THE SCRIPTURE/20 Minutes. Read Luke 24:13-35 and discuss.

1. Why did the two men take off for Emmaus?
   a. scared stiff
   b. work the next day
   c. running away
   d. disillusionment over the events of the last week

2. Why didn't the two men recognize Jesus when he joined them?
   a. they refused to believe their eyes
   b. they were too occupied
   c. Jesus was invisible in his resurrection body
   d. they didn't look up to see who it was
   e. they were kept from recognizing him

3. When they heard the report from the women about the empty tomb, what did they assume?
   a. the worst
   b. Jesus was alive
   c. someone had stolen the body
   d. the authorities were arresting everybody

4. Why did Jesus begin with Moses and the prophets in explaining what happened?
   a. the guys knew about them
   b. Moses gave the Law and the prophets predicted the coming Messiah
   c. to understand Jesus, you have to understand the Old Testament
   d. to show them they were on the right track about Jesus

5. What opened the eyes of the two men?
   a. burst of insight
   b. the way Jesus "took bread . . . and broke it"
   c. the Holy Spirit
   d. putting two and two together

6. Why did the two men want to return to Jerusalem?
   a. to join the party
   b. to confirm the women's report
   c. to make amends
   d. to be with their friends
   e. to tell everybody the good news
   f. to rejoin Jesus' team they had quit

MY OWN STORY/25 Minutes.

1. Take a moment and indicate from 1 to 10 how you would cope with the following stress situations. 1 is NO ANXIETY; 10 is HIGH ANXIETY.

_____ DEATH: Your closest friend suddenly dies
_____ SECURITY: One day your boss tells you that you are fired
_____ HOPE SHATTERED: The dreams you had for the future are dashed
_____ LODGING: You don't have a place to sleep tonight
_____ REPUTATION: You risked everything and the cause you believed in turns sour
_____ FRIENDS: The old gang breaks up, including most of your friends
_____ SUICIDE: One of your friends hangs himself
_____ BETRAYAL: You feel let down by the one person in the world you trusted
_____ SHAME: The people in town laugh at you and think you've wasted your life

2. Have you ever felt like running away or throwing in the towel spiritually?
   a. maybe once or twice
   b. often
   c. never

3. What is the thing that triggers a spiritual crisis in your experience?
   a. financial panic
   b. anger with God over personal tragedy
   c. disappointment in a relationship
   d. domestic problems/hassles
   e. questions/doubts about my faith
   f. disillusionment with my church
   g. lack of direction from God

4. What has helped you recognize Jesus walking alongside you when you are down spiritually?
   a. time alone with God
   b. talking it out with someone
   c. fellowship with other strugglers
   d. getting away from the situation
   e. Communion
   f. reading familiar Scripture
   g. a favorite hymn

REFLECT: 1. Where is your "Road to Emmaus" – the place where Jesus surprised you recently? What happened? 2. When have you felt that Jesus intervened and revealed himself to you when you were in the process of talking to someone else? What happened? What did you learn from the experience? 3. How well do you think you can explain the life, death and resurrection of Jesus Christ and how a person can have a relationship with him? Try rehearsing or role playing this in your group. Who could you communicate these truths with "for real" today? 4. What questions would you ask Jesus if he spent the evening with you?

OPEN: What favorite slogan or "pep" talk do you recall from your school coach? How did that coach treat you when you "bombed"?

DIG: 1. How does Jesus press peace into this situation? Into their awareness? 2. Why are the disciples having such difficulty believing: Not using their eyes? Not enough evidence? Not enough faith? Too much joy? 3. What interpretation from Jesus helps them to believe? 4. What do the Scriptures reveal about Christ? 5. What task does he give them? With what promise?

REFLECT: 1. What doubts have troubled you this week? How could Jesus bring peace to you in this situation? 2. What does Jesus need to do for you so that you could have a stronger faith in him? How has he revealed himself to you in the past? 3. Where is your Jerusalem – your beginning point, the place where you began your ministry and recognized God's power?

OPEN: How are you at saying "goodbye" to those you love?

DIG: How do the disciples react this time to Jesus being taken away from them? What is the difference between the absence caused by the Crucifixion and the absence caused by the Ascension?

REFLECT: What has been the high-point in this study for you?

---

²⁸As they approached the village to which they were going, Jesus acted as if he were going farther. ²⁹But they urged him strongly, "Stay with us, for it is nearly evening; the day is almost over." So he went in to stay with them.

³⁰When he was at the table with them, he took bread, gave thanks, broke it and began to give it to them. ³¹Then their eyes were opened and they recognized him, and he disappeared from their sight. ³²They asked each other, "Were not our hearts burning within us while he talked with us on the road and opened the Scriptures to us?"

³³They got up and returned at once to Jerusalem. There they found the Eleven and those with them, assembled together ³⁴and saying, "It is true! The Lord has risen and has appeared to Simon." ³⁵Then the two told what had happened on the way, and how Jesus was recognized by them when he broke the bread.

Jesus Appears to the Disciples

³⁶While they were still talking about this, Jesus himself stood among them and said to them, "Peace be with you."

³⁷They were startled and frightened, thinking they saw a ghost. ³⁸He said to them, "Why are you troubled, and why do doubts rise in your minds? ³⁹Look at my hands and my feet. It is I myself! Touch me and see; a ghost does not have flesh and bones, as you see I have."

⁴⁰When he had said this, he showed them his hands and feet. ⁴¹And while they still did not believe it because of joy and amazement, he asked them, "Do you have anything here to eat?" ⁴²They gave him a piece of broiled fish, ⁴³and he took it and ate it in their presence.

⁴⁴He said to them, "This is what I told you while I was still with you: Everything must be fulfilled that is written about me in the Law of Moses, the Prophets and the Psalms."

⁴⁵Then he opened their minds so they could understand the Scriptures. ⁴⁶He told them, "This is what is written: The Christ will suffer and rise from the dead on the third day, ⁴⁷and repentance and forgiveness of sins will be preached in his name to all nations, beginning at Jerusalem. ⁴⁸You are witnesses of these things. ⁴⁹I am going to send you what my Father has promised; but stay in the city until you have been clothed with power from on high."

The Ascension

⁵⁰When he had led them out to the vicinity of Bethany, he lifted up his hands and blessed them. ⁵¹While he was blessing them, he left them and was taken up into heaven. ⁵²Then they worshiped him and returned to Jerusalem with great joy. ⁵³And they stayed continually at the temple, praising God.

JOHN

INTRODUCTION

Author—The Disciple Whom Jesus Loved

The writer of the fourth Gospel does not name himself in the text. Like the other three gospels, the fourth Gospel is anonymous. The inscription "The Gospel According to John" or "According to John" (as found in some ancient manuscripts) was added to the text by early Christians.

Yet in a curious way the fourth Gospel is less anonymous than the other three because the writer identifies himself in the final chapter by way of a title. He calls himself "the disciple whom Jesus loved" (21:20-24; see also 13:23-25; 19:26-27; 20:2-8; 21:7). Who then is this mysterious disciple who wanted to be known only in terms of his relationship to Jesus?

One of the Twelve

He must have been one of the twelve original disciples because he was present at the Last Supper (13:23-25; 21:20). In fact, the beloved disciple was "reclining next to" Jesus (13:23). This gives us a valuable clue as to his identity: He was probably one of the three (occasionally four) disciples who were closest to Jesus—Peter, James, John and sometimes Andrew. We know that the person reclining next to Jesus was not Peter, because Peter asked this disciple a question (13:24). The person was probably not Andrew, since Andrew is explicitly named several times in the text (1:40, 44; 6:8; 12:22); it would be strange to name a disciple in some places and to list him anonymously in others as "the disciple whom Jesus loved." Most of the other disciples are also named in this gospel. Some have suggested Lazarus as author of the fourth Gospel because in 11:5 Jesus is said to have loved him, but Lazarus is named in chapters 11-12. Of all the possible candidates, only the sons of Zebedee (James and John) are not named in the fourth Gospel. The beloved disciple could not have been James, since he died at the hands of Herod Agrippa I (Acts 12:2) early in the development of the church, and the fourth Gospel was written years after his death. Therefore, the most likely candidate is his brother John.

Indeed, early church tradition is unanimous that John the apostle, the son of Zebedee, wrote the fourth Gospel. For example, toward the end of the second century Irenaeus wrote: "Afterwards, John, the disciple of the Lord, who also had leaned upon His breast, did himself publish a Gospel during his residence at Ephesus in Asia."

John's Biography

What, then, do we know about John the apostle? First, we know that he and his brother James, along with Peter and his brother Andrew, were the first four disciples called by Jesus (Mark 1:19). Furthermore, James and John seem inseparable. On only one occasion is John recorded as acting alone (Luke 9:49-50). Together the two brothers want to call down fire on a village (Luke 9:54). Together they earn the title from Jesus of "Sons of Thunder" (Mark 3:17). The two of them request to be seated on Jesus' right and left in the coming kingdom (Mark 10:37). They are both with Jesus on the Mount of Transfiguration (Mark 9:2), in Gethsemane (Mark 14:33), and when Jairus' daughter is raised from the dead (Mark 5:37). John is right at the heart of Jesus' life and ministry. He of all the disciples is qualified to give the world a glimpse of Jesus' deepest thoughts and profound concerns.

Date

As is so often the case with books of the Bible, it is not possible to give an exact date for the writing of John's gospel. Most scholars agree that it was the last of the four gospels to be written. It was probably composed in A.D. 80 or 90, though it may have been written shortly after the fall of Jerusalem in A.D. 70.

Characteristics

For those familiar with the synoptic Gospels (Matthew, Mark, Luke), what strikes one so forcibly about John's gospel is how *different* it is. Despite their different emphases, the Synoptics tell the same story (probably because Matthew and Luke both build upon Mark's account). They are telling one part of Jesus' story. John, however, tells another part of that story. This is not to say that John's account contradicts the Synoptics. Rather, John makes explicit what Matthew, Mark, and Luke only hint. He leaves out a lot of material covered in the Synoptics, but he adds information about aspects of Jesus' ministry not discussed elsewhere. And he records for us not just Jesus' pithy statements, so prominent in the Synoptics, but also his longer discourses.

The Omissions

In John's gospel, we find no information about Jesus' birth; His baptism is only alluded to; and His temptation is not even mentioned. In the fourth Gospel, Jesus casts out no demons, cures no lepers, almost never speaks in parables, and does not emphasize the idea of the kingdom of God. John does not mention the institution of the Lord's Supper or Jesus' agony in the Garden of Gethsemane.

The Conclusion

Instead, in John's gospel we are told about portions of Jesus' ministry not discussed in the Synoptics. We hear about Jesus' ministry before John the Baptist's imprisonment. We hear of Jesus' visits to Jerusalem before His final visit when He was crucified. Perhaps most importantly, in the fourth Gospel we are given details of Jesus' ministry in Judea (the Synoptic gospels focus on his Galilean ministry). John's gospel is particularly rich when it comes to the teachings of Jesus. Here we find His long discourses on great themes such as light, love, life, truth, and abiding. Here in the great *I Am* sections we listen to Jesus reveal who He is.

John also records for us some of the most beloved stories about Jesus. Only in the fourth Gospel can we read about the wedding feast at Cana of Galilee (2:1-11), the night visit of Nicodemus (3:1-15), the conversation with the woman at the well (4:4-42), the raising of Lazarus from the dead (11:1-44), and the washing of the disciples' feet (13:1-17). In John's gospel, we find the bulk of our Lord's teaching about the Holy Spirit and here the mysterious "I" in the Sermon on the Mount ("You have heard that it was said . . . but I tell you. . . .") becomes the majestic "I am" who is God's own Son.

Style

John writes in very simple Greek. He does not use a wide range of vocabulary. He often repeats words and phrases. Yet the end result is a compelling document whose very simplicity makes it impressive.

The fourth Gospel was written by a man with an adequate but not extensive education in Greek. In fact, some scholars suggest that this Greek sounds acquired, not native. Furthermore, the writing has a strong Jewish flavoring. This is exactly what one would expect of John, the son of Zebedee—a Jew who had lived for a long time in Galilee, an area whose population included more Gentiles than Jews.

Theme

Why did John write as he did about Jesus? What was his purpose in gathering together this account? Two of his own statements provide the answer to this question.

First, John asserts in his first epistle: "This we proclaim concerning the Word of life. The life appeared; we have seen it and testify to it. . . . We proclaim to you what we have seen and heard, so that you also may have fellowship with us" (1 John 1:1-3). Second, John states at the end of his gospel: "These are written that you may believe that Jesus is the Christ, the Son of God, and that by believing you may have life in his name" (John 20:31). John's gospel, therefore, like the other three gospels, is a witness document. He tells us Jesus' story so that we will understand who Jesus is, put our faith in him as the unique Son of God, and so experience life in Christ and fellowship with other believers.

Structure

It is not clear how John's gospel ought to be subdivided. It is an incredibly rich, complex, and fluid piece of writing in which various themes operate at different levels.

Still, most scholars agree that John's Gospel begins with a distinct prologue (1:1-18) and then divides into two major parts. The first part of the gospel concentrates on Jesus' *public ministry*. It is organized around his miracles, "signs" that reveal who he really is. This part covers most of the three years of Jesus' ministry.

In the second part, the focus shifts from the crowds to the disciples and Jesus' *private ministry* among them. The theme in this section is *glory*, that is revealed in Jesus' crucifixion and resurrection. The time period of this part is short: from the Thursday night of the Last Supper through Jesus' postresurrection appearances.

Additional themes run through the book. For example, the material is grouped around the major Jewish feasts. Also, the idea of the passion of Jesus is present throughout. The chart below illustrates the structural complexity of this gospel.

Overview Study Questions

1. The author of the fourth Gospel never names himself. Yet you can figure out who he is. Look up all the references given above in the section entitled "Author" and then summarize how we know John wrote this book.
2. Read the stories about John in Mark's gospel and write a short biography. See Mark 1:16-20; 3:13-19; 5:37; 9:2-13; 9:38-41; 10:35-45; 13:3-4; and 14:32-42.
3. Skim John's gospel. What picture of Jesus emerges from these pages?

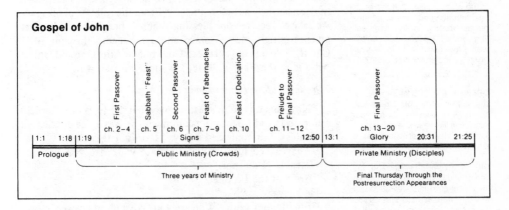

John

OPEN : 1. What is your full name? How did your parents come up with your name? **2.** What is your "nick name"? Where did you get that? **3.** What do you think is the best way to let someone get to know what you are like? **4.** Have you ever tried to express your love in "words"?

DIG: 1. What point in time begins this gospel story? Why then and there? **2.** What identifies "the Word" (vv. 1-5,10-18)? How is Jesus God's final word? **3.** How is Jesus like "light"? Who witnesses the light (vv. 6-8)? Who or what fails to comprehend the light (vv. 5,10,11)? Why? **4.** How does one become a child of God? Define each pregnant phrase in verses 12-13. **5.** What truths about Jesus would strike those who believe "God" would never mix with humanity? **6.** How are John the Babtist and Moses given "second billing"? **7.** How can one "know" God?

REFLECT: 1. In your own life, where have you allowed Jesus to make his "dwelling place" with you? Would you say that you have kept him at the door? Let him into the living room? Or given him the keys to the whole house? **2.** If this passage were the director's script for a movie, what music and stage setting would help you narrate this text? How could this movie symbolize your own spiritual roots?

OPEN: 1. If a CBS news reporter stopped you on the street and asked who you were and what your mission in life was, what would you say? **2.** Have you ever been mistaken for a famous person? Who was it?

DIG: 1. What questions do the priests and Levites ask John? What do these questions reveal about why they were sent? **2.** Why do you think John responds so abruptly? What would you have said in his situation? **3.** What is John's goal and mission in life (vv. 22-23, 26-27; see also Isaiah 40:3-5)? **4.** Since baptism only applied to Gentile converts to Judaism, what is behind the Pharisees' cynical question (vv. 24-25) and John's evasive answer (vv. 26-27)? **5.** In what sense would you call the Baptist the last of the Old Testament prophets?

REFLECT: 1. What is your goal and mission in life? How would you com-

The Word Became Flesh

1 In the beginning was the Word, and the Word was with God, and the Word was God. [2]He was with God in the beginning.

[3]Through him all things were made; without him nothing was made that has been made. [4]In him was life, and that life was the light of men. [5]The light shines in the darkness, but the darkness has not understood[a] it.

[6]There came a man who was sent from God; his name was John. [7]He came as a witness to testify concerning that light, so that through him all men might believe. [8]He himself was not the light; he came only as a witness to the light. [9]The true light that gives light to every man was coming into the world.[b]

[10]He was in the world, and though the world was made through him, the world did not recognize him. [11]He came to that which was his own, but his own did not receive him. [12]Yet to all who received him, to those who believed in his name, he gave the right to become children of God— [13]children born not of natural descent,[c] nor of human decision or a husband's will, but born of God.

[14]The Word became flesh and made his dwelling among us. We have seen his glory, the glory of the One and Only,[d] who came from the Father, full of grace and truth.

[15]John testifies concerning him. He cries out, saying, "This was he of whom I said, 'He who comes after me has surpassed me because he was before me.' " [16]From the fullness of his grace we have all received one blessing after another. [17]For the law was given through Moses; grace and truth came through Jesus Christ. [18]No one has ever seen God, but God the One and Only,[d] [e]who is at the Father's side, has made him known.

John the Baptist Denies Being the Christ

[19]Now this was John's testimony when the Jews of Jerusalem sent priests and Levites to ask him who he was. [20]He did not fail to confess, but confessed freely, "I am not the Christ.[f]"

[21]They asked him, "Then who are you? Are you Elijah?"
He said, "I am not."
"Are you the Prophet?"
He answered, "No."

[22]Finally they said, "Who are you? Give us an answer to take back to those who sent us. What do you say about yourself?"

[23]John replied in the words of Isaiah the prophet, "I am the voice of one calling in the desert, 'Make straight the way for the Lord.' "[g]

[24]Now some Pharisees who had been sent [25]questioned him,

---

a5 Or darkness, and the darkness has not overcome   b9 Or This was the true light that gives light to every man who comes into the world   c13 Greek of bloods   d14,18 Or the Only Begotten   e18 Some manuscripts but the only (or only begotten) Son   f20 Or Messiah. "The Christ" (Greek) and "the Messiah" (Hebrew) both mean "the Anointed One"; also in verse 25.   g23 Isaiah 40:3

LOOKING INTO THE SCRIPTURE/20 Minutes. Read John 1:1-18 and discuss.

1. If you really wanted to explain to someone how much you loved them, what would you do?
   - a. rent a billboard
   - b. send a video
   - c. flood the city with leaflets
   - d. send someone to explain
   - e. go myself

2. How would you describe the opening of this gospel?
   - a. looking down the barrel of time
   - b. the curtain rising on a great drama
   - c. the music from a space odyssey
   - d. walking into a movie that has already started
   - e. reading the last page of a great novel before you read the book

3. What do you think is the theme of this introduction?
   - a. the Creator of the world has come to redeem his creation
   - b. God who created the world has become flesh
   - c. the battle for the control of the world has started
   - d. life and salvation is for everyone

4. How would you describe John the Baptist's role?
   - a. pre-game show
   - b. press box announcer
   - c. first act
   - d. the clue to the mystery
   - e. a footnote in history

5. What is the invitation in verse 12?
   - a. to live a good life
   - b. to learn how to be successful
   - c. to get yourself together
   - d. to join the family of God

6. When does this life begin?
   - a. when you die and go to heaven
   - b. whenever you take God at his word
   - c. when you win the lottery
   - d. when you clean up your life

7. What impresses me most about God is that:
   - a. he has always existed
   - b. he is the light (nothing is hidden from him)
   - c. he sent his son to live with us as a human being (the Incarnation)
   - d. he gave us the right to become his children
   - e. he really wants us to know him
   - f. he is the Creator & Sustainer of life

MY OWN STORY/25 Minutes.

1. When did Jesus become the Word of God to you?
   - a. years ago
   - b. just recently
   - c. never has
   - d. not sure what you mean

2. If you had to compare your relationship with God right now to a ball game, where would you be?
   - a. sitting in the grandstands
   - b. on the team/benchwarming
   - c. playing defense
   - d. playing offense
   - e. on the injury list
   - f. halftime in the locker room
   - g. trying to figure out the game
   - h. giving it all I've got

3. What if Jesus told you that you were his personal representative in the world today. How would that make you feel?
   - a. you've got to be kidding
   - b. scared
   - c. OK, if I'm not the only one
   - d. OK, but I don't like the idea that those closest to me might not accept me
   - e. I'm not ready to be a servant
   - f. not sure what this means
   - g. eager to start

pare your goals to a cooked steak: Half cooked? Medium rare? Medium well? Well done? **3.** How could you get a little help in setting your goals from John the Baptist?

OPEN: How do you react in a job interview? What if you have a day to think over the questions?

DIG: 1. How does John the Baptist finally answer the question about why he baptized? **2.** What does John mean by "Lamb of God" (see Ex. 12:1-13; Is. 53:7)? **3.** What proof does John offer that Jesus is the Son of God?

REFLECT: 1. If you were asked to testify in court that Jesus is the Son of God, what would you say? **2.** How could John the Baptist help you?

OPEN: Who is the most famous person you have ever met? What were the circumstances?

DIG: 1. In light of verses 30-31, how do you think John felt when his disciples left him to follow Jesus? What does this say about John? **2.** From verse 38, what motivated the disciples of John to follow Jesus? After spending some time with Jesus, what motivated Andrew to tell his brother Simon about Jesus? **3.** What are the titles used in this passage to describe Jesus? **4.** How do you think Simon felt when Jesus changed his name to Cephas (meaning "rock")?

REFLECT: 1. What was your motive for originally following Jesus? **2.** Who was the Andrew in your life who first brought you to Jesus?

OPEN: 1. As a kid, were you more likely to be picked for a ball team or a spelling bee? **2.** If you were asked to pick the future leaders of the church, where would you look? What qualities would you seek?

DIG: 1. What did Philip have in common with Andrew? What insight about Jesus excites Philip? **2.** What type of person is Nathanael? Why do you think he could find it hard to believe Philip's statement? **3.** Why do you think Jesus called Philip and Nathanael in such different ways? How do you think Nathanael felt

"Why then do you baptize if you are not the Christ, nor Elijah, nor the Prophet?"

[26]"I baptize with[h] water," John replied, "but among you stands one you do not know. [27]He is the one who comes after me, the thongs of whose sandals I am not worthy to untie."

[28]This all happened at Bethany on the other side of the Jordan, where John was baptizing.

Jesus the Lamb of God

[29]The next day John saw Jesus coming toward him and said, "Look, the Lamb of God, who takes away the sin of the world! [30]This is the one I meant when I said, 'A man who comes after me has surpassed me because he was before me.' [31]I myself did not know him, but the reason I came baptizing with water was that he might be revealed to Israel."

[32]Then John gave this testimony: "I saw the Spirit come down from heaven as a dove and remain on him. [33]I would not have known him, except that the one who sent me to baptize with water told me, 'The man on whom you see the Spirit come down and remain is he who will baptize with the Holy Spirit.' [34]I have seen and I testify that this is the Son of God."

Jesus' First Disciples

[35]The next day John was there again with two of his disciples. [36]When he saw Jesus passing by, he said, "Look, the Lamb of God!"

[37]When the two disciples heard him say this, they followed Jesus. [38]Turning around, Jesus saw them following and asked, "What do you want?"

They said, "Rabbi" (which means Teacher), "where are you staying?"

[39]"Come," he replied, "and you will see."

So they went and saw where he was staying, and spent that day with him. It was about the tenth hour.

[40]Andrew, Simon Peter's brother, was one of the two who heard what John had said and who had followed Jesus. [41]The first thing Andrew did was to find his brother Simon and tell him, "We have found the Messiah" (that is, the Christ). [42]And he brought him to Jesus.

Jesus looked at him and said, "You are Simon son of John. You will be called Cephas" (which, when translated, is Peter[i]).

Jesus Calls Philip and Nathanael

[43]The next day Jesus decided to leave for Galilee. Finding Philip, he said to him, "Follow me."

[44]Philip, like Andrew and Peter, was from the town of Bethsaida. [45]Philip found Nathanael and told him, "We have found the one Moses wrote about in the Law, and about whom the prophets also wrote—Jesus of Nazareth, the son of Joseph."

[46]"Nazareth! Can anything good come from there?" Nathanael asked.

---

[h]26 Or in; also in verses 31 and 33 mean rock.   [i]42 Both Cephas (Aramaic) and Peter (Greek)

LOOKING INTO THE SCRIPTURE/20 Minutes. Read the Scripture passage aloud in your group, then answer the questions below.

1. What was John the Baptist saying about Jesus when he described him as the "Lamb of God"?
   a. he was to be the ruler of the restored kingdom of Judah
   b. he was the promised sacrifice for the sin of the world
   c. he was meek and gentle like a sheep

2. How do you react to the disciples following Jesus for the day?
   a. they were irresponsible
   b. Jesus must have been irresistable
   c. they didn't have anything better to do
   d. etiquette was not their strong point
   e. they had no idea what they were in for

3. What is Jesus inviting the two disciples of John the Baptist to do?
   a. switch their allegiance to him
   b. examine the evidence for themselves
   c. tag along for the fun of it
   d. give him a chance to prove himself

4. "We have found the Messiah." What was Andrew, Simon Peter's brother, really saying?
   a. Jesus will help them to overthrow the Roman Empire
   b. Jesus is a great teacher
   c. Jesus is the future king of Israel
   d. Jesus will take away their sin

5. "You are Simon son of John. You will be Cephas." Why did Jesus change his name from Simon (meaning "sinking sand") to Peter (meaning "the rock")?
   a. he wanted Simon to feel good about himself
   b. he saw a strength in Simon that justified changing his name
   c. he wanted to start the process of changing Simon's self image
   d. he saw ahead to what Simon would be some day

MY OWN STORY/25 Minutes.

1. What was your name when you first felt drawn to Jesus?
   a. Desperate David
   b. Guilty Gus
   c. Much Afraid
   d. Lonely Larry
   e. Confused Connie
   f. _____

2. What was it about Jesus that drew you to him?
   a. historical evidence
   b. being around my parents
   c. my own personal yearning
   d. the changed life of a friend
   e. peer pressure
   f. search for the truth
   g. desire to find meaning for my life

3. If you were given a "nickname" right now to describe your spiritual condition, what would it be?
   a. Slippery: on a greasy slide going downhill
   b. Rocky II: the comeback kid
   c. Barely: never triumphant/just somehow
   d. Refrigerator: taking it all in
   e. Grace: thankful for what God did
   f. Patience: God is doing his thing
   g. Spacey: out to lunch
   h. _____

4. What is the biggest obstacle to your spiritual growth right now?
   a. not knowing what God wants
   b. keeping a daily discipline
   c. feeling all alone
   d. fear of failing
   e. _____

when Jesus spoke to him? **4.** Of the five people in verses 35-48 to follow Jesus, (a) How was the contact made for each one? (b) How much did each one know about Jesus when he decided to follow Jesus?

REFLECT: 1. What were the circumstances surrounding your first encounter with Jesus? **2.** How much did you know about Jesus when you decided to follow him?

OPEN: 1. What is the funniest thing that happened at a wedding you attended? **2.** How are you at wedding receptions, especially if you do not know the bride or groom?

DIG: 1. What did the wedding invitation say: Who? What? Where? When? Why? **2.** Given the importance of social customs, what problem has arisen? **3.** What's going on here between Jesus and his mother (vv. 3-5)? Between Jesus and the servants (vv. 5, 7-9)? The MC and the bridegroom (vv. 9-10)? The water and the wine (note that "ceremonial washing jars" are spotlessly clean)? How do you feel about Jesus' extravagance (note today's price of 150 gallons of wine)? **4.** As a "sign" of deeper significance (v. 11), what is going on beneath this simple surface story: To what "time" is Jesus referring (v. 4; see also John 7: 6, 8, 12:23; 17:1)? Why do the disciples believe (v. 11)?

REFLECT: Where is the wine level (zest for life) in your life right now: Full? Half full? Empty? What is draining you? Where do you need to see a miracle?

OPEN: 1. How are you at keeping your room clean? **2.** What visiting guest would cause you to get busy and clean house: The "boss"? Your pastor? Your college roomate? A celebrity? Your in-laws? **2.** Do you have a "short fuse" or a "long fuse"?

DIG: 1. Why are sellers and money changers needed at the temple: Jews left home without American Express? Or what? Why has this once-useful practice deteriorated into racketeering? Why is Jesus so upset (see Ex. 12:21-28; Nu. 28:16-19)? **2.** As one of the sellers, how would you feel about Jesus' cleaning house? As one of the disciples, how would you later reflect upon

"Come and see," said Philip.

⁴⁷When Jesus saw Nathanael approaching, he said of him, "Here is a true Israelite, in whom there is nothing false."

⁴⁸"How do you know me?" Nathanael asked.

Jesus answered, "I saw you while you were still under the fig tree before Philip called you."

⁴⁹Then Nathanael declared, "Rabbi, you are the Son of God; you are the King of Israel."

⁵⁰Jesus said, "You believeʲ because I told you I saw you under the fig tree. You shall see greater things than that." ⁵¹He then added, "I tell youᵏ the truth, youᵏ shall see heaven open, and the angels of God ascending and descending on the Son of Man."

Jesus Changes Water to Wine

2 On the third day a wedding took place at Cana in Galilee. Jesus' mother was there, ²and Jesus and his disciples had also been invited to the wedding. ³When the wine was gone, Jesus' mother said to him, "They have no more wine."

⁴"Dear woman, why do you involve me?" Jesus replied, "My time has not yet come."

⁵His mother said to the servants, "Do whatever he tells you."

⁶Nearby stood six stone water jars, the kind used by the Jews for ceremonial washing, each holding from twenty to thirty gallons.ˡ

⁷Jesus said to the servants, "Fill the jars with water"; so they filled them to the brim.

⁸Then he told them, "Now draw some out and take it to the master of the banquet."

They did so, ⁹and the master of the banquet tasted the water that had been turned into wine. He did not realize where it had come from, though the servants who had drawn the water knew. Then he called the bridegroom aside ¹⁰and said, "Everyone brings out the choice wine first and then the cheaper wine after the guests have had too much to drink; but you have saved the best till now."

¹¹This, the first of his miraculous signs, Jesus performed at Cana of Galilee. He thus revealed his glory, and his disciples put their faith in him.

Jesus Clears the Temple

¹²After this he went down to Capernaum with his mother and brothers and his disciples. There they stayed for a few days.

¹³When it was almost time for the Jewish Passover, Jesus went up to Jerusalem. ¹⁴In the temple courts he found men selling cattle, sheep and doves, and others sitting at tables exchanging money. ¹⁵So he made a whip out of cords, and drove all from the temple area, both sheep and cattle; he scattered the coins of the money changers and overturned their tables. ¹⁶To those who sold doves he said, "Get these out of here! How dare you turn my Father's house into a market!"

ʲ50 Or *Do you believe . . . ?*   ᵏ51 The Greek is plural.   ˡ6 Greek *two to three metretes* (probably about 75 to 115 liters)

LOOKING INTO THE SCRIPTURE/20 Minutes. Read John 2:1-11 and discuss.

1. If you could choose any miracle to start you off in a new job or ministry, what would it be?
   a. healing the multitudes
   b. negotiating a peace treaty between superpowers
   c. paying off the national debt in one day at no one's expense
   d. raising a sunken ship and saving the passengers
   e. leading a national revival
   f. _____

2. Why do you think Jesus went to the wedding?
   a. to please his mother
   b. the whole village was invited
   c. it was the fun place to be
   d. to perform a miracle

3. When they ran out of wine, why did the mother of Jesus try to get Jesus involved?
   a. concern for the guests
   b. to get the bridegroom out of a jam
   c. she was catering the party
   d. she knew Jesus could do something

4. How do you think Jesus felt?
   a. upset
   b. annoyed
   c. embarrassed
   d. reluctant
   e. willing

5. Why did Jesus go about solving the problem as he did?
   a. to keep from embarrassing the groom
   b. to remain anonymous
   c. he didn't know if it would work
   d. to surprise everyone

6. How do you think the bridegroom felt when he heard about the new wine?
   a. perplexed
   b. intrigued
   c. delighted
   d. amazed

7. Why do you think Jesus performed his first miracle at a wedding feast?
   a. it just happened that way
   b. his mother asked him
   c. he saw a need and met it
   d. wine had special significance
   e. weddings had special significance

MY OWN STORY/25 Minutes.

1. Where do you need to see the water turned into wine in your life right now? Choose two or three.
   ☐ SELF-ESTEEM: feeling blah, worthless, useless, and out of it
   ☐ FAMILY: feeling hassled, haggard, strung out, and put through the wringer
   ☐ WORK/SCHOOL: feeling pushed, pressed, and overloaded
   ☐ APPEARANCE: feeling ugly, zits, braces, frizzy hair, and overweight
   ☐ SPIRITUAL LIFE: feeling lonely, dry, and out of sync with God and his family
   ☐ PHYSICAL LIFE: feeling worn out, used up, drained, and ready to retire
   ☐ MENTAL LIFE: feeling dumb, stupid, like my brain has taken a vacation

2. In the most difficult area above that you checked, how would you describe your situation in terms of the story of the Scripture?
   a. the wine has run out completely
   b. there's new wine available but I'm not drinking
   c. I've tried the new wine and nothing has changed
   d. I'm not sure the new wine is any better

3. What role do you see individual members of your group playing to make the miracle happen in your life?
   a. JESUS' MOTHER: Intercessor
   b. SERVANTS: Labor under Jesus' direction
   c. BANQUET MAITRE D': Witness of the change
   d. DISCIPLES: Walking the road with me
   e. JESUS: Resource manager

this episode? **3.** How is Jesus then challenged? Why? **4.** Why does Jesus not entrust himself to the crowds in verses 23-25? What is "in a man" that caused him to be so cautious?

REFLECT: If you compare your spiritual life to the rooms of a house, which room do you think could use some spring-cleaning: (a) Library - the reading room, (b) Dining room - appetites, desires, (c) Workshop - where you keep your gifts, skills and talents, (d) Recreation room - where you hang out after work, (e) Family room - where most of your relationships are lived out, or (f) Closet - where your hang-ups are?

OPEN: 1. Where were you told that babies came from by your parents or friends? **2.** What do you think about husbands assisting in the birthing process in the delivery room? **3.** What is your best story about husbands in the "waiting room" of the maternity ward?

DIG: 1. What can you find out about Nicodemus in verses 1-2? What is significant about his coming to Jesus? Why do you think he came at night? Why do think Jesus was so direct with him? **2.** What two ideas about birth are Jesus and Nicodemus thinking of? How does Jesus further explain what he means in verses 5-7? What point is Jesus making by comparing spiritual birth to the wind? How does Jesus account for Nicodemus' lack of understanding? **3.** What does Jesus claim about himself in verses 13-15? From Numbers 31:4-9, what was the role of the snake in the desert? How is Jesus serving in a similar role? How does he clarify what is needed to be born again? **4.** From verses 16-18, what stands out to you about God and what he wants to do? What response is required of us? How do you think verses 19-20 relate to the time Nicodemus came to Jesus (v. 2)? According to verse 21, how will belief show itself? **5.** How is Jesus' use of the words "born again" similar and different from the way it is used today? How would you define what it means to a person from outer space who had never heard the phrase?

REFLECT: 1. What caused you to first consider the claims of Jesus? **2.** How would you compare your own search for God to those of Nicodemus: More intellectual? More straight-forward? Different but

[17]His disciples remembered that it is written: "Zeal for your house will consume me." [m]

[18]Then the Jews demanded of him, "What miraculous sign can you show us to prove your authority to do all this?"

[19]Jesus answered them, "Destroy this temple, and I will raise it again in three days."

[20]The Jews replied, "It has taken forty-six years to build this temple, and you are going to raise it in three days?" [21]But the temple he had spoken of was his body. [22]After he was raised from the dead, his disciples recalled what he had said. Then they believed the Scripture and the words that Jesus had spoken.

[23]Now while he was in Jerusalem at the Passover Feast, many people saw the miraculous signs he was doing and believed in his name. [n] [24]But Jesus would not entrust himself to them, for he knew all men. [25]He did not need man's testimony about man, for he knew what was in a man.

Jesus Teaches Nicodemus

3 Now there was a man of the Pharisees named Nicodemus, a member of the Jewish ruling council. [2]He came to Jesus at night and said, "Rabbi, we know you are a teacher who has come from God. For no one could perform the miraculous signs you are doing if God were not with him."

[3]In reply Jesus declared, "I tell you the truth, no one can see the kingdom of God unless he is born again. [o]"

[4]"How can a man be born when he is old?" Nicodemus asked. "Surely he cannot enter a second time into his mother's womb to be born!"

[5]Jesus answered, "I tell you the truth, no one can enter the kingdom of God unless he is born of water and the Spirit. [6]Flesh gives birth to flesh, but the Spirit [p] gives birth to spirit. [7]You should not be surprised at my saying, 'You [q] must be born again.' [8]The wind blows wherever it pleases. You hear its sound, but you cannot tell where it comes from or where it is going. So it is with everyone born of the Spirit."

[9]"How can this be?" Nicodemus asked.

[10]"You are Israel's teacher," said Jesus, "and do you not understand these things? [11]I tell you the truth, we speak of what we know, and we testify to what we have seen, but still you people do not accept our testimony. [12]I have spoken to you of earthly things and you do not believe; how then will you believe if I speak of heavenly things? [13]No one has ever gone into heaven except the one who came from heaven—the Son of Man. [r] [14]Just as Moses lifted up the snake in the desert, so the Son of Man must be lifted up, [15]that everyone who believes in him may have eternal life. [s]

[16]"For God so loved the world that he gave his one and only Son, [t] that whoever believes in him shall not perish but have eternal life. [17]For God did not send his Son into the world to condemn the world, but to save the world through him. [18]Who-

---

[m]17 Psalm 69:9 [n]23 Or *and believed in him* [o]3 Or *born from above*; also in verse 7 [p]6 Or *but spirit* [q]7 The Greek is plural. [r]13 Some manuscripts *Man, who is in heaven* [s]15 Or *believes may have eternal life in him* [t]16 Or *his only begotten Son*

JESUS TEACHES NICODEMUS

LOOKING INTO THE SCRIPTURE/20 Minutes. Read John 3:1-21 and discuss.

1. Why did Nicodemus come to Jesus by night?
   a. he couldn't wait until morning
   b. he worked during the day
   c. he was afraid of being seen
   d. he wanted time alone with Jesus

2. Of the three levels of communication, how did the conversation start out?
   a. mouth to mouth—polite talk
   b. head to head—intellectual talk
   c. heart to heart—deep sharing

3. When Jesus explained, ". . . unless a man is born again . . ." what happened?
   a. Nicodemus got defensive
   b. Nicodemus got curious
   c. Nicodemus got interested
   d. Nicodemus got confused

4. In the conversation that followed, what is the issue?
   a. religion versus new life
   b. what Jesus' kingdom is all about
   c. why religious people don't understand
   d. how to get into the kingdom

5. "Just as Moses lifted up the snake in the desert, so the Son of Man must be lifted up. . . ." To what is Jesus referring here?
   a. Numbers 21:4-9 in the Old Testament
   b. the death of Jesus on the cross
   c. the resurrection of Jesus
   d. the second coming of Jesus

6. What is the condition for obtaining eternal life according to verses 16-18?
   a. feeling sorry for yourself
   b. feeling sorry for your sins
   c. living a clean life
   d. going to church every Sunday
   e. receiving God's free gift by faith

7. How do you think Nicodemus came away from this conversation with Jesus?
   a. totally confused
   b. enlightened
   c. a silent follower of Jesus
   d. intellectually convinced
   e. with "food" for thought

8. Do you think Jesus could have been more kind to the religion teacher?   ☐ Yes ☐ No

MY OWN STORY/25 Minutes.

1. The chart below shows thirteen stages of conversion in the spiritual journey of a person. Where are you now in your own spiritual journey?

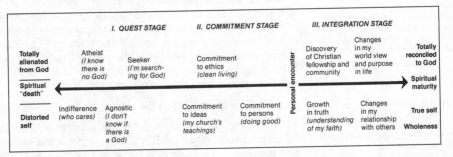

2. What is the Spirit's "wind" like in your life right now?
   a. still as a summer night
   b. a few little gusts
   c. howling
   d. full sail
   e. _____

3. Where is the "wind" of the Spirit carrying you?
   a. to a safe harbor
   b. out to the rough waters
   c. I'm not sure, but it is exciting
   d. nowhere that I know
   e. _____

just as real? Not sure? **3.** Where are you right now in your understanding of spiritual life: Still in the dark? Closer, but not completely sure? Getting it together? **3.** What would be your advice for someone who has a lot of questions?

OPEN: 1. How did your parents resolve arguments between your brother or sister? **2.** At family reunions, what subject (such as politics or religion) is bound to start an argument?

DIG: 1. Reading between the lines, what do you think had happened at the river? What do you think the "certain Jew" had said? How would you have felt if you had been one of John's disciples at this point? **2.** How does John the Baptist respond? What is the point of the allegory or story about the bride and bridegroom? What does John's response tell you about John? **3.** What facts about Jesus does John bring out in verses 31-36? **4.** How does the phrase "rejecting the Son" stand in contrast to what "belief" really means? What are the results of each response to him?

REFLECT: 1. How would the principle that John the Baptist explains work in the business world today? What would happen if you applied this in your situation? **2.** Do you think that a person can know for sure that he possesses eternal life? In a scientific world in which everything must be measured or proved, what proof can you put forward?

OPEN: 1. When you were growing up, who were the people you were told not to associate with? What part of the city or country would you be warned about? What would have happened if you had gone there? **2.** Where was the "watering hole" in your home town, where everybody went to "hang out"?

DIG: 1. What evidence in 1:19-28 and 3:22-26 could explain why Jesus decided to "get out of town" in a hurry? **2.** As one of the disciples growing up in a good Jewish home and being taught to despise the Samaritans because they were "half-breeds" (who intermarried with the wrong families), how would you feel when Jesus decided to go

ever believes in him is not condemned, but whoever does not believe stands condemned already because he has not believed in the name of God's one and only Son." [19]This is the verdict: Light has come into the world, but men loved darkness instead of light because their deeds were evil. [20]Everyone who does evil hates the light, and will not come into the light for fear that his deeds will be exposed. [21]But whoever lives by the truth comes into the light, so that it may be seen plainly that what he has done has been done through God." [v]

John the Baptist's Testimony About Jesus

[22]After this, Jesus and his disciples went out into the Judean countryside, where he spent some time with them, and baptized. [23]Now John also was baptizing at Aenon near Salim, because there was plenty of water, and people were constantly coming to be baptized. [24](This was before John was put in prison.) [25]An argument developed between some of John's disciples and a certain Jew[w] over the matter of ceremonial washing. [26]They came to John and said to him, "Rabbi, that man who was with you on the other side of the Jordan—the one you testified about—well, he is baptizing, and everyone is going to him."

[27]To this John replied, "A man can receive only what is given him from heaven. [28]You yourselves can testify that I said, 'I am not the Christ[x] but am sent ahead of him.' [29]The bride belongs to the bridegroom. The friend who attends the bridegroom waits and listens for him, and is full of joy when he hears the bridegroom's voice. That joy is mine, and it is now complete. [30]He must become greater; I must become less.

[31]"The one who comes from above is above all; the one who is from the earth belongs to the earth, and speaks as one from the earth. The one who comes from heaven is above all. [32]He testifies to what he has seen and heard, but no one accepts his testimony. [33]The man who has accepted it has certified that God is truthful. [34]For the one whom God has sent speaks the words of God, for God[y] gives the Spirit without limit. [35]The Father loves the Son and has placed everything in his hands. [36]Whoever believes in the Son has eternal life, but whoever rejects the Son will not see life, for God's wrath remains on him." [z]

Jesus Talks With a Samaritan Woman

4 The Pharisees heard that Jesus was gaining and baptizing more disciples than John, [2]although in fact it was not Jesus who baptized, but his disciples. [3]When the Lord learned of this, he left Judea and went back once more to Galilee.

[4]Now he had to go through Samaria. [5]So he came to a town in Samaria called Sychar, near the plot of ground Jacob had given to his son Joseph. [6]Jacob's well was there, and Jesus, tired as he was from the journey, sat down by the well. It was about the sixth hour.

---

[u]18 Or *God's only begotten Son*   [v]21 Some interpreters end the quotation after verse 15.
[w]25 Some manuscripts *and certain Jews*   [x]28 Or *Messiah*   [y]34 Greek *he*
[z]36 Some interpreters end the quotation after verse 30.

JESUS TALKS WITH A SAMARITAN WOMAN

LOOKING INTO THE SCRIPTURE/15 Minutes. Read John 4:1-26 and walk through the spiritual encounter with the Samaritan woman.

1. What was the Samaritan woman really saying in reply to Jesus' question, "will you give me a drink?"
   a. do you know who I am (an outcast)?
   b. why would you talk to me?
   c. you're giving me too much attention. What do you want?
   d. you're threatening me

2. What was the woman's response when Jesus said, "If you knew the gift of God and who it is that asks you for a drink, you would have asked him and he would have given you living water."
   a. stumbling for an answer at first
   b. arousing of a spiritual desire for something
   c. curious: "Is it possible this is the thing I've been looking for?"
   d. skeptical: "Who do you think you are?"

3. How does the woman respond when Jesus explains, ". . . the water I give will become a spring of water welling up to eternal life . . ."
   a. puzzled: "Are you kidding me?"
   b. desirous: "I'd love to have it."
   c. open: "I'm ready."

4. Why didn't the woman give up on this conversation when Jesus told her, "Go, call your husband and come back?"
   a. she was intrigued by his willingness to talk
   b. she realized she had nothing to hide
   c. what Jesus offered appealed to her
   d. he treated her with respect
   e. she knew he spoke the truth and that he could help her
   f. she didn't want to lose the chance to get her questions answered

5. When Jesus declared that "the time is coming . . . when true worshipers will worship the Father in spirit and truth . . ." what was her response?
   a. deep desire: "I want that myself"
   b. awareness: "I think I understand"
   c. commitment: "I'm sold"
   d. clarification: "What are you trying to say?"

6. What do you imagine was the look on her face when Jesus said, "I who speak to you am he."
   a. mouth open: surprise
   b. furrowed brow: puzzlement
   c. flashing eyes: anger
   d. laughter: delight

MY OWN STORY/25 Minutes. Share your own experience.

1. How do you respond when someone speaks to you unexpectedly?
   a. pretend I didn't hear
   b. try to be courteous
   c. look around at who's there
   d. move away quickly
   e. answer any questions

2. How would you compare your own spiritual beginnings with God to that of the woman at the well?
   a. more intellectual
   b. different, but just as real
   c. even more crazy
   d. I'll have to think about that

3. In your own experience, do you think the circumstances surrounding your own encounter were coincidental or part of the plan and purpose of God?
   a. purely coincidental
   b. more than coincidental
   c. still trying to figure this out

4. If Jesus were to stop by the "watering hole" where you hang out, what would he probably ask you right now? (be honest).
   a. what are you doing with your life?
   b. are you satisfied with what you're doing?
   c. are you looking for the real thing?
   d. other _____

5. How would you describe the way God is working in your life right now?
   a. master architect
   b. construction foreman
   c. coach on sidelines
   d. big boss in grandstands
   e. trainer
   f. cheerleader
   g. blocker/running interference
   h. Monday morning quarterback
   i. sculptor

through Samaria instead of the long way home? **3.** If you knew that "nice" girls did not come to the water well at noon time ("the sixth hour"), why do think Jesus risked his reputation to ask a favor of this woman? **4.** How would you describe the woman's response? **5.** How did Jesus turn the tables on her in verse 10? **6.** In the woman's reply, what is she really saying? How does she remind you of Nicodemus and his question? **7.** Why does Jesus so abruptly change the focus on the conversation to her personal life (v. 16)? What strikes you about the way he responds to her claim not to have a husband? If you met a stranger who suddenly let you know he knew all your private life, what would you do? **8.** Why do you think this woman changes the conversation to a more religious topic? In the context of this scene, what does Jesus mean by telling her that God is interested in worshippers who will do so in "spirit and truth"? **9.** What is significant about Jesus choosing this occasion to reveal for the first time who he is?

REFLECT: 1. How would you begin to talk about God with a pagan prostitute from a group of people you were raised to despise? What social, ethic, or religious barriers are difficult for you to break through? How would Jesus relate to these people you find difficult? **2.** What aspects of Jesus' conversation could you use as a model for your own discussions with searching friends?

OPEN: What causes you to skip a meal unknowingly? To eat too much unknowingly?

DIG: 1. Why were the disciples surprised to find Jesus with this woman? **2.** What does "leaving her water jar" reveal about Jesus' impact on the woman? How did she impact others? **3.** Given Jesus' tendency to be misunderstood (2:19; 3:3 - 4:10), why does he do it again (vv. 32-34)? What's the paradox of "food"? **4.** How does the parable of harvesting apply to the future? To evangelism?

[7]When a Samaritan woman came to draw water, Jesus said to her, "Will you give me a drink?" [8](His disciples had gone into the town to buy food.)

[9]The Samaritan woman said to him, "You are a Jew and I am a Samaritan woman. How can you ask me for a drink?" (For Jews do not associate with Samaritans. [a])

[10]Jesus answered her, "If you knew the gift of God and who it is that asks you for a drink, you would have asked him and he would have given you living water."

[11]"Sir," the woman said, "you have nothing to draw with and the well is deep. Where can you get this living water? [12]Are you greater than our father Jacob, who gave us the well and drank from it himself, as did also his sons and his flocks and herds?"

[13]Jesus answered, "Everyone who drinks this water will be thirsty again, [14]but whoever drinks the water I give him will never thirst. Indeed, the water I give him will become in him a spring of water welling up to eternal life."

[15]The woman said to him, "Sir, give me this water so that I won't get thirsty and have to keep coming here to draw water."

[16]He told her, "Go, call your husband and come back."

[17]"I have no husband," she replied.

Jesus said to her, "You are right when you say you have no husband. [18]The fact is, you have had five husbands, and the man you now have is not your husband. What you have just said is quite true."

[19]"Sir," the woman said, "I can see that you are a prophet. [20]Our fathers worshiped on this mountain, but you Jews claim that the place where we must worship is in Jerusalem."

[21]Jesus declared, "Believe me, woman, a time is coming when you will worship the Father neither on this mountain nor in Jerusalem. [22]You Samaritans worship what you do not know; we worship what we do know, for salvation is from the Jews. [23]Yet a time is coming and has now come when the true worshipers will worship the Father in spirit and truth, for they are the kind of worshipers the Father seeks. [24]God is spirit, and his worshipers must worship in spirit and in truth."

[25]The woman said, "I know that Messiah" (called Christ) "is coming. When he comes, he will explain everything to us."

[26]Then Jesus declared, "I who speak to you am he."

The Disciples Rejoin Jesus

[27]Just then his disciples returned and were surprised to find him talking with a woman. But no one asked, "What do you want?" or "Why are you talking with her?"

[28]Then, leaving her water jar, the woman went back to the town and said to the people, [29]"Come, see a man who told me everything I ever did. Could this be the Christ [b]?" [30]They came out of the town and made their way toward him.

[31]Meanwhile his disciples urged him, "Rabbi, eat something."

---

[a]9 Or *do not use dishes Samaritans have used*   [b]29 Or *Messiah*

³²But he said to them, "I have food to eat that you know nothing about."

³³Then his disciples said to each other, "Could someone have brought him food?"

³⁴"My food," said Jesus, "is to do the will of him who sent me and to finish his work. ³⁵Do you not say, 'Four months more and then the harvest'? I tell you, open your eyes and look at the fields! They are ripe for harvest. ³⁶Even now the reaper draws his wages, even now he harvests the crop for eternal life, so that the sower and the reaper may be glad together. ³⁷Thus the saying 'One sows and another reaps' is true. ³⁸I sent you to reap what you have not worked for. Others have done the hard work, and you have reaped the benefits of their labor."

Many Samaritans Believe

³⁹Many of the Samaritans from that town believed in him because of the woman's testimony, "He told me everything I ever did." ⁴⁰So when the Samaritans came to him, they urged him to stay with them, and he stayed two days. ⁴¹And because of his words many more became believers.

⁴²They said to the woman, "We no longer believe just because of what you said; now we have heard for ourselves, and we know that this man really is the Savior of the world."

Jesus Heals the Official's Son

⁴³After the two days he left for Galilee. ⁴⁴(Now Jesus himself had pointed out that a prophet has no honor in his own country.) ⁴⁵When he arrived in Galilee, the Galileans welcomed him. They had seen all that he had done in Jerusalem at the Passover Feast, for they also had been there.

⁴⁶Once more he visited Cana in Galilee, where he had turned the water into wine. And there was a certain royal official whose son lay sick at Capernaum. ⁴⁷When this man heard that Jesus had arrived in Galilee from Judea, he went to him and begged him to come and heal his son, who was close to death.

⁴⁸"Unless you people see miraculous signs and wonders," Jesus told him, "you will never believe."

⁴⁹The royal official said, "Sir, come down before my child dies."

⁵⁰Jesus replied, "You may go. Your son will live."

The man took Jesus at his word and departed. ⁵¹While he was still on the way, his servants met him with the news that his boy was living. ⁵²When he inquired as to the time when his son got better, they said to him, "The fever left him yesterday at the seventh hour."

⁵³Then the father realized that this was the exact time at which Jesus had said to him, "Your son will live." So he and all his household believed.

⁵⁴This was the second miraculous sign that Jesus performed, having come from Judea to Galilee.

REFLECT: 1. Thinking about your life this week, have you been more like the disciples with their concern for physical needs? Or more like the woman with enthusiasm for spiritual things? What distracts you from spiritual things? **2.** How does doing the will of God supply the same essentials in your life that food does? **3.** What is the "harvest" around you that is ready for picking?

OPEN: Who is the last person you would expect to "get saved"?

DIG: What led these folk to believe? What role did follow-up play?

REFLECT: 1. What does this whole episode (4:1-42) teach you? **2.** How is the gospel to break through to the outcasts where you live?

OPEN: 1. When you were a child, what was the most serious illness or injury you ever had? **2.** With your kids, what is the scariest illness or injury you can remember?

DIG: 1. Now that Jesus is back home again, what motivates the people to welcome him? **2.** How do you account for the contrast between the crowd's welcome (v. 45) and Jesus' comments in verses 44 and 48? How are the Galileans like and unlike the Samaritans in verses 39-42? Why? **3.** What motivates a royal official to travel so far? Considering his response to Jesus in verse 50, how is he an exception to "the people" Jesus speaks of in verse 48? How would you have responded to what Jesus told him to do? What was the result of his action? **4.** What does a "miraculous sign" point to about Jesus? How does it add to what was demonstrated by his first sign (vv. 2:1-11)?

REFLECT: 1. Where are you more likely to be ignored or discounted: In your own community? Or in a foreign land? Why? **2.** When you bring your problem to God, such as a sickness in the family, do you tend to accept his word or keep fretting and fussing? **3.** When have you taken God at his word (even though the circumstances were seemingly impossible) and discovered that God did exactly what he promised?

OPEN: 1. If you were sick in bed and a friend offered you two tickets to the Super Bowl, what would you do? **2.** What occasion causes you to get "sick" even though you are perfectly fit?

DIG: 1. Where does the action jump to in this fast-moving documentary on Jesus' ministry? What happened one time before in this place (see 2:12-25)? **2.** How would you re-create the setting of this story from verses 2-4 for a stage plan? What is the smell? The noises? The atmosphere? How would you feel if you were in the audience? **3.** Focusing in on one person, describe him (v. 5). **4.** As Jesus approaches, what does he say? What is Jesus really asking? **5.** What is the response (v. 7)? **6.** Why were the religious leaders so upset? **7.** Why did Jesus warn this person (v. 14)? Was this person really sick? How so?

REFLECT: 1. What is the connection between some forms of illness and spiritual or emotional problems? When have you found yourself getting physically sick over problems that you refuse to deal with? **2.** Who has a tendency to "rain on your parade" because you offended their religious scruples?

OPEN: 1. Where have you picked up some of the mannerisms of your parents, such as sitting habits, eating habits, talking habits, etc.? **2.** As you get older, do you find yourself becoming more like your parents or less like your parents?

DIG: 1. What was the result for Jesus of his healing the man in verses 1-15? **2.** How did the way he answered the Jewish leaders only heighten their opposition? Why would Jesus do this? **3.** From verses 19-23, in what way does Jesus say he is equal with the Father? What terms are used to show the kind of relationship between Jesus and the Father? How does this relate to John 1:1 and 1:18? **4.** What claims does Jesus make about himself in verse 24? What is the promise? When does someone start to possess this promise? **5.** Looking over verses 24-30 again, what happens to those who do hear and believe? To those who do not? **6.** How would you describe the business that God the Father and God the Son are in? What exactly is the offer God is making to humanity?

The Healing at the Pool

5 Some time later, Jesus went up to Jerusalem for a feast of the Jews. [2]Now there is in Jerusalem near the Sheep Gate a pool, which in Aramaic is called Bethesda[c] and which is surrounded by five covered colonnades. [3]Here a great number of disabled people used to lie—the blind, the lame, the paralyzed.[d] [5]One who was there had been an invalid for thirty-eight years. [6]When Jesus saw him lying there and learned that he had been in this condition for a long time, he asked him, "Do you want to get well?"

[7]"Sir," the invalid replied, "I have no one to help me into the pool when the water is stirred. While I am trying to get in, someone else goes down ahead of me."

[8]Then Jesus said to him, "Get up! Pick up your mat and walk." [9]At once the man was cured; he picked up his mat and walked.

The day on which this took place was a Sabbath, [10]and so the Jews said to the man who had been healed, "It is the Sabbath; the law forbids you to carry your mat."

[11]But he replied, "The man who made me well said to me, 'Pick up your mat and walk.' "

[12]So they asked him, "Who is this fellow who told you to pick it up and walk?"

[13]The man who was healed had no idea who it was, for Jesus had slipped away into the crowd that was there.

[14]Later Jesus found him at the temple and said to him, "See, you are well again. Stop sinning or something worse may happen to you." [15]The man went away and told the Jews that it was Jesus who had made him well.

Life Through the Son

[16]So, because Jesus was doing these things on the Sabbath, the Jews persecuted him. [17]Jesus said to them, "My Father is always at his work to this very day, and I, too, am working." [18]For this reason the Jews tried all the harder to kill him; not only was he breaking the Sabbath, but he was even calling God his own Father, making himself equal with God.

[19]Jesus gave them this answer: "I tell you the truth, the Son can do nothing by himself; he can do only what he sees his Father doing, because whatever the Father does the Son also does. [20]For the Father loves the Son and shows him all he does. Yes, to your amazement he will show him even greater things than these. [21]For just as the Father raises the dead and gives them life, even so the Son gives life to whom he is pleased to give it. [22]Moreover, the Father judges no one, but has entrusted all judgment to the Son, [23]that all may honor the Son just as they honor the Father. He who does not honor the Son does not honor the Father, who sent him.

---

c2 Some manuscripts Bethzatha; other manuscripts Bethsaida   *d3 Some less important manuscripts paralyzed—and they waited for the moving of the waters. 4From time to time an angel of the Lord would come down and stir up the waters. The first one into the pool after each such disturbance would be cured of whatever disease he had.*

THE HEALING AT THE POOL

LOOKING INTO THE SCRIPTURE/20 Minutes. Read John 5:1-15 and discuss.

1. Do you think the paralytic was really sick or playing sick?
   a. he was really sick
   b. he thought he was sick
   c. he was sick to avoid taking responsibility for his life
   d. he was sick, but it was in his mind

2. Who do you think brought this man to the pool each morning?
   a. family/friends
   b. wife/children
   c. community volunteers
   d. people who felt sorry for him

3. Why do you think this man wanted to go to the pool?
   a. to meet his buddies
   b. to be in the place of healing
   c. to be healed
   d. to get away from responsibility

4. When Jesus asked him the question, "Do you want to get well?", how would you paraphrase his answer?
   a. are you crazy? Would I be lying here for 38 years if I could walk?
   b. oh, poor me! I'm really so helpless
   c. others that I rely on have failed me
   d. I've been sick so long I don't think I can accept responsibility for my life

5. How would you paraphrase Jesus' reply?
   a. if you really want to get well, you can
   b. don't blame others for your problems
   c. I'm sick of your whining. Move it
   d. getting well may cost you your excuses. Are you willing to risk it?

6. Do you think Jesus was being harsh or cruel with this man?
   a. yes
   b. no

MY OWN STORY/25 Minutes.

1. Honestly, how many years have you been lying next to your healing place while manipulating others with your problems?
   a. now, wait a minute. I don't do that
   b. not sure what you mean
   c. I don't know how to get over my paralysis
   d. quite a few

2. What is your favorite excuse for avoiding responsibility for your life?
   a. I've got an inferiority complex
   b. my parents overprotected me
   c. I never got any breaks
   d. I've had a bad year
   e. the last time I tried, I failed
   f. I don't have any support at home
   g. my church isn't going anywhere
   h. nobody else will join me

3. If Jesus were to pass by your "pool" today, what would he say or do if he knew your deepest need at the moment?
   a. stop and be with me
   b. ask me "what's going on?"
   c. assure me that "it's okay"
   d. put his arms around me
   e. tell me to "get off my duff"
   f. get me started in his "Word"
   g. lift me into the healing pool
   h. remove the thing that is crippling me
   i. help me to deal with the thing that is crippling me
   j. get me out of the situation I'm in
   k. crack a few jokes
   l. throw away my crutches
   m. tell me "he's proud to have me on his team"
   n. pass on without saying a word

REFLECT: 1. If you had to explain to someone from outer space what verse 24 means in your own words, how would you put it? **2.** In your own spiritual journey, when did you come to understand this truth? How did it effect your self image? Your lifestyle? Your life goals?

OPEN: 1. Who was one of your heroes when you were a kid that is still someone you admire? Who was one of your heroes that has since turned out to be a disappointment? **2.** Have you ever encountered a fraud in business – who made a whole lot of claims about himself or herself that were out-right lies?

DIG: 1. Have someone read aloud verses 24-30, pretentiously making those self-assertions. How does this person make the rest of you feel? **2.** How does Jesus defend his claims? How do you think the religious leaders felt when Jesus refers to these witnesses (already discounted by these authorities)? **3.** How does Jesus throw back at the religious leaders their own Scriptures? What is the true purpose for Bible study? Since their problem was not lack of information, what was it?

REFLECT: 1. If Jesus claims to be God in the flesh, what are the two choices we are faced with? **2.** If Jesus is a fraud, how could he also be a good teacher, like many of the cults teach? If he is not a fraud, what does this demand of us?

OPEN: How do you react when plans for a quiet evening at home are suddenly interrupted by the surprise arrival of people demanding something from you?

DIG: 1. From verses 1-3, why did Jesus sail to the far side of the lake? Why did the crowd follow after? **2.** What do you think was the nature of the test that Jesus was using on Philip? How do you think the wed-

²⁴"I tell you the truth, whoever hears my word and believes him who sent me has eternal life and will not be condemned; he has crossed over from death to life. ²⁵I tell you the truth, a time is coming and has now come when the dead will hear the voice of the Son of God and those who hear will live. ²⁶For as the Father has life in himself, so he has granted the Son to have life in himself. ²⁷And he has given him authority to judge because he is the Son of Man.

²⁸"Do not be amazed at this, for a time is coming when all who are in their graves will hear his voice ²⁹and come out—those who have done good will rise to live, and those who have done evil will rise to be condemned. ³⁰By myself I can do nothing; I judge only as I hear, and my judgment is just, for I seek not to please myself but him who sent me.

Testimonies About Jesus

³¹"If I testify about myself, my testimony is not valid. ³²There is another who testifies in my favor, and I know that his testimony about me is valid.

³³"You have sent to John and he has testified to the truth. ³⁴Not that I accept human testimony; but I mention it that you may be saved. ³⁵John was a lamp that burned and gave light, and you chose for a time to enjoy his light.

³⁶"I have testimony weightier than that of John. For the very work that the Father has given me to finish, and which I am doing, testifies that the Father has sent me. ³⁷And the Father who sent me has himself testified concerning me. You have never heard his voice nor seen his form, ³⁸nor does his word dwell in you, for you do not believe the one he sent. ³⁹You diligently study* the Scriptures because you think that by them you possess eternal life. These are the Scriptures that testify about me, ⁴⁰yet you refuse to come to me to have life.

⁴¹"I do not accept praise from men, ⁴²but I know you. I know that you do not have the love of God in your hearts. ⁴³I have come in my Father's name, and you do not accept me; but if someone else comes in his own name, you will accept him. ⁴⁴How can you believe if you accept praise from one another, yet make no effort to obtain the praise that comes from the only God*?

⁴⁵"But do not think I will accuse you before the Father. Your accuser is Moses, on whom your hopes are set. ⁴⁶If you believed Moses, you would believe me, for he wrote about me. ⁴⁷But since you do not believe what he wrote, how are you going to believe what I say?"

Jesus Feeds the Five Thousand

6 Some time after this, Jesus crossed to the far shore of the Sea of Galilee (that is, the Sea of Tiberias), ²and a great crowd of people followed him because they saw the miraculous signs he had performed on the sick. ³Then Jesus went up on a mountainside and sat down with his disciples. ⁴The Jewish Passover Feast was near.

*39 Or *Study diligently* (the imperative)   *44 Some early manuscripts *the Only One*

5When Jesus looked up and saw a great crowd coming toward him, he said to Philip, "Where shall we buy bread for these people to eat?" 6He asked this only to test him, for he already had in mind what he was going to do.

7Philip answered him, "Eight months' wages* would not buy enough bread for each one to have a bite!"

8Another of his disciples, Andrew, Simon Peter's brother, spoke up, 9"Here is a boy with five small barley loaves and two small fish, but how far will they go among so many?"

10Jesus said, "Have the people sit down." There was plenty of grass in that place, and the men sat down, about five thousand of them. 11Jesus then took the loaves, gave thanks, and distributed to those who were seated as much as they wanted. He did the same with the fish.

12When they had all had enough to eat, he said to his disciples, "Gather the pieces that are left over. Let nothing be wasted." 13So they gathered them and filled twelve baskets with the pieces of the five barley loaves left over by those who had eaten.

14After the people saw the miraculous sign that Jesus did, they began to say, "Surely this is the Prophet who is to come into the world." 15Jesus, knowing that they intended to come and make him king by force, withdrew again to a mountain by himself.

Jesus Walks on the Water

16When evening came, his disciples went down to the lake, 17where they got into a boat and set off across the lake for Capernaum. By now it was dark, and Jesus had not yet joined them. 18A strong wind was blowing and the waters grew rough. 19When they had rowed three or three and a half miles,* they saw Jesus approaching the boat, walking on the water; and they were terrified. 20But he said to them, "It is I; don't be afraid." 21Then they were willing to take him into the boat, and immediately the boat reached the shore where they were heading.

22The next day the crowd that had stayed on the opposite shore of the lake realized that only one boat had been there, and that Jesus had not entered it with his disciples, but that they had gone away alone. 23Then some boats from Tiberias landed near the place where the people had eaten the bread after the Lord had given thanks. 24Once the crowd realized that neither Jesus nor his disciples were there, they got into the boats and went to Capernaum in search of Jesus.

Jesus the Bread of Life

25When they found him on the other side of the lake, they asked him, "Rabbi, when did you get here?"

26Jesus answered, "I tell you the truth, you are looking for me, not because you saw miraculous signs but because you ate the loaves and had your fill. 27Do not work for food that spoils, but for food that endures to eternal life, which the Son of Man will give you. On him God the Father has placed his seal of approval."

g7 Greek two hundred denarii   *h19 Greek rowed twenty-five or thirty|stadia (about 5 or 6 kilometers)*

ding at Cana (2:1-11) could be a factor in this test? What does Philip's response indicate about how he did on the previous test? How about Andrew's response? 3. What is the significance of the fact that there was more left over after the feeding than there was food to start with? What truths about Jesus does this miracle show? 4. How do you think the nearness of the Passover feast (when Jews from all over the empire would flock to Jerusalem) would fuel the desires of the people in verses 14-15? What does Jesus' response indicate about his idea of his kingship?

REFLECT: 1. When have you experienced a time when God seemed to stretch your limited resources (physically and emotionally) far beyond what you could have imagined? 2. In what ways are you like Philip and Andrew, failing to remember something about Jesus when you face a difficult situation?

OPEN: Growing up, what was one of your greatest fears: High places? Darkness? Picked last on a team? Water? How fearful are you now?

DIG: 1. On a dark and stormy night, weary from rowing, afraid of capsizing, how would you have reacted when you saw and then heard Jesus on the water? Any changes (in the story and in your heart) once Jesus is aboard? 2. What did the disciples fail to see in feeding 5,000 that might have helped them here? How do you think they felt about Jesus at days' end?

REFLECT: 1. How do you respond when storms whip up in your life? 2. Where are you going through a little choppy water right now? How are you handling this?

OPEN: 1. What memories do you have as a child of your mother baking bread? What was her favorite recipe? What was your favorite bread? 2. Who is the easiest person in your family for you to communicate with? With what person do you need to work on communication because you are often misunderstood?

DIG: 1. Why are the crowds still searching for Jesus (vv. 24-26)? 2. How does Jesus respond to the crowd's question? How are his interests different from theirs? 3. From verses 27-29, how does

Jesus say they are to work for the food that leads to eternal life? **4.** What does the crowd ask Jesus to do so that they can believe him? What does the sign they request show about their real interest? **5.** In verses 32-33, how does Jesus use their interest in food to illustrate what he wants them to understand? What does bread do physically for us that is like what he can do spiritually? **6.** What claims does Jesus make in verses 35-40? What is the will of the Father? How does this section show what he means by saying he is the "Bread of Life"? **7.** In verses 41-42, how do the crowds respond to his claims? How is the principle Jesus mentioned in 4:43 played out here? **8.** What do verses 44-45 teach about what God does and what people do in the process of coming to know Jesus? What promise is repeated three times for those who do come to Him? Why the emphasis on this? **9.** How is the "bread" he gives greater than that of Moses (vv. 32 and 49)? **10.** On what level are the people responding to his comments? **11.** In light of their misunderstanding, why does Jesus develop the illustration even more graphically in verses 53-58? In light of the passage as a whole, what does Jesus mean by "eating his flesh" and "drinking his blood" (compare v. 40 with v. 54)? How does the image of eating and drinking clarify what he means by believing in him? **12.** What is the central truth in this passage concerning Jesus?

REFLECT: 1. In our culture, what is the main reason for following Jesus? What was your orginal motive? **2.** How would you describe your daily spiritual diet: Junk food? Frozen food? Baby food? TV microwave food? Left-overs? Meat and potatoes? Pure bread and wine? **3.** Has your "familiarity" with Jesus (raised on Sunday School stories, going to parochial school, etc.) ever kept you from really seeing who he is? What can help remove the blinders?

---

²⁸Then they asked him, "What must we do to do the works God requires?"

²⁹Jesus answered, "The work of God is this: to believe in the one he has sent."

³⁰So they asked him, "What miraculous sign then will you give that we may see it and believe you? What will you do? ³¹Our forefathers ate the manna in the desert; as it is written: 'He gave them bread from heaven to eat.'ⁱ"

³²Jesus said to them, "I tell you the truth, it is not Moses who has given you the bread from heaven, but it is my Father who gives you the true bread from heaven. ³³For the bread of God is he who comes down from heaven and gives life to the world."

³⁴"Sir," they said, "from now on give us this bread."

³⁵Then Jesus declared, "I am the bread of life. He who comes to me will never go hungry, and he who believes in me will never be thirsty. ³⁶But as I told you, you have seen me and still you do not believe. ³⁷All that the Father gives me will come to me, and whoever comes to me I will never drive away. ³⁸For I have come down from heaven not to do my will but to do the will of him who sent me. ³⁹And this is the will of him who sent me, that I shall lose none of all that he has given me, but raise them up at the last day. ⁴⁰For my Father's will is that everyone who looks to the Son and believes in him shall have eternal life, and I will raise him up at the last day."

⁴¹At this the Jews began to grumble about him because he said, "I am the bread that came down from heaven." ⁴²They said, "Is this not Jesus, the son of Joseph, whose father and mother we know? How can he now say, 'I came down from heaven'?"

⁴³"Stop grumbling among yourselves," Jesus answered. ⁴⁴"No one can come to me unless the Father who sent me draws him, and I will raise him up at the last day. ⁴⁵It is written in the Prophets: 'They will all be taught by God.'ʲ Everyone who listens to the Father and learns from him comes to me. ⁴⁶No one has seen the Father except the one who is from God; only he has seen the Father. ⁴⁷I tell you the truth, he who believes has everlasting life. ⁴⁸I am the bread of life. ⁴⁹Your forefathers ate the manna in the desert, yet they died. ⁵⁰But here is the bread that comes down from heaven, which a man may eat and not die. ⁵¹I am the living bread that came down from heaven. If anyone eats of this bread, he will live forever. This bread is my flesh, which I will give for the life of the world."

⁵²Then the Jews began to argue sharply among themselves, "How can this man give us his flesh to eat?"

⁵³Jesus said to them, "I tell you the truth, unless you eat the flesh of the Son of Man and drink his blood, you have no life in you. ⁵⁴Whoever eats my flesh and drinks my blood has eternal life, and I will raise him up at the last day. ⁵⁵For my flesh is real food and my blood is real drink. ⁵⁶Whoever eats my flesh and drinks my blood remains in me, and I in him. ⁵⁷Just as the living Father sent me and I live because of the Father, so the one who

ⁱ31 Exodus 16:4; Neh. 9:15; Psalm 78:24,25   *ʲ45* Isaiah 54:13

feeds on me will live because of me. [58]This is the bread that came down from heaven. Your forefathers ate manna and died, but he who feeds on this bread will live forever." [59]He said this while teaching in the synagogue in Capernaum.

Many Disciples Desert Jesus

[60]On hearing it, many of his disciples said, "This is a hard teaching. Who can accept it?"

[61]Aware that his disciples were grumbling about this, Jesus said to them, "Does this offend you? [62]What if you see the Son of Man ascend to where he was before! [63]The Spirit gives life; the flesh counts for nothing. The words I have spoken to you are spirit[k] and they are life. [64]Yet there are some of you who do not believe." For Jesus had known from the beginning which of them did not believe and who would betray him. [65]He went on to say, "This is why I told you that no one can come to me unless the Father has enabled him."

[66]From this time many of his disciples turned back and no longer followed him.

[67]"You do not want to leave too, do you?" Jesus asked the Twelve.

[68]Simon Peter answered him, "Lord, to whom shall we go? You have the words of eternal life. [69]We believe and know that you are the Holy One of God."

[70]Then Jesus replied, "Have I not chosen you, the Twelve? Yet one of you is a devil!" [71](He meant Judas, the son of Simon Iscariot, who, though one of the Twelve, was later to betray him.)

Jesus Goes to the Feast of Tabernacles

7 After this, Jesus went around in Galilee, purposely staying away from Judea because the Jews there were waiting to take his life. [2]But when the Jewish Feast of Tabernacles was near, [3]Jesus' brothers said to him, "You ought to leave here and go to Judea, so that your disciples may see the miracles you do. [4]No one who wants to become a public figure acts in secret. Since you are doing these things, show yourself to the world." [5]For even his own brothers did not believe in him.

[6]Therefore Jesus told them, "The right time for me has not yet come; for you any time is right. [7]The world cannot hate you, but it hates me because I testify that what it does is evil. [8]You go to the Feast. I am not yet[l] going up to this Feast, because for me the right time has not yet come." [9]Having said this, he stayed in Galilee.

[10]However, after his brothers had left for the Feast, he went also, not publicly, but in secret. [11]Now at the Feast the Jews were watching for him and asking, "Where is that man?"

[12]Among the crowds there was widespread whispering about him. Some said, "He is a good man."

Others replied, "No, he deceives the people." [13]But no one would say anything publicly about him for fear of the Jews.

OPEN: 1. Have you ever received a "Dear John" letter? **2.** Have you ever found yourself at the top of the opinion polls one day, only to be deserted by the same folk the next?

DIG: 1. Looking back at 6:54-56, what is the hard teaching that many of Jesus' followers found so unacceptable? How has their attitude changed since verses 14-15? Since this is the last major event the author records about Jesus' ministry in Galilee, what does it mean: How does Jesus fare on the last opinion poll taken of the people? **2.** Do you think they turned away because they did, or did not, really understand what he meant? Why? **3.** Why do you think Peter and the others decided to stay? How does this relate to verse 65?

REFLECT: 1. What keeps you from junking your faith and going on to something else? **2.** How many people have made Jesus into an "errand boy" to meet their own personal agendas?

OPEN: 1. When you were a kid, were you ever dared by your brothers or sisters to do something that turned out to be dangerous? **2.** When your family gets together for a reunion, what is the chief topic of conversation?

DIG: 1. From 5:18, what were the reasons the religious leaders were out to kill Jesus? **2.** In light of 6:42 and 6:66, why do you think his brothers want Jesus to go to this feast where Jews from all over the empire would gather? Do you think they are being sincere or sarcastic? Why? **3.** What does Jesus say is the difference between him and his brothers? What does Jesus realize about public reaction to him? **4.** What are some of the rumors going around about Jesus in Jerusalem? Given these rumors, why do you think he chose to go secretly?

REFLECT: 1. Do you face any family opposition or ridicule to your faith? How do you deal with it? What do you find here from Jesus' experience? **2.** Are you more likely to be cautious, or daring, in sharing your faith with your family? Why?

[k]63 Or *Spirit*   [l]8 Some early manuscripts do not have *yet.*

OPEN: 1. When are you more impressed by an untrained lay person than an "expert" in the field? 2. Who often says: "My mind is made up. Don't confuse me with the facts"?

DIG: 1. Why all this opposition to Jesus (see also 5:18)? 2. Given the risk, why does Jesus go to the Passover anyway (see 7:1-11)? 3. How do the people react to Jesus' teaching (vv. 15, 20, 23-24)? Why? 4. What do Jesus' responses reveal about his own authority? About their authority? Their integrity? Their objections to his healing? Their judgments? 5. If you were one of the crowd with vested interests, how would you be responding now? 6. What main point are the Jewish leaders missing?

REFLECT: 1. When have you found yourself at odds with the religious establishment because you had to follow your own conscience? What happened? 2. How does this passage deal with the agnostic who says that he does not have enough evidence to make a decision about God?

OPEN: 1. When you go on a hike, how much water do you take along? What is the thirstiest you have been? How did you feel? What happened? 2. What would you choose as the most beautiful and refreshing stream you have ever visited?

DIG: 1. Who is saying what about Jesus in this passage? What is causing the confusion? 2. Why does Jesus' teaching in verses 23-29 provoke the response of verse 30? How is he once again misunderstood? 4. Given that every day at this feast water would be poured out as a symbol of thanks for God's provision, how is Jesus' statement in verse 37-38 especially powerful? Comparing verses 37-38 with 4:13-14, what are some ways that the Spirit's work relates to the work of Christ? 5. How does the confusion over Jesus' birthplace cloud the issue of his identity even more?

REFLECT: 1. Has the flow of the Spirit in your life lately felt more like a refreshing spring or a clogged faucet? 2. What have you found helpful in releasing the stream of the Spirit's water in your life? 3. What is the relationship for you between acting on your belief in Christ and your experiencing the refreshing power of the Holy Spirit?

Jesus Teaches at the Feast

[14]Not until halfway through the Feast did Jesus go up to the temple courts and begin to teach. [15]The Jews were amazed and asked, "How did this man get such learning without having studied?"

[16]Jesus answered, "My teaching is not my own. It comes from him who sent me. [17]If anyone chooses to do God's will, he will find out whether my teaching comes from God or whether I speak on my own. [18]He who speaks on his own does so to gain honor for himself, but he who works for the honor of the one who sent him is a man of truth; there is nothing false about him. [19]Has not Moses given you the law? Yet not one of you keeps the law. Why are you trying to kill me?"

[20]"You are demon-possessed," the crowd answered. "Who is trying to kill you?"

[21]Jesus said to them, "I did one miracle, and you are all astonished. [22]Yet, because Moses gave you circumcision (though actually it did not come from Moses, but from the patriarchs), you circumcise a child on the Sabbath. [23]Now if a child can be circumcised on the Sabbath so that the law of Moses may not be broken, why are you angry with me for healing the whole man on the Sabbath? [24]Stop judging by mere appearances, and make a right judgment."

Is Jesus the Christ?

[25]At that point some of the people of Jerusalem began to ask, "Isn't this the man they are trying to kill? [26]Here he is, speaking publicly, and they are not saying a word to him. Have the authorities really concluded that he is the Christ[m]? [27]But we know where this man is from; when the Christ comes, no one will know where he is from."

[28]Then Jesus, still teaching in the temple courts, cried out, "Yes, you know me, and you know where I am from. I am not here on my own, but he who sent me is true. You do not know him, [29]but I know him because I am from him and he sent me."

[30]At this they tried to seize him, but no one laid a hand on him, because his time had not yet come. [31]Still, many in the crowd put their faith in him. They said, "When the Christ comes, will he do more miraculous signs than this man?"

[32]The Pharisees heard the crowd whispering such things about him. Then the chief priests and the Pharisees sent temple guards to arrest him.

[33]Jesus said, "I am with you for only a short time, and then I go to the one who sent me. [34]You will look for me, but you will not find me; and where I am, you cannot come."

[35]The Jews said to one another, "Where does this man intend to go that we cannot find him? Will he go where our people live scattered among the Greeks, and teach the Greeks? [36]What did he mean when he said, 'You will look for me, but you will not find me,' and 'Where I am, you cannot come'?"

[37]On the last and greatest day of the Feast, Jesus stood and

[m]26 Or Messiah; also in verses 27, 31, 41 and 42

said in a loud voice, "If anyone is thirsty, let him come to me and drink. [38]Whoever believes in me, as " the Scripture has said, streams of living water will flow from within him." [39]By this he meant the Spirit, whom those who believed in him were later to receive. Up to that time the Spirit had not been given, since Jesus had not yet been glorified.

[40]On hearing his words, some of the people said, "Surely this man is the Prophet."

[41]Others said, "He is the Christ."

Still others asked, "How can the Christ come from Galilee? [42]Does not the Scripture say that the Christ will come from David's family° and from Bethlehem, the town where David lived?" [43]Thus the people were divided because of Jesus. [44]Some wanted to seize him, but no one laid a hand on him.

Unbelief of the Jewish Leaders

[45]Finally the temple guards went back to the chief priests and Pharisees, who asked them, "Why didn't you bring him in?"

[46]"No one ever spoke the way this man does," the guards declared.

[47]"You mean he has deceived you also?" the Pharisees retorted. [48]"Has any of the rulers or of the Pharisees believed in him? [49]No! But this mob that knows nothing of the law—there is a curse on them."

[50]Nicodemus, who had gone to Jesus earlier and who was one of their own number, asked, [51]"Does our law condemn anyone without first hearing him to find out what he is doing?"

[52]They replied, "Are you from Galilee, too? Look into it, and you will find that a prophet^P does not come out of Galilee."

———————

[The earliest and most reliable manuscripts and other ancient witnesses do not have John 7:53-8:11.]

[53]Then each went to his own home.

8 But Jesus went to the Mount of Olives. [2]At dawn he appeared again in the temple courts, where all the people gathered around him, and he sat down to teach them. [3]The teachers of the law and the Pharisees brought in a woman caught in adultery. They made her stand before the group [4]and said to Jesus, "Teacher, this woman was caught in the act of adultery. [5]In the Law Moses commanded us to stone such women. Now what do you say?" [6]They were using this question as a trap, in order to have a basis for accusing him.

But Jesus bent down and started to write on the ground with his finger. [7]When they kept on questioning him, he straightened up and said to them, "If any one of you is without sin, let him be the first to throw a stone at her." [8]Again he stooped down and wrote on the ground.

———————

OPEN: **1.** When has someone jumped to a wrong conclusion about you based on wrong info? **2.** How did your parents handle tattling? How do you handle it now with your kids?

DIG: **1.** Why do the guards keep hands off: Fear? Faith? Frustration? Deception? Wrong timing (see 7:30)? **2.** What tensions can you feel here? **3.** What justification do the Pharisees offer in refuting the guards? In refuting Nicodemus? Who is "right" in this debate? Why do you think Nicodemus risked defending Jesus?

REFLECT: **1.** When have you been ridiculed because of your faith? What did you do? **2.** In crisis, when slander is rampant and reputations are at stake, what do you do?

———————

OPEN: Have you ever been sent to the principal's office? Or jail? Or had your driver's licence revoked? In each case, what for? Were you guilty or innocent?

DIG: **1.** Do you think the woman was set up for this situation? Why or why not? **2.** How would this situation be a trap for Jesus? What would the Pharisees accuse Jesus of if he told them to let her go? If he told them to stone her? **3.** How does his response to them spring the trap? What do you think he wrote in the sand that would add to the effect of his statement? **4.** If you were the woman, what emotions would you have felt up to verse 8? What then would be the significance of Jesus asking her the question in verse 10? **5.** How does Jesus' response to the woman contrast with what the Pharisees said the law required? How does his word exemplify "grace and truth" (1:17)?

---

n37,38 Or / If anyone is thirsty, let him come to me. / And let him drink, 38who believes in me. / As   *o42 Greek seed*   *p52 Two early manuscripts the Prophet*

LOOKING INTO THE SCRIPTURE/20 Minutes. Read John 7:58-8:11 and discuss.

1. Which to you is the grossest sin?
   a. cheating on income tax
   b. having premarital/extramarital sex
   c. selling pornography
   d. cutting shady business deals
   e. child abuse

2. Who would you have trouble forgiving?
   a. a rapist
   b. a drug dealer
   c. a crooked politician
   d. an adulterer
   e. a Nazi war criminal

3. If you had been in the crowd when the woman caught in adultery was brought to Jesus, what would you have done?
   a. blushed
   b. stood up for the woman
   c. looked the other way
   d. picked up a stone
   e. prayed for the woman

4. Why do you think Jesus bent down and wrote on the ground?
   a. to let the men think
   b. to take the attention away from the woman
   c. to write something for the teachers to read—like their names

d. to collect his thoughts
e. to doodle something
f. to keep from getting so angry with the accusers

5. What was Jesus really saying by these words, "If any one of you is without sin, let him be the first to throw a stone at her"?
   a. deal with your own sin first
   b. judgmentalism is a worse sin
   c. everyone of you has committed adultery
   d. you see in others your own sin

6. In the last thing Jesus said to the woman, what was the tone in his voice and what did it mean?
   a. guilt trip: You've been bad, and I'm ashamed of you
   b. warning: I'll let you off this time but don't do it again
   c. affirmation: You're a beautiful person and you don't have to put yourself down
   d. support: You may fail again and again, but let's go for it
   e. understanding: You're free to live differently

MY OWN STORY/25 Minutes.

1. What's the hardest thing about forgiving?
   a. they might think I'm condoning their behavior
   b. when their sin is something I don't have trouble with
   c. fear they might consider me a patsy
   d. resisting the temptation to take revenge
   e. letting go of the hurt feelings

2. Why do you think more people confess their sins to the bartender than a pastor/priest?
   a. it's easier to talk when you're drunk
   b. bartenders are more understanding
   c. people are more at home in a bar
   d. bartenders never judge you
   e. everybody in a bar has failed

3. When it comes to forgiving yourself when you blow it, put a dot on the line to indicate where you are between these two extremes.

I ALWAYS PUT   I HAVE LEARNED TO ACCEPT
MYSELF DOWN _____ GOD'S FORGIVENESS

4. What do you do when you blow it?
   a. crawl into a hole
   b. try to be extra good
   c. confess it to God and move on
   d. confess it to my pastor or priest
   e. shrug it off

5. Who are the people in your life that accept you no matter what you've done?
   a. my parents
   b. my friends
   c. one special person
   d. my support group

⁹At this, those who heard began to go away one at a time, the older ones first, until only Jesus was left, with the woman still standing there. ¹⁰Jesus straightened up and asked her, "Woman, where are they? Has no one condemned you?"

¹¹"No one, sir," she said.

"Then neither do I condemn you," Jesus declared. "Go now and leave your life of sin."

The Validity of Jesus' Testimony

¹²When Jesus spoke again to the people, he said, "I am the light of the world. Whoever follows me will never walk in darkness, but will have the light of life."

¹³The Pharisees challenged him, "Here you are, appearing as your own witness; your testimony is not valid."

¹⁴Jesus answered, "Even if I testify on my own behalf, my testimony is valid, for I know where I came from and where I am going. But you have no idea where I come from or where I am going. ¹⁵You judge by human standards; I pass judgment on no one. ¹⁶But if I do judge, my decisions are right, because I am not alone. I stand with the Father, who sent me. ¹⁷In your own Law it is written that the testimony of two men is valid. ¹⁸I am one who testifies for myself; my other witness is the Father, who sent me."

¹⁹Then they asked him, "Where is your father?"

"You do not know me or my Father," Jesus replied. "If you knew me, you would know my Father also." ²⁰He spoke these words while teaching in the temple area near the place where the offerings were put. Yet no one seized him, because his time had not yet come.

²¹Once more Jesus said to them, "I am going away, and you will look for me, and you will die in your sin. Where I go, you cannot come."

²²This made the Jews ask, "Will he kill himself? Is that why he says, 'Where I go, you cannot come'?"

²³But he continued, "You are from below; I am from above. You are of this world; I am not of this world. ²⁴I told you that you would die in your sins; if you do not believe that I am ₍the one I claim to be₎,ᵠ you will indeed die in your sins."

²⁵"Who are you?" they asked.

"Just what I have been claiming all along," Jesus replied. ²⁶"I have much to say in judgment of you. But he who sent me is reliable, and what I have heard from him I tell the world."

²⁷They did not understand that he was telling them about his Father. ²⁸So Jesus said, "When you have lifted up the Son of Man, then you will know that I am ₍the one I claim to be₎ and that I do nothing on my own but speak just what the Father has taught me. ²⁹The one who sent me is with me; he has not left me alone, for I always do what pleases him." ³⁰Even as he spoke, many put their faith in him.

ᵠ24 Or *I am he*; also in verse 28

REFLECT: 1. How does the way Jesus treated this woman help you to deal with some of the sins you struggle with? **2.** How does Jesus' acceptance of you "as you are" free you to change, rather than simply reinforce your bad behavior? **3.** What can you learn from Jesus helps a friend who has fallen?

OPEN: 1. What is your most vivid memory as a child of going into a dark place? What feelings do you associate with darkness? **2.** Have you ever had to appear as a witness in court? Have you ever had to testify on your behalf?

DIG: 1. What is Jesus' claim in verse 12? What is the promise? What does Jesus mean by "light" and "darkness"? **2.** How do the Pharisees react to his claim? Given the discussion from 5:31-40 about witnesses, how does Jesus here bolster his claim? In light of 7:41-42, what does it matter that Jesus knows where he comes from? **3.** What does the Pharisees' misunderstanding in verse 19 reveal about their relationship with the Father? **4.** Compare verses 21-22 with 7:34-36: How are they misunderstanding Jesus now? **5.** From verses 23-24, what are the ways Jesus is different than these religious leaders? What is at stake in this difference? How is verse 25 the critical question for the Pharisees? In light of their question, what is the importance of his repeating the phrase "he who sent me" (vv. 16,18,26,29)? **6.** What does Jesus claim about his relationship with the Father in verses 27-29? What does he mean in verse 28? How will this show people he is the Christ? What is the significance of verse 30 in light of the total misunderstanding of the Pharisees in this passage? How do the Pharisees exemplify darkness in this scene?

REFLECT: 1. In your travels have you ever visited a country where the "light" of the gospel has never really penetrated? How did it feel? **2.** When the "lights" go out in some of the old Western countries where Jesus was once strong, what usually takes its place? **3.** How about the country where you live now? How would you describe the "lights" right now? **4.** What is God saying to you through all of this?

221

The Children of Abraham

³¹To the Jews who had believed him, Jesus said, "If you hold to my teaching, you are really my disciples. ³²Then you will know the truth, and the truth will set you free."

³³They answered him, "We are Abraham's descendants' and have never been slaves of anyone. How can you say that we shall be set free?"

³⁴Jesus replied, "I tell you the truth, everyone who sins is a slave to sin. ³⁵Now a slave has no permanent place in the family, but a son belongs to it forever. ³⁶So if the Son sets you free, you will be free indeed. ³⁷I know you are Abraham's descendants. Yet you are ready to kill me, because you have no room for my word. ³⁸I am telling you what I have seen in the Father's presence, and you do what you have heard from your father.'"

³⁹"Abraham is our father," they answered.

"If you were Abraham's children," said Jesus, "then you would' do the things Abraham did. ⁴⁰As it is, you are determined to kill me, a man who has told you the truth that I heard from God. Abraham did not do such things. ⁴¹You are doing the things your own father does."

"We are not illegitimate children," they protested. "The only Father we have is God himself."

The Children of the Devil

⁴²Jesus said to them, "If God were your Father, you would love me, for I came from God and now am here. I have not come on my own; but he sent me. ⁴³Why is my language not clear to you? Because you are unable to hear what I say. ⁴⁴You belong to your father, the devil, and you want to carry out your father's desire. He was a murderer from the beginning, not holding to the truth, for there is no truth in him. When he lies, he speaks his native language, for he is a liar and the father of lies. ⁴⁵Yet because I tell the truth, you do not believe me! ⁴⁶Can any of you prove me guilty of sin? If I am telling the truth, why don't you believe me? ⁴⁷He who belongs to God hears what God says. The reason you do not hear is that you do not belong to God."

The Claims of Jesus About Himself

⁴⁸The Jews answered him, "Aren't we right in saying that you are a Samaritan and demon-possessed?"

⁴⁹"I am not possessed by a demon," said Jesus, "but I honor my Father and you dishonor me. ⁵⁰I am not seeking glory for myself; but there is one who seeks it, and he is the judge. ⁵¹I tell you the truth, if anyone keeps my word, he will never see death."

⁵²At this the Jews exclaimed, "Now we know that you are demon-possessed! Abraham died and so did the prophets, yet you say that if anyone keeps your word, he will never taste

---

ʳ33 Greek seed; also in verse 37   ˢ38 Or|presence. Therefore do what you have heard from the Father.   ᵗ39 Some early|manuscripts "If you are Abraham's children," said Jesus, "then

death. ⁵³Are you greater than our father Abraham? He died, and so did the prophets. Who do you think you are?"

⁵⁴Jesus replied, "If I glorify myself, my glory means nothing. My Father, whom you claim as your God, is the one who glorifies me. ⁵⁵Though you do not know him, I know him. If I said I did not, I would be a liar like you, but I do know him and keep his word. ⁵⁶Your father Abraham rejoiced at the thought of seeing my day; he saw it and was glad."

⁵⁷"You are not yet fifty years old," the Jews said to him, "and you have seen Abraham!"

⁵⁸"I tell you the truth," Jesus answered, "before Abraham was born, I am!" ⁵⁹At this, they picked up stones to stone him, but Jesus hid himself, slipping away from the temple grounds.

Jesus Heals a Man Born Blind

9 As he went along, he saw a man blind from birth. ²His disciples asked him, "Rabbi, who sinned, this man or his parents, that he was born blind?"

³"Neither this man nor his parents sinned," said Jesus, "but this happened so that the work of God might be displayed in his life. ⁴As long as it is day, we must do the work of him who sent me. Night is coming, when no one can work. ⁵While I am in the world, I am the light of the world."

⁶Having said this, he spit on the ground, made some mud with the saliva, and put it on the man's eyes. ⁷"Go," he told him, "wash in the Pool of Siloam" (this word means Sent). So the man went and washed, and came home seeing.

⁸His neighbors and those who had formerly seen him begging asked, "Isn't this the same man who used to sit and beg?" ⁹Some claimed that he was.

Others said, "No, he only looks like him."

But he himself insisted, "I am the man."

¹⁰"How then were your eyes opened?" they demanded.

¹¹He replied, "The man they call Jesus made some mud and put it on my eyes. He told me to go to Siloam and wash. So I went and washed, and then I could see."

¹²"Where is this man?" they asked him.

"I don't know," he said.

The Pharisees Investigate the Healing

¹³They brought to the Pharisees the man who had been blind. ¹⁴Now the day on which Jesus had made the mud and opened the man's eyes was a Sabbath. ¹⁵Therefore the Pharisees also asked him how he had received his sight. "He put mud on my eyes," the man replied, "and I washed, and now I see."

¹⁶Some of the Pharisees said, "This man is not from God, for he does not keep the Sabbath."

But others asked, "How can a sinner do such miraculous signs?" So they were divided.

¹⁷Finally they turned again to the blind man, "What have you to say about him? It was your eyes he opened."

The man replied, "He is a prophet."

¹⁸The Jews still did not believe that he had been blind and had received his sight until they sent for the man's parents. ¹⁹"Is this

here? Looking at Exodus 3:14, why did Jesus' final claim cause such outrage?

REFLECT: 1. Either Jesus is all that he said he is, or Jesus is the biggest fraud that ever lived. Which is it for you? **2.** For a seeker who honestly wants to know the truth about Jesus, what would you suggest? How could you help this person from your own spiritual pilgrimage?

OPEN: 1. When you were young, what was the most fun thing you did with mud? **2.** If you were blind, what would you miss seeing the most?

DIG: 1. What idea lies behind the disciples question (v. 1): Curiosity? Guilt-tripping? A trap? Compassion? **2.** What does Jesus' answer (vv. 3-5) reveal: Jesus' empathy? God's work? Their calling? A cover-up? **3.** In this story, what is the "work of God" (v. 3)? The "night" that is coming (v. 4)? The "light of the world" (v. 5)? How are sin and suffering related (also 5:14)? Likewise, how are faith and action related? (Hint: What if the man had refused to go. . .?)

REFLECT: 1. As you look back over your life, what so-called handicap (like dyslexia, stuttering, learning disability, or physical problem) has turned into an opportunity for God to demonstrate his power? **2.** When you hear about another person's misfortune, how do you react: More like the disciples (he must have done something wrong)? Or like Jesus (here is chance to show God's mercy)?

OPEN: Who is your favorite detective in the movies or literature: Sherlock Holmes? Inspector Clouseau? Miss Marple? Lord Peter Wimmsey? The Hardy Boys? Nancy Drew? Or James Bond?

DIG: 1. What convinces some of the Pharisees to conclude against Jesus (v. 16; see also 5:9-10, 23)? What question bothers others? Why does Jesus keep healing on the Sabbath when it upsets the Pharisees so much? **2.** In light of their divided opinion, why do the Pharisees question the man's parents? How would you feel if you were his father or mother: Embarassed? Defensive? Proud? Afraid (v. 22)? **3.** Note the many conflicting claims to knowledge and certainty on the part of the Pharasees, the parents and the man born blind. What is each party sure of? Not sure of? **4.** In the course of this investigation, what is the once-blind man able to see and conclude about Jesus (vv. 12, 17, 25, 27, 30-33; also 36, 38)? How is the man's attitude changing as well: From defensive to offensive? Patience to impatience? Fear to faith? Ignorance to insight? **5.** In contrast to the man's growing spiritual insight, how are the Pharisees progressing: In frustration? Anger? Stubbornness? Openness to convert (v. 27)? Openness to converse? **6.** What is the Pharisee's real motive in questioning the man: To certify a genuine healing? To give glory to God? To trap Jesus? To defend their traditional form of faith?

REFLECT: 1. If you were severely questioned about your faith, what would you say? **2.** What have you found most helpful in dealing with people who ridicule your faith? **3.** Has your faith in Jesus led to your exclusion from any group? How has this hurt or helped you?

OPEN: If you could choose one day in your life for the "roller- coaster" award (most highs and lows in 24 hours), what day qualifies: Being fired and finding new work the same day? Or what?

DIG: 1. How would you feel if you had just been healed of blindness? If you were then thrown out of church for breaking the rules? If you later met the man who healed you? **2.** Why does Jesus wait until now to fully present himself? How is the man, only now, able to affirm Jesus as Lord? **3.** In this chapter, how have the Pharisees become blind? How has the man gained real sight? What blindness is the result of sin (vv. 1:39-41)? How do such guilty people "see" again?

REFLECT: How would you score your own spiritual sight right now: 20-20? 20/800? Color blind? A few "blind spots"? Why? What could correct this?

your son?" they asked. "Is this the one you say was born blind? How is it that now he can see?"

²⁰"We know he is our son," the parents answered, "and we know he was born blind. ²¹But how he can see now, or who opened his eyes, we don't know. Ask him. He is of age; he will speak for himself." ²²His parents said this because they were afraid of the Jews, for already the Jews had decided that anyone who acknowledged that Jesus was the Christ ᵘ would be put out of the synagogue. ²³That was why his parents said, "He is of age; ask him."

²⁴A second time they summoned the man who had been blind. "Give glory to God,ᵛ" they said. "We know this man is a sinner."

²⁵He replied, "Whether he is a sinner or not, I don't know. One thing I do know. I was blind but now I see!"

²⁶Then they asked him, "What did he do to you? How did he open your eyes?"

²⁷He answered, "I have told you already and you did not listen. Why do you want to hear it again? Do you want to become his disciples, too?"

²⁸Then they hurled insults at him and said, "You are this fellow's disciple! We are disciples of Moses! ²⁹We know that God spoke to Moses, but as for this fellow, we don't even know where he comes from."

³⁰The man answered, "Now that is remarkable! You don't know where he comes from, yet he opened my eyes. ³¹We know that God does not listen to sinners. He listens to the godly man who does his will. ³²Nobody has ever heard of opening the eyes of a man born blind. ³³If this man were not from God, he could do nothing."

³⁴To this they replied, "You were steeped in sin at birth; how dare you lecture us!" And they threw him out.

Spiritual Blindness

³⁵Jesus heard that they had thrown him out, and when he found him, he said, "Do you believe in the Son of Man?"

³⁶"Who is he, sir?" the man asked. "Tell me so that I may believe in him."

³⁷Jesus said, "You have now seen him; in fact, he is the one speaking with you."

³⁸Then the man said, "Lord, I believe," and he worshiped him.

³⁹Jesus said, "For judgment I have come into this world, so that the blind will see and those who see will become blind."

⁴⁰Some Pharisees who were with him heard him say this and asked, "What? Are we blind too?"

⁴¹Jesus said, "If you were blind, you would not be guilty of sin; but now that you claim you can see, your guilt remains.

ᵘ22 Or *Messiah*   ᵛ24 A solemn charge to tell the truth (see Joshua 7:19)

The Shepherd and His Flock

10 "I tell you the truth, the man who does not enter the sheep pen by the gate, but climbs in by some other way, is a thief and a robber. ²The man who enters by the gate is the shepherd of his sheep. ³The watchman opens the gate for him, and the sheep listen to his voice. He calls his own sheep by name and leads them out. ⁴When he has brought out all his own, he goes on ahead of them, and his sheep follow him because they know his voice. ⁵But they will never follow a stranger; in fact, they will run away from him because they do not recognize a stranger's voice." ⁶Jesus used this figure of speech, but they did not understand what he was telling them.

⁷Therefore Jesus said again, "I tell you the truth, I am the gate for the sheep. ⁸All who ever came before me were thieves and robbers, but the sheep did not listen to them. ⁹I am the gate; whoever enters through me will be saved. ʷHe will come in and go out, and find pasture. ¹⁰The thief comes only to steal and kill and destroy; I have come that they may have life, and have it to the full.

¹¹"I am the good shepherd. The good shepherd lays down his life for the sheep. ¹²The hired hand is not the shepherd who owns the sheep. So when he sees the wolf coming, he abandons the sheep and runs away. Then the wolf attacks the flock and scatters it. ¹³The man runs away because he is a hired hand and cares nothing for the sheep.

¹⁴"I am the good shepherd; I know my sheep and my sheep know me— ¹⁵just as the Father knows me and I know the Father—and I lay down my life for the sheep. ¹⁶I have other sheep that are not of this sheep pen. I must bring them also. They too will listen to my voice, and there shall be one flock and one shepherd. ¹⁷The reason my Father loves me is that I lay down my life—only to take it up again. ¹⁸No one takes it from me, but I lay it down of my own accord. I have authority to lay it down and authority to take it up again. This command I received from my Father."

¹⁹At these words the Jews were again divided. ²⁰Many of them said, "He is demon-possessed and raving mad. Why listen to him?"

²¹But others said, "These are not the sayings of a man possessed by a demon. Can a demon open the eyes of the blind?"

The Unbelief of the Jews

²²Then came the Feast of Dedication ˣ at Jerusalem. It was winter, ²³and Jesus was in the temple area walking in Solomon's Colonnade. ²⁴The Jews gathered around him, saying, "How long will you keep us in suspense? If you are the Christ,ʸ tell us plainly."

²⁵Jesus answered, "I did tell you, but you do not believe. The miracles I do in my Father's name speak for me, ²⁶but you do not believe because you are not my sheep. ²⁷My sheep listen to my voice; I know them, and they follow me. ²⁸I give them

ʷ9 Or *kept safe*   ˣ22 That is, Hanukkah   ʸ24 Or *Messiah*

OPEN: Growing up, what was your favorite pet? How did this pet respond when it heard your voice? Did your pet respond to one family member more than others?

DIG: 1. In this parable, what do the sheep, shepherd, and stranger represent? How does the story in chapter 9 provide one example of what this parable is about? **2.** What is the relationship of the shepherd to his sheep? How do the sheep respond to the true shepherd? How does this relate to the difficulty of the Pharisees in understanding Jesus? **3.** What does Jesus mean by likening himself to a gate for the sheepfold? How is he not like the "thieves and robbers" (vv. 8-10)? In this context, who are these "thieves and robbers"? **4.** How does Jesus identify himself unmistakably with the "good shepherd" (vv. 11-15)? How does Jesus' giving of his life relate to his promise of giving abundant life to others (v. 10)? **5.** Who are the "other sheep" (v. 16) he must bring also? What characterizes his flock (vv. 14-16)? **6.** What provocative claim does Jesus make (vv. 17-18)? Why are his listeners so provoked and divided (vv. 19-21)? Had you been there, how would you have responded?

REFLECT: 1. Looking back, what turning point was significant for you spiritually in terms of hearing "God's voice" and responding? **2.** With so many conflicting "voices" (cults, materialism, mood-altering drugs) vying for your attention, how do you discern true from false? **3.** Being counted among Jesus' other sheep (v. 16), how does that make you feel?

OPEN: 1. What is the important "feast day" in the year for your family? Who generally comes? What is served? What is the big "pastime"? **2.** What family traditions are you going to preserve for your kids?

DIG: 1. Given the meaning of this Hanukkah feast (when Jews celebrate their deliverance from the Persian threat in Queen Esther's day), Why are the people pressuring Jesus to declare His "candidacy" plainly and publicly? **2.** Judging from Jesus' reply (vv. 25-30), is he open with them? Evasive? Provocative? Why? How have the people been responding to Jesus' miracles so far (see 7:23; 9:24; 10:19-21)? Why do some listen, while others do not: God's election? Human stubbornness? Blindness? More miracles required for this "show me" state? **3.** Judging from their murderous intentions, how did the Jews interpret Jesus' claim to be one with God (vv. 30-33)? How would you react to a friend making such an egocentric claim? **4.** How does Jesus' answer (v. 34, quoting Psalm 8:26) sidetrack his opposition? Is Jesus here using Scripture as a shield to hide behind, or as a sword to cut two ways? How do Jesus' words and deeds together prove his main point (v. 30)? How do you account for the way Jesus was received across the Jordan?

REFLECT: 1. What things have convinced you that Jesus is the Messiah? Did you have to overcome any preconceived ideas that kept you from faith? **2.** What difference does it make to you that Jesus really is God and not just a man? Would the promise of verse 28 mean much otherwise?

OPEN: 1. What is the saddest funeral you ever witnessed–where a friend, family member or national figure was taken suddenly and unexpectedly? How did you feel at the time? **2.** When have you had to be the bearer of such sad news? Did you speak euphemistically, or get right to the point?

DIG: 1. How would you describe Jesus' relationship with this family (vv. 1-5)? **2.** Why does Jesus deliberately delay (v. 6): To rest up for the long journey? More important priorities? Lazarus was not sick enough? The people had not grieved enough? Jesus did not care enough? Jesus was waiting for a more dramatic moment? **3.** Given his disciples' objection (v. 8), what do you think Jesus means by his parable (vv. 9-10)? **4.** Why is Jesus returning to Lazarus at this time (vv. 11-15)? What do the disciples fear instead (vv. 8, 16)?

REFLECT: 1. Have you ever felt like God was not listening when you prayed? How did you deal with this? **2.** How does the way in which Jesus postponed his response to the sisters' request help you in understanding your own prayer life? **3.** Have you, like Thomas, ever felt Jesus was calling you to do some-

eternal life, and they shall never perish; no one can snatch them out of my hand. ²⁹My Father, who has given them to me, is greater than all*z*; no one can snatch them out of my Father's hand. ³⁰I and the Father are one."

³¹Again the Jews picked up stones to stone him, ³²but Jesus said to them, "I have shown you many great miracles from the Father. For which of these do you stone me?"

³³"We are not stoning you for any of these," replied the Jews, "but for blasphemy, because you, a mere man, claim to be God."

³⁴Jesus answered them, "Is it not written in your Law, 'I have said you are gods'*a*? ³⁵If he called them 'gods,' to whom the word of God came—and the Scripture cannot be broken— ³⁶what about the one whom the Father set apart as his very own and sent into the world? Why then do you accuse me of blasphemy because I said, 'I am God's Son'? ³⁷Do not believe me unless I do what my Father does. ³⁸But if I do it, even though you do not believe me, believe the miracles, that you may know and understand that the Father is in me, and I in the Father." ³⁹Again they tried to seize him, but he escaped their grasp.

⁴⁰Then Jesus went back across the Jordan to the place where John had been baptizing in the early days. Here he stayed ⁴¹and many people came to him. They said, "Though John never performed a miraculous sign, all that John said about this man was true." ⁴²And in that place many believed in Jesus.

The Death of Lazarus

11 Now a man named Lazarus was sick. He was from Bethany, the village of Mary and her sister Martha. ²This Mary, whose brother Lazarus now lay sick, was the same one who poured perfume on the Lord and wiped his feet with her hair. ³So the sisters sent word to Jesus, "Lord, the one you love is sick."

⁴When he heard this, Jesus said, "This sickness will not end in death. No, it is for God's glory so that God's Son may be glorified through it." ⁵Jesus loved Martha and her sister and Lazarus. ⁶Yet when he heard that Lazarus was sick, he stayed where he was two more days.

⁷Then he said to his disciples, "Let us go back to Judea."

⁸"But Rabbi," they said, "a short while ago the Jews tried to stone you, and yet you are going back there?"

⁹Jesus answered, "Are there not twelve hours of daylight? A man who walks by day will not stumble, for he sees by this world's light. ¹⁰It is when he walks by night that he stumbles, for he has no light."

¹¹After he had said this, he went on to tell them, "Our friend Lazarus has fallen asleep; but I am going there to wake him up."

¹²His disciples replied, "Lord, if he sleeps, he will get better." ¹³Jesus had been speaking of his death, but his disciples thought he meant natural sleep.

z29 Many early manuscripts *What my Father has given me is greater than all*
a34 Psalm 82:6

LOOKING INTO THE SCRIPTURE/20 Minutes. Read John 11:1-44 and discuss.

1. If your best friend did not come when you needed him/her, how would you feel?
   a. very angry
   b. deserted
   c. hurt
   d. assume there was good reason
   e. terrible, but I would never show it

2. Why do you think Jesus delayed two days before setting out to see Lazarus?
   a. he knew he couldn't make it before Lazarus' death
   b. he was warned that people were out to kill him
   c. he needed time to prepare himself
   d. God had a greater purpose in mind

3. Why do you think Jesus told his disciples that Lazarus was sleeping at first when he knew Lazarus was dead?
   a. he didn't want to deal with their shock
   b. he wanted to deal with their shock at a later time
   c. he needed time to work through his own feelings first
   d. he didn't want them to think the situation was hopeless

4. Jesus did not cry when he got word of Lazarus' death, but he did cry when he went with Mary to the tomb. Why?
   a. he knew he could raise Lazarus, but he felt for the mourners
   b. the reality didn't sink in until he saw the tomb personally
   c. he was glad Lazarus was dead so he could show his power, but death is horrible even so
   d. he cried because Mary was crying

5. Of the five stages of grief, where were (1) Thomas, (2) Martha on his arrival, (3) Mary at the tomb, (4) some of the Jews (v. 37)?
   a. denial/isolation: He is not really dead
   b. anger: He's dead and you let him die
   c. bargaining: If you'll do this, I'll do that
   d. depression: I don't want to talk about it
   e. acceptance: He's dead and there's nothing we can do about it

6. If you had been there and saw Jesus crying, how would you have felt?
   a. embarrassed for him: Grown men don't cry
   b. relieved: It's okay to cry
   c. awkward: Let's get on with it
   d. mad: You could have done something if you had gotten here earlier and now all you can do is blubber
   e. comforted: He really cared

7. Why did Jesus ask the friends to "Take away the stone" (v. 38) and "Take off the grave clothes and let him go"?
   a. he needed their help
   b. he didn't like the smell
   c. he wanted to convince them that Lazarus had really been dead
   d. he wanted them to be part of the healing process
   e. he always works in cooperation with human instruments

MY OWN STORY/25 Minutes. Share how this story touches on some of your own experience.

1. How do you handle grief—particularly unexpected death?
   a. pretend nothing has happened
   b. keep everything inside
   c. get angry at God
   d. isolate myself from everybody
   e. call my friends and talk, talk, talk
   f. try to put on a brave front
   g. keep busy
   h. let it all out

2. What have you found helpful when you are called upon to help a friend who is undergoing grief?
   a. share some Scripture
   b. just be present and say nothing
   c. wait three days and call
   d. bring food/flowers/book
   e. take this person away for a day in the mountains
   f. do a lot of hugging/touching
   g. listen to their reminiscences
   h. encourage them to say what they're really feeling

thing very risky (like returning to "Jerusalem" where you had nearly been stoned)? What happened?

OPEN: 1. As a child, how did you feel at Christmas having to wait around for your parents to get up before you could open the presents? 2. What funeral was the hardest for you to go through? Which funeral was more like a glorious celebration?

DIG: 1. How long had Lazarus been dead by the time Jesus arrived? How would you feel if you were Martha or Mary when you heard that Jesus finally had come? What would you say to him knowing he had received your message in plenty of time? 2. What do you learn about Martha from the way she talks with Jesus in verses 21-27? How does Jesus stretch her faith by his claim in verse 25? How does this relate to his claim in 10:9? How does her response in verse 27 show that she really did understand what he said in verses 25-26? 3. How is Mary's greeting similar and different from Martha's? In light of the fact that Jesus knew he was going to raise Lazarus (11:11), what do you think would account for his strong emotional response in verse 33-35? What does this scene teach you about him? 4. What feelings or questions lie behind the comments of the mourners in verses 36-37?

REFLECT: 1. When have you been faced with a tough decision recently that ended up stretching your faith? What would have been different for you if that struggle had simply been avoided? 2. Have you ever attended a funeral where there was no sense of hope or the promise of eternal life in verses 25-26? How did you go away from that experience?

OPEN: What is the worst odor you can remember: Dead fish? Rotten eggs? Amonia? Tear gas?

DIG: 1. Why does Martha object to removing the stone? Where did her confidence go (vv. 22-24, 40)? Where would yours be? 2. Why does Jesus pray (see v.22)? 3. Putting yourself into the drama of verses 41-44, how would you be feeling as Lazarus? As Jesus? Martha? Mary? The mourners?

[14]So then he told them plainly, "Lazarus is dead, [15]and for your sake I am glad I was not there, so that you may believe. But let us go to him."

[16]Then Thomas (called Didymus) said to the rest of the disciples, "Let us also go, that we may die with him."

Jesus Comforts the Sisters

[17]On his arrival, Jesus found that Lazarus had already been in the tomb for four days. [18]Bethany was less than two miles[b] from Jerusalem, [19]and many Jews had come to Martha and Mary to comfort them in the loss of their brother. [20]When Martha heard that Jesus was coming, she went out to meet him, but Mary stayed at home.

[21]"Lord," Martha said to Jesus, "if you had been here, my brother would not have died. [22]But I know that even now God will give you whatever you ask."

[23]Jesus said to her, "Your brother will rise again."

[24]Martha answered, "I know he will rise again in the resurrection at the last day."

[25]Jesus said to her, "I am the resurrection and the life. He who believes in me will live, even though he dies; [26]and whoever lives and believes in me will never die. Do you believe this?"

[27]"Yes, Lord," she told him, "I believe that you are the Christ,[c] the Son of God, who was to come into the world."

[28]And after she had said this, she went back and called her sister Mary aside. "The Teacher is here," she said, "and is asking for you." [29]When Mary heard this, she got up quickly and went to him. [30]Now Jesus had not yet entered the village, but was still at the place where Martha had met him. [31]When the Jews who had been with Mary in the house, comforting her, noticed how quickly she got up and went out, they followed her, supposing she was going to the tomb to mourn there.

[32]When Mary reached the place where Jesus was and saw him, she fell at his feet and said, "Lord, if you had been here, my brother would not have died."

[33]When Jesus saw her weeping, and the Jews who had come along with her also weeping, he was deeply moved in spirit and troubled. [34]"Where have you laid him?" he asked.

"Come and see, Lord," they replied.

[35]Jesus wept.

[36]Then the Jews said, "See how he loved him!"

[37]But some of them said, "Could not he who opened the eyes of the blind man have kept this man from dying?"

Jesus Raises Lazarus From the Dead

[38]Jesus, once more deeply moved, came to the tomb. It was a cave with a stone laid across the entrance. [39]"Take away the stone," he said.

"But, Lord," said Martha, the sister of the dead man, "by this time there is a bad odor, for he has been there four days."

[40]Then Jesus said, "Did I not tell you that if you believed, you would see the glory of God?"

[b]18 Greek fifteen stadia (about 3 kilometers)   [c]27 Or Messiah

⁴¹So they took away the stone. Then Jesus looked up and said, "Father, I thank you that you have heard me. ⁴²I knew that you always hear me, but I said this for the benefit of the people standing here, that they may believe that you sent me."

⁴³When he had said this, Jesus called in a loud voice, "Lazarus, come out!" ⁴⁴The dead man came out, his hands and feet wrapped with strips of linen, and a cloth around his face.

Jesus said to them, "Take off the grave clothes and let him go."

The Plot to Kill Jesus

⁴⁵Therefore many of the Jews who had come to visit Mary, and had seen what Jesus did, put their faith in him. ⁴⁶But some of them went to the Pharisees and told them what Jesus had done. ⁴⁷Then the chief priests and the Pharisees called a meeting of the Sanhedrin.

"What are we accomplishing?" they asked. "Here is this man performing many miraculous signs. ⁴⁸If we let him go on like this, everyone will believe in him, and then the Romans will come and take away both our place ᵈ and our nation."

⁴⁹Then one of them, named Caiaphas, who was high priest that year, spoke up, "You know nothing at all! ⁵⁰You do not realize that it is better for you that one man die for the people than that the whole nation perish."

⁵¹He did not say this on his own, but as high priest that year he prophesied that Jesus would die for the Jewish nation, ⁵²and not only for that nation but also for the scattered children of God, to bring them together and make them one. ⁵³So from that day on they plotted to take his life.

⁵⁴Therefore Jesus no longer moved about publicly among the Jews. Instead he withdrew to a region near the desert, to a village called Ephraim, where he stayed with his disciples.

⁵⁵When it was almost time for the Jewish Passover, many went up from the country to Jerusalem for their ceremonial cleansing before the Passover. ⁵⁶They kept looking for Jesus, and as they stood in the temple area they asked one another, "What do you think? Isn't he coming to the Feast at all?" ⁵⁷But the chief priests and Pharisees had given orders that if anyone found out where Jesus was, he should report it so that they might arrest him.

Jesus Anointed at Bethany

12 Six days before the Passover, Jesus arrived at Bethany, where Lazarus lived, whom Jesus had raised from the dead. ²Here a dinner was given in Jesus' honor. Martha served, while Lazarus was among those reclining at the table with him. ³Then Mary took about a pint ᵉ of pure nard, an expensive perfume; she poured it on Jesus' feet and wiped his feet with her hair. And the house was filled with the fragrance of the perfume.

⁴But one of his disciples, Judas Iscariot, who was later to betray him, objected, ⁵"Why wasn't this perfume sold and the

ᵈ48 Or *temple*   ᵉ3 Greek *a litra* (probably about 0.5 liter)

REFLECT: 1. Comparing your spiritual life to Lazarus' experience, where are you right now: Still in the grave? Alive, but still in grave clothes? Alive and completely unwrapped? **2.** Who helped to unwrap the grave clothes in your life? Why not thank them?

OPEN: 1. Have you ever been in the council chambers where the governing body of your city meet? Have you ever seen this body in session? **2.** Have you ever been caught in a situation where you were expected to keep the peace, even at the sacrifice of your own principles?

DIG: 1. What response does the miracle with Lazarus produce? Why do you think some of the people went to the Pharisees with the news? What does it show about their view of Jesus? **2.** What are the chief concerns of the leaders? What do they fail to see in this story? How does Caiaphas propose to solve "the Jesus problem"? How does Caiaphas' murderous threat unwittingly convey prophetic truth regarding the effect of Jesus death? **3.** How does Jesus respond to this new situation? What do you think the crowds would be expecting as Passover approached?

REFLECT: 1. How does it make you feel when political considerations are given priority over truth and justice? What would you have done if you had been on the Sanhedrin? **2.** Are you more likely to over-react, or under-react, when you see truth and justice ignored?

OPEN: If you had a year's wages to blow on friends, which would you choose: (a) a big party for all, (b) a glorious trip for a few, or (c) an extravagant gift for one?

DIG: 1. Given the occasion for this dinner party, how does Mary's action seem: Thoughtful, but misguided? Tasteful, but extravagant? Wasteful, no buts about it? Honoring to the nth degree? Why? **2.** What are Judas' public and private objections? Do you think the perfume could have been spent for better purposes? Why? **3.** How does Jesus interpret Mary's action and apply it to Judas? **4.** Given that "you will always have the poor among you," what does that mean for today's poverty relief programs?

REFLECT: 1. If you had a year's salary to use for Christ, how would you use it? How is that reflected in your budget now? **2.** If you could take a year off and use your time as a gift to God, what would you do? How is that reflected in your prioriities now? **3.** If you could combine your group's resources in one common cause for Christ, what would you do?

OPEN: 1. What famous person have you seen in a parade? **2.** If you could review any parade in the world, what would you choose?

DIG: 1. How would you set this opening scene for TV? What "flashbacks" (e.g., Lazarus' resurrection) would you use as the TV producer to show the crowd now so whipped up, but once so confused and divided (as in 7:40-43; 10:19-21)? **2.** How could you tie in their hope that Jesus will do at this Passover what God did at the first Passover? **3.** Why a lowly donkey for Jesus (see Zech. 9:9)? **4.** According to your script, what would the crowds, the disciples and Jewish leaders be feeling about now? One week later? Had you been there, what would you be feeling: fanaticism, fickleness, faith or fear? Why?

REFLECT: 1. What is the lesson here for you? How do you feel about religious surveys and opinion polls? **2.** Is your worship life like a hero's victory or a funeral dirge? Why?

OPEN: 1. In your family, who can predict the weather? How does stormy weather affect you emotionally **2.** Are you more likely to panic in the *big* crises or the *little* ones?

DIG: 1. What would motivate these Gentiles in verse 20 to come to Jerusalem during a special time of Jewish patriotism? **2.** What was so unique about their request that Philip would filter it through Andrew instead of just going right to Jesus? **3.** Jesus has said several times that "his time had not yet come" (2:4; 7:6, 30). What about this request caused him to say that now his time has come? **4.** In his parable in (v. 24), who is the kernel of wheat? How is this request related to the request of these Gentiles? **5.** What then is he calling his disciples to do

money given to the poor? It was worth a year's wages. *ⁱ* " ⁶He did not say this because he cared about the poor but because he was a thief; as keeper of the money bag, he used to help himself to what was put into it.

⁷"Leave her alone," Jesus replied. "It was intended that she should save this perfume for the day of my burial. ⁸You will always have the poor among you, but you will not always have me."

⁹Meanwhile a large crowd of Jews found out that Jesus was there and came, not only because of him but also to see Lazarus, whom he had raised from the dead. ¹⁰So the chief priests made plans to kill Lazarus as well, ¹¹for on account of him many of the Jews were going over to Jesus and putting their faith in him.

The Triumphal Entry

¹²The next day the great crowd that had come for the Feast heard that Jesus was on his way to Jerusalem. ¹³They took palm branches and went out to meet him, shouting,

"Hosanna!*ᵍ*"

"Blessed is he who comes in the name of the Lord!" *ʰ*

"Blessed is the King of Israel!"

¹⁴Jesus found a young donkey and sat upon it, as it is written,

¹⁵"Do not be afraid, O Daughter of Zion;
see, your king is coming,
seated on a donkey's colt." *ⁱ*

¹⁶At first his disciples did not understand all this. Only after Jesus was glorified did they realize that these things had been written about him and that they had done these things to him.

¹⁷Now the crowd that was with him when he called Lazarus from the tomb and raised him from the dead continued to spread the word. ¹⁸Many people, because they had heard that he had given this miraculous sign, went out to meet him. ¹⁹So the Pharisees said to one another, "See, this is getting us nowhere. Look how the whole world has gone after him!"

Jesus Predicts His Death

²⁰Now there were some Greeks among those who went up to worship at the Feast. ²¹They came to Philip, who was from Bethsaida in Galilee, with a request. "Sir," they said, "we would like to see Jesus." ²²Philip went to tell Andrew; Andrew and Philip in turn told Jesus.

²³Jesus replied, "The hour has come for the Son of Man to be glorified. ²⁴I tell you the truth, unless a kernel of wheat falls to the ground and dies, it remains only a single seed. But if it dies, it produces many seeds. ²⁵The man who loves his life will lose it, while the man who hates his life in this world will keep

ⁱ5 Greek *three hundred denarii*   *ᵍ13* A Hebrew expression meaning "Save!" which became an exclamation of praise   *ʰ13* Psalm 118:25, 26   *ⁱ15* Zech. 9:9

it for eternal life. ²⁶Whoever serves me must follow me; and where I am, my servant also will be. My Father will honor the one who serves me.

²⁷"Now my heart is troubled, and what shall I say? 'Father, save me from this hour'? No, it was for this very reason I came to this hour. ²⁸Father, glorify your name!"

Then a voice came from heaven, "I have glorified it, and will glorify it again." ²⁹The crowd that was there and heard it said it had thundered; others said an angel had spoken to him. ³⁰Jesus said, "This voice was for your benefit, not mine. ³¹Now is the time for judgment on this world; now the prince of this world will be driven out. ³²But I, when I am lifted up from the earth, will draw all men to myself." ³³He said this to show the kind of death he was going to die.

³⁴The crowd spoke up, "We have heard from the Law that the Christʲ will remain forever, so how can you say, 'The Son of Man must be lifted up'? Who is this 'Son of Man'?"

³⁵Then Jesus told them, "You are going to have the light just a little while longer. Walk while you have the light, before darkness overtakes you. The man who walks in the dark does not know where he is going. ³⁶Put your trust in the light while you have it, so that you may become sons of light." When he had finished speaking, Jesus left and hid himself from them.

The Jews Continue in Their Unbelief

³⁷Even after Jesus had done all these miraculous signs in their presence, they still would not believe in him. ³⁸This was to fulfill the word of Isaiah the prophet:

> "Lord, who has believed our message
> and to whom has the arm of the Lord been
> revealed?"ᵏ

³⁹For this reason they could not believe, because, as Isaiah says elsewhere:

> ⁴⁰"He has blinded their eyes
> and deadened their hearts,
> so they can neither see with their eyes,
> nor understand with their hearts,
> nor turn—and I would heal them."ˡ

⁴¹Isaiah said this because he saw Jesus' glory and spoke about him.

⁴²Yet at the same time many even among the leaders believed in him. But because of the Pharisees they would not confess their faith for fear they would be put out of the synagogue; ⁴³for they loved praise from men more than praise from God.

⁴⁴Then Jesus cried out, "When a man believes in me, he does not believe in me only, but in the one who sent me. ⁴⁵When he looks at me, he sees the one who sent me. ⁴⁶I have come into the world as a light, so that no one who believes in me should stay in darkness.

in verse 25-26? What promise do they receive? **6.** In verses 27-32, "new" is repeated three times. What things are about to occur? How do these realities affect Jesus? How does he deal with the anxiety? **7.** What causes the crowd's confidence in 11:13 to begin to waver in verses 32-34? What do you think might be happening to the celebration at this point? **8.** How is Jesus' death (v. 32) related to his being glorified (v. 23)?

REFLECT: **1.** If you knew that you only had a few more days to live, what would you do differently? **2.** From verses 24-26, where is Jesus calling you to "die" so that you may really "live"? What do you tend to hold on to rather than follow Jesus? **3.** How does Jesus' example in verse 27 give you the courage to deal with some of your ambiguous feelings?

OPEN: **1.** When a salesman comes to your door, do you feel more gullible, or more skeptical, than most people? Cite examples. **2.** Who are your heroes because they say what they mean and mean what they say?

DIG: **1.** What are some of the miraculous signs that Jesus has done that the author has described in this gospel? How do the prophecies from Isaiah 5:31 and Isaiah 6:10 account for the people's disbelief in spite of these signs? Do you think the prophecy from Isaiah 6:10 is a statement of irony, or of God's intent? Why? **2.** What is the author implying about Jesus in verse 41? How does it fit with 8:58? **3.** What inhibited the leaders from speaking up in spite of their belief in Jesus? How does this illustrate 11:25-26? If you were in their shoes, what would you be saying to yourself as you faced this dilemma? **4.** What is Jesus claiming in verses 44-45? How do verses 44-46 relate to 1:1-5? How is Jesus like a light? **5.** What does Jesus emphasize in verse 47-50? Why is this especially appropriate since this is his last public statement? How is it that Jesus' words can either judge a person, or lead him/her to life?

REFLECT: **1.** Where do you find it most difficult to live your faith: At home or work? **2.** When are you most timid or afraid to share your faith? **3.** What have you found most

---

ʲ34 Or *Messiah*   ᵏ38 Isaiah 53:1   ˡ40 Isaiah 6:10

---

⁴⁷"As for the person who hears my words but does not keep them, I do not judge him. For I did not come to judge the world, but to save it. ⁴⁸There is a judge for the one who rejects me and does not accept my words; that very word which I spoke will condemn him at the last day. ⁴⁹For I did not speak of my own accord, but the Father who sent me commanded me what to say and how to say it. ⁵⁰I know that his command leads to eternal life. So whatever I say is just what the Father has told me to say."

Jesus Washes His Disciples' Feet

13 It was just before the Passover Feast. Jesus knew that the time had come for him to leave this world and go to the Father. Having loved his own who were in the world, he now showed them the full extent of his love.ᵐ

²The evening meal was being served, and the devil had already prompted Judas Iscariot, son of Simon, to betray Jesus. ³Jesus knew that the Father had put all things under his power, and that he had come from God and was returning to God; ⁴so he got up from the meal, took off his outer clothing, and wrapped a towel around his waist. ⁵After that, he poured water into a basin and began to wash his disciples' feet, drying them with the towel that was wrapped around him.

⁶He came to Simon Peter, who said to him, "Lord, are you going to wash my feet?"

⁷Jesus replied, "You do not realize now what I am doing, but later you will understand."

⁸"No," said Peter, "you shall never wash my feet."

Jesus answered, "Unless I wash you, you have no part with me."

⁹"Then, Lord," Simon Peter replied, "not just my feet but my hands and my head as well!"

¹⁰Jesus answered, "A person who has had a bath needs only to wash his feet; his whole body is clean. And you are clean, though not every one of you." ¹¹For he knew who was going to betray him, and that was why he said not every one was clean.

¹²When he had finished washing their feet, he put on his clothes and returned to his place. "Do you understand what I have done for you?" he asked them. ¹³"You call me 'Teacher' and 'Lord,' and rightly so, for that is what I am. ¹⁴Now that I, your Lord and Teacher, have washed your feet, you also should wash one another's feet. ¹⁵I have set you an example that you should do as I have done for you. ¹⁶I tell you the truth, no servant is greater than his master, nor is a messenger greater than the one who sent him. ¹⁷Now that you know these things, you will be blessed if you do them.

ᵐ*1 Or* he loved them|to the last

John 13:1-17   **JESUS WASHES HIS DISCIPLES' FEET**

LOOKING INTO THE SCRIPTURE/20 Minutes. Read John 13:1-17 and discuss.

1. What do you look for in a leader? Rank these qualities in order of their importance from 1 to 10. Then go back and put an * next to those qualities you think Peter would demonstrate as a leader.

_____ toleration: accepts differences of opinion

_____ motivation: able too inspire confidence

_____ courage: willing to take risks

_____ initiative: self-starter

_____ intelligence: high I.Q.

_____ task oriented: dedicated to reaching goals

_____ unselfish: puts others first

_____ flexible: able to make midcourse corrections

_____ pragmatic: practical and resourceful

_____ action oriented: try anything once

2. Assuming the disciples were aware of the custom of footwashing, why didn't they wash their feet when entering the home?
   a. you can't wash your own feet
   b. they forgot
   c. it was the servant's job
   d. it would be humiliating

3. Why do you think Jesus washed his disciples' feet?
   a. to shame them
   b. to show his deep love for them
   c. to teach them a lesson in servanthood
   d. to give them a new model for their lives together
   e. to show them real leadership

4. Why was Peter so upset with Jesus?
   a. he felt guilty
   b. he didn't want to see Jesus degrading himself
   c. he thought one of the other disciples should do it
   d. he thought his feet were clean enough
   e. he didn't understand what Jesus was doing

5. "A person who has had a bath needs only to wash his feet; his whole body is clean. . . ." What is the point Jesus is making here?
   a. this is just a ritual to observe
   b. your feet are the important part of the body
   c. If you've taken a bath before starting out, all you need to clean are your feet
   d. spiritually, once you have been cleansed of sin, all you need to have is the feet washed of daily dirt.

6. How did Jesus expect the disciples to follow his example?
   a. by washing each other's feet
   b. by serving each other and those for whom the message is intended
   c. by counting themselves no better than Jesus
   d. by being willing to suffer all the shame Jesus would suffer

---

MY OWN STORY/25 Minutes.

1. If Jesus were to wash your feet today in a new and meaningful way (knowing your needs as he does), what would Jesus do?
   a. wash my feet
   b. ask "how can I help you?" and do it
   c. tell me he was proud to have me on the team
   d. put his arms around me and hold me
   e. forgive my sin

2. Why do you think people in the church do not regularly practice the equivalent of footwashing?
   a. we don't want to get too close
   b. we're too busy meeting our own needs
   c. it's not really okay to have needs
   d. overwhelmed and don't know where to start
   e. we're too proud to serve one another

3. In your family relationships, what would it mean to practice footwashing?
   a. to be available to meet needs
   b. to consider no job too menial
   c. to be sensitive to someone who is having a bad day
   d. to show our affection more
   e. to spend time just listening
   f. to be patient and forgiving

233

OPEN: 1. Which childhood hero later let you down? Why? **2.** What movie actor would you choose to depict Judas? **3.** Who would you choose as the saddest character in modern history? Why?

DIG: 1. If you were a movie director, how would you capture the real drama of verse 18-22? If you had been sitting at this table, what would you be feeling? Saying? **2.** In foretelling his betrayal (vv. 18-21), what do you sense in Jesus: Resolution? Resignation? Remorse? Resistance? Restlessness? What do you sense in his disciples? In Judas? **3.** Is Judas to be excused or held responsible, when "the Devil made him do it" (v. 27; also 6:70; 12:4-6; 13:2)? **4.** What irony do you find here in the reference to "the poor" and to "night"?

REFLECT: 1. If you knew ahead of time that someone would stab you in the back, how would you treat that person? **2.** Given three years of most intimate fellowship with Jesus, how could Judas turn around and betray him? **3.** Once betrayed in a relationship, how do you then trust again?

OPEN: 1. If you knew that you were about to die, how would you break the news to your close friends? What would you do if your friends tried to deny it, or couldn't handle it? **2.** What would you do if a friend tried to put up the "big brave front"?

DIG: 1. Why do you think Jesus waited until Judas had gone to share what he does here? **2.** Since Jesus is about to depart, what does he call the disciples to do? From his example in 13:1-17, how would you define what he means by love? From John 3:16 and 13:1, why is love the best evidence that they are Jesus' followers? **3.** From what you see of Peter in 13:6-9 and 13:36-37, what type of person do you think he is? **4.** How do you think Peter felt when Jesus made the prediction in verse 38?

REFLECT: 1. How would you compare your own spiritual "good intentions" to Simon Peter's? **2.** How do you set yourself up for spiritual "letdowns"? **3.** On a scale from 1 to 10, how would you rank your own spiritual community against the standard of love in verses 34-35?

Jesus Predicts His Betrayal

[18]"I am not referring to all of you; I know those I have chosen. But this is to fulfill the scripture: 'He who shares my bread has lifted up his heel against me.'[n]

[19]"I am telling you now before it happens, so that when it does happen you will believe that I am He. [20]I tell you the truth, whoever accepts anyone I send accepts me; and whoever accepts me accepts the one who sent me."

[21]After he had said this, Jesus was troubled in spirit and testified, "I tell you the truth, one of you is going to betray me."

[22]His disciples stared at one another, at a loss to know which of them he meant. [23]One of them, the disciple whom Jesus loved, was reclining next to him. [24]Simon Peter motioned to this disciple and said, "Ask him which one he means."

[25]Leaning back against Jesus, he asked him, "Lord, who is it?"

[26]Jesus answered, "It is the one to whom I will give this piece of bread when I have dipped it in the dish." Then, dipping the piece of bread, he gave it to Judas Iscariot, son of Simon. [27]As soon as Judas took the bread, Satan entered into him.

"What you are about to do, do quickly," Jesus told him, [28]but no one at the meal understood why Jesus said this to him. [29]Since Judas had charge of the money, some thought Jesus was telling him to buy what was needed for the Feast, or to give something to the poor. [30]As soon as Judas had taken the bread, he went out. And it was night.

Jesus Predicts Peter's Denial

[31]When he was gone, Jesus said, "Now is the Son of Man glorified and God is glorified in him. [32]If God is glorified in him,[o] God will glorify the Son in himself, and will glorify him at once.

[33]"My children, I will be with you only a little longer. You will look for me, and just as I told the Jews, so I tell you now: Where I am going, you cannot come.

[34]"A new command I give you: Love one another. As I have loved you, so you must love one another. [35]By this all men will know that you are my disciples, if you love one another."

[36]Simon Peter asked him, "Lord, where are you going?"

Jesus replied, "Where I am going, you cannot follow now, but you will follow later."

[37]Peter asked, "Lord, why can't I follow you now? I will lay down my life for you."

[38]Then Jesus answered, "Will you really lay down your life for me? I tell you the truth, before the rooster crows, you will disown me three times!

---

n18 Psalm 41:9   *o32* Many early manuscripts do not have *If God is glorified in|him.*

Jesus Comforts His Disciples

14 "Do not let your hearts be troubled. Trust in God[p]; trust
also in me. [2]In my Father's house are many rooms; if it
were not so, I would have told you. I am going there to prepare
a place for you. [3]And if I go and prepare a place for you, I will
come back and take you to be with me that you also may be
where I am. [4]You know the way to the place where I am going."

Jesus the Way to the Father

[5]Thomas said to him, "Lord, we don't know where you are
going, so how can we know the way?"
[6]Jesus answered, "I am the way and the truth and the life. No
one comes to the Father except through me. [7]If you really knew
me, you would know[q] my Father as well. From now on, you do
know him and have seen him."
[8]Philip said, "Lord, show us the Father and that will be
enough for us."
[9]Jesus answered: "Don't you know me, Philip, even after I
have been among you such a long time? Anyone who has seen
me has seen the Father. How can you say, 'Show us the Father'?
[10]Don't you believe that I am in the Father, and that the Father
is in me? The words I say to you are not just my own. Rather,
it is the Father, living in me, who is doing his work. [11]Believe
me when I say that I am in the Father and the Father is in me;
or at least believe on the evidence of the miracles themselves.
[12]I tell you the truth, anyone who has faith in me will do what
I have been doing. He will do even greater things than these,
because I am going to the Father. [13]And I will do whatever you
ask in my name, so that the Son may bring glory to the Father.
[14]You may ask me for anything in my name, and I will do it.

Jesus Promises the Holy Spirit

[15]"If you love me, you will obey what I command. [16]And I will
ask the Father, and he will give you another Counselor to be
with you forever— [17]the Spirit of truth. The world cannot
accept him, because it neither sees him nor knows him. But you
know him, for he lives with you and will be[r] in you. [18]I will not
leave you as orphans; I will come to you. [19]Before long, the
world will not see me anymore, but you will see me. Because I
live, you also will live. [20]On that day you will realize that I am
in my Father, and you are in me, and I am in you. [21]Whoever
has my commands and obeys them, he is the one who loves me.
He who loves me will be loved by my Father, and I too will love
him and show myself to him."
[22]Then Judas (not Judas Iscariot) said, "But, Lord, why do
you intend to show yourself to us and not to the world?"
[23]Jesus replied, "If anyone loves me, he will obey my teaching. My Father will love him, and we will come to him and make

[p]1 Or *You trust in God* [q]7 Some early manuscripts *If you really have known me, you will know* [r]17 Some early manuscripts *and is*

OPEN: What is your favorite room in the house? Why do you worry?

DIG: How does Jesus comfort his disciples? What is this "house"? Do they understand (see v. 5)?

REFLECT: In troubled times, what has given you hope and courage?

OPEN: When you were a kid, can you remember a time when you got lost? What happened?

DIG: 1. Look at Peter's question in 13:36, Thomas' queston in 14:5, Philip's question in 14:8 and Judas' question in 14:22. What problems are the disciples struggling with? **2.** How would you put Jesus' statement in 14:6-7 in your own words? What is the force of the claims Jesus makes here? **3.** How does 1:18 relate to what Jesus says in 14:9? What evidence does Jesus give for his claims? **4.** Do you feel the promises Jesus makes in verses 12-14 are "blank check" promises about prayer? Or are there some conditions to them?

REFLECT: 1. If Jesus is the way, do you feel you are on a bumpy dead-end street or a four lane highway? **2.** In light of 14:6, how would you respond to someone who said "there are many ways to God"?

OPEN: Who was the best counselor you ever had inside or outside of the school? What was it about this person that made this person so special?

DIG: 1. In 13:34, how are the disciples to show love to each other? In 14:15, how are they to show love to Jesus? Why is this idea repeated four times (vv. 15, 21, 23, 24)? **2.** How does Jesus set the example for us in verse 31? Of all of the promises given in this passage (vv. 16-18, 21, 23, 26-27), which one means to most to you? **3.** What do you learn about the Spirit in verses 16-17 and 25-27? What is the relationship of the Father, Jesus, and the Spirit to the believer? To each other? **4.** How would you define the difference between how Jesus and the world gives peace? **5.** Since verse 30 says Satan has no power over Jesus, why must Jesus die? How do verses 3:14-15, 6:53-54 and 10:15-18 answer this question?

REFLECT: 1. How would you describe the "peace" quotient in your life right now from 1 to 10 (1 = "smooth sailing", 10 = furious storm)? **2.** How would you counsel from your own experience a person who is going through a painful storm right now? **3.** How "at home" are the Father, Son and Spirit in your life? Are they more like owners, or temporary guests?

OPEN: **1.** Who has a "green thumb" in your family? **2.** If you could plant an orchard, what fruit trees or vines would you plant? What experience have you had with pruning trees or vines?

DIG: **1.** Imagine yourself as a branch on a vine. How would you feel as you saw the gardener approaching you with a knife? What does the Father use as his pruning tools? How would what the disciples are experiencing right now (in 13:18-21, 13:36-38, 14:5-8) be an example of this process? **2.** "Remain in me", "love", and "bearing fruit" are all phrases repeated several times in this passage. What are some of the relationships between these words? **3.** How do verses 9 and 12 tie together? How is love the essential dynamic of the Christian life? How do verses 12-13 take Jesus' command to love even further than 13:34-35? **4.** Compare 14:13-14 with 15:7 and 15:16. What do you learn about the connection between obedience and prayer? **5.** How does this call to love relate to Jesus' statement in verse 15? How does our relationship with Jesus change once we start practicing this example of love?

REFLECT: **1.** If you were an apple tree, how would you describe the fruit in your life lately: Grade A-1? Juicy? Green? Wormy? Fermented? **2.** Using the vine-tender image in this passage, what do you think Jesus would do if he could get his hands on you right now?

our home with him. ²⁴He who does not love me will not obey my teaching. These words you hear are not my own; they belong to the Father who sent me.

²⁵"All this I have spoken while still with you. ²⁶But the Counselor, the Holy Spirit, whom the Father will send in my name, will teach you all things and will remind you of everything I have said to you. ²⁷Peace I leave with you; my peace I give you. I do not give to you as the world gives. Do not let your hearts be troubled and do not be afraid.

²⁸"You heard me say, 'I am going away and I am coming back to you.' If you loved me, you would be glad that I am going to the Father, for the Father is greater than I. ²⁹I have told you now before it happens, so that when it does happen you will believe. ³⁰I will not speak with you much longer, for the prince of this world is coming. He has no hold on me, ³¹but the world must learn that I love the Father and that I do exactly what my Father has commanded me.

"Come now; let us leave.

The Vine and the Branches

15 "I am the true vine, and my Father is the gardener. ²He cuts off every branch in me that bears no fruit, while every branch that does bear fruit he prunes* so that it will be even more fruitful. ³You are already clean because of the word I have spoken to you. ⁴Remain in me, and I will remain in you. No branch can bear fruit by itself; it must remain in the vine. Neither can you bear fruit unless you remain in me.

⁵"I am the vine; you are the branches. If a man remains in me and I in him, he will bear much fruit; apart from me you can do nothing. ⁶If anyone does not remain in me, he is like a branch that is thrown away and withers; such branches are picked up, thrown into the fire and burned. ⁷If you remain in me and my words remain in you, ask whatever you wish, and it will be given you. ⁸This is to my Father's glory, that you bear much fruit, showing yourselves to be my disciples.

⁹"As the Father has loved me, so have I loved you. Now remain in my love. ¹⁰If you obey my commands, you will remain in my love, just as I have obeyed my Father's commands and remain in his love. ¹¹I have told you this so that my joy may be in you and that your joy may be complete. ¹²My command is this: Love each other as I have loved you. ¹³Greater love has no one than this, that he lay down his life for his friends. ¹⁴You are my friends if you do what I command. ¹⁵I no longer call you servants, because a servant does not know his master's business. Instead, I have called you friends, for everything that I learned from my Father I have made known to you. ¹⁶You did not choose me, but I chose you and appointed you to go and bear fruit—fruit that will last. Then the Father will give you whatever you ask in my name. ¹⁷This is my command: Love each other.

*2 The Greek for *prunes* also means *cleans*.

THE VINE AND THE BRANCHES

LOOKING INTO THE SCRIPTURE/20 Minutes. Read John 15:1-17 and discuss.

1. Take this test and share your answers TRUE or FALSE.
T F The life of the grape is in the branch
T F You can't judge a grapevine by its looks
T F A good gardener is a tough pruner
T F Pruning a vine will not hurt it
T F It's the job of the branch to stay connected to the vine
T F A vine without fruit is worthless

2. Why did Jesus use the illustration of a vine?
   a. everybody could understand
   b. to explain spiritual principles
   c. to threaten spiritual non-producers
   d. he was passing through a vineyard

3. Where does this illustration fit into the larger discourse on the Holy Spirit's ministry?
   a. it explains how the Father, Son, and Holy Spirit work together
   b. it shows the Father as a loving caretaker
   c. it shows the Son as the vine
   d. it shows the importance of the believer abiding in the vine

4. What do the branch that bears no fruit and the fruitful branch have in common?
   a. they both start out tapped into the vine
   b. they both get cut off, but for different reasons
   c. one is dead, the other is growing
   d. neither bears fruit because the buds are cut off

5. If you had been one of the disciples hearing this illustration for the first time, what would you have learned?
   a. very little at the time
   b. to cling to Christ
   c. to trust God
   d. to depend upon the Holy Spirit
   e. life brings with it humbling experiences

6. What is the Christian promised for remaining in the vine?
   a. success in everything he/she does
   b. a life full of happiness
   c. the fragrance of Christ in his/her life
   d. eternal life
   e. the ability to do God's work

MY OWN STORY/25 Minutes.

1. What kind of fruit would you like to see in your Christian life?
   a. love for my family
   b. compassion for the needy
   c. obedience to God
   d. willingness to serve others
   e. ability to share my faith

2. On those days when your vine is wilted, how do you get your spiritual energy back?
   a. drink some water: spend time alone with God
   b. cultivate the soil: seek encouragement from friends
   c. fertilize: sign up for a retreat or Bible study
   d. take out of the hot sun: get away from the stress
   e. submit to pruning: admit where I've been wrong
   f. wait for evening's cool: get some sleep

3. If God could get his hands on you, what would he do?
   a. I'm afraid to think
   b. prune off a few things
   c. do some radical surgery
   d. care for me very tenderly
   e. nothing

4. Where do you struggle to "remain in the vine?"
   a. busy: no time for cultivation
   b. distracted: my work/school comes first
   c. tired: the fruit is too heavy
   d. disappointed: God hasn't come through in my life
   e. defeated: it's hard to be obedient to God's will
   f. lonely: I feel like I'm the only branch on the vine

The World Hates the Disciples

[18] "If the world hates you, keep in mind that it hated me first. [19] If you belonged to the world, it would love you as its own. As it is, you do not belong to the world, but I have chosen you out of the world. That is why the world hates you. [20] Remember the words I spoke to you: 'No servant is greater than his master.'[t] If they persecuted me, they will persecute you also. If they obeyed my teaching, they will obey yours also. [21] They will treat you this way because of my name, for they do not know the One who sent me. [22] If I had not come and spoken to them, they would not be guilty of sin. Now, however, they have no excuse for their sin. [23] He who hates me hates my Father as well. [24] If I had not done among them what no one else did, they would not be guilty of sin. But now they have seen these miracles, and yet they have hated both me and my Father. [25] But this is to fulfill what is written in their Law: 'They hated me without reason.'[u]

[26] "When the Counselor comes, whom I will send to you from the Father, the Spirit of truth who goes out from the Father, he will testify about me. [27] And you also must testify, for you have been with me from the beginning.

16 "All this I have told you so that you will not go astray. [2] They will put you out of the synagogue; in fact, a time is coming when anyone who kills you will think he is offering a service to God. [3] They will do such things because they have not known the Father or me. [4] I have told you this, so that when the time comes you will remember that I warned you. I did not tell you this at first because I was with you.

The Work of the Holy Spirit

[5] "Now I am going to him who sent me, yet none of you asks me, 'Where are you going?' [6] Because I have said these things, you are filled with grief. [7] But I tell you the truth: It is for your good that I am going away. Unless I go away, the Counselor will not come to you; but if I go, I will send him to you. [8] When he comes, he will convict the world of guilt[v] in regard to sin and righteousness and judgment: [9] in regard to sin, because men do not believe in me; [10] in regard to righteousness, because I am going to the Father, where you can see me no longer; [11] and in regard to judgment, because the prince of this world now stands condemned.

[12] "I have much more to say to you, more than you can now bear. [13] But when he, the Spirit of truth, comes, he will guide you into all truth. He will not speak on his own; he will speak only what he hears, and he will tell you what is yet to come. [14] He will bring glory to me by taking from what is mine and making it known to you. [15] All that belongs to the Father is mine. That is why I said the Spirit will take from what is mine and make it known to you.

[16] "In a little while you will see me no more, and then after a little while you will see me."

[t]20 John 13:16   [u]25 Psalms 35:19; 69:4   [v]8 Or will expose the guilt of the world

238

The Disciples' Grief Will Turn to Joy

¹⁷Some of his disciples said to one another, "What does he mean by saying, 'In a little while you will see me no more, and then after a little while you will see me,' and 'Because I am going to the Father'?" ¹⁸They kept asking, "What does he mean by 'a little while'? We don't understand what he is saying."

¹⁹Jesus saw that they wanted to ask him about this, so he said to them, "Are you asking one another what I meant when I said, 'In a little while you will see me no more, and then after a little while you will see me'? ²⁰I tell you the truth, you will weep and mourn while the world rejoices. You will grieve, but your grief will turn to joy. ²¹A woman giving birth to a child has pain because her time has come; but when her baby is born she forgets the anguish because of her joy that a child is born into the world. ²²So with you: Now is your time of grief, but I will see you again and you will rejoice, and no one will take away your joy. ²³In that day you will no longer ask me anything. I tell you the truth, my Father will give you whatever you ask in my name. ²⁴Until now you have not asked for anything in my name. Ask and you will receive, and your joy will be complete.

²⁵"Though I have been speaking figuratively, a time is coming when I will no longer use this kind of language but will tell you plainly about my Father. ²⁶In that day you will ask in my name. I am not saying that I will ask the Father on your behalf. ²⁷No, the Father himself loves you because you have loved me and have believed that I came from God. ²⁸I came from the Father and entered the world; now I am leaving the world and going back to the Father."

²⁹Then Jesus' disciples said, "Now you are speaking clearly and without figures of speech. ³⁰Now we can see that you know all things and that you do not even need to have anyone ask you questions. This makes us believe that you came from God."

³¹"You believe at last!"ʷ Jesus answered. ³²"But a time is coming, and has come, when you will be scattered, each to his own home. You will leave me all alone. Yet I am not alone, for my Father is with me.

³³"I have told you these things, so that in me you may have peace. In this world you will have trouble. But take heart! I have overcome the world."

Jesus Prays for Himself

17 After Jesus said this, he looked toward heaven and prayed:

"Father, the time has come. Glorify your Son, that your Son may glorify you. ²For you granted him authority over all people that he might give eternal life to all those you have given him. ³Now this is eternal life: that they may know you, the only true God, and Jesus Christ, whom you have sent. ⁴I have brought you glory on earth by completing the

ʷ31 Or *"Do you now believe?"*

OPEN: 1. How scattered is your family? How often do you get together for family reunions? **2.** Did your parents ever tell you about your own birth experience? What was it like for them? Do you think they felt it was worth it?

DIG: 1. What tones of voice do you hear in the disciples' conversation in verses 17-18? If you were there, would Jesus' answer encourage you, or confuse you more? **2.** What event is Jesus referring to in verses 20-22? In what ways does the world's "joy" (v. 20) contrast with the joy the disciples will experience (v. 22)? How is this similar to what Jesus said about peace in 14:27? **3.** From verses 23-27, what things characterize the relationship we can have with the Father because of Jesus? **4.** Do you think the disciples really grasp what Jesus says in verse 28? Why? **5.** What do you learn from verse 33 about Jesus' mission and its effect for us? How have you seen this in your life?

REFLECT: 1. How do you deal with change? Moves? Job transfers? Transitions from one stage in your life to another? How has "pain" helped you to grow up? **2.** From your experience, how could you comfort someone going through change? **3.** From your experience, how could you verify verses 23-24 are true?

OPEN: What was the biggest decision you ever made (e.g., to get married)? How did it alter the rest of your life (kids, etc.)?

DIG: 1. Looking back (see 2:4; 7:6,8; 12:23; 13:1) what event is it now "time" to occur? **2.** What does Jesus request in this prayer? What does it mean to "glorify" someone? How has Jesus done that for the Father? And vice versa, the Father for Jesus? How is Jesus' diety emphasized here? **3.** What has been Jesus' mission?

REFLECT: 1. Do you "know" you have eternal life? **2.** Whose glory does your life reflect most? Your own? Your earthly father's? Your Heavenly Father's? Be honest.

OPEN: 1. Who taught you most about the meaning of prayer? **2.** What was the first prayer you were ever taught?

DIG: 1. While Jesus prays for himself in verses 1-5, who is the focal point of his prayer here? Why? If you had to file a report to the Father on Jesus' activities, how would you illustrate verse 6-8 from earlier passages in this gospel? **2.** What are Jesus' requests for the disciples (v. 11, 15 and 16)? How would you feel hearing Jesus pray these things for you? How would you feel after the resurrection? **3.** How does God's Word act in the process of setting us apart for his mission?

REFLECT: 1. If you had to sum up in one or two phrases what your goal has been over the past year, what would you say? How does this relate to God's purpose? **2.** How are your prayers for others like and unlike Jesus' prayer? Do your prayers reflect the short-term urgent, or the long-term important needs people have? If Jesus prayed only for the urgent needs of his disciples, how would this prayer be different?

OPEN: 1. At 3:00 AM, who do you call to share a deep personal problem? **2.** What would it take for your friends outside the church to really notice what's going on inside?

DIG: 1. Now who is the focus of Jesus' prayer? Toward what end? What kind of unity exists between God and Jesus that we should be like them? **2.** How should this unity affect others (vv. 21, 23)? In your experience, where has this loving unity attracted those ouside the church? When have they been repelled? **3.** What does Jesus' ultimate desire (v. 24) reveal about His love for us? **4.** How do verses 25-26 sum up some on the major concerns of Jesus in chapters 13-16?

REFLECT: If paid $10.00/hour for consciously working at loving others, and docked the same for working against love, how much money would you have made (or lost) this past week? Why the shortfall?

work you gave me to do. ⁵And now, Father, glorify me in your presence with the glory I had with you before the world began.

Jesus Prays for His Disciples

⁶"I have revealed youˣ to those whom you gave me out of the world. They were yours; you gave them to me and they have obeyed your word. ⁷Now they know that everything you have given me comes from you. ⁸For I gave them the words you gave me and they accepted them. They knew with certainty that I came from you, and they believed that you sent me. ⁹I pray for them. I am not praying for the world, but for those you have given me, for they are yours. ¹⁰All I have is yours, and all you have is mine. And glory has come to me through them. ¹¹I will remain in the world no longer, but they are still in the world, and I am coming to you. Holy Father, protect them by the power of your name—the name you gave me—so that they may be one as we are one. ¹²While I was with them, I protected them and kept them safe by that name you gave me. None has been lost except the one doomed to destruction so that Scripture would be fulfilled.

¹³"I am coming to you now, but I say these things while I am still in the world, so that they may have the full measure of my joy within them. ¹⁴I have given them your word and the world has hated them, for they are not of the world any more than I am of the world. ¹⁵My prayer is not that you take them out of the world but that you protect them from the evil one. ¹⁶They are not of the world, even as I am not of it. ¹⁷Sanctify ʸ them by the truth; your word is truth. ¹⁸As you sent me into the world, I have sent them into the world. ¹⁹For them I sanctify myself, that they too may be truly sanctified.

Jesus Prays for All Believers

²⁰"My prayer is not for them alone. I pray also for those who will believe in me through their message, ²¹that all of them may be one, Father, just as you are in me and I am in you. May they also be in us so that the world may believe that you have sent me. ²²I have given them the glory that you gave me, that they may be one as we are one: ²³I in them and you in me. May they be brought to complete unity to let the world know that you sent me and have loved them even as you have loved me.

²⁴"Father, I want those you have given me to be with me where I am, and to see my glory, the glory you have given me because you loved me before the creation of the world. ²⁵"Righteous Father, though the world does not know you, I know you, and they know that you have sent me. ²⁶I have made you known to them, and will continue to make you known in order that the love you have for me may be in them and that I myself may be in them.''

ˣ6 Greek *your name;* also in verse 26   ʸ17 Greek *hagiazo (set apart for sacred use or make holy);* also in verse 19

Jesus Arrested

18 When he had finished praying, Jesus left with his disciples and crossed the Kidron Valley. On the other side there was an olive grove, and he and his disciples went into it.

²Now Judas, who betrayed him, knew the place, because Jesus had often met there with his disciples. ³So Judas came to the grove, guiding a detachment of soldiers and some officials from the chief priests and Pharisees. They were carrying torches, lanterns and weapons.

⁴Jesus, knowing all that was going to happen to him, went out and asked them, "Who is it you want?"

⁵"Jesus of Nazareth," they replied.

"I am he," Jesus said. (And Judas the traitor was standing there with them.) ⁶When Jesus said, "I am he," they drew back and fell to the ground.

⁷Again he asked them, "Who is it you want?"

And they said, "Jesus of Nazareth."

⁸"I told you that I am he," Jesus answered. "If you are looking for me, then let these men go." ⁹This happened so that the words he had spoken would be fulfilled: "I have not lost one of those you gave me."ᶻ

¹⁰Then Simon Peter, who had a sword, drew it and struck the high priest's servant, cutting off his right ear. (The servant's name was Malchus.)

¹¹Jesus commanded Peter, "Put your sword away! Shall I not drink the cup the Father has given me?"

Jesus Taken to Annas

¹²Then the detachment of soldiers with its commander and the Jewish officials arrested Jesus. They bound him ¹³and brought him first to Annas, who was the father-in-law of Caiaphas, the high priest that year. ¹⁴Caiaphas was the one who had advised the Jews that it would be good if one man died for the people.

Peter's First Denial

¹⁵Simon Peter and another disciple were following Jesus. Because this disciple was known to the high priest, he went with Jesus into the high priest's courtyard, ¹⁶but Peter had to wait outside at the door. The other disciple, who was known to the high priest, came back, spoke to the girl on duty there and brought Peter in.

¹⁷"You are not one of this man's disciples, are you?" the girl at the door asked Peter.

He replied, "I am not."

¹⁸It was cold, and the servants and officials stood around a fire they had made to keep warm. Peter also was standing with them, warming himself.

OPEN: 1. Where do you go when you need to prepare yourself for a very stressful time? **2.** Have you ever seen a "death row" where people awaited their final sentence? How did you feel?

DIG: 1. Why do you suppose the Pharisees want to take advantage of the "night" (see 13:30) to arrest Jesus (see also 3:19-20; 12:35)? **2.** How would you react if you were one of the disciples who saw these menacing-looking people coming? How do you account for the mob's deference (v. 6; see also 1:5)? **3.** Seeing how Jesus deals with the mob (vv. 4, 8) and Peter (v. 11), what do you learn about him? **4.** What do you learn from Peter's reaction: He is a skilled swordsman? Loyal to Jesus? Short-fused? Confused? **5.** What is "the cup" which Jesus must drink?

REFLECT; 1. When you see injustice taking place, how do you react? **2.** In the Holocaust, the innocent did nothing and they were slaughtered. When is it right to stand up for justice and when is it better to leave the judgment to God?

OPEN: When have you been before a judge? What for?

DIG: Why was Jesus taken to Annas so quickly? Given his pacifism (vv. 6, 11), why is Jesus bound?

REFLECT: Have you ever been "set up" to incriminate yourself?

OPEN: 1. Do you suffer from "hoof-in-mouth" disease? How so? **2.** What is your latest blooper?

DIG: 1. Since several disciples have already been named in the gospel, who do you think this "other disciple" might be? **2.** What do you think he and Peter are hoping to do? **3.** How does Peter's reaction to the girl differ from his episode in the garden (18:10)? How do you account for this difference?

REFLECT: 1. When is it hardest for you to admit that you are a disciple of Jesus? Why? **2.** How do you handle it when you realize that you have denied Jesus by your actions, word or attitudes?

ᶻ9 John 6:39

OPEN: If you could take one page out of the history books when the church smeared Christ's name, what page would you tear out?

DIG: How does Jesus turn the other cheek and expose this trial as a mockery? What galls you here? What do you feel like doing on Jesus' behalf?

REFLECT: 1. Have you ever felt you were unjustly treated by leaders of the institutional church? How did you handle it? 2. Have you been able to forgive these people, or are you still holding a grudge?

OPEN: When you blow it, what then?

DIG: What does Peter need: Better alibi? Stronger denials? Silent rooster? Amnesia? Confession? Why?

REFLECT: Peter probably told this story about his denial on himself. Why didn't he keep it to himself?

OPEN: Have you ever been pulled over by the police? Accused of speeding when you were not? Taken to the police station and mistreated? What happened?

DIG: 1. Where is Jesus brought next? When? Why are the Jewish leaders rushing this trial through so fast? 2. What is so ironic about the religious leaders in verse 28? How do their actions serve to illustrate Jesus' charges against them in 5:39-40 and 7:24? 3. From verse 33, what reason do they finally give to Pilate for bringing Jesus to him? Why would Pilate take this seriously? How are Pilate's fears similar to those of the Jewish leaders in 11:48? 4. What do you think Pilate meant by what he said in verse 38? Why do you think he said it? 5. What is Pilate's conclusion? Why doesn't Pilate just release Jesus? From this episode, what type of person do you think Pilate is?

REFLECT: 1. Today, Peter is held in esteem and Pilate is scorned. Why do you judge these two so differently when they both "caved in" under pressure? 2. Barabbas (a deserving criminal) gets off free and Jesus (an innocent victim) is condemnned. What is the lesson here for you?

The High Priest Questions Jesus

[19]Meanwhile, the high priest questioned Jesus about his disciples and his teaching.

[20]"I have spoken openly to the world," Jesus replied. "I always taught in synagogues or at the temple, where all the Jews come together. I said nothing in secret. [21]Why question me? Ask those who heard me. Surely they know what I said."

[22]When Jesus said this, one of the officials nearby struck him in the face. "Is this the way you answer the high priest?" he demanded.

[23]"If I said something wrong," Jesus replied, "testify as to what is wrong. But if I spoke the truth, why did you strike me?" [24]Then Annas sent him, still bound, to Caiaphas the high priest. [a]

Peter's Second and Third Denials

[25]As Simon Peter stood warming himself, he was asked, "You are not one of his disciples, are you?"

He denied it, saying, "I am not."

[26]One of the high priest's servants, a relative of the man whose ear Peter had cut off, challenged him, "Didn't I see you with him in the olive grove?" [27]Again Peter denied it, and at that moment a rooster began to crow.

Jesus Before Pilate

[28]Then the Jews led Jesus from Caiaphas to the palace of the Roman governor. By now it was early morning, and to avoid ceremonial uncleanness the Jews did not enter the palace; they wanted to be able to eat the Passover. [29]So Pilate came out to them and asked, "What charges are you bringing against this man?"

[30]"If he were not a criminal," they replied, "we would not have handed him over to you."

[31]Pilate said, "Take him yourselves and judge him by your own law."

"But we have no right to execute anyone," the Jews objected. [32]This happened so that the words Jesus had spoken indicating the kind of death he was going to die would be fulfilled.

[33]Pilate then went back inside the palace, summoned Jesus and asked him, "Are you the king of the Jews?"

[34]"Is that your own idea," Jesus asked, "or did others talk to you about me?"

[35]"Am I a Jew?" Pilate replied. "It was your people and your chief priests who handed you over to me. What is it you have done?"

[36]Jesus said, "My kingdom is not of this world. If it were, my servants would fight to prevent my arrest by the Jews. But now my kingdom is from another place."

[37]"You are a king, then!" said Pilate.

[a]24 Or (Now Annas had sent him, still bound, to Caiaphas the high priest.)

Jesus answered, "You are right in saying I am a king. In fact, for this reason I was born, and for this I came into the world, to testify to the truth. Everyone on the side of truth listens to me."

³⁸"What is truth?" Pilate asked. With this he went out again to the Jews and said, "I find no basis for a charge against him. ³⁹But it is your custom for me to release to you one prisoner at the time of the Passover. Do you want me to release 'the king of the Jews'?"

⁴⁰They shouted back, "No, not him! Give us Barabbas!" Now Barabbas had taken part in a rebellion.

Jesus Sentenced to be Crucified

19 Then Pilate took Jesus and had him flogged. ²The soldiers twisted together a crown of thorns and put it on his head. They clothed him in a purple robe ³and went up to him again and again, saying, "Hail, king of the Jews!" And they struck him in the face.

⁴Once more Pilate came out and said to the Jews, "Look, I am bringing him out to you to let you know that I find no basis for a charge against him." ⁵When Jesus came out wearing the crown of thorns and the purple robe, Pilate said to them, "Here is the man!"

⁶As soon as the chief priests and their officials saw him, they shouted, "Crucify! Crucify!"

But Pilate answered, "You take him and crucify him. As for me, I find no basis for a charge against him."

⁷The Jews insisted, "We have a law, and according to that law he must die, because he claimed to be the Son of God."

⁸When Pilate heard this, he was even more afraid, ⁹and he went back inside the palace. "Where do you come from?" he asked Jesus, but Jesus gave him no answer. ¹⁰"Do you refuse to speak to me?" Pilate said. "Don't you realize I have power either to free you or to crucify you?"

¹¹Jesus answered, "You would have no power over me if it were not given to you from above. Therefore the one who handed me over to you is guilty of a greater sin."

¹²From then on, Pilate tried to set Jesus free, but the Jews kept shouting, "If you let this man go, you are no friend of Caesar. Anyone who claims to be a king opposes Caesar."

¹³When Pilate heard this, he brought Jesus out and sat down on the judge's seat at a place known as the Stone Pavement (which in Aramaic is Gabbatha). ¹⁴It was the day of Preparation of Passover Week, about the sixth hour.

"Here is your king," Pilate said to the Jews.

¹⁵But they shouted, "Take him away! Take him away! Crucify him!"

"Shall I crucify your king?" Pilate asked.

"We have no king but Caesar," the chief priests answered.

¹⁶Finally Pilate handed him over to them to be crucified.

OPEN: 1. What is the closest you have come to being responsible for keeping the peace in a situation that got "ugly"? Have you ever been in a crowd that got carried along by a few hot-headed leaders? **2.** Have you ever visited or been in a country where individual rights were ignored?

DIG: 1. In view of Pilate's conviction in 18:38, 19:4 and 19:6, why would he allow Jesus to be beaten? Put yourself in the place of one of the soldiers in verses 1:3. Are you just being cruel or are there deeper hates and fears involved? **2.** What charge do the Jewish leaders claim is the reason for Jesus to be crucified? What does Pilate's fearful response to that charge show about him? How might his conversation with Jesus in 18:33-37 contribute to this growing fear? **3.** Why do you think Jesus refused to answer Pilate's question? How do Pilate's actions so far back up his claim in verse 10? Why do you think Jesus responds to that claim but not his question in verse 9? **4.** What additional pressure do the leaders bring upon Pilate in verse 12? What is their implied threat to him? **5.** When Pilate appeals to them in verse 15, what does the priests' reply indicate about their spiritual condition? In light of 8:33 and 8:41, why is this especially ironic? **6.** Pretend you are Pilate. How would you explain to your wife that night why you finally let Jesus be killed?

REFLECT: 1. Recall a time at work or in your community, where you were put in Pilate's situation of having to make a decision based either on personal ambition and fear, or on what you know is right? What is the lesson for you here? **2.** If you were asked to put in a good word for Pilate, what would it be?

243

OPEN: 1. What movie or book (such as "Jesus Christ SuperStar", "Godspell" or "Ben Hur") brought home to you most vividly the events of the crucifixion? 2. When you were a child, what did you associate with the crucifixion: A stain glass window? Jewelry someone wore? An Easter pageant? Or what?

DIG: 1. According to the sign on Jesus' cross, for what "official" reason was he crucified? What various meanings does this title have for Pilate (18:33-37)? For the soldiers (19:14-15)? For Jews (19:12)? The chief priests (19:14-15)? Is this title being used here sincerely or mockingly? Why then in all three common languages (see also 12:32)? 2. As Jesus may have recited Psalm 22 from the cross, what meaning do you suppose it has for him? And consequently for you? 3. Given Jesus' mother's faith in him at the outset of his public ministry (see John 2:3-5), what must she be feeling now at the end? Judging from verses 26-27, what are Jesus' last wishes for his mother?

REFLECT: 1. If Jesus were to come to our generation today and preach the same gospel that he preached to the first century, how do you think the average person on the street would respond? 2. How could you explain the need for the crucifixion to someone who really wanted to understand (see also John 3:16)?

OPEN: 1. Which of these assassinations affected you the most: John F. Kennedy? Martin Luther King? Or John Lennon? What do you remember about the tragedy? 2. Have you ever had any broken bones? How did it happen?

DIG: 1. From here and throughout John's gospel, we see that Jesus' death has special pardoxical meaning: In what sense was Jesus' death necessary yet voluntary? Triumphant yet tragic? Pre-ordained yet avoidable? Lifted up yet laid down? Unjust yet just? Finished yet ongoing? 2. What evidence and testimony certify Jesus' death? 3. What else could "the flow of blood and water" mean (see Exodus 12:7, 12-13; John 4:10; 7:37-38)?

REFLECT: 1. In your own spiritual journey, when did you come to understand the meaning of the death of Christ? What did you think the death of Christ was all about before this? 2. In a few words, how has the death of Jesus Christ affected your

The Crucifixion

So the soldiers took charge of Jesus. [17]Carrying his own cross, he went out to the place of the Skull (which in Aramaic is called Golgotha). [18]Here they crucified him, and with him two others—one on each side and Jesus in the middle.

[19]Pilate had a notice prepared and fastened to the cross. It read: JESUS OF NAZARETH, THE KING OF THE JEWS. [20]Many of the Jews read this sign, for the place where Jesus was crucified was near the city, and the sign was written in Aramaic, Latin and Greek. [21]The chief priests of the Jews protested to Pilate, "Do not write 'The King of the Jews,' but that this man claimed to be king of the Jews."

[22]Pilate answered, "What I have written, I have written."

[23]When the soldiers crucified Jesus, they took his clothes, dividing them into four shares, one for each of them, with the undergarment remaining. This garment was seamless, woven in one piece from top to bottom.

[24]"Let's not tear it," they said to one another. "Let's decide by lot who will get it."

This happened that the scripture might be fulfilled which said,

"They divided my garments among them
    and cast lots for my clothing."[b]

So this is what the soldiers did.

[25]Near the cross of Jesus stood his mother, his mother's sister, Mary the wife of Clopas, and Mary Magdalene. [26]When Jesus saw his mother there, and the disciple whom he loved standing nearby, he said to his mother, "Dear woman, here is your son," [27]and to the disciple, "Here is your mother." From that time on, this disciple took her into his home.

The Death of Jesus

[28]Later, knowing that all was now completed, and so that the Scripture would be fulfilled, Jesus said, "I am thirsty." [29]A jar of wine vinegar was there, so they soaked a sponge in it, put the sponge on a stalk of the hyssop plant, and lifted it to Jesus' lips. [30]When he had received the drink, Jesus said, "It is finished." With that, he bowed his head and gave up his spirit.

[31]Now it was the day of Preparation, and the next day was to be a special Sabbath. Because the Jews did not want the bodies left on the crosses during the Sabbath, they asked Pilate to have the legs broken and the bodies taken down. [32]The soldiers therefore came and broke the legs of the first man who had been crucified with Jesus, and then those of the other. [33]But when they came to Jesus and found that he was already dead, they did not break his legs. [34]Instead, one of the soldiers pierced Jesus' side with a spear, bringing a sudden flow of blood and water. [35]The man who saw it has given testimony, and his testimony is true. He knows that he tells the truth, and he testifies so that

[b]24 Psalm 22:18

you also may believe. [36]These things happened so that the scripture would be fulfilled: "Not one of his bones will be broken,"[c] [37]and, as another scripture says, "They will look on the one they have pierced."[d]

The Burial of Jesus

[38]Later, Joseph of Arimathea asked Pilate for the body of Jesus. Now Joseph was a disciple of Jesus, but secretly because he feared the Jews. With Pilate's permission, he came and took the body away. [39]He was accompanied by Nicodemus, the man who earlier had visited Jesus at night. Nicodemus brought a mixture of myrrh and aloes, about seventy-five pounds.[e] [40]Taking Jesus' body, the two of them wrapped it, with the spices, in strips of linen. This was in accordance with Jewish burial customs. [41]At the place where Jesus was crucified, there was a garden, and in the garden a new tomb, in which no one had ever been laid. [42]Because it was the Jewish day of Preparation and since the tomb was nearby, they laid Jesus there.

The Empty Tomb

20 Early on the first day of the week, while it was still dark, Mary Magdalene went to the tomb and saw that the stone had been removed from the entrance. [2]So she came running to Simon Peter and the other disciple, the one Jesus loved, and said, "They have taken the Lord out of the tomb, and we don't know where they have put him!"

[3]So Peter and the other disciple started for the tomb. [4]Both were running, but the other disciple outran Peter and reached the tomb first. [5]He bent over and looked in at the strips of linen lying there but did not go in. [6]Then Simon Peter, who was behind him, arrived and went into the tomb. He saw the strips of linen lying there, [7]as well as the burial cloth that had been around Jesus' head. The cloth was folded up by itself, separate from the linen. [8]Finally the other disciple, who had reached the tomb first, also went inside. He saw and believed. [9](They still did not understand from Scripture that Jesus had to rise from the dead.)

Jesus Appears to Mary Magdalene

[10]Then the disciples went back to their homes, [11]but Mary stood outside the tomb crying. As she wept, she bent over to look into the tomb [12]and saw two angels in white, seated where Jesus' body had been, one at the head and the other at the foot.

[13]They asked her, "Woman, why are you crying?"

"They have taken my Lord away," she said, "and I don't know where they have put him." [14]At this, she turned around and saw Jesus standing there, but she did not realize that it was Jesus.

[15]"Woman," he said, "why are you crying? Who is it you are looking for?"

OPEN: reason for living? (Read Romans 5:6-8 and 6:19-23.)

OPEN: What kind of burial would you like? Where?

DIG: 1. As a secret believer like Joseph or Nicodemus, why would you risk public exposure now? **2.** Some say Jesus really did not die, but revived in the tomb. How would 19:1,18,32-34 and verse 40 argue against this idea?

REFLECT: 1. How does your fear of others and your love for Jesus sometimes conflict? **2.** In spite of past failures and fears, what will you do this week to make amends?

OPEN: After you bury someone you love, how do you deal with your grief? Do you find comfort in going out to the cemetary? Why?

DIG: 1. As Mary, having seen Jesus' torturous death, what is your emotional state two days later? Would you be sleepless? Why else would you visit the tomb so early? Realizing the body is gone, how do you react? **2.** What does "the other disciple" (likely John, the author) believe? Why?

REFLECT: 1. When you bury someone you dearly love, how does the fact of the resurrection of Jesus from the dead help you to deal with your own pain? **2.** What do you rely on for evidence that Jesus is the Son of God and that he rose from the dead?

OPEN: What do you believe about UFO's and extra terrestrial phenomena? Ever seen any?

DIG: 1. Given the disciples response in verse 8, why is Mary crying? Would you have responded more like Mary, or like the men? Why? **2.** From her response to the angels and to Jesus, would you say she is quietly grieving, or more hysterical? Why? **3.** What finally breaks through her grief and confusion? How does her return to the disciples here contrast to that in verse 2? **4.** What term does Jesus use for his disciples here? How does this relate to what he said in 15:15? What is new in their relationship from now on?

---

[c]36 Exodus 12:46; Num. 9:12; Psalm 34:20   [d]37 Zech. 12:10   [e]39 Greek *a hundred litrai* (about 34 kilograms)

REFLECT: **1.** When someone you dearly loved died (such as your father or a close friend), how did you feel right afterward? What was your next feeling? The next? etc. **2.** How did God meet you in this process and bring about healing?

OPEN: When you were a kid, where was your hiding place?

DIG: **1.** Why are the disciples especially fearful now? **2.** Of all things Jesus must have said at this time, why do think the author records "peace be with you" twice? **3.** What does this peace lead to? How does this relate to their fears?

REFLECT: Into what current situation is Jesus pressing his peace? What would that "peace" mean to you?

OPEN: What do you do on Super Bowl Sunday? What would you do if there were "network difficulties" and you missed the last two minutes and the score was tied?

DIG: **1.** Considering Mary in verse 13 and the other disciples in verses 9 and 19, do you think Thomas was like, or unlike them? Would you be more like Thomas, or like Peter and John in verse 8? How do you think Thomas and the others got along during the week between verse 19 and 26? **2.** How does Jesus deal with Thomas' doubt? What is significant about his response to Jesus? What does Thomas call Jesus which no one yet called him in this gospel? **3.** What does the author say is the purpose for writing this gospel?

REFLECT: **1.** When have you struggled with spiritual doubts? What caused your doubts? How did God deal with you in this time? **2.** What questions are you struggling with the most right now? **3.** What have you found most helpful in dealing with your doubts?

Thinking he was the gardener, she said, "Sir, if you have carried him away, tell me where you have put him, and I will get him."

¹⁶Jesus said to her, "Mary."

She turned toward him and cried out in Aramaic, "Rabboni!" (which means Teacher).

¹⁷Jesus said, "Do not hold on to me, for I have not yet returned to the Father. Go instead to my brothers and tell them, 'I am returning to my Father and your Father, to my God and your God.' "

¹⁸Mary Magdalene went to the disciples with the news: "I have seen the Lord!" And she told them that he had said these things to her.

Jesus Appears to His Disciples

¹⁹On the evening of that first day of the week, when the disciples were together, with the doors locked for fear of the Jews, Jesus came and stood among them and said, "Peace be with you!" ²⁰After he said this, he showed them his hands and side. The disciples were overjoyed when they saw the Lord.

²¹Again Jesus said, "Peace be with you! As the Father has sent me, I am sending you." ²²And with that he breathed on them and said, "Receive the Holy Spirit. ²³If you forgive anyone his sins, they are forgiven; if you do not forgive them, they are not forgiven."

Jesus Appears to Thomas

²⁴Now Thomas (called Didymus), one of the Twelve, was not with the disciples when Jesus came. ²⁵So the other disciples told him, "We have seen the Lord!"

But he said to them, "Unless I see the nail marks in his hands and put my finger where the nails were, and put my hand into his side, I will not believe it."

²⁶A week later his disciples were in the house again, and Thomas was with them. Though the doors were locked, Jesus came and stood among them and said, "Peace be with you!" ²⁷Then he said to Thomas, "Put your finger here; see my hands. Reach out your hand and put it into my side. Stop doubting and believe."

²⁸Thomas said to him, "My Lord and my God!"

²⁹Then Jesus told him, "Because you have seen me, you have believed; blessed are those who have not seen and yet have believed."

³⁰Jesus did many other miraculous signs in the presence of his disciples, which are not recorded in this book. ³¹But these are written that you may^f believe that Jesus is the Christ, the Son of God, and that by believing you may have life in his name.

f31 Some manuscripts may continue to

LOOKING INTO THE SCRIPTURE/20 Minutes. Read John 20:24-31 and discuss these questions.

1. How do you feel when you find the last page of your mystery novel missing?
   a. cheated
   b. agitated
   c. indifferent
   d. creative: (write my own ending)
   e. driven: (who else has read it?)
   f. inconvenienced: (have to go to the library)
   g. defeated

2. Why do you think Thomas was not with the rest of the disciples on Easter night when Jesus appeared to them in the Upper Room?
   a. he had run away
   b. he was a loner
   c. he was sorting out things
   d. he thought it was all over

3. "Unless I see the nail marks in his hands and put my finger where the nails were, and put my hand into his side, I will not believe." What is Thomas saying here?
   a. you guys are crazy
   b. I want to believe, but . . .
   c. don't break my heart a second time . . .
   d. I need proof (seeing is believing)

4. Why did Jesus wait seven days to appear to Thomas?
   a. he was busy
   b. he wanted Thomas to think about it
   c. he wanted to wait until Thomas was ready
   d. he gave his disciples a chance to convince him

5. How did Jesus deal with Thomas?
   a. tenderly
   b. in his own way
   c. with the evidence he asked for

6. What did Jesus mean when he said, "blessed are those who have not seen and yet have believed"?
   a. those who do not doubt will be happier
   b. you don't have to see to believe
   c. God calls us to be faithful even when we can't see
   d. you blew it, Thomas

MY OWN STORY/25 Minutes.

1. When you have spiritual doubts, what does that indicate?
   a. my faith is weak
   b. I need some more information
   c. growth may be taking place
   d. someone needs to understand me
   e. I need a spiritual "check up"

2. What kind of spiritual "proof" do you need?
   a. pragmatic—if it works, it must be true
   b. empirical—firsthand experience
   c. faith—a leap in the dark
   d. historical—evidence of his working in the past
   e. rational—it makes sense

3. If you could ask God one question about your own faith, what would it be?
   a. how do you deal with doubt
   b. what happens when you don't feel like a Christian
   c. how do you know when you have "touched" God
   d. do I have faith even when I don't think about God during the day?

4. What have you found helpful in times of doubt?
   a. the fact the Bible says it
   b. the evidence of past miracles
   c. historical evidence
   d. the faith of others
   e. go back to the bare essentials

OPEN: 1. What has been the best fishing trip you have ever been on? **2.** Where is your favorite spot for a "cook out"?

DIG: 1. Where are these seven disciples now? How far away (in miles and time) from the place where Jesus was killed and rose again? **2.** In view of the type of fishing they are doing (all night, using nets), do you think Peter's statement in verse 3 is an indication of just wanting something to do, or a return to his old business? **3.** Compare this story with Luke 5:1-11. Why do you think Jesus might repeat this type of miracle now? What effect would it especially have on Peter? What does Peter's response tell you about this effect? **4.** Where did Jesus get the fish in verse 9? How would you feel when you saw them if you had been fishing with the disciples all night? How does his preparing them breakfast reinforce what he did for them in 13:1-17?

REFLECT: 1. Where do you go to get away from it all? How does God meet you there? **2.** What does God use to get your attention and get through to you when he needs to reestablish contact: A crow-bar? A sledge hammer? A good night of rest? A serendipity?

OPEN: 1. Have you ever been kicked off the team or out of school? Why? **2.** What were your chores around the house when you were a kid? How did your parents deal with you when the chores were not done?

DIG: 1. Why do you think Jesus repeated the same question and charge to Peter three times? How is Peter supposed to demonstrate his love and loyalty to Jesus now? In light of 10:15, what would Jesus' shepherd image mean to Peter? **2.** What does Jesus mean by his prediction in verse 18? How would you feel if you knew you were going to one day face a torturous death? Why did he ask right away about John? **3.** What does Jesus' response to Peter in verse 22 show regarding what Jesus feels is critical? How is this linked with verses 15-17?

Jesus and the Miraculous Catch of Fish

21 Afterward Jesus appeared again to his disciples, by the Sea of Tiberias.[g] It happened this way: [2]Simon Peter, Thomas (called Didymus), Nathanael from Cana in Galilee, the sons of Zebedee, and two other disciples were together. [3]"I'm going out to fish," Simon Peter told them, and they said, "We'll go with you." So they went out and got into the boat, but that night they caught nothing.

[4]Early in the morning, Jesus stood on the shore, but the disciples did not realize that it was Jesus.

[5]He called out to them, "Friends, haven't you any fish?"

"No," they answered.

[6]He said, "Throw your net on the right side of the boat and you will find some." When they did, they were unable to haul the net in because of the large number of fish.

[7]Then the disciple whom Jesus loved said to Peter, "It is the Lord!" As soon as Simon Peter heard him say, "It is the Lord," he wrapped his outer garment around him (for he had taken it off) and jumped into the water. [8]The other disciples followed in the boat, towing the net full of fish, for they were not far from shore, about a hundred yards.[h] [9]When they landed, they saw a fire of burning coals there with fish on it, and some bread.

[10]Jesus said to them, "Bring some of the fish you have just caught."

[11]Simon Peter climbed aboard and dragged the net ashore. It was full of large fish, 153, but even with so many the net was not torn. [12]Jesus said to them, "Come and have breakfast." None of the disciples dared ask him, "Who are you?" They knew it was the Lord. [13]Jesus came, took the bread and gave it to them, and did the same with the fish. [14]This was now the third time Jesus appeared to his disciples after he was raised from the dead.

Jesus Reinstates Peter

[15]When they had finished eating, Jesus said to Simon Peter, "Simon son of John, do you truly love me more than these?"

"Yes, Lord," he said, "you know that I love you."

Jesus said, "Feed my lambs."

[16]Again Jesus said, "Simon son of John, do you truly love me?"

He answered, "Yes, Lord, you know that I love you."

Jesus said, "Take care of my sheep."

[17]The third time he said to him, "Simon son of John, do you love me?"

Peter was hurt because Jesus asked him the third time, "Do you love me?" He said, "Lord, you know all things; you know that I love you."

---

[g]1 That is, Sea of Galilee   [h]8 Greek|*about two hundred cubits* (about 90 meters)

LOOKING INTO THE SCRIPTURE/20 Minutes. Read John 21:15-25 and discuss.

1. Why do you think John included this story in his gospel?
   a. to explain how Jesus forgave his friend Peter
   b. to explain where Peter got his motivation to spread the Good News
   c. to explain why he lived to a ripe old age when Peter didn't

2. From the previous story, why do you think Peter was back fishing again?
   a. for recreation
   b. it was his livelihood
   c. he was waiting for further instructions
   d. he had given up on his commitment to follow Christ

3. Why did Jesus press Peter three times with the question, "Do you love me unconditionally . . . truly love me unconditionally . . . do you love me (like a brother)?"
   a. he was trying to make a point
   b. to get his attention
   c. to rub it in
   d. to shame him with his past failure

4. If you had been Peter by the end of the third question, how would you have felt?
   a. mad
   b. hurt
   c. humiliated
   d. like a buck private

5. "Feed my lambs . . . Take care of my sheep . . . Feed my sheep." What is Jesus saying here?
   a. your job is to take care of my followers
   b. show me that you love me
   c. keep the movement going
   d. don't blow it again

6. At this point in Peter's life, would you have nominated Peter to be a leader in the church?
   a. absolutely not
   b. maybe, but on probation
   c. I think so, because he learned from his failure
   d. I hope so, because I have done worse

MY OWN STORY/25 Minutes.

1. If you were asked the same question that Jesus asked Peter, how would you respond?
   a. yes—all of the time
   b. yes—most of the time
   c. yes—some of the time
   d. huh?
   e. ask me tomorrow

2. "Take care of my sheep." If Jesus said this to you three times, what would this mean for you now?
   a. get going
   b. I'm counting on you
   c. get your eyes off yourself
   d. consider the whole world
   e. seek first the kingdom of God

3. When you blow it, how do you feel afterwards?
   a. like running away
   b. like returning to familiar surroundings
   c. like trying again
   d. like committing myself even more next time
   e. I chalk it up to experience
   f. doubt—like maybe God is changing my direction because of my failure in one area
   g. angry at myself

4. How do you think God can help you overcome a recent failure in your life?
   a. by sending me friends who've gone through the same thing
   b. by showing where I went wrong so I learn from it
   c. by helping me face the consequences
   d. by just loving me
   e. by giving me a new job to do
   f. he can't do anything

5. In the past few months, where have you seen the most progress in your life?
   a. personal discipline
   b. spiritual development
   c. self-confidence
   d. concern for others
   e. family relationships
   f. moral courage
   g. Bible understanding
   h. openness to God's will
   i. change in priorities
   j. attitude about work/school
   k. ability to relax/unwind
   l. _____

REFLECT: **1.** Why do you think the author included this story in his gospel? **2.** What is the closest you have come to blowing it so badly that you thought God was never going to speak to you again? What did you discover about God in this experience? **3.** When have you compared yourself with someone else and wondered why his or her life was the way it was? What did God teach you in that situation? **4.** Who do you know that needs to feel forgiven by God? What could you do this week to remind this person that God is a God of forgiveness? **5.** If Jesus is able to forgive Peter and to forgive us, how should we act toward those who have wronged us? Who do you know who needs to feel forgiven by you? What will you do today to tell them they are forgiven? **6.** What has been the highpoint in this study for you? Why?

Jesus said, "Feed my sheep. [18]I tell you the truth, when you were younger you dressed yourself and went where you wanted; but when you are old you will stretch out your hands, and someone else will dress you and lead you where you do not want to go." [19]Jesus said this to indicate the kind of death by which Peter would glorify God. Then he said to him, "Follow me!"

[20]Peter turned and saw that the disciple whom Jesus loved was following them. (This was the one who had leaned back against Jesus at the supper and had said, "Lord, who is going to betray you?") [21]When Peter saw him, he asked, "Lord, what about him?"

[22]Jesus answered, "If I want him to remain alive until I return, what is that to you? You must follow me." [23]Because of this, the rumor spread among the brothers that this disciple would not die. But Jesus did not say that he would not die; he only said, "If I want him to remain alive until I return, what is that to you?"

[24]This is the disciple who testifies to these things and who wrote them down. We know that his testimony is true.

[25]Jesus did many other things as well. If every one of them were written down, I suppose that even the whole world would not have room for the books that would be written.

ACTS

INTRODUCTION

Author

Although Luke is nowhere named within Acts as author, there is a strong and ancient tradition that he did, indeed, write this book as a companion piece to the third Gospel.

Little is known of Luke. He is mentioned only three times in the New Testament (Col. 4:14; Philem. 24; 2 Tim. 4:11). From these references, it can be deduced that Luke was a physician, a valued companion of Paul, and a Gentile.

A Physician

Luke's medical background is corroborated by his use of medical terms (especially in his gospel), for example, in recounting the story of the camel and the needle's eye. "For the word needle both Mark and Matthew use the Greek word *raphis,* which is the ordinary word for a tailor's or a household needle. Luke alone uses the word *belone,* which is the technical word for a surgeons' needle" (William Barclay, *The Acts of the Apostles,* p. XIV).

Paul's Companion

Luke's role as Paul's traveling companion is evident in the Book of Acts. In the four so-called *we* sections, the author suddenly switches from saying "They did this" to "We did that" (Acts 16:10-17; 20: 5-6; 21:1-18; 27:1-28:16). At these points in Paul's journeys, Luke joined him as a colleague in ministry.

A Gentile

We learn that Luke was a Gentile from the list of greetings with which Paul concludes Colossians. First Paul records the greetings sent by "the only Jews among my fellow workers" (Col. 4:10-11). Then in verse 12 he begins a second set of greetings presumably from the Gentiles in the party. Luke's name is included in this latter list.

Characteristics

The Book of Acts is the bridge between the Gospels and the Epistles. It is no accident that modern Bibles are arranged with the life of Jesus on one side of Acts and the correspondence of the apostles on the other. This is because, on the one hand, Acts completes the story of Jesus. It shows how his life, death, and resurrection brought a whole new community into existence: the church. On the other hand, Acts sets the stage for the correspondence to this church; the letters make up the rest of the New Testament. At many points it would be difficult to get the full sense of what the Epistles are saying without the data found in Acts.

Luke tells the story of the development of the church, not by strictly chronicling every event that occurred as the church spread from Jerusalem to Rome — the sheer volume of the data prevented this — but rather by opening a series of windows that allows us to glimpse important (and representative) developments in its growth.

1. Key Figure—The Holy Spirit

One thing that characterizes the entire story is the work of the Holy Spirit. There is little question in Luke's mind how the church spread: The Holy Spirit did it. So we see the church come into being as a result of the baptism of the Holy Spirit (2:38-41). First as only a handful of disciples, it turned suddenly into a full-fledged movement. We then see the Holy Spirit gently but directly guide the early church (13:2 and 16:7). In fact, the presence of the Holy Spirit signals that a church is authentic and not spurious (19:1-6). Some have suggested that this book ought to have been labeled *The Acts of the Holy Spirit* and not *The Acts of the Apostles!*

2. Leading Roles—Peter and Paul

This latter designation is inaccurate for yet another reason. The whole apostolic band is not really in view here. The Book of Acts is the story of only two apostles — Peter and Paul. Peter's story is told first. In the initial 12 chapters, he is the central figure. But in chapter 13, the spotlight shifts to Paul, and he holds center stage until Acts concludes.

The stories of these two men are not dissimilar. In fact, there are a surprising number of common elements. Both heal cripples (3:1-10; 14:8-12); both have the experience of seeing cures brought about in unusual ways (5:15-16; 19:11-12); both bring people back to life (9:36-42; 20:9-12); both meet a magician (8:9-25; 13:6-12); and both are released from prison as the result of a miracle (12:7; 16:26-28).

The reason for this focus on Peter and on Paul is not hard to guess. They were the key leaders of the two main elements of the early church: Peter was the chief apostle to the Jews, while Paul was the chief apostle to the Gentiles. So in hearing their stories, we hear the story of the unfolding of the whole church.

3. Key Sources

Where did Luke get his information about the growth of the church? The source of the second half of the book (chapters 13-28) is clear. Luke got this information directly from his friend and companion Paul. We know Luke was actually with Paul during some of this period (the *we* sections), and he may well have kept a journal. We can also guess that during the long days of travel, and during Paul's confinement in prison, the great apostle probably recounted his many adventures to Luke. But what about the first twelve chapters that center around Peter? Here is where Luke's skill as a historian is especially evident. Luke tells us in his prologue to the third Gospel that he "carefully investigated everything from the beginning" (Luke 1:3). How? Probably by talking to many individuals he may have met via Paul. For example, Luke knew Mark. Both men were with Paul when he wrote Colossians (Col. 4:10, 14). From Mark he would have received valuable information about the growth of the church in Jerusalem and about Peter's role in this. (Many feel Mark's gospel reflects Peter's perspective.) And certainly Luke would have listened to the stories about Peter that were repeated in the churches he visited. Finally, he may well have had access to the official records (written and oral) of the key churches mentioned in the first twelve chapters — the church at Jerusalem (from Mark and others); the church at Caesarea (Philip and his daughters entertained Luke and Paul according to Acts 21:8, and Philip was associated with Stephen and the events of Acts 6:1-8:3); and the church at Antioch (many feel Luke's home was Antioch).

4. Keen Historian

Luke's accuracy as a historian was called into question by certain scholars until the archaeological research of Sir William Ramsay demonstrated Luke's exact and detailed knowledge of the political and social conditions of the times. For example, although a number of different titles were given to Roman officials, Luke always seems to have got it right. When Paul was in Cyprus (Acts 13:7), Luke tells us a proconsul was in charge, although this was only briefly the case. At Malta (Acts 28:7), the ruler is correctly called the "chief man" or "chief official" *protos*. At Ephesus (Acts 19:35), Luke identifies the official who quieted the crowd as the "city clerk" *grammateus*. In Thessolonica (Acts 17:6), he identifies the leaders as "city officials" *politarches*, even though this was an unusual office with no parallel elsewhere in the Roman Empire and only recently verified by inscriptions. Luke had the mind of a researcher: He was careful and paid attention to details. Thus when reading his story of the early church, we have confidence that what Luke tells us is just what happened.

Theme

Why did Luke write the Book of Acts? One reason must have been his desire to commend Christianity to the Gentile world in general and to the Roman government in particular. Certainly there was much about Christianity that would have appealed to Gentiles. For one thing, Jesus came for all people and not just for his Jewish kinfolk. So one finds in Acts the same universality present in Luke's gospel. The good news about Jesus is not just for Jews but for all people. Not surprisingly, therefore, we find in Acts not only Jews turning to Jesus (three thousand on the Day of Pentecost, Acts 2:41) but also Gentiles. We see Peter (the Apostle to the Jews) welcoming Cornelius, the Roman centurion, into the church. We see Philip preaching to the Samaritans and Jewish believers and evangelizing Gentiles in Antioch. In particular, we find Paul called by Christ to be the Apostle to the Gentiles, setting up churches across the Roman Empire. Finally in Acts 15, there is formal affirmation that Gentiles are accepted in the church of Jesus Christ on equal terms with Jews (they do not first have to become Jewish converts). Acts is an eloquent testimony to the universal appeal of Jesus.

Luke's response to the Roman government is fascinating. He seemed to go out of his way to show that Christians were loyal citizens and not lawbreakers and criminals (18:14; 19:37; 23:29; 25:25). He also took pains to point out that Roman officials had always treated Christians fairly and courteously (13:12; 16:35-40; 18:12-17; 19:31). This was important to state lest Christianity be perceived as a political movement and therefore a threat to the Roman Empire. His writing did, after all, talk about the kingdom and about Jesus as Lord (the imperial title).

However, commending Christianity to Gentiles was probably not Luke's central aim. His main purpose is implicit in 1:8. "But you will receive power when the Holy Spirit comes on you; and you will be my witnesses in Jerusalem, and in all Judea and Samaria, and to the ends of the earth." Luke's aim was to show how, in thirty short years, Christianity had spread from Jerusalem to Rome.

Structure

Luke accomplished his purpose by describing six phases of growth (as charted by C. H. Turner and noted in Barclay, *The Acts of the Apostles*, p. xviii):

1. *The church at Jerusalem* (1:1-6:7). Summary statement: "So the word of God spread. The number of disciples in Jerusalem increased rapidly, and a large number of priests became obedient to the faith" (6:7).
2. *From Jerusalem to Palestine* (6:8-9:31). Summary statement: "Then the church throughout Judea, Galilee and Samaria enjoyed a time of peace . . . it grew in numbers . . ." (9:31).
3. *From Palestine to Antioch, gateway to the Gentile world* (9:32-12:24). Summary statement: "The word of God continued to increase and spread" (12:24).
4. *From Antioch to Asia* (12:25-16:5). Summary statement: "So the churches were strengthened in the faith and grew daily in numbers" (16:5).
5. *From Asia to Europe* (16:6-19:20). Summary statement: "In this way the word of the Lord spread widely and grew in power" (19:20).
6. *From Europe in general to Rome in particular* (19:21-28:31). Summary statement: "Therefore I want you to know that God's salvation has been sent to the Gentiles, and they will listen!" (28:28).

Acts

OPEN: Which book or movie sequel was, for you, as good or better than the original? Which book or movie do you wish would produce a sequel? How would you script that? What part would you cast for yourself?

DIG: 1. How does this sequel pick up where Luke 24:45-53 leaves off? **2.** What do the disciples anticipate is going to happen when they receive the Spirit (v. 6)? What are some major ways their idea of the kingdom differs from his (vv. 7-8)? **3.** As a disciple, how would you feel when you heard this? When you then saw Jesus go into heaven (v. 9)? When you heard the angels' promise (v. 11)? When you recalled the words of Jesus in John 16:5-15?

REFLECT: 1. What proofs do you have of Jesus' resurrection that would make sense to your non-believing friends? **2.** How have you narrowed your view of God's kingdom so that it fits in with your type of people? What can help you break out of this box? **3.** What is your Jerusalem to which you are called to bear witness? In what ways do you sense a need for the Spirit to help you do so?

OPEN: When your family has to make a major decision, how do you usually go about it?

DIG: 1. Who is present in this meeting? From Mark 3:20-21, 31-35 and John 7:1-5, how do you account for this change in Jesus' "family"? **2.** In light of Peter's denial of Jesus, how might the others feel about his leadership? How might John 21:15-19 calm any fears they have? **3.** Given verses 6-8, how would you be praying if you were in this group? What emotions would you feel? **4.** What is the role of Scripture, prayer, discussion, qualifications and trust in God regarding the process for choosing a replacement for Judas?

REFLECT: 1. What have been your best experiences in group prayer? How might joining in prayer with others around a common mission that is way beyond your natural ability enhance your own prayer life? How does verse 8 provide that for you? **2.** How does the pattern of decision-making here compare with

Jesus Taken Up Into Heaven

1 In my former book, Theophilus, I wrote about all that Jesus began to do and to teach [2]until the day he was taken up to heaven, after giving instructions through the Holy Spirit to the apostles he had chosen. [3]After his suffering, he showed himself to these men and gave many convincing proofs that he was alive. He appeared to them over a period of forty days and spoke about the kingdom of God. [4]On one occasion, while he was eating with them, he gave them this command: "Do not leave Jerusalem, but wait for the gift my Father promised, which you have heard me speak about. [5]For John baptized with[a] water, but in a few days you will be baptized with the Holy Spirit."

[6]So when they met together, they asked him, "Lord, are you at this time going to restore the kingdom to Israel?"

[7]He said to them: "It is not for you to know the times or dates the Father has set by his own authority. [8]But you will receive power when the Holy Spirit comes on you; and you will be my witnesses in Jerusalem, and in all Judea and Samaria, and to the ends of the earth."

[9]After he said this, he was taken up before their very eyes, and a cloud hid him from their sight.

[10]They were looking intently up into the sky as he was going, when suddenly two men dressed in white stood beside them. [11]"Men of Galilee," they said, "why do you stand here looking into the sky? This same Jesus, who has been taken from you into heaven, will come back in the same way you have seen him go into heaven."

Matthias Chosen to Replace Judas

[12]Then they returned to Jerusalem from the hill called the Mount of Olives, a Sabbath day's walk[b] from the city. [13]When they arrived, they went upstairs to the room where they were staying. Those present were Peter, John, James and Andrew; Philip and Thomas, Bartholomew and Matthew; James son of Alphaeus and Simon the Zealot, and Judas son of James. [14]They all joined together constantly in prayer, along with the women and Mary the mother of Jesus, and with his brothers.

[15]In those days Peter stood up among the believers[c] (a group numbering about a hundred and twenty) [16]and said, "Brothers, the Scripture had to be fulfilled which the Holy Spirit spoke long ago through the mouth of David concerning Judas, who served as guide for those who arrested Jesus— [17]he was one of our number and shared in this ministry."

[18](With the reward he got for his wickedness, Judas bought a field; there he fell headlong, his body burst open and all his intestines spilled out. [19]Everyone in Jerusalem heard about this, so they called that field in their language Akeldama, that is, Field of Blood.)

[a]5 Or *in*   [b]12 That is, about 3/4 mile (about 1,100 meters)   [c]15 Greek *brothers*

[20]"For," said Peter, "it is written in the book of Psalms,

" 'May his place be deserted;
let there be no one to dwell in it,'[d]

and,

" 'May another take his place of leadership.'[e]

[21]Therefore it is necessary to choose one of the men who have been with us the whole time the Lord Jesus went in and out among us, [22]beginning from John's baptism to the time when Jesus was taken up from us. For one of these must become a witness with us of his resurrection."

[23]So they proposed two men: Joseph called Barsabbas (also known as Justus) and Matthias. [24]Then they prayed, "Lord, you know everyone's heart. Show us which of these two you have chosen [25]to take over this apostolic ministry, which Judas left to go where he belongs." [26]Then they cast lots, and the lot fell to Matthias; so he was added to the eleven apostles.

The Holy Spirit Comes at Pentecost

2 When the day of Pentecost came, they were all together in one place. [2]Suddenly a sound like the blowing of a violent wind came from heaven and filled the whole house where they were sitting. [3]They saw what seemed to be tongues of fire that separated and came to rest on each of them. [4]All of them were filled with the Holy Spirit and began to speak in other tongues[f] as the Spirit enabled them.

[5]Now there were staying in Jerusalem God-fearing Jews from every nation under heaven. [6]When they heard this sound, a crowd came together in bewilderment, because each one heard them speaking in his own language. [7]Utterly amazed, they asked: "Are not all these men who are speaking Galileans? [8]Then how is it that each of us hears them in his own native language? [9]Parthians, Medes and Elamites; residents of Mesopotamia, Judea and Cappadocia, Pontus and Asia, [10]Phrygia and Pamphylia, Egypt and the parts of Libya near Cyrene; visitors from Rome [11](both Jews and converts to Judaism); Cretans and Arabs—we hear them declaring the wonders of God in our own tongues!" [12]Amazed and perplexed, they asked one another, "What does this mean?"

[13]Some, however, made fun of them and said, "They have had too much wine.[g]"

Peter Addresses the Crowd

[14]Then Peter stood up with the Eleven, raised his voice and addressed the crowd: "Fellow Jews and all of you who live in Jerusalem, let me explain this to you; listen carefully to what I say. [15]These men are not drunk, as you suppose. It's only nine in the morning! [16]No, this is what was spoken by the prophet Joel:

---

[d]20 Psalm 69:25   [e]20 Psalm 109:8   [f]4 Or *languages*; also in verse 11
[g]13 Or *sweet wine*

how you make important decisions? Which of the ingredients listed here do you need to utilize more?

OPEN: In school, were foreign languages easy or hard for you? Why?

DIG: 1. Given that Pentecost was quite the harvest festival (Dt. 16:9-10), why does God choose this day to give the Holy Spirit? If you had been in that room, what would you have seen, heard and felt? **2.** Using a Bible map and a contemporary map, from how far away are these pilgrims in verses 9 -11? What attracts this crowd to the disciples? **3.** Looking at 1:8, how is that promise already beginning to be fulfilled here? **4.** If you were one of the crowd, would you respond more like those in verse 12, or those in verse 13? Why?

REFLECT: 1. When have you experienced an empowering from God to witness about Christ? **2.** What do you think was God's part and Jesus' followers part in this event? What will you do this week to be better prepared for God's use?

OPEN: What's the largest crowd you've ever spoken to? How did you feel just before you spoke? How well did you do?

DIG: 1. Compare Peter and the other disciples in John 18:25-27 and 20:19 with their actions here: What accounts for the great difference? **2.** How do you see Luke 24:44-49 reflected in this sermon? Given the audience, why would Peter use so many quotes from the Old Testament? **3.** What is the major point Peter wants the people to understand about what is happening (vv. 13, 17, 19)? Since the prophets often used dramatic figurative language to indicate God was going to deal with his people in a new way, how does verse 21 sum up the "new way" that Peter says is now? **4.** How familiar were these people with the events of Jesus' life? How might they be dealing with the rumors of the empty tomb? Given that, why does Peter emphasize the resurrection (vv. 24, 31, 32)? **5.** What are the implications of the resurrection and ascension for Jesus (vv. 24, 30-31, 33-36)? For the people? What would it mean to the people that Jesus is a spiritual king far greater than their greatest earthly king ever was? How might this account for their reaction in verse 37? **6.** If you were to use Peter's answer (vv. 38-40) to their question to explain to someone what it means to become a Christian, what would you say? What is required? What is promised? **7.** Remembering that these 3,000 included people visiting from the places mentioned in verses 8-11, how do you see Acts 1:8 partially fulfilled even here? What news will the people be bringing home with them?

REFLECT: **1.** When was the last time you seized an opportunity to witness for Jesus? What happened? Who stood with you at that time? What impresses you most about Peter in this section: His courage? His knowledge? Or what? **2.** How are you like Peter? Unlike him? What encourages you as you watch Peter? Why? **3.** From Peter's sermon, what facts about Jesus would be important for non-believers to understand? **4.** What difference does it make to you that Jesus really is the reigning King over all? How does that truth impact your daily life? **5.** When did you make your initial commitment to Christ? Who was influential in that process? What convinced you of your need for him? **6.** To repent and be baptized in Jesus name meant to turn away from all other loyalties and affirm allegiance to Jesus: In what ways does that call still present a challenge to you? How have you experienced the reality of God's promises to those who answer that call? **7.** Looking over chapter 2, what was the apostles part and God's part in this witnessing situation? How does that encourage you as you seek to be a witness for Christ?

17" 'In the last days, God says,
  I will pour out my Spirit on all people.
Your sons and daughters will prophesy,
  your young men will see visions,
  your old men will dream dreams.
18Even on my servants, both men and women,
  I will pour out my Spirit in those days,
  and they will prophesy.
19I will show wonders in the heaven above
  and signs on the earth below,
  blood and fire and billows of smoke.
20The sun will be turned to darkness
  and the moon to blood
  before the coming of the great and glorious day of the
    Lord.
21And everyone who calls
  on the name of the Lord will be saved.ʰ

22"Men of Israel, listen to this: Jesus of Nazareth was a man accredited by God to you by miracles, wonders and signs, which God did among you through him, as you yourselves know. 23This man was handed over to you by God's set purpose and foreknowledge; and you, with the help of wicked men,ⁱ put him to death by nailing him to the cross. 24But God raised him from the dead, freeing him from the agony of death, because it was impossible for death to keep its hold on him. 25David said about him:

  " 'I saw the Lord always before me.
  Because he is at my right hand,
    I will not be shaken.
26Therefore my heart is glad and my tongue rejoices;
  my body also will live in hope,
27because you will not abandon me to the grave,
  nor will you let your Holy One see decay.
28You have made known to me the paths of life;
  you will fill me with joy in your presence.'ʲ

29"Brothers, I can tell you confidently that the patriarch David died and was buried, and his tomb is here to this day. 30But he was a prophet and knew that God had promised him on oath that he would place one of his descendants on his throne. 31Seeing what was ahead, he spoke of the resurrection of the Christ,ᵏ that he was not abandoned to the grave, nor did his body see decay. 32God has raised this Jesus to life, and we are all witnesses of the fact. 33Exalted to the right hand of God, he has received from the Father the promised Holy Spirit and has poured out what you now see and hear. 34For David did not ascend to heaven, and yet he said,

  " 'The Lord said to my Lord:
  "Sit at my right hand

_h21_ Joel 2:28-32   _i23_ Or _of those not having the law_ (that is, Gentiles)
_j28_ Psalm 16:8-11   _k31_ Or _Messiah._ "The Christ" (Greek) and "the Messiah" (Hebrew) both mean "the Anointed One"; also in verse 36.

³⁵until I make your enemies
a footstool for your feet." '¹

³⁶"Therefore let all Israel be assured of this: God has made this Jesus, whom you crucified, both Lord and Christ."

³⁷When the people heard this, they were cut to the heart and said to Peter and the other apostles, "Brothers, what shall we do?"

³⁸Peter replied, "Repent and be baptized, every one of you, in the name of Jesus Christ for the forgiveness of your sins. And you will receive the gift of the Holy Spirit. ³⁹The promise is for you and your children and for all who are far off—for all whom the Lord our God will call."

⁴⁰With many other words he warned them; and he pleaded with them, "Save yourselves from this corrupt generation." ⁴¹Those who accepted his message were baptized, and about three thousand were added to their number that day.

The Fellowship of the Believers

⁴²They devoted themselves to the apostles' teaching and to the fellowship, to the breaking of bread and to prayer. ⁴³Everyone was filled with awe, and many wonders and miraculous signs were done by the apostles. ⁴⁴All the believers were together and had everything in common. ⁴⁵Selling their possessions and goods, they gave to anyone as he had need. ⁴⁶Every day they continued to meet together in the temple courts. They broke bread in their homes and ate together with glad and sincere hearts, ⁴⁷praising God and enjoying the favor of all the people. And the Lord added to their number daily those who were being saved.

Peter Heals the Crippled Beggar

3 One day Peter and John were going up to the temple at the time of prayer—at three in the afternoon. ²Now a man crippled from birth was being carried to the temple gate called Beautiful, where he was put every day to beg from those going into the temple courts. ³When he saw Peter and John about to enter, he asked them for money. ⁴Peter looked straight at him, as did John. Then Peter said, "Look at us!" ⁵So the man gave them his attention, expecting to get something from them.

⁶Then Peter said, "Silver or gold I do not have, but what I have I give you. In the name of Jesus Christ of Nazareth, walk." ⁷Taking him by the right hand, he helped him up, and instantly the man's feet and ankles became strong. ⁸He jumped to his feet and began to walk. Then he went with them into the temple courts, walking and jumping, and praising God. ⁹When all the people saw him walking and praising God, ¹⁰they recognized him as the same man who used to sit begging at the temple gate called Beautiful, and they were filled with wonder and amazement at what had happened to him.

OPEN: What would you have to change in your church if 3,000 new converts suddenly showed up next Sunday?

REFLECT: How is your church fellowship similar to and different from the fellowship described in these verses? How does this make you feel? What could you do to help your church be more like this? How will this example affect how you pray for your church?

OPEN: When was the last time you jumped for joy? What happened?

DIG: 1. Put yourself in the place of the cripple: What would you write in your diary as a description of a typical day in your life? How do you feel about yourself? **2.** When Peter first spoke to you and surprised you by grabbing your hand, what thoughts would race through your mind? **3.** Describe or role-play what verses 8-10 must have looked like. What do you as the ex-cripple write in your diary that night? **4.** From 2:19, 22, 43 and this story, what do you think was the purpose of signs and miracles at this time?

REFLECT: 1. How has Jesus brought healing to some crippled area of your life? How has that changed you? **2.** In Peter's stiuation, would you do the same thing as Peter did and believe God to work miraculously through you? Or would you ask John for a dime? Why? What might increase your trust in God to work in and through you?

¹⁵ Psalm 110:1

Peter Speaks to the Onlookers

[11] While the beggar held on to Peter and John, all the people were astonished and came running to them in the place called Solomon's Colonnade. [12] When Peter saw this, he said to them: "Men of Israel, why does this surprise you? Why do you stare at us as if by our own power or godliness we had made this man walk? [13] The God of Abraham, Isaac and Jacob, the God of our fathers, has glorified his servant Jesus. You handed him over to be killed, and you disowned him before Pilate, though he had decided to let him go. [14] You disowned the Holy and Righteous One and asked that a murderer be released to you. [15] You killed the author of life, but God raised him from the dead. We are witnesses of this. [16] By faith in the name of Jesus, this man whom you see and know was made strong. It is Jesus' name and the faith that comes through him that has given this complete healing to him, as you can all see.

[17] "Now, brothers, I know that you acted in ignorance, as did your leaders. [18] But this is how God fulfilled what he had foretold through all the prophets, saying that his Christ[m] would suffer. [19] Repent, then, and turn to God, so that your sins may be wiped out, that times of refreshing may come from the Lord, [20] and that he may send the Christ, who has been appointed for you—even Jesus. [21] He must remain in heaven until the time comes for God to restore everything, as he promised long ago through his holy prophets. [22] For Moses said, 'The Lord your God will raise up for you a prophet like me from among your own people; you must listen to everything he tells you. [23] Anyone who does not listen to him will be completely cut off from among his people.'[n]

[24] "Indeed, all the prophets from Samuel on, as many as have spoken, have foretold these days. [25] And you are heirs of the prophets and of the covenant God made with your fathers. He said to Abraham, 'Through your offspring all peoples on earth will be blessed.'[o] [26] When God raised up his servant, he sent him first to you to bless you by turning each of you from your wicked ways."

Peter and John Before the Sanhedrin

4 The priests and the captain of the temple guard and the Sadducees came up to Peter and John while they were speaking to the people. [2] They were greatly disturbed because the apostles were teaching the people and proclaiming in Jesus the resurrection of the dead. [3] They seized Peter and John, and because it was evening, they put them in jail until the next day. [4] But many who heard the message believed, and the number of men grew to about five thousand.

[5] The next day the rulers, elders and teachers of the law met in Jerusalem. [6] Annas the high priest was there, and so were Caiaphas, John, Alexander and the other men of the high priest's family. [7] They had Peter and John brought before them and began to question them: "By what power or what name did you do this?"

[m]18 Or *Messiah*; also in verse 20   [n]23 Deut. 18:15,18,19   [o]25 Gen. 22:18; 26:4

8Then Peter, filled with the Holy Spirit, said to them: "Rulers and elders of the people! 9If we are being called to account today for an act of kindness shown to a cripple and are asked how he was healed, 10then know this, you and all the people of Israel: It is by the name of Jesus Christ of Nazareth, whom you crucified but whom God raised from the dead, that this man stands before you healed. 11He is

" 'the stone you builders rejected,
which has become the capstone.' *q*

12Salvation is found in no one else, for there is no other name under heaven given to men by which we must be saved."

13When they saw the courage of Peter and John and realized that they were unschooled, ordinary men, they were astonished and they took note that these men had been with Jesus. 14But since they could see the man who had been healed standing there with them, there was nothing they could say. 15So they ordered them to withdraw from the Sanhedrin and then conferred together. 16"What are we going to do with these men?" they asked. "Everybody living in Jerusalem knows they have done an outstanding miracle, and we cannot deny it. 17But to stop this thing from spreading any further among the people, we must warn these men to speak no longer to anyone in this name."

18Then they called them in again and commanded them not to speak or teach at all in the name of Jesus. 19But Peter and John replied, "Judge for yourselves whether it is right in God's sight to obey you rather than God. 20For we cannot help speaking about what we have seen and heard."

21After further threats they let them go. They could not decide how to punish them, because all the people were praising God for what had happened. 22For the man who was miraculously healed was over forty years old.

The Believers' Prayer

23On their release, Peter and John went back to their own people and reported all that the chief priests and elders had said to them. 24When they heard this, they raised their voices together in prayer to God. "Sovereign Lord," they said, "you made the heaven and the earth and the sea, and everything in them. 25You spoke by the Holy Spirit through the mouth of your servant, our father David:

" 'Why do the nations rage
and the peoples plot in vain?
26The kings of the earth take their stand
and the rulers gather together
against the Lord
and against his Anointed One.' *'*

27Indeed Herod and Pontius Pilate met together with the Gentiles and the people' of Israel in this city to conspire against your holy servant Jesus, whom you anointed. 28They did what your

---

3. If you were one of the authorities, what would be your reaction to Peter's bold answer? What does it mean here that Peter was filled with the Holy Spirit (vv. 18-12)? How does that compare with the purpose of filling in 2:4? How does this scene play out what Jesus said in Luke 21:12-15? **4.** How is the response of the leaders similar to their response in the incident with Lazarus (see John 11:45-53; 12:10-11)? Why are they continuing to respond like this? What does it say about them?

REFLECT: 1. What was the most persecution you have ever experienced because of your faith? What did you do? **2.** On a scale of 1 (low) to 10 (high), how sure are you of Peter's statement in verse 12? What has built your assurance the most? What doubts still linger? **3.** How has knowing Jesus shaped your character so that people might notice you had "been with Jesus"? **4.** When, if ever, do you feel Peter's response to his political and religious leaders might be appropriate for a Christian today? How do you reconcile this passage with Romans 13:1-4? **5.** What examples show religious systems actually block people from God?

OPEN: What was the first experience of sincere, heart-felt prayer you can recall? What happened?

DIG: 1. Given how the Sanhedrin (4:15-17) and the disciples each respond to problems, what does that reveal about their view of themselves? Of God? **2.** Why might the disciples begin the prayer by recalling God's sovereignty (vv. 24-28)? **3.** Compare 2:23, 3:17-18 and 4:28. What difference does it make to the disciples that Jesus' death was not simply the plan of his enemies? Why do you think God sometimes uses evil people to fulfill his plans? **4.** How might Acts 1:8 be shaping the disciples' prayer in verses 29-30? **5.** What seems to be one major purpose of the Spirit's filling (see 2:4, 4:8, 31)?

REFLECT: 1. How are your prayers in crisis times similar to and different from this prayer? What benefit might it be in those times to recall God's character and actions in his-

---

p11 Or cornerstone   q11 Psalm 118:22   r26 That is, Christ or Messiah
s26 Psalm 2:1,2   t27 The Greek is plural.

tory? **2.** In times of trouble, do you respond more like the Sanhedrin (trying to figure out for yourself what to do)? Or like the disciples (coming to God in earnest prayer)? What would help your trust in God to increase in those times?

DIG: Compare verses 32-35 with 2:42-47. What strikes you about the church in Acts? How well would you fit into it?

REFLECT: 1. If you were to describe your church, which of the phrases here could you use to do so? Which ones would not fit now? Why? **2.** How well does verse 32 fit your relationship with others in your church? What would have to change in you for such sharing to be more possible?

OPEN: 1. Growing up, what religious practices did you do just because everybody else did it that way? **2.** When have you been a pall bearer?

DIG: 1. Were Ananias and Sapphira required to sell the land and lay all the money at the apostles feet? Why or why not? What was their sin? **2.** What would Ananias and Sapphira gain by lying about the money they received? How is your answer related to verses 32-37? **3.** Given that we all do bad things, why do you think God punished Ananias and Sapphira so severely? How might great fear be useful to God's plan at this point?

REFLECT: 1. If you had been one of the young men who buried Ananias and Sapphira, how do you think you would have felt? Why? **2.** When have you been like Ananias and Sapphira and tried to fool God? What happened? What did you learn in that situation? How did God discipline you? How has your life changed since then? **3.** How have you experienced the fear of the Lord? What has been its influence in your life since then?

DIG: 1. How would you describe this church from what is mentioned here? **2.** How might the incident in 5:1-11 cause merely curious people not to join with the believers? What words would describe how outsiders might look upon the church?

power and will had decided beforehand should happen. ²⁹Now, Lord, consider their threats and enable your servants to speak your word with great boldness. ³⁰Stretch out your hand to heal and perform miraculous signs and wonders through the name of your holy servant Jesus."

³¹After they prayed, the place where they were meeting was shaken. And they were all filled with the Holy Spirit and spoke the word of God boldly.

The Believers Share Their Possessions

³²All the believers were one in heart and mind. No one claimed that any of his possessions was his own, but they shared everything they had. ³³With great power the apostles continued to testify to the resurrection of the Lord Jesus, and much grace was upon them all. ³⁴There were no needy persons among them. For from time to time those who owned lands or houses sold them, brought the money from the sales ³⁵and put it at the apostles' feet, and it was distributed to anyone as he had need.

³⁶Joseph, a Levite from Cyprus, whom the apostles called Barnabas (which means Son of Encouragement), ³⁷sold a field he owned and brought the money and put it at the apostles' feet.

Ananias and Sapphira

5 Now a man named Ananias, together with his wife Sapphira, also sold a piece of property. ²With his wife's full knowledge he kept back part of the money for himself, but brought the rest and put it at the apostles' feet.

³Then Peter said, "Ananias, how is it that Satan has so filled your heart that you have lied to the Holy Spirit and have kept for yourself some of the money you received for the land? ⁴Didn't it belong to you before it was sold? And after it was sold, wasn't the money at your disposal? What made you think of doing such a thing? You have not lied to men but to God."

⁵When Ananias heard this, he fell down and died. And great fear seized all who heard what had happened. ⁶Then the young men came forward, wrapped up his body, and carried him out and buried him.

⁷About three hours later his wife came in, not knowing what had happened. ⁸Peter asked her, "Tell me, is this the price you and Ananias got for the land?"

"Yes," she said, "that is the price."

⁹Peter said to her, "How could you agree to test the Spirit of the Lord? Look! The feet of the men who buried your husband are at the door, and they will carry you out also."

¹⁰At that moment she fell down at his feet and died. Then the young men came in and, finding her dead, carried her out and buried her beside her husband. ¹¹Great fear seized the whole church and all who heard about these events.

The Apostles Heal Many

¹²The apostles performed many miraculous signs and wonders among the people. And all the believers used to meet together in Solomon's Colonnade. ¹³No one else dared join them, even though they were highly regarded by the people.

[14]Nevertheless, more and more men and women believed in the Lord and were added to their number. [15]As a result, people brought the sick into the streets and laid them on beds and mats so that at least Peter's shadow might fall on some of them as he passed by. [16]Crowds gathered also from the towns around Jerusalem, bringing their sick and those tormented by evil[u] spirits, and all of them were healed.

The Apostles Persecuted

[17]Then the high priest and all his associates, who were members of the party of the Sadducees, were filled with jealousy. [18]They arrested the apostles and put them in the public jail. [19]But during the night an angel of the Lord opened the doors of the jail and brought them out. [20]"Go, stand in the temple courts," he said, "and tell the people the full message of this new life."

[21]At daybreak they entered the temple courts, as they had been told, and began to teach the people.

When the high priest and his associates arrived, they called together the Sanhedrin—the full assembly of the elders of Israel—and sent to the jail for the apostles. [22]But on arriving at the jail, the officers did not find them there. So they went back and reported, [23]"We found the jail securely locked, with the guards standing at the doors; but when we opened them, we found no one inside." [24]On hearing this report, the captain of the temple guard and the chief priests were puzzled, wondering what would come of this.

[25]Then someone came and said, "Look! The men you put in jail are standing in the temple courts teaching the people." [26]At that, the captain went with his officers and brought the apostles. They did not use force, because they feared that the people would stone them.

[27]Having brought the apostles, they made them appear before the Sanhedrin to be questioned by the high priest. [28]"We gave you strict orders not to teach in this name," he said. "Yet you have filled Jerusalem with your teaching and are determined to make us guilty of this man's blood."

[29]Peter and the other apostles replied: "We must obey God rather than men! [30]The God of our fathers raised Jesus from the dead—whom you had killed by hanging him on a tree. [31]God exalted him to his own right hand as Prince and Savior that he might give repentance and forgiveness of sins to Israel. [32]We are witnesses of these things, and so is the Holy Spirit, whom God has given to those who obey him."

[33]When they heard this, they were furious and wanted to put them to death. [34]But a Pharisee named Gamaliel, a teacher of the law, who was honored by all the people, stood up in the Sanhedrin and ordered that the men be put outside for a little while. [35]Then he addressed them: "Men of Israel, consider carefully what you intend to do to these men. [36]Some time ago Theudas appeared, claiming to be somebody, and about four hundred men rallied to him. He was killed, all his followers were dis-

[u]16 Greek unclean

REFLECT: To what extent is your church seen by others as a place for healing to occur? What could help that to be more true?

OPEN: 1. What was the most intimidating group of people you ever had to face? What happened? 2. If you were in jail, depending on your own wits to get out, what ruses would you try?

DIG: 1. How do you account for the jealousy of the Sadducees? 2. How would you, as an apostle, feel during the events described in verses 18-21? What might you expect to happen next? 3. Cast people in your group to be the high priest, an officer (v. 22), the captain, and the "someone" of verse 25. Have each role play the scene described in verses 21-26 (everyone else plays the role of the full assembly). What are the leaders feeling as the events proceed? 4. Of what do they accuse the apostles in verse 28? How is this different from what bothered them in 4:2? How could they miss the impact of these miracles? 5. What things in Peter's response would rouse their fury? In light of 4:1-12, why is Peter being so direct? How might what happened in 5:19-20 encourage him? 6. Prior to Jesus' coming, there were many Jewish zealots who led rebellions against Rome: What is Gamaliel's point in recalling two such leaders? Do you think Gamaliel might be one of the secret believers mentioned in John 12:42? Or a political opportunist not wanting to rouse the public? Why? How do you think Peter's statement in verse 29 (and 4:19) may have influenced Gamaliel? 7. Flogging was a severe punishment which sometimes resulted in death. How would you respond to such treatment if you were an apostle? How would you respond if, when God freed you from jail, that only led to more severe punishment? What does the actual response of the apostles show about them? How do you think the Sanhedrin feels realizing its threats and punishments have not worked? 8. In sum, what things motivate the Sanhedrin? The church?

REFLECT: 1. How do you think you would feel if you were sent to jail for what you believe? How would your family feel? 2. What would this do to your life? What kind of disgrace have you suffered because you follow Jesus? Whom do you know who has been persecuted for his or her faith? What have you learned from their persecution? **3.** How have you experienced God setting you free so you can honor him more fully? **4.** What is the ultimate authority in your life? When does this create problems for you? What can you do to overcome these problems? **5.** When have you rejoiced in suffering? How does this relate to your ultimate authority? **6.** How do you account for the fact that sometimes God does deliver you out of hardships, but at other times he allows you to go through them?

OPEN: What are some things an ideal pastor should be able to do?

DIG: 1. Given 2:44-45 and 4:32, how do you account for the problem described in 6:1? **2.** How do the apostles show that they view this as a serious problem? Why would the church decide to choose Greek-speaking Jews to fill all seven slots? **3.** Looking at 6:7, 5:42, 4:32-35, and 2:42-47, how would you sum up what has happened in Acts so far? How does this relate to 1:8?

REFLECT: 1. What roles does your church expect your pastor(s) to perform? How might your pastor(s) be relieved of some of those duties in order to teach, preach and pray? **2.** What is the most pressing problem facing your church? How might the principles described here help the church in dealing with it?

OPEN: What was the worst lie anyone ever told about you? What made it the worst? Why do you think this person lied about you? How do you feel about this person today?

DIG: 1. Given verses 8 and 10, what do you think Stephen must have been like? What would you expect in a person described like this? **2.** Immigrant Jews often formed their own synagogues in Jerusalem: What is significant about their opposition to Stephen? How is it like and unlike the opposition the apostles received from the Sanhedrin (5:27-28)? **3.** Look at John 2:13-21 and 5:21-24. How might these teachings of Jesus form the background for the accusations against Stephen in verses 13-14?

persed, and it all came to nothing. [37]After him, Judas the Galilean appeared in the days of the census and led a band of people in revolt. He too was killed, and all his followers were scattered. [38]Therefore, in the present case I advise you: Leave these men alone! Let them go! For if their purpose or activity is of human origin, it will fail. [39]But if it is from God, you will not be able to stop these men; you will only find yourselves fighting against God."

[40]His speech persuaded them. They called the apostles in and had them flogged. Then they ordered them not to speak in the name of Jesus, and let them go.

[41]The apostles left the Sanhedrin, rejoicing because they had been counted worthy of suffering disgrace for the Name. [42]Day after day, in the temple courts and from house to house, they never stopped teaching and proclaiming the good news that Jesus is the Christ. [v]

The Choosing of the Seven

6 In those days when the number of disciples was increasing, the Grecian Jews among them complained against the Hebraic Jews because their widows were being overlooked in the daily distribution of food. [2]So the Twelve gathered all the disciples together and said, "It would not be right for us to neglect the ministry of the word of God in order to wait on tables. [3]Brothers, choose seven men from among you who are known to be full of the Spirit and wisdom. We will turn this responsibility over to them [4]and will give our attention to prayer and the ministry of the word."

[5]This proposal pleased the whole group. They chose Stephen, a man full of faith and of the Holy Spirit; also Philip, Procorus, Nicanor, Timon, Parmenas, and Nicolas from Antioch, a convert to Judaism. [6]They presented these men to the apostles, who prayed and laid their hands on them.

[7]So the word of God spread. The number of disciples in Jerusalem increased rapidly, and a large number of priests became obedient to the faith.

Stephen Seized

[8]Now Stephen, a man full of God's grace and power, did great wonders and miraculous signs among the people. [9]Opposition arose, however, from members of the Synagogue of the Freedmen (as it was called)—Jews of Cyrene and Alexandria as well as the provinces of Cilicia and Asia. These men began to argue with Stephen, [10]but they could not stand up against his wisdom or the Spirit by whom he spoke.

[11]Then they secretly persuaded some men to say, "We have heard Stephen speak words of blasphemy against Moses and against God."

[12]So they stirred up the people and the elders and the teachers of the law. They seized Stephen and brought him before the Sanhedrin. [13]They produced false witnesses, who testified, "This fellow never stops speaking against this holy place and

[v]42 Or Messiah   [w]3 Gen. 12:1   [x]7 Gen. 15:13,14

against the law. [14]For we have heard him say that this Jesus of Nazareth will destroy this place and change the customs Moses handed down to us."

[15]All who were sitting in the Sanhedrin looked intently at Stephen, and they saw that his face was like the face of an angel.

Stephen's Speech to the Sanhedrin

7 Then the high priest asked him, "Are these charges true?" [2]To this he replied: "Brothers and fathers, listen to me! The God of glory appeared to our father Abraham while he was still in Mesopotamia, before he lived in Haran. [3]'Leave your country and your people,' God said, 'and go to the land I will show you.' [w]

[4]"So he left the land of the Chaldeans and settled in Haran. After the death of his father, God sent him to this land where you are now living. [5]He gave him no inheritance here, not even a foot of ground. But God promised him that he and his descendants after him would possess the land, even though at that time Abraham had no child. [6]God spoke to him in this way: 'Your descendants will be strangers in a country not their own, and they will be enslaved and mistreated four hundred years. [7]But I will punish the nation they serve as slaves,' God said, 'and afterward they will come out of that country and worship me in this place.' [x] [8]Then he gave Abraham the covenant of circumcision. And Abraham became the father of Isaac and circumcised him eight days after his birth. Later Isaac became the father of Jacob, and Jacob became the father of the twelve patriarchs.

[9]"Because the patriarchs were jealous of Joseph, they sold him as a slave into Egypt. But God was with him [10]and rescued him from all his troubles. He gave Joseph wisdom and enabled him to gain the goodwill of Pharaoh king of Egypt; so he made him ruler over Egypt and all his palace.

[11]"Then a famine struck all Egypt and Canaan, bringing great suffering, and our fathers could not find food. [12]When Jacob heard that there was grain in Egypt, he sent our fathers on their first visit. [13]On their second visit, Joseph told his brothers who he was, and Pharaoh learned about Joseph's family. [14]After this, Joseph sent for his father Jacob and his whole family, seventy-five in all. [15]Then Jacob went down to Egypt, where he and our fathers died. [16]Their bodies were brought back to Shechem and placed in the tomb that Abraham had bought from the sons of Hamor at Shechem for a certain sum of money.

[17]"As the time drew near for God to fulfill his promise to Abraham, the number of our people in Egypt greatly increased. [18]Then another king, who knew nothing about Joseph, became ruler of Egypt. [19]He dealt treacherously with our people and oppressed our forefathers by forcing them to throw out their newborn babies so that they would die.

[20]"At that time Moses was born, and he was no ordinary child. [y] For three months he was cared for in his father's house. [21]When he was placed outside, Pharaoh's daughter took him and brought him up as her own son. [22]Moses was educated in all the wisdom of the Egyptians and was powerful in speech and action.

y20 Or was fair in the sight of God

REFLECT: What two or three adjectives best describe your spiritual life? What would have to be different for you to be reorganized as "full of grace and power?

OPEN: As a child, who was the best storyteller you ever heard? What made that person so effective?

DIG: 1. From 6:13-14, how would you write up the formal charges against Stephen? **2.** Why does Stephen reply to the high priest's question by a history lesson? What would this show about his respect for the law? **3.** Why does Stephen spend the bulk of his history lesson talking about Moses? What parallels does he make between Moses and Jesus? How does this relate to the charges against him in 6:13-14? How does his quote in verse 37 begin to turn the tables on his accusers regarding who really is rejecting Moses? **4.** From verses 44-50, what is his point about the temple and God's presence? How is he turning the tables against his accusers once again? **5.** Look at Deuteronomy 10:16 and 30:4. What does Stephen mean by the phrase "uncircumcised hearts and ears"? Especially in the context of Deuteronomy 10, what is Stephen really saying by his use of this phrase about the Sanhedrin's regard for Moses and the law? **6.** Of what does he accuse them in verses 51-53? What does his charge show about why he gave them this history lesson? **7.** Considering this situation, what type of person is Stephen?

REFLECT: 1. Would you say that the Old Testament is more like a stranger, or a close friend, to you? How does this speech show the importance of the Old Testament to the early Christians? What will you do to let its importance grow for you? **2.** Since the Sanhedrin knew their history every bit as much as Stephen, how do you account for their radically different response to Jesus? What is needed in your life besides knowledge to really understand Jesus? **3.** When Jesus was brought to trial, he was basically quiet before the Sanhedrin, yet Stephen spoke very boldly. How do you decide when to speak and when to be quiet before opposition? **4.** In what ways could the charges Stephen makes against the leaders be made against you? How has resistance to God been shown in your life this week? How will you begin to bow to him in that area now? **5.** In what ways do people hold on to religious rituals and heroes today, while missing the whole point of what those ceremonies and people represent? How does this tendency affect you?

23"When Moses was forty years old, he decided to visit his fellow Israelites. 24He saw one of them being mistreated by an Egyptian, so he went to his defense and avenged him by killing the Egyptian. 25Moses thought that his own people would realize that God was using him to rescue them, but they did not. 26The next day Moses came upon two Israelites who were fighting. He tried to reconcile them by saying, 'Men, you are brothers; why do you want to hurt each other?'

27"But the man who was mistreating the other pushed Moses aside and said, 'Who made you ruler and judge over us? 28Do you want to kill me as you killed the Egyptian yesterday?'ᵃ 29When Moses heard this, he fled to Midian, where he settled as a foreigner and had two sons.

30"After forty years had passed, an angel appeared to Moses in the flames of a burning bush in the desert near Mount Sinai. 31When he saw this, he was amazed at the sight. As he went over to look more closely, he heard the Lord's voice: 32'I am the God of your fathers, the God of Abraham, Isaac and Jacob.'ᵃ Moses trembled with fear and did not dare to look.

33"Then the Lord said to him, 'Take off your sandals; the place where you are standing is holy ground. 34I have indeed seen the oppression of my people in Egypt. I have heard their groaning and have come down to set them free. Now come, I will send you back to Egypt.'ᵇ

35"This is the same Moses whom they had rejected with the words, 'Who made you ruler and judge?' He was sent to be their ruler and deliverer by God himself, through the angel who appeared to him in the bush. 36He led them out of Egypt and did wonders and miraculous signs in Egypt, at the Red Seaᶜ and for forty years in the desert.

37This is that Moses who told the Israelites, 'God will send you a prophet like me from your own people.'ᵈ 38He was in the assembly in the desert, with the angel who spoke to him on Mount Sinai, and with our fathers; and he received living words to pass on to us.

39"But our fathers refused to obey him. Instead, they rejected him and in their hearts turned back to Egypt. 40They told Aaron, 'Make us gods who will go before us. As for this fellow Moses who led us out of Egypt—we don't know what has happened to him!'ᵉ 41That was the time they made an idol in the form of a calf. They brought sacrifices to it and held a celebration in honor of what their hands had made. 42But God turned away and gave them over to the worship of the heavenly bodies. This agrees with what is written in the book of the prophets:

" 'Did you bring me sacrifices and offerings
    forty years in the desert, O house of Israel?
43You have lifted up the shrine of Molech
    and the star of your god Rephan,
    the idols you made to worship.
Therefore I will send you into exile'ᶠ beyond Babylon.

ᵃ28 Exodus 2:14   ᵃ32 Exodus 3:6   ᵇ34 Exodus 3:5,7,8,10
ᶜ36 That is, Sea of Reeds   ᵈ37 Deut. 18:15   ᵉ40 Exodus 32:1
ᶠ43 Amos 5:25-27

44"Our forefathers had the tabernacle of the Testimony with them in the desert. It had been made as God directed Moses, according to the pattern he had seen. 45Having received the tabernacle, our fathers under Joshua brought it with them when they took the land from the nations God drove out before them. It remained in the land until the time of David, 46who enjoyed God's favor and asked that he might provide a dwelling place for the God of Jacob.ᵍ 47But it was Solomon who built the house for him.

48"However, the Most High does not live in houses made by men. As the prophet says:

49" 'Heaven is my throne,
　　and the earth is my footstool.
What kind of house will you build for me?
　　　　　　　　　　　　　　says the Lord.
　　Or where will my resting place be?
50Has not my hand made all these things?'ʰ

51"You stiff-necked people, with uncircumcised hearts and ears! You are just like your fathers: You always resist the Holy Spirit! 52Was there ever a prophet your fathers did not persecute? They even killed those who predicted the coming of the Righteous One. And now you have betrayed and murdered him— 53you who have received the law that was put into effect through angels but have not obeyed it."

The Stoning of Stephen

54When they heard this, they were furious and gnashed their teeth at him. 55But Stephen, full of the Holy Spirit, looked up to heaven and saw the glory of God, and Jesus standing at the right hand of God. 56"Look," he said, "I see heaven open and the Son of Man standing at the right hand of God."

57At this they covered their ears and, yelling at the top of their voices, they all rushed at him, 58dragged him out of the city and began to stone him. Meanwhile, the witnesses laid their clothes at the feet of a young man named Saul.

59While they were stoning him, Stephen prayed, "Lord Jesus, receive my spirit." 60Then he fell on his knees and cried out, "Lord, do not hold this sin against them." When he had said this, he fell asleep.

8 And Saul was there, giving approval to his death.

The Church Persecuted and Scattered

On that day a great persecution broke out against the church at Jerusalem, and all except the apostles were scattered throughout Judea and Samaria. 2Godly men buried Stephen and mourned deeply for him. 3But Saul began to destroy the church. Going from house to house, he dragged off men and women and put them in prison.

OPEN: What would be your last words before you die? Be brief!

DIG: 1. Why are Stephen's listeners so enraged (see Dan. 7:13-14)? **2.** Stephen's death was probably illegal (see John 18:31). What does that reveal about the desperation of the Sanhedrin?

REFLECT: 1. How could Stephen face such persecution with a forgiving heart? How does Stephen's "secret" encourage you? **2.** Peter's strong speech in Acts 2 led to mass conversion, while Stephen's speech led to his death. What does that fact teach you about how we are to evaluate success in our service to God?

OPEN: If all the Christians in your community were suddenly subject to arrest, what would happen in your church?

DIG: Look at Acts 8:1. How is this an example of God using the evil people for his plan? How is it similar to 2:23 and 3:15-18?

REFLECT: What is the worst thing that ever happened to you? Can you see now how God has used it for good in your life?

ᵍ46 Some early manuscripts *the house of Jacob*　ʰ50 Isaiah 66:1,2

OPEN: What do you do for attention?

DIG: 1. How does Philip gain the crowd's attention? How does persecution (8:1-3) spread joy (v. 8)? **2.** As this event marks the beginning of phase two in God's master plan (1:8), how would you sum up the "Jerusalem phase" (chapters 2-7)?

OPEN: Who is the most powerful personality you know? What type of influence does she or he have on you?

DIG: 1. What do Simon and Philip have in common (vv. 9- 11)? How are they different? How has the crowd responded to both men in the past (see v. 6)? **2.** Given that the Samaritans were considered as outcasts and heretics by the Jews (see John 4:9 and 19-22), why would Peter and John come to them? **3.** In light of the Jewish-Samaritan division, why might the Father delay pouring out his Spirit until Peter and John were on the scene? Do you think this was more of a lesson for the Samaritans or the apostles? Why? **4.** In what ways does Simon's reaction to the apostles in verses 18-19 show his deep misunderstanding about the gospel? **5.** Do you think that Simon's words in verse 24 reveal a change in his heart? Why or why not?

REFLECT: 1. What was your primary motivation in receiving Jesus Christ as Savior? What's your primary motivation for continuing in the faith? **2.** Has your personal influence declined or increased since you became a Christian? How? Why? **3.** What cultural or ethnic prejudices were you brought up with? How is the gospel breaking through those prejudices in your life? **4.** How has jealousy of other Christians gotten in the way of your faith?

OPEN: For you, what "funny thing happened on the way to _____"?

DIG: 1. How does 2:11 account for the eunich's visit to Jerusalem? **2.** The eunich was reading Isaiah 53. Read that passage and note all the ways Jesus fits the picture of the one described there. If you were Philip using Isaiah 53, what would you emphasize about the gospel? **3.** Make a list of the things God did

Philip in Samaria

⁴Those who had been scattered preached the word wherever they went. ⁵Philip went down to a city in Samaria and proclaimed the Christ¹ there. ⁶When the crowds heard Philip and saw the miraculous signs he did, they all paid close attention to what he said. ⁷With shrieks, evilʲ spirits came out of many, and many paralytics and cripples were healed. ⁸So there was great joy in that city.

Simon the Sorcerer

⁹Now for some time a man named Simon had practiced sorcery in the city and amazed all the people of Samaria. He boasted that he was someone great, ¹⁰and all the people, both high and low, gave him their attention and exclaimed, "This man is the divine power known as the Great Power." ¹¹They followed him because he had amazed them for a long time with his magic. ¹²But when they believed Philip as he preached the good news of the kingdom of God and the name of Jesus Christ, they were baptized, both men and women. ¹³Simon himself believed and was baptized. And he followed Philip everywhere, astonished by the great signs and miracles he saw.

¹⁴When the apostles in Jerusalem heard that Samaria had accepted the word of God, they sent Peter and John to them. ¹⁵When they arrived, they prayed for them that they might receive the Holy Spirit, ¹⁶because the Holy Spirit had not yet come upon any of them; they had simply been baptized intoᵏ the name of the Lord Jesus. ¹⁷Then Peter and John placed their hands on them, and they received the Holy Spirit.

¹⁸When Simon saw that the Spirit was given at the laying on of the apostles' hands, he offered them money ¹⁹and said, "Give me also this ability so that everyone on whom I lay my hands may receive the Holy Spirit."

²⁰Peter answered: "May your money perish with you, because you thought you could buy the gift of God with money! ²¹You have no part or share in this ministry, because your heart is not right before God. ²²Repent of this wickedness and pray to the Lord. Perhaps he will forgive you for having such a thought in your heart. ²³For I see that you are full of bitterness and captive to sin."

²⁴Then Simon answered, "Pray to the Lord for me so that nothing you have said may happen to me."

²⁵When they had testified and proclaimed the word of the Lord, Peter and John returned to Jerusalem, preaching the gospel in many Samaritan villages.

Philip and the Ethiopian

²⁶Now an angel of the Lord said to Philip, "Go south to the road—the desert road—that goes down from Jerusalem to Gaza." ²⁷So he started out, and on his way he met an Ethiopianˡ eunuch, an important official in charge of all the treasury of Candace, queen of the Ethiopians. This man had gone to Jerusa-

ⁱ5 Or *Messiah* ʲ7 Greek *unclean* ᵏ16 Or *in* ˡ27 That is, from the upper Nile region

lem to worship, [28]and on his way home was sitting in his chariot reading the book of Isaiah the prophet. [29]The Spirit told Philip, "Go to that chariot and stay near it."

[30]Then Philip ran up to the chariot and heard the man reading Isaiah the prophet. "Do you understand what you are reading?" Philip asked.

[31]"How can I," he said, "unless someone explains it to me?" So he invited Philip to come up and sit with him.

[32]The eunuch was reading this passage of Scripture:

"He was led like a sheep to the slaughter,
and as a lamb before the shearer is silent,
so he did not open his mouth.
[33]In his humiliation he was deprived of justice.
Who can speak of his descendants?
For his life was taken from the earth." [m]

[34]The eunuch asked Philip, "Tell me, please, who is the prophet talking about, himself or someone else?" [35]Then Philip began with that very passage of Scripture and told him the good news about Jesus.

[36]As they traveled along the road, they came to some water and the eunuch said, "Look, here is water. Why shouldn't I be baptized?" [n] [38]And he gave orders to stop the chariot. Then both Philip and the eunuch went down into the water and Philip baptized him. [39]When they came up out of the water, the Spirit of the Lord suddenly took Philip away, and the eunuch did not see him again, but went on his way rejoicing. [40]Philip, however, appeared at Azotus and traveled about, preaching the gospel in all the towns until he reached Caesarea.

Saul's Conversion

9 Meanwhile, Saul was still breathing out murderous threats against the Lord's disciples. He went to the high priest [2]and asked him for letters to the synagogues in Damascus, so that if he found any there who belonged to the Way, whether men or women, he might take them as prisoners to Jerusalem. [3]As he neared Damascus on his journey, suddenly a light from heaven flashed around him. [4]He fell to the ground and heard a voice say to him, "Saul, Saul, why do you persecute me?"

[5]"Who are you, Lord?" Saul asked.

"I am Jesus, whom you are persecuting," he replied. [6]"Now get up and go into the city, and you will be told what you must do."

[7]The men traveling with Saul stood there speechless; they heard the sound but did not see anyone. [8]Saul got up from the ground, but when he opened his eyes he could see nothing. So they led him by the hand into Damascus. [9]For three days he was blind, and did not eat or drink anything.

[10]In Damascus there was a disciple named Ananias. The Lord called to him in a vision, "Ananias!"

"Yes, Lord," he answered.

---

in this passage to prepare the way for his message. What is the relationship between this preparation and human initiative in this story? What does this teach you about how God operates through people? **4.** What is the significance of this story in light of the fact that the church is being persecuted in Jerusalem? **5.** From what you have seen in chapter 8, what has been the effect of Stephen's death upon Philip? Upon the church as a whole?

REFLECT: 1. What has been your "Gaza Road"—a place where you shared the good news in an unusual way? **2.** From this story, as well as Acts 3:6-16 and 2:5-14, how does God set up opportunities to witness? How can this awareness free you from fears in evangelism? What do these stories show about the context in which evangelism is to happen? **3.** Deep down, do you really feel successful, important people need the gospel as much as poor beggars (3:2)? Why or why not? **4.** Had you been Philip, would you know the Bible well enough to speak directly to the eunuch's questions? How will you grow in your understanding of the faith so you might be prepared for surprise opportunities?

OPEN: As a child, of whom were you most afraid? Why?

DIG: 1. Saul traveled 150 miles to Damascus in order to expand what started as a local persecution against believers in Jerusalem (8:1)? What does that tell you about Saul? **2.** Saul's former teacher was Gamaliel (see Acts 22:8). What had Gamaliel advised the Sanhedrin regarding Christians in 5:34-39? How is Saul responding to this advise? What does this show about Saul? **3.** Describe what happened in verses 3-9 from the viewpoint of one of Saul's companions. **4.** How do you think Saul felt when confronted by Jesus (vv. 4-6)? What might he be thinking about during those three days of blindness in light of his previous activities? **5.** How would you feel in Ananias' place? Since Jesus had already appeared to Saul directly, why this time would he want a person to go to Saul? What is significant about the way Ananias addresses Saul? Saul becomes famous again: Why did God involve him at all?

---

[m]33 Isaiah 53:7,8 [n]36 Some late manuscripts *baptized?" [37]Philip said, "If you believe with all your heart, you may." The eunuch answered, "I believe that Jesus Christ is the Son of God."*

REFLECT: 1. How did the Lord first get your attention? Was it in some dramatic way like this or a quieter, more natural form? 2. What types of people do you assume are beyond God's reach so that, if God spoke to you about them, you would question him? How does this story challenge these assumptions? 3. When have you, like Annanias, obeyed the Lord even when you had doubts about it? What happened? 4. Who has played the role of Ananias in your life? To whom does the Lord want you to play that role?

[11]The Lord told him, "Go to the house of Judas on Straight Street and ask for a man from Tarsus named Saul, for he is praying. [12]In a vision he has seen a man named Ananias come and place his hands on him to restore his sight."

[13]"Lord," Ananias answered, "I have heard many reports about this man and all the harm he has done to your saints in Jerusalem. [14]And he has come here with authority from the chief priests to arrest all who call on your name."

[15]But the Lord said to Ananias, "Go! This man is my chosen instrument to carry my name before the Gentiles and their kings and before the people of Israel. [16]I will show him how much he must suffer for my name."

[17]Then Ananias went to the house and entered it. Placing his hands on Saul, he said, "Brother Saul, the Lord—Jesus, who appeared to you on the road as you were coming here—has sent me so that you may see again and be filled with the Holy Spirit." [18]Immediately, something like scales fell from Saul's eyes, and he could see again. He got up and was baptized, [19]and after taking some food, he regained his strength.

Saul in Damascus and Jerusalem

Saul spent several days with the disciples in Damascus. [20]At once he began to preach in the synagogues that Jesus is the Son of God. [21]All those who heard him were astonished and asked, "Isn't he the man who raised havoc in Jerusalem among those who call on this name? And hasn't he come here to take them as prisoners to the chief priests?" [22]Yet Saul grew more and more powerful and baffled the Jews living in Damascus by proving that Jesus is the Christ.[o]

OPEN: If you knew that all doors of this building were being guarded by people wanting to kill you, how would you try to sneak out of here?

DIG: 1. If you were a member of one of the synagogues who knew why Saul had come to Damascus, what would you expect him to say when he came to your synagogue? Describe your reaction as he proceeds to preach for Christ. How would you account for the change? 2. The events of verses 23-28 probably occurred about 2-3 years after Saul's conversion (see Gal 1:15-18). How has the Lord totally changed things for Saul during this time? 3. Given 8:3 and 9:1, why might the Jerusalem disciples still be afraid of Saul? What risk is Barnabas taking? 4. Compare 9:29 with 7:9-10 and 8:1. How have things come around full circle for Saul? Why would both the people in Damascus and Jerusalem want to kill him? What does that show about Saul? Given what happened after Stephen angered the Jews in Jerusalem (8:1), why might the disciples have sent Paul 400 miles away to his home town? 5. How is the story of Saul related to 1:8? What do you think Acts will be about from here on?

REFLECT: 1. What changes has knowing Jesus brought into your life? How have other people responded? 2. Who has been a Barnabas to you? How? To whom have you served as a Barnabas?

[23]After many days had gone by, the Jews conspired to kill him, [24]but Saul learned of their plan. Day and night they kept close watch on the city gates in order to kill him. [25]But his followers took him by night and lowered him in a basket through an opening in the wall.

[26]When he came to Jerusalem, he tried to join the disciples, but they were all afraid of him, not believing that he really was a disciple. [27]But Barnabas took him and brought him to the apostles. He told them how Saul on his journey had seen the Lord and that the Lord had spoken to him, and how in Damascus he had preached fearlessly in the name of Jesus. [28]So Saul stayed with them and moved about freely in Jerusalem, speaking boldly in the name of the Lord. [29]He talked and debated with the Grecian Jews, but they tried to kill him. [30]When the brothers learned of this, they took him down to Caesarea and sent him off to Tarsus.

[31]Then the church throughout Judea, Galilee and Samaria enjoyed a time of peace. It was strengthened; and encouraged by the Holy Spirit, it grew in numbers, living in the fear of the Lord.

[o]22 Or Messiah

Aeneas and Dorcas

³²As Peter traveled about the country, he went to visit the saints in Lydda. ³³There he found a man named Aeneas, a paralytic who had been bedridden for eight years. ³⁴"Aeneas," Peter said to him, "Jesus Christ heals you. Get up and take care of your mat." Immediately Aeneas got up. ³⁵All those who lived in Lydda and Sharon saw him and turned to the Lord.

³⁶In Joppa there was a disciple named Tabitha (which, when translated, is Dorcas*p*), who was always doing good and helping the poor. ³⁷About that time she became sick and died, and her body was washed and placed in an upstairs room. ³⁸Lydda was near Joppa; so when the disciples heard that Peter was in Lydda, they sent two men to him and urged him, "Please come at once!"

³⁹Peter went with them, and when he arrived he was taken upstairs to the room. All the widows stood around him, crying and showing him the robes and other clothing that Dorcas had made while she was still with them.

⁴⁰Peter sent them all out of the room; then he got down on his knees and prayed. Turning toward the dead woman, he said, "Tabitha, get up." She opened her eyes, and seeing Peter she sat up. ⁴¹He took her by the hand and helped her to her feet. Then he called the believers and the widows and presented her to them alive. ⁴²This became known all over Joppa, and many people believed in the Lord. ⁴³Peter stayed in Joppa for some time with a tanner named Simon.

Cornelius Calls for Peter

10 At Caesarea there was a man named Cornelius, a centurion in what was known as the Italian Regiment. ²He and all his family were devout and God-fearing; he gave generously to those in need and prayed to God regularly. ³One day at about three in the afternoon he had a vision. He distinctly saw an angel of God, who came to him and said, "Cornelius!"

⁴Cornelius stared at him in fear. "What is it, Lord?" he asked.

The angel answered, "Your prayers and gifts to the poor have come up as a memorial offering before God. ⁵Now send men to Joppa to bring back a man named Simon who is called Peter. ⁶He is staying with Simon the tanner, whose house is by the sea."

⁷When the angel who spoke to him had gone, Cornelius called two of his servants and a devout soldier who was one of his attendants. ⁸He told them everything that had happened and sent them to Joppa.

Peter's Vision

⁹About noon the following day as they were on their journey and approaching the city, Peter went up on the roof to pray. ¹⁰He became hungry and wanted something to eat, and while the meal was being prepared, he fell into a trance. ¹¹He saw heaven opened and something like a large sheet being let down to earth by its four corners. ¹²It contained all kinds of four-footed ani-

*p*36 Both *Tabitha* (Aramaic) and *Dorcas* (Greek) mean *gazelle*.

OPEN: What example can you give of how quickly gossip spreads in your community?

DIG: What do verses 35, 41-42, 5:12-14, 4:30, 2:43 and 2:22 teach about the purpose of these signs and wonders? **3.** Although Peter had healed many people, he had never raised anyone from death. What might he be feeling as he goes to Tabitha's home? Why would he want to be alone during this time? **4.** Which of Jesus' miracles do these two incidents remind you of? How is Peter now like Jesus?

REFLECT: 1. How have you experienced God's healing in your life? What resulted from this healing for you? For others? **2.** How is God stretching your faith these days? In what new areas are you having to trust him more **3.** Why is it that Tabitha could be raised, but Stephen died and was buried, even though Peter was there too (8:2)? How would you explain God's ways to Stephen's widow or mother? How might what happened as a result of Stephen's death and Tabitha's resurrection help you to understand?

OPEN: If you were in the army now, of what would you daydream?

DIG: 1. Since Cornelius is part of an occupying army, what is especially unusual about him? About his encounter with God? **2.** What might the three men talk about along their 30-mile trek to Joppa?

REFLECT: 1. How would verse 2 serve as a description of your spiritual life? If someone had to evaluate your spiritual life by how you treated others this week, what would they say? **2.** What type of memorial offering does your lifestyle present before God?

OPEN: What is the strangest dream you have had recently?

DIG: 1. Look at Leviticus 11:4-7, 13-19 and 29-30. With these restrictions, how do you think Peter must have felt when he heard the voice telling him to eat these animals? Why was it repeated three times? What would the new principle given in verse 15 mean to him? How does it fit in the context of Cornelius? **2.** What might Peter be feeling when the men sent by Cornelius showed up? 3. How might the example of Jesus in Luke 7:1-10 also encourage Peter to listen to these men?

REFLECT: 1. What are some principles or beliefs you have held on to that God has modified? 2. What new relationships has God given you recently? How has he brought these people into your life? How have you influenced each other?

OPEN: When was the first time you remember encountering prejudice? How did you feel at the time? How did this occurrence affect your life?

DIG: 1. Given Peter's experience in verses 9-23 and what you see of Cornelius here, what do you imagine each man was feeling as they greeted each other? 2. Jews regarded even people like Cornelius as pagans unless they fully submitted to Jewish practices (see 11:3). Knowing that, what would verse 28 have meant for Peter? For Cornelius? How do verses 28, 34-35 and 43 show why the story of Cornelius is so important in Acts? 3. What is the main point in Peter's sermon? How does that compare with his sermon in 2:36-39 and 3:17-23? From these three sermons, what do you see as central to the gospel message? 4. In light of the astonished reaction of the Jews (v. 45), what was the purpose of these Gentiles speaking in tongues? How does this reinforce the private vision of Peter in 10:9-23?

REFLECT: 1. Using this story, how would you respond to the question: "Can people who have never heard the gospel be saved"? If your answer is "yes", why then did God send Peter to preach (see also 11:14)? If it is "no", how do you explain verses 34-35? 2. Against what types of people do you feel pre-

mals, as well as reptiles of the earth and birds of the air. 13Then a voice told him, "Get up, Peter. Kill and eat."

14"Surely not, Lord!" Peter replied. "I have never eaten anything impure or unclean."

15The voice spoke to him a second time, "Do not call anything impure that God has made clean."

16This happened three times, and immediately the sheet was taken back to heaven.

17While Peter was wondering about the meaning of the vision, the men sent by Cornelius found out where Simon's house was and stopped at the gate. 18They called out, asking if Simon who was known as Peter was staying there.

19While Peter was still thinking about the vision, the Spirit said to him, "Simon, three*q* men are looking for you. 20So get up and go downstairs. Do not hesitate to go with them, for I have sent them."

21Peter went down and said to the men, "I'm the one you're looking for. Why have you come?"

22The men replied, "We have come from Cornelius the centurion. He is a righteous and God-fearing man, who is respected by all the Jewish people. A holy angel told him to have you come to his house so that he could hear what you have to say." 23Then Peter invited the men into the house to be his guests.

Peter at Cornelius' House

The next day Peter started out with them, and some of the brothers from Joppa went along. 24The following day he arrived in Caesarea. Cornelius was expecting them and had called together his relatives and close friends. 25As Peter entered the house, Cornelius met him and fell at his feet in reverence. 26But Peter made him get up. "Stand up," he said, "I am only a man myself."

27Talking with him, Peter went inside and found a large gathering of people. 28He said to them: "You are well aware that it is against our law for a Jew to associate with a Gentile or visit him. But God has shown me that I should not call any man impure or unclean. 29So when I was sent for, I came without raising any objection. May I ask why you sent for me?"

30Cornelius answered: "Four days ago I was in my house praying at this hour, at three in the afternoon. Suddenly a man in shining clothes stood before me 31and said, 'Cornelius, God has heard your prayer and remembered your gifts to the poor. 32Send to Joppa for Simon who is called Peter. He is a guest in the home of Simon the tanner, who lives by the sea.' 33So I sent for you immediately, and it was good of you to come. Now we are all here in the presence of God to listen to everything the Lord has commanded you to tell us."

34Then Peter began to speak: "I now realize how true it is that God does not show favoritism 35but accepts men from every nation who fear him and do what is right. 36You know the message God sent to the people of Israel, telling the good news of peace through Jesus Christ, who is Lord of all. 37You know

q19 One early manuscript *two*; other manuscripts do not have the number.

what has happened throughout Judea, beginning in Galilee after the baptism that John preached— [38]how God anointed Jesus of Nazareth with the Holy Spirit and power, and how he went around doing good and healing all who were under the power of the devil, because God was with him.

[39]"We are witnesses of everything he did in the country of the Jews and in Jerusalem. They killed him by hanging him on a tree, [40]but God raised him from the dead on the third day and caused him to be seen. [41]He was not seen by all the people, but by witnesses whom God had already chosen—by us who ate and drank with him after he rose from the dead. [42]He commanded us to preach to the people and to testify that he is the one whom God appointed as judge of the living and the dead. [43]All the prophets testify about him that everyone who believes in him receives forgiveness of sins through his name."

[44]While Peter was still speaking these words, the Holy Spirit came on all who heard the message. [45]The circumcised believers who had come with Peter were astonished that the gift of the Holy Spirit had been poured out even on the Gentiles. [46]For they heard them speaking in tongues[r] and praising God.

Then Peter said, [47]"Can anyone keep these people from being baptized with water? They have received the Holy Spirit just as we have." [48]So he ordered that they be baptized in the name of Jesus Christ. Then they asked Peter to stay with them for a few days.

Peter Explains His Actions

11 The apostles and the brothers throughout Judea heard that the Gentiles also had received the word of God. [2]So when Peter went up to Jerusalem, the circumcised believers criticized him [3]and said, "You went into the house of uncircumcised men and ate with them."

[4]Peter began and explained everything to them precisely as it had happened: [5]"I was in the city of Joppa praying, and in a trance I saw a vision. I saw something like a large sheet being let down from heaven by its four corners, and it came down to where I was. [6]I looked into it and saw four-footed animals of the earth, wild beasts, reptiles, and birds of the air. [7]Then I heard a voice telling me, 'Get up, Peter. Kill and eat.'

[8]"I replied, 'Surely not, Lord! Nothing impure or unclean has ever entered my mouth.'

[9]"The voice spoke from heaven a second time, 'Do not call anything impure that God has made clean.' [10]This happened three times, and then it was all pulled up to heaven again.

[11]"Right then three men who had been sent to me from Caesarea stopped at the house where I was staying. [12]The Spirit told me to have no hesitation about going with them. These six brothers also went with me, and we entered the man's house. [13]He told us how he had seen an angel appear in his house and say, 'Send to Joppa for Simon who is called Peter. [14]He will bring you a message through which you and all your household will be saved.'

[r]46 Or *other languages*

juduced? How has that developed? What evidence is there that the lesson of Peter's vision has broken through to you with respect to these people? **3.** Consider the make-up of your community and of your church. Are there some types of people (ethnically, socially, politically, age-wise, etc.) who would just assume that your church is not for them? Are there some forms or practices you could change to remove those barriers? How would you feel about making those changes?

OPEN: As a teen, what, if anything, turned you off about the church? Likewise, what turned you on?

DIG: 1. How do the Jewish believers here demonstrate the same error as the apostles did in 1:6? Given 10:14, how do you think Peter would have responded if some other believer had first been sent to the Gentiles? **2.** Why might Luke have taken the time and space to record the events of 10:9-46 all over again? What is he trying to communicate to his readers? **3.** Of what importance is the gift of the Holy Spirit in Peter's argument? Why would this have such a strong effect on the Jerusalem believers? **4.** Why do you think God chose Peter to be the first to go to the Gentiles? Do you think any other disciple would have been as successful in both Caesaria and Jerusalem? Why or why not? **5.** What do you sense is the attitude and tone of voice of Peter's audience in verse 2? How about in verse 18? How does this story open the way for Acts 1:8 to be fulfilled in a new way?

REFLECT: 1. How have you been criticized for breaking the religious traditions of your church? Why did you do so? How have you judged others for doing so? What did you feel was at stake? **2.** Galatians

271

2:11-14 shows that the lesson of 10:34-35 and 11:18 was not easily learned, even by Peter. What might have happened to the Christian mission if the early church denied the new principle (10:15, 28 and 11:9) which God taught Peter? **3.** How might this principle affect how you treat people you find "unacceptable"?

OPEN: What one person has encouraged you most in the faith? How has this built your faith?

DIG: 1. Antioch was the third largest city in the Roman empire. What might the apostles feel as they hear the gospel is taking root there? **2.** From 4:36-37, 9:27-28 and 11:22-26, what would you write about Barnabas if you had to prepare a character reference for him? Considering 9:22 and 28-29, why might Barnabas have decided to recruit Saul for this work? **3.** What do you learn about the nature of the Antioch church when they send aid to the Jerusalem church?

REFLECT: 1. With what people do you rub shoulders that no minister or priest would normally contact? How might you share the gospel with them? **2.** Would these people be comfortable in your church as it now is? Why or why not? How should you address this issue? **3.** Who do you know that is like Barnabas? In what ways would you like to be more like him? **4.** What would you consider to be evidence of the grace of God at work in your life? In your church?

OPEN: When have you had a dream that seemed so real that you wondered afterwards whether the experience might have actually happened? What was it about?

DIG: 1. This Herod is the nephew of the Herod who ruled in Jesus' day. What do you learn about his character in verses 1-3? Why would this action please the Jewish leaders? Why do you think Herod, as a Roman official, would now join in the Jewish opposition to the church? **2.** How might James' death (v. 2) relate to the unbelief of the church (v. 15)? When Rhoda came announcing who was at the door, what would you have said if you were there? **3.** How do you feel about the fact that God saved Peter but not James? In light of John 21:18-19, how might Peter respond

[15]"As I began to speak, the Holy Spirit came on them as he had come on us at the beginning. [16]Then I remembered what the Lord had said: 'John baptized with[s] water, but you will be baptized with the Holy Spirit.' [17]So if God gave them the same gift as he gave us, who believed in the Lord Jesus Christ, who was I to think that I could oppose God?''

[18]When they heard this, they had no further objections and praised God, saying, "So then, God has granted even the Gentiles repentance unto life.''

The Church in Antioch

[19]Now those who had been scattered by the persecution in connection with Stephen traveled as far as Phoenicia, Cyprus and Antioch, telling the message only to Jews. [20]Some of them, however, men from Cyprus and Cyrene, went to Antioch and began to speak to Greeks also, telling them the good news about the Lord Jesus. [21]The Lord's hand was with them, and a great number of people believed and turned to the Lord.

[22]News of this reached the ears of the church at Jerusalem, and they sent Barnabas to Antioch. [23]When he arrived and saw the evidence of the grace of God, he was glad and encouraged them all to remain true to the Lord with all their hearts. [24]He was a good man, full of the Holy Spirit and faith, and a great number of people were brought to the Lord.

[25]Then Barnabas went to Tarsus to look for Saul, [26]and when he found him, he brought him to Antioch. So for a whole year Barnabas and Saul met with the church and taught great numbers of people. The disciples were called Christians first at Antioch.

[27]During this time some prophets came down from Jerusalem to Antioch. [28]One of them, named Agabus, stood up and through the Spirit predicted that a severe famine would spread over the entire Roman world. (This happened during the reign of Claudius.) [29]The disciples, each according to his ability, decided to provide help for the brothers living in Judea. [30]This they did, sending their gift to the elders by Barnabas and Saul.

Peter's Miraculous Escape From Prison

12 It was about this time that King Herod arrested some who belonged to the church, intending to persecute them. [2]He had James, the brother of John, put to death with the sword. [3]When he saw that this pleased the Jews, he proceeded to seize Peter also. This happened during the Feast of Unleavened Bread. [4]After arresting him, he put him in prison, handing him over to be guarded by four squads of four soldiers each. Herod intended to bring him out for public trial after the Passover.

[5]So Peter was kept in prison, but the church was earnestly praying to God for him.

[6]The night before Herod was to bring him to trial, Peter was sleeping between two soldiers, bound with two chains, and sentries stood guard at the entrance. [7]Suddenly an angel of the

[s]16 Or in

Lord appeared and a light shone in the cell. He struck Peter on the side and woke him up. "Quick, get up!" he said, and the chains fell off Peter's wrists.

[8]Then the angel said to him, "Put on your clothes and sandals." And Peter did so. "Wrap your cloak around you and follow me," the angel told him. [9]Peter followed him out of the prison, but he had no idea that what the angel was doing was really happening; he thought he was seeing a vision. [10]They passed the first and second guards and came to the iron gate leading to the city. It opened for them by itself, and they went through it. When they had walked the length of one street, suddenly the angel left him.

[11]Then Peter came to himself and said, "Now I know without a doubt that the Lord sent his angel and rescued me from Herod's clutches and from everything the Jewish people were anticipating."

[12]When this had dawned on him, he went to the house of Mary the mother of John, also called Mark, where many people had gathered and were praying. [13]Peter knocked at the outer entrance, and a servant girl named Rhoda came to answer the door. [14]When she recognized Peter's voice, she was so overjoyed she ran back without opening it and exclaimed, "Peter is at the door!"

[15]"You're out of your mind," they told her. When she kept insisting that it was so, they said, "It must be his angel."

[16]But Peter kept on knocking, and when they opened the door and saw him, they were astonished. [17]Peter motioned with his hand for them to be quiet and described how the Lord had brought him out of prison. "Tell James and the brothers about this," he said, and then he left for another place.

[18]In the morning, there was no small commotion among the soldiers as to what had become of Peter. [19]After Herod had a thorough search made for him and did not find him, he crossexamined the guards and ordered that they be executed.

Herod's Death

Then Herod went from Judea to Caesarea and stayed there a while. [20]He had been quarreling with the people of Tyre and Sidon; they now joined together and sought an audience with him. Having secured the support of Blastus, a trusted personal servant of the king, they asked for peace, because they depended on the king's country for their food supply.

[21]On the appointed day Herod, wearing his royal robes, sat on his throne and delivered a public address to the people. [22]They shouted, "This is the voice of a god, not of a man." [23]Immediately, because Herod did not give praise to God, an angel of the Lord struck him down, and he was eaten by worms and died.

[24]But the word of God continued to increase and spread.

[25]When Barnabas and Saul had finished their mission, they returned from[t] Jerusalem, taking with them John, also called Mark.

to this question? **4.** Who is the James of verse 17 (see Galatians 1:18-19)? Why do you think he is mentioned specifically? What does this tell you about his importance in the Jerusalem church? **5.** Putting yourself in the place of the soldiers (v. 18), what would you say to each other in the morning?

REFLECT: **1.** Who really has power here: Herod or the Lord of the church? What does this tell about how Christians ought to deal with opposition and persecution? **2.** How are you like the people in the prayer meeting in this story? What are some of your prayers that you'd be surprised if God answered affirmatively? **3.** Although Peter was miraculously rescued from prison, he went into hiding to avoid Herod. How does this illustrate an overlap between God's power and human common sense? Do you think Peter showed a lack of faith by leaving Jerusalem? Why or why not?

OPEN: What do you think a person of power should look like?

DIG: **1.** What do you learn here about the contrast between Herod's power and God's? **2.** Josephus, a Jewish historian, dates Herod's sudden death at 44 AD. In the 11 years since the events of Acts 1, what types of persecutions has the church encountered? How far has it expanded? **3.** Since the Jerusalem church is facing intense opposition, what does the return of Saul and Barnabas to Antioch indicate may be the next wave of expansion for the church?

REFLECT: What worldly forces seem all-powerful to you? How does Herod's experience put them into perspective for you?

[t]25 Some manuscripts *to*

OPEN: Could your company afford to lose 40% of its senior staff in one swoop? Could your church? How?

DIG: What was the scene when the Spirit spoke to the leaders at Antioch? How do you think he may have spoken? How could the Spirit speak in your worship times?

OPEN: What name changes have you taken on over the years? What for?

DIG: 1. Cyprus is about a 150-mile sail from Seleucia and was Barnabas' home (4:36). What might these two men be thinking and feeling as they go? **2.** Since Gentiles were already welcome in the church (11:18), why would Barnabas and Saul go to the synagogue? **3.** Put yourself in Elymas' place. Why and how would you oppose these missionaries? If you were Sergius Paulus, what would be your response to the missionaries after the events of verses 9-12? Likewise, if you were the proconsul?

REFLECT: 1. With what types of people do you feel most comfortable talking about the Lord? Why? **2.** When have people tried to turn you from your faith? What happened? How do you deal with such pressures?

OPEN: Of all the great speeches in history—by presidents and popes, mom and dad, your boss and secretary, civil rights activists and the street corner preacher—which one most vividly sticks in your memory? Why? Which one would you sooner forget but can't?

DIG: 1. From Cyprus to Pisidian Antioch is about 350 miles by sea and land. What does their willingness to travel so far show about Paul and Barnabas? Why do you think John (Mark 12:12) may have left them to go back to his home? **2.** Compare verse 15 with verse 5: Why are they using this strategy? **3.** What is significant about Paul's audience? **4.** From verses 17-23, list all the things Paul says God has done. How do God's actions in 17-22 prepare the way for Paul to speak about Jesus in verse 23? **5.** Compare verses 22-23 and 36-37 with Romans 1:3 and Acts 2:29-31: What is the connection between

Barnabas and Saul Sent Off

13 In the church at Antioch there were prophets and teachers: Barnabas, Simeon called Niger, Lucius of Cyrene, Manaen (who had been brought up with Herod the tetrarch) and Saul. [2]While they were worshiping the Lord and fasting, the Holy Spirit said, "Set apart for me Barnabas and Saul for the work to which I have called them." [3]So after they had fasted and prayed, they placed their hands on them and sent them off.

On Cyprus

[4]The two of them, sent on their way by the Holy Spirit, went down to Seleucia and sailed from there to Cyprus. [5]When they arrived at Salamis, they proclaimed the word of God in the Jewish synagogues. John was with them as their helper.

[6]They traveled through the whole island until they came to Paphos. There they met a Jewish sorcerer and false prophet named Bar-Jesus, [7]who was an attendant of the proconsul, Sergius Paulus. The proconsul, an intelligent man, sent for Barnabas and Saul because he wanted to hear the word of God. [8]But Elymas the sorcerer (for that is what his name means) opposed them and tried to turn the proconsul from the faith. [9]Then Saul, who was also called Paul, filled with the Holy Spirit, looked straight at Elymas and said, [10]"You are a child of the devil and an enemy of everything that is right! You are full of all kinds of deceit and trickery. Will you never stop perverting the right ways of the Lord? [11]Now the hand of the Lord is against you. You are going to be blind, and for a time you will be unable to see the light of the sun."

Immediately mist and darkness came over him, and he groped about, seeking someone to lead him by the hand. [12]When the proconsul saw what had happened, he believed, for he was amazed at the teaching about the Lord.

In Pisidian Antioch

[13]From Paphos, Paul and his companions sailed to Perga in Pamphylia, where John left them to return to Jerusalem. [14]From Perga they went on to Pisidian Antioch. On the Sabbath they entered the synagogue and sat down. [15]After the reading from the Law and the Prophets, the synagogue rulers sent word to them, saying, "Brothers, if you have a message of encouragement for the people, please speak."

[16]Standing up, Paul motioned with his hand and said: "Men of Israel and you Gentiles who worship God, listen to me! [17]The God of the people of Israel chose our fathers; he made the people prosper during their stay in Egypt, with mighty power he led them out of that country, [18]he endured their conduct[u] for about forty years in the desert, [19]he overthrew seven nations in Canaan and gave their land to his people as their inheritance. [20]All this took about 450 years.

"After this, God gave them judges until the time of Samuel the prophet. [21]Then the people asked for a king, and he gave them Saul son of Kish, of the tribe of Benjamin, who ruled forty

[u]18 Some manuscripts *and cared for them*

years. ²²After removing Saul, he made David their king. He testified concerning him: 'I have found David son of Jesse a man after my own heart; he will do everything I want him to do.'

²³"From this man's descendants God has brought to Israel the Savior Jesus, as he promised. ²⁴Before the coming of Jesus, John preached repentance and baptism to all the people of Israel. ²⁵As John was completing his work, he said: 'Who do you think I am? I am not that one. No, but he is coming after me, whose sandals I am not worthy to untie.'

²⁶"Brothers, children of Abraham, and you God-fearing Gentiles, it is to us that this message of salvation has been sent. ²⁷The people of Jerusalem and their rulers did not recognize Jesus, yet in condemning him they fulfilled the words of the prophets that are read every Sabbath. ²⁸Though they found no proper ground for a death sentence, they asked Pilate to have him executed. ²⁹When they had carried out all that was written about him, they took him down from the tree and laid him in a tomb. ³⁰But God raised him from the dead, ³¹and for many days he was seen by those who had traveled with him from Galilee to Jerusalem. They are now his witnesses to our people.

³²"We tell you the good news: What God promised our fathers ³³he has fulfilled for us, their children, by raising up Jesus. As it is written in the second Psalm:

" 'You are my Son;
today I have become your Father.'ᵛ ʷ

³⁴The fact that God raised him from the dead, never to decay, is stated in these words:

" 'I will give you the holy and sure blessings promised to David.'ˣ

³⁵So it is stated elsewhere:

" 'You will not let your Holy One see decay.'ʸ

³⁶"For when David had served God's purpose in his own generation, he fell asleep; he was buried with his fathers and his body decayed. ³⁷But the one whom God raised from the dead did not see decay.

³⁸"Therefore, my brothers, I want you to know that through Jesus the forgiveness of sins is proclaimed to you. ³⁹Through him everyone who believes is justified from everything you could not be justified from by the law of Moses. ⁴⁰Take care that what the prophets have said does not happen to you:

⁴¹" 'Look, you scoffers,
wonder and perish,
for I am going to do something in your days
that you would never believe,
even if someone told you.'ᶻ"

⁴²As Paul and Barnabas were leaving the synagogue, the people invited them to speak further about these things on the

David and Jesus? Why is this so important to Paul and Peter? **6.** What things about Jesus is Paul emphasizing by his use of the three quotes in verses 33, 34 and 35? The resurrection is mentioned four times in verses 30-37. How does the resurrection confirm the meaning of these quotes? **7.** In verses 38-39, what does Paul say is the central meaning of the resurrection for his listeners? Compare verse 39 with Romans 3:20-24 and 8:3-4. From these verses, how would you explain what Paul means by being "justified"? **8.** Why would Paul end his sermon with an Old Testament quote warning of judgment? **9.** What feelings and emotions are created by this sermon in the various groups of people mentioned in verses 42-51? How do you account for such variety of responses?

REFLECT: **1.** If you were to emphasize one central truth about the gospel, what would it be? Why? **2.** What difference would it make to your faith if there was no Easter to celebrate but only a Good Friday to remember? **3.** How do you think Paul would respond to a modern-day skeptic who felt Jesus was a noble, but misguided, martyr? What role would the Old Testament play in his answer? How would knowing the Old Testament help you understand your faith better? **4.** What kind of opposition have you faced because of your faith? How do you usually respond to opposition? Does it make you stronger? Why? Would it be tougher for you to face opposition from community leaders or from family members? Why?

---

v33 Or *have begotten you*   w33 Psalm 2:7   x34 Isaiah 55:3   y35 Psalm 16:10   z41 Hab. 1:5

next Sabbath. ⁴³When the congregation was dismissed, many of the Jews and devout converts to Judaism followed Paul and Barnabas, who talked with them and urged them to continue in the grace of God.

⁴⁴On the next Sabbath almost the whole city gathered to hear the word of the Lord. ⁴⁵When the Jews saw the crowds, they were filled with jealousy and talked abusively against what Paul was saying.

⁴⁶Then Paul and Barnabas answered them boldly: "We had to speak the word of God to you first. Since you reject it and do not consider yourselves worthy of eternal life, we now turn to the Gentiles. ⁴⁷For this is what the Lord has commanded us:

" 'I have made youᵃ a light for the Gentiles,
    that youᵃ may bring salvation to the ends of the
        earth.'ᵇ"

⁴⁸When the Gentiles heard this, they were glad and honored the word of the Lord; and all who were appointed for eternal life believed.

⁴⁹The word of the Lord spread through the whole region. ⁵⁰But the Jews incited the God-fearing women of high standing and the leading men of the city. They stirred up persecution against Paul and Barnabas, and expelled them from their region. ⁵¹So they shook the dust from their feet in protest against them and went to Iconium. ⁵²And the disciples were filled with joy and with the Holy Spirit.

In Iconium

14 At Iconium Paul and Barnabas went as usual into the Jewish synagogue. There they spoke so effectively that a great number of Jews and Gentiles believed. ²But the Jews who refused to believe stirred up the Gentiles and poisoned their minds against the brothers. ³So Paul and Barnabas spent considerable time there, speaking boldly for the Lord, who confirmed the message of his grace by enabling them to do miraculous signs and wonders. ⁴The people of the city were divided; some sided with the Jews, others with the apostles. ⁵There was a plot afoot among the Gentiles and Jews, together with their leaders, to mistreat them and stone them. ⁶But they found out about it and fled to the Lycaonian cities of Lystra and Derbe and to the surrounding country, ⁷where they continued to preach the good news.

In Lystra and Derbe

⁸In Lystra there sat a man crippled in his feet, who was lame from birth and had never walked. ⁹He listened to Paul as he was speaking. Paul looked directly at him, saw that he had faith to be healed ¹⁰and called out, "Stand up on your feet!" At that, the man jumped up and began to walk.

¹¹When the crowd saw what Paul had done, they shouted in the Lycaonian language, "The gods have come down to us in human form!" ¹²Barnabas they called Zeus, and Paul they called

OPEN: Have "sticks and stones" ever hurt you? How about "names"?

DIG: 1. How does their experience in Iconium differ from Antioch? How is it similar? **2.** What is the purpose of signs and wonders here (see also 6:8)? Why are the people divided (v. 4)?

REFLECT: 1. How would you feel if you were constantly under siege like Paul and Barnabas? What advice would you have given them as they were run out of town? Why? **2.** When you face difficulties, how do you decide if you should give up, or if you should tough it out?

OPEN: What was one embarrassing case of mistaken identity you can recall making?

DIG: 1. What was religious life like in Lystra? **2.** Compare verses 8-15 with 3:1-2. How are the two stories alike and different? What results from each healing? **3.** What does Paul emphasize about God in his speech? How is his speech to this crowd different from his sermon in the synagogue in 13:17-41? Why? What do these differences teach you about sharing your faith with

ᵃ47 The Greek is singular.   ᵇ47 Isaiah 49:6

Hermes because he was the chief speaker. [13]The priest of Zeus, whose temple was just outside the city, brought bulls and wreaths to the city gates because he and the crowd wanted to offer sacrifices to them.

[14]But when the apostles Barnabas and Paul heard of this, they tore their clothes and rushed out into the crowd, shouting: [15]"Men, why are you doing this? We too are only men, human like you. We are bringing you good news, telling you to turn from these worthless things to the living God, who made heaven and earth and sea and everything in them. [16]In the past, he let all nations go their own way. [17]Yet he has not left himself without testimony: He has shown kindness by giving you rain from heaven and crops in their seasons; he provides you with plenty of food and fills your hearts with joy." [18]Even with these words, they had difficulty keeping the crowd from sacrificing to them.

[19]Then some Jews came from Antioch and Iconium and won the crowd over. They stoned Paul and dragged him outside the city, thinking he was dead. [20]But after the disciples had gathered around him, he got up and went back into the city. The next day he and Barnabas left for Derbe.

The Return to Antioch in Syria

[21]They preached the good news in that city and won a large number of disciples. Then they returned to Lystra, Iconium and Antioch, [22]strengthening the disciples and encouraging them to remain true to the faith. "We must go through many hardships to enter the kingdom of God," they said. [23]Paul and Barnabas appointed elders[c] for them in each church and, with prayer and fasting, committed them to the Lord, in whom they had put their trust. [24]After going through Pisidia, they came into Pamphylia, [25]and when they had preached the word in Perga, they went down to Attalia.

[26]From Attalia they sailed back to Antioch, where they had been committed to the grace of God for the work they had now completed. [27]On arriving there, they gathered the church together and reported all that God had done through them and how he had opened the door of faith to the Gentiles. [28]And they stayed there a long time with the disciples.

The Council at Jerusalem

15 Some men came down from Judea to Antioch and were teaching the brothers: "Unless you are circumcised, according to the custom taught by Moses, you cannot be saved." [2]This brought Paul and Barnabas into sharp dispute and debate with them. So Paul and Barnabas were appointed, along with some other believers, to go up to Jerusalem to see the apostles and elders about this question. [3]The church sent them on their way, and as they traveled through Phoenicia and Samaria, they told how the Gentiles had been converted. This news made all the brothers very glad. [4]When they came to Jerusalem, they were welcomed by the church and the apostles and elders, to

---

c23 Or Barnabas ordained elders; or Barnabas had elders elected

---

various types of people? **4.** Since Antioch was 100 miles away, what does that tell you about the nature of Paul's opposition? **5.** After reading verses 19-20, how would you characterize Paul? His supporters? How do you feel about John's desertion at Perga (13:14) after reading these verses?

REFLECT: 1. What was one of the biggest misunderstandings about Christianity you had to overcome before you could really believe? **2.** How do people with whom you have shared the gospel read it through their own prejudices or beliefs? How have you tried to correct their misunderstandings? **3.** In what areas are you most easily swayed by other people's opinions? How does this affect your Christian faith? What can you do to remain strong in your faith? How will you begin strengthening your faith this week?

OPEN: What was the longest trip you ever took? What was your reason to do so?

DIG: 1. After the treatment Paul and Barnabas received, do you think the believers in those cities expected them to return? How would you feel if you were one of these new believers when you had heard they had come back? **2.** From what they have seen in Paul and Barnabas, what would these new elders realize about their job? **3.** Reviewing this journey of about 1100 miles (13:1-14:26), what do you learn about Paul? About the gospel?

REFLECT: Seeing Paul and Barnabas' courage, faith and endurance, how are you challenged to serve the Lord more completely?

OPEN: How does your family or church usually decide what to do when areas of controversy arise?

DIG: 1. Looking at the concerns of the Pharisees in Mark 2:16, 18, 24 and 7:6, what other things may these teachers be saying are necessary for the Gentiles to do? If you were one of the Gentiles hearing that these regulations were required, how would you feel about your faith? As a strict Jew, why would these things be important for you? **2.** The letter of Paul to the Galatians was probably written after the journey described in chapters 13-14 but before the events of chapter 15. From Galatians 2:21, 3:5 and

---

3:10-14, what is the main issue as Paul sees it? If these regulations were accepted, what would that do to all converts so far ? **3.** Compare Acts 10:28, plus 34-35 and Galatians 2:11-13 with Acts 15:7-11. How would you describe Peter's struggle with this issue? How does Paul's teaching in Galatians 2:15-16 show its influence upon Peter in his address here? **4.** Knowing Paul's Pharisaic background (26:5) and Peter's desire to keep the law (10:14), how might the testimony of these two men be especially weighty for the council? **5.** What is James' position in the matter (vv. 13-21; also Gal. 1:19)? What has led him to change his mind? **6.** What is the significance of the council's decision in light of Acts 1:8? Given Paul's advice about a similar controversy in I Corinthians 8:1-13, why were the conditions of verse 20 included?

REFLECT: 1. Reviewing verses 1-21, what roles do you see played by experience, theology and practical considerations in the decision-making process of the council? What issues trouble your church? Which might be resolved by looking at them with these three realities in mind? **2.** Is there some area of your faith where you feel like Peter—going back and forth because you are not sure of what is right? How might verse 11 relate to this concern? **3.** In what ways do you or your church add on to the gospel in your relations with non-Christians or new believers? How have these add-ons gotten in the way of your faith? How will you free yourself from them? **4.** In light of this section, does Galatians 5:6 seem like a good summary of what it really means to be a Christian? Why or why not?

OPEN: How do you feel about other Christians whose worship or lifestyle is historically very different from yours (i.e., Catholic - Protestant, black-white, pentecostal-nonpentecostal)?

DIG: 1. Why would a letter and representatives from the Jerusalem church be a good way to communicate the apostles' decision? **2.** What is the tone of the letter? What would verse 24 communicate to the readers? Verses 25-27? Verses 28-29? **3.** How do Judas and Silas personally add to this letter? How are the unity and harmony of the primarily Jewish church in Jerusalem and the

whom they reported everything God had done through them.

⁵Then some of the believers who belonged to the party of the Pharisees stood up and said, "The Gentiles must be circumcised and required to obey the law of Moses."

⁶The apostles and elders met to consider this question. ⁷After much discussion, Peter got up and addressed them: "Brothers, you know that some time ago God made a choice among you that the Gentiles might hear from my lips the message of the gospel and believe. ⁸God, who knows the heart, showed that he accepted them by giving the Holy Spirit to them, just as he did to us. ⁹He made no distinction between us and them, for he purified their hearts by faith. ¹⁰Now then, why do you try to test God by putting on the necks of the disciples a yoke that neither we nor our fathers have been able to bear? ¹¹No! We believe it is through the grace of our Lord Jesus that we are saved, just as they are."

¹²The whole assembly became silent as they listened to Barnabas and Paul telling about the miraculous signs and wonders God had done among the Gentiles through them. ¹³When they finished, James spoke up: "Brothers, listen to me. ¹⁴Simon*d* has described to us how God at first showed his concern by taking from the Gentiles a people for himself. ¹⁵The words of the prophets are in agreement with this, as it is written:

¹⁶" 'After this I will return
　　and rebuild David's fallen tent.
　Its ruins I will rebuild,
　　and I will restore it,
¹⁷that the remnant of men may seek the Lord,
　　and all the Gentiles who bear my name,
　says the Lord, who does these things'*e*
¹⁸　that have been known for ages.*f*

¹⁹"It is my judgment, therefore, that we should not make it difficult for the Gentiles who are turning to God. ²⁰Instead we should write to them, telling them to abstain from food polluted by idols, from sexual immorality, from the meat of strangled animals and from blood. ²¹For Moses has been preached in every city from the earliest times and is read in the synagogues on every Sabbath."

The Council's Letter to Gentile Believers

²²Then the apostles and elders, with the whole church, decided to choose some of their own men and send them to Antioch with Paul and Barnabas. They chose Judas (called Barsabbas) and Silas, two men who were leaders among the brothers. ²³With them they sent the following letter:

The apostles and elders, your brothers,

To the Gentile believers in Antioch, Syria and Cilicia:

Greetings.

---

d14 Greek *Simeon,* a variant of *Simon;* that is, Peter　　*e17* Amos 9:11,12
f17,18 Some manuscripts *things'*— / *18known to the Lord for ages is his work*

²⁴We have heard that some went out from us without our authorization and disturbed you, troubling your minds by what they said. ²⁵So we all agreed to choose some men and send them to you with our dear friends Barnabas and Paul— ²⁶men who have risked their lives for the name of our Lord Jesus Christ. ²⁷Therefore we are sending Judas and Silas to confirm by word of mouth what we are writing. ²⁸It seemed good to the Holy Spirit and to us not to burden you with anything beyond the following requirements: ²⁹You are to abstain from food sacrificed to idols, from blood, from the meat of strangled animals and from sexual immorality. You will do well to avoid these things.

Farewell.

³⁰The men were sent off and went down to Antioch, where they gathered the church together and delivered the letter. ³¹The people read it and were glad for its encouraging message. ³²Judas and Silas, who themselves were prophets, said much to encourage and strengthen the brothers. ³³After spending some time there, they were sent off by the brothers with the blessing of peace to return to those who had sent them.ᵍ ³⁵But Paul and Barnabas remained in Antioch, where they and many others taught and preached the word of the Lord.

Disagreement Between Paul and Barnabas

³⁶Some time later Paul said to Barnabas, "Let us go back and visit the brothers in all the towns where we preached the word of the Lord and see how they are doing." ³⁷Barnabas wanted to take John, also called Mark, with them, ³⁸but Paul did not think it wise to take him, because he had deserted them in Pamphylia and had not continued with them in the work. ³⁹They had such a sharp disagreement that they parted company. Barnabas took Mark and sailed for Cyprus, ⁴⁰but Paul chose Silas and left, commended by the brothers to the grace of the Lord. ⁴¹He went through Syria and Cilicia, strengthening the churches.

Timothy Joins Paul and Silas

16 He came to Derbe and then to Lystra, where a disciple named Timothy lived, whose mother was a Jewess and a believer, but whose father was a Greek. ²The brothers at Lystra and Iconium spoke well of him. ³Paul wanted to take him along on the journey, so he circumcised him because of the Jews who lived in that area, for they all knew that his father was a Greek. ⁴As they traveled from town to town, they delivered the decisions reached by the apostles and elders in Jerusalem for the people to obey. ⁵So the churches were strengthened in the faith and grew daily in numbers.

primarily Gentile church in Antioch illustrated in verses 30-33? How might their relationship have turned out differently if the people in 15:5 had won their way?

REFLECT: 1. From the debate, the resulting letter and the way in which it was delivered, what do you learn about the way to solve disagreements among Christians? How is your style of handling disagreements similar to the way the issue was handled in chapter 15? Different from it? 2. In your community's churches, what are the ethnic, social and racial lines of division? What is your relationship like with believers in these different churches? How might verses 30-33 be a model for unity within diversity among these churches? In light of Acts 1:8, how important is it to work for this type of relationship?

OPEN: What "break-up" was hardest for you? What happened? Why?

DIG: Role play how you think Paul and Barnabus agreed to split up. With which one would you have sided? Why?

REFLECT: Are you more "person-oriented" or "task-oriented"? What are the strengths and weaknesses of your type?

OPEN: When have you felt a "double standard" was applied to you at work? At home? In the church? What for?

DIG: 1. Given the decision to reject the teachings of those in 15:1, why did Paul turn around and circumcise Timothy? How might this "double standard" be justified (see I Cor. 9:19-23)? 2. What was the effect of the council's decision on these young churches?

REFLECT: 1. How has your parents' heritage affected your faith? Why? 2. When have you given up some personal rights in order to better represent Christ to others? How might you need to do so now? 3. What do you learn from Paul's action here, and his belief in 15:1-2, about balancing truth and love?

ᵍ33 Some manuscripts *them,* ³⁴*but Silas decided to remain there*

OPEN: How is politics like a "revolving door"? Likewise, your life?

DIG: 1. Note the change from "they" to "we" in verse 10: How does this relate to Luke 1:3-4? **2.** How is this closed door (v. 7) pivotal?

REFLECT: 1. When has God closed a door in your life? What happened? How did you feel then? Now? **2.** Where do you see an open door now? What is it? What are your plans for this opportunity?

OPEN: If you were to lead a mission thrust into a new area, how would you start?

DIG: Compare verse 13 with 14:1 and 17:2. What does the fact that there was no synagogue in Philippi mean regarding the Jewish community there? How did that affect Paul's strategy for mission?

REFLECT: How did the Lord open your heart to respond to the gospel? What people did he use as part of the process?

OPEN: When you are discouraged, what type of music do you like to listen to? Why?

DIG: 1. How would you feel if this servant-girl was following you around making this announcement? What influence might her true statement actually be having on these missionaries' effectiveness? **2.** Retell verses 17-21 from the perspective of the owners of the girl: What do you feel about your girl? About your money? About these missionaries? **3.** Since there apparently was no synagogue in Philippi (v. 13), and since the Gentile missionaries (Luke and Timothy) were not seized, how might racism be a factor in the actions described in verses 19-24? What might be meant by the charge against them? **4.** If you were falsely accused, severely beaten and thrown into a dark group jail, would you still trust your sense that God had called you to go to this place (16:9-10)? Why or why not? **5.** What does the response of Paul and Silas show about them? If you were the jailer, what would you think of Paul and Silas as you heard them singing? How about after the events of verses 26-28? **6.** In what ways does

Paul's Vision of the Man of Macedonia

[6]Paul and his companions traveled throughout the region of Phrygia and Galatia, having been kept by the Holy Spirit from preaching the word in the province of Asia. [7]When they came to the border of Mysia, they tried to enter Bithynia, but the Spirit of Jesus would not allow them to. [8]So they passed by Mysia and went down to Troas. [9]During the night Paul had a vision of a man of Macedonia standing and begging him, "Come over to Macedonia and help us." [10]After Paul had seen the vision, we got ready at once to leave for Macedonia, concluding that God had called us to preach the gospel to them.

Lydia's Conversion in Philippi

[11]From Troas we put out to sea and sailed straight for Samothrace, and the next day on to Neapolis. [12]From there we traveled to Philippi, a Roman colony and the leading city of that district of Macedonia. And we stayed there several days.

[13]On the Sabbath we went outside the city gate to the river, where we expected to find a place of prayer. We sat down and began to speak to the women who had gathered there. [14]One of those listening was a woman named Lydia, a dealer in purple cloth from the city of Thyatira, who was a worshiper of God. The Lord opened her heart to respond to Paul's message. [15]When she and the members of her household were baptized, she invited us to her home. "If you consider me a believer in the Lord," she said, "come and stay at my house." And she persuaded us.

Paul and Silas in Prison

[16]Once when we were going to the place of prayer, we were met by a slave girl who had a spirit by which she predicted the future. She earned a great deal of money for her owners by fortune-telling. [17]This girl followed Paul and the rest of us, shouting, "These men are servants of the Most High God, who are telling you the way to be saved." [18]She kept this up for many days. Finally Paul became so troubled that he turned around and said to the spirit, "In the name of Jesus Christ I command you to come out of her!" At that moment the spirit left her.

[19]When the owners of the slave girl realized that their hope of making money was gone, they seized Paul and Silas and dragged them into the marketplace to face the authorities. [20]They brought them before the magistrates and said, "These men are Jews, and are throwing our city into an uproar [21]by advocating customs unlawful for us Romans to accept or practice."

[22]The crowd joined in the attack against Paul and Silas, and the magistrates ordered them to be stripped and beaten. [23]After they had been severely flogged, they were thrown into prison, and the jailer was commanded to guard them carefully. [24]Upon receiving such orders, he put them in the inner cell and fastened their feet in the stocks.

[25]About midnight Paul and Silas were praying and singing hymns to God, and the other prisoners were listening to them. [26]Suddenly there was such a violent earthquake that the founda-

tions of the prison were shaken. At once all the prison doors flew open, and everybody's chains came loose. 27The jailer woke up, and when he saw the prison doors open, he drew his sword and was about to kill himself because he thought the prisoners had escaped. 28But Paul shouted, "Don't harm yourself! We are all here!"

29The jailer called for lights, rushed in and fell trembling before Paul and Silas. 30He then brought them out and asked, "Sirs, what must I do to be saved?"

31They replied, "Believe in the Lord Jesus, and you will be saved—you and your household." 32Then they spoke the word of the Lord to him and to all the others in his house. 33At that hour of the night the jailer took them and washed their wounds; then immediately he and all his family were baptized. 34The jailer brought them into his house and set a meal before them; he was filled with joy because he had come to believe in God—he and his whole family.

35When it was daylight, the magistrates sent their officers to the jailer with the order: "Release those men." 36The jailer told Paul, "The magistrates have ordered that you and Silas be released. Now you can leave. Go in peace."

37But Paul said to the officers: "They beat us publicly without a trial, even though we are Roman citizens, and threw us into prison. And now do they want to get rid of us quietly? No! Let them come themselves and escort us out."

38The officers reported this to the magistrates, and when they heard that Paul and Silas were Roman citizens, they were alarmed. 39They came to appease them and escorted them from the prison, requesting them to leave the city. 40After Paul and Silas came out of the prison, they went to Lydia's house, where they met with the brothers and encouraged them. Then they left.

In Thessalonica

17 When they had passed through Amphipolis and Apollonia, they came to Thessalonica, where there was a Jewish synagogue. 2As his custom was, Paul went into the synagogue, and on three Sabbath days he reasoned with them from the Scriptures, 3explaining and proving that the Christ *h* had to suffer and rise from the dead. "This Jesus I am proclaiming to you is the Christ, *h*" he said. 4Some of the Jews were persuaded and joined Paul and Silas, as did a large number of God-fearing Greeks and not a few prominent women.

5But the Jews were jealous; so they rounded up some bad characters from the marketplace, formed a mob and started a riot in the city. They rushed to Jason's house in search of Paul and Silas in order to bring them out to the crowd. *i* 6But when they did not find them, they dragged Jason and some other brothers before the city officials, shouting: "These men who have caused trouble all over the world have now come here, 7and Jason has welcomed them into his house. They are all defying Caesar's decrees, saying that there is another king, one called

*h*3 Or *Messiah*   *i*5 Or *the assembly of the people*

the jailer express his new faith in Jesus? How is this like Cornelius (10:44-48) and the Ethiopian official (8:36-39)? **7.** Given the charge against them (v. 20-21), why might Paul insist on his rights as a Roman citizen? (Note: Most residents in the Roman empire did not have the privilege of citizenship.) How would this diffuse tensions which might have arisen for this young Philippian church?

REFLECT: 1. The girl's owners rejected the gospel because it cost them financially. What financial concerns keep some people from faith today? Are any of these concerns a factor for you? **2.** About 12 years after these events, Paul wrote the letter to the Philippians from another prison. How does Philippians 4:4-7, 12-13 account for Paul's behavior in Acts 16:25? What can you learn from his example about knowing peace and joy even in hard times? **3.** If a person asked you, "What must I do to be saved?", how would you answer? **4.** In Acts, the disciples are sometimes freed from hard situations, but other times they have to go through them. What can you learn from their experiences that will help you as you encounter difficult times?

OPEN: When you were growing up, how often did your family move? How did you feel about these moves?

DIG: 1. Thessalonica was a wealthy trading city on a major road going from the Adriatic Sea to present day Istanbul by the Black Sea. How is Paul received at Thessalonica (see also 1 Thess. 1:40-10; 3:1-4)? **2.** What types of accusations has Paul encountered so far (vv. 5-7; also 16:20-21)? What motivations lay behind these accusations? **3.** Since his conversion in Acts 9, this is the sixth time Paul had been forced to leave an area because of persecution. How would you feel about your mission if that happened to you? How does your view compare with Paul's view on this (see 1 Thess. 2:1-6)?

REFLECT: 1. Whether Jesus or Caesar was Lord became a real issue for Christians a few years later. When has your faith in Christ led to conflict with other authorities claiming your loyalty?

Jesus." [8]When they heard this, the crowd and the city officials were thrown into turmoil. [9]Then they made Jason and the others post bond and let them go.

In Berea

[10]As soon as it was night, the brothers sent Paul and Silas away to Berea. On arriving there, they went to the Jewish synagogue. [11]Now the Bereans were of more noble character than the Thessalonians, for they received the message with great eagerness and examined the Scriptures every day to see if what Paul said was true. [12]Many of the Jews believed, as did also a number of prominent Greek women and many Greek men.

[13]When the Jews in Thessalonica learned that Paul was preaching the word of God at Berea, they went there too, agitating the crowds and stirring them up. [14]The brothers immediately sent Paul to the coast, but Silas and Timothy stayed at Berea. [15]The men who escorted Paul brought him to Athens and then left with instructions for Silas and Timothy to join him as soon as possible.

In Athens

[16]While Paul was waiting for them in Athens, he was greatly distressed to see that the city was full of idols. [17]So he reasoned in the synagogue with the Jews and the God-fearing Greeks, as well as in the marketplace day by day with those who happened to be there. [18]A group of Epicurean and Stoic philosophers began to dispute with him. Some of them asked, "What is this babbler trying to say?" Others remarked, "He seems to be advocating foreign gods." They said this because Paul was preaching the good news about Jesus and the resurrection. [19]Then they took him and brought him to a meeting of the Areopagus, where they said to him, "May we know what this new teaching is that you are presenting? [20]You are bringing some strange ideas to our ears, and we want to know what they mean." [21](All the Athenians and the foreigners who lived there spent their time doing nothing but talking about and listening to the latest ideas.)

[22]Paul then stood up in the meeting of the Areopagus and said: "Men of Athens! I see that in every way you are very religious. [23]For as I walked around and looked carefully at your objects of worship, I even found an altar with this inscription: TO AN UNKNOWN GOD. Now what you worship as something unknown I am going to proclaim to you.

[24]"The God who made the world and everything in it is the Lord of heaven and earth and does not live in temples built by hands. [25]And he is not served by human hands, as if he needed anything, because he himself gives all men life and breath and everything else. [26]From one man he made every nation of men, that they should inhabit the whole earth; and he determined the times set for them and the exact places where they should live. [27]God did this so that men would seek him and perhaps reach out for him and find him, though he is not far from each one of us. [28]'For in him we live and move and have our being.' As some of your own poets have said, 'We are his offspring.'

OPEN: When your pastor preaches, do you examine the Scriptures? The furnishings? The pretty faces? Your nose?

DIG: 1. Compared with the Thessalonians (vv. 2-4), how do the Bereans receive the gospel (vv. 11-12)? **2.** What missions strategy do you see here (vv. 14-15): "Cut and run"? "Divide and conquer"? "Different strokes for different folks"? Or what?

REFLECT: 1. In terms of time, consistency and intensity, how would you rate your Bible study? **2.** How might your small group split up to pilot new groups among different folks? What people or task would you be best suited for?

OPEN: How do you feel around philosophy majors? Why? Do others feel likewise about you? Why not?

DIG: 1. What does the fact that Paul was so noticed by these Greek philosophers tell you about the extent of his activity in Athens? **2.** What do you sense is the general attitude of these philosophers (vv. 18-21)? How do you think Luke felt about them? Since they thought "Jesus" and "Resurrection" were two gods, what is their prior understanding of Christianity? **3.** The Stoics believed "god" was in everything and so everything was "god" (pantheism), while the Epicureans had little or no belief in "god" at all. How would you begin to tell people like this about the gospel? **4.** What does Paul begin telling them about God (vv. 23-30)? How does Paul use his familiarity with their culture to help them see the weaknesses in the way they relate to deity? **5.** How is the emphasis of this sermon different from that in 13:16-41? Why? Is his lack of using Scripture in Acts 17 a strength or a weakness? Why? How are the sermons alike in terms of what they call people to do? **6.** Since the Greeks believed that body was earthly and evil, how would the idea of the resurrection of Jesus strike them? **7.** How might verse 21 account for the differences of response in Athens compared to Berea (17:12) and Thessalonica (17:4)?

REFLECT: 1. What distresses you spiritually about the area in which you live? What specific needs do

²⁹"Therefore since we are God's offspring, we should not think that the divine being is like gold or silver or stone—an image made by man's design and skill. ³⁰In the past God overlooked such ignorance, but now he commands all people everywhere to repent. ³¹For he has set a day when he will judge the world with justice by the man he has appointed. He has given proof of this to all men by raising him from the dead."

³²When they heard about the resurrection of the dead, some of them sneered, but others said, "We want to hear you again on this subject." ³³At that, Paul left the Council. ³⁴A few men became followers of Paul and believed. Among them was Dionysius, a member of the Areopagus, also a woman named Damaris, and a number of others.

In Corinth

18 After this, Paul left Athens and went to Corinth. ²There he met a Jew named Aquila a native of Pontus, who had recently come from Italy with his wife Priscilla, because Claudius had ordered all the Jews to leave Rome. Paul went to see them, ³and because he was a tentmaker as they were, he stayed and worked with them. ⁴Every Sabbath he reasoned in the synagogue, trying to persuade Jews and Greeks.

⁵When Silas and Timothy came from Macedonia, Paul devoted himself exclusively to preaching, testifying to the Jews that Jesus was the Christ.ʲ ⁶But when the Jews opposed Paul and became abusive, he shook out his clothes in protest and said to them, "Your blood be on your own heads! I am clear of my responsibility. From now on I will go to the Gentiles."

⁷Then Paul left the synagogue and went next door to the house of Titius Justus, a worshiper of God. ⁸Crispus, the synagogue ruler, and his entire household believed in the Lord; and many of the Corinthians who heard him believed and were baptized.

⁹One night the Lord spoke to Paul in a vision: "Do not be afraid; keep on speaking, do not be silent. ¹⁰For I am with you, and no one is going to attack and harm you, because I have many people in this city." ¹¹So Paul stayed for a year and a half, teaching them the word of God.

¹²While Gallio was proconsul of Achaia, the Jews made a united attack on Paul and brought him into court. ¹³"This man," they charged, "is persuading the people to worship God in ways contrary to the law."

¹⁴Just as Paul was about to speak, Gallio said to the Jews, "If you Jews were making a complaint about some misdemeanor or serious crime, it would be reasonable for me to listen to you. ¹⁵But since it involves questions about words and names and your own law—settle the matter yourselves. I will not be a judge of such things." ¹⁶So he had them ejected from the court. ¹⁷Then they all turned on Sosthenes the synagogue ruler and beat him in front of the court. But Gallio showed no concern whatever.

you see? What do you feel God is calling you to do about them? **2.** Who do you know that has very little or no background in the gospel? How would your witness be different than to someone out of a Christian background? **3.** Paul uses idols and Greek poetry as points of contact between these people and the gospel. How might you use movies, books, TV shows, music, etc., as a way of relating the gospel more effectively to others today?

OPEN: Do you think it would help or hurt the church if the government monitored its activity more closely? Why?

DIG: 1. Claudius' order was given about 50 AD after a Jewish riot in Rome over the preaching of Christ there. How does that, plus verses 12-17, show the official Roman attitude toward Christianity? Would this help or hinder Christians in their witness? **2.** How did Paul's ministry change after Timothy and Silas came to him? How might Philippians 4:15-16 account for this change? **3.** Given the abusive opposition from Jews to anyone associated with Paul (v. 6, also 17:5-9), what would it be like for Crispus and his household to convert and be baptized (v. 8)? What happened to Crispus' successor, Sosthenes (v. 17, also 1 Cor. 1:1)? What effect might these two conversions have on the Jewish community in Corinth? **4.** How would Paul feel about the start-up of his ministry at Corinth (see 1 Cor. 2:3)? What has happened so far on this trip (Acts 16ff.) to cause Paul such fear and trembling? How might the vision from God (vv. 9-10) and the gift from the Philipians encourage Paul in his weakness?

REFLECT: 1. With what missionaries have you entered into financial partnership? What difference would it make if they were not supported by other Christians? If you have not yet done so, how might you begin to encourage some missionaries in this way? **2.** When have you felt at the end of your ability to cope? How has God brought encouragement to you?

ʲ5 Or *Messiah;* also in verse 28

OPEN: What do you like best about returning home after a long trip?

DIG: 1. Verses 18-22 sum up a lot of traveling (see a Bible map): How far did Paul travel at this time? 2. From verses 24-26, what type of person was Apollos? How about Priscilla and Aquilla? 3. Comparing verses 27-28 with I Corinthians 3:4-6, what type of influence did Apollos have in Corinth (part of Achaia)? How would he be especially effective in the intellectual circles found in Athens and Corinth?

REFLECT: 1. Who was very helpful to you when you were young and enthusiastic about the faith? How did this person help? 2. For what circles do you sense God has equipped you to serve? How can you do so this week? 3. How does your church balance evangelism with the strengthening and equipping of believers?

OPEN: Why are so many people attracted to ouija boards, tarot cards, astrology and the like? When have you encountered these things?

DIG: 1. From 18:19-21, why do you think Paul headed right to Ephesus on his next trip? 2. Apollos was from Egypt (18:24), and these disciples were about 800 miles from Jerusalem. What does the fact that they were both followers of John the Baptist tell you about the extent of his influence? How would their awareness of John be good preparation for them to hear the gospel (see John 1:19-34)? 3. Since Paul had to teach these people about Jesus (v. 4), they apparently had not heard about him or the Spirit (v. 2). From 2:38 and 10:43-44, as well as this section, what do you learn about the relationship between faith in Jesus and receiving the Spirit? 4. What seems to be the signal throughout Acts for Paul to stop teaching in the synagogue? Why do you think this is so? What do these "stop and go" signals teach you about ministry in general? 5. Compare verses 8-9 with 13-15: How do these two groups of Jews view Jesus differently? If you were one

Priscilla, Aquila and Apollos

[18]Paul stayed on in Corinth for some time. Then he left the brothers and sailed for Syria, accompanied by Priscilla and Aquila. Before he sailed, he had his hair cut off at Cenchrea because of a vow he had taken. [19]They arrived at Ephesus, where Paul left Priscilla and Aquila. He himself went into the synagogue and reasoned with the Jews. [20]When they asked him to spend more time with them, he declined. [21]But as he left, he promised, "I will come back if it is God's will." Then he set sail from Ephesus. [22]When he landed at Caesarea, he went up and greeted the church and then went down to Antioch.

[23]After spending some time in Antioch, Paul set out from there and traveled from place to place throughout the region of Galatia and Phrygia, strengthening all the disciples.

[24]Meanwhile a Jew named Apollos, a native of Alexandria, came to Ephesus. He was a learned man, with a thorough knowledge of the Scriptures. [25]He had been instructed in the way of the Lord, and he spoke with great fervor[k] and taught about Jesus accurately, though he knew only the baptism of John. [26]He began to speak boldly in the synagogue. When Priscilla and Aquila heard him, they invited him to their home and explained to him the way of God more adequately.

[27]When Apollos wanted to go to Achaia, the brothers encouraged him and wrote to the disciples there to welcome him. On arriving, he was a great help to those who by grace had believed. [28]For he vigorously refuted the Jews in public debate, proving from the Scriptures that Jesus was the Christ.

Paul in Ephesus

19 While Apollos was at Corinth, Paul took the road through the interior and arrived at Ephesus. There he found some disciples [2]and asked them, "Did you receive the Holy Spirit when[l] you believed?"

They answered, "No, we have not even heard that there is a Holy Spirit."

[3]So Paul asked, "Then what baptism did you receive?"

"John's baptism," they replied.

[4]Paul said, "John's baptism was a baptism of repentance. He told the people to believe in the one coming after him, that is, in Jesus." [5]On hearing this, they were baptized into[m]the name of the Lord Jesus. [6]When Paul placed his hands on them, the Holy Spirit came on them, and they spoke in tongues[n] and prophesied. [7]There were about twelve men in all.

[8]Paul entered the synagogue and spoke boldly there for three months, arguing persuasively about the kingdom of God. [9]But some of them became obstinate; they refused to believe and publicly maligned the Way. So Paul left them. He took the disciples with him and had discussions daily in the lecture hall of Tyrannus. [10]This went on for two years, so that all the Jews and Greeks who lived in the province of Asia heard the word of the Lord.

k25 Or *with fervor in the Spirit*   l2 Or *after*   m5 Or *in*   n6 Or *other languages*

¹¹God did extraordinary miracles through Paul, ¹²so that even handkerchiefs and aprons that had touched him were taken to the sick, and their illnesses were cured and the evil spirits left them.

¹³Some Jews who went around driving out evil spirits tried to invoke the name of the Lord Jesus over those who were demon-possessed. They would say, "In the name of Jesus, whom Paul preaches, I command you to come out." ¹⁴Seven sons of Sceva, a Jewish chief priest, were doing this. ¹⁵One day, the evil spirit answered them, "Jesus I know, and I know about Paul, but who are you?" ¹⁶Then the man who had the evil spirit jumped on them and overpowered them all. He gave them such a beating that they ran out of the house naked and bleeding.

¹⁷When this became known to the Jews and Greeks living in Ephesus, they were all seized with fear, and the name of the Lord Jesus was held in high honor. ¹⁸Many of those who believed now came and openly confessed their evil deeds. ¹⁹A number who had practiced sorcery brought their scrolls together and burned them publicly. When they calculated the value of the scrolls, the total came to fifty thousand drachmas.ᵒ ²⁰In this way the word of the Lord spread widely and grew in power.

²¹After all this had happened, Paul decided to go to Jerusalem, passing through Macedonia and Achaia. "After I have been there," he said, "I must visit Rome also." ²²He sent two of his helpers, Timothy and Erastus, to Macedonia, while he stayed in the province of Asia a little longer.

The Riot in Ephesus

²³About that time there arose a great disturbance about the Way. ²⁴A silversmith named Demetrius, who made silver shrines of Artemis, brought in no little business for the craftsmen. ²⁵He called them together, along with the workmen in related trades, and said: "Men, you know we receive a good income from this business. ²⁶And you see and hear how this fellow Paul has convinced and led astray large numbers of people here in Ephesus and in practically the whole province of Asia. He says that man-made gods are no gods at all. ²⁷There is danger not only that our trade will lose its good name, but also that the temple of the great goddess Artemis will be discredited, and the goddess herself, who is worshiped throughout the province of Asia and the world, will be robbed of her divine majesty."

²⁸When they heard this, they were furious and began shouting: "Great is Artemis of the Ephesians!" ²⁹Soon the whole city was in an uproar. The people seized Gaius Aristarchus, Paul's traveling companions from Macedonia, and rushed as one man into the theater. ³⁰Paul wanted to appear before the crowd, but the disciples would not let him. ³¹Even some of the officials of the province, friends of Paul, sent him a message begging him not to venture into the theater.

³²The assembly was in confusion: Some were shouting one thing, some another. Most of the people did not even know why

ᵒ19 A drachma was a silver coin worth about a day's wages.

of Sceva's sons, what would you say about Jesus after verse 16? **6.** From the reaction of the crowd in verses 17-19, how would you describe the general response to Jesus prior to verses 13-16? Why would those events change people's ideas so much?

REFLECT: **1.** Suppose God did not give his Spirit to those who believe in Jesus: How would your life be different? **2.** How do people today try to use Jesus for their own purposes? What is the difference between that and real faith in Christ? **3.** What did you have to change in your lifestyle when you first began to follow Jesus? Are there some things now you are reluctant to burn in order to be really honest with God? What would it cost you to burn them?

OPEN: Have you ever been caught in a riot or mob scene? What happened? What do you think causes such behavior?

DIG: **1.** Look at 17:24-29. If you were Demetrius, how would you counter Paul's teaching against idol-making and idol worship? **2.** From verses 25 and 27, what reasons does Demetrius use to rally people against Paul? Given that the temple of Artemis was considered one of the seven wonders of the world, what trades and business would be affected if large numbers of people believed Paul? **3.** Appoint a group member to be a TV reporter interviewing others who are part of the crowd described in verses 32-34. What do they see and hear? Why are they there? Why are the Jews trying to get a speaker (Alexander) to represent them? Why would he be shouted down by the crowd? **4.** How does the concern of the city clerk differ from that of Demetrius?

REFLECT: **1.** Success, money and independence are examples of some "sacred idols" (values most people accept without question) in our culture. What other contemporary idols come to mind? How has your faith in Christ affected your relationship with these idols? What changes would occur in our culture if large numbers of Christians challenged these idols? **2.** Could Demetrius have become a Christian and still kept his business? Why or why not? Can you think of parallel situations today where someone in a "respectable" trade would be forced to choose between that trade and Christ? What pressures would that cause a person? **3.** How have you seen religious and patriotic loyalties used as a cover for economic concerns? What does it really mean to follow Jesus at these times? **4.** What originally started as Artemis-worship became Artemis-business. How might Christians fall into the same trap and make Jesus-worship into the Jesus-business?

OPEN: What do you do best with money: Earn it? Keep it? Lose it? Spend it? Give it away?

DIG: One reason for this trip was to collect for Christians in Judea (see Ro. 15:25-29). Why then might Paul want companions for this task (see 2 Cor. 8:16-23; 1 Cor. 16:1-4)? Why else might Paul want these Gentiles along for the presentation in Jerusalem (see Acts 15)?

REFLECT: Paul's companions provide protection against anyone accusing Paul of misusing the funds. How might "faith ministries" today be helped by such accountability?

OPEN: How have you seen someone's drowsiness in church cause problems? When was the last time you were caught nodding off during a sermon? what happened?

DIG: 1. What can you learn from the church in Troas and about Paul from this lengthy meeting? **2.** In 9:37-41, Luke tells how Peter raised a dead person to life. Why would he tell a similar story about Paul?

REFLECT: On a scale of 1 (low) to 10 (high), how eager are you to grow spiritually? What are you willing to give up in order to have more time to do so?

---

they were there. ³³The Jews pushed Alexander to the front, and some of the crowd shouted instructions to him. He motioned for silence in order to make a defense before the people. ³⁴But when they realized he was a Jew, they all shouted in unison for about two hours: "Great is Artemis of the Ephesians!"

³⁵The city clerk quieted the crowd and said: "Men of Ephesus, doesn't all the world know that the city of Ephesus is the guardian of the temple of the great Artemis and of her image, which fell from heaven? ³⁶Therefore, since these facts are undeniable, you ought to be quiet and not do anything rash. ³⁷You have brought these men here, though they have neither robbed temples nor blasphemed our goddess. ³⁸If, then, Demetrius and his fellow craftsmen have a grievance against anybody, the courts are open and there are proconsuls. They can press charges. ³⁹If there is anything further you want to bring up, it must be settled in a legal assembly. ⁴⁰As it is, we are in danger of being charged with rioting because of today's events. In that case we would not be able to account for this commotion, since there is no reason for it." ⁴¹After he had said this, he dismissed the assembly.

Through Macedonia and Greece

20 When the uproar had ended, Paul sent for the disciples and, after encouraging them, said good-by and set out for Macedonia. ²He traveled through that area, speaking many words of encouragement to the people, and finally arrived in Greece, ³where he stayed three months. Because the Jews made a plot against him just as he was about to sail for Syria, he decided to go back through Macedonia. ⁴He was accompanied by Sopater son of Pyrrhus from Berea, Aristarchus and Secundus from Thessalonica, Gaius from Derbe, Timothy also, Tychicus and Trophimus from the province of Asia. ⁵These men went on ahead and waited for us at Troas. ⁶But we sailed from Philippi after the Feast of Unleavened Bread, and five days later joined the others at Troas, where we stayed seven days.

Eutychus Raised From the Dead at Troas

⁷On the first day of the week we came together to break bread. Paul spoke to the people and, because he intended to leave the next day, kept on talking until midnight. ⁸There were many lamps in the upstairs room where we were meeting. ⁹Seated in a window was a young man named Eutychus, who was sinking into a deep sleep as Paul talked on and on. When he was sound asleep, he fell to the ground from the third story and was picked up dead. ¹⁰Paul went down, threw himself on the young man and put his arms around him. "Don't be alarmed," he said. "He's alive!" ¹¹Then he went upstairs again and broke bread and ate. After talking until daylight, he left. ¹²The people took the young man home alive and were greatly comforted.

Paul's Farewell to the Ephesian Elders

[13]We went on ahead to the ship and sailed for Assos, where we were going to take Paul aboard. He had made this arrangement because he was going there on foot. [14]When he met us at Assos, we took him aboard and went on to Mitylene. [15]The next day we set sail from there and arrived off Kios. The day after that we crossed over to Samos, and on the following day arrived at Miletus. [16]Paul had decided to sail past Ephesus to avoid spending time in the province of Asia, for he was in a hurry to reach Jerusalem, if possible, by the day of Pentecost.

[17]From Miletus, Paul sent to Ephesus for the elders of the church. [18]When they arrived, he said to them: "You know how I lived the whole time I was with you, from the first day I came into the province of Asia. [19]I served the Lord with great humility and with tears, although I was severely tested by the plots of the Jews. [20]You know that I have not hesitated to preach anything that would be helpful to you but have taught you publicly and from house to house. [21]I have declared to both Jews and Greeks that they must turn to God in repentance and have faith in our Lord Jesus.

[22]"And now, compelled by the Spirit, I am going to Jerusalem, not knowing what will happen to me there. [23]I only know that in every city the Holy Spirit warns me that prison and hardships are facing me. [24]However, I consider my life worth nothing to me, if only I may finish the race and complete the task the Lord Jesus has given me—the task of testifying to the gospel of God's grace.

[25]"Now I know that none of you among whom I have gone about preaching the kingdom will ever see me again. [26]Therefore, I declare to you today that I am innocent of the blood of all men. [27]For I have not hesitated to proclaim to you the whole will of God. [28]Keep watch over yourselves and all the flock of which the Holy Spirit has made you overseers.[p] Be shepherds of the church of God,[q] which he bought with his own blood. [29]I know that after I leave, savage wolves will come in among you and will not spare the flock. [30]Even from your own number men will arise and distort the truth in order to draw away disciples after them. [31]So be on your guard! Remember that for three years I never stopped warning each of you night and day with tears.

[32]"Now I commit you to God and to the word of his grace, which can build you up and give you an inheritance among all those who are sanctified. [33]I have not coveted anyone's silver or gold or clothing. [34]You yourselves know that these hands of mine have supplied my own needs and the needs of my companions. [35]In everything I did, I showed you that by this kind of hard work we must help the weak, remembering the words the Lord Jesus himself said: 'It is more blessed to give than to receive.' "

[36]When he had said this, he knelt down with all of them and

---

p28 Traditionally *bishops*   *q28* Many manuscripts *of the Lord* prayed. [37]They all wept as they embraced him and kissed him. [38]What grieved them most was his statement that they would never see his face again. Then they accompanied him to the ship.

On to Jerusalem

21 After we had torn ourselves away from them, we put out to sea and sailed straight to Cos. The next day we went to Rhodes and from there to Patara. [2]We found a ship crossing over to Phoenicia, went on board and set sail. [3]After sighting Cyprus and passing to the south of it, we sailed on to Syria. We landed at Tyre, where our ship was to unload its cargo. [4]Finding the disciples there, we stayed with them seven days. Through the Spirit they urged Paul not to go on to Jerusalem. [5]But when our time was up, we left and continued on our way. All the disciples and their wives and children accompanied us out of the city, and there on the beach we knelt to pray. [6]After saying good-by to each other, we went aboard the ship, and they returned home.

[7]We continued our voyage from Tyre and landed at Ptolemais, where we greeted the brothers and stayed with them for a day. [8]Leaving the next day, we reached Caesarea and stayed at the house of Philip the evangelist, one of the Seven. [9]He had four unmarried daughters who prophesied.

[10]After we had been there a number of days, a prophet named Agabus came down from Judea. [11]Coming over to us, he took Paul's belt, tied his own hands and feet with it and said, "The Holy Spirit says, 'In this way the Jews of Jerusalem will bind the owner of this belt and will hand him over to the Gentiles.' "

[12]When we heard this, we and the people there pleaded with Paul not to go up to Jerusalem. [13]Then Paul answered, "Why are you weeping and breaking my heart? I am ready not only to be bound, but also to die in Jerusalem for the name of the Lord Jesus." [14]When he would not be dissuaded, we gave up and said, "The Lord's will be done."

[15]After this, we got ready and went up to Jerusalem. [16]Some of the disciples from Caesarea accompanied us and brought us to the home of Mnason, where we were to stay. He was a man from Cyprus and one of the early disciples.

Paul's Arrival at Jerusalem

[17]When we arrived at Jerusalem, the brothers received us warmly. [18]The next day Paul and the rest of us went to see James, and all the elders were present. [19]Paul greeted them and reported in detail what God had done among the Gentiles through his ministry.

[20]When they heard this, they praised God. Then they said to Paul: "You see, brother, how many thousands of Jews have believed, and all of them are zealous for the law. [21]They have been informed that you teach all the Jews who live among the Gentiles to turn away from Moses, telling them not to circumcise their children or live according to our customs. [22]What shall we do? They will certainly hear that you have come, [23]so do what we tell you. There are four men with us who have made a vow. [24]Take these men, join in their purification rites and pay their

---

OPEN: What piece of clothing that you are wearing (belt, hat, shoes, etc.) best represents your lifestyle now? Why?

DIG: 1. Compare verses 4 and 10-13 with 20:22-23. How might Paul be interpreting these warnings differently than his friends do? Why does he not listen to their advice? **2.** How would you be feeling by now if you were one of Paul's companions during this trip? Are you impressed with his courage? Or do you think he is being foolish? Why? **3.** How is Paul's situation as he travels to Jerusalem similar to that of Jesus' unwavering determination to go to Jerusalem (see Luke 13:31-33)?

REFLECT:1. In your eyes, did Paul make the right decision to go to Jerusalem even though godly people through the Spirit urged him not to go? Why or why not? **2.** When have you made decisions against the wishes of people you admired and trusted? What happened? In retrospect, was your decision a wise one? Why or why not?

OPEN: When you were in grade school, was your favorite teacher flexible or rigid regarding classroom rules? What impact did that have on you?

DIG: 1. What pressure do James and the elders face as Paul comes to Jerusalem? How might Paul's teaching, as illustrated in Galatians 5:2-6, cause strict Jews to be upset? **2.** This issue was supposedly settled at least 6 years earlier at the council described in Acts 15. How do you account for the fact that these tensions still were so strong among the Jerusalem believers? **3.** How would James' suggestion to Paul solve the problem for both of them? Why would it be espe-

expenses, so that they can have their heads shaved. Then everybody will know there is no truth in these reports about you, but that you yourself are living in obedience to the law. 25As for the Gentile believers, we have written to them our decision that they should abstain from food sacrificed to idols, from blood, from the meat of strangled animals and from sexual immorality."

26The next day Paul took the men and purified himself along with them. Then he went to the temple to give notice of the date when the days of purification would end and the offering would be made for each of them.

Paul Arrested

27When the seven days were nearly over, some Jews from the province of Asia saw Paul at the temple. They stirred up the whole crowd and seized him, 28shouting, "Men of Israel, help us! This is the man who teaches all men everywhere against our people and our law and this place. And besides, he has brought Greeks into the temple area and defiled this holy place." 29(They had previously seen Trophimus the Ephesian in the city with Paul and assumed that Paul had brought him into the temple area.)

30The whole city was aroused, and the people came running from all directions. Seizing Paul, they dragged him from the temple, and immediately the gates were shut. 31While they were trying to kill him, news reached the commander of the Roman troops that the whole city of Jerusalem was in an uproar. 32He at once took some officers and soldiers and ran down to the crowd. When the rioters saw the commander and his soldiers, they stopped beating Paul.

33The commander came up and arrested him and ordered him to be bound with two chains. Then he asked who he was and what he had done. 34Some in the crowd shouted one thing and some another, and since the commander could not get at the truth because of the uproar, he ordered that Paul be taken into the barracks. 35When Paul reached the steps, the violence of the mob was so great he had to be carried by the soldiers. 36The crowd that followed kept shouting, "Away with him!"

Paul Speaks to the Crowd

37As the soldiers were about to take Paul into the barracks, he asked the commander, "May I say something to you?"

"Do you speak Greek?" he replied. 38"Aren't you the Egyptian who started a revolt and led four thousand terrorists out into the desert some time ago?"

39Paul answered, "I am a Jew, from Tarsus in Cilicia, a citizen of no ordinary city. Please let me speak to the people."

40Having received the commander's permission, Paul stood on the steps and motioned to the crowd. When they were all 22 silent, he said to them in Aramaicʳ: 1"Brothers and fathers, listen now to my defense."

2When they heard him speak to them in Aramaic, they became very quiet.

ʳ40 Or possibly *Hebrew;* also in 22:2

cially important for Paul's Gentile companions to be reminded of what they should do (see 15:20)? **4.** How does Paul's action in verses 24-26 illustrate his principle in I Corinthians 9:19-20?

REFLECT: How do you decide when you should bend for the sake of others, and when you should insist on your principles?

___

OPEN: What was one of the most raucous crowd scenes you have ever been a part of? How did you feel as part of it?

DIG: 1. Paul spent more time in Ephesus than anywhere else in his travels (19:8-10). Why might they be especially upset when they saw Paul? Gentiles were forbidden from the temple under penalty of death. How would the accusation of verse 28 fuel the suspicions of James (v. 21)? **2.** Compare the reaction against Paul in verse 30-31 with that against Stephen in 6:11-13, which occurred 20 years earlier. What does this tell you about Christian-Jewish relationships in Jerusalem during this period? **3.** In light of 20:23 and 21:13, and the parallel experience of Jesus, what would you be feeling if you were Paul hearing the shouts of this lynch mob?

REFLECT: What one group do you think is most critical of the church today? What could be done to lessen the misunderstanding between the two? What can you do to help this process?

___

OPEN: When have you been in a position where you wished you could understand another language more?

DIG: 1. From 21:30-36, why might the commander think Paul was this Egyptian revolutionary? **2.** Under the circumstances, why did Paul think it so important to address this hostile crowd? How would Jewish-Christian relationships erode even further if the charges of 21:28 were left unanswered? **3.** Many foreign-born Jews did not know Aramaic well. How does Paul's use of this language along with the content of his speech force these Jews to listen? **4.** This speech recounts the events of 9:1-18. Skimming 22:1-10, in how many ways does Paul point out how much alike he and the crowd are? What is he hoping to achieve by doing so? **5.** Why does Paul's reference to the Gentiles (v. 21) so upset the crowd (v. 22), whereas they did not react to his speaking about Jesus? What does this show was the real sticking point about the gospel for the Jews at this time?

REFLECT: 1. Paul used a personal testimony in addressing this group. What would have happened if he had preached a sermon? Why are personal testimonies effective? When do you find your story most effective and helpful to others? **2.** How has your faith in Jesus redirected your life in a surprising way? In what ways do you struggle against that redirection (like Paul did in vv. 19-20)? In what ways have you embraced some of these changes for yourself?

Then Paul said: [3]"I am a Jew, born in Tarsus of Cilicia, but brought up in this city. Under Gamaliel I was thoroughly trained in the law of our fathers and was just as zealous for God as any of you are today. [4]I persecuted the followers of this Way to their death, arresting both men and women and throwing them into prison, [5]as also the high priest and all the Council can testify. I even obtained letters from them to their brothers in Damascus, and went there to bring these people as prisoners to Jerusalem to be punished.

[6]"About noon as I came near Damascus, suddenly a bright light from heaven flashed around me. [7]I fell to the ground and heard a voice say to me, 'Saul! Saul! Why do you persecute me?'

[8]"'Who are you, Lord?' I asked.

"'I am Jesus of Nazareth, whom you are persecuting,' he replied. [9]My companions saw the light, but they did not understand the voice of him who was speaking to me.

[10]"'What shall I do, Lord?' I asked.

"'Get up,' the Lord said, 'and go into Damascus. There you will be told all that you have been assigned to do.' [11]My companions led me by the hand into Damascus, because the brilliance of the light had blinded me.

[12]"A man named Ananias came to see me. He was a devout observer of the law and highly respected by all the Jews living there. [13]He stood beside me and said, 'Brother Saul, receive your sight!' And at that very moment I was able to see him.

[14]"Then he said: 'The God of our fathers has chosen you to know his will and to see the Righteous One and to hear words from his mouth. [15]You will be his witness to all men of what you have seen and heard. [16]And now what are you waiting for? Get up, be baptized and wash your sins away, calling on his name.'

[17]"When I returned to Jerusalem and was praying at the temple, I fell into a trance [18]and saw the Lord speaking. 'Quick!' he said to me. 'Leave Jerusalem immediately, because they will not accept your testimony about me.'

[19]"'Lord,' I replied, 'these men know that I went from one synagogue to another to imprison and beat those who believe in you. [20]And when the blood of your martyr[ˢ] Stephen was shed, I stood there giving my approval and guarding the clothes of those who were killing him.'

[21]"Then the Lord said to me, 'Go; I will send you far away to the Gentiles.' "

Paul the Roman Citizen

[22]The crowd listened to Paul until he said this. Then they raised their voices and shouted, "Rid the earth of him! He's not fit to live!"

[23]As they were shouting and throwing off their cloaks and flinging dust into the air, [24]the commander ordered Paul to be taken into the barracks. He directed that he be flogged and questioned in order to find out why the people were shouting at him like this. [25]As they stretched him out to flog him, Paul said to the centurion standing there, "Is it legal for you to flog

OPEN: How did your brothers and sisters deliberately antagonize you when you were growing up? How successful were they? How would you usually get even?

DIG: 1. Why does the crowd ultimately turn against Paul? What does this have to do with the charges against Paul? Why would Paul's statement make them so angry? **2.** Compare verses 25-29 with 16:37-38: How was Paul's status as a Roman citizen an asset in his ministry to Gentiles?

ˢ20 Or *witness*

a Roman citizen who hasn't even been found guilty?"

²⁶When the centurion heard this, he went to the commander and reported it. "What are you going to do?" he asked. "This man is a Roman citizen."

²⁷The commander went to Paul and asked, "Tell me, are you a Roman citizen?"

"Yes, I am," he answered.

²⁸Then the commander said, "I had to pay a big price for my citizenship."

"But I was born a citizen," Paul replied.

²⁹Those who were about to question him withdrew immediately. The commander himself was alarmed when he realized that he had put Paul, a Roman citizen, in chains.

Before the Sanhedrin

³⁰The next day, since the commander wanted to find out exactly why Paul was being accused by the Jews, he released him and ordered the chief priests and all the Sanhedrin to assemble. Then he brought Paul and had him stand before them.

23 Paul looked straight at the Sanhedrin and said, "My brothers, I have fulfilled my duty to God in all good conscience to this day." ²At this the high priest Ananias ordered those standing near Paul to strike him on the mouth. ³Then Paul said to him, "God will strike you, you whitewashed wall! You sit there to judge me according to the law, yet you yourself violate the law by commanding that I be struck!"

⁴Those who were standing near Paul said, "You dare to insult God's high priest?"

⁵Paul replied, "Brothers, I did not realize that he was the high priest; for it is written: 'Do not speak evil about the ruler of your people.'ᶦ"

⁶Then Paul, knowing that some of them were Sadducees and the others Pharisees, called out in the Sanhedrin, "My brothers, I am a Pharisee, the son of a Pharisee. I stand on trial because of my hope in the resurrection of the dead." ⁷When he said this, a dispute broke out between the Pharisees and the Sadducees, and the assembly was divided. ⁸(The Sadducees say that there is no resurrection, and that there are neither angels nor spirits, but the Pharisees acknowledge them all.)

⁹There was a great uproar, and some of the teachers of the law who were Pharisees stood up and argued vigorously. "We find nothing wrong with this man," they said. "What if a spirit or an angel has spoken to him?" ¹⁰The dispute became so violent that the commander was afraid Paul would be torn to pieces by them. He ordered the troops to go down and take him away from them by force and bring him into the barracks.

¹¹The following night the Lord stood near Paul and said, "Take courage! As you have testified about me in Jerusalem, so you must also testify in Rome."

REFLECT: 1. After having been whipped before, what would you have felt if you were Paul when the soldiers began to prepare you for this punishment? What is one of the hardest things you have had to experience because of your faith? **2.** What opportunities do you have for the spread of the gospel by being a citizen of your country? How might you capitalize on these opportunities more effectively?

OPEN: If you were a "prisoner of conscience", would you prefer to be tried before a secular court or a church body? Why? Where wuld you expect to get a fairer trial?

DIG: 1. Given the rumors and accusations against Paul (21:21, 28), why would the high priest react so violently to Paul's statement in verse 1? **2.** In verses 1-5, how does Paul show his respect and zeal for the Jewish law? Why does he make such a point of doing so? **3.** Why does Paul change the focus of attention from whether he has kept the law to his hope in the resurrection? Given the tensions on this issue between the Pharisees and Sadducees, describe what you think the next few minutes of the assembly must have been like. **4.** What effect does the split have on Paul's case? If you were the commander, what would you conclude after this meeting? **5.** Given the small probability of a fair hearing, do you think the result of this meeting is what Paul hoped for or not? Why? **6.** The last time we heard God speak to Paul was in 18:9-10, after he had experienced a series of setbacks. How would the Lord's message to him here (v. 11) help Paul again? How might this help Paul recall what the Lord said about him to Ananias in 9:15-16?

REFLECT: 1. When facing death, what duty before God do you want to say you have fulfilled? How can you pursue that course this week? **2.** How has the Lord encouraged you during hard times? **3.** What might be your "Rome"—the next important step in your spiritual journey? Why do you think so?

ᶦ5 Exodus 22:28

OPEN: When you were growing up, who was one of your favorite uncles? Why? Your favorite nephew or niece? Why?

DIG: 1. How do you explain the fierce determination of these men to kill Paul? How might this illustrate Romans 10:2? Why do they think he is so dangerous? **2.** Given verse 11, how would you feel if you were Paul when you heard the news from your nephew? By sending his nephew to the commander, is Paul showing a lack of faith in God's promise? Why or why not?

REFLECT: 1. How have you seen examples of irrational hatred motivating people? What might be a way to break through that? When is it better just to get away from them? **2.** What risks did Paul's nephew take in this story? How might you be called upon this week to risk yourself by standing up for someone that others dislike?

OPEN: If Adolph Hitler had lived to face his accusers at the Nuremberg trials for Nazi war criminals, what kind of security measures would have been necessary to protect him from lynch mobs and assassination attempts? Would you have been willing to protect Hitler from his enemies? Why not?

DIG: 1. How does the way the commander provided for Paul contrast with the way Pilate dealt with Jesus? Why do you think this is the case? **2.** How has the commander decided to deal with the "Paul problem"? How does all this relate to Jesus' words in 9:15? **3.** How would you feel if you were one of the men in verses 12-13 when you found out the next day that Paul was gone?

REFLECT: 1. How do Paul's experiences with Roman authority here shed light on his comments in Romans 13:1-7? How does this contrast with Peter's experience with the Jewish authorities in Acts 3:19-20? **2.** What do these two incidents show you about the Christian's

The Plot to Kill Paul

12The next morning the Jews formed a conspiracy and bound themselves with an oath not to eat or drink until they had killed Paul. 13More than forty men were involved in this plot. 14They went to the chief priests and elders and said, "We have taken a solemn oath not to eat anything until we have killed Paul. 15Now then, you and the Sanhedrin petition the commander to bring him before you on the pretext of wanting more accurate information about his case. We are ready to kill him before he gets here."

16But when the son of Paul's sister heard of this plot, he went into the barracks and told Paul.

17Then Paul called one of the centurions and said, "Take this young man to the commander; he has something to tell him." 18So he took him to the commander.

The centurion said, "Paul, the prisoner, sent for me and asked me to bring this young man to you because he has something to tell you."

19The commander took the young man by the hand, drew him aside and asked, "What is it you want to tell me?"

20He said: "The Jews have agreed to ask you to bring Paul before the Sanhedrin tomorrow on the pretext of wanting more accurate information about him. 21Don't give in to them, because more than forty of them are waiting in ambush for him. They have taken an oath not to eat or drink until they have killed him. They are ready now, waiting for your consent to their request."

22The commander dismissed the young man and cautioned him, "Don't tell anyone that you have reported this to me."

Paul Transferred to Caesarea

23Then he called two of his centurions and ordered them, "Get ready a detachment of two hundred soldiers, seventy horsemen and two hundred spearmen " to go to Caesarea at nine tonight. 24Provide mounts for Paul so that he may be taken safely to Governor Felix."

25He wrote a letter as follows:

26Claudius Lysias,

To His Excellency, Governor Felix:

Greetings.

27This man was seized by the Jews and they were about to kill him, but I came with my troops and rescued him, for I had learned that he is a Roman citizen. 28I wanted to know why they were accusing him, so I brought him to their Sanhedrin. 29I found that the accusation had to do with questions about their law, but there was no charge against him that deserved death or imprisonment. 30When I was informed of a plot to be carried out against the man,

---

ᵘ23 The meaning of the Greek for this word is uncertain.

I sent him to you at once. I also ordered his accusers to present to you their case against him.

³¹So the soldiers, carrying out their orders, took Paul with them during the night and brought him as far as Antipatris. ³²The next day they let the cavalry go on with him, while they returned to the barracks. ³³When the cavalry arrived in Caesarea, they delivered the letter to the governor and handed Paul over to him. ³⁴The governor read the letter and asked what province he was from. Learning that he was from Cilicia, ³⁵he said, "I will hear your case when your accusers get here." Then he ordered that Paul be kept under guard in Herod's palace.

The Trial Before Felix

24 Five days later the high priest Ananias went down to Caesarea with some of the elders and a lawyer named Tertullus, and they brought their charges against Paul before the governor. ²When Paul was called in, Tertullus presented his case before Felix: "We have enjoyed a long period of peace under you, and your foresight has brought about reforms in this nation. ³Everywhere and in every way, most excellent Felix, we acknowledge this with profound gratitude. ⁴But in order not to weary you further, I would request that you be kind enough to hear us briefly.

⁵"We have found this man to be a troublemaker, stirring up riots among the Jews all over the world. He is a ringleader of the Nazarene sect ⁶and even tried to desecrate the temple; so we seized him. ⁸By⁰ examining him yourself you will be able to learn the truth about all these charges we are bringing against him."

⁹The Jews joined in the accusation, asserting that these things were true.

¹⁰When the governor motioned for him to speak, Paul replied: "I know that for a number of years you have been a judge over this nation; so I gladly make my defense. ¹¹You can easily verify that no more than twelve days ago I went up to Jerusalem to worship. ¹²My accusers did not find me arguing with anyone at the temple, or stirring up a crowd in the synagogues or anywhere else in the city. ¹³And they cannot prove to you the charges they are now making against me. ¹⁴However, I admit that I worship the God of our fathers as a follower of the Way, which they call a sect. I believe everything that agrees with the Law and that is written in the Prophets, ¹⁵and I have the same hope in God as these men, that there will be a resurrection of both the righteous and the wicked. ¹⁶So I strive always to keep my conscience clear before God and man.

¹⁷"After an absence of several years, I came to Jerusalem to bring my people gifts for the poor and to present offerings. ¹⁸I was ceremonially clean when they found me in the temple courts doing this. There was no crowd with me, nor was I involved in any disturbance. ¹⁹But there are some Jews from the province

relationship with civil authority? Where do you need to show your support of government authority? Where should you be challenging it?

_____

OPEN: Has there ever been a famous trial or legal case that has caught your attention? What was it? Why did it interest you?

DIG: 1. Felix had a reputation of violently suppressing rebellions against Rome: How might Tertullus hope this would compensate for the lack of evidence he could offer? **2.** How might all the charges in verses 5-6 seem true to Ananias and Tertullus? What does their reference to Christians as the "Nazarene sect" show about their view of Christians? **3.** How then does Paul defend himself (vv. 11-19)? In light of the riot in Jerusalem over Paul, if you were Felix and only had Lysias' letter (23:26-30), the accusations of the Jews, and Paul's word to go on, what would you do? **4.** Given what happened in Corinth (18:12-16), why might Paul want to shift the focus of the controversy to his belief in the resurrection? **5.** What do you learn about Felix form verses 22-26? If he had been in Pilate's place, what do you think he would have done with Jesus? In light of 23:11, what must Paul be feeling as time wears on and no progress at all is made?

REFLECT: 1. How has your desire to serve Christ been misunderstood by others? How did you feel? **2.** What's the difference between being "well acquainted with the Way" and being a believer? How long were you well acquainted before you became a believer? **3.** Have you ever felt there was a period in your life that was "dead time"—time when nothing seemed to be happening at all? Why do you think God allows such times in our lives?

ᵛ6-8 Some manuscripts _him and wanted to judge him according to our law._ ⁷_But the commander, Lysias, came and with the use of much force snatched him from our hands_ ⁸_and ordered his accusers to come before you. By_

of Asia, who ought to be here before you and bring charges if they have anything against me. ²⁰Or these who are here should state what crime they found in me when I stood before the Sanhedrin— ²¹unless it was this one thing I shouted as I stood in their presence: 'It is concerning the resurrection of the dead that I am on trial before you today.' "

²²Then Felix, who was well acquainted with the Way, adjourned the proceedings. "When Lysias the commander comes," he said, "I will decide your case." ²³He ordered the centurion to keep Paul under guard but to give him some freedom and permit his friends to take care of his needs.

²⁴Several days later Felix came with his wife Drusilla, who was a Jewess. He sent for Paul and listened to him as he spoke about faith in Christ Jesus. ²⁵As Paul discoursed on righteousness, self-control and the judgment to come, Felix was afraid and said, "That's enough for now! You may leave. When I find it convenient, I will send for you." ²⁶At the same time he was hoping that Paul would offer him a bribe, so he sent for him frequently and talked with him.

²⁷When two years had passed, Felix was succeeded by Porcius Festus, but because Felix wanted to grant a favor to the Jews, he left Paul in prison.

The Trial Before Festus

25 Three days after arriving in the province, Festus went up from Caesarea to Jerusalem, ²where the chief priests and Jewish leaders appeared before him and presented the charges against Paul. ³They urgently requested Festus, as a favor to them, to have Paul transferred to Jerusalem, for they were preparing an ambush to kill him along the way. ⁴Festus answered, "Paul is being held at Caesarea, and I myself am going there soon. ⁵Let some of your leaders come with me and press charges against the man there, if he has done anything wrong."

⁶After spending eight or ten days with them, he went down to Caesarea, and the next day he convened the court and ordered that Paul be brought before him. ⁷When Paul appeared, the Jews who had come down from Jerusalem stood around him, bringing many serious charges against him, which they could not prove.

⁸Then Paul made his defense: "I have done nothing wrong against the law of the Jews or against the temple or against Caesar."

⁹Festus, wishing to do the Jews a favor, said to Paul, "Are you willing to go up to Jerusalem and stand trial before me there on these charges?"

¹⁰Paul answered: "I am now standing before Caesar's court, where I ought to be tried. I have not done any wrong to the Jews, as you yourself know very well. ¹¹If, however, I am guilty of doing anything deserving death, I do not refuse to die. But if the charges brought against me by these Jews are not true, no one has the right to hand me over to them. I appeal to Caesar!"

¹²After Festus had conferred with his council, he declared: "You have appealed to Caesar. To Caesar you will go!"

OPEN: When you were in high school, how did your class respond when you had a substitute teacher?

DIG: 1. Seeing how much time (two years) has passed since the trial in Acts 24, what does the request here show about the strength of the Jewish leaders' desires against Paul? How might the contrast between Paul now and in Acts 9:1-2 account in part for their animosity? **2.** From 24:27 and 25:9, how is Paul being used as a pawn by these Roman officials? How might this account for his decision to appeal to Caesar?

REFLECT: 1. What do you do when you feel that no matter what you say you will not really be heard by another person? **2.** What was one circumstance that threatened to ambush you in your spiritual life? How did you deal with it? **3.** If someone wanted to prove you were a Christian, what evidence from this past week could they use?

Festus Consults King Agrippa

¹³A few days later King Agrippa and Bernice arrived at Caesarea to pay their respects to Festus. ¹⁴Since they were spending many days there, Festus discussed Paul's case with the king. He said: "There is a man here whom Felix left as a prisoner. ¹⁵When I went to Jerusalem, the chief priests and elders of the Jews brought charges against him and asked that he be condemned.

¹⁶"I told them that it is not the Roman custom to hand over any man before he has faced his accusers and has had an opportunity to defend himself against their charges. ¹⁷When they came here with me, I did not delay the case, but convened the court the next day and ordered the man to be brought in. ¹⁸When his accusers got up to speak, they did not charge him with any of the crimes I had expected. ¹⁹Instead, they had some points of dispute with him about their own religion and about a dead man named Jesus who Paul claimed was alive. ²⁰I was at a loss how to investigate such matters; so I asked if he would be willing to go to Jerusalem and stand trial there on these charges. ²¹When Paul made his appeal to be held over for the Emperor's decision, I ordered him held until I could send him to Caesar."

²²Then Agrippa said to Festus, "I would like to hear this man myself."

He replied, "Tomorrow you will hear him."

Paul Before Agrippa

²³The next day Agrippa and Bernice came with great pomp and entered the audience room with the high ranking officers and the leading men of the city. At the command of Festus, Paul was brought in. ²⁴Festus said: "King Agrippa, and all who are present with us, you see this man! The whole Jewish community has petitioned me about him in Jerusalem and here in Caesarea, shouting that he ought not to live any longer. ²⁵I found he had done nothing deserving of death, but because he made his appeal to the Emperor I decided to send him to Rome. ²⁶But I have nothing definite to write to His Majesty about him. Therefore I have brought him before all of you, and especially before you, King Agrippa, so that as a result of this investigation I may have something to write. ²⁷For I think it is unreasonable to send on a prisoner without specifying the charges against him."

26 Then Agrippa said to Paul, "You have permission to speak for yourself."

So Paul motioned with his hand and began his defense: ²"King Agrippa, I consider myself fortunate to stand before you today as I make my defense against all the accusations of the Jews, ³and especially so because you are well acquainted with all the Jewish customs and controversies. Therefore, I beg you to listen to me patiently.

⁴"The Jews all know the way I have lived ever since I was a child, from the beginning of my life in my own country, and also in Jerusalem. ⁵They have known me for a long time and can testify, if they are willing, that according to the strictest sect of our religion, I lived as a Pharisee. ⁶And now it is because of my hope in what God has promised our fathers that I am on trial today. ⁷This is the promise our twelve tribes are hoping to see

OPEN: If you could be king or queen for a day, what new law would you enact?

DIG: 1. How fair is Festus in describing the case? How much does he seem to know about Judaism? About Christianity? How would this have affected any decision he would have made in the case? Do you think he is honestly trying to find the truth in this matter? **2.** This Agrippa was the son of the Herod in 12:1-23. Why might he be especially interested in hearing from Paul?

REFLECT: When you have questions about your faith, to whom do you turn? Why? How else do you seek input?

OPEN: Who is the most important or most powerful person you have had to speak to? How did you feel as you thought about what to say beforehand?

DIG: 1. What is the problem Festus faces? Why doesn't he just let Paul go free? From 26:3, how would he hope Agrippa might help? **2.** From 23:6, 24:21 and 26:6-8, what is the issue Paul continually says is the real source of his conflict with the Jewish leaders? Why do you think his adversaries never directly bring this out (see 18:15)? How does his conviction about the resurrection differ from that of the Pharisees, who in theory believed in a general resurrection as well? **3.** In verses 6-7, 22-23 and 27, why does he refer to the law and prophets to support his case? **4.** Compare 26:20 with 20:21. How could you tell someone what it means to be a Christian from these two verses? **5.** Would you describe Paul's speech as a defense or a personal testimony? How are the two related? Do you think Paul's primary goal in this speech is to convince Agrippa of his innocence? Or to convince Agrippa of the truth of Christianity's claims? Why? **6.** From 25:19 and 26:24, how much credence does Festus have regarding the resurrection of Jesus? How might Paul's response in verses 25-27 surprise Festus? **7.** If you were in this hall, what impressions would you have of Paul as he concluded his speech? **8.** Up to this point, the Romans considered Christians and Jews basically as one and the same. Within five years the emperor Nero was aware enough of the differences to violently persecute Christians in Rome. From this speech, what might the Romans begin to see as some of the differences?

REFLECT: **1.** What differences does it make to you that Jesus really rose from the dead? What would be different about your faith if that was not the case? **2.** How does verse 18 fit as a description of your spiritual journey? What other images describe what coming to faith was like for you? **3.** In verse 14, Paul adds a comment not found in his conversion story in chapters 9 or 22. When has God pointed out to you that you have been struggling against him? How has he redirected you since then? **4.** Paul considered himself a servant and a witness. In what way is God's call to you similar to his call to Paul? Different? **5.** What difference does it make to you that the events around the life of Jesus were public knowledge, things "not done in a corner"? How does that fact negate charges some people make today that the disciples made up all those stories about Jesus? **6.** How has Christ brought light into your life? How can you pass on that light to someone else this week?

fulfilled as they earnestly serve God day and night. O king, it is because of this hope that the Jews are accusing me. ⁸Why should any of you consider it incredible that God raises the dead?

⁹"I too was convinced that I ought to do all that was possible to oppose the name of Jesus of Nazareth. ¹⁰And that is just what I did in Jerusalem. On the authority of the chief priests I put many of the saints in prison, and when they were put to death, I cast my vote against them. ¹¹Many a time I went from one synagogue to another to have them punished, and I tried to force them to blaspheme. In my obsession against them, I even went to foreign cities to persecute them.

¹²"On one of these journeys I was going to Damascus with the authority and commission of the chief priests. ¹³About noon, O king, as I was on the road, I saw a light from heaven, brighter than the sun, blazing around me and my companions. ¹⁴We all fell to the ground, and I heard a voice saying to me in Aramaic,ʷ 'Saul, Saul, why do you persecute me? It is hard for you to kick against the goads.'

¹⁵"Then I asked, 'Who are you, Lord?'

" 'I am Jesus, whom you are persecuting,' the Lord replied. ¹⁶'Now get up and stand on your feet. I have appeared to you to appoint you as a servant and as a witness of what you have seen of me and what I will show you. ¹⁷I will rescue you from your own people and from the Gentiles. I am sending you to them ¹⁸to open their eyes and turn them from darkness to light, and from the power of Satan to God, so that they may receive forgiveness of sins and a place among those who are sanctified by faith in me.'

¹⁹"So then, King Agrippa, I was not disobedient to the vision from heaven. ²⁰First to those in Damascus, then to those in Jerusalem and in all Judea, and to the Gentiles also, I preached that they should repent and turn to God and prove their repentance by their deeds. ²¹That is why the Jews seized me in the temple courts and tried to kill me. ²²But I have had God's help to this very day, and so I stand here and testify to small and great alike. I am saying nothing beyond what the prophets and Moses said would happen— ²³that the Christˣ would suffer and, as the first to rise from the dead, would proclaim light to his own people and to the Gentiles."

²⁴At this point Festus interrupted Paul's defense. "You are out of your mind, Paul!" he shouted. "Your great learning is driving you insane."

²⁵"I am not insane, most excellent Festus," Paul replied. "What I am saying is true and reasonable. ²⁶The king is familiar with these things, and I can speak freely to him. I am convinced that none of this has escaped his notice, because it was not done in a corner. ²⁷King Agrippa, do you believe the prophets? I know you do."

²⁸Then Agrippa said to Paul, "Do you think that in such a short time you can persuade me to be a Christian?"

²⁹Paul replied, "Short time or long—I pray God that not only

ʷ14 Or Hebrew   ˣ23 Or Messiah

you but all who are listening to me today may become what I am, except for these chains."

³⁰The king rose, and with him the governor and Bernice and those sitting with them. ³¹They left the room, and while talking with one another, they said, "This man is not doing anything that deserves death or imprisonment."

³²Agrippa said to Festus, "This man could have been set free if he had not appealed to Caesar."

Paul Sails for Rome

27 When it was decided that we would sail for Italy, Paul and some other prisoners were handed over to a centurion named Julius, who belonged to the Imperial Regiment. ²We boarded a ship from Adramyttium about to sail for ports along the coast of the province of Asia, and we put out to sea. Aristarchus, a Macedonian from Thessalonica, was with us.

³The next day we landed at Sidon; and Julius, in kindness to Paul, allowed him to go to his friends so they might provide for his needs. ⁴From there we put out to sea again and passed to the lee of Cyprus because the winds were against us. ⁵When we had sailed across the open sea off the coast of Cilicia and Pamphylia, we landed at Myra in Lycia. ⁶There the centurion found an Alexandrian ship sailing for Italy and put us on board. ⁷We made slow headway for many days and had difficulty arriving off Cnidus. When the wind did not allow us to hold our course, we sailed to the lee of Crete, opposite Salmone. ⁸We moved along the coast with difficulty and came to a place called Fair Havens, near the town of Lasea.

⁹Much time had been lost, and sailing had already become dangerous because by now it was after the Fast.ʸ So Paul warned them, ¹⁰"Men, I can see that our voyage is going to be disastrous and bring great loss to ship and cargo, and to our own lives also." ¹¹But the centurion, instead of listening to what Paul said, followed the advice of the pilot and of the owner of the ship. ¹²Since the harbor was unsuitable to winter in, the majority decided that we should sail on, hoping to reach Phoenix and winter there. This was a harbor in Crete, facing both southwest and northwest.

The Storm

¹³When a gentle south wind began to blow, they thought they had obtained what they wanted; so they weighed anchor and sailed along the shore of Crete. ¹⁴Before very long, a wind of hurricane force, called the "northeaster," swept down from the island. ¹⁵The ship was caught by the storm and could not head into the wind; so we gave way to it and were driven along. ¹⁶As we passed to the lee of a small island called Cauda, we were hardly able to make the lifeboat secure. ¹⁷When the men had hoisted it aboard, they passed ropes under the ship itself to hold it together. Fearing that they would run aground on the sandbars of Syrtis, they lowered the sea anchor and let the ship be driven along. ¹⁸We took such a violent battering from the storm

OPEN: If you could take a "honeymooners' cruise" anywhere, where would you go? Why?

DIG: 1. From verses 1-3 and 43, what do you know about the centurion in charge? How might his concern for Paul indicate how Paul used his time while imprisoned in Caesarea? **2.** If you were the ship's owner or pilot, how would you react to Paul warning about the 50-mile trip they wanted to make? Would you have responded any differently than Julius did to Paul's concern?

REFLECT: 1. From where did unexpected kindness come to Paul in this story? How has unexpected kindness come to you in the past month? **2.** Who are some new and different people in your life who have made a difference this year? How? **3.** Whose advice do you wish you had followed at one time in your life? What happened because you didn't? How did God continue to work with you despite your unwise decision?

OPEN: What is one of the most memorable storms you have experienced? What makes it stand out for you?

DIG: 1. What things in verses 13-20 show how severe this storm was? Verse 27 indicates this situation lasted 2 weeks. How would you be feeling by the end of the first week? **2.** As a sailor on board, how would you feel about Paul's message in verses 21-26? **3.** After being in Caesarea for at least two years, why might Paul especially need to hear the promise of 23:11 repeated at this time (v. 24)?

ʸ9 That is, the Day of Atonement (Yom Kippur)

REFLECT: **1.** When have you felt caught in a northeaster, driven along by the wind? What happened? What did you learn from the situation? **2.** In terms of a weather report, how would you describe your life at present? Five years ago? **3.** When have you reacted in a crisis as Paul did?

OPEN: Suppose the "ship" of your life was put in danger of being shipwrecked by stormy circumstances. Your only hope of survival is "four anchors", which you must drop very carefully. Upon what four rock bottom articles of the Christian faith will you drop anchor? Why those four?

DIG: **1.** If you had been on board, how would you have felt at this point? **2.** Compare verse 31 with verse 11: What do you think the centurion feels about Paul now? About the God Paul serves? **3.** How do Paul's words and example serve to encourage the others? How would your estimation of Paul have changed during the two weeks of the storm?

REFLECT: **1.** How do Paul's attitudes and actions compare with those of the sailors? To what would you attribute Paul's ability to remain calm under pressure? **2.** What is the greatest pressure situation you're facing now? How can Paul's example and the principles you've learned from this story help you in your situation? What is your part and what is God's part in the resolution of your storm? **3.** When have you been tempted to bail out of a stormy situation, to sneak away in a life boat? What happened? What did you learn?

that the next day they began to throw the cargo overboard. [19]On the third day, they threw the ship's tackle overboard with their own hands. [20]When neither sun nor stars appeared for many days and the storm continued raging, we finally gave up all hope of being saved.

[21]After the men had gone a long time without food, Paul stood up before them and said: "Men, you should have taken my advice not to sail from Crete; then you would have spared yourselves this damage and loss. [22]But now I urge you to keep up your courage, because not one of you will be lost; only the ship will be destroyed. [23]Last night an angel of the God whose I am and whom I serve stood beside me [24]and said, 'Do not be afraid, Paul. You must stand trial before Caesar; and God has graciously given you the lives of all who sail with you.' [25]So keep up your courage, men, for I have faith in God that it will happen just as he told me. [26]Nevertheless, we must run aground on some island."

The Shipwreck

[27]On the fourteenth night we were still being driven across the Adriatic[z] Sea, when about midnight the sailors sensed they were approaching land. [28]They took soundings and found that the water was a hundred and twenty feet[a] deep. A short time later they took soundings again and found it was ninety feet[b] deep. [29]Fearing that we would be dashed against the rocks, they dropped four anchors from the stern and prayed for daylight. [30]In an attempt to escape from the ship, the sailors let the lifeboat down into the sea, pretending they were going to lower some anchors from the bow. [31]Then Paul said to the centurion and the soldiers, "Unless these men stay with the ship, you cannot be saved." [32]So the soldiers cut the ropes that held the lifeboat and let it fall away.

[33]Just before dawn Paul urged them all to eat. "For the last fourteen days," he said, "you have been in constant suspense and have gone without food—you haven't eaten anything. [34]Now I urge you to take some food. You need it to survive. Not one of you will lose a single hair from his head." [35]After he said this, he took some bread and gave thanks to God in front of them all. Then he broke it and began to eat. [36]They were all encouraged and ate some food themselves. [37]Altogether there were 276 of us on board. [38]When they had eaten as much as they wanted, they lightened the ship by throwing the grain into the sea.

[39]When daylight came, they did not recognize the land, but they saw a bay with a sandy beach, where they decided to run the ship aground if they could. [40]Cutting loose the anchors, they left them in the sea and at the same time untied the ropes that held the rudders. Then they hoisted the foresail to the wind and made for the beach. [41]But the ship struck a sandbar and ran aground. The bow stuck fast and would not move, and the stern was broken to pieces by the pounding of the surf.

---

[z]27 In ancient times the name referred to an area extending well south of Italy.
[a]28 Greek *twenty orguias* (about 37 meters)   [b]28 Greek *fifteen orguias* (about 27 meters)

⁴²The soldiers planned to kill the prisoners to prevent any of them from swimming away and escaping. ⁴³But the centurion wanted to spare Paul's life and kept them from carrying out their plan. He ordered those who could swim to jump overboard first and get to land. ⁴⁴The rest were to get there on planks or on pieces of the ship. In this way everyone reached land in safety.

Ashore on Malta

28 Once safely on shore, we found out that the island was called Malta. ²The islanders showed us unusual kindness. They built a fire and welcomed us all because it was raining and cold. ³Paul gathered a pile of brushwood and, as he put it on the fire, a viper, driven out by the heat, fastened itself on his hand. ⁴When the islanders saw the snake hanging from his hand, they said to each other, "This man must be a murderer; for though he escaped from the sea, Justice has not allowed him to live." ⁵But Paul shook the snake off into the fire and suffered no ill effects. ⁶The people expected him to swell up or suddenly fall dead, but after waiting a long time and seeing nothing unusual happen to him, they changed their minds and said he was a god.

⁷There was an estate nearby that belonged to Publius, the chief official of the island. He welcomed us to his home and for three days entertained us hospitably. ⁸His father was sick in bed, suffering from fever and dysentery. Paul went in to see him and, after prayer, placed his hands on him and healed him. ⁹When this had happened, the rest of the sick on the island came and were cured. ¹⁰They honored us in many ways and when we were ready to sail, they furnished us with the supplies we needed.

Arrival at Rome

¹¹After three months we put out to sea in a ship that had wintered in the island. It was an Alexandrian ship with the figurehead of the twin gods Castor and Pollux. ¹²We put in at Syracuse and stayed there three days. ¹³From there we set sail and arrived at Rhegium. The next day the south wind came up, and on the following day we reached Puteoli. ¹⁴There we found some brothers who invited us to spend a week with them. And so we came to Rome. ¹⁵The brothers there had heard that we were coming, and they traveled as far as the Forum of Appius and the Three Taverns to meet us. At the sight of these men Paul thanked God and was encouraged. ¹⁶When we got to Rome, Paul was allowed to live by himself, with a soldier to guard him.

Paul Preaches at Rome Under Guard

¹⁷Three days later he called together the leaders of the Jews. When they had assembled, Paul said to them: "My brothers, although I have done nothing against our people or against the customs of our ancestors, I was arrested in Jerusalem and handed over to the Romans. ¹⁸They examined me and wanted to release me, because I was not guilty of any crime deserving death. ¹⁹But when the Jews objected, I was compelled to appeal to Caesar—not that I had any charge to bring against my own people. ²⁰For this reason I have asked to see you and talk with

OPEN: When have you received unexpected hospitality at a time you needed it?

DIG: 1. In light of the fact God did intend for Paul to get to Rome, why do you think he allowed all the events of 27:1-28:9 to happen? What stories might the centurion tell his fellow officers once they arrive? **2.** How might this set the stage for when Paul writes how his imprisonment at Rome served to advance the gospel (see Phil. 1:12-13)? How do you see Acts 1:8 still being demonstrated?

REFLECT: 1. How has God used a disaster in your life for ministry? What have you learned from this? **2.** Whom is God prompting you to see or write? What could you do this week to reach out to that person? **3.** How difficult is it for you to accept hospitality and to receive help? What makes you that way?

OPEN: For what recently appointed task or personal resolve have you said, "Better late than never!"? What happened once you "arrived"?

DIG: Given the long delay, his shipwreck at sea, his continuing prisoner status, and serendipitous fellowship (v. 15), how might Paul feel upon finally arriving in Rome?

REFLECT: 1. In what area of your life has God given you special encouragement this week? How important is this kind of encouragement for you? **2.** This week how will you go the "extra mile" to provide "serendipity" for your spiritual leaders?

OPEN: How would you feel if in your morning paper you read that a prominent local pastor or priest had been jailed for anti-government activities?

DIG: 1. Why might Paul take the initiative to call this meeting with the Jewish leaders in Rome? Four times since this episode began in chapter 21, Paul's innocence has been clearly stated. Why does Luke emphasize this point so strongly?

2. How do Paul's statements in 23:6, 24:21, 26:8 and 28:20 illustrate what he means by Ephesians 4:1, Colossians 4:3 and Philemon 1? How does the existence of these letters demonstrate how Paul made the best of his situation? **3.** In light of all Paul has been through, how do you think he felt when he heard the Jews' response in verse 21? How is their attitude different from that of the Jews in Jerusalem? How do you account for that difference? Why do you think the Jerusalem Jews did not pursue the case after it left their area? **4.** How do verses 25-28 serve as a thematic bridge which, after crossing over, Christianity is no longer viewed as a narrow Jewish sect (v. 24), but as a faith for all peoples (v. 28)? **5.** How does this bridge relate to Acts 1:8? To Acts 9:15-16? To Acts 26:22-23? **6.** Verse 31 is similar to other summary verses in Acts (see 6:7, 9:31, 12:24, 16:5, 19:20, etc.). What does this ending show about Luke's central concern in writing Acts?

REFLECT: 1. How would you characterize the ministry you have in your home? What do you like best about using your home to reach out to others? How do you think you could use it more effectively? **2.** What are some things that bother your non-Christian friends about the faith? How do you help them to overcome those barriers? **3.** How do you think Paul, who traveled so extensively and worked so hard, felt about being housebound for another two years? How did he serve Christ even with that limitation? What limitations do you feel placed upon you by circumstances beyond your control? How do you react to those limits? How can you serve the Lord even with these limits? **4.** How does verse 31 set the stage for how your life should be a continuation of Acts? In what way would you like to contribute to this movement of God the next two years? **5.** Probably within a few years of this section, Paul was killed by the emperor Nero. How would verse 31 serve as a fitting epithet on Paul's grave? What do you need to build into your life now, so that your faith in Christ will be what people recall about you at death?

you. It is because of the hope of Israel that I am bound with this chain."

²¹They replied, "We have not received any letters from Judea concerning you, and none of the brothers who have come from there has reported or said anything bad about you. ²²But we want to hear what your views are, for we know that people everywhere are talking against this sect."

²³They arranged to meet Paul on a certain day, and came in even larger numbers to the place where he was staying. From morning till evening he explained and declared to them the kingdom of God and tried to convince them about Jesus from the Law of Moses and from the Prophets. ²⁴Some were convinced by what he said, but others would not believe. ²⁵They disagreed among themselves and began to leave after Paul had made this final statement: "The Holy Spirit spoke the truth to your forefathers when he said through Isaiah the prophet:

²⁶" 'Go to this people and say,
"You will be ever hearing but never understanding;
   you will be ever seeing but never perceiving."
²⁷For this people's heart has become calloused;
   they hardly hear with their ears,
   and they have closed their eyes.
Otherwise they might see with their eyes,
   hear with their ears,
   understand with their hearts
and turn, and I would heal them.' ᶜ

²⁸"Therefore I want you to know that God's salvation has been sent to the Gentiles, and they will listen!" ᵈ

³⁰For two whole years Paul stayed there in his own rented house and welcomed all who came to see him. ³¹Boldly and without hindrance he preached the kingdom of God and taught about the Lord Jesus Christ.

ᶜ27 Isaiah 6:9,10   ᵈ28 Some manuscripts *listen!"* ²⁹*After he said this, the Jews left, arguing vigorously among themselves.*

ROMANS

INTRODUCTION

Date and Audience

For nearly ten years Paul had been at work evangelizing the Gentile territories ringing the Aegean Sea. Now that there were established churches throughout the region, he turns his eyes to fresh fields. He would go to Spain, the oldest Roman colony in the West. But first there was unfinished business: He had taken up a collection to aid the poor in Jerusalem—a fine gesture on the part of the newer churches—and now he had to take this to Jerusalem, though he did so with some misgiving (Rom. 15:31).

After Jerusalem, he planned to travel to Spain, stopping enroute to fulfill a long-held dream. He would visit Rome—the capital of the world. In anticipation of that visit, he wrote the Letter to the Romans by way of introduction (the Roman Christians did not know him, though, as chapter 16 reveals, he had friends there). He was also eager to assure the Roman Christians, contrary to false rumors they might have heard, that the gospel he was preaching was, indeed, the gospel of Jesus Christ. Paul wrote his letter during a three-month period spent in Corinth at the home of his friend and convert Gaius (Rom. 16:23). It was winter. The time was probably A.D. 56-57 (though it was certainly sometime between A.D. 54-59).

Paul's plan did not work as he intended. He would visit Rome, but not for three more years, and then he would come not as a tourist but as a prisoner. His misgivings about his Jerusalem trip proved accurate. Once there he was quickly arrested and eventually sent to Rome for trial. Paul remained in Rome under house arrest for at least two years. Ultimately, according to reliable tradition, he was executed at a place just outside Rome. He never went to Spain.

It is not known how the Roman church began. It is not unlikely that some Roman Jews, converted on the Day of Pentecost (Acts 2:10), began the church. The Roman historian Suetonius writes that Jews were expelled from Rome about A.D. 50 for rioting, probably as a result of preaching Jesus in synagogues. As for the Gentile Christians in Rome, it is known that other Christian missionaries besides Paul were active in founding churches.

Characteristics

Romans is Paul's most complete theological statement—carefully written, precise, and painstakingly logical (though its logic is "rabbinic" and somewhat baffling to modern readers). This is not to say, however, that Romans is dull and ponderous. Quite the contrary, it is alive and vital, full of surprises and paradox, colorful, compassionate, and sweeping in scope. In fact, the very magnitude of its themes makes Romans, at times, heavy going. Even the apostle Peter sometimes found Paul's writing hard to understand (2 Peter 3:16)!

Theme

At issue is the question of how God will judge each of us on the final day. Will it be on the basis of how "good" we were, that is, how well we kept the Law? If so, our life would be full of unending tension. Acutely aware of repeated failure, we would never have any assurance of acquittal. The Law would then be a cursed thing to us—a constant reminder of our inadequacy.

But this is not how God intends life to be. Here the great theme of Romans emerges: We can have assurance of right standing before God and hence know we will be given a positive verdict on Judgment Day. Such confidence does not come because of what we have done. It comes because of what God does—thanks to Christ's death in our place, he freely offers us his grace. Salvation is a gift, which we cannot earn; we can only receive it by faith with such gratitude that our whole life changes.

Paul sets this theme against the teaching of certain Jewish Christians, legalists who would add circumcision to grace (thus nullifying grace). If we have to do anything to deserve it, salvation is not an unearned gift freely given by God. In the course of his argument, Paul sets up a series of antitheses: faith versus works, Spirit versus flesh, and liberty versus bondage.

In answering the question of how we gain right standing before God, Paul argues first that both pagans and religious people stand condemned before God (1:18-3:20), that right standing comes only by God's grace shown in Christ's sacrificial death and acceptance by faith (3:21-5:21), and that such righteousness leads to a whole new lifestyle (6:1-8:39). He then deals with the question of why Israel rejected Christ (9:1-11:36), ending with practical exhortations for a life of faith (12:1-15:13).

Such a rich and complex piece of writing deserves repeated study. Still the major themes are readily visible and the key words are obvious.

The Importance of Romans

The impact of Romans on the history of the church can hardly be overstated. Many great advances occurred as the result of a fresh reading of this book. In A.D. 386, Augustine was converted by reading Romans 13:13-14. He then went on to write his definitive analysis of human nature and original sin (based on Romans 5 and 7), which shaped Western theology for centuries. By 1516, Martin Luther had grasped the doctrine of justification by faith alone, and so the Protestant Reformation was born. In 1738, John Wesley was converted upon hearing someone read Luther's preface to Romans, and so the evangelical revival in England was launched. In 1918, Karl Barth published his commentary on Romans, which fell like a "bomb on the playground of the theologians" (Karl Adam, quoted in *The Epistle to the Romans,* F. F. Bruce, p. 60), and so the modern period of theology was inaugurated.

Luther wrote: "This Epistle is really the chief part of the New Testament and the very purest Gospel, and is worthy not only that every Christian should know it word for word, by heart, but occupy himself with it everyday, as the bread of the soul" (*Commentary on Romans,* trans. by J. Theodore Mueller, p. xiii). Calvin wrote that "if we understand this Epistle, we have a passage opened to us to the understanding of the whole Scripture" (*The Epistles of Paul the Apostle to the Romans and the Thessalonians,* trans. by R. MacKenzie, p. 2).

Romans

1 Paul, a servant of Christ Jesus, called to be an apostle and set apart for the gospel of God— ²the gospel he promised beforehand through his prophets in the Holy Scriptures ³regarding his Son, who as to his human nature was a descendant of David, ⁴and who through the Spirit^a of holiness was declared with power to be the Son of God^b by his resurrection from the dead: Jesus Christ our Lord. ⁵Through him and for his name's sake, we received grace and apostleship to call people from among all the Gentiles to the obedience that comes from faith. ⁶And you also are among those who are called to belong to Jesus Christ.

⁷To all in Rome who are loved by God and called to be saints:

Grace and peace to you from God our Father and from the Lord Jesus Christ.

Paul's Longing to Visit Rome

⁸First, I thank my God through Jesus Christ for all of you, because your faith is being reported all over the world. ⁹God, whom I serve with my whole heart in preaching the gospel of his Son, is my witness how constantly I remember you ¹⁰in my prayers at all times; and I pray that now at last by God's will the way may be opened for me to come to you.

¹¹I long to see you so that I may impart to you some spiritual gift to make you strong— ¹²that is, that you and I may be mutually encouraged by each other's faith. ¹³I do not want you to be unaware, brothers, that I planned many times to come to you (but have been prevented from doing so until now) in order that I might have a harvest among you, just as I have had among the other Gentiles.

¹⁴I am obligated both to Greeks and non-Greeks, both to the wise and the foolish. ¹⁵That is why I am so eager to preach the gospel also to you who are at Rome.

¹⁶I am not ashamed of the gospel, because it is the power of God for the salvation of everyone who believes: first for the Jew, then for the Gentile. ¹⁷For in the gospel a righteousness from God is revealed, a righteousness that is by faith from first to last,^{c} just as it is written: "The righteous will live by faith."^{d}

God's Wrath Against Mankind

¹⁸The wrath of God is being revealed from heaven against all the godlessness and wickedness of men who suppress the truth by their wickedness, ¹⁹since what may be known about God is plain to them, because God has made it plain to them. ²⁰For since the creation of the world God's invisible qualities—his eternal power and divine nature—have been clearly seen, being understood from what has been made, so that men are without excuse.

$a4$ Or who as to his spirit $b4$ Or was appointed to be the Son of God with power $c17$ Or is from faith to faith $d17$ Hab. 2:4

OPEN: 1. What kinds of letters do you save? Why? 2. If your life were a letter, to whom would you send it? What would "you" say? How would you sign it?

DIG: 1. What does Paul's introduction reveal about himself? About the gospel? 2. From Paul's use of "call" and "called" (vv. 5-7), what does it mean to be a Christian?

REFLECT: 1. How did God call you to Christ? How has that call affected your ambitions and goals? 2. To what mission or task do you sense God is calling you five years from now?

OPEN: What special friends do you pray for often? What has made them so close to you?

DIG: 1. How would you feel if you received this letter as you read verses 8-13? 2. How might Paul rewrite verse 14 if he were addressing people in your community? 3. What excites Paul about the gospel? Pretend one of your group members is turned off to religious words and skeptical about Christianity: How would you explain verse 17 to her or him?

REFLECT: 1. How "mutually encouraged" are you by your church or fellowship group? What could help? 2. This past week, with what percent of your heart did you serve God? How can verses 16-17 strengthen your desire to do so? 3. Who are the people in your world toward whom you sense an obligation to reach for Christ? How is this reflected in your prayers and actions?

OPEN: What is your most vivid childhood memory of being disciplined? How did you feel about it then? Now?

DIG: 1. If verse 17 is the solution, how do verses 18-21 describe the problem? 2. From verses 19-21 (also Psalm 8:3-4; 19:1; 139:13-15), what do you know about God through nature? 3. What phrases in verses 18, 21-23, 25, and 28 describe attitudes or actions which lie behind the various acts of evil? 4. How does God respond to these evil attitudes? How might giving people

303

over to this evil (vv. 24, 26, and 28) be a part of their punishment? How does their "freedom" actually become a trap?

REFLECT: 1. How have you seen examples of a futile mind and a darkened heart in your own life? When has your freedom to resist God only ended up hurting you? 2. How would you use this section to talk with someone who believes all people are basically good? 3. In reading through the list of sins in verses 29-32, how do you feel having some of your faults listed right along with the "really awful" sins others commit?

OPEN: Who laid down the law in your home when you were growing up? How did you feel about it? Was it fair, just, or kind?

DIG: 1. From 2:17, who is the "you" Paul specifically addresses here in 2:1? Given that the Roman church was a mix of Jewish and Gentile converts, what tensions might exist in this church (vv. 1-5)? Since idolatry (1:28) and homosexuality (1:27) were considered very scandalous sins by the Jewish community, how would they feel reading 2:1-4? In what ways might they be guilty of the same basic causes of sin Paul describes in 1:18 and 21? 2. Given verse 3, what type of judgments about others might still be legitimate? What type of judgment is forbidden here? 3. What evidence do you see in verses 5-13 that God's kindness to these people has led to presumption rather than repentance? How are they in the same boat as the people in 1:18-32? 4. How do you reconcile 1:17, where Paul says righteousness is by faith, with what he says about doing good (2:7) and obeying the law (2:13)? What is Paul's point in each section?

²¹For although they knew God, they neither glorified him as God nor gave thanks to him, but their thinking became futile and their foolish hearts were darkened. ²²Although they claimed to be wise, they became fools ²³and exchanged the glory of the immortal God for images made to look like mortal man and birds and animals and reptiles.

²⁴Therefore God gave them over in the sinful desires of their hearts to sexual impurity for the degrading of their bodies with one another. ²⁵They exchanged the truth of God for a lie, and worshiped and served created things rather than the Creator— who is forever praised. Amen.

²⁶Because of this, God gave them over to shameful lusts. Even their women exchanged natural relations for unnatural ones. ²⁷In the same way the men also abandoned natural relations with women and were inflamed with lust for one another. Men committed indecent acts with other men, and received in themselves the due penalty for their perversion.

²⁸Furthermore, since they did not think it worthwhile to retain the knowledge of God, he gave them over to a depraved mind, to do what ought not to be done. ²⁹They have become filled with every kind of wickedness, evil, greed and depravity. They are full of envy, murder, strife, deceit and malice. They are gossips, ³⁰slanderers, God-haters, insolent, arrogant and boastful; they invent ways of doing evil; they disobey their parents; ³¹they are senseless, faithless, heartless, ruthless. ³²Although they know God's righteous decree that those who do such things deserve death, they not only continue to do these very things but also approve of those who practice them.

God's Righteous Judgment

2 You, therefore, have no excuse, you who pass judgment on someone else, for at whatever point you judge the other, you are condemning yourself, because you who pass judgment do the same things. ²Now we know that God's judgment against those who do such things is based on truth. ³So when you, a mere man, pass judgment on them and yet do the same things, do you think you will escape God's judgment? ⁴Or do you show contempt for the riches of his kindness, tolerance and patience, not realizing that God's kindness leads you towards repentance?

⁵But because of your stubbornness and your unrepentant heart, you are storing up wrath against yourself for the day of God's wrath, when his righteous judgment will be revealed. ⁶God "will give to each person according to what he has done." ᵉ ⁷To those who by persistence in doing good seek glory, honor and immortality, he will give eternal life. ⁸But for those who are self-seeking and who reject the truth and follow evil, there will be wrath and anger. ⁹There will be trouble and distress for every human being who does evil: first for the Jew, then for the Gentile; ¹⁰but glory, honor and peace for everyone who does good: first for the Jew, then for the Gentile. ¹¹For God does not show favoritism.

¹²All who sin apart from the law will also perish apart from

ᵉ6 Psalm 62:12; Prov. 24:12

the law, and all who sin under the law will be judged by the law. [13]For it is not those who hear the law who are righteous in God's sight, but it is those who obey the law who will be declared righteous. [14](Indeed, when Gentiles, who do not have the law, do by nature things required by the law, they are a law for themselves, even though they do not have the law, [15]since they show that the requirements of the law are written on their hearts, their consciences also bearing witness, and their thoughts now accusing, now even defending them.) [16]This will take place on the day when God will judge men's secrets through Jesus Christ, as my gospel declares.

The Jews and the Law

[17]Now you, if you call yourself a Jew; if you rely on the law and brag about your relationship to God; [18]if you know his will and approve of what is superior because you are instructed by the law; [19]if you are convinced that you are a guide for the blind, a light for those who are in the dark, [20]an instructor of the foolish, a teacher of infants, because you have in the law the embodiment of knowledge and truth— [21]you, then, who teach others, do you not teach yourself? You who preach against stealing, do you steal? [22]You who say that people should not commit adultery, do you commit adultery? You who abhor idols, do you rob temples? [23]You who brag about the law, do you dishonor God by breaking the law? [24]As it is written: "God's name is blasphemed among the Gentiles because of you."[f]

[25]Circumcision has value if you observe the law, but if you break the law, you have become as though you had not been circumcised. [26]If those who are not circumcised keep the law's requirements, will they not be regarded as though they were circumcised? [27]The one who is not circumcised physically and yet obeys the law will condemn you who, even though you have the[g] written code and circumcision, are a lawbreaker.

[28]A man is not a Jew if he is only one outwardly, nor is circumcision merely outward and physical. [29]No, a man is a Jew if he is one inwardly; and circumcision is circumcision of the heart, by the Spirit, not by the written code. Such a man's praise is not from men, but from God.

God's Faithfulness

3 What advantage, then, is there in being a Jew, or what value is there in circumcision? [2]Much in every way! First of all, they have been entrusted with the very words of God.

[3]What if some did not have faith? Will their lack of faith nullify God's faithfulness? [4]Not at all! Let God be true, and every man a liar. As it is written:

"So that you may be proved right when you speak
and prevail when you judge."[h]

[5]But if our unrighteousness brings out God's righteousness more clearly, what shall we say? That God is unjust in bringing his wrath on us? (I am using a human argument.) [6]Certainly not!

REFLECT: 1. How does the emphasis here on God's judgment make a difference in how you view your life before God? **2.** Has God's kindness led you toward real love for him? How so? Or do you now take the relationship for granted? Why? **3.** Do you see yourself more as a "gross sinner" (1:18-32)? Or as a "respectable sinner" (2:1-16)? What difference does it make with God?

OPEN: What's your most vivid memory of religious training as a child? How do you feel about this training?

DIG: 1. If you were one of the Jewish people in verses 17-24, what would you write about yourself as a character sketch on a job application? What type of reference would your Gentile neighbor write? What accounts for the difference? **2.** How is the intent of the law and of circumcision (the Old Testament sign for being part of God's family, see Gen. 17:1-14) being twisted? **3.** From Deuteronomy 10:16; 30:6 and Jeremiah 4:4; 9:25-26, what does Paul mean by "circumcision of the heart" (v. 29)? What is the real mark of God's family?

REFLECT: 1. When have you ever realized that the finger pointed at the Jews in 17-24 could also be pointed at you as well? **2.** When did your faith become more than a ritual? **3.** What religious rituals and symbols are twisted today like this? Paraphrase what Paul is saying in verses 25-29, using the Christian symbol of baptism.

OPEN: What advantages did you gain by being brought up in your area of the country and in your particular home? What disadvantages did you face?

DIG: Have one person take the role of someone protesting Paul's conclusion in 2:28-29. That person reads the questions in verses 1,3,5 and 7. Have another person read Paul's responses in verses 2,4,6 and 8. What is the issue in each objection? How do the questions continue the practice of misapplying God's teachings?

REFLECT: 1. What responsibilities come to Christians who have the advantage of possessing God's

---

f24 Isaiah 52:5; Ezek. 36:22   g27 Or who, by means of a   h4 Psalm 51:4

Word? **2.** How have you encountered people twisting God's teaching for their own use? How did you respond?

OPEN: When has someone spilled the beans on your past actions which you wanted to hide? How did you feel about yourself afterwards?

DIG: 1. Although the Jewish Christians in Rome apparently felt superior to the Gentiles (2:1, 3:1), what does Paul say they have in common? **2.** From verses 10-18, list what is said regarding human thought, direction, speech, and action. How does this list make you feel? **3.** How do verses 19 and 1:20 prove Paul's point that the whole world is accountable to God? **4.** From verse 20, would you say that the law is *descriptive"* (more like a doctor's thermometer)? Or *prescriptive"* (more like medicine to a sick patient)?

REFLECT: 1. Suppose this letter ended with verse 20, how would you feel about yourself? About God? **2.** When did you first really sense your sin and need for God? What motivated you to turn to God? **3.** What can you learn about witnessing from Paul's example in chapters 2-3? What types of people today may need to be approached like this?

OPEN: What was one of your favorite stories as a child? Why?

DIG: 1. Have different people look up "justification", "redemption" and sacrifice of "atonement" in a dictionary. How would you translate these terms into everyday English to explain what God did for us in Jesus? How can you illustrate them by examples of the freedom, forgiveness and acceptance you have found in Jesus? **2.** How does Paul continue to break down barriers between the Jewish and Gentile believers? What objection is raised in verse 31? Why would this be a serious problem for the Jews (see 3:8)?

REFLECT: 1. If you had to explain the gospel from this passage alone, what would you say? **2.** When did the message of God's grace become real to you? What difference is it making in your life right now? **3.** What prejudices and barriers exist in the church today? How could you help to break them down?

If that were so, how could God judge the world? [7]Someone might argue, "If my falsehood enhances God's truthfulness and so increases his glory, why am I still condemned as a sinner?" [8]Why not say—as we are being slanderously reported as saying and as some claim that we say—"Let us do evil that good may result"? Their condemnation is deserved.

No One Is Righteous

[9]What shall we conclude then? Are we any better[i]? Not at all! We have already made the charge that Jews and Gentiles alike are all under sin. [10]As it is written:

> "There is no one righteous, not even one;
> [11] there is no one who understands,
>   no one who seeks God.
> [12]All have turned away,
>   they have together become worthless;
> there is no one who does good,
>   not even one."[j]
> [13]"Their throats are open graves;
>   their tongues practice deceit."[k]
> "The poison of vipers is on their lips."[l]
> [14] "Their mouths are full of cursing and bitterness."[m]
> [15]"Their feet are swift to shed blood;
> [16] ruin and misery mark their ways,
> [17]and the way of peace they do not know."[n]
> [18] "There is no fear of God before their eyes."[o]

[19]Now we know that whatever the law says, it says to those who are under the law, so that every mouth may be silenced and the whole world held accountable to God. [20]Therefore no one will be declared righteous in his sight by observing the law; rather, through the law we become conscious of sin.

Righteousness Through Faith

[21]But now a righteousness from God, apart from law, has been made known, to which the Law and the Prophets testify. [22]This righteousness from God comes through faith in Jesus Christ to all who believe. There is no difference, [23]for all have sinned and fall short of the glory of God, [24]and are justified freely by his grace through the redemption that came by Christ Jesus. [25]God presented him as a sacrifice of atonement,[p] through faith in his blood. He did this to demonstrate his justice, because in his forbearance he had left the sins committed beforehand unpunished — [26]he did it to demonstrate his justice at the present time, so as to be just and the one who justifies those who have faith in Jesus.

[27]Where, then, is boasting? It is excluded. On what principle? On that of observing the law? No, but on that of faith. [28]For we maintain that a man is justified by faith apart from observing the law. [29]Is God the God of Jews only? Is he not the God of Gentiles too? Yes, of Gentiles too, [30]since there is only one God, who will

[i]9 Or *worse* [j]12 Psalms 14:1-3; 53:1-3; Eccles. 7:20 [k]13 Psalm 5:9
[l]13 Psalm 140:3 [m]14 Psalm 10:7 [n]17 Isaiah 59:7,8 [o]18 Psalm 36:1
[p]25 Or *as the one who would turn aside his wrath, taking away sin*

justify the circumcised by faith and the uncircumcised through that same faith. [31]Do we, then, nullify the law by this faith? Not at all! Rather, we uphold the law.

Abraham Justified by Faith

4 What then shall we say that Abraham, our forefather, discovered in this matter? [2]If, in fact, Abraham was justified by works, he had something to boast about—but not before God. [3]What does the Scripture say? "Abraham believed God, and it was credited to him as righteousness."[q]

[4]Now when a man works, his wages are not credited to him as a gift, but as an obligation. [5]However, to the man who does not work but trusts God who justifies the wicked, his faith is credited as righteousness. [6]David says the same thing when he speaks of the blessedness of the man to whom God credits righteousness apart from works:

[7]"Blessed are they
   whose transgressions are forgiven,
   whose sins are covered.
[8]Blessed is the man
   whose sin the Lord will never count against him."[r]

[9]Is this blessedness only for the circumcised, or also for the uncircumcised? We have been saying that Abraham's faith was credited to him as righteousness. [10]Under what circumstances was it credited? Was it after he was circumcised, or before? It was not after, but before! [11]And he received the sign of circumcision, a seal of the righteousness that he had by faith while he was still uncircumcised. So then, he is the father of all who believe but have not been circumcised, in order that righteousness might be credited to them. [12]And he is also the father of the circumcised who not only are circumcised but who also walk in the footsteps of the faith that our father Abraham had before he was circumcised.

[13]It was not through law that Abraham and his offspring received the promise that he would be heir of the world, but through the righteousness that comes by faith. [14]For if those who live by law are heirs, faith has no value and the promise is worthless, [15]because law brings wrath. And where there is no law there is no transgression.

[16]Therefore, the promise comes by faith, so that it may be by grace and may be guaranteed to all Abraham's offspring—not only to those who are of the law but also to those who are of the faith of Abraham. He is the father of us all. [17]As it is written: "I have made you a father of many nations."[s] He is our father in the sight of God, in whom he believed—the God who gives life to the dead and calls things that are not as though they were.

[18]Against all hope, Abraham in hope believed and so became the father of many nations, just as it had been said to him, "So shall your offspring be."[t] [19]Without weakening in his faith, he faced the fact that his body was as good as dead—since he was about a hundred years old—and that Sarah's womb was also

---

OPEN: If God actually spoke directly to you and promised to give you something you wanted with all your heart, how would you feel? How would you feel 25 years later if nothing had happened yet?

DIG: 1. Since some of the Jewish converts believed they were set right with God by the law, why does Paul go back to the examples of Abraham and David? **2.** How does 4:3-8 illustrate what is said in 3:27-28? From verses 3-8, on what basis is a right relationship with God given or credited to us? **3.** What is Paul's point in stressing that Abraham was counted as right with God before he was circumcised? How do verses 9-17 support Paul's statement in 3:29-31? **4.** As you walk by faith in the footsteps of Abraham's faith (vv. 18-21), how do you feel? What do you learn about faith? **5.** How do verses 17 and 21 sum up specifically what Abraham believed about God? How do these truths relate to what Paul calls us to believe in verses 23-25? **6.** How would you sum up the gospel from verses 23-25?

REFLECT: 1. Who are some other Biblical characters that you respect as an example of faith? Who are some Christians alive now that set the pace for you about trusting in God? What is most important about these persons to you? **2.** What practical, personal or emotional differences does it make to you whether a right relationship with God is a gift, or something you have to work for? **3.** Since this right relationship is a gift, how would you use Abraham's example to argue against a presumptuous attitude toward God? **4.** Where are you being stretched in your ability to trust God's promises to you? What can you learn from Abraham's example to encourage you?

---

q3 Gen. 15:6; also in verse 22   r8 Psalm 32:1,2   s17 Gen. 17:5   t18 Gen. 15:5

dead. [20]Yet he did not waver through unbelief regarding the promise of God, but was strengthened in his faith and gave glory to God, [21]being fully persuaded that God had power to do what he had promised. [22]This is why "it was credited to him as righteousness." [23]The words "it was credited to him" were written not for him alone, [24]but also for us, to whom God will credit righteousness—for us who believe in him who raised Jesus our Lord from the dead. [25]He was delivered over to death for our sins and was raised to life for our justification.

Peace and Joy

5 Therefore, since we have been justified through faith, we[u] have peace with God through our Lord Jesus Christ, [2]through whom we have gained access by faith into this grace in which we now stand. And we[u] rejoice in the hope of the glory of God. [3]Not only so, but we[u] also rejoice in our sufferings, because we know that suffering produces perseverance; [4]perseverance, character; and character, hope. [5]And hope does not disappoint us, because God has poured out his love into our hearts by the Holy Spirit, whom he has given us.

[6]You see, at just the right time, when we were still powerless, Christ died for the ungodly. [7]Very rarely will anyone die for a righteous man, though for a good man someone might possibly dare to die. [8]But God demonstrates his own love for us in this: While we were still sinners, Christ died for us.

[9]Since we have now been justified by his blood, how much more shall we be saved from God's wrath through him! [10]For if, when we were God's enemies, we were reconciled to him through the death of his Son, how much more, having been reconciled, shall we be saved through his life! [11]Not only is this so, but we also rejoice in God through our Lord Jesus Christ, through whom we have now received reconciliation.

Death Through Adam, Life Through Christ

[12]Therefore, just as sin entered the world through one man, and death through sin, and in this way death came to all men, because all sinned— [13]for before the law was given, sin was in the world. But sin is not taken into account when there is no law. [14]Nevertheless, death reigned from the time of Adam to the time of Moses, even over those who did not sin by breaking a command, as did Adam, who was a pattern of the one to come.

[15]But the gift is not like the trespass. For if the many died by the trespass of the one man, how much more did God's grace and the gift that came by the grace of the one man, Jesus Christ, overflow to the many! [16]Again, the gift of God is not like the result of the one man's sin: The judgment followed one sin and brought condemnation, but the gift followed many trespasses and brought justification. [17]For if, by the trespass of the one man, death reigned through that one man, how much more will those who receive God's abundant provision of grace and of the gift of righteousness reign in life through the one man, Jesus Christ.

[u]1,2,3 Or *let us*

OPEN: Whom do you know that rejoices in suffering? Why do they?

DIG: 1. In your own words, what does it mean to be "justified through faith" (v. 1)? **2.** What benefits are ours as a result of being justified by faith (vv. 1-5)? How are suffering, hope and God's love interrelated? **3.** What words in verses 6, 8 and 10 describe what we once were in God's eyes? How does the death of Christ change this relationship? **4.** As you read verses 9-11, what tone of voice do you hear Paul using? Why? **5.** Compare verse 9 with 3:25 and Leviticus 16:3-16: How does this Old Testament ritual illustrate what Christ did on the cross for believers?

REFLECT: 1. What is the worst suffering you've experienced? What has God taught you through it? **2.** What three words best describe your life before you were a Christian? How about now? Why the change?

OPEN: What personality traits do you have from each of your parents? If you are a parent, how do you see yourself reflected in your own children?

DIG: 1. How does Paul sum up the "bad news" of the Bible in verses 12-14? Think of a decision you made that affected others in a bad way: How does this help you understand verse 12? **2.** From verses 15-19, list in two columns the comparisons and contrasts between Adam and Jesus: What results from each one? What do you learn about the work of Christ from this list? **3.** From 5:1-21, what do you note about what God has done through Jesus for us? How does this help you understand the meaning of God's grace (vv. 1, 15, 17, 20, 21)? How does this chapter illustrate why "Grace and Peace to you" (1:7) is such an apt greeting for Christians?

REFLECT: 1. Does the gospel message excite you as it does

[18]Consequently, just as the result of one trespass was condemnation for all men, so also the result of one act of righteousness was justification that brings life for all men. [19]For just as through the disobedience of the one man the many were made sinners, so also through the obedience of the one man the many will be made righteous.

[20]The law was added so that the trespass might increase. But where sin increased, grace increased all the more, [21]so that, just as sin reigned in death, so also grace might reign through righteousness to bring eternal life through Jesus Christ our Lord.

Dead to Sin, Alive in Christ

6 What shall we say, then? Shall we go on sinning so that grace may increase? [2]By no means! We died to sin; how can we live in it any longer? [3]Or don't you know that all of us who were baptized into Christ Jesus were baptized into his death? [4]We were therefore buried with him through baptism into death in order that, just as Christ was raised from the dead through the glory of the Father, we too may live a new life.

[5]If we have been united with him like this in his death, we will certainly also be united with him in his resurrection. [6]For we know that our old self was crucified with him so that the body of sin might be done away with,[v] that we should no longer be slaves to sin— [7]because anyone who has died has been freed from sin.

[8]Now if we died with Christ, we believe that we will also live with him. [9]For we know that since Christ was raised from the dead, he cannot die again; death no longer has mastery over him. [10]The death he died, he died to sin once for all; but the life he lives, he lives to God.

[11]In the same way, count yourselves dead to sin but alive to God in Christ Jesus. [12]Therefore do not let sin reign in your mortal body so that you obey its evil desires. [13]Do not offer the parts of your body to sin, as instruments of wickedness, but rather offer yourselves to God, as those who have been brought from death to life; and offer the parts of your body to him as instruments of righteousness. [14]For sin shall not be your master, because you are not under law, but under grace.

Slaves to Righteousness

[15]What then? Shall we sin because we are not under law but under grace? By no means! [16]Don't you know that when you offer yourselves to someone to obey him as slaves, you are slaves to the one whom you obey—whether you are slaves to sin, which leads to death, or to obedience, which leads to righteousness? [17]But thanks be to God that, though you used to be slaves to sin, you wholeheartedly obeyed the form of teaching to which you were entrusted. [18]You have been set free from sin and have become slaves to righteousness.

[19]I put this in human terms because you are weak in your natural selves. Just as you used to offer the parts of your body in slavery to impurity and to ever-increasing wickedness, so now

[v]6 Or be rendered powerless

Paul? Why or why not? What could help you feel anew it's life and vitality? **2.** Write a thank-you letter to Jesus reflecting on what he has done for you, as portrayed by Paul in chapter 5. **3.** Read these letters as closing prayers.

OPEN: When the time comes, how do you prefer to die: By accident? Of natural causes? A martyr's death? By your own hand? Why?

DIG: 1. From 3:8 and 6:1, how are some people misusing Paul's emphasis on God's grace (5:20-21)? What do they hear Paul saying? **2.** How would you paraphrase Paul's brief answer in verse 2? The idea of death is mentioned 15 times in this section: How does Christ's death and resurrection tie into our relationship with sin? **3.** What actions does Paul call us to perform in verses 11-13? How do these relate to his general statement in verse 3? What motivation does he give us for doing so (v.13)?

REFLECT: 1. How have you experienced Christ's death and resurrection in your life? **2.** What do you do when you hear voices from your former life? **3.** From verses 11-13, what specifically do you need to do this week to count yourself dead to sin but alive to Christ? **4.** If you could dig a grave and put one thing in it to be buried with Christ forever what would it be? **5.** As you struggle with sin, what from this passage gives you hope?

OPEN: From your cultural and social history, what images and feelings do you associate with "slavery": Civil rights? Filthy habits? Tyrannical boss? Apron strings? "Puppy love"? God's curse?

DIG: 1. How is the question in verse 15 another attempt to misuse Paul's teaching on grace (see v. 1)? **2.** Whereas death was the image used in 1-14, what image does Paul use here? What is the "cost and benefit" of each type of slavery? How does one become a "slave" to Christ? **3.** From verse 19, how are we to live out our freedom from sin?

REFLECT: 1. In your own spiritual life, when did you realize that you did not have to be a slave to old desires? **2.** In which areas of your life do you feel trapped like a slave? **3.** How would seeing yourself as God's willing servant have made a difference in your actions and attitudes this past week?

OPEN: What images and feelings do you associate with "marriage": Kitchen slave? Bedroom athlete? Lifelong vow? Adultery?

DIG: 1. After "death and life" and "slavery and freedom," what new image is used here? How does this image help you understand your relationship with Christ? **2.** What did the law actually produce in those who tried to live by it? How has Jesus changed this? **3.** What would "fruits for death" look like compared to "fruit to God"?

REFLECT: 1. Do you feel more "married" to the living Christ who frees us, or to some religious code that reminds you how you have failed? **2.** In your life's vineyard, what would "fruit to God" look like compared with "fruit for death"?

OPEN: During your teen years, what was one of your biggest struggles? How have you handled this struggle since?

DIG: 1. What is the significance of the shift in pronouns from 7:1-6 and this section? How does Paul's example in verses 7-11 illustrate what he meant in verse 5? Give an example of this principle in your life. **2.** How is it that the law which was supposed to lead to life actually leads to death? How do verses 14-20 answer this question? **3.** Prior to Paul's conversion, how must he have felt about the inner turmoil described here? How did he try to deal with it then (see Philippians 3:4-6)? What has he found in Christ? **4.** Why do you think God's law was given for us to follow: A means to follow in order to be saved? A guide to follow once we are saved by grace? A stumbling block, impossible to follow, which only points the sinner to God's grace? How do verses 10, 12 and 22 support your answer?

REFLECT: 1. In light of your own struggles with sin, how do you feel reading about Paul's conflict? How is this a model for a healthy, realistic self-image? **2.** If you were comparing

offer them in slavery to righteousness leading to holiness. [20]When you were slaves to sin, you were free from the control of righteousness. [21]What benefit did you reap at that time from the things you are now ashamed of? Those things result in death! [22]But now that you have been set free from sin and have become slaves to God, the benefit you reap leads to holiness, and the result is eternal life. [23]For the wages of sin is death, but the gift of God is eternal life in[w] Christ Jesus our Lord.

An Illustration From Marriage

7 Do you not know, brothers—for I am speaking to men who know the law—that the law has authority over a man only as long as he lives? [2]For example, by law a married woman is bound to her husband as long as he is alive, but if her husband dies, she is released from the law of marriage. [3]So then, if she marries another man while her husband is still alive, she is called an adulteress. But if her husband dies, she is released from that law and is not an adulteress, even though she marries another man.

[4]So, my brothers, you also died to the law through the body of Christ, that you might belong to another, to him who was raised from the dead, in order that we might bear fruit to God. [5]For when we were controlled by the sinful nature,[x] the sinful passions aroused by the law were at work in our bodies, so that we bore fruit for death. [6]But now, by dying to what once bound us, we have been released from the law so that we serve in the new way of the Spirit, and not in the old way of the written code.

Struggling With Sin

[7]What shall we say, then? Is the law sin? Certainly not! Indeed I would not have known what sin was except through the law. For I would not have known what coveting really was if the law had not said, "Do not covet."[y] [8]But sin, seizing the opportunity afforded by the commandment, produced in me every kind of covetous desire. For apart from law, sin is dead. [9]Once I was alive apart from law; but when the commandment came, sin sprang to life and I died. [10]I found that the very commandment that was intended to bring life actually brought death. [11]For sin, seizing the opportunity afforded by the commandment, deceived me, and through the commandment put me to death. [12]So then, the law is holy, and the commandment is holy, righteous and good.

[13]Did that which is good, then, become death to me? By no means! But in order that sin might be recognized as sin, it produced death in me through what was good, so that through the commandment sin might become utterly sinful.

[14]We know that the law is spiritual; but I am unspiritual, sold as a slave to sin. [15]I do not understand what I do. For what I want to do I do not do, but what I hate I do. [16]And if I do what I do not want to do, I agree that the law is good. [17]As it is, it is no longer I myself who do it, but it is sin living in me. [18]I know that nothing good lives in me, that is, in my sinful nature.[z] For

---

w23 Or *through*   *x5* Or *the flesh;* also in verse 25   *y7* Exodus 20:17; Deut. 5:21
z18 Or *my flesh*

I have the desire to do what is good, but I cannot carry it out. ¹⁹For what I do is not the good I want to do; no, the evil I do not want to do—this I keep on doing. ²⁰Now if I do what I do not want to do, it is no longer I who do it, but it is sin living in me that does it.

²¹So I find this law at work: When I want to do good, evil is right there with me. ²²For in my inner being I delight in God's law; ²³but I see another law at work in the members of my body, waging war against the law of my mind and making me a prisoner of the law of sin at work within my members. ²⁴What a wretched man I am! Who will rescue me from this body of death? ²⁵Thanks be to God—through Jesus Christ our Lord!

So then, I myself in my mind am a slave to God's law, but in the sinful nature a slave to the law of sin.

Life Through the Spirit

8 Therefore, there is now no condemnation for those who are in Christ Jesus,ᵃ ²because through Christ Jesus the law of the Spirit of life set me free from the law of sin and death. ³For what the law was powerless to do in that it was weakened by the sinful nature,ᵇ God did by sending his own Son in the likeness of sinful man to be a sin offering.ᶜ And so he condemned sin in sinful man,ᵈ ⁴in order that the righteous requirements of the law might be fully met in us, who do not live according to the sinful nature but according to the Spirit.

⁵Those who live according to the sinful nature have their minds set on what that nature desires; but those who live in accordance with the Spirit have their minds set on what the Spirit desires. ⁶The mind of sinful manᵉ is death, but the mind controlled by the Spirit is life and peace; ⁷the sinful mindᶠ is hostile to God. It does not submit to God's law, nor can it do so. ⁸Those controlled by the sinful nature cannot please God.

⁹You, however, are controlled not by the sinful nature but by the Spirit, if the Spirit of God lives in you. And if anyone does not have the Spirit of Christ, he does not belong to Christ. ¹⁰But if Christ is in you, your body is dead because of sin, yet your spirit is alive because of righteousness. ¹¹And if the Spirit of him who raised Jesus from the dead is living in you, he who raised Christ from the dead will also give life to your mortal bodies through his Spirit, who lives in you.

¹²Therefore, brothers, we have an obligation—but it is not to the sinful nature, to live according to it. ¹³For if you live according to the sinful nature, you will die; but if by the Spirit you put to death the misdeeds of the body, you will live, ¹⁴because those who are led by the Spirit of God are sons of God. ¹⁵For you did not receive a spirit that makes you a slave again to fear, but you received the Spirit of sonship.ᵍ And by him we cry, *"Abba,ʰ* Father.'' ¹⁶The Spirit himself testifies with our spirit that we are God's children. ¹⁷Now if we are children, then we are heirs—heirs of God and co-heirs with Christ, if indeed we share in his sufferings in order that we may also share in his glory.

your spiritual life to a football game, what would the score be? What quarter is it? Are you now on offense or defense? What is your game plan? How does knowing Christ make a difference? **3.** When have you experienced the sense of Jesus rescuing you from sin or situations that were way too big for you to handle? How does Jesus help you now?

OPEN: When you were a child, who let you off the hook when you knew you deserved to be punished for something done wrong? How did you feel toward them?

DIG: 1. From 3:22-24, 4:23-24, 5:9 and 8:1-4, how would you explain the gospel to someone struggling with his or her own sense of failure to be "good enough" for God? How is "no condemnation" related to the idea of "justification" (3:24, 5:1)? **2.** Using verses 5-11, make a list comparing what Paul says about living according to the sinful nature and according to the Spirit. What is the relationship of each to the Law of God? **3.** Since we are not set right with God by doing good works, what is the motive for changing our lives? How do verses 13-14, 6:13 and 6:19 together show how we are to deal with our sinful nature? What does he mean by the phrase "by the Spirit" (vv. 13-14)? **4.** What does it mean to you that you are not God's slave but his child?

REFLECT: 1. In light of verse 1, how should you handle feelings of guilt and unworthiness before God? What truths here can help at these times? **2.** What mostly occupies your time? Why? Is there anything you wish occupied more of your time? Why? **3.** What mostly occupies your thoughts? How much in harmony with your faith are your thoughts and time? What would help put them in tune? **4.** When bad memories or unhealthy thoughts enter your mind, what have you found most helpful in dealing with them? **5.** When did you first realize you needed to turn control of your life over to the Holy Spirit? What happened?

ᵃ1 Some later manuscripts Jesus, who do not live according to the sinful nature but according to the Spirit, *ᵇ3 Or the flesh; also in verses 4, 5, 8, 9, 12 and 13* *ᶜ3 Or man, for sin* *ᵈ3 Or in the flesh* *ᵉ6 Or mind set on the flesh* *ᶠ7 Or the mind set on the flesh* *ᵍ15 Or adoption* *ʰ15 Aramaic for Father*

OPEN: What person in your family seems best able to cope with trouble and hardship? What is this person's secret?

DIG: 1. From 8:17, what type of suffering does Paul have in view here? What do you think he means by the glory to come? How does this relate to what he says about creation in 19-23? **2.** What would a world like ours be like if there was no decay or death? How is this a picture of glory? **3.** How can the hope in verses 22-25 help you during times of trial?

REFLECT: 1. What frustrates you most about living in a fallen world? **2.** What is the difference between hope and wishful thinking? How has your hope in Christ helped you this week? **3.** When was the last time you did not know how to pray? How did the Holy Spirit help you?

OPEN: On an optimist-pessimist scale, where would you position yourself? Why?

DIG: 1. What confidence does verse 28 give you about events that occur in your life? How does this relate to the idea of suffering in verse 18? **2.** In verses 29-30, what 5 verbs describe God's role in our coming to know him? How do these add to a Christian's confidence? How does verse 29 define God's good purposes for us? **3.** In verses 31-39, how does Paul settle the fears of those who may still be asking questions about the security of God's love for us? **4.** How might the forces mentioned in verses 38-39 try to unsettle our trust in God's love? What does Paul's ringing assurance do for your fears? How do verses 31-39 sum up Paul's message in Romans thus far?

REFLECT: 1. When has it been hardest for you to believe Romans 8:28? **2.** How is God putting you through the school of hard knocks now? In the midst of the knocks, how do you see God at work? **3.** Of the enemies mentioned in verses 38-39, which one is the most real to you? **4.** What will you claim from this passage to help you through the week? How could your group pray specifically for you this week?

Future Glory

[18]I consider that our present sufferings are not worth comparing with the glory that will be revealed in us. [19]The creation waits in eager expectation for the sons of God to be revealed. [20]For the creation was subjected to frustration, not by its own choice, but by the will of the one who subjected it, in hope [21]that[i] the creation itself will be liberated from its bondage to decay and brought into the glorious freedom of the children of God.

[22]We know that the whole creation has been groaning as in the pains of childbirth right up to the present time. [23]Not only so, but we ourselves, who have the firstfruits of the Spirit, groan inwardly as we wait eagerly for our adoption as sons, the redemption of our bodies. [24]For in this hope we were saved. But hope that is seen is no hope at all. Who hopes for what he already has? [25]But if we hope for what we do not yet have, we wait for it patiently.

[26]In the same way, the Spirit helps us in our weakness. We do not know what we ought to pray for, but the Spirit himself intercedes for us with groans that words cannot express. [27]And he who searches our hearts knows the mind of the Spirit, because the Spirit intercedes for the saints in accordance with God's will.

More Than Conquerors

[28]And we know that in all things God works for the good of those who love him,[j] who[k] have been called according to his purpose. [29]For those God foreknew he also predestined to be conformed to the likeness of his Son, that he might be the firstborn among many brothers. [30]And those he predestined, he also called; those he called, he also justified; those he justified, he also glorified.

[31]What, then, shall we say in response to this? If God is for us, who can be against us? [32]He who did not spare his own Son, but gave him up for us all—how will he not also, along with him, graciously give us all things? [33]Who will bring any charge against those whom God has chosen? It is God who justifies. [34]Who is he that condemns? Christ Jesus, who died—more than that, who was raised to life—is at the right hand of God and is also interceding for us. [35]Who shall separate us from the love of Christ? Shall trouble or hardship or persecution or famine or nakedness or danger or sword? [36]As it is written:

> "For your sake we face death all day long;
>   we are considered as sheep to be slaughtered."[l]

[37]No, in all these things we are more than conquerors through him who loved us. [38]For I am convinced that neither death nor life, neither angels nor demons,[m] neither the present nor the future, nor any powers, [39]neither height nor depth, nor anything else in all creation, will be able to separate us from the love of God that is in Christ Jesus our Lord.

---

*i*20,21 Or *subjected it in hope.* *21For*   *j*28 Some manuscripts *And we know that all things work together for good to those who love God*   *k*28 Or *works together with those who love him to bring about* what *is good—with those who heavenly rulers*   *l*36 Psalm 44:22   *m*38 Or *nor*

God's Sovereign Choice

9 I speak the truth in Christ—I am not lying, my conscience confirms it in the Holy Spirit— ²I have great sorrow and unceasing anguish in my heart. ³For I could wish that I myself were cursed and cut off from Christ for the sake of my brothers, those of my own race, ⁴the people of Israel. Theirs is the adoption as sons; theirs the divine glory, the covenants, the receiving of the law, the temple worship and the promises. ⁵Theirs are the patriarchs, and from them is traced the human ancestry of Christ, who is God over all, forever praised!ⁿ Amen.

⁶It is not as though God's word had failed. For not all who are descended from Israel are Israel. ⁷Nor because they are his descendants are they all Abraham's children. On the contrary, "It is through Isaac that your offspring will be reckoned."ᵒ ⁸In other words, it is not the natural children who are God's children, but it is the children of the promise who are regarded as Abraham's offspring. ⁹For this was how the promise was stated: "At the appointed time I will return, and Sarah will have a son."ᵖ

¹⁰Not only that, but Rebekah's children had one and the same father, our father Isaac. ¹¹Yet, before the twins were born or had done anything good or bad—in order that God's purpose in election might stand: ¹²not by works but by him who calls—she was told, "The older will serve the younger."�q ¹³Just as it is written: "Jacob I loved, but Esau I hated."ʳ

¹⁴What then shall we say? Is God unjust? Not at all! ¹⁵For he says to Moses,

"I will have mercy on whom I have mercy,
   and I will have compassion on whom I have
      compassion."ˢ

¹⁶It does not, therefore, depend on man's desire or effort, but on God's mercy. ¹⁷For the Scripture says to Pharaoh: "I raised you up for this very purpose, that I might display my power in you and that my name might be proclaimed in all the earth."ᵗ ¹⁸Therefore God has mercy on whom he wants to have mercy, and he hardens whom he wants to harden.

¹⁹One of you will say to me: "Then why does God still blame us? For who resists his will?" ²⁰But who are you, O man, to talk back to God? "Shall what is formed say to him who formed it, 'Why did you make me like this?' "ᵘ ²¹Does not the potter have the right to make out of the same lump of clay some pottery for noble purposes and some for common use?

²²What if God, choosing to show his wrath and make his power known, bore with great patience the objects of his wrath—prepared for destruction? ²³What if he did this to make the riches of his glory known to the objects of his mercy, whom he prepared in advance for glory— ²⁴even us, whom he also called, not only from the Jews but also from the Gentiles? ²⁵As he says in Hosea:

OPEN: 1. What about your family background helped you toward faith in Christ? What hindered you? **2.** Supposing salvation did depend on human desire and effort, what grade would God give you: "E" for effort? "C" for creative? "A" for accomplishment? "F" for failure to follow directions? If God graded on a "curve", would you have a better chance of passing his life-long course? Why or why not? Would "crib sheets" help? How about remedial education? Going back to pre-school? Polishing a few apples and becoming the Teacher's pet?

DIG: 1. Given Paul's assurance in 8:39, why would he turn from that to discuss the problem of widespread Jewish unbelief? From verse 6, what question does unbelief raise for some persons? **2.** In verses 1-3, what phrases show Paul's deep concern for his people? **3.** How should each of the benefits he mentions in verses 4 -5 have drawn the Jewish people to Christ? How does he account for their unbelief in spite of these advantages? How does what he wrote in 4:12 fit in here? How does this explain who the "children of the promise" are? **4.** How would verse 8 and 4:11-12 help resolve conflicts between Jews and Gentiles in the Roman church? **5.** In light of verse 11, how does Paul maintain God's justice? What does 3:9-20 imply would be just and fair for each of us to receive from God? According to 5:9-10, on what basis does God relate to us? How does this tie in with 9:15-16? **6.** How does Paul respond to further questions about God's fairness in choosing some but not others? What is God's overriding purpose? How do the Old Testament quotes in verses 25-29 relate to Paul's argument here? How would these be effective in solving tensions between Jewish and Gentile Christians?

REFLECT: 1. If you could ask Paul for clarification on this passage, what would you ask him? Why? How do you think he would answer? **2.** Where are you growing in your understanding of God's will for your life? What questions would you like to ask God about this? **3.** How deeply do you hurt for unbelievers? Why? **4.** How do you feel about verse 16? Have you ever wondered about why God chose you to be part of his plan for the universe? What have you concluded? What work do you think God created you for? **5.** Using a piece of pottery as a metaphor, describe who you are (a water pitcher, a coffee mug, etc.)

ⁿ5 Or Christ, who is over all. God be forever praised! Or Christ. God who is over all be forever praised!   ᵒ7 Gen. 21:12   ᵖ9 Gen. 18:10,14   q12 Gen. 25:23   ʳ13 Mal. 1:2,3   ˢ15 Exodus 33:19   ᵗ17 Exodus 9:16   ᵘ20 Isaiah 29:16; 45:9

and how God wants to use you. **6.** Who are some non-Christians God has used to help you toward spiritual maturity? How has God used them? **7.** What are five benefits to your spiritual life that have come to you because of where you live? How might these benefits blind you to aspects of God's saving grace? What will you do to insure that this does not happen?

OPEN: Would you rather raise your children in a pagan society where you have to fight for what you believe? Or in a religious society where everyone believes as you do? Why? What do you think are the main strengths and weaknesses of raising children in each type of society?

DIG: 1. In what characteristic way did Jews seek to be right with God? From 3:20 and 7:7-11, what was the basic problem in this approach? How do you see people trying this same way today? **2.** On the basis of 10:1-2, how would you respond to someone who said, "What you believe doesn't matter as long as you are sincere"? How can zeal for God sometimes get in the way of knowing him? **3.** How would the attitude of a person coming to God on the basis of his or her performance (v. 5) be different from that of someone coming to him by faith in Christ (vv. 8-9)? **4.** What does it mean to confess "Jesus is Lord"? How would you illustrate this from earlier chapters in Romans? How does this tie in with belief? **5.** Look at 3:23-23: How does the phrase, "there is no difference", in that context compare with its use here in 10:12? What hope is given here? **6.** What is the purpose of Paul's series of questions in verses 14-15? How do these verses plus verse 17 emphasize the importance of evangelism? **7.** Although Israel heard the message, Gentiles under-

"I will call them 'my people' who are not my people;
  and I will call her 'my loved one' who is not my loved one," [v]

²⁶and,

"It will happen that in the very place where it was said to them,
  'You are not my people,'
they will be called 'sons of the living God.' " [w]

²⁷Isaiah cries out concerning Israel:

"Though the number of the Israelites be like the sand by the sea,
  only the remnant will be saved.
²⁸For the Lord will carry out
  his sentence on earth with speed and finality." [x]

²⁹It is just as Isaiah said previously:

"Unless the Lord Almighty
  had left us descendants,
we would have become like Sodom,
  we would have been like Gomorrah." [y]

Israel's Unbelief

³⁰What then shall we say? That the Gentiles, who did not pursue righteousness, have obtained it, a righteousness that is by faith; ³¹but Israel, who pursued a law of righteousness, has not attained it. ³²Why not? Because they pursued it not by faith but as if it were by works. They stumbled over the "stumbling stone." ³³As it is written:

"See, I lay in Zion a stone that causes men to stumble
  and a rock that makes them fall,
and the one who trusts in him will never be put to shame." [z]

10 Brothers, my heart's desire and prayer to God for the Israelites is that they may be saved. ²For I can testify about them that they are zealous for God, but their zeal is not based on knowledge. ³Since they did not know the righteousness that comes from God and sought to establish their own, they did not submit to God's righteousness. ⁴Christ is the end of the law so that there may be righteousness for everyone who believes.

⁵Moses describes in this way the righteousness that is by the law: "The man who does these things will live by them." [a] ⁶But the righteousness that is by faith says: "Do not say in your heart, 'Who will ascend into heaven?' [b] " (that is, to bring Christ down) ⁷"or 'Who will descend into the deep?' [c]" (that is, to bring Christ up from the dead). ⁸But what does it say? "The word is near you; it is in your mouth and in your heart," [d] that is, the word of faith we are proclaiming: ⁹That if you confess with your mouth, "Jesus is Lord," and believe in your heart that God raised him

v25 Hosea 2:23   w26 Hosea 1:10   x28 Isaiah 10:22,23   y29 Isaiah 1:9
z33 Isaiah 8:14; 28:16   a5 Lev. 18:5   b6 Deut. 30:12   c7 Deut. 30:13
d8 Deut. 30:14

from the dead, you will be saved. [10]For it is with your heart that you believe and are justified, and it is with your mouth that you confess and are saved. [11]As the Scripture says, "Anyone who trusts in him will never be put to shame."[e] [12]For there is no difference between Jew and Gentile—the same Lord is Lord of all and richly blesses all who call on him, [13]for, "Everyone who calls on the name of the Lord will be saved."[f]

[14]How, then, can they call on the one they have not believed in? And how can they believe in the one of whom they have not heard? And how can they hear without someone preaching to them? [15]And how can they preach unless they are sent? As it is written, "How beautiful are the feet of those who bring good news!"[g]

[16]But not all the Israelites accepted the good news. For Isaiah says, "Lord, who has believed our message?"[h] [17]Consequently, faith comes from hearing the message, and the message is heard through the word of Christ. [18]But I ask: Did they not hear? Of course they did:

"Their voice has gone out into all the earth,
their words to the ends of the world."[i]

[19]Again I ask: Did Israel not understand? First, Moses says,

"I will make you envious by those who are not a nation;
I will make you angry by a nation that has no
understanding."[j]

[20]And Isaiah boldly says,

"I was found by those who did not seek me;
I revealed myself to those who did not ask for me."[k]

[21]But concerning Israel he says,

"All day long I have held out my hands
to a disobedient and obstinate people."[l]

The Remnant of Israel

11 I ask then: Did God reject his people? By no means! I am an Israelite myself, a descendant of Abraham, from the tribe of Benjamin. [2]God did not reject his people, whom he foreknew. Don't you know what the Scripture says in the passage about Elijah—how he appealed to God against Israel: [3]"Lord, they have killed your prophets and torn down your altars; I am the only one left, and they are trying to kill me"[m]? [4]And what was God's answer to him? "I have reserved for myself seven thousand who have not bowed the knee to Baal."[n] [5]So too, at the present time there is a remnant chosen by grace. [6]And if by grace, then it is no longer by works; if it were, grace would no longer be grace.[o]

[7]What then? What Israel sought so earnestly it did not obtain, but the elect did. The others were hardened, [8]as it is written:

stood it: What does Paul's emphasis on this in verses 18-21 tell you about the importance of the Jew-Gentile division in the Roman church?

REFLECT: 1. If a friend asked you to explain the difference between Christianity and other religions, how would 9:30-31 help you answer? **2.** What is one major way your confession of Christ as Lord has influenced your life? **3.** The central affirmation of the early church was "Jesus is Lord"; everyone else was saying "Caesar is Lord". Who or what are some gods that compete with your allegiance to Christ? **4.** What are the stumbling stones in your walk with God? Has the need to have faith been a stumbling stone or a stepping stone for you? **5.** How might you bring the good news into the lives of your family and friends this week?

OPEN: When have you felt rejected by God? What broke the ice?

DIG: 1. How might Paul's comments in 9:25 and 10:21 lead someone to ask the question in 11:1? How do the examples he gives answer that concern? How does his answer illustrate 9:6-7 and 8:29? **2.** On what basis are Paul and others of the remnant chosen? Given what he has said in 10:3, why would this be so difficult for his fellow Israelites to grasp? How do you see church people today continuing to rely more on their performance of religious rituals than on God's grace?

REFLECT: 1. When have you felt like the only one left who seems to care about God? What were the circumstances? How did God respond? **2.** How is it possible for someone to try so hard to please God that they resist his love for them? When have you experienced this?

e11 Isaiah 28:16   *f13* Joel 2:32   *g15* Isaiah 52:7   *h16* Isaiah 53:1
i18 Psalm 19:4   *j19* Deut. 32:21   *k20* Isaiah 65:1   *l21* Isaiah 65:2
m3 1 Kings 19:10,14   *n4* 1 Kings 19:18   *o6* Some manuscripts *by grace. But if by works, then it is no longer grace; if it were, work* would no longer be work.

"God gave them a spirit of stupor,
eyes so that they could not see
and ears so that they could not hear,
to this very day."[p]

9And David says:

"May their table become a snare and a trap,
a stumbling block and a retribution for them.
10May their eyes be darkened so they cannot see,
and their backs be bent forever."[q]

OPEN: As a child, when did your desire to be like one of your heroes help you to change and grow?

DIG: 1. How does Paul's question in verse 11 relate to the question in verse 1? What hope does he give in his answer? **2.** In what ways would God's grace toward Gentiles break through the walls of presumption which the Jews had built toward God? **3.** Up to now, Paul has been dealing with the tendency of Jewish believers to feel superior to Gentiles: How does his image of an olive tree deal with the other side of the coin in verses 13-24? **4.** What phrases indicate what the Gentile believers were thinking? What attitude ought they to have toward their acceptance by God? How does this section emphasize the point Paul has been trying to make all along (that there is no difference between Jew and Gentile before God)? **5.** How would you reconcile verse 22 with 8:38-39?

REFLECT: 1. How has arrogance between types of Christians hurt your church experience? **2.** What modern illustration would you use to replace the grafted olive branch? Where would you fit within this new analogy? **3.** When someone else receives God's blessing and grace in their lives, does that spur you on to seek God all the more, or does it make you upset? Why?

Ingrafted Branches.

11Again I ask: Did they stumble so as to fall beyond recovery?
Not at all! Rather, because of their transgression, salvation has
come to the Gentiles to make Israel envious. 12But if their
transgression means riches for the world, and their loss means
riches for the Gentiles, how much greater riches will their fullness bring!

13I am talking to you Gentiles. Inasmuch as I am the apostle
to the Gentiles, I make much of my ministry 14in the hope that
I may somehow arouse my own people to envy and save some
of them. 15For if their rejection is the reconciliation of the world,
what will their acceptance be but life from the dead? 16If the part
of the dough offered as firstfruits is holy, then the whole batch
is holy; if the root is holy, so are the branches.

17If some of the branches have been broken off, and you,
though a wild olive shoot, have been grafted in among the others
and now share in the nourishing sap from the olive root, 18do
not boast over those branches. If you do, consider this: You do
not support the root, but the root supports you. 19You will say
then, "Branches were broken off so that I could be grafted in."
20Granted. But they were broken off because of unbelief, and
you stand by faith. Do not be arrogant, but be afraid. 21For if
God did not spare the natural branches, he will not spare you
either.

22Consider therefore the kindness and sternness of God: sternness to those who fell, but kindness to you, provided that you
continue in his kindness. Otherwise, you also will be cut off.
23And if they do not persist in unbelief, they will be grafted in,
for God is able to graft them in again. 24After all, if you were
cut out of an olive tree that is wild by nature, and contrary to
nature were grafted into a cultivated olive tree, how much more
readily will these, the natural branches, be grafted into their
own olive tree!

OPEN: How much do you enjoy a mystery? What is your favorite mystery? When did you read, see or experience it?

DIG: 1. Why does Paul want his Gentile readers to be aware of God's plan here? Why might pride become a danger to them? **2.** How would you paraphrase God's purpose in verses 25-26 and verses 30-31? How would this diffuse ten-

All Israel Will Be Saved

25I do not want you to be ignorant of this mystery, brothers,
so that you may not be conceited: Israel has experienced a
hardening in part until the full number of the Gentiles has come
in. 26And so all Israel will be saved, as it is written:

"The deliverer will come from Zion;
he will turn godlessness away from Jacob.

p8 Deut. 29:4; Isaiah 29:10 *q10* Psalm 69:22,23

²⁷And this is ʳ my covenant with them
when I take away their sins.''ˢ

²⁸As far as the gospel is concerned, they are enemies on your account; but as far as election is concerned, they are loved on account of the patriarchs, ²⁹for God's gifts and his call are irrevocable. ³⁰Just as you who were at one time disobedient to God have now received mercy as a result of their disobedience, ³¹so they too have now become disobedient in order that they too may nowᵗ receive mercy as a result of God's mercy to you. ³²For God has bound all men over to disobedience so that he may have mercy on them all.

Doxology

³³Oh, the depth of the riches of the wisdom andᵘ
knowledge of God!
How unsearchable his judgments,
and his paths beyond tracing out!
³⁴"Who has known the mind of the Lord?
Or who has been his counselor?"ᵛ
³⁵"Who has ever given to God,
that God should repay him?"ʷ
³⁶For from him and through him and to him are all
things.
To him be the glory forever! Amen.

Living Sacrifices

12 Therefore, I urge you, brothers, in view of God's mercy, to offer your bodies as living sacrifices, holy and pleasing to God—this is your spiritualˣ act of worship. ²Do not conform any longer to the pattern of this world, but be transformed by the renewing of your mind. Then you will be able to test and approve what God's will is—his good, pleasing and perfect will.

³For by the grace given me I say to every one of you: Do not think of yourself more highly than you ought, but rather think of yourself with sober judgment, in accordance with the measure of faith God has given you. ⁴Just as each of us has one body with many members, and these members do not all have the same function, ⁵so in Christ we who are many form one body, and each member belongs to all the others. ⁶We have different gifts, according to the grace given us. If a man's gift is prophesying, let him use it in proportion to hisʸ faith. ⁷If it is serving, let him serve; if it is teaching, let him teach; ⁸if it is encouraging, let him encourage; if it is contributing to the needs of others, let him give generously; if it is leadership, let him govern diligently; if it is showing mercy, let him do it cheerfully.

Love

⁹Love must be sincere. Hate what is evil; cling to what is good. ¹⁰Be devoted to one another in brotherly love. Honor one another above yourselves. ¹¹Never be lacking in zeal, but keep your spiritual fervor, serving the Lord. ¹²Be joyful in hope,

---

sions between the two groups? **3.** What is the ultimate hope for Israel (v. 26-27)? For Gentiles (v. 32)? How does this tie in to Paul's teaching in 3:21-24?

REFLECT: 1. When have you been conceited about yourself or your faith? How has God dealt with this conceit? **2.** How has God's mercy toward others spurred you on in faith?

OPEN: When simply told, "Praise the Lord anyway," do you? Or do you first need your questions answered? Why are you like that?

DIG: 1. How does this song of praise relate to Paul's argument in verses 25-32? **2.** What attributes of God does Paul celebrate here? Why these? How are any unanswered questions that may be raised by chapters 9-11 quieted by the Old Testament quotes in verses 33-36? **3.** Why is this a good place for doxology, Paul's and yours?

OPEN: What task would be most frustrating if your right and left hands refused to work together?

DIG: 1. How does this section flow from Paul's emphasis on God's mercy in 11:30-32? **2.** Along with 6:13, 19; 8:13, what does 12:1 add to your understanding of true worship? **3.** Given the tensions between Jews and Gentiles in this church, why would Paul begin his discussion of God's will for us with a discussion of gifts and their interdependence (vv. 3-8)?

REFLECT: 1. In what ways do you tend to conform to the world? What are some of the world's major influences on your life? How have you tried to break away from them? **2.** What does it mean for you to be a sacrifice to God? How can you present your body as a living sacrifice in everyday life? How does this relate to using your own personal spiritual gift within your church?

OPEN: 1. In the ideal church, what three attitudes would you expect to find in people? **2.** And if you found the "perfect" church, and then you joined it, guess what? . . .

DIG: 1. What would you entitle this section? Why? **2.** How does this section continue to unfold what Paul

---

ʳ27 Or *will be do not have now.*   ˢ27 Isaiah 59:20,21; 27:9; Jer. 31:33,34   ᵗ31 Some manuscripts
ᵘ33 Or *riches and the wisdom and the*   ᵛ34 Isaiah 40:13
ʷ35 Job 41:11   ˣ1 Or *reasonable*   ʸ6 Or *in agreement with the*

means in verses 1-2? **3.** What attitudes and actions is Paul encouraging here?

REFLECT: 1. What can you do this week, in a practical way, to honor someone who irritates you? **2.** Of the commands listed in verses 9-21, which two are easiest for you to keep? Which two are the most difficult? Why? **3.** Where have you seen the greatest growth in your Christian community? **4.** If you could have three wishes for your church, what would they be? What can you do now to be making these wishes come true?

OPEN: What law of your country do you object to most? How do you think God feels about it?

DIG: 1. In light of Paul's teaching about freedom in Christ, why might this section be important for the church in Rome? How does he view government in relationship to God? **2.** How are government leaders seen as God's servants? How does this section challenge the world's view of relating to governing authority? **3.** Compare this passage with Acts 5:27-32. What overriding principles do you find in these passages for guiding the Christian's relationship with authority?

REFLECT: Do you have more trouble submitting to authority, or serving God rather than men? How does this passage help you?

OPEN: What are your favorite clothes? "Wear" did you get them? How do you feel and act when you wear them?

DIG: 1. From verses 8-10, how does the law help us know what it means to love? How does this differ from what love means to many people today? **2.** How do verses 13-14 spell out his light and darkness theme (v. 12)? **3.** What does the "clothing" of verse 14 mean in practical terms for you? How would you use this section to explain what holiness is all about?

REFLECT: 1. How would your life

patient in affliction, faithful in prayer. [13]Share with God's people who are in need. Practice hospitality.

[14]Bless those who persecute you; bless and do not curse. [15]Rejoice with those who rejoice; mourn with those who mourn. [16]Live in harmony with one another. Do not be proud, but be willing to associate with people of low position.[z] Do not be conceited.

[17]Do not repay anyone evil for evil. Be careful to do what is right in the eyes of everybody. [18]If it is possible, as far as it depends on you, live at peace with everyone. [19]Do not take revenge, my friends, but leave room for God's wrath, for it is written: "It is mine to avenge; I will repay,"[a] says the Lord. [20]On the contrary:

> "If your enemy is hungry, feed him;
>   if he is thirsty, give him something to drink.
> In doing this, you will heap burning coals on his
>   head."[b]

[21]Do not be overcome by evil, but overcome evil with good.

Submission to the Authorities

13 Everyone must submit himself to the governing authorities, for there is no authority except that which God has established. The authorities that exist have been established by God. [2]Consequently, he who rebels against the authority is rebelling against what God has instituted, and those who do so will bring judgment on themselves. [3]For rulers hold no terror for those who do right, but for those who do wrong. Do you want to be free from fear of the one in authority? Then do what is right and he will commend you. [4]For he is God's servant to do you good. But if you do wrong, be afraid, for he does not bear the sword for nothing. He is God's servant, an agent of wrath to bring punishment on the wrongdoer. [5]Therefore, it is necessary to submit to the authorities, not only because of possible punishment but also because of conscience.

[6]This is also why you pay taxes, for the authorities are God's servants, who give their full time to governing. [7]Give everyone what you owe him: If you owe taxes, pay taxes; if revenue, then revenue; if respect, then respect; if honor, then honor.

Love, for the Day Is Near

[8]Let no debt remain outstanding, except the continuing debt to love one another, for he who loves his fellowman has fulfilled the law. [9]The commandments, "Do not commit adultery," "Do not murder," "Do not steal," "Do not covet,"[c] and whatever other commandment there may be, are summed up in this one rule: "Love your neighbor as yourself."[d] [10]Love does no harm to its neighbor. Therefore love is the fulfillment of the law.

[11]And do this, understanding the present time. The hour has come for you to wake up from your slumber, because our salvation is nearer now than when we first believed. [12]The night is nearly over; the day is almost here. So let us put aside the deeds

z16 Or willing to do menial work *a19 Deut. 32:35* *b20 Prov. 25:21,22* *c9 Exodus 20:13-15,17; Deut. 5:17-19,21* *d9 Lev. 19:18*

of darkness and put on the armor of light. ¹³Let us behave decently, as in the daytime, not in orgies and drunkenness, not in sexual immorality and debauchery, not in dissension and jealousy. ¹⁴Rather, clothe yourselves with the Lord Jesus Christ, and do not think about how to gratify the desires of the sinful nature.ᵉ

The Weak and the Strong

14 Accept him whose faith is weak, without passing judgment on disputable matters. ²One man's faith allows him to eat everything, but another man, whose faith is weak, eats only vegetables. ³The man who eats everything must not look down on him who does not, and the man who does not eat everything must not condemn the man who does, for God has accepted him. ⁴Who are you to judge someone else's servant? To his own master he stands or falls. And he will stand, for the Lord is able to make him stand.

⁵One man considers one day more sacred than another; another man considers every day alike. Each one should be fully convinced in his own mind. ⁶He who regards one day as special, does so to the Lord. He who eats meat, eats to the Lord, for he gives thanks to God; and he who abstains, does so to the Lord and gives thanks to God. ⁷For none of us lives to himself alone and none of us dies to himself alone. ⁸If we live, we live to the Lord; and if we die, we die to the Lord. So, whether we live or die, we belong to the Lord.

⁹For this very reason, Christ died and returned to life so that he might be the Lord of both the dead and the living. ¹⁰You, then, why do you judge your brother? Or why do you look down on your brother? For we will all stand before God's judgment seat. ¹¹It is written:

" 'As surely as I live,' says the Lord,
'every knee will bow before me;
every tongue will confess to God.' "ᶠ

¹²So then, each of us will give an account of himself to God.

¹³Therefore let us stop passing judgment on one another. Instead, make up your mind not to put any stumbling block or obstacle in your brother's way. ¹⁴As one who is in the Lord Jesus, I am fully convinced that no foodᵍ is unclean in itself. But if anyone regards something as unclean, then for him it is unclean. ¹⁵If your brother is distressed because of what you eat, you are no longer acting in love. Do not by your eating destroy your brother for whom Christ died. ¹⁶Do not allow what you consider good to be spoken of as evil. ¹⁷For the kingdom of God is not a matter of eating and drinking, but of righteousness, peace and joy in the Holy Spirit, ¹⁸because anyone who serves Christ in this way is pleasing to God and approved by men.

¹⁹Let us therefore make every effort to do what leads to peace and to mutual edification. ²⁰Do not destroy the work of God for the sake of food. All food is clean, but it is wrong for a man to eat anything that causes someone else to stumble. ²¹It is better

ᵉ14 Or *the flesh*   ᶠ11 Isaiah 45:23   ᵍ14 Or *that nothing*

---

be different today if you had consciously tried to "wear" Jesus Christ? What will you have to change to insure a better fit? **2.** When have you been slumbering in your faith? How did you wake up?

OPEN: When you were a child, how did you settle arguments with your brothers and sisters or close friends?

DIG: 1. Given the Jewish dietary laws and Sabbath regulations, how might the issues Paul addresses here be causing disunity in the church at Rome? **2.** What attitudes and motivations do you see here (14:3, 7, 8, 10, 13, 19, 22; 15:2, 7) which guide our relationship toward those with whom we disagree? **3.** From these examples, how would you define what Paul means by "disputable matters" in verse 1? What might be such an issue today? **4.** What kind of judgment is Paul calling for? What principles here should guide us when we are dealing with differences of opinion on matters that do not violate the moral law? **5.** Instead of judging, what do 14:13 and 15:2 say should occupy our energy? How does this relate to verse 17? **6.** What does Paul mean by the words "stumble" and "fall" in verses 20-21? How might this happen in the Roman situation? In your situation? **7.** How does 15:3 and 7 sum up the essential motivation for this lifestyle of putting others' concerns first? **8.** What can you learn from 14:17 and 15:13 about what should characterize the church? How would living out what Paul calls us to do here contribute to this goal?

REFLECT: 1. Using an illustration from nature, how weak or strong are you in the faith? Are you like a lion in a zoo who looks strong but has never been tested? Or are you like a palm tree, not very strong but having a solid root structure? Or what? **2.** Would you be more like the weak or the strong in this passage? Why? Contemporize the issues which divide the so-called "strong" (libertarians) and "weak" (legalists): Which "gray area" issues divide your church or fellowship group? Agree on an issue to debate and role play your version of verses 2-6. **3.** When has your freedom been a stumbling block to someone else? What happened? **4.** As you've matured in the faith, how has your sensitivity to the consciences of other Christians changed? **5.** What kind of account

(14:12) do you think you will be able to give to God? How does it make you feel to know you will have to give an account of your life? **6.** What have you done in the past six months that has led "to peace and to mutual edification" among people in your church? **7.** Where do you draw the line on trying to please everyone?

not to eat meat or drink wine or to do anything else that will cause your brother to fall.

²²So whatever you believe about these things keep between yourself and God. Blessed is the man who does not condemn himself by what he approves. ²³But the man who has doubts is condemned if he eats, because his eating is not from faith; and everything that does not come from faith is sin.

15 We who are strong ought to bear with the failings of the weak and not to please ourselves. ²Each of us should please his neighbor for his good, to build him up. ³For even Christ did not please himself but, as it is written: "The insults of those who insult you have fallen on me."ʰ ⁴For everything that was written in the past was written to teach us, so that through endurance and the encouragement of the Scriptures we might have hope.

⁵May the God who gives endurance and encouragement give you a spirit of unity among yourselves as you follow Christ Jesus, ⁶so that with one heart and mouth you may glorify the God and Father of our Lord Jesus Christ.

⁷Accept one another, then, just as Christ accepted you, in order to bring praise to God. ⁸For I tell you that Christ has become a servant of the Jewsⁱ on behalf of God's truth, to confirm the promises made to the patriarchs ⁹so that the Gentiles may glorify God for his mercy, as it is written:

"Therefore I will praise you among the Gentiles;
I will sing hymns to your name."ʲ

¹⁰Again, it says,

"Rejoice, O Gentiles, with his people."ᵏ

¹¹And again,

"Praise the Lord, all you Gentiles,
and sing praises to him, all you peoples."ˡ

¹²And again, Isaiah says,

"The Root of Jesse will spring up,
one who will arise to rule over the nations;
the Gentiles will hope in him."ᵐ

¹³May the God of hope fill you with all joy and peace as you trust in him, so that you may overflow with hope by the power of the Holy Spirit.

Paul the Minister to the Gentiles

¹⁴I myself am convinced, my brothers, that you yourselves are full of goodness, complete in knowledge and competent to instruct one another. ¹⁵I have written you quite boldly on some points, as if to remind you of them again, because of the grace God gave me ¹⁶to be a minister of Christ Jesus to the Gentiles with the priestly duty of proclaiming the gospel of God, so that the Gentiles might become an offering acceptable to God, sanctified by the Holy Spirit.

OPEN: What is the furthest you've ever been away from home? What is the most significant memory you have of that trip?

DIG: 1. From your reading of Romans, what are some of the major points Paul has stressed? **2.** How does Paul define his ministry? What motivates and inspires him? Illyricum (v. 19) is in present day Yugoslavia: How far is that from Jerusalem? What does this tell you about Paul?

ʰ3 Psalm 69:9   ⁱ8 Greek *circumcision*   ʲ9 2 Samuel 22:50; Psalm 18:49
ᵏ10 Deut. 32:43   ˡ11 Psalm 117:1   ᵐ12 Isaiah 11:10

[17]Therefore I glory in Christ Jesus in my service to God. [18]I will not venture to speak of anything except what Christ has accomplished through me in leading the Gentiles to obey God by what I have said and done— [19]by the power of signs and miracles, through the power of the Spirit. So from Jerusalem all the way around to Illyricum, I have fully proclaimed the gospel of Christ. [20]It has always been my ambition to preach the gospel where Christ was not known, so that I would not be building on someone else's foundation. [21]Rather, as it is written:

"Those who were not told about him will see,
and those who have not heard will understand."[n]

[22]This is why I have often been hindered from coming to you.

Paul's Plan to Visit Rome

[23]But now that there is no more place for me to work in these regions, and since I have been longing for many years to see you, [24]I plan to do so when I go to Spain. I hope to visit you while passing through and to have you assist me on my journey there, after I have enjoyed your company for a while. [25]Now, however, I am on my way to Jerusalem in the service of the saints there. [26]For Macedonia and Achaia were pleased to make a contribution for the poor among the saints in Jerusalem. [27]They were pleased to do it, and indeed they owe it to them. For if the Gentiles have shared in the Jews' spiritual blessings, they owe it to the Jews to share with them their material blessings. [28]So after I have completed this task and have made sure that they have received this fruit, I will go to Spain and visit you on the way. [29]I know that when I come to you, I will come in the full measure of the blessing of Christ.

[30]I urge you, brothers, by our Lord Jesus Christ and by the love of the Spirit, to join me in my struggle by praying to God for me. [31]Pray that I may be rescued from the unbelievers in Judea and that my service in Jerusalem may be acceptable to the saints there, [32]so that by God's will I may come to you with joy and together with you be refreshed. [33]The God of peace be with you all. Amen.

Personal Greetings

16 I commend to you our sister Phoebe, a servant[o] of the church in Cenchrea. [2]I ask you to receive her in the Lord in a way worthy of the saints and to give her any help she may need from you, for she has been a great help to many people, including me.

[3]Greet Priscilla[p] and Aquila, my fellow workers in Christ Jesus. [4]They risked their lives for me. Not only I but all the churches of the Gentiles are grateful to them. [5]Greet also the church that meets at their house.

Greet my dear friend Epenetus, who was the first convert to Christ in the province of Asia. [6]Greet Mary, who worked very hard for you. [7]Greet Andronicus and Junias, my relatives who have been in

[n]21 Isaiah 52:15   [o]1 Or *deaconess*   [p]3 Greek *Prisca*, a variant of *Priscilla*

OPEN: To what "hot spot" in the world would you gladly accept a round-trip ticket for two? To what "hot spot" would you refuse to go, even if all expenses were paid? Why?

DIG: 1. Why was a collection taken? What principles about giving can be learned from the example of the Macedonians and Achaians? **2.** What two prayer requests does Paul make? Why does he mention these requests to the Christians at Rome? **3.** How would you describe Paul's ministry from this passage and the one before it?

REFLECT: 1. When you hear the word "missionary", what are your first thoughts? **2.** How would you compare Paul's concern for God's work with your own concern? **3.** How much do you know about world needs? World missions? How could you increase your interest in and knowledge of both?

OPEN: When you die, how would you like others to describe your Christian life and service?

DIG: 1. Go through verses 1-16, listing all the things for which Paul commends these people. What does this show about how we ought to measure a person's success in life? **2.** If you received this letter, how would you treat Phoebe when she arrived? How many other women are named here? (In v. 7, "Junias" is most probably really "Junia", a woman's name). What roles do these women play in the church? **3.** Although Paul had never been to Rome, what does this greeting show about his awareness of their church? **4.** How might Paul's concern in 17-20 be reflected in the issues he has dealt with in 3:8, 6:1,

15, 7:7 and 9:14 (see also Galatians 5:2-6)? How are these false teachers contradicting Paul's main point about serving Christ (v. 18, see 14:17-18)? **5.** What do verses 25-27 show you about the purpose and plan of God throughout history?

REFLECT: 1. Who are some people you know whom you consider real servants of Christ **2.** What are some of the teachings that are dividing the church today? How do you work for balance between a desire for unity and a desire to maintain truth? **3.** What does it mean to you that in these final chapters God is described as the "God of hope" (15:13) and the "God of peace" (15:33, 16:20)? How would you sum up how it is we can know God like this, especially when Paul started off this letter by showing us the God of wrath? **4.** What will you do to increase your participation in God's plan to lead all nations to believe and obey him? Do you view this task more as a grim duty or as a tremendous privilege? What does this show about your heart attitude toward the gospel?

prison with me. They are outstanding among the apostles, and they were in Christ before I was.

[8]Greet Ampliatus, whom I love in the Lord.

[9]Greet Urbanus, our fellow worker in Christ, and my dear friend Stachys.

[10]Greet Apelles, tested and approved in Christ.

Greet those who belong to the household of Aristobulus.

[11]Greet Herodion, my relative.

Greet those in the household of Narcissus who are in the Lord.

[12]Greet Tryphena and Tryphosa, those women who work hard in the Lord.

Greet my dear friend Persis, another woman who has worked very hard in the Lord.

[13]Greet Rufus, chosen in the Lord, and his mother, who has been a mother to me, too.

[14]Greet Asyncritus, Phlegon, Hermes, Patrobas, Hermas and the brothers with them.

[15]Greet Philologus, Julia, Nereus and his sister, and Olympas and all the saints with them.

[16]Greet one another with a holy kiss.

All the churches of Christ send greetings.

[17]I urge you, brothers, to watch out for those who cause divisions and put obstacles in your way that are contrary to the teaching you have learned. Keep away from them. [18]For such people are not serving our Lord Christ, but their own appetites. By smooth talk and flattery they deceive the minds of naive people. [19]Everyone has heard about your obedience, so I am full of joy over you; but I want you to be wise about what is good, and innocent about what is evil.

[20]The God of peace will soon crush Satan under your feet. The grace of our Lord Jesus be with you.

[21]Timothy, my fellow worker, sends his greetings to you, as do Lucius, Jason and Sosipater, my relatives.

[22]I, Tertius, who wrote down this letter, greet you in the Lord.

[23]Gaius, whose hospitality I and the whole church here enjoy, sends you his greetings.

Erastus, who is the city's director of public works, and our brother Quartus send you their greetings. [q]

[25]Now to him who is able to establish you by my gospel and the proclamation of Jesus Christ, according to the revelation of the mystery hidden for long ages past, [26]but now revealed and made known through the prophetic writings by the command of the eternal God, so that all nations might believe and obey him— [27]to the only wise God be glory forever through Jesus Christ! Amen.

q23 Some manuscripts their greetings. [24]May the grace of our Lord Jesus Christ be with all of you. Amen.

1 CORINTHIANS

INTRODUCTION

Audience

Corinth the City

Corinth was an unusual city. After its capture by the Roman legions in 146 B.C., the city was leveled. It lay in waste for nearly a hundred years until Julius Caesar rebuilt it in 44 B.C. Then it grew rapidly, thanks largely to its unique geographical location. Because it lay at the neck of a narrow isthmus connecting the Peloponnesus with central Greece, it controlled all north-south land traffic. To the east and the west of the city were two fine harbors. Both goods and ships were hauled across the four-mile-wide Isthmus of Corinth. Thus Corinth also controlled most east-west sea routes. This strategic location commanded wealth and influence. By the time of Paul's visit some one hundred years after its rebuilding, Corinth had become the capital of the province of Achaia and the third most important city in the Roman Empire, after Rome and Alexandria.

In this wealthy young city, excess seemed to be the norm. The city was stocked with art purchased from around the Roman Empire. It became a center of philosophy, though apparently few citizens were seriously interested in studying philosophy, preferring rather to listen to stirring orations on faddish topics delivered by the city's numerous itinerant philosophers. Even in religion, this excess was obvious. The Greek author Pausanias describes twenty-six pagan shrines and temples including the great temples of Apollo and Aphrodite. In Old Corinth, a thousand temple prostitutes had served Aphrodite, the goddess of love, and New Corinth continued this tradition of sexual worship practices. The city developed a worldwide reputation for vice and debauchery.

Luxury was the hallmark of Corinth. Because storms in the Aegean Sea were frequent and treacherous, sailors preferred to put into one of the harbors and transship to the other, despite the exorbitant prices charged by the Corinthians. Consequently, goods from around the world passed through Corinthian ports, and some 400,000 slaves were kept in the city to provide the labor for this arduous job.

Into Corinth flowed people from around the Roman Empire. There were "Greek adventurers and Roman bourgeois, with a tainting infusion of Phoenicians, a mass of Jews, ex-soldiers, philosophers, merchants, sailors, freed men, slaves, tradespeople, hucksters and agents of every form of vice" (Farrar, quoted by William Barclay, *The Letters to the Corinthians*, p. 4.). Rootless, proud, independent, egalitarian, individualistic, rich—together the Corinthians shaped their new city into the cosmopolitan capital that it was in Paul's day. Not surprisingly, it was in Corinth that Paul had to fight this battle to prevent Christianity from succumbing to debilitating enticements offered by paganism.

Paul and the Corinthians

Paul visited Corinth during his second missionary journey, probably in A.D. 50. Having been in some peril in Macedonia, he fled by ship to Athens (Acts 17:5-15). Not meeting with great success there (Acts 17:16-34), he then journeyed the short distance to Corinth where he met Priscilla and Aquila (Acts 18:1-3). At first he preached in the synagogue with some success (even the ruler of the synagogue was won to Christ). But then the Jews forced him to leave, so he moved next door into the home of a Gentile. Hoping to silence him, the Jews eventually hauled Paul before the governor Gallio, but Gallio threw the case out of court as having no merit. After some eighteen months (his longest stay anywhere except Ephesus), Paul left and continued his missionary work in Syria.

Two events sparked the writing of 1 Corinthians some three or four years later. First, Paul heard that a divisive spirit was loose in the church (1 Cor. 1:11). Second, he received a letter in which the Corinthians asked him questions about marriage and other matters (1 Cor. 7:1). In addition, a delegation from Corinth completed his knowledge of the problems there (1 Cor. 16:15-17). Being unable to visit Corinth personally, Paul sought to deal with the issues by letter. Thus the Corinthian correspondence was begun.

Theme

First Corinthians is a practical, issue-oriented letter in which Paul tells his readers what they ought or ought not to do. Paul's typical pattern in other letters is to begin with a strong theological statement and then to follow up by applying this insight to daily life. But this is not the case in 1 Corinthians. Here we find little direct theological teaching. Rather Paul discusses, in turn, a number of behavioral issues.

The problem was that these proud, materialistic, independent ex-pagans were having a most difficult time learning how to live as Christians. It was at this level of lifestyle that paganism directed its attack on the newly emerging Christian faith. *Christian behavior was the underlying issue.* Where were the lines to be drawn? How much of one's culture had to be abandoned to become a Christian? Residual paganism was mounting a frontal attack on Christianity. If Christianity lost in Corinth, its existence would be threatened throughout the Roman Empire. So just as he did in Galatians, when residual Judaism attacked Christianity over the issue of the Law, here in 1 Corinthians Paul struck back decisively and directly.

The Structure of 1 Corinthians

The problem in understanding 1 Corinthians is that we only have Paul's responses. We don't know with certainty what questions and problems he is addressing. These have to be deduced. Still, it is clear that there are two major divisions in the letter. In chapters 1-6, Paul responds to four problems of which he has become aware. Then in chapters 7-15, he responds to a series of specific questions raised in a letter the Corinthians have sent him.

Outline

An outline of 1 Corinthians looks like this:
1. Problems Reported to Paul (1:10-6:20)
    A. Divisions in the Church (1:10-4:21)
    B. Incest (5:1-13)
    C. Lawsuits among Believers (6:1-11)
    D. Sexual Immorality (6:12-20)
2. Questions asked of Paul (7:1-15:58)
    A. Marriage (7:1-24)
    B. Virgins (7:25-40)
    C. Food Sacrificed to Idols (8:1-11:1)
    D. Propriety in Worship (11:2-16)
    E. The Lord's Supper (11:17-34)
    F. Spiritual Gifts (12:1-14:40)
    G. The Resurrection (15:1-58)
In 1:1-9, Paul begins this letter in usual fashion; in chapter 16, he writes a concluding note.

1 Corinthians

1 Paul, called to be an apostle of Christ Jesus by the will of God, and our brother Sosthenes,

²To the church of God in Corinth, to those sanctified in Christ Jesus and called to be holy, together with all those everywhere who call on the name of our Lord Jesus Christ—their Lord and ours:

³Grace and peace to you from God our Father and the Lord Jesus Christ.

Thanksgiving

⁴I always thank God for you because of his grace given you in Christ Jesus. ⁵For in him you have been enriched in every way—in all your speaking and in all your knowledge— ⁶because our testimony about Christ was confirmed in you. ⁷Therefore you do not lack any spiritual gift as you eagerly wait for our Lord Jesus Christ to be revealed. ⁸He will keep you strong to the end, so that you will be blameless on the day of our Lord Jesus Christ. ⁹God, who has called you into fellowship with his Son Jesus Christ our Lord, is faithful.

Divisions in the Church

¹⁰I appeal to you, brothers, in the name of our Lord Jesus Christ, that all of you agree with one another so that there may be no divisions among you and that you may be perfectly united in mind and thought. ¹¹My brothers, some from Chloe's household have informed me that there are quarrels among you. ¹²What I mean is this: One of you says, "I follow Paul"; another, "I follow Apollos"; another, "I follow Cephas*"; still another, "I follow Christ."

¹³Is Christ divided? Was Paul crucified for you? Were you baptized into* the name of Paul? ¹⁴I am thankful that I did not baptize any of you except Crispus and Gaius, ¹⁵so no one can say that you were baptized into my name. ¹⁶(Yes, I also baptized the household of Stephanas; beyond that, I don't remember if I baptized anyone else.) ¹⁷For Christ did not send me to baptize, but to preach the gospel—not with words of human wisdom, lest the cross of Christ be emptied of its power.

Christ the Wisdom and Power of God

¹⁸For the message of the cross is foolishness to those who are perishing, but to us who are being saved it is the power of God. ¹⁹For it is written:

"I will destroy the wisdom of the wise;
　the intelligence of the intelligent I will frustrate."*

²⁰Where is the wise man? Where is the scholar? Where is the philosopher of this age? Has not God made foolish the wisdom of the world? ²¹For since in the wisdom of God the world

*12 That is, Peter　　*13 Or *in*; also in verse 15　　*19 Isaiah 29:14

OPEN: 1. If you could choose a title for yourself, what would it be? What would it say about you? **2.** Would you like your spouse to be both smarter and more gifted than you, with fewer faults? Why or why not?

DIG: 1. Why do you think Paul stresses that he is an apostle? **2.** How does he address this church? **3.** Why does he remind them of their calling? If you had been the founding pastor of this problematic church, how would you have begun this letter? **4.** Why is Paul thankful for these things if they might cause him problems?

REFLECT: How does your thankfulness and confidence level compare with Paul's? What do you think would give you more confidence and a more grateful heart?

OPEN: How did your parents handle squabbles on family trips?

DIG: 1. What have the unresolved quarrels in the Corinthian church produced? **2.** What causes or gifts might each of these factions represent (v. 12)? **3.** Why are these differences so dangerous? **4.** How does Paul use his relationship with the Corinthians to narrow these differences?

REFLECT: 1. What religious party "labels" do you espouse (defend)? Which do you eschew (deny)? **2.** Can you think of a quarrel you had recently that greatly affected your life? What are some of the ways that you have worked towards resolving the quarrel?

OPEN: On a scale of 1-10, how important are the following qualities to you: Great wealth? Personal power? Physical beauty? Immense intellect? Why? Which does your spouse excel in? How do you feel about that?

DIG: 1. What qualities were most important to the Greeks and Jews of Paul's day? **2.** What has God done to the wisdom of the world? Why do the "wise" so often miss the significance of Christ and the

325

cross? What has it become for them? How does God show both wisdom and power? **3.** Describe the Corinthian church? Why did God choose them? What is their boast? **4.** How did Paul's ministry *demonstrate* the distinction between the wisdom and power of the world and that of God? What was a priority for Paul? Why? **5.** What does a ministry *devoid* of God's wisdom and power look like? Sound like? Feel like?

REFLECT: 1. How is your society like and unlike the one pictured in this passage? Where do your colleagues confuse God's wisdom and power from the world's? In whom or what does your family trust? Why do we Christians so often miss the significance of Christ and the cross? **2.** Can you think of any situation today where God uses the foolish, the weak, the lowly or the despised to build his kingdom? Explain your answer? **3.** How has God demonstrated his wisdom and power in your life recently? How does this make you feel?

OPEN: When as a child were you asked to keep a secret from a member of your family? Were you able to keep it? How hard was that for you? Are you one in whom others readily confide? Why or why not?

DIG: 1. In what way is God's wisdom a secret? **2.** Who are the "mature", (v. 6) the "rulers of this age", (vv. 6, 8) the "man without the Spirit" (v. 14)? "the spiritual man" (v. 15), and the "we" of verse 16? Who of these groups understands God's wisdom, and who does not? Why? **3.** What benefits does the Spirit bring to the believer? How? **4.** According to Paul, what is the nature of true wisdom?

REFLECT: 1. If you asked your closest friends to describe a wise person, what do you think they would say? How would their wisdom compare with God's? **2.** What has God prepared for you who love him? What does that make you want to do?

---

through its wisdom did not know him, God was pleased through the foolishness of what was preached to save those who believe. ²²Jews demand miraculous signs and Greeks look for wisdom, ²³but we preach Christ crucified: a stumbling block to Jews and foolishness to Gentiles, ²⁴but to those whom God has called, both Jews and Greeks, Christ the power of God and the wisdom of God. ²⁵For the foolishness of God is wiser than man's wisdom, and the weakness of God is stronger than man's strength.

²⁶Brothers, think of what you were when you were called. Not many of you were wise by human standards; not many were influential; not many were of noble birth. ²⁷But God chose the foolish things of the world to shame the wise; God chose the weak things of the world to shame the strong. ²⁸He chose the lowly things of this world and the despised things—and the things that are not—to nullify the things that are, ²⁹so that no one may boast before him. ³⁰It is because of him that you are in Christ Jesus, who has become for us wisdom from God—that is, our righteousness, holiness and redemption. ³¹Therefore, as it is written: "Let him who boasts boast in the Lord."*d*

2 When I came to you, brothers, I did not come with eloquence or superior wisdom as I proclaimed to you the testimony about God.*e* ²For I resolved to know nothing while I was with you except Jesus Christ and him crucified. ³I came to you in weakness and fear, and with much trembling. ⁴My message and my preaching were not with wise and persuasive words, but with a demonstration of the Spirit's power, ⁵so that your faith might not rest on men's wisdom, but on God's power.

Wisdom From the Spirit

⁶We do, however, speak a message of wisdom among the mature, but not the wisdom of this age or of the rulers of this age, who are coming to nothing. ⁷No, we speak of God's secret wisdom, a wisdom that has been hidden and that God destined for our glory before time began. ⁸None of the rulers of this age understood it, for if they had, they would not have crucified the Lord of glory. ⁹However, as it is written:

> "No eye has seen,
>   no ear has heard,
> no mind has conceived
>   what God has prepared for those who love him"*f*—

¹⁰but God has revealed it to us by his Spirit.

The Spirit searches all things, even the deep things of God. ¹¹For who among men knows the thoughts of a man except the man's spirit within him? In the same way no one knows the thoughts of God except the Spirit of God. ¹²We have not received the spirit of the world but the Spirit who is from God, that we may understand what God has freely given us. ¹³This is what we speak, not in words taught us by human wisdom but in words taught by the Spirit, expressing spiritual truths in spiritual words.*g* ¹⁴The man without the Spirit does not accept

---

d31 Jer. 9:24   *e1* Some manuscripts *as I proclaimed to you God's mystery*
f9 Isaiah 64:4   *g13* Or *Spirit, interpreting spiritual truths to spiritual men*

the things that come from the Spirit of God, for they are foolishness to him, and he cannot understand them, because they are spiritually discerned. [15]The spiritual man makes judgments about all things, but he himself is not subject to any man's judgment:

[16]"For who has known the mind of the Lord
 that he may instruct him?"[h]

But we have the mind of Christ.

On Divisions in the Church

3 Brothers, I could not address you as spiritual but as worldly—mere infants in Christ. [2]I gave you milk, not solid food, for you were not yet ready for it. Indeed, you are still not ready. [3]You are still worldly. For since there is jealousy and quarreling among you, are you not worldly? Are you not acting like mere men? [4]For when one says, "I follow Paul," and another, "I follow Apollos," are you not mere men?

[5]What, after all, is Apollos? And what is Paul? Only servants, through whom you came to believe—as the Lord has assigned to each his task. [6]I planted the seed, Apollos watered it, but God made it grow. [7]So neither he who plants nor he who waters is anything, but only God, who makes things grow. [8]The man who plants and the man who waters have one purpose, and each will be rewarded according to his own labor. [9]For we are God's fellow workers; you are God's field, God's building.

[10]By the grace God has given me, I laid a foundation as an expert builder, and someone else is building on it. But each one should be careful how he builds. [11]For no one can lay any foundation other than the one already laid, which is Jesus Christ. [12]If any man builds on this foundation using gold, silver, costly stones, wood, hay or straw, [13]his work will be shown for what it is, because the Day will bring it to light. It will be revealed with fire, and the fire will test the quality of each man's work. [14]If what he has built survives, he will receive his reward. [15]If it is burned up, he will suffer loss; he himself will be saved, but only as one escaping through the flames.

[16]Don't you know that you yourselves are God's temple and that God's Spirit lives in you? [17]If anyone destroys God's temple, God will destroy him; for God's temple is sacred, and you are that temple.

[18]Do not deceive yourselves. If any one of you thinks he is wise by the standards of this age, he should become a "fool" so that he may become wise. [19]For the wisdom of this world is foolishness in God's sight. As it is written: "He catches the wise in their craftiness"[i]; [20]and again, "The Lord knows that the thoughts of the wise are futile."[j] [21]So then, no more boasting about men! All things are yours, [22]whether Paul or Apollos or Cephas[k] or the world or life or death or the present or the future—all are yours, [23]and you are of Christ, and Christ is of God.

OPEN: When "choosing up sides" for teams in school, were you chosen first, last or somewhere in the middle? How did this make you feel?

DIG: 1. In what way has the Corinthian church "chosen sides?" What does this demonstrate about them? **2.** How should they regard their leaders? Who gives the growth? **3.** What is the foundation of the church? How does our building affect the lives of others now? How will the quality of our work be revealed in the future? What will be the consequences of our actions? **4.** What images does Paul use to describe our work? What does each image mean? **5.** What is God's view of the wisdom of this world? What kind of wisdom has been demonstrated in the Corinthian church? How does becoming a "fool" make one wise? What is the roll of the intellect in Christian faith? **6.** In what sense is the statement "all things are yours" (vv. 21-23) true?

REFLECT: 1. What does it mean to be worldly? How do we express the world's wisdom in our lives, families and churches? What specific steps can we take to change this? **2.** Who were the planters and waterers in your spiritual journey? In whose lives have you planted and watered within the past year? Within the past week? **3.** What kind of a builder are you? What do you think will be left standing when your work is tested? **4.** How does it make you feel to be God's friend? God's building? God's temple? What affect does that have on the way you view yourself? On the way you view others? **5.** What does it mean for you to become a "fool" for Christ?

---

[h]16 Isaiah 40:13   [i]19 Job 5:13   [j]20 Psalm 94:11   [k]22 That is, Peter

Apostles of Christ

4 So then, men ought to regard us as servants of Christ and as those entrusted with the secret things of God. ²Now it is required that those who have been given a trust must prove faithful. ³I care very little if I am judged by you or by any human court; indeed, I do not even judge myself. ⁴My conscience is clear, but that does not make me innocent. It is the Lord who judges me. ⁵Therefore judge nothing before the appointed time; wait till the Lord comes. He will bring to light what is hidden in darkness and will expose the motives of men's hearts. At that time each will receive his praise from God.

⁶Now, brothers, I have applied these things to myself and Apollos for your benefit, so that you may learn from us the meaning of the saying, "Do not go beyond what is written." Then you will not take pride in one man over against another. ⁷For who makes you different from anyone else? What do you have that you did not receive? And if you did receive it, why do you boast as though you did not?

⁸Already you have all you want! Already you have become rich! You have become kings—and that without us! How I wish that you really had become kings so that we might be kings with you! ⁹For it seems to me that God has put us apostles on display at the end of the procession, like men condemned to die in the arena. We have been made a spectacle to the whole universe, to angels as well as to men. ¹⁰We are fools for Christ, but you are so wise in Christ! We are weak, but you are strong! You are honored, we are dishonored! ¹¹To this very hour we go hungry and thirsty, we are in rags, we are brutally treated, we are homeless. ¹²We work hard with our own hands. When we are cursed, we bless; when we are persecuted, we endure it; ¹³when we are slandered, we answer kindly. Up to this moment we have become the scum of the earth, the refuse of the world.

¹⁴I am not writing this to shame you, but to warn you, as my dear children. ¹⁵Even though you have ten thousand guardians in Christ, you do not have many fathers, for in Christ Jesus I became your father through the gospel. ¹⁶Therefore I urge you to imitate me. ¹⁷For this reason I am sending to you Timothy, my son whom I love, who is faithful in the Lord. He will remind you of my way of life in Christ Jesus, which agrees with what I teach everywhere in every church.

¹⁸Some of you have become arrogant, as if I were not coming to you. ¹⁹But I will come to you very soon, if the Lord is willing, and then I will find out not only how these arrogant people are talking, but what power they have. ²⁰For the kingdom of God is not a matter of talk but of power. ²¹What do you prefer? Shall I come to you with a whip, or in love and with a gentle spirit?

l5 Or *that his body;* or *that the flesh*   *m13* Deut. 17:7; 19:19; 21:21; 22:21,24; 24:7

Expel the Immoral Brother!

5 It is actually reported that there is sexual immorality among you, and of a kind that does not occur even among pagans: A man has his father's wife. [2]And you are proud! Shouldn't you rather have been filled with grief and have put out of your fellowship the man who did this? [3]Even though I am not physically present, I am with you in spirit. And I have already passed judgment on the one who did this, just as if I were present. [4]When you are assembled in the name of our Lord Jesus and I am with you in spirit, and the power of our Lord Jesus is present, [5]hand this man over to Satan, so that the sinful nature[l] may be destroyed and his spirit saved on the day of the Lord.

[6]Your boasting is not good. Don't you know that a little yeast works through the whole batch of dough? [7]Get rid of the old yeast that you may be a new batch without yeast—as you really are. For Christ, our Passover lamb, has been sacrificed. [8]Therefore let us keep the Festival, not with the old yeast, the yeast of malice and wickedness, but with bread without yeast, the bread of sincerity and truth.

[9]I have written you in my letter not to associate with sexually immoral people— [10]not at all meaning the people of this world who are immoral, or the greedy and swindlers, or idolaters. In that case you would have to leave this world. [11]But now I am writing you that you must not associate with anyone who calls himself a brother but is sexually immoral or greedy, an idolater or a slanderer, a drunkard or a swindler. With such a man do not even eat.

[12]What business is it of mine to judge those outside the church? Are you not to judge those inside? [13]God will judge those outside. "Expel the wicked man from among you."[m]

Lawsuits Among Believers

6 If any of you has a dispute with another, dare he take it before the ungodly for judgment instead of before the saints? [2]Do you not know that the saints will judge the world? And if you are to judge the world, are you not competent to judge trivial cases? [3]Do you not know that we will judge angels? How much more the things of this life! [4]Therefore, if you have disputes about such matters, appoint as judges even men of little account in the church![n] [5]I say this to shame you. Is it possible that there is nobody among you wise enough to judge a dispute between believers? [6]But instead, one brother goes to law against another—and this in front of unbelievers!

[7]The very fact that you have lawsuits among you means you have been completely defeated already. Why not rather be wronged? Why not rather be cheated? [8]Instead, you yourselves cheat and do wrong, and you do this to your brothers.

[9]Do you not know that the wicked will not inherit the kingdom of God? Do not be deceived: Neither the sexually immoral nor idolaters nor adulterers nor male prostitutes nor homosexual offenders [10]nor thieves nor the greedy nor drunkards nor slanderers nor swindlers will inherit the kingdom of God. [11]And that

n4 Or matters, do you appoint as judges men of little account in the church?

OPEN: 1. What was the closest you ever came to being expelled from school? What for? **2.** How has incest touched your family or circle of friends? Likewise, AIDS? Do you avoid the victims or offenders?

DIG: 1. What actions does Paul tell the Corinthians to take toward this church member? Why? What was he doing? **2.** What is the purpose of excommunication? What does it do for the offender? For the victim? For the church? How accurately does Paul's image of old and new yeast describe the situation? **3.** How do you reconcile Paul's teaching in chapter 5 with that in 4:3-5? What is he saying in these two sections? **4.** How many different ways does Paul describe what the church must do with the offender? Why does he repeat himself?

REFLECT: 1. Under what conditions would you expel someone from the church? How would you feel about your actions? How well does your church provide discipline for its members? **2.** When have you been "broad-minded" about sin? How did this attitude "work its way through your life"? What affect did it have on others? **3.** How seriously should believers feel about sin in their life? Why? How have fellow believers helped you take sin seriously (compare Matthew 18:15-17)?

OPEN: When was the last time you felt cheated? Did you do anything about it? What?

DIG: 1. How have the believers in Corinth handled their dispute? Why is it wrong for believers to sue one another? What alternative does Paul offer? What qualifies the church to provide this alternative? **2.** Why do lawsuits among believers cast an atmosphere of defeat on the church? How should the Corinthians settle their disputes? **3.** How do verses 9-11 relate to this discussion of lawsuits among believers?

REFLECT: 1. What was the last dispute you had with a fellow believer? How did you resolve it? How do you feel when you confront someone over an action on their part? **2.** Do you agree with Paul that it is better to be cheated than to go to court against a believer? Why or why not? Have you ever done this? What happened? **3.** How well do we distinguish between cultural and Christian norms? What is most effective—whip, love or gentle spirit—in confronting believers cought up in a destructive lifestlye?

OPEN: With food, do you "eat to live"? Or "live to eat"? As you grow older, which do you think will go first: Your appetite for food, books, or sex? Why?

DIG: 1. In verses 12-13, who is Paul quoting: His own point of view? Or someone else's? Why do you think so? 2. In verses 13-17, what does Paul teach about the body? How does Paul preclude sexual immorality for the Christian? 3. What does Paul say is the *one* sexual choice for the Christian single? Why?

REFLECT: 1. What other options, if any, do you consider beneficial for the Christian single handling the sex drive: Suppression? Sublimation? Look, but don't touch? Or what? Explain your answer. 2. What else drives you? What, if anything, is mastering you? How can the Spirit within help you honor God in all aspects of your "body"?

OPEN: 1. (If married) If you were suddenly single tomorrow, how do you think you would handle the dating scene the second time around? Why? 2. (If single) If you were suddenly married tomorrow (to someone you loved), what would you miss most about your singleness? What would you miss the least? Why?

DIG: 1. In verses 1-9, why does Paul think it is good for a man not to marry? How has immorality complicated this matter for Paul and the Corinthian church? What are the sexual responsibilities of husbands and wives in marriage? 2. In verses 10-16, how does Paul emphasize the scaredness of the marriage vows? What does he say about the Christian and divorce? 3. What difference does it make whether the separating spouse is a believer or not? 4. In verses 17-24, what is the rule Paul lays down "in all the churches"? How does this rule apply to changing one's religious affiliation? Changing one's professional career? Changing an unjust situation? 5. In verses 25-28, how does Paul apply this rule to married and single persons? Why? 6. What is "the present crisis" (vv. 26, 29-31)? Was it limited to the first century outlook and thus Paul's rule no longer applies except in similar

is what some of you were. But you were washed, you were sanctified, you were justified in the name of the Lord Jesus Christ and by the Spirit of our God.

Sexual Immorality

12"Everything is permissible for me"—but not everything is beneficial. "Everything is permissible for me"—but I will not be mastered by anything. 13"Food for the stomach and the stomach for food"—but God will destroy them both. The body is not meant for sexual immorality, but for the Lord, and the Lord for the body. 14By his power God raised the Lord from the dead, and he will raise us also. 15Do you not know that your bodies are members of Christ himself? Shall I then take the members of Christ and unite them with a prostitute? Never! 16Do you not know that he who unites himself with a prostitute is one with her in body? For it is said, "The two will become one flesh."*o* 17But he who unites himself with the Lord is one with him in spirit.

18Flee from sexual immorality. All other sins a man commits are outside his body, but he who sins sexually sins against his own body. 19Do you not know that your body is a temple of the Holy Spirit, who is in you, whom you have received from God? You are not your own; 20you were bought at a price. Therefore honor God with your body.

Marriage

7 Now for the matters you wrote about: It is good for a man not to marry.*p* 2But since there is so much immorality, each man should have his own wife, and each woman her own husband. 3The husband should fulfill his marital duty to his wife, and likewise the wife to her husband. 4The wife's body does not belong to her alone but also to her husband. In the same way, the husband's body does not belong to him alone but also to his wife. 5Do not deprive each other except by mutual consent and for a time, so that you may devote yourselves to prayer. Then come together again so that Satan will not tempt you because of your lack of self-control. 6I say this as a concession, not as a command. 7I wish that all men were as I am. But each man has his own gift from God; one has this gift, another has that.

8Now to the unmarried and the widows I say: It is good for them to stay unmarried, as I am. 9But if they cannot control themselves, they should marry, for it is better to marry than to burn with passion.

10To the married I give this command (not I, but the Lord): A wife must not separate from her husband. 11But if she does, she must remain unmarried or else be reconciled to her husband. And a husband must not divorce his wife.

12To the rest I say this (I, not the Lord): If any brother has a wife who is not a believer and she is willing to live with him, he must not divorce her. 13And if a woman has a husband who is not a believer and he is willing to live with her, she must not divorce him. 14For the unbelieving husband has been sanctified

o16 Gen. 2:24   *p1* Or "*It is good for a man not to have sexual relations with a woman.*"

through his wife, and the unbelieving wife has been sanctified through her believing husband. Otherwise your children would be unclean, but as it is, they are holy.

¹⁵But if the unbeliever leaves, let him do so. A believing man or woman is not bound in such circumstances; God has called us to live in peace. ¹⁶How do you know, wife, whether you will save your husband? Or, how do you know, husband, whether you will save your wife?

¹⁷Nevertheless, each one should retain the place in life that the Lord assigned to him and to which God has called him. This is the rule I lay down in all the churches. ¹⁸Was a man already circumcised when he was called? He should not become uncircumcised. Was a man uncircumcised when he was called? He should not be circumcised. ¹⁹Circumcision is nothing and uncircumcision is nothing. Keeping God's commands is what counts. ²⁰Each one should remain in the situation which he was in when God called him. ²¹Were you a slave when you were called? Don't let it trouble you—although if you can gain your freedom, do so. ²²For he who was a slave when he was called by the Lord is the Lord's freedman; similarly, he who was a free man when he was called is Christ's slave. ²³You were bought at a price; do not become slaves of men. ²⁴Brothers, each man, as responsible to God, should remain in the situation God called him to.

²⁵Now about virgins: I have no command from the Lord, but I give a judgment as one who by the Lord's mercy is trustworthy. ²⁶Because of the present crisis, I think that it is good for you to remain as you are. ²⁷Are you married? Do not seek a divorce. Are you unmarried? Do not look for a wife. ²⁸But if you do marry, you have not sinned; and if a virgin marries, she has not sinned. But those who marry will face many troubles in this life, and I want to spare you this.

²⁹What I mean, brothers, is that the time is short. From now on those who have wives should live as if they had none; ³⁰those who mourn, as if they did not; those who are happy, as if they were not; those who buy something, as if it were not theirs to keep; ³¹those who use the things of the world, as if not engrossed in them. For this world in its present form is passing away.

³²I would like you to be free from concern. An unmarried man is concerned about the Lord's affairs—how he can please the Lord. ³³But a married man is concerned about the affairs of this world—how he can please his wife— ³⁴and his interests are divided. An unmarried woman or virgin is concerned about the Lord's affairs: Her aim is to be devoted to the Lord in both body and spirit. But a married woman is concerned about the affairs of this world—how she can please her husband. ³⁵I am saying this for your own good, not to restrict you, but that you may live in a right way in undivided devotion to the Lord.

³⁶If anyone thinks he is acting improperly toward the virgin he is engaged to, and if she is getting along in years and he feels he ought to marry, he should do as he wants. He is not sinning. They should get married. ³⁷But the man who has settled the matter in his own mind, who is under no compulsion but has control over his own will, and who has made up his mind not to marry the virgin—this man also does the right thing. ³⁸So

crisis situations? Or is time always "short" from the foreshortened biblical perspective? Why or why not? **7.** In verses 32-35, to what actions and attitudes does Paul appeal in order to free the Christian from concern? How is the Christian who fails to heed this advice divided in his or her devotion to the Lord? **8.** In verses 36-38, how is Paul's advice to the engaged couple different than what he has said earlier in chapter 7? Who do you know that fits this description or is facing this dilemma? **9.** In verses 39-40, is Paul's advice about remarriage any different that what he said about marriage? Why or why not? While Paul says that a widow(er) is free to remarry only after the spouse dies, what about divorcées: Must they wait until their former spouse dies in order to freely remarry? Why or why not?

REFLECT: **1.** What are the advantages of being single? Of being married? What do you like best and least about your situation? What changes would you make? **2.** How has singleness or marriage helped your service for Christ? Hurt it? **3.** What change, if any, ought Christian faith bring to your marriage? If married, how has your spouse helped you to grow spiritually? **4.** What advice would you give someone considering marriage? Divorce? Remarriage? **5.** If you've gone through a divorce and remarriage, or if a close friend has, what did you learn from this experience? **6.** What do you think God is specifically saying to you in this passage? What changes will you make this week because of it?

then, he who marries the virgin does right, but he who does not marry her does even better. *q*

³⁹A woman is bound to her husband as long as he lives. But if her husband dies, she is free to marry anyone she wishes, but he must belong to the Lord. ⁴⁰In my judgment, she is happier if she stays as she is—and I think that I too have the Spirit of God.

Food Sacrificed to Idols

8 Now about food sacrificed to idols: We know that we all possess knowledge. *r* Knowledge puffs up, but love builds up. ²The man who thinks he knows something does not yet know as he ought to know. ³But the man who loves God is known by God.

⁴So then, about eating food sacrificed to idols: We know that an idol is nothing at all in the world and that there is no God but one. ⁵For even if there are so-called gods, whether in heaven or on earth (as indeed there are many "gods" and many "lords"), ⁶yet for us there is but one God, the Father, from whom all things came and for whom we live; and there is but one Lord, Jesus Christ, through whom all things came and through whom we live.

⁷But not everyone knows this. Some people are still so accustomed to idols that when they eat such food they think of it as having been sacrificed to an idol, and since their conscience is weak, it is defiled. ⁸But food does not bring us near to God; we are no worse if we do not eat, and no better if we do.

⁹Be careful, however, that the exercise of your freedom does not become a stumbling block to the weak. ¹⁰For if anyone with a weak conscience sees you who have this knowledge eating in an idol's temple, won't he be emboldened to eat what has been sacrificed to idols? ¹¹So this weak brother, for whom Christ died, is destroyed by your knowledge. ¹²When you sin against your brothers in this way and wound their weak conscience, you sin against Christ. ¹³Therefore, if what I eat causes my brother to fall into sin, I will never eat meat again, so that I will not cause him to fall.

The Rights of an Apostle

9 Am I not free? Am I not an apostle? Have I not seen Jesus our Lord? Are you not the result of my work in the Lord? ²Even though I may not be an apostle to others, surely I am to you! For you are the seal of my apostleship in the Lord.

³This is my defense to those who sit in judgment on me. ⁴Don't we have the right to food and drink? ⁵Don't we have the right to take a believing wife along with us, as do the other apostles and the Lord's brothers and Cephas *s*? ⁶Or is it only I and Barnabas who must work for a living?

OPEN: Would you be willing to go to a slaughter house and kill a pig or cow or chicken? Why or why not? Why do you eat meat? Or don't you?

DIG: 1. Why is eating meat sacrificed to idols a sin for some people (v. 11) and not a sin for others (v. 8)? How would the Corinthians' background cause them problems with this issue? **2.** What is the guiding principle in this chapter? What contemporary applications do you see? **3.** How can the exercise of our freedom cause others to stumble? How serious is this issue?

REFLECT: 1. As a member of the Corinthian church, would your conscience have been weak or strong? Why? **2.** What were the biggest stumbling blocks for you growing up? What are the biggest stumbling blocks to you now? **3.** When have you done something that didn't bother you, but caused someone else to stumble? How did you feel about this? **4.** What criteria do you use to make decisions about your behavior? What is the balance between knowledge and love? What recent decision illustrates this process?

OPEN: 1. When have you been so fulfilled that you thought "I don't care if they pay me or not—I love this job"? **2.** How would you react if suddenly your pay were cut and you were expected to work joyfully, but for nothing? **3.** When has your volunteer ministry been more important to you than what you did for a living?

DIG: 1. Why does Paul make such a big deal about being an apostle? What is the implied answer to each of his questions in verse 1? What are the proofs of his apostleship? **2.** What rights does he have as an apostle? In verses 7-12, how does Paul illustrate his right to financial support? Why doesn't Paul claim this right? What does this say about

q36-38 Or ³⁶If anyone thinks he is not treating his daughter properly, and if she is getting along in years, and he feels she ought to marry, he should do as he wants. He is not sinning. He should let her get married. ³⁷But the man who has settled the matter in his own mind, who is under no compulsion but has control over his own will, and who has made up his mind to keep the virgin unmarried—this man also does the right thing. ³⁸So then, he who gives his virgin in marriage does right, but he who does not give her in marriage does even better.   *r1 Or "We all possess knowledge," as you say*   *s5 That is, Peter*

⁷Who serves as a soldier at his own expense? Who plants a vineyard and does not eat of its grapes? Who tends a flock and does not drink of the milk? ⁸Do I say this merely from a human point of view? Doesn't the Law say the same thing? ⁹For it is written in the Law of Moses: "Do not muzzle an ox while it is treading out the grain."ʲ Is it about oxen that God is concerned? ¹⁰Surely he says this for us, doesn't he? Yes, this was written for us, because when the plowman plows and the thresher threshes, they ought to do so in the hope of sharing in the harvest. ¹¹If we have sown spiritual seed among you, is it too much if we reap a material harvest from you? ¹²If others have this right of support from you, shouldn't we have it all the more?

But we did not use this right. On the contrary, we put up with anything rather than hinder the gospel of Christ. ¹³Don't you know that those who work in the temple get their food from the temple, and those who serve at the altar share in what is offered on the altar? ¹⁴In the same way, the Lord has commanded that those who preach the gospel should receive their living from the gospel.

¹⁵But I have not used any of these rights. And I am not writing this in the hope that you will do such things for me. I would rather die than have anyone deprive me of this boast. ¹⁶Yet when I preach the gospel, I cannot boast, for I am compelled to preach. Woe to me if I do not preach the gospel! ¹⁷If I preach voluntarily, I have a reward; if not voluntarily, I am simply discharging the trust committed to me. ¹⁸What then is my reward? Just this: that in preaching the gospel I may offer it free of charge, and so not make use of my rights in preaching it.

¹⁹Though I am free and belong to no man, I make myself a slave to everyone, to win as many as possible. ²⁰To the Jews I became like a Jew, to win the Jews. To those under the law I became like one under the law (though I myself am not under the law), so as to win those under the law. ²¹To those not having the law I became like one not having the law (though I am not free from God's law but am under Christ's law), so as to win those not having the law. ²²To the weak I became weak, to win the weak. I have become all things to all men so that by all possible means I might save some. ²³I do all this for the sake of the gospel, that I may share in its blessings.

²⁴Do you not know that in a race all the runners run, but only one gets the prize? Run in such a way as to get the prize. ²⁵Everyone who competes in the games goes into strict training. They do it to get a crown that will not last; but we do it to get a crown that will last forever. ²⁶Therefore I do not run like a man running aimlessly; I do not fight like a man beating the air. ²⁷No, I beat my body and make it my slave so that after I have preached to others, I myself will not be disqualified for the prize.

Paul? 3. What compels Paul to preach the gospel? What is his reward or prize for faithful service (vv. 16-18, 23-27)? 4. In verses 19-23, what is Paul's missionary strategy? Why is this strategy successful? How does being "all things to all people" (v. 22) free up Paul to be truly himself? 5. What is the point of the foot race imagery (vv. 24-27)? To what in the Christian life does the "race" refer? The "prize" or "crown"? The "strict training"? "Beating my body"? "Disqualification"? 6. How would you summarize this chapter in a sentence or two?

REFLECT: 1. What are some of your obvious rights? When did you recently give them up for someone else? How did you feel about it? **2.** What are some of the rights of your leaders? How do you respect, obey, support and love them? **3.** How well do you think your church provides materially for its leaders? What criteria do you use to determine this support? **4.** How closely would you be willing to identify with someone to win them to Christ? Would you willingly worship with Jews on Saturday or Moslems on Friday in order to win them over to Christ? Would you take a lower-paying job or move to the inner city in order to win over those with less opportunity to hear the gospel? Would you remain single for the same reason? Can you think of a situation in which you did something like this? Who are the people in your community who need to be won to Christ? **5.** In racing terms, how would you describe your training and the race you're running for Christ? Of 100 Christians picked at random who started this race together, where are you today in relation to the rest of the pack? Why?

*9 Deut. 25:4

OPEN: What is one of your family's holiday traditions? How does your family try to remember the past?

DIG: **1.** In verses 1-5, to what era in Israel's history is Paul referring (see Exodus 13-17)? How are these experiences similar to Christian sacraments? Did Israel's sacramental history protect all the Israelites? Why or why not? What truth does this history teach believers? **2.** What four examples from Israel's history does Paul select? How do they relate to four Corinthian problems Paul has dealt with? What is Paul's point? **3.** How does God demonstrate his faithfulness in temptation? How do you feel about this?

REFLECT: **1.** Do you think the examples in this passage could also serve as warnings to Christians today? Why or why not? What affect does this have on your attitudes and actions? **2.** What have you learned from the temptations you faced successfully? Not successfully? From which you grown more? Why? **3.** What temptations have you faced victoriously this week? Did you sense God's activity as described in verse 13? In what way?

OPEN: If you had to flee your burning home, what three things would you take with you? Why?

DIG: **1.** What is the relationship between idols and demons? Which is more dangerous? Why? **2.** How does participation in the Lord's Supper compare with Paul's teaching about idol sacrifices? **3.** What decision does Paul say the Corinthians have to make? What are the consequences of this decision?

REFLECT: What false gods do people in the twentieth century worship? Which ones tempt you? To find out, go through a group values clarification exercise until you see which value emerges at the apex of your hierarchy.

OPEN: How old were you when you got your driver's license? How did you feel when you passed the driver's exam? Where was the first place you drove? Who was the first person you told?

DIG: **1.** What is Paul's solution to the believer's freedom in regard to eating meat sacrificed to idols? **2.** When is it permissible to eat idol

Warnings From Israel's History

10 For I do not want you to be ignorant of the fact, brothers, that our forefathers were all under the cloud and that they all passed through the sea. ²They were all baptized into Moses in the cloud and in the sea. ³They all ate the same spiritual food ⁴and drank the same spiritual drink; for they drank from the spiritual rock that accompanied them, and that rock was Christ. ⁵Nevertheless, God was not pleased with most of them; their bodies were scattered over the desert.

⁶Now these things occurred as examples" to keep us from setting our hearts on evil things as they did. ⁷Do not be idolaters, as some of them were; as it is written: "The people sat down to eat and drink and got up to indulge in pagan revelry."ᵛ ⁸We should not commit sexual immorality, as some of them did—and in one day twenty-three thousand of them died. ⁹We should not test the Lord, as some of them did—and were killed by snakes. ¹⁰And do not grumble, as some of them did—and were killed by the destroying angel.

¹¹These things happened to them as examples and were written down as warnings for us, on whom the fulfillment of the ages has come. ¹²So, if you think you are standing firm, be careful that you don't fall! ¹³No temptation has seized you except what is common to man. And God is faithful; he will not let you be tempted beyond what you can bear. But when you are tempted, he will also provide a way out so that you can stand up under it.

Idol Feasts and the Lord's Supper

¹⁴Therefore, my dear friends, flee from idolatry. ¹⁵I speak to sensible people; judge for yourselves what I say. ¹⁶Is not the cup of thanksgiving for which we give thanks a participation in the blood of Christ? And is not the bread that we break a participation in the body of Christ? ¹⁷Because there is one loaf, we, who are many, are one body, for we all partake of the one loaf.

¹⁸Consider the people of Israel: Do not those who eat the sacrifices participate in the altar? ¹⁹Do I mean then that a sacrifice offered to an idol is anything, or that an idol is anything? ²⁰No, but the sacrifices of pagans are offered to demons, not to God, and I do not want you to be participants with demons. ²¹You cannot drink the cup of the Lord and the cup of demons too; you cannot have a part in both the Lord's table and the table of demons. ²²Are we trying to arouse the Lord's jealousy? Are we stronger than he?

The Believer's Freedom

²³"Everything is permissible"—but not everything is beneficial. "Everything is permissible"—but not everything is constructive. ²⁴Nobody should seek his own good, but the good of others.

²⁵Eat anything sold in the meat market without raising questions of conscience, ²⁶for, "The earth is the Lord's, and everything in it."ʷ

ᵘ6 Or *types*; also in verse 11   ᵛ7 Exodus 32:6   ʷ26 Psalm 24:1

²⁷If some unbeliever invites you to a meal and you want to go, eat whatever is put before you without raising questions of conscience. ²⁸But if anyone says to you, "This has been offered in sacrifice," then do not eat it, both for the sake of the man who told you and for conscience' sake ˣ— ²⁹the other man's conscience, I mean, not yours. For why should my freedom be judged by another's conscience? ³⁰If I take part in the meal with thankfulness, why am I denounced because of something I thank God for?

³¹So whether you eat or drink or whatever you do, do it all for the glory of God. ³²Do not cause anyone to stumble, whether Jews, Greeks or the church of God— ³³even as I try to please everybody in every way. For I am not seeking my own good but

11 the good of many, so that they may be saved. ¹Follow my example, as I follow the example of Christ.

Propriety in Worship

²I praise you for remembering me in everything and for holding to the teachings,ʸ just as I passed them on to you.

³Now I want you to realize that the head of every man is Christ, and the head of the woman is man, and the head of Christ is God. ⁴Every man who prays or prophesies with his head covered dishonors his head. ⁵And every woman who prays or prophesies with her head uncovered dishonors her head—it is just as though her head were shaved. ⁶If a woman does not cover her head, she should have her hair cut off; and if it is a disgrace for a woman to have her hair cut or shaved off, she should cover her head. ⁷A man ought not to cover his head,ᶻ since he is the image and glory of God; but the woman is the glory of man. ⁸For man did not come from woman, but woman from man; ⁹neither was man created for woman, but woman for man. ¹⁰For this reason, and because of the angels, the woman ought to have a sign of authority on her head.

¹¹In the Lord, however, woman is not independent of man, nor is man independent of woman. ¹²For as woman came from man, so also man is born of woman. But everything comes from God. ¹³Judge for yourselves: Is it proper for a woman to pray to God with her head uncovered? ¹⁴Does not the very nature of things teach you that if a man has long hair, it is a disgrace to him, ¹⁵but that if a woman has long hair, it is her glory? For long hair is given to her as a covering. ¹⁶If anyone wants to be contentious about this, we have no other practice—nor do the churches of God.

meat? When is it not permissible to do so? On what basis? **3.** What four principles guide Paul's decision-making process?

REFLECT: 1. What is one thing for you in today's culture that corresponds to the problem of idol meat in Paul's culture? Can you apply Paul's solution to this problem? Why or why not? **2.** What brings glory to God? In this matter of glorifying God by seeking the good of others, what is the example of Christ? The example of Paul? To what extent do you do things "for the glory of God"?

OPEN: How did you wear your hair for your senior picture in high school? Would you wear the same hair style today? Why or why not?

DIG: 1. In the culture to which Paul is writing, prostitutes did not cover their heads. What specific problems does this practice create for unveiled women in the Corinthian church? **2.** What is Paul's solution? What reasons does he give? **3.** What does "headship" mean here: *Source* (as in *head*waters)? Or *authority* (as in *head*waiter? How does this definition of headship relate to the question of propiety in worship? To the question of the creation order (vv. 7-10)? To the question of God and Christ in the Trinity (v. 3)? **4.** Here (vv. 5, 13) Paul evidently permits women to pray and prophesy (albeit with their head covered). Elsewhere (14:34-35; also I Tim. 2:9-15), Paul prohibits (certain) women from speaking publically in worship. How do you reconcile these two teachings? What is their common point? **5.** Why do you think we should follow cultural norms in worship? How is this situational teaching important to people of any culture? **6.** Does Paul's firm "bottom line" (v. 16) contradict our freedom in Christ? Why or why not?

REFLECT: 1. What cultural norms are practiced in your church's worship service? Do they enhance or hinder worship of God? **2.** What are some specific ways that women share in worship equally with men? **3.** How do you prepare for worship? What changes will you make because of this passage?

ˣ28 Some manuscripts *conscience' sake, for "the earth is the Lord's and everything in it"* ʸ2 Or *traditions* ᶻ4-7 Or *⁴Every man who prays or prophesies with long hair dishonors his head. ⁵And every woman who prays or prophesies with no covering of hair, on her head dishonors her head—she is just like one of the "shorn women." ⁶If a woman has no covering, let her be for now with short hair, but since it is a disgrace for a woman to have her hair shorn or shaved, she should grow it again. ⁷A man ought not to have long hair*

OPEN: When was the last time you "pigged out" at a church pot-luck? When did you get your "firsts", leaving someone else the "crumbs"? How did you feel about this?

DIG: 1. How was the Lord's Supper celebrated by the Corinthians? How did their actions actually distort its intended meaning? 2. Why does Paul repeat the words used in the Lord's Supper (vv. 23-26)? What is a person doing when he or she participates in the Lord's Supper? 3. Other than "pigging out" or "getting drunk" (vv. 21-22), what sin might disqualify one from taking Communion? What is the "unworthy manner" or the "unexamined life" in this context (vv. 27-34)? In your church circles? 4. Why is the Lord's Supper so important for the believer?

REFLECT: 1. The specific "Corinthian disorders" identified by Paul were disunity, lack of love, gluttony and drunkenness. In what ways do we distort the meaning of the Lord's Supper in the modern church? Are we divided? Do we lack love? Do we allow some members to go without food or drink? Do we prohibit certain "sinners" from even taking Communion? 2. When you hear the words, "This is my body", what do you think? Why? When you hear the words, "This is the new covenant in my blood", what do you think? Why? 3. How do you examine yourself in preparation for Lord's Supper? How could the Lord's Supper take on more significance in your life?

OPEN: What was the best gift you ever received? You ever gave?

DIG: 1. What criteria does Paul give here to discern that one is speaking by the Spirit of God? Why is this important? 2. In verses 4-6, are "gifts" distinct from "service"? From "working"? What is the same in each case? What is the point here? 3. What does Paul teach about spiritual gifts in this passage? Who has them? For what purpose? What nine different gifts are mentioned? How does each contribute to the common good? Is this list exhaustive (see Ro. 12 and Eph. 4)?

REFLECT: 1. How are spiritual gifts discovered, developed and used in your church? What specific things can the church, even your group, do to encourage this? 2. What are your spiritual gifts? In what area of .

The Lord's Supper

[17]In the following directives I have no praise for you, for your meetings do more harm than good. [18]In the first place, I hear that when you come together as a church, there are divisions among you, and to some extent I believe it. [19]No doubt there have to be differences among you to show which of you have God's approval. [20]When you come together, it is not the Lord's Supper you eat, [21]for as you eat, each of you goes ahead without waiting for anybody else. One remains hungry, another gets drunk. [22]Don't you have homes to eat and drink in? Or do you despise the church of God and humiliate those who have nothing? What shall I say to you? Shall I praise you for this? Certainly not!

[23]For I received from the Lord what I also passed on to you: The Lord Jesus, on the night he was betrayed, took bread, [24]and when he had given thanks, he broke it and said, "This is my body, which is for you; do this in remembrance of me." [25]In the same way, after supper he took the cup, saying, "This cup is the new covenant in my blood; do this, whenever you drink it, in remembrance of me." [26]For whenever you eat this bread and drink this cup, you proclaim the Lord's death until he comes.

[27]Therefore, whoever eats the bread or drinks the cup of the Lord in an unworthy manner will be guilty of sinning against the body and blood of the Lord. [28]A man ought to examine himself before he eats of the bread and drinks of the cup. [29]For anyone who eats and drinks without recognizing the body of the Lord eats and drinks judgment on himself. [30]That is why many among you are weak and sick, and a number of you have fallen asleep. [31]But if we judged ourselves, we would not come under judgment. [32]When we are judged by the Lord, we are being disciplined so that we will not be condemned with the world.

[33]So then, my brothers, when you come together to eat, wait for each other. [34]If anyone is hungry, he should eat at home, so that when you meet together it may not result in judgment. And when I come I will give further directions.

Spiritual Gifts

12 Now about spiritual gifts, brothers, I do not want you to be ignorant. [2]You know that when you were pagans, somehow or other you were influenced and led astray to mute idols. [3]Therefore I tell you that no one who is speaking by the Spirit of God says, "Jesus be cursed," and no one can say, "Jesus is Lord," except by the Holy Spirit.

[4]There are different kinds of gifts, but the same Spirit. [5]There are different kinds of service, but the same Lord. [6]There are different kinds of working, but the same God works all of them in all men.

[7]Now to each one the manifestation of the Spirit is given for the common good. [8]To one there is given through the Spirit the message of wisdom, to another the message of knowledge by means of the same Spirit, [9]to another faith by the same Spirit, to another gifts of healing by that one Spirit, [10]to another miraculous powers, to another prophecy, to another distinguishing between spirits, to another speaking in different kinds of

tongues,*a* and to still another the interpretation of tongues.*a* ¹¹All these are the work of one and the same Spirit, and he gives them to each one, just as he determines.

One Body, Many Parts

¹²The body is a unit, though it is made up of many parts; and though all its parts are many, they form one body. So it is with Christ. ¹³For we were all baptized by*b* one Spirit into one body—whether Jews or Greeks, slave or free—and we were all given the one Spirit to drink.

¹⁴Now the body is not made up of one part but of many. ¹⁵If the foot should say, "Because I am not a hand, I do not belong to the body," it would not for that reason cease to be part of the body. ¹⁶And if the ear should say, "Because I am not an eye, I do not belong to the body," it would not for that reason cease to be part of the body. ¹⁷If the whole body were an eye, where would the sense of hearing be? If the whole body were an ear, where would the sense of smell be? ¹⁸But in fact God has arranged the parts in the body, every one of them, just as he wanted them to be. ¹⁹If they were all one part, where would the body be? ²⁰As it is, there are many parts, but one body.

²¹The eye cannot say to the hand, "I don't need you!" And the head cannot say to the feet, "I don't need you!" ²²On the contrary, those parts of the body that seem to be weaker are indispensable, ²³and the parts that we think are less honorable we treat with special honor. And the parts that are unpresentable are treated with special modesty, ²⁴while our presentable parts need no special treatment. But God has combined the members of the body and has given greater honor to the parts that lacked it, ²⁵so that there should be no division in the body, but that its parts should have equal concern for each other. ²⁶If one part suffers, every part suffers with it; if one part is honored, every part rejoices with it.

²⁷Now you are the body of Christ, and each one of you is a part of it. ²⁸And in the church God has appointed first of all apostles, second prophets, third teachers, then workers of miracles, also those having gifts of healing, those able to help others, those with gifts of administration, and those speaking in different kinds of tongues. ²⁹Are all apostles? Are all prophets? Are all teachers? Do all work miracles? ³⁰Do all have gifts of healing? Do all speak in tongues*c*? Do all interpret? ³¹But eagerly desire*d* the greater gifts.

Love

And now I will show you the most excellent way.

13 If I speak in the tongues*e* of men and of angels, but have not love, I am only a resounding gong or a clanging cymbal. ²If I have the gift of prophecy and can fathom all mysteries and all knowledge, and if I have a faith that can move mountains, but have not love, I am nothing. ³If I give all I possess to the poor and surrender my body to the flames,*f* but have not love, I gain nothing.

a10 Or languages; also in verse 28   b13 Or with; or in   c30 Or other languages   d31 Or But you are eagerly desiring   e1 Or languages f3 Some early manuscripts body that I may boast

OPEN: service do you use these gifts?

OPEN: Of these body parts, which is more important to you: Your feet, your hands, your eyes or your ears? Why? If you had to lose one of these body parts, which would you give up? Why?

DIG: 1. In verses 12-13, what four ways does Paul stress the unity of believers? **2.** In verses 14-15, how does Paul use the body imagery to make a different point? What if Paul had said, "If the whole body were a *tongue,...*"? **3.** What in the church's body life would be the equivalent of the "eye"? The "foot"? The "weaker"? The "less honorable"? The "unpresentable"? The "presentable parts"? **4.** How is each part to be treated, respectively? Why? How does that fit God's design for the church's body life and your personal life? **5.** How does a common cold affect your whole body? What analogy do you draw from that experience (v. 26)? **6.** What specific gifts are listed in verses 28-30? What is the function of each?

REFLECT: 1. Paul asks rhetorically, "Do *all* have gifts of healing?" etc. Today Paul might ask, "Do *any* have gifts of...?" How would you answer for your church? **2.** Suppose your church were organized around spiritual gifts: What would it look like? What would it take to develop such a church? **3.** Which gift mentioned in verses 28-30 do you have? Why do you think God gave you this gift? How can you use your gift to unify the body of Christ?

OPEN: If you could wake up tomorrow with one new gift or ability, what would you want it to be? What would you do with this new found quality?

DIG: 1. What are three "spiritual gifts" that Paul compares in importance to love in verses 1-3? Why is each useless without love? **2.** What is love? List the eight characteristics of what love "*is*" and the seven characteristics that love "*is not*" in verses 4-7? **3.** What contrast does Paul make in verses 8-12? Why will spiritual gifts cease to be relevant? Which three carry over into the new age? Why is love the greatest?

REFLECT: 1. When has someone loved you in the way Paul describes? What facets of this kind of love have you experienced recently? 2. When have you been hurt in a love relationship? What went wrong? How was the love in that relationship different from that described in chapter 13? 3. Rewrite this chapter, substituting the name *Jesus* for the word *love* everywhere it occurs: What new vision of love does this give you?

_____

OPEN: 1. What foreign language(s) have you studied? What memories do you have of this? When has language gotten in the way of understanding for you? What were the consequences? 2. When was the last time you sang to yourself? To someone else?

DIG: 1. How does chapter 14 relate to what Paul has said in chapters 12 and 13 about spiritual gifts (see 12:1 and 13:1)? 2. What are the three commands Paul gives in verse 1? Why does he give the commands in that order? 3. Why do you think Paul chooses to contrast the gift of prophecy and the gift of tongues? How would you define each gift? What are two values of each gift? 4. In verses 13-19, how does Paul stress the value and use of gifts to edify the church? What does it mean, "in regard to evil, be infants" (v. 20): Innocent of evil? Ignorant of evil? Or what? 5. Likewise, "in your thinking be adults"—what does this imply: Intellectual capacity? Mature wisdom? The more excellent way (v. 12, see 13:1)? Or what? 6. In verses 21-25, why does Paul caution about the use of tongues in church worship? Why does Paul favor prophecy or preaching in public meetings? 7. Is Paul saying in this chapter that tongues are bad? Why or why not? 8. How would you summarize this passage in one sentence (see 14:1)?

REFLECT: 1. In what ways have you experienced the power and presence of God—"God is really among you!"—both as individuals and as a church? 2. Who is someone you identify with the gift of prophecy? With the gift of tongues? How did these people contribute to your own spiritual growth? 3. Using

⁴Love is patient, love is kind. It does not envy, it does not boast, it is not proud. ⁵It is not rude, it is not self-seeking, it is not easily angered, it keeps no record of wrongs. ⁶Love does not delight in evil but rejoices with the truth. ⁷It always protects, always trusts, always hopes, always perseveres.

⁸Love never fails. But where there are prophecies, they will cease; where there are tongues, they will be stilled; where there is knowledge, it will pass away. ⁹For we know in part and we prophesy in part, ¹⁰but when perfection comes, the imperfect disappears. ¹¹When I was a child, I talked like a child, I thought like a child, I reasoned like a child. When I became a man, I put childish ways behind me. ¹²Now we see but a poor reflection as in a mirror; then we shall see face to face. Now I know in part; then I shall know fully, even as I am fully known.

¹³And now these three remain: faith, hope and love. But the greatest of these is love.

Gifts of Prophecy and Tongues

14 Follow the way of love and eagerly desire spiritual gifts, especially the gift of prophecy. ²For anyone who speaks in a tongue*g* does not speak to men but to God. Indeed, no one understands him; he utters mysteries with his spirit.*h* ³But everyone who prophesies speaks to men for their strengthening, encouragement and comfort. ⁴He who speaks in a tongue edifies himself, but he who prophesies edifies the church. ⁵I would like every one of you to speak in tongues,*i* but I would rather have you prophesy. He who prophesies is greater than one who speaks in tongues,*i* unless he interprets, so that the church may be edified.

⁶Now, brothers, if I come to you and speak in tongues, what good will I be to you, unless I bring you some revelation or knowledge or prophecy or word of instruction? ⁷Even in the case of lifeless things that make sounds, such as the flute or harp, how will anyone know what tune is being played unless there is a distinction in the notes? ⁸Again, if the trumpet does not sound a clear call, who will get ready for battle? ⁹So it is with you. Unless you speak intelligible words with your tongue, how will anyone know what you are saying? You will just be speaking into the air. ¹⁰Undoubtedly there are all sorts of languages in the world, yet none of them is without meaning. ¹¹If then I do not grasp the meaning of what someone is saying, I am a foreigner to the speaker, and he is a foreigner to me. ¹²So it is with you. Since you are eager to have spiritual gifts, try to excel in gifts that build up the church.

¹³For this reason anyone who speaks in a tongue should pray that he may interpret what he says. ¹⁴For if I pray in a tongue, my spirit prays, but my mind is unfruitful. ¹⁵So what shall I do? I will pray with my spirit, but I will also pray with my mind; I will sing with my spirit, but I will also sing with my mind. ¹⁶If you are praising God with your spirit, how can one who finds himself among those who do not understand*j* say "Amen" to

_____

*g*2 Or *another language;* also in verses 4, 13, 14, 19, 26 and 27   *h*2 Or *by the Spirit*
*i*5 Or *other languages;* also in verses 6, 18, 22, 23 and 39   *j*16 Or *among the inquirers*

your thanksgiving, since he does not know what you are saying? [17]You may be giving thanks well enough, but the other man is not edified.

[18]I thank God that I speak in tongues more than all of you. [19]But in the church I would rather speak five intelligible words to instruct others than ten thousand words in a tongue.

[20]Brothers, stop thinking like children. In regard to evil be infants, but in your thinking be adults. [21]In the Law it is written:

> "Through men of strange tongues
>   and through the lips of foreigners
> I will speak to this people,
>   but even then they will not listen to me,"[k]

says the Lord.

[22]Tongues, then, are a sign, not for believers but for unbelievers; prophecy, however, is for believers, not for unbelievers. [23]So if the whole church comes together and everyone speaks in tongues, and some who do not understand[l] or some unbelievers come in, will they not say that you are out of your mind? [24]But if an unbeliever or someone who does not understand[m] comes in while everybody is prophesying, he will be convinced by all that he is a sinner and will be judged by all, [25]and the secrets of his heart will be laid bare. So he will fall down and worship God, exclaiming, "God is really among you!"

Orderly Worship

[26]What then shall we say, brothers? When you come together, everyone has a hymn, or a word of instruction, a revelation, a tongue or an interpretation. All of these must be done for the strengthening of the church. [27]If anyone speaks in a tongue, two—or at the most three—should speak, one at a time, and someone must interpret. [28]If there is no interpreter, the speaker should keep quiet in the church and speak to himself and God.

[29]Two or three prophets should speak, and the others should weigh carefully what is said. [30]And if a revelation comes to someone who is sitting down, the first speaker should stop. [31]For you can all prophesy in turn so that everyone may be instructed and encouraged. [32]The spirits of prophets are subject to the control of prophets. [33]For God is not a God of disorder but of peace.

As in all the congregations of the saints, [34]women should remain silent in the churches. They are not allowed to speak, but must be in submission, as the Law says. [35]If they want to inquire about something, they should ask their own husbands at home; for it is disgraceful for a woman to speak in the church.

[36]Did the word of God originate with you? Or are you the only people it has reached? [37]If anybody thinks he is a prophet or spiritually gifted, let him acknowledge that what I am writing to you is the Lord's command. [38]If he ignores this, he himself will be ignored.[n]

OPEN: What was the most meaningful part of the worship service for you as a child? As an adult? Why this part of the service?

DIG: 1. What picture of worship is given in this passage? How does this relate to God's nature (v. 33)? 2. What guidelines for worship does Paul give here? Why would these guidelines be helpful? By what standard might the congregation "weigh carefully" the prophecy? 3. Paul here (vv. 34-35) prohibits women from "speaking" in the churches. But elsewhere (11:5, 13) Paul clearly permits women to "pray and prophesy" (albeit with their head covered)? Why? What is the common principle? 4. How does Paul address directly the inflated view the Corinthians have of their own spiritual gifts (vv. 36-40)?

REFLECT: 1. In what ways does our worship experience parallel what Paul says here? How does it differ? 2. What was the most helpful aspect of the last worship service you attended? Who helped you the most: The pastor, the choir, an usher or someone sitting nearby? How did they help? 3. How close have you come to sharing in a fellowship like the one described in verses 26-33? What ever became of this fellowship? What would you like to bring from that experience to your church today?

an age category, ranging from infant to adult, where would you rank yourself with regard to evil? With regard to thinking? 4. Suppose if you were paid $10/hour for consciously excelling at love, and docked $10/hour for consciously pursuing other ways. How rich (or poor) would you be at week's end? What did you learn by following this more excellent way?

---

k21 Isaiah 28:11,12   l23 Or some inquirers   m24 Or or some inquirer
n38 Some manuscripts *If he is ignorant of this, let him be ignorant*

39Therefore, my brothers, be eager to prophesy, and do not
forbid speaking in tongues. 40But everything should be done in
a fitting and orderly way.

OPEN: What is one important truth your grandparents passed on to you? What is one important truth you could pass on to your kids?

DIG: 1. What are the main points of the gospel Paul preached to the Corinthians? What words of explanation does Paul make about these points? **2.** These points are "what I received" and "of first importance". How does that emphasis relate to verses 1-2? **3.** Why do you think Paul mentions all the people who saw the risen Christ? **4.** What effect does the resurrection of Christ have on Paul's apostleship and ministry? How is this evident by what he has written in the rest of this letter?

REFLECT: 1. If you had to explain to an interested friend who Jesus Christ is, what would you say? **2.** Of the facts in verses 3-8, which is most important to you? Why?

The Resurrection of Christ

15 Now, brothers, I want to remind you of the gospel I
preached to you, which you received and on which you
have taken your stand. 2By this gospel you are saved, if you hold
firmly to the word I preached to you. Otherwise, you have
believed in vain.
3For what I received I passed on to you as of first importance[o]:
that Christ died for our sins according to the Scriptures, 4that
he was buried, that he was raised on the third day according to
the Scriptures, 5and that he appeared to Peter,[p] and then to the
Twelve. 6After that, he appeared to more than five hundred of
the brothers at the same time, most of whom are still living,
though some have fallen asleep. 7Then he appeared to James,
then to all the apostles, 8and last of all he appeared to me also,
as to one abnormally born.
9For I am the least of the apostles and do not even deserve to
be called an apostle, because I persecuted the church of God.
10But by the grace of God I am what I am, and his grace to me
was not without effect. No, I worked harder than all of them—
yet not I, but the grace of God that was with me. 11Whether,
then, it was I or they, this is what we preach, and this is what
you believed.

OPEN: 1. If you could write your own epitaph or inscription for your tombstone what would it say? **2.** At your funeral, is it important for you that people mourn your death? Why? What would they miss most about you?

DIG: 1. What would life be like, according to Paul (vv. 12-19), if there were *no* ressurrection of the dead? What proofs does Paul offer that this is not the case? **2.** What imagery and analogy does Paul use to describe Christ's resurrection (vv. 20-23)? What are the implications for the Christian that Christ *did* rise from the dead (vv. 21-28)? What happens when "the end" finally comes? **3.** What are three present activities that are absurd if there is no future resurrection (verses 29-34)? **4.** What does Paul mean in verse 31? How is this an argument for the resurrection?

REFLECT: 1. When did you come to the point in your own spiritual life that you connected the resurrection of Christ with your own victory over death? Who told you? How did you feel? **2.** How do you think your life would change if Christ had not been

The Resurrection of the Dead

12But if it is preached that Christ has been raised from the
dead, how can some of you say that there is no resurrection of
the dead? 13If there is no resurrection of the dead, then not even
Christ has been raised. 14And if Christ has not been raised, our
preaching is useless and so is your faith. 15More than that, we
are then found to be false witnesses about God, for we have
testified about God that he raised Christ from the dead. But he
did not raise him if in fact the dead are not raised. 16For if the
dead are not raised, then Christ has not been raised either. 17And
if Christ has not been raised, your faith is futile; you are still in
your sins. 18Then those also who have fallen asleep in Christ are
lost. 19If only for this life we have hope in Christ, we are to be
pitied more than all men.
20But Christ has indeed been raised from the dead, the firstfruits of those who have fallen asleep. 21For since death came
through a man, the resurrection of the dead comes also through
a man. 22For as in Adam all die, so in Christ all will be made
alive. 23But each in his own turn: Christ, the firstfruits; then,
when he comes, those who belong to him. 24Then the end will
come, when he hands over the kingdom to God the Father after
he has destroyed all dominion, authority and power. 25For he
must reign until he has put all his enemies under his feet. 26The
last enemy to be destroyed is death. 27For he "has put everything
under his feet."[q] Now when it says that "everything" has been

[o]3 Or *you at the first* [p]5 Greek *Cephas* [q]27 Psalm 8:6

put under him, it is clear that this does not include God himself, who put everything under Christ. ²⁸When he has done this, then the Son himself will be made subject to him who put everything under him, so that God may be all in all.

²⁹Now if there is no resurrection, what will those do who are baptized for the dead? If the dead are not raised at all, why are people baptized for them? ³⁰And as for us, why do we endanger ourselves every hour? ³¹I die every day—I mean that, brothers—just as surely as I glory over you in Christ Jesus our Lord. ³²If I fought wild beasts in Ephesus for merely human reasons, what have I gained? If the dead are not raised,

"Let us eat and drink,
for tomorrow we die."ʳ

³³Do not be misled: "Bad company corrupts good character." ³⁴Come back to your senses as you ought, and stop sinning; for there are some who are ignorant of God—I say this to your shame.

The Resurrection Body

³⁵But someone may ask, "How are the dead raised? With what kind of body will they come?" ³⁶How foolish! What you sow does not come to life unless it dies. ³⁷When you sow, you do not plant the body that will be, but just a seed, perhaps of wheat or of something else. ³⁸But God gives it a body as he has determined, and to each kind of seed he gives its own body. ³⁹All flesh is not the same: Men have one kind of flesh, animals have another, birds another and fish another. ⁴⁰There are also heavenly bodies and there are earthly bodies; but the splendor of the heavenly bodies is one kind, and the splendor of the earthly bodies is another. ⁴¹The sun has one kind of splendor, the moon another and the stars another; and star differs from star in splendor.

⁴²So will it be with the resurrection of the dead. The body that is sown is perishable, it is raised imperishable; ⁴³it is sown in dishonor, it is raised in glory; it is sown in weakness, it is raised in power; ⁴⁴it is sown a natural body, it is raised a spiritual body.

If there is a natural body, there is also a spiritual body. ⁴⁵So it is written: "The first man Adam became a living being"ˢ; the last Adam, a life-giving spirit. ⁴⁶The spiritual did not come first, but the natural, and after that the spiritual. ⁴⁷The first man was of the dust of the earth, the second man from heaven. ⁴⁸As was the earthly man, so are those who are of the earth; and as is the man from heaven, so also are those who are of heaven. ⁴⁹And just as we have borne the likeness of the earthly man, so shall weᵗ bear the likeness of the man from heaven.

⁵⁰I declare to you, brothers, that flesh and blood cannot inherit the kingdom of God, nor does the perishable inherit the imperishable. ⁵¹Listen, I tell you a mystery: We will not all sleep, but we will all be changed— ⁵²in a flash, in the twinkling of an eye, at the last trumpet. For the trumpet will sound, the dead will be raised imperishable, and we will be changed. ⁵³For

raised from the dead? Why? **3.** When have you felt that your faith was futile and life was without hope? How did this effect your attitude and actions? How useful is your faith now? **4.** What are some practical ways that you can show and tell your unbelieving friends and relatives that Christ is alive and can be known? How can you do this without being unpleasant or manipulative?

OPEN: Suppose someone you loved died and came back to tell you about life beyond the grave: Would this person be recognizable? How so? Would you believe him or her? How come? Would you yearn to exchange places? Why?

DIG: 1. How will the resurrected body be different from the earthly body? How does the analogy of the seed in (vv. 36-38, 42-44) clarify the difference? Why does Paul place so much emphasis on this difference? **2.** What is the point in comparing Adam and Christ (vv. 45-49)? In this regard, what does verse 49 mean? **3.** How does the final resurrection fulfill Hosea 13:14, quoted in verses 54-55? How is the Law the power of sin? What is Christ's victory? Who cannot inherit the Kingdom of God? Who can? **4.** What are the implications of Christ's victory for the Christian's life and ministry?

REFLECT: 1. In verses 35-58, what words are most comforting to one who has lost a loved one in death? What words are most encouraging to one who considers his ministry futile? What words are most mind-boggling to the skeptic, even the believer? **2.** What has been the toughest death for you to experience? Why was it so painful? What did you learn from that experience? **3.** How firmly do you stand on the truth of verse 58? What motivates you to give yourself fully to the Lord's work? **4.** How important is it for Christians to share the truths of this passage with others? Why? With whom will you share them this week?

_____

the perishable must clothe itself with the imperishable, and the mortal with immortality. [54]When the perishable has been clothed with the imperishable, and the mortal with immortality, then the saying that is written will come true: "Death has been swallowed up in victory." [u]

[55]"Where, O death, is your victory?
Where, O death, is your sting?" [v]

[56]The sting of death is sin, and the power of sin is the law. [57]But thanks be to God! He gives us the victory through our Lord Jesus Christ.

[58]Therefore, my dear brothers, stand firm. Let nothing move you. Always give yourselves fully to the work of the Lord, because you know that your labor in the Lord is not in vain.

The Collection for God's People

16 Now about the collection for God's people: Do what I told the Galatian churches to do. [2]On the first day of every week, each one of you should set aside a sum of money in keeping with his income, saving it up, so that when I come no collections will have to be made. [3]Then, when I arrive, I will give letters of introduction to the men you approve and send them with your gift to Jerusalem. [4]If it seems advisable for me to go also, they will accompany me.

Personal Requests

[5]After I go through Macedonia, I will come to you—for I will be going through Macedonia. [6]Perhaps I will stay with you awhile, or even spend the winter, so that you can help me on my journey, wherever I go. [7]I do not want to see you now and make only a passing visit; I hope to spend some time with you, if the Lord permits. [8]But I will stay on at Ephesus until Pentecost, [9]because a great door for effective work has opened to me, and there are many who oppose me.

[10]If Timothy comes, see to it that he has nothing to fear while he is with you, for he is carrying on the work of the Lord, just as I am. [11]No one, then, should refuse to accept him. Send him on his way in peace so that he may return to me. I am expecting him along with the brothers.

[12]Now about our brother Apollos: I strongly urged him to go to you with the brothers. He was quite unwilling to go now, but he will go when he has the opportunity.

[13]Be on your guard; stand firm in the faith; be men of courage; be strong. [14]Do everything in love.

[15]You know that the household of Stephanas were the first converts in Achaia, and they have devoted themselves to the service of the saints. I urge you, brothers, [16]to submit to such as these and to everyone who joins in the work, and labors at it. [17]I was glad when Stephanas, Fortunatus and Achaicus arrived, because they have supplied what was lacking from you. [18]For they refreshed my spirit and yours also. Such men deserve recognition.

OPEN: When, if ever, has a person given you money unsolicited?

DIG: 1. What are Paul's instructions concerning the collection for the poor? **2.** Why do you think he gives such careful instructions? **3.** Why would Paul entrust financial accountability and responsibility to men approved by the Corinthian believers themselves? Explain?

_____

OPEN: What personal characteristics would you look for in someone you wanted to represent you on a business trip? What would be the most important quality?

DIG: 1. What are Paul's plans according to verses 5-9? Why does Paul want to stay on in Ephesus and not visit the Corinthians right now? **2.** What are Timothy's plans? What might he fear in Corinth? Why do you think it wise that Apollos not visit Corinth right now? **3.** What is the relationship of Stephanas and his family to the church in Corinth? To Paul? How do you think their service relates to Paul's instructions in verses 13-14?

REFLECT: 1. What's been the greatest door for effective work ever opened to you? Did you walk through and serve? Did you face much opposition? **2.** What situation in your life right now requires great vigilance, firmness, courage and strength? How difficult is it for you to "Do everything in love"? Why? **3.** How does Paul's way of relating to his friends in the ministry compare to your way of relating to friends and co-workers? How well do you submit to others? How much recognition do you give them?

_____

[u]54 Isaiah 25:8   [v]55 Hosea 13:14

Final Greetings

¹⁹The churches in the province of Asia send you greetings. Aquila and Priscilla*greet you warmly in the Lord, and so does the church that meets at their house. ²⁰All the brothers here send you greetings. Greet one another with a holy kiss.

²¹I, Paul, write this greeting in my own hand.

²²If anyone does not love the Lord—a curse be on him. Come, O Lord*!

²³The grace of the Lord Jesus be with you.

²⁴My love to all of you in Christ Jesus. Amen.*

OPEN: When was the last time you had difficulty saying good-bye to close friends? What did you say? What made it so difficult?

DIG: 1. What sort of relationship seems to exist between this church and Paul? Why? How will this relationship help the Corinthians deal in the future with the major issues Paul has raised? **2.** How does the tone Paul began this letter with (1:1-9) compare with the one he ends with? Why?

REFLECT: 1. How would you feel after reading this letter if it had been addressed to you? What kind of a relationship would you now have with Paul? **2.** What is the most important thing you've learned in this study of I Corinthians? How has it changed your life?

---

w19 Greek *Prisca,* a variant of *Priscilla*   *x22* In Aramaic the expression *Come, O Lord* is *Marana tha.*   *y24* Some manuscripts do not have *Amen.*

2 CORINTHIANS

INTRODUCTION

Audience

See the introductory notes to 1 Corinthians.

The Occasion

C. K. Barrett says that 2 Corinthians is "surely the most difficult book in the New Testament" (*The Second Epistle to the Corinthians: Harper New Testament Commentaries*). Part of its difficulty is that one cannot understand the epistle without understanding what happened during the period between the writing of 1 and 2 Corinthians, since much of the epistle is devoted to Paul's explanation of his actions then. Unfortunately, no one really knows what happened. What follows is a "best guess" based on the work of Barrett and Fee (Gordon D. Fee, *Corinthians: A Study Guide*).

Paul's visits to Corinth

Paul's first visit to Corinth took place during his second missionary journey. It was then that he founded the Corinthian church. In 2 Corinthians 13:1, Paul proposes a third visit to the city. It seems that his second visit was the cause of much trouble and the reason he wrote 2 Corinthians.

This second visit had been promised in 1 Corinthians 16:1-9. Paul wrote that he would leave Ephesus, journey to Macedonia, and then come down to Corinth en route to Jerusalem with the collection. (See map, Plan A.) As the time drew near to the trip, Paul changed to Plan B, in which he went straight to Corinth, intending to go from there up to Macedonia and then back to Corinth once again. (See map, Plan B.) He thought this would bring the Christians in Corinth great pleasure, since he would be with them twice instead of just once (1:15-16). Instead his unexpected visit proved so painful (because of a conflict with false apostles), he cancelled his return trip from Macedonia. Instead he went back to Ephesus, then north again to Troas, and finally back once more to Macedonia. (See map, Actual Trip.) At Macedonia, he wrote 2 Corinthians to prepare them for a third visit.

Paul's letters to the Corinthians

Reconstructing the events surrounding the writing of 2 Corinthians is further complicated because Paul wrote at least two other letters to the Corinthians that have not been preserved (see 1 Cor. 5:9; 2 Cor. 2:3-4, 9; 7:8-13). Paul wrote one of these letters prior to 1 Corinthians and another (the "sorrowful" letter) in between 1 and 2 Corinthians, probably to explain why he was not returning to Corinth from Macedonia (1:23; 2:4).

Second Corinthians may itself be not one but two letters: The fierce tone of chapters 10-13 stands in sharp contrast to the gentle, reconciling tone of chapters 1-9. According to this conjecture, the first nine chapters (Paul's fourth letter) seem to be based on the report of Titus (7:6-16) that the situation in Corinth had been rectified. But when Titus returned to Corinth with Chapters 1-9, he found to his horror that the "super-apostles" were back in charge, so he beat a hasty retreat back to Macedonia. Reacting to the new situation, Paul penned chapters 10-13 (his fifth letter). The fourth and fifth letters were later copied together, since they were so closely related in subject matter, and they became what we know as 2 Corinthians.

344

Paul's new opponents

Who, then, opposed Paul with such vigor during his second "painful" visit? The best guess (and it is only that) is that the troublemakers were not from the Corinthian church itself. Rather, they were a band of outside "apostles" (called cynically by Paul "super-apostles" in 11:5 and 12:11), probably Jewish Christians from Palestine who sought to conform the Corinthian church to Jewish law. In any case, they attacked Paul vigorously, calling him two-faced (10:1-11); they questioned his credentials as an apostle; and they criticized him for drawing no financial support from the Corinthians (the way a real apostle would). Apparently Paul's real pain came because the Corinthians did not rally to his support in this conflict. They remained on the sidelines, supporting neither party.

Paul's pain

In many ways, 2 Corinthians is Paul's most personal letter. He reveals his pain and his joy, his outrage and his suffering, his love and his convictions. 2 Corinthians is filled with profound feeling. As C. K. Barrett said: "Writing 2 Corinthians must have come near to breaking Paul, and . . . a church that is prepared to read it with him and understand it, may find itself broken too" (*The Second Epistle to the Corinthians: Harper New Testament Commentaries*).

But not only is Paul's pain evident in this letter; but also his toughness. He was willing to fight tooth and nail to wrest the Corinthians from the corrupting influence of the false apostles. "It would have been natural for Paul simply to give up the ungrateful, unruly, unloving, unintelligent Corinthians and leave them to their destiny. There is no indication that this thought ever crossed his mind" (Barrett, *The Second Epistle*, pp. 32-33). The reason for his tenacity is found in the strength of his calling. He was an apostle—called by God to bring men and women into the kingdom. No band of petty pretenders was going to defeat him in that God-given purpose. He was an apostle and so, of course, he had to write as he did.

Structure

2 Corinthians can be divided into three major sections:
1. Paul's travel plans (chapters 1-7), with a long digression on the nature of ministry (2:14-7:3).
2. The Corinthian collection (chapters 8-9).
3. Paul's defense of his apostleship and exposure of the false apostles (chapters 10-13).

2 Corinthians

OPEN: 1. When you were sick or hurt as a child, to whom did you most often turn for comfort? **2.** When was the last time you felt like you were in a "pressure cooker" situation? What happened?

DIG: 1. What in the opening of this letter is so typical of Paul? Which phrase here stands out as a possible "bumper sticker" of Paul's? How do "grace and peace" sum up what the gospel is all about? **2.** What's the relationship between God's ability to comfort us and our ability to comfort others? **3.** How are Christ's and Paul's sufferings related to the Corinthians? What pressures do you suppose Paul is facing that would cause him to despair even of life? **4.** What reaction is Paul trying to solicit from the Corinthians (vv. 6-7, 10-11)?

REFLECT: 1. Paul found that intense pressures led him to depend on God all the more (v. 9): How do you respond to pressures that seem beyond your ability to handle? **2.** Whom do you know that is under intense pressure now? How does this passage suggest you should pray for them this week?

OPEN: 1. What was one accomplishment as a teenager that you felt really proud of? **2.** When do you recall relying on someone else's repeated promise which he or she reneged on? (Perhaps a promised fishing trip or a business arrangement that fell through?) How did you feel then?

DIG: 1. In what does Paul boast? What is the basis for his integrity? **2.** How is "worldly wisdom" (v. 12, 17) recognizable? Likewise, "God's grace"? **3.** From verses 15-17, of what may Paul have been accused by some of the Corinthians? How does he account for his change of plans (1:23-2:2)? **4.** What does it mean that Jesus is the "Yes" of God's promise to us? What promises of God do you know, for which Christ is the fulfillment? **5.** Corinth was the commercial center of the empire: What would the three trading metaphors in verse 22 mean for

1 Paul, an apostle of Christ Jesus by the will of God, and Timothy our brother,

To the church of God in Corinth, together with all the saints throughout Achaia:

²Grace and peace to you from God our Father and the Lord Jesus Christ.

The God of All Comfort

³Praise be to the God and Father of our Lord Jesus Christ, the Father of compassion and the God of all comfort, ⁴who comforts us in all our troubles, so that we can comfort those in any trouble with the comfort we ourselves have received from God. ⁵For just as the sufferings of Christ flow over into our lives, so also through Christ our comfort overflows. ⁶If we are distressed, it is for your comfort and salvation; if we are comforted, it is for your comfort, which produces in you patient endurance of the same sufferings we suffer. ⁷And our hope for you is firm, because we know that just as you share in our sufferings, so also you share in our comfort.

⁸We do not want you to be uninformed, brothers, about the hardships we suffered in the province of Asia. We were under great pressure, far beyond our ability to endure, so that we despaired even of life. ⁹Indeed, in our hearts we felt the sentence of death. But this happened that we might not rely on ourselves but on God, who raises the dead. ¹⁰He has delivered us from such a deadly peril, and he will deliver us. On him we have set our hope that he will continue to deliver us, ¹¹as you help us by your prayers. Then many will give thanks on our*ᵃ* behalf for the gracious favor granted us in answer to the prayers of many.

Paul's Change of Plans

¹²Now this is our boast: Our conscience testifies that we have conducted ourselves in the world, and especially in our relations with you, in the holiness and sincerity that are from God. We have done so not according to worldly wisdom but according to God's grace. ¹³For we do not write you anything you cannot read or understand. And I hope that, ¹⁴as you have understood us in part, you will come to understand fully that you can boast of us just as we will boast of you in the day of the Lord Jesus.

¹⁵Because I was confident of this, I planned to visit you first so that you might benefit twice. ¹⁶I planned to visit you on my way to Macedonia and to come back to you from Macedonia, and then to have you send me on my way to Judea. ¹⁷When I planned this, did I do it lightly? Or do I make my plans in a worldly manner so that in the same breath I say, "Yes, yes" and "No, no"?

¹⁸But as surely as God is faithful, our message to you is not "Yes" and "No." ¹⁹For the Son of God, Jesus Christ, who was

ᵃ11 Many manuscripts your

preached among you by me and Silas[b] and Timothy, was not "Yes" and "No," but in him it has always been "Yes." [20]For no matter how many promises God has made, they are "Yes" in Christ. And so through him the "Amen" is spoken by us to the glory of God. [21]Now it is God who makes both us and you stand firm in Christ. He anointed us, [22]set his seal of ownership on us, and put his Spirit in our hearts as a deposit, guaranteeing what is to come.

[23]I call God as my witness that it was in order to spare you that I did not return to Corinth. [24]Not that we lord it over your faith, but we work with you for your joy, because it is by faith you stand firm. 2 [1]So I made up my mind that I would not make another painful visit to you. [2]For if I grieve you, who is left to make me glad but you whom I have grieved? [3]I wrote as I did so that when I came I should not be distressed by those who ought to make me rejoice. I had confidence in all of you, that you would all share my joy. [4]For I wrote you out of great distress and anguish of heart and with many tears, not to grieve you but to let you know the depth of my love for you.

Forgiveness for the Sinner

[5]If anyone has caused grief, he has not so much grieved me as he has grieved all of you, to some extent—not to put it too severely. [6]The punishment inflicted on him by the majority is sufficient for him. [7]Now instead, you ought to forgive and comfort him, so that he will not be overwhelmed by excessive sorrow. [8]I urge you, therefore, to reaffirm your love for him. [9]The reason I wrote you was to see if you would stand the test and be obedient in everything. [10]If you forgive anyone, I also forgive him. And what I have forgiven—if there was anything to forgive—I have forgiven in the sight of Christ for your sake, [11]in order that Satan might not outwit us. For we are not unaware of his schemes.

Ministers of the New Covenant

[12]Now when I went to Troas to preach the gospel of Christ and found that the Lord had opened a door for me, [13]I still had no peace of mind, because I did not find my brother Titus there. So I said good-by to them and went on to Macedonia.

[14]But thanks be to God, who always leads us in triumphal procession in Christ and through us spreads everywhere the fragrance of the knowledge of him. [15]For we are to God the aroma of Christ among those who are being saved and those who are perishing. [16]To the one we are the smell of death; to the other, the fragrance of life. And who is equal to such a task? [17]Unlike so many, we do not peddle the word of God for profit. On the contrary, in Christ we speak before God with sincerity, like men sent from God.

3 Are we beginning to commend ourselves again? Or do we need, like some people, letters of recommendation to you or from you? [2]You yourselves are our letter, written on our hearts, known and read by everybody. [3]You show that you are a letter from Christ, the result of our ministry, written not with

[b]19 Greek *Silvanus*, a variant of *Silas*

the Corinthian Christians? 6. From this section how would you describe the relationship between Paul and the Corinthian chruch?

REFLECT: 1. Where have you felt the tension between living by worldly wisdom and living by God's grace? 2. How has the consistent lifestyle of some Christian leader you respect influenced you? Have you ever been hurt by what you have perceived as a lack of integrity in a Christian leader? What do these examples mean for you in terms of how you ought to relate to others?

OPEN: What was one of the most effective punishments your parents used on you as a child?

DIG: 1. Paul's grievous letter must have been about what (vv. 3-8, see 7:8-12)? 2. From verse 6-8, what do you think has happened since the letter was received? What does this passage teach about the nature and purpose of church discipline? 3. How might their continuation of punishment be a scheme of Satan?

OPEN: Swap resumés in your group: What do they reveal about yourselves?

DIG: 1. Until Titus returns with "good news" (see 7:6ff), Paul has "no peace of mind": What does that reveal about Paul's concern for this church? 2. How can the same gospel be either the smell of death or the fragrance of life? 3. What do the contrasts in 2:17-3:1 show about what may be happening in Corinth? Although preachers often had letters of recommendation when they traveled to new areas (Acts 18:27; III John 5-8), why does Paul say he needs no such letter for the Corinthians? How does this relate to Acts 18:1-11? 4. What is Paul's point in transitioning from the letter of commendation to the "letter that kills" (v. 6)? 5. To sum up verses 1:1-3:6, what reasons does Paul use for why the Corinthians should listen to him?

ink but with the Spirit of the living God, not on tablets of stone but on tablets of human hearts.

[4]Such confidence as this is ours through Christ before God. [5]Not that we are competent in ourselves to claim anything for ourselves, but our competence comes from God. [6]He has made us competent as ministers of a new covenant—not of the letter but of the Spirit; for the letter kills, but the Spirit gives life.

The Glory of the New Covenant

[7]Now if the ministry that brought death, which was engraved in letters on stone, came with glory, so that the Israelites could not look steadily at the face of Moses because of its glory, fading though it was, [8]will not the ministry of the Spirit be even more glorious? [9]If the ministry that condemns men is glorious, how much more glorious is the ministry that brings righteousness! [10]For what was glorious has no glory now in comparison with the surpassing glory. [11]And if what was fading away came with glory, how much greater is the glory of that which lasts!

[12]Therefore, since we have such a hope, we are very bold. [13]We are not like Moses, who would put a veil over his face to keep the Israelites from gazing at it while the radiance was fading away. [14]But their minds were made dull, for to this day the same veil remains when the old covenant is read. It has not been removed, because only in Christ is it taken away. [15]Even to this day when Moses is read, a veil covers their hearts. [16]But whenever anyone turns to the Lord, the veil is taken away. [17]Now the Lord is the Spirit, and where the Spirit of the Lord is, there is freedom. [18]And we, who with unveiled faces all reflect[c] the Lord's glory, are being transformed into his likeness with ever-increasing glory, which comes from the Lord, who is the Spirit.

Treasures in Jars of Clay

4 Therefore, since through God's mercy we have this ministry, we do not lose heart. [2]Rather, we have renounced secret and shameful ways; we do not use deception, nor do we distort the word of God. On the contrary, by setting forth the truth plainly we commend ourselves to every man's conscience in the sight of God. [3]And even if our gospel is veiled, it is veiled to those who are perishing. [4]The god of this age has blinded the minds of unbelievers, so that they cannot see the light of the gospel of the glory of Christ, who is the image of God. [5]For we do not preach ourselves, but Jesus Christ as Lord, and ourselves as your servants for Jesus' sake. [6]For God, who said, "Let light shine out of darkness,"[d] made his light shine in our hearts to give us the light of the knowledge of the glory of God in the face of Christ.

[7]But we have this treasure in jars of clay to show that this all-surpassing power is from God and not from us. [8]We are hard pressed on every side, but not crushed; perplexed, but not in despair; [9]persecuted, but not abandoned; struck down, but not destroyed. [10]We always carry around in our body the death of

c18 Or contemplate   *d6 Gen. 1:3*

Jesus, so that the life of Jesus may also be revealed in our body. ¹¹For we who are alive are always being given over to death for Jesus' sake, so that his life may be revealed in our mortal body. ¹²So then, death is at work in us, but life is at work in you.

¹³It is written: "I believed; therefore I have spoken."ᶜ With that same spirit of faith we also believe and therefore speak, ¹⁴because we know that the one who raised the Lord Jesus from the dead will also raise us with Jesus and present us with you in his presence. ¹⁵All this is for your benefit, so that the grace that is reaching more and more people may cause thanksgiving to overflow to the glory of God.

¹⁶Therefore we do not lose heart. Though outwardly we are wasting away, yet inwardly we are being renewed day by day. ¹⁷For our light and momentary troubles are achieving for us an eternal glory that far outweighs them all. ¹⁸So we fix our eyes not on what is seen, but on what is unseen. For what is seen is temporary, but what is unseen is eternal.

Our Heavenly Dwelling

5 Now we know that if the earthly tent we live in is destroyed, we have a building from God, an eternal house in heaven, not built by human hands. ²Meanwhile we groan, longing to be clothed with our heavenly dwelling, ³because when we are clothed, we will not be found naked. ⁴For while we are in this tent, we groan and are burdened, because we do not wish to be unclothed but to be clothed with our heavenly dwelling, so that what is mortal may be swallowed up by life. ⁵Now it is God who has made us for this very purpose and has given us the Spirit as a deposit, guaranteeing what is to come.

⁶Therefore we are always confident and know that as long as we are at home in the body we are away from the Lord. ⁷We live by faith, not by sight. ⁸We are confident, I say, and would prefer to be away from the body and at home with the Lord. ⁹So we make it our goal to please him, whether we are at home in the body or away from it. ¹⁰For we must all appear before the judgment seat of Christ, that each one may receive what is due him for the things done while in the body, whether good or bad.

The Ministry of Reconciliation

¹¹Since, then, we know what it is to fear the Lord, we try to persuade men. What we are is plain to God, and I hope it is also plain to your conscience. ¹²We are not trying to commend ourselves to you again, but are giving you an opportunity to take pride in us, so that you can answer those who take pride in what is seen rather than in what is in the heart. ¹³If we are out of our mind, it is for the sake of God; if we are in our right mind, it is for you. ¹⁴For Christ's love compels us, because we are convinced that one died for all, and therefore all died. ¹⁵And he died for all, that those who live should no longer live for themselves but for him who died for them and was raised again.

¹⁶So from now on we regard no one from a worldly point of view. Though we once regarded Christ in this way, we do so no

ᶜ13 Psalm 116:10

How has that made a difference in your life? **2.** How well does verse 5 serve as a description of your ministry to others? Why is being a servant to others essential for sharing the gospel? What is one way you could be more of a servant to someone you are concerned about now? **3.** How do verses 7-12 and 16-18 help you cope with your present difficulties and anxieties? **4.** How does this section challenge common ideas of what makes a person a "success" or "failure"? What comfort might "parents in pain" take from this chapter?

OPEN: 1. What things would you like to see included in your dream house? **2.** Where is "home" for you?

DIG: 1. How does Paul's confidence in his future relate to what he said in 4:16-18 and demonstrate what Jesus said in John 14:1-3? **2.** What images do you see as you consider with Paul "our heavenly dwelling"? **3.** Why such confidence about the future (v.5; also 1:21-22)? What role does faith play in this? How does Paul's vision impact his daily living (vv. 6-10)? **4.** What motivates him more: Desire to be with Christ (v. 8)? Or fear of judgment (v. 10)? Which motivates you more?

REFLECT: How much of Paul's vision is reflected in your outlook? How is God's purpose (v. 5) and pleasure (v. 9) reflected in your confidence level and daily priorities?

OPEN: If you were to be appointed as ambassador for your country, where would you like to be sent? What would you need to know before you were sent there?

DIG: 1. In verses 10-11, what is Paul's motive for evangelism? How about in verse 14? How do those two motives fit together? How would someone motivated by these values stand in contrast to someone motivated by those mentioned in 2:17 and 5:12? **2.** What does Paul say here (vv. 15-17) about Christ and our response to him? **3.** What does "reconciliation" mean? What is its opposite? What story from your life might illustrate Paul's use of this word? **4.** What does God do through Christ (v. 18)? Through us

(v. 20)? For us (vv. 17-18)? **6.** Role play in your group the message and ministry of reconciliation. Be sure to convey how it feels to "implore" or urge someone, also how it feels for someone else to take the rap for you (v. 21)? "Now" is the time to do this.

REFLECT: 1. What motivates you to share your faith? If you rarely do so, what inhibits you? **2.** What is one area in which you have recently struggled in terms of living for yourself rather than for Christ? **3.** Knowing what it is like to be alienated and reconciled in other relationships, how is it going in your relationship with God: Still a family feud? Or is now the time of God's favor?

OPEN: 1. Whom do you consider a great Christian leader today? Why? **2.** For whom besides your dentist do you "open wide"?

DIG: 1. How does Paul defend the authenticity of his ministry here? **2.** Paul could have appealed to his radical conversion, special revelations, or miracles (see 12:12), but he doesn't: Why not? What do you find most convincing about the evidence presented here instead? **3.** What is Paul asking the Corinthians (and us) to do in verses 11-13?

REFLECT: 1. By what standards do you guage a successful ministry: Number of converts? Blessings? Miracles? Honor awards? Books published? Friends in high places? **2.** Would Paul be a success by your standards? Would you? **3.** For whom do you open wide your heart?

OPEN: 1. Given the choice of anyone you've never met, whom would you want as your dinner guest? As your close friend? **2.** What type of environmental pollution has most affected you? How so?

DIG: 1. Given a possible misapplication of what Paul has just said (vv. 11-13), what is Paul commanding here and why? **2.** Read Paul's quotations in their original context: Why does having God as our Father obligate and enable us to separate from other competing loyalties and sexually immoral people (see also I Cor. 5:9-11)? **3.** Try answering some of Paul's rhetorical questions (vv.14-16): What commonalities, if any, do you find?

longer. [17]Therefore, if anyone is in Christ, he is a new creation; the old has gone, the new has come! [18]All this is from God, who reconciled us to himself through Christ and gave us the ministry of reconciliation: [19]that God was reconciling the world to himself in Christ, not counting men's sins against them. And he has committed to us the message of reconciliation. [20]We are therefore Christ's ambassadors, as though God were making his appeal through us. We implore you on Christ's behalf: Be reconciled to God. [21]God made him who had no sin to be sin[f] for us, so that in him we might become the righteousness of God.

6 As God's fellow workers we urge you not to receive God's grace in vain. [2]For he says,

"In the time of my favor I heard you,
    and in the day of salvation I helped you."[g]

I tell you, now is the time of God's favor, now is the day of salvation.

Paul's Hardships

[3]We put no stumbling block in anyone's path, so that our ministry will not be discredited. [4]Rather, as servants of God we commend ourselves in every way: in great endurance; in troubles, hardships and distresses; [5]in beatings, imprisonments and riots; in hard work, sleepless nights and hunger; [6]in purity, understanding, patience and kindness; in the Holy Spirit and in sincere love; [7]in truthful speech and in the power of God; with weapons of righteousness in the right hand and in the left; [8]through glory and dishonor, bad report and good report; genuine, yet regarded as impostors; [9]known, yet regarded as unknown; dying, and yet we live on; beaten, and yet not killed; [10]sorrowful, yet always rejoicing; poor, yet making many rich; having nothing, and yet possessing everything.

[11]We have spoken freely to you, Corinthians, and opened wide our hearts to you. [12]We are not withholding our affection from you, but you are withholding yours from us. [13]As a fair exchange—I speak as to my children—open wide your hearts also.

Do Not Be Yoked With Unbelievers

[14]Do not be yoked together with unbelievers. For what do righteousness and wickedness have in common? Or what fellowship can light have with darkness? [15]What harmony is there between Christ and Belial[h]? What does a believer have in common with an unbeliever? [16]What agreement is there between the temple of God and idols? For we are the temple of the living God. As God has said: "I will live with them and walk among them, and I will be their God, and they will be my people."[i]

[17]"Therefore come out from them
    and be separate,

                says the Lord.

---

f21 Or *be a sin offering*   *g2* Isaiah 49:8   *h15* Greek *Beliar,* a variant of *Belial*
i16 Lev. 26:12; Jer. 32:38; Ezek. 37:27

Touch no unclean thing,
   and I will receive you." [j]
[18]"I will be a Father to you,
   and you will be my sons and daughters,
                 says the Lord Almighty." [k]

7 Since we have these promises, dear friends, let us purify ourselves from everything that contaminates body and spirit, perfecting holiness out of reverence for God.

Paul's Joy

[2]Make room for us in your hearts. We have wronged no one, we have corrupted no one, we have exploited no one. [3]I do not say this to condemn you; I have said before that you have such a place in our hearts that we would live or die with you. [4]I have great confidence in you; I take great pride in you. I am greatly encouraged; in all our troubles my joy knows no bounds.

[5]For when we came into Macedonia, this body of ours had no rest, but we were harassed at every turn—conflicts on the outside, fears within. [6]But God, who comforts the downcast, comforted us by the coming of Titus, [7]and not only by his coming but also by the comfort you had given him. He told us about your longing for me, your deep sorrow, your ardent concern for me, so that my joy was greater than ever.

[8]Even if I caused you sorrow by my letter, I do not regret it. Though I did regret it—I see that my letter hurt you, but only for a little while— [9]yet now I am happy, not because you were made sorry, but because your sorrow led you to repentance. For you became sorrowful as God intended and so were not harmed in any way by us. [10]Godly sorrow brings repentance that leads to salvation and leaves no regret, but worldly sorrow brings death. [11]See what this godly sorrow has produced in you: what earnestness, what eagerness to clear yourselves, what indignation, what alarm, what longing, what concern, what readiness to see justice done. At every point you have proved yourselves to be innocent in this matter. [12]So even though I wrote to you, it was not on account of the one who did the wrong or of the injured party, but rather that before God you could see for yourselves how devoted to us you are. [13]By all this we are encouraged.

In addition to our own encouragement, we were especially delighted to see how happy Titus was, because his spirit has been refreshed by all of you. [14]I had boasted to him about you, and you have not embarrassed me. But just as everything we said to you was true, so our boasting about you to Titus has proved to be true as well. [15]And his affection for you is all the greater when he remembers that you were all obedient, receiving him with fear and trembling. [16]I am glad I can have complete confidence in you.

REFLECT: 1. Of the different relationships Paul has in view here, which one(s) apply to you? **2.** What does it mean to you that you are the dwelling place of God? What contaminants might affect your body? Your spirit? Is there something contaminating you now from which you should separate?

OPEN: When you want to communicate with someone without being misunderstood, what do you do? When you get sidetracked, what do you do? When a major breakdown in communications occurs, what do you do then?

DIG: 1. From 7:1-4 and 6:11-13, what would you say has been the relationship between Paul and this church? **2.** In 7:5, Paul picks up the account of his travels which he left off in 2:12-13: How does his account in 7:5-7 illustrate why he began this letter with thanks to God for his comfort (1:3-7)? **3.** In light of his appeal in 7:2, do you think Titus' report was entirely positive? Why or why not? **4.** What is the result of Paul's previous letter to them (see also 2:3-4)? What intentions does Paul clarify in verses 8-13? What does Paul regret? Not regret? Why? Give an example of how godly sorrow differs from worldly sorrow? **5.** What tone or feeling do you sense Paul had as he wrote 7:16? In light of his previous letter, why would he so underscore his present joy and confidence? If you were in this church, how would you feel as you read this?

REFLECT: 1. Have you ever been confronted by someone who loves you regarding something wrong you have done? How did you feel towards that person at the time? **2.** How do you decide when it is more loving to confront someone with their sin than to ignore it? What attitudes are needed to make loving confrontation different than being judgmental? How do you see those attitudes in Paul? **3.** Would you share a time when godly sorrow motivated you to make a real change in your life? How do you feel about that change now?

---

[j]17 Isaiah 52:11; Ezek. 20:34,41   [k]18 2 Samuel 7:14; 7:8

Generosity Encouraged

8 And now, brothers, we want you to know about the grace that God has given the Macedonian churches. [2]Out of the most severe trial, their overflowing joy and their extreme poverty welled up in rich generosity. [3]For I testify that they gave as much as they were able, and even beyond their ability. Entirely on their own, [4]they urgently pleaded with us for the privilege of sharing in this service to the saints. [5]And they did not do as we expected, but they gave themselves first to the Lord and then to us in keeping with God's will. [6]So we urged Titus, since he had earlier made a beginning, to bring also to completion this act of grace on your part. [7]But just as you excel in everything—in faith, in speech, in knowledge, in complete earnestness and in your love for us[l]—see that you also excel in this grace of giving.

[8]I am not commanding you, but I want to test the sincerity of your love by comparing it with the earnestness of others. [9]For you know the grace of our Lord Jesus Christ, that though he was rich, yet for your sakes he became poor, so that you through his poverty might become rich.

[10]And here is my advice about what is best for you in this matter: Last year you were the first not only to give but also to have the desire to do so. [11]Now finish the work, so that your eager willingness to do it may be matched by your completion of it, according to your means. [12]For if the willingness is there, the gift is acceptable according to what one has, not according to what he does not have.

[13]Our desire is not that others might be relieved while you are hard pressed, but that there might be equality. [14]At the present time your plenty will supply what they need, so that in turn their plenty will supply what you need. Then there will be equality, [15]as it is written: "He who gathered much did not have too much, and he who gathered little did not have too little."[m]

Titus Sent to Corinth

[16]I thank God, who put into the heart of Titus the same concern I have for you. [17]For Titus not only welcomed our appeal, but he is coming to you with much enthusiasm and on his own initiative. [18]And we are sending along with him the brother who is praised by all the churches for his service to the gospel. [19]What is more, he was chosen by the churches to accompany us as we carry the offering, which we administer in order to honor the Lord himself and to show our eagerness to help. [20]We want to avoid any criticism of the way we administer this liberal gift. [21]For we are taking pains to do what is right, not only in the eyes of the Lord but also in the eyes of men.

[22]In addition, we are sending with them our brother who has often proved to us in many ways that he is zealous, and now even more so because of his great confidence in you. [23]As for Titus, he is my partner and fellow worker among you; as for our brothers, they are representatives of the churches and an honor to Christ. [24]Therefore show these men the proof of your love and the reason for our pride in you, so that the churches can see it.

l7 Some manuscripts/in our love for you   m15 Exodus 16:18

9 There is no need for me to write to you about this service to the saints. [2]For I know your eagerness to help, and I have been boasting about it to the Macedonians, telling them that since last year you in Achaia were ready to give; and your enthusiasm has stirred most of them to action. [3]But I am sending the brothers in order that our boasting about you in this matter should not prove hollow, but that you may be ready, as I said you would be. [4]For if any Macedonians come with me and find you unprepared, we—not to say anything about you—would be ashamed of having been so confident. [5]So I thought it necessary to urge the brothers to visit you in advance and finish the arrangements for the generous gift you had promised. Then it will be ready as a generous gift, not as one grudgingly given.

Sowing Generously

[6]Remember this: Whoever sows sparingly will also reap sparingly, and whoever sows generously will also reap generously. [7]Each man should give what he has decided in his heart to give, not reluctantly or under compulsion, for God loves a cheerful giver. [8]And God is able to make all grace abound to you, so that in all things at all times, having all that you need, you will abound in every good work. [9]As it is written:

"He has scattered abroad his gifts to the poor;
his righteousness endures forever." [n]

[10]Now he who supplies seed to the sower and bread for food will also supply and increase your store of seed and will enlarge the harvest of your righteousness. [11]You will be made rich in every way so that you can be generous on every occasion, and through us your generosity will result in thanksgiving to God.

[12]This service that you perform is not only supplying the needs of God's people but is also overflowing in many expressions of thanks to God. [13]Because of the service by which you have proved yourselves, men will praise God for the obedience that accompanies your confession of the gospel of Christ, and for your generosity in sharing with them and with everyone else. [14]And in their prayers for you their hearts will go out to you, because of the surpassing grace God has given you. [15]Thanks be to God for his indescribable gift!

Paul's Defense of His Ministry

10 By the meekness and gentleness of Christ, I appeal to you—I, Paul, who am "timid" when face to face with you, but "bold" when away! [2]I beg you that when I come I may not have to be as bold as I expect to be toward some people who think that we live by the standards of this world. [3]For though we live in the world, we do not wage war as the world does. [4]The weapons we fight with are not the weapons of the world. On the contrary, they have divine power to demolish strongholds. [5]We demolish arguments and every pretension that sets itself up against the knowledge of God, and we take captive every thought to make it obedient to Christ. [6]And we will be ready to

n9 Psalm 112:9

came to visit you, would they find your generosity lacking or overflowing? With what else besides money are you generous? **3.** For you to become more generous, what would have to change—your job, time priorities, spending habits, mission vision, or what?

OPEN: 1. What is the most hilarious thing about you? **2.** What is one lesson about money you can recall learning from your parents?

DIG: 1. By using the image of sowing and reaping, is Paul saying that, if you give $100, you will get $1,000? Why or why not? **2.** With giving away money, how is that a source of hilarity or cheer for the giver (v.8)? **3.** What do you make of the *all*ness in verse 8? **4.** How is "righteousness" reaped (vv. 9-10): By whom? Through whom? To what extent? **5.** How is thanksgiving increased (vv. 11-13)? Likewise, whose thanksgiving is this? **6.** How is giving contagious? Who really gives to whom? Is it possible to out-give God (vv. 14-15)?

REFLECT: 1. In what way have you reaped by being generous to others in need? **2.** Given the promise of verse 8, with what steps of obedience and seeds of generosity will you begin? Where? When? For whose sake? **3.** Try writing thank-you notes to God for his "indescribable gift" to you?

OPEN: Is "authority" more of a positive or negative word to you? Why?

DIG: 1. Why the sudden shift in tone and subject matter (as if chapters 10-13 were a separate letter)? **2.** Things have improved in Corinth since Paul wrote his last letter (7:8-16), but not altogether: How is Paul discredited here (vv. 1-2, 9-11)? How is Paul's gentleness and meekness being misunderstood? **3.** Where have you seen, instead, Paul's strength and other-centeredness demonstrated most judiciously and compassionately? **4.** How is Paul's exercise of authority (vv. 3-8) different than his usurpers, the so-called "super-apostles"

(11:5, 20)? What kind of authority do you suppose the Corinthians want? What must change before Paul comes to visit again (vv. 5-7, 11)? **5.** What is wrong with commending ourselves and comparing ourselves with others (vv. 12-18)? What are the proper limits of boasting and Christian ambition? **6.** If you were the Corinthians, who would you listen to at this point and why?

REFLECT: 1. From Paul's example here, what is supposed to be the "normal" way Christians exercise leadership over one another? On a scale from 1-10, how well does your leadership of those for whom you are responsible demonstrate Christ's gentleness and meekness? **2.** What will you work on this week that demonstrates your interest in building others up and not tearing them down? **3.** When is it right to show "tough love" as Paul does here by demanding that someone change? What risks does that involve? **4.** As an act of "tough love", what worldly, anti-God thoughts prevail in your circle of friends, which you might "take captive" and "make obedient to Christ", as Paul does (v. 5)?

OPEN: What picture springs to mind when you hear the word "Satan"?

DIG: 1. What is happening in Corinth that is upsetting Paul? From verses 4-7, what can you learn about these "super-apostles"? How does this relate to his command in 6:14? **2.** Why do you think Paul refused to be supported by the Corinthians while he was with them? Why would he accept help from the Macedonian churches? How is this servant-attitude of Paul's being distorted by the false apostles? How do their motives compare with this (see 2:17)? **3.** What is Paul's final conclusion about these teachers (vv. 13-15)? What tensions would you feel as a Corinthian Christian when you read this accusation by Paul? **4.** Given the criticisms of Paul by these "super-apostles", is this not a case of "tit-for-tat" or "the pot calling the kettle 'black'"? Is not Paul violating his own standards in 10:12? Why or why not? (See Paul's admission of this in 11:16ff.)

punish every act of disobedience, once your obedience is complete.

[7]You are looking only on the surface of things. [o] If anyone is confident that he belongs to Christ, he should consider again that we belong to Christ just as much as he. [8]For even if I boast somewhat freely about the authority the Lord gave us for building you up rather than pulling you down, I will not be ashamed of it. [9]I do not want to seem to be trying to frighten you with my letters. [10]For some say, "His letters are weighty and forceful, but in person he is unimpressive and his speaking amounts to nothing." [11]Such people should realize that what we are in our letters when we are absent, we will be in our actions when we are present.

[12]We do not dare to classify or compare ourselves with some who commend themselves. When they measure themselves by themselves and compare themselves with themselves, they are not wise. [13]We, however, will not boast beyond proper limits, but will confine our boasting to the field God has assigned to us, a field that reaches even to you. [14]We are not going too far in our boasting, as would be the case if we had not come to you, for we did get as far as you with the gospel of Christ. [15]Neither do we go beyond our limits by boasting of work done by others. [p] Our hope is that, as your faith continues to grow, our area of activity among you will greatly expand, [16]so that we can preach the gospel in the regions beyond you. For we do not want to boast about work already done in another man's territory. [17]But, "Let him who boasts boast in the Lord." [q] [18]For it is not the one who commends himself who is approved, but the one whom the Lord commends.

Paul and the False Apostles

11 I hope you will put up with a little of my foolishness; but you are already doing that. [2]I am jealous for you with a godly jealousy. I promised you to one husband, to Christ, so that I might present you as a pure virgin to him. [3]But I am afraid that just as Eve was deceived by the serpent's cunning, your minds may somehow be led astray from your sincere and pure devotion to Christ. [4]For if someone comes to you and preaches a Jesus other than the Jesus we preached, or if you receive a different spirit from the one you received, or a different gospel from the one you accepted, you put up with it easily enough. [5]But I do not think I am in the least inferior to those "super-apostles." [6]I may not be a trained speaker, but I do have knowledge. We have made this perfectly clear to you in every way.

[7]Was it a sin for me to lower myself in order to elevate you

---

[o]7 Or *Look at the obvious facts*   [p]13-15 Or *[13]We, however, will not boast about things that cannot be measured, but|we will boast according to the standard of measurement that the God of measure has assigned us—a measurement that relates even to you. [14] . . . . [15]Neither do we boast about things that cannot be measured in regard to the work done by others.*   [q]17 Jer. 9:24

by preaching the gospel of God to you free of charge? [8]I robbed other churches by receiving support from them so as to serve you. [9]And when I was with you and needed something, I was not a burden to anyone, for the brothers who came from Macedonia supplied what I needed. I have kept myself from being a burden to you in any way, and will continue to do so. [10]As surely as the truth of Christ is in me, nobody in the regions of Achaia will stop this boasting of mine. [11]Why? Because I do not love you? God knows I do! [12]And I will keep on doing what I am doing in order to cut the ground from under those who want an opportunity to be considered equal with us in the things they boast about.

[13]For such men are false apostles, deceitful workmen, masquerading as apostles of Christ. [14]And no wonder, for Satan himself masquerades as an angel of light. [15]It is not surprising, then, if his servants masquerade as servants of righteousness. Their end will be what their actions deserve.

Paul Boasts About His Sufferings

[16]I repeat: Let no one take me for a fool. But if you do, then receive me just as you would a fool, so that I may do a little boasting. [17]In this self-confident boasting I am not talking as the Lord would, but as a fool. [18]Since many are boasting in the way the world does, I too will boast. [19]You gladly put up with fools since you are so wise! [20]In fact, you even put up with anyone who enslaves you or exploits you or takes advantage of you or pushes himself forward or slaps you in the face. [21]To my shame I admit that we were too weak for that!

What anyone else dares to boast about—I am speaking as a fool—I also dare to boast about. [22]Are they Hebrews? So am I. Are they Israelites? So am I. Are they Abraham's descendants? So am I. [23]Are they servants of Christ? (I am out of my mind to talk like this.) I am more. I have worked much harder, been in prison more frequently, been flogged more severely, and been exposed to death again and again. [24]Five times I received from the Jews the forty lashes minus one. [25]Three times I was beaten with rods, once I was stoned, three times I was shipwrecked, I spent a night and a day in the open sea, [26]I have been constantly on the move. I have been in danger from rivers, in danger from bandits, in danger from my own countrymen, in danger from Gentiles; in danger in the city, in danger in the country, in danger at sea; and in danger from false brothers. [27]I have labored and toiled and have often gone without sleep; I have known hunger and thirst and have often gone without food; I have been cold and naked. [28]Besides everything else, I face daily the pressure of my concern for all the churches. [29]Who is weak, and I do not feel weak? Who is led into sin, and I do not inwardly burn?

[30]If I must boast, I will boast of the things that show my weakness. [31]The God and Father of the Lord Jesus, who is to be praised forever, knows that I am not lying. [32]In Damascus the governor under King Aretas had the city of the Damascenes guarded in order to arrest me. [33]But I was lowered in a basket from a window in the wall and slipped through his hands.

REFLECT: 1. Spiritually, you have been promised to one husband who is Christ (v. 2). How are you getting ready for that upcoming wedding? **2.** What "different gospel" has at one point or another caught your attention? How did it pull you away from Jesus? How did you become aware of its deceitfulness? **3.** Someone has said, "Sin rarely approaches us as evil, but as virtue in disguise": What is one time you were deceived by thinking something evil really was all right? From what Paul says here in verses 2-5, how can you guard yourself against this strategy of Satan?

OPEN: Where was the last place you felt you were really in danger of being hurt? Would you put yourself in that position again?

DIG: 1. Paul has flipped his wig! In 10:1, Paul made it clear how he would like to appeal to them, so why here does he sarcastically resort to "boasting" as the false apostles were doing? What is the irony that galls Paul (see also 12:11-13)? **2.** From 1:12, 9:2, 10:8 and 11:10, of what things has Paul already boasted? How does this differ from that of the false teachers? **3.** The false teachers were apparently Palestinean Jews (11:22) preaching a distorted gospel (11:4): How does Paul validate his claim to be far more a servant of Christ than they? How is his suffering a more eloquent witness to his authority than fine speech (11:6)? **4.** What strikes you about Paul as you read verses 23-33? How would you regard a minister coming to your church who had been through this type of experience? Would you feel grateful or guilty or what?

REFLECT: 1. For both Jesus and Paul, their gentleness was misunderstood as weakness. When have you ever felt your good intentions were distorted? What happened? **2.** Would Paul have been better received if he had pushed his weight around more? How would that have misrepresented the gospel? **3.** In your own witness, where are you caught "between a rock and a hard place"? How can others pray for you this week in that regard?

355

Paul's Vision and His Thorn

12 I must go on boasting. Although there is nothing to be gained, I will go on to visions and revelations from the Lord. [2]I know a man in Christ who fourteen years ago was caught up to the third heaven. Whether it was in the body or out of the body I do not know—God knows. [3]And I know that this man—whether in the body or apart from the body I do not know, but God knows— [4]was caught up to paradise. He heard inexpressible things, things that man is not permitted to tell. [5]I will boast about a man like that, but I will not boast about myself, except about my weaknesses. [6]Even if I should choose to boast, I would not be a fool, because I would be speaking the truth. But I refrain, so no one will think more of me than is warranted by what I do or say.

[7]To keep me from becoming conceited because of these surpassingly great revelations, there was given me a thorn in my flesh, a messenger of Satan, to torment me. [8]Three times I pleaded with the Lord to take it away from me. [9]But he said to me, "My grace is sufficient for you, for my power is made perfect in weakness." Therefore I will boast all the more gladly about my weaknesses, so that Christ's power may rest on me. [10]That is why, for Christ's sake, I delight in weaknesses, in insults, in hardships, in persecutions, in difficulties. For when I am weak, then I am strong.

Paul's Concern for the Corinthians

[11]I have made a fool of myself, but you drove me to it. I ought to have been commended by you, for I am not in the least inferior to the "super-apostles," even though I am nothing. [12]The things that mark an apostle—signs, wonders and miracles—were done among you with great perseverance. [13]How were you inferior to the other churches, except that I was never a burden to you? Forgive me this wrong!

[14]Now I am ready to visit you for the third time, and I will not be a burden to you, because what I want is not your possessions but you. After all, children should not have to save up for their parents, but parents for their children. [15]So I will very gladly spend for you everything I have and expend myself as well. If I love you more, will you love me less? [16]Be that as it may, I have not been a burden to you. Yet, crafty fellow that I am, I caught you by trickery! [17]Did I exploit you through any of the men I sent you? [18]I urged Titus to go to you and I sent our brother with him. Titus did not exploit you, did he? Did we not act in the same spirit and follow the same course?

[19]Have you been thinking all along that we have been defending ourselves to you? We have been speaking in the sight of God as those in Christ; and everything we do, dear friends, is for your strengthening. [20]For I am afraid that when I come I may not find you as I want you to be, and you may not find me as you want me to be. I fear that there may be quarreling, jealousy, outbursts of anger, factions, slander, gossip, arrogance and disorder. [21]I am afraid that when I come again my God will humble me before you, and I will be grieved over many who have sinned earlier

and have not repented of the impurity, sexual sin and debauchery in which they have indulged.

Final Warnings

13 This will be my third visit to you. "Every matter must be established by the testimony of two or three witnesses."[r] [2]I already gave you a warning when I was with you the second time. I now repeat it while absent: On my return I will not spare those who sinned earlier or any of the others, [3]since you are demanding proof that Christ is speaking through me. He is not weak in dealing with you, but is powerful among you. [4]For to be sure, he was crucified in weakness, yet he lives by God's power. Likewise, we are weak in him, yet by God's power we will live with him to serve you.

[5]Examine yourselves to see whether you are in the faith; test yourselves. Do you not realize that Christ Jesus is in you—unless, of course, you fail the test? [6]And I trust that you will discover that we have not failed the test. [7]Now we pray to God that you will not do anything wrong. Not that people will see that we have stood the test but that you will do what is right even though we may seem to have failed. [8]For we cannot do anything against the truth, but only for the truth. [9]We are glad whenever we are weak but you are strong; and our prayer is for your perfection. [10]This is why I write these things when I am absent, that when I come I may not have to be harsh in my use of authority—the authority the Lord gave me for building you up, not for tearing you down.

Final Greetings

[11]Finally, brothers, good-by. Aim for perfection, listen to my appeal, be of one mind, live in peace. And the God of love and peace will be with you.

[12]Greet one another with a holy kiss. [13]All the saints send their greetings.

[14]May the grace of the Lord Jesus Christ, and the love of God, and the fellowship of the Holy Spirit be with you all.

OPEN: 1. In high school or college, what did you do to help yourself and others get ready for big exams? **2.** Have you kissed any frog princes lately? Who? What happened?

DIG: 1. Acts 18 records Paul's first visit to Corinth and Acts 20:2-3 alludes to what must have been his third visit. Given that he stayed away from Corinth three months between letters or visits, what do you think happened as a result of this letter? **2.** Paul prefers to come to them in "the gentleness and meekness of Christ" (10:1) and the possessiveness of a loving parent (12:14-15). How will he come, instead, if repentance has not occured? How does this relate to the ministry of Jesus? **3.** While they have been negatively examining Paul's "credentials" as an apostle all along, what does he call them to do in verse 5? Whether or not they approve of him, what does he pray for them in verses 7-9? **4.** What do verses 10-11 show about his hope as he considers his upcoming visit? How does he want them to see his authority? **5.** Considering the problems of this church, how would his benediction in verse 14 be especially appropriate?

REFLECT: 1. Misunderstanding gentleness and compassion as negative traits was a real problem in Corinth: How is that same problem seen in our society? In your church? **2.** People often want strong, attractive, assertive leaders for their churches: How would Paul fit that profile? **3.** If you were searching for a new pastor or new small group leaders, what leadership profile modelled by Paul would you look for instead? How do *you* fit that profile? **4.** In what area of your spiritual life will you aim for "perfection" this week? How can others encourage and pray to that end for you? **5.** Close your group session by "kissing" (as in v. 12) and discovering if there are any frog princes in your group?

[r]1 Deut. 19:15

357

GALATIANS

INTRODUCTION

Audience

Paul tells us he is writing "to the churches in Galatia" (1:2). But where are these churches located? This is a problem because in 25 B.C. the Romans created a new imperial province that they named Galatia. This new province was made up of the original kingdom of Galatia plus a new region to the south forged out of territory originally belonging to six other regions. So when a first-century writer speaks of Galatia, it is not always clear whether he is referring to the original territory in the north or the new province extending southward. In these notes, though scholarly opinion is divided at this point, the view is taken that Paul was writing to the churches he planted in South Galatia (Pisidian Antioch, Iconium, Lystra, and Derbe) during his first missionary journey described in Acts 13-14.

Date

The date of Paul's Epistle depends on whether he was writing to churches in North or South Galatia. If Paul had been writing to congregations in North Galatia, the letter could not have been written before his third missionary expedition after the journey mentioned in Acts 16:6 and 18:23, around A.D. 55. On the other hand, if Paul were writing to the churches in the southern region, as we are assuming, the Epistle to the Galatians is his earliest letter written in A.D. 48 or 49, possibly while he was in Syrian Antioch just prior to the Council in Jerusalem (Acts 15:6-21).

Theme

The Issue

Paul was furious and he didn't care who knew it. "You foolish Galatians!" he cried, "who has bewitched you?" (3:1). He felt so strongly because the issue he was addressing in this letter was not a minor matter of church policy. It struck right to the heart of the gospel.

Apparently some legalistic Jewish-Christians (Judaizers) had been stirring up trouble. They had twisted the gospel into something Jesus never intended, and then they had cast aspersions on Paul. "Who is that fellow, anyway. He wasn't one of the Twelve. He is a self-appointed apostle. No wonder he left out some crucial parts of the message. Let us set you straight. . . ." And the Galatians were taken in, so it seems. Paul wrote, "I am astonished that you are so quickly deserting the one who called you by the grace of Christ and are turning to a different gospel" (1:6).

What were the Judaizers saying? At first glance, they seemed to be adding only a little to the message. "Believe in Christ," they were saying (they were Christians), "but also be circumcised" (6:12). Now to be circumcised was not such a high requirement, but Paul saw the implications. If the Galatians let themselves be circumcised, it would be but the first step back to keeping the whole Law (5:3). This is slavery (4:9). This is bondage (5:1). This is not the gospel. The gospel is that salvation is a free gift, by grace. If you add anything else to grace, salvation is no longer free. It then becomes a matter of doing the "other thing."

The core issue in Galatians is justification. How does a person gain right standing before God? The Judaizers said that Christ (grace) plus circumcision (law keeping) equals right standing. Paul's equation was different: Christ (grace) plus *nothing else* equals right standing. Works are excluded from Paul's equation. "Know that a man is not justified by observing the law, but by faith in Jesus Christ. So we, too, have put our faith in Christ Jesus that we may be justified by faith in Christ and not by observing the law, because by observing the law no one will be justified" (2:16). This key verse sums up Paul's argument.

The Implications

To the modern reader, it may seem, at times, as if Paul is getting worked up over a relatively small issue. After all, the important thing is to believe in Jesus, and all the parties agreed to that. But in fact, as history demonstrated, this issue was profound. Paul's concerns were more than validated. The underlying issue related to the universality of Christianity. Was Christianity for all people in all cultures (as Paul was arguing), or was it only a Jewish sect? To be a Christian, did you first have to become a Jew (which is the implication of the Judaizers' argument)? Did you have to accept Jewish customs, live a Jewish lifestyle, and submit to Jewish laws? If so, if the Judaizers had won, Christianity would probably have died out in the first century.

As we know, Christianity did not disappear along with all the Palestinian sects. Rather, the church was able to expand into the Graeco-Roman world because the gospel was truly universal. It was not tied to temple sacrifice and the law of Moses, about which most pagans neither knew nor cared. The Judaizers wanted a Christianity circumscribed by Jewish exclusiveness, taboos, and customs — in which, perforce, Gentile believers would always be second-class citizens. Paul fought this with vehemence and passion, as had other believers from Stephen onward; so Christianity became the transcultural world religion Christ intended (Matt. 28:19-20).

The Relationship between Galatians and Romans

It is obvious that there is a close thematic connection between Galatians and Romans. Galatians appears to be Paul's first attempt at wrestling with the issue of justification by faith alone. Paul does so in the context of having to deal with a local problem. Romans, on the other hand, is a more studied consideration of the same issue. It is an eloquent, carefully stated, logical argument, which stands as one of the finest pieces of theological writing ever penned. Paul lifts the core of his argument from Galatians and shapes and refines it into a theological whole in Romans. As J. B. Lightfoot wrote: "The Epistle to the Galatians stands in relation to the Roman letter, as the rough model to the finished statue" (*St. Paul's Epistle to the Galatians*, p. 49).

Structure

After a terse greeting (1:1-5) and pronouncement of anathema against the troublemaker (1:6-10), Paul launches into his first major theme: his *personal defense* in which he deals with the charge that he is not a real apostle (1:11-2:21). This is followed by a *doctrinal defense* in which he shows that Christianity lived under the law is inferior to Christianity lived by faith (3:1-4:31). On the basis of these two arguments, he then shows what true Christian freedom is (5:1-6:10), ending with an unusual conclusion written in his own hand (6:11-18).

Galatians

OPEN: 1. Who contributed to your spiritual beginnings? How so? **2.** How do you respond to anger?

DIG: 1. How does Paul assert his authority (v. 1)? Why does he do so (v. 6)? What is happening to these churches which Paul himself had begun (Acts 13-14)? **2.** Given the situation in Galatia, what elements of the gospel does Paul stress and why? Otherwise, what might happen due to the distorted gospel (see 4:8-11, 17; 6:12-13)? **3.** What accusation is Paul refuting in verse 10? How might Paul be contrued as a "people-pleaser"? A "loose cannon"? **4.** With this opening gauntlet thrown down, what do you expect to find in this red-hot epistle?

REFLECT: What is one of today's "distorted gospels"? What difference does it make in those who believe it? How might Galations help you refute it? In doing so, how will you keep from being either a "people-pleaser" or a "loose cannon" (see 1 Cor. 9:19-23)?

OPEN: At age 18, where was "home"? What career were you preparing for then? Now? Back then, how long were you in the "cocoon" stage before you were ready to fly?

DIG: 1. In light of verses 6-7, why does Paul stress where his message came from (vv. 11-12)? **2.** Skim Acts 9:1-31: What do Paul's comments here add to his conversion story? Why is it so important that the Galations understand that he is not just passing on second-hand information to them? How does this section validate his claim to be an apostle (v. 1)? **3.** What does the fact that Paul preached so extensively without formal approval by the apostles in Jerusalem tell you about him? How do you feel about him as a result?

REFLECT: 1. If you had to argue for the reality of the gospel by giving one example of how you have changed as a result of your faith, what would you share? How is your personal experience of Christ an important part of your witness to others? **2.** Whom do you know who was once very hostile to Christ, but is now his follower? What brought about that change?

1 Paul, an apostle—sent not from men nor by man, but by Jesus Christ and God the Father, who raised him from the dead— ²and all the brothers with me,

To the churches in Galatia:

³Grace and peace to you from God our Father and the Lord Jesus Christ, ⁴who gave himself for our sins to rescue us from the present evil age, according to the will of our God and Father, ⁵to whom be glory for ever and ever. Amen.

No Other Gospel

⁶I am astonished that you are so quickly deserting the one who called you by the grace of Christ and are turning to a different gospel— ⁷which is really no gospel at all. Evidently some people are throwing you into confusion and are trying to pervert the gospel of Christ. ⁸But even if we or an angel from heaven should preach a gospel other than the one we preached to you, let him be eternally condemned! ⁹As we have already said, so now I say again: If anybody is preaching to you a gospel other than what you accepted, let him be eternally condemned!

¹⁰Am I now trying to win the approval of men, or of God? Or am I trying to please men? If I were still trying to please men, I would not be a servant of Christ.

Paul Called by God

¹¹I want you to know, brothers, that the gospel I preached is not something that man made up. ¹²I did not receive it from any man, nor was I taught it; rather, I received it by revelation from Jesus Christ.

¹³For you have heard of my previous way of life in Judaism, how intensely I persecuted the church of God and tried to destroy it. ¹⁴I was advancing in Judaism beyond many Jews of my own age and was extremely zealous for the traditions of my fathers. ¹⁵But when God, who set me apart from birth*a* and called me by his grace, was pleased ¹⁶to reveal his Son in me so that I might preach him among the Gentiles, I did not consult any man, ¹⁷nor did I go up to Jerusalem to see those who were apostles before I was, but I went immediately into Arabia and later returned to Damascus.

¹⁸Then after three years, I went up to Jerusalem to get acquainted with Peter*b* and stayed with him fifteen days. ¹⁹I saw none of the other apostles—only James, the Lord's brother. ²⁰I assure you before God that what I am writing you is no lie. ²¹Later I went to Syria and Cilicia. ²²I was personally unknown to the churches of Judea that are in Christ. ²³They only heard the report: "The man who formerly persecuted us is now preaching the faith he once tried to destroy." ²⁴And they praised God because of me.

a15 Or *from my mother's womb*   *b18* Greek *Cephas*

Paul Accepted by the Apostles

2 Fourteen years later I went up again to Jerusalem, this time with Barnabas. I took Titus along also. ²I went in response to a revelation and set before them the gospel that I preach among the Gentiles. But I did this privately to those who seemed to be leaders, for fear that I was running or had run my race in vain. ³Yet not even Titus, who was with me, was compelled to be circumcised, even though he was a Greek. ⁴This matter arose, because some false brothers had infiltrated our ranks to spy on the freedom we have in Christ Jesus and to make us slaves. ⁵We did not give in to them for a moment, so that the truth of the gospel might remain with you.

⁶As for those who seemed to be important—whatever they were makes no difference to me; God does not judge by external appearance—those men added nothing to my message. ⁷On the contrary, they saw that I had been entrusted with the task of preaching the gospel to the Gentiles,ᶜ just as Peter had been to the Jews.ᵈ ⁸For God, who was at work in the ministry of Peter as an apostle to the Jews, was also at work in my ministry as an apostle to the Gentiles. ⁹James, Peterᵉ and John, those reputed to be pillars, gave me and Barnabas the right hand of fellowship when they recognized the grace given to me. They agreed that we should go to the Gentiles, and they to the Jews. ¹⁰All they asked was that we should continue to remember the poor, the very thing I was eager to do.

Paul Opposes Peter

¹¹When Peter came to Antioch, I opposed him to his face, because he was clearly in the wrong. ¹²Before certain men came from James, he used to eat with the Gentiles. But when they arrived, he began to draw back and separate himself from the Gentiles because he was afraid of those who belonged to the circumcision group. ¹³The other Jews joined him in his hypocrisy, so that by their hypocrisy even Barnabas was led astray.

¹⁴When I saw that they were not acting in line with the truth of the gospel, I said to Peter in front of them all, "You are a Jew, yet you live like a Gentile and not like a Jew. How is it, then, that you force Gentiles to follow Jewish customs?

¹⁵"We who are Jews by birth and not 'Gentile sinners' ¹⁶know that a man is not justified by observing the law, but by faith in Jesus Christ. So we, too, have put our faith in Christ Jesus that we may be justified by faith in Christ and not by observing the law, because by observing the law no one will be justified.

¹⁷"If, while we seek to be justified in Christ, it becomes evident that we ourselves are sinners, does that mean that Christ promotes sin? Absolutely not! ¹⁸If I rebuild what I destroyed, I prove that I am a lawbreaker. ¹⁹For through the law I died to the law so that I might live for God. ²⁰I have been crucified with Christ and I no longer live, but Christ lives in me. The life I live in the body, I live by faith in the Son of God, who loved me and

OPEN: In gaining entrance into your chosen field, what judgment bar did you pass? How did you make it?

DIG: 1. Here, (also Acts 11:18; 15:1) how does Paul confront those who believe Gentiles had to first become Jewish to be really Christian? **2.** How did the decision about Titus confirm the validity of Paul's message? Given the charges against him (1:10), why was this such a critical issue for Paul? **3.** Given the position of Peter, James, and John as the leaders of the Jerusalem church, how would their approval of Paul's message validate his claim in 1:11-12? **4.** From verse 10 (also Acts 11:25-30), how does caring for the poor relate to preaching the gospel?

REFLECT: 1. How do you feel when your beliefs run counter to popular opinions? What would you have done in Paul's position? **2.** Who are the people God has entrusted to you with whom you might share the gospel? How can you do so this week? **3.** How does *your* caring for the poor relate to preaching the gospel?

OPEN: If God was like Santa Clause, checking his list twice to see who was good enough, would you get "your heart's desire" or a "lump of coal"?

DIG: 1. Read Acts 11:1-18. In light of this experience, how do you account for Peter's actions here when he comes to Antioch? **2.** How is the word "justified" commonly used today? How does Paul use the term, as compared with his opponents (vv. 15-16)? What's at stake here (see also Acts 13:38-39)? **3.** What's happening in verses 17-20: Is "justification by faith" a legal fiction? An excuse to keep on sinning? Or a new reality that leads us away from sin? Why? **4.** In verse 21, how does Paul turn the tables on his rule-keeping opponents?

REFLECT: 1. What Christian brother or sister have you clashed with recently? Over what personalities or issues? How did you resolve things? **2.** What difference would it make to you if Paul's gospel was wrong, and you did have to earn your way to God by keeping the Jewish laws?

ᶜ7 Greek *uncircumcised*   ᵈ7 Greek *circumcised*; also in verses 8 and 9   ᵉ9 Greek *Cephas*; also in verses 11 and 14

gave himself for me. [21]I do not set aside the grace of God, for if righteousness could be gained through the law, Christ died for nothing!"[f]

OPEN: What "family ties" (blessings and curses) have been handed down to you?

DIG: 1. How does Paul's appeal to their experience in the six questions of verses 1-5 validate what he argued for in 2:15-16? **2.** Paul appeals to their suffering (v. 4), their experience (vv. 2-5), and Christ's death (2:21)—Why? How does all that add up to expose the foolishness and futility of human effort? **3.** How does the example of Abraham (vv. 6-9) extend Paul's argument? How is our faith in Christ a fulfillment of God's promise to Abraham? **4.** How do each of these four Old Testament references (vv. 10-13) expose the problem of trying to be right with God by trusting in one's ability to keep his law? **5.** How does Jesus solve this problem for us (vv. 13-14)?

REFLECT: 1. How have you faced that tension of trusting in Christ's work or your own? What "Christian" rules seem to be important in your circle? Why? **2.** How would you explain the promised "rightousness" (v. 6), "blessing" (vv. 8-9, 14), "curse" (v. 10) and Spirit (v. 14) to a prospective convert? Would you say anything different to a new believer? Why?

OPEN: If you could choose the sex, mental capacity, and physical health of your soon-to-be-born child, would you do it? Why or why not?

DIG: 1. What is the distinction here between seeds and Seed? What is the parallel Paul wants to make between the types of covenants (wills) people make, and the covenant promise (3:8) God made to Abraham? **2.** Since the law was not to take the place of the promise, how do verses 19 and 23 explain what the law's purpose actually is (see also Romans 3:20)? **3.** Relating to God by the law like what: Being kept in prison? Scolded by a harsh disciplinarian? Tutored by a remedial ed teacher? All three? **4.** How does Christ change all this? Why then would anyone go back to the law?

REFLECT: 1. How do Paul's various arguments here touch your everyday life? Why might they seem obscure? **2.** How could you

Faith or Observance of the Law

3 You foolish Galatians! Who has bewitched you? Before your very eyes Jesus Christ was clearly portrayed as crucified. [2]I would like to learn just one thing from you: Did you receive the Spirit by observing the law, or by believing what you heard? [3]Are you so foolish? After beginning with the Spirit, are you now trying to attain your goal by human effort? [4]Have you suffered so much for nothing—if it really was for nothing? [5]Does God give you his Spirit and work miracles among you because you observe the law, or because you believe what you heard?

[6]Consider Abraham: "He believed God, and it was credited to him as righteousness."[g] [7]Understand, then, that those who believe are children of Abraham. [8]The Scripture foresaw that God would justify the Gentiles by faith, and announced the gospel in advance to Abraham: "All nations will be blessed through you."[h] [9]So those who have faith are blessed along with Abraham, the man of faith.

[10]All who rely on observing the law are under a curse, for it is written: "Cursed is everyone who does not continue to do everything written in the Book of the Law."[i] [11]Clearly no one is justified before God by the law, because, "The righteous will live by faith."[j] [12]The law is not based on faith; on the contrary, "The man who does these things will live by them."[k] [13]Christ redeemed us from the curse of the law by becoming a curse for us, for it is written: "Cursed is everyone who is hung on a tree."[l] [14]He redeemed us in order that the blessing given to Abraham might come to the Gentiles through Christ Jesus, so that by faith we might receive the promise of the Spirit.

The Law and the Promise

[15]Brothers, let me take an example from everyday life. Just as no one can set aside or add to a human covenant that has been duly established, so it is in this case. [16]The promises were spoken to Abraham and to his seed. The Scripture does not say "and to seeds," meaning many people, but "and to your seed,"[m] meaning one person, who is Christ. [17]What I mean is this: The law, introduced 430 years later, does not set aside the covenant previously established by God and thus do away with the promise. [18]For if the inheritance depends on the law, then it no longer depends on a promise; but God in his grace gave it to Abraham through a promise.

[19]What, then, was the purpose of the law? It was added because of transgressions until the Seed to whom the promise referred had come. The law was put into effect through angels by a mediator. [20]A mediator, however, does not represent just one party; but God is one.

[21]Is the law, therefore, opposed to the promises of God?

f21 Some interpreters end the quotation after verse 14.　g6 Gen. 15:6
h8 Gen. 12:3; 18:18; 22:18　i10 Deut. 27:26　j11 Hab. 2:4　k12 Lev. 18:5
l13 Deut. 21:23　m16 Gen. 12:7; 13:15; 24:7

Absolutely not! For if a law had been given that could impart life, then righteousness would certainly have come by the law. [22]But the Scripture declares that the whole world is a prisoner of sin, so that what was promised, being given through faith in Jesus Christ, might be given to those who believe.

[23]Before this faith came, we were held prisoners by the law, locked up until faith should be revealed. [24]So the law was put in charge to lead us to Christ" that we might be justified by faith. [25]Now that faith has come, we are no longer under the supervision of the law.

Sons of God

[26]You are all sons of God through faith in Christ Jesus, [27]for all of you who were baptized into Christ have clothed yourselves with Christ. [28]There is neither Jew nor Greek, slave nor free, male nor female, for you are all one in Christ Jesus. [29]If you belong to Christ, then you are Abraham's seed, and heirs according to the promise.

4 What I am saying is that as long as the heir is a child, he is no different from a slave, although he owns the whole estate. [2]He is subject to guardians and trustees until the time set by his father. [3]So also, when we were children, we were in slavery under the basic principles of the world. [4]But when the time had fully come, God sent his Son, born of a woman, born under law, [5]to redeem those under law, that we might receive the full rights of sons. [6]Because you are sons, God sent the Spirit of his Son into our hearts, the Spirit who calls out, "Abba,° Father." [7]So you are no longer a slave, but a son; and since you are a son, God has made you also an heir.

Paul's Concern for the Galatians

[8]Formerly, when you did not know God, you were slaves to those who by nature are not gods. [9]But now that you know God—or rather are known by God—how is it that you are turning back to those weak and miserable principles? Do you wish to be enslaved by them all over again? [10]You are observing special days and months and seasons and years! [11]I fear for you, that somehow I have wasted my efforts on you.

[12]I plead with you, brothers, become like me, for I became like you. You have done me no wrong. [13]As you know, it was because of an illness that I first preached the gospel to you. [14]Even though my illness was a trial to you, you did not treat me with contempt or scorn. Instead, you welcomed me as if I were an angel of God, as if I were Christ Jesus himself. [15]What has happened to all your joy? I can testify that, if you could have done so, you would have torn out your eyes and given them to me. [16]Have I now become your enemy by telling you the truth?

[17]Those people are zealous to win you over, but for no good. What they want is to alienate you ⎣from us⎦, so that you may be zealous for them. [18]It is fine to be zealous, provided the purpose is good, and to be so always and not just when I am with you. [19]My dear children, for whom I am again in the pains of child-

clarify Paul's arguments for someone who could care less about such fine distinctions? How would you use this passage with someone who thought that keeping the Golden Rule or the Ten Commandments is enough to get right with God? **3.** What experience helped you see your need to let the rules drive you to Jesus to find mercy?

OPEN: Given the ability to project yourself "back to the future"—into the past but not return, would you do so? Where would you go? What would you do if your actions might alter human history?

DIG: 1. How does being "clothed with Christ" (v. 27) eliminate major cultural barriers (v. 28)? Or does it? **2.** How is being under the Law like that of an heir who is still a minor (vv. 1-3)? **3.** How has God entered time to alter human history and make us adult heirs?

REFLECT: 1. What difference, if any, has your "baptism into Christ" made? **2.** Are you still under the custody of the Law? Or an adult heir of the King? Why?

OPEN: 1. What are your most compulsive habits? How do you try to break them? **2.** Would you willingly lose both eyes if it guaranteed the health and safety of your children? Why or why not?

DIG: 1. Prior to their conversion to Christ, the Galations followed the customs of honoring the Greek gods (Acts 14:11-13). How are they now doing the same with Jewish festivals (v. 10)? **2.** What is the difference between celebrating religious holidays (Christmas or Easter) and what the Galations were doing? **3.** In 4:12-20 what are the differences in attitudes and goals between Paul (v. 9) and the other teachers (v. 17)? Why is Paul so perplexed?

REFLECT: 1. Where has the "fizz" in your Christian life gone? Are you as joyful and zealous for Christ now as you were when you first came to him? Why or why not? **2.** Have you slipped back into any bad habits, from which Christ once delivered you? Which ones? **3.** What differ-

---

n24 Or charge until Christ came   *o6 Aramaic for Father* ence does knowing God—or rather being known by him—make?

OPEN: 1. Where were you born: In a hospital? At home? What city? What "story" do your parents tell about your birth? 2. How would you like to be married to two women or be the wife of a man with two wives?

DIG: 1. Read Genesis 16:1-4; 18:10-14; 21:1-10. What were the differences in the births of these two sons of Abraham? How does this story relate to his argument in 3:7 and 4:7? 2. Normally, the Jews would regard Sarah as their spiritual mother and Hagar as the spiritual mother of Gentiles: Why does Paul reverse the picture? 3. How are the spiritual descendents of Sarah distinguished from the other line of descent?

REFLECT: 1. Has your experience as a Christian been more of a growing into freedom or coming under rules? Why? 2. Has your joy in Christ ever been crushed by someone's sense that you were breaking traditions or rules? How have you imposed standards on others limiting their freedom? 3. How do you feel knowing that God's promises of justification and the fullness of the Spirit are yours? What difference will these promises make in your life and witness this week?

OPEN: You notice a friend doing something self-destructive, but without any self-awareness. Do you point it out? What happened the last time you tried?

DIG: 1. What's at stake here (vv. 1-4)? What does Paul mean by "yoke of slavery"? 2. If rule-keeping doesn't count for anything (v. 2), but dooms one to fail (vv. 3-4), what does count (vv. 5-6)? Why only faith? 3. What is Paul's tone in verses 7-12? Why does this issue move him so strongly? 4. In verses 13-15, how does Paul navigate between the danger of legalism on the one side and total license on the other? 5. Paul says: a) we are not "under the law" anymore; b) we are to fulfill it. How can both be true at once? Hint: What are we free from? What are we free for?

REFLECT: 1. What "spiritual yardstick" does your church circle use to see who measures up? What

birth until Christ is formed in you, [20]how I wish I could be with you now and change my tone, because I am perplexed about you!

Hagar and Sarah

[21]Tell me, you who want to be under the law, are you not aware of what the law says? [22]For it is written that Abraham had two sons, one by the slave woman and the other by the free woman. [23]His son by the slave woman was born in the ordinary way; but his son by the free woman was born as the result of a promise.

[24]These things may be taken figuratively, for the women represent two covenants. One covenant is from Mount Sinai and bears children who are to be slaves: This is Hagar. [25]Now Hagar stands for Mount Sinai in Arabia and corresponds to the present city of Jerusalem, because she is in slavery with her children. [26]But the Jerusalem that is above is free, and she is our mother. [27]For it is written:

"Be glad, O barren woman,
  who bears no children;
break forth and cry aloud,
  you who have no labor pains;
because more are the children of the desolate woman
  than of her who has a husband." [p]

[28]Now you, brothers, like Isaac, are children of promise. [29]At that time the son born in the ordinary way persecuted the son born by the power of the Spirit. It is the same now. [30]But what does the Scripture say? "Get rid of the slave woman and her son, for the slave woman's son will never share in the inheritance with the free woman's son." [q] [31]Therefore, brothers, we are not children of the slave woman, but of the free woman.

Freedom in Christ

5 It is for freedom that Christ has set us free. Stand firm, then, and do not let yourselves be burdened again by a yoke of slavery.

[2]Mark my words! I, Paul, tell you that if you let yourselves be circumcised, Christ will be of no value to you at all. [3]Again I declare to every man who lets himself be circumcised that he is obligated to obey the whole law. [4]You who are trying to be justified by law have been alienated from Christ; you have fallen away from grace. [5]But by faith we eagerly await through the Spirit the righteousness for which we hope. [6]For in Christ Jesus neither circumcision nor uncircumcision has any value. The only thing that counts is faith expressing itself through love.

[7]You were running a good race. Who cut in on you and kept you from obeying the truth? [8]That kind of persuasion does not come from the one who calls you. [9]"A little yeast works through the whole batch of dough." [10]I am confident in the Lord that you will take no other view. The one who is throwing you into confusion will pay the penalty, whoever he may be. [11]Brothers,

---

p27 Isaiah 54:1 . q30 Gen. 21:10

if I am still preaching circumcision, why am I still being persecuted? In that case the offense of the cross has been abolished. [12]As for those agitators, I wish they would go the whole way and emasculate themselves!

[13]You, my brothers, were called to be free. But do not use your freedom to indulge the sinful nature[r]; rather, serve one another in love. [14]The entire law is summed up in a single command: "Love your neighbor as yourself."[s] [15]If you keep on biting and devouring each other, watch out or you will be destroyed by each other.

Life by the Spirit

[16]So I say, live by the Spirit, and you will not gratify the desires of the sinful nature. [17]For the sinful nature desires what is contrary to the Spirit, and the Spirit what is contrary to the sinful nature. They are in conflict with each other, so that you do not do what you want. [18]But if you are led by the Spirit, you are not under law.

[19]The acts of the sinful nature are obvious: sexual immorality, impurity and debauchery; [20]idolatry and witchcraft; hatred, discord, jealousy, fits of rage, selfish ambition, dissensions, factions [21]and envy; drunkenness, orgies, and the like. I warn you, as I did before, that those who live like this will not inherit the kingdom of God.

[22]But the fruit of the Spirit is love, joy, peace, patience, kindness, goodness, faithfulness, [23]gentleness and self-control. Against such things there is no law. [24]Those who belong to Christ Jesus have crucified the sinful nature its passions and desires. [25]Since we live by the Spirit, let us keep in step with the Spirit. [26]Let us not become conceited, provoking and envying each other.

Doing Good to All

6 Brothers, if someone is caught in a sin, you who are spiritual should restore him gently. But watch yourself, or you also may be tempted. [2]Carry each other's burdens, and in this way you will fulfill the law of Christ. [3]If anyone thinks he is something when he is nothing, he deceives himself. [4]Each one should test his own actions. Then he can take pride in himself, without comparing himself to somebody else, [5]for each one should carry his own load.

[6]Anyone who receives instruction in the word must share all good things with his instructor.

[7]Do not be deceived: God cannot be mocked. A man reaps what he sows. [8]The one who sows to please his sinful nature, from that nature[t] will reap destruction; the one who sows to please the Spirit, from the Spirit will reap eternal life. [9]Let us not become weary in doing good, for at the proper time we will reap a harvest if we do not give up. [10]Therefore, as we have opportunity, let us do good to all people, especially to those who belong to the family of believers.

---

[r]13 Or *the flesh;* also in verses 16, 17, 19 and 24   [s]14 Lev. 19:18   [t]8 Or *his flesh, from the flesh*

"yokes" have been imposed on you? How have you been freed from the same? Whose yoke have you taken on instead (see Mt. 11:28-30)? **2.** How have you seen Christian freedom abused? How is Galatians an antidote to those who think their freedom in Christ gives them license to do anything they wish?

OPEN: What does your garden grow without your help? With your help?

DIG: 1. According to Paul, if you were made alive by the Spirit, how come you still struggle with sin? **2.** Since we are not under the law, what is wrong with indulging our sinful nature once in a while? If not by rule-keeping, how then do we grow spiritually? How do these fruit (vv. 22-23) flesh out what Paul means by "Christ formed in you" (4:19)? **4.** Illustrate practically what it means to "crucify" the sinful nature and "keep in step" with the Spirit?

REFLECT: 1. Which spiritual fruit are "blossoming" for you? In the "bud" stage? **2.** Which sinful acts are "dead and buried"? Which are Mortally wounded"? "Alive and well"? **3.** How can you and the Spirit grow the one and kill the other?

OPEN: Supposing your group goes backpacking together, who carries the heavy stuff? Why? What load does each person carry on their own? Why?

DIG: 1. How do verses 1-2 illustrate practical ways of helping someone else "keep in step with the Spirit" (v. 5:25)? What is the "law of Christ" (see 5:14)? **2.** How does one restore a brother caught in sin without falling victim or puffing himself up (vv. 3-5)? **3.** In this teaching on mutual responsibility, does verse 5 contradict verse 2? Why or why not? **3.** How are verses 7-10 a summary of Paul's teaching about the Spirit-filled life? How do these verses relate to the question of circumcision?

REFLECT: 1. What sorts of burdens do your friends carry? How could you help them with these burdens? **2.** As you reflect on what you have sown this year, what will the harvest look like? What specifically will you do this week to "sow to please the Spirit" now?

OPEN: 1. As a child, were you a troublemaker or peacemaker? **2.** What is one thing you'd be proud enough to boast about?

DIG: 1. How does Paul sum up the motives of the false teachers (vv. 12-13)? His own motives (v. 11)? **2.** Ultimately, why is the matter of keeping the Jewish rules irrelevant? From key passages in Galations, how would you describe what this "new creation" is all about? **3.** Why does Paul call these Gentile Galatians the "Israel of God" (see 3:6-9)? How is that a final rebuke to those who would compel these believers to obey Jewish rules first? **4.** What does Paul mean by bearing on his body the marks of Jesus and boasting only in cross of Jesus (vv. 14, 17; see 2 Cor. 11: 23-30)? How is Paul's willingness to suffer a further rebuke to the false teachers?

REFLECT: 1. In what ways do people tamper with the gospel today to make it less "offensive"? How have you been tempted to do so? **2.** How has your coming to Christ changed your attitudes toward the common values and ideas of the world? Where do you find these things still a pressure upon you? **3.** What does it mean for you to boast in the cross? In proportion to the other things you boast about, how can you express more your identification with the cross this week? In closing your session, how can you do that as a group?

Not Circumcision but a New Creation

[11]See what large letters I use as I write to you with my own hand!

[12]Those who want to make a good impression outwardly are trying to compel you to be circumcised. The only reason they do this is to avoid being persecuted for the cross of Christ. [13]Not even those who are circumcised obey the law, yet they want you to be circumcised that they may boast about your flesh. [14]May I never boast except in the cross of our Lord Jesus Christ, through which " the world has been crucified to me, and I to the world. [15]Neither circumcision nor uncircumcision means anything; what counts is a new creation. [16]Peace and mercy to all who follow this rule, even to the Israel of God.

[17]Finally, let no one cause me trouble, for I bear on my body the marks of Jesus.

[18]The grace of our Lord Jesus Christ be with your spirit, brothers. Amen.

---

u*14* Or *whom*

EPHESIANS

INTRODUCTION

Characteristics

William Barclay called Ephesians "The Queen of the Epistles" (*The Letters to the Galatians and Ephesians,* p. 83). Samuel Taylor Coleridge, the English poet, said it was "the divinest composition of man" (Barclay, p. 71). Indeed, there is a breathtaking grandeur about Paul's letter to the Ephesians as it sketches the reconciling work of God in Christ — making one of all peoples of the earth, subduing the hostile cosmic powers, and creating a new humanity and a new society. It is with not a little awe that one approaches Ephesians, the "greatest" and "the most relevant of all Paul's works" (John Mackay, *God's Order: The Ephesian Letter and This Present Time,* pp. 9-10).

The Captivity Letters

Paul is in prison once again, and Epaphras has come to visit him bearing disturbing news about the church at Colossae. Since Paul is about to send back the runaway slave Onesimus (now converted) to his owner Philemon, a member of the Colossian Church, he takes this opportunity to send along a letter in which he addresses the Colossian heresy. He also writes two more letters: one to Philemon and one to a neighboring area, the Letter to the Ephesians. These three epistles form the core of what we now know as the Prison Epistles or the Captivity Letters. The fourth Prison Epistle, Philippians, was written in prison on another occasion.

Ephesians and Colossians are more similar in language and content than any other two letters in the New Testament. Seventy-five of the 155 verses in Ephesians are found in parallel form in Colossians. It seems that Paul first developed those themes in Colossians while dealing with a local problem, and then expanded them, explained them, and cast them into a universal setting in Ephesians.

Place and Date of Writing

It is unclear from which city Paul wrote. It seems that he spent time in prisons throughout the Roman Empire (see 2 Cor. 11:23). While Caesarea (Acts 24) and Ephesus have been suggested as possible sites, the most likely place was Rome (Acts 28). In that case, the letter to the Ephesians was written in the early sixties, some thirty years after Jesus' crucifixion and only a few years before Paul's death.

Structure

Between an introductory greeting (1:1-2) and a concluding salutation (6:21-24) — both typical of letters written in Paul's day — the material falls easily into two parts. Part 1 (chaps. 1-3) concerns *doctrine*, while part 2 (chaps. 4-6) is about *ethics*. In part 1, Paul preaches about the new life and the new society God has brought into being through Jesus Christ. In part 2, he teaches about the new standards and new relationships expected of believers. In other words, he moves from theory to practice, from the indicative ("This is the way things are") to the imperative ("Therefore, do this"). Throughout, the emphasis is on *unity*. In part 1, Paul extols the great reconciling work of Christ who through the Cross overcame the demonic powers (chap. 1), thus breaking down the wall between God and the human race (2:1-10) and the walls between people themselves (2:11-22). In part 2, the imperatives are largely exhortations for unity in relationships.

Ephesians

OPEN: What is the best medicine for you when you get down in the dumps?

DIG: 1. Skimming through this passage, what would you say is Paul's tone? **2.** In your own words, how would you describe the "blessings in Christ" mentioned in verses 3-9? How do they relate to praising God? **3.** From verses 3-14, list the activities and descriptive words relating to the work of the Father, Jesus, and the Holy Spirit. What does this show you about God? About his relationship to us? His goals for us? **4.** How does his initiative in choosing us (v. 4) relate to our believing (v. 13)? How do you know if you are "chosen" or "adopted" or "predestined"? **5.** What phrases from this section could you use to define your purpose as a Christian?

REFLECT: 1. From this passage, what motivates you to praise God the most? Why? **2.** What are some of the greatest benefits of God's grace to you? How does the reality of his grace make a difference in how you see yourself? What part of God's plan most confuses you? Most encourages you? **3.** What would you need to change in your lifestlye to live for the praise of his glory this week?

OPEN: What do you remember most about Thanksgiving Day when you were a child?

DIG: 1. What did Paul pray for the Ephesians? What motivated his prayers? People for whom such prayers are answered—what do they look like? Sound like? **2.** How are each of these resources—faith, love, spiritual awareness, hope, riches, power—illustrated and applied here in Paul's prayer? **3.** Specifically, how is the fullness of Christ (v. 23) related to the fulfillment of God's purpose for the church (vv. 12, 22)? How would you describe Jesus from this passage? How is his position related to our hope and power (v. 18)?

REFLECT: 1. How would you expect to change if your small group prayed verses 17-19 into your life? **2.** In light of the power available to

1 Paul, an apostle of Christ Jesus by the will of God,

To the saints in Ephesus,[a] the faithful[b] in Christ Jesus:

[2]Grace and peace to you from God our Father and the Lord Jesus Christ.

Spiritual Blessings in Christ

[3]Praise be to the God and Father of our Lord Jesus Christ, who has blessed us in the heavenly realms with every spiritual blessing in Christ. [4]For he chose us in him before the creation of the world to be holy and blameless in his sight. In love [5]he[c] predestined us to be adopted as his sons through Jesus Christ, in accordance with his pleasure and will— [6]to the praise of his glorious grace, which he has freely given us in the One he loves. [7]In him we have redemption through his blood, the forgiveness of sins, in accordance with the riches of God's grace [8]that he lavished on us with all wisdom and understanding. [9]And he[d] made known to us the mystery of his will according to his good pleasure, which he purposed in Christ, [10]to be put into effect when the times will have reached their fulfillment—to bring all things in heaven and on earth together under one head, even Christ.

[11]In him we were also chosen,[e] having been predestined according to the plan of him who works out everything in conformity with the purpose of his will, [12]in order that we, who were the first to hope in Christ, might be for the praise of his glory. [13]And you also were included in Christ when you heard the word of truth, the gospel of your salvation. Having believed, you were marked in him with a seal, the promised Holy Spirit, [14]who is a deposit guaranteeing our inheritance until the redemption of those who are God's possession—to the praise of his glory.

Thanksgiving and Prayer

[15]For this reason, ever since I heard about your faith in the Lord Jesus and your love for all the saints, [16]I have not stopped giving thanks for you, remembering you in my prayers. [17]I keep asking that the God of our Lord Jesus Christ, the glorious Father, may give you the Spirit[f] of wisdom and revelation, so that you may know him better. [18]I pray also that the eyes of your heart may be enlightened in order that you may know the hope to which he has called you, the riches of his glorious inheritance in the saints, [19]and his incomparably great power for us who believe. That power is like the working of his mighty strength, [20]which he exerted in Christ when he raised him from the dead and seated him at his right hand in the heavenly realms, [21]far above all rule and authority, power and dominion, and every title that can be given, not only in the present age but also in

---

a1 Some early manuscripts do not have *in Ephesus.*   *b1* Or *believers who are* *c4,5* Or *sight in love.* *5He*   *d8,9* Or *us. With all wisdom and understanding,* *9he* *e11* Or *were made heirs*   *f17* Or *a spirit*

the one to come. ²²And God placed all things under his feet and appointed him to be head over everything for the church, ²³which is his body, the fullness of him who fills everything in every way.

Made Alive in Christ

2 As for you, you were dead in your transgressions and sins, ²in which you used to live when you followed the ways of this world and of the ruler of the kingdom of the air, the spirit who is now at work in those who are disobedient. ³All of us also lived among them at one time, gratifying the cravings of our sinful nature^g and following its desires and thoughts. Like the rest, we were by nature objects of wrath. ⁴But because of his great love for us, God, who is rich in mercy, ⁵made us alive with Christ even when we were dead in transgressions—it is by grace you have been saved. ⁶And God raised us up with Christ and seated us with him in the heavenly realms in Christ Jesus, ⁷in order that in the coming ages he might show the incomparable riches of his grace, expressed in his kindness to us in Christ Jesus. ⁸For it is by grace you have been saved, through faith—and this not from yourselves, it is the gift of God— ⁹not by works, so that no one can boast. ¹⁰For we are God's workmanship, created in Christ Jesus to do good works, which God prepared in advance for us to do.

One in Christ

¹¹Therefore, remember that formerly you who are Gentiles by birth and called "uncircumcised" by those who call themselves "the circumcision" (that done in the body by the hands of men)— ¹²remember that at that time you were separate from Christ, excluded from citizenship in Israel and foreigners to the covenants of the promise, without hope and without God in the world. ¹³But now in Christ Jesus you who once were far away have been brought near through the blood of Christ.

¹⁴For he himself is our peace, who has made the two one and has destroyed the barrier, the dividing wall of hostility, ¹⁵by abolishing in his flesh the law with its commandments and regulations. His purpose was to create in himself one new man out of the two, thus making peace, ¹⁶and in this one body to reconcile both of them to God through the cross, by which he put to death their hostility. ¹⁷He came and preached peace to you who were far away and peace to those who were near. ¹⁸For through him we both have access to the Father by one Spirit.

¹⁹Consequently, you are no longer foreigners and aliens, but fellow citizens with God's people and members of God's household, ²⁰built on the foundation of the apostles and prophets, with Christ Jesus himself as the chief cornerstone. ²¹In him the whole building is joined together and rises to become a holy temple in the Lord. ²²And in him you too are being built together to become a dwelling in which God lives by his Spirit.

Christians (v. 19) what is your favorite excuse for "operating on one or two cylinders"? Why not all four or eight?

OPEN: What was one of the best gifts you received as a child? What made it so special to you?

DIG: 1. What does it mean to be "dead in sin": Helpless? Guilty? Lifeless? What has caused this death? 2. What has God done to fix the problem? Why must he take the initiative? What comparisons does Paul make between Christ's experience (1:20-23) and ours (vv. 5-7)? 3. From verses 8-10, which is more important: Grace or works? Why? Is "faith" itself a "work" or a "gift"? Why?

REFLECT: 1. If you had to climb your way to heaven up some ladder of good works, what rung would you be on? Why? 2. Accepting God's solution to your sin problem, what good works do you think God has in store for you? Why?

OPEN: What country did your ancestors come from? Do you think citizenship in this country meant more to them than to you? When have you felt like an alien?

DIG: 1. What problems faced the Gentiles before Christ? What benefits result from being "in Christ"? 2. What is the bomb that Jesus dropped on the religious "class system" of his day? What impact would applying verses 14-18 have on the longstanding divisions between Jews and Gentiles? 3. What was the difference between Hitler's idea of a super race and Paul's idea of "one body"? How do Paul's pictures of the new citizenship, a new family, and a new temple help explain the reconciling work of Christ (vv. 19-22)? 4. From verses 18 and 22, what can you learn about the work of the Father, Son and Spirit in our lives?

REFLECT: 1. When asked to join a group or club, what guidelines from Paul will you use? 2. What relationship in your life still needs the wall of hostility knocked down? How will that happen? 3. Although God's grace is personal (2:8), what social barriers should it be affecting in your community? What is your role in that process?

^g3 Or *our flesh*

369

Paul the Preacher to the Gentiles

3 For this reason I, Paul, the prisoner of Christ Jesus for the sake of you Gentiles— ²Surely you have heard about the administration of God's grace that was given to me for you, ³that is, the mystery made known to me by revelation, as I have already written briefly. ⁴In reading this, then, you will be able to understand my insight into the mystery of Christ, ⁵which was not made known to men in other generations as it has now been revealed by the Spirit to God's holy apostles and prophets. ⁶This mystery is that through the gospel the Gentiles are heirs together with Israel, members together of one body, and sharers together in the promise in Christ Jesus.

⁷I became a servant of this gospel by the gift of God's grace given me through the working of his power. ⁸Although I am less than the least of all God's people, this grace was given me: to preach to the Gentiles the unsearchable riches of Christ, ⁹and to make plain to everyone the administration of this mystery, which for ages past was kept hidden in God, who created all things. ¹⁰His intent was that now, through the church, the manifold wisdom of God should be made known to the rulers and authorities in the heavenly realms, ¹¹according to his eternal purpose which he accomplished in Christ Jesus our Lord. ¹²In him and through faith in him we may approach God with freedom and confidence. ¹³I ask you, therefore, not to be discouraged because of my sufferings for you, which are your glory.

A Prayer for the Ephesians

¹⁴For this reason I kneel before the Father, ¹⁵from whom his whole family*ʰ* in heaven and on earth derives its name. ¹⁶I pray that out of his glorious riches he may strengthen you with power through his Spirit in your inner being, ¹⁷so that Christ may dwell in your hearts through faith. And I pray that you, being rooted and established in love, ¹⁸may have power, together with all the saints, to grasp how wide and long and high and deep is the love of Christ, ¹⁹and to know this love that surpasses knowledge— that you may be filled to the measure of all the fullness of God.

²⁰Now to him who is able to do immeasurably more than all we ask or imagine, according to his power that is at work within us, ²¹to him be glory in the church and in Christ Jesus throughout all generations, for ever and ever! Amen.

Unity in the Body of Christ

4 As a prisoner for the Lord, then, I urge you to live a life worthy of the calling you have received. ²Be completely humble and gentle; be patient, bearing with one another in love. ³Make every effort to keep the unity of the Spirit through the bond of peace. ⁴There is one body and one Spirit— just as you were called to one hope when you were called— ⁵one Lord, one faith, one baptism; ⁶one God and Father of all, who is over all and through all and in all.

ʰ15 Or whom all fatherhood

[7]But to each one of us grace has been given as Christ apportioned it. [8]This is why it[i] says:

"When he ascended on high,
he led captives in his train
and gave gifts to men."[j]

[9](What does "he ascended" mean except that he also descended to the lower, earthly regions[k]? [10]He who descended is the very one who ascended higher than all the heavens, in order to fill the whole universe.) [11]It was he who gave some to be apostles, some to be prophets, some to be evangelists, and some to be pastors and teachers, [12]to prepare God's people for works of service, so that the body of Christ may be built up [13]until we all reach unity in the faith and in the knowledge of the Son of God and become mature, attaining to the whole measure of the fullness of Christ.

[14]Then we will no longer be infants, tossed back and forth by the waves, and blown here and there by every wind of teaching and by the cunning and craftiness of men in their deceitful scheming. [15]Instead, speaking the truth in love, we will in all things grow up into him who is the Head, that is, Christ. [16]From him the whole body, joined and held together by every supporting ligament, grows and builds itself up in love, as each part does its work.

Living as Children of Light

[17]So I tell you this, and insist on it in the Lord, that you must no longer live as the Gentiles do, in the futility of their thinking. [18]They are darkened in their understanding and separated from the life of God because of the ignorance that is in them due to the hardening of their hearts. [19]Having lost all sensitivity, they have given themselves over to sensuality so as to indulge in every kind of impurity, with a continual lust for more.

[20]You, however, did not come to know Christ that way. [21]Surely you heard of him and were taught in him in accordance with the truth that is in Jesus. [22]You were taught, with regard to your former way of life, to put off your old self, which is being corrupted by its deceitful desires; [23]to be made new in the attitude of your minds; [24]and to put on the new self, created to be like God in true righteousness and holiness.

[25]Therefore each of you must put off falsehood and speak truthfully to his neighbor, for we are all members of one body. [26]"In your anger do not sin"[l]: Do not let the sun go down while you are still angry, [27]and do not give the devil a foothold. [28]He who has been stealing must steal no longer, but must work, doing something useful with his own hands, that he may have something to share with those in need.

[29]Do not let any unwholesome talk come out of your mouths, but only what is helpful for building others up according to their needs, that it may benefit those who listen. [30]And do not grieve the Holy Spirit of God, with whom you were sealed for the day of redemption. [31]Get rid of all bitterness, rage and anger, brawl-

3. Since the church is to live in unity as the body of Christ, what is the purpose (vv. 12-13) of the various gifts in verses 8-11? **4.** What are the differences between the unity that already exists (vv. 3-6) and that which has yet to be (vv. 13-16)? **5.** What is the climactic point of this whole passage? How will this happen?

REFLECT: 1. Of the five qualities listed in verse 2, which one do you feel most needs to be developed in your life? What relationship do you need to apply it to the most? **2.** As opposed to love without truth or truth without love, what does it mean to "speak the truth in love" in the church? **3.** How could your study group help you discover, develop and use your spiritual gift in building up the body of Christ? **4.** From this passage, what is the problem with trying to live the Christian life apart from the church? In what way do you need others? What strength can you give others?

OPEN: At what age did Mom let you start choosing your own clothes to wear, or does she still know what looks best on you? Which of your clothes in your current wardrobe have you held on to the longest? Why?

DIG: 1. According to verses 17-19 how do the mind, heart, and conscience influence the actions of nonbelievers? How are Christians to deal with these realities? How does putting on the "new self" lead to inner change? **2.** According to Paul, is it possible to change conduct without a transformation of the heart? Likewise, can the heart be changed without a resulting change of conduct? Why? **3.** According to Paul, what specific behaviors distinguish the Christian lifestyle from the pagan lifestyle (4:25-5:4)? What type of speech and actions should characterize Christians? How does this relate to 4:24 and 32? **4.** In 4:1, Paul calls us to model our lives in accordance with our high calling as God's people. In 5:1, what is the model he holds up for us? How about in 5:8? **5.** In what sense is darkness a good description of the life controlled by the Spirit? What incentives does he give in 5:2-21 to live according to these models? **6.** What is the difference between foolish talk or coarse joking and a good "belly laugh" story? Between

[i]8 Or *God*   [j]8 Psalm 68:18   [k]9 Or *the depths of the earth*   [l]26 Psalm 4:4

"the fruitless deeds of darkness" and good honest fun? **7.** What contrasts does he draw between the old and new life in 5:15-21? What is the difference between "being careful how you live" (v. 15) and being the life of the party? What sights, sounds, tastes and feelings describe a person living out this new life?

REFLECT: **1.** What is one way you have seen the contrast of the "old" and the "new" in your life? What piece of "old life" clothing seems to be skin tight and hard to remove now? How might replacing the "old garment" with a new one (vv. 25-32) help you? **2.** What are the positive and/or negative motivations which prompt you to live a Christian life? **3.** If God could put a pollution control on your mind, where would he start? **4.** Where do you feel you are making progress in your Christian life at the moment? **5.** Of the different pictures of what it means to live as a Christian—putting off, putting on, imitating God, and being light instead of darkness—which means the most to you? Why? **6.** From this section, what would you say characterizes a Spirit-filled life? Comparing that with your life, how full have you been with the Spirit this week? What do you want to work on so that he may fill you more?

OPEN: **1.** Suppose your fiancée suddenly and tragically became a quadraplegic: Would you back out of the marriage gracefully? Or would you go through with it faithfully? Why? **2.** What was the most maddening thing your parents did when you were a child?

DIG: **1.** How does the relationship between Christ and the church help explain what Paul means by "submission"? How does that relationship help explain the role of the husband in marriage? **2.** To what expression of "headship"—Christ's and the husband's—is the wife asked to submit: The sacrificial kind? The bossy kind? Or both? **3.** Can a wife's respect for her husband (5:33) be commanded? Or must it be earned? Why? Likewise,

ing and slander, along with every form of malice. [32]Be kind and compassionate to one another, forgiving each other, just as in Christ God forgave you.

5 Be imitators of God, therefore, as dearly loved children [2]and live a life of love, just as Christ loved us and gave himself up for us as a fragrant offering and sacrifice to God.

[3]But among you there must not be even a hint of sexual immorality, or of any kind of impurity, or of greed, because these are improper for God's holy people. [4]Nor should there be obscenity, foolish talk or coarse joking, which are out of place, but rather thanksgiving. [5]For of this you can be sure: No immoral, impure or greedy person—such a man is an idolater—has any inheritance in the kingdom of Christ and of God.[m][6]Let no one deceive you with empty words, for because of such things God's wrath comes on those who are disobedient. [7]Therefore do not be partners with them.

[8]For you were once darkness, but now you are light in the Lord. Live as children of light [9](for the fruit of the light consists in all goodness, righteousness and truth) [10]and find out what pleases the Lord. [11]Have nothing to do with the fruitless deeds of darkness, but rather expose them. [12]For it is shameful even to mention what the disobedient do in secret. [13]But everything exposed by the light becomes visible, [14]for it is light that makes everything visible. This is why it is said:

"Wake up, O sleeper,
  rise from the dead,
and Christ will shine on you."

[15]Be very careful, then, how you live—not as unwise but as wise, [16]making the most of every opportunity, because the days are evil. [17]Therefore do not be foolish, but understand what the Lord's will is. [18]Do not get drunk on wine, which leads to debauchery. Instead, be filled with the Spirit. [19]Speak to one another with psalms, hymns and spiritual songs. Sing and make music in your heart to the Lord, [20]always giving thanks to God the Father for everything, in the name of our Lord Jesus Christ.

[21]Submit to one another out of reverence for Christ.

Wives and Husbands

[22]Wives, submit to your husbands as to the Lord. [23]For the husband is the head of the wife as Christ is the head of the church, his body, of which he is the Savior. [24]Now as the church submits to Christ, so also wives should submit to their husbands in everything.

[25]Husbands, love your wives, just as Christ loved the church and gave himself up for her [26]to make her holy, cleansing[n] her by the washing with water through the word, [27]and to present her to himself as a radiant church, without stain or wrinkle or any other blemish, but holy and blameless. [28]In this same way, husbands ought to love their wives as their own bodies. He who loves his wife loves himself. [29]After all, no one ever hated his

[m]5 Or *kingdom of the Christ and God*   [n]26 Or *having cleansed*

own body, but he feeds and cares for it, just as Christ does the church— [30]for we are members of his body. [31]"For this reason a man will leave his father and mother and be united to his wife, and the two will become one flesh."[o] [32]This is a profound mystery—but I am talking about Christ and the church. [33]However, each one of you also must love his wife as he loves himself, and the wife must respect her husband.

Children and Parents

6 Children, obey your parents in the Lord, for this is right. [2]"Honor your father and mother"—which is the first commandment with a promise— [3]"that it may go well with you and that you may enjoy long life on the earth."[p]

[4]Fathers, do not exasperate your children; instead, bring them up in the training and instruction of the Lord.

Slaves and Masters

[5]Slaves, obey your earthly masters with respect and fear, and with sincerity of heart, just as you would obey Christ. [6]Obey them not only to win their favor when their eye is on you, but like slaves of Christ, doing the will of God from your heart. [7]Serve wholeheartedly, as if you were serving the Lord, not men, [8]because you know that the Lord will reward everyone for whatever good he does, whether he is slave or free.

[9]And masters, treat your slaves in the same way. Do not threaten them, since you know that he who is both their Master and yours is in heaven, and there is no favoritism with him.

The Armor of God

[10]Finally, be strong in the Lord and in his mighty power. [11]Put on the full armor of God so that you can take your stand against the devil's schemes. [12]For our struggle is not against flesh and blood, but against the rulers, against the authorities, against the powers of this dark world and against the spiritual forces of evil in the heavenly realms. [13]Therefore put on the full armor of God, so that when the day of evil comes, you may be able to stand your ground, and after you have done everything, to stand. [14]Stand firm then, with the belt of truth buckled around your waist, with the breastplate of righteousness in place, [15]and with your feet fitted with the readiness that comes from the gospel of peace. [16]In addition to all this, take up the shield of faith, with which you can extinguish all the flaming arrows of the evil one. [17]Take the helmet of salvation and the sword of the Spirit, which is the word of God. [18]And pray in the Spirit on all occasions with all kinds of prayers and requests. With this in mind, be alert and always keep on praying for all the saints.

[19]Pray also for me, that whenever I open my mouth, words may be given me so that I will fearlessly make known the mystery of the gospel, [20]for which I am an ambassador in chains. Pray that I may declare it fearlessly, as I should.

children's respect for their parents? A worker's respect for the employer? How might 5:1 and 5:21 relate to these relationships? **4.** What does it mean to bring up children in the Lord without exasperating them (6:4)? Give examples from your own experience. **5.** How is Christ central to Paul's instructions about slaves and masters? What problems would be avoided if his instructions were heeded? **6.** In summary, how does 5:21 apply to the types of relationships found in this section? What are the mutual obligations involved in these relationships? In what ways could Paul's instructions be misinterpreted apart from the context of 5:21? How have you been affected by these misinterpretations?

REFLECT: **1.** How does Paul's teaching about marriage challenge common ideas today? Which affect you? What principles flowing from this section can you work on to help you be a better spouse (or potential spouse)? **2.** What does it mean for you as an adult to honor your parents? How might this help improve relationships with them? **3.** Applying Paul's teaching in 6:5-9 to your work environment, what will you do differently this week?

OPEN: Growing up, what were some of your favorite Halloween costumes, and why?

DIG: **1.** From 1:19-21, where is Christ now? How does this give us hope as we encounter the evil forces described here? From what you have read in Ephesians (2:1-3,14; 4:14,17-19,26-27; 5:3-18), how are these forces demonstrated in our lives? **2.** ow? How does this give us hope as we encounter the evil forces described here? From what you have read in Ephesians (2:1-3,14; 4:14,17-19,26-27; 5:3-18), how are these forces demonstrated in our lives? **2.** What do verses 11-14 say about how we are to respond to these forces? To resist evil what six pieces of equipment are needed (vv. 14-17)? Which piece is the only offensive weapon listed? **3.** Where does prayer fit in (v. 18)? What does Paul pray for (vv. 19-20)? Why? What does this tell you about spiritual warfare? **4.** From verse 23, how do the words "peace", "love", "faith", and "grace" sum up Paul's teaching in this letter?

o31 Gen. 2:24   p3 Deut. 5:16

REFLECT: 1. As you consider your armor, what parts are in good shape? What is moldy and rusty? What do you need to do to get ready for battle? What is at stake if you don't? 2. Paul was on the front lines of the battle (v. 20). What role do you think you play in the church's resistance movement against Satan? What evidence do you see of the battle around you? 3. What can you learn from Paul's prayers (1:16-18, 3:14-19, and 6:19-20) about how you should pray for others? How can your group practice this? 4. Of the four summary words in verse 23 (peace, love, faith, and grace), which means the most to you now? Why?

Final Greetings

²¹Tychicus, the dear brother and faithful servant in the Lord, will tell you everything, so that you also may know how I am and what I am doing. ²²I am sending him to you for this very purpose, that you may know how we are, and that he may encourage you.

²³Peace to the brothers, and love with faith from God the Father and the Lord Jesus Christ. ²⁴Grace to all who love our Lord Jesus Christ with an undying love.

PHILIPPIANS

INTRODUCTION

Audience

Setting

Located in the Roman province of Macedonia (a territory corresponding to northern Greece and parts of several other Balkan countries), Philippi was a historic city. Founded by Alexander the Great's father in 360 B.C. so he could mine its gold to pay for his army, Philippi eventually came to prominence as the result of two battles. In 42 B.C. on the plains of Philippi, the Caesarean forces of Anthony and Octavian defeated the Republican forces led by the assassins of Julius Caesar—Brutus and Cassius. Then in 31 B.C., Octavian (who later became the Emperor Caesar Augustus) became sole ruler by defeating his former colleague Anthony, who was in alliance with the Egyptian Queen Cleopatra. Veterans from these conflicts were given land in Philippi, and Octavian declared it to be a Roman colony with all the rights, tax breaks, and privileges thereof. To be in Philippi was to be in a miniature Rome.

Paul and the Philippian Church

Philippi was certainly one of Paul's favorite churches. There was such a warm feeling of mutual care and concern that Paul called the Philippians his "joy and crown" (4:1).

Paul had founded the church around A.D. 50 as the result of a night vision in which a "man of Macedonia" beckoned him to "come over . . . and help us" (Acts 16:9). He sailed immediately from Asia, thus launching Christianity in Europe. Paul's stay at Philippi was marked by joy and trial. On the positive side was the conversion of Lydia, the dealer in purple cloth, as well as the conversion of the jailer and his family after an earthquake unexpectedly released Paul from prison. On the negative side, in Philippi the first recorded conflict between Christians and Gentiles occurred, and Paul was thrown in jail for casting out a demon from a fortuneteller's slave girl.

This letter to the largely Gentile church was written some twelve or thirteen years later, probably around A.D. 63 or 64.

Theme

Paul is in prison (probably in Rome) when Epaphroditus, an old friend from Philippi, arrives bearing yet another gift from the church. Unfortunately, Epaphroditus falls gravely ill. His home church hears about it and is grieved. In due course he recovers, and Paul is anxious for him to return home and relieve their fears. This affords Paul an opportunity to send along a letter.

So he writes these old friends in the warmest and most personal of his epistles. There is no need for him to assert his apostolity, as he usually does when beginning a letter. There is no formality in his outline either. Paul puts down ideas as they occur to him, often with strong declarations of emotion.

Basically, Philippians is a letter of thanksgiving (1:3-11 and 4:14-20) and a report on his imprisonment (1:12-26; 2:19-30; 4:10-13). Still, Paul has two concerns: a tendency in the church toward disunity (1:27-2:18 and 4:2-3) and potential dangers from Judaizers (3:2-16) and false teachers (3:17-21).

Philippians

OPEN: 1. Who taught you to send thank you notes? **2.** When you care about someone, are you more likely to send a funny card or a touching one?

DIG: 1. What feelings does Paul have for the Phillipians (vv. 3-8)? What concerns (vv. 9-11)? Why? **2.** What is the "good work" which will be completed when the Lord returns? **3.** What is the "grace" in which the Phillipians share? **4.** Does Paul love these Phillipians because he has been praying for them? Or does he pray for them because of his love?

REFLECT: 1. What grade would you give yourself on expressing your feelings: To God in prayer? To your family? **2.** Who was the "Paul" in your life who wrote letters to you? To whom can you extend "grace and peace" this week? Pray that God will press his peace into their situation and yours.

OPEN: 1. What is the closest you have come to facing death? **2.** Who do you admire for turning misfortune into a springboard for sharing their faith? **3.** What radio or TV preacher do you listen to? Who do you "turn off"?

DIG: 1. How does Paul determine whether an event is good or bad? What criterion does he use? How would Paul's example encourage the brothers in the Lord? **2.** Why would Paul's imprisonment encourage others to preach more fearlessly? What benefits would there be to this increased activity? What does this say about how God works through circumstances? **3.** How do you think preaching done with evil motives can effectively spread the gospel? **4.** What is the difference between Paul's desire for death and thoughts of suicide? How would you explain verse 21? **5.** What do you think is the theme of verse 27? Why? Why is this aspect of Christianity so important to Paul? **6.** Why is suffering to be considered a benefit granted by God? How does this relate to Paul's joy in trying circumstances? What does this tell you about the nature of the Christian life?

1 Paul and Timothy, servants of Christ Jesus,

To all the saints in Christ Jesus at Philippi, together with the overseers[a] and deacons:

[2]Grace and peace to you from God our Father and the Lord Jesus Christ.

Thanksgiving and Prayer

[3]I thank my God every time I remember you. [4]In all my prayers for all of you, I always pray with joy [5]because of your partnership in the gospel from the first day until now, [6]being confident of this, that he who began a good work in you will carry it on to completion until the day of Christ Jesus.

[7]It is right for me to feel this way about all of you, since I have you in my heart; for whether I am in chains or defending and confirming the gospel, all of you share in God's grace with me. [8]God can testify how I long for all of you with the affection of Christ Jesus.

[9]And this is my prayer: that your love may abound more and more in knowledge and depth of insight, [10]so that you may be able to discern what is best and may be pure and blameless until the day of Christ, [11]filled with the fruit of righteousness that comes through Jesus Christ—to the glory and praise of God.

Paul's Chains Advance the Gospel

[12]Now I want you to know, brothers, that what has happened to me has really served to advance the gospel. [13]As a result, it has become clear throughout the whole palace guard[b] and to everyone else that I am in chains for Christ. [14]Because of my chains, most of the brothers in the Lord have been encouraged to speak the word of God more courageously and fearlessly.

[15]It is true that some preach Christ out of envy and rivalry, but others out of good will. [16]The latter do so in love, knowing that I am put here for the defense of the gospel. [17]The former preach Christ out of selfish ambition, not sincerely, supposing that they can stir up trouble for me while I am in chains.[c] [18]But what does it matter? The important thing is that in every way, whether from false motives or true, Christ is preached. And because of this I rejoice.

Yes, and I will continue to rejoice, [19]for I know that through your prayers and the help given by the Spirit of Jesus Christ, what has happened to me will turn out for my deliverance.[d] [20]I eagerly expect and hope that I will in no way be ashamed, but will have sufficient courage so that now as always Christ will be exalted in my body, whether by life or by death. [21]For to me, to live is Christ and to die is gain. [22]If I am to go on living in the body, this will mean fruitful labor for me. Yet what shall I choose? I do not know! [23]I am torn between the two: I desire to depart and be with Christ, which is better by far; [24]but it is

---

a1 Traditionally *bishops*   *b13* Or *whole palace*   *c16,17* Some late manuscripts have verses 16 and 17 in reverse order.   *d19* Or *salvation*

more necessary for you that I remain in the body. ²⁵Convinced of this, I know that I will remain, and I will continue with all of you for your progress and joy in the faith, ²⁶so that through my being with you again your joy in Christ Jesus will overflow on account of me.

²⁷Whatever happens, conduct yourselves in a manner worthy of the gospel of Christ. Then, whether I come and see you or only hear about you in my absence, I will know that you stand firm in one spirit, contending as one man for the faith of the gospel ²⁸without being frightened in any way by those who oppose you. This is a sign to them that they will be destroyed, but that you will be saved—and that by God. ²⁹For it has been granted to you on behalf of Christ not only to believe on him, but also to suffer for him, ³⁰since you are going through the same struggle you saw I had, and now hear that I still have.

Imitating Christ's Humility

2 If you have any encouragement from being united with Christ, if any comfort from his love, if any fellowship with the Spirit, if any tenderness and compassion, ²then make my joy complete by being like-minded, having the same love, being one in spirit and purpose. ³Do nothing out of selfish ambition or vain conceit, but in humility consider others better than yourselves. ⁴Each of you should look not only to your own interests, but also to the interests of others.

⁵Your attitude should be the same as that of Christ Jesus:

⁶Who, being in very nature᷄ God,
did not consider equality with God something to be grasped,
⁷but made himself nothing,
taking the very nature ᶠ of a servant,
being made in human likeness.
⁸And being found in appearance as a man,
he humbled himself
and became obedient to death—
even death on a cross!
⁹Therefore God exalted him to the highest place
and gave him the name that is above every name,
¹⁰that at the name of Jesus every knee should bow,
in heaven and on earth and under the earth,
¹¹and every tongue confess that Jesus Christ is Lord,
to the glory of God the Father.

Shining as Stars

¹²Therefore, my dear friends, as you have always obeyed—not only in my presence, but now much more in my absence—continue to work out your salvation with fear and trembling, ¹³for it is God who works in you to will and to act according to his good purpose.

¹⁴Do everything without complaining or arguing, ¹⁵so that you may become blameless and pure, children of God without fault in a crooked and depraved generation, in which you shine

ᵉ6 Or *in the form of*   ᶠ7 Or *the form*

REFLECT: 1. Paul had the ability to see opportunity in every misfortune. How about you? **2.** If you were to die today, what would you like to have said about you at the funeral? In your obituary? **3.** What is your greatest motive for staying alive? **4.** How do you feel about being kept alive mechanically in the hospital?

OPEN: If you had a second life to live in unselfish service to mankind, what would you like to do?

DIG: 1. Reading between the lines, what do you think was the problem with the church in Philippi? **2.** What are four motives for living in unity? How is this unity related to humility? To witness? To suffering? **3.** How can you consider a person "better than" yourself when you know you are "better than" they are? **4.** How could Jesus Christ become a "man" and still be God? Was he only play-acting? Did he have two part-time jobs? Use a telephone booth to change roles? If he was fully God, how could he suffer "death" on the cross? In becoming human, which of the "divine attributes" (e.g., knowing everything, being everywhere) did Jesus give up? Which did he retain? **5.** What is the "therefore" (v. 9) there for? What new actors, movements and results are signaled by this pivotal word?

REFLECT: If you threw a party for these people who helped shape your life by their unselfish caring, who would you invite to your party?

OPEN: What time of day are you most alive? Most grumpy? What gets you going when stalled?

DIG: 1. In the context of chapter 2, what does it mean to "work out your (plural) salvation"? Individually get right with God? Or collectively become whole and healthy? What part of this salvation is up to God? Up to you? **2.** Which slogan best explains Paul's statement in verses 12-13: "God helps those that help themselves" or "Let go and let God"?

REFLECT: Do you consider "working out your salvation" a full-time job or more of a hobby?

OPEN: 1. When you were in grade school, who was your best friend? Why did you like this person so much? 2. If you had to turn your business or family affairs over to one person outside of your family, who would you choose right now?

DIG: 1. What kind of praise and instruction is Paul giving Timothy and Epaphroditus? What impact would this have on those who received this letter? 2. Which of the Philippians' problems (see 1:17, 2:3 and 14; 3:2 and 4:3) are these two messengers best suited to handle? 3. In bringing out the best in these people (Timothy, Epaphroditus, the Philippian church members, Euodia and Syntyche), what is Paul's secret?

REFLECT: How do you bring out the best in people you work with? What aspects of Paul's psychology and strategy could you adopt?

OPEN: 1. If you had to brag about one thing that you can do better than anyone else, what would it be?

DIG: 1. How could Paul "rejoice" in the Lord (v. 1) and not complain (2:14) amidst so many problems? Is joy a choice or an emotion? Why? 2. What does "confidence in the flesh" mean: Good looks? Good works? Reputation? The right schooling? A "cut" above the rest? Or what? 3. How does Paul regard his own rank, accomplishments and heritage? Why? How does this compare with the example of the Lord (v. 10, also 2:6-11)? 4. In shifting the basis for his confidence form personal striving and privilege to Christ's work and grace, what did it cost Paul? What did he gain?

REFLECT: What value do you place on your own religious upbringing? Your schooling? Job seniority? Trophies? If all this was taken away from you, would you be less valuable as a person?

like stars in the universe [16]as you hold out[g] the word of life—in order that I may boast on the day of Christ that I did not run or labor for nothing. [17]But even if I am being poured out like a drink offering on the sacrifice and service coming from your faith, I am glad and rejoice with all of you. [18]So you too should be glad and rejoice with me.

Timothy and Epaphroditus

[19]I hope in the Lord Jesus to send Timothy to you soon, that I also may be cheered when I receive news about you. [20]I have no one else like him, who takes a genuine interest in your welfare. [21]For everyone looks out for his own interests, not those of Jesus Christ. [22]But you know that Timothy has proved himself, because as a son with his father he has served with me in the work of the gospel. [23]I hope, therefore, to send him as soon as I see how things go with me. [24]And I am confident in the Lord that I myself will come soon.

[25]But I think it is necessary to send back to you Epaphroditus, my brother, fellow worker and fellow soldier, who is also your messenger, whom you sent to take care of my needs. [26]For he longs for all of you and is distressed because you heard he was ill. [27]Indeed he was ill, and almost died. But God had mercy on him, and not on him only but also on me, to spare me sorrow upon sorrow. [28]Therefore I am all the more eager to send him, so that when you see him again you may be glad and I may have less anxiety. [29]Welcome him in the Lord with great joy, and honor men like him, [30]because he almost died for the work of Christ, risking his life to make up for the help you could not give me.

No Confidence in the Flesh

3 Finally, my brothers, rejoice in the Lord! It is no trouble for me to write the same things to you again, and it is a safeguard for you.
[2]Watch out for those dogs, those men who do evil, those mutilators of the flesh. [3]For it is we who are the circumcision, we who worship by the Spirit of God, who glory in Christ Jesus, and who put no confidence in the flesh— [4]though I myself have reasons for such confidence.

If anyone else thinks he has reasons to put confidence in the flesh, I have more: [5]circumcised on the eighth day, of the people of Israel, of the tribe of Benjamin, a Hebrew of Hebrews; in regard to the law, a Pharisee; [6]as for zeal, persecuting the church; as for legalistic righteousness, faultless.

[7]But whatever was to my profit I now consider loss for the sake of Christ. [8]What is more, I consider everything a loss compared to the surpassing greatness of knowing Christ Jesus my Lord, for whose sake I have lost all things. I consider them rubbish, that I may gain Christ [9]and be found in him, not having a righteousness of my own that comes from the law, but that which is through faith in Christ—the righteousness that comes from God and is by faith. [10]I want to know Christ and the power

g16 Or hold on to

of his resurrection and the fellowship of sharing in his sufferings, becoming like him in his death, ¹¹and so, somehow, to attain to the resurrection from the dead.

Pressing on Toward the Goal

¹²Not that I have already obtained all this, or have already been made perfect, but I press on to take hold of that for which Christ Jesus took hold of me. ¹³Brothers, I do not consider myself yet to have taken hold of it. But one thing I do: Forgetting what is behind and straining toward what is ahead, ¹⁴I press on toward the goal to win the prize for which God has called me heavenward in Christ Jesus.

¹⁵All of us who are mature should take such a view of things. And if on some point you think differently, that too God will make clear to you. ¹⁶Only let us live up to what we have already attained.

¹⁷Join with others in following my example, brothers, and take note of those who live according to the pattern we gave you. ¹⁸For, as I have often told you before and now say again even with tears, many live as enemies of the cross of Christ. ¹⁹Their destiny is destruction, their god is their stomach, and their glory is in their shame. Their mind is on earthly things. ²⁰But our citizenship is in heaven. And we eagerly await a Savior from there, the Lord Jesus Christ, ²¹who, by the power that enables him to bring everything under his control, will transform our lowly bodies so that they will be like his glorious body.

4 Therefore, my brothers, you whom I love and long for, my joy and crown, that is how you should stand firm in the Lord, dear friends!

Exhortations

²I plead with Euodia and I plead with Syntyche to agree with each other in the Lord. ³Yes, and I ask you, loyal yokefellow,ʰ help these women who have contended at my side in the cause of the gospel, along with Clement and the rest of my fellow workers, whose names are in the book of life.

⁴Rejoice in the Lord always. I will say it again: Rejoice! ⁵Let your gentleness be evident to all. The Lord is near. ⁶Do not be anxious about anything, but in everything, by prayer and petition, with thanksgiving, present your requests to God. ⁷And the peace of God, which transcends all understanding, will guard your hearts and your minds in Christ Jesus.

⁸Finally, brothers, whatever is true, whatever is noble, whatever is right, whatever is pure, whatever is lovely, whatever is admirable—if anything is excellent or praiseworthy—think about such things. ⁹Whatever you have learned or received or heard from me, or seen in me—put it into practice. And the God of peace will be with you.

OPEN: 1. What's the best prize or award you've ever received? If you could win any award, what would you like to win? Why? **2.** When it comes to your dream of the ideal lifestyle, are you more like the pioneer (always pushing on) or the settler (settling down)?

DIG: 1. Using the imagery of a track race, where does Paul picture himself in his spiritual life? What prize is he after? How's he going to reach his goal? **2.** Is perfectionism attainable for the Christian? Why or why not? **3.** How are Christians supposed to resolve differences among themselves (vv. 15-17)? Likewise, differences with "enemies" (3:18; 4:1)? What are those differences? Who are these enemies?

REFLECT: 1. What are some of the hurdles you have successfully cleared this past year in your race toward the prize? What is the hurdle which looms immediately before you? **2.** Compare your life right now to a track race. Are you sitting on the sidelines? Warming up? At the starting blocks? Gutting it out?

OPEN: Where do you go, or what do you do, to get one hour's reprieve from the day's problems?

DIG: 1. What does it take for these two female church leaders to "agree in the Lord"? And who's responsibility is it to be the "loyal yokefellows" (v. 3) **2.** Which attitudes enable people to cope successfully in difficult times? **3.** Of these attitudes and virtues endorsed by Paul, which are uniquely Christian? Which represent the best of first century pagan culture (and 20th century pop psychology)? **4.** In this matter of resolving conflicts, why does Paul point to himself as an example to follow (v. 9)? What kind of an example is Paul (see also 1:15-18; 3:2, or 17-18)?

REFLECT: 1. On a scale of 1 to 10, what is the anxiety level in your life right now? **2.** What are some of the "excellent or praiseworthy" things that you can be thinking on this week?

ʰ3 Or loyal Syzygus

Thanks for Their Gifts

[10]I rejoice greatly in the Lord that at last you have renewed your concern for me. Indeed, you have been concerned, but you had no opportunity to show it. [11]I am not saying this because I am in need, for I have learned to be content whatever the circumstances. [12]I know what it is to be in need, and I know what it is to have plenty. I have learned the secret of being content in any and every situation, whether well fed or hungry, whether living in plenty or in want. [13]I can do everything through him who gives me strength.

[14]Yet it was good of you to share in my troubles. [15]Moreover, as you Philippians know, in the early days of your acquaintance with the gospel, when I set out from Macedonia, not one church shared with me in the matter of giving and receiving, except you only; [16]for even when I was in Thessalonica, you sent me aid again and again when I was in need. [17]Not that I am looking for a gift, but I am looking for what may be credited to your account. [18]I have received full payment and even more; I am amply supplied, now that I have received from Epaphroditus the gifts you sent. They are a fragrant offering, an acceptable sacrifice, pleasing to God. [19]And my God will meet all your needs according to his glorious riches in Christ Jesus.

[20]To our God and Father be glory for ever and ever. Amen.

Final Greetings

[21]Greet all the saints in Christ Jesus. The brothers who are with me send greetings. [22]All the saints send you greetings, especially those who belong to Caesar's household.

[23]The grace of the Lord Jesus Christ be with your spirit. Amen. [i]

---

i23 Some manuscripts do not have Amen.

COLOSSIANS

INTRODUCTION

Date

Tradition has it that Paul wrote Colossians, Ephesians, and Philemon during his imprisonment in Rome. This would mean these letters were written in the early sixties. However, other sites including Caesarea and Ephesus have been proposed as the place of Paul's confinement, so that neither date nor place is certain.

Audience

The City of Colossae

About a hundred miles west of Ephesus in the Lycus River valley stood the city of Colossae. In Paul's time, it was located in the Roman province of Asia (in what today is Turkey). It was one of three major population centers that had flourished in the region. Hierapolis and Laodicea (4:13) stood on opposite sides of the River Lycus, about six miles apart, while Colossae straddled the river some twelve miles upstream.

Since it was located on a major trade route from Ephesus, Colossae was considered a great city in the days of Xerxes, the Persian general (fifth century B.C.). A hundred years later, it had developed into a prosperous commerical center on account of its weaving industry. In fact, Colossian came to mean a certain color of dyed wool.

By the time of Paul, however, Colossae's prominence had diminished, though its sister cities, Laodicea and Hierapolis, were still prospering. Laodicea had become the seat of Roman government in the region, and Heirapolis was famous for its healing waters. But Colossae, when Paul wrote, was no longer even a city. In fact, as Lightfoot notes, Colossae was the least important town to which Paul ever wrote (*St. Paul's Epistles to the Colossians and Philemon*, p. 16).

The Church of Colossae

Paul did not found this church, at least not directly. It was probably established as a result of his ministry in Ephesus, since during Paul's two or three years in Ephesus the whole province of Asia was evangelized (Acts 19:10). Paul, however, never visited the churches at Colossae or Laodicea (2:1).

Epaphras probably founded the Colossian church. A native of Colossae (4:12), he worked hard on behalf of the church there (4:13). In fact, in 1:6-7 Paul says: "All over the world this gospel is producing fruit and growing . . . You learned it from Epaphras. . . ." Paul then commends Epaphras as his dear friend and a faithful minister of Christ. In fact, because of their friendship, Epaphras stayed with Paul during his imprisonment (Philem. 23) and so was unable to deliver the letter to the Colossians personally.

We meet the church at Colossae in another of Paul's letters. Paul wrote to one of its members, Philemon, asking that he accept back the runaway slave Onesimus converted through Paul's ministry.

The church at Colossae was probably mainly Gentile in composition. In 1:21 Paul speaks of the Colossian Christians as having once been "alienated from God" and "enemies in your minds"—phrases he uses elsewhere to describe those who are not part of God's covenant with Israel. Then in 1:27, he talks about making the mystery of God clear to the Gentiles; the reference is obviously to the Colossians. Finally in 3:5-7, Paul lists their past sins that are characteristic of Gentiles rather than Jews.

Religion in Colossae

A large number of Jews had lived in the region of Colossae, ever since the second century B.C. when Antiochus III brought two thousand Jews from Mesopotamia and Babylon to settle there. By Paul's time there may have been as many as fifty thousand Jews living in the region and practicing their religion. However, their synagogues had a "reputation for laxity and openness to speculation drifting in from the hellenistic world" (Ralph P. Martin, *Colossians and Philemon: New Century Bible Commentary,* p. 18)

But freethinking Judaism was not the major religious force in the Lycus valley. The Greek religions also flourished there. The cult of Cybele, for example, was highly popular. This was a fertility cult characterized by ecstasy and excessive enthusiasm, though it also had an ascetic side. Throughout the Roman Empire, the worship of Isis, Apollo, Dionysus, Asclepius, and other gods was widespread. In particular, the cult of Mithras, a mystery religion based on astrology and sacrifice, abounded in Colossae.

The church at Colossae, therefore, grew up in an atmosphere that blended a variety of religious traditions that may have been sources of heresy within the church. "In the Colossian church we appear to be in touch with a meeting-place where the freethinking Judaism of the dispersion and the speculative ideas of Greek mystery-religion are in close contact. Out of this interchange and fusion comes a syncretism, which is theologically novel (bringing Christ into a hierarchy and a system) and ethically conditioned (advocating a rigorous discipline and an ecstatic visionary reward). On both counts, in Paul's eyes, it is a deadly danger to the incipient church" (Martin, *Colossians and Philemon,* pp. 18-19).

The Colossian Heresy

Something was wrong in the church. Although Epaphras had good news to report to Paul (1:4-8; 2:5), Paul knew there was also a problem of some sort. Apparently the young church had been exposed to an attractive but heretical teaching which threatened its growth and existence. We do not know exactly what this heresy was. Nowhere does Paul define the problem. It is only by inferences from his arguments against the heresy that we begin to piece together its character.

Apparently it had something to do with astrology. Paul talks about the *stoicheia* or "basic principles of this world" (2:8, 20), understood by Greeks as "immortal lords of creation, existing in their own right, and as astrological tyrants who laid claim to control men's lives as the playthings of fate" (Martin). These star-deities were kept at bay by ascetic practices. In fact, a life of abstinence and self-punishment was thought to lead to salvation (Paul probably refers to such ascetic practices in 2:20-23).

In contrast, Paul insists that Jesus alone is Lord of the universe (1:15-18; 2:9-10) and that rules and regulations are not the path to salvation (2:20, 23).

Theme

As Paul does so often, he begins his letter with a strong doctrinal statement and concludes it by drawing out the behavioral implications of the doctrine. Here his doctrinal emphasis is on the cosmic nature of Jesus Christ. Jesus is the divine Lord of the universe who reconciles all things to himself through his death. Paul sets this strong statement of Christ's deity (1:13-2:7) over against the speculative, ritual-oriented, ascetic faith of the false teachers (2:8-23). Once the truth about Christ is stated, Paul turns to the implications of Christ's cosmic lordship and describes how those in union with him ought to live (3:1-4:6). As Barclay has written: "It remains a strange and wonderful fact that Paul wrote the letter which contains the highest reach of his thought to so unimportant a town as Colossae then was. But in doing so he checked a tendency, which, if it had been allowed to develop, would have wrecked Asian Christianity, and which might well have done irreparable damage to the faith of the whole Church" (*The Letters to the Philippians, Colossians, and Thessalonians,* p. 122).

The Epistle to the Colossians begins, like most of Paul's letters, with a lengthy introduction (1:1-12). In the first major division on doctrine, Paul establishes the preeminence of Christ (1:13-2:23). He follows this with an exhortation to the Colossians to live in union with Christ (3:1-4:6). He concludes with personal greetings (4:7-18).

Colossians

1 Paul, an apostle of Christ Jesus by the will of God, and Timothy our brother,

²To the holy and faithful* brothers in Christ at Colosse:

Grace and peace to you from God our Father.*

Thanksgiving and Prayer

³We always thank God, the Father of our Lord Jesus Christ, when we pray for you, ⁴because we have heard of your faith in Christ Jesus and of the love you have for all the saints— ⁵the faith and love that spring from the hope that is stored up for you in heaven and that you have already heard about in the word of truth, the gospel ⁶that has come to you. All over the world this gospel is bearing fruit and growing, just as it has been doing among you since the day you heard it and understood God's grace in all its truth. ⁷You learned it from Epaphras, our dear fellow servant, who is a faithful minister of Christ on our* behalf, ⁸and who also told us of your love in the Spirit.

⁹For this reason, since the day we heard about you, we have not stopped praying for you and asking God to fill you with the knowledge of his will through all spiritual wisdom and understanding. ¹⁰And we pray this in order that you may live a life worthy of the Lord and may please him in every way: bearing fruit in every good work, growing in the knowledge of God, ¹¹being strengthened with all power according to his glorious might so that you may have great endurance and patience, and joyfully ¹²giving thanks to the Father, who has qualified you* to share in the inheritance of the saints in the kingdom of light. ¹³For he has rescued us from the dominion of darkness and brought us into the kingdom of the Son he loves, ¹⁴in whom we have redemption,* the forgiveness of sins.

The Supremacy of Christ

¹⁵He is the image of the invisible God, the firstborn over all creation. ¹⁶For by him all things were created: things in heaven and on earth, visible and invisible, whether thrones or powers or rulers or authorities; all things were created by him and for him. ¹⁷He is before all things, and in him all things hold together. ¹⁸And he is the head of the body, the church; he is the beginning and the firstborn from among the dead, so that in everything he might have the supremacy. ¹⁹For God was pleased to have all his fullness dwell in him, ²⁰and through him to reconcile to himself all things, whether things on earth or things in heaven, by making peace through his blood, shed on the cross.

OPEN: What attracts you to certain strangers: Are they just "friends you haven't met"? What about the members of your study group: What have you heard that prepares you to like them? What might you have in common?

DIG: 1. Paul hasn't met these believers (2:1), yet he is attracted to them. Why? What qualities of this church would attract you the most? **2.** If faith, hope and love are the fruit of the gospel (vv. 5-6), then what does this fruit look like? Feel like? Taste like? **3.** What is "God's grace in all its truth" (v. 6)? What aspects of grace do you see in verses 12-14? What aspects do you not understand, for which Paul's prayer (vv. 9-12) applies to you as well? **4.** Reading between the lines here (also 2:4, 8, 18), what concerns Paul about the Colossians?

REFLECT: 1. How do your prayers for others compare with Paul's intensity, thankfulness, and clarity? Where do you get "stuck" in prayer? What might help you get "unstuck"? How might God's "power" (v. 11) help you get "unstuck"? **2.** In the field of your life and those you pray for, are the fruits of faith, love and hope being cultivated? How so? Or are those fields neglected in drought? How will you tend to those neglected fields this week?

OPEN: 1. As a kid, what "superhuman" character, on TV or in real life, did you look up to? Why? **2.** Who is the "Rock of Gilbrator" in your family now?

DIG: 1. What does "firstborn" mean in relation to "creation" (v. 15) and "the dead" (v. 18)? **2.** Given Christ's supreme role in creation (vv. 15-17), what does that imply for the church (v. 18)? For heavenly beings (v. 20)? For all earthly powers and authority (also 2:10)? **3.** Regarding Christ's reconciling work (vv. 20-22), who benefits? How so? Toward what end?

REFLECT: 1. What does it mean to you knowing that it was Jesus, the Creator and Lord of all, who died on the cross for you? How have you begun to experience the peace with God he has won? **2..** What forces

---

*²Or *believing*   *²Some manuscripts *Father and the Lord Jesus Christ*
*⁷Some manuscripts *your*   *¹²Some manuscripts *us*   *¹⁴A few late manuscripts *redemption through his blood*

or people sometimes seem to be more powerful that Jesus? Why? How do you respond to hearing that even these things are under Christ's authority? **3.** Which do you have more difficulty with: Understanding how Christ is supreme? Or yielding your life to his supremacy? What will you do about that this week?

OPEN: 1. When you were young, what mystery stories did you enjoy: Hardy Boys? Nancy Drew? Or what? **2.**When was the last time you felt taken in by a smooth talker?

DIG: 1. In what sense are Paul's sufferings a continuation of Jesus' sufferings? Why would this lead him to rejoice (see 2 Cor. 12:9-10)? **2.** Colossae would be familiar with "mystery" religions, the "fullness" of which was only experienced after rigorous training. By contrast, what "mystery" of God is now fully revealed in the gospel (1:26, 27, 2:2)?

REFLECT: 1. In your life and witness, do you have Paul's *ardor* (fervency)? Or the Colossian's *order* (firmness, 1:23; 2:5)? How might knowing "Christ in you" help you be both fervent and firm in your faith? **2.** Is Paul's stated purpose (1:28; 2:2) a reality in your life? Or are you still somewhere along the way? How far along the way are you? **3.** What "fine sounding arguments" hinder you by saying there is more to life than him? How does Paul's argument speak to your concerns?

OPEN: 1. When you were young, what did you think a "religious" person must be like? How did you feel about that type of person? **2.** What animal to you most symbolizes freedom? How are you like that animal?

DIG: 1. According to verses 6-8, how are we to counteract the growth of worldly philosophy in the church? What does "rooted and built up" imply to you? **2.** Is it possible for Christ to be the first step and something else the second step in the Christian life? How do verses 9-12 answer that question? **3.** What kind of circumcision is done by Christ (v. 11)? How did he do it (vv. 12-15)? **4.** How do you reconcile Christ's "cancelling" of the "written code" (v. 14) with his statements in Matthew 5:17-20, where he "fulfills" the "Law and the Prophets"? **5.** What is wrong with adding Jewish practices

²¹Once you were alienated from God and were enemies in your minds because of*ᶠ* your evil behavior. ²²But now he has reconciled you by Christ's physical body through death to present you holy in his sight, without blemish and free from accusation— ²³if you continue in your faith, established and firm, not moved from the hope held out in the gospel. This is the gospel that you heard and that has been proclaimed to every creature under heaven, and of which I, Paul, have become a servant.

Paul's Labor for the Church

²⁴Now I rejoice in what was suffered for you, and I fill up in my flesh what is still lacking in regard to Christ's afflictions, for the sake of his body, which is the church. ²⁵I have become its servant by the commission God gave me to present to you the word of God in its fullness— ²⁶the mystery that has been kept hidden for ages and generations, but is now disclosed to the saints. ²⁷To them God has chosen to make known among the Gentiles the glorious riches of this mystery, which is Christ in you, the hope of glory.

²⁸We proclaim him, admonishing and teaching everyone with all wisdom, so that we may present everyone perfect in Christ. ²⁹To this end I labor, struggling with all his energy, which so powerfully works in me.

2 I want you to know how much I am struggling for you and for those at Laodicea, and for all who have not met me personally. ²My purpose is that they may be encouraged in heart and united in love, so that they may have the full riches of complete understanding, in order that they may know the mystery of God, namely, Christ, ³in whom are hidden all the treasures of wisdom and knowledge. ⁴I tell you this so that no one may deceive you by fine-sounding arguments. ⁵For though I am absent from you in body, I am present with you in spirit and delight to see how orderly you are and how firm your faith in Christ is.

Freedom From Human Regulations Through Life With Christ

⁶So then, just as you received Christ Jesus as Lord, continue to live in him, ⁷rooted and built up in him, strengthened in the faith as you were taught, and overflowing with thankfulness.

⁸See to it that no one takes you captive through hollow and deceptive philosophy, which depends on human tradition and the basic principles of this world rather than on Christ.

⁹For in Christ all the fullness of the Deity lives in bodily form, ¹⁰and you have been given fullness in Christ, who is the head over every power and authority. ¹¹In him you were also circumcised, in the putting off of the sinful nature,*ᵍ* not with a circumcision done by the hands of men but with the circumcision done by Christ, ¹²having been buried with him in baptism and raised with him through your faith in the power of God, who raised him from the dead.

ᶠ21 Or minds, as shown by   *ᵍ11 Or the flesh*

[13]When you were dead in your sins and in the uncircumcision of your sinful nature,[h] God made you[i] alive with Christ. He forgave us all our sins, [14]having canceled the written code, with its regulations, that was against us and that stood opposed to us; he took it away, nailing it to the cross. [15]And having disarmed the powers and authorities, he made a public spectacle of them, triumphing over them by the cross.[j]

[16]Therefore do not let anyone judge you by what you eat or drink, or with regard to a religious festival, a New Moon celebration or a Sabbath day. [17]These are a shadow of the things that were to come; the reality, however, is found in Christ. [18]Do not let anyone who delights in false humility and the worship of angels disqualify you for the prize. Such a person goes into great detail about what he has seen, and his unspiritual mind puffs him up with idle notions. [19]He has lost connection with the Head, from whom the whole body, supported and held together by its ligaments and sinews, grows as God causes it to grow. [20]Since you died with Christ to the basic principles of this world, why, as though you still belonged to it, do you submit to its rules: [21]"Do not handle! Do not taste! Do not touch!"? [22]These are all destined to perish with use, because they are based on human commands and teachings. [23]Such regulations indeed have an appearance of wisdom, with their self-imposed worship, their false humility and their harsh treatment of the body, but they lack any value in restraining sensual indulgence.

Rules for Holy Living

3 Since, then, you have been raised with Christ, set your hearts on things above, where Christ is seated at the right hand of God. [2]Set your minds on things above, not on earthly things. [3]For you died, and your life is now hidden with Christ in God. [4]When Christ, who is your[k] life, appears, then you also will appear with him in glory.

[5]Put to death, therefore, whatever belongs to your earthly nature: sexual immorality, impurity, lust, evil desires and greed, which is idolatry. [6]Because of these, the wrath of God is coming.[l] [7]You used to walk in these ways, in the life you once lived. [8]But now you must rid yourselves of all such things as these: anger, rage, malice, slander, and filthy language from your lips. [9]Do not lie to each other, since you have taken off your old self with its practices [10]and have put on the new self, which is being renewed in knowledge in the image of its Creator. [11]Here there is no Greek or Jew, circumcised or uncircumcised, barbarian, Scythian, slave or free, but Christ is all, and is in all.

[12]Therefore, as God's chosen people, holy and dearly loved, clothe yourselves with compassion, kindness, humility, gentleness and patience. [13]Bear with each other and forgive whatever grievances you may have against one another. Forgive as the Lord forgave you. [14]And over all these virtues put on love, which binds them all together in perfect unity.

to faith in Christ (vv. 16-17)? Likewise, what's wrong with basing your faith on private visions and spiritual experiences (vv. 18-19)? Or on abstinence, self-punishment and other ascetic practices (vv. 20-23)? **6.** What then *is* of value in "restraining sensual indulgence" (v. 23; see vv. 6-7)?

REFLECT: **1.** When have you felt like the "roots" of your faith in Christ were barely below the surface? What helps you to sink those roots deeper? **2.** What "second steps" or additions to faith in Christ have you encountered from people trying to encourage you to be "more spiritual"? How do you see these "additions" really denying the truth that Jesus has saved you? In light of 2:9-10, 16-19, how would you respond to these pressures now? **3.** What evidence have you seen that trying to live up to religious rules in and of itself does not help change you on the inside? What is the source of real change and growth? Where do you want to apply Paul's solution this week?

OPEN: What clothes do you wear when you want to really look your best? How about when you don't care what you look like?

DIG: **1.** Now what does Paul say is the focus of true spirituality (vv. 1-2)? How is setting your mind and heart on Christ related to what he has already done for us (v. 1)? To what he will do for us (v. 2)? **2.** How is that Christian mind-set different than one's "earthly nature" (vv. 5-10)? What do the new set of "clothes" (vv. 12-15) look like compared to these old ones? **3.** What does all this "putting off" and "putting on" actually involve: A quick-change act? A disguise? A burial service? A shopping spree? **4.** In shopping or swapping a new "spiritual wardrobe," look again at verses 10-11, 15-17, noting the verbs, their subjects and objects: Who is doing what to whom to ensure that "Christ is all"? How does Christ tailor-fit his clothes for you?

REFLECT: **1.** How would you characterize your last week: Too heavenly-minded to be any earthly good? Or too earthly-minded to be any heavenly good? Next week what will occupy your mind, and what good will you do, as a result of this study? **2.** Given verse 11,

---

[h]13 Or *your flesh* [i]13 Some manuscripts *us* [j]15 Or *them in him* [k]4 Some
manuscripts *our* [l]6 Some early manuscripts *coming on those who are disobedient*

and this new Christ-like clothing we all wear, shall we then all look like? Why or why not?

OPEN: Who has been one of your best employers? What did you appreciate about him or her?

DIG: 1. What do you see here which indicates that all these relationships are to be built around Christ? **2.** How do each of these Christ-centered relationships happen? How is your answer supported by Paul's principles in 3:1-17?

REFLECT: 1. As a wife or husband, child or parent, how do you wish to grow towards Paul's teaching here? **2.** How does the slave-master teaching relate to your work situation? What difference would it make if you actually worked as if it was Jesus for whom you were working?

DIG: In advancing the gospel, what role is played by prayer? By watchfulness? Thankfulness? Open doors? Closed doors or chains? Wise actions? Opportunism? Graceful talk? Salty talk?

REFLECT: In proportion to other concerns, how much do you talk to Christ about a brother? How much do you talk to your brother about Christ?

Colossians 4:7-18

OPEN: 1. In high school, who were two of your best friends? What was one quality about them that stands out to you? **2.** What is your reaction to unsigned formal Christmas newsletters? What difference does the personal greeting make? Why?

DIG: 1. From Acts 20:4, Eph. 6:21, 2 Tim. 4:12, Titus 3:12 and verses 7-8 here, what type of man is Tychicus? **2.** Onesimus (see Philemon 10-16) was a runaway slave from Colossae whom Paul was sending back to his master, Philemon. In light of 3:22-4:1, how might the Colossians be feeling towards him? **3.** Aristarchus, (Acts 19:29, 27:2, Philemon 24), Mark (Acts 12:12, 13:5, 13, 15:36-40 and the author of Mark), Luke (the author of Luke-Acts), and Demas (Philemon

[15]Let the peace of Christ rule in your hearts, since as members of one body you were called to peace. And be thankful. [16]Let the word of Christ dwell in you richly as you teach and admonish one another with all wisdom, and as you sing psalms, hymns and spiritual songs with gratitude in your hearts to God. [17]And whatever you do, whether in word or deed, do it all in the name of the Lord Jesus, giving thanks to God the Father through him.

Rules for Christian Households

[18]Wives, submit to your husbands, as is fitting in the Lord. [19]Husbands, love your wives and do not be harsh with them. [20]Children, obey your parents in everything, for this pleases the Lord.

[21]Fathers, do not embitter your children, or they will become discouraged.

[22]Slaves, obey your earthly masters in everything; and do it, not only when their eye is on you and to win their favor, but with sincerity of heart and reverence for the Lord. [23]Whatever you do, work at it with all your heart, as working for the Lord, not for men, [24]since you know that you will receive an inheritance from the Lord as a reward. It is the Lord Christ you are serving. [25]Anyone who does wrong will be repaid for his wrong, and there is no favoritism.

4 Masters, provide your slaves with what is right and fair, because you know that you also have a Master in heaven.

Further Instructions

[2]Devote yourselves to prayer, being watchful and thankful. [3]And pray for us, too, that God may open a door for our message, so that we may proclaim the mystery of Christ, for which I am in chains. [4]Pray that I may proclaim it clearly, as I should. [5]Be wise in the way you act toward outsiders; make the most of every opportunity. [6]Let your conversation be always full of grace, seasoned with salt, so that you may know how to answer everyone.

Final Greetings

[7]Tychicus will tell you all the news about me. He is a dear brother, a faithful minister and fellow servant in the Lord. [8]I am sending him to you for the express purpose that you may know about our[m] circumstances and that he may encourage your hearts. [9]He is coming with Onesimus, our faithful and dear brother, who is one of you. They will tell you everything that is happening here.

[10]My fellow prisoner Aristarchus sends you his greetings, as does Mark, the cousin of Barnabas. (You have received instructions about him; if he comes to you, welcome him.) [11]Jesus, who is called Justus, also sends greetings. These are the only Jews among my fellow workers for the kingdom of God, and they

---

m8 Some manuscripts *that he may know about your*

have proved a comfort to me. [12]Epaphras, who is one of you and a servant of Christ Jesus, sends greetings. He is always wrestling in prayer for you, that you may stand firm in all the will of God, mature and fully assured. [13]I vouch for him that he is working hard for you and for those at Laodicea and Hierapolis. [14]Our dear friend Luke, the doctor, and Demas send greetings. [15]Give my greetings to the brothers at Laodicea, and to Nympha and the church in her house.

[16]After this letter has been read to you, see that it is also read in the church of the Laodiceans and that you in turn read the letter from Laodicea.

[17]Tell Archippus: "See to it that you complete the work you have received in the Lord."

[18]I, Paul, write this greeting in my own hand. Remember my chains. Grace be with you.

24, 2 Tim. 4:10) were all with Paul at various times. Why would he include them in his greetings to the church? **4.** In light of the influence of the false teachers, why would Paul's commendation of Epaphras be especially important (1:7, 4:12-13)? **5.** What role does Nympha and Archippus (Philemon 1) play in these churches?

REFLECT: 1. Seeing how Paul operated with a team of fellow Christians, what does that mean for your life? For your small group **2.** Of the qualities used to describe these men, which one would you most like others to say about you in five years? How do 2:6-7 and 3:1-2 indicate you can get moving in that direction?

1 THESSALONIANS

INTRODUCTION

Date

First Thessalonians may well be the first document in what eventually became the New Testament. Many scholars believe that it is Paul's earliest letter, although a few say that Galatians has that honor. In any case, it is generally agreed that 1 Thessalonians was written about A.D. 50, during Paul's second missionary journey not long after the founding of the church in Thessalonica. Paul probably wrote from Corinth, where he went after he left Athens. Timothy had returned with news from Thessalonica, and this letter was Paul's response to his report.

Audience

The City of Thessalonica

Thessalonica was a great city. Originally named Therme, its famous harbor became the base for the Persian fleet during Xerxes' invasion of Europe. In 315 B.C., Cassander, the Macedonian king, renamed the city Thessalonica after his wife, the half-sister of Alexander the Great. In 146 B.C. after Rome had taken over Greece, Thessalonica was made the capital of the Roman province of Macedonia. In 42 B.C., Rome granted it the status of a free city, which gave Thessalonica a high degree of autonomy.

The key to its importance was Thessalonica's location astride the famous *Via Egnatia* — the great Roman military road across northern Greece, which stretched from the Adriatic Sea on the west to Constantinople in the east. Hence trade between Rome and Asia Minor and points farther east flowed through Thessalonica, making it very wealthy. This was a crucial site for a church if Christianity were to spread throughout the world.

The Church

When Paul crossed over into Macedonia in A.D. 50, a new era began for Christianity. Now the gospel had spread to Europe and only in a matter of time would it flow west, through Greece, into Italy, on to Spain and the limits of the Roman Empire. After the night vision that sent Paul across the Aegean Sea to Philippi, in due course he came to Thessalonica, which turned out to be a key stop in his pioneering work in Europe.

His stay in Thessalonica was brief and stormy. After he had preached in the synagogue for three Sabbaths, the Jews were so jealous of his success that they organized a mob by rounding up "some bad characters from the marketplace" (Acts 17:5). The mob then rushed around looking for Paul and Silas. Failing to find them, they dragged Jason (at whose home Paul was staying) and a few other Christians before the city officials. They claimed that these men were cohorts of Paul who was preaching that Jesus, not Caesar, was king. That night after Jason and the others were released on bail, Paul and Silas slipped away to Berea.

The Concerns

Could three weeks of ministry produce a viable church at Thessalonica? Apparently this question troubled Paul. After ministering in Berea, Paul had gone on to Athens. He attempted to return to Thessalonica, but his efforts were frustrated (2:17-18). In his place he sent Timothy to see how they were doing and to give them what help he could (2:17-3:5).

What Timothy found was twofold. Generally the news was good. The converts were standing fast in their faith despite persecution and Paul's hasty departure from the city. In fact, they were even doing evangelistic work on their own. On the other hand, there were (not unexpectedly) some problems. Some of the converts had not fully understood the ethical implications of the gospel. In particular, there was laxity in sexual matters (4:3-8). Some felt it unnecessary to work and had become a burden to the others (4:11-12; 5:14). There was also misunderstanding about the Second Coming. They knew Christ would return again and rescue them from the "coming wrath" (1:1-10; 5:9-10). But some worried about those Christians who died prior to the Lord's return (4:13-14). Quite possibly Paul and the others had departed from Thessalonica before their teaching on this subject was complete. So Paul assures them that the dead in Christ were at no disadvantage. In fact, the first event of the Second Coming would be the resurrection of the dead (4:16).

In his letter to them, Paul expresses his relief and joy at their good progress in the gospel. They have become, he says "a model to all the believers in Macedonia and Achaia" (1:7). Paul goes on to explain why he never returned to them. He ends his letter with further instruction about the life of holiness they ought to be leading and about the Second Coming.

The Converts

Who were these believers? Luke says (in Acts 17) that the church had its roots in the Jewish community. Some members of the synagogue, where Paul preached along with a large number of God-fearing Greeks — Gentiles who worshiped at the synagogue — and several prominent women, had become convinced that Jesus was the Messiah and so became Christians. These included Jason who opened his home to Paul and his companions, and Aristarchus who was later Paul's traveling companion and prison mate (Col. 4:10; Philem. 24; Acts 19:29; 20:4, 27:2).

In fact, throughout Paul's ministry in Macedonia, many prominent women were converted. Lydia, the businesswoman, was his first convert in Philippi (Acts 16:14). Many "prominent Greek women" were converted in Berea (Acts 17:12). Unlike most other women in the first century, the women in Macedonia had been noted for their competence and for the active role they played in society. As it turns out, they were crucial to the growth of the church in Europe.

The greater part of the church, however, seems to have been made up of converted pagans, as Paul's comment in 1:9 indicates: "You turned to God from idols."

1 Thessalonians

OPEN: 1. When the neighborhood kids chose up teams for a game, what were you most often: A captain? Picked first? Picked last? Overlooked?

DIG: 1. What do you know about the Thessalonian church from Paul's experiences in Thessalonica (see Acts 17:1-9)? **2.** What convinced Paul that the Thessalonians were, indeed, chosen by God? **3.** How did the Thessalonians first become imitators of and then models for the faith (vv. 6-10)? What does this tell you about their growth in Christ? **4.** In an age without mass media, how do you suppose their faith became so legendary "everywhere"?

REFLECT: 1. What kind of "model" are you for those around you? Still on the drawing board? A work in progress? Secured in a private collection? On puplic display at the National Museum? **2.** Which of the qualities in verse 3 do you most wish to see develop in your life now? How might others in the group help you?

OPEN: What was one of your most memorable failures experienced in junior or senior high school?

DIG: 1. From verses 1-6, what rumors about Paul have been spread by his opposition? How do his assurances speak to the concerns some may have had about his integrity? **2.** From verses 1-11, what does ethical evangelism look like? What do the images of being a mother (v. 7) and father (v. 11) teach about ministry? **3.** What difficulties were the Thessalonians facing (v. 14-15)? How dangerous would this be to the faith of new Christians? Why? How would Paul's example of preserverance in the face of persecution encourage them? **4.** What do you suppose is the secret to Paul's faithful response to hostile opposition? How might verses 13-15 provide encouragement to both Paul and his readers?

REFLECT: 1. What really turns you off about the way some people present the gospel? How are you attempting to avoid these mistakes and yet still maintain a strong witness? **2.** What is your secret for per-

1 Paul, Silas[a] and Timothy,

To the church of the Thessalonians in God the Father and the Lord Jesus Christ:

Grace and peace to you.[b]

Thanksgiving for the Thessalonians' Faith

[2]We always thank God for all of you, mentioning you in our prayers. [3]We continually remember before our God and Father your work produced by faith, your labor prompted by love, and your endurance inspired by hope in our Lord Jesus Christ.

[4]For we know, brothers loved by God, that he has chosen you, [5]because our gospel came to you not simply with words, but also with power, with the Holy Spirit and with deep conviction. You know how we lived among you for your sake. [6]You became imitators of us and of the Lord; in spite of severe suffering, you welcomed the message with the joy given by the Holy Spirit. [7]And so you became a model to all the believers in Macedonia and Achaia. [8]The Lord's message rang out from you not only in Macedonia and Achaia—your faith in God has become known everywhere. Therefore we do not need to say anything about it, [9]for they themselves report what kind of reception you gave us. They tell how you turned to God from idols to serve the living and true God, [10]and to wait for his Son from heaven, whom he raised from the dead—Jesus, who rescues us from the coming wrath.

Paul's Ministry in Thessalonica

2 You know, brothers, that our visit to you was not a failure. [2]We had previously suffered and been insulted in Philippi, as you know, but with the help of our God we dared to tell you his gospel in spite of strong opposition. [3]For the appeal we make does not spring from error or impure motives, nor are we trying to trick you. [4]On the contrary, we speak as men approved by God to be entrusted with the gospel. We are not trying to please men but God, who tests our hearts. [5]You know we never used flattery, nor did we put on a mask to cover up greed—God is our witness. [6]We were not looking for praise from men, not from you or anyone else.

As apostles of Christ we could have been a burden to you, [7]but we were gentle among you, like a mother caring for her little children. [8]We loved you so much that we were delighted to share with you not only the gospel of God but our lives as well, because you had become so dear to us. [9]Surely you remember, brothers, our toil and hardship; we worked night and day in order not to be a burden to anyone while we preached the gospel of God to you.

---

[a]1 Greek *Silvanus*, a variant of *Silas*   [b]1 Some early manuscripts *you from God*
our Father and the Lord Jesus Christ

¹⁰You are witnesses, and so is God, of how holy, righteous and blameless we were among you who believed. ¹¹For you know that we dealt with each of you as a father deals with his own children, ¹²encouraging, comforting and urging you to live lives worthy of God, who calls you into his kingdom and glory.

¹³And we also thank God continually because, when you received the word of God, which you heard from us, you accepted it not as the word of men, but as it actually is, the word of God, which is at work in you who believe. ¹⁴For you, brothers, became imitators of God's churches in Judea, which are in Christ Jesus: You suffered from your own countrymen the same things those churches suffered from the Jews, ¹⁵who killed the Lord Jesus and the prophets and also drove us out. They displease God and are hostile to all men ¹⁶in their effort to keep us from speaking to the Gentiles so that they may be saved. In this way they always heap up their sins to the limit. The wrath of God has come upon them at last.ᶜ

Paul's Longing to See the Thessalonians

¹⁷But, brothers, when we were torn away from you for a short time (in person, not in thought), out of our intense longing we made every effort to see you. ¹⁸For we wanted to come to you—certainly I, Paul, did, again and again—but Satan stopped us. ¹⁹For what is our hope, our joy, or the crown in which we will glory in the presence of our Lord Jesus when he comes? Is it not you? ²⁰Indeed, you are our glory and joy.

3 So when we could stand it no longer, we thought it best to be left by ourselves in Athens. ²We sent Timothy, who is our brother and God's fellow workerᵈ in spreading the gospel of Christ, to strengthen and encourage you in your faith, ³so that no one would be unsettled by these trials. You know quite well that we were destined for them. ⁴In fact, when we were with you, we kept telling you that we would be persecuted. And it turned out that way, as you well know. ⁵For this reason, when I could stand it no longer, I sent to find out about your faith. I was afraid that in some way the tempter might have tempted you and our efforts might have been useless.

Timothy's Encouraging Report

⁶But Timothy has just now come to us from you and has brought good news about your faith and love. He has told us that you always have pleasant memories of us and that you long to see us, just as we also long to see you. ⁷Therefore, brothers, in all our distress and persecution we were encouraged about you because of your faith. ⁸For now we really live, since you are standing firm in the Lord. ⁹How can we thank God enough for you in return for all the joy we have in the presence of our God because of you? ¹⁰Night and day we pray most earnestly that we may see you again and supply what is lacking in your faith.

¹¹Now may our God and Father himself and our Lord Jesus clear the way for us to come to you. ¹²May the Lord make your

ᶜ16 Or *them fully*   ᵈ2 Some manuscripts *brother and fellow worker;* other manuscripts *brother and God's servant*

severing in the face of opposition to your Christian faith? Who can you share that special encouragement with this week? **3.** Who has influenced you positively for godly living? What characterizes their life? How can you be more like that person for the sake of someone else this week? **4.** Make a list of all the characteristics of a faithful Christian worker given in this passage. Of these, which do you possess? Which of these do you want to work at developing

---

OPEN: As a kid, when and where did homesickness strike you the hardest? What did you do about it?

DIG: 1. Why do you think Paul called the Thessalonian church his "hope", "joy", and "crown"? **2.** If Paul promised the Thessalonian Christians trials and persecution when he was with them (v. 4), why do you think he is having to write to them about it now?

REFLECT: 1. If someone were to tell you that God promises a trouble-free life to those who are true Christians, how would you respond to them? **2.** How prepared are you to hang in there when Satan stops you? Are you more likely to press on, no matter what? Or re-group and plan a new attack? Or go home, saying "I'm tired"?

OPEN: What room in your childhood home fills you with the most pleasant memories? What happened there?

DIG: 1. What was it about Timothy's report which particularly encourages Paul? Why? What does this tell you about Paul's desires and concerns for the Thessalonians? **2.** What guidelines can you find in Paul's desires, concerns and prayers for those who disciple new Christians today?

REFLECT: 1. In what specific ways have you been encouraged by someone else's faith? Have you told them about it? **2.** Which of Paul's prayer requests would you want someone to pray for you right now? Do likewise for someone else in your small group.

---

love increase and overflow for each other and for everyone else, just as ours does for you. [13]May he strengthen your hearts so that you will be blameless and holy in the presence of our God and Father when our Lord Jesus comes with all his holy ones.

Living to Please God

4 Finally, brothers, we instructed you how to live in order to please God, as in fact you are living. Now we ask you and urge you in the Lord Jesus to do this more and more. [2]For you know what instructions we gave you by the authority of the Lord Jesus.

[3]It is God's will that you should be sanctified: that you should avoid sexual immorality; [4]that each of you should learn to control his own body* in a way that is holy and honorable, [5]not in passionate lust like the heathen, who do not know God; [6]and that in this matter no one should wrong his brother or take advantage of him. The Lord will punish men for all such sins, as we have already told you and warned you. [7]For God did not call us to be impure, but to live a holy life. [8]Therefore, he who rejects this instruction does not reject man but God, who gives you his Holy Spirit.

[9]Now about brotherly love we do not need to write to you, yourselves have been taught by God to love each other. [10]And in fact, you do love all the brothers throughout Macedonia. Yet we urge you, brothers, to do so more and more.

[11]Make it your ambition to lead a quiet life, to mind your own business and to work with your hands, just as we told you, [12]so that your daily life may win the respect of outsiders and so that you will not be dependent on anybody.

The Coming of the Lord

[13]Brothers, we do not want you to be ignorant about those who fall asleep, or to grieve like the rest of men, who have no hope. [14]We believe that Jesus died and rose again and so we believe that God will bring with Jesus those who have fallen asleep in him. [15]According to the Lord's own word, we tell you that we who are still alive, who are left till the coming of the Lord, will certainly not precede those who have fallen asleep. [16]For the Lord himself will come down from heaven, with a loud command, with the voice of the archangel and with the trumpet call of God, and the dead in Christ will rise first. [17]After that, we who are still alive and are left will be caught up together with them in the clouds to meet the Lord in the air. And so we will be with the Lord forever. [18]Therefore encourage each other with these words.

5 Now, brothers, about times and dates we do not need to write to you, [2]for you know very well that the day of the Lord will come like a thief in the night. [3]While people are saying, "Peace and safety," destruction will come on them suddenly, as labor pains on a pregnant woman, and they will not escape.

---

*4 Or *learn to live with his own wife; or learn to acquire a wife*

⁴But you, brothers, are not in darkness so that this day should surprise you like a thief. ⁵You are all sons of the light and sons of the day. We do not belong to the night or to the darkness. ⁶So then, let us not be like others, who are asleep, but let us be alert and self-controlled. ⁷For those who sleep, sleep at night, and those who get drunk, get drunk at night. ⁸But since we belong to the day, let us be self-controlled, putting on faith and love as a breastplate, and the hope of salvation as a helmet. ⁹For God did not appoint us to suffer wrath but to receive salvation through our Lord Jesus Christ. ¹⁰He died for us so that, whether we are awake or asleep, we may live together with him. ¹¹Therefore encourage one another and build each other up, just as in fact you are doing.

Final Instructions

¹²Now we ask you, brothers, to respect those who work hard among you, who are over you in the Lord and who admonish you. ¹³Hold them in the highest regard in love because of their work. Live in peace with each other. ¹⁴And we urge you, brothers, warn those who are idle, encourage the timid, help the weak, be patient with everyone. ¹⁵Make sure that nobody pays back wrong for wrong, but always try to be kind to each other and to everyone else.

¹⁶Be joyful always; ¹⁷pray continually; ¹⁸give thanks in all circumstances, for this is God's will for you in Christ Jesus.

¹⁹Do not put out the Spirit's fire; ²⁰do not treat prophecies with contempt. ²¹Test everything. Hold on to the good. ²²Avoid every kind of evil.

²³May God himself, the God of peace, sanctify you through and through. May your whole spirit, soul and body be kept blameless at the coming of our Lord Jesus Christ. ²⁴The one who calls you is faithful and he will do it.

²⁵Brothers, pray for us. ²⁶Greet all the brothers with a holy kiss. ²⁷I charge you before the Lord to have this letter read to all the brothers.

²⁸The grace of our Lord Jesus Christ be with you.

How can you as a group better help one another to put on faith, love, and hope?

OPEN: What causes you to "blow a gasket": Traffic jams? Christmas shopping? Bickering children? Burnt dinners? Or what?

DIG: 1. What's the connection here between the various elements of the Christian community (the pastors, the disreputable, the idle, the timid, the weak, those who like to get even, the grumpy, the ungrateful, the spiritual wet-blankets, the spiritual counterfeiters, the evildoers) and the commands Paul gives? **2.** When the Christian life of peace and order begins to sound impossible, what (or who) do you fall back on? How does this relate to verse 24?

REFLECT: 1. Of the various elements listed above, and the commands related to each, which ones are most relevant to your church? To your small group? To your life last week? Which ones do you feel you are practicing pretty well? **2.** If Paul were writing to you, would he add another command? Why? What would it be? **3.** Of these various exhortations, which one will you work on doing something about this week? **4.** What have you most appreciated about 1 Thessalonians? Why?

---

2 THESSALONIANS

INTRODUCTION

Characteristics

Why a Second Letter?

First and Second Thessalonians are very much alike. In fact, 2 Thessalonians covers almost the same ground as 1 Thessalonians, although in a more perfunctory fashion. There is thanksgiving for the faith and love of the Thessalonians, encouragement to them in the midst of their persecution, teaching about the Second Coming, and a warning against idleness. Furthermore, 2 Thessalonians was probably written within months, if not weeks, of 1 Thessalonians. Why was it necessary?

The answer may well be that Paul's first letter to these young, untaught Christians produced a serious misunderstanding that necessitated a second, clarifying letter. Specifically, his teaching that "the day of the Lord will come like a thief in the night" (1 Thess. 5:2) may have encouraged people to abandon normal pursuits to prepare for the Second Coming. Thus, he wrote 2 Thessalonians 2:1-12, outlining the events that must take place *prior to* the return of Christ. "The Second Coming is imminent," he seems to be saying, "but not so imminent that you have to stop everything else." Then he goes on to reiterate what he said in his earlier letter: Stand firm and do not be idle.

Amplifying a Theme

In fact, 1 and 2 Thessalonians compliment one another concerning the Second Coming. Paul's teaching in 1 Thessalonians "is mainly on a personal level: It is given in response to questions about the lot of believers who have died before the *Parousia*. This is followed by a brief reference to the Day of the Lord as it affects men and women in general: It will take the ungodly by surprise, but believers, being children of light, will be awake and prepared for it. In 2 Thessalonians believers are told further how they may be prepared for the great day. They will recognize the events which signal its approach" (F. F. Bruce, *1 and 2 Thessalonians: Word Biblical Commentary* Vol. 45 p. xliii).

"The Secret Power of Lawlessness"

Paul was not unaware of what was happening around him. To this point, the peaceful conditions in the Roman Empire had been of great value to the spread of Christianity. But "there were disquieting straws in the wind." There was mounting unrest in Judea, and this unrest had repercussions elsewhere, he and his colleagues learned in Thessalonica, where they were branded as men who had 'subverted the world.' By the time they had arrived in Corinth, they had heard of the expulsion of Jews from Rome. The troubles which had driven him from one Macedonian city after another were fresh in Paul's mind when 2 Thessalonians was written. Probably Gallio's encouraging judgment at Corinth had not yet been given. Roman law and order were still in control, but it was only too clear that the 'hidden power of lawlessness' was already at work, and it would probably continue to work until it erupted violently and swept all before it. When the Thessalonians were told that the Day of the Lord cannot arrive until the great rebellion has broken out, the Day is not being postponed to the indefinite future: the great rebellion might well break out within a few years. "If they paid heed to what they were being told, they would be ready—well informed as well as morally alert" (Bruce, *1 and 2 Thessalonians, p. xliii*).

The Audience

See the notes on 1 Thessalonians for further details about this church.

2 Thessalonians

1 Paul, Silas[a] and Timothy,

To the church of the Thessalonians in God our Father and the Lord Jesus Christ:

[2]Grace and peace to you from God the Father and the Lord Jesus Christ.

Thanksgiving and Prayer

[3]We ought always to thank God for you, brothers, and rightly so, because your faith is growing more and more, and the love every one of you has for each other is increasing. [4]Therefore, among God's churches we boast about your perseverance and faith in all the persecutions and trials you are enduring.

[5]All this is evidence that God's judgment is right, and as a result you will be counted worthy of the kingdom of God, for which you are suffering. [6]God is just: He will pay back trouble to those who trouble you [7]and give relief to you who are troubled, and to us as well. This will happen when the Lord Jesus is revealed from heaven in blazing fire with his powerful angels. [8]He will punish those who do not know God and do not obey the gospel of our Lord Jesus. [9]They will be punished with everlasting destruction and shut out from the presence of the Lord and from the majesty of his power [10]on the day he comes to be glorified in his holy people and to be marveled at among all those who have believed. This includes you, because you believed our testimony to you.

[11]With this in mind, we constantly pray for you, that our God may count you worthy of his calling, and that by his power he may fulfill every good purpose of yours and every act prompted by your faith. [12]We pray this so that the name of our Lord Jesus may be glorified in you, and you in him, according to the grace of our God and the Lord Jesus Christ.[b]

The Man of Lawlessness

2 Concerning the coming of our Lord Jesus Christ and our being gathered to him, we ask you, brothers, [2]not to become easily unsettled or alarmed by some prophecy, report or letter supposed to have come from us, saying that the day of the Lord has already come. [3]Don't let anyone deceive you in any way, for that day will not come, until the rebellion occurs and the man of lawlessness[c] is revealed, the man doomed to destruction. [4]He will oppose and will exalt himself over everything that is called God or is worshiped, so that he sets himself up in God's temple, proclaiming himself to be God.

[5]Don't you remember that when I was with you I used to tell you these things? [6]And now you know what is holding him back, so that he may be revealed at the proper time. [7]For the secret

a1 Greek *Silvanus*, a variant of *Silas*   *b12* Or *God and Lord, Jesus Christ*
c3 Some manuscripts *sin*

REFLECT: **1.** What do you think would be the result of choosing to "love the truth"? **2.** Do you see the church today any better informed or morally alert for the end times? What do we need to do in order not to be deceived?

OPEN: If I want you to remember something, should I tell you or should I write it down? Why?

REFLECT: **1.** How has God taken the initiative in our salvation? What does he continue to do for us? What are we to do? What specific steps could you take to continue to stand firm? **2.** Where do you need the most encouragement and strength right now?

REFLECT: What part does prayer play in the spread of the gospel? In protecting us from evil? Are you one who works at prayer or do you let prayer work on you? Why? Are you more likely to talk to a brother about Christ or to Christ about a brother? Why? How are God's love and Christ's perseverance needed now in your life?

OPEN: **1.** What was your first paid job? How hard did you work at it? What did you do with your money? **2.** What kind of rules did your family have about eating? What happened if you broke the rules?

DIG: **1.** How might I Thess. 5:1-3 have been misunderstood by these people leading to the problem Paul addresses here? How does he use his own example to correct them? **2.** From I Thess. 4:11, why would Paul view idleness as a serious problem? What is the purpose of disciplining the offenders?

REFLECT: **1.** What do you think idleness has to do with a person's relationship to Christ? Why? What is the place of daily work and mundane tasks in the life of a Christian?

power of lawlessness is already at work; but the one who now holds it back will continue to do so till he is taken out of the way. [8]And then the lawless one will be revealed, whom the Lord Jesus will overthrow with the breath of his mouth and destroy by the splendor of his coming. [9]The coming of the lawless one will be in accordance with the work of Satan displayed in all kinds of counterfeit miracles, signs and wonders, [10]and in every sort of evil that deceives those who are perishing. They perish because they refused to love the truth and so be saved. [11]For this reason God sends them a powerful delusion so that they will believe the lie [12]and so that all will be condemned who have not believed the truth but have delighted in wickedness.

Stand Firm

[13]But we ought always to thank God for you, brothers loved by the Lord, because from the beginning God chose you[d] to be saved through the sanctifying work of the Spirit and through belief in the truth. [14]He called you to this through our gospel, that you might share in the glory of our Lord Jesus Christ. [15]So then, brothers, stand firm and hold to the teachings[e] we passed on to you, whether by word of mouth or by letter.

[16]May our Lord Jesus Christ himself and God our Father, who loved us and by his grace gave us eternal encouragement and good hope, [17]encourage your hearts and strengthen you in every good deed and word.

Request for Prayer

3 Finally, brothers, pray for us that the message of the Lord may spread rapidly and be honored, just as it was with you. [2]And pray that we may be delivered from wicked and evil men, for not everyone has faith. [3]But the Lord is faithful, and he will strengthen and protect you from the evil one. [4]We have confidence in the Lord that you are doing and will continue to do the things we command. [5]May the Lord direct your hearts into God's love and Christ's perseverance.

Warning Against Idleness

[6]In the name of the Lord Jesus Christ, we command you, brothers, to keep away from every brother who is idle and does not live according to the teaching[f] you received from us. [7]For you yourselves know how you ought to follow our example. We were not idle when we were with you, [8]nor did we eat anyone's food without paying for it. On the contrary, we worked night and day, laboring and toiling so that we would not be a burden to any of you. [9]We did this, not because we do not have the right to such help, but in order to make ourselves a model for you to follow. [10]For even when we were with you, we gave you this rule: "If a man will not work, he shall not eat."

[11]We hear that some among you are idle. They are not busy; they are busybodies. [12]Such people we command and urge in the Lord Jesus Christ to settle down and earn the bread they eat.

---

d13 Some manuscripts *because God chose you as his firstfruits*   *e15* Or *traditions*   *f6* Or *tradition*

¹³And as for you, brothers, never tire of doing what is right.

¹⁴If anyone does not obey our instruction in this letter, take special note of him. Do not associate with him, in order that he may feel ashamed. ¹⁵Yet do not regard him as an enemy, but warn him as a brother.

Final Greetings

¹⁶Now may the Lord of peace himself give you peace at all times and in every way. The Lord be with all of you.

¹⁷I, Paul, write this greeting in my own hand, which is the distinguishing mark in all my letters. This is how I write.

¹⁸The grace of our Lord Jesus Christ be with you all.

2. If an adult family member or friend sponged off you constantly, what would you do?

OPEN: What would a handwriting analysis reveal about your personality: Are you more lake a doctor (illegible writing)? Or an English teacher (model penmanship)? Or a nerd (totally computerized)?

DIG: Why does Paul have to emphasize the closing of this letter in his own hand (see 2:2)? How is the close of the letter similar to its beginning? What does Paul emphasize in both places? Why do you think he emphasizes this? What does it tell you about God's will for us? Considering the hard things Paul has to say in the middle between the two ends, what impact do you think his letter had on the original readers?

REFLECT: 1. On a peace-rating scale of 1-10 (1 is "Blissfully peacefull", 10 is "High anxiety"), where would you rate your sense of over-all peace? Where in particular do you need this group to pray for you to have peace right now? **2.** If you were to sum up 2 Thessalonians in your own words what would you say to someone who is suffering persecution? To someone who is idle? To someone who is lacking faith?

---

1 TIMOTHY

INTRODUCTION

The Pastoral Letters

In 1726, Paul Anton of Halle gave a series of lectures about 1 and 2 Timothy and Titus that he entitled "The Pastoral Epistles." Ever since, this name has stuck to these three books—with unfortunate results. Because of the title, these books have come to be viewed, in Anton's words, as consisting "mostly of advice to younger ministers." They are understood to be church manuals in which one finds instructions on church organization and guidelines for ministry.

There are real problems with this view, not the least of which is that denominations as diverse as Roman Catholics, Plymouth Brethren, and Presbyterians all claim to have found their organizational guidelines within the Pastoral Epistles (Gordon Fee, *1 and 2 Timothy, Titus: A Good News Commentary*, p. xxxii). The dramatically different structures in these three denominations proves that whatever the Pastoral Epistles might be, they are not primarily guides to church order.

"First Timothy is not intended to *establish* church order, but to *respond* in a very *ad hoc* way to the Ephesian situation with its straying elders. To put it another way: What we learn about church order in 1 Timothy is not so much organizational as reformational. We see *reflections* of church structure, not organizational charts; paradigms, not imperatives; qualifications, not duties; the correcting of error and abuse, not a 'How to' manual on church organization" (Gordon Fee, "The Sticky Wicket: Intentionality and Particularity/Externality," an unpublished paper, pp. 8-9)

The Audience

Timothy—Paul's Friend and Colleague

When Paul first met Timothy, he was living at Lystra in the Roman province of Galatia (modern Turkey). Timothy was the child of a mixed marriage. His father was a Gentile and his mother was Jewish (Acts 16:1). Timothy, along with his mother Eunice and his grandmother Lois, was probably converted during Paul's first missionary journey (Acts 14:8-25; compare 2 Tim. 3:10-11). By the time of Paul's second visit to the area a year or two later, Timothy had matured so much as a Christian that the local church recommended Timothy to Paul as a traveling companion (Acts 16:2). However, Paul decided that Timothy must be circumcised first to legitimize him in the eyes of Paul's Jewish critics. Without circumcision, they would have considered him a Gentile (because of his Greek father), even though he had been brought up in his mother's religion.

From this point on, Timothy seems to be associated with Paul's ministry in one way or another. He was a co-worker with Paul (Rom. 16:21; 1 Thess. 3:2; 1 Cor. 16:10; Phil. 2:22). He collaborated in the writing of six of Paul's letters (1 and 2 Thess., 2 Cor., Phil., Col., and Philem.). He was Paul's trusted representative on three missions before this one in Ephesus (to Thessalonica around A.D. 50; to Corinth between A.D. 53 and 54; and to Philippi around A.D. 60-62).

Timothy was not just a colleague of Paul's; he was a beloved friend. Paul called him "my son whom I love, who is faithful in the Lord" (1 Cor. 4:17). In Philippians 2:20-22, the aging apostle says: "I have no one else like him . . . Timothy has proved himself, because as a son with his father he has served with me in the work of the gospel."

A Personal Letter

The three so-called Pastoral Epistles (plus Philemon) are set apart from the other letters written by Paul; they are addressed to persons, not churches. In the case of 1 Timothy, however, it seems that Paul intended to write his instructions directly to the church but was unable to do so, since the local leadership was itself the problem. Consequently, he wrote to the church via his envoy, Timothy. There are few personal remarks in 1 Timothy, and all of these are directed toward Timothy's commission to restore proper order in the church (see 1:18-19; 4:6-16; 6:11-21).

Theme

Paul tells us why he wrote 1 Timothy:

As I urged you when I went into Macedonia, stay there in Ephesus so that you may command certain men not to teach false doctrines any longer. . . . (1:3).

Although I hope to come to you soon, I am writing you these instructions so that, if I am delayed, you will know how people ought to conduct themselves in God's household, which is the church of the living God, the pillar and foundation of the truth (3:14-15).

Timothy had been left in Ephesus for one purpose: to prevent those who had "shipwrecked their [own] faith" (1:19) from corrupting the rest of the church (see 2 Tim. 2:17-18). He was Paul's apostolic delegate, taking temporary charge of the Ephesian church during the crises it was facing.

The False Teachers

Who were these false teachers who had so upset the Ephesian church? Were they outsiders who had infiltrated the church? Were they philosophers unaffiliated with the church, but whose ideas were being listened to nevertheless? Or were these false teachers members of the church itself?

The best guess is that these troubling teachers were *elders* of the Ephesian church! A careful reading of 1 Timothy seems to indicate this. First of all, it is clear that the teaching in Ephesians was done by the elders (3:2; 5:17). Furthermore, Paul devotes considerable space to outlining the qualifications for leaders in the church. These qualifications contrast sharply with what he says about the false teachers. For example, the false teachers "forbid people to marry" (4:3). Paul says that an overseer (elder), in contrast, "must be . . . the husband of but one wife" and "must manage his own family well" (3:2, 4-5; see also 3:12). The false teachers "think that godliness is a means to financial gain" (6:5); whereas an elder must "not [be] a lover of money" (3:3). In other words, Paul is saying: "Here is what true elders are like, in contrast to your erring elders." Finally in 5:17-25, he outlines the process of selection and discipline of elders "who sin" (v. 20).

Paul had a sense that this might happen in Ephesus. In his farewell address he said, "Even from your own number men will arise and distort the truth in order to draw away disciples after them" (Acts 20:30).

Two further notes: From various references (2:9-15; 5:11-15; 2 Tim. 3:6-7), it appears that these false teachers were listened to, supported, and encouraged by some of the women in the church, especially younger widows. Second, it is likely that the church in Ephesus was not a single large body that met together on Sunday. Rather, it consisted of a number of house churches some of which had been taken over by the false teachers.

The Nature of the False Teaching

As is often the case, since we have only Paul's response to the problem and not a clear exposition of it, we are forced to deduce the nature of the heresy. From the text, it seems that the false teachers were involved in esoteric speculation rather than the exposition of accepted Christian teaching. Furthermore, the teachers were proud, arrogant, disputatious, and greedy. They used religion to make money and gain power. Their false teaching was connected with the Old Testament, but it also had an ascetic component and a strong Greek element. It appears to be much like the false teaching in the Lycus valley churches (see the introduction to Colossians).

1 Timothy

OPEN: What chores were you assigned at home? Who was put in charge of things when your parents left on a trip? How did your parents settle disputes between you and your brother/sister?

DIG: 1. What assignment is Timothy given? On what authority? For what purpose? How do you suppose Timothy feels about being left in charge? Left behind? Being left in conflict? Affirmed "my true son"? **2.** What three blessings (v. 2), personal qualities (v. 5), and theological resources (vv. 8, 11) did Paul remind Timothy to appropriate for this task? **3.** What should be the basis for settling disputes: truth, love, faith, law, sincerity? Why? **4.** How and for whom does one use the law "properly"?

REFLECT: 1. Who was the Bible teacher, if anyone, who grounded you in the faith? **2.** Have you ever been in a situation where sound "doctrine" was not balanced with "pure heart, good concience and sincere faith"? What happened? **3.** How would you describe your own balance in these four areas?

OPEN: 1. Who holds the record in your group for the most speeding tickets? The most days of playing hookey from school? **2.** Between your Mom and Dad, who was the disciplinarian?

DIG: 1. Why do you think Paul took the time to explain his "past life" to Timothy? **2.** How is Paul's testimony like a teeter-totter (balancing sin and grace, self and Christ, etc.)? **3.** How is Paul's testimony like sailing? (How does one avoid being ship wrecked? Which is the sail and the rudder?) **4.** In what sense are Paul, Hymenaeus, and Alexander each an example of God's patience and mercy?

REFLECT: 1. When has your faith come the closest to being "ship wrecked"? What did you learn from this? **2.** What word would you use to describe your life before you became a Christian? Since then? **3.** From your own experience, what could you say to a seeker about God's "patience and mercy"?

1 Paul, an apostle of Christ Jesus by the command of God our Savior and of Christ Jesus our hope,

²To Timothy my true son in the faith:

Grace, mercy and peace from God the Father and Christ Jesus our Lord.

Warning Against False Teachers of the Law

³As I urged you when I went into Macedonia, stay there in Ephesus so that you may command certain men not to teach false doctrines any longer ⁴nor to devote themselves to myths and endless genealogies. These promote controversies rather than God's work—which is by faith. ⁵The goal of this command is love, which comes from a pure heart and a good conscience and a sincere faith. ⁶Some have wandered away from these and turned to meaningless talk. ⁷They want to be teachers of the law, but they do not know what they are talking about or what they so confidently affirm.

⁸We know that the law is good if one uses it properly. ⁹We also know that law*ᵃ* is made not for the righteous but for lawbreakers and rebels, the ungodly and sinful, the unholy and irreligious; for those who kill their fathers or mothers, for murderers, ¹⁰for adulterers and perverts, for slave traders and liars and perjurers—and for whatever else is contrary to the sound doctrine ¹¹that conforms to the glorious gospel of the blessed God, which he entrusted to me.

The Lord's Grace to Paul

¹²I thank Christ Jesus our Lord, who has given me strength, that he considered me faithful, appointing me to his service. ¹³Even though I was once a blasphemer and a persecutor and a violent man, I was shown mercy because I acted in ignorance and unbelief. ¹⁴The grace of our Lord was poured out on me abundantly, along with the faith and love that are in Christ Jesus.

¹⁵Here is a trustworthy saying that deserves full acceptance: Christ Jesus came into the world to save sinners—of whom I am the worst. ¹⁶But for that very reason I was shown mercy so that in me, the worst of sinners, Christ Jesus might display his unlimited patience as an example for those who would believe on him and receive eternal life. ¹⁷Now to the King eternal, immortal, invisible, the only God, be honor and glory for ever and ever. Amen.

¹⁸Timothy, my son, I give you this instruction in keeping with the prophecies once made about you, so that by following them you may fight the good fight, ¹⁹holding on to faith and a good conscience. Some have rejected these and so have shipwrecked their faith. ²⁰Among them are Hymenaeus and Alexander, whom I have handed over to Satan to be taught not to blaspheme.

ᵃ9 Or that the law

Instructions on Worship

2 I urge, then, first of all, that requests, prayers, intercession and thanksgiving be made for everyone— ²for kings and all those in authority, that we may live peaceful and quiet lives in all godliness and holiness. ³This is good, and pleases God our Savior, ⁴who wants all men to be saved and to come to a knowledge of the truth. ⁵For there is one God and one mediator between God and men, the man Christ Jesus, ⁶who gave himself as a ransom for all men—the testimony given in its proper time. ⁷And for this purpose I was appointed a herald and an apostle—I am telling the truth, I am not lying—and a teacher of the true faith to the Gentiles.

⁸I want men everywhere to lift up holy hands in prayer, without anger or disputing.

⁹I also want women to dress modestly, with decency and propriety, not with braided hair or gold or pearls or expensive clothes, ¹⁰but with good deeds, appropriate for women who profess to worship God.

¹¹A woman should learn in quietness and full submission. ¹²I do not permit a woman to teach or to have authority over a man; she must be silent. ¹³For Adam was formed first, then Eve. ¹⁴And Adam was not the one deceived; it was the woman who was deceived and became a sinner. ¹⁵But women *ᵇ* will be saved *ᶜ* through childbearing—if they continue in faith, love and holiness with propriety.

Overseers and Deacons

3 Here is a trustworthy saying: If anyone sets his heart on being an overseer, *ᵈ* he desires a noble task. ²Now the overseer must be above reproach, the husband of but one wife, temperate, self-controlled, respectable, hospitable, able to teach, ³not given to drunkenness, not violent but gentle, not quarrelsome, not a lover of money. ⁴He must manage his own family well and see that his children obey him with proper respect. ⁵(If anyone does not know how to manage his own family, how can he take care of God's church?) ⁶He must not be a recent convert, or he may become conceited and fall under the same judgment as the devil. ⁷He must also have a good reputation with outsiders, so that he will not fall into disgrace and into the devil's trap.

⁸Deacons, likewise, are to be men worthy of respect, sincere, not indulging in much wine, and not pursuing dishonest gain. ⁹They must keep hold of the deep truths of the faith with a clear conscience. ¹⁰They must first be tested; and then if there is nothing against them, let them serve as deacons.

¹¹In the same way, their wives *ᵉ* are to be women worthy of respect, not malicious talkers but temperate and trustworthy in everything.

¹²A deacon must be the husband of but one wife and must manage his children and his household well. ¹³Those who have served well gain an excellent standing and great assurance in their faith in Christ Jesus.

ᵇ15 Greek *she*   *ᶜ15* Or *restored*   *ᵈ1* Traditionally *bishop*; also in verse 2
ᵉ11 Or *way*, *deaconesses*

OPEN: Where did you go to church when you were a kid? What could you do, and not do, on Sundays? Who tucked you in at night and heard your prayers?

DIG: 1. What reasons does Paul assert to justify the universal scope and number one priority of prayer? **2.** What is the relation here between godliness and prayer? Between prayer and salvation? Between pregnancy and salvation (v. 15)? Between certain women in public ministry and their affect on the prayers of men? **3.** In this context, what is Paul specifically prohibiting: Both women teaching and women having authority over men? Or just women teaching in a domineering (usurping) way over men? What is "cultural" (limited application) and what is "universal" (wide application) in this passage? What is the basis for your opinion?

REFLECT: 1. With regard to your prayer life, what hinders you? Helps you? **2.** What have you found helpful in affirming your personhood in a church and society that often treats people unequally?

OPEN: 1. Recall a "PK" (Preacher's Kid) you know. What were the special "expectations" put on this person. **2.** Were you a "little angel" or a "big brat" when left with a new babysitter? Why?

DIG: 1. Since the Ephesian church already had leaders, why is Timothy given this list of qualifications for leadership? Why a list of qualifications only, and not duties also? What, if anything, is distinctly Christian about these qualifications? Why are all these qualifications outward, not inward, in orientation? **2.** How do you interpret "the husband of one wife"? Does that mean the overseer must not be single? Divorced? Widowed? Remarried? A polygamist? Or does it demand sexual fidelity if married (see also 5:9)? **3.** What kind of "test" do you suppose the deacons are given? Why? **4.** What is Paul's main purpose for writing these instructions to Timothy?

REFLECT: How could your church profit from a network of house group leaders with these qualifications? Supposing you were on the search committee for your church, responsible for finding ten people (or couples) who would meet these qualifications, who comes to mind?

¹⁴Although I hope to come to you soon, I am writing you these instructions so that, ¹⁵if I am delayed, you will know how people ought to conduct themselves in God's household, which is the church of the living God, the pillar and foundation of the truth. ¹⁶Beyond all question, the mystery of godliness is great:

> He*ᶠ* appeared in a body,*ᵍ*
>> was vindicated by the Spirit,
> was seen by angels,
>> was preached among the nations,
> was believed on in the world,
>> was taken up in glory.

Instructions to Timothy

4 The Spirit clearly says that in later times some will abandon the faith and follow deceiving spirits and things taught by demons. ²Such teachings come through hypocritical liars, whose consciences have been seared as with a hot iron. ³They forbid people to marry and order them to abstain from certain foods, which God created to be received with thanksgiving by those who believe and who know the truth. ⁴For everything God created is good, and nothing is to be rejected if it is received with thanksgiving, ⁵because it is consecrated by the word of God and prayer.

⁶If you point these things out to the brothers, you will be a good minister of Christ Jesus, brought up in the truths of the faith and of the good teaching that you have followed. ⁷Have nothing to do with godless myths and old wives' tales; rather, train yourself to be godly. ⁸For physical training is of some value, but godliness has value for all things, holding promise for both the present life and the life to come.

⁹This is a trustworthy saying that deserves full acceptance ¹⁰(and for this we labor and strive), that we have put our hope in the living God, who is the Savior of all men, and especially of those who believe.

¹¹Command and teach these things. ¹²Don't let anyone look down on you because you are young, but set an example for the believers in speech, in life, in love, in faith and in purity. ¹³Until I come, devote yourself to the public reading of Scripture, to preaching and to teaching. ¹⁴Do not neglect your gift, which was given you through a prophetic message when the body of elders laid their hands on you.

¹⁵Be diligent in these matters; give yourself wholly to them, so that everyone may see your progress. ¹⁶Watch your life and doctrine closely. Persevere in them, because if you do, you will save both yourself and your hearers.

Advice About Widows, Elders and Slaves

5 Do not rebuke an older man harshly, but exhort him as if he were your father. Treat younger men as brothers, ²older women as mothers, and younger women as sisters, with absolute purity.

³Give proper recognition to those widows who are really in

OPEN: 1. What parting words did your parents always say when you were leaving home? **2.** What do you do to keep in shape physically? **3.** What "rites of passage" did you have to pass through as an adolescent to prove your manhood or womanhood?

DIG: 1. How does Paul combat the false teachings at Ephesus? Why is it hypocritical to preach abstinence from marriage and certain foods? **2.** What analogy and promises does Paul give to help Timothy train to be godly? **3.** Will Timothy's hearers be more convinced of the truth by the life he lives? Or by the Scriptures he reads? Or the spiritual gift he exercises? Or the company he keeps? Or by dressing for success? Why?

REFLECT: 1. What lies are currently being taught in your Christian circles about what a Christian can and can't do? If your friend was being swayed by these teachings what would you say? Do? **2.** If you were to design a spiritual fitness training program comparable to the one you use to keep physically fit, what would it consist of? Why?

OPEN: 1. When you were growing up, did your family ever struggle financially? What did you do to compensate? **2.** Today what do you do if, and when, there's consistently more month left at the end of the money? Who would you turn to for help? Why or why not?

ᶠ16 Some manuscripts God   *ᵍ16 Or in the flesh*

need. ⁴But if a widow has children or grandchildren, these should learn first of all to put their religion into practice by caring for their own family and so repaying their parents and grandparents, for this is pleasing to God. ⁵The widow who is really in need and left all alone puts her hope in God and continues night and day to pray and to ask God for help. ⁶But the widow who lives for pleasure is dead even while she lives. ⁷Give the people these instructions, too, so that no one may be open to blame. ⁸If anyone does not provide for his relatives, and especially for his immediate family, he has denied the faith and is worse than an unbeliever.

⁹No widow may be put on the list of widows unless she is over sixty, has been faithful to her husband,ʰ ¹⁰and is well known for her good deeds, such as bringing up children, showing hospitality, washing the feet of the saints, helping those in trouble and devoting herself to all kinds of good deeds.

¹¹As for younger widows, do not put them on such a list. For when their sensual desires overcome their dedication to Christ, they want to marry. ¹²Thus they bring judgment on themselves, because they have broken their first pledge. ¹³Besides, they get into the habit of being idle and going about from house to house. And not only do they become idlers, but also gossips and busybodies, saying things they ought not to. ¹⁴So I counsel younger widows to marry, to have children, to manage their homes and to give the enemy no opportunity for slander. ¹⁵Some have in fact already turned away to follow Satan.

¹⁶If any woman who is a believer has widows in her family, she should help them and not let the church be burdened with them, so that the church can help those widows who are really in need.

¹⁷The elders who direct the affairs of the church well are worthy of double honor, especially those whose work is preaching and teaching. ¹⁸For the Scripture says, "Do not muzzle the ox while it is treading out the grain,"ⁱ and "The worker deserves his wages."ʲ ¹⁹Do not entertain an accusation against an elder unless it is brought by two or three witnesses. ²⁰Those who sin are to be rebuked publicly, so that the others may take warning.

²¹I charge you, in the sight of God and Christ Jesus and the elect angels, to keep these instructions without partiality, and to do nothing out of favoritism.

²²Do not be hasty in the laying on of hands, and do not share in the sins of others. Keep yourself pure.

²³Stop drinking only water, and use a little wine because of your stomach and your frequent illnesses.

²⁴The sins of some men are obvious, reaching the place of judgment ahead of them; the sins of others trail behind them. ²⁵In the same way, good deeds are obvious, and even those that are not cannot be hidden.

6 All who are under the yoke of slavery should consider their masters worthy of full respect, so that God's name and our teaching may not be slandered. ²Those who have believing masters are not to show less respect for them because they are

DIG: 1. From what you read between the lines, what was the problem concerning widows in this church? What distinguishes the various kinds of widows? How differently is the church to respond to each kind (see also Acts 6:1-6)? How might this welfare system become corrupted? How might Paul's strategy (v. 9-15) eliminate the dangers of corruption? **2.** What are some applicable principles from this passage that bear on the church and government welfare programs of today? **3.** Why are church elders in general especially liable to "double honor"? To public rebuke? To hidden sins? **4.** How would the early church protect a leader from a frivolous or malicious charge (v. 19-20)? **5.** Why might a Christian slave's lack of respect for his master result in the slander of God's name and Christian teaching? **6.** Do you think these verses promote the institution of slavery? Why or why not?

REFLECT: 1. How many widows are there in your extended family? At present, how are their needs met? **2.** When, if ever, have you suddenly become single? What was that time like? **3.** How would you evaluate what your church is doing now for those in need? **4.** Of these various instructions, which one has your name on it? Why?

ʰ9 Or has had but one husband   ⁱ18 Deut. 25:4   ʲ18 Luke 10:7

brothers. Instead, they are to serve them even better, because those who benefit from their service are believers, and dear to them. These are the things you are to teach and urge on them.

Love of Money

³If anyone teaches false doctrines and does not agree to the sound instruction of our Lord Jesus Christ and to godly teaching, ⁴he is conceited and understands nothing. He has an unhealthy interest in controversies and quarrels about words that result in envy, strife, malicious talk, evil suspicions ⁵and constant friction between men of corrupt mind, who have been robbed of the truth and who think that godliness is a means to financial gain.

⁶But godliness with contentment is great gain. ⁷For we brought nothing into the world, and we can take nothing out of it. ⁸But if we have food and clothing, we will be content with that. ⁹People who want to get rich fall into temptation and a trap and into many foolish and harmful desires that plunge men into ruin and destruction. ¹⁰For the love of money is a root of all kinds of evil. Some people, eager for money, have wandered from the faith and pierced themselves with many griefs.

Paul's Charge to Timothy

¹¹But you, man of God, flee from all this, and pursue righteousness, godliness, faith, love, endurance and gentleness. ¹²Fight the good fight of the faith. Take hold of the eternal life to which you were called when you made your good confession in the presence of many witnesses. ¹³In the sight of God, who gives life to everything, and of Christ Jesus, who while testifying before Pontius Pilate made the good confession, I charge you ¹⁴to keep this command without spot or blame until the appearing of our Lord Jesus Christ, ¹⁵which God will bring about in his own time—God, the blessed and only Ruler, the King of kings and Lord of lords, ¹⁶who alone is immortal and who lives in unapproachable light, whom no one has seen or can see. To him be honor and might forever. Amen.

¹⁷Command those who are rich in this present world not to be arrogant nor to put their hope in wealth, which is so uncertain, but to put their hope in God, who richly provides us with everything for our enjoyment. ¹⁸Command them to do good, to be rich in good deeds, and to be generous and willing to share. ¹⁹In this way they will lay up treasure for themselves as a firm foundation for the coming age, so that they may take hold of the life that is truly life.

²⁰Timothy, guard what has been entrusted to your care. Turn away from godless chatter and the opposing ideas of what is falsely called knowledge, ²¹which some have professed and in so doing have wandered from the faith.

Grace be with you.

OPEN: If your house caught on fire, and you could only rescue the children and three material items, what three would you choose and why?

DIG: 1. What motivates these false teachers? With what results? **2.** What is the "great gain" in "godliness with contentment" (v. 6)?

REFLECT: 1. How important is it to you to win word battles with your spouse? Your peers? **2.** If you could reduce your financial commitments and simplify your lifestyle, would you do it? What's holding you back? How could your small group help one another go forward in this area?

OPEN: 1. When you were growing up, did your parents tend to overprotect you, or push you beyond your limits? **2.** With your kids, what are you going to do differently when it comes to risk-taking versus playing it safe?

DIG: 1. Of the four commands and several character traits by which Paul begins his final appeal to Timothy (vv. 11-12), which ones sound the most encouraging? Why? **2.** What does Paul's "fight" imagery tell you about the nature of the Christian life? **3.** What is Paul saying about the already wealthy: That their wealth is sinful? That it's a temptation? A great responsibility to help others? A great means to attain heavenly riches for oneself? Or what? **4.** Given Paul's lengthy stay and comprehensive teaching at Ephesus, why is that church easily side-tracked by irrelevancies (6:20; also 5:3-5; 4:1-3) and susceptible to false teachers (also Acts 20:27-31)? **5.** How would you rate Paul as a "fight coach" for Timothy?

REFLECT: 1. Using the allegory of a "fight", how would you compare your spiritual life to a 15-round championship match: Are you winning? Losing? Tied? Going strong? Winded? Down for the count? **2.** As you look back, who was the "Paul" who served as a spiritual fight coach in your life and gave you the strong advice when you needed it? **3.** Who is a "Timothy" in your life for whom you can be a "Paul"?

2 TIMOTHY

INTRODUCTION

The Last Letter

Second Timothy is probably the last epistle Paul ever wrote. He is an old man now, in prison once again, deserted by most all of his friends, and facing the likely prospect of death. "For I am already being poured out like a drink offering, and the time has come for my departure. I have fought the good fight, I have finished the race, I have kept the faith. Now there is in store for me the crown of righteousness" (4:6-8). Bishop Handley Moule once said that he found it difficult to read 2 Timothy "without finding something like a mist gathering in the eyes" (*The Second Epistle to Timothy: The Devotional Commentary*, p. 16).

Audience

Timothy's Time

Indeed, 2 Timothy is deeply moving as Paul writes the younger man, imploring him to come and be with him in the waning days of his life. In 2 Timothy, the urgency of the problem in Ephesus is the background. Paul's more pressing need is to have Timothy at his side once again. Even more than personal comfort, Paul wants to pass on the torch of his ministry to Timothy.

Timothy was the logical choice for this new responsibility. He had been Paul's trusted colleague for over fifteen years, and he really cared for the welfare of the churches (Phil. 2:20-22). This was a crucial time for the churches in Europe and Asia. They seemed fragile in the face of the forces pressing against them. For one thing, Rome had turned against Christianity. Nero seemed bent on destroying the church. Furthermore, in Asia there had been widespread apostasy (1:15). Only a generation after Christ's resurrection, "Christianity . . . trembled, humanly speaking, on the verge of annihilation" (Moule, *The Second Epistle to Timothy*, p. 18). But Paul's ministry was over. No longer could he travel through the Roman Empire putting out fires, correcting errors, establishing order. Now it was up to Timothy and the others.

To lay this responsibility on Timothy was not easy. In many ways he was an unlikely leader. He was relatively young by Roman standards, in his mid-thirties (1 Tim. 4:12; 2 Tim. 2:22). He was prone to illness (1 Tim. 5:23). And he was, apparently, somewhat shy and in need of encouragement (2 Tim. 1:7-8; 2:1, 3; 3:12-14; 4:15); to his credit, Timothy overcame his natural inclination and tackled risky assignments for Paul (e.g., in Corinth).

If Timothy did not make it to Rome in time, these instructions in 2 Timothy would have to suffice. Paul's last letter was a crucial one.

Paul's Situation

It is difficult to trace Paul's movements during the period when he wrote the Pastoral Epistles. The best guess is that after being released from the house arrest in Rome (described at the end of Acts), Paul went on another preaching tour taking with him Timothy and Titus. In the course of their travels, they came to Crete. When it came time to move on, Paul left Titus behind to appoint proper leaders for the new church there. Paul and Timothy went to Macedonia via Ephesus. At Ephesus, Paul discovered that heresy was rotting away the church. So he excommunicated Hymenaeus and Alexander, two of the erring leaders (1 Tim. 1:19-20), and he left Timothy behind to help the church through its difficulties (1 Tim. 1:3-4). Paul himself went on to Macedonia. Once there he wrote both 1 Timothy and Titus (hence the similarity between the two letters).

Paul wintered in the Adriatic seacoast town of Nicopolis where he was (presumably) joined by Titus. In the spring, Paul started back to Ephesus, only to be arrested along the way—

probably at Troas at the instigation of Alexander the metalworker (2 Tim. 4:13-15).

Paul was eventually taken back to Rome and thrown into prison. This time he was not allowed the relative comfort of a rented house with twenty-four-hour-a-day guards, as was the case during his first imprisonment. Instead he was chained and thrown into a dark, damp dungeon (1:16), "like a criminal" (2:9). Onesiphorus was able to find Paul only after a long search (1:17). Paul was cold ("bring the cloak," 4:13), bored ("bring . . . my scrolls, especially the parchments," 4:13), and lonely ("only Luke is with me," 4:11). He had already had a preliminary hearing (4:16-17). His full trial was yet to come, and he did not expect to be acquitted. Nero's insane persecution of the Christians was at its height.

So Paul wrote Timothy to come to him in Rome. He sent this letter (2 Timothy) via Tychicus, who was to replace Timothy in Ephesus. (See also Fee, *1 and 2 Timothy, Titus,* p. xix.)

Characteristics

Although 2 Timothy is similar in content and focus to both 1 Timothy and Titus, there are some marked differences. Second Timothy is far more personal than 1 Timothy. First Timothy has the feel of a business letter containing important instructions to be heeded by the local congregation. But in 2 Timothy, Paul is writing to Timothy and not to the church, and he reminisces about the work he and Timothy did together. His primary purpose is not combating heresy (although that is a background concern), but to call Timothy to join him in Rome.

In fact, it is Paul's altered situation that gives 2 Timothy its distinct flavor. There is an urgency to his writing. His ministry is over. He tells Timothy to "fan into flame the gift of God, which is in you" (1:6). Timothy must "not be ashamed to testify about our Lord" (1:8). He must "guard the good deposit that was entrusted" to him (1:14). "Preach the Word" (4:2), Paul says, "in season and out of season." So Paul instructs his heir apparent.

Second Timothy is also characterized, somewhat surprisingly, by a note of triumph. Paul knows that despite all the difficulties he is facing, despite the pressure on the church, the gospel will prevail. It cannot be chained even if he is chained (2:9). Nor will the church ultimately be hampered. It, too, will prevail (2:11-13; 4:8). Therefore, Paul writes to Timothy to carry on the work of the gospel despite persecution, despite Paul's death, because God's kingdom will prevail (3:10-4:8).

2 Timothy

1 Paul, an apostle of Christ Jesus by the will of God, according to the promise of life that is in Christ Jesus,

²To Timothy, my dear son:

Grace, mercy and peace from God the Father and Christ Jesus our Lord.

Encouragement to Be Faithful

³I thank God, whom I serve, as my forefathers did, with a clear conscience, as night and day I constantly remember you in my prayers. ⁴Recalling your tears, I long to see you, so that I may be filled with joy. ⁵I have been reminded of your sincere faith, which first lived in your grandmother Lois and in your mother Eunice and, I am persuaded, now lives in you also. ⁶For this reason I remind you to fan into flame the gift of God, which is in you through the laying on of my hands. ⁷For God did not give us a spirit of timidity, but a spirit of power, of love and of self-discipline.

⁸So do not be ashamed to testify about our Lord, or ashamed of me his prisoner. But join with me in suffering for the gospel, by the power of God, ⁹who has saved us and called us to a holy life—not because of anything we have done but because of his own purpose and grace. This grace was given us in Christ Jesus before the beginning of time, ¹⁰but it has now been revealed through the appearing of our Savior, Christ Jesus, who has destroyed death and has brought life and immortality to light through the gospel. ¹¹And of this gospel I was appointed a herald and an apostle and a teacher. ¹²That is why I am suffering as I am. Yet I am not ashamed, because I know whom I have believed, and am convinced that he is able to guard what I have entrusted to him for that day.

¹³What you heard from me, keep as the pattern of sound teaching, with faith and love in Christ Jesus. ¹⁴Guard the good deposit that was entrusted to you—guard it with the help of the Holy Spirit who lives in us.

¹⁵You know that everyone in the province of Asia has deserted me, including Phygelus and Hermogenes.

¹⁶May the Lord show mercy to the household of Onesiphorus, because he often refreshed me and was not ashamed of my chains. ¹⁷On the contrary, when he was in Rome, he searched hard for me until he found me. ¹⁸May the Lord grant that he will find mercy from the Lord on that day! You know very well in how many ways he helped me in Ephesus.

2 You then, my son, be strong in the grace that is in Christ Jesus. ²And the things you have heard me say in the presence of many witnesses entrust to reliable men who will also be qualified to teach others. ³Endure hardship with us like a good soldier of Christ Jesus. ⁴No one serving as a soldier gets involved in civilian affairs—he wants to please his commanding officer. ⁵Similarly, if anyone competes as an athlete, he does not receive the victor's crown unless he competes according to the rules.

OPEN: 1. What physical traits have you inherited from your father's side of the family? From you mother's side? **2.** What teacher or coach had a knack for bringing out the best in you?

DIG: 1. Why do you think Paul reminds Timothy of the heritage of his grandmother and mother, but not his father (see also Acts 16:1-3)? Why the reminder about Timothy's gift and three-fold spirit, which are from God (1:6-7)? **2.** From verse 8, what pressures may Paul fear would cause Timothy to be afraid of ministry? Why might a dying Paul be especially concerned about this? Why does Paul remind Timothy of the content of the gospel (1:9-10)? How would this help him to not be ashamed of it? **3.** What did Paul's three roles – herald, apostle, and teacher of the gospel – mean in his day? In our day? **4.** Why do you think Paul is so concerned about so many of his friends deserting him? Is it for their sake? His own sake? Or the gospel's sake? **5.** What is the secret to maintaining the principle of multiplication in spreading the gospel (2:1-2)? **6.** What do the lives of the soldier, the athlete, and the farmer teach about the Christian life? Why can't Paul's chains stop the message even if they can stop the messenger? How would these images of endurance and reward encourage Timothy to steadfastly face his own suffering? **7.** What are the key themes of this whole unit and how are they pulled together in the hymn cited here (2:11-13)?

REFLECT: 1. If you were a missionary with six months left before you had to leave where you worked, where (who, how) would you invest your energy? What would you want your legacy to be? **2.** Who have been some key family members in your own spiritual heritage? How have they influenced you? **3.** In what areas are you gifted? How could you "fan into flame" these gifts? How can your small group help you in discerning and developing your spiritual gift? **4.** When you hear that God has given you a spirit not of timidity but of power, of love, and of self discipline, how do you feel? If you believed this more, how would your life change? Why? **5.** What do you have in common with the soldier, the athlete, and the farmer in verses 1-7? What don't you have in common with them? **7.** What role are suffering and endurance playing in your life right now?

OPEN: 1. What is the one topic sure to provoke an argument at large family gatherings? Who "baits" whom? Who intervenes? Where does the argument usually end? **2.** For special company or occasions do you bring out the good china? Why?

DIG: 1. What's the difference between "godless", "foolish", and "stupid" arguments (vv. 16, 23) and defending the faith (vv. 24-26)? **2.** From this passage, make a list of those things which a Christian should pursue. How would each of the items on this list help to produce a godly life? Make a second list from this passage of those things a Christian should flee from. How would the items in this list deflect the Christian's attempt to build a godly life? **3.** How does the analogy in verses 20-21 reflect these lists? **4.** In this context (vv. 22-26), how does repentance involve the mind? The will? The conscience?

REFLECT: 1. On a scale of 1 ("this needs work") to 10 (I'm doing great in this"), how would you rate yourself in the areas of Christian conversation/godless chatter? In godly/ungodly lifestyle? **2.** How can you begin polishing up some of the dusty, mundane articles in your life for God's special use (vv. 20-21)? Of the four goals Paul calls us to pursue in verse 22, which one do you sense a need to work on this week? How will you do so?

[6]The hardworking farmer should be the first to receive a share of the crops. [7]Reflect on what I am saying, for the Lord will give you insight into all this.

[8]Remember Jesus Christ, raised from the dead, descended from David. This is my gospel, [9]for which I am suffering even to the point of being chained like a criminal. But God's word is not chained. [10]Therefore I endure everything for the sake of the elect, that they too may obtain the salvation that is in Christ Jesus, with eternal glory.

[11]Here is a trustworthy saying:

If we died with him,
we will also live with him;
[12]if we endure,
we will also reign with him.
If we disown him,
he will also disown us;
[13]if we are faithless,
he will remain faithful,
for he cannot disown himself.

A Workman Approved by God

[14]Keep reminding them of these things. Warn them before God against quarreling about words; it is of no value, and only ruins those who listen. [15]Do your best to present yourself to God as one approved, a workman who does not need to be ashamed and who correctly handles the word of truth. [16]Avoid godless chatter, because those who indulge in it will become more and more ungodly. [17]Their teaching will spread like gangrene. Among them are Hymenaeus and Philetus, [18]who have wandered away from the truth. They say that the resurrection has already taken place, and they destroy the faith of some. [19]Nevertheless, God's solid foundation stands firm, sealed with this inscription: "The Lord knows those who are his,"[a] and, "Everyone who confesses the name of the Lord must turn away from wickedness."

[20]In a large house there are articles not only of gold and silver, but also of wood and clay; some are for noble purposes and some for ignoble. [21]If a man cleanses himself from the latter, he will be an instrument for noble purposes, made holy, useful to the Master and prepared to do any good work.

[22]Flee the evil desires of youth, and pursue righteousness, faith, love and peace, along with those who call on the Lord out of a pure heart. [23]Don't have anything to do with foolish and stupid arguments, because you know they produce quarrels. [24]And the Lord's servant must not quarrel; instead, he must be kind to everyone, able to teach, not resentful. [25]Those who oppose him he must gently instruct, in the hope that God will grant them repentance leading them to a knowledge of the truth, [26]and that they will come to their senses and escape from the trap of the devil, who has taken them captive to do his will.

[a]19 Num. 16:5 (see Septuagint)

Godlessness in the Last Days

3 But mark this: There will be terrible times in the last days. [2]People will be lovers of themselves, lovers of money, boastful, proud, abusive, disobedient to their parents, ungrateful, unholy, [3]without love, unforgiving, slanderous, without self-control, brutal, not lovers of the good, [4]treacherous, rash, conceited, lovers of pleasure rather than lovers of God— [5]having a form of godliness but denying its power. Have nothing to do with them.

[6]They are the kind who worm their way into homes and gain control over weak-willed women, who are loaded down with sins and are swayed by all kinds of evil desires, [7]always learning but never able to acknowledge the truth. [8]Just as Jannes and Jambres opposed Moses, so also these men oppose the truth—men of depraved minds, who, as far as the faith is concerned, are rejected. [9]But they will not get very far because, as in the case of those men, their folly will be clear to everyone.

Paul's Charge to Timothy

[10]You, however, know all about my teaching, my way of life, my purpose, faith, patience, love, endurance, [11]persecutions, sufferings—what kinds of things happened to me in Antioch, Iconium and Lystra, the persecutions I endured. Yet the Lord rescued me from all of them. [12]In fact, everyone who wants to live a godly life in Christ Jesus will be persecuted, [13]while evil men and impostors will go from bad to worse, deceiving and being deceived. [14]But as for you, continue in what you have learned and have become convinced of, because you know those from whom you learned it, [15]and how from infancy you have known the holy Scriptures, which are able to make you wise for salvation through faith in Christ Jesus. [16]All Scripture is God-breathed and is useful for teaching, rebuking, correcting and training in righteousness, [17]so that the man of God may be thoroughly equipped for every good work.

4 In the presence of God and of Christ Jesus, who will judge the living and the dead, and in view of his appearing and his kingdom, I give you this charge: [2]Preach the Word; be prepared in season and out of season; correct, rebuke and encourage—with great patience and careful instruction. [3]For the time will come when men will not put up with sound doctrine. Instead, to suit their own desires, they will gather around them a great number of teachers to say what their itching ears want to hear. [4]They will turn their ears away from the truth and turn aside to myths. [5]But you, keep your head in all situations, endure hardship, do the work of an evangelist, discharge all the duties of your ministry.

[6]For I am already being poured out like a drink offering, and the time has come for my departure. [7]I have fought the good fight, I have finished the race, I have kept the faith. [8]Now there is in store for me the crown of righteousness, which the Lord, the righteous Judge, will award to me on that day—and not only to me, but also to all who have longed for his appearing.

OPEN: What do you do when the movie gets scary?

DIG: 1. Of the 19-odd items in this catalogue of vices, which one seems to be the basic sin, from which all the other sins flow? Why? **2.** What does it mean to have a form of godliness but deny its power? How does this relate to verse 7? Why would these people be especially dangerous?

REFLECT: 1. Where do you draw the line between living in the world, but not allowing it to squeeze you into its mold? **2.** How do you reconcile 2:25-26 with 3:5 in dealing with those who oppose you?

OPEN: 1. What is your dad's occupation? Your mom's? Yours? What tools of the trade are involved in each? **2.** What do you like most about missionary slide shows? What do you like least? Why?

DIG: 1. Why does Paul begin his "missionary presentation" to Timothy emphasizing his character and suffering? From Acts 13:13-14:20, if Paul's narrative were accompanied with slides, what images come into view? **2.** Is persecution necessarily a result of godliness? Is godliness necessarily a virtue of those who are persecuted? Why or why not? **3.** What does Paul say about the origin and purpose of Scripture that is especially relevant to Timothy's situation? **4.** Why is it such a temptation to tell people what they want to hear rather than what they need to hear? Why might this be a special problem for Timothy (see 2 Tim 1:7)? How might Paul's words in 4:6-8 encourage Timothy to endure in his ministry?

REFLECT: 1. Using Paul's comparison of the Christian life to an Olympic race, where would you say you are? Just getting started? Running well? Tuckered out? Coming into the home stretch? **2.** Given Paul's final charge (4:1-5), your temperament, and the social situations you find yourself in, how will you resist the temptation to say only things people want to hear and instead be faithful in representing Jesus? **3.** Since the Bible is so important to Christian living what are you doing to build it into your life?

OPEN: If you left home without anything, what would be the first thing you'd ask to have sent to you? Why?

DIG: 1. What clues do you pick up from between the lines about how Paul is feeling? **2.** If you remember, Mark was kicked off the team by Paul on the second missionary journey (Acts 15:36-41). What does verse 11 (20 years later) reveal? What is the lesson here for you? **3.** How does Paul in his last words echo Jesus in Gethsemane and on the cross?

REFLECT: 1. Who are some people you really need? How do they minister to you? Who are your teammates? Why do you work well together? **2.** When have you felt especially protected by God? What sense of confidence did it give you? **3.** What do you find in Paul's philosophy of endurance that is a particular inspiration to you? Is there a theme verse which best summarizes that point for you? Memorize it this week. **4.** Write a self-addressed letter reminding yourself of the key things you feel committed to doing in the next six months as a result of your study of Paul's letter(s) to Timothy. Give that letter to your group leader for delivery six months from now. **5.** If one of those key things is the application of 2 Timothy 2:2, answer the who, where, when, how, what and "what if" questions related to your intended discipleship program or "Operation Timothy".

Personal Remarks

⁹Do your best to come to me quickly, ¹⁰for Demas, because he loved this world, has deserted me and has gone to Thessalonica. Crescens has gone to Galatia, and Titus to Dalmatia. ¹¹Only Luke is with me. Get Mark and bring him with you, because he is helpful to me in my ministry. ¹²I sent Tychicus to Ephesus. ¹³When you come, bring the cloak that I left with Carpus at Troas, and my scrolls, especially the parchments.

¹⁴Alexander the metalworker did me a great deal of harm. The Lord will repay him for what he has done. ¹⁵You too should be on your guard against him, because he strongly opposed our message.

¹⁶At my first defense, no one came to my support, but everyone deserted me. May it not be held against them. ¹⁷But the Lord stood at my side and gave me strength, so that through me the message might be fully proclaimed and all the Gentiles might hear it. And I was delivered from the lion's mouth. ¹⁸The Lord will rescue me from every evil attack and will bring me safely to his heavenly kingdom. To him be glory for ever and ever. Amen.

Final Greetings

¹⁹Greet Priscilla*b* and Aquila and the household of Onesiphorus. ²⁰Erastus stayed in Corinth, and I left Trophimus sick in Miletus. ²¹Do your best to get here before winter. Eubulus greets you, and so do Pudens, Linus, Claudia and all the brothers.

²²The Lord be with your spirit. Grace be with you.

---

b19 Greek *Prisca*, a variant of *Priscilla*

TITUS

INTRODUCTION

Audience
The Church on Crete

Paul and Titus, along with Timothy, went to Crete as part of a preaching tour following Paul's release from his first imprisonment in Rome. When Paul and Timothy left for Macedonia, Titus stayed behind to establish firmly the new church on Crete. When Paul reached Macedonia he wrote two letters — one to Timothy who had remained in Ephesus and the other to Titus.

In his letter to Titus, Paul reminds the younger man of his role: to appoint good leaders who will guide the church wisely. He also urges Titus to combat the false teachers found on the island. Finally, he tells him that either Artemas or Tychicus will come to relieve him (3:12), after which he is to join Paul for the winter. (See details of Paul's itinerary during this period in the introduction to 2 Timothy.)

Crete

Crete is a large island in the Mediterranean, southeast of Greece. The Minoan civilization flourished there before the time of Christ. A Jewish colony existed on the island. On the Day of Pentecost, Jews from Crete were in Jerusalem and witnessed the coming of the Holy Spirit (Acts 2:11). During his voyage to Rome, the ship on which Paul sailed skimmed the coast of Crete before being caught by a storm and driven to Malta (Acts 27:7-21).

Titus

Titus was a Greek (Gal. 2:3) who was probably converted through Paul's ministry. He accompanied Paul on his crucial second visit to Jerusalem when the inflammatory question was raised about whether Gentiles had to become Jews before they could become Christians (Gal. 2:1-10). Paul used Titus as a test case, refusing to allow him to be circumcised despite the insistence of the Judaizers.

Titus was a trusted colleague of Paul's and one of his special envoys sent on difficult assignments. For example, when the conflict between Paul and the Corinthian church had reached a breaking point, it was Titus who delivered Paul's "harsh" letter and restored order in that community. After reporting back to Paul that he had succeeded in this mission (2 Cor. 7:5-7), Titus was sent back to Corinth. This time he carried with him the letter known as 2 Corinthians (2 Cor. 8:6). On the second trip he was also charged with arranging for the collection to be given to the poor in Jerusalem.

Titus (presumably) left Crete when his replacement Artemas arrived, and he spent the winter with Paul at Nicopolis. In the spring, Paul left for Ephesus, was arrested and then sent to prison in Rome. At some point, Titus was sent to Dalmatia (modern Yugoslavia) for yet another mission.

In short, Titus was a valued friend and a trusted colleague of Paul's, one whom he called "my true son in our common faith" (1:4).

Characteristics

Titus is strikingly similar to 1 Timothy. Apart from the greeting and two pieces of theological writing in 2:11-14 and 3:3-7 (which appear to be creeds), all the material is parallel to 1 Timothy.

Still, the differences are notable. The main difference is found in the contrasting situation of Titus and Timothy. Timothy had been left to straighten out a mess in an already established church. Titus, on the other hand, had the job of appointing elders in a new church. As a result, there is less intensity in Titus. There are few imperatives ("Do this"); there is no mention of endurance (as one finds in 1 Timothy); and there are no appeals to "keep the faith." Establishing order in a new church was quite different from restoring order to an established church.

Titus

OPEN: If a friend was introducing you to her parents, which of your credentials would she mention?

DIG: What does Paul say here about his primary role? His relationship to God? To Titus?

REFLECT: To what ministry has God called you? How are you sure of that calling: By God's election? By your own action? By confirming results? By luck of the draw?

OPEN: If your local newspaper wanted to interview a Christian for a feature article, who would you recommend? Why?

DIG: 1. Why is Titus given a list of leadership qualifications where the emphasis is mostly on "being" and not "doing"? How do you account for the similarities between this list and the one in 1 Timothy 3:2-7? How do you account for the differences? **2.** How do you interpret "the husband of one wife"? **3.** What should disqualify someone from church leadership? **4.** What's going on at Crete that Titus should appoint such elders? **5.** What is Paul's main purpose for writing these instructions?

REFLECT: 1. Suppose you were on a search committee for your church, responsible for finding ten people or couples who would meet these qualifications, who comes to mind? Would you nominate yourself? **2.** Of the controversies buzzing around your church and community, which one should your leadership tackle first? Second? Third?

OPEN: 1. What did your mother warn you about prior to your getting married? What happened anyway? **2.** What is the "no-no" that you have the most problems just saying "no" to? Why?

DIG: 1. In Paul's discipleship program, who is to teach whom and what are they to teach? What difference does age make in dealing with the subject matter and the teachers/trainers assigned? Why the re-

1 Paul, a servant of God and an apostle of Jesus Christ for the faith of God's elect and the knowledge of the truth that leads to godliness— [2]a faith and knowledge resting on the hope of eternal life, which God, who does not lie, promised before the beginning of time, [3]and at his appointed season he brought his word to light through the preaching entrusted to me by the command of God our Savior,

[4]To Titus, my true son in our common faith:

Grace and peace from God the Father and Christ Jesus our Savior.

Titus' Task on Crete

[5]The reason I left you in Crete was that you might straighten out what was left unfinished and appoint[a] elders in every town, as I directed you. [6]An elder must be blameless, the husband of but one wife, a man whose children believe and are not open to the charge of being wild and disobedient. [7]Since an overseer[b] is entrusted with God's work, he must be blameless—not overbearing, not quick-tempered, not given to drunkenness, not violent, not pursuing dishonest gain. [8]Rather he must be hospitable, one who loves what is good, who is self-controlled, upright, holy and disciplined. [9]He must hold firmly to the trustworthy message as it has been taught, so that he can encourage others by sound doctrine and refute those who oppose it.

[10]For there are many rebellious people, mere talkers and deceivers, especially those of the circumcision group. [11]They must be silenced, because they are ruining whole households by teaching things they ought not to teach—and that for the sake of dishonest gain. [12]Even one of their own prophets has said, "Cretans are always liars, evil brutes, lazy gluttons." [13]This testimony is true. Therefore, rebuke them sharply, so that they will be sound in the faith [14]and will pay no attention to Jewish myths or to the commands of those who reject the truth. [15]To the pure, all things are pure, but to those who are corrupted and do not believe, nothing is pure. In fact, both their minds and consciences are corrupted. [16]They claim to know God, but by their actions they deny him. They are detestable, disobedient and unfit for doing anything good.

What Must Be Taught to Various Groups

2 You must teach what is in accord with sound doctrine. [2]Teach the older men to be temperate, worthy of respect, self-controlled, and sound in faith, in love and in endurance.

[3]Likewise, teach the older women to be reverent in the way they live, not to be slanderers or addicted to much wine, but to teach what is good. [4]Then they can train the younger women to love their husbands and children, [5]to be self-controlled and

---

a5 Or ordain   *b7 Traditionally bishop*

pure, to be busy at home, to be kind, and to be subject to their husbands, so that no one will malign the word of God.

⁶Similarly, encourage the young men to be self-controlled. ⁷In everything set them an example by doing what is good. In your teaching show integrity, seriousness ⁸and soundness of speech that cannot be condemned, so that those who oppose you may be ashamed because they have nothing bad to say about us.

⁹Teach slaves to be subject to their masters in everything, to try to please them, not to talk back to them, ¹⁰and not to steal from them, but to show that they can be fully trusted, so that in every way they will make the teaching about God our Savior attractive.

¹¹For the grace of God that brings salvation has appeared to all men. ¹²It teaches us to say "No" to ungodliness and worldly passions, and to live self-controlled, upright and godly lives in this present age, ¹³while we wait for the blessed hope—the glorious appearing of our great God and Savior, Jesus Christ, ¹⁴who gave himself for us to redeem us from all wickedness and to purify for himself a people that are his very own, eager to do what is good.

¹⁵These, then, are the things you should teach. Encourage and rebuke with all authority. Do not let anyone despise you.

Doing What Is Good

3 Remind the people to be subject to rulers and authorities, to be obedient, to be ready to do whatever is good, ²to slander no one, to be peaceable and considerate, and to show true humility toward all men.

³At one time we too were foolish, disobedient, deceived and enslaved by all kinds of passions and pleasures. We lived in malice and envy, being hated and hating one another. ⁴But when the kindness and love of God our Savior appeared, ⁵he saved us, not because of righteous things we had done, but because of his mercy. He saved us through the washing of rebirth and renewal by the Holy Spirit, ⁶whom he poured out on us generously through Jesus Christ our Savior, ⁷so that, having been justified by his grace, we might become heirs having the hope of eternal life. ⁸This is a trustworthy saying. And I want you to stress these things, so that those who have trusted in God may be careful to devote themselves to doing what is good. These things are excellent and profitable for everyone.

⁹But avoid foolish controversies and genealogies and arguments and quarrels about the law, because these are unprofitable and useless. ¹⁰Warn a divisive person once, and then warn him a second time. After that, have nothing to do with him. ¹¹You may be sure that such a man is warped and sinful; he is self-condemned.

Final Remarks

¹²As soon as I send Artemas or Tychicus to you, do your best to come to me at Nicopolis, because I have decided to winter there. ¹³Do everything you can to help Zenas the lawyer and Apollos on their way and see that they have everything they need. ¹⁴Our people must learn to devote themselves to doing

peated emphasis on teaching "self-control" (vv. 1:6, 10; 2:2, 5, 6, 12; 3:3) and doing "what is good" (vv. 3, 6, 14; also 3:1, 8)? **2.** Who has the harder job: The one teaching self-control, or the one just learning it? Why? **3.** What is the main purpose of all this sound teaching: To become master students? Busybodies? Do-gooders? Model workers? Trustworthy evangelists? Authoritative Bible-bangers? Or to give us hope beyond this life?

REFLECT: 1. Which age-category and subject material apply to you? **2.** Who are your teachers in this regard? Your audience? **3.** How closely does your teaching and learning adhere to the main purpose given to Titus?

OPEN: In your post-high school days, how did you regard those in authority, such as: Clergy? Policemen? Anyone over thirty? Why? Are you more radical today or more mellow?

DIG: 1. Why do you suppose Paul stresses "doing what is good" (vv. 1, 8)? What is it about human nature that makes such reminders necessary (v. 3)? Or are they futile? **2.** What (or who) enables people to do anything good at all (vv. 4-7)? Of the ingredients listed here, which is key to our salvation: God's kindness? Human righteousness? "Washing" (baptism)? A spiritual rebirth? Outpouring of the Holy Spirit? Good works? **3.** How are the people to treat heretics: Avoid them? Argue with them? Admonish them? Condemn them? Why?

REFLECT: 1. What were you like before God showed you his mercy? Afterwards? **2.** How does knowing the "before Christ" and "after Christ" difference encourage you to do whatever is good right now?

OPEN: If you could spend the winter anywhere you wanted, where would you spend it?

DIG: What further encouragement do you receive here for doing good?

REFLECT: 1. Which is your "hot button" that moves you to "do good": The call of duty? The needs of others? The example of others? The resources to do your best? A simple reminder is enough? Fear of consequences if you don't? **2.** What "good" are you around the house? Around the church? Around town? Or are you up to "no good"? **3.** Where in your last five years as a Christian do you feel you have been most productive for the Lord?

what is good, in order that they may provide for daily necessities and not live unproductive lives.

¹⁵Everyone with me sends you greetings. Greet those who love us in the faith.

Grace be with you all.

PHILEMON

INTRODUCTION

Characteristics

Philemon is the shortest of Paul's New Testament letters and it is his only private letter preserved in Scripture. All his other letters, whether to churches or to co-workers, relate to Paul's ministry. But Philemon is a personal note written to a friend about a private matter—the fate of Onesimus, the runaway slave. As such, it gives us a valuable glimpse into Paul's personality. He is deeply sympathetic to the plight of Onesimus, so much so that he is willing to deprive himself of Onesimus' help and to pay Philemon for any loss Onesimus has caused him (v. 19). This is certainly Christian compassion in action.

Slaves in the Roman Empire

We cannot understand the Epistle to Philemon without understanding something about the status of slaves in the first-century Roman world. First, slaves were considered property, not people. Therefore, they were under the absolute control of their master or mistress. A slave owner could beat or even kill a slave if he or she chose, although, in all fairness, many slaves fared quite well. Pliny, a Roman official, tells that Vedius Pollio ordered that a slave who had dropped a crystal goblet be thrown into the fishpond. There he was torn to pieces by lamprey (William Barclay, *Letters to Timothy, Titus, Philemon*, p. 316).

Onesimus had run away from his owner, Philemon. As a fugitive, he was subject to severe punishment or even death if caught. For Paul to send him back was an inconsiderable risk. Philemon had every right to brand Onesimus with the Letter F on his forehead (for *fugitivus* or runaway) or do even worse.

We often wonder why Paul does not simply condemn slavery on this occasion. This would have been a fine time to do so. Yet, as Lightfoot says, "The word 'emancipation' seems to be trembling on his lips, and yet he does not once utter it" (*Saint Paul and Epistles to the Colossians and to Philemon*, p. 321). The reason is partly clear: social conditions were not yet right for such a massive upheaval. There were sixty million slaves in the Roman Empire when Paul wrote. The social and economic structure of Rome was built around them. The Romans would never have voluntarily freed their slaves, and any revolt would have been crushed savagely. Emancipation did eventually come, spearheaded by Christian effort, but it was hundreds of years away.

In the meantime, Paul struck the first blow in that direction by declaring to the church at Colossae in his companion letter that "there is no Greek or Jew, circumcised or uncircumcised, barbarian, Scythian, slave or free, but Christ is all, and is in all" (Col. 3:11). In this private letter to Philemon, he said that Onesimus was returning "no longer as a slave, but better than a slave, as a dear brother" (v. 16).

Thus the master-slave relationship was transformed, and so the seeds were sown that led eventually to the abolition of slavery.

Onesimus

He was a slave. He may well have been a thief ("if he has done you any wrong or owes you anything, charge it to me," v. 18). He was certainly a fugitive. But he had become a Christian. Somehow he had met up with Paul. Perhaps he had gone to Rome to try to escape notice in that vast city, and his path had crossed Paul's. Or perhaps he had been caught and imprisoned alongside Paul. In any case, he was now a new man—living proof of Christ's power about which Paul writes to the Colossians.

The outcome of this story is never told. We do not know whether Paul's letter had the impact he hoped. But a curious piece of historical information might shed light on what happened. Some fifty years after Paul wrote Philemon, Ignatius, the bishop of Antioch, was being taken to Rome to be executed. Along the way at Smyrna, he wrote a letter to the church at Ephesus. In this letter he extolled their wonderful bishop, whose name was Onesimus! He referred to this man exactly as Paul did by making a pun on his name. Onesimus means "useful" or "profitable." "Formerly he was useless to you, but now he has become useful," Paul said (v. 11). Ignatius commented that "he is Onesimus by name and Onesimus by nature, the profitable one to Christ. It may well be that Onesimus, the runaway slave, had become with the passing years none other than Onesimus, the great bishop of Ephesus" (Barclay, *Letters to Timothy, Titus, Philemon,* p. 316).

If this was the case, it would explain how the letter to Philemon got into the New Testament. Many scholars feel that the first collection of Paul's letters was made at Ephesus at about the time Onesimus was bishop. He may have included this note as a vivid demonstration of how the great Christ can change and use even a fugitive slave like himself.

Philemon

[1]Paul, a prisoner of Christ Jesus, and Timothy our brother,

To Philemon our dear friend and fellow worker, [2]to Apphia our sister, to Archippus our fellow soldier and to the church that meets in your home:

[3]Grace to you and peace from God our Father and the Lord Jesus Christ.

Thanksgiving and Prayer

[4]I always thank my God as I remember you in my prayers, [5]because I hear about your faith in the Lord Jesus and your love for all the saints. [6]I pray that you may be active in sharing your faith, so that you will have a full understanding of every good thing we have in Christ. [7]Your love has given me great joy and encouragement, because you, brother, have refreshed the hearts of the saints.

Paul's Plea for Onesimus

[8]Therefore, although in Christ I could be bold and order you to do what you ought to do, [9]yet I appeal to you on the basis of love. I then, as Paul—an old man and now also a prisoner of Christ Jesus— [10]I appeal to you for my son Onesimus,[a] who became my son while I was in chains. [11]Formerly he was useless to you, but now he has become useful both to you and to me.

[12]I am sending him—who is my very heart—back to you. [13]I would have liked to keep him with me so that he could take your place in helping me while I am in chains for the gospel. [14]But I did not want to do anything without your consent, so that any favor you do will be spontaneous and not forced. [15]Perhaps the reason he was separated from you for a little while was that you might have him back for good— [16]no longer as a slave, but better than a slave, as a dear brother. He is very dear to me but even dearer to you, both as a man and as a brother in the Lord.

[17]So if you consider me a partner, welcome him as you would welcome me. [18]If he has done you any wrong or owes you anything, charge it to me. [19]I, Paul, am writing this with my own hand. I will pay it back—not to mention that you owe me your very self. [20]I do wish, brother, that I may have some benefit from you in the Lord; refresh my heart in Christ. [21]Confident of your obedience, I write to you, knowing that you will do even more than I ask.

[22]And one thing more: Prepare a guest room for me, because I hope to be restored to you in answer to your prayers.

[23]Epaphras, my fellow prisoner in Christ Jesus, sends you greetings. [24]And so do Mark, Aristarchus, Demas and Luke, my fellow workers.

[25]The grace of the Lord Jesus Christ be with your spirit.

[a]10 Onesimus means useful.

OPEN: When you write to someone requesting a big favor, do you "butter them up" first, or get to the point?

DIG: If Paul's goal was to affirm Philemon and his family, do you think he succeeded? Why? What did he say that was the most affirming and was the basis for Paul's appeal (v. 8)?

REFLECT: How are you doing at affirming and encouraging those around you? What effect do you think more affirmation and encouragement would have on your family? On your work associates? On those who need reconciliation?

OPEN: What name were you given at birth? What nick names have you been given since? What do they mean? How are you living up to their meaning?

DIG: 1. Given the seriousness of the crime committed by Onesimus (see Introduction to Philemon), what impact will Onesimus' return have on Philemon's household? On Paul's relationship with Philemon? On Onesimus himself? **2.** Does the fact that Onesimus' has become a Christian lessen the seriousness of his crime? **3.** What is radical about Paul's view of Onesimus (vv. 10-18)? **4.** Given Paul's concern and need for Onesimus, why does Paul return Onesimus to Philemon anyway? Why doesn't Paul exert his apostolic authority and declare Onesimus free and keep him as a partner in the gospel? Or is Paul using "reverse psychology" here, still hoping for the services of Philemon and/or the freedom of slaves? **5.** What do you think are the chances that Philemon will do what Paul asks? In what way might Philemon be right to refuse Paul?

REFLECT: 1. Like Onesimus, do you have something you need to return to and make right? Do you have someone like Paul who can help you do that? **2.** When do you feel obligated to forgive someone: When they confess their sin? When they later change their behavior? When someone else intercedes for the offending party?

HEBREWS

INTRODUCTION

Author

No one knows who wrote the Epistle to the Hebrews. The author is nowhere named within it, nor is there any strong external evidence pointing to one particular person. These facts have not deterred speculation, however. At least eight good candidates for the role of author have been proposed.

A favorite choice has been Paul, probably because the King James translation wrongly lists him as author, even though such a designation is found in none of the ancient manuscripts. It is unlikely that Paul wrote Hebrews. The style and language of this epistle is quite unlike Paul's, although this fact is more evident in the Greek original than in the English translation. The Epistle to the Hebrews is a polished piece of writing. Its transitions are neatly in place and its argument carefully spelled out. This is in sharp contrast to Paul's more ragged style. He had the habit of losing the thread of his argument because he would become excited about some new piece of God's revelation before he had drawn to a logical conclusion the case he originally started to build.

Other suggested authors include Barnabas, Luke, Priscilla, Silvanus (1 Peter 5:12), Apollos, and Clement of Rome. Origen, a third-century Christian scholar, had the last word on this issue: He wrote that as to the identity of the author "only God knows certainly" (recorded in Eusebius, *Historia Ecclesiastica*).

Audience

The title "To the Hebrews" can be traced back to manuscripts of the late second century. Even though it was not a part of the original document, it seems an accurate designation given the very Jewish flavor of the epistle. This letter was probably written to a particular assembly of Jewish-Christian believers (perhaps a house church) that was part of a larger community, quite possibly in Rome.

Whoever these people were, it is clear that they had suffered great persecution (10:32-34) and that they were being tempted to abandon Christianity. What is less clear is the nature of the pressures weighing against them. Perhaps the constant indignities they suffered as Christians were beginning to take their toll. Or perhaps they were facing the prospect of severe persecution in the near future. Or the problem may have been internal. Maybe they were being enticed away from Christ by false teaching that seemed to offer relief from their struggles. They might have been considering a return to a form of Judaism as one way to bring community acceptance and thus lessen tensions.

In any case, the temptation to apostasy or reversion was severe enough that the letter to the Hebrews had to be written to encourage these beleaguered Christians to "hold on" (3:6), to "persevere" (10:36), and to "hold unswervingly to the hope we profess" (10:23) lest they compromise Christ and lose all the enormous blessings of the New Covenant.

Date

As with so much else about this epistle, it is difficult to be certain about its date of composition. If the persecution referred to is that of Nero, then Hebrews was written after A.D. 64. Some hold that it must have been written prior to the fall of Jerusalem and the destruction of the temple in A.D. 70, for such an unprecedented event would probably have been mentioned by the book's author as the sure sign of the end of the sacrificial system. Others argue for a later date. If the fall of Jerusalem were recent, they reason, it would be so gigantic and so fresh in the minds of the readers that it need not be mentioned. In that case, the book could have been written prior to the persecution by Emperor Domitian in A.D. 85, probably somewhere around A.D. 80.

Characteristics

To many modern readers, Hebrews is a strange book filled with references to ancient practices, with the presuppositions of a wholly different culture, and with images that evoke no recognition in the twentieth century. It is true that to understand Hebrews, the reader must understand the Old Testament. Yet for all its strangeness, the book of Hebrews continues to fascinate modern readers because of its vivid images, its relentless argument that refuses to detour from the main point, its stirring remembrances of the heroes of the faith, and most of all its almost breathtaking portrait of Jesus — the ultimate priest who, for ourselves for a time, was made a little lower than the angels. This Jesus captivates the mind and imagination of the twentieth-century person — this Jesus who not only gave strength to those enduring persecution two thousand years ago, but who still today gives strength to those facing the possibility of nuclear annihilation.

Themes

How does one write to suffering Christians and tell them to stay faithful despite the price they are paying? The author wisely begins not by considering their difficult circumstances nor by simply telling them, "This is the right thing to do, so do it." Instead, he points them to Jesus, the only one who is worth such costly allegiance. As a result, in the Book of Hebrews, we get a marvelous portrait of Christ — the prophet, priest, and king whose New Covenant is so superior to the Old Covenant that to fall away from him should be unthinkable. The central theme of Hebrews, therefore, is the superiority of Christ. He is superior to the great religious leaders of the past such as Moses, Joshua, and Aaron. He is superior to the great supernatural powers like angels. The New Covenant he established and the new order he inaugurated are superior to the old beliefs and practices of the Jewish religion.

Structure

This particular New Testament book has been called an epistle but in fact, it lacks several key features of a true letter. It has no introductory greeting, nor does it name either the sender or the recipients. Its ending is typical of a letter, however, with personal greetings and a standard conclusion.

If Hebrews is not a true letter, then what is it? Some have suggested that Hebrews is a written sermon. Certainly the book frequently has the feel of a sermon (e.g., 11:32), and it is written in the style of a sermon. Its method of argument is sermonic in nature. Structurally, its closest New Testament parallel is 1 John, which also seems to be a sermon.

Outline

Given its theme of Christ's superiority contrasted with warnings not to depart from him, the Book of Hebrews may be outlined as follows (adapted from Philip Edgcumbe Hughes, *A Commentary on the Epistle to the Hebrews,* pp. ix-x):
1. Christ is superior to the prophets (1:1-3)
2. Christ is superior to angels (1:4-2:18)
   (Warning 1: 2:1-4)
3. Christ is superior to Moses (3:1-4:13)
   (Warning 2: 3:7-4:2)
4. Christ is superior to the old priesthood (4:14-10:18)
   (Warning 3: 5:11-6:8)
5. Christ is superior as the new and living way (10:19-13:25)
   (Warning 4: 10:26-31)
   (Warning 5: 12:14-17)
   (Warning 6: 12:25-29)

Hebrews

OPEN: 1. What strength or personality trait did you receive from your father? Your mother? Who do you take after on musical ability? Mechanical ability? Athletic ability? **2.** What does your father do? Your grandfather? How would you like to take over your father's job or business? **3.** If you could be an angel for a day, what would you like to do?

DIG: 1. To what two groups of people is Jesus compared in chapter 1 (e.g., vv. 1 , 4)? **2.** What was the function of the Old Testament prophets (v. 1)? In what ways was Jesus' function similar (v. 2)? Different (vv. 2-3)? How is Jesus superior to the prophets? What is the difference between the "past" and "these last days"? **3.** According to verses 1-3, who is Jesus? What has he done? Where is he now? What two metaphors are used to describe his relationship with God (v. 3)? What is the author struggling here to tell us about Jesus? **4.** In what ways is Jesus superior to angels (vv. 4-14)? **5.** In verses 5-14, what new facts does the author add to his portrait of Jesus? What is Jesus' title (v. 5)? His role (vv. 8-9, 13)? What does the comparison with creation reveal about his nature (vv. 10-12)? **6.** What is taught here about the nature and function of angels (vv. 6, 7, 14)? **7.** What do you suppose was problematic about the way the recipients of Hebrews viewed angels that would cause the author to write as he does? **8.** By what means does the author prove each of his points? How does this demonstrate his understanding of the role of the prophets as expressed in verse 1? Whose words does one find in the Bible? Check out each quotation as to its original context and meaning. How is each quotation used by the author?

REFLECT: 1. When did Jesus Christ become more than just a name to you? **2.** Who is one of the people you look upon as your spiritual "forefather"? How important is your spiritual heritage: A little? A lot? More all the time? **3.** Of all the qualities of Jesus given in verses 2-4, which one are you beginning to realize more and more? **4.** Of what help is it for the Christian that God has indeed spoken "at many times and in various ways"? Why not in just one way? **5.** In what ways does it matter how we view the nature of Jesus Christ? Does it

The Son Superior to Angels

1 In the past God spoke to our forefathers through the prophets at many times and in various ways, [2] but in these last days he has spoken to us by his Son, whom he appointed heir of all things, and through whom he made the universe. [3] The Son is the radiance of God's glory and the exact representation of his being, sustaining all things by his powerful word. After he had provided purification for sins, he sat down at the right hand of the Majesty in heaven. [4] So he became as much superior to the angels as the name he has inherited is superior to theirs.

[5] For to which of the angels did God ever say,

"You are my Son;
today I have become your Father[a]"[b]?

Or again,

"I will be his Father,
and he will be my Son"[c]?

[6] And again, when God brings his firstborn into the world, he says,

"Let all God's angels worship him."[d]

[7] In speaking of the angels he says,

"He makes his angels winds,
his servants flames of fire."[e]

[8] But about the Son he says,

"Your throne, O God, will last for ever and ever,
and righteousness will be the scepter of your kingdom.
[9] You have loved righteousness and hated wickedness;
therefore God, your God, has set you above your companions
by anointing you with the oil of joy."[f]

[10] He also says,

"In the beginning, O Lord, you laid the foundations of the earth,
and the heavens are the work of your hands.
[11] They will perish, but you remain;
they will all wear out like a garment.
[12] You will roll them up like a robe;
like a garment they will be changed.
But you remain the same,
and your years will never end."[g]

[13] To which of the angels did God ever say,

---

a5 Or *have begotten you*   *b5* Psalm 2:7   *c5* 2 Samuel 7:14; 1 Chron. 17:13
d6 Deut. 32:43 (see Dead Sea Scrolls and Septuagint)   *e7* Psalm 104:4
f9 Psalm 45:6,7   *g12* Psalm 102:25-27

"Sit at my right hand
until I make your enemies
a footstool for your feet" *h*?

¹⁴Are not all angels ministering spirits sent to serve those who will inherit salvation?

Warning to Pay Attention

2 We must pay more careful attention, therefore, to what we have heard, so that we do not drift away. ²For if the message spoken by angels was binding, and every violation and disobedience received its just punishment, ³how shall we escape if we ignore such a great salvation? This salvation, which was first announced by the Lord, was confirmed to us by those who heard him. ⁴God also testified to it by signs, wonders and various miracles, and gifts of the Holy Spirit distributed according to his will.

Jesus Made Like His Brothers

⁵It is not to angels that he has subjected the world to come, about which we are speaking. ⁶But there is a place where someone has testified:

"What is man that you are mindful of him,
the son of man that you care for him?
⁷You made him a little' lower than the angels;
you crowned him with glory and honor
⁸ and put everything under his feet." *j*

In putting everything under him, God left nothing that is not subject to him. Yet at present we do not see everything subject to him. ⁹But we see Jesus, who was made a little lower than the angels, now crowned with glory and honor because he suffered death, so that by the grace of God he might taste death for everyone.

¹⁰In bringing many sons to glory, it was fitting that God, for whom and through whom everything exists, should make the author of their salvation perfect through suffering. ¹¹Both the one who makes men holy and those who are made holy are of the same family. So Jesus is not ashamed to call them brothers. ¹²He says,

"I will declare your name to my brothers;
in the presence of the congregation I will sing your praises." *k*

¹³And again,

"I will put my trust in him." *l*

And again he says,

"Here am I, and the children God has given me." *m*

¹⁴Since the children have flesh and blood, he too shared in their humanity so that by his death he might destroy him who holds the power of death—that is, the devil— ¹⁵and free those

make any difference that he was the Son rather than just a prophet or angel?

OPEN: In what class in school was it the hardest to pay attention?

DIG: 1. In light of the previous chapter, what is it that might prompt the readers to drift away? **2.** What does it mean to drift away? **3.** For the reader, what confirmed the truth of the message of the gospel?

REFLECT: 1. When, if ever, did you drift away from the faith? Why?

OPEN: 1. When your parents were gone, who were you "subject to" as a kid? How did you look upon this person? Who do you leave in charge of your affairs when you are away? **2.** Of your brothers/sisters, to whom do you feel closest?

DIG: 1. In contrast to the popular expectation of that day (v. 5) to whom does God subject the world (vv. 6-8a)? Why is the rule of man not yet complete or universal (v. 8)? Who rules instead? **2.** In comparing men and angels (vv. 5-8), how are men "lower"? Higher? What is the ultimate destiny of humanity? **3.** What does the phrase 'the world to come' refer to? How can the Messianic age be both present and future? **4.** In what respects was Jesus "made lower than the angels" (v. 9)? What elevated him above them? Which two respects does Jesus share with humanity (vv. 7, 9)? In which respect is Jesus unique? **5.** Who are Jesus' "brothers" (vv. 10-13): Men or angels? Why? Why did we need someone with flesh and blood like us - not an angel - to die in our place (vv. 14-18)? What did Jesus accomplish by his death as one of us? **6.** What was necessary for our salvation to come through Jesus (v. 10)? What is the goal of our salvation (vv. 10-11)? And its author? What does it mean to call Jesus "the author . . . of salvation"? **7.** What is the difference between the way Jesus made atonement (v. 17) and the way the priests mediate atonement?

REFLECT: 1. When do you find yourself tempted to "throw in the towel" on your faith: Just after a big disappointment? When you are away from spiritual fellowship with others? When you have intellectual doubts? When things are not going your way? When you are around people that laugh at Christianity? **2.** How do the accomplishments and examples of Jesus described here encourage you when you are tempted to sin or tested in your faith?

OPEN: What is your favorite style of house? Would you like to build your own home? Why?

DIG: 1. Which key word twice describes Moses and Jesus? As both are faithful, what distinguishes Jesus from Moses (vv. 5-6)? **2.** How does fixing one's thoughts on Jesus help overcome fear?

REFLECT: What keeps you on your toes spiritually? When do you need to "hold on"?

OPEN: 1. If you lost your way on a trip, what would you do: Stop and ask directions? Check the map? Drive around until you found the way? **2.** What is the longest trip you took with your family in a car? Who decided who would sit where in the car? How did your parents handle griping from the "back seat"?

DIG: 1. What new warning is given (vv. 8, 12)? How does this compare with 3:6 and 2:1-4? **2.** To what incident does the quotation from Psalms (vv. 7-11) refer? See Numbers 14: How did the people of Israel harden their hearts? With what results (vv. 10-11)? **3.** What does it mean to turn away from the living God (v. 12)? What role does the Christian community play in keeping us true to God (v. 13)? What will be the outcome of faithfulness (v. 14)? **4.** What is the answer to each question in verses 16-18? What is the point of the questions (v. 19)? **5.** What does it mean today to harden our hearts against God?

REFLECT: 1. What has been one of the most rebellious times in your spiritual life? What resulted from it? Who or what helped to bring you back? **2.** How would you describe your heart now: Soft? Hard? Cold? Warm? **3.** Where do you think hardness of heart comes from? **4.** Who deserves the Good Samaritan Award for helping you when you were nearly dead spiritually?

who all their lives were held in slavery by their fear of death. [16]For surely it is not angels he helps, but Abraham's descendants. [17]For this reason he had to be made like his brothers in every way, in order that he might become a merciful and faithful high priest in service to God, and that he might make atonement for[n] the sins of the people. [18]Because he himself suffered when he was tempted, he is able to help those who are being tempted.

Jesus Greater Than Moses

3 Therefore, holy brothers, who share in the heavenly calling, fix your thoughts on Jesus, the apostle and high priest whom we confess. [2]He was faithful to the one who appointed him, just as Moses was faithful in all God's house. [3]Jesus has been found worthy of greater honor than Moses, just as the builder of a house has greater honor than the house itself. [4]For every house is built by someone, but God is the builder of everything. [5]Moses was faithful as a servant in all God's house, testifying to what would be said in the future. [6]But Christ is faithful as a son over God's house. And we are his house, if we hold on to our courage and the hope of which we boast.

Warning Against Unbelief

[7]So, as the Holy Spirit says:

"Today, if you hear his voice,
[8] do not harden your hearts
as you did in the rebellion,
during the time of testing in the desert,
[9]where your fathers tested and tried me
and for forty years saw what I did.
[10]That is why I was angry with that generation,
and I said, 'Their hearts are always going astray,
and they have not known my ways.'
[11]So I declared on oath in my anger,
'They shall never enter my rest.' "[o]

[12]See to it, brothers, that none of you has a sinful, unbelieving heart that turns away from the living God. [13]But encourage one another daily, as long as it is called Today, so that none of you may be hardened by sin's deceitfulness. [14]We have come to share in Christ if we hold firmly till the end the confidence we had at first. [15]As has just been said:

"Today, if you hear his voice,
do not harden your hearts
as you did in the rebellion."[p]

[16]Who were they who heard and rebelled? Were they not all those Moses led out of Egypt? [17]And with whom was he angry for forty years? Was it not with those who sinned, whose bodies fell in the desert? [18]And to whom did God swear that they would never enter his rest if not to those who disobeyed[q]? [19]So we see that they were not able to enter, because of their unbelief.

---

[n]17 Or and that he might turn aside God's wrath, taking away   [o]11 Psalm 95:7-11
[p]15 Psalm 95:7,8   [q]18 Or disbelieved

A Sabbath-Rest for the People of God

4 Therefore, since the promise of entering his rest still stands, let us be careful that none of you be found to have fallen short of it. ²For we also have had the gospel preached to us, just as they did; but the message they heard was of no value to them, because those who heard did not combine it with faith.ʳ ³Now we who have believed enter that rest, just as God has said,

"So I declared on oath in my anger,
'They shall never enter my rest.' "ˢ

And yet his work has been finished since the creation of the world. ⁴For somewhere he has spoken about the seventh day in these words: "And on the seventh day God rested from all his work."ᵗ ⁵And again in the passage above he says, "They shall never enter my rest."

⁶It still remains that some will enter that rest, and those who formerly had the gospel preached to them did not go in, because of their disobedience. ⁷Therefore God again set a certain day, calling it Today, when a long time later he spoke through David, as was said before:

"Today, if you hear his voice,
do not harden your hearts."ᵘ

⁸For if Joshua had given them rest, God would not have spoken later about another day. ⁹There remains, then, a Sabbath-rest for the people of God; ¹⁰for anyone who enters God's rest also rests from his own work, just as God did from his. ¹¹Let us, therefore, make every effort to enter that rest, so that no one will fall by following their example of disobedience.

¹²For the word of God is living and active. Sharper than any double-edged sword, it penetrates even to dividing soul and spirit, joints and marrow; it judges the thoughts and attitudes of the heart. ¹³Nothing in all creation is hidden from God's sight. Everything is uncovered and laid bare before the eyes of him to whom we must give account.

Jesus the Great High Priest

¹⁴Therefore, since we have a great high priest who has gone through the heavens,ᵛ Jesus the Son of God, let us hold firmly to the faith we profess. ¹⁵For we do not have a high priest who is unable to sympathize with our weaknesses, but we have one who has been tempted in every way, just as we are—yet was without sin. ¹⁶Let us then approach the throne of grace with confidence, so that we may receive mercy and find grace to help us in our time of need.

5 Every high priest is selected from among men and is appointed to represent them in matters related to God, to offer gifts and sacrifices for sins. ²He is able to deal gently with those who are ignorant and are going astray, since he himself is subject to weakness. ³This is why he has to offer sacrifices for his own sins, as well as for the sins of the people.

ʳ2 Many manuscripts *because they did not share in the faith of those who obeyed*
ˢ3 Psalm 95:11; also in verse 5   ᵗ4 Gen. 2:2   ᵘ7 Psalm 95:7,8   ᵛ14 Or *gone into heaven*

OPEN: What is your favorite way to spend a restful Sunday afternoon?

DIG: 1. From the story of Israel's rebellion, what conclusion are we to draw (v. 1)? What promise still stands? Why? **2.** How do the Israelites in the desert (3:7-19) parallel Christians in the first century (4:1-13)? What "message" (v. 2) was given each community (see Ex. 3:7; Nu. 14:7-9)? With what reception and results? Why is hearing not enough (v. 2)? **3.** What is this "rest" promised by God: The promised land? Sunday off? Heaven? How do verses 3b-10 support your answer? Likewise, how does your answer demonstrate that rest is still accessible (vv. 1-3)? **4.** How is 4:1-11 an explanation of 4:19? What does verse 11 tell us is the proper response to the warning in verse 1? **5.** When told that a heavenly rest awaits you and must be entered into by faith, how do you respond? **6.** What is the "Word of God" (v. 12)? Spoken by whom (1:1, 2; 2:2; 3:5)? Described how? With what impact? What does it mean that God's Word is Living? Active? That it penetrates? Judges? How has the author used the "Word of God" thus far?

REFLECT: 1. How would you explain the heavenly rest to someone who is not a Christian? **2.** Would it ever be accurate to say that only the weary will find rest? Why or why not? **3.** What evidence do you have that the Word of God is living and active today? How do you react to this view of the Word of God: encouraged, frightened, or sobered?

OPEN: If on the pastor search committee of your church, what three qualities would you look for?

DIG: 1. What are we to conclude from Jesus' priesthood? How does this relate to his previous warnings (e.g., 2:1-3; 3:1, 12-15; 4:1, 11)? **2.** What about Jesus' priesthood is encouraging (vv. 14-15)? How so? What is the significance of Jesus' full humanity here? Likewise, his sinlessness? How shall we then respond (v. 16)? How differently might the Jews have responded? **3.** What is the significance of the titles ascribed to Jesus (v. 14)? What else has the author said about Jesus' high priesthood (2:17; 3:1)? **4.** How does the role of the Jewish high priest compare to Jesus' role (5:1-10)? In terms of how each is chosen? How each relates to sinners?

How each intercedes with God? **5.** How do Jesus' prayers in verse 7 (see also Mk. 14:32-36), demonstrate Jesus' humanity? How does God answer those prayers (vv. 8-10; also 2:10)? **6.** What two qualities of a high priest does Jesus possess (5:1-10) to be designated high priest in the line of Melchizedek (vv. 6, 10; for additional details see chapter 7)?

REFLECT: 1. Why is it hard for many people to trust the love of God? **2.** What kind of situations lead folks to consider turning back from Christ? **3.** What advantage is it to you to see one of the roles of Jesus as being the great high priest? **4.** How would you explain the priesthood of Jesus without reference to the Old Testament sacrificial system?

OPEN: If you could take it hot out of the oven to eat with a glass of cold milk, what would you choose — chocolate chip cookies, pound cake or homemade bread with butter? What is your favorite junk food?

DIG: 1. Why does the author hesitate to give his readers further details about the Melchizedek order (vv. 10-12)? What distinguishes the immature believers (vv. 11-14)? **2.** How does a Christian mature (5:14-6:3)? What are these foundational truths that mature Christians already know? What do you know about repentance and faith? Baptism? Laying on of hands? Resurrection of the dead? Judgment? **3.** What does the author once again warn is "impossible" (vv. 4-6)? What five phrases distinguish those who are tempted to fall? To what experience does each phrase refer? Is their potential fate (v. 6) reversible? Why (see also Mt. 10:33)? How is your answer supported by the agricultural analogy (vv. 7-8)? **4.** Having issued such a stern warning directed to others, how does the author then encourage his readers to do "better" (vv. 9-12)? What "parental logic" do you see here? Positive incentives? Negative ones? Praising? Prodding?

REFLECT: 1. How would you describe your spiritual diet at the moment? **2.** Do you think it's "impossible" for a person who has once been "enlightened" and who has genuinely "fallen away" to repent again and walk with God? Why or why not? **3.** What response does it bring about in you when people have confidence in you (v. 9)? **4.** What factors tend to promote spiritual laziness in your life?

[4]No one takes this honor upon himself; he must be called by God, just as Aaron was. [5]So Christ also did not take upon himself the glory of becoming a high priest. But God said to him,

> "You are my Son;
>   today I have become your Father. [w]' [x]

[6]And he says in another place,

> "You are a priest forever,
>   in the order of Melchizedek." [y]

[7]During the days of Jesus' life on earth, he offered up prayers and petitions with loud cries and tears to the one who could save him from death, and he was heard because of his reverent submission. [8]Although he was a son, he learned obedience from what he suffered [9]and, once made perfect, he became the source of eternal salvation for all who obey him [10]and was designated by God to be high priest in the order of Melchizedek.

Warning Against Falling Away

[11]We have much to say about this, but it is hard to explain because you are slow to learn. [12]In fact, though by this time you ought to be teachers, you need someone to teach you the elementary truths of God's word all over again. You need milk, not solid food! [13]Anyone who lives on milk, being still an infant, is not acquainted with the teaching about righteousness. [14]But solid food is for the mature, who by constant use have trained themselves to distinguish good from evil.

6 Therefore let us leave the elementary teachings about Christ and go on to maturity, not laying again the foundation of repentance from acts that lead to death, [z] and of faith in God, [2]instruction about baptisms, the laying on of hands, the resurrection of the dead, and eternal judgment. [3]And God permitting, we will do so.

[4]It is impossible for those who have once been enlightened, who have tasted the heavenly gift, who have shared in the Holy Spirit, [5]who have tasted the goodness of the word of God and the powers of the coming age, [6]if they fall away, to be brought back to repentance, because [a] to their loss they are crucifying the Son of God all over again and subjecting him to public disgrace.

[7]Land that drinks in the rain often falling on it and that produces a crop useful to those for whom it is farmed receives the blessing of God. [8]But land that produces thorns and thistles is worthless and is in danger of being cursed. In the end it will be burned.

[9]Even though we speak like this, dear friends, we are confident of better things in your case—things that accompany salvation. [10]God is not unjust; he will not forget your work and the love you have shown him as you have helped his people and continue to help them. [11]We want each of you to show this same diligence to the very end, in order to make your hope sure. [12]We do not want you to become lazy, but to imitate those who through faith and patience inherit what has been promised.

---

[w]5 Or *have begotten you*   [x]5 Psalm 2:7   [y]6 Psalm 110:4   [z]1 Or *from useless rituals*   [a]6 Or *repentance while*

The Certainty of God's Promise

[13]When God made his promise to Abraham, since there was no one greater for him to swear by, he swore by himself, [14]saying, "I will surely bless you and give you many descendants."[b] [15]And so after waiting patiently, Abraham received what was promised.

[16]Men swear by someone greater than themselves, and the oath confirms what is said and puts an end to all argument. [17]Because God wanted to make the unchanging nature of his purpose very clear to the heirs of what was promised, he confirmed it with an oath. [18]God did this so that, by two unchangeable things in which it is impossible for God to lie, we who have fled to take hold of the hope offered to us may be greatly encouraged. [19]We have this hope as an anchor for the soul, firm and secure. It enters the inner sanctuary behind the curtain, [20]where Jesus, who went before us, has entered on our behalf. He has become a high priest forever, in the order of Melchizedek.

Melchizedek the Priest

7 This Melchizedek was king of Salem and priest of God Most High. He met Abraham returning from the defeat of the kings and blessed him, [2]and Abraham gave him a tenth of everything. First, his name means "king of righteousness"; then also, "king of Salem" means "king of peace." [3]Without father or mother, without genealogy, without beginning of days or end of life, like the Son of God he remains a priest forever.

[4]Just think how great he was: Even the patriarch Abraham gave him a tenth of the plunder! [5]Now the law requires the descendants of Levi who become priests to collect a tenth from the people—that is, their brothers—even though their brothers are descended from Abraham. [6]This man, however, did not trace his descent from Levi, yet he collected a tenth from Abraham and blessed him who had the promises. [7]And without doubt the lesser person is blessed by the greater. [8]In the one case, the tenth is collected by men who die; but in the other case, by him who is declared to be living. [9]One might even say that Levi, who collects the tenth, paid the tenth through Abraham, [10]because when Melchizedek met Abraham, Levi was still in the body of his ancestor.

Jesus Like Melchizedek

[11]If perfection could have been attained through the Levitical priesthood (for on the basis of it the law was given to the people), why was there still need for another priest to come—one in the order of Melchizedek, not in the order of Aaron? [12]For when there is a change of the priesthood, there must also be a change of the law. [13]He of whom these things are said belonged to a different tribe, and no one from that tribe has ever served at the altar. [14]For it is clear that our Lord descended from Judah, and in regard to that tribe Moses said nothing about priests. [15]And what we have said is even more clear if another priest like

[b]14 Gen. 22:17

OPEN: In which of the following do you have the most difficulty "waiting patiently": (a) for elevators, (b) for food in a restaurant, (c) in traffic jams, (d) for Christmas?

DIG: 1. What crisis were the Hebrews facing (see 3:13. 6:6)? **2.** Why would it be helpful to be reminded of Abraham? **3.** What part does Jesus now play for Christians? Tie in how Jesus helps in our crisis and how his presence helps us be certain of God's promise.

REFLECT: 1. What areas of your life are the hardest for you to trust God? The easiest? Why? **2.** Why do we want God to respond to our needs more quickly? **3.** In what sense do God's promises from the past act as an anchor for you today?

OPEN: When you were a child, who were some of your heroes? What made them heroes? How did you spend (or save) your allowance as a child?

DIG: 1. From this passage what do we know about Melchizedek? About his meeting with Abraham? **2.** What additional information about this event is found in Genesis 14:17-20? **3.** How does Abraham regard Melchizedek? What do the receiving of the tithe and the blessing signal about Melchizedek? **4.** What does the author suggest in comparing Melchizedek with Levi and the Levitical priests?

REFLECT: 1. What importance do you attach to some of the obscure Old Testament characters like Melchizedek? **2.** Is the Old Testament largely a closed book for you? Why or why not?

OPEN: How would you describe the perfect omelette? The perfect child? The perfect evening? The perfect pastor? The perfect you?

DIG: 1. Who is the new priest? Why was he necessary (v. 11)? In which priestly line does he stand? Why (vv. 12-13)? **2.** On what basis did Jesus become a priest (vv. 15-16)? How is it he could become a priest 'forever'? **3.** Why was the law set aside (vv. 18-19)? In what senses had the law failed? How does the argument in verse 18 parallel that in verse 11? What then are the two features of the Jewish religious system that have been superceded? **4.** What is the author's next reason that Jesus' priesthood is superior (vv. 20-22)? By what oath did he become priest (vv. 20-21)? With what result (v. 22)? **5.** What is the advantage of a permanent priesthood (vv. 23-25)? **6.** In what final way is Jesus superior as a high priest (vv. 26-28)? What is the fourfold contrast between the two types of priests (v. 28)? **7.** In what ways is Melchizedek superior to Levi (vv. 11-28)? On the basis of what Old Testament passage does the author to the Hebrews argue the superiority of Melchizedek? The superiority of Jesus?

REFLECT: 1. Is there a chance that you will be perfect in this life? How often are you tempted to earn your salvation through attempting perfection? **2.** How secure do you feel in having Jesus as your high priest? **3.** Since Jesus, our high priest, meets our needs, how can we better appropriate this reality in our daily lives? **4.** Supposing we did have a faith which required perfection, which emotion would dominate your life: false pride or true despair? Why? What good news from this passage speaks to you in this regard?

OPEN: 1. What are you best at forgetting? **2.** By the year 2050, what current necessities do you think might be obsolete? **3.** What is one thing you wish was obsolete right now? Why?

DIG: 1. What is the point of the previous argument (vv. 1-2)? How would this offer a strong incentive not to turn away from Christianity as some of these readers are tempted to do? Who is Jesus (v. 1)? What does he do? (v. 2)? Where does he do it? What contrast is made between tabernacles (vv. 2, 5)? **2.** How does the author further specify the work of a high priest (v. 7)? Why would Jesus have not been a priest on earth (vv. 3-4; also 7:27)? **3.** Contrast the location, nature and function of the two priesthoods described in verses 1-5. **4.** Why is Jesus' ministry superior (v. 6)? What is a covenant? What is a mediator? What was the old covenant that was administered by the priests (Ex. 19:5-6; 24:1-8)? What is the new covenant mediated by Jesus (vv. 10-12)? **5.** Why was a

Melchizedek appears, ¹⁶one who has become a priest not on the basis of a regulation as to his ancestry but on the basis of the power of an indestructible life. ¹⁷For it is declared:

"You are a priest forever,
in the order of Melchizedek." ᶜ

¹⁸The former regulation is set aside because it was weak and useless ¹⁹(for the law made nothing perfect), and a better hope is introduced, by which we draw near to God.

²⁰And it was not without an oath! Others became priests without any oath, ²¹but he became a priest with an oath when God said to him:

"The Lord has sworn
and will not change his mind:
'You are a priest forever.' " ᶜ

²²Because of this oath, Jesus has become the guarantee of a better covenant.

²³Now there have been many of those priests, since death prevented them from continuing in office; ²⁴but because Jesus lives forever, he has a permanent priesthood. ²⁵Therefore he is able to save completely ᵈ those who come to God through him, because he always lives to intercede for them.

²⁶Such a high priest meets our need—one who is holy, blameless, pure, set apart from sinners, exalted above the heavens. ²⁷Unlike the other high priests, he does not need to offer sacrifices day after day, first for his own sins, and then for the sins of the people. He sacrificed for their sins once for all when he offered himself. ²⁸For the law appoints as high priests men who are weak; but the oath, which came after the law, appointed the Son, who has been made perfect forever.

The High Priest of a New Covenant

8 The point of what we are saying is this: We do have such a high priest, who sat down at the right hand of the throne of the Majesty in heaven, ²and who serves in the sanctuary, the true tabernacle set up by the Lord, not by man.

³Every high priest is appointed to offer both gifts and sacrifices, and so it was necessary for this one also to have something to offer. ⁴If he were on earth, he would not be a priest, for there are already men who offer the gifts prescribed by the law. ⁵They serve at a sanctuary that is a copy and shadow of what is in heaven. This is why Moses was warned when he was about to build the tabernacle: "See to it that you make everything according to the pattern shown you on the mountain." ᵉ ⁶But the ministry Jesus has received is as superior to theirs as the covenant of which he is mediator is superior to the old one, and it is founded on better promises.

⁷For if there had been nothing wrong with that first covenant, no place would have been sought for another. ⁸But God found fault with the people and said ᶠ:

ᶜ17,21 Psalm 110:4   ᵈ25 Or *forever*   ᵉ5 Exodus 25:40   ᶠ8 Some manuscripts may be translated *fault and said to the people.*

"The time is coming, declares the Lord,
    when I will make a new covenant
with the house of Israel
    and with the house of Judah.
⁹It will not be like the covenant
    I made with their forefathers
when I took them by the hand
    to lead them out of Egypt,
because they did not remain faithful to my covenant,
    and I turned away from them,
                                    declares the Lord.
¹⁰This is the covenant I will make with the house of Israel
    after that time, declares the Lord.
I will put my laws in their minds
    and write them on their hearts.
I will be their God,
    and they will be my people.
¹¹No longer will a man teach his neighbor,
    or a man his brother, saying, 'Know the Lord,'
because they will all know me,
    from the least of them to the greatest.
¹²For I will forgive their wickedness
    and will remember their sins no more."ᵍ

¹³By calling this covenant "new," he has made the first one obsolete; and what is obsolete and aging will soon disappear.

Worship in the Earthly Tabernacle

9 Now the first covenant had regulations for worship and also an earthly sanctuary. ²A tabernacle was set up. In its first room were the lampstand, the table and the consecrated bread; this was called the Holy Place. ³Behind the second curtain was a room called the Most Holy Place, ⁴which had the golden altar of incense and the gold-covered ark of the covenant. This ark contained the gold jar of manna, Aaron's staff that had budded, and the stone tablets of the covenant. ⁵Above the ark were the cherubim of the Glory, overshadowing the atonement cover.ʰ But we cannot discuss these things in detail now.

⁶When everything had been arranged like this, the priests entered regularly into the outer room to carry on their ministry. ⁷But only the high priest entered the inner room, and that only once a year, and never without blood, which he offered for himself and for the sins the people had committed in ignorance. ⁸The Holy Spirit was showing by this that the way into the Most Holy Place had not yet been disclosed as long as the first tabernacle was still standing. ⁹This is an illustration for the present time, indicating that the gifts and sacrifices being offered were not able to clear the conscience of the worshiper. ¹⁰They are only a matter of food and drink and various ceremonial washings—external regulations applying until the time of the new order.

new covenant necessary (vv. 7-9)? What four promises does God make in the new covenant (vv. 10-12)? What does the new covenant imply as to the fate of Judaism (v. 13)?

REFLECT: 1. Which aspects of the new covenant are the greatest source of joy for you? **2.** What is the difference between "knowing" someone and "knowing about" that person? In which sense do you "know" the president of your country? By contrast, at what level do you "know" your earthly father? Your Heavenly Father? **3.** How difficult is it for you to believe God will remember your sins no more? Which sins of the past have you yet to forgive yourself for, even though God has? Why pray for forgiveness to be complete when you can worry all the more instead?

OPEN: In your childhood home where was the "Holy of Holies"—that place where you were forbidden to go or not allowed to touch?

DIG: 1. From verses 1-5, how do you picture this earthly sanctuary with all its key elements? What is the significance of each item in the Holy Place? In the Most Holy Place? Why do you think one is holier? Which item was Indiana Jones searching for? Why? If such an archeological treasure were actually found today, what difference would that make for your faith? **2.** If you do want to "discuss these things in detail now," read Exodus 25-31, 35-40. **3.** Regarding the regulaltions for worship (vv. 6-10), what do you observe? What goes on in the outer room? In the inner room (see also Lev. 16:14f)? Why? What did *not* happen here at this time (vv. 8-9)? Why were their gifts and sacrifices not sufficient to clear their consciences? What would later prove sufficient?

REFLECT: 1. Where do you find worship most meaningful? **2.** What matters most to you about the order of service or the elements of worship? Why? What matters least? Why? What is most confusing? **3.** How do you clear your concience?

ᵍ12 Jer. 31:31-34   ʰ5 Traditionally *the mercy seat*

OPEN: 1. What event or experience have you gone through "once" but never want to go through again? **2.** How do you react to the sight of your own blood? To someone else's? Why?

DIG: 1. What kind of cleansing did the old system provide (v. 13)? **2.** Jesus' priesthood is exercised here in what setting? By what right (v. 12)? How often? **3.** How is the priesthood of Christ distinguished from the old system (vv. 3:12-14)? What types of cleansing did the two sacrificial systems bring about (vv. 13-14)? Why does Christ's sacrifice have the more significant, everlasting result? **4.** How is Christ's mediation like a "ransom" (v. 15): Who are the hostages? Hostage to what? What is the ransom price? What about those who lived and died before Christ: Is their sin somehow covered by this ransom, too (see also Ro. 3:25)? **5.** How is Christ's death like a "will" made good (vv. 16-18): Who are the beneficiaries? What is their inheritance? What puts the will in force? **6.** How is Christ's sacrifice like the old covenant in its emphasis on the shed blood (vv. 19-22): Whose blood? What for? How extensive is the application? How effective? **7.** What are the "copies" in this next analogy (vv. 23-24)? What then is the real thing? What makes that reality "better" than the copy, or the one sacrifice of Christ better than the many made by others (vv. 24-26)? **8.** In the last analogy here (vv. 27-28), how is the once-and-for-allness of Christ's death illustrated?

REFLECT: What argument, if any, can you find to counter this assertion in chapter 9 that Christ's death is unique, superior, effitive for salvation? Is it necessary to buy into all the Old Testament typologies to understand the blood of Christ? Why? How else do you explain the blood?

OPEN: What repetitious activity do you dislike most: (a) cleaning the bathroom? (b) mowing the lawn? (c) shaving? (d) driving to and from work? (e) doing the dishes? (f) getting out of bed? Why?

DIG: 1. Why is the law insufficient? Knowing how a shadow is produced, how then is the law a

The Blood of Christ

[11]When Christ came as high priest of the good things that are already here,[i] he went through the greater and more perfect tabernacle that is not man-made, that is to say, not a part of this creation. [12]He did not enter by means of the blood of goats and calves; but he entered the Most Holy Place once for all by his own blood, having obtained eternal redemption. [13]The blood of goats and bulls and the ashes of a heifer sprinkled on those who are ceremonially unclean sanctify them so that they are outwardly clean. [14]How much more, then, will the blood of Christ, who through the eternal Spirit offered himself unblemished to God, cleanse our consciences from acts that lead to death,[j] so that we may serve the living God!

[15]For this reason Christ is the mediator of a new covenant, that those who are called may receive the promised eternal inheritance—now that he has died as a ransom to set them free from the sins committed under the first covenant.

[16]In the case of a will,[k] it is necessary to prove the death of the one who made it, [17]because a will is in force only when somebody has died; it never takes effect while the one who made it is living. [18]This is why even the first covenant was not put into effect without blood. [19]When Moses had proclaimed every commandment of the law to all the people, he took the blood of calves, together with water, scarlet wool and branches of hyssop, and sprinkled the scroll and all the people. [20]He said, "This is the blood of the covenant, which God has commanded you to keep."[l] [21]In the same way, he sprinkled with the blood both the tabernacle and everything used in its ceremonies. [22]In fact, the law requires that nearly everything be cleansed with blood, and without the shedding of blood there is no forgiveness.

[23]It was necessary, then, for the copies of the heavenly things to be purified with these sacrifices, but the heavenly things themselves with better sacrifices than these. [24]For Christ did not enter a man-made sanctuary that was only a copy of the true one; he entered heaven itself, now to appear for us in God's presence. [25]Nor did he enter heaven to offer himself again and again, the way the high priest enters the Most Holy Place every year with blood that is not his own. [26]Then Christ would have had to suffer many times since the creation of the world. But now he has appeared once for all at the end of the ages to do away with sin by the sacrifice of himself. [27]Just as man is destined to die once, and after that to face judgment, [28]so Christ was sacrificed once to take away the sins of many people; and he will appear a second time, not to bear sin, but to bring salvation to those who are waiting for him.

Christ's Sacrifice Once for All

10 The law is only a shadow of the good things that are coming—not the realities themselves. For this reason it can never, by the same sacrifices repeated endlessly year after year, make perfect those who draw near to worship. [2]If it could, would they not have stopped being offered? For the worshipers

[i]11 Some early manuscripts *are to come*   [j]14 Or *from useless rituals*
[k]16 Same Greek word as *covenant*; also in verse 17   [l]20 Exodus 24:8

would have been cleansed once for all, and would no longer have felt guilty for their sins. [3]But those sacrifices are an annual reminder of sins, [4]because it is impossible for the blood of bulls and goats to take away sins.

[5]Therefore, when Christ came into the world, he said:

"Sacrifice and offering you did not desire,
but a body you prepared for me;
[6]with burnt offerings and sin offerings
you were not pleased.
[7]Then I said, 'Here I am—it is written about me in the scroll—
I have come to do your will, O God.' "[m]

[8]First he said, "Sacrifices and offerings, burnt offerings and sin offerings you did not desire, nor were you pleased with them" (although the law required them to be made). [9]Then he said, "Here I am, I have come to do your will." He sets aside the first to establish the second. [10]And by that will, we have been made holy through the sacrifice of the body of Jesus Christ once for all.

[11]Day after day every priest stands and performs his religious duties; again and again he offers the same sacrifices, which can never take away sins. [12]But when this priest had offered for all time one sacrifice for sins, he sat down at the right hand of God. [13]Since that time he waits for his enemies to be made his footstool, [14]because by one sacrifice he has made perfect forever those who are being made holy.

[15]The Holy Spirit also testifies to us about this. First he says:

[16]"This is the covenant I will make with them
after that time, says the Lord.
I will put my laws in their hearts,
and I will write them on their minds."[n]

[17]Then he adds:

"Their sins and lawless acts
I will remember no more."[o]

[18]And where these have been forgiven, there is no longer any sacrifice for sin.

A Call to Persevere

[19]Therefore, brothers, since we have confidence to enter the Most Holy Place by the blood of Jesus, [20]by a new and living way opened for us through the curtain, that is, his body, [21]and since we have a great priest over the house of God, [22]let us draw near to God with a sincere heart in full assurance of faith, having our hearts sprinkled to cleanse us from a guilty conscience and having our bodies washed with pure water. [23]Let us hold unswervingly to the hope we profess, for he who promised is faithful. [24]And let us consider how we may spur one another on toward love and good deeds. [25]Let us not give up meeting together, as some are in the habit of doing, but let us encourage one another—and all the more as you see the Day approaching.

[m]7 Psalm 40:6-8 (see Septuagint) [n]16 Jer. 31:33 [o]17 Jer. 31:34

"shadow" of reality? Where is true reality? **2.**What is one positive function of the annual animal sacrifice? **3.** In what ways does Christ replace the inadequate sacrifices of the law? How are Jesus' obedience and our holiness connected? **4.** What contrasts are listed in verses 11-13 between the old sacrificial system and the new? **5.** Why was Jesus' once and for all sacrifice made future sacrifice no longer necessary? **6.** In what sense are Christians already made perfect (or holy) while still in the process of being made holy (or perfect)?

REFLECT: 1. How much of your time is spent with a gnawing and vague sense of guilt: (a) all the time? (b) most of the time? (c) a little of the time? (d) a fraction of the time? **2.** In what sense are you now perfect (see v. 14)? In what way is God calling you to the practice of greater holiness? **3.** If you were asked to memorize one verse from this section, which would you choose and why?

OPEN: 1. How did you meet your spouse or "friend"? What was your dating like? Likewise, your courtship? The Day?

DIG: 1. Upon what two great realities does the author rest his case (vv. 19-21)? **2.** Given this great motive and means, what four-part challenge does the author give (vv. 21-25)? How does this passage parallel 4:14-16? **3.** What does it mean to "draw near to God" (v. 22)? How does inner cleansing and the outer rite of baptism make it possible to truly worship God? **4.** What hope are we to hold unswervingly? On what basis? Why has it been wavering for the original readers?

5. The author's call to fellowship in action and in worship is given a sense of urgency by what coming event? If they habitually reject Christ in favor of sin, what do they forfeit (v. 26; also 3:14; 6:4-6)? What can they expect instead (vv. 27, 30-31)? Why is this fate not so unexpected (vv. 28-29; also Dt. 17:2-6)? In rejecting Christ, of what three grievous sins would they be guilty? **7.** How does all of the above logic support the author's clinching statement in verse 31 (compare with 4:12-13; 6:8)? **8.** After such a dire warning, how does the author then encourage the Hebrews (vv. 32-39)? What previous testing had they faced (vv. 32-34)? What present course of action and future consequences is theirs to choose (vv. 35-36)? What future event ought to encourage them to persevere (vv. 37-38)? Why (vv. 38-39)?

REFLECT: 1. In what specific ways could you spur another Christian on toward love and good deeds? What (or who) spurs you on? **2.** What is the difference between deliberate sinning and "accidental" sinning? **3.** How much persecution do you experience because you are a believer? Do you think your spiritual strength would increase if you were persecuted? Why or why not?

OPEN: Who sticks in your memory as the greatest person of faith that you have personally known?

DIG: 1. What are the connections between what the author has just said in 10:35-39 and the themes of chapter 11? **2.** In his definition of faith in verse 1, what two verbs describe faith? What is the object of both of these verbs? Is our faith directed toward the future, toward the present, or toward both? Why do you conclude this? Write your own expanded definition of faith as you try to capture the meaning of verse 1. **3.** How does verse 6 exemplify this understanding of faith? **4.** How does verse 3 illustrate faith as the certainty "of what we do not see?" Why is faith necessary to see the Creator behind the creation? When we understand God to be the Creator, how does that effect our view of "life issues" today—abortion, nuclear war, and genetic engineering? When we affirm "chance plus time" as the creator, what happens then to the value we place on life? **5.** How come Abel's sacrifice

²⁶If we deliberately keep on sinning after we have received the knowledge of the truth, no sacrifice for sins is left, ²⁷but only a fearful expectation of judgment and of raging fire that will consume the enemies of God. ²⁸Anyone who rejected the law of Moses died without mercy on the testimony of two or three witnesses. ²⁹How much more severely do you think a man deserves to be punished who has trampled the Son of God under foot, who has treated as an unholy thing the blood of the covenant that sanctified him, and who has insulted the Spirit of grace? ³⁰For we know him who said, "It is mine to avenge; I will repay,"ᵖ and again, "The Lord will judge his people."ᑫ ³¹It is a dreadful thing to fall into the hands of the living God.

³²Remember those earlier days after you had received the light, when you stood your ground in a great contest in the face of suffering. ³³Sometimes you were publicly exposed to insult and persecution; at other times you stood side by side with those who were so treated. ³⁴You sympathized with those in prison and joyfully accepted the confiscation of your property, because you knew that you yourselves had better and lasting possessions.

³⁵So do not throw away your confidence; it will be richly rewarded. ³⁶You need to persevere so that when you have done the will of God, you will receive what he has promised. ³⁷For in just a very little while,

> "He who is coming will come and will not delay.
> ³⁸ But my righteous oneʳ will live by faith.
> And if he shrinks back,
> I will not be pleased with him."ˢ

³⁹But we are not of those who shrink back and are destroyed, but of those who believe and are saved.

By Faith

11 Now faith is being sure of what we hope for and certain of what we do not see. ²This is what the ancients were commended for.

³By faith we understand that the universe was formed at God's command, so that what is seen was not made out of what was visible.

⁴By faith Abel offered God a better sacrifice than Cain did. By faith he was commended as a righteous man, when God spoke well of his offerings. And by faith he still speaks, even though he is dead.

⁵By faith Enoch was taken from this life, so that he did not experience death; he could not be found, because God had taken him away. For before he was taken, he was commended as one who pleased God. ⁶And without faith it is impossible to please God, because anyone who comes to him must believe that he exists and that he rewards those who earnestly seek him.

⁷By faith Noah, when warned about things not yet seen, in holy fear built an ark to save his family. By his faith he condemned the world and became heir of the righteousness that comes by faith.

p30 Deut. 32:35   *q30* Deut. 32:36; Psalm 135:14   *r38* One early manuscript
But the righteous   *s38* Hab. 2:3,4

⁸By faith Abraham, when called to go to a place he would later receive as his inheritance, obeyed and went, even though he did not know where he was going. ⁹By faith he made his home in the promised land like a stranger in a foreign country; he lived in tents, as did Isaac and Jacob, who were heirs with him of the same promise. ¹⁰For he was looking forward to the city with foundations, whose architect and builder is God.

¹¹By faith Abraham, even though he was past age—and Sarah herself was barren—was enabled to become a father because he¹ considered him faithful who had made the promise. ¹²And so from this one man, and he as good as dead, came descendants as numerous as the stars in the sky and as countless as the sand on the seashore.

¹³All these people were still living by faith when they died. They did not receive the things promised; they only saw them and welcomed them from a distance. And they admitted that they were aliens and strangers on earth. ¹⁴People who say such things show that they are looking for a country of their own. ¹⁵If they had been thinking of the country they had left, they would have had opportunity to return. ¹⁶Instead, they were longing for a better country—a heavenly one. Therefore God is not ashamed to be called their God, for he has prepared a city for them.

¹⁷By faith Abraham, when God tested him, offered Isaac as a sacrifice. He who had received the promises was about to sacrifice his one and only son, ¹⁸even though God had said to him, "It is through Isaac that your offspring" will be reckoned."ᵛ ¹⁹Abraham reasoned that God could raise the dead, and figuratively speaking, he did receive Isaac back from death.

²⁰By faith Isaac blessed Jacob and Esau in regard to their future.

²¹By faith Jacob, when he was dying, blessed each of Joseph's sons, and worshiped as he leaned on the top of his staff.

²²By faith Joseph, when his end was near, spoke about the exodus of the Israelites from Egypt and gave instructions about his bones.

²³By faith Moses' parents hid him for three months after he was born, because they saw he was no ordinary child, and they were not afraid of the king's edict.

²⁴By faith Moses, when he had grown up, refused to be known as the son of Pharaoh's daughter. ²⁵He chose to be mistreated along with the people of God rather than to enjoy the pleasures of sin for a short time. ²⁶He regarded disgrace for the sake of Christ as of greater value than the treasures of Egypt, because he was looking ahead to his reward. ²⁷By faith he left Egypt, not fearing the king's anger; he persevered because he saw him who is invisible. ²⁸By faith he kept the Passover and the sprinkling of blood, so that the destroyer of the firstborn would not touch the firstborn of Israel.

²⁹By faith the people passed through the Red Seaʷ as on dry land; but when the Egyptians tried to do so, they were drowned.

³⁰By faith the walls of Jericho fell, after the people had marched around them for seven days.

is regarded as better than Cain's (see Gen. 4:1-12)? How did Abel's sacrifice prefigure the whole sacrificial system and Christ's ultimate sacrifice in a way Cain's did not (recall ch. 9-10)? **6.** What aspect of faith (v. 1) is demonstrated by Enoch (v. 5; see Gen. 5:21-24)? By Noah (v. 7; see Gen. 6:5-22; 7:11-12)? By Noah's mocking neighbors? **7.** How do each of the three examples from Abraham's life illustrate faith (vv. 8-10, 11-12, 17-19)? What do the verbs tell you in each instance? Likewise, the obstacles to be overcome? The resulting life-changes for himself? For his family? For believers today? **8.** If such ultimate results could not be foreseen by Abraham (v. 13), what kind of faith must he have had? What does it mean to be "aliens and strangers on earth", seeking the "city of God" in heaven (vv. 13-16)? **9.** What group of people does the author next use to illustrate faith (vv. 17-31)? Recall each Old Testament story which is referred to: What do the stories in verses 17-22 have in common? What five acts of faith are next mentioned (vv. 23-31)? **10.** What is the significance of Moses' suffering disgrace "for the sake of Christ" (v. 26)? For example, how does this bolster the author's use elsewhere of Old Testament passages in regard to Christ? **13.** What additional heroes of the faith are noted (vv. 32-38)? What great achievements were accomplished as a result of faith? What price was paid for such faith? What came of such faith (vv. 39-40)?

REFLECT: 1. How would you define "faith"? **2.** What are some verbs that describe your own faith? Why these? **3.** Of the people mentioned in this section, with whom do you feel you have the most in common? Why? With whom do you have the least in common? Why? Which situation would have been the most difficult for you to face? Why? **4.** How has your life changed as a result of your faith in God? What has your faith cost you? How has your faith affected your neighbors? **5.** What does it mean to you to be an alien and a stranger on earth? In what ways do you feel like a stranger in this world?

ᵗ11 Or *By faith even Sarah, who was past age, was enabled to bear children because she* ᵘ18 Greek *seed* ᵛ18 Gen. 21:12 ʷ29 That is, Sea of Reeds

³¹By faith the prostitute Rahab, because she welcomed the spies, was not killed with those who were disobedient. ˣ

³²And what more shall I say? I do not have time to tell about Gideon, Barak, Samson, Jephthah, David, Samuel and the prophets, ³³who through faith conquered kingdoms, administered justice, and gained what was promised; who shut the mouths of lions, ³⁴quenched the fury of the flames, and escaped the edge of the sword; whose weakness was turned to strength; and who became powerful in battle and routed foreign armies. ³⁵Women received back their dead, raised to life again. Others were tortured and refused to be released, so that they might gain a better resurrection. ³⁶Some faced jeers and flogging, while still others were chained and put in prison. ³⁷They were stonedʸ; they were sawed in two; they were put to death by the sword. They went about in sheepskins and goatskins, destitute, persecuted and mistreated— ³⁸the world was not worthy of them. They wandered in deserts and mountains, and in caves and holes in the ground.

³⁹These were all commended for their faith, yet none of them received what had been promised. ⁴⁰God had planned something better for us so that only together with us would they be made perfect.

God Disciplines His Sons

12 Therefore, since we are surrounded by such a great cloud of witnesses, let us throw off everything that hinders and the sin that so easily entangles, and let us run with perseverance the race marked out for us. ²Let us fix our eyes on Jesus, the author and perfecter of our faith, who for the joy set before him endured the cross, scorning its shame, and sat down at the right hand of the throne of God. ³Consider him who endured such opposition from sinful men, so that you will not grow weary and lose heart.

⁴In your struggle against sin, you have not yet resisted to the point of shedding your blood. ⁵And you have forgotten that word of encouragement that addresses you as sons:

"My son, do not make light of the Lord's discipline,
and do not lose heart when he rebukes you,
⁶because the Lord disciplines those he loves,
and he punishes everyone he accepts as a son."ᶻ

⁷Endure hardship as discipline; God is treating you as sons. For what son is not disciplined by his father? ⁸If you are not disciplined (and everyone undergoes discipline), then you are illegitimate children and not true sons. ⁹Moreover, we have all had human fathers who disciplined us and we respected them for it. How much more should we submit to the Father of our spirits and live! ¹⁰Our fathers disciplined us for a little while as they thought best; but God disciplines us for our good, that we may share in his holiness. ¹¹No discipline seems pleasant at the time, but painful. Later on, however, it produces a harvest of righteousness and peace for those who have been trained by it.

OPEN: 1. Of all your life experiences to date, which brought you the most discipline. Which one exposed an area where you have little discipline? **2.** Of all the races and contests you've been in, which ones were significant because of the crowd's reaction to you in particular?

DIG: 1. What "three" actions in verses 1-2 are Christians commanded to do as they run the race? Of what practical help are the cloud of witnesses (a sample of which were described in ch. 11)? **2.** Drawing from their example and your own experience, what does it mean to throw off sin and hindrances? To run with preseverence? To fix our eyes on Jesus? **3.** What does hardship demonstrate about a person's relationship to God? How should a person respond to God when disciplined? How does Christ's discipline differ from human discipline? What benefit does discipline bring?

REFLECT: 1. What comfort do you get from knowing that a cloud of witnesses is watching you run the Christian race? **2.** What are two obstacles that hinder and entangle you in your race? Why? **3.** What have you discovered that helps you keep your eyes fixed on Jesus? **4.** How has God disciplined you in the past? What did you learn from that? **5.** What's the hardest thing you're going through right now? How is God using this in your life, now and in your future?

ˣ31 Or *unbelieving*   ʸ37 Some early manuscripts *stoned; they were put to the test;*   ᶻ6 Prov. 3:11,12

[12]Therefore, strengthen your feeble arms and weak knees. [13]"Make level paths for your feet,"[a] so that the lame may not be disabled, but rather healed.

Warning Against Refusing God

[14]Make every effort to live in peace with all men and to be holy; without holiness no one will see the Lord. [15]See to it that no one misses the grace of God and that no bitter root grows up to cause trouble and defile many. [16]See that no one is sexually immoral, or is godless like Esau, who for a single meal sold his inheritance rights as the oldest son. [17]Afterward, as you know, when he wanted to inherit this blessing, he was rejected. He could bring about no change of mind, though he sought the blessing with tears.

[18]You have not come to a mountain that can be touched and that is burning with fire; to darkness, gloom and storm; [19]to a trumpet blast or to such a voice speaking words that those who heard it begged that no further word be spoken to them, [20]because they could not bear what was commanded: "If even an animal touches the mountain, it must be stoned."[b] [21]The sight was so terrifying that Moses said, "I am trembling with fear."[c]

[22]But you have come to Mount Zion, to the heavenly Jerusalem, the city of the living God. You have come to thousands upon thousands of angels in joyful assembly, [23]to the church of the firstborn, whose names are written in heaven. You have come to God, the judge of all men, to the spirits of righteous men made perfect, [24]to Jesus the mediator of a new covenant, and to the sprinkled blood that speaks a better word than the blood of Abel.

[25]See to it that you do not refuse him who speaks. If they did not escape when they refused him who warned them on earth, how much less will we, if we turn away from him who warns us from heaven? [26]At that time his voice shook the earth, but now he has promised, "Once more I will shake not only the earth but also the heavens."[d] [27]The words "once more" indicate the removing of what can be shaken—that is, created things—so that what cannot be shaken may remain.

[28]Therefore, since we are receiving a kingdom that cannot be shaken, let us be thankful, and so worship God acceptably with reverence and awe, [29]for our "God is a consuming fire."[e]

Concluding Exhortations

13 Keep on loving each other as brothers. [2]Do not forget to entertain strangers, for by so doing some people have entertained angels without knowing it. [3]Remember those in prison as if you were their fellow prisoners, and those who are mistreated as if you yourselves were suffering.

[4]Marriage should be honored by all, and the marriage bed kept pure, for God will judge the adulterer and all the sexually immoral. [5]Keep your lives free from the love of money and be content with what you have, because God has said,

OPEN: What most impresses you about the mountains: Their majesty? Tranquility? How they got there? How you got to their summit? How some mountains defy conquering? Which ones would you like to visit? Why?

DIG: 1. What six instructions does the author give (vv. 14-17)? How do these admonitions relate to disciplining your weaker members (vv. 12-13)? To not refusing God (v. 25)? **2.** In our Christian lives why is peace important? Holiness? Grace? How does bitterness affect our lives? Sexual immorality? Godlessness? What key principle, especially important to the Hebrews, does Esau illustrate (see also Gen. 25: 29-34; 27). **3.**What two "mountains" are contrasted here (vv. 18-21, 22-24)? What is the point of this comparison? How approachable is God on Mt. Sinai versus Mount Zion? In each case, who speaks? Trembles? Rejoices? Encourages you? **4.** What two ways of divine revelation and human response are contrasted in verses 25-29? What is the point here? What happens to those who refuse God's voice from Mt. Sinai (vv. 19, 25; also 3:17)? From heaven (vv. 25-27)? How has God spoken to us from heaven (see 1:2)? What is our reward and appropriate response (v. 28)?

REFLECT: 1. With whom are you not living in peace? What would it take to resolve that one? **2.** Likewise, what "bitter root" of the past threatens trouble today? What will it take to uproot it? **3.** What in this passage comforts you? What makes you uneasy? Why?

OPEN: 1. If you could use just one or two words to describe the relationship you had with your brothers and sisters when you were growing up, what would you say ("the big chill", "war and peace", "the James' gang".) **2.**What is your most memorable encounter with a stranger? Why?

DIG: 1. What topics does the author touch upon in verses 1-19? Why? How does all this relate together and to the situation of the Hebrews? **2.** What five personal qualities should characterize Christians (vv. 1-6)? What happens to us when

---

[a]13 Prov. 4:26   [b]20 Exodus 19:12,13   [c]21 Deut. 9:19   [d]26 Haggai 2:6
[e]29 Deut. 4:24

we neglect any of these areas? **3.** Which leaders is he probably referring to in verse 7? (see verse 11)? What is the significance of Jesus' changelessness? **4.** What "strange teaching" in particular, was a temptation to Hebrew Christians (vv. 9-10)? What rituals, mores, and other forms of legalism tempt us? Why? **5.** What is the point of the argument in verses 9-12? Based on his argument, what ought Christians then to do (vv. 13-16)? **6.** What is the relationship between a congregation and its leadership (v. 17)? Why does the author desire their prayers (vv. 18-19)? What does he pray for them (v. 20-21)? **7.** What is the author's final appeal (v. 23)? What personal notes does he add (v. 23-24)?

REFLECT: **1.** In which one of these five areas have you made the most progress: loving one another as brothers, entertaining strangers, remembering those in prison, keeping your marriage strong or staying free from the love of money? Which do you need the most work on? **2.** In which of these five areas is your church the strongest? The weakest? What happens when we neglect any of these areas? **3.** What's been the most significant thing you've learned from studying Hebrews? How has this affected your life?

> "Never will I leave you;
>   never will I forsake you."[f]

6So we say with confidence,

> "The Lord is my helper; I will not be afraid.
>   What can man do to me?"[g]

7Remember your leaders, who spoke the word of God to you. Consider the outcome of their way of life and imitate their faith. 8Jesus Christ is the same yesterday and today and forever.

9Do not be carried away by all kinds of strange teachings. It is good for our hearts to be strengthened by grace, not by ceremonial foods, which are of no value to those who eat them. 10We have an altar from which those who minister at the tabernacle have no right to eat.

11The high priest carries the blood of animals into the Most Holy Place as a sin offering, but the bodies are burned outside the camp. 12And so Jesus also suffered outside the city gate to make the people holy through his own blood. 13Let us, then, go to him outside the camp, bearing the disgrace he bore. 14For here we do not have an enduring city, but we are looking for the city that is to come.

15Through Jesus, therefore, let us continually offer to God a sacrifice of praise—the fruit of lips that confess his name. 16And do not forget to do good and to share with others, for with such sacrifices God is pleased.

17Obey your leaders and submit to their authority. They keep watch over you as men who must give an account. Obey them so that their work will be a joy, not a burden, for that would be of no advantage to you.

18Pray for us. We are sure that we have a clear conscience and desire to live honorably in every way. 19I particularly urge you to pray so that I may be restored to you soon.

20May the God of peace, who through the blood of the eternal covenant brought back from the dead our Lord Jesus, that great Shepherd of the sheep, 21equip you with everything good for doing his will, and may he work in us what is pleasing to him, through Jesus Christ, to whom be glory for ever and ever. Amen.

22Brothers, I urge you to bear with my word of exhortation, for I have written you only a short letter.

23I want you to know that our brother Timothy has been released. If he arrives soon, I will come with him to see you.

24Greet all your leaders and all God's people. Those from Italy send you their greetings.

25Grace be with you all.

f5 Deut. 31:6   *g6* Psalm 118:6,7

JAMES

INTRODUCTION

Authorship

In the New Testament there are apparently five men by the name of James, but only two who might conceivably have written this epistle — either James the apostle, or James the brother of Jesus. Since it is almost certain that the apostle James (the son of Zebedee) was killed by Herod in A.D. 44 (before the epistle could have been written), traditionally the author has been assumed to be James, the leader of the church in Jerusalem and the brother of Jesus (Mark 6:3).

The pilgrimage of James to faith is fascinating. At first Jesus' family was hostile to his ministry (John 7:5) and, in fact, tried to stop it at one point (Mark 3:21). Yet after Jesus' ascension, Jesus' mother and brothers are listed among the early believers (Acts 1:14). For James, this coming to faith may have resulted from Jesus' postresurrection appearance to him (1 Cor. 15:7).

Apart from the fact that they were closely related, James' relationship to Jesus is not totally clear. Some maintained that they were cousins (the New Testament word for "brother" is looser in meaning than the modern equivalent). Some suggest he was a half-brother to Jesus, a son of Mary and Joseph. Others say that James might have been an older stepbrother of Jesus by a (conjectural) marriage of Joseph previous to his marriage to Mary. The latter view, which excludes any blood relationship to Jesus, might better explain the failure of Jesus' brother to believe in Him during His lifetime (Mark 3:21, John 7:2-8); and James' lack of concern for Mary because she was only their stepmother might also explain why Jesus, from the cross, committed His mother to the apostle John (John 19:25-27). But the reason may have been that Mary's discipleship alienated her from her other children, who still did not believe in Jesus. (Robert H. Gundrey, *A Survey of the New Testament,* p. 324)

A Church Leader

In any case, James emerged as the leader of the church in Jerusalem. It was to James that Peter reported after his miraculous escape from Herod's prison (Acts 12:17). James presided over the first Jerusalem Council which decided the important question of whether to admit Gentiles to the church (Acts 15, especially vv. 13-21). James was consulted by Paul during his first trip to Jerusalem after his conversion (Gal. 1:19), and then James joined in the official recognition of Paul's call as Apostle to the Gentiles (Gal. 2:8-10). It is to James that Paul later brought the collection for the poor (Acts 21:17-25).

A Jew

We also know that James was a strict Jew who adhered to the Mosaic Law (Gal. 2:12), yet unlike the Judaizers, he supported Paul's ministry to the Gentiles (Acts 21:17-26). Later accounts indicate that James was martyred in A.D. 62.

The question of who wrote the book of James is, however, still somewhat of a puzzle primarily because Jesus and his saving work is mentioned so little — a curious omission if the author was Jesus' brother. This question baffled even the ancient church. Both the Latin Father Jerome and the church historian Eusebius (as well as others) observe that not all accept James as having been written by our Lord's brother.

Audience

James is one of the Catholic (general) Epistles (along with 1 and 2 Peter, John's epistles, and Jude), so called because it has no single destination. Thus, it is not clear to whom James is addressing his comments. At first glance, it appears that he is writing to Jewish Christians dispersed around the Greek world: "to the twelve tribes scattered among the nations" (1:1). But since Peter uses the same sort of inscription (1 Peter 1:1-2) when he is clearly addressing Gentile Christians who consider themselves the New Israel, James' destination remains unclear. In fact, a strong case can be made (see Sophie Laws, *The Epistle of James: Harper New Testament Commentaries,* pp. 32-38) that James was writing for a community of "God-fearers," that is, Gentiles who had been deeply attracted to Judaism. That such folk were then drawn to Christianity is clear from examples in Acts, such as Cornelius (Acts 10:2, 22), Lydia (Acts 16:14), Titius Justus (Acts 18:7), and others. This would help to explain the convergence of Jewish, Greek, and Christian elements in the book of James.

Date

It is difficult to date the Book of James. Some place it very early, around A.D. 45, making it the first New Testament book. Others date it quite late.

Characteristics

Among the New Testament books, James is an oddity. It is written in quite a different style from the others, more like the Book of Proverbs than Paul's epistles. But even more than its style, its contents set James apart. It does not treat many of those themes we have come to expect in the New Testament.

Its Omissions

There is no mention of the Holy Spirit and no reference to the redemptive work or resurrection of Christ. In fact, it contains only two references to the name Jesus Christ (1:1 and 2:1). Furthermore, when examples are given, they are drawn from the lives of Old Testament prophets, not from the experiences of Jesus. Although the title *Lord* appears eleven times, it generally refers to the name of God (in Old Testament fashion) and not to the kingly authority of Jesus. Indeed, it is God the Father who is the focus of the Book of James.

Thus, Martin Luther wrote in his preface to the New Testament that "St. John's Gospel and his first epistle, St. Paul's epistles, especially Romans, Galatians, and Ephesians, and St. Peter's first epistle are the books that show you Christ and teach you all that is necessary and salvatory for you to know, even if you were never to see or hear any other book or doctrine. Therefore St. James' epistle is really an epistle of straw, compared to these others, for it has nothing of the nature of the gospel about it."

Its Contributions

Luther notwithstanding, James is clearly a Christian piece of writing. Full of wisdom, it is based solidly on the teaching of Jesus and is a genuine product of first-century Christianity. To be sure, it is not as directly theological as many other New Testament Epistles, but then James' concern is not doctrinal (which he seems to assume) but rather ethical — how the Christian faith is to be lived on a day-by-day basis. As Johann Gottfrieds Herder wrote, "If the Epistle is of straw, then there is within that straw a very hearty, firm, nourishing . . . grain" (*Briefe Zweener Brüder Jesu in unserem Kanon,* in *Herders sömmtliche Werke* ed. Bernard Suphan, Vol 7, p. 500, n. 2).

Background

James draws his language, images, and ideas from three worlds: Judaism, Greek culture, and early Christianity. From Christianity, he uses the language of eschatology (5:7-9), common patterns of Christian ethical instruction, which parallel those in 1 Peter (1:2-4, 21; 4:7-10), and especially, the teachings of Jesus (1:5, 17; 2:5, 8, 19; 4:3; 5:12). From Judaism, he draws his insistence on the unity of God, concern for keeping law, and quotations from Jewish Scriptures (2:8, 11, 21-25; 4:6; 5:11, 17-18) along with his use of Jewish terms (e.g., the word translated "hell" in 3:6 is the Hebrew Gehenna). Christianity and Judaism shared his concern for the poor and oppressed. From the Greek-speaking world—"the shared culture of the eastern Mediterranean area within the Roman Empire that resulted from the conquests of Alexander the Great" (Laws, *The Epistle of James,* p. 5), he takes the language (which he uses with skill), the source of his Old Testament quotations (he uses the Greek Old Testament, not the Hebrew version), Greek forms of composition, and metaphors drawn from Greek and Latin sources (e.g., the horse and the ship in 3:3-4).

Structure

Written in epistle (letter) form, James is loosely structured and rambling in style. It seems to jump from one idea to another without any overall plan, apart from that of providing a manual of Christian conduct. In fact, the Book of James shares many characteristics of the sermonic style of both Greek philosophers and Jewish rabbis. As in Greek sermons, James carries on a conversation with a hypothetical opponent (2:18-26; 5:13-16), switches subjects by means of a question (2:14; 4:1), uses many commands (60 of the 108 verses in James are imperatives), relies on vivid images from everyday life (3:3-6; 5:7), illustrates points by reference to famous people (2:21-23, 25; 5:11, 17), uses vivid antitheses in which the right way is set alongside the wrong way (2:13, 26), begins the sermon with a striking paradox that captures the hearers' attention (1:2, "consider it pure joy . . . whenever you face trials"), is quite stern (2:20; 4:4), and clinches a point by means of a quotation (1:11, 17; 4:6; 5:11, 20) (Ropes and Barclay). It should be noted, as William Barclay writes:

> The main aim of these ancient preachers, it must be remembered, was not to investigate new truth; it was to awaken sinners to the error of their ways, and to compel them to see truths which they knew but deliberately neglected or had forgotten (*The Letters of James and Peter,* pp. 33-34).

Jewish sermons had many of the same characteristics. But rabbis also had the habit, as did James, of constructing sermons that were deliberately disconnected—a series of moral truths and exhortations strung together like beads.

Theme

While James clearly stands in the tradition of other Christian writers, he has some special concerns. The relationship between rich and poor crops up at various points (1:9-11; 5:1-4)—an issue of special significance to the modern affluent West. He is concerned about the use and abuse of speech (1:19, 22-24, 26; 2:12; 3:3-12; 5:12). He gives instruction on prayer (1:5-8; 4:2-3; 5:13-18). Above all, he is concerned with ethical behavior. How believers act, he says, has eschatological significance; future reward or punishment depends on it. In this regard, James bemoans the inconsistence of human behavior (1:6-8, 22-24; 2:14-17; 4:1, 3). Human beings are "double-minded" (1:8; 4:8) in sharp contrast to God, who is one (2:19).

James has been incorrectly understood by some to be contradicting Paul's doctrine of justification by faith (2:14-26). In fact if James had Paul in mind at all, he was addressing himself to those who had perverted Paul's message—insisting that it doesn't matter what you do, as long as you have faith. James responded by asserting that works are the outward evidence of inner faith. Works make faith visible to others. In contrast, Paul was concerned with our standing before God. As is evident from Romans 12-15, Paul certainly agreed with James that faith in Christ has direct implications for how believers live.

James

OPEN: 1. Is it harder to go through tough times for yourself, or watch someone you love go through hard times? **2.** What is your favorite garage sale purchase? Who is your favorite underdog?

DIG: 1. How is it possible to rejoice in difficult circumstances? Does perseverence here imply active overcoming or passive acceptance? Does wisdom here imply exceptional knowledge or moral insight? **2.** What is the big challenge here to Christians facing doubt? Is doubt to be expressed or suppressed or what? Why? **3.** In your opinion, what would a brother in humble circumstances have to take pride in? What is low about a rich man's position? **4.** What is the practical difference between trials and temptations? How is the birth process an apt metaphor to distinguish the source, the steps and the end result of temptation? How does one go about resisting temptation?

REFLECT: 1. When have you felt like giving up: In marriage? With your kids? At work? Then what did you do? **2.** What kind of pain is the hardest for you to endure: Physical suffering or emotional loss? **3.** What sustains you most in times of stress and trial? **4.** What is a "good and perfect gift" that you are thankful for?

OPEN: When you look at yourself in the morning, what "little things" do you try to cover up for appearance sake?

DIG: 1. How are we to "listen": Let the other person speak first? Don't respond in anger? Engage the mind before the mouth? Show we listen by what we do? Turn up the volume on our spiritual receiver to hear what God is saying through the other person and God's word? **2.** What characterizes true religion: Action or belief? Acts of charity or acts of piety? Why do you think this is so? **3.** How can one attain "pure

1 James, a servant of God and of the Lord Jesus Christ,

To the twelve tribes scattered among the nations:

Greetings.

Trials and Temptations

²Consider it pure joy, my brothers, whenever you face trials of many kinds, ³because you know that the testing of your faith develops perseverance. ⁴Perseverance must finish its work so that you may be mature and complete, not lacking anything. ⁵If any of you lacks wisdom, he should ask God, who gives generously to all without finding fault, and it will be given to him. ⁶But when he asks, he must believe and not doubt, because he who doubts is like a wave of the sea, blown and tossed by the wind. ⁷That man should not think he will receive anything from the Lord; ⁸he is a double-minded man, unstable in all he does.

⁹The brother in humble circumstances ought to take pride in his high position. ¹⁰But the one who is rich should take pride in his low position, because he will pass away like a wild flower. ¹¹For the sun rises with scorching heat and withers the plant; its blossom falls and its beauty is destroyed. In the same way, the rich man will fade away even while he goes about his business.

¹²Blessed is the man who perseveres under trial, because when he has stood the test, he will receive the crown of life that God has promised to those who love him.

¹³When tempted, no one should say, "God is tempting me." For God cannot be tempted by evil, nor does he tempt anyone; ¹⁴but each one is tempted when, by his own evil desire, he is dragged away and enticed. ¹⁵Then, after desire has conceived, it gives birth to sin; and sin, when it is full-grown, gives birth to death.

¹⁶Don't be deceived, my dear brothers. ¹⁷Every good and perfect gift is from above, coming down from the Father of the heavenly lights, who does not change like shifting shadows. ¹⁸He chose to give us birth through the word of truth, that we might be a kind of firstfruits of all he created.

Listening and Doing

¹⁹My dear brothers, take note of this: Everyone should be quick to listen, slow to speak and slow to become angry, ²⁰for man's anger does not bring about the righteous life that God desires. ²¹Therefore, get rid of all moral filth and the evil that is so prevalent and humbly accept the word planted in you, which can save you.

²²Do not merely listen to the word, and so deceive yourselves. Do what it says. ²³Anyone who listens to the word but does not do what it says is like a man who looks at his face in a mirror ²⁴and, after looking at himself, goes away and immediately forgets what he looks like. ²⁵But the man who looks intently into the perfect law that gives freedom, and continues to do this, not

forgetting what he has heard, but doing it—he will be blessed in what he does.

²⁶If anyone considers himself religious and yet does not keep a tight rein on his tongue, he deceives himself and his religion is worthless. ²⁷Religion that God our Father accepts as pure and faultless is this: to look after orphans and widows in their distress and to keep oneself from being polluted by the world.

Favoritism Forbidden

2 My brothers, as believers in our glorious Lord Jesus Christ, don't show favoritism. ²Suppose a man comes into your meeting wearing a gold ring and fine clothes, and a poor man in shabby clothes also comes in. ³If you show special attention to the man wearing fine clothes and say, "Here's a good seat for you," but say to the poor man, "You stand there" or "Sit on the floor by my feet," ⁴have you not discriminated among yourselves and become judges with evil thoughts?

⁵Listen, my dear brothers: Has not God chosen those who are poor in the eyes of the world to be rich in faith and to inherit the kingdom he promised those who love him? ⁶But you have insulted the poor. Is it not the rich who are exploiting you? Are they not the ones who are dragging you into court? ⁷Are they not the ones who are slandering the noble name of him to whom you belong?

⁸If you really keep the royal law found in Scripture, "Love your neighbor as yourself,"ᵃ you are doing right. ⁹But if you show favoritism, you sin and are convicted by the law as law-breakers. ¹⁰For whoever keeps the whole law and yet stumbles at just one point is guilty of breaking all of it. ¹¹For he who said, "Do not commit adultery,"ᵇ also said, "Do not murder."ᶜ If you do not commit adultery but do commit murder, you have become a lawbreaker.

¹²Speak and act as those who are going to be judged by the law that gives freedom, ¹³because judgment without mercy will be shown to anyone who has not been merciful. Mercy triumphs over judgment!

Faith and Deeds

¹⁴What good is it, my brothers, if a man claims to have faith but has no deeds? Can such faith save him? ¹⁵Suppose a brother or sister is without clothes and daily food. ¹⁶If one of you says to him, "Go, I wish you well; keep warm and well fed," but does nothing about his physical needs, what good is it? ¹⁷In the same way, faith by itself, if it is not accompanied by action, is dead.

¹⁸But someone will say, "You have faith; I have deeds."

Show me your faith without deeds, and I will show you my faith by what I do. ¹⁹You believe that there is one God. Good! Even the demons believe that—and shudder.

²⁰You foolish man, do you want evidence that faith without deedsᵈ is useless? ²¹Was not our ancestor Abraham considered righteous for what he did when he offered his son Isaac on the

religion" (v. 27) and the "righteous life" (v. 20) God desires?

REFLECT: 1. When did you get serious about applying God's Word to your life? 2. What typically gets your goat? Why? 3. Who are the needy in your community? What are you doing to help them?

OPEN: 1. For what sporting or musical event would you buy the "best seats"? 2. Who in your family tree would come the closest to being a millionaire? 3. Have you ever been to a third world country where there are only two classes—rich and poor?

DIG: 1. On what principle should we challenge discrimination in any form? In what places (the church, the courts, housing, employment, etc.) should we apply this principle? 2. If rich and poor (black and white, male and female) are saved on the same basis (belief in Jesus), on what basis are they each judged? 3. While believers are not to show favoritism, does not God seem partial to widows, orphans, the poor and oppressed? Why or why not? 4. Is it possible to keep this royal law of neighbor love (v. 8)? Or is everyone bound to stumble at one point (v. 10)? In which case, is mercy or judgment called for? Why?

REFLECT: Speaking for your church, what kind of people (hippies, yuppies, elderly, divorced, un-educated, blue collar workers) tend not to be "your kind of folk"? What would James have to say about that situation?

OPEN: 1. Are you a doer or a thinker? Are you more likely to act without thinking or think without acting? 2. What was the nicest thing a stranger ever did for you recently?

DIG: 1. What kind of "faith" is James criticizing: Intellectual faith? Invisible faith? Inconsistent faith? Orthodox faith? Incomplete faith? Ignorant faith? Inward faith? Why? 2. What kind of "faith" is James commending: Ritual-keeping, works-oriented faith? Saving faith? Sanctifying faith? Faith toward God? Faith toward people? Why? 3. From what you know about Abraham and Rahab (the Jericho prostitute that allowed the Israel spies to hide in her home), how do these heroes of the faith prove James' point (vv. 20-26)? 4. If

---

ᵃ8 Lev. 19:18   *ᵇ11* Exodus 20:14; Deut. 5:18   *ᶜ11* Exodus 20:13; Deut. 5:17
ᵈ20 Some early manuscripts *dead*

altar? ²²You see that his faith and his actions were working together, and his faith was made complete by what he did. ²³And the scripture was fulfilled that says, "Abraham believed God, and it was credited to him as righteousness,"*e* and he was called God's friend. ²⁴You see that a person is justified by what he does and not by faith alone.

²⁵In the same way, was not even Rahab the prostitute considered righteous for what she did when she gave lodging to the spies and sent them off in a different direction? ²⁶As the body without the spirit is dead, so faith without deeds is dead.

Taming the Tongue

3 Not many of you should presume to be teachers, my brothers, because you know that we who teach will be judged more strictly. ²We all stumble in many ways. If anyone is never at fault in what he says, he is a perfect man, able to keep his whole body in check.

³When we put bits into the mouths of horses to make them obey us, we can turn the whole animal. ⁴Or take ships as an example. Although they are so large and are driven by strong winds, they are steered by a very small rudder wherever the pilot wants to go. ⁵Likewise the tongue is a small part of the body, but it makes great boasts. Consider what a great forest is set on fire by a small spark. ⁶The tongue also is a fire, a world of evil among the parts of the body. It corrupts the whole person, sets the whole course of his life on fire, and is itself set on fire by hell.

⁷All kinds of animals, birds, reptiles and creatures of the sea are being tamed and have been tamed by man, ⁸but no man can tame the tongue. It is a restless evil, full of deadly poison.

⁹With the tongue we praise our Lord and Father, and with it we curse men, who have been made in God's likeness. ¹⁰Out of the same mouth come praise and cursing. My brothers, this should not be. ¹¹Can both fresh water and salt*f* water flow from the same spring? ¹²My brothers, can a fig tree bear olives, or a grapevine bear figs? Neither can a salt spring produce fresh water.

Two Kinds of Wisdom

¹³Who is wise and understanding among you? Let him show it by his good life, by deeds done in the humility that comes from wisdom. ¹⁴But if you harbor bitter envy and selfish ambition in your hearts, do not boast about it or deny the truth. ¹⁵Such "wisdom" does not come down from heaven but is earthly, unspiritual, of the devil. ¹⁶For where you have envy and selfish ambition, there you find disorder and every evil practice.

¹⁷But the wisdom that comes from heaven is first of all pure; then peace-loving, considerate, submissive, full of mercy and good fruit, impartial and sincere. ¹⁸Peacemakers who sow in peace raise a harvest of righteousness.

e23 Gen. 15:6   *f11* Greek *bitter* (see also verse 14)

Submit Yourselves to God

4 What causes fights and quarrels among you? Don't they come from your desires that battle within you? ²You want something but don't get it. You kill and covet, but you cannot have what you want. You quarrel and fight. You do not have, because you do not ask God. ³When you ask, you do not receive, because you ask with wrong motives, that you may spend what you get on your pleasures.

⁴You adulterous people, don't you know that friendship with the world is hatred toward God? Anyone who chooses to be a friend of the world becomes an enemy of God. ⁵Or do you think Scripture says without reason that the spirit he caused to live in us envies intensely?ᵍ ⁶But he gives us more grace. That is why Scripture says:

"God opposes the proud
but gives grace to the humble."ʰ

⁷Submit yourselves, then, to God. Resist the devil, and he will flee from you. ⁸Come near to God and he will come near to you. Wash your hands, you sinners, and purify your hearts, you double-minded. ⁹Grieve, mourn and wail. Change your laughter to mourning and your joy to gloom. ¹⁰Humble yourselves before the Lord, and he will lift you up.

¹¹Brothers, do not slander one another. Anyone who speaks against his brother or judges him speaks against the law and judges it. When you judge the law, you are not keeping it, but sitting in judgment on it. ¹²There is only one Lawgiver and Judge, the one who is able to save and destroy. But you—who are you to judge your neighbor?

Boasting About Tomorrow

¹³Now listen, you who say, "Today or tomorrow we will go to this or that city, spend a year there, carry on business and make money." ¹⁴Why, you do not even know what will happen tomorrow. What is your life? You are a mist that appears for a little while and then vanishes. ¹⁵Instead, you ought to say, "If it is the Lord's will, we will live and do this or that." ¹⁶As it is, you boast and brag. All such boasting is evil. ¹⁷Anyone, then, who knows the good he ought to do and doesn't do it, sins.

Warning to Rich Oppressors

5 Now listen, you rich people, weep and wail because of the misery that is coming upon you. ²Your wealth has rotted, and moths have eaten your clothes. ³Your gold and silver are corroded. Their corrosion will testify against you and eat your flesh like fire. You have hoarded wealth in the last days. ⁴Look! The wages you failed to pay the workmen who mowed your fields are crying out against you. The cries of the harvesters have reached the ears of the Lord Almighty. ⁵You have lived on earth

OPEN: 1. Over what and with whom did you quarrel most when you were a kid? **2.** Did you ever get caught "two-timing" your steady? How did you get out of it?

DIG: 1. From what does this strife come: From persecution? Possessiveness? Private pleasures? Misguided prayer? Frustrated desire (see 1:14)? How accurate is James' diagnosis? **2.** How is James' tenfold prescription (vv. 7-10) an effective antidote? **3.** What is meant by "adulterous people" (v. 4), "friendship with the world" (v. 4), and submission to God (vv. 7-10)? **4.** Is such total submission or repentance toward God essential for all Christians or only some? Why or why not? **5.** How then shall we "judge" (vv. 11-12)?

REFLECT: 1. What is your usual response when your desires are frustrated? Where does that get you? **2.** How have you been guilty of "two-timing" God? **3.** When you pray, do you find yourself telling, asking, or praising God? **4.** Have you taken the cure prescribed by James?

OPEN: Are you a long range-planner, or do you take one day at a time?

DIG: 1. Regarding "tomorrows", what's wrong with planning? With "boasting"? With profit-making? **2.** What or who is overlooked here?

REFLECT: What then are you going to do with your appointment calendar and God's will?

OPEN: What experience most affected your social conscience?

DIG: 1. What is James saying about wealth: Is it sinful? Is it illusory? Hazardous to your health? A burdensome responsibility? A way to heaven? To hell? **2.** Who is James addressing as "rich people": Christian businessmen (as in 4:13-17)? Secular landowners? Today's multi-national corporations?

REFLECT: What abuses by the rich occur in the late 20th century? How could your church, or even your

---

ᵍ5 Or *that God jealously longs for the spirit that he made to live in us; or that the Spirit he caused to live in us longs jealously* ʰ6 Prov. 3:34

small group, use its resources to help overcome such inequity?

OPEN: What do you think of as "the good ole days" in your life? Were they really that good?

DIG: 1. Instead of retaliation or vengence, what does James urge the poor to do? Why? 2. What lessons are provided the Christian by the farmer? By the returning Judge? By the prophets? By Job? 3. How does honesty without oath-taking (v. 12) relate to perseverance without grumbling (vv. 7-11) and to health through prayer (vv. 13-18)?

REFLECT: Have you ever gone through a period when you doubted God's presence in the midst of hardship and suffering? Explain.

OPEN: As a child, did you pray before you went to bed at night? Did you pray the same prayer every night? Who taught you to pray?

DIG: 1. What is the connection between the spiritual, emotional, physical, vocational and relational areas in our lives? Can you be sick or sinful in one area and completely whole in the others? Why or why not? 2. How does the Body of Christ participate in the ministry of healing for one another? 3. If the prayer of a righteous person is so effective (v. 16), why do more people go to the bartender than the church to confess their sins? 4. In faith healing, is there a right way to pray (see also 1:5-8 and 4:3)? A right person to pray (prophet, saint or "a man just like us", vv. 16-17)? A right answer to such prayers (vv. 15-18; 4:15)? Why or why not?

REFLECT: 1. When have you come the closest to wandering from the faith? How did it happen? Who helped bring you back? How would you go about helping someone else who has wandered from the faith? 2. The Book of James can polarize those who grapple with it, leaving groups pulling in opposite directions. Which way do you find yourself leaning: Guilty or inspired? Resistant or repentant? Wavering or single-minded? Passing the buck to the rich, or passing out bucks to the poor?

in luxury and self-indulgence. You have fattened yourselves in the day of slaughter.[i] 6You have condemned and murdered innocent men, who were not opposing you.

Patience in Suffering

7Be patient, then, brothers, until the Lord's coming. See how the farmer waits for the land to yield its valuable crop and how patient he is for the autumn and spring rains. 8You too, be patient and stand firm, because the Lord's coming is near. 9Don't grumble against each other, brothers, or you will be judged. The Judge is standing at the door!

10Brothers, as an example of patience in the face of suffering, take the prophets who spoke in the name of the Lord. 11As you know, we consider blessed those who have persevered. You have heard of Job's perseverance and have seen what the Lord finally brought about. The Lord is full of compassion and mercy.

12Above all, my brothers, do not swear—not by heaven or by earth or by anything else. Let your "Yes" be yes, and your "No," no, or you will be condemned.

The Prayer of Faith

13Is any one of you in trouble? He should pray. Is anyone happy? Let him sing songs of praise. 14Is any one of you sick? He should call the elders of the church to pray over him and anoint him with oil in the name of the Lord. 15And the prayer offered in faith will make the sick person well; the Lord will raise him up. If he has sinned, he will be forgiven. 16Therefore confess your sins to each other and pray for each other so that you may be healed. The prayer of a righteous man is powerful and effective.

17Elijah was a man just like us. He prayed earnestly that it would not rain, and it did not rain on the land for three and a half years. 18Again he prayed, and the heavens gave rain, and the earth produced its crops.

19My brothers, if one of you should wander from the truth and someone should bring him back, 20remember this: Whoever turns a sinner from the error of his way will save him from death and cover over a multitude of sins.

---

i5 Or *yourselves as in a day of feasting*

1 PETER

INTRODUCTION

The General Epistles

The so-called Catholic or General Epistles consist of 1 and 2 Peter, Jude, James, and 1, 2, and 3 John. These documents were given this title because they seemed to be universal in scope. They were written to all churches and not just to one particular church or person, as were Paul's letters. This designation is not completely accurate, however. James and 1 Peter are written to specific, albeit widely scattered groups of Christians, while 2 and 3 John have a specific audience.

Audience

Its Location

First Peter is a circular letter to Christians living in the northwest section of Asia Minor (in what is now modern Turkey). Pontus, Galatia, Cappadocia, Asia, and Bithynia (1:1) are all Roman provinces. This area had a large population, and the fact that Christians were living throughout the region testifies to the success of early Christian missionaries.

That these Christians were mainly Gentiles is clear from the way Peter describes their preconversion life; he uses categories and phrases typically applied to pagans but not to Jews (1:14; 2:9-10; 4:3-4). Peter also uses the Greek form of his name, Cephas, in this letter, and not Simon, his Jewish name.

Its Need

On July 19 A.D. 64, Rome caught fire. For three days and three nights the fire blazed out of control. Ancient temples and landmarks were swept away. Homes were destroyed. Ten of the fourteen city wards suffered damage; three wards were reduced to rubble. The people of Rome were distraught and angry, especially because it was widely believed that if Emperor Nero had not actually set the fire, he certainly had done nothing to contain it. In fact, certain of Nero's chamberlains were caught with firebrands trying to rekindle the waning fire. Many felt that Nero's passion for building caused him to want the city destroyed so he might rebuild it. No matter what Nero did to refute this rumor—and he aided the homeless extensively— nothing allayed the suspicion that the fire was his doing. Clearly he needed a scapegoat on which to blame the fire.

The Christians were nominated for this dubious honor. Up to this time, they were thought to be simply a Jewish sect and were hardly noticed by Roman authorities. In fact, the Roman courts protected Christians against the wrath of the synagogue and others. But now all this changed. Nero introduced the church to martyrdom. What began in Rome would soon wash across the Roman Empire.

Under Roman law there were two types of religious systems: those that were legal, such as Judaism, and those that were forbidden. Anyone who practiced a forbidden religion was considered a criminal and was subject to harsh penalties. After the great fire, Christianity was judged to be distinct from Judaism, and it was quickly prohibited. This meant that throughout the Roman Empire, Christians were now technically outlaws and thus subject to persecution. Just such persecution was taking place in Asia Minor among the Christians to whom Peter writes (4:12).

Theme

In the midst of the "painful trial" (4:12) they are suffering, Peter writes to comfort and encourage. "Rejoice that you participate in the sufferings of Christ" (4:13), he says. How can they rejoice at such a difficult time? Because of the great *hope* they have as Christians. Hope is the theme of Peter's letter to these suffering believers.

Author

Peter was one of the first disciples called by Jesus. From Galilee, he was by trade a fisherman. His father was Jonah. His brother was Andrew the apostle. He was married, and his wife accompanied him on some of his preaching tours. Peter quickly became one of the leaders among the twelve apostles; later, he was a leader of the church in Jerusalem. He was the Apostle to the Jews, yet because of his response to a vision, the first Gentile convert, Cornelius, was admitted to the church (Acts 10).

Tradition says that Peter perished in Rome, around A.D. 68, by crucifixion upside down.

Characteristics

Sources

When reading 1 Peter, one keeps hearing echoes from other parts of the Bible. Certainly the Old Testament is present. Peter quotes a number of passages, particularly from Isaiah. For example in 1:24-25, he quotes Isaiah 40:6-8; in 2:6, Isaiah 28:16; in 2:8, Isaiah 8:14; and in 2:22, Isaiah 53:9. Furthermore, he frequently alludes to Old Testament ideas and stories.

Peter is also familiar with Paul's writings. This letter contains parallels to Romans and, in particular, Ephesians. For example, compare 1:3 with Ephesians 1:3 and 1:20 with Ephesians 1:4. Note also similarity between Peter and Paul in their instructions to family members and slaves (1 Peter 1:18-3:7; Eph. 5:21-6:9; Col. 3:18-25). In addition, there are parallels to Hebrews, James, and not surprisingly, to Peter's own sermons in Acts.

Of course, this does not necessarily mean that Peter was consciously quoting from New Testament documents. It may simply be that there was a common pattern of teaching in the early church and that Peter is tapping into this as did other New Testament writers.

Style

First Peter is written in excellent Greek, so much so that some have questioned whether a Galilean fisherman like Peter could have had such a sophisticated command of the language. First Peter contains some of the best Greek in the New Testament. Its style is smoother even than Paul's with his years of training; its rhythmic structure is not unlike that of the Greek masters.

The answer to this question is found in 5:12: "With the help of Silas . . . I have written to you." The Greek here indicates that Silas was more than just a stenographer. In fact, he could well be the source of the excellent style as he helped Peter draft the letter and polish up the language.

1 Peter

1 Peter, an apostle of Jesus Christ,

To God's elect, strangers in the world, scattered throughout Pontus, Galatia, Cappadocia, Asia and Bithynia, ²who have been chosen according to the foreknowledge of God the Father, through the sanctifying work of the Spirit, for obedience to Jesus Christ and sprinkling by his blood:

Grace and peace be yours in abundance.

Praise to God for a Living Hope

³Praise be to the God and Father of our Lord Jesus Christ! In his great mercy he has given us new birth into a living hope through the resurrection of Jesus Christ from the dead, ⁴and into an inheritance that can never perish, spoil or fade—kept in heaven for you, ⁵who through faith are shielded by God's power until the coming of the salvation that is ready to be revealed in the last time. ⁶In this you greatly rejoice, though now for a little while you may have had to suffer grief in all kinds of trials. ⁷These have come so that your faith—of greater worth than gold, which perishes even though refined by fire—may be proved genuine and may result in praise, glory and honor when Jesus Christ is revealed. ⁸Though you have not seen him, you love him; and even though you do not see him now, you believe in him and are filled with an inexpressible and glorious joy, ⁹for you are receiving the goal of your faith, the salvation of your souls.

¹⁰Concerning this salvation, the prophets, who spoke of the grace that was to come to you, searched intently and with the greatest care, ¹¹trying to find out the time and circumstances to which the Spirit of Christ in them was pointing when he predicted the sufferings of Christ and the glories that would follow. ¹²It was revealed to them that they were not serving themselves but you, when they spoke of the things that have now been told you by those who have preached the gospel to you by the Holy Spirit sent from heaven. Even angels long to look into these things.

Be Holy

¹³Therefore, prepare your minds for action; be self-controlled; set your hope fully on the grace to be given you when Jesus Christ is revealed. ¹⁴As obedient children, do not conform to the evil desires you had when you lived in ignorance. ¹⁵But just as he who called you is holy, so be holy in all you do; ¹⁶for it is written: "Be holy, because I am holy." ᵃ

¹⁷Since you call on a Father who judges each man's work impartially, live your lives as strangers here in reverent fear. ¹⁸For you know that it was not with perishable things such as silver or gold that you were redeemed from the empty way of life handed down to you from your forefathers, ¹⁹but with the precious blood of Christ, a lamb without blemish or defect. ²⁰He

ᵃ16 Lev. 11:44,45; 19:2; 20:7

OPEN: 1. If you couldn't live in this country, where would you choose to live? Why? **2.** When you were a teen, what kinds of things were you chosen to do? How did it feel?

DIG: 1. What circumstances do you think the original recipients faced that would cause Peter to write like this? **2.** What kind of work is each person (Father, Son, and Spirit) doing in our lives? **3.** What basis does Peter give his readers for having a living hope? **4.** What qualities of a Christian last forever? **5.** What words, phrases or ideas would you list under "already available" to a Christian? What ones would you list under "not yet but glad they are coming"? How do the ones on the "not yet" support the "already" list? Are some on both lists? Why? **6.** What does this passage ask us to believe, and what does this passage ask us to do because of these beliefs?

REFLECT: 1. Imagining your faith as a mountain climb, what situations in your life now would be faith cliff hangers, easy trails, thirsty moments, great views or just walking up the path? What would you pull out of your 1 Peter pack in these situations? **2.** The prophets struggled to know more. What aspect of your faith are you struggling to know more? **3.** Under what fiery circumstances and situations has your faith become more genuine through melting it down to essentials?

OPEN: 1. What did you do as a child that got you into the most trouble? **2.** What toy did you enjoy the most when you were younger? What happened to it? Would you play with it now if you had it? Be honest!

DIG: 1. From the five commands Peter gives in verses 13-15, how would you define "holy"? **2.** What reasons does Peter give for his commands (see also vv. 3-12)? How can those reasons move us to obey? **3.** What were these people like before they discovered faith in Christ? What happened to them when they believed? What commands does Peter give them now that they believe? **4.** After digging

445

a deep hole, what words and phrases from this passage would you fill it with to help you love more deeply? What characteristics would fall into the hole that would need to be removed regularly?

REFLECT 1. Are you more like a stranger, a pilgrim, an explorer, or a landowner on this earth? Why? **2.** How does "holiness" behave at home, work, church, neighborhood, etc.? Give specific examples. **3.** If you were to write insurance for your life and everything in it, list the perishable things you have and do. What "forever" things do you have and do that wouldn't need insurance? According to the amount of time, effort, and money you spend on each, which items come first, the perishable or "forever" ones?

OPEN: If someone asked you to oversee the building and staffing of a community center, what services would it contain? What would the staff do? What kind of people would you get to staff it?

DIG: 1. What similarities does Peter show between Christ's experience and the Christian's experience? **2.** How could you repaint in practical terms what Peter meant by the pictures he gives us in verses 5 and 9? **3.** What does a cornerstone do? How is Christ a cornerstone? Why would people stumble over the stone rather than build their lives on it? **4.** In what ways would it be difficult for Peter's readers to think of themselves in the terms used in verses 9-10? Is this what Peter thinks they will become, or are they all these things now? Why?

REFLECT: 1. Suppose you are a war correspondent reporting live from the front, how would you describe the war going on within yourself represented by verses 9-10 and verse 11? **2.** In what dark rooms of your life has God turned on a light? **3.** How does it make you feel to be chosen, royalty, and God's possession? When is it most difficult to remember what God has made you? **4.** If you were to build a spiritual house from the living stones in your group, where would each member be positioned to realize best his or her own pattern of giftedness, (walls, roof, telephone line, etc)? How does this fit who you are in Christ?

was chosen before the creation of the world, but was revealed in these last times for your sake. ²¹Through him you believe in God, who raised him from the dead and glorified him, and so your faith and hope are in God.

²²Now that you have purified yourselves by obeying the truth so that you have sincere love for your brothers, love one another deeply, from the heart. *b* ²³For you have been born again, not of perishable seed, but of imperishable, through the living and enduring word of God. ²⁴For,

> "All men are like grass,
> and all their glory is like the flowers of the field;
> the grass withers and the flowers fall,
> ²⁵ but the word of the Lord stands forever."*c*

And this is the word that was preached to you.

2 Therefore, rid yourselves of all malice and all deceit, hypocrisy, envy, and slander of every kind. ²Like newborn babies, crave pure spiritual milk, so that by it you may grow up in your salvation, ³now that you have tasted that the Lord is good.

The Living Stone and a Chosen People

⁴As you come to him, the living Stone—rejected by men but chosen by God and precious to him— ⁵you also, like living stones, are being built into a spiritual house to be a holy priesthood, offering spiritual sacrifices acceptable to God through Jesus Christ. ⁶For in Scripture it says:

> "See, I lay a stone in Zion,
> a chosen and precious cornerstone,
> and the one who trusts in him
> will never be put to shame."*d*

⁷Now to you who believe, this stone is precious. But to those who do not believe,

> "The stone the builders rejected
> has become the capstone,*e*"*f*

⁸and,

> "A stone that causes men to stumble
> and a rock that makes them fall."*g*

They stumble because they disobey the message—which is also what they were destined for.

⁹But you are a chosen people, a royal priesthood, a holy nation, a people belonging to God, that you may declare the praises of him who called you out of darkness into his wonderful light. ¹⁰Once you were not a people, but now you are the people of God; once you had not received mercy, but now you have received mercy.

¹¹Dear friends, I urge you, as aliens and strangers in the world, to abstain from sinful desires, which war against your

---

b22 Some early manuscripts from a pure heart   *c25 Isaiah 40:6-8*   *d6 Isaiah 28:16*
e7 Or cornerstone   *f7 Psalm 118:22*   *g8 Isaiah 8:14*

soul. [12]Live such good lives among the pagans that, though they accuse you of doing wrong, they may see your good deeds and glorify God on the day he visits us.

Submission to Rulers and Masters

[13]Submit yourselves for the Lord's sake to every authority instituted among men: whether to the king, as the supreme authority, [14]or to governors, who are sent by him to punish those who do wrong and to commend those who do right. [15]For it is God's will that by doing good you should silence the ignorant talk of foolish men. [16]Live as free men, but do not use your freedom as a cover-up for evil; live as servants of God. [17]Show proper respect to everyone: Love the brotherhood of believers, fear God, honor the king.

[18]Slaves, submit yourselves to your masters with all respect, not only to those who are good and considerate, but also to those who are harsh. [19]For it is commendable if a man bears up under the pain of unjust suffering because he is conscious of God. [20]But how is it to your credit if you receive a beating for doing wrong and endure it? But if you suffer for doing good and you endure it, this is commendable before God. [21]To this you were called, because Christ suffered for you, leaving you an example, that you should follow in his steps.

[22]"He committed no sin,
  and no deceit was found in his mouth." [h]

[23]When they hurled their insults at him, he did not retaliate; when he suffered, he made no threats. Instead, he entrusted himself to him who judges justly. [24]He himself bore our sins in his body on the tree, so that we might die to sins and live for righteousness; by his wounds you have been healed. [25]For you were like sheep going astray, but now you have returned to the Shepherd and Overseer of your souls.

Wives and Husbands

3 Wives, in the same way be submissive to your husbands so that, if any of them do not believe the word, they may be won over without words by the behavior of their wives, [2]when they see the purity and reverence of your lives. [3]Your beauty should not come from outward adornment, such as braided hair and the wearing of gold jewelry and fine clothes. [4]Instead, it should be that of your inner self, the unfading beauty of a gentle and quiet spirit, which is of great worth in God's sight. [5]For this is the way the holy women of the past who put their hope in God used to make themselves beautiful. They were submissive to their own husbands, [6]like Sarah, who obeyed Abraham and called him her master. You are her daughters if you do what is right and do not give way to fear.

[7]Husbands, in the same way be considerate as you live with your wives, and treat them with respect as the weaker partner and as heirs with you of the gracious gift of life, so that nothing will hinder your prayers.

[h]22 Isaiah 53:9

OPEN: When you were growing up, what authority figure was toughest for you to respect? Why?

DIG: 1. Given verse 16 plus the reality of government persecution, why is submission to authority a concern for Peter? What is its purpose? 2. How do the verbs in verse 17 help define what Peter means by submission? 3. How is their relationship with God to influence how they deal with human authority? How might the description of Christ in verses 21-25 be especially helpful in situations way beyond our control?

REFLECT: 1. What "authorities" are over you? How do you apply verses 16-17 in those relationships? 2. If your company sent you someplace where you had no protection from harassment as a Christian, how would this passage shape your response? 3. Compare Paul's assertive actions in Acts 16:35-37 with Peter's call to submission here: When is it better to oppose injustice?

OPEN: As a child, how did you picture your "Prince Charming" or "girl of your dreams"?

DIG: 1. How is the submission called for in verses 1-2 similar in purpose to that in 2:13-15? What qualities are included? 2. How would you put Peter's "beauty program" into practice? 3. In what way is Peter saying husbands are to live "in the same way" as their wives? What would you expect to see in a marriage built on mutual submission and consideration?

REFLECT: 1. Married or not, what qualities here would you like to build into your life? Why? 2. How is the call of verses 1 and 7 an example of applying 2:16 to marriage? What other principles for marriage flow from 2:16? 3. Does this passage advocate spouses staying in cruel situations? Why or why not?

OPEN: If you were to write the headlines in a newspaper describing your local church, what would they be?

DIG: 1. Using examples from your church, how would you illustrate the qualities in verse 8? **2.** How does the quote from Psalm 34 sum up all Peter has said in 2:11-3:15? As opposed to being afraid of what the world fears (v. 14), what does he mean by setting apart Christ as Lord (v. 15)? How will this affect their behavior? **3.** What are some of the reasons for their hope which Peter has already given in this letter? **4.** How does the story of the flood along with baptism give hope to these readers? **5.** How does the example of Christ's life give encouragement in times of suffering?

REFLECT: 1. What were the circumstances surrounding you the last time you asked God, "Why?"? **2.** How does hope change your everyday behavior and make people ask about it? **3.** What situation seemed hopeless to you when God brought hope? **3.** Choose one difficult relationship in which you are currently involved. How could you bless that person this week? What would you need to do? **4.** When was the last time you had an opportunity to talk about your faith with a nonbeliever? What happened? How did you feel afterward? In what ways could you have done better? **5.** As you reflect upon your fellowship or church, are you "in harmony" or "out of tune"? Why? What can you do to strengthen the harmony?

OPEN: What was one of the worst things you were caught doing wrong when you were young? What were the consequences?

DIG: 1. As you imagine a specific compromising situation that Peter's readers may find themselves in, what would the pagans be saying to them? What things does Peter tell them in this section to think about in the situation? **2.** How are the reality of judgment (vv. 5-7) and Christ's glory (v. 11) to influence the daily behavior of these Christians? **3.** How do the actions described in verses 8-11 show what love is all about? How would this strengthen people facing suffering?

Suffering for Doing Good

[8]Finally, all of you, live in harmony with one another; be sympathetic, love as brothers, be compassionate and humble. [9]Do not repay evil with evil or insult with insult, but with blessing, because to this you were called so that you may inherit a blessing. [10]For,

> "Whoever would love life
>   and see good days
> must keep his tongue from evil
>   and his lips from deceitful speech.
> [11]He must turn from evil and do good;
>   he must seek peace and pursue it.
> [12]For the eyes of the Lord are on the righteous
>   and his ears are attentive to their prayer,
> but the face of the Lord is against those who do evil."[i]

[13]Who is going to harm you if you are eager to do good? [14]But even if you should suffer for what is right, you are blessed. "Do not fear what they fear[j]; do not be frightened."[k] [15]But in your hearts set apart Christ as Lord. Always be prepared to give an answer to everyone who asks you to give the reason for the hope that you have. But do this with gentleness and respect, [16]keeping a clear conscience, so that those who speak maliciously against your good behavior in Christ may be ashamed of their slander. [17]It is better, if it is God's will, to suffer for doing good than for doing evil. [18]For Christ died for sins once for all, the righteous for the unrighteous, to bring you to God. He was put to death in the body but made alive by the Spirit, [19]through whom[l] also he went and preached to the spirits in prison [20]who disobeyed long ago when God waited patiently in the days of Noah while the ark was being built. In it only a few people, eight in all, were saved through water, [21]and this water symbolizes baptism that now saves you also—not the removal of dirt from the body but the pledge[m] of a good conscience toward God. It saves you by the resurrection of Jesus Christ, [22]who has gone into heaven and is at God's right hand—with angels, authorities and powers in submission to him.

Living for God

4 Therefore, since Christ suffered in his body, arm yourselves also with the same attitude, because he who has suffered in his body is done with sin. [2]As a result, he does not live the rest of his earthly life for evil human desires, but rather for the will of God. [3]For you have spent enough time in the past doing what pagans choose to do—living in debauchery, lust, drunkenness, orgies, carousing and detestable idolatry. [4]They think it strange that you do not plunge with them into the same flood of dissipation, and they heap abuse on you. [5]But they will have to give account to him who is ready to judge the living and the dead. [6]For this is the reason the gospel was preached even to those who

---

[i]12 Psalm 34:12-16   [j]14 Or *not fear their threats*   [k]14 Isaiah 8:12
[l]18,19 Or *alive in the spirit,* [19]*through which*   [m]21 Or *response*

are now dead, so that they might be judged according to men in regard to the body, but live according to God in regard to the spirit.

[7]The end of all things is near. Therefore be clear minded and self-controlled so that you can pray. [8]Above all, love each other deeply, because love covers over a multitude of sins. [9]Offer hospitality to one another without grumbling. [10]Each one should use whatever gift he has received to serve others, faithfully administering God's grace in its various forms. [11]If anyone speaks, he should do it as one speaking the very words of God. If anyone serves, he should do it with the strength God provides, so that in all things God may be praised through Jesus Christ. To him be the glory and the power for ever and ever. Amen.

Suffering for Being a Christian

[12]Dear friends, do not be surprised at the painful trial you are suffering, as though something strange were happening to you. [13]But rejoice that you participate in the sufferings of Christ, so that you may be overjoyed when his glory is revealed. [14]If you are insulted because of the name of Christ, you are blessed, for the Spirit of glory and of God rests on you. [15]If you suffer, it should not be as a murderer or thief or any other kind of criminal, or even as a meddler. [16]However, if you suffer as a Christian, do not be ashamed, but praise God that you bear that name. [17]For it is time for judgment to begin with the family of God; and if it begins with us, what will the outcome be for those who do not obey the gospel of God? [18]And,

"If it is hard for the righteous to be saved,
　what will become of the ungodly and the sinner?"[n]

[19]So then, those who suffer according to God's will should commit themselves to their faithful Creator and continue to do good.

To Elders and Young Men

5 To the elders among you, I appeal as a fellow elder, a witness of Christ's sufferings and one who also will share in the glory to be revealed: [2]Be shepherds of God's flock that is under your care, serving as overseers—not because you must, but because you are willing, as God wants you to be; not greedy for money, but eager to serve; [3]not lording it over those entrusted to you, but being examples to the flock. [4]And when the Chief Shepherd appears, you will receive the crown of glory that will never fade away.

[5]Young men, in the same way be submissive to those who are older. All of you, clothe yourselves with humility toward one another, because,

"God opposes the proud
　but gives grace to the humble."[o]

REFLECT: 1. When you remembered a time that someone made fun of you, how did it feel? What in this passage might help in working through those feelings? **2.** Which commands in verses 7-11 do you need to pay special attention to this week? **3.** What is one gift you think each of the members of this group has? How could that gift be used to show love?

OPEN: If you were an army officer who must command his troops to enter a tough battle, how would you motivate them?

DIG: 1. In what sense are the Christians suffering part of Christ's suffering? Why should the Christian find joy in this? **2.** When Peter asks them to continue to do good (v. 19), what reasons does he give for continuing?

REFLECT: 1. When you feel like giving up and not continuing, what keeps you going? **2.** If you were asked to tell a group of new believers what to expect in the Christian life, what are some things you would tell them? Why? **3.** In a society where Christians are not persecuted a great deal by their government, how does suffering for Christ come? How have you suffered? How has suffering purified, changed, molded or matured you?

OPEN: 1. If you had won the *Church Game Show* and received the grand prize of becoming a pastor for a week, what would you do with your time?

DIG: 1. What good and bad motives does Peter give for being in leadership? Why would the motivation and conduct of elders be especially important in a church undergoing persecution? What qualities does Peter encourage elders to cultivate? How would each of these help in times of persecution? **2.** What connections do you see between submissiveness, humility and anxiety? What anxieties do these people face? What would replace their fears as they followed verses 6-7? **3.** What is the role of the Devil in persecution? What does he hope will be the result of persecution? What result does hope in God bring instead?

[n]18 Prov. 11:31   [o]5 Prov. 3:34

REFLECT: 1. In what area of your life would you like God to restore and make you strong, firm and steadfast? 2. What leadership responsibilities do you have? (We all have some!) How do you score on Peter's leadership test? How can you improve your score? 3. In your life, is the lion just looking for you, nibbling at your heels, or chewing you up? How can your group help you resist him?

OPEN: If Jesus was betrayed by Judas' "kiss of death", what would be the equivelent meaning of someone's "kiss of love"? Have you kissed any "frog princes" lately? Who? What happened?

DIG: 1. Skimming this letter, how has Peter encouraged these believers? What has he stressed about God's grace? About Christian hope? Personal holiness? Service and submission to others? Perseverence in doing good? 2. Given that Babylon was one of the main enemies of Israel in the Old Testament, and given that Peter is writing this letter from Rome, what does he mean by verse 13? How does that sum up the pressures these believers were facing?

REFLECT: 1. What pictures of Christ has Peter drawn in this letter? How do those pictures bring peace to you? 2. What is a pressure you face that causes you to waver in your trust in Christ? What from this letter has helped you? 3. If you haven't kissed any "frog princes" lately, and even if you have, close your group session by greeting one another with a "kiss of love" (v. 14).

[6]Humble yourselves, therefore, under God's mighty hand, that he may lift you up in due time. [7]Cast all your anxiety on him because he cares for you.

[8]Be self-controlled and alert. Your enemy the devil prowls around like a roaring lion looking for someone to devour. [9]Resist him, standing firm in the faith, because you know that your brothers throughout the world are undergoing the same kind of sufferings.

[10]And the God of all grace, who called you to his eternal glory in Christ, after you have suffered a little while, will himself restore you and make you strong, firm and steadfast. [11]To him be the power for ever and ever. Amen.

Final Greetings

[12]With the help of Silas,[p] whom I regard as a faithful brother, I have written to you briefly, encouraging you and testifying that this is the true grace of God. Stand fast in it.

[13]She who is in Babylon, chosen together with you, sends you her greetings, and so does my son Mark. [14]Greet one another with a kiss of love.

Peace to all of you who are in Christ.

p12 Greek Silvanus, a variant of Silas

2 PETER

INTRODUCTION

The Neglected Book

In contrast to 1 Peter, which is "the best known and loved, the most read" of the General Epistles; 2 Peter "is one of the neglected books of the New Testament" (Barclay, *The Letters of James and Peter*, p. 335). Few people seem to have read and studied it. One commentator has called 2 Peter "the least valuable of the New Testament writings" (E. F. Scott in Barclay, *The Letters of James and Peter*, p. 335). Several others have called for it to be deleted from the New Testament. Why is this? What is the problem with 2 Peter?

Second Peter's difficulties are not new. In fact, it almost did not make it into the New Testament. Luther calls it second-class Scripture; Calvin had doubts about it; and Erasmus rejected it altogether.

Author

The problem is that a lot of people question whether Peter actually wrote this particular letter. It was not uncommon in the first century to attribute pieces of writing to famous people. In fact, Peter's name is attached to several other books that clearly were not written by him (e.g., the Gospel of Peter, the Preaching of Peter, and the Apocalypse of Peter).

So questions arise when the language and thought of 1 and 2 Peter are compared. In their original Greek form, these two books are strikingly different. Could the same man have written both? This difference in style, of course, may simply be the result of Peter's use of two different secretaries. Peter indicates in his first letter that Silas helped him write it (1 Peter 5:12), and it is known that Peter had other secretaries (e.g., Mark and Glaucias). As Michael Green has shown, the case against Peter's authorship is not nearly as conclusive as might be supposed (*The Second Epistle of Peter and the Epistles of Jude: Tyndale New Testament Commentaries*). In any case, 2 Peter is a part of the New Testament, and it has a valuable message for the twentieth century which is important to recover.

Theme

Second Peter is a very important book for the twentieth century because it deals with the very issues confronting the modern church: laxity of lifestyle based on defective doctrine. Some church members in Peter's time were arguing that the doctrine of the Second Coming had to be reconsidered. "The plain fact is that Christ has not returned yet," they said, "and he probably won't" (see 3:4, 9). In fact, they suggested that this doctrine may have been invented by the apostles rather than revealed by God (1:16), perhaps to keep Christians in line. The doctrine of the Second Coming was sort of a moral club used to inhibit one's lifestyle. In contrast, the false teachers were saying that behavior does not matter. "Freedom" was their catchword, and evidently they felt free to indulge in sexual immorality, drunkenness, and sensual excesses generally (2:2, 10, 13-14, 18) (Richard Bauckham, *Jude, 2 Peter: Word Biblical Commentary*, p. 155).

"Not so!" roars Peter in this letter. And it is his "not so" that we need to hear in this day of speculative theology and hedonistic lifestyles. We, too, need to remain firmly established within the truth we received from the prophets and from our Lord (chap. 1). We, too, need to be warned against those who would lead people away from that truth (chap. 2). And we, too, need to be reminded (in a passage that is chillingly real in this nuclear age) that the world will one day end when the Lord returns (chap. 3).

Audience

On the basis of 1:1 it appears that there were no specific recipients of the letter. It seems to be for all Christians everywhere (hence its description as a General Epistle). However, in the body of the letter it becomes clear that 2 Peter was sent to a church or group of churches that had received 1 Peter (3:1). This would make the recipients Gentile Christians in Asia Minor. Furthermore, the tone of the letter makes it clear that a specific problem and specific false teachers are in view. All of this indicates that this is a letter to particular people living in a particular area.

Structure

Second Peter is a letter like other New Testament letters. It calls itself a letter (3:1). It begins like a typical first-century letter (1:1-2) by identifying sender and recipients and offering a Christian greeting. And then, in typical fashion, it announces its theme (1:3-11) and tells the occasion of writing (1:12-15). The only thing 2 Peter lacks is personal greetings at the end, but these were not characteristic of all first-century letters.

Second Peter is also a farewell speech or a testament. It sounds like the last words of a great leader. There are many examples of this form of literature in the first century. In the New Testament, Paul's farewell speech to the Ephesian elders had this character (Acts 20:17-35), as does the Book of 2 Timothy.

In 1:12-15, Peter says that his death is soon to take place, and the way he writes his letter is typical of testament literature in general. The letter contains ethical instructions in which the author summarizes his views, and then he makes predictions about the future (Bauckham, *Jude, 2 Peter*).

2 Peter

1 Simon Peter, a servant and apostle of Jesus Christ,

To those who through the righteousness of our God and Savior Jesus Christ have received a faith as precious as ours:

²Grace and peace be yours in abundance through the knowledge of God and of Jesus our Lord.

Making One's Calling and Election Sure

³His divine power has given us everything we need for life and godliness through our knowledge of him who called us by his own glory and goodness. ⁴Through these he has given us his very great and precious promises, so that through them you may participate in the divine nature and escape the corruption in the world caused by evil desires.

⁵For this very reason, make every effort to add to your faith goodness; and to goodness, knowledge; ⁶and to knowledge, self-control; and to self-control, perseverance; and to perseverance, godliness; ⁷and to godliness, brotherly kindness; and to brotherly kindness, love. ⁸For if you possess these qualities in increasing measure, they will keep you from being ineffective and unproductive in your knowledge of our Lord Jesus Christ. ⁹But if anyone does not have them, he is nearsighted and blind, and has forgotten that he has been cleansed from his past sins.

¹⁰Therefore, my brothers, be all the more eager to make your calling and election sure. For if you do these things, you will never fall, ¹¹and you will receive a rich welcome into the eternal kingdom of our Lord and Savior Jesus Christ.

Prophecy of Scripture

¹²So I will always remind you of these things, even though you know them and are firmly established in the truth you now have. ¹³I think it is right to refresh your memory as long as I live in the tent of this body, ¹⁴because I know that I will soon put it aside, as our Lord Jesus Christ has made clear to me. ¹⁵And I will make every effort to see that after my departure you will always be able to remember these things.

¹⁶We did not follow cleverly invented stories when we told you about the power and coming of our Lord Jesus Christ, but we were eyewitnesses of his majesty. ¹⁷For he received honor and glory from God the Father when the voice came to him from the Majestic Glory, saying, "This is my Son, whom I love; with him I am well pleased."ᵃ ¹⁸We ourselves heard this voice that came from heaven when we were with him on the sacred mountain.

¹⁹And we have the word of the prophets made more certain, and you will do well to pay attention to it, as to a light shining in a dark place, until the day dawns and the morning star rises in your hearts. ²⁰Above all, you must understand that no proph-

ᵃ17 Matt. 17:5; Mark 9:7; Luke 9:35

OPEN: As a teenager what did you most desire to do, career-wise? Sports-wise? Academic-wise? Relationship-wise? How have these four desires changed in the decade since then? Which of these desires is still dominant today?

DIG: 1. From verses 1-4, what is "everything we need for life"? **2.** With "everything" given to us, for what reason must we then add to our faith? And with what effort (vv. 5, 10)? **3.** What seven qualities or equipment are we to zealously desire? How does each fit with the one mentioned before it? **4.** Why is this moral progress and productive knowledge (v. 8) so desirable for believers (vv. 4, 10-11)?

REFLECT: 1. According to verse 1, is this letter written to you? Why? **2.** Of the seven qualities in verses 5-7, which two do you feel you possess in the greatest measure? What are some specific efforts you can make to add to what you have in each area? **3.** With God's power and your effort, are you engaged in a tug-of-war? Or are you rowing the same boat? Why?

OPEN: How is your life like a tent: Always picking up stakes and moving on? Resistant to winds of change? Cozy with some, cold to others?

DIG: 1. What events of Jesus' life does Peter recall (vv. 12-13, 16-18)? If you were Peter, what other favorite stories of Jesus come to mind? **2.** Why does Peter forcefully establish his eyewitness credentials? What problem does this imply that his readers may have been facing? **3.** Likewise, why does Peter defend the authority and inspiration of the prophets? How could a harmony of Peter's message and the prophets' message help Peter's cause (v. 19)? If so much prophecy has already been fulfilled in Christ's first coming, how then are we to regard the prophecies yet to be fulfilled?

REFLECT: 1. If you could have been with Jesus at any one event in his life, which would you choose? Why? **2.** If a non-Christian asked you to "prove" the Scriptures are God's Word, on what would you base your answer? **3.** Given that the Scriptures are true and trustworthy, how will that effect your Bible study habit? And your witness?

———————

OPEN: 1. If people like pets who are like them in some way, what could one learn about you from your choice of pet? **2.** What "beasts" and other "things which go bump in the night" are you afraid of? Why?

DIG: 1. Having just commended true prophets (1:12-21), who does Peter now condemn? Why? **2.** If it is so plain that judgment awaits these false teachers, why does anyone follow them (vv. 2-3, 14, 18-19)? **3.** Likewise, if they are so evil, why do you think God allows them to teach in his church? Is not God's goodness, or God's greatness, brought into question by delaying their judgment? **4.** In response to that implied question, Peter gives God's track record in dealing with evil: What examples are cited in verses 4-9? **5.** If not even angels, the ancient world, and Sodom and Gomorrah are spared God's wrath against sin, who *does* God protect from judgment? Why? How is that a particular comfort to Peter's fearful audience? **6.** In verses 13-16, what new information does Peter present? What examples does Peter use to describe God's past performance (vv. 4-9)? What do you know about these examples? How does Peter summarize this paragraph (vv. 9-10)? **7.** What other imagery does Peter use to further denounce the seductive character of these false prophets (vv. 17-19)? **8.** What "freedom" do they promise: Freedom from sin? From laws? From judgment? From ethical obligations to others and to Christ? All of the above? **9.** How would you paraphrase verses 20-21? What do you think this is saying about salvation? How does verse 22 support your answer?

REFLECT: 1. How do you know when a TV evangelist or radio preacher is "exploiting you with stories they have made up" or feeding you empty promises as "springs without water"? **2.** Do such false teachers upset you as much as Peter? Why or why not? **3.** What modern cult leader would you give the "Golden Fleece Award" for greed and ripping off the public? **4.** Which preacher do you trust more than others? Why? **5.** In what ways are you better off knowing the Lord? In what ways are you worse off?

ecy of Scripture came about by the prophet's own interpretation. ²¹For prophecy never had its origin in the will of man, but men spoke from God as they were carried along by the Holy Spirit.

False Teachers and Their Destruction

2 But there were also false prophets among the people, just as there will be false teachers among you. They will secretly introduce destructive heresies, even denying the sovereign Lord who bought them—bringing swift destruction on themselves. ²Many will follow their shameful ways and will bring the way of truth into disrepute. ³In their greed these teachers will exploit you with stories they have made up. Their condemnation has long been hanging over them, and their destruction has not been sleeping.

⁴For if God did not spare angels when they sinned, but sent them to hell,*ᵇ* putting them into gloomy dungeons*ᶜ* to be held for judgment; ⁵if he did not spare the ancient world when he brought the flood on its ungodly people, but protected Noah, a preacher of righteousness, and seven others; ⁶if he condemned the cities of Sodom and Gomorrah by burning them to ashes, and made them an example of what is going to happen to the ungodly; ⁷and if he rescued Lot, a righteous man, who was distressed by the filthy lives of lawless men ⁸(for that righteous man, living among them day after day, was tormented in his righteous soul by the lawless deeds he saw and heard)— ⁹if this is so, then the Lord knows how to rescue godly men from trials and to hold the unrighteous for the day of judgment, while continuing their punishment.*ᵈ* ¹⁰This is especially true of those who follow the corrupt desire of the sinful nature*ᵉ* and despise authority.

Bold and arrogant, these men are not afraid to slander celestial beings; ¹¹yet even angels, although they are stronger and more powerful, do not bring slanderous accusations against such beings in the presence of the Lord. ¹²But these men blaspheme in matters they do not understand. They are like brute beasts, creatures of instinct, born only to be caught and destroyed, and like beasts they too will perish.

¹³They will be paid back with harm for the harm they have done. Their idea of pleasure is to carouse in broad daylight. They are blots and blemishes, reveling in their pleasures while they feast with you.*ᶠ* ¹⁴With eyes full of adultery, they never stop sinning; they seduce the unstable; they are experts in greed—an accursed brood! ¹⁵They have left the straight way and wandered off to follow the way of Balaam son of Beor, who loved the wages of wickedness. ¹⁶But he was rebuked for his wrongdoing by a donkey—a beast without speech—who spoke with a man's voice and restrained the prophet's madness.

¹⁷These men are springs without water and mists driven by a storm. Blackest darkness is reserved for them. ¹⁸For they

———————

ᵇ4 Greek *Tartarus*   *ᶜ4* Some manuscripts *into chains of darkness*
ᵈ9 Or *unrighteous for punishment until the day of judgment*   *ᵉ10* Or *the flesh*
ᶠ13 Some manuscripts *in their love feasts*

mouth empty, boastful words and, by appealing to the lustful desires of sinful human nature, they entice people who are just escaping from those who live in error. ¹⁹They promise them freedom, while they themselves are slaves of depravity—for a man is a slave to whatever has mastered him. ²⁰If they have escaped the corruption of the world by knowing our Lord and Savior Jesus Christ and are again entangled in it and overcome, they are worse off at the end than they were at the beginning. ²¹It would have been better for them not to have known the way of righteousness, than to have known it and then to turn their backs on the sacred command that was passed on to them. ²²Of them the proverbs are true: "A dog returns to its vomit,"ᵍ and, "A sow that is washed goes back to her wallowing in the mud."

The Day of the Lord

3 Dear friends, this is now my second letter to you. I have written both of them as reminders to stimulate you to wholesome thinking. ²I want you to recall the words spoken in the past by the holy prophets and the command given by our Lord and Savior through your apostles.

³First of all, you must understand that in the last days scoffers will come, scoffing and following their own evil desires. ⁴They will say, "Where is this 'coming' he promised? Ever since our fathers died, everything goes on as it has since the beginning of creation." ⁵But they deliberately forget that long ago by God's word the heavens existed and the earth was formed out of water and by water. ⁶By these waters also the world of that time was deluged and destroyed. ⁷By the same word the present heavens and earth are reserved for fire, being kept for the day of judgment and destruction of ungodly men.

⁸But do not forget this one thing, dear friends: With the Lord a day is like a thousand years, and a thousand years are like a day. ⁹The Lord is not slow in keeping his promise, as some understand slowness. He is patient with you, not wanting anyone to perish, but everyone to come to repentance.

¹⁰But the day of the Lord will come like a thief. The heavens will disappear with a roar; the elements will be destroyed by fire, and the earth and everything in it will be laid bare. ʰ

¹¹Since everything will be destroyed in this way, what kind of people ought you to be? You ought to live holy and godly lives ¹²as you look forward to the day of God and speed its coming. ⁱ That day will bring about the destruction of the heavens by fire, and the elements will melt in the heat. ¹³But in keeping with his promise we are looking forward to a new heaven and a new earth, the home of righteousness.

¹⁴So then, dear friends, since you are looking forward to this, make every effort to be found spotless, blameless and at peace with him. ¹⁵Bear in mind that our Lord's patience means salvation, just as our dear brother Paul also wrote you with the wisdom that God gave him. ¹⁶He writes the same way in all his

OPEN: 1. When did your dad promise a fishing trip, or a ball game, or a graduation present, and then fail to deliver? How did that make you feel? **2.** When told, "Wait until your birthday", or "Christmas isn't here yet", and "You'd better be good until then", how did that affect your behavior in the meantime?

DIG: 1. Following the digression of chapter 2, to what themes does Peter now return? **2.** What "must" the readers first understand (see also 1:20-21)? **3.** Why does God's creation of the earth support Peter's contention that he will also destroy the earth? Why is it so difficult for people to believe? What does this tell you about their perception of God? **4.** What frustrations does God's patience produce? How is God's patience a benefit (vv. 9, 15)? **5.** How does God's view of time differ from the readers' view? How does this viewpoint affect belief about the six "days" of creation? The "soon" return of Christ? **6.** In this context (vv. 10-16), is Peter addressing the certainty, or the timing, or the manner of Christ's coming? **7.** How is that an effective inducement to godly living now? **8.** How does Peter's reference to Paul likewise encourage his readers to right behavior? **9.** What is Peter's final antidote to the false teachers of his day (vv. 17-18)?

REFLECT: 1. If you were in charge of the world's clock, would you slow it down or speed it up? Why? **2.** If you were in charge of creating, destroying, and redeeming the world, which would you take more "time" doing? Why? **3.** In football strategy "the best defense is a good offense", meaning if the other team never gets the ball they can't score against you. How is Peter's strategy like that in his defense against those who would lead us away from the truth?

ᵍ22 Prov. 26:11   ʰ10 Some manuscripts *be burned up*   ⁱ12 Or *as you wait eagerly* *for the day of God to|come*

letters, speaking in them of these matters. His letters contain some things that are hard to understand, which ignorant and unstable people distort, as they do the other Scriptures, to their own destruction.

[17]Therefore, dear friends, since you already know this, be on your guard so that you may not be carried away by the error of lawless men and fall from your secure position. [18]But grow in the grace and knowledge of our Lord and Savior Jesus Christ. To him be glory both now and forever! Amen.

1 JOHN

INTRODUCTION

Author

Despite the fact that the author is nowhere named in the epistle, it is highly probable that he is none other than the beloved apostle John, now an old man living in Asia Minor and pastoring the churches in and around Ephesus. There are a number of reasons for attributing this anonymous epistle to John, including the following:

1. A strong tradition dating back to the early days of the church holds that John is the author.
2. There are many similarities in style and content between the Gospel of John and this epistle. The same sharp contrasts appear in both — light and darkness, truth and falsehood, love and hate. The differences between them can be traced to differences in purpose and to the length of time that elapsed between the composition of each.
3. The internal information in the epistle points to John. For example, the author tells us that he was one of the original eyewitnesses of Jesus (1:1-2). Also, the author writes with the air of authority that would be expected of an apostle (4:6).

Date

There is little clear evidence by which to date this letter accurately. Although it can be dated as early as A.D. 60, it was probably written toward the end of the New Testament era (A.D. 90-95), by which time the gnosticlike heresy had flourished.

Characteristics

First John is written in the simplest Greek of all the New Testament. (It is usually the first book seminary students learn to translate.) Although 5,437 different Greek words appear in the New Testament, only 303 are used in the three Johannine epistles — less than six percent of the total. This is not to say, however, that 1 John is a superficial book. On the contrary, here the apostle John, now an old man, is writing a distillation of all he has learned. "This is what Christianity is all about," he is saying. "This is what it all boils down to: God is light (1:5); God is love (4:16); Jesus is the Messiah (2:22); the Son of God (4:15), who has come in the flesh (4:2), and we are to be his children (3:1). As such we have eternal life (2:25). We do not continue in sin (2:1), but we love one another (3:11). I repeat we are to love one another (4:7-12)."

A story is told by Jerome of "blessed John the evangelist," an extremely old man, "being carried into the congregation at Ephesus, unable to say anything except 'Little children, love one another.' Having heard this same thing so often, they ask 'Master, why do you always say this?' 'Because,' he replied, 'it is the Lord's command, and if this only is done, it is enough.'" (J. R. W. Stott, *The Epistles of John*, p. 49).

Luther wrote: "I have never read a book written in simpler words than this one, and yet the words are inexpressible" (*Luther's Werke*, 28, 183).

Theme

The problem was heresy. Apparently a group of Christians got involved in false teaching, split off from the church (2:19), and were now hassling their former friends, probably trying to convince them to espouse their new and "advanced" views (2:26). This deeply troubled the church and thus John, as pastor, wrote to assure the Christians in and around Ephesus that they were, indeed, true Christians with the assurance of eternal life.

The nature of the heresy is not completely clear. John wasted no time defining the false position. The recipients of his letter knew well enough what was being taught. Still, by the nature of John's defense of orthodox Christianity, certain features of the heresy emerge.

Deficient Doctrine

For one thing, the false teacher's doctrine was seriously deficient. In particular, they had a low view of Jesus. They did not believe he was the Messiah (2:22, 5:1). They did not believe he was the Son of God (5:5). They denied that Jesus had come in the flesh (4:2). They apparently claimed they did not need Jesus because they already knew God (2:4) and had fellowship with him (1:6). They did not believe that sin separated a person from God (1:6, 8, 10), and thus they had no need of Jesus' atoning death (5:6) to provide foreigveness and a way back to God. It is not by accident that John calls them "antichrists." (2:22).

Spiritual Elitism

This group had come to think of themselves as some sort of spiritual elite, claiming that they had a "deeper" understanding of Christianity, probably by direct revelation (4:1-6). As an antidote to such spiritual pride, John reminded his readers over and over that Christians are called to love one another, not to look down on their brothers and sisters who do not measure up to their own supposed, superior insight.

It is not clear what labels to affix to this group of false teachers. They were probably related to what later became Gnosticism — a philosophy in which matter (including the body) was impure and spirit was all that counted. Therefore, these false teachers denied that Christ was fully human. They kept his deity, but at the expense of his humanity. To them, salvation came by illumination. Thus, esoteric "knowledge" was eagerly sought, often at the expense of apostolic doctrine.

Discerning Authenticity

John's central concerns are quite clear. He wants to define the marks of a true Christian against the claims of the false teachers. He wants his congregation to have assurance that they have eternal life (5:13). He wants them to know the characteristics of a true Christian: right belief (the doctrinal test), righteousness (the moral test), and love (the social test).

Structure

It is very difficult to outline John's first epistle, to trace the flow of his thought and put it into neat categories (as one can do with Romans, for example). Rather, it seems that John (much like James) would write a paragraph and then be reminded of a related topic that he would then deal with in the next paragraph. This, in turn, would spark a further consideration. The ideas are focused and related; they hang together, but not with a Western style of logic. The structure is almost *spiral*, "for the development of a theme often brings us back almost to the starting point; almost but not quite, for there is a slight shift which provides a transiition to a fresh theme; or it may be to a theme which had apparently been dismissed at an earlier point and now comes up for consideration from a slightly different angle" (C. H. Dodd, *The Johannine Epistles: The Moffatt New Testament Commentaries,* p. xxi).

First John is not an epistle like 2 and 3 John or most of Paul's writings. It lacks identification of writer and recipients, a salutation, and a final greeting. Still, it is not a generalized document written to all Christians. John has a specific audience in mind, probably the churches in his charge in Asia Minor. Despite the lack of usual greetings, he writes in personal terms. Many see 1 John as a tract, perhaps intended to be read as a sermon, in which John deals with a specific problem.

1 John

The Word of Life

1 That which was from the beginning, which we have heard, which we have seen with our eyes, which we have looked at and our hands have touched—this we proclaim concerning the Word of life. ²The life appeared; we have seen it and testify to it, and we proclaim to you the eternal life, which was with the Father and has appeared to us. ³We proclaim to you what we have seen and heard, so that you also may have fellowship with us. And our fellowship is with the Father and with his Son, Jesus Christ. ⁴We write this to make our*ᵃ* joy complete.

Walking in the Light

⁵This is the message we have heard from him and declare to you: God is light; in him there is no darkness at all. ⁶If we claim to have fellowship with him yet walk in the darkness, we lie and do not live by the truth. ⁷But if we walk in the light, as he is in the light, we have fellowship with one another, and the blood of Jesus, his Son, purifies us from all*ᵇ* sin.

⁸If we claim to be without sin, we deceive ourselves and the truth is not in us. ⁹If we confess our sins, he is faithful and just and will forgive us our sins and purify us from all unrighteousness. ¹⁰If we claim we have not sinned, we make him out to be a liar and his word has no place in our lives.

2 My dear children, I write this to you so that you will not sin. But if anybody does sin, we have one who speaks to the Father in our defense—Jesus Christ, the Righteous One. ²He is the atoning sacrifice for our sins, and not only for ours but also for*ᶜ* the sins of the whole world.

³We know that we have come to know him if we obey his commands. ⁴The man who says, "I know him," but does not do what he commands is a liar, and the truth is not in him. ⁵But if anyone obeys his word, God's love*ᵈ* is truly made complete in him. This is how we know we are in him: ⁶Whoever claims to live in him must walk as Jesus did.

⁷Dear friends, I am not writing you a new command but an old one, which you have had since the beginning. This old command is the message you have heard. ⁸Yet I am writing you a new command; its truth is seen in him and you, because the darkness is passing and the true light is already shining.

⁹Anyone who claims to be in the light but hates his brother is still in the darkness. ¹⁰Whoever loves his brother lives in the light, and there is nothing in him*ᵉ* to make him stumble. ¹¹But whoever hates his brother is in the darkness and walks around in the darkness; he does not know where he is going, because the darkness has blinded him.

ᵃ4 Some manuscripts your *ᵇ7 Or every* *ᶜ2 Or He is the one who turns aside God's wrath, taking away our sins, and not only ours but also* *ᵈ5 Or word, love for God* *ᵉ10 Or it*

need to do this week to improve your fellowship with other people? With God?

OPEN: Growing up, what did you crave that was either "illegal, immoral or fattening"? If you could have it all, what would "it" be?

DIG: "The world"—what did this mean for John's first readers? For you? Are human desires and God's will always opposite? Explain.

OPEN: When you were a kid, who coaxed you to "get into trouble"? Who tried to keep you on the "straight and narrow"?

DIG: 1. How would you recognize and resist an "antichrist" if you met one (see also 4:3)? How do the many antichrists foreshadow the one Antichrist to come? What danger do they pose for the church today? **2.** What is the "anointing from the Holy One" (vv. 20, 27; see also John 14:17; 15:26; 16:13)? How is this anointing related to knowing truth? And to "what you have heard from the beginning" (apostolic doctrine)? **3.** Why is adherence to apostolic teaching necessary for remaining in Christ (v. 24)? Why is the Heavenly Teacher equally important? Likewise, fellowship with other Christians (v. 19)? **4.** What are the only two options when it comes to Jesus? Why only two? If one just believes in God and not Jesus, is that person a non-Christian? An uncommitted Christian? A counterfeit Christian? Or even an antichrist? Why?

REFLECT: 1. Who was a spiritual parent to you, caring enough to warn you when you went astray? **2.** Who or what do you look to now to help you sort out truth from lies?

[12]I write to you, dear children,
  because your sins have been forgiven on account of
    his name.
[13]I write to you, fathers,
  because you have known him who is from the
    beginning.
I write to you, young men,
  because you have overcome the evil one.
I write to you, dear children,
  because you have known the Father.
[14]I write to you, fathers,
  because you have known him who is from the
    beginning.
I write to you, young men,
  because you are strong,
  and the word of God lives in you,
  and you have overcome the evil one.

Do Not Love the World

[15]Do not love the world or anything in the world. If anyone loves the world, the love of the Father is not in him. [16]For everything in the world—the cravings of sinful man, the lust of his eyes and the boasting of what he has and does—comes not from the Father but from the world. [17]The world and its desires pass away, but the man who does the will of God lives forever.

Warning Against Antichrists

[18]Dear children, this is the last hour; and as you have heard that the antichrist is coming, even now many antichrists have come. This is how we know it is the last hour. [19]They went out from us, but they did not really belong to us. For if they had belonged to us, they would have remained with us; but their going showed that none of them belonged to us. [20]But you have an anointing from the Holy One, and all of you know the truth.[f] [21]I do not write to you because you do not know the truth, but because you do know it and because no lie comes from the truth. [22]Who is the liar? It is the man who denies that Jesus is the Christ. Such a man is the antichrist—he denies the Father and the Son. [23]No one who denies the Son has the Father; whoever acknowledges the Son has the Father also.

[24]See that what you have heard from the beginning remains in you. If it does, you also will remain in the Son and in the Father. [25]And this is what he promised us—even eternal life.

[26]I am writing these things to you about those who are trying to lead you astray. [27]As for you, the anointing you received from him remains in you, and you do not need anyone to teach you. But as his anointing teaches you about all things and as that anointing is real, not counterfeit—just as it has taught you, remain in him.

---

f20 Some manuscripts *and you know all things*

Children of God

²⁸And now, dear children, continue in him, so that when he appears we may be confident and unashamed before him at his coming.

²⁹If you know that he is righteous, you know that everyone who does what is right has been born of him.

3 How great is the love the Father has lavished on us, that we should be called children of God! And that is what we are! The reason the world does not know us is that it did not know him. ²Dear friends, now we are children of God, and what we will be has not yet been made known. But we know that when he appears,^g we shall be like him, for we shall see him as he is. ³Everyone who has this hope in him purifies himself, just as he is pure.

⁴Everyone who sins breaks the law; in fact, sin is lawlessness. ⁵But you know that he appeared so that he might take away our sins. And in him is no sin. ⁶No one who lives in him keeps on sinning. No one who continues to sin has either seen him or known him.

⁷Dear children, do not let anyone lead you astray. He who does what is right is righteous, just as he is righteous. ⁸He who does what is sinful is of the devil, because the devil has been sinning from the beginning. The reason the Son of God appeared was to destroy the devil's work. ⁹No one who is born of God will continue to sin, because God's seed remains in him; he cannot go on sinning, because he has been born of God. ¹⁰This is how we know who the children of God are and who the children of the devil are: Anyone who does not do what is right is not a child of God; nor is anyone who does not love his brother.

Love One Another

¹¹This is the message you heard from the beginning: We should love one another. ¹²Do not be like Cain, who belonged to the evil one and murdered his brother. And why did he murder him? Because his own actions were evil and his brother's were righteous. ¹³Do not be surprised, my brothers, if the world hates you. ¹⁴We know that we have passed from death to life, because we love our brothers. Anyone who does not love remains in death. ¹⁵Anyone who hates his brother is a murderer, and you know that no murderer has eternal life in him.

¹⁶This is how we know what love is: Jesus Christ laid down his life for us. And we ought to lay down our lives for our brothers. ¹⁷If anyone has material possessions and sees his brother in need but has no pity on him, how can the love of God be in him? ¹⁸Dear children, let us not love with words or tongue but with actions and in truth. ¹⁹This then is how we know that we belong to the truth, and how we set our hearts at rest in his presence ²⁰whenever our hearts condemn us. For God is greater than our hearts, and he knows everything.

²¹Dear friends, if our hearts do not condemn us, we have confidence before God ²²and receive from him anything we ask,

^{g2} Or *when it is made known*

OPEN: 1. For which guests would you bother to clean your house: Your parents? Your pastor? Your in-laws? A celebrity? **2.** Do you think parents should try to keep their children out of trouble after age fifteen? Why?

DIG: 1. What additional incentives does John, the author, give for remaining in Christ and being a child of God? **2.** What does it mean to be a child of God: Freed from all sin? Accepted in spite of our sin? Childishly dependent? Just naughty every now and then? **3.** Why are God's children not received by the world (3:1, 2, 6, 9, 10)? **4.** What does John say about sin and the sinner: That a Christian "cannot" sin? That a Christian "will not deliberately" sin? That a Christian "does not habitually" sin? That sin for the Christian is impossible? Incompatible? Incongruous? **5.** What are the two false teachings about sin that John attacks in this letter (see 1:6-2:2 and 3:3-10)?

REFLECT: 1. What motivates you to live a clean and holy life? **2.** As you get older, do you find the old sinful desires easier or harder to resist? **3.** When you blow it, what have you found most helpful in making it right with God and getting on with life?

OPEN: 1. Who was your first "true love"? **2.** Who gave you your first kiss outside of the family? **3.** What person really taught you what love is all about? How?

DIG: 1. How does the story of Cain and Abel (Genisis 4:1-8) illustrate the meaning of "love one another"? How does the cross of Christ illustrate the same point? **2.** How does John's definition of love (vv. 16-18) differ from your experience and expression of love in dating relationships? In your family? In your church? **3.** Does obedience result in answered prayer (vv. 21-22)? Or does obedience move us to pray? Why? **4.** Does obedience result from union with God (v. 24)? Or does union with God result from obedience? Why? **5.** How does God meet our need for assurance (vv. 14, 16, 19, 20 24)?

REFLECT: Goaded by the examples of John, the command of Christ and the honesty of Peanuts ("I love mankind; it's people I can't stand"), who are the people you can not get along with? What can you do about it this week? Are you willing to try?

OPEN: What concerns you more: The way-out cults? Or subtle immitations that look like Christianity?

DIG: 1. If the Holy Spirit bears witness as to who are actually Christians (3:24), what happens when false religionists claim the same Spirit (4:1)? How can one distinguish between rival claims to religious truth (see also 2:20-23)? **2.** How does one resist a false prophet (vv. 4-6)?

REFLECT: 1. Why do so many people from good religious backgrounds fall for cults? **2.** How equipped are you to deal with false prophets (vv. 4-6)?

OPEN: 1. What characteristics or strengths did you get from your father? Your mother? **2.** What family event or experience stands out as an example of your family at their closest?

DIG: 1. What is this love that John mentions 32 times in this unit: A warm feeling? Brotherly obligation? Sacrificial action? Material giving? Absence of malice? Forgiveness of sins? All of these? **2.** How does this message that "God is love" (4:8, 16) relate to the other main teaching that "God is light" (1:5)? **3.** How is God's love expressed through Jesus? Through humans? **4.** How is such love suppressed through fear? Through hatred? **5.** How is such love made "complete" (vv. 12, 17) or "perfect" (v. 18)?

REFLECT: 1. What experience have you had where love cast out fear? Where fear cast out love? **2.** Where do you have the greatest trouble loving people: At church? At the office? Or at home? Why?

---

because we obey his commands and do what pleases him. [23]And this is his command: to believe in the name of his Son, Jesus Christ, and to love one another as he commanded us. [24]Those who obey his commands live in him, and he in them. And this is how we know that he lives in us: We know it by the Spirit he gave us.

Test the Spirits

4 Dear friends, do not believe every spirit, but test the spirits to see whether they are from God, because many false prophets have gone out into the world. [2]This is how you can recognize the Spirit of God: Every spirit that acknowledges that Jesus Christ has come in the flesh is from God, [3]but every spirit that does not acknowledge Jesus is not from God. This is the spirit of the antichrist, which you have heard is coming and even now is already in the world.

[4]You, dear children, are from God and have overcome them, because the one who is in you is greater than the one who is in the world. [5]They are from the world and therefore speak from the viewpoint of the world, and the world listens to them. [6]We are from God, and whoever knows God listens to us; but whoever is not from God does not listen to us. This is how we recognize the Spirit[h] of truth and the spirit of falsehood.

God's Love and Ours

[7]Dear friends, let us love one another, for love comes from God. Everyone who loves has been born of God and knows God. [8]Whoever does not love does not know God, because God is love. [9]This is how God showed his love among us: He sent his one and only Son[i] into the world that we might live through him. [10]This is love: not that we loved God, but that he loved us and sent his Son as an atoning sacrifice for[j] our sins. [11]Dear friends, since God so loved us, we also ought to love one another. [12]No one has ever seen God; but if we love one another, God lives in us and his love is made complete in us.

[13]We know that we live in him and he in us, because he has given us of his Spirit. [14]And we have seen and testify that the Father has sent his Son to be the Savior of the world. [15]If anyone acknowledges that Jesus is the Son of God, God lives in him and he in God. [16]And so we know and rely on the love God has for us.

God is love. Whoever lives in love lives in God, and God in him. [17]In this way, love is made complete among us so that we will have confidence on the day of judgment, because in this world we are like him. [18]There is no fear in love. But perfect love drives out fear, because fear has to do with punishment. The one who fears is not made perfect in love.

[19]We love because he first loved us. [20]If anyone says, "I love God," yet hates his brother, he is a liar. For anyone who does not love his brother, whom he has seen, cannot love God, whom he has not seen. [21]And he has given us this command: Whoever loves God must also love his brother.

---

h6 Or *spirit*   *i9* Or *his only begotten Son*   *j10* Or *as the one who would turn aside his wrath, taking away*

Faith in the Son of God

5 Everyone who believes that Jesus is the Christ is born of God, and everyone who loves the father loves his child as well. [2]This is how we know that we love the children of God: by loving God and carrying out his commands. [3]This is love for God: to obey his commands. And his commands are not burdensome, [4]for everyone born of God overcomes the world. This is the victory that has overcome the world, even our faith. [5]Who is it that overcomes the world? Only he who believes that Jesus is the Son of God.

[6]This is the one who came by water and blood—Jesus Christ. He did not come by water only, but by water and blood. And it is the Spirit who testifies, because the Spirit is the truth. [7]For there are three that testify: [8]the [k] Spirit, the water and the blood; and the three are in agreement. [9]We accept man's testimony, but God's testimony is greater because it is the testimony of God, which he has given about his Son. [10]Anyone who believes in the Son of God has this testimony in his heart. Anyone who does not believe God has made him out to be a liar, because he has not believed the testimony God has given about his Son. [11]And this is the testimony: God has given us eternal life, and this life is in his Son. [12]He who has the Son has life; he who does not have the Son of God does not have life.

Concluding Remarks

[13]I write these things to you who believe in the name of the Son of God so that you may know that you have eternal life. [14]This is the confidence we have in approaching God: that if we ask anything according to his will, he hears us. [15]And if we know that he hears us—whatever we ask—we know that we have what we asked of him.

[16]If anyone sees his brother commit a sin that does not lead to death, he should pray and God will give him life. I refer to those whose sin does not lead to death. There is a sin that leads to death. I am not saying that he should pray about that. [17]All wrongdoing is sin, and there is sin that does not lead to death.

[18]We know that anyone born of God does not continue to sin; the one who was born of God keeps him safe, and the evil one cannot harm him. [19]We know that we are children of God, and that the whole world is under the control of the evil one. [20]We know also that the Son of God has come and has given us understanding, so that we may know him who is true. And we are in him who is true—even in his Son Jesus Christ. He is the true God and eternal life.

[21]Dear children, keep yourselves from idols.

OPEN: 1. When you were a child, what chore did you have that was a real burden? **2.** Have you ever had to testify in court? If so, what did your testimony have to be in agreement with?

DIG 1. John ends here where he began (1:1-4)—with what similar themes? **2.** What is the "victory that has overcome the world": Christ's death and resurrection? Our conversion or baptism? **3.** How does one come to faith in Jesus? **4.** What is meant by "water and the blood": Christ's baptism and death? Our purification and redemption? The sacraments? **5.** How are belief, love and obedience interconnected?

REFLECT: 1. Which of the commands in this letter do you find most difficult to do? Most enlightening? Most central? **2.** When in your spiritual pilgrimage did you come to understand the meaning of God's gift of eternal life? Or are you still somewhere along the way? Where?

OPEN: 1. What came closest to being the "unpardonable sin" in your family: Playing cards? Hogging the bathroom? Tying up the phone? Leaving your room a mess? Picking your nose in public? **2.** As a child, who did you idolize? How do you feel about that person now?

DIG: 1. What assurance does John offer his readers as their pastor? On what basis are we assured of eternal life? Of answered prayer? Of deliverance from habitual sin? Of knowing truth? **2.** What might be the sin that leads to death (see Mark 3:22-30)? Why does the very fear that you might have committed this sin prove that you have not done so? **3.** What does it mean to "pray according to his will"?

REFLECT: 1. Have you ever felt like your prayers were "bouncing off the ceiling"? What did you do? **2.** What prayer has God answered recently that you waited on for a long time? **3.** What prayer is still on hold? **4.** What are some "God-substitutes" (idols) which have crept into your Christian life: Golf on Sunday? Snack food instead of quiet time? Extra hours at work getting ahead instead of time helping others find faith? Or what? **5.** What is the most important thing you have learned from this book in the Bible?

---

[k]7,8 Late manuscripts of the Vulgate *testify in|heaven: the Father, the Word and the Holy Spirit, and these three are one.* [8]*And|there are three that testify on earth: the* (not found in any Greek manuscript before|the sixteenth century)

2 JOHN
3 JOHN

INTRODUCTION

Characteristics

Second and Third John are the shortest letters in the New Testament; so short, in fact, that virtually everyone concedes that they are genuine. (Who would bother to fake such brief and unassuming documents?) Their length is determined by the size of a standard papyrus sheet (8 x 10 inches). Each letter would fit exactly on one sheet.

Author

There is much similarity of style and content between 2 and 3 John. (For example, compare 2 John 1 and 3 John 1; 2 John 4 and 3 John 4; 2 John 12 and 3 John 13-14). Undoubtedly both were written by the same person. There is also a close connection between 1 John and these two shorter letters (compare, for example, 1 John 4:3 and 2 John 7). All three epistles seem to deal with the same situation. Therefore, it seems very likely that the "elder" who wrote 2 and 3 John is, indeed, the apostle John.

Theme

The issue addressed by 2 and 3 John is that of wandering missionaries. In a time when Roman inns were notorious for being dirty and flea-infested, visiting Christian teachers would turn to the local church for hospitality. The problem was that some of the people seeking room and board were false teachers, expounding erroneous doctrines; others were phony, pretending to be true prophets to get free hospitality. Even a pagan Greek author like Lucian noticed this sort of abuse. In his satirical work *Peregrinus,* he wrote about a religious charlatan who lived off the generosity of the church simply as a way to avoid working. In an attempt to cope with this problem, the *Didache,* an early church manual, laid down a series of regulations guiding the reception of itinerant ministers. It said, for example, that true prophets were indeed to be entertained—for a day or two. But if a prophet stayed three days, this was a sign that he was false. Likewise, if a prophet under the inspiration of the Spirit asked for money, he was a false prophet.

These concerns are found in 2 and 3 John. In 2 John, the author worries about false prophets who are teaching erroneous doctrine. "Do not welcome such," he says (2 John 10). But in 3 John, he addresses the opposite problem: Christians who failed to provide hospitality for genuine teachers.

2 John

¹The elder,

To the chosen lady and her children, whom I love in the truth—and not I only, but also all who know the truth— ²because of the truth, which lives in us and will be with us forever:

³Grace, mercy and peace from God the Father and from Jesus Christ, the Father's Son, will be with us in truth and love.

⁴It has given me great joy to find some of your children walking in the truth, just as the Father commanded us. ⁵And now, dear lady, I am not writing you a new command but one we have had from the beginning. I ask that we love one another. ⁶And this is love: that we walk in obedience to his commands. As you have heard from the beginning, his command is that you walk in love.

⁷Many deceivers, who do not acknowledge Jesus Christ as coming in the flesh, have gone out into the world. Any such person is the deceiver and the antichrist. ⁸Watch out that you do not lose what you have worked for, but that you may be rewarded fully. ⁹Anyone who runs ahead and does not continue in the teaching of Christ does not have God; whoever continues in the teaching has both the Father and the Son. ¹⁰If anyone comes to you and does not bring this teaching, do not take him into your house or welcome him. ¹¹Anyone who welcomes him shares in his wicked work.

¹²I have much to write to you, but I do not want to use paper and ink. Instead, I hope to visit you and talk with you face to face, so that our joy may be complete.

¹³The children of your chosen sister send their greetings.

OPEN: 1. When you were growing up, where did you gather for family reunions? What was special about those times? Where did the guests stay? **2.** Whose home could you drop in on and know that you would be welcome—even without calling?

DIG: 1. How are John's twin themes of truth and love interconnected here? Which is easier for you to do "Walk in truth" or "walk in love"? **2.** Is the lady addressed in this letter erring on the side of truth, or on the side of love, if she were to show hospitality to these false traveling teachers? Why? What's wrong with welcoming such wandering missionaries? **3.** How do John's exhortations to true believers (vv. 4-6) help them resist the deception and wickedness of the religious frauds (vv. 7-11)?

REFLECT: 1. Have you ever been involved in a deep relationship that had to be terminated because of an overriding issue involving your faith? What happened? **2.** Who do you open your home to? Who do you refuse? **3.** When is the last time you had someone over who was really hurting, lonely or needing help? Should you do this more often? What's stopping you?

3 John

OPEN: 1. Did you ever run out of money when you were away from home? What did you do? **2.** Who extended loving hospitality to you when you needed it most?

DIG: 1. What do you think was going on that caused John to write this letter? How does this letter tackle the hospitality issue differently from the previous letter? How is this letter and the previous letter similar? Different? **2.** Why is this letter urging that genuine teachers be taken in and provided for along their journey? **3.** Who does the hospitality of Gaius and the hostility of Diotrephes remind you of in your church circles? Who are you more like?

REFLECT: 1. In choosing close friends (like Gaius was to John), what do you look for? **2.** Do you find opening your home easy or difficult? Why do you think this is? **3.** If you could start a Bible study group for new people, who would you want to invite and why?

¹The elder,

To my dear friend Gaius, whom I love in the truth.

²Dear friend, I pray that you may enjoy good health and that all may go well with you, even as your soul is getting along well. ³It gave me great joy to have some brothers come and tell about your faithfulness to the truth and how you continue to walk in the truth. ⁴I have no greater joy than to hear that my children are walking in the truth.

⁵Dear friend, you are faithful in what you are doing for the brothers, even though they are strangers to you. ⁶They have told the church about your love. You will do well to send them on their way in a manner worthy of God. ⁷It was for the sake of the Name that they went out, receiving no help from the pagans. ⁸We ought therefore to show hospitality to such men so that we may work together for the truth.

⁹I wrote to the church, but Diotrephes, who loves to be first, will have nothing to do with us. ¹⁰So if I come, I will call attention to what he is doing, gossiping maliciously about us. Not satisfied with that, he refuses to welcome the brothers. He also stops those who want to do so and puts them out of the church.

¹¹Dear friend, do not imitate what is evil but what is good. Anyone who does what is good is from God. Anyone who does what is evil has not seen God. ¹²Demetrius is well spoken of by everyone—and even by the truth itself. We also speak well of him, and you know that our testimony is true.

¹³I have much to write you, but I do not want to do so with pen and ink. ¹⁴I hope to see you soon, and we will talk face to face.

Peace to you. The friends here send their greetings. Greet the friends there by name.

JUDE

INTRODUCTION

Author

In the New Testament there are five people by the name of Jude or Judas (Mark 6:3; Luke 6:16; John 14:22; Acts 9:11; 15:22, 27, 32), but only one is a serious candidate as author: Jude, the brother of Jesus.

Little is known about Jude. He was one of four brothers (Matt. 13:55; Mark 6:3). He was probably not a follower of Jesus during the years of his brother's ministry (Mark 3:21, 31-35; John 7:5). It was only after the Resurrection that Jude became a believer (Acts 1:14).

The brothers of Jesus eventually became itinerant missionaries (1 Cor. 9:5). Tradition has it that they spread the gospel throughout Palestine. Jude's brother, James the Just, was leader of the church in Jerusalem.

So in the book of Jude, a reader comes in touch with "those original Palestinian Christian circles in which Jesus' own blood relatives were leaders" (Richard Bauckham, *Jude, 2 Peter: Word Biblical Commentary*, p. xi).

Characteristics

Another Neglected Book

Most people know Jude only because of its benediction (vv. 24-25):

Now unto him that is able to keep you from falling, and to present you faultless before the presence of his glory with exceeding joy, to the only wise God our Saviour, be glory and majesty, dominion and power, both now and ever. Amen. (KJV)

Like 2 Peter, Jude is widely unread because of doubts about its pedigree and because of its frequent unfamiliar images. To its first readers, however, Jude was anything but obscure. It was heard as a fiery call to defend the faith against the heretics who had wormed their way into the church (v. 4).

The Texts Jude Expounds

This is a sermon, and in true sermonic fashion, Jude quotes (or alludes to) various texts and then explains them. What sets Jude's sermon apart from contemporary Christian sermons is his choice of texts. His first references are to Old Testament stories (vv. 5-7, 11), and his concluding reference is to "what the apostles of our Lord Jesus Christ foretold" (v. 17). This is familiar material. But in between, Jude quotes *1 Enoch* (vv. 14-15), a Jewish apocryphal book, and alludes to the *Assumption of Moses* in verse 9, probably to the *Testament of Naphtali* (v. 7) and to the *Testament of Asher* (v. 8).

The Apocryphal books Jude quotes were written during the time between the Old and New Testament. They were not accepted as orthodox and so never became part of the Bible itself.

Certain of the church fathers concluded (wrongly) that any book that used apocryphal literature as Jude did could not be genuine. But this view says more about the presuppositions of those theologians than it does about what can and cannot be included within Scripture.

Certainly other New Testament authors used nonbiblical Jewish writing in 1 Corinthians 10:4 and 2 Timothy 3:8. Paul quotes the heathen poets in Acts 17:28; 1 Corinthians 15:32-33; and Titus 1:12. The author of Hebrews echoes the works of Philo; James makes reference to nonbiblical sources. The issue is not where the specific words came from but how the New Testament writer used these words to reveal God's truth.

Relationship to 2 Peter

It is clear that Jude and 2 Peter are somehow related. Of the twenty-five verses in Jude, fifteen appear in whole or in part in 2 Peter. The question is: What is the nature of the relationship between Jude and 2 Peter? Did Jude quote from 2 Peter? Or was the reverse true? Or did they both quote from the same outside source? The answer to this question is by no means certain.

Theme

Jude gives an overview of his book in verses 3-4. He makes two points. First, Christians are "to contend for the faith"; second, they are to do so against false Christians who "have secretly slipped in among [them]." The rest of the book develops these two points. In verses 5-19, the nature of the false teachers is explained. Jude makes it exceedingly clear that this is not a new problem and furthermore, their condemnation is sure. In verses 20-23, Jude gets to his main point: He appeals to the Christians to hold on to the Christian faith despite false teachers.

The False Teachers

Jude's opponents are a band of smooth-talking teachers who go from church to church, receiving hospitality in return for their instruction. Such itinerant teachers were often a source of trouble in the early church (Matt. 7:15; 2 Cor. 10-11; 1 John 4:1; 2 John 10). In this case, the teachers were *antinomians,* that is, they rejected all moral standards (since they misunderstood grace) and indulged in all manner of immoral behavior, particularly of a sexual sort. Their teaching was derived largely from individual ecstatic experience ("God told me"), and they considered themselves the sole judge of their own actions.

Structure

Jude is a genuine letter. It has a standard opening (vv. 1-2), and in verses 3-4 the theme and occasion of the epistle are defined — again typical of a letter. But Jude is also a short sermon. The bulk of the book (vv. 5-25) consists of an exposition of certain texts as related to a particular problem facing the church. Thus, Jude is a sermon sent by mail to be read before the congregation(s).

The Book of Jude is a painstakingly crafted document. Jude packs a lot of content into a few words by carefully choosing his words and images. Verses 11-13 are particularly vivid in imagery, evoking a wide range of associations in remarkably few words.

Jude

[1]Jude, a servant of Jesus Christ and a brother of James,

To those who have been called, who are loved by God the Father and kept by[a] Jesus Christ:

[2]Mercy, peace and love be yours in abundance.

The Sin and Doom of Godless Men

[3]Dear friends, although I was very eager to write to you about the salvation we share, I felt I had to write and urge you to contend for the faith that was once for all entrusted to the saints. [4]For certain men whose condemnation was written about[b] long ago have secretly slipped in among you. They are godless men, who change the grace of our God into a license for immorality and deny Jesus Christ our only Sovereign and Lord.

[5]Though you already know all this, I want to remind you that the Lord[c] delivered his people out of Egypt, but later destroyed those who did not believe. [6]And the angels who did not keep their positions of authority but abandoned their own home— these he has kept in darkness, bound with everlasting chains for judgment on the great Day. [7]In a similar way, Sodom and Gomorrah and the surrounding towns gave themselves up to sexual immorality and perversion. They serve as an example of those who suffer the punishment of eternal fire.

[8]In the very same way, these dreamers pollute their own bodies, reject authority and slander celestial beings. [9]But even the archangel Michael, when he was disputing with the devil about the body of Moses, did not dare to bring a slanderous accusation against him, but said, "The Lord rebuke you!" [10]Yet these men speak abusively against whatever they do not understand; and what things they do understand by instinct, like unreasoning animals—these are the very things that destroy them.

[11]Woe to them! They have taken the way of Cain; they have rushed for profit into Balaam's error; they have been destroyed in Korah's rebellion.

[12]These men are blemishes at your love feasts, eating with you without the slightest qualm—shepherds who feed only themselves. They are clouds without rain, blown along by the wind; autumn trees, without fruit and uprooted—twice dead. [13]They are wild waves of the sea, foaming up their shame; wandering stars, for whom blackest darkness has been reserved forever.

[14]Enoch, the seventh from Adam, prophesied about these men: "See, the Lord is coming with thousands upon thousands of his holy ones [15]to judge everyone, and to convict all the ungodly of all the ungodly acts they have done in the ungodly way, and of all the harsh words ungodly sinners have spoken against him." [16]These men are grumblers and faultfinders; they follow their own evil desires; they boast about themselves and flatter others for their own advantage.

---

[a]1 Or *for; or in*   [b]4 Or *men who were marked out for condemnation*
[c]5 Some early manuscripts *Jesus*

A Call to Persevere

[17]But, dear friends, remember what the apostles of our Lord Jesus Christ foretold. [18]They said to you, "In the last times there will be scoffers who will follow their own ungodly desires." [19]These are the men who divide you, who follow mere natural instincts and do not have the Spirit.

[20]But you, dear friends, build yourselves up in your most holy faith and pray in the Holy Spirit. [21]Keep yourselves in God's love as you wait for the mercy of our Lord Jesus Christ to bring you to eternal life.

[22]Be merciful to those who doubt; [23]snatch others from the fire and save them; to others show mercy, mixed with fear—hating even the clothing stained by corrupted flesh.

Doxology

[24]To him who is able to keep you from falling and to present you before his glorious presence without fault and with great joy— [25]to the only God our Savior be glory, majesty, power and authority, through Jesus Christ our Lord, before all ages, now and forevermore! Amen.

REVELATION

INTRODUCTION

Apocalyptic Literature

The Book of Revelation is unique. It is the only apocalyptic book in the New Testament. What makes this so unusual is that while the New Testament books were written, apocalyptic literature flourished. In fact, during the period between the Old and New Testaments, apocalyptic literature was the most common type of Jewish religious writing.

At the heart of apocalyptic literature was *hope*—hope that God would right wrongs and rescue the righteous. The Jews knew that they were God's chosen people, yet they had been subject to ungodly rules for so long. As a result, they longed for that great day when God would intervene in history and bring about what he promised. They gave shape to these longings in the so-called apocalyptic writings (*apocalypse* is a Greek word meaning an "unveiling" or "uncovering" of future events or hidden realms, like heaven).

Apocalyptic literature dealt with the details of God's return: how he would burst into history, whom he would destroy, how he would set up his kingdom. These books were, of necessity, the products of dreams and visions. Consequently, they were filled with swirling images and vivid pictures of death, supernatural places and creatures, destruction and redemption, and so on. Since the events described were unlike anything that had ever happened, they could only be alluded to, often in cryptic language. The resulting mystery surrounding such writing was further compounded by the need for secrecy. Were these books to fall into the hands of the rulers (the ones singled out for destruction), they would be considered seditious and would land their authors in jail or worse. So the books were written in code. They could be understood only by those on the writer's side who had the key to the code. Outsiders, such as the police, would find them unintelligible. Of course, this is why we have a problem today in deciphering apocalyptic literature. In many cases, we have lost the key.

The Apocalyptic World View

Underlying both Jewish and Christian apocalyptic literature was the view that history is divided into two ages. The present age is evil and corrupt and it will be destroyed. The age-to-come is characterized by goodness and by God's presence and power. The central turning point in history, on which apocalyptic writers often focused, is the Day of the Lord, when the present age will give way to the new age.

Christian writers understood this to be the day of Christ's return—the Second Coming. He had come once, as a baby in Bethlehem, and by his first coming had set in motion the events that would draw the present age to a close. When he came again, it would not be as an infant but as a king before whom the whole creation would bow. For the moment, however, Christians live in the in-between time. Christ's ultimate victory was secured at the Cross; Satan was defeated. But the victory had yet to be claimed in its fullness. Satan still pretended that he was in charge and would do so until the Second Coming.

What is striking is how similar the pattern is in Christian and Jewish apocalyptic literature. Beyond the obvious difference over the role of Christ, the same outline is found in Jewish literature as in Revelation. Specifically:

1. The Messiah will be the central figure in the Day of the Lord.
2. The coming of the new age will be preceded by a terrible time in history filled with war, famine, and calamity of all sorts. In fact, the elements themselves will disintegrate, and hatred and anger will prevail in human affairs.
3. The Day of the Lord will be the time when judgment is rendered.

4. Following judgment, there will be a time of great peace and joy. The New Jerusalem will descend. The dead will rise and the Messiah will reign.

Characteristics

Not only is Revelation strange; it is also difficult. The world of the Book of Revelation is so remote from the modern world that one hardly knows where to begin in trying to understand it. It is a world filled with weird beasts who have ten horns and seven heads; a world of seals and trumpets and bowls that bring disaster; a world populated with angels and demons, with lions and lambs, with horses and dragons. Who can make sense out of all this?

As a result, we often either ignore Revelation or distort it. Barclay calls Revelation "the playground of religious eccentrics" (*The Revelation of John: Daily Study Bible,* Vol. 1, p. 1). Indeed some wild notions have been extracted from Revelation and claimed to have divine sanction. On the other hand, as Philip Carrington has said:

> In the case of the *Revelation* we are dealing with an artist greater than Stevenson or Coleridge or Bach. St. John has a better sense of the right word than Stevenson; he has a greater command of unearthly supernatural loveliness than Coleridge; he has a richer sense of melody and rhythm and composition than Bach . . . It is the only masterpiece of pure art in the New Testament (*The Meaning of Revelation,* pp. xvii, xix).

The Book of Revelation is well worth reading, but it must be approached with humility and caution. To pin one's whole theology on details in the Book of Revelation is dangerous indeed. With prayer and patience, the reader needs to work at understanding the text.

Revelation is written in the worst Greek of any book of the New Testament. There are mistakes in grammar and stylistic errors such as a schoolboy would make. Yet R. H. Charles, an expert on apocalyptic literature, considers the bad grammar deliberate. According to Charles, John wrote this way for emphasis. His clumsy Greek style reflects his attempt to translate Old Testament passages — the author was thinking in Hebrew but writing in Greek. Furthermore, a vision such as John had can never be adequately captured by mere words. John had to push language to its limits even to approximate what he had seen. The poor Greek may also have resulted from John's imprisonment on Patmos, where he probably had no secretary to smooth out his style. (*A Critical Exegetical Commentary on the Revelation of St. John: International Critical Commentary,* pp. x-xi).

Author

Although the author only refers to himself as "John" (1:4), it has traditionally been assumed that he was none other than John the apostle. In fact, this simple designation "John" is strong proof in itself that the apostle was the writer. Typically apocalyptic literature claimed to be authored by famous heroes of the past (e.g., Abraham, Ezra, Enoch, and Baruch). But John writes in his own name, and only a person of the stature of an apostle could expect to have such a work received as authoritative. Furthermore, when Revelation is compared to the Gospel of John and the three letters of John, there are striking similarities in ideas, theology, and language.

John wrote from the island of Patmos, a rocky, barren island in the Aegean Sea (ten miles long and five miles wide), where he had been exiled because of his Christian witness. Tradition says that he was eventually released from Patmos and spent the remaining years of his long life in Ephesus.

Date

Most scholars feel that the Book of Revelation was written toward the end of the reign of Domitian, that is, around A.D. 90-95. This is what Irenaeus, a second-century bishop, claimed. Still, this dating is not conclusive. Evidence has been offered that it might have been written during the last years of Nero's reign (between A.D. 65 and 68) or when Vespasian was emperor (A.D. 69-79).

Audience

The Book of Revelation was addressed to seven churches in the western part of the Roman province of Asia (see map). The order in which these churches are addressed is the order in which a messenger from Patmos would come to each church if he followed the great circular Roman road connecting the cities.

Theme

Rome is a central and consistently negative image in the Book of Revelation. This view of the Roman government stands in sharp contrast to the rest of the New Testament, where Rome is seen as the protector of Christianity. In the early days of missionary activity, Roman judges protected Christians from Jewish mobs (Acts 18:1-17; 19:13-41). It was Roman justice to which Paul turned in his time of need (Acts 23:12-35; 25:10-11). As a result, the apostles urged submission to Rome (Rom. 13:1-7; 1 Peter 2:13-17). But in Revelation, the attitude is quite different. Rome is seen as a whore, drunk with the blood of Christians (17:5-6), deserving nothing but destruction.

This shift in attitude is due to one thing — Caesar worship. Although Roman rulers were long considered divine, their centrality in Roman civil religion was not enforced until the end of the first century. Then it became obligatory for citizens all across the Roman Empire to appear once a year before a magistrate to burn a pinch of incense and declare, "Caesar is Lord." This was more an act of loyalty to Rome than a religious statement, but Christians simply could not bring themselves to declare that anyone except Jesus was Lord. As a result, they were hounded mercilessly by civil authorities. This is the situation to which Revelation speaks. It attempts to encourage Christians by giving them the long view. They may suffer now while Caesar pretends to be Lord, but ahead lies unimaginable glory when Jesus, the true Lord, comes in power. This kind of vision would give harassed Christians the strength to endure.

Structure

John begins with a description of the vision from which the Book of Revelation came (chap. 1). Chapters 2 and 3 contain specific messages to seven churches in Asia Minor. Chapters 4 and 5 describe a vision of God and of Christ. Then in chapters 6-19 various plagues of judgment are described. The book is concluded (chaps. 20-22) by a description of the coming kingdom.

While the overall structure is clear, how it all fits together varies with the reader's interpretive posture.

Interpretation

There are widely varying ways to interpret Revelation. Some limit its meaning to the first-century struggle between the church and Rome. Others see Revelation as a collection of symbols that predict future events (e.g., the locusts from the bottomless pit represent the invasion of Europe by Islam). In fact, the Book of Revelation probably speaks both to the immediate first-century struggle of Christians and to the future when the Lord will return.

Revelation

OPEN: 1. What kind of book are you: Mystery? Sports? Technical? Adventure? Poetry? Unreadable? Sealed book? X-Rated? Why? **2.** What book has "blessed" you recently? Why?

DIG: What is revelation? In this case, who is revealed? By whom? To whom? For what purpose?

OPEN: Would you be better as a king, a priest, or a servant? Why? What would your spouse or roommate say is your typical role?

DIG: 1. Who is John? Identify these seven churches (1:11) and locate them on a map. **2.** How is God the Son described in verses 5-6? What is the meaning of each title? What three things does Christ do for us? **3.** What theme of the Book of Revelation is foreshadowed in verse 7? What is significant about the fact that every eye shall see him?

REFLECT: If you were asked to tell someone three facts about Jesus that are especially significant to you, what would you say? Why are these facts so important to you?

OPEN: What is the most bizarre dream you have ever had? How did it make you feel?

DIG: 1. Why was John on Patmos? What do you know about his assignment there? **2.** On what day does he receive this message? In what condition was he when he heard the voice? What's significant about the day and the condition? **3.** Describe the attributes of the "son of man". What does each aspect of this description suggest about Christ? **4.** What is the meaning of the seven stars? The seven lampstands? In what way are stars and lampstands similar? What does it mean for a church to be a light? **5.** Close your eyes and have someone read slowly verses 12-18, several times if necessary. Meditate on what you see in this imagery. Describe your experience. How does this help you

Prologue

1 The revelation of Jesus Christ, which God gave him to show his servants what must soon take place. He made it known by sending his angel to his servant John, ²who testifies to everything he saw—that is, the word of God and the testimony of Jesus Christ. ³Blessed is the one who reads the words of this prophecy, and blessed are those who hear it and take to heart what is written in it, because the time is near.

Greetings and Doxology

⁴John,

To the seven churches in the province of Asia:

Grace and peace to you from him who is, and who was, and who is to come, and from the seven spirits*a* before his throne, ⁵and from Jesus Christ, who is the faithful witness, the firstborn from the dead, and the ruler of the kings of the earth.

To him who loves us and has freed us from our sins by his blood, ⁶and has made us to be a kingdom and priests to serve his God and Father—to him be glory and power for ever and ever! Amen.

⁷Look, he is coming with the clouds,
    and every eye will see him,
even those who pierced him;
    and all the peoples of the earth will mourn because of him.
                                    So shall it be! Amen.

⁸"I am the Alpha and the Omega," says the Lord God, "who is, and who was, and who is to come, the Almighty."

One Like a Son of Man

⁹I, John, your brother and companion in the suffering and kingdom and patient endurance that are ours in Jesus, was on the island of Patmos because of the word of God and the testimony of Jesus. ¹⁰On the Lord's Day I was in the Spirit, and I heard behind me a loud voice like a trumpet, ¹¹which said: "Write on a scroll what you see and send it to the seven churches: to Ephesus, Smyrna, Pergamum, Thyatira, Sardis, Philadelphia and Laodicea."

¹²I turned around to see the voice that was speaking to me. And when I turned I saw seven golden lampstands, ¹³and among the lampstands was someone "like a son of man,"*b* dressed in a robe reaching down to his feet and with a golden sash around his chest. ¹⁴His head and hair were white like wool, as white as snow, and his eyes were like blazing fire. ¹⁵His feet were like

a4 Or the sevenfold Spirit   *b13 Daniel 7:13*

bronze glowing in a furnace, and his voice was like the sound of rushing waters. ¹⁶In his right hand he held seven stars, and out of his mouth came a sharp double-edged sword. His face was like the sun shining in all its brilliance.

¹⁷When I saw him, I fell at his feet as though dead. Then he placed his right hand on me and said: "Do not be afraid. I am the First and the Last. ¹⁸I am the Living One; I was dead, and behold I am alive for ever and ever! And I hold the keys of death and Hades.

¹⁹"Write, therefore, what you have seen, what is now and what will take place later. ²⁰The mystery of the seven stars that you saw in my right hand and of the seven golden lampstands is this: The seven stars are the angels^c of the seven churches, and the seven lampstands are the seven churches.

To the Church in Ephesus

2 "To the angel^d of the church in Ephesus write:

These are the words of him who holds the seven stars in his right hand and walks among the seven golden lampstands: ²I know your deeds, your hard work and your perseverance. I know that you cannot tolerate wicked men, that you have tested those who claim to be apostles but are not, and have found them false. ³You have persevered and have endured hardships for my name, and have not grown weary.

⁴Yet I hold this against you: You have forsaken your first love. ⁵Remember the height from which you have fallen! Repent and do the things you did at first. If you do not repent, I will come to you and remove your lampstand from its place. ⁶But you have this in your favor: You hate the practices of the Nicolaitans, which I also hate.

⁷He who has an ear, let him hear what the Spirit says to the churches. To him who overcomes, I will give the right to eat from the tree of life, which is in the paradise of God.

To the Church in Smyrna

⁸"To the angel of the church in Smyrna write:

These are the words of him who is the First and the Last, who died and came to life again. ⁹I know your afflictions and your poverty—yet you are rich! I know the slander of those who say they are Jews and are not, but are a synagogue of Satan. ¹⁰Do not be afraid of what you are about to suffer. I tell you, the devil will put some of you in prison to test you, and you will suffer persecution for ten days. Be faithful, even to the point of death, and I will give you the crown of life.

¹¹He who has an ear, let him hear what the Spirit says to the churches. He who overcomes will not be hurt at all by the second death.

to understand what John has experienced?

REFLECT: 1. If you were to use the analogy of a lighting fixture to describe your church, what kind would you choose (a chandelier, a nightlight, etc.)? In what condition is it? Why? **2.** If someone like the man described in this chapter visited you, what would be your response? What does this reveal about you? **3.** Are you right now "on Patmos" (suffering) or "in the Spirit" (reigning)? Why?

OPEN: What kind of letters do you like to write? To receive? Why?

DIG: 1. What do you know about the church at Ephesus (see Acts 19, 1 Tim.; Eph.)? **2.** What good things characterize this church? How might its strengths have been the cause of its failure? What do you think Sunday worship was like in this church? **3.** What is repentance? Why is it necessary for the Ephesian church?

REFLECT: 1. Of the positive qualities mentioned about this group, which best decribes you? Why? **2.** Of these qualities, which best desribes your church? Why? **3.** What did you do at first in your relationship with Christ that you don't do now? In what ways have you lost the first love? What secrets have you found to keep that love alive?

OPEN: If you were rich, what would you like to do?

DIG: 1. What problems is this church facing? How can they be both poor and rich? Why is the title by which Jesus reveals himself especially significant for this church? Why? **2.** What does this passage teach about the nature of suffering? About the power of Satan?

REFLECT: 1. In what kind of economic condition have you found it most difficult to live out your faith: When you've been poor? Or when you've had enough money? Why? **2.** In what ways do you feel rich? **3.** What are some prisons in which you find yourself? How do you think you got in them? What is God's message to you in prison? Does it help you to know that Jesus is first and last? Why?

---

c20 Or messengers   *d1 Or messenger; also in verses 8, 12 and 18*

To the Church in Pergamum

¹²"To the angel of the church in Pergamum write:

These are the words of him who has the sharp, double-edged sword. ¹³I know where you live—where Satan has his throne. Yet you remain true to my name. You did not renounce your faith in me, even in the days of Antipas, my faithful witness, who was put to death in your city—where Satan lives.

¹⁴Nevertheless, I have a few things against you: You have people there who hold to the teaching of Balaam, who taught Balak to entice the Israelites to sin by eating food sacrificed to idols and by committing sexual immorality. ¹⁵Likewise you also have those who hold to the teaching of the Nicolaitans. ¹⁶Repent therefore! Otherwise, I will soon come to you and will fight against them with the sword of my mouth.

¹⁷He who has an ear, let him hear what the Spirit says to the churches. To him who overcomes, I will give some of the hidden manna. I will also give him a white stone with a new name written on it, known only to him who receives it.

To the Church in Thyatira

¹⁸"To the angel of the church in Thyatira write:

These are the words of the Son of God, whose eyes are like blazing fire and whose feet are like burnished bronze. ¹⁹I know your deeds, your love and faith, your service and perseverance, and that you are now doing more than you did at first.

²⁰Nevertheless, I have this against you: You tolerate that woman Jezebel, who calls herself a prophetess. By her teaching she misleads my servants into sexual immorality and the eating of food sacrificed to idols. ²¹I have given her time to repent of her immorality, but she is unwilling. ²²So I will cast her on a bed of suffering, and I will make those who commit adultery with her suffer intensely, unless they repent of her ways. ²³I will strike her children dead. Then all the churches will know that I am he who searches hearts and minds, and I will repay each of you according to your deeds. ²⁴Now I say to the rest of you in Thyatira, to you who do not hold to her teaching and have not learned Satan's so-called deep secrets (I will not impose any other burden on you): ²⁵Only hold on to what you have until I come.

²⁶To him who overcomes and does my will to the end, I will give authority over the nations—

²⁷'He will rule them with an iron scepter;
    he will dash them to pieces like pottery'—

just as I have received authority from my Father. ²⁸I will also give him the morning star. ²⁹He who has an ear, let him hear what the Spirit says to the churches.

ᶜ27 Psalm 2:9

To the Church in Sardis

3 "To the angel[f] of the church in Sardis write:

These are the words of him who holds the seven spirits[g] of God and the seven stars. I know your deeds; you have a reputation of being alive, but you are dead. [2]Wake up! Strengthen what remains and is about to die, for I have not found your deeds complete in the sight of my God. [3]Remember, therefore, what you have received and heard; obey it, and repent. But if you do not wake up, I will come like a thief, and you will not know at what time I will come to you.

[4]Yet you have a few people in Sardis who have not soiled their clothes. They will walk with me, dressed in white, for they are worthy. [5]He who overcomes will, like them, be dressed in white. I will never blot out his name from the book of life, but will acknowledge his name before my Father and his angels. [6]He who has an ear, let him hear what the Spirit says to the churches.

To the Church in Philadelphia

[7]"To the angel of the church in Philadelphia write:

These are the words of him who is holy and true, who holds the key of David. What he opens no one can shut, and what he shuts no one can open. [8]I know your deeds. See, I have placed before you an open door that no one can shut. I know that you have little strength, yet you have kept my word and have not denied my name. [9]I will make those who are of the synagogue of Satan, who claim to be Jews though they are not, but are liars—I will make them come and fall down at your feet and acknowledge that I have loved you. [10]Since you have kept my command to endure patiently, I will also keep you from the hour of trial that is going to come upon the whole world to test those who live on the earth.

[11]I am coming soon. Hold on to what you have, so that no one will take your crown. [12]Him who overcomes I will make a pillar in the temple of my God. Never again will he leave it. I will write on him the name of my God and the name of the city of my God, the new Jerusalem, which is coming down out of heaven from my God; and I will also write on him my new name. [13]He who has an ear, let him hear what the Spirit says to the churches.

To the Church in Laodicea

[14]"To the angel of the church in Laodicea write:

These are the words of the Amen, the faithful and true witness, the ruler of God's creation. [15]I know your deeds, that you are neither cold nor hot. I wish you were either one or the other! [16]So, because you are lukewarm—neither hot nor cold—I am about to spit you out of my mouth. [17]You say, 'I am rich; I have acquired wealth and do not need a

[f]1 Or *messenger*; also in verses 7 and 14   [g]1 Or *the sevenfold Spirit*

OPEN: What is an example where a group's reputation fell miserably short of reality in your experience.

DIG: 1. What is the contrast between reputation and reality in Sardis? What dangers exist for Christians in resting on an image instead of nurturing a genuine spiritual life? 2. What is the only hope for the survival of the Sardis church?

REFLECT: 1. What is your reputation in your church? In your community? With your family? How accurate are these reputations? How would you like to see them changed? Why? 2. How alert is your present spiritual state? 3. How does this passage apply to your group? What will you do to help your group to "overcome"?

OPEN: What is a maddening experience where you've been locked out?

DIG: 1. What is the "key of David" (see Isa. 22:20-25; 26:2; Matt. 16:19; 23:13)? What is the "open door" (see 1 Cor. 16:9; 2 Cor. 2:12; Rev. 3:20; 4:1)? How do these relate to each other and to the Christian life? 2. What is so special about the perseverance of the Philadelphians? Describe their enemies.

REFLECT: 1. What open doors has Christ placed before you? How have you taken advantage of the pathways he's made available to you? 2. What are some closed doors he's placed in your career path? In your social life? In your schooling? How have you responded to each of these closed doors? 3. In what ways are you like the Christians in Philadelphia? Unlike them? Why? 4. What is the Spirit saying to you? How will you act on this today?

OPEN: Who is the most significant dinner guest you have hosted in the last year? How did the presence of that honored person make you feel?

DIG: 1. What does the "faithful and true witness" see when he looks at the Laodicean church? How does the church view itself? What is its true state? 2. What does Jesus tell the Laodiceans to do in verse 18? Why? How does this explain the nature of true wealth? 3. List the attri-

477

butes of Christ found in chapters 2 and 3. How would you describe Christ based on what you have read so far in this book? How does this amplify the picture of Jesus in the Gospels?

REFLECT: 1. If Jesus took your spiritual temperature today, what would he find? Why? 2. What is Jesus waiting for at the door of your life? How long have you kept him on the threshold? Why? 3. What is the Spirit saying to you?

___

OPEN: What is the most memorable storm you have ever been in? What happened?

DIG: 1. Where does this scene "in heaven" actually take place: In the after-life? Or in the region where the stars shine? Or some perfect order of things after this world has passed away? Or on the level of spiritual reality here and now (as in Eph. 2:6), where good and evil are unmasked to be seen for what they really are? 2. Who is the figure on the throne? What is he like? What are the 24 elders like? (Note: 24 seems to represent all of God's people, steming from the 12 tribes before Christ and the 12 apostles after Christ; see Rev. 21:12-14). 3. What does the scene around the throne include? Note its many Old Testament images (Gen. 9:12-17; Exod. 19: 16-19; 25:31-40; 2 Chron. 4:2-6, Ezek. 1). 4. How does John envision the four living creatures (a likely reference to nature, throbbing with the eternal power and deity of God)? What kind of response does the central figure elicit from the elders and the creatures? Why? 5. What does this say about who God is and how he relates to his creation?

REFLECT: 1. What invitation has Jesus extended to you this week? How did you respond? 2. When would you say you were "in the Spirit" this week? What does that term mean to you? 3. How have you worshiped God today? How good do you feel about the way you worship God? Why? What needs to happen in your life for you to feel better? 4. Likewise, how do you feel about your small group worship?

thing.' But you do not realize that you are wretched, pitiful, poor, blind and naked. [18]I counsel you to buy from me gold refined in the fire, so you can become rich; and white clothes to wear, so you can cover your shameful nakedness; and salve to put on your eyes, so you can see.

[19]Those whom I love I rebuke and discipline. So be earnest, and repent. [20]Here I am! I stand at the door and knock. If anyone hears my voice and opens the door, I will come in and eat with him, and he with me.

[21]To him who overcomes, I will give the right to sit with me on my throne, just as I overcame and sat down with my Father on his throne. [22]He who has an ear, let him hear what the Spirit says to the churches."

The Throne in Heaven

4 After this I looked, and there before me was a door standing open in heaven. And the voice I had first heard speaking to me like a trumpet said, "Come up here, and I will show you what must take place after this." [2]At once I was in the Spirit, and there before me was a throne in heaven with someone sitting on it. [3]And the one who sat there had the appearance of jasper and carnelian. A rainbow, resembling an emerald, encircled the throne. [4]Surrounding the throne were twenty-four other thrones, and seated on them were twenty-four elders. They were dressed in white and had crowns of gold on their heads. [5]From the throne came flashes of lightning, rumblings and peals of thunder. Before the throne, seven lamps were blazing. These are the seven spirits[h] of God. [6]Also before the throne there was what looked like a sea of glass, clear as crystal.

In the center, around the throne, were four living creatures, and they were covered with eyes, in front and in back. [7]The first living creature was like a lion, the second was like an ox, the third had a face like a man, the fourth was like a flying eagle. [8]Each of the four living creatures had six wings and was covered with eyes all around, even under his wings. Day and night they never stop saying:

"Holy, holy, holy
is the Lord God Almighty,
who was, and is, and is to come."

[9]Whenever the living creatures give glory, honor and thanks to him who sits on the throne and who lives for ever and ever, [10]the twenty-four elders fall down before him who sits on the throne, and worship him who lives for ever and ever. They lay their crowns before the throne and say:

[11]"You are worthy, our Lord and God,
to receive glory and honor and power,
for you created all things,
and by your will they were created
and have their being."

h5 Or the sevenfold Spirit

The Scroll and the Lamb

5 Then I saw in the right hand of him who sat on the throne a scroll with writing on both sides and sealed with seven seals. ²And I saw a mighty angel proclaiming in a loud voice, "Who is worthy to break the seals and open the scroll?" ³But no one in heaven or on earth or under the earth could open the scroll or even look inside it. ⁴I wept and wept because no one was found who was worthy to open the scroll or look inside. ⁵Then one of the elders said to me, "Do not weep! See, the Lion of the tribe of Judah, the Root of David, has triumphed. He is able to open the scroll and its seven seals."

⁶Then I saw a Lamb, looking as if it had been slain, standing in the center of the throne, encircled by the four living creatures and the elders. He had seven horns and seven eyes, which are the seven spirits¹ of God sent out into all the earth. ⁷He came and took the scroll from the right hand of him who sat on the throne. ⁸And when he had taken it, the four living creatures and the twenty-four elders fell down before the Lamb. Each one had a harp and they were holding golden bowls full of incense, which are the prayers of the saints. ⁹And they sang a new song:

"You are worthy to take the scroll
    and to open its seals,
because you were slain,
    and with your blood you purchased men for God
    from every tribe and language and people and nation.
¹⁰You have made them to be a kingdom and priests to
        serve our God,
    and they will reign on the earth."

¹¹Then I looked and heard the voice of many angels, numbering thousands upon thousands, and ten thousand times ten thousand. They encircled the throne and the living creatures and the elders. ¹²In a loud voice they sang:

"Worthy is the Lamb, who was slain,
to receive power and wealth and wisdom and strength
and honor and glory and praise!"

¹³Then I heard every creature in heaven and on earth and under the earth and on the sea, and all that is in them, singing:

"To him who sits on the throne and to the Lamb
be praise and honor and glory and power,
        for ever and ever!"

¹⁴The four living creatures said, "Amen," and the elders fell down and worshiped.

The Seals

6 I watched as the Lamb opened the first of the seven seals. Then I heard one of the four living creatures say in a voice like thunder, "Come!" ²I looked, and there before me was a white horse! Its rider held a bow, and he was given a crown, and he rode out as a conqueror bent on conquest.

¹6 Or *the sevenfold Spirit*

OPEN: 1. What was the best choir or musical group in which you ever participated? What was most memorable about the group? 2. Are you more like a lion or a lamb? Why?

DIG: 1. What do you think makes the scroll so significant? What dilemma does the sealed scroll pose? 2. Who is the one worthy person? What titles are used to describe Christ? How can he be both the Lion and the Lamb? Where does he appear? What is the significance of this? 3. What is the response to his receipt of the scroll? Analyze the three songs: How is the Lamb described? What qualifies him to open the scroll (see also John 1:29)? Who are the true kings and priests on earth? How is the Lamb praised?

REFLECT: 1. How would you capture this scene of praise and adoration via a poem, a sketch, a piece of music, a prayer, etc.? To do this, put yourself into the scene, seeing and feeling what John saw and felt. Collect these praise items from your group into a united concert of prayer and praise. 2. What would the visions in chapters 4 and 5 have meant to the persecuted Christians of Asia? What does this vision say to us in the twentieth century as we view our out-of-control world? Based on this, what actions will you take this week?

OPEN: 1. What kind of horse are you most like: A Clydesdale? A Kentucky thoroughbred? An Arabian stallion? Or a Texas quarter horse? Why? 2. How is your group like a team of four horsemen — each pulling in a different direction, or the same? Why?

DIG: 1. How would you describe

each of the four horsemen? Accordingly, who or what might each of these represent? (E.g., Does the first horseman refer to earthy warfare or to the conquering gospel? fare or to the conquering gospel?) Why? **2.** Compare and contrast the horsemen rides, what happens? When the luxury items (wine and oil) are still available, but the basic foodstuffs are scarce and costly, what does that tell you about their economic situation? **3.** In what sense do the first three horsemen lead to the fourth? How have each of these forces (conquest, strife, scarcity & death) operated throughout history? How do they prevail today? **4.** What is revealed by the opening of the fifth seal? What is the cry of these martyrs? How is it answered? How is this related to the suffering of the Christians in John's day? **5.** What event occurs when the sixth seal is broken (see Mark 13)? What elements of the Day of Judgment are described here? Compare this account to Matthew 24. **5.** Indeed, who can stand under the wrath of God? How?

REFLECT: 1. Which seal opening makes the greatest impression on you? Why? **2.** What's the worst thing that has happened to you because of your faithfulness to the Word of God? Do you think there will come a day in your society in the next twenty years when people will be tortured and killed for their beliefs? Why or why not? **3.** In what area of your life are you trying to hide from God? What do you need to do to be able to come out of hiding? How will you begin to accomplish this today? **4.** How does this passage make you feel about the end times? Why? How will this affect your actions?

OPEN: What kind of wind (a warm, gentle breeze, a cold north wind, etc.) best symbolizes your life? Why?

DIG: 1. Do you think the work of the four angels is a "new" woe or a restatement of the events in chapter 6? Why? Likewise, in what sense do the events of chapter 7 come "after" the events in chapter 6: In the actual chronology of history? Or in the constantly refocussing of John's vision? **2.** What is the message of the fifth angel? Who is sealed? When, in the chronology of these events, does this sealing occur? What does it mean to be sealed as a servant of God (see

³When the Lamb opened the second seal, I heard the second living creature say, "Come!" ⁴Then another horse came out, a fiery red one. Its rider was given power to take peace from the earth and to make men slay each other. To him was given a large sword.

⁵When the Lamb opened the third seal, I heard the third living creature say, "Come!" I looked, and there before me was a black horse! Its rider was holding a pair of scales in his hand. ⁶Then I heard what sounded like a voice among the four living creatures, saying, "A quart^j of wheat for a day's wages,^{k} and three quarts of barley for a day's wages,^{k} and do not damage the oil and the wine!"

⁷When the Lamb opened the fourth seal, I heard the voice of the fourth living creature say, "Come!" ⁸I looked, and there before me was a pale horse! Its rider was named Death, and Hades was following close behind him. They were given power over a fourth of the earth to kill by sword, famine and plague, and by the wild beasts of the earth.

⁹When he opened the fifth seal, I saw under the altar the souls of those who had been slain because of the word of God and the testimony they had maintained. ¹⁰They called out in a loud voice, "How long, Sovereign Lord, holy and true, until you judge the inhabitants of the earth and avenge our blood?" ¹¹Then each of them was given a white robe, and they were told to wait a little longer, until the number of their fellow servants and brothers who were to be killed as they had been was completed.

¹²I watched as he opened the sixth seal. There was a great earthquake. The sun turned black like sackcloth made of goat hair, the whole moon turned blood red, ¹³and the stars in the sky fell to earth, as late figs drop from a fig tree when shaken by a strong wind. ¹⁴The sky receded like a scroll, rolling up, and every mountain and island was removed from its place.

¹⁵Then the kings of the earth, the princes, the generals, the rich, the mighty, and every slave and every free man hid in caves and among the rocks of the mountains. ¹⁶They called to the mountains and the rocks, "Fall on us and hide us from the face of him who sits on the throne and from the wrath of the Lamb! ¹⁷For the great day of their wrath has come, and who can stand?"

144,000 Sealed

7 After this I saw four angels standing at the four corners of the earth, holding back the four winds of the earth to prevent any wind from blowing on the land or on the sea or on any tree. ²Then I saw another angel coming up from the east, having the seal of the living God. He called out in a loud voice to the four angels who had been given power to harm the land and the sea: ³"Do not harm the land or the sea or the trees until we put a seal on the foreheads of the servants of our God." ⁴Then I heard the number of those who were sealed: 144,000 from all the tribes of Israel.

j6 Greek a choinix (probably about a liter)   *k6 Greek a denarius*

⁵From the tribe of Judah 12,000 were sealed,
from the tribe of Reuben 12,000,
from the tribe of Gad 12,000,
⁶from the tribe of Asher 12,000,
from the tribe of Naphtali 12,000,
from the tribe of Manasseh 12,000,
⁷from the tribe of Simeon 12,000,
from the tribe of Levi 12,000,
from the tribe of Issachar 12,000,
⁸from the tribe of Zebulun 12,000,
from the tribe of Joseph 12,000,
from the tribe of Benjamin 12,000.

The Great Multitude in White Robes

⁹After this I looked and there before me was a great multitude that no one could count, from every nation, tribe, people and language, standing before the throne and in front of the Lamb. They were wearing white robes and were holding palm branches in their hands. ¹⁰And they cried out in a loud voice:

"Salvation belongs to our God,
who sits on the throne,
and to the Lamb."

¹¹All the angels were standing around the throne and around the elders and the four living creatures. They fell down on their faces before the throne and worshiped God, ¹²saying:

"Amen!
Praise and glory
and wisdom and thanks and honor
and power and strength
be to our God for ever and ever.
Amen!"

¹³Then one of the elders asked me, "These in white robes—who are they, and where did they come from?"

¹⁴I answered, "Sir, you know."

And he said, "These are they who have come out of the great tribulation; they have washed their robes and made them white in the blood of the Lamb. ¹⁵Therefore,

"they are before the throne of God
and serve him day and night in his temple;
and he who sits on the throne will spread his tent over
them.
¹⁶Never again will they hunger;
never again will they thirst.
The sun will not beat upon them,
nor any scorching heat.
¹⁷For the Lamb at the center of the throne will be their
shepherd;
he will lead them to springs of living water.
And God will wipe away every tear from their eyes."

Gen. 4:15; Ezek. 9:4-6; Eph. 1:13-14)? **3.** Is this "144,000" a symbol (concerned with style, scale and election) or a statistic (concerned with accuracy)? Why (see also Rev. 7:9; 14:1-5)?

REFLECT: 1. How have you sensed God's protection and fresh wind in the last six months? Before that? **2.** What sort of seal has God placed on your life? How is this seal evident to others?

OPEN: 1. If you could have been a member of any tribe in history, which tribe would you choose? Why? **2.** What could you carry in your hand that would symbolize one of your favorite activities? Why did you choose this?

DIG: 1. What does John see next? How does he characterize the size of the crowd? Is this innumerable, mixed multitude the same as the 144,000 Isrealites/servants of God? Why or why not? What are they doing, wearing, carrying? What's the significance of the white robes, the palm branches and the washing? What does all this say about God's kingdom and Christ's sacrifice? **2.** When the multitude cries out, how do the angels, elders, and the four living creatures respond? **3.** What qualifies this white-robed crowd to stand before God? What is their new role? What is "the great tribulation" — a particular event or a general experience? **4.** Regarding the safety, security and service of these Christians, is this a present life experience for them? Or only a promise to be realized in some vague distant future? Or both?

REFLECT: 1. Have each group member take a different one of the praise words ascribed to God to meditate on and reflect back to him as part of your group's devotion to God. **2.** What is your greatest tribulation or persecution? How difficult does that seem next to that faced by the people of John's day? Why? How difficult does it seem next to the majesty of God seen in this passage? Why? How will you incorporate this glimpse of heavenly worship into your earthly walk? **3.** If your group were suddenly transported to this throne of God and transformed by what you saw there, what new apparrel, attitudes and activities would you each take on?

OPEN: What does extended silence sound like? Feel like?

DIG: 1. In the drama of seals and trumpets, why this silence (v. 1)? Why the golden censer? Where does each fit? **2.** What do alters and incense teach you about prayer (vv. 3-5; compare 5:8; 6:9-10; 9:13)?

REFLECT: 1. Does this imagery seem far removed from your everyday experience? Why? **2.** When was the last time you tried silent meditation or cried for justice? What happened?

OPEN: 1. What is one of the most excruciating pains you've ever experienced? What happened? **2.** What color would you use to describe your past week? Why? To describe your past year? Why?

DIG: 1. What are the events that follow the sounding of each of the first four trumpets? What do the trumpets signify: Triumph or doom? Life or death? Or what? **2.** How do these sets of events of the first four trumpets compare with the events inaugurated by the first six seals? **3.** Likewise, how do these sets of events compare with the plagues in Exodus 7-10 and Joel 2:1-11? **4.** What parallels or repeated patterns do you see between the opening of the seals and sounding of the trumpets, suggesting these two scenes are in reality two sides of the same coin? (Note how the trumpets focus on what will happen to the unbelieving world, whereas the seals focus on what will happen to the church.) **5.** Do these seals and trumpets refer to datable, sequential events? Or to aspects of the world condition, which may be true at any point in history? Why? Why? **6.** What happens when the fifth trumpet sounds? Who might the fallen star be (see Luke 10:18; Isa. 14:12)? What power do the locusts have? Describe them. **7.** What events are inaugurated by the sixth trumpet? What response ought to woe elict from the unbelieving world? Why? Why then do you suppose this woe failed to bring the majority to repentance, as intended?

REFLECT: 1. How do you feel when you read this account of stranger-than-fiction events? **2.** How has the star named "Wormwood," or "Bitterness," affected your life? How has your bitterness affected others? What have

The Seventh Seal and the Golden Censer

8 When he opened the seventh seal, there was silence in heaven for about half an hour.

²And I saw the seven angels who stand before God, and to them were given seven trumpets.

³Another angel, who had a golden censer, came and stood at the altar. He was given much incense to offer, with the prayers of all the saints, on the golden altar before the throne. ⁴The smoke of the incense, together with the prayers of the saints, went up before God from the angel's hand. ⁵Then the angel took the censer, filled it with fire from the altar, and hurled it on the earth; and there came peals of thunder, rumblings, flashes of lightning and an earthquake.

The Trumpets

⁶Then the seven angels who had the seven trumpets prepared to sound them.

⁷The first angel sounded his trumpet, and there came hail and fire mixed with blood, and it was hurled down upon the earth. A third of the earth was burned up, a third of the trees were burned up, and all the green grass was burned up.

⁸The second angel sounded his trumpet, and something like a huge mountain, all ablaze, was thrown into the sea. A third of the sea turned into blood, ⁹a third of the living creatures in the sea died, and a third of the ships were destroyed.

¹⁰The third angel sounded his trumpet, and a great star, blazing like a torch, fell from the sky on a third of the rivers and on the springs of water— ¹¹the name of the star is Wormwood.¹ A third of the waters turned bitter, and many people died from the waters that had become bitter.

¹²The fourth angel sounded his trumpet, and a third of the sun was struck, a third of the moon, and a third of the stars, so that a third of them turned dark. A third of the day was without light, and also a third of the night.

¹³As I watched, I heard an eagle that was flying in midair call out in a loud voice: "Woe! Woe! Woe to the inhabitants of the earth, because of the trumpet blasts about to be sounded by the other three angels!"

9 The fifth angel sounded his trumpet, and I saw a star that had fallen from the sky to the earth. The star was given the key to the shaft of the Abyss. ²When he opened the Abyss, smoke rose from it like the smoke from a gigantic furnace. The sun and sky were darkened by the smoke from the Abyss. ³And out of the smoke locusts came down upon the earth and were given power like that of scorpions of the earth. ⁴They were told not to harm the grass of the earth or any plant or tree, but only those people who did not have the seal of God on their foreheads. ⁵They were not given power to kill them, but only to torture them for five months. And the agony they suffered was like that of the sting of a scorpion when it strikes a man. ⁶During those days men will seek death, but will not find it; they will long to die, but death will elude them.

¹11 That is, Bitterness

[7]The locusts looked like horses prepared for battle. On their heads they wore something like crowns of gold, and their faces resembled human faces. [8]Their hair was like women's hair, and their teeth were like lions' teeth. [9]They had breastplates like breastplates of iron, and the sound of their wings was like the thundering of many horses and chariots rushing into battle. [10]They had tails and stings like scorpions, and in their tails they had power to torment people for five months. [11]They had as king over them the angel of the Abyss, whose name in Hebrew is Abaddon, and in Greek, Apollyon.*m*

[12]The first woe is past; two other woes are yet to come.

[13]The sixth angel sounded his trumpet, and I heard a voice coming from the horns*n* of the golden altar that is before God. [14]It said to the sixth angel who had the trumpet, "Release the four angels who are bound at the great river Euphrates." [15]And the four angels who had been kept ready for this very hour and day and month and year were released to kill a third of mankind. [16]The number of the mounted troops was two hundred million. I heard their number.

[17]The horses and riders I saw in my vision looked like this: Their breastplates were fiery red, dark blue, and yellow as sulfur. The heads of the horses resembled the heads of lions, and out of their mouths came fire, smoke and sulfur. [18]A third of mankind was killed by the three plagues of fire, smoke and sulfur that came out of their mouths. [19]The power of the horses was in their mouths and in their tails; for their tails were like snakes, having heads with which they inflict injury.

[20]The rest of mankind that were not killed by these plagues still did not repent of the work of their hands; they did not stop worshiping demons, and idols of gold, silver, bronze, stone and wood—idols that cannot see or hear or walk. [21]Nor did they repent of their murders, their magic arts, their sexual immorality or their thefts.

The Angel and the Little Scroll

10 Then I saw another mighty angel coming down from heaven. He was robed in a cloud, with a rainbow above his head; his face was like the sun, and his legs were like fiery pillars. [2]He was holding a little scroll, which lay open in his hand. He planted his right foot on the sea and his left foot on the land, [3]and he gave a loud shout like the roar of a lion. When he shouted, the voices of the seven thunders spoke. [4]And when the seven thunders spoke, I was about to write; but I heard a voice from heaven say, "Seal up what the seven thunders have said and do not write it down."

[5]Then the angel I had seen standing on the sea and on the land raised his right hand to heaven. [6]And he swore by him who lives for ever and ever, who created the heavens and all that is in them, the earth and all that is in it, and the sea and all that is in it, and said, "There will be no more delay! [7]But in the days when the seventh angel is about to sound his trumpet, the mystery of God will be accomplished, just as he announced to his servants the prophets."

---

m11 Abaddon and Apollyon mean Destroyer.   *n13 That is, projections*

you discovered as an antidote to bitterness? **3.** When have you wanted to die? Why? **4.** What comfort or discomfort would this passage bring to someone wanting to die? **5.** What do you have in common with the people mentioned in verse 20-21? What will you do about this today? **6.** What do you think about Christians praying for trouble to strike the unbelieving world? And what do you think of God's answer to such prayers? What modern-day images does the imagery of these plagues bring to mind for you (e.g., volcanic eruptions, atomic fallout, 'natural' disasters, environmental pollution, lunar and solar eclipses, AIDS, tank and plane warfare)? Or do you find all this quite difficult, if not impossible, to visualize "how" all this takes place (except in sci fi literature)? **7.** While the "how" question may elude you, do you see the "who" and the "why" behind these "stranger-than-fiction" events?

OPEN: Who was one of your fictional heroes when you were a child: Buck Rogers? The Lone Ranger? The Roadrunner? Why?

DIG: 1. What is the angel like that announces the coming of the seventh trumpet. In what ways does this picture contrast with the traditional view of angels? Why might John be forbidden to record the words of the seven thunders (see also 2 Corinthians 12:4)? **2.** What purposes have the disasters of the first six trumpets served? What do you anticipate the seventh trumpet to bring forth? What is the "mystery of God" in verse 7 (see Rom. 11:25-36; 16:25-27; Eph. 1:9-14)? **3.** What happens to the small scroll? How can a revelation from God be both sweet and bitter?

REFLECT: 1. How in the past year or two has God led you into a project that you probably wouldn't have selected yourself? What happened? **2.** What is an experience you once savored for a moment, but that later turned sour? **3.** How has God's Word been both sweet and sour to you?

OPEN: What have been the three greatest years of your life? Why?

DIG: 1. What is John commanded to do? Why? Who will be "measured" (that is, protected) and why? Who are these two indestructible, universal witnesses? And their enemies? **2.** What happens to these two witnesses? Why? What results from their death and resurrection? **3.** If God's witness will be faithfully maintained for "1260 days" to counter-balance the "42 months", which are the times of the Gentiles (or nations), then what do the "3 and ½ days" mean?

REFLECT 1. Who have been two of the most important people in your spiritual development? How have they witnessed to you? **2.** What do you learn in this passage about what it means to be a witness? **3.** What has been toughest about living out your faith at work? At School? At home? Why such difficulty? **4.** How have you felt especially empowered by God in the last six months?

OPEN: What was the most rewarding job you ever had? Why was it so?

DIG: 1. What long-foretold event occurs with the seventh trumpet? How is Christ's second coming a "good news/bad news" event? For whom? Why? **2.** For what reasons is God thanked and praised? What does this tell you about God's

⁸Then the voice that I had heard from heaven spoke to me once more: "Go, take the scroll that lies open in the hand of the angel who is standing on the sea and on the land."

⁹So I went to the angel and asked him to give me the little scroll. He said to me, "Take it and eat it. It will turn your stomach sour, but in your mouth it will be as sweet as honey." ¹⁰I took the little scroll from the angel's hand and ate it. It tasted as sweet as honey in my mouth, but when I had eaten it, my stomach turned sour. ¹¹Then I was told, "You must prophesy again about many peoples, nations, languages and kings."

The Two Witnesses

11 I was given a reed like a measuring rod and was told, "Go and measure the temple of God and the altar, and count the worshipers there. ²But exclude the outer court; do not measure it, because it has been given to the Gentiles. They will trample on the holy city for 42 months. ³And I will give power to my two witnesses, and they will prophesy for 1,260 days, clothed in sackcloth." ⁴These are the two olive trees and the two lampstands that stand before the Lord of the earth. ⁵If anyone tries to harm them, fire comes from their mouths and devours their enemies. This is how anyone who wants to harm them must die. ⁶These men have power to shut up the sky so that it will not rain during the time they are prophesying; and they have power to turn the waters into blood and to strike the earth with every kind of plague as often as they want.

⁷Now when they have finished their testimony, the beast that comes up from the Abyss will attack them, and overpower and kill them. ⁸Their bodies will lie in the street of the great city, which is figuratively called Sodom and Egypt, where also their Lord was crucified. ⁹For three and a half days men from every people, tribe, language and nation will gaze on their bodies and refuse them burial. ¹⁰The inhabitants of the earth will gloat over them and will celebrate by sending each other gifts, because these two prophets had tormented those who live on the earth.

¹¹But after the three and a half days a breath of life from God entered them, and they stood on their feet, and terror struck those who saw them. ¹²Then they heard a loud voice from heaven saying to them, "Come up here." And they went up to heaven in a cloud, while their enemies looked on.

¹³At that very hour there was a severe earthquake and a tenth of the city collapsed. Seven thousand people were killed in the earthquake, and the survivors were terrified and gave glory to the God of heaven.

¹⁴The second woe has passed; the third woe is coming soon.

The Seventh Trumpet

¹⁵The seventh angel sounded his trumpet, and there were loud voices in heaven, which said:

> "The kingdom of the world has become the kingdom of
>   our Lord and of his Christ,
> and he will reign for ever and ever."

¹⁶And the twenty-four elders, who were seated on their thrones

before God, fell on their faces and worshiped God, ¹⁷saying:

"We give thanks to you, Lord God Almighty,
  the One who is and who was,
because you have taken your great power
  and have begun to reign.
¹⁸The nations were angry;
  and your wrath has come.
The time has come for judging the dead,
  and for rewarding your servants the prophets
and your saints and those who reverence your name,
  both small and great—
and for destroying those who destroy the earth."

¹⁹Then God's temple in heaven was opened, and within his temple was seen the ark of his covenant. And there came flashes of lightning, rumblings, peals of thunder, an earthquake and a great hailstorm.

The Woman and the Dragon

12 A great and wondrous sign appeared in heaven: a woman clothed with the sun, with the moon under her feet and a crown of twelve stars on her head. ²She was pregnant and cried out in pain as she was about to give birth. ³Then another sign appeared in heaven: an enormous red dragon with seven heads and ten horns and seven crowns on his heads. ⁴His tail swept a third of the stars out of the sky and flung them to the earth. The dragon stood in front of the woman who was about to give birth, so that he might devour her child the moment it was born. ⁵She gave birth to a son, a male child, who will rule all the nations with an iron scepter. And her child was snatched up to God and to his throne. ⁶The woman fled into the desert to a place prepared for her by God, where she might be taken care of for 1,260 days.

⁷And there was war in heaven. Michael and his angels fought against the dragon, and the dragon and his angels fought back. ⁸But he was not strong enough, and they lost their place in heaven. ⁹The great dragon was hurled down—that ancient serpent called the devil or Satan, who leads the whole world astray. He was hurled to the earth, and his angels with him.

¹⁰Then I heard a loud voice in heaven say:

"Now have come the salvation and the power and the
    kingdom of our God,
  and the authority of his Christ.
For the accuser of our brothers,
  who accuses them before our God day and night,
  has been hurled down.
¹¹They overcame him
  by the blood of the Lamb
  and by the word of their testimony;
they did not love their lives so much
  as to shrink from death.
¹²Therefore rejoice, you heavens
  and you who dwell in them!
But woe to the earth and the sea,

power? **3.** Where, in the thematic development of Revelation, does the unveiling of God's heavenly temple and ark of the covenant best fit? (Note: Some or all of the phenomena occuring here in 11:19 also occur in 4:5 and 8:5 as the "musical overture" to a shift in scene.)

REFLECT: 1. Do you cringe as you imagine God's power over an unbelieving world—to hurt them (trumpet 5 or 1st woe), to kill them (trumpet 6 or 2nd woe), to damn them (trumpet 7 or 3rd woe)? Why do you feel that way? **2.** As God displays this awesome power in response to prayers (8:4), how do you feel about what he has called you to do? What will you pray? Why?

OPEN: When you were a child, who was the most important woman in your life besides your mother? Why?

DIG: 1. Describe the woman, the dragon, and the child. Who does the woman represent: The dragon? The child? **2.** Where does the next conflict occur? Who are the protagonists? What's the outcome of this conflict? What is the significance of this outcome for the earth? For Christians? What Old Testament and New Testament events parallel this passage? **3.** When do you see this heavenly battle occurring: At some particular time and place in history? Pre-history? Or post-history? Or do you see this vision depicting the always-in-progress heavenly battle between the Kingdom of God and the Kingdom of Satan, and as such, taking place in the spiritual realm which is behind all of this world's history? Why?

REFLECT: 1. What do you learn here about conflict between the Christian church and demonic evil? **2.** How real do you think Satan is? When has he seemed most real to you? Why? **3.** How do you overcome Satan (see v. 11)? How could you apply these tactics in your own life? What do you need to do to become stronger for spiritual battle? **4.** How could your Christian friends pray for you in battles you are facing? Likewise, how could you pray for then? Do this in your group.

because the devil has gone down to you!
He is filled with fury,
    because he knows that his time is short.''

[13]When the dragon saw that he had been hurled to the earth, he pursued the woman who had given birth to the male child. [14]The woman was given the two wings of a great eagle, so that she might fly to the place prepared for her in the desert, where she would be taken care of for a time, times and half a time, out of the serpent's reach. [15]Then from his mouth the serpent spewed water like a river, to overtake the woman and sweep her away with the torrent. [16]But the earth helped the woman by opening its mouth and swallowing the river that the dragon had spewed out of his mouth. [17]Then the dragon was enraged at the woman and went off to make war against the rest of her offspring—those who obey God's commandments and hold to the testimony of Jesus. [1]And the dragon[o] stood on the shore of the sea.

13

The Beast out of the Sea

And I saw a beast coming out of the sea. He had ten horns and seven heads, with ten crowns on his horns, and on each head a blasphemous name. [2]The beast I saw resembled a leopard, but had feet like those of a bear and a mouth like that of a lion. The dragon gave the beast his power and his throne and great authority. [3]One of the heads of the beast seemed to have had a fatal wound, but the fatal wound had been healed. The whole world was astonished and followed the beast. [4]Men worshiped the dragon because he had given authority to the beast, and they also worshiped the beast and asked, "Who is like the beast? Who can make war against him?"

[5]The beast was given a mouth to utter proud words and blasphemies and to exercise his authority for forty-two months. [6]He opened his mouth to blaspheme God, and to slander his name and his dwelling place and those who live in heaven. [7]He was given power to make war against the saints and to conquer them. And he was given authority over every tribe, people, language and nation. [8]All inhabitants of the earth will worship the beast—all whose names have not been written in the book of life belonging to the Lamb that was slain from the creation of the world.[p]

[9]He who has an ear, let him hear.

[10]If anyone is to go into captivity,
    into captivity he will go.
If anyone is to be killed[q] with the sword,
    with the sword he will be killed.

This calls for patient endurance and faithfulness on the part of the saints.

OPEN: 1. Who do you think is one of the most charismatic leaders living today? How do you think charisma has helped him or her to lead? **2.** When you were growing up, who was the most patient person in your family? What impressed you most about his or her patience?

DIG: 1. What is this beast from the sea like? What is the source of its power? How does it use its power? What is the extent of its power? What is the relationship between the beast and the dragon? **2.** Who worships the beast? **3.** Who do you think the first-century Christians would have identified as this beast (see Dan. 7 and Rom. 13:1)? **4.** What impact will this beast have on the Christians? How ought they to respond? Why?

REFLECT: 1. Who are some of the beasts or idols in your life — people, forces, institutions, etc. — that are testing your allegiance to Christ alone? How have you been swayed from your allegiance to Christ by talk of "patriotism" and "tradition"? How is God helping you deal with them? **2.** Is your name written in the Book of Life? How do you know? **3.** What kind of grade would you give yourself on patient endurance and faithfulness? Why?

o1 Some late manuscripts And I   p8 Or written from the creation of the world in the book of life belonging to the Lamb that was slain   q10 Some manuscripts anyone kills

The Beast out of the Earth

[11]Then I saw another beast, coming out of the earth. He had two horns like a lamb, but he spoke like a dragon. [12]He exercised all the authority of the first beast on his behalf, and made the earth and its inhabitants worship the first beast, whose fatal wound had been healed. [13]And he performed great and miraculous signs, even causing fire to come down from heaven to earth in full view of men. [14]Because of the signs he was given power to do on behalf of the first beast, he deceived the inhabitants of the earth. He ordered them to set up an image in honor of the beast who was wounded by the sword and yet lived. [15]He was given power to give breath to the image of the first beast, so that it could speak and cause all who refused to worship the image to be killed. [16]He also forced everyone, small and great, rich and poor, free and slave, to receive a mark on his right hand or on his forehead, [17]so that no one could buy or sell unless he had the mark, which is the name of the beast or the number of his name.

[18]This calls for wisdom. If anyone has insight, let him calculate the number of the beast, for it is man's number. His number is 666.

The Lamb and the 144,000

14 Then I looked, and there before me was the Lamb, standing on Mount Zion, and with him 144,000 who had his name and his Father's name written on their foreheads. [2]And I heard a sound from heaven like the roar of rushing waters and like a loud peal of thunder. The sound I heard was like that of harpists playing their harps. [3]And they sang a new song before the throne and before the four living creatures and the elders. No one could learn the song except the 144,000 who had been redeemed from the earth. [4]These are those who did not defile themselves with women, for they kept themselves pure. They follow the Lamb wherever he goes. They were purchased from among men and offered as firstfruits to God and the Lamb. [5]No lie was found in their mouths; they are blameless.

The Three Angels

[6]Then I saw another angel flying in midair, and he had the eternal gospel to proclaim to those who live on the earth—to every nation, tribe, language and people. [7]He said in a loud voice, "Fear God and give him glory, because the hour of his judgment has come. Worship him who made the heavens, the earth, the sea and the springs of water."

[8]A second angel followed and said, "Fallen! Fallen is Babylon the Great, which made all the nations drink the maddening wine of her adulteries."

[9]A third angel followed them and said in a loud voice: "If anyone worships the beast and his image and receives his mark on the forehead or on the hand, [10]he, too, will drink of the wine of God's fury, which has been poured full strength into the cup of his wrath. He will be tormented with burning sulfur in the presence of the holy angels and of the Lamb. [11]And the smoke of their torment rises for ever and ever. There is no rest day or night for those who worship the beast and his image, or for

---

OPEN: 1. Pick a number from 1-1000. Why did you pick that number? **2.** What Halloween costume, worn by your party friends, was unusually deceptive?

DIG: 1. What is this beast from the earth like? **2.** If the first beast exersises political power, what authority does this second beast exercise? How are true government and religion connected and mimicked by these two beasts? In first-century Rome, how was this done (see introduction to the Book of Revelation)? **3.** Why "666" as a symbol for false religion? How does the mark of the beast compare with the mark of God? (7:3)? **4.** Compare the view of the Roman Empire in chapter 13 with that in Mark 12:13-17. How had Rome changed over the years that might account for these two views?

REFLECT: How then shall we wisely discern false government? False religion?

OPEN: What kind of singer are you: Off-Broadway? Off-key? Off-color?

DIG: 1. Given the chaos described in chapters 12-13, what comfort do you find in this passage? What sights? Sounds? Feelings? **2.** Who is the Lamb? What has he done? Why are the people following him?

REFLECT: 1. What do you have in common with the 144,000? How are you different? **2.** How has your relationship with Christ enabled you to endure recent hardships in your life?

OPEN: Tell the group a "good news/bad news" joke. Analyze it for what's so good about the good news.

DIG: 1. What is the essence of the "eternal gospel" proclaimed by the angel of grace? Who will hear it? Has this vision yet been fulfilled? What response to the gospel is called for? **2.** By contrast, what message does the angel of doom spread? Who is Babylon that has fallen? Who has been infected by the spirit of Babylon? **3.** How does Satan's system (13:2-10) differ from God's church (14:1-5)? How does Satan's ideology (13:11-18) differ from God's truth (14:6-13)?

REFLECT: 1. What are you doing to help proclaim the gospel to every nation, tribe, language, and people? What has been your experience sharing the Good News with people from other cultures? **2.** How do you look upon death: As a rest? A reward? A new phase in the journey? Or what? **3.** What would you like to be doing when God calls you home?

OPEN: What is one memory you have of harvesting something? What were you harvesting? How hard did you work? Did you enjoy this work? Why or why not?

DIG: 1. Identify the four supernatural beings in this fifth vision. What is the role of each? **2.** What are the differences between the two parts of the vision (vv. 14-16 and 17-20)? What is the nature of the judgment that will occur (see Matt. 13:30, 39)? **3.** Who might the first figure be (see Dan. 7:13)?

REFLECT: How ripe do you think the world is now? Do you feel that the end of the world is close at hand? Why or why not? How does this affect your lifestyle? Why?

OPEN: 1. When you were a child, what is one thing you liked about going to your favorite body of water? **2.** If you could have a bowl full of anything right now, what would you want? Why?

DIG: 1. What new sign does John see? How does he describe the sign? Why does he say these are the last plagues? **2.** What picture does he paint in verse 2? What is the nature of the praise given to God? Who offers it? Compare and contrast Moses' song of deliverance from Egypt (Exod. 15:1-18) with the song sung by those delivered from the beast. **3.** What does John see next? How does the angels' attire contrast with what they are given to do? **4.** What does the temple in heaven mean: A haven of rest and playing harps for those who die? Or a time to reckon with God's holiness and wrath unveiled in that very temple? (Is there no rest for the wicked anywhere?) Why?

REFLECT: 1. How does this passage make you feel? Why? What does it make you want to do? Why? **2.** What great and mighty deeds has God done in your life for which you

anyone who receives the mark of his name." [12]This calls for patient endurance on the part of the saints who obey God's commandments and remain faithful to Jesus.

[13]Then I heard a voice from heaven say, "Write: Blessed are the dead who die in the Lord from now on."

"Yes," says the Spirit, "they will rest from their labor, for their deeds will follow them."

The Harvest of the Earth

[14]I looked, and there before me was a white cloud, and seated on the cloud was one "like a son of man"[r] with a crown of gold on his head and a sharp sickle in his hand. [15]Then another angel came out of the temple and called in a loud voice to him who was sitting on the cloud, "Take your sickle and reap, because the time to reap has come, for the harvest of the earth is ripe." [16]So he who was seated on the cloud swung his sickle over the earth, and the earth was harvested.

[17]Another angel came out of the temple in heaven, and he too had a sharp sickle. [18]Still another angel, who had charge of the fire, came from the altar and called in a loud voice to him who had the sharp sickle, "Take your sharp sickle and gather the clusters of grapes from the earth's vine, because its grapes are ripe." [19]The angel swung his sickle on the earth, gathered its grapes and threw them into the great winepress of God's wrath. [20]They were trampled in the winepress outside the city, and blood flowed out of the press, rising as high as the horses' bridles for a distance of 1,600 stadia.[s]

Seven Angels With Seven Plagues

15 I saw in heaven another great and marvelous sign: seven angels with the seven last plagues—last, because with them God's wrath is completed. [2]And I saw what looked like a sea of glass mixed with fire and, standing beside the sea, those who had been victorious over the beast and his image and over the number of his name. They held harps given them by God [3]and sang the song of Moses the servant of God and the song of the Lamb:

"Great and marvelous are your deeds,
   Lord God Almighty.
Just and true are your ways,
   King of the ages.
[4]Who will not fear you, O Lord,
   and bring glory to your name?
For you alone are holy.
All nations will come
   and worship before you,
for your righteous acts have been revealed."

[5]After this I looked and in heaven the temple, that is, the tabernacle of the Testimony, was opened. [6]Out of the temple came the seven angels with the seven plagues. They were

r14 Daniel 7:13   *s20* That is, about 180 miles (about 300 kilometers)

dressed in clean, shining linen and wore golden sashes around their chests. ⁷Then one of the four living creatures gave to the seven angels seven golden bowls filled with the wrath of God, who lives for ever and ever. ⁸And the temple was filled with smoke from the glory of God and from his power, and no one could enter the temple until the seven plagues of the seven angels were completed.

The Seven Bowls of God's Wrath

16 Then I heard a loud voice from the temple saying to the seven angels, "Go, pour out the seven bowls of God's wrath on the earth."

²The first angel went and poured out his bowl on the land, and ugly and painful sores broke out on the people who had the mark of the beast and worshiped his image.

³The second angel poured out his bowl on the sea, and it turned into blood like that of a dead man, and every living thing in the sea died.

⁴The third angel poured out his bowl on the rivers and springs of water, and they became blood. ⁵Then I heard the angel in charge of the waters say:

"You are just in these judgments,
    you who are and who were, the Holy One,
    because you have so judged;
⁶for they have shed the blood of your saints and
        prophets,
    and you have given them blood to drink as they
        deserve."

⁷And I heard the altar respond:

"Yes, Lord God Almighty,
    true and just are your judgments."

⁸The fourth angel poured out his bowl on the sun, and the sun was given power to scorch people with fire. ⁹They were seared by the intense heat and they cursed the name of God, who had control over these plagues, but they refused to repent and glorify him.

¹⁰The fifth angel poured out his bowl on the throne of the beast, and his kingdom was plunged into darkness. Men gnawed their tongues in agony ¹¹and cursed the God of heaven because of their pains and their sores, but they refused to repent of what they had done.

¹²The sixth angel poured out his bowl on the great river Euphrates, and its water was dried up to prepare the way for the kings from the East. ¹³Then I saw three evil¹ spirits that looked like frogs; they came out of the mouth of the dragon, out of the mouth of the beast and out of the mouth of the false prophet. ¹⁴They are spirits of demons performing miraculous signs, and they go out to the kings of the whole world, to gather them for the battle on the great day of God Almighty.

¹13 Greek *unclean*

OPEN: 1. What firsthand experience have you had with a natural disaster? What happened? What are your most vivid memories about it? 2. What would be the worst plague for you to experience: Sores all over your body? Intense heat without air conditioning? Total darkness? Or great thirst with very little water? Why?

will praise him today? How appropriate is the song in this passage to your experience with God? Why?

DIG: 1. What contents are in each bowl of wrath? Why are these plagues worse than those ushered in by the trumpets (contrast, for example, 8:8 with 16:3)? What was the function of the trumpet plagues? What is the function of the plagues in this passage? 2. Why does the angel (speaking on behalf of nature) react to the outpouring of God's wrath, not with pain or sorrow, but with recognition of divine justice? 3. What is described in the interlude (vv. 13-16) between the sixth and seventh bowls? What function did the frogs perform? What will happen at the battle of Armageddon (i.e., "hill of Megiddo," an historic crossroads of the Middle East)? 4. How will the just purposes of God and the evil purposes of Satan finally and awfully converge at Armageddon? With what result (vv. 17-21)? 5. Compare the seven seals, seven trumpets and seven bowls to each other and to the ten plagues of Egypt (Exod. 7-10). What examples of contrast (e.g., "not only . . . but . . .") can you find in each section? 6. What is the connection between the three scenes (of seals, trumpets and bowls)? Is it chronological or logical or what? Why? How would these seals, trumpets and bowls each be a comfort to John's original readers?

REFLECT: 1. What has God done in your life to help you repent? How receptive are you to admitting your guilt and repenting when you sin? 2. "War is Hell." How would this quotation be especially appropriate to this passage? What does this tell you about God's judgment? 3. What are the frogs that are battling with you? How is the battle going? 4. How is the Book of Revelation making you feel? Why? What has surprised you about God or about this book? How would you explain the necessity of these plagues to someone who is not a Christian?

OPEN: 1. If you could be famous for one hour, for what would you like to be known? Why? **2.** What bumper sticker or sign best sums up your life now? Why?

DIG: 1. Who is the central figure in the next scene, who appears to be "off-stage"? In what sense is she influencial? Evil? Attractive? Repulsive? Who is she (see also 14:8 and 16:19)? How is the woman and this beast like the first and second beasts of chapter 13? **2.** Is this passage condemning physical adultery, or spiritual adultery, as the ultimate sin? Why? **3.** How does the beast she is riding compare with the two beasts of chapter 13? What does the angel say about the origin of the beast? Its history? Its future? How do you interpret this? What kind of response does the beast elicit? Why? **4.** Geographically, historically and spiritually—what do you think the beast's seven heads and ten horns represent (see also Dan. 7:15-28)? Why do the kings and the beast join forces? With what result? How can evil turn on itself, Satan in effect casting out Satan? How does God's greater purpose triumph in all this? **5.** How are the readers of Revelation comforted here by the many "definitions" of the symbols? Do these correspondences explain the meaning of the symbolism, or beg further explanation? Do they simply refocus, even rivet, our attention on a single object from a different angle? Why?

REFLECT: 1. How does Babylon in this passage symbolize what is wrong in society today? For example, what worldly institutions have been overthrown by revolution, only

¹⁵"Behold, I come like a thief! Blessed is he who stays awake and keeps his clothes with him, so that he may not go naked and be shamefully exposed."

¹⁶Then they gathered the kings together to the place that in Hebrew is called Armageddon.

¹⁷The seventh angel poured out his bowl into the air, and out of the temple came a loud voice from the throne, saying, "It is done!" ¹⁸Then there came flashes of lightning, rumblings, peals of thunder and a severe earthquake. No earthquake like it has ever occurred since man has been on earth, so tremendous was the quake. ¹⁹The great city split into three parts, and the cities of the nations collapsed. God remembered Babylon the Great and gave her the cup filled with the wine of the fury of his wrath. ²⁰Every island fled away and the mountains could not be found. ²¹From the sky huge hailstones of about a hundred pounds each fell upon men. And they cursed God on account of the plague of hail, because the plague was so terrible.

The Woman on the Beast

17 One of the seven angels who had the seven bowls came and said to me, "Come, I will show you the punishment of the great prostitute, who sits on many waters. ²With her the kings of the earth committed adultery and the inhabitants of the earth were intoxicated with the wine of her adulteries."

³Then the angel carried me away in the Spirit into a desert. There I saw a woman sitting on a scarlet beast that was covered with blasphemous names and had seven heads and ten horns. ⁴The woman was dressed in purple and scarlet, and was glittering with gold, precious stones and pearls. She held a golden cup in her hand, filled with abominable things and the filth of her adulteries. ⁵This title was written on her forehead:

MYSTERY

BABYLON THE GREAT

THE MOTHER OF PROSTITUTES

AND OF THE ABOMINATIONS OF THE EARTH.

⁶I saw that the woman was drunk with the blood of the saints, the blood of those who bore testimony to Jesus.

When I saw her, I was greatly astonished. ⁷Then the angel said to me: "Why are you astonished? I will explain to you the mystery of the woman and of the beast she rides, which has the seven heads and ten horns. ⁸The beast, which you saw, once was, now is not, and will come up out of the Abyss and go to his destruction. The inhabitants of the earth whose names have not been written in the book of life from the creation of the world will be astonished when they see the beast, because he once was, now is not, and yet will come.

⁹"This calls for a mind with wisdom. The seven heads are seven hills on which the woman sits. ¹⁰They are also seven kings. Five have fallen, one is, the other has not yet come; but when he does come, he must remain for a little while. ¹¹The beast who once was, and now is not, is an eighth king. He belongs to the seven and is going to his destruction.

[12]"The ten horns you saw are ten kings who have not yet received a kingdom, but who for one hour will receive authority as kings along with the beast. [13]They have one purpose and will give their power and authority to the beast. [14]They will make war against the Lamb, but the Lamb will overcome them because he is Lord of lords and King of kings—and with him will be his called, chosen and faithful followers."

[15]Then the angel said to me, "The waters you saw, where the prostitute sits, are peoples, multitudes, nations and languages. [16]The beast and the ten horns you saw will hate the prostitute. They will bring her to ruin and leave her naked; they will eat her flesh and burn her with fire. [17]For God has put it into their hearts to accomplish his purpose by agreeing to give the beast their power to rule, until God's words are fulfilled. [18]The woman you saw is the great city that rules over the kings of the earth."

The Fall of Babylon

18 After this I saw another angel coming down from heaven. He had great authority, and the earth was illuminated by his splendor. [2]With a mighty voice he shouted:

"Fallen! Fallen is Babylon the Great!
She has become a home for demons
and a haunt for every evil[u] spirit,
a haunt for every unclean and detestable bird.
[3]For all the nations have drunk
the maddening wine of her adulteries.
The kings of the earth committed adultery with her,
and the merchants of the earth grew rich from her
excessive luxuries."

[4]Then I heard another voice from heaven say:

"Come out of her, my people,
so that you will not share in her sins,
so that you will not receive any of her plagues;
[5]for her sins are piled up to heaven,
and God has remembered her crimes.
[6]Give back to her as she has given;
pay her back double for what she has done.
Mix her a double portion from her own cup.
[7]Give her as much torture and grief
as the glory and luxury she gave herself.
In her heart she boasts,
'I sit as queen; I am not a widow,
and I will never mourn.'
[8]Therefore in one day her plagues will overtake her:
death, mourning and famine.
She will be consumed by fire,
for mighty is the Lord God who judges her.

[u]2 Greek *unclean*

to be replaced by new leaderships who succumb to the same godless ideology? **2.** Of society's wrongs, which ones have entrapped you from time to time? How has God enabled you to escape or avoid the snares of "the great prostitute? **3.** Surely by now you are "calling for a mind with wisdom." What wisdom do you need in the next few weeks? What wisdom do you need in understanding the message of Revelation? **4.** If you have not grasped the full meaning of the various beasts, have you at least been frightened by the power of evil? And what will you do with your fear?

OPEN: If you were a piece of merchandise, would you be made of precious stones, fine linens or costly woods? Why? **2.** Remember as a child when you built a tower of dominoes or blocks, only to have it all fall down—what did you like best about it? Least? Why? **3.** If you could be captain of any kind of ship, what kind would you want? Why?

DIG: 1. As compelling as the power of evil is, a more compelling authority shouts an overriding double-edged message: one edge cutting Babylon and her followers, the other exhorting God's people. What are two voices, the two messages, and the two responses called forth from the two audiences? How does God's perspective on Babylon (vv. 2-6) differ from Babylon's self-understanding (v. 7). **2.** How do the voices from the world greet the fall of Babylon (vv. 9-20)? Contemporize each of their laments—make them your own. Why do they mourn? Why would you mourn if you were in their situation? **3.** Compare this passage with the following Old Testament prophecies about the fall of great cities. How is each city a historical example of this greater spiritual reality, the fall of Babylon the Great: Sodom and Gomorrah (see Genesis 19)? Babylon (see Isaiah 13, 1, 47)? Tyre (see Ezekiel 27-28)? **4.** What conclusions do you draw concerning the destruction of Babylon from this comparison? What do you learn about God?

REFLECT: 1. If you were going to describe your life in terms of a city, what would you say? What kinds of cargoes are coming into it? What activities occur within its walls? How does it compare with Babylon? What would be a fitting name for your city? Why that name? What do you do to keep the evils listed in this passage out of your city or life? 2.When has an important part of your life collapsed? What did other individuals have to say about this demise? What perspective did God bring to your fallen situation? 3. What is the most important lesson you learned from this passage? Why this? What actions will you take today based on this learning?

---

[9]"When the kings of the earth who committed adultery with her and shared her luxury see the smoke of her burning, they will weep and mourn over her. [10]Terrified at her torment, they will stand far off and cry:

" 'Woe! Woe, O great city,
O Babylon, city of power!
In one hour your doom has come!'

[11]"The merchants of the earth will weep and mourn over her because no one buys their cargoes any more— [12]cargoes of gold, silver, precious stones and pearls; fine linen, purple, silk and scarlet cloth; every sort of citron wood, and articles of every kind made of ivory, costly wood, bronze, iron and marble; [13]cargoes of cinnamon and spice, of incense, myrrh and frankincense, of wine and olive oil, of fine flour and wheat; cattle and sheep; horses and carriages; and bodies and souls of men.

[14]"They will say, 'The fruit you longed for is gone from you. All your riches and splendor have vanished, never to be recovered.' [15]The merchants who sold these things and gained their wealth from her will stand far off, terrified at her torment. They will weep and mourn [16]and cry out:

" 'Woe! Woe, O great city,
dressed in fine linen, purple and scarlet,
and glittering with gold, precious stones and pearls!
[17]In one hour such great wealth has been brought to
ruin!'

"Every sea captain, and all who travel by ship, the sailors, and all who earn their living from the sea, will stand far off. [18]When they see the smoke of her burning, they will exclaim, 'Was there ever a city like this great city?' [19]They will throw dust on their heads, and with weeping and mourning cry out:

" 'Woe! Woe, O great city,
where all who had ships on the sea
became rich through her wealth!
In one hour she has been brought to ruin!
[20]Rejoice over her, O heaven!
Rejoice, saints and apostles and prophets!
God has judged her for the way she treated you.' "

[21]Then a mighty angel picked up a boulder the size of a large millstone and threw it into the sea, and said:

"With such violence
the great city of Babylon will be thrown down,
never to be found again.
[22]The music of harpists and musicians, flute players and
trumpeters,
will never be heard in you again.
No workman of any trade
will ever be found in you again.
The sound of a millstone
will never be heard in you again.

²³The light of a lamp
  will never shine in you again.
The voice of bridegroom and bride
  will never be heard in you again.
Your merchants were the world's great men.
  By your magic spell all the nations were led astray.
²⁴In her was found the blood of prophets and of the
    saints,
  and of all who have been killed on the earth."

Hallelujah!

19 After this I heard what sounded like the roar of a great
multitude in heaven shouting:

"Hallelujah!
Salvation and glory and power belong to our God,
² for true and just are his judgments.
He has condemned the great prostitute
  who corrupted the earth by her adulteries.
He has avenged on her the blood of his servants."

³And again they shouted:

"Hallelujah!
The smoke from her goes up for ever and ever."

⁴The twenty-four elders and the four living creatures fell
down and worshiped God, who was seated on the throne. And
they cried:

"Amen, Hallelujah!"

⁵Then a voice came from the throne, saying:

"Praise our God,
  all you his servants,
you who fear him,
  both small and great!"

⁶Then I heard what sounded like a great multitude, like the
roar of rushing waters and like loud peals of thunder, shouting:

"Hallelujah!
  For our Lord God Almighty reigns.
⁷Let us rejoice and be glad
  and give him glory!
For the wedding of the Lamb has come,
  and his bride has made herself ready.
⁸Fine linen, bright and clean,
  was given her to wear."

(Fine linen stands for the righteous acts of the saints.)

⁹Then the angel said to me, "Write: 'Blessed are those who
are invited to the wedding supper of the Lamb!'" And he
added, "These are the true words of God."

¹⁰At this I fell at his feet to worship him. But he said to me,
"Do not do it! I am a fellow servant with you and with your
brothers who hold to the testimony of Jesus. Worship God! For
the testimony of Jesus is the spirit of prophecy."

OPEN: 1. When was the last time your city's favorite ball team finally won it all? Tell the group about any ticker-tape parades and other local celebrations you may have witnessed. **2.** What was the most festive wedding and reception you ever attended? **3.** What funeral have you attended where the eulogy was most memorable for its praise of God's salvation?

DIG: 1. In contrast to the silence that comes with the fall of Babylon (18:22), what characterizes the new scene in heaven? Who participates in this praise? **2.** Compare and contrast the five songs of praise: What is the most frequent refrain? What do we learn about God's character? **3.** Contrast the prostitute of chapters 17 and 18 with the bride of verses 6-9 (see also Eph. 5:25-27). What do you find most interesting about this contrast? Why? **4.** How is John (and how might we be) tempted to worship the angel or messenger of the good news? **5.** How is the witness of Jesus related to prophecy?

REFLECT: 1. What are four things for which you are extremely grateful to God? How do you usually express your gratitude to him about these four things? **2.** How has your interest in worshipping God increased or decreased in the last year? Since beginning your study of Revelation? Why? **3.** What are some sounds of worship that you really appreciate? Why? How will you use these this week to worship God? **4.** Seeing spiritual Babylon defeated and condemned and the Lord God triumphant and glorious— how does that affect your overall view of your problems here and now? What is one problem you will now manage more confidently and joyfully as a result of your study of Revelation.

OPEN: When you were young, how much did you want a horse? Why? Who was your favorite real or fictional horse? Why?

DIG: 1. What about the horse, the rider and the setting commands your attention? What description, titles and names from the rest of Revelation help you unmistakably identify the rider? **2.** Who is following Christ: Is this the "church militant" (still on earth)? Or the "church triumphant" (now in heaven)? Angels or birds or what? Why? **3.** What weapon does the rider wield and why? Does this remind you of certain Bible-bangers? Why? **4.** How does this great supper (vv. 17-18) compare with the wedding supper (19:9)? Which meal would you prefer? Why? **5.** Who are the combatants in this war (vv. 19-21)? Who wins? What happens to the enemy leaders? To the army? **6.** How does this "last battle" compare to "previous" ones (16:12-16; 17:14-16) and a "later" one (20:7-10)? Do you think these are different accounts of the same battle? Why?

REFLECT: What hopes and fears, noble desires and worst instincts, does this triumphant picture bring out in you? Why? How has Jesus been your deliverer this year?

OPEN: When was the last time you "lost your head"? What happened?

DIG: 1. What deed is described here? By whom? How? Why is Satan bound? **2.** Where and when will this 1000-year reign begin: On earth or in heaven? Beginning when Christ first came? Or when he comes again? Why? **3.** What will life be like without Satan deceiving the nations but with the church reigning instead? In what sense is that already true? And not yet true? **4.** What role do the martyrs play on earth? In heaven? **5.** What is the first resurrection? The second death (see also 20:11-15)? What do these mean to Christians? To the rest of the dead?

REFLECT: 1. What are some dragons you have slain? How? What part did God play in these victories? **2.** How would you feel about being a martyr for Christ? Why? What comfort and strength does this passage give you?

The Rider on the White Horse

[11]I saw heaven standing open and there before me was a white horse, whose rider is called Faithful and True. With justice he judges and makes war. [12]His eyes are like blazing fire, and on his head are many crowns. He has a name written on him that no one knows but he himself. [13]He is dressed in a robe dipped in blood, and his name is the Word of God. [14]The armies of heaven were following him, riding on white horses and dressed in fine linen, white and clean. [15]Out of his mouth comes a sharp sword with which to strike down the nations. "He will rule them with an iron scepter." [v] He treads the winepress of the fury of the wrath of God Almighty. [16]On his robe and on his thigh he has this name written:

KING OF KINGS AND LORD OF LORDS.

[17]And I saw an angel standing in the sun, who cried in a loud voice to all the birds flying in midair, "Come, gather together for the great supper of God, [18]so that you may eat the flesh of kings, generals, and mighty men, of horses and their riders, and the flesh of all people, free and slave, small and great."

[19]Then I saw the beast and the kings of the earth and their armies gathered together to make war against the rider on the horse and his army. [20]But the beast was captured, and with him the false prophet who had performed the miraculous signs on his behalf. With these signs he had deluded those who had received the mark of the beast and worshiped his image. The two of them were thrown alive into the fiery lake of burning sulfur. [21]The rest of them were killed with the sword that came out of the mouth of the rider on the horse, and all the birds gorged themselves on their flesh.

The Thousand Years

20 And I saw an angel coming down out of heaven, having the key to the Abyss and holding in his hand a great chain. [2]He seized the dragon, that ancient serpent, who is the devil, or Satan, and bound him for a thousand years. [3]He threw him into the Abyss, and locked and sealed it over him, to keep him from deceiving the nations anymore until the thousand years were ended. After that, he must be set free for a short time.

[4]I saw thrones on which were seated those who had been given authority to judge. And I saw the souls of those who had been beheaded because of their testimony for Jesus and because of the word of God. They had not worshiped the beast or his image and had not received his mark on their foreheads or their hands. They came to life and reigned with Christ a thousand years. [5](The rest of the dead did not come to life until the thousand years were ended.) This is the first resurrection. [6]Blessed and holy are those who have part in the first resurrection. The second death has no power over them, but they will be priests of God and of Christ and will reign with him for a thousand years.

[v]15 Psalm 2:9

Satan's Doom

[7]When the thousand years are over, Satan will be released from his prison [8]and will go out to deceive the nations in the four corners of the earth—Gog and Magog—to gather them for battle. In number they are like the sand on the seashore. [9]They marched across the breadth of the earth and surrounded the camp of God's people, the city he loves. But fire came down from heaven and devoured them. [10]And the devil, who deceived them, was thrown into the lake of burning sulfur, where the beast and the false prophet had been thrown. They will be tormented day and night for ever and ever.

The Dead Are Judged

[11]Then I saw a great white throne and him who was seated on it. Earth and sky fled from his presence, and there was no place for them. [12]And I saw the dead, great and small, standing before the throne, and books were opened. Another book was opened, which is the book of life. The dead were judged according to what they had done as recorded in the books. [13]The sea gave up the dead that were in it, and death and Hades gave up the dead that were in them, and each person was judged according to what he had done. [14]Then death and Hades were thrown into the lake of fire. The lake of fire is the second death. [15]If anyone's name was not found written in the book of life, he was thrown into the lake of fire.

The New Jerusalem

21 Then I saw a new heaven and a new earth, for the first heaven and the first earth had passed away, and there was no longer any sea. [2]I saw the Holy City, the new Jerusalem, coming down out of heaven from God, prepared as a bride beautifully dressed for her husband. [3]And I heard a loud voice from the throne saying, "Now the dwelling of God is with men, and he will live with them. They will be his people, and God himself will be with them and be their God. [4]He will wipe every tear from their eyes. There will be no more death or mourning or crying or pain, for the old order of things has passed away."

[5]He who was seated on the throne said, "I am making everything new!" Then he said, "Write this down, for these words are trustworthy and true."

[6]He said to me: "It is done. I am the Alpha and the Omega, the Beginning and the End. To him who is thirsty I will give to drink without cost from the spring of the water of life. [7]He who overcomes will inherit all this, and I will be his God and he will be my son. [8]But the cowardly, the unbelieving, the vile, the murderers, the sexually immoral, those who practice magic arts, the idolaters and all liars—their place will be in the fiery lake of burning sulfur. This is the second death."

[9]One of the seven angels who had the seven bowls full of the seven last plagues came and said to me, "Come, I will show you the bride, the wife of the Lamb." [10]And he carried me away in the Spirit to a mountain great and high, and showed me the Holy City, Jerusalem, coming down out of heaven from God. [11]It shone with the glory of God, and its brilliance was like that of

DIG: 1. Why do you think Satan will again try to deceive the nations? Why do you suppose God unbound him and let him out of the Abyss? 2. Describe this version of the last battle, comparing it to the other versions in Revelation and in Ezekiel 38-39. What is the final fate of the beast and the false prophet?

REFLECT: What is your biggest spiritual battle today? How is it like previous ones? What is the outcome so far?

OPEN: How do you judge a book?

DIG: Who is exempted, and who is exhumed, in the great white throne judgement? On what basis?

REFLECT: Imagine a book made of your life, with every thought and deed recorded, then read by all. How would you feel? If Christ edited that book by substituting his works for yours, how would you feel then? How will you then live today?

OPEN: 1. Where is one of the most beautiful places you have ever been? What impressed you the most about that place? 2. What was one of the most beautiful spots in your hometown when you were growing up? 3. How do you think your city would be different if God were the mayor?

DIG: 1. Where will the new age be lived out—on earth or in heaven? Why do you think so? 2. Who will be the "residents" of the New Jerusalem, the "wife" of the Lamb? Whose presence is the vision caught up with? What's missing from this picture? Why? 3. What do you think it will be like living without fear, pain or death and with the continual and direct presence of God? Will this new world coming be recognizable? How so? 4. What is the significance of the names ascribed to God, especially for those who "overcome" and those who do not? 5.What is it about the city that John and his readers are meant to notice in particular and why? Of its central figure, its light, its construction, its foundation, its gates, its measurements and its beauty—what impresses you the most and why? 6.Compare John's vision of reality here with the related visions in Ezekiel 40-48 and Isaiah 60-66. Accordingly, what was the function of the temple in the old Jerusalem? Why is there no need for a temple in the New Jerusalem? **7.** How do you decide which is a symbol and which is not, and what is the reality to which the symbol points? Is it by how mind-boggling or humanly inconceivable a thing is? And what is more "real": The spiritual things visualized here in the New Jerusalem? Or the physical objects of the Old Jerusalem?

REFLECT: 1. Does the New Jerusalem come close to your idea of beauty? Why or why not? How do you feel about the fact that the Holy City will be your hometown? How do you feel about the fact that this is what Jesus has prepared you for? **2.** What has caused you mourning, crying, and pain in the past year? What does it mean to you to know that this will pass away? **3.** How must the early Christians have greeted this vision of what lay in store for them? How do you respond to this same hope? **4.** Create your own worship service based on Revelation 21. **5.** Imagine yourself at the wedding feast with Christ: Are you the happy bride, or a lady-in-waiting? A direct participant, or a distant spectator? Why?

a very precious jewel, like a jasper, clear as crystal. [12]It had a great, high wall with twelve gates, and with twelve angels at the gates. On the gates were written the names of the twelve tribes of Israel. [13]There were three gates on the east, three on the north, three on the south and three on the west. [14]The wall of the city had twelve foundations, and on them were the names of the twelve apostles of the Lamb.

[15]The angel who talked with me had a measuring rod of gold to measure the city, its gates and its walls. [16]The city was laid out like a square, as long as it was wide. He measured the city with the rod and found it to be 12,000 stadia[w] in length, and as wide and high as it is long. [17]He measured its wall and it was 144 cubits[x] thick,[y] by man's measurement, which the angel was using. [18]The wall was made of jasper, and the city of pure gold, as pure as glass. [19]The foundations of the city walls were decorated with every kind of precious stone. The first foundation was jasper, the second sapphire, the third chalcedony, the fourth emerald, [20]the fifth sardonyx, the sixth carnelian, the seventh chrysolite, the eighth beryl, the ninth topaz, the tenth chrysoprase, the eleventh jacinth, and the twelfth amethyst.[z] [21]The twelve gates were twelve pearls, each gate made of a single pearl. The great street of the city was of pure gold, like transparent glass.

[22]I did not see a temple in the city, because the Lord God Almighty and the Lamb are its temple. [23]The city does not need the sun or the moon to shine on it, for the glory of God gives it light, and the Lamb is its lamp. [24]The nations will walk by its light, and the kings of the earth will bring their splendor into it. [25]On no day will its gates ever be shut, for there will be no night there. [26]The glory and honor of the nations will be brought into it. [27]Nothing impure will ever enter it, nor will anyone who does what is shameful or deceitful, but only those whose names are written in the Lamb's book of life.

The River of Life

22 Then the angel showed me the river of the water of life, as clear as crystal, flowing from the throne of God and of the Lamb [2]down the middle of the great street of the city. On each side of the river stood the tree of life, bearing twelve crops of fruit, yielding its fruit every month. And the leaves of the tree are for the healing of the nations. [3]No longer will there be any curse. The throne of God and of the Lamb will be in the city, and his servants will serve him. [4]They will see his face, and his name will be on their foreheads. [5]There will be no more night. They will not need the light of a lamp or the light of the sun, for the Lord God will give them light. And they will reign for ever and ever.

[6]The angel said to me, "These words are trustworthy and true. The Lord, the God of the spirits of the prophets, sent his angel to show his servants the things that must soon take place."

OPEN: If you could begin your life over again, and re-write your personal history, how far back would you go and why? What turning points would you re-write in your teenage years? In your child-rearing years? In your retirement?

DIG: 1. What new features of the New Jerusalem are found? Trace the origin of the river and tree of life from its source to its fruit. **2.** Where else do we see these same features (see Gen. 1-3; Ezek. 47:1-2; Joel 3:18; Zech. 14:8)? **3.** What does this comparison suggest about the unity of Scripture? The completeness of God's salvation?

REFLECT: What difficulties of comprehension does this eternal city, the river of life, and the immediacy of these events pose for you? What bearing, if any, do these realities have on your present lifestyle? Why?

---

[w]16 That is, about 1,400 miles (about 2,200 kilometers)   [x]17 That is, about 200 feet (about 65 meters)   [y]17 Or *high*   [z]20 The precise identification of some of these precious stones is uncertain.

Jesus Is Coming

[7]"Behold, I am coming soon! Blessed is he who keeps the words of the prophecy in this book."

[8]I, John, am the one who heard and saw these things. And when I had heard and seen them, I fell down to worship at the feet of the angel who had been showing them to me. [9]But he said to me, "Do not do it! I am a fellow servant with you and with your brothers the prophets and of all who keep the words of this book. Worship God!"

[10]Then he told me, "Do not seal up the words of the prophecy of this book, because the time is near. [11]Let him who does wrong continue to do wrong; let him who is vile continue to be vile; let him who does right continue to do right; and let him who is holy continue to be holy."

[12]"Behold, I am coming soon! My reward is with me, and I will give to everyone according to what he has done. [13]I am the Alpha and the Omega, the First and the Last, the Beginning and the End.

[14]"Blessed are those who wash their robes, that they may have the right to the tree of life and may go through the gates into the city. [15]Outside are the dogs, those who practice magic arts, the sexually immoral, the murderers, the idolaters and everyone who loves and practices falsehood.

[16]"I, Jesus, have sent my angel to give you[a] this testimony for the churches. I am the Root and the Offspring of David, and the bright Morning Star."

[17]The Spirit and the bride say, "Come!" And let him who hears say, "Come!" Whoever is thirsty, let him come; and whoever wishes, let him take the free gift of the water of life.

[18]I warn everyone who hears the words of the prophecy of this book: If anyone adds anything to them, God will add to him the plagues described in this book. [19]And if anyone takes words away from this book of prophecy, God will take away from him his share in the tree of life and in the holy city, which are described in this book.

[20]He who testifies to these things says, "Yes, I am coming soon."

Amen. Come, Lord Jesus.

[21]The grace of the Lord Jesus be with God's people. Amen.

OPEN: 1. What breed of dog best typifies the kind of week you've had? Why? **2.** If you could give yourself a new name, typifying the legacy your family gave you, or the God-given potential you have, or some hidden aspiration you have yet to realize, what name would you choose? Why?

DIG: 1. What words of Christ are repeated three times in this closing (vv. 7, 12, 20)? How do these words sum up the theme of Revelation? **2.** What do John (v. 8), the angel (vv. 9-10) and Jesus (vv. 7,16) say about the value, validity and vehicle of God's self-revelation? **3.** What significance do you attribute to Jesus' claims and names in verses 12-17? Regarding these claims, how is the final state of humanity determined: By some arbitrary reward system, fixed from eternity? Or by what we have done in this present life? Or by our response to his univeral ("whoever thirsts") and undeserved ("free gift") invitation to simply "come"? **4.** What then do you make of God's summary of human destiny: Is it ever too late for people to change their ways or come to Christ? Why or why not? **5.** In the contrast between those "inside" the city and those "outside" (vv. 14-15), what is implied about the basis for our salvation and judgment? What does it mean to "wash" one's "robe"? **6.** What is the meaning of God's final curse in verses 18-19? Knowing what you now do about the seven plagues, the tree of life, and the Holy City, how seriously do you take this warning?

REFLECT: 1. Collect one-sentence summaries from your group on the book of Revelation. **2.** How have you prepared yourself for Christ's second coming? Do you feel more ready, or less ready, after reading Revelation than you did beforehand? Why? **3.** How do you want your worship of God to change in the next six months? Why? **4.** How have your perceptions of Jesus Christ, Satan, heaven, and hell changed since you've read this book? **5.** What has been the most important thing you have learned in your study of this book? Why?

[a]16 The Greek is plural.

SUBJECT INDEX

This index can be considered a combination of a regular book index and a Bible concordance. It is obviously not intended to be comprehensive, but it will help the reader locate significant persons, places, events, and concepts of the New Testament.

Entries and subentries appear in **boldface type.**

Scripture reference follow in lightface type.

Aaron, Acts 7:40; Hebrews 5:
4; 7:11; 9:4
Abel, Matthew 23:25;
Luke 11:51; Hebrews 11:4;
12:24; 1 John 3:12
Abraham, Matthew 1:1; 3:9;
Luke 3:8; 16:22-31; John 8:
33-41,52-58; Acts 7:2;
Romans 4:1-22; 9:6-9;
Galatians 3:6-18;
Hebrews 6:13-15; 7:1-9; 11:
8-19; James 2:21-23
Adoption, spiritual,
Matthew 5:9,45; 12:50;
Luke 6:35; John 1:12,13;
11:52; Romans 4:16,17; 8:
14-29; 9:4-8,24-26;
2 Corinthians 6:16-18;
Galatians 3:7,26-29; 4:1-7;
Ephesians 1:5; 2:19;
Philippians 2:15;
Hebrews 2:10-13; 12:5-10;
1 John 3:1,2,10;
Revelation 21:7
Aeneas, Acts 9:32-35
Agrippa. *See* **Herod Agrippa**
II.
Ananias and Sapphira,
Acts 5:1-11
Ananias of Damascus,
Acts 9:10-17; 22:12-16
Ananias the High Priest,
Acts 23:2-5; 24:1
Andrew, Matthew 4:18; 10:2;
Mark 1:16; 3:18; 13:3,4;
Luke 6:14; John 1:40-42,44;
6:8; 12:22; Acts 1:13
Angels, Matthew 1:20,21; 2:
13,19,20; 4:11; 13:39-42;
16:27; 18:10; 22:30; 24:
31,36; 25:31; 26:53; 28:2-7;
Mark 1:13; 8:38; 12:25; 13:
32; Luke 1:11-20,26-38; 2:
9-15; 15:10; 16:22; 20:36;
22:43; 24:23; John 1:51; 5:
3; 20:12,13; Acts 1:10,11; 5:
19,20; 7:30,35,38,53; 8:26;
10:3-5,22; 12:7-11,23; 23:8;
27:23,24; 1 Corinthians 6:3;
Colossians 2:18;
1 Thessalonians 4:16;

2 Thessalonians 1:7;
1 Timothy 3:16; 5:21;
Hebrews 1:4-14; 2:2,5-9,16;
12:22; Jude 6,9;
Revelation 1:1,20; 2:
1,8,12,18; 3:1,5,7,14; 5:
2,11,12; 7:1-3,11,12; 8:
1-12; 9:1,13-15; 10:1-10;
11:15; 12:7-9; 14:
6-10,15-19; 15:1,6-8; 16:
1-12,17; 17:1,7,15; 18:1,21;
19:9,10,17; 20:1; 21:9-17;
22:1,6-11,16
Anna, Luke 2:36-38
Annas, Luke 3:2; John 18:
13,24; Acts 4:6
Antichrist, 1 John 2:18,22; 4:
3; 2 John 7
Antioch, Pisidian, Acts 13:
14-52; 14:19-22; 18:22
Antioch, Syrian, Acts 11:
19-30; 13:1; 14:26-28; 15:
22,23,35; Galatians 2:11;
2 Timothy 3:11
Apollos, Acts 18:24-28; 19:1;
1 Corinthians 1:12; 3:
4-7,22; 4:6; 16:12; Titus 3:
13
Apostles, chosen,
Matthew 4:18-22; 9:9; 10:
2-4; Mark 1:16-20; 2:13,14;
3:13-19; Luke 5:27,28; 6:
13-16; John 1:35-51
commissioned, Matthew 10:
1-42; 28:19,20; Mark 3:
14,15; 6:7-11; 16:15-18;
Luke 9:1-6; 22:28-30;
John 20:21-23; 21:15-19;
Acts 1:4-8; 10:42
list of, Matthew 10:2-4;
Mark 3:16-19; Luke 6:13-16;
Acts 1:13,26
Aquila, Acts 18:2,18,26;
Romans 16:3,4;
1 Corinthians 16:19;
2 Timothy 4:19
Ascension of Christ, John 6:
62; 7:33; 14:2,28; 16:5,7;
20:17; Acts 2:33;
Romans 8:34; Ephesians 1:
20,21; 4:8-10; Hebrews 6:

20; 9:12,24; 10:12;
1 Peter 3:22 *See also*
Jesus, events in life of.
Athens, Acts 17:15-34; 18:1;
1 Thessalonians 3:1

Babylon, Matthew 1:11,12,
17; Acts 7:43; 1 Peter 5:13;
Revelation 14:8; 16:9; 17:5;
18:2,10,21
Baptism, by Jesus, John 3:
22; 4:1,2
by John, Matthew 3:5-17;
21:25; Mark 1:4-11; 11:30;
Luke 3:2-22; 7:29; 20:4;
John 3:23; Acts 13:24; 18:
25; 19:3,4
Christian, Matthew 28:19,
20; Mark 16:15,16; John 3:
3-6; Acts 2:38,41;8:36-38;
9:18; 10:47,48; 16:15,33;
18:8; 19:4,5; 22:16;
Romans 6:3,4;
1 Corinthians 1:13-17; 12:
13; Galatians 3:27;
Ephesians 4:5;
Colossians 2:12; Titus 3:5;
1 Peter 3:20,21
with the Holy Spirit,
Matthew 3:11; John 1:33; 3:
5; 20:22; Acts 1:5; 2:
1-4,38,39; 10:44-46; 11:16;
19:2-6; 1 Corinthians 12:13;
Titus 3:5,6
Barabbas, Matthew 27:16-26;
Mark 15:7-15; Luke 23:
18-25; John 18:40; Acts 3:
14
Barnabas, Acts 4:36,37; 9:27;
11:22-26,30; 12:25; 13:
1-3,42-50; 14:1-23; 15:
2-4,12,22-41;
1 Corinthians 9:6;
Galatians 2:1-9,13;
Colossians 4:10
Bartholomew, Matthew 10:3;
Mark 3:18; Luke 6:14;
Acts 1:13
Bartimaeus, Mark 10:46
Beatitudes, Matthew 5:3-11;
Luke 6:20-22